I've travelled the world twice over,
Met the famous: saints and sinners,
Poets and artists, kings and queens,
Old stars and hopeful beginners,
I've been where no-one's been before,
Learned secrets from writers and cooks
All with one library ticket
To the wonderful world of books.

© JANICE JAMES.

# SONS AND LOVERS

This is the novel with which Lawrence established himself in the eyes of his generation, and it has remained ever since his best known and most widely read book. In setting down the story of Paul Morel, Lawrence was painfully recapitulating his own experiences. Walter Morel, the miner, Mrs. Morel, quieter and more refined than her husband and possessive towards her sons, and Miriam, the girl who fights a long and puzzling battle with his mother for supremacy in Paul's affections, repeat in the book the pattern that took place in real life.

# D. H. LAWRENCE

# SONS
# AND LOVERS

# CHARNWOOD
*Leicester*

First published 1913 by
William Heinemann Ltd., London


First Charnwood Edition
published November 1981
by arrangement with
William Heinemann Ltd., London


Reprinted 1992

### British Library CIP Data

Lawrence, D. H.
  Sons and lovers.— Large print ed.
  (Charnwood library series)
  I. Title    II. Series
  823'.912 [F]

  ISBN 0-7089-8008-2

Published by
F. A. Thorpe (Publishing) Ltd.
Anstey, Leicestershire

Printed and Bound in Great Britain by
T. J. Press (Padstow) Ltd., Padstow, Cornwall

# Part 1

# 1

## THE EARLY MARRIED LIFE
## OF THE MORELS

"THE BOTTOMS" succeeded to "Hell Row". Hell Row was a block of thatched, bulging cottages that stood by the brookside on Greenhill Lane. There lived the colliers who worked in the little gin-pits two fields away. The brook ran under the alder trees, scarcely soiled by these small mines, whose coal was drawn to the surface by donkeys that plodded wearily in a circle round a gin. And all over the countryside were these same pits, some of which had been worked in the time of Charles II, the few colliers and the donkeys burrowing down like ants into the earth, making queer mounds and little black places among the corn-fields and the meadows. And the cottages of these coal-miners, in blocks and pairs here and there, together with odd farms and homes of the stockingers, straying over the parish, formed the village of Bestwood.

Then, some sixty years ago, a sudden change took place. The gin-pits were elbowed aside by the large mines of the financiers. The coal and iron field of Nottinghamshire and Derbyshire was discovered. Carston, Waite and Co. appeared. Amid tremen-

3

dous excitement, Lord Palmerston formally opened the company's first mine at Spinney Park, on the edge of Sherwood Forest.

About this time the notorious Hell Row, which through growing old had acquired an evil reputation, was burned down, and much dirt was cleansed away.

Carston, Waite & Co. found they had struck on a good thing, so, down the valleys of the brooks from Selby and Nuttall, new mines were sunk, until soon there were six pits working. From Nuttall, high up on the sandstone among the woods, the railway ran, past the ruined priory of the Carthusians and past Robin Hood's Well, down to Spinney Park, then on to Minton, a large mine among corn-fields; from Minton across the farmlands of the valleyside to Bunker's Hill, branching off there, and running north to Beggarlee and Selby, that looks over at Crich and the hills of Derbyshire: six mines like black studs on the countryside, linked by a loop of fine chain, the railway.

To accommodate the regiments of miners, Carston, Waite and Co. built the Squares, great quadrangles of dwellings on the hillside of Bestwood, and then, in the brook valley, on the site of Hell Row, they erected the Bottoms.

The Bottoms consisted of six blocks of miners' dwellings, two rows of three, like the dots on a blank-six domino, and twelve houses in a block. This double row of dwellings sat at the front of the rather sharp slope from Bestwood, and looked out, from the attic windows at least, on the slow climb of the valley towards Selby.

The houses themselves were substantial and very decent. One could walk all round, seeing little front gardens with auriculas and saxifrage in the shadow of the bottom block, sweet-williams and pinks in the sunny top block; seeing neat front windows, little porches, little privet hedges, and dormer windows for the attics. But that was outside; that was the view on to the uninhabited parlours of all the colliers' wives. The dwelling-room, the kitchen, was at the back of the house, facing inward between the blocks, looking at a scrubby back garden, and then at the ash-pits. And between the rows, between the long lines of ash-pits, went the alley, where the children played and the women gossiped and the men smoked. So, the actual conditions of living in the Bottoms, that was so well built and that looked so nice, were quite unsavoury because people must live in the kitchen, and the kitchens opened on to that nasty alley of ash-pits.

Mrs. Morel was not anxious to move into the Bottoms, which was already twelve years old and on the downward path, when she descended to it from Bestwood. But it was the best she could do. Moreover, she had an end house in one of the top blocks, and thus had only one neighbour; on the other side an extra strip of garden. And, having an end house, she enjoyed a kind of aristocracy among the other women of the "between" houses, because her rent was five shillings and sixpence instead of

5

five shillings a week. But this superiority in station was not much consolation to Mrs. Morel.

She was thirty-one years old, and had been married eight years. A rather small woman, of delicate mould but resolute bearing, she shrank a little from the first contact with the Bottoms women. She came down in the July, and in the September expected her third baby.

Her husband was a miner. They had only been in their new home three weeks when the wakes, or fair, began. Morel, she knew, was sure to make a holiday of it. He went off early on the Monday morning, the day of the fair. The two children were highly excited. William, a boy of seven, fled off immediately after breakfast, to prowl round the wakes ground, leaving Annie, who was only five, to whine all morning to go also. Mrs. Morel did her work. She scarcely knew her neighbours yet, and knew no one with whom to trust the little girl. So she promised to take her to the wakes after dinner.

William appeared at half-past twelve. He was a very active lad, fair-haired, freckled, with a touch of the Dane or Norwegian about him.

"Can I have my dinner, mother?" he cried, rushing in with his cap on. " 'Cause it begins at half-past one, the man says so."

"You can have your dinner as soon as it's done," replied the mother.

"Isn't it done?" he cried, his blue eyes staring at her in indignation. "Then I'm goin' be-out it."

6

"You'll do nothing of the sort. It will be done in five minutes. It is only half-past twelve."

"They'll be beginnin'," the boy half cried, half shouted.

"You won't die if they do," said the mother. "Besides, it's only half-past twelve, so you've a full hour."

The lad began hastily to lay the table, and directly the three sat down. They were eating batter-pudding and jam, when the boy jumped off his chair and stood perfectly still. Some distance away could be heard the first small braying of a merry-go-round, and the tooting of a horn. His face quivered as he looked at his mother.

"I told you!" he said, running to the dresser for his cap.

"Take your pudding in your hand—and it's only five past one, so you were wrong—you haven't got your twopence," cried the mother in a breath.

The boy came back, bitterly disappointed, for his twopence, then went off without a word.

"I want to go, I want to go," said Annie, beginning to cry.

"Well, and you shall go, whining, wizzening little stick!" said the mother. And later in the afternoon she trudged up the hill under the tall hedge with her child. The hay was gathered from the fields, and cattle were turned on to the eddish. It was warm, peaceful.

Mrs. Morel did not like the wakes. There were two sets of horses, one going by steam, one pulled

7

round by a pony; three organs were grinding, and there came odd cracks of pistol-shots, fearful screeching of the cocoanut man's rattle, shouts of the Aunt Sally man, screeches from the peep-show lady. The mother perceived her son gazing enraptured outside the Lion Wallace booth, at the pictures of this famous lion that had killed a negro and maimed for life two white men. She left him alone, and went to get Annie a spin of toffee. Presently the lad stood in front of her, wildly excited.

"You never said you was coming—isn't the' a lot of things?—that lion's killed three men—I've spent my tuppence—an' look here."

He pulled from his pocket two egg-cups, with pink moss-roses on them.

"I got these from that stall where y'ave ter get them marbles in them holes. An' I got these two in two goes—'aepenny a go—they've got moss-roses on, look here. I wanted these."

She knew he wanted them for her.

"H'm!" she said, pleased. "They *are* pretty!"

"Shall you carry 'em, 'cause I'm frightened o' breakin' 'em?"

He was tipful of excitement now she had come, led her about the ground, showed her everything. Then, at the peep-show, she explained the pictures, in a sort of story, to which he listened as if spellbound. He would not leave her. All the time he stuck close to her, bristling with a small boy's pride of her. For no other woman looked such a lady as she did, in her little black bonnet and her cloak. She

8

smiled when she saw women she knew. When she was tired she said to her son:

"Well, are you coming now, or later?"

"Are you goin' a'ready?" he cried, his face full of reproach.

"Already? It is past four, I know."

"What are you goin' a'ready for?" he lamented.

"You needn't come if you don't want," she said.

And she went slowly away with her little girl, whilst her son stood watching her, cut to the heart to let her go, and yet unable to leave the wakes. As she crossed the open ground in front of the Moon and Stars she heard men shouting, and smelled the beer, and hurried a little, thinking her husband was probably in the bar.

At about half-past six her son came home, tired now, rather pale, and somewhat wretched. He was miserable, though he did not know it, because he had let her go alone. Since she had gone, he had not enjoyed his wakes.

"Has my dad been?" he asked.

"No," said the mother.

"He's helping to wait at the Moon and Stars. I seed him through that black tin stuff wi' holes in, on the window, wi' his sleeves rolled up."

"Ha!" exclaimed the mother shortly. "He's got no money. An' he'll be satisfied if he gets his 'lowance, whether they give him more or not."

When the light was fading, and Mrs. Morel could see no more to sew, she rose and went to the door. Everywhere was the sound of excitement, the rest-

9

lessness of the holiday, that at last infected her. She went out into the side garden. Women were coming home from the wakes, the children hugging a white lamb with green legs, or a wooden horse. Occasionally a man lurched past, almost as full as he could carry. Sometimes a good husband came along with his family, peacefully. But usually the women and children were alone. The stay-at-home mothers stood gossiping at the corners of the alley, as the twilight sank, folding their arms under their white aprons.

Mrs. Morel was alone, but she was used to it. Her son and her little girl slept upstairs; so, it seemed, her home was there behind her, fixed and stable. But she felt wretched with the coming child. The world seemed a dreary place, where nothing else would happen for her—at least until William grew up. But for herself, nothing but this dreary endurance—till the children grew up. And the children! She could not afford to have this third. She did not want it. The father was serving beer in a public house, swilling himself drunk. She despised him, and was tied to him. This coming child was too much for her. If it were not for William and Annie, she was sick of it, the struggle with poverty and ugliness and meanness.

She went into the front garden, feeling too heavy to take herself out, yet unable to stay indoors. The heat suffocated her. And looking ahead, the prospect of her life made her feel as if she were buried alive.

The front garden was a small square with a privet hedge. There she stood, trying to soothe herself with the scent of flowers and the fading, beautiful evening. Opposite her small gate was the stile that led uphill, under the tall hedge between the burning glow of the cut pastures. The sky overhead throbbed and pulsed with light. The glow sank quickly off the field; the earth and the hedges smoked dusk. As it drew dark, a ruddy glare came out on the hilltop, and out of the glare the diminished commotion of the fair.

Sometimes, down the trough of darkness formed by the path under the hedges, men came lurching home. One young man lapsed into a run down the steep bit that ended the hill, and went with a crash into the stile. Mrs. Morel shuddered. He picked himself up, swearing viciously, rather pathetically, as if he thought the stile had wanted to hurt him.

She went indoors, wondering if things were never going to alter. She was beginning by now to realise that they would not. She seemed so far away from her girlhood, she wondered if it were the same person walking heavily up the back garden at the Bottoms as had run so lightly up the breakwater at Sheerness ten years before.

"What have *I* to do with it?" she said to herself. "What have I to do with all this? Even the child I am going to have! It doesn't seem as if *I* were taken into account."

Sometimes life takes hold of one, carries the body along, accomplishes one's history, and yet is not real, but leaves oneself as it were slurred over.

"I wait," Mrs. Morel said to herself—"I wait, and what I wait for can never come."

Then she straightened the kitchen, lit the lamp, mended the fire, looked out the washing for the next day, and put it to soak. After which she sat down to her sewing. Through the long hours her needle flashed regularly through the stuff. Occasionally she sighed, moving to relieve herself. And all the time she was thinking how to make the most of what she had, for the children's sakes.

At half-past eleven her husband came. His cheeks were very red and very shiny above his black moustache. His head nodded slightly. He was pleased with himself.

"Oh! Oh! waitin' for me, lass? I've bin 'elpin' Anthony, an' what's think he's gen me? Nowt b'r a lousy hae'f-crown, an' that's ivry penny——"

"He thinks you've made the rest up in beer," she said shortly.

"An' I 'aven't—that I 'aven't. You b'lieve me, I've 'ad very little this day, I have an' all." His voice went tender. "Here, an' I browt thee a bit o' brandysnap, an' a cocoanut for th' children." He laid the gingerbread and the cocoanut, a hairy object, on the table. "Nay, tha niver said thankyer for nowt i' thy life, did ter?"

As a compromise, she picked up the cocoanut and shook it, to see if it had any milk.

"It's a good 'un, you may back yer life o' that. I got it fra' Bill Hodgkisson. 'Bill,' I says, 'tha non

12

wants them three nuts, does ter? Arena ter for gi'ein' me one for my bit of a lad an' wench?' 'I ham, Walter, my lad,' 'e says; 'ta'e which on 'em ter's a mind.' An' so I took one, an' thanked 'im. I didn't like ter shake it afore 'is eyes, but 'e says, 'Tha'd better ma'e sure it's a good un, Walt.' An' so, yer see, I knowed it was. He's a nice chap, is Bill Hodgkisson, 'e's a nice chap!"

"A man will part with anything so long as he's drunk, and you're drunk along with him," said Mrs. Morel.

"Eh, tha mucky little 'ussy, who's drunk, I sh'd like ter know?" said Morel. He was extraordinarily pleased with himself, because of his day's helping to wait in the Moon and Stars. He chattered on.

Mrs. Morel, very tired, and sick of his babble, went to bed as quickly as possible, while he raked the fire.

Mrs. Morel came of a good old burgher family, famous independents who had fought with Colonel Hutchinson, and who remained stout Congregationalists. Her grandfather had gone bankrupt in the lace-market at a time when so many lace-manufacturers were ruined in Nottingham. Her father, George Coppard, was an engineer—a large, handsome, haughty man, proud of his fair skin and blue eyes, but more proud still of his integrity. Gertrude resembled her mother in her small build. But her temper, proud and unyielding, she had from the Coppards.

George Coppard was bitterly galled by his own

13

poverty. He became foreman of the engineers in the dockyard at Sheerness. Mrs. Morel—Gertrude—was the second daughter. She favoured her mother, loved her mother best of all; but she had the Coppards' clear, defiant blue eyes and their broad brow. She remembered to have hated her father's overbearing manner towards her gentle, humorous, kindly-souled mother. She remembered running over the breakwater at Sheerness and finding the boat. She remembered to have been petted and flattered by all the men when she had gone to the dockyard, for she was a delicate, rather proud child. She remembered the funny old mistress, whose assistant she had become, whom she had loved to help in the private school. And she still had the Bible that John Field had given her. She used to walk home from chapel with John Field when she was nineteen. He was the son of a well-to-do tradesman, had been to college in London, and was to devote himself to business.

She could always recall in detail a September Sunday afternoon, when they had sat under the vine at the back of her father's house. The sun came through the chinks of the vine-leaves and made beautiful patterns, like a lace scarf, falling on her and on him. Some of the leaves were clean yellow, like yellow flat flowers.

"Now sit still," he had cried. "Now your hair, I don't know what it *is* like! It's as bright as copper and gold, as red as burnt copper, and it has gold threads when the sun shines on it. Fancy their say-

14

ing it's brown. Your mother calls it mouse-colour."

She had met his brilliant eyes, but her clear face scarcely showed the elation which rose within her.

"But you say you don't like business," she pursued.

"I don't. I hate it!" he cried hotly.

"And you would like to go into the ministry," she half implored.

"I should. I should love it, if I thought I could make a first-rate preacher."

"Then why don't you—why *don't* you?" Her voice rang with defiance. "If *I* were a man, nothing would stop me."

She held her head erect. He was rather timid before her.

"But my father's so stiff-necked. He means to put me into the business, and I know he'll do it."

"But if you're a *man*?" she had cried.

"Being a man isn't everything," he replied, frowning with puzzled helplessness.

Now, as she moved about her work at the Bottoms, with some experience of what being a man meant, she knew that it was *not* everything.

At twenty, owing to her health, she had left Sheerness. Her father had retired home to Nottingham. John Field's father had been ruined; the son had gone as a teacher in Norwood. She did not hear of him until, two years later, she made determined inquiry. He had married his landlady, a woman of forty, a widow with property.

And still Mrs. Morel preserved John Field's Bible.

She did not now believe him to be—— Well, she understood pretty well what he might or might not have been. So she preserved his Bible, and kept his memory intact in her heart, for her own sake. To her dying day, for thirty-five years, she did not speak of him.

When she was twenty-three years old, she met, at a Christmas party, a young man from the Erewash Valley. Morel was then twenty-seven years old. He was well set-up, erect, and very smart. He had wavy black hair that shone again, and a vigorous black beard that had never been shaved. His cheeks were ruddy, and his red, moist mouth was noticeable because he laughed so often and so heartily. He had that rare thing, a rich, ringing laugh. Gertrude Coppard had watched him, fascinated. He was so full of colour and animation, his voice ran so easily into comic grotesque, he was so ready and so pleasant with everybody. Her own father had a rich fund of humour, but it was satiric. This man's was different: soft, non-intellectual, warm, a kind of gambolling.

She herself was opposite. She had a curious, receptive mind which found much pleasure and amusement in listening to other folk. She was clever in leading folk to talk. She loved ideas, and was considered very intellectual. What she liked most of all was an argument on religion or philosophy or politics with some educated man. This she did not often enjoy. So she always had people tell her about themselves, finding her pleasure so.

16

In her person she was rather small and delicate, with a large brow, and dropping bunches of brown silk curls. Her blue eyes were very straight, honest, and searching. She had the beautiful hands of the Coppards. Her dress was always subdued. She wore dark blue silk, with a peculiar silver chain of silver scallops. This, and a heavy brooch of twisted gold, was her only ornament. She was still perfectly intact, deeply religious, and full of beautiful candour.

Walter Morel seemed melted away before her. She was to the miner that thing of mystery and fascination, a lady. When she spoke to him, it was with a southern pronounciation and a purity of English which thrilled him to hear. She watched him. He danced well, as if it were natural and joyous in him to dance. His grandfather was a French refugee who had married an English barmaid—if it had been a marriage. Gertrude Coppard watched the young miner as he danced, a certain subtle exultation like glamour in his movement, and his face the flower of his body, ruddy, with tumbled black hair, and laughing alike whatever partner he bowed above. She thought him rather wonderful, never having met anyone like him. Her father was to her the type of all men. And George Coppard, proud in his bearing, handsome, and rather bitter; who preferred theology in reading, and who drew near in sympathy only to one man, the Apostle Paul; who was harsh in government, and in familiarity ironic; who ignored all sensuous pleasure:—he was very different from the miner.

17

Gertrude herself was rather contemptuous of dancing; she had not the slightest inclination towards that accomplishment, and had never learned even a Roger de Coverley. She was puritan, like her father, high-minded, and really stern. Therefore the dusky, golden softness of this man's sensuous flame of life, that flowed off his flesh like the flame from a candle, not baffled and gripped into incandescence by thought and spirit as her life was, seemed to her something wonderful, beyond her.

He came and bowed above her. A warmth radiated through her as if she had drunk wine.

"Now do come and have this one wi' me," he said caressively. "It's easy, you know. I'm pining to see you dance."

She had told him before she could not dance. She glanced at his humility and smiled. Her smile was very beautiful. It moved the man so that he forgot everything.

"No, I won't dance," she said softly. Her words came clean and ringing.

Not knowing what he was doing—he often did the right thing by instinct—he sat beside her, inclining reverentially.

"But you mustn't miss your dance," she reproved.

"Nay, I don't want to dance that—it's not one as I care about."

"Yet you invited me to it."

He laughed very heartily at this.

"I never thought o' that. Tha'rt not long in taking the curl out of me."

It was her turn to laugh quickly.

"You don't look as if you'd come much uncurled," she said.

"I'm like a pig's tail, I curl because I canna help it," he laughed, rather boisterously.

"And you are a miner!" she exclaimed in surprise.

"Yes. I went down when I was ten."

She looked at him in wondering dismay.

"When you were ten! And wasn't it very hard?" she asked.

"You soon get used to it. You live like th' mice, an' you pop out at night to see what's going on."

"It makes me feel blind," she frowned.

"Like a moudiwarp!" he laughed. "Yi, an' there's some chaps as does go round like moudiwarps." He thrust his face forward in the blind, snout-like way of a mole, seeming to sniff and peer for direction. "They dun though!" he protested naïvely. "Tha niver seed such a way they get in. But tha mun let me ta'e thee down some time, an' tha can see for thysen."

She looked at him, startled. This was a new tract of life suddenly opened before her. She realised the life of the miners, hundreds of them toiling below earth and coming up at evening. He seemed to her noble. He risked his life daily, and with gaiety. She looked at him, with a touch of appeal in her pure humility.

"Shouldn't ter like it?" he asked tenderly. " 'Appen not, it 'ud dirty thee."

She had never been "thee'd" and "thou'd" before.

The next Christmas they were married, and for three months she was perfectly happy: for six months she was very happy.

He had signed the pledge, and wore the blue ribbon of a tee-totaller: he was nothing if not showy. They lived, she thought, in his own house. It was small, but convenient enough, and quite nicely furnished, with solid, worthy stuff that suited her honest soul. The women, her neighbours, were rather foreign to her, and Morel's mother and sisters were apt to sneer at her ladylike ways. But she could perfectly well live by herself, so long as she had her husband close.

Sometimes, when she herself wearied of love-talk, she tried to open her heart seriously to him. She saw him listen deferentially, but without understanding. This killed her efforts at a finer intimacy, and she had flashes of fear. Sometimes he was restless of an evening: it was not enough for him just to be near her, she realised. She was glad when he set himself to little jobs.

He was a remarkably handy man—could make or mend anything. So she would say:

"I do like that coal-rake of your mother's—it is small and natty."

"Does ter, my wench? Well, I made that, so I can make thee one!"

"What! why, it's a steel one!"

"An' what if it is! Tha s'lt ha'e one very similar, if not exactly same."

She did not mind the mess, nor the hammering and noise. He was busy and happy.

But in the seventh month, when she was brushing his Sunday coat, she felt papers in the breast pocket, and, seized with a sudden curiosity, took them out to read. He very rarely wore the frock-coat he was married in: and it had not occurred to her before to feel curious concerning the papers. They were the bills of the household furniture, still unpaid.

"Look here," she said at night, after he was washed and had had his dinner. "I found these in the pocket of your wedding-coat. Haven't you settled the bills yet?"

"No. I haven't had a chance."

"But you told me all was paid. I had better go into Nottingham on Saturday and settle them. I don't like sitting on another man's chairs and eating from an unpaid table."

He did not answer.

"I can have your bank-book, can't I?"

"Tha can ha'e it, for what good it'll be to thee."

"I thought——" she began. He had told her he had a good bit of money left over. But she realised it was no use asking questions. She sat rigid with bitterness and indignation.

The next day she went down to see his mother.

"Didn't you buy the furniture for Walter?" she asked.

21

"Yes, I did," tartly retorted the elder woman.

"And how much did he give you to pay for it?"

The elder woman was stung with fine indignation.

"Eighty pound, if you're so keen on knowin'," she replied.

"Eighty pounds! But there are forty-two pounds still owing!"

"I can't help that."

"But where has it all gone?"

"You'll find all the papers, I think, if you look—beside ten pound as he owed me, an' six pound as the wedding cost down here."

"Six pounds!" echoed Gertrude Morel. It seemed to her monstrous that, after her own father had paid so heavily for her wedding, six pounds more should have been squandered in eating and drinking at Walter's parents' house, at his expense.

"And how much has he sunk in his houses?" she asked.

"His houses—which houses?"

Gertrude Morel went white to the lips. He had told her the house he lived in, and the next one, was his own.

"I thought the house we live in——" she began.

"They're my houses, those two," said the mother-in-law. "And not clear either. It's as much as I can do to keep the mortgage interest paid."

Gertrude sat white and silent. She was her father now.

"Then we ought to be paying you rent," she said coldly.

22

"Walter is paying me rent," replied the mother.

"And what rent?" asked Gertrude.

"Six and six a week," retorted the mother.

It was more than the house was worth. Gertrude held her head erect, looked straight before her.

"It is lucky to be you," said the elder woman, bitingly, "to have a husband as takes all the worry of the money, and leaves you a free hand."

The young wife was silent.

She said very little to her husband, but her manner had changed towards him. Something in her proud, honourable soul had crystallised out hard as rock.

When October came in, she thought only of Christmas. Two years ago, at Christmas, she had met him. Last Christmas she had married him. This Christmas she would bear him a child.

"You don't dance yourself, do you, missis?" asked her nearest neighbour, in October, when there was great talk of opening a dancing-class over the Brick and Tile Inn at Bestwood.

"No—I never had the least inclination to," Mrs. Morel replied.

"Fancy! An' how funny as you should ha' married your Mester. You know he's quite a famous one for dancing."

"I didn't know he was famous," laughed Mrs. Morel.

"Yea, he is though! Why, he ran that dancing-class in the Miners' Arms club-room for over five year."

"Did he?"

"Yes, he did." The other woman was defiant. "An' it was thronged every Tuesday, and Thursday, an' Sat'day—an' there *was* carryin's-on, accordin' to all accounts."

This kind of thing was gall and bitterness to Mrs. Morel, and she had a fair share of it. The women did not spare her, at first; for she was superior, though she could not help it.

He began to be rather late in coming home.

"They're working very late now, aren't they?" she said to her washer-woman.

"No later than they allers do, I don't think. But they stop to have their pint at Ellen's, an' they get talkin', an' there you are! Dinner stone cold—an' it serves 'em right."

"But Mr. Morel does not take any drink."

The woman dropped the clothes, looked at Mrs. Morel, then went on with her work, saying nothing.

Gertrude Morel was very ill when the boy was born. Morel was good to her, as good as gold. But she felt very lonely, miles away from her own people. She felt lonely with him now, and his presence only made it more intense.

The boy was small and frail at first, but he came on quickly. He was a beautiful child, with dark gold ringlets, and dark-blue eyes which changed gradually to a clear grey. His mother loved him passionately. He came just when her own bitterness of disillusion was hardest to bear; when her faith in life was shaken, and her soul felt dreary and lonely. She

24

made much of the child, and the father was jealous.

At last Mrs. Morel despised her husband. She turned to the child; she turned from the father. He had begun to neglect her; the novelty of his own home was gone. He had no grit, she said bitterly to herself. What he felt just at the minute, that was all to him. He could not abide by anything. There was nothing at the back of all his show.

There began a battle between the husband and wife—a fearful, bloody battle that ended only with the death of one. She fought to make him undertake his own responsibilities, to make him fulfil his obligations. But he was too different from her. His nature was purely sensuous, and she strove to make him moral, religious. She tried to force him to face things. He could not endure it—it drove him out of his mind.

While the baby was still tiny, the father's temper had become so irritable that it was not to be trusted. The child had only to give a little trouble when the man began to bully. A little more, and the hard hands of the collier hit the baby. Then Mrs. Morel loathed her husband, loathed him for days; and he went out and drank; and she cared very little what he did. Only, on his return, she scathed him with her satire.

The estrangement between them caused him, knowingly or unknowingly, grossly to offend her where he would not have done.

William was only one year old, and his mother was proud of him, he was so pretty. She was not well off now, but her sisters kept the boy in clothes. Then, with his little white hat curled with an ostrich feather, and his white coat, he was a joy to her, the twining wisps of hair clustering round his head. Mrs. Morel lay listening, one Sunday morning, to the chatter of the father and child downstairs. Then she dozed off. When she came downstairs, a great fire glowed in the grate, the room was hot, the breakfast was roughly laid, and seated in his arm-chair, against the chimney-piece, sat Morel, rather timid; and standing between his legs, the child—cropped like a sheep, with such an odd round poll—looking wondering at her; and on a newspaper spread out upon the hearthrug, a myriad of crescent-shaped curls, like the petals of a marigold scattered in the reddening firelight.

Mrs. Morel stood still. It was her first baby. She went very white, and was unable to speak.

"What dost think o' 'im?" Morel laughed uneasily.

She gripped her two fists, lifted them, and came forward. Morel shrank back.

"I could kill you, I could!" she said. She choked with rage, her two fists uplifted.

"Yer non want ter make a wench on 'im," Morel said, in a frightened tone, bending his head to shield his eyes from hers. His attempt at laughter had vanished.

The mother looked down at the jagged, close-clipped head of her child. She put her hands on his hair, and stroked and fondled his head.

"Oh—my boy!" she faltered. Her lip trembled,

26

her face broke, and, snatching up the child, she buried her face in his shoulder and cried painfully. She was one of those women who cannot cry; whom it hurts as it hurts a man. It was like ripping something out of her, her sobbing.

Morel sat with his elbows on his knees, his hands gripped together till the knuckles were white. He gazed in the fire, feeling almost stunned, as if he could not breathe.

Presently she came to an end, soothed the child and cleared away the breakfast-table. She left the newspaper, littered with curls, spread upon the hearth-rug. At last her husband gathered it up and put it at the back of the fire. She went about her work with closed mouth and very quiet. Morel was subdued. He crept about wretchedly, and his meals were a misery that day. She spoke to him civilly, and never alluded to what he had done. But he felt something final had happened.

Afterwards she said she had been silly, that the boy's hair would have had to be cut, sooner or later. In the end, she even brought herself to say to her husband it was just as well he had played barber when he did. But she knew, and Morel knew, that that act had caused something momentous to take place in her soul. She remembered the scene all her life, as one in which she had suffered the most intensely.

This act of masculine clumsiness was the spear through the side of her love for Morel. Before, while she had striven against him bitterly, she had fretted after him, as if he had gone astray from her. Now she ceased to fret for his love: he was an outsider to her. This made life much more bearable.

Nevertheless, she still continued to strive with him. She still had her high moral sense, inherited from generations of Puritans. It was now a religious instinct, and she was almost a fanatic with him, because she loved him, or had loved him. If he sinned, she tortured him. If he drank, and lied, was often a poltroon, sometimes a knave, she wielded the lash unmercifully.

The pity was, she was too much his opposite. She could not be content with the little he might be; she would have him the much that he ought to be. So, in seeking to make him nobler than he could be, she destroyed him. She injured and hurt and scarred herself, but she lost none of her worth. She also had the children.

He drank rather heavily, though not more than many miners, and always beer, so that whilst his health was affected, it was never injured. The weekend was his chief carouse. He sat in the Miners' Arms until turning-out time every Friday, every Saturday, and every Sunday evening. On Monday and Tuesday he had to get up and reluctantly leave towards ten o'clock. Sometimes he stayed at home on Wednesday and Thursday evenings, or was only out for an hour. He practically never had to miss work owing to his drinking.

But although he was very steady at work, his wages fell off. He was blab-mouthed, a tonguewagger. Authority was hateful to him, therefore he could only abuse the pit-managers. He would say, in the Palmerston:

"Th' gaffer come down to our stall this morning, an' 'e says, 'You know, Walter, this 'ere'll not do. What about these props?' An' I says to him, 'Why, what art talkin' about? What d'st mean about th' props?' 'It'll never do, this 'ere,' 'e says. 'You'll be havin' th' roof in, one o' these days.' An' I says, 'Tha'd better stan' on a bit o' clunch, then, an' hold it up wi' thy 'ead.' So 'e wor that mad, 'e cossed an' 'e swore, an' t'other chaps they did laugh." Morel was a good mimic. He imitated the manager's fat, squeaky voice, with its attempt at good English.

" 'I shan't have it, Walter. Who knows more about it, me or you?' So I says, 'I've niver fun out how much tha' knows, Alfred. It'll 'appen carry thee ter bed an' back.' "

So Morel would go on to the amusement of his boon companions. And some of this would be true. The pit-manager was not an educated man. He had been a boy along with Morel, so that, while the two disliked each other, they more or less took each other for granted. But Alfred Charlesworth did not forgive the butty these public-house sayings. Consequently, although Morel was a good miner, sometimes earning as much as five pounds a week when he married, he came gradually to have worse and worse stalls, where the coal was thin, and hard to get, and unprofitable.

Also, in summer the pits are slack. Often, on

29

bright sunny mornings, the men are seen trooping home again at ten, eleven, or twelve o'clock. No empty trucks stand at the pit-mouth. The women on the hillside look across as they shake the hearth-rug against the fence, and count the wagons the engine is taking along the line up the valley. And the children, as they come from school at dinner-time, looking down the fields and seeing the wheels on the headstocks standing, say:

"Minton's knocked off. My dad'll be at home."

And there is a sort of shadow over all, women and children and men, because money will be short at the end of the week.

Morel was supposed to give his wife thirty shillings a week, to provide everything—rent, food, clothes, clubs, insurance, doctors. Occasionally, if he were flush, he gave her thirty-five. But these occasions by no means balanced those when he gave her twenty-five. In winter, with a decent stall, the miner might earn fifty or fifty-five shillings a week. Then he was happy. On Friday night, Saturday, and Sunday, he spent royally, getting rid of his sovereign or thereabouts. And out of so much, he scarcely spared the children an extra penny or bought them a pound of apples. It all went in drink. In the bad times, matters were more worrying, but he was not so often drunk, so that Mrs. Morel used to say:

"I'm not sure I wouldn't rather be short, for when he's flush, there isn't a minute of peace."

If he earned forty shillings he kept ten; from

thirty-five he kept five; from thirty-two he kept four; from twenty-eight he kept three; from twenty-four he kept two; from twenty he kept one-and-six; from eighteen he kept a shilling; from sixteen he kept sixpence. He never saved a penny, and he gave his wife no opportunity of saving; instead, she had occasionally to pay his debts; not public-house debts, for those never were passed on to the women, but debts when he had bought a canary, or a fancy walking-stick.

At the wakes time Morel was working badly, and Mrs. Morel was trying to save against her confinement. So it galled her bitterly to think he should be out taking his pleasure and spending money, whilst she remained at home, harassed. There were two days' holiday. On the Tuesday morning Morel rose early. He was in good spirits. Quite early, before six o'clock, she heard him whistling away to himself downstairs. He had a pleasant way of whistling, lively and musical. He nearly always whistled hymns. He had been a choir-boy with a beautiful voice, and had taken solos in Southwell cathedral. His morning whistling alone betrayed it.

His wife lay listening to him tinkering away in the garden, his whistling ringing out as he sawed and hammered away. It always gave her a sense of warmth and peace to hear him thus as she lay in bed, the children not yet awake, in the bright early morning, happy in his man's fashion.

At nine o'clock, while the children with bare legs and feet were sitting playing on the sofa, and the mother was washing up, he came in from his carpentry, his sleeves rolled up, his waistcoat hanging open. He was still a good-looking man, with black, wavy hair, and a large black moustache. His face was perhaps too much inflamed, and there was about him a look almost of peevishness. But now he was jolly. He went straight to the sink where his wife was washing up.

"What, are thee there!" he said boisterously. "Sluthe off an' let me wesh mysen."

"You may wait till I've finished," said his wife.

"Oh, mun I? An' what if I shonna?"

This good-humoured threat amused Mrs. Morel.

"Then you can go and wash yourself in the soft-water tub."

"Ha! I can' an' a', tha mucky little 'ussy."

With which he stood watching her a moment, then went away to wait for her.

When he chose he could still make himself again a real gallant. Usually he preferred to go out with a scarf round his neck. Now, however, he made a toilet. There seemed so much gusto in the way he puffed and swilled as he washed himself, so much alacrity with which he hurried to the mirror in the kitchen, and, bending because it was too low for him, scrupulously parted his wet black hair, that it irritated Mrs. Morel. He put on a turn-down collar, a black bow, and wore his Sunday tail-coat. As such, he looked spruce, and what his clothes would not do, his instinct for making the most of his good looks would.

At half-past nine Jerry Purdy came to call for his pal. Jerry was Morel's bosom friend, and Mrs. Morel disliked him. He was a tall, thin man, with a rather foxy face, the kind of face that seems to lack eyelashes. He walked with a stiff, brittle dignity, as if his head were on a wooden spring. His nature was cold and shrewd. Generous where he intended to be generous, he seemed to be very fond of Morel, and more or less to take charge of him.

Mrs. Morel hated him. She had known his wife, who had died of consumption, and who had, at the end, conceived such a violent dislike of her husband, that if he came into her room it caused her hæmorrhage. None of which Jerry had seemed to mind. And now his eldest daughter, a girl of fifteen, kept a poor house for him, and looked after the two younger children.

"A mean, wizzen-hearted stick!" Mrs. Morel said of him.

"I've never known Jerry mean in *my* life," protested Morel. "A opener-handed and more freer chap you couldn't find anywhere, accordin' to my knowledge."

"Open-handed to you," retorted Mrs. Morel. "But his fist is shut tight enough to his children, poor things."

"Poor things! And what for are they poor things, I should like to know."

But Mrs. Morel would not be appeased on Jerry's score.

The subject of argument was seen, craning his

thin neck over the scullery curtain. He caught Mrs. Morel's eye.

"Mornin', missis! Mester in?"

"Yes—he is."

Jerry entered unasked, and stood by the kitchen doorway. He was not invited to sit down, but stood there, coolly asserting the rights of men and husbands.

"A nice day," he said to Mrs. Morel.

"Yes."

"Grand out this morning—grand for a walk."

"Do you mean *you're* going for a walk?" she asked.

"Yes. We mean walkin' to Nottingham," he replied.

"H'm!"

The two men greeted each other, both glad: Jerry, however, full of assurance, Morel rather subdued, afraid to seem too jubilant in presence of his wife. But he laced his boots quickly, with spirit. They were going for a ten-mile walk across the fields to Nottingham. Climbing the hillside from the Bottoms, they mounted gaily into the morning. At the Moon and Stars they had their first drink, then on to the Old Spot. Then a long five miles of drought to carry them into Bulwell to a glorious pint of bitter. But they stayed in a field with some haymakers whose gallon bottle was full, so that, when they came in sight of the city, Morel was sleepy. The town spread upwards before them, smoking vaguely in the midday glare, fridging the crest away to the south with spires and factory bulks and chimneys.

In the last field Morel lay down under an oak tree and slept soundly for over an hour. When he rose to go forward he felt queer.

The two had dinner in the Meadows, with Jerry's sister, then repaired to the Punch Bowl, where they mixed in the excitement of pigeon racing. Morel never in his life played cards, considering them as having some occult, malevolent power—"the devil's pictures," he called them! But he was a master of skittles and of dominoes. He took a challenge from a Newark man, on skittles. All the men in the old, long bar took sides, betting either one way or the other. Morel took off his coat. Jerry held the hat containing the money. The men at the tables watched. Some stood with their mugs in their hands. Morel felt his big wooden ball carefully, then launched it. He played havoc among the nine-pins, and won half a crown, which restored him to solvency.

By seven o'clock the two were in good condition. They caught the 7.30 train home.

In the afternoon the Bottoms was intolerable. Every inhabitant remaining was out of doors. The women, in twos and threes, bareheaded and in white aprons, gossiped in the alley between the blocks. Men, having a rest between drinks, sat on their heels and talked. The place smelled stale; the slate roofs glistered in the arid heat.

Mrs. Morel took the little girl down to the brook in the meadows, which were not more than two hundred yards away. The water ran quickly over stones and broken pots. Mother and child leaned on the rail of the old sheep-bridge, watching. Up at the dipping-hole, at the other end of the meadow, Mrs. Morel could see the naked forms of boys flashing round the deep yellow water, or an occasional bright figure dart glittering over the blackish stagnant meadow. She knew William was at the dipping-hole, and it was the dread of her life lest he should get drowned. Annie played under the tall old hedge, picking up alder cones, that she called currants. The child required much attention, and the flies were teasing.

The children were put to bed at seven o'clock. Then she worked awhile.

When Walter Morel and Jerry arrived at Bestwood they felt a load off their minds; a railway journey no longer impended, so they could put the finishing touches to a glorious day. They entered the Nelson with the satisfaction of returned travellers.

The next day was a work-day, and the thought of it put a damper on the men's spirits. Most of them, moreover, had spent their money. Some were already rolling dismally home, to sleep in preparation for the morrow. Mrs. Morel, listening to their mournful singing, went indoors. Nine o'clock passed, and ten, and still "the pair" had not returned. On a doorstep somewhere a man was singing loudly, in a drawl: "Lead, kindly Light." Mrs. Morel was always indignant with the drunken men that they must sing that hymn when they got maudlin.

"As if 'Genevieve' weren't good enough," she said.

The kitchen was full of the scent of boiled herbs and hops. On the hob a large black saucepan steamed slowly. Mrs. Morel took a panchion, a great bowl of thick red earth, streamed a heap of white sugar into the bottom, and then, straining herself to the weight, was pouring in the liquor.

Just then Morel came in. He had been very jolly in the Nelson, but coming home had grown irritable. He had not quite got over the feeling of irritability and pain, after having slept on the ground when he was so hot; and a bad conscience afflicted him as he neared the house. He did not know he was angry. But when the garden gate resisted his attempts to open it, he kicked it and broke the latch. He entered just as Mrs. Morel was pouring the infusion of herbs out of the saucepan. Swaying slightly, he lurched against the table. The boiling liquor pitched. Mrs. Morel started back.

"Good gracious," she cried, "coming home in his drunkenness!"

"Comin' home in his what?" he snarled, his hat over his eye.

Suddenly her blood rose in a jet.

"Say you're *not* drunk!" she flashed.

She had put down her saucepan, and was stirring the sugar into the beer. He dropped his two hands heavily on the table, and thrust his face forwards at her.

" 'Say you're not drunk,' " he repeated. "Why,

nobody but a nasty little bitch like you 'ud 'ave such a thought."

He thrust his face forward at her.

"There's money to bezzle with, if there's money for nothing else."

"I've not spent a two-shillin' bit this day," he said.

"You don't get as drunk as a lord on nothing," she replied. "And," she cried, flashing into sudden fury, "if you've been sponging on your beloved Jerry, why, let him look after his children, for they need it."

"It's a lie, it's a lie. Shut your face, woman."

They were now at battle-pitch. Each forgot everything save the hatred of the other and the battle between them. She was fiery and furious as he. They went on till he called her a liar.

"No," she cried, starting up, scarce able to breathe. "Don't call me that—you, the most despicable liar that ever walked in shoe-leather." She forced the last words out of suffocated lungs.

"You're a liar!" he yelled, banging the table with his fist. "You're a liar, you're a liar."

She stiffened herself, with clenched fists.

"The house is filthy with you," she cried.

"Then get out on it—it's mine. Get out on it!" he shouted. "It's me as brings th' money whoam, not thee. It's my house, not thine. Then ger out on't—ger out on't!"

"And I would," she cried, suddenly shaken into tears of impotence. "Ah, wouldn't I, wouldn't I

38

have gone long ago, but for those children. Ay, haven't I repented not going years ago, when I'd only the one"—suddenly drying into rage. "Do you think it's for *you* I stop—do you think I'd stop one minute for *you*?"

"Go then," he shouted, beside himself. "Go!"

"No!" She faced round. "No," she cried loudly, "you shan't have it *all* your own way; you shan't do *all* you like. I've got those children to see to. My word," she laughed, "I should look well to leave them to you."

"Go," he cried thickly, lifting his fist. He was afraid of her. "Go!"

"I should be only too glad. I should laugh, laugh, my lord, if I could get away from you," she replied.

He came up to her, his red face, with its bloodshot eyes, thrust forward, and gripped her arms. She cried in fear of him, struggled to be free. Coming slightly to himself, panting, he pushed her roughly to the outer door, and thrust her forth, slotting the bolt behind her with a bang. Then he went back into the kitchen, dropped into his arm-chair, his head, bursting full of blood, sinking between his knees. Thus he dipped gradually into a stupor, from exhaustion and intoxication.

The moon was high and magnificent in the August night. Mrs. Morel, seared with passion, shivered to find herself out there in a great white light, that fell cold on her, and gave a shock to her inflamed soul. She stood for a few moments helplessly staring at the glistening great rhubarb leaves near the door. Then she got the air into her breast. She walked down the garden path, trembling in every limb, while the child boiled within her. For a while she could not control her consciousness; mechanically she went over the last scene, then over it again, certain phrases, certain moments coming each time like a brand red-hot down on her soul; and each time she enacted again the past hour, each time the brand came down at the same points, till the mark was burnt in, and the pain burnt out, and at last she came to herself. She must have been half an hour in this delirious condition. Then the presence of the night came again to her. She glanced round in fear. She had wandered to the side garden, where she was walking up and down the path beside the currant bushes under the long wall. The garden was a narrow strip, bounded from the road, that cut transversely between the blocks, by a thick thorn hedge.

She hurried out of the side garden to the front, where she could stand as if in an immense gulf of white light, the moon streaming high in face of her, the moonlight standing up from the hills in front, and filling the valley where the Bottoms crouched, almost blindingly. There, panting and half weeping in reaction from the stress, she murmured to herself over and over again: "The nuisance! the nuisance!"

She became aware of something about her. With an effort she roused herself to see what it was that penetrated her consciousness. The tall white lilies were reeling in the moonlight, and the air was

40

charged with their perfume, as with a presence. Mrs. Morel gasped slightly in fear. She touched the big, pallid flowers on their petals, then shivered. They seemed to be stretching in the moonlight. She put her hand into one white bin: the gold scarcely showed on her fingers by moonlight. She bent down to look at the binful of yellow pollen; but it only appeared dusky. Then she drank a deep draught of the scent. It almost made her dizzy.

Mrs. Morel leaned on the garden gate, looking out, and she lost herself awhile. She did not know what she thought. Except for a slight feeling of sickness, and her consciousness in the child, herself melted out like scent into the shiny, pale air. After a time the child, too, melted with her in the mixing-pot of moonlight, and she rested with the hills and lilies and houses, all swum together in a kind of swoon.

When she came to herself she was tired for sleep. Languidly she looked about her; the clumps of white phlox seemed like bushes spread with linen; a moth ricochetted over them, and right across the garden. Following it with her eye roused her. A few whiffs of the raw, strong scent of phlox invigorated her. She passed along the path, hesitating at the white rose-bush. It smelled sweet and simple. She touched the white ruffles of the roses. Their fresh scent and cool, soft leaves reminded her of the morning-time and sunshine. She was very fond of them. But she was tired, and wanted to sleep. In the mysterious out-of-doors she felt forlorn.

41

There was no noise anywhere. Evidently the children had not been wakened, or had gone to sleep again. A train, three miles away, roared across the valley. The night was very large, and very strange, stretching its hoary distances infinitely. And out of the silver-grey fog of darkness came sounds vague and hoarse: a corncrake not far off, sound of a train like a sigh, and distant shouts of men.

Her quietened heart beginning to beat quickly again, she hurried down the side garden to the back of the house. Softly she lifted the latch; the door was still bolted, and hard against her. She rapped gently, waited, then rapped again. She must not rouse the children, nor the neighbours. He must be asleep, and he would not wake easily. Her heart began to burn to be indoors. She clung to the door-handle. Now it was cold; she would take a chill, and in her present condition!

Putting her apron over her head and her arms, she hurried again to the side garden, to the window of the kitchen. Leaning on the sill, she could just see, under the blind, her husband's arms spread out on the table, and his black head on the board. He was sleeping with his face lying on the table. Something in his attitude made her feel tired of things. The lamp was burning smokily; she could tell by the copper colour of the light. She tapped at the window more and more noisily. Almost it seemed as if the glass would break. Still he did not wake up.

After vain efforts, she began to shiver, partly from contact with the stone, and from exhaustion.

Fearful always for the unborn child, she wondered what she could do for warmth. She went down to the coal-house, where there was an old hearth-rug she had carried out for the rag-man the day before. This she wrapped over her shoulders. It was warm, if grimy. Then she walked up and down the garden path, peeping every now and then under the blind, knocking, and telling herself that in the end the very strain of his position must waken him.

At last, after about an hour, she rapped long and low at the window. Gradually the sound penetrated to him. When, in despair, she had ceased to tap, she saw him stir, then lift his face blindly. The labouring of his heart hurt him into consciousness. She rapped imperatively at the window. He started awake. Instantly she saw his fists set and his eyes glare. He had not a grain of physical fear. If it had been twenty burglars, he would have gone blindly for them. He glared round, bewildered, but prepared to fight.

"Open the door, Walter," she said coldly.

His hands relaxed. It dawned on him what he had done. His head dropped, sullen and dogged. She saw him hurry to the door, heard the bolt chock. He tried the latch. It opened—and there stood the silver-grey night, fearful to him, after the tawny light of the lamp. He hurried back.

When Mrs. Morel entered, she saw him almost running through the door to the stairs. He had ripped his collar off his neck in his haste to be gone ere she came in, and there it lay with bursten button-holes. It made her angry.

She warmed and soothed herself. In her weariness forgetting everything, she moved about at the little tasks that remained to be done, set his breakfast, rinsed his pit-bottle, put his pit-clothes on the hearth to warm, set his pit-boots beside them, put him out a clean scarf and snap-bag and two apples, raked the fire, and went to bed. He was already dead asleep. His narrow black eyebrows were drawn up in a sort of peevish misery into his forehead while his cheeks' down-strokes, and his sulky mouth, seemed to be saying: "I don't care who you are nor what you are, I *shall* have my own way."

Mrs. Morel knew him too well to look at him. As she unfastened her brooch at the mirror, she smiled faintly to see her face all smeared with the yellow dust of lilies. She brushed it off, and at last lay down. For some time her mind continued snapping and jetting sparks, but she was asleep before her husband awoke from the first sleep of his drunkenness.

# 2

## THE BIRTH OF PAUL,
## AND ANOTHER BATTLE

AFTER such a scene as the last, Walter Morel was for some days abashed and ashamed, but he soon regained his old bullying indifference. Yet there was a slight shrinking, a diminishing in his assurance. Physically even, he shrank, and his fine full presence waned. He never grew in the least stout, so that, as he sank from his erect, assertive bearing, his physique seemed to contract along with his pride and moral strength.

But now he realised how hard it was for his wife to drag about at her work, and, his sympathy quickened by penitence, hastened forward with his help. He came straight home from the pit, and stayed in at evening till Friday, and then he could not remain at home. But he was back again by ten o'clock, almost quite sober.

He always made his own breakfast. Being a man who rose early and had plenty of time he did not, as some miners do, drag his wife out of bed at six o'clock. At five, sometimes earlier, he woke, got straight out of bed, and went downstairs. When she could not sleep, his wife lay waiting for this time, as for a period of peace. The only real rest seemed to be when he was out of the house.

He went downstairs in his shirt and then struggled into his pit-trousers, which were left on the hearth to warm all night. There was always a fire, because Mrs. Morel raked. And the first sound in the house was the bang, bang of the poker against the raker, as Morel smashed the remainder of the coal to make the kettle, which was filled and left on the hob, finally boil. His cup and knife and fork, all he wanted except just the food, was laid ready on the table on a newspaper. Then he got his breakfast, made the tea, packed the bottom of the doors with rugs to shut out the draught, piled a big fire, and sat down to an hour of joy. He toasted his bacon on a fork and caught the drops of fat on his bread; then he put the rasher on his thick slice of bread, and cut off chunks with a clasp-knife, poured his tea into his saucer, and was happy. With his family about, meals were never so pleasant. He loathed a fork: it is a modern introduction which has still scarcely reached common people. What Morel preferred was a clasp-knife. Then, in solitude, he ate and drank, often sitting, in cold weather, on a little stool with his back to the warm chimney-piece, his food on the fender, his cup on the hearth. And then he read the last night's newspaper—what of it he could—spelling it over laboriously. He preferred to keep the blinds down and the candle lit even when it was daylight; it was the habit of the mine.

At a quarter to six he rose, cut two thick slices of

46

bread and butter, and put them in the white calico snap-bag. He filled his tin bottle with tea. Cold tea without milk or sugar was the drink he preferred for the pit. Then he pulled off his shirt, and put on his pit-singlet, a vest of thick flannel cut low round the neck, and with short sleeves like a chemise.

Then he went upstairs to his wife with a cup of tea because she was ill, and because it occurred to him.

"I've brought thee a cup o' tea, lass," he said.

"Well, you needn't, for you know I don't like it," she replied.

"Drink it up; it'll pop thee off to sleep again."

She accepted the tea. It pleased him to see her take it and sip it.

"I'll back my life there's no sugar in," she said.

"Yi—there's one big 'un," he replied, injured.

"It's a wonder," she said, sipping again.

She had a winsome face when her hair was loose. He loved her to grumble at him in this manner. He looked at her again, and went, without any sort of leave-taking. He never took more than two slices of bread and butter to eat in the pit, so an apple or an orange was a treat to him. He always liked it when she put one out for him. He tied a scarf round his neck, put on his great, heavy boots, his coat, with the big pocket, that carried his snap-bag and his bottle of tea, and went forth into the fresh morning air, closing, without locking, the door behind him. He loved the early morning, and the walk across the fields. So he appeared at the pit-top, often with a

47

stalk from the hedge between his teeth, which he chewed all day to keep his mouth moist, down the mine, feeling quite as happy as when he was in the field.

Later, when the time for the baby grew nearer, he would bustle round in his slovenly fashion, poking out the ashes, rubbing the fireplace, sweeping the house before he went to work. Then, feeling very self-righteous, he went upstairs.

"Now I'm cleaned up for thee: tha's no 'casions ter stir a peg all day, but sit and read thy books."

Which made her laugh, in spite of her indignation.

"And the dinner cooks itself?" she answered.

"Eh, I know nowt about th' dinner."

"You'd know if there weren't any."

"Ay, 'appen so," he answered, departing.

When she got downstairs, she would find the house tidy, but dirty. She could not rest until she had thoroughly cleaned; so she went down to the ash-pit with her dust-pan. Mrs. Kirk, spying her, would contrive to have to go to her own coal-place at that minute. Then, across the wooden fence, she would call:

"So you keep wagging on, then?"

"Ay," answered Mrs. Morel deprecatingly. "There's nothing else for it."

"Have you seen Hose?" called a very small woman from across the road. It was Mrs. Anthony, a black-haired, strange little body, who always wore a brown velvet dress, tight-fitting.

"I haven't," said Mrs. Morel.

"Eh, I wish he'd come. I've got a copperful of clothes, an' I'm sure I heered his bell."

"Hark! He's at the end."

The two women looked down the alley. At the end of the Bottoms a man stood in a sort of old-fashioned trap, bending over bundles of cream-coloured stuff; while a cluster of women held up their arms to him, some with bundles. Mrs. Anthony herself had a heap of creamy, undyed stockings hanging over her arm.

"I've done ten dozen this week," she said proudly to Mrs. Morel.

"T-t-t!" went the other. "I don't know how you can find time."

"Eh!" said Mrs. Anthony. "You can find time if you make time."

"I don't know how you do it," said Mrs. Morel. "And how much shall you get for those many?"

"Tuppence-ha'penny a dozen," replied the other.

"Well," said Mrs. Morel. "I'd starve before I'd sit down and seam twenty-four stockings for twopence ha'penny."

"Oh, I don't know," said Mrs. Anthony. "You can rip along with 'em."

Hose was coming along, ringing his bell. Women were waiting at the yard-ends with their seamed stockings hanging over their arms. The man, a common fellow, made jokes with them, tried to swindle them, and bullied them. Mrs. Morel went up her yard disdainfully.

It was an understood thing that if one woman wanted her neighbour, she should put the poker in the fire and bang at the back of the fireplace, which, as the fires were back to back, would make a great noise in the adjoining house. One morning Mrs. Kirk, mixing a pudding, nearly started out of her skin as she heard the thud, thud, in her grate. With her hands all floury, she rushed to the fence.

"Did you knock, Mrs. Morel?"

"If you wouldn't mind, Mrs. Kirk."

Mrs. Kirk climbed on to her copper, got over the wall on to Mrs. Morel's copper, and ran in to her neighbour.

"Eh, dear, how are you feeling?" she cried in concern.

"You might fetch Mrs. Bower," said Mrs. Morel.

Mrs. Kirk went into the yard, lifted up her strong, shrill voice, and called:

"Ag-gie—Ag-gie!"

The sound was heard from one end of the Bottoms to the other. At last Aggie came running up, and was sent for Mrs. Bower, whilst Mrs. Kirk left her pudding and stayed with her neighbour.

Mrs. Morel went to bed. Mrs. Kirk had Annie and William for dinner. Mrs. Bower, fat and waddling, bossed the house.

"Hash some cold meat up for the master's dinner, and make him an apple-charlotte pudding," said Mrs. Morel.

"He may go without pudding *this* day," said Mrs. Bower.

50

Morel was not as a rule one of the first to appear at the bottom of the pit, ready to come up. Some men were there before four o'clock, when the whistle blew loose-all; but Morel, whose stall, a poor one, was at this time about a mile and a half away from the bottom, worked usually till the first mate stopped, then he finished also. This day, however, the miner was sick of the work. At two o'clock he looked at his watch, by the light of the green candle—he was in a safe working—and again at half-past two. He was hewing at a piece of rock that was in the way for the next day's work. As he sat on his heels, or kneeled, giving hard blows with his pick, "Uszza—uszza!" he went.

"Shall ter finish, Sorry?"* cried Barker, his fellow butty.

"Finish? Niver while the world stands!" growled Morel.

And he went on striking. He was tired.

"It's a heart-breaking job," said Barker.

But Morel was too exasperated, at the end of his tether, to answer. Still he struck and hacked with all his might.

"Tha might as well leave it, Walter," said Barker. "It'll do tomorrow, without thee hackin' thy guts out."

"I'll lay no b—— finger on this tomorrow, Isr'el!" cried Morel.

* "Sorry" is a common form of address. It is, perhaps, a corruption of "sirrah".

51

"Oh, well, if tha wunna, someb'dy else 'll ha'e to," said Israel.

Then Morel continued to strike.

"Hey-up there—*loose-a'*!" cried the men, leaving the next stall.

Morel continued to strike.

"Tha'll happen catch me up," said Barker, departing.

When he had gone, Morel, left alone, felt savage. He had not finished his job. He had overworked himself into a frenzy. Rising, wet with sweat, he threw his tool down, pulled on his coat, blew out his candle, took his lamp, and went. Down the main road the lights of the other men went swinging. There was a hollow sound of many voices. It was a long, heavy tramp underground.

He sat at the bottom of the pit, where the great drops of water fell plash. Many colliers were waiting their turns to go up, talking noisily. Morel gave his answers short and disagreeable.

"It's rainin', Sorry," said old Giles, who had had the news from the top.

Morel found one comfort. He had his old umbrella, which he loved, in the lamp cabin. At last he took his stand on the chair, and was at the top in a moment. Then he handed in his lamp and got his umbrella, which he had bought at an auction for one-and-six. He stood on the edge of the pit-bank for a moment, looking out over the fields; grey rain was falling. The trucks stood full of wet, bright coal. Water ran down the sides of the waggons, over the white "C.W. and Co.". Colliers, walking indifferent to the rain, were streaming down the line and up the field, a grey, dismal host. Morel put up his umbrella, and took pleasure from the peppering of the drops thereon.

All along the road to Bestwood the miners tramped, wet and grey and dirty, but their red mouths talking with animation. Morel also walked with a gang, but he said nothing. He frowned peevishly as he went. Many men passed into the Prince of Wales or into Ellen's. Morel, feeling sufficiently disagreeable to resist temptation, trudged along under the dripping trees that overhung the park wall, and down the mud of Greenhill Lane.

Mrs. Morel lay in bed, listening to the rain, and the feet of the colliers from Minton, their voices, and the bang, bang of the gates as they went through the stile up the field.

"There's some herb beer behind the pantry door," she said. "Th' master 'll want a drink, if he doesn't stop."

But he was late, so she concluded he had called for a drink, since it was raining. What did he care about the child or her?

She was very ill when her children were born.

"What is it?" she asked, feeling sick to death.

"A boy."

And she took consolation in that. The thought of being the mother of men was warming to her heart. She looked at the child. It had blue eyes, and a lot of fair hair, and was bonny. Her love came up hot, in

53

spite of everything. She had it in bed with her.

Morel, thinking nothing, dragged his way up the garden path, wearily and angrily. He closed his umbrella, and stood it in the sink; then he sluthered his heavy boots into the kitchen. Mrs. Bower appeared in the inner doorway.

"Well," she said, "she's about as bad as she can be. It's a boy childt."

The miner grunted, put his empty snap-bag and his tin bottle on the dresser, went back into the scullery and hung up his coat, then came and dropped into his chair.

"Han yer got a drink?" he asked.

The woman went into the pantry. There was heard the pop of a cork. She set the mug, with a little, disgusted rap, on the table before Morel. He drank, gasped, wiped his big moustache on the end of his scarf, drank, gasped, and lay back in his chair. The woman would not speak to him again. She set his dinner before him, and went upstairs.

"Was that the master?" asked Mrs. Morel.

"I've gave him his dinner," replied Mrs. Bower.

After he had sat with his arms on the table—he resented the fact that Mrs. Bower put no cloth on for him, and gave him a little plate, instead of a full-sized dinner-plate—he began to eat. The fact that his wife was ill, that he had another boy, was nothing to him at that moment. He was too tired; he wanted his dinner; he wanted to sit with his arms lying on the board; he did not like having Mrs. Bower about. The fire was too small to please him.

54

After he had finished his meal, he sat for twenty minutes; then he stoked up a big fire. Then, in his stockinged feet, he went reluctantly upstairs. It was a struggle to face his wife at this moment, and he was tired. His face was black, and smeared with sweat. His singlet had dried again, soaking the dirt in. He had a dirty woollen scarf round his throat. So he stood at the foot of the bed.

"Well, how are ter, then?" he asked.

"I s'll be all right," she answered.

"H'm!"

He stood at a loss what to say next. He was tired, and this bother was rather a nuisance to him, and he didn't quite know where he was.

"A lad, tha says," he stammered.

She turned down the sheet and showed the child.

"Bless him!" he murmured. Which made her laugh, because he blessed by rote—pretending paternal emotion, which he did not feel just then.

"Go now," she said.

"I will, my lass," he answered, turning away.

Dismissed, he wanted to kiss her, but he dared not. She half wanted him to kiss her, but could not bring herself to give any sign. She only breathed freely when he was gone out of the room again, leaving behind him a faint smell of pit-dirt.

Mrs. Morel had a visit every day from the Congregational clergyman. Mr. Heaton was young, and very poor. His wife had died at the birth of his first baby, so he remained alone in the manse. He was a Bachelor of Arts of Cambridge, very shy, and no

55

preacher. Mrs. Morel was fond of him, and he depended on her. For hours he talked to her, when she was well. He became the god-parent of the child.

Occasionally the minister stayed to tea with Mrs. Morel. Then she laid the cloth early, got out her best cups, with a little green rim, and hoped Morel would not come too soon; indeed, if he stayed for a pint, she would not mind this day. She had always two dinners to cook, because she believed children should have their chief meal at midday, whereas Morel needed his at five o'clock. So Mr. Heaton would hold the baby, whilst Mrs. Morel beat up a batter-pudding or peeled the potatoes, and he, watching her all the time, would discuss his next sermon. His ideas were quaint and fantastic. She brought him judiciously to earth. It was a discussion of the wedding at Cana.

"When He changed the water into wine at Cana," he said, "that is a symbol that the ordinary life, even the blood, of the married husband and wife, which had before been uninspired, like water, became filled with the Spirit, and was as wine, because, when love enters, the whole spiritual constitution of a man changes, is filled with the Holy Ghost, and almost his form is altered."

Mrs. Morel thought to herself:

"Yes, poor fellow, his young wife is dead; that is why he makes his love into the Holy Ghost."

They were halfway down their first cup of tea when they heard the sluther of pit-boots.

56

"Good gracious!" exclaimed Mrs. Morel, in spite of herself.

The minister looked rather scared. Morel entered. He was feeling rather savage. He nodded a "How d'yer do" to the clergyman, who rose to shake hands with him.

"Nay," said Morel, showing his hand, "look thee at it! Tha niver wants ter shake hands wi' a hand like that, does ter? There's too much pick-haft and shovel-dirt on it."

The minister flushed with confusion, and sat down again. Mrs. Morel rose, carried out the steaming saucepan. Morel took off his coat, dragged his armchair to table, and sat down heavily.

"Are you tired?" asked the clergyman.

"Tired? I ham that," replied Morel. "*You* don't know what it is to be tired, as *I'm* tired."

"No," replied the clergyman.

"Why, look yer 'ere," said the miner, showing the shoulders of his singlet. "It's a bit dry now, but it's wet as a clout with sweat even yet. Feel it."

"Goodness!" cried Mrs. Morel. "Mr. Heaton doesn't want to feel your nasty singlet."

The clergyman put out his hand gingerly.

"No, perhaps he doesn't," said Morel; "but it's all come out of me, whether or not. An' iv'ry day alike my singlet's wringin' wet. 'Aven't you got a drink, Missis, for a man when he comes home barkled up from the pit."

"You know you drank all the beer," said Mrs. Morel, pouring out his tea.

"An' was there no more to be got?" Turning to the clergyman—"A man gets that caked up wi' th' dust, you know,—that clogged up down a coal-mine, he *needs* a drink when he comes home."

"I am sure he does," said the clergyman.

"But it's ten to one if there's owt for him."

"There's water—and there's tea," said Mrs. Morel.

"Water! It's not water as'll clear his throat."

He poured out a saucerful of tea, blew it, and sucked it up through his great black moustache, sighing afterwards. Then he poured out another saucerful, and stood his cup on the table.

"My cloth!" said Mrs. Morel, putting it on a plate.

"A man as comes home as I do 's too tired to care about cloths," said Morel.

"Pity!" exclaimed his wife sarcastically.

The room was full of the smell of meat and vegetables and pit-clothes.

He leaned over to the minister, his great moustache thrust forward, his mouth very red in his black face.

"Mr. Heaton," he said, "a man as has been down the black hole all day, dingin' away at a coal-face, yi, a sight harder than that wall——"

"Needn't make a moan of it," put in Mrs. Morel.

She hated her husband because, whenever he had an audience, he whined and played for sympathy. William, sitting nursing the baby, hated him, with a boy's hatred for false sentiment, and for the stupid treatment of his mother. Annie had never liked him; she merely avoided him.

When the minister had gone, Mrs. Morel looked at her cloth.

"A fine mess!" she said.

"Dos't think I'm goin' to sit wi' my arms danglin', cos tha's got a parson for tea wi' thee?" he bawled.

They were both angry, but she said nothing. The baby began to cry, and Mrs. Morel, picking up a saucepan from the hearth, accidentally knocked Annie on the head, whereupon the girl began to whine, and Morel to shout at her. In the midst of this pandemonium, William looked up at the big glazed text over the mantelpiece and read distinctly:

"God Bless Our Home!"

Whereupon Mrs. Morel, trying to soothe the baby, jumped up, rushed at him, boxed his ears, saying:

"What are *you* putting in for?"

And then she sat down and laughed, till tears ran over her cheeks, while William kicked the stool he had been sitting on, and Morel growled:

"I canna see what there is so much to laugh at."

One evening, directly after the parson's visit, feeling unable to bear herself after another display from her husband, she took Annie and the baby and went out. Morel had kicked William, and the mother would never forgive him.

She went over the sheep-bridge and across a corner of the meadow to the cricket-ground. The meadows seemed one space of ripe, evening light, whispering with the distant mill-race. She sat on a seat under the alders in the cricket-ground, and fronted the evening. Before her, level and solid, spread the big green cricket-field, like the bed of a sea of light. Children played in the bluish shadow of the pavilion. Many rooks, high up, came cawing home across the softly-woven sky. They stooped in a long curve down into the golden glow, concentrating, cawing, wheeling, like black flakes on a slow vortex, over a tree clump that made a dark boss among the pasture.

A few gentlemen were practising, and Mrs. Morel could hear the chock of the ball, and the voices of men suddenly roused; could see the white forms of men shifting silently over the green, upon which already the under shadows were smouldering. Away at the grange, one side of the haystacks was lit up, the other sides blue-grey. A waggon of sheaves rocked small across the melting yellow light.

The sun was going down. Every open evening, the hills of Derbyshire were blazed over with red sunset. Mrs. Morel watched the sun sink from the glistening sky, leaving a soft flower-blue overhead, while the western space went red, as if all the fire had swum down there, leaving the bell cast flawless blue. The mountain-ash berries across the field stood fierily out from the dark leaves, for a moment. A few shocks of corn in a corner of the fallow stood up as if alive; she imagined them bowing; perhaps her son would be a Joseph. In the east, a mirrored sunset floated pink opposite the west's scarlet. The big haystacks on the hillside, that butted into the glare, went cold.

With Mrs. Morel it was one of those still moments when the small frets vanish, and the beauty of things stands out, and she had the peace and the strength to see herself. Now and again, a swallow cut close to her. Now and again, Annie came up with a handful of alder-currants. The baby was restless on his mother's knee, clambering with his hands at the light.

Mrs. Morel looked down at him. She had dreaded this baby like a catastrophe, because of her feeling for her husband. And now she felt strangely towards the infant. Her heart was heavy because of the child, almost as if it were unhealthy, or malformed. Yet it seemed quite well. But she noticed the peculiar knitting of the baby's brows, and the peculiar heaviness of its eyes, as if it were trying to understand something that was pain. She felt, when she looked at her child's dark, brooding pupils, as if a burden were on her heart.

"He looks as if he was thinking about something—quite sorrowful," said Mrs. Kirk.

Suddenly, looking at him, the heavy feeling at the mother's heart melted into passionate grief. She bowed over him, and a few tears shook swiftly out of her very heart. The baby lifted his fingers.

"My lamb!" she cried softly.

61

And at that moment she felt, in some far inner place of her soul, that she and her husband were guilty.

The baby was looking up at her. It had blue eyes like her own, but its look was heavy, steady, as if it had realised something that had stunned some point of its soul.

In her arms lay the delicate baby. Its deep blue eyes, always looking up at her unblinking, seemed to draw her innermost thoughts out of her. She no longer loved her husband; she had not wanted this child to come, and there it lay in her arms and pulled at her heart. She felt as if the navel string that had connected its frail little body with hers had not been broken. A wave of hot love went over her to the infant. She held it close to her face and breast. With all her force, with all her soul she would make up to it for having brought it into the world unloved. She would love it all the more now it was here; carry it in her love. Its clear, knowing eyes gave her pain and fear. Did it know all about her? When it lay under her heart, had it been listening then? Was there a reproach in the look? She felt the marrow melt in her bones, with fear and pain.

Once more she was aware of the sun lying red on the rim of the hill opposite. She suddenly held up the child in her hands.

"Look!" she said. "Look, my pretty!"

She thrust the infant forward to the crimson, throbbing sun, almost with relief. She saw him lift his little fist. Then she put him to her bosom again, ashamed almost of her impulse to give him back again whence he came.

"If he lives," she thought to herself, "what will become of him—what will he be?"

Her heart was anxious.

"I will call him Paul," she said suddenly; she knew not why.

After a while she went home. A fine shadow was flung over the deep green meadow, darkening all.

As she expected, she found the house empty. But Morel was home by ten o'clock, and that day, at least, ended peacefully.

Walter Morel was, at this time, exceedingly irritable. His work seemed to exhaust him. When he came home he did not speak civilly to anybody. If the fire were rather low he bullied about that; he grumbled about his dinner; if the children made a chatter he shouted at them in a way that made their mother's blood boil, and made them hate him.

On the Friday he was not home by eleven o'clock. The baby was unwell, and was restless, crying if he were put down. Mrs. Morel, tired to death, and still weak, was scarcely under control.

"I wish the nuisance would come," she said wearily to herself.

The child at last sank down to sleep in her arms. She was too tired to carry him to the cradle.

"But I'll say nothing, whatever time he comes," she said. "It only works me up; I won't say anything. But I know if he does anything it'll make my blood boil," she added to herself.

She sighed, hearing him coming, as if it were something she could not bear. He, taking his revenge, was nearly drunk. She kept her head bent over the child as he entered, not wishing to see him. But it went through her like a flash of hot fire when, in passing, he lurched against the dresser, setting the tins rattling, and clutched at the white pot knobs for support. He hung up his hat and coat, then returned, stood glowering from a distance at her, as she sat bowed over the child.

"Is there nothing to eat in the house?" he asked, insolently, as if to a servant. In certain stages of his intoxication he affected the clipped, mincing speech of the towns. Mrs. Morel hated him most in this condition.

"You know what there is in the house," she said, so coldly, it sounded impersonal.

He stood and glared at her without moving a muscle.

"I asked a civil question, and I expect a civil answer," he said affectedly.

"And you got it," she said, still ignoring him.

He glowered again. Then he came unsteadily forward. He leaned on the table with one hand, and with the other jerked at the table drawer to get a knife to cut bread. The drawer stuck because he pulled sideways. In a temper he dragged it, so that it flew out bodily, and spoons, forks, knives, a hundred metallic things, splashed with a clatter and a clang upon the brick floor. The baby gave a little convulsed start.

"What are you doing, clumsy, drunken fool?" the mother cried.

"Then tha should get the flamin' thing thysen. Tha should get up, like other women have to, an' wait on a man."

"Wait on you—wait on you?" she cried. "Yes, I see myself."

"Yis, an' I'll learn thee tha's got to. Wait on *me*, yes tha sh'lt wait on me——"

"Never, milord. I'd wait on a dog at the door first."

"What—what?"

He was trying to fit in the drawer. At her last speech he turned round. His face was crimson, his eyes bloodshot. He stared at her one silent second in threat.

"P-h!" she went quickly, in contempt.

He jerked at the drawer in his excitement. It fell, cut sharply on his shin, and on the reflex he flung it at her.

One of the corners caught her brow as the shallow drawer crashed into the fireplace. She swayed, almost fell stunned from her chair. To her very soul she was sick; she clasped the child tightly to her bosom. A few moments elapsed; then, with an effort, she brought herself to. The baby was crying plaintively. Her left brow was bleeding rather profusely. As she glanced down at the child, her brain reeling, some drops of blood soaked into its white shawl; but the baby was at least not hurt. She

65

balanced her head to keep equilibrium, so that the blood ran into her eye.

Walter Morel remained as he had stood, leaning on the table with one hand, looking blank. When he was sufficiently sure of his balance, he went across to her, swayed, caught hold of the back of her rocking-chair, almost tipping her out; then leaning forward over her, and swaying as he spoke, he said, in a tone of wondering concern:

"Did it catch thee?"

He swayed again, as if he would pitch on to the child. With the catastrophe he had lost all balance.

"Go away," she said, struggling to keep her presence of mind.

He hiccoughed. "Let's—let's look at it," he said, hiccoughing again.

"Go away!" she cried.

"Lemme—lemme look at it, lass."

She smelled him of drink, felt the unequal pull of his swaying grasp on the back of her rocking-chair.

"Go away," she said, and weakly she pushed him off.

He stood, uncertain in balance, gazing upon her. Summoning all her strength she rose, the baby on one arm. By a cruel effort of will, moving as if in sleep, she went across to the scullery, where she bathed her eye for a minute in cold water; but she was too dizzy. Afraid lest she should swoon, she returned to her rocking-chair, trembling in every fibre. By instinct, she kept the baby clasped.

Morel, bothered, had succeeded in pushing the

drawer back into its cavity, and was on his knees, groping, with numb paws, for the scattered spoons.

Her brow was still bleeding. Presently Morel got up and came craning his neck towards her.

"What has it done to thee, lass?" he asked, in a very wretched, humble tone.

"You can see what it's done," she answered.

He stood, bending forward, supported on his hands, which grasped his legs just above the knee. He peered to look at the wound. She drew away from the thrust of his face with its great moustache, averting her own face as much as possible. As he looked at her, who was cold and impassive as stone, with mouth shut tight, he sickened with feebleness and hopelessness of spirit. He was turning drearily away, when he saw a drop of blood fall from the averted wound into the baby's fragile, glistening hair. Fascinated, he watched the heavy dark drop hang in the glistening cloud, and pull down the gossamer. Another drop fell. It would soak through to the baby's scalp. He watched, fascinated, feeling it soak in; then, finally, his manhood broke.

"What of this child?" was all his wife said to him. But her low, intense tones brought his head lower. She softened: "Get me some wadding out of the middle drawer," she said.

He stumbled away very obediently, presently returning with a pad, which she singed before the fire, then put on her forehead, as she sat with the baby on her lap.

"Now that clean pit-scarf."

67

Again he rummaged and fumbled in the drawer, returning presently with a red, narrow scarf. She took it, and with trembling fingers proceeded to bind it round her head.

"Let me tie it for thee," he said humbly.

"I can do it myself," she replied. When it was done she went upstairs, telling him to rake the fire and lock the door.

In the morning Mrs. Morel said:

"I knocked against the latch of the coal-place, when I was getting a raker in the dark, because the candle blew out." Her two small children looked up at her with wide, dismayed eyes. They said nothing, but their parted lips seemed to express the unconscious tragedy they felt.

Walter Morel lay in bed next day until nearly dinner-time. He did not think of the previous evening's work. He scarcely thought of anything, but he would not think of that. He lay and suffered like a sulking dog. He had hurt himself most; and he was the more damaged because he would never say a word to her, or express his sorrow. He tried to wriggle out of it. "It was her own fault," he said to himself. Nothing, however, could prevent his inner consciousness inflicting on him the punishment which ate into his spirit like rust, and which he could only alleviate by drinking.

He felt as if he had not the initiative to get up, or to say a word, or to move, but could only lie like a log. Moreover, he had himself violent pains in the head. It was Saturday. Towards noon he rose, cut himself food in the pantry, ate it with his head dropped, then pulled on his boots, and went out, to return at three o'clock slightly tipsy and relieved; then once more straight to bed. He rose again at six in the evening, had tea and went straight out.

Sunday was the same: bed till noon, the Palmerston Arms till 2.30, dinner, and bed; scarcely a word spoken. When Mrs. Morel went upstairs, towards four o'clock, to put on her Sunday dress, he was fast asleep. She would have felt sorry for him, if he had once said, "Wife, I'm sorry." But no; he insisted to himself it was her fault. And so he broke himself. So she merely left him alone. There was this deadlock of passion between them, and she was stronger.

The family began tea. Sunday was the only day when all sat down to meals together.

"Isn't my father going to get up?" asked William.

"Let him lie," the mother replied.

There was a feeling of misery over all the house. The children breathed the air that was poisoned, and they felt dreary. They were rather disconsolate, did not know what to do, what to play at.

Immediately Morel woke he got straight out of bed. That was characteristic of him all his life. He was all for activity. The prostrated inactivity of two mornings was stifling him.

It was near six o'clock when he got down. This time he entered without hesitation, his wincing sensitiveness having hardened again. He did not care any longer what the family thought or felt.

The tea-things were on the table. William was

reading aloud from "The Child's Own", Annie listening and asking eternally "why?" Both children hushed into silence as they heard the approaching thud of their father's stockinged feet, and shrank as he entered. Yet he was usually indulgent to them.

Morel made the meal alone, brutally. He ate and drank more noisily than he had need. No one spoke to him. The family life withdrew, shrank away, and became hushed as he entered. But he cared no longer about his alienation.

Immediately he had finished tea he rose with alacrity to go out. It was this alacrity, this haste to be gone, which so sickened Mrs. Morel. As she heard him sousing heartily in cold water, heard the eager scratch of the steel comb on the side of the bowl, as he wetted his hair, she closed her eyes in disgust. As he bent over, lacing his boots, there was a certain vulgar gusto in his movement that divided him from the reserved, watchful rest of the family. He always ran away from the battle with himself. Even in his own heart's privacy, he excused himself, saying, "If she hadn't said so-and-so, it would never have happened. She asked for what she's got." The children waited in restraint during his preparations. When he had gone, they sighed with relief.

He closed the door behind him, and was glad. It was a rainy evening. The Palmerston would be the cosier. He hastened forward in anticipation. All the slate roofs of the Bottoms shone black with wet.

The roads, always dark with coal-dust, were full of blackish mud. He hastened along. The Palmerston windows were steamed over. The passage was paddled with wet feet. But the air was warm, if foul, and full of the sound of voices and the smell of beer and smoke.

"What shollt ha'e, Walter?" cried a voice, as soon as Morel appeared in the doorway.

"Oh, Jim, my lad, wheriver has thee sprung frae?"

The men made a seat for him, and took him in warmly. He was glad. In a minute or two they had thawed all responsibility out of him, all shame, all trouble, and he was clear as a bell for a jolly night.

On the Wednesday following, Morel was penniless. He dreaded his wife. Having hurt her, he hated her. He did not know what to do with himself that evening, having not even twopence with which to go to the Palmerston, and being already rather deeply in debt. So, while his wife was down the garden with the child, he hunted in the top drawer of the dresser where she kept her purse, found it, and looked inside. It contained a half-crown, two halfpennies, and a sixpence. So he took the sixpence, put the purse carefully back, and went out.

The next day, when she wanted to pay the greengrocer, she looked in the purse for her sixpence, and her heart sank to her shoes. Then she sat down and thought: "*Was* there a sixpence? I hadn't spent it, had I? And I hadn't left it anywhere else?"

She was much put about. She hunted round

everywhere for it. And, as she sought, the conviction came into her heart that her husband had taken it. What she had in her purse was all the money she possessed. But that he should sneak it from her thus was unbearable. He had done so twice before. The first time she had not accused him, and at the weekend he had put the shilling again into her purse. So that was how she had known he had taken it. The second time he had not paid back.

This time she felt it was too much. When he had had his dinner—he came home early that day—she said to him coldly:

"Did you take sixpence out of my purse last night?"

"Me!" he said, looking up in an offended way. "No, I didna! I niver clapped eyes on your purse."

But she could detect the lie.

"Why, you know you did," she said quietly.

"I tell you I didna," he shouted. "Yer at me again, are yer? I've had about enough on't."

"So you filch sixpence out of my purse while I'm taking the clothes in."

"I'll may yer pay for this," he said, pushing back his chair in desperation. He bustled and got washed, then went determinedly upstairs. Presently he came down dressed, and with a big bundle in a blue-checked, enormous handkerchief.

"And now," he said, "you'll see me again when you do."

"It'll be before I want to," she replied; and at that he marched out of the house with his bundle. She

72

sat trembling slightly, but her heart brimming with contempt. What would she do if he went to some other pit, obtained work, and got in with another woman? But she knew him too well—he couldn't. She was dead sure of him. Nevertheless her heart was gnawed inside her.

"Where's my dad?" said William, coming in from school.

"He says he's run away," replied the mother.

"Where to?"

"Eh, I don't know. He's taken a bundle in the blue handkerchief, and says he's not coming back."

"What shall we do?" cried the boy.

"Eh, never trouble, he won't go far."

"But if he doesn't come back," wailed Annie.

And she and William retired to the sofa and wept. Mrs. Morel sat and laughed.

"You pair of gabeys!" she exclaimed. "You'll see him before the night's out."

But the children were not to be consoled. Twilight came on. Mrs. Morel grew anxious from very weariness. One part of her said it would be a relief to see the last of him; another part fretted because of keeping the children; and inside her, as yet, she could not quite let him go. At the bottom, she knew very well he could *not* go.

When she went down to the coal-place at the end of the garden, however, she felt something behind the door. So she looked. And there in the dark lay the big blue bundle. She sat on a piece of coal and laughed. Every time she saw it, so fat and yet so ig-

73

nominious, slunk into its corner in the dark, with its ends flopping like dejected ears from the knots, she laughed again. She was relieved.

Mrs. Morel sat waiting. He had not any money, she knew, so if he stopped he was running up a bill. She was very tired of him—tired to death. He had not even the courage to carry his bundle beyond the yard-end.

As she meditated, at about nine o'clock, he opened the door and came in, slinking, and yet sulky. She said not a word. He took off his coat, and slunk to his arm-chair, where he began to take off his boots.

"You'd better fetch your bundle before you take your boots off," she said quietly.

"You may thank your stars I've come back tonight," he said, looking up from under his dropped head, sulkily, trying to be impressive.

"Why, where should you have gone? You daren't even get your parcel through the yard-end," she said.

He looked such a fool she was not even angry with him. He continued to take his boots off and prepare for bed.

"I don't know what's in your blue handkerchief," she said. "But if you leave it the children shall fetch it in the morning."

Whereupon he got up and went out of the house, returning presently and crossing the kitchen with averted face, hurrying upstairs. As Mrs. Morel saw him slink quickly through the inner doorway, holding his bundle, she laughed to herself: but her heart was bitter, because she had loved him.

74

# 3

## THE CASTING OFF OF MOREL—
## THE TAKING ON OF WILLIAM

D URING the next week Morel's temper was almost unbearable. Like all miners, he was a great lover of medicines, which, strangely enough, he would often pay for himself.

"You mun get me a drop o' laxy vitral," he said. "It's a winder as we canna ha'e a sup i' th' 'ouse."

So Mrs. Morel bought him elixir of vitriol, his favourite first medicine. And he made himself a jug of wormwood tea. He had hanging in the attic great bunches of dried herbs: wormwood, rue, horehound, elder flowers, parsley-purt, marsh-mallow, hyssop, dandelion, and centaury. Usually there was a jug of one or other decoction standing on the hob, from which he drank largely.

"Grand!" he said, smacking his lips after wormwood. "Grand!" And he exhorted the children to try.

"It's better than any of your tea or your cocoa stews," he vowed. But they were not to be tempted.

This time, however, neither pills nor vitriol nor all his herbs would shift the "nasty peens in his head". He was sickening for an attack of an inflammation of the brain. He had never been well since his sleeping on the ground when he went with Jerry to Nottingham. Since then he had drunk and stormed. Now he fell seriously ill, and Mrs. Morel had him to nurse. He was one of the worst patients imaginable. But, in spite of all, and putting aside the fact that he was bread-winner, she never quite wanted him to die. Still there was one part of her wanted him for herself.

The neighbours were very good to her: occasionally some had the children in to meals, occasionally some would do the downstairs work for her, one would mind the baby for a day. But it was a great drag, nevertheless. It was not every day the neighbours helped. Then she had nursing of baby and husband, cleaning and cooking, everything to do. She was quite worn out, but she did what was wanted of her.

And the money was just sufficient. She had seventeen shillings a week from clubs, and every Friday Barker and the other butty put by a portion of the stall's profits for Morel's wife. And the neighbours made broths, and gave eggs, and such invalids' trifles. If they had not helped her so generously in those times, Mrs. Morel would never have pulled through, without incurring debts that would have dragged her down.

The weeks passed. Morel, almost against hope, grew better. He had a fine constitution, so that, once on the mend, he went straight forward to recovery. Soon he was pottering about downstairs. During his illness his wife had spoilt him a little.

Now he wanted her to continue. He often put his hand to his head, pulled down the corners of his mouth, and shammed pains he did not feel. But there was no deceiving her. At first she merely smiled to herself. Then she scolded him sharply.

"Goodness, man, don't be so lachrymose."

That wounded him slightly, but still he continued to feign sickness.

"I wouldn't be such a mardy baby," said the wife shortly.

Then he was indignant, and cursed under his breath, like a boy. He was forced to resume a normal tone, and to cease to whine.

Nevertheless, there was a state of peace in the house for some time. Mrs. Morel was more tolerant of him, and he, depending on her almost like a child, was rather happy. Neither knew that she was more tolerant because she loved him less. Up till this time, in spite of all, he had been her husband and her man. She had felt that, more or less, what he did to himself he did to her. Her living depended on him. There were many, many stages in the ebbing of her love for him, but it was always ebbing.

Now, with the birth of this third baby, her self no longer set towards him, helplessly, but was like a tide that scarcely rose, standing off from him. After this she scarcely desired him. And, standing more aloof from him, not feeling him so much part of herself, but merely part of her circumstances, she did not mind so much what he did, could leave him alone.

77

There was the halt, the wistfulness about the ensuing year, which is like autumn in a man's life. His wife was casting him off, half regretfully, but relentlessly; casting him off and turning now for love and life to the children. Henceforward he was more or less a husk. And he himself acquiesced, as so many men do, yielding their place to their children.

During his recuperation, when it was really over between them, both made an effort to come back somewhat to the old relationship of the first months of their marriage. He sat at home and, when the children were in bed, and she was sewing—she did all her sewing by hand, made all shirts and children's clothing—he would read to her from the newspaper, slowly pronouncing and delivering the words like a man pitching quoits. Often she hurried him on, giving him a phrase in anticipation. And then he took her words humbly.

The silences between them were peculiar. There would be the swift, slight "cluck" of her needle, the sharp "pop" of his lips as he let out the smoke, the warmth, the sizzle on the bars as he spat in the fire. Then her thoughts turned to William. Already he was getting a big boy. Already he was top of the class, and the master said he was the smartest lad in the school. She saw him a man, young, full of vigour, making the world glow again for her.

And Morel sitting there, quite alone, and having nothing to think about, would be feeling vaguely uncomfortable. His soul would reach out in its blind way to her and find her gone. He felt a sort of emptiness, almost like a vacuum in his soul. He was unsettled and restless. Soon he could not live in that atmosphere, and he affected his wife. Both felt an oppression on their breathing when they were left together for some time. Then he went to bed and she settled down to enjoy herself alone, working, thinking, living.

Meanwhile another infant was coming, fruit of this little peace and tenderness between the separating parents. Paul was seventeen months old when the new baby was born. He was then a plump, pale child, quiet, with heavy blue eyes, and still the peculiar slight knitting of the brows. The last child was also a boy, fair and bonny. Mrs. Morel was sorry when she knew she was with child, both for economic reasons and because she did not love her husband; but not for the sake of the infant.

They called the baby Arthur. He was very pretty, with a mop of gold curls, and he loved his father from the first. Mrs. Morel was glad this child loved the father. Hearing the miner's footsteps, the baby would put up his arms and crow. And if Morel were in a good temper, he called back immediately, in his hearty, mellow voice:

"What then, my beauty? I sh'll come to thee in a minute."

And as soon as he had taken off his pit-coat, Mrs. Morel would put an apron round the child, and give him to his father.

"What a sight the lad looks!" she would exclaim sometimes, taking back the baby, that was smutted on the face from his father's kisses and play. Then Morel laughed joyfully.

"He's a little collier, bless his bit o' mutton!" he exclaimed.

And these were the happy moments of her life now, when the children included the father in her heart.

Meanwhile William grew bigger and stronger and more active, while Paul, always rather delicate and quiet, got slimmer, and trotted after his mother like her shadow. He was usually active and interested, but sometimes he would have fits of depression. Then the mother would find the boy of three or four crying on the sofa.

"What's the matter?" she asked, and got no answer.

"What's the matter?" she insisted, getting cross.

"I don't know," sobbed the child.

So she tried to reason him out of it, or to amuse him, but without effect. It made her feel beside herself. Then the father, always impatient, would jump from his chair and shout:

"If he doesn't stop, I'll smack him till he does."

"You'll do nothing of the sort," said the mother coldly. And then she carried the child into the yard, plumped him into his little chair, and said: "Now cry there, Misery!"

And then a butterfly on the rhubarb-leaves perhaps caught his eye, or at last he cried himself to

80

sleep. These fits were not often, but they caused a shadow in Mrs. Morel's heart, and her treatment of Paul was different from that of the other children.

Suddenly one morning as she was looking down the alley of the Bottoms for the barm-man, she heard a voice calling her. It was the thin little Mrs. Anthony in brown velvet.

"Here, Mrs. Morel, I want to tell you about your Willie."

"Oh, do you?" replied Mrs. Morel. "Why, what's the matter?"

"A lad as gets 'old of another an' rips his clothes off'n 'is back," Mrs. Anthony said, "wants showing something."

"Your Alfred's as old as my William," said Mrs. Morel.

" 'Appen 'e is, but that doesn't give him a right to get hold of the boy's collar, an' fair rip it clean off his back."

"Well," said Mrs. Morel. "I don't thrash my children, and even if I did, I should want to hear their side of the tale."

"They'd happen be a bit better if they did get a good hiding," retorted Mrs. Anthony. "When it comes ter rippin' a lad's clean collar off'n 'is back a-purpose——"

"I'm sure he didn't do it on purpose," said Mrs. Morel.

"Make me a liar!" shouted Mrs. Anthony.

Mrs. Morel moved away and closed her gate. Her hand trembled as she held her mug of barm.

"But I s'll let your mester know," Mrs. Anthony cried after her.

At dinner-time, when William had finished his meal and wanted to be off again—he was then eleven years old—his mother said to him:

"What did you tear Alfred Anthony's collar for?"

"When did I tear his collar?"

"I don't know when, but his mother says you did."

"Why—it was yesterday—an' it was torn a'ready."

"But you tore it more."

"Well, I'd got a cobbler as 'ad licked seventeen—an' Alfy Ant'ny 'e says:

'Adam an' Eve an' pinch-me,
    Went down to a river to bade.
Adam an' Eve got drownded,
    Who do yer think got saved?'

An' so I says: 'Oh, Pinch-*you*,' an' so I pinched 'im, an' 'e was mad, an' so he snatched my cobbler an' run off with it. An' so I run after 'im, an' when I was gettin' hold of 'im, 'e dodged, an' it ripped 'is collar. But I got my cobbler——"

He pulled from his pocket a black old horse-chestnut hanging on a string. This old cobbler had "cobbled"—hit and smashed—seventeen other cobblers on similar strings. So the boy was proud of his veteran.

82

"Well," said Mrs. Morel, "you know you've got no right to rip his collar."

"Well, our mother!" he answered. "I never meant tr'a done it—an' it was on'y an old indirrubber collar as was torn a'ready."

"Next time," said his mother, "*you* be more careful. I shouldn't like it if you came home with your collar torn off."

"I don't care, our mother; I never did it a-purpose."

The boy was rather miserable at being reprimanded.

"No—well, you be more careful."

William fled away, glad to be exonerated. And Mrs. Morel, who hated any bother with the neighbours, thought she would explain to Mrs. Anthony, and the business would be over.

But that evening Morel came in from the pit looking very sour. He stood in the kitchen and glared round, but did not speak for some minutes. Then:

"Wheer's that Willy?" he asked.

"What do you want *him* for?" asked Mrs. Morel, who had guessed.

"I'll let 'im know when I get him," said Morel, banging his pit-bottle on to the dresser.

"I suppose Mrs. Anthony's got hold of you and been yarning to you about Alfy's collar," said Mrs. Morel, rather sneering.

"Niver mind who's got hold of me," said Morel. "When I get hold of '*im* I'll make his bones rattle."

"It's a poor tale," said Mrs. Morel, "that you're

83

so ready to side with any snipey vixen who likes to come telling tales against your own children."

"I'll learn 'im!" said Morel. "It none matters to me whose lad 'e is; 'e's none goin' rippin' an' tearin' about just as he's a mind."

" 'Ripping and tearing about!' " repeated Mrs. Morel. "He was running after that Alfy, who'd taken his cobbler, and he accidentally got hold of his collar, because the other dodged—as an Anthony would."

"I know!" shouted Morel threateningly.

"You would, before you're told," replied his wife bitingly.

"Niver you mind," stormed Morel. "I know my business."

"That's more than doubtful," said Mrs. Morel, "supposing some loud-mouthed creature had been getting you to thrash your own children."

"I know," repeated Morel.

And he said no more, but sat and nursed his bad temper. Suddenly William ran in, saying:

"Can I have my tea, mother?"

"Tha can ha'e more than that!" shouted Morel.

"Hold your noise, man," said Mrs. Morel; "and don't look so ridiculous."

"He'll look ridiculous before I've done wi' him!" shouted Morel, rising from his chair and glaring at his son.

William, who was a tall lad for his years, but very sensitive, had gone pale, and was looking in a sort of horror at his father.

"Go out!" Mrs. Morel commanded her son.

William had not the wit to move. Suddenly Morel clenched his fist, and crouched.

"I'll *gi'e* him 'go out'!" he shouted like an insane thing.

"What!" cried Mrs. Morel, panting with rage. "You shall not touch him for *her* telling, you shall not!"

"Shonna I?" shouted Morel. "Shonna I?"

And, glaring at the boy, he ran forward. Mrs. Morel sprang in between them, with her fist lifted.

"Don't you *dare!*" she cried.

"What!" he shouted, baffled for the moment. "What!"

She spun round to her son.

"*Go* out of the house!" she commanded him in fury.

The boy, as if hypnotised by her, turned suddenly and was gone. Morel rushed to the door, but was too late. He returned, pale under his pit-dirt with fury. But now his wife was fully roused.

"Only dare!" she said in a loud, ringing voice. "Only dare, milord, to lay a finger on that child! You'll regret it for ever."

He was afraid of her. In a towering rage, he sat down.

When the children were old enough to be left, Mrs. Morel joined the Women's Guild. It was a little club of women attached to the Co-operative Wholesale Society, which met on Monday night in the long room over the grocery shop of the Bestwood

"Co-op". The women were supposed to discuss the benefits to be derived from co-operation, and other social questions. Sometimes Mrs. Morel read a paper. It seemed queer to the children to see their mother, who was always busy about the house, sitting writing in her rapid fashion, thinking, referring to books, and writing again. They felt for her on such occasions the deepest respect.

But they loved the Guild. It was the only thing to which they did not grudge their mother—and that partly because she enjoyed it, partly because of the treats they derived from it. The Guild was called by some hostile husbands, who found their wives getting too independent, the "clat-fart" shop—that is, the gossip-shop. It is true, from off the basis of the Guild, the women could look at their homes, at the conditions of their own lives, and find fault. So the colliers found their women had a new standard of their own, rather disconcerting. And also, Mrs. Morel always had a lot of news on Monday nights, so that the children liked William to be in when their mother came home, because she told him things.

Then, when the lad was thirteen, she got him a job in the "Co-op." office. He was a very clever boy, frank, with rather rough features and real viking blue eyes.

"What dost want ter ma'e a stool-harsed Jack on 'im for?" said Morel. "All he'll do is to wear his britches behind out, an' earn nowt. What's 'e startin' wi'?"

"It doesn't matter what he's starting with," said Mrs. Morel.

"It wouldna! Put 'im i' th' pit we me, an' 'e'll earn a easy ten shillin' a wik from th' start. But six shillin' wearin' his truck-end out on a stool's better than ten shillin' i' th' pit wi' me, I know."

"He is *not* going in the pit," said Mrs. Morel, "and there's an end of it."

"It wor good enough for me, but it's non good enough for 'im."

"If your mother put you in the pit at twelve, it's no reason why I should do the same with my lad."

"Twelve! It wor a sight afore that!"

"Whenever it was," said Mrs. Morel.

She was very proud of her son. He went to the night school, and learned shorthand, so that by the time he was sixteen he was the best shorthand clerk and book-keeper on the place, except one. Then he taught in the night schools. But he was so fiery that only his good-nature and his size protected him.

All the things that men do—the decent things—William did. He could run like the wind. When he was twelve he won a first prize in a race; an inkstand of glass, shaped like an anvil. It stood proudly on the dresser, and gave Mrs. Morel a keen pleasure. The boy only ran for her. He flew home with his anvil, breathless, with a "Look, mother!" That was the first real tribute to herself. She took it like a queen.

"How pretty!" she exclaimed.

Then he began to get ambitious. He gave all his

money to his mother. When he earned fourteen shillings a week, she gave him back two for himself, and, as he never drank, he felt himself rich. He went about with the bourgeois of Bestwood. The townlet contained nothing higher than the clergyman. Then came the bank manager, then the doctors, then the tradespeople, and after that the hosts of colliers. William began to consort with the sons of the chemist, the schoolmaster, and the tradesmen. He played billiards in the Mechanics' Hall. Also he danced—this in spite of his mother. All the life that Bestwood offered he enjoyed, from the sixpenny-hops down Church Street, to sports and billiards.

Paul was treated to dazzling descriptions of all kinds of flower-like ladies, most of whom lived like cut blooms in William's heart for a brief fortnight.

Occasionally some flame would come in pursuit of her errant swain. Mrs. Morel would find a strange girl at the door, and immediately she sniffed the air.

"Is Mr. Morel in?" the damsel would ask appealingly.

"My husband is at home," Mrs. Morel replied.

"I—I mean *young* Mr. Morel," repeated the maiden painfully.

"Which one? There are several."

Whereupon much blushing and stammering from the fair one.

"I—I met Mr. Morel—at Ripley," she explained.

"Oh—at a dance!"

"Yes."

"I don't approve of the girls my son meets at dances. And he is *not* at home."

Then he came home angry with his mother for having turned the girl away so rudely. He was a careless, yet eager-looking fellow, who walked with long strides, sometimes frowning, often with his cap pushed jollily to the back of his head. Now he came in frowning. He threw his cap on to the sofa, and took his strong jaw in his hand, and glared down at his mother. She was small, with her hair taken straight back from her forehead. She had a quiet air of authority, and yet of rare warmth. Knowing her son was angry, she trembled inwardly.

"Did a lady call for me yesterday, mother?" he asked.

"I don't know about a lady. There was a girl came."

"And why didn't you tell me?"

"Because I forgot, simply."

He fumed a little.

"A good-looking girl—seemed a lady?"

"I didn't look at her."

"Big brown eyes?"

"I did *not* look. And tell your girls, my son, that when they're running after you, they're not to come and ask your mother for you. Tell them that—brazen baggages you meet at dancing-classes."

"I'm sure she was a nice girl."

"And I'm sure she wasn't."

There ended the altercation. Over the dancing

there was a great strife between the mother and the son. The grievance reached its height when William said he was going to Hucknall Torkard—considered a low town—to a fancy-dress ball. He was to be a Highlander. There was a dress he could hire, which one of his friends had had, and which fitted him perfectly. The Highland suit came home. Mrs. Morel received it coldly and would not unpack it.

"My suit come?" cried William.

"There's a parcel in the front room."

He rushed in and cut the string.

"How do you fancy your son in this!" he said, enraptured, showing her the suit.

"You know I don't want to fancy you in it."

On the evening of the dance, when he had come home to dress, Mrs. Morel put on her coat and bonnet.

"Aren't you going to stop and see me, mother?" he asked.

"No; I don't want to see you," she replied.

She was rather pale, and her face was closed and hard. She was afraid of her son's going the same way as his father. He hesitated a moment, and his heart stood still with anxiety. Then he caught sight of the Highland bonnet with its ribbons. He picked it up gleefully, forgetting her. She went out.

When he was nineteen he suddenly left the Co-op. office and got a situation in Nottingham. In his new place he had thirty shillings a week instead of eighteen. This was indeed a rise. His mother and his father were brimmed up with pride. Everybody praised William. It seemed he was going to get on rapidly. Mrs. Morel hoped, with his aid, to help her younger sons. Annie was now studying to be a teacher. Paul, also very clever, was getting on well, having lessons in French and German from his godfather, the clergyman who was still a friend to Mrs. Morel. Arthur, a spoilt and very good-looking boy, was at the Board school, but there was talk of his trying to get a scholarship for the High School in Nottingham.

William remained a year at his new post in Nottingham. He was studying hard, and growing serious. Something seemed to be fretting him. Still he went out to the dances and the river parties. He did not drink. The children were all rabid teetotallers. He came home very late at night, and sat yet longer studying. His mother implored him to take more care, to do one thing or another.

"Dance, if you want to dance, my son; but don't think you can work in the office, and then amuse yourself, and *then* study on top of all. You can't; the human frame won't stand it. Do one thing or the other—amuse yourself or learn Latin; but don't try to do both."

Then he got a place in London, at a hundred and twenty a year. This seemed a fabulous sum. His mother doubted almost whether to rejoice or to grieve.

"They want me in Lime Street on Monday week,

mother," he cried, his eyes blazing as he read the letter. Mrs. Morel felt everything go silent inside her. He read the letter: " 'And will you reply by Thursday whether you accept. Yours faithfully——' They want me, mother, at a hundred and twenty a year, and don't even ask to see me. Didn't I tell you I could do it! Think of me in London! And I can give you twenty pounds a year, mater. We s'll all be rolling in money."

"We shall, my son," she answered sadly.

It never occurred to him that she might be more hurt at his going away than glad of his success. Indeed, as the days drew near for his departure, her heart began to close and grow dreary with despair. She loved him so much! More than that, she hoped in him so much. Almost she lived by him. She liked to do things for him: she liked to put a cup for his tea and to iron his collars, of which he was so proud. It was a joy to her to have him proud of his collars. There was no laundry. So she used to rub away at them with her little convex iron, to polish them, till they shone from the sheer pressure of her arm. Now she would not do it for him. Now he was going away. She felt almost as if he were going as well out of her heart. He did not seem to leave her inhabited with himself. That was the grief and the pain to her. He took nearly all himself away.

A few days before his departure—he was just twenty—he burned his love-letters. They had hung on a file at the top of the kitchen cupboard. From some of them he had read extracts to his mother.

Some of them she had taken the trouble to read herself. But most were too trivial.

Now, on the Saturday morning he said:

"Come on, 'Postle, let's go through my letters, and you can have the birds and flowers."

Mrs. Morel had done her Saturday's work on the Friday, because he was having a last day's holiday. She was making him a rice cake, which he loved, to take with him. He was scarcely conscious that she was so miserable.

He took the first letter off the file. It was mauve-tinted, and had purple and green thistles. William sniffed the page.

"Nice scent! Smell."

And he thrust the sheet under Paul's nose.

"Um!" said Paul, breathing in. "What d'you call it? Smell, mother."

His mother ducked her small, fine nose down to the paper.

"*I* don't want to smell their rubbish," she said, sniffing.

"This girl's father," said William, "is as rich as Crœsus. He owns property without end. She calls me Lafayette, because I know French. 'You will see, I've forgiven you'—I like *her* forgiving me. 'I told mother about you this morning, and she will have much pleasure if you come to tea on Sunday, but she will have to get father's consent also. I sincerely hope he will agree. I will let you know how it transpires. If, however, you——' "

93

" 'Let you know how it' what?" interrupted Mrs. Morel.

" 'Transpires'—oh yes!"

" 'Transpires!' " repeated Mrs. Morel mockingly. "I thought she was so well educated!"

William felt slightly uncomfortable, and abandoned this maiden, giving Paul the corner with the thistles. He continued to read extracts from his letters, some of which amused his mother, some of which saddened her and made her anxious for him.

"My lad," she said, "they're very wise. They know they've only got to flatter your vanity, and you press up to them like a dog that has its head scratched."

"Well, they can't go on scratching for ever," he replied. "And when they've done, I trot away."

"But one day you'll find a string round your neck that you can't pull off," she answered.

"Not me! I'm equal to any of 'em, mater, they needn't flatter themselves."

"You flatter *yourself*," she said quietly.

Soon there was a heap of twisted black pages, all that remained of the file of scented letters, except that Paul had thirty or forty pretty tickets from the corners of the notepaper—swallows and forget-me-nots and ivy sprays. And William went to London, to start a new life.

# 4

## THE YOUNG LIFE OF PAUL

PAUL would be built like his mother, slightly and rather small. His fair hair went reddish, and then dark brown; his eyes were grey. He was a pale, quiet child, with eyes that seemed to listen, and with a full, dropping underlip.

As a rule he seemed old for his years. He was so conscious of what other people felt, particularly his mother. When she fretted he understood, and could have no peace. His soul seemed always attentive to her.

As he grew older he became stronger. William was too far removed from him to accept him as a companion. So the smaller boy belonged at first almost entirely to Annie. She was a tomboy and a "flybie-skybie", as her mother called her. But she was intensely fond of her second brother. So Paul was towed round at the heels of Annie, sharing her game. She raced wildly at lerky with the other young wild-cats of the Bottoms. And always Paul flew beside her, living her share of the game, having as yet no part of his own. He was quiet and not noticeable. But his sister adored him. He always seemed to care for things if she wanted him to.

She had a big doll of which she was fearfully

95

proud, though not so fond. So she laid the doll on the sofa, and covered it with an antimacassar, to sleep. Then she forgot it. Meantime Paul must practise jumping off the sofa arm. So he jumped crash into the face of the hidden doll. Annie rushed up, uttered a loud wail, and sat down to weep a dirge. Paul remained quite still.

"You couldn't tell it was there, mother; you couldn't tell it was there," he repeated over and over. So long as Annie wept for the doll he sat helpless with misery. Her grief wore itself out. She forgave her brother—he was so much upset. But a day or two afterwards she was shocked.

"Let's make a sacrifice of Arabella," he said. "Let's burn her."

She was horrified, yet rather fascinated. She wanted to see what the boy would do. He made an altar of bricks, pulled some of the shavings out of Arabella's body, put the waxen fragments into the hollow face, poured on a little paraffin, and set the whole thing alight. He watched with wicked satisfaction the drops of wax melt off the broken forehead of Arabella, and drop like sweat into the flame. So long as the stupid big doll burned he rejoiced in silence. At the end he poked among the embers with a stick, fished out the arms and legs, all blackened, and smashed them under stones.

"That's the sacrifice of Missis Arabella," he said. "An' I'm glad there's nothing left of her."

Which disturbed Annie inwardly, although she

96

could say nothing. He seemed to hate the doll so intensely, because he had broken it.

All the children, but particularly Paul, were peculiarly *against* their father, along with their mother. Morel continued to bully and to drink. He had periods, months at a time, when he made the whole life of the family a misery. Paul never forgot coming home from the Band of Hope one Monday evening and finding his mother with her eye swollen and discoloured, his father standing on the hearth-rug, feet astride, his head down, and William, just home from work, glaring at his father. There was a silence as the young children entered, but none of the elders looked round.

William was white to the lips, and his fists were clenched. He waited until the children were silent, watching with children's rage and hate; then he said:

"You coward, you daren't do it when I was in."

But Morel's blood was up. He swung round on his son. William was bigger, but Morel was hard-muscled, and mad with fury.

"Dossn't I?" he shouted. "Dossn't I? Ha'e much more o' they chelp, my young jockey, an' I'll rattle my fist about thee. Ay, an' I sholl that, dost see?"

Morel crouched at the knees and showed his fist in an ugly, almost beast-like fashion. William was white with rage.

"Will yer?" he said, quiet and intense. "It 'ud be the last time, though."

Morel danced a little nearer, crouching, drawing

97

back his fist to strike. William put his fists ready. A light came into his blue eyes, almost like a laugh. He watched his father. Another word, and the men would have begun to fight. Paul hoped they would. The three children sat pale on the sofa.

"Stop it, both of you," cried Mrs. Morel in a hard voice. "We've had enough for *one* night. And *you*," she said, turning on to her husband, "look at your children!"

Morel glanced at the sofa.

"Look at the children, you nasty little bitch!" he sneered. "Why, what have *I* done to the children, I should like to know? But they're like yourself; you've put 'em up to your own tricks and nasty ways—you've learned 'em in it, you 'ave."

She refused to answer him. No one spoke. After a while he threw his boots under the table and went to bed.

"Why didn't you let me have a go at him?" said William, when his father was upstairs. "I could easily have beaten him."

"A nice thing—your own father," she replied.

" '*Father!*' " repeated William. "Call *him my* father!"

"Well, he is—and so——"

"But why don't you let me settle him? I could do, easily."

"The idea!" she cried. "It hasn't come to *that* yet."

"No," he said, "it's come to worse. Look at yourself. *Why* don't you let me give it him?"

"Because I couldn't bear it, so never think of it," she cried quickly.

And the children went to bed, miserably.

When William was growing up, the family moved from the Bottoms to a house on the brow of the hill, commanding a view of the valley, which spread out like a convex cockle-shell, or a clamp-shell, before it. In front of the house was a huge old ash-tree. The west wind, sweeping from Derbyshire, caught the houses with full force, and the tree shrieked again. Morel liked it.

"It's music," he said. "It sends me to sleep."

But Paul and Arthur and Annie hated it. To Paul it became almost a demoniacal noise. The winter of their first year in the new house their father was very bad. The children played in the street, on the brim of the wide, dark valley, until eight o'clock. Then they went to bed. Their mother sat sewing below. Having such a great space in front of the house gave the children a feeling of night, of vastness, and of terror. This terror came in from the shrieking of the tree and the anguish of the home discord. Often Paul would wake up, after he had been asleep a long time, aware of thuds downstairs. Instantly he was wide awake. Then he heard the booming shouts of his father, come home nearly drunk, then the sharp replies of his mother, then the bang, bang of his father's fist on the table, and the nasty snarling shout as the man's voice got higher. And then the whole was drowned in a piercing medley of shrieks and cries from the great, wind-swept ash-tree. The children lay silent in suspense, waiting for a lull in the wind to hear what their father was doing. He might hit their mother again. There was a feeling of horror, a kind of bristling in the darkness, and a sense of blood. They lay with their hearts in the grip of an intense anguish. The wind came through the tree fiercer and fiercer. All the cords of the great harp hummed, whistled, and shrieked. And then came the horror of the sudden silence, silence everywhere, outside and downstairs. What was it? Was it a silence of blood? What had he done?

The children lay and breathed the darkness. And then, at last, they heard their father throw down his boots and tramp upstairs in his stockinged feet. Still they listened. Then at last, if the wind allowed, they heard the water of the tap drumming into the kettle, which their mother was filling for morning, and they could go to sleep in peace.

So they were happy in the morning—happy, very happy playing, dancing at night round the lonely lamp-post in the midst of the darkness. But they had one tight place of anxiety in their hearts, one darkness in their eyes, which showed all their lives.

Paul hated his father. As a boy he had a fervent private religion.

"Make him stop drinking," he prayed every night. "Lord, let my father die," he prayed very often. "Let him not be killed at pit," he prayed when, after tea, the father did not come home from work.

That was another time when the family suffered intensely. The children came from school and had their teas. On the hob the big black saucepan was simmering, the stew-jar was in the oven, ready for Morel's dinner. He was expected at five o'clock. But for months he would stop and drink every night on his way from work.

In the winter nights, when it was cold, and grew dark early, Mrs. Morel would put a brass candlestick on the table, light a tallow candle to save the gas. The children finished their bread-and-butter, or dripping, and were ready to go out to play. But if Morel had not come they faltered. The sense of his sitting in all his pit-dirt, drinking, after a long day's work, not coming home and eating and washing, but sitting, getting drunk, on an empty stomach, made Mrs. Morel unable to bear herself. From her the feeling was transmitted to the other children. She never suffered alone any more: the children suffered with her.

Paul went out to play with the rest. Down in the great trough of twilight, tiny clusters of lights burned where the pits were. A few last colliers straggled up the dim field path. The lamplighter came along. No more colliers came. Darkness shut down over the valley; work was done. It was night.

Then Paul ran anxiously into the kitchen. The one candle still burned on the table, the big fire glowed red. Mrs. Morel sat alone. On the hob the saucepan steamed; the dinner-plate lay waiting on the table. All the room was full of the sense of waiting, waiting for the man who was sitting in his pit-dirt, dinnerless, some mile away from home, across the darkness, drinking himself drunk. Paul stood in the doorway.

"Has my dad come?" he asked.

"You can see he hasn't," said Mrs. Morel, cross with the futility of the question.

Then the boy dawdled about near his mother. They shared the same anxiety. Presently Mrs. Morel went out and strained the potatoes.

"They're ruined and black," she said; "but what do I care?"

Not many words were spoken. Paul almost hated his mother for suffering because his father did not come home from work.

"What do you bother yourself for?" he said. "If he wants to stop and get drunk, why don't you let him?"

"Let him!" flashed Mrs. Morel. "You may well say 'let him!'."

She knew that the man who stops on the way home from work is on a quick way to ruining himself and his home. The children were yet young, and depended on the breadwinner. William gave her the sense of relief, providing her at last with someone to turn to if Morel failed. But the tense atmosphere of the room on these waiting evenings was the same.

The minutes ticked away. At six o'clock still the cloth lay on the table, still the dinner stood waiting, still the same sense of anxiety and expectation in the room. The boy could not stand it any longer. He could not go out and play. So he ran in to Mrs. Inger, next door but one, for her to talk to him. She had no children. Her husband was good to her, but was in a shop, and came home late. So, when she saw the lad at the door, she called:

"Come in, Paul."

The two sat talking for some time, when suddenly the boy rose, saying:

"Well, I'll be going and seeing if my mother wants an errand doing."

He pretended to be perfectly cheerful, and did not tell his friend what ailed him. Then he ran indoors.

Morel at these times came in churlish and hateful.

"This is a nice time to come home," said Mrs. Morel.

"Wha's it matter to yo' what time I come whoam?" he shouted.

And everybody in the house was still, because he was dangerous. He ate his food in the most brutal manner possible, and, when he had done, pushed all the pots in a heap away from him, to lay his arms on the table. Then he went to sleep.

Paul hated his father so. The collier's small, mean head, with its black hair slightly soiled with grey, lay on the bare arms, and the face, dirty and in-flamed, with a fleshy nose and thin, paltry brows, was turned sideways, asleep with beer and weari-ness and nasty temper. If anyone entered suddenly, or a noise were made, the man looked up and shouted:

"I'll lay my fist about thy y'ead, I'm tellin' thee, if tha doesna stop that clatter! Dost hear?"

And the two last words, shouted in a bullying fashion, usually at Annie, made the family writhe with hate of the man.

He was shut out from all family affairs. No one told him anything. The children, alone with their mother, told her all about the day's happenings, everything. Nothing had really taken place in them until it was told to their mother. But as soon as the father came in, everything stopped. He was like the scotch in the smooth, happy machinery of the home. And he was always aware of this fall of silence on his entry, the shutting off of life, the unwelcome. But now it was gone too far to alter.

He would dearly have liked the children to talk to him, but they could not. Sometimes Mrs. Morel would say:

"You ought to tell your father."

Paul won a prize in a competition in a child's paper. Everybody was highly jubilant.

"Now you'd better tell your father when he comes in," said Mrs. Morel. "You know how he carries on and says he's never told anything."

"All right," said Paul. But he would almost rather have forfeited the prize than have to tell his father.

"I've won a prize in a competition, dad," he said.

Morel turned round to him.

"Have you, my boy? What sort of a competition?"

"Oh, nothing—about famous women."

"And how much is the prize, then, as you've got?"

"It's a book."

"Oh, indeed!"

"About birds."

"Hm—hm!"

And that was all. Conversation was impossible between the father and any other member of the family. He was an outsider. He had denied the God in him.

The only times when he entered again into the life of his own people was when he worked, and was happy at work. Sometimes, in the evening, he cobbled the boots or mended the kettle or his pit-bottle. Then he always wanted several attendants, and the children enjoyed it. They united with him in the work, in the actual doing of something, when he was his real self again.

He was a good workman, dexterous, and one who, when he was in a good humour, always sang. He had whole periods, months, almost years, of friction and nasty temper. Then sometimes he was jolly again. It was nice to see him run with a piece of red-hot iron into the scullery, crying:

"Out of my road—out of my road!"

Then he hammered the soft, red-glowing stuff on his iron goose, and made the shape he wanted. Or he sat absorbed for a moment, soldering. Then the children watched with joy as the metal sank suddenly molten, and was shoved about against the nose of the soldering-iron, while the room was full of a scent of burnt resin and hot tin, and Morel was silent and intent for a minute. He always sang when he mended boots because of the jolly sound of hammering. And he was rather happy when he sat putting great patches on his moleskin pit trousers, which he would often do, considering them too dirty, and the stuff too hard, for his wife to mend.

But the best time for the young children was when he made fuses. Morel fetched a sheaf of long sound wheat-straws from the attic. These he cleaned with his hand, till each one gleamed like a stalk of gold, after which he cut the straws into lengths of about six inches, leaving, if he could, a notch at the bottom of each piece. He always had a beautifully sharp knife that could cut a straw clean without hurting it. Then he set in the middle of the table a heap of gunpowder, a little pile of black grains upon the white-scrubbed board. He made and trimmed the straws while Paul and Annie filled and plugged them. Paul loved to see the black grains trickle down a crack in his palm into the mouth of the straw, peppering jollily downwards till the straw was full. Then he bunged up the mouth with a bit of soap—which he got on his thumb-nail from a pat in a saucer—and the straw was finished.

"Look, dad!" he said.

"That's right, my beauty," replied Morel, who was peculiarly lavish of endearments to his second son. Paul popped the fuse into the powder-tin, ready for the morning, when Morel would take it to the pit, and use it to fire a shot that would blast the coal down.

Meantime Arthur, still fond of his father, would lean on the arm of Morel's chair and say:

"Tell us about down pit, daddy."

This Morel loved to do.

"Well, there's one little 'oss—we call 'im Taffy," he would begin. "An' he's a fawce 'un!"

Morel had a warm way of telling a story. He made one feel Taffy's cunning.

"He's a brown 'un," he would answer, "an' not very high. Well, he comes i' th' stall wi' a rattle, an' then yo' 'ear 'im sneeze.

" 'Ello, Taff,' you say, 'what art sneezin' for? Bin ta'ein' some snuff?'

"An' 'e sneezes again. Then he slives up an' shoves 'is 'ead on yer, that cadin'.

" 'What's want, Taff?' yo' say."

"And what does he?" Arthur always asked.

"He wants a bit o' bacca, my duckie."

This story of Taffy would go on interminably, and everybody loved it.

Or sometimes it was a new tale.

"An' what dost think, my darlin'? When I went to put my coat on at snap-time, what should go runnin' up my arm but a mouse.

" 'Hey up, theer!' I shouts.

"An' I wor just in time ter get 'im by th' tail."

"And did you kill it?"

"I did, for they're a nuisance. The place is fair snied wi' 'em."

"An' what do they live on?"

"The corn as the 'osses drops—an' they'll get in your pocket an' eat your snap, if you'll let 'em—no matter where yo' hing your coat—the slivin', nibblin' little nuisances, for they are."

These happy evenings could not take place unless Morel had some job to do. And then he always went to bed very early, often before the children. There was nothing remaining for him to stay up for, when he had finished tinkering, and had skimmed the headlines of the newspaper.

And the children felt secure when their father was in bed. They lay and talked softly a while. Then they started as the lights went suddenly sprawling over the ceiling from the lamps that swung in the hands of the colliers tramping by outside, going to take the nine o'clock shift. They listened to the voices of the men, imagined them dipping down into the dark valley. Sometimes they went to the window and watched the three or four lamps growing tinier and tinier, swaying down the fields in the darkness. Then it was a joy to rush back to bed and cuddle closely in the warmth.

Paul was rather a delicate boy, subject to bronchitis. The others were all quite strong; so this was another reason for his mother's difference in feeling for him. One day he came home at dinner-time feeling ill. But it was not a family to make any fuss.

108

"What's the matter with *you*?" his mother asked sharply.

"Nothing," he replied.

But he ate no dinner.

"If you eat no dinner, you're not going to school," she said.

"Why?" he asked.

"That's why."

So after dinner he lay down on the sofa, on the warm chintz cushions the children loved. Then he fell into a kind of doze. That afternoon Mrs. Morel was ironing. She listened to the small, restless noise the boy made in his throat as she worked. Again rose in her heart the old, almost weary feeling towards him. She had never expected him to live. And yet he had a great vitality in his young body. Perhaps it would have been a little relief to her if he had died. She always felt a mixture of anguish in her love for him.

He, in his semi-conscious sleep, was vaguely aware of the clatter of the iron on the iron-stand, of the faint thud, thud on the ironing-board. Once roused, he opened his eyes to see his mother standing on the hearth-rug with the hot iron near her cheek, listening, as it were, to the heat. Her still face, with the mouth closed tight from suffering and disillusion and self-denial, and her nose the smallest bit on one side, and her blue eyes so young, quick, and warm, made his heart contract with love. When she was quiet, so, she looked brave and rich with life, but as if she had been done out of her rights. It hurt the boy keenly, this feeling about her that she had never had her life's fulfilment: and his own incapability to make up to her hurt him with a sense of impotence, yet made him patiently dogged inside. It was his childish aim.

She spat on the iron, and a little ball of spit bounded, raced off the dark, glossy surface. Then, kneeling, she rubbed the iron on the sack lining of the hearth-rug vigorously. She was warm in the ruddy firelight. Paul loved the way she crouched and put her head on one side. Her movements were light and quick. It was always a pleasure to watch her. Nothing she ever did, no movement she ever made, could have been found fault with by her children. The room was warm and full of the scent of hot linen. Later on the clergyman came and talked softly with her.

Paul was laid up with an attack of bronchitis. He did not mind much. What happened happened, and it was no good kicking against the pricks. He loved the evenings, after eight o'clock, when the light was put out, and he could watch the fire-flames spring over the darkness of the walls and ceiling; could watch huge shadows waving and tossing, till the room seemed full of men who battled silently.

On retiring to bed, the father would come into the sickroom. He was always very gentle if anyone were ill. But he disturbed the atmosphere for the boy.

"Are ter asleep, my darlin'?" Morel asked softly.

"No; is my mother comin'?"

"She's just finishin' foldin' the clothes. Do you

110

want anything?" Morel rarely "thee'd" his son.

"I don't want nothing. But how long will she be?"

"Not long, my duckie."

The father waited undecidedly on the hearth-rug for a moment or two. He felt his son did not want him. Then he went to the top of the stairs and said to his wife:

"This childt's axin' for thee; how long art goin' to be?"

"Until I've finished, good gracious! Tell him to go to sleep."

"She says you're to go to sleep," the father repeated gently to Paul.

"Well, I want *her* to come," insisted the boy.

"He says he can't go off till you come," Morel called downstairs.

"Eh, dear! I shan't be long. And do stop shouting downstairs. There's the other children——"

Then Morel came again and crouched before the bedroom fire. He loved a fire dearly.

"She says she won't be long," he said.

He loitered about indefinitely. The boy began to get feverish with irritation. His father's presence seemed to aggravate all his sick impatience. At last Morel, after having stood looking at his son awhile, said softly:

"Good-night, my darling."

"Good-night," Paul replied, turning round in relief to be alone.

Paul loved to sleep with his mother. Sleep is still

most perfect, in spite of hygienists, when it is shared with a beloved. The warmth, the security and peace of soul, the utter comfort from the touch of the other, knits the sleep, so that it takes the body and soul completely in its healing. Paul lay against her and slept, and got better; whilst she, always a bad sleeper, fell later on into a profound sleep that seemed to give her faith.

In convalescence he would sit up in bed, see the fluffy horses feeding at the troughs in the field, scattering their hay on the trodden yellow snow; watch the miners troop home—small, black figures trailing slowly in gangs across the white field. Then the night came up in dark blue vapour from the snow.

In convalescence everything was wonderful. The snowflakes, suddenly arriving on the window-pane, clung there a moment like swallows, then were gone, and a drop of water was crawling down the glass. The snowflakes whirled round the corner of the house, like pigeons dashing by. Away across the valley the little black train crawled doubtfully over the great whiteness.

While they were so poor, the children were delighted if they could do anything to help economically. Annie and Paul and Arthur went out early in the morning, in summer, looking for mushrooms, hunting through the wet grass, from which the larks were rising, for the white-skinned, wonderful naked bodies crouched secretly in the green. And if they got half a pound they felt exceedingly happy: there was the joy of finding something, the joy of accepting something straight from the hand of Nature, and the joy of contributing to the family exchequer.

But the most important harvest, after gleaning for frumenty, was the blackberries. Mrs. Morel must buy fruit for puddings on the Saturdays; also she liked blackberries. So Paul and Arthur scoured the coppices and woods and old quarries, so long as a blackberry was to be found, every week-end going on their search. In that region of mining villages blackberries became a comparative rarity. But Paul hunted far and wide. He loved being out in the country, among the bushes. But he also could not bear to go home to his mother empty. That, he felt, would disappoint her, and he would have died rather.

"Good gracious!" she would exclaim as the lads came in, late, and tired to death, and hungry, "wherever have you been?"

"Well," replied Paul, "there wasn't any, so we went over Misk Hills. And look here, our mother!"

She peeped into the basket.

"Now, those are fine ones!" she exclaimed.

"And there's over two pounds—isn't there over two pounds?"

She tried the basket.

"Yes," she answered doubtfully.

Then Paul fished out a little spray. He always brought her one spray, the best he could find.

"Pretty!" she said, in a curious tone, of a woman accepting a love-token.

113

The boy walked all day, went miles and miles, rather than own himself beaten and come home to her empty-handed. She never realised this, whilst he was young. She was a woman who waited for her children to grow up. And William occupied her chiefly.

But when William went to Nottingham, and was not so much at home, the mother made a companion of Paul. The latter was unconsciously jealous of his brother, and William was jealous of him. At the same time, they were good friends.

Mrs. Morel's intimacy with her second son was more subtle and fine, perhaps not so passionate as with her eldest. It was the rule that Paul should fetch the money on Friday afternoons. The colliers of the five pits were paid on Fridays, but not individually. All the earnings of each stall were put down to the chief butty, as contractor, and he divided the wages again, either in the public-house or in his own home. So that the children could fetch the money, school closed early on Friday afternoons. Each of the Morel children—William, then Annie, then Paul—had fetched the money on Friday afternoons, until they went themselves to work. Paul used to set off at half-past three, with a little calico bag in his pocket. Down all the paths, women, girls, children, and men were seen trooping to the offices.

These offices were quite handsome: a new, red-brick building, almost like a mansion, standing in its own grounds at the end of Greenhill Lane. The waiting-room was the hall, a long, bare room paved

114

with blue brick, and having a seat all round, against the wall. Here sat the colliers in their pit-dirt. They had come up early. The women and children usually loitered about on the red gravel paths. Paul always examined the grass border, and the big grass bank, because in it grew tiny pansies and tiny forget-me-nots. There was a sound of many voices. The women had on their Sunday hats. The girls chattered loudly. Little dogs ran here and there. The green shrubs were silent all around.

Then from inside came the cry "Spinney Park—Spinney Park." All the folk for Spinney Park trooped inside. When it was time for Bretty to be paid, Paul went in among the crowd. The pay-room was quite small. A counter went across, dividing it into half. Behind the counter stood two men—Mr. Braithwaite and his clerk, Mr. Winterbottom. Mr. Braithwaite was large, somewhat of the stern patriarch in appearance, having a rather thin white beard. He was usually muffled in an enormous silk neckerchief, and right up to the hot summer a huge fire burned in the open grate. No window was open. Sometimes in winter the air scorched the throats of the people, coming in from the freshness. Mr. Winterbottom was rather small and fat, and very bald. He made remarks that were not witty, whilst his chief launched forth patriarchal admonitions against the colliers.

The room was crowded with miners in their pit-dirt, men who had been home and changed, and women, and one or two children, and usually a dog.

115

Paul was quite small, so it was often his fate to be jammed behind the legs of the men, near the fire which scorched him. He knew the order of the names—they went according to stall number.

"Holliday," came the ringing voice of Mr. Braithwaite. Then Mrs. Holliday stepped silently forward, was paid, drew aside.

"Bower—John Bower."

A boy stepped to the counter. Mr. Braithwaite, large and irascible, glowered at him over his spectacles.

"John Bower!" he repeated.

"It's me," said the boy.

"Why, you used to 'ave a different nose than that," said glossy Mr. Winterbottom, peering over the counter. The people tittered, thinking of John Bower senior.

"How is it your father's not come!" said Mr. Braithwaite, in a large and magisterial voice.

"He's badly," piped the boy.

"You should tell him to keep off the drink," pronounced the great cashier.

"An' niver mind if he puts his foot through yer," said a mocking voice from behind.

All the men laughed. The large and important cashier looked down at his next sheet.

"Fred Pilkington!" he called, quite indifferent.

Mr. Braithwaite was an important shareholder in the firm.

Paul knew his turn was next but one, and his heart began to beat. He was pushed against the

116

chimney-piece. His calves were burning. But he did not hope to get through the wall of men.

"Walter Morel!" came the ringing voice.

"Here!" piped Paul, small and inadequate.

"Morel—Walter Morel!" the cashier repeated, his finger and thumb on the invoice, ready to pass on.

Paul was suffering convulsions of self-consciousness, and could not or would not shout. The backs of the men obliterated him. Then Mr. Winterbottom came to the rescue.

"He's here. Where is he? Morel's lad?"

The fat, red, bald little man peered round with keen eyes. He pointed at the fireplace. The colliers looked round, moved aside, and disclosed the boy.

"Here he is!" said Mr. Winterbottom.

Paul went to the counter.

"Seventeen pounds eleven and fivepence. Why don't you shout up when you're called?" said Mr. Braithwaite. He banged on to the invoice a five-pound bag of silver, then in a delicate and pretty movement, picked up a little ten-pound column of gold, and plumped it beside the silver. The gold slid in a bright stream over the paper. The cashier finished counting off the money; the boy dragged the whole down the counter to Mr. Winterbottom, to whom the stoppages for rent and tools must be paid. Here he suffered again.

"Sixteen an' six," said Mr. Winterbottom.

The lad was too much upset to count. He pushed forward some loose silver and half a sovereign.

"How much do you think you've given me?" asked Mr. Winterbottom.

The boy looked at him, but said nothing. He had not the faintest notion.

"Haven't you got a tongue in your head?"

Paul bit his lip, and pushed forward some more silver.

"Don't they teach you to count at the Board-school?" he asked.

"Nowt but algibbra an' French," said a collier.

"An' cheek an' impidence," said another.

Paul was keeping someone waiting. With trembling fingers he got his money into the bag and slid out. He suffered the tortures of the damned on these occasions.

His relief, when he got outside, and was walking along the Mansfield Road, was infinite. On the park wall the mosses were green. There were some gold and some white fowls pecking under the apple trees of an orchard. The colliers were walking home in a stream. The boy went near the wall, self-consciously. He knew many of the men, but could not recognise them in their dirt. And this was a new torture to him.

When he got down to the New Inn, at Bretty, his father was not yet come. Mrs. Wharmby, the landlady, knew him. His grandmother, Morel's mother, had been Mrs. Wharmby's friend.

"Your father's not come yet," said the landlady, in the peculiar half-scornful, half-patronising voice of a woman who talks chiefly to grown men. "Sit you down."

Paul sat down on the edge of the bench in the bar. Some colliers were "reckoning"—sharing out their money—in a corner; others came in. They all glanced at the boy without speaking. At last Morel came; brisk, and with something of an air, even in his blackness.

"Hello!" he said rather tenderly to his son. "Have you bested me? Shall you have a drink of something?"

Paul and all the children were bred up fierce anti-alcoholists, and he would have suffered more in drinking a lemonade before all the men than in having a tooth drawn.

The landlady looked at him *de haut en bas*, rather pitying, and at the same time, resenting his clear, fierce morality. Paul went home, glowering. He entered the house silently. Friday was baking day, and there was usually a hot bun. His mother put it before him.

Suddenly he turned on her in a fury, his eyes flashing:

"I'm *not* going to the office any more," he said.

"Why, what's the matter?" his mother asked in surprise. His sudden rages rather amused her.

"I'm *not* going any more," he declared.

"Oh, very well, tell your father so."

He chewed his bun as if he hated it.

"I'm not—I'm not going to fetch the money."

"Then one of Carlin's children can go; they'd be

119

glad enough of the sixpence," said Mrs. Morel.

This sixpence was Paul's only income. It mostly went in buying birthday presents; but it *was* an income, and he treasured it. But——

"They can have it, then!" he said. "I don't want it."

"Oh, very well," said his mother. "But you needn't bully *me* about it."

"They're hateful, and common, and hateful, they are, and I'm not going any more. Mr. Braithwaite drops his 'h's', an' Mr. Winterbottom says 'You was'."

"And is that why you won't go any more?" smiled Mrs. Morel.

The boy was silent for some time. His face was pale, his eyes dark and furious. His mother moved about at her work, taking no notice of him.

"They always stan' in front of me, so's I can't get out," he said.

"Well, my lad, you've only to *ask* them," she replied.

"An' then Alfred Winterbottom says, 'What do they teach you at the Board-school?' "

"They never taught *him* much," said Mrs. Morel, "that is a fact—neither manners nor wit—and his cunning he was born with."

So, in her own way, she soothed him. His ridiculous hypersensitiveness made her heart ache. And sometimes the fury in his eyes roused her, made her sleeping soul lift up its head a moment, surprised.

"What was the cheque?" she asked.

"Seventeen pounds eleven and fivepence, and sixteen and six stoppages," replied the boy. "It's a good week; and only five shillings stoppages for my father."

So she was able to calculate how much her husband had earned, and could call him to account if he gave her short money. Morel always kept to himself the secret of the week's amount.

Friday was the baking night and market night. It was the rule that Paul should stay at home and bake. He loved to stop in and draw or read; he was very fond of drawing. Annie always "gallivanted" on Friday nights; Arthur was enjoying himself as usual. So the boy remained alone.

Mrs. Morel loved her marketing. In the tiny market-place on the top of the hill, where four roads, from Nottingham and Derby, Ilkeston and Mansfield, meet, many stalls were erected. Brakes ran in from surrounding villages. The market-place was full of women, the streets packed with men. It was amazing to see so many men everywhere in the streets. Mrs. Morel usually quarrelled with her lace woman, sympathised with her fruit man—who was a gabey, but his wife was a bad 'un—laughed with the fish man—who was a scamp but so droll—put the linoleum man in his place, was cold with the odd-wares man, and only went to the crockery man when she was driven—or drawn by the cornflowers on a little dish; then she was coldly polite.

121

"I wondered how much that little dish was," she said.

"Sevenpence to you."

"Thank you."

She put the dish down and walked away; but she could not leave the market-place without it. Again she went by where the pots lay coldly on the floor, and she glanced at the dish furtively, pretending not to.

She was a little woman, in a bonnet and a black costume. Her bonnet was in its third year; it was a great grievance to Annie.

"Mother!" the girl implored, "don't wear that nubbly little bonnet."

"Then what else shall I wear," replied the mother tartly. "And I'm sure it's right enough."

It had started with a tip; then had had flowers; now was reduced to black lace and a bit of jet.

"It looks rather come down," said Paul. "Couldn't you give it a pick-me-up?"

"I'll jowl your head for impudence," said Mrs. Morel, and she tied the strings of the black bonnet valiantly under her chin.

She glanced at the dish again. Both she and her enemy, the pot man, had an uncomfortable feeling, as if there were something between them. Suddenly he shouted:

"Do you want it for fivepence?"

She started. Her heart hardened; but then she stooped and took up her dish.

"I'll have it," she said.

"Yer'll do me the favour, like?" he said. "Yer'd better spit in it, like yer do when y'ave something give yer."

Mrs. Morel paid him the fivepence in a cold manner.

"I don't see you give it me," she said. "You wouldn't let me have it for fivepence if you didn't want to."

"In this flamin', scrattlin' place you may count yerself lucky if you can give your things away," he growled.

"Yes; there are bad times, and good," said Mrs. Morel.

But she had forgiven the pot man. They were friends. She dare now finger his pots. So she was happy.

Paul was waiting for her. He loved her home-coming. She was always her best so—triumphant, tired, laden with parcels, feeling rich in spirit. He heard her quick, light step in the entry and looked up from his drawing.

"Oh!" she sighed, smiling at him from the door-way.

"My word, you *are* loaded!" he exclaimed, putting down his brush.

"I am!" she gasped. "That brazen Annie said she'd meet me. *Such* a weight!"

She dropped her string bag and her packages on the table.

"Is the bread done?" she asked, going to the oven.

"The last one is soaking," he replied. "You needn't look, I've not forgotten it."

"Oh, that pot man!" she said, closing the oven door. "You know what a wretch I've said he was? Well, I don't think he's quite so bad."

"Don't you?"

The boy was attentive to her. She took off her little black bonnet.

"No. I think he can't make any money—well, it's everybody's cry alike nowadays—and it makes him disagreeable."

"It would *me*," said Paul.

"Well, one can't wonder at it. And he let me have—how much do you think he let me have *this* for?"

She took the dish out of its rag of newspaper, and stood looking on it with joy.

"Show me!" said Paul.

The two stood together gloating over the dish.

"I *love* cornflowers on things," said Paul.

"Yes, and I thought of the teapot you bought me——"

"One and three," said Paul.

"Fivepence!"

"It's not enough, mother."

"No. Do you know, I fairly sneaked off with it. But I'd been extravagant, I couldn't afford any more. And he needn't have let me have it if he hadn't wanted to."

"No, he needn't, need he," said Paul, and the two

124

comforted each other from the fear of having robbed the pot man.

"We c'n have stewed fruit in it," said Paul.

"Or custard, or a jelly," said his mother.

"Or radishes and lettuce," said he.

"Don't forget that bread," she said, her voice bright with glee.

Paul looked in the oven; tapped the loaf on the base.

"It's done," he said, giving it to her.

She tapped it also.

"Yes," she replied, going to unpack her bag. "Oh, and I'm a wicked, extravagant woman. I know I s'll come to want."

He hopped to her side eagerly, to see her latest extravagance. She unfolded another lump of newspaper and disclosed some roots of pansies and of crimson daisies.

"Four penn'orth!" she moaned.

"How *cheap*!" he cried.

"Yes, but I couldn't afford it *this* week of all weeks."

"But lovely!" he cried.

"Aren't they!" she exclaimed, giving way to pure joy. "Paul, look at this yellow one, isn't it—and a face just like an old man!"

"Just!" cried Paul, stooping to sniff. "And smells that nice! But he's a bit splashed."

He ran in the scullery, came back with the flannel, and carefully washed the pansy.

"*Now* look at him now he's wet!" he said.

"Yes!" she exclaimed, brimful of satisfaction.

The children of Scargill Street felt quite select. At the end where the Morels lived there were not many young things. So the few were more united. Boys and girls played together, the girls joining in the fights and the rough games, the boys taking part in the dancing games and rings and make-belief of the girls.

Annie and Paul and Arthur loved the winter evenings, when it was not wet. They stayed indoors till the colliers were all gone home, till it was thick dark, and the street would be deserted. Then they tied their scarves round their necks, for they scorned overcoats, as all the colliers' children did, and went out. The entry was very dark, and at the end the whole great night opened out, in a hollow, with a little tangle of lights below where Minton pit lay, and another far away opposite for Selby. The farthest tiny lights seemed to stretch out the darkness for ever. The children looked anxiously down the road at the one lamp-post, which stood at the end of the field path. If the little, luminous space were deserted, the two boys felt genuine desolation. They stood with their hands in their pockets under the lamp, turning their backs on the night, quite miserable, watching the dark houses. Suddenly a pinafore under a short coat was seen, and a long-legged girl came flying up.

"Where's Billy Pillins an' your Annie an' Eddie Dakin?"

126

"I don't know."

But it did not matter so much—there were three now. They set up a game round the lamp-post, till the others rushed up, yelling. Then the play went fast and furious.

There was only this one lamp-post. Behind was the great scoop of darkness, as if all the night were there. In front, another wide, dark way opened over the hill brow. Occasionally somebody came out of this way and went into the field down the path. In a dozen yards the night had swallowed them. The children played on.

They were brought exceedingly close together owing to their isolation. If a quarrel took place, the whole play was spoilt. Arthur was very touchy, and Billy Pillins—really Philips—was worse. Then Paul had to side with Arthur, and on Paul's side went Alice, while Billy Pillins always had Emmie Limb and Eddie Dakin to back him up. Then the six would fight, hate with a fury of hatred, and flee home in terror. Paul never forgot, after one of these fierce internecine fights, seeing a big red moon lift itself up, slowly, between the waste road over the hill-top, steadily, like a great bird. And he thought of the Bible, that the moon should be turned to blood. And the next day he made haste to be friends with Billy Pillins. And then the wild, intense games went on again under the lamp-post, surrounded by so much darkness. Mrs. Morel, going into her parlour, would hear the children singing away:

"My shoes are made of Spanish leather,
  My socks are made of silk;
I wear a ring on every finger,
  I wash myself in milk."

They sounded so perfectly absorbed in the game as their voices came out of the night, that they had the feel of wild creatures singing. It stirred the mother; and she understood when they came in at eight o'clock, ruddy, with brilliant eyes, and quick, passionate speech.

They all loved the Scargill Street house for its openness, for the great scallop of the world it had in view. On summer evenings the women would stand against the field fence, gossiping, facing the west, watching the sunsets flare quickly out, till the Derbyshire hills ridged across the crimson far away, like the black crest of a newt.

In this summer season the pits never turned full time, particularly the soft coal. Mrs. Dakin, who lived next door to Mrs. Morel, going to the field fence to shake her hearth-rug, would spy men coming slowly up the hill. She saw at once they were colliers. Then she waited, a tall, thin, shrew-faced woman, standing on the hill brow, almost like a menace to the poor colliers who were toiling up. It was only eleven o'clock. From the far-off wooded hills the haze that hangs like fine black crape at the back of a summer morning had not yet dissipated. The first man came to the stile. "Chock-chock!" went the gate under his thrust.

128

"What, han' yer knocked off?" cried Mrs. Dakin.

"We han, missis."

"It's a pity as they letn yer goo," she said sarcastically.

"It is that," replied the man.

"Nay, you know you're flig to come up again," she said.

And the man went on. Mrs. Dakin, going up her yard, spied Mrs. Morel taking the ashes to the ashpit.

"I reckon Minton's knocked off, missis," she cried.

"Isn't it sickenin'!" exclaimed Mrs. Morel in wrath.

"Ha! But I'n just seed Jont Hutchby."

"They might as well have saved their shoeleather," said Mrs. Morel. And both women went indoors disgusted.

The colliers, their faces scarcely blackened, were trooping home again. Morel hated to go back. He loved the sunny morning. But he had gone to pit to work, and to be sent home again spoilt his temper.

"Good gracious, at this time!" exclaimed his wife, as he entered.

"Can I help it, woman?" he shouted.

"And I've not done half enough dinner."

"Then I'll eat my bit o' snap as I took with me," he bawled pathetically. He felt ignominious and sore.

And the children, coming home from school, would wonder to see their father eating with his dinner the two thick slices of rather dry and dirty bread-and-butter that had been to pit and back.

"What's my dad eating his snap for now?" asked Arthur.

"I should ha'e it holled at me if I didna," snorted Morel.

"What a story!" exclaimed his wife.

"An' is it goin' to be wasted?" said Morel. "I'm not such a extravagant mortal as you lot, with your waste. If I drop a bit of bread at pit, in all the dust an' dirt, I pick it up an' eat it."

"The mice would eat it," said Paul. "It wouldn't be wasted."

"Good bread-an'-butter's not for mice, either," said Morel. "Dirty or not dirty, I'd eat it rather than it should be wasted."

"You might leave it for the mice and pay for it out of your next pint," said Mrs. Morel.

"Oh, might I?" he exclaimed.

They were very poor that autumn. William had just gone away to London, and his mother missed his money. He sent ten shillings once or twice, but he had many things to pay for at first. His letters came regularly once a week. He wrote a good deal to his mother, telling her all his life, how he made friends, and was exchanging lessons with a Frenchman, how he enjoyed London. His mother felt again he was remaining to her just as when he was at home. She wrote to him every week her direct, rather witty letters. All day long, as she cleaned the house, she thought of him. He was in London: he

130

would do well. Almost, he was like her knight who wore *her* favour in the battle.

He was coming at Christmas for five days. There had never been such preparations. Paul and Arthur scoured the land for holly and evergreens. Annie made the pretty paper hoops in the old-fashioned way. And there was unheard-of extravagance in the larder. Mrs. Morel made a big and magnificent cake. Then, feeling queenly, she showed Paul how to blanch almonds. He skinned the long nuts reverently, counting them all, to see not one was lost. It was said that eggs whisked better in a cold place. So the boy stood in the scullery, where the temperature was nearly at freezing-point, and whisked and whisked, and flew in excitement to his mother as the white of egg grew stiffer and more snowy.

"Just look, mother! Isn't it lovely?"

And he balanced a bit on his nose, then blew it in the air.

"Now, don't waste it," said the mother.

Everybody was mad with excitement. William was coming on Christmas Eve. Mrs. Morel surveyed her pantry. There was a big plum cake, and a rice cake, jam tarts, lemon tarts, and mince-pies—two enormous dishes. She was finishing cooking—Spanish tarts and cheese-cakes. Everywhere was decorated. The kissing bunch of berried holly hung with bright and glittering things, spun slowly over Mrs. Morel's head as she trimmed her little tarts in the kitchen. A great fire roared. There was a scent of cooked pastry. He was due at seven o'clock, but he would be late. The three children had gone to meet him. She was alone. But at a quarter to seven Morel came in again. Neither wife nor husband spoke. He sat in his arm-chair, quite awkward with excitement, and she quietly went on with her baking. Only by the careful way in which she did things could it be told how much moved she was. The clock ticked on.

"What time dost say he's coming?" Morel asked for the fifth time.

"The train gets in at half-past six," she replied emphatically.

"Then he'll be here at ten past seven."

"Eh, bless you, it'll be hours late on the Midland," she said indifferently. But she hoped, by expecting him late, to bring him early. Morel went down the entry to look for him. Then he came back.

"Goodness, man!" she said. "You're like an ill-sitting hen."

"Hadna yo better be gettin' him summat t' eat ready?" asked the father.

"There's plenty of time," she answered.

"There's not so much as _I_ can see on," he answered, turning crossly in his chair. She began to clear her table. The kettle was singing. They waited and waited.

Meantime the three children were on the platform at Sethley Bridge, on the Midland main line, two miles from home. They waited one hour. A train came—he was not there. Down the line the red and green lights shone. It was very dark and very cold.

"Ask him if the London train's come," said Paul to Annie, when they saw a man in a tip cap.

"I'm not," said Annie. "You be quiet—he might send us off."

But Paul was dying for the man to know they were expecting someone by the London train: it sounded so grand. Yet he was much too much scared of broaching any man, let alone one in a peaked cap, to dare to ask. The three children could scarcely go into the waiting-room for fear of being sent away, and for fear something should happen whilst they were off the platform. Still they waited in the dark and cold.

"It's an hour an' a half late," said Arthur pathetically.

"Well," said Annie, "it's Christmas Eve."

They all grew silent. He wasn't coming. They looked down the darkness of the railway. There was London! It seemed the uttermost of distance. They thought anything might happen if one came from London. They were all too troubled to talk. Cold, and unhappy, and silent, they huddled together on the platform.

At last, after more than two hours, they saw the lights of an engine peering round, away down the darkness. A porter ran out. The children drew back with beating hearts. A great train, bound for Manchester, drew up. Two doors opened, and from one of them, William. They flew to him. He handed

133

parcels to them cheerily, and immediately began to explain that this great train had stopped for *his* sake at such a small station as Sethley Bridge: it was not booked to stop.

Meanwhile the parents were getting anxious. The table was set, the chop was cooked, everything was ready. Mrs. Morel put on her black apron. She was wearing her best dress. Then she sat, pretending to read. The minutes were a torture to her.

"H'm!" said Morel. "It's an hour an' a ha'ef."

"And those children waiting!" she said.

"Th' train canna ha' come in yet," he said.

"I tell you, on Christmas Eve they're *hours* wrong."

They were both a bit cross with each other, so gnawed with anxiety. The ash tree moaned outside in a cold, raw wind. And all that space of night from London home! Mrs. Morel suffered. The slight click of the works inside the clock irritated her. It was getting so late; it was getting unbearable.

At last there was a sound of voices, and a footstep in the entry.

"Ha's here!" cried Morel, jumping up.

Then he stood back. The mother ran a few steps towards the door and waited. There was a rush and a patter of feet, the door burst open. William was there. He dropped his Gladstone bag and took his mother in his arms.

"Mater!" he said.

"My boy!" she cried.

And for two seconds, no longer, she clasped him

and kissed him. Then she withdrew and said, trying to be quite normal:

"But how late you are!"

"Aren't I!" he cried, turning to his father. "Well, dad!"

The two men shook hands.

"Well, my lad!"

Morel's eyes were wet.

"We thought tha'd niver be commin'," he said.

"Oh, I'd come!" exclaimed William.

Then the son turned round to his mother.

"But you look well," she said proudly, laughing.

"Well!" he exclaimed. "I should think so—coming home!"

He was a fine fellow, big, straight, and fearless-looking. He looked round at the evergreens and the kissing bunch, and the little tarts that lay in their tins on the hearth.

"By jove! mother, it's not different!" he said, as if in relief.

Everybody was still for a second. Then he suddenly sprang forward, picked a tart from the hearth, and pushed it whole into his mouth.

"Well, did iver you see such a parish oven!" the father exclaimed.

He had brought them endless presents. Every penny he had he had spent on them. There was a sense of luxury overflowing in the house. For his mother there was an umbrella with gold on the pale handle. She kept it to her dying day, and would have lost anything rather than that. Everybody had something gorgeous, and besides, there were pounds of unknown sweets: Turkish delight, crystallised pineapple, and such-like things which, the children thought, only the splendour of London could provide. And Paul boasted of these sweets among his friends.

"Real pineapple, cut off in slices, and then turned into crystal—fair grand!"

Everybody was mad with happiness in the family. Home was home, and they loved it with a passion of love, whatever the suffering had been. There were parties, there were rejoicings. People came in to see William, to see what difference London had made to him. And they all found him "such a gentleman, and *such* a fine fellow, my word"!

When he went away again the children retired to various places to weep alone. Morel went to bed in misery, and Mrs. Morel felt as if she were numbed by some drug, as if her feelings were paralysed. She loved him passionately.

He was in the office of a lawyer connected with a large shipping firm, and at the midsummer his chief offered him a trip in the Mediterranean on one of the boats, for quite a small cost. Mrs. Morel wrote: "Go, go, my boy. You may never have a chance again, and I should love to think of you cruising there in the Mediterranean almost better than to have you at home." But William came home for his fortnight's holiday. Not even the Mediterranean, which pulled at all his young man's desire to travel, and at his poor man's wonder at the glamorous south, could take him away when he might come home. That compensated his mother for much.

# 5

## PAUL LAUNCHES INTO LIFE

MOREL was rather a heedless man, careless of danger. So he had endless accidents. Now, when Mrs. Morel heard the rattle of an empty coal-cart cease at the entry-end, she ran into the parlour to look, expecting almost to see her husband seated in the wagon, his face grey under his dirt, his body limp and sick with some hurt or other. If it were he, she would run out to help.

About a year after William went to London, and just after Paul had left school, before he got work, Mrs. Morel was upstairs and her son was painting in the kitchen—he was very clever with his brush—when there came a knock at the door. Crossly he put down his brush to go. At the same moment his mother opened a window upstairs and looked down.

A pit-lad in his dirt stood on the threshold.

"Is this Walter Morel's?" he asked.

"Yes," said Mrs. Morel. "What is it?"

But she had guessed already.

"Your mester's got hurt," he said.

"Eh, dear me!" she exclaimed. "It's a wonder if he hadn't, lad. And what's he done this time?"

"I don't know for sure, but it's 'is leg somewhere. They ta'ein' 'im ter th' 'ospital."

"Good gracious me!" she exclaimed. "Eh, dear, what a one he is! There's not five minutes of peace, I'll be hanged if there is! His thumb's nearly better, and now— Did you see him?"

"I seed him at th' bottom. An' I seed 'em bring 'im up in a tub, an' 'e wor in a dead faint. But he shouted like anythink when Doctor Fraser examined him i' th' lamp cabin—an' cossed an' swore, an' said as 'e wor goin' to be ta'en whoam—'e worn't goin' ter th' 'ospital."

The boy faltered to an end.

"He *would* want to come home, so that I can have all the bother. Thank you, my lad. Eh, dear, if I'm not sick—sick and surfeited, I am!"

She came downstairs. Paul had mechanically resumed his painting.

"And it must be pretty bad if they've taken him to the hospital," she went on. "But what a *careless* creature he is! Other men don't have all these accidents. Yes, he *would* want to put all the burden on me. Eh, dear, just as we *were* getting easy a bit at last. Put those things away, there's no time to be painting now. What time is there a train? I know I s'll have to go trailing to Keston. I s'll have to leave that bedroom."

"I can finish it," said Paul.

"You needn't. I shall catch the seven o'clock back, I should think. Oh, my blessed heart, the fuss and commotion he'll make! And those granite setts at Tinder Hill—he might well call them kidney pebbles—they'll jolt him almost to bits. I wonder why they can't mend them, the state they're in, an' all the men as go across in that ambulance. You'd think they'd have a hospital here. The men bought the ground, and, my sirs, there'd be accidents enough to keep it going. But no, they must trail them ten miles in a slow ambulance to Nottingham. It's a crying shame! Oh, and the fuss he'll make! I know he will! I wonder who's with him. Barker, I s'd think. Poor beggar, he'll wish himself anywhere rather. But he'll look after him, I know. Now there's no telling how long he'll be stuck in that hospital—and *won't* he hate it! But if it's only his leg it's not so bad."

All the time she was getting ready. Hurriedly taking off her bodice, she crouched at the boiler while the water ran slowly into her lading-can.

"I wish this boiler was at the bottom of the sea!" she exclaimed, wriggling the handle impatiently. She had very handsome, strong arms, rather surprising on a smallish woman.

Paul cleared away, put on the kettle, and set the table.

"There isn't a train till four-twenty," he said. "You've time enough."

"Oh no, I haven't!" she cried, blinking at him over the towel as she wiped her face.

"Yes, you have. You must drink a cup of tea at any rate. Should I come with you to Keston?"

"Come with me? What for, I should like to know? Now, what have I to take him? Eh, dear! His clean shirt—and it's a blessing it *is* clean. But it had better

140

be aired. And stockings—he won't want them—and a towel, I suppose; and handkerchiefs. Now what else?"

"A comb, a knife and fork and spoon," said Paul. His father had been in the hospital before.

"Goodness knows what sort of state his feet were in," continued Mrs. Morel, as she combed her long brown hair, that was fine as silk, and was touched now with grey. "He's very particular to wash himself to the waist, but below he thinks doesn't matter. But there, I suppose they see plenty like it."

Paul had laid the table. He cut his mother one or two pieces of very thin bread and butter.

"Here you are," he said, putting her cup of tea in her place.

"I can't be bothered!" she exclaimed crossly.

"Well, you've got to, so there, now it's put out ready," he insisted.

So she sat down and sipped her tea, and ate a little, in silence. She was thinking.

In a few minutes she was gone, to walk the two and a half miles to Keston Station. All the things she was taking him she had in her bulging string bag. Paul watched her go up the road between the hedges—a little, quick-stepping figure, and his heart ached for her, that she was thrust forward again into pain and trouble. And she, tripping so quickly in her anxiety, felt at the back of her her son's heart waiting on her, felt him bearing what part of the burden he could, even supporting her. And when she was at the hospital, she thought: "It *will* upset that lad when I tell him how bad it is. I'd better be careful." And when she was trudging home again, she felt he was coming to share her burden.

"Is it bad?" asked Paul, as soon as she entered the house.

"It's bad enough," she replied.

"What?"

She sighed and sat down, undoing her bonnet-strings. Her son watched her face as it was lifted, and her small, work-hardened hands fingering at the bow under her chin.

"Well," she answered, "it's not really dangerous, but the nurse says it's a dreadful smash. You see, a great piece of rock fell on his leg—here—and it's a compound fracture. There are pieces of bone sticking through——"

"Ugh—how horrid!" exclaimed the children.

"And," she continued, "of course he says he's going to die—it wouldn't be him if he didn't. 'I'm done for, my lass!' he said, looking at me. 'Don't be so silly,' I said to him. 'You're not going to die of a broken leg, however badly it's smashed.' 'I s'll niver come out of 'ere but in a wooden box,' he groaned. 'Well,' I said, 'if you want them to carry you into the garden in a wooden box, when you're better, I've no doubt they will.' 'If we think it's good for him,' said the Sister. She's an awfully nice Sister, but rather strict."

Mrs. Morel took off her bonnet. The children waited in silence.

"Of course, he *is* bad," she continued, "and he will be. It's a great shock, and he's lost a lot of blood; and, of course, it *is* a very dangerous smash. It's not at all sure that it will mend so easily. And then there's the fever and the mortification—if it took bad ways he'd quickly be gone. But there, he's a clean-blooded man, with wonderful healing flesh, and so I see no reason why it *should* take bad ways. Of course there's a wound——"

She was pale now with emotion and anxiety. The three children realised that it was very bad for their father, and the house was silent, anxious.

"But he always gets better," said Paul after a while.

"That's what I tell him," said the mother.

Everybody moved about in silence.

"And he really looked nearly done for," she said. "But the Sister says that is the pain."

Annie took away her mother's coat and bonnet.

"And he looked at me when I came away! I said: 'I s'll have to go now, Walter, because of the train—and the children.' And he looked at me. It seems hard."

Paul took up his brush again and went on painting. Arthur went outside for some coal. Annie sat looking dismal. And Mrs. Morel, in her little rocking-chair that her husband had made for her when the first baby was coming, remained motionless, brooding. She was grieved, and bitterly sorry for the man who was hurt so much. But still,

143

in her heart of hearts, where the love should have burned, there was a blank. Now, when all her woman's pity was roused to its full extent, when she would have slaved herself to death to nurse him and to save him, when she would have taken the pain herself, if she could, somewhere far away inside her, she felt indifferent to him and to his suffering. It hurt her most of all, this failure to love him, even when he roused her strong emotions. She brooded a while.

"And there," she said suddenly, "when I'd got half-way to Keston, I found I'd come out in my working boots—and *look* at them." They were an old pair of Paul's, brown and rubbed through at the toes. "I didn't know what to do with myself, for shame," she added.

In the morning, when Annie and Arthur were at school, Mrs. Morel talked again to her son, who was helping her with her housework.

"I found Barker at the hospital. He did look bad, poor little fellow! 'Well,' I said to him, 'what sort of a journey did you have with him?' 'Dunna ax me, missis!' he said. 'Ay,' I said, 'I know what he'd be.' 'But it *wor* bad for him, Mrs. Morel, it *wor* that!' he said. 'I know,' I said. 'At ivry jolt I thought my 'eart would ha' flown clean out o' my mouth,' he said. 'An' the scream 'e gives sometimes! Missis, not for a fortune would I go through wi' it again.' 'I can quite understand it,' I said. 'It's a nasty job, though,' he said, 'an one as'll be a long while afore it's right again.' 'I'm afraid it will,' I said. I like Mr.

Barker—I *do* like him. There's something so manly about him."

Paul resumed his task silently.

"And of course," Mrs. Morel continued, "for a man like your father, the hospital *is* hard. He *can't* understand rules and regulations. And he won't let anybody else touch him, not if he can help it. When he smashed the muscles of his thigh, and it had to be dressed four times a day, *would* he let anybody but me or his mother do it? He wouldn't. So, of course, he'll suffer in there with the nurses. And I didn't like leaving him. I'm sure, when I kissed him an' came away, it seemed a shame."

So she talked to her son, almost as if she were thinking aloud to him, and he took it in as best he could, by sharing her trouble to lighten it. And in the end she shared almost everything with him without knowing.

Morel had a very bad time. For a week he was in a critical condition. Then he began to mend. And then, knowing he was going to get better, the whole family sighed with relief, and proceeded to live happily.

They were not badly off whilst Morel was in the hospital. There were fourteen shillings a week from the pit, ten shillings from the sick club, and five shillings from the Disability Fund; and then every week the butties had something for Mrs. Morel— five or seven shillings—so that she was quite well to do. And whilst Morel was progressing favourably in the hospital, the family was extraordinarily happy

145

and peaceful. On Saturdays and Wednesdays Mrs. Morel went to Nottingham to see her husband. Then she always brought back some little thing: a small tube of paints for Paul, or some thick paper; a couple of postcards for Annie, that the whole family rejoiced over for days before the girl was allowed to send them away; or a fret-saw for Arthur, or a bit of pretty wood. She described her adventures into the big shops with joy. Soon the folk in the picture-shop knew her, and knew about Paul. The girl in the book-shop took a keen interest in her. Mrs. Morel was full of information when she got home from Nottingham. The three sat round till bed-time, listening, putting in, arguing. Then Paul often raked the fire.

"I'm the man in the house now," he used to say to his mother with joy. They learned how perfectly peaceful the home could be. And they almost re-gretted—though none of them would have owned to such callousness—that their father was soon coming back.

Paul was now fourteen, and was looking for work. He was a rather small and rather finely-made boy, with dark brown hair and light blue eyes. His face had already lost its youthful chubbiness, and was becoming somewhat like William's—rough-featured, almost rugged—and it was extraordinarily mobile. Usually he looked as if he saw things, was full of life, and warm; then his smile, like his mother's, came suddenly and was very lovable; and then, when there was any clog in his soul's quick running, his face went stupid and ugly. He was the sort of boy that becomes a clown and a lout as soon as he is not understood, or feels himself held cheap; and, again, is adorable at the first touch of warmth.

He suffered very much from the first contact with anything. When he was seven, the starting school had been a nightmare and a torture to him. But afterwards he liked it. And now that he felt he had to go out into life, he went through agonies of shrinking self-consciousness. He was quite a clever painter for a boy of his years, and he knew some French and German and mathematics that Mr. Heaton had taught him. But nothing he had was of any commercial value. He was not strong enough for heavy manual work, his mother said. He did not care for making things with his hands, preferred racing about, or making excursions into the country, or reading, or painting.

"What do you want to be?" his mother asked.

"Anything."

"That is no answer," said Mrs. Morel.

But it was quite truthfully the only answer he could give. His ambition, as far as this world's gear went, was quietly to earn his thirty or thirty-five shillings a week somewhere near home, and then, when his father died, have a cottage with his mother, paint and go out as he liked, and live happy ever after. That was his programme as far as doing things went. But he was proud within himself, measuring people against himself, and placing them, inexorably. And he thought that *perhaps* he might also make a painter, the real thing. But that he left alone.

"Then," said his mother, "you must look in the paper for the advertisements."

He looked at her. It seemed to him a bitter humiliation and an anguish to go through. But he said nothing. When he got up in the morning, his whole being was knotted up over this one thought:

"I've got to go and look for advertisements for a job."

It stood in front of the morning, that thought, killing all joy and even life, for him. His heart felt like a tight knot.

And then, at ten o'clock, he set off. He was supposed to be a queer, quiet child. Going up the sunny street of the little town, he felt as if all the folk he met said to themselves: "He's going to the Co-op. reading-room to look in the papers for a place. He can't get a job. I suppose he's living on his mother." Then he crept up the stone stairs behind the drapery shop at the Co-op., and peeped in the reading-room. Usually one or two men were there, either old, useless fellows, or colliers "on the club". So he entered, full of shrinking and suffering when they looked up, seated himself at the table, and pretended to scan the news. He knew they would think: "What does a lad of thirteen want in a reading-room with a newspaper?" and he suffered.

Then he looked wistfully out of the window. Already he was a prisoner of industrialism. Large sunflowers stared over the old red wall of the

148

garden opposite, looking in their jolly way down on the women who were hurrying with something for dinner. The valley was full of corn, brightening in the sun. Two collieries, among the fields, waved their small white plumes of steam. Far off on the hills were the woods of Annesley, dark and fascinating. Already his heart went down. He was being taken into bondage. His freedom in the beloved home valley was going now.

The brewers' waggons came rolling up from Keston with enormous barrels, four a side, like beans in a burst bean-pod. The waggoner, throned aloft, rolling massively in his seat, was not so much below Paul's eye. The man's hair, on his small, bullet head, was bleached almost white by the sun, and on his thick red arms, rocking idly on his sack apron, the white hairs glistened. His red face shone and was almost asleep with sunshine. The horses, handsome and brown, went on by themselves, looking by far the masters of the show.

Paul wished he were stupid. "I wish," he thought to himself, "I was fat like him, and like a dog in the sun. I wish I was a pig and a brewer's waggoner."

Then, the room being at last empty, he would hastily copy an advertisement on a scrap of paper, then another, and slip out in immense relief. His mother would scan over his copies.

"Yes," she said, "you may try."

William had written out a letter of application, couched in admirable business language, which Paul copied, with variations. The boy's handwriting was execrable, so that William, who did all things well, got into a fever of impatience.

The elder brother was becoming quite swanky. In London he found that he could associate with men far above his Bestwood friends in station. Some of the clerks in the office had studied for the law, and were more or less going through a kind of apprenticeship. William always made friends among men wherever he went, he was so jolly. Therefore he was soon visiting and staying in houses of men who, in Bestwood, would have looked down on the unapproachable bank manager, and would merely have called indifferently on the Rector. So he began to fancy himself as a great gun. He was, indeed, rather surprised at the ease with which he became a gentleman.

His mother was glad, he seemed so pleased. And his lodging in Walthamstow was so dreary. But now there seemed to come a kind of fever into the young man's letters. He was unsettled by all the change, he did not stand firm on his own feet, but seemed to spin rather giddily on the quick current of the new life. His mother was anxious for him. She could feel him losing himself. He had danced and gone to the theatre, boated on the river, been out with friends; and she knew he sat up afterwards in his cold bedroom grinding away at Latin, because he intended to get on in his office, and in the law as much as he could. He never sent his mother any money now. It was all taken, the little he had, for his own life. And she did not want any, except sometimes, when she was in a tight corner, and when ten shillings would have saved her much worry. She still dreamed of William, and of what he would do, with herself behind him. Never for a minute would she admit to herself how heavy and anxious her heart was because of him.

Also he talked a good deal now of a girl he had met at a dance, a handsome brunette, quite young, and a lady, after whom the men were running thick and fast.

"I wonder if you would run, my boy," his mother wrote to him, "unless you saw all the other men chasing her too. You feel safe enough and vain enough in a crowd. But take care, and see how you feel when you find yourself alone, and in triumph."

William resented these things, and continued the chase. He had taken the girl on the river. "If you saw her, mother, you would know how I feel. Tall and elegant, with the clearest of clear, transparent olive complexions, hair as black as jet, and such grey eyes—bright, mocking, like lights on water at night. It is all very well to be a bit satirical till you see her. And she dresses as well as any woman in London. I tell you, your son doesn't half put his head up when she goes walking down Piccadilly with him."

Mrs. Morel wondered, in her heart, if her son did not go walking down Piccadilly with an elegant figure and fine clothes, rather than with a woman who was near to him. But she congratulated him in her doubtful fashion. And, as she stood over the washing-tub, the mother brooded over her son. She saw him saddled with an elegant and expensive wife, earning little money, dragging along and getting draggled in some small, ugly house in a suburb. "But there," she told herself, "I am very likely a silly—meeting trouble half-way." Nevertheless, the load of anxiety scarcely ever left her heart, lest William should do the wrong thing by himself.

Presently, Paul was bidden call upon Thomas Jordan, Manufacturer of Surgical Appliances, at 21, Spaniel Row, Nottingham. Mrs. Morel was all joy.

"There, you see!" she cried, her eyes shining. "You've only written four letters, and the third is answered. You're lucky, my boy, as I always said you were."

Paul looked at the picture of a wooden leg, adorned with elastic stockings and other appliances, that figured on Mr. Jordan's notepaper, and he felt alarmed. He had not known that elastic stockings existed. And he seemed to feel the business world, with its regulated system of values, and its impersonality, and he dreaded it. It seemed monstrous also that a business could be run on wooden legs.

Mother and son set off together one Tuesday morning. It was August and blazing hot. Paul walked with something screwed up tight inside him. He would have suffered much physical pain rather than this unreasonable suffering at being exposed to strangers, to be accepted or rejected. Yet he chattered away with his mother. He would never have confessed to her how he suffered over these things, and she only partly guessed. She was gay, like a sweetheart. She stood in front of the ticket-office at Bestwood, and Paul watched her take from her purse the money for the tickets. As he saw her hands in their old black kid gloves getting the silver out of the worn purse, his heart contracted with pain of love of her.

She was quite excited, and quite gay. He suffered because she *would* talk aloud in presence of the other travellers.

"Now look at that silly cow!" she said, "careering round as if it thought it was a circus."

"It's most likely a bottfly," he said very low.

"A what?" she asked brightly and unashamed.

They thought a while. He was sensible all the time of having her opposite him. Suddenly their eyes met, and she smiled to him—a rare, intimate smile, beautiful with brightness and love. Then each looked out of the window.

The sixteen slow miles of railway journey passed. The mother and son walked down Station Street, feeling the excitement of lovers having an adventure together. In Carrington Street they stopped to hang over the parapet and look at the barges on the canal below.

"It's just like Venice," he said, seeing the sunshine on the water that lay between high factory walls.

"Perhaps," she answered, smiling.

They enjoyed the shops immensely.

"Now you see that blouse," she would say,

153

"wouldn't that just suit our Annie? And for one-and-eleven-three. Isn't that cheap?"

"And made of needlework as well," he said.

"Yes."

They had plenty of time so they did not hurry. The town was strange and delightful to them. But the boy was tied up inside in a knot of apprehension. He dreaded the interview with Thomas Jordan.

It was nearly eleven o'clock by St. Peter's Church. They turned up a narrow street that led to the Castle. It was gloomy and old-fashioned, having low dark shops and dark green house doors with brass knockers, and yellow-ochred doorsteps projecting on to the pavement; then another old shop whose small window looked like a cunning, half-shut eye. Mother and son went cautiously, looking everywhere for "Thomas Jordan and Son". It was like hunting in some wild place. They were on tip-toe of excitement.

Suddenly they spied a big, dark archway, in which were names of various firms, Thomas Jordan among them.

"Here it is!" said Mrs. Morel. "But now *where* is it?"

They looked round. On one side was a queer, dark, cardboard factory, on the other a Commercial Hotel.

"It's up the entry," said Paul.

And they ventured under the archway, as into the jaws of the dragon. They emerged into a wide yard, like a well, with buildings all round. It was littered with straw and boxes, and cardboard. The sunshine actually caught one crate whose straw was streaming on to the yard like gold. But elsewhere the place was like a pit. There were several doors, and two flights of steps. Straight in front, on a dirty glass door at the top of a staircase, loomed the ominous words "Thomas Jordan and Son—Surgical Appliances." Mrs. Morel went first, her son followed her. Charles I mounted his scaffold with a lighter heart than had Paul Morel as he followed his mother up the dirty steps to the dirty door.

She pushed open the door, and stood in pleased surprise. In front of her was a big warehouse, with creamy paper parcels everywhere, and clerks, with their shirt-sleeves rolled back, were going about in an at-home sort of way. The light was subdued, the glossy cream parcels seemed luminous, the counters were of dark brown wood. All was quiet and very homely. Mrs. Morel took two steps forward, then waited. Paul stood behind her. She had on her Sunday bonnet and a black veil; he wore a boy's broad white collar and a Norfolk suit.

One of the clerks looked up. He was thin and tall, with a small face. His way of looking was alert. Then he glanced round to the other end of the room, where was a glass office. And then he came forward. He did not say anything, but leaned in a gentle, inquiring fashion towards Mrs. Morel.

"Can I see Mr. Jordan?" she asked.

"I'll fetch him," answered the young man.

He went down to the glass office. A red-faced,

white-whiskered old man looked up. He reminded Paul of a pomeranian dog. Then the same little man came up the room. He had short legs, was rather stout, and wore an alpaca jacket. So, with one ear up, as it were, he came stoutly and inquiringly down the room.

"Good morning!" he said, hesitating before Mrs. Morel, in doubt as to whether she were a customer or not.

"Good morning. I came with my son, Paul Morel. You asked him to call this morning."

"Come this way," said Mr. Jordan, in a rather snappy little manner intended to be business-like.

They followed the manufacturer into a grubby little room, upholstered in black American leather, glossy with the rubbing of many customers. On the table was a pile of trusses, yellow wash-leather hoops tangled together. They looked new and living. Paul sniffed the odour of new wash-leather. He wondered what the things were. By this time he was so much stunned that he only noticed the outside things.

"Sit down!" said Mr. Jordan, irritably pointing Mrs. Morel to a horse-hair chair. She sat on the edge in an uncertain fashion. Then the little old man fidgeted and found a paper.

"Did you write this letter?" he snapped, thrusting what Paul recognised as his own notepaper in front of him.

"Yes," he answered.

At that moment he was occupied in two ways:

156

first, in feeling guilty for telling a lie, since William had composed the letter; second, in wondering why his letter seemed so strange and different, in the fat, red hand of the man, from what it had been when it lay on the kitchen table. It was like part of himself, gone astray. He resented the way the man held it.

"Where did you learn to write?" said the old man crossly.

Paul merely looked at him shamedly, and did not answer.

"He *is* a bad writer," put in Mrs. Morel apologetically. Then she pushed up her veil. Paul hated her for not being prouder with this common little man, and he loved her face clear of the veil.

"And you say you know French?" inquired the little man, still sharply.

"Yes," said Paul.

"What school did you go to?"

"The Board-school."

"And did you learn it there?"

"No—I——" The boy went crimson and got no farther.

"His godfather gave him lessons," said Mrs. Morel, half pleading and rather distant.

Mr. Jordan hesitated. Then, in his irritable manner—he always seemed to keep his hands ready for action—he pulled another sheet of paper from his pocket, unfolded it. The paper made a crackling noise. He handed it to Paul.

"Read that," he said.

It was a note in French, in thin, flimsy foreign

157

handwriting that the boy could not decipher. He stared blankly at the paper.

" 'Monsieur,' " he began; then he looked in great confusion at Mr. Jordan. "It's the—it's the——"

He wanted to say "handwriting", but his wits would no longer work even sufficiently to supply him with the word. Feeling an utter fool, and hating Mr. Jordan, he turned desperately to the paper again.

" 'Sir,—Please send me'—er—er—I can't tell the—er—'two pairs—*gris fil bas*—grey thread stockings'—er—er—'*sans*—without'—er—I can't tell the words—er—'*doigts*—fingers'—er—I can't tell the——"

He wanted to say "handwriting", but the word still refused to come. Seeing him stuck, Mr. Jordan snatched the paper from him.

" 'Please send by return two pairs grey thread stockings without *toes*.' "

"Well," flashed Paul, " '*doigts*' means 'fingers'—as well—as a rule——"

The little man looked at him. He did not know whether "*doigts*" meant "fingers"; he knew that for all *his* purposes it meant "toes".

"Fingers to stockings!" he snapped.

"Well, it *does* mean fingers," the boy persisted.

He hated the little man, who made such a clod of him. Mr. Jordan looked at the pale, stupid, defiant boy, then at the mother, who sat quiet and with that peculiar shut-off look of the poor who have to depend on the favour of others.

"And when could he come?" he asked.

"Well," said Mrs. Morel, "as soon as you wish. He has finished school now."

"He would live in Bestwood?"

"Yes; but he could be in—at the station—at a quarter to eight."

"H'm!"

It ended by Paul's being engaged as junior spiral clerk at eight shillings a week. The boy did not open his mouth to say another word, after having insisted that "*doigts*" meant "fingers". He followed his mother down the stairs. She looked at him with her bright blue eyes full of love and joy.

"I think you'll like it," she said.

" '*Doigts*' does mean 'fingers', mother, and it was the writing. I couldn't read the writing."

"Never mind, my boy. I'm sure he'll be all right, and you won't see much of him. Wasn't that first young fellow nice? I'm sure you'll like them."

"But wasn't Mr. Jordan common, mother? Does he own it all?"

"I suppose he was a workman who has got on," she said. "You mustn't mind people so much. They're not being disagreeable to *you*—it's their way. You always think people are meaning things for you. But they don't."

It was very sunny. Over the big desolate space of the market-place the blue sky shimmered, and the granite cobbles of the paving glistened. Shops down the Long Row were deep in obscurity, and the shadow was full of colour. Just where the horse

159

trams trundled across the market was a row of fruit stalls, with fruit blazing in the sun—apples and piles of reddish oranges, small greengage plums and bananas. There was a warm scent of fruit as mother and son passed. Gradually his feeling of ignominy and of rage sank.

"Where should we go for dinner?" asked the mother.

It was felt to be a reckless extravagance. Paul had only been in an eating-house once or twice in his life, and then only to have a cup of tea and a bun. Most of the people of Bestwood considered that tea and bread-and-butter, and perhaps potted beef, was all they could afford to eat in Nottingham. Real cooked dinner was considered great extravagance. Paul felt rather guilty.

They found a place that looked quite cheap. But when Mrs. Morel scanned the bill of fare, her heart was heavy, things were so dear. So she ordered kidney-pies and potatoes as the cheapest available dish.

"We oughtn't to have come here, mother," said Paul.

"Never mind," she said. "We won't come again."

She insisted on his having a small currant tart, because he liked sweets.

"I don't want it, mother," he pleaded.

"Yes," she insisted; "you'll have it."

And she looked round for the waitress. But the waitress was busy, and Mrs. Morel did not like to

160

bother her then. So the mother and son waited for the girl's pleasure, whilst she flirted among the men.

"Brazen hussy!" said Mrs. Morel to Paul. "Look now, she's taking that man *his* pudding, and he came long after us."

"It doesn't matter, mother," said Paul.

Mrs. Morel was angry. But she was too poor, and her orders were too meagre, so that she had not the courage to insist on her rights just then. They waited and waited.

"Should we go, mother?" he said.

Then Mrs. Morel stood up. The girl was passing near.

"Will you bring one currant tart?" said Mrs. Morel clearly.

The girl looked round insolently.

"Directly," she said.

"We have waited quite long enough," said Mrs. Morel.

In a moment the girl came back with the tart. Mrs. Morel asked coldly for the bill. Paul wanted to sink through the floor. He marvelled at his mother's hardness. He knew that only years of battling had taught her to insist even so little on her rights. She shrank as much as he.

"It's the last time I go *there* for anything!" she declared, when they were outside the place, thankful to be clear.

"We'll go," she said, "and look at Keep's and Boot's, and one or two places, shall we?"

They had discussions over the pictures, and Mrs.

Morel wanted to buy him a little sable brush that he hankered after. But this indulgence he refused. He stood in front of milliners' shops and drapers' shops almost bored, but content for her to be interested. They wandered on.

"Now, just look at those black grapes!" she said. "They make your mouth water. I've wanted some of those for years, but I s'll have to wait a bit before I get them."

Then she rejoiced in the florists, standing in the doorway sniffing.

"Oh! oh! Isn't it simply lovely!"

Paul saw, in the darkness of the shop, an elegant young lady in black peering over the counter curiously.

"They're looking at you," he said, trying to draw his mother away.

"But what is it?" she exclaimed, refusing to be moved.

"Stocks!" he answered, sniffing hastily. "Look, there's a tubful."

"So there is—red and white. But really, I never knew stocks to smell like it!" And, to his great relief, she moved out of the doorway, but only to stand in front of the window.

"Paul!" she cried to him, who was trying to get out of sight of the elegant young lady in black—the shop-girl. "Paul! Just look here!"

He came reluctantly back.

"Now, just look at that fuchsia!" she exclaimed, pointing.

"H'm!" He made a curious, interested sound. "You'd think every second as the flowers was going to fall off, they hang so big an' heavy."

"And such an abundance!" she cried.

"And the way they drop downwards with their threads and knots!"

"Yes!" she exclaimed. "Lovely!"

"I wonder who'll buy it!" he said.

"I wonder!" she answered. "Not us."

"It would die in our parlour."

"Yes, beastly cold, sunless hole; it kills every bit of a plant you put in, and the kitchen chokes them to death."

They bought a few things, and set off towards the station. Looking up the canal, through the dark pass of the buildings, they saw the Castle on its bluff of brown, green-bushed rock, in a positive miracle of delicate sunshine.

"Won't it be nice for me to come out at dinner-times?" said Paul. "I can go all round here and see everything. I s'll love it."

"You will," assented his mother.

He had spent a perfect afternoon with his mother. They arrived home in the mellow evening, happy, and glowing, and tired.

In the morning he filled in the form for his season-ticket and took it to the station. When he got back, his mother was just beginning to wash the floor. He sat crouched up on the sofa.

"He says it'll be here on Saturday," he said.

"And how much will it be?"

"About one pound eleven," he said.

She went on washing her floor in silence.

"Is it a lot?" he asked.

"It's no more than I thought," she answered.

"An' I s'll earn eight shillings a week," he said.

She did not answer, but went on with her work. At last she said:

"That William promised me, when he went to London, as he'd give me a pound a month. He has given me ten shillings—twice; and now I know he hasn't a farthing if I asked him. Not that I want it. Only just now you'd think he might be able to help with this ticket, which I'd never expected."

"He earns a lot," said Paul.

"He earns a hundred and thirty pounds. But they're all alike. They're large in promises, but it's precious little fulfilment you get."

"He spends over fifty shillings a week on himself," said Paul.

"And I keep this house on less than thirty," she replied; "and am supposed to find money for extras. But they don't care about helping you, once they've gone. He'd rather spend it on that dressed-up creature."

"She should have her own money if she's so grand," said Paul.

"She should, but she hasn't. I asked him. And I know he doesn't buy her a gold bangle for nothing. I wonder whoever bought me a gold bangle."

William was succeeding with his "Gipsy", as he called her. He asked the girl—her name was Louisa

164

Lily Denys Western—for a photograph to send to his mother. The photo came—a handsome brunette, taken in profile, smirking slightly—and, it might be, quite naked, for on the photograph not a scrap of clothing was to be seen, only a naked bust.

"Yes," wrote Mrs. Morel to her son, "the photograph of Louie is very striking, and I can see she must be attractive. But do you think, my boy, it was very. good taste of a girl to give her young man that photo to send to his mother—the first? Certainly the shoulders are beautiful, as you say. But I hardly expected to see so much of them at the first view."

Morel found the photograph standing on the chiffonier in the parlour. He came out with it between his thick thumb and finger.

"Who dost reckon this is?" he asked of his wife.

"It's the girl our William is going with," replied Mrs. Morel.

"H'm! 'Er's a bright spark, from th' look on 'er, an' one as wunna do him owermuch good neither. Who is she?"

"Her name is Louisa Lily Denys Western."

"An' come again to-morrer!" exclaimed the miner. 'An' is 'er an actress?"

"She is not. She's supposed to be a lady."

"I'll bet!" he exclaimed, still staring at the photo. "A lady, is she? An' how much does she reckon ter keep up this sort o' game on?"

"On nothing. She lives with an old aunt, whom she hates, and takes what bit of money's given her."

"H'm!" said Morel, laying down the photograph.

165

"Then he's a fool to ha' ta'en up wi' such a one as that."

"Dear Mater," William replied. "I'm sorry you didn't like the photograph. It never occurred to me when I sent it, that you mightn't think it decent. However, I told Gyp that it didn't quite suit your prim and proper notions, so she's going to send you another, that I hope will please you better. She's always being photographed; in fact, the photographers *ask* her if they may take her for nothing."

Presently the new photograph came, with a little silly note from the girl. This time the young lady was seen in a black satin evening bodice, cut square, with little puff sleeves, and black lace hanging down her beautiful arms.

"I wonder if she ever wears anything except evening clothes," said Mrs. Morel sarcastically. "I'm sure I *ought* to be impressed."

"You are disagreeable, mother," said Paul. "I think the first one with bare shoulders is lovely."

"Do you?" answered his mother. "Well, I don't."

On the Monday morning the boy got up at six to start work. He had the season-ticket, which had cost such bitterness, in his waistcoat pocket. He loved it with its bars of yellow across. His mother packed his dinner in a small, shut-up basket, and he set off at a quarter to seven to catch the 7.15 train. Mrs. Morel came to the entry-end to see him off.

It was a perfect morning. From the ash tree the slender green fruits that the children call "pigeons" were twinkling gaily down on a little breeze, into the front gardens of the houses. The valley was full of a lustrous dark haze, through which the ripe corn shimmered, and in which the steam from Minton pit melted swiftly. Puffs of wind came. Paul looked over the high woods of Aldersley, where the country gleamed, and home had never pulled at him so powerfully.

"Good-morning, mother," he said, smiling, but feeling very unhappy.

"Good-morning," she replied cheerfully and tenderly.

She stood in her white apron on the open road, watching him as he crossed the field. He had a small, compact body that looked full of life. She felt, as she saw him trudging over the field, that where he determined to go he would get. She thought of William. He would have leaped the fence instead of going round the stile. He was away in London, doing well. Paul would be working in Nottingham. Now she had two sons in the world. She could think of two places, great centres of industry, and feel that she had put a man into each of them, that these men would work out what *she* wanted; they were derived from her, they were of her, and their works also would be hers. All the morning long she thought of Paul.

At eight o'clock he climbed the dismal stairs of Jordan's Surgical Appliance Factory, and stood helplessly against the first great parcel-rack, waiting for somebody to pick him up. The place was still not awake. Over the counters were great dust

167

sheets. Two men only had arrived, and were heard talking in a corner, as they took off their coats and rolled up their shirt-sleeves. It was ten past eight. Evidently there was no rush of punctuality. Paul listened to the voices of the two clerks. Then he heard someone cough, and saw in the office at the end of the room an old, decaying clerk, in a round smoking-cap of black velvet embroidered with red and green, opening letters. He waited and waited. One of the junior clerks went to the old man, greeted him cheerily and loudly. Evidently the old "chief" was deaf. Then the young fellow came striding importantly down to his counter. He spied Paul.

"Hello!" he said. "You the new lad?"

"Yes," said Paul.

"H'm! What's your name?"

"Paul Morel."

"Paul Morel? All right, you come on round here."

Paul followed him round the rectangle of counters. The room was second storey. It had a great hole in the middle of the floor, fenced as with a wall of counters, and down this wide shaft the lifts went, and the light for the bottom storey. Also there was a corresponding big, oblong hole in the ceiling, and one could see above, over the fence of the top floor, some machinery; and right away overhead was the glass roof, and all light for the three storeys came downwards, getting dimmer, so that it was always night on the ground floor and rather gloomy on the second floor. The factory was the top floor, the warehouse the second, the storehouse the ground floor. It was an insanitary, ancient place.

Paul was led round to a very dark corner.

"This is the 'Spiral' corner," said the clerk. "You're Spiral, with Pappleworth. He's your boss, but he's not come yet. He doesn't get here till half-past eight. So you can fetch the letters, if you like, from Mr. Melling down there."

The young man pointed to the old clerk in the office.

"All right," said Paul.

"Here's a peg to hang your cap on. Here are your entry ledgers. Mr. Pappleworth won't be long."

And the thin young man stalked away with long, busy strides over the hollow wooden floor.

After a minute or two Paul went down and stood in the door of the glass office. The old clerk in the smoking-cap looked down over the rim of his spectacles.

"Good-morning," he said, kindly and impressively. "You want the letters for the Spiral department, Thomas?"

Paul resented being called "Thomas". But he took the letters and returned to his dark place, where the counter made an angle, where the great parcel-rack came to an end, and where there were three doors in the corner. He sat on a high stool and read the letters—those whose handwriting was not too difficult. They ran as follows:

"Will you please send me at once a pair of lady's

169

silk spiral thigh-hose, without feet, such as I had from you last year; length, thigh to knee, etc." Or, "Major Chamberlain wishes to repeat his previous order for a silk non-elastic suspensory bandage."

Many of these letters, some of them in French or Norwegian, were a great puzzle to the boy. He sat on his stool nervously awaiting the arrival of his "boss". He suffered tortures of shyness when, at half-past eight, the factory girls for upstairs trooped past him.

Mr. Pappleworth arrived, chewing a chlorodyne gum, at about twenty to nine, when all the other men were at work. He was a thin, sallow man with a red nose, quick, staccato, and smartly but stiffly dressed. He was about thirty-six years old. There was something rather "doggy", rather smart, rather 'cute and shrewd, and something warm, and something slightly contemptible about him.

"You my new lad?" he said.

Paul stood up and said he was.

"Fetched the letters?"

Mr. Pappleworth gave a chew to his gum.

"Yes."

"Copied 'em?"

"No."

"Well, come on then, let's look slippy. Changed your coat?"

"No."

"You want to bring an old coat and leave it here." He pronounced the last words with the chlorodyne gum between his side teeth. He vanished into the

170

darkness behind the great parcel-rack, reappeared coatless, turning up a smart striped shirt-cuff over a thin and hairy arm. Then he slipped into his coat. Paul noticed how thin he was, and that his trousers were in folds behind. He seized a stool, dragged it beside the boy's, and sat down.

"Sit down," he said.

Paul took a seat.

Mr. Pappleworth was very close to him. The man seized the letters, snatched a long entry-book out of a rack in front of him, flung it open, seized a pen, and said:

"Now look here. You want to copy these letters in here." He sniffed twice, gave a quick chew at his gum, stared fixedly at a letter, then went very still and absorbed, and wrote the entry rapidly, in a beautiful flourishing hand. He glanced quickly at Paul.

"See that?"

"Yes."

"Think you can do it all right?"

"Yes."

"All right then, let's see you."

He sprang off his stool. Paul took a pen. Mr. Pappleworth disappeared. Paul rather liked copying the letters, but he wrote slowly, laboriously, and exceedingly badly. He was doing the fourth letter, and feeling quite busy and happy, when Mr. Pappleworth reappeared.

"Now then, how'r' yer getting on? Done 'em?"

He leaned over the boy's shoulder, chewing, and smelling of chlorodyne.

"Strike my bob, lad, but you're a beautiful writer!" he exclaimed satirically. "Ne'er mind, how many h'yer done? Only three! I'd 'a eaten 'em. Get on, my lad, an' put numbers on 'em. Here, look! Get on!"

Paul ground away at the letters, whilst Mr. Pappleworth fussed over various jobs. Suddenly the boy started as a shrill whistle sounded near his ear. Mr. Pappleworth came, took a plug out of a pipe, and said, in an amazingly cross and bossy voice:

"Yes?"

Paul heard a faint voice, like a woman's, out of the mouth of the tube. He gazed in wonder, never having seen a speaking-tube before.

"Well," said Mr. Pappleworth disagreeably into the tube "you'd better get some of your back work done, then."

Again the woman's tiny voice was heard, sounding pretty and cross.

"I've not time to stand here while you talk," said Mr. Pappleworth, and he pushed the plug into the tube.

"Come, my lad," he said imploringly to Paul, "there's Polly crying out for them orders. Can't you buck up a bit? Here, come out!"

He took the book, to Paul's immense chagrin, and began the copying himself. He worked quickly and well. This done, he seized some strips of long

172

yellow paper, about three inches wide, and made out the day's orders for the work-girls.

"You'd better watch me," he said to Paul, working all the while rapidly. Paul watched the weird little drawings of legs, and thighs, and ankles, with the strokes across and the numbers, and the few brief directions which his chief made upon the yellow paper. Then Mr. Pappleworth finished and jumped up.

"Come on with me," he said, and the yellow papers flying in his hands, he dashed through a door and down some stairs, into the basement where the gas was burning. They crossed the cold, damp storeroom, then a long, dreary room with a long table on trestles, into a smaller, cosy apartment, not very high, which had been built on to the main building. In this room a small woman with a red serge blouse, and her black hair done on top of her head, was waiting like a proud little bantam.

"Here y'are!" said Pappleworth.

"I think it is 'here you are'!" exclaimed Polly. "The girls have been here nearly half an hour waiting. Just think of the time wasted!"

"*You* think of getting your work done and not talking so much," said Mr. Pappleworth. "You could ha' been finishing off."

"You know quite well we finished everything off on Saturday!" cried Polly, flying at him, her dark eyes flashing.

"Tu-tu-tu-tu-terterter!" he mocked. "Here's your new lad. Don't ruin him as you did the last."

173

"As we did the last!" repeated Polly. "Yes, *we* do a lot of ruining, we do. My word, a lad would *take* some ruining after he'd been with you."

"It's time for work now, not for talk," said Mr. Pappleworth severely and coldly.

"It was time for work some time back," said Polly, marching away with her head in the air. She was an erect little body of forty.

In that room were two round spiral machines on the bench under the window. Through the inner doorway was another longer room, with six more machines. A little group of girls, nicely dressed in white aprons, stood talking together.

"Have you nothing else to do but talk?" said Mr. Pappleworth.

"Only wait for you," said one handsome girl, laughing.

"Well, get on, get on," he said. "Come on, my lad. You'll know your road down here again."

And Paul ran upstairs after his chief. He was given some checking and invoicing to do. He stood at the desk, labouring in his execrable handwriting. Presently Mr. Jordan came strutting down from the glass office and stood behind him, to the boy's great discomfort. Suddenly a red and fat finger was thrust on the form he was filling in.

"*Mr.* J. A. Bates, Esquire!" exclaimed the cross voice just behind his ear.

Paul looked at "Mr. J. A. Bates, Esquire" in his own vile writing, and wondered what was the matter now.

"Didn't they teach you any better than *that* while they were at it? If you put 'Mr.' you don't put 'Esquire'—a man can't be both at once."

The boy regretted his too-much generosity in disposing of honours, hesitated, and with trembling fingers, scratched out the "Mr." Then all at once Mr. Jordan snatched away the invoice.

"Make another! Are you going to send *that* to a gentleman?" And he tore up the blue form irritably.

Paul, his ears red with shame, began again. Still Mr. Jordan watched.

"I don't know what they *do* teach in schools. You'll have to write better than that. Lads learn nothing nowadays, but how to recite poetry and play the fiddle. Have you seen his writing?" he asked of Mr. Pappleworth.

"Yes; prime, isn't it?" replied Mr. Pappleworth indifferently.

Mr. Jordan gave a little grunt, not unamiable. Paul divined that his master's bark was worse than his bite. Indeed, the little manufacturer, although he spoke bad English, was quite gentleman enough to leave his men alone and to take no notice of trifles. But he knew he did not look like the boss and owner of the show, so he had to play his rôle of proprietor at first, to put things on a right footing.

"Let's see, *what's* your name?" asked Mr. Pappleworth of the boy.

"Paul Morel."

It is curious that children suffer so much at having to pronounce their own names.

"Paul Morel, is it? All right, you Paul-Morel through them things there, and then——"

Mr. Pappleworth subsided on to a stool, and began writing. A girl came up from out of a door just behind, put some newly-pressed elastic web appliances on the counter, and returned. Mr. Pappleworth picked up the whitey-blue knee-band, examined it, and its yellow order-paper quickly, and put it on one side. Next was a flesh-pink "leg". He went through the few things, wrote out a couple of orders, and called to Paul to accompany him. This time they went through the door whence the girl had emerged. There Paul found himself at the top of a little wooden flight of steps, and below him saw a room with windows round two sides, and at the farther end half a dozen girls sitting bending over the benches in the light from the window, sewing. They were singing together "Two Little Girls in Blue". Hearing the door opened, they all turned round, to see Mr. Pappleworth and Paul looking down on them from the far end of the room. They stopped singing.

"Can't you make a bit less row?" said Mr. Pappleworth. "Folk'll think we keep cats."

A hunchback woman on a high stool turned her long, rather heavy face towards Mr. Pappleworth, and said, in a contralto voice:

"They're all tom-cats then."

In vain Mr. Pappleworth tried to be impressive for Paul's benefit. He descended the steps into the finishing-off room, and went to the hunchback

Fanny. She had such a short body on her high stool that her head, with its great bands of bright brown hair, seemed over large, as did her pale, heavy face. She wore a dress of green-black cashmere, and her wrists, coming out of the narrow cuffs, were thin and flat, as she put down her work nervously. He showed her something that was wrong with a knee-cap.

"Well," she said, "you needn't come blaming it on to me. It's not my fault." Her colour mounted to her cheek.

"I never said it *was* your fault. Will you do as I tell you?" replied Mr. Pappleworth shortly.

"You don't say it's my fault, but you'd like to make out as it was," the hunchback woman cried, almost in tears. Then she snatched the knee-cap from her "boss", saying: "Yes, I'll do it for you, but you needn't be snappy."

"Here's your new lad," said Mr. Pappleworth.

Fanny turned, smiling very gently on Paul.

"Oh!" she said.

"Yes; don't make a softy of him between you."

"It's not us as 'ud make a softy of him," she said indignantly.

"Come on then, Paul," said Mr. Pappleworth.

"*Au revoy*, Paul," said one of the girls.

There was a titter of laughter. Paul went out, blushing deeply, not having spoken a word.

The day was very long. All morning the work-people were coming to speak to Mr. Pappleworth. Paul was writing or learning to make up parcels, ready for the midday post. At one o'clock, or, rather, at a quarter to one, Mr. Pappleworth disappeared to catch his train: he lived in the suburbs. At one o'clock, Paul, feeling very lost, took his dinner-basket down into the stockroom in the basement, that had the long table on trestles, and ate his meal hurriedly, alone in that cellar of gloom and desolation. Then he went out of doors. The brightness and the freedom of the streets made him feel adventurous and happy. But at two o'clock he was back in the corner of the big room. Soon the work-girls went trooping past, making remarks. It was the commoner girls who worked upstairs at the heavy tasks of truss-making and the finishing of artificial limbs. He waited for Mr. Pappleworth, not knowing what to do, sitting scribbling on the yellow order-paper. Mr. Pappleworth came at twenty minutes to three. Then he sat and gossiped with Paul, treating the boy entirely as an equal, even in age.

In the afternoon there was never very much to do, unless it were near the week-end, and the accounts had to be made up. At five o'clock all the men went down into the dungeon with the table on trestles, and there they had tea, eating bread-and-butter on the bare, dirty boards, talking with the same kind of ugly haste and slovenliness with which they ate their meal. And yet upstairs the atmosphere among them was always jolly and clear. The cellar and the trestles affected them.

After tea, when all the gases were lighted, *work*

went more briskly. There was the big evening post to get off. The hose came up warm and newly pressed from the workrooms. Paul had made out the invoices. Now he had the packing up and addressing to do, then he had to weigh his stock of parcels on the scales. Everywhere voices were calling weights, there was the chink of metal, the rapid snapping of string, the hurrying to old Mr. Melling for stamps. And at last the postman came with his sack, laughing and jolly. Then everything slacked off, and Paul took his dinner-basket and ran to the station to catch the eight-twenty train. The day in the factory was just twelve hours long.

His mother sat waiting for him rather anxiously. He had to walk from Keston, so was not home until about twenty past nine. And he left the house before seven in the morning. Mrs. Morel was rather anxious about his health. But she herself had had to put up with so much that she expected her children to take the same odds. They must go through with what came. And Paul stayed at Jordan's, although all the time he was there his health suffered from the darkness and lack of air and the long hours.

He came in pale and tired. His mother looked at him. She saw he was rather pleased, and her anxiety all went.

"Well, and how was it?" she asked.

"Ever so funny, mother," he replied. "You don't have to work a bit hard, and they're nice with you."

"And did you get on all right?"

"Yes: they only say my writing's bad. But Mr.

179

Pappleworth—he's my man—said to Mr. Jordan I should be all right. I'm Spiral, mother; you must come and see. It's ever so nice."

Soon he liked Jordan's. Mr. Pappleworth, who had a certain "saloon bar" flavour about him, was always natural, and treated him as if he had been a comrade. Sometimes the "Spiral boss" was irritable, and chewed more lozenges than ever. Even then, however, he was not offensive, but one of those people who hurt themselves by their own irritability more than they hurt other people.

"Haven't you done that *yet*?" he would cry. "Go on, be a month of Sundays."

Again, and Paul could understand him least then, he was jocular and in high spirits.

"I'm going to bring my little Yorkshire terrier bitch tomorrow," he said jubilantly to Paul.

"What's a Yorkshire terrier?"

"*Don't* know what a Yorkshire terrier is? *Don't know a Yorkshire*——" Mr. Pappleworth was aghast.

"Is it a little silky one—colours of iron and rusty silver?"

"*That's* it, my lad. She's a gem. She's had five pounds' worth of pups already, and she's worth over seven pounds herself; and she doesn't weigh twenty ounces."

The next day the bitch came. She was a shivering, miserable morsel. Paul did not care for her; she seemed so like a wet rag that would never dry. Then a man called for her, and began to make coarse

180

jokes. But Mr. Pappleworth nodded his head in the direction of the boy, and the talk went on *sotto voce*.

Mr. Jordan only made one more excursion to watch Paul, and then the only fault he found was seeing the boy lay his pen on the counter.

"Put your pen in your ear, if you're going to be a clerk. Pen in your ear!" And one day he said to the lad: "Why don't you hold your shoulders straighter? Come down here," when he took him into the glass office and fitted him with special braces for keeping the shoulders square.

But Paul liked the girls best. The men seemed common and rather dull. He liked them all, but they were uninteresting. Polly, the little brisk overseer downstairs, finding Paul eating in the cellar, asked him if she could cook him anything on her little stove. Next day his mother gave him a dish that could be heated up. He took it into the pleasant, clean room to Polly. And very soon it grew to be an established custom that he should have dinner with her. When he came in at eight in the morning he took his basket to her, and when he came down at one o'clock she had his dinner ready.

He was not very tall, and palc, with thick chestnut hair, irregular features, and a wide, full mouth. She was like a small bird. He often called her a "robinet". Though naturally rather quiet, he would sit and chatter with her for hours telling her about his home. The girls all liked to hear him talk. They often gathered in a little circle while he sat on a bench, and held forth to them, laughing. Some of

181

them regarded him as a curious little creature, so serious, yet so bright and jolly, and always so delicate in his way with them. They all liked him, and he adored them. Polly he felt he belonged to. Then Connie, with her mane of red hair, her face of apple-blossom, her murmuring voice, such a lady in her shabby black frock, appealed to his romantic side.

"When you sit winding," he said, "it looks as if you were spinning at a spinning-wheel—it looks ever so nice. You remind me of Elaine in the 'Idylls of the King'. I'd draw you if I could."

And she glanced at him blushing shyly. And later on he had a sketch he prized very much: Connie sitting on the stool before the wheel, her flowing mane of red hair on her rusty black frock, her red mouth shut and serious, running the scarlet thread off the hank on to the reel.

With Louie, handsome and brazen, who always seemed to thrust her hip at him, he usually joked.

Emma was rather plain, rather old, and condescending. But to condescend to him made her happy, and he did not mind.

"How do you put needles in?" he asked.

"Go away and don't bother."

"But I ought to know how to put needles in."

She ground at her machine all the while steadily.

"There are many things you ought to know," she replied.

"Tell me, then, how to stick needles in the machine."

"Oh, the boy, what a nuisance he is! Why, *this* is how you do it."

He watched her attentively. Suddenly a whistle piped. Then Polly appeared, and said in a clear voice:

"Mr. Pappleworth wants to know how much longer you're going to be down here playing with the girls, Paul."

Paul flew upstairs, calling "Goodbye!" and Emma drew herself up.

"It wasn't *me* who wanted him to play with the machine," she said.

As a rule, when all the girls came back at two o'clock, he ran upstairs to Fanny, the hunchback, in the finishing-off room. Mr. Pappleworth did not appear till twenty to three, and he often found his boy sitting beside Fanny, talking, or drawing, or singing with the girls.

Often, after a minute's hesitation, Fanny would begin to sing. She had a fine contralto voice. Everybody joined in the chorus, and it went well. Paul was not at all embarrassed, after a while, sitting in the room with the half a dozen work-girls.

At the end of the song Fanny would say:

"I know you've been laughing at me."

"Don't be so soft, Fanny!" cried one of the girls.

Once there was mention of Connie's red hair.

"Fanny's is better, to my fancy," said Emma.

"You needn't try to make a fool of me," said Fanny, flushing deeply.

"No, but she has, Paul; she's got beautiful hair."

183

"It's a treat of a colour," said he. "That coldish colour like earth, and yet shiny. It's like bog-water."

"Goodness me!" exclaimed one girl, laughing.

"How I do but get criticised!" said Fanny.

"But you should see it down, Paul," cried Emma earnestly. "It's simply beautiful. Put it down for him, Fanny, if he wants something to paint."

Fanny would not, and yet she wanted to.

"Then I'll take it down myself," said the lad.

"Well, you can if you like," said Fanny.

And he carefully took the pins out of the knot, and the rush of hair, of uniform dark brown, slid over the humped back.

"What a lovely lot!" he exclaimed.

The girls watched. There was silence. The youth shook the hair loose from the coil.

"It's splendid!" he said, smelling its perfume. "I'll bet it's worth pounds."

"I'll leave it you when I die, Paul," said Fanny, half joking.

"You look just like anybody else, sitting drying their hair," said one of the girls to the long-legged hunchback.

Poor Fanny was morbidly sensitive, always imagining insults. Polly was curt and business-like. The two departments were for ever at war, and Paul was always finding Fanny in tears. Then he was made the recipient of all her woes, and he had to plead her case with Polly.

So the time went along happily enough. The factory had a homely feel. No one was rushed or driven. Paul always enjoyed it when the work got faster, towards post-time, and all the men united in labour. He liked to watch his fellow-clerks at work. The man was the work and the work was the man, one thing, for the time being. It was different with the girls. The real woman never seemed to be there at the task, but as if left out, waiting.

From the train going home at night he used to watch the lights of the town, sprinkled thick on the hills, fusing together in a blaze in the valleys. He felt rich in life and happy. Drawing farther off, there was a patch of lights at Bulwell like myriad petals shaken to the ground from the shed stars; and beyond was the red glare of the furnaces, playing like hot breath on the clouds.

He had to walk two and more miles from Keston home, up two long hills, down two short hills. He was often tired, and he counted the lamps climbing the hill above him, how many more to pass. And from the hill-top, on pitch-dark nights, he looked round on the villages five or six miles away, that shone like swarms of glittering living things, almost a heaven against his feet. Marlpool and Heanor scattered the far-off darkness with brilliance. And occasionally the black valley space between was traced, violated by a great train rushing south to London or north to Scotland. The trains roared by like projectiles level on the darkness, fuming and burning, making the valley clang with their passage. They were gone, and the lights of the towns and villages glittered in silence.

And then he came to the corner at home, which faced the other side of the night. The ash-tree seemed a friend now. His mother rose with gladness as he entered. He put his eight shillings proudly on the table.

"It'll help, mother?" he asked wistfully.

"There's precious little left," she answered, "after your ticket and dinners and such are taken off."

Then he told her the budget of the day. His life-story, like an Arabian Nights, was told night after night to his mother. It was almost as if it were her own life.

186

# 6

## DEATH IN THE FAMILY

ARTHUR MOREL was growing up. He was a quick, careless, impulsive boy, a good deal like his father. He hated study, made a great moan if he had to work, and escaped as soon as possible to his sport again.

In appearance he remained the flower of the family, being well made, graceful, and full of life. His dark brown hair and fresh colouring, and his exquisite dark blue eyes shaded with long lashes, together with his generous manner and fiery temper, made him a favourite. But as he grew older his temper became uncertain. He flew into rages over nothing, seemed unbearably raw and irritable.

His mother, whom he loved, wearied of him sometimes. He thought only of himself. When he wanted amusement, all that stood in his way he hated, even if it were she. When he was in trouble he moaned to her ceaselessly.

"Goodness, boy!" she said, when he groaned about a master who, he said, hated him, "if you don't like it, alter it, and if you can't alter it, put up with it."

And his father, whom he had loved and who had worshipped him, he came to detest. As he grew older Morel fell into a slow ruin. His body, which had been beautiful in movement and in being, shrank, did not seem to ripen with the years, but to get mean and rather despicable. There came over him a look of meanness and of paltriness. And when the mean-looking elderly man bullied or ordered the boy about, Arthur was furious. Moreover, Morel's manners got worse and worse, his habits somewhat disgusting. When the children were growing up and in the crucial stage of adolescence, the father was like some ugly irritant to their souls. His manners in the house were the same as he used among the colliers down pit.

"Dirty nuisance!" Arthur would cry, jumping up and going straight out of the house when his father disgusted him. And Morel persisted the more because his children hated it. He seemed to take a kind of satisfaction in disgusting them, and driving them nearly mad, while they were so irritably sensitive at the age of fourteen or fifteen. So that Arthur, who was growing up when his father was degenerate and elderly, hated him worst of all.

Then, sometimes, the father would seem to feel the contemptuous hatred of his children.

"There's not a man tries harder for his family!" he would shout. "He does his best for them, and then gets treated like a dog. But I'm not going to stand it, I tell you!"

But for the threat and the fact that he did not try so hard as he imagined, they would have felt sorry. As it was, the battle now went on nearly all between father and children, he persisting in his dirty and disgusting ways, just to assert his independence. They loathed him.

Arthur was so inflamed and irritable at last, that when he won a scholarship for the Grammar School in Nottingham, his mother decided to let him live in town, with one of her sisters, and only come home at week-ends.

Annie was still a junior teacher in the Board-school, earning about four shillings a week. But soon she would have fifteen shillings, since she had passed her examination, and there would be financial peace in the house.

Mrs. Morel clung now to Paul. He was quiet and not brilliant. But still he stuck to his painting, and still he stuck to his mother. Everything he did was for her. She waited for his coming home in the evening, and then she unburdened herself of all she had pondered, or of all that had occurred to her during the day. He sat and listened with his earnestness. The two shared lives.

William was engaged now to his brunette, and had bought her an engagement ring that cost eight guineas. The children gasped at such a fabulous price.

"Eight guineas!" said Morel. "More fool him! If he'd gen me some on't, it 'ud ha' looked better on 'im."

"Given *you* some of it!" cried Mrs. Morel. "Why give *you* some of it!"

She remembered *he* had bought no engagement

ring at all, and she preferred William, who was not mean, if he were foolish. But now the young man talked only of the dances to which he went with his betrothed, and the different resplendent clothes she wore; or he told his mother with glee how they went to the theatre like great swells.

He wanted to bring the girl home. Mrs. Morel said she should come at the Christmas. This time William arrived with a lady, but with no presents. Mrs. Morel had prepared supper. Hearing footsteps, she rose and went to the door. William entered.

"Hello, mother!" He kissed her hastily, then stood aside to present a tall, handsome girl, who was wearing a costume of fine black-and-white check, and furs.

"Here's Gyp!"

Miss Western held out her hand and showed her teeth in a small smile.

"Oh, how do you do, Mrs. Morel!" she exclaimed.

"I am afraid you will be hungry," said Mrs. Morel.

"Oh no, we had dinner on the train. Have you got my gloves, Chubby?"

William Morel, big and raw-boned, looked at her quickly.

"How should I?" he said.

"Then I've lost them. Don't be cross with me."

A frown went over his face, but he said nothing. She glanced round the kitchen. It was small and curious to her, with its glittering kissing-bunch, its evergreens behind the pictures, its wooden chairs and little deal table. At that moment Morel came in.

"Hello, dad!"

"Hello, my son! Tha's let on me!"

The two shook hands, and William presented the lady. She gave the same smile that showed her teeth.

"How do you do, Mr. Morel?"

Morel bowed obsequiously.

"I'm very well, and I hope so are you. You must make yourself very welcome."

"Oh, thank you," she replied, rather amused.

"You will like to go upstairs," said Mrs. Morel.

"If you don't mind; but not if it is any trouble to you."

"It is no trouble. Annie will take you. Walter, carry up this box."

"And don't be an hour dressing yourself up," said William to his betrothed.

Annie took a brass candlestick, and, too shy almost to speak, preceded the young lady to the front bedroom, which Mr. and Mrs. Morel had vacated for her. It, too, was small and cold by candle-light. The colliers' wives only lit fires in bedrooms in case of extreme illness.

"Shall I unstrap the box?" asked Annie.

"Oh, thank you very much!"

Annie played the part of maid, then went downstairs for hot water.

"I think she's rather tired, mother," said William. "It's a beastly journey, and we had such a rush."

"Is there anything I can give her?" asked Mrs. Morel.

"Oh no, she'll be all right."

But there was a chill in the atmosphere. After half an hour Miss Western came down, having put on a purplish-coloured dress, very fine for the collier's kitchen.

"I told you you'd no need to change," said William to her.

"Oh, Chubby!" Then she turned with that sweetish smile to Mrs. Morel. "Don't you think he's always grumbling, Mrs. Morel?"

"Is he?" said Mrs. Morel. "That's not very nice of him."

"It isn't, really!"

"You are cold," said the mother. "Won't you come near the fire?"

Morel jumped out of his arm-chair.

"Come and sit you here!" he cried. "Come and sit you here!"

"No, dad, keep your own chair. Sit on the sofa, Gyp," said William.

"No, no!" cried Morel. "This cheer's warmest. Come and sit here, Miss Wesson."

"Thank you *so* much," said the girl, seating herself in the collier's arm-chair, the place of honour. She shivered, feeling the warmth of the kitchen penetrate her.

"Fetch me a hanky, Chubby dear!" she said, putting up her mouth to him, and using the same intimate tone as if they were alone; which made the

192

rest of the family feel as if they ought not to be present. The young lady evidently did not realise them as people: they were creatures to her for the present. William winced.

In such a household, in Streatham, Miss Western would have been a lady condescending to her inferiors. These people were to her, certainly clownish—in short, the working classes. How was she to adjust herself?

"I'll go," said Annie.

Miss Western took no notice, as if a servant had spoken. But when the girl came downstairs again with the handkerchief, she said: "Oh, thank you!" in a gracious way.

She sat and talked about the dinner on the train, which had been so poor; about London, about dances. She was really very nervous, and chattered from fear. Morel sat all the time smoking his thick twist tobacco, watching her, and listening to her glib London speech, as he puffed. Mrs. Morel, dressed up in her best black silk blouse, answered quietly and rather briefly. The three children sat round in silence and admiration. Miss Western was the princess. Everything of the best was got out for her: the best cups, the best spoons, the best table cloth, the best coffee-jug. The children thought she must find it quite grand. She felt strange, not able to realize the people, not knowing how to treat them. William joked, and was slightly uncomfortable.

At about ten o'clock he said to her:

"Aren't you tired, Gyp?"

"Rather, Chubby," she answered, at once in the intimate tones and putting her head slightly on one side.

"I'll light her the candle, mother," he said.

"Very well," replied the mother.

Miss Western stood up, held out her hand to Mrs. Morel.

"Good-night, Mrs. Morel," she said.

Paul sat at the boiler, letting the water run from the tap into a stone beer-bottle. Annie swathed the bottle in an old flannel pit-singlet, and kissed her mother good-night. She was to share the room with the lady, because the house was full.

"You wait a minute," said Mrs. Morel to Annie. And Annie sat nursing the hot-water bottle. Miss Western shook hands all round, to everybody's discomfort, and took her departure, preceded by William. In five minutes he was downstairs again. His heart was rather sore; he did not know why. He talked very little till everybody had gone to bed, but himself and his mother. Then he stood with his legs apart, in his old attitude on the hearth-rug, and said hesitatingly:

"Well, mother?"

"Well, my son?"

She sat in the rocking-chair, feeling somehow hurt and humiliated, for his sake.

"Do you like her?"

"Yes," came the slow answer.

"She's shy yet, mother. She's not used to it. It's

different from her aunt's house, you know."

"Of course it is, my boy; and she must find it difficult."

"She does." Then he frowned swiftly. "If only she wouldn't put on her *blessed* airs!"

"It's only her first awkwardness, my boy. She'll be all right."

"That's it, mother," he replied gratefully. But his brow was gloomy. "You know, she's not like you, mother. She's not serious, and she can't think."

"She's young, my boy."

"Yes; and she's had no sort of show. Her mother died when she was a child. Since then she's lived with her aunt, whom she can't bear. And her father was a rake. She's had no love."

"No! Well, you must make up to her."

"And so—you have to forgive her a lot of things."

"*What* do you have to forgive her, my boy?"

"I dunno. When she seems shallow, you have to remember she's never had anybody to bring her deeper side out. And she's *fearfully* fond of me."

"Anybody can see that."

"But you know, mother—she's—she's different from us. Those sort of people, like those she lives amongst, they don't seem to have the same principles."

"You mustn't judge too hastily," said Mrs. Morel.

But he seemed uneasy within himself.

In the morning, however, he was up singing and larking round the house.

195

"Hello!" he called, sitting on the stairs. "Are you getting up?"

"Yes," her voice called faintly.

"Merry Christmas!" he shouted to her.

Her laugh, pretty and tinkling, was heard in the bedroom. She did not come down in half an hour.

"Was she *really* getting up when she said she was?" he asked of Annie.

"Yes, she was," replied Annie.

He waited a while, then went to the stairs again.

"Happy New Year," he called.

"Thank you, Chubby dear!" came the laughing voice, far away.

"Buck up!" he implored.

It was nearly an hour, and still he was waiting for her. Morel, who always rose before six, looked at the clock.

"Well, it's a winder!" he exclaimed.

The family had breakfasted, all but William. He went to the foot of the stairs.

"Shall I have to send you an Easter egg up there?" he called, rather crossly. She only laughed. The family expected, after that time of preparation, something like magic. At last she came, looking very nice in a blouse and skirt.

"Have you *really* been all this time getting ready?" he asked.

"Chubby dear! That question is not permitted, is it, Mrs. Morel?"

She played the grand lady at first. When she went with William to chapel, he in his frock-coat and silk hat, she in her furs and London-made costume, Paul and Arthur and Annie expected everybody to bow to the ground in admiration. And Morel, standing in his Sunday suit at the end of the road, watching the gallant pair go, felt he was the father of princes and princesses.

And yet she was not so grand. For a year now she had been a sort of secretary or clerk in a London office. But while she was with the Morels she queened it. She sat and let Annie or Paul wait on her as if they were her servants. She treated Mrs. Morel with a certain glibness and Morel with patronage. But after a day or so she began to change her tune.

William always wanted Paul or Annie to go along with them on their walks. It was so much more interesting. And Paul really *did* admire "Gipsy" whole-heartedly; in fact, his mother scarcely forgave the boy for the adulation with which he treated the girl.

On the second day, when Lily said: "Oh, Annie, do you know where I left my muff?" William replied:

"You know it is in your bedroom. Why do you ask Annie?"

And Lily went upstairs with a cross, shut mouth. But it angered the young man that she made a servant of his sister.

On the third evening William and Lily were sitting together in the parlour by the fire in the dark. At a quarter to eleven Mrs. Morel was heard raking the fire. William came out to the kitchen, followed by his beloved.

"Is it as late as that, mother?" he said. She had been sitting alone.

"It is not *late*, my boy, but it is as late as I usually sit up."

"Won't you go to bed, then?" he asked.

"And leave you two? No, my boy, I don't believe in it."

"Can't you trust us, mother?"

"Whether I can or not, I won't do it. You can stay till eleven if you like, and I can read."

"Go to bed, Gyp," he said to his girl. "We won't keep mater waiting."

"Annie has left the candle burning, Lily," said Mrs. Morel; "I think you will see."

"Yes, thank you. Good-night, Mrs. Morel."

William kissed his sweetheart at the foot of the stairs, and she went. He returned to the kitchen.

"Can't you trust us, mother?" he repeated, rather offended.

"My boy, I tell you I don't *believe* in leaving two young things like you alone downstairs when everyone else is in bed."

And he was forced to take this answer. He kissed his mother good-night.

At Easter he came over alone. And then he discussed his sweetheart endlessly with his mother.

"You know, mother, when I'm away from her I don't care for her a bit. I shouldn't care if I never saw her again. But, then, when I'm with her in the evenings I am awfully fond of her."

"It's a queer sort of love to marry on," said Mrs. Morel, "if she holds you no more than that!"

"It *is* funny!" he exclaimed. It worried and perplexed him. "But yet—there's so much between us now I couldn't give her up."

"You know best," said Mrs. Morel. "But if it is as you say, I wouldn't call it *love*—at any rate, it doesn't look much like it."

"Oh, I don't know, mother. She's an orphan, and——"

They never came to any sort of conclusion. He seemed puzzled and rather fretted. She was rather reserved. All his strength and money went in keeping this girl. He could scarcely afford to take his mother to Nottingham when he came over.

Paul's wages had been raised at Christmas to ten shillings, to his great joy. He was quite happy at Jordan's, but his health suffered from the long hours and the confinement. His mother, to whom he became more and more significant, thought how to help.

His half-day holiday was on Monday afternoon. On a Monday morning in May, as the two sat alone at breakfast, she said:

"I think it will be a fine day."

He looked up in surprise. This meant something.

"You know Mr. Leivers has gone to live on a new farm. Well, he asked me last week if I wouldn't go and see Mrs. Leivers, and I promised to bring you on Monday if it's fine. Shall we go?"

"I say, little woman, how lovely!" he cried. "And we'll go this afternoon?"

Paul hurried off to the station jubilant. Down Derby Road was a cherry-tree that glistened. The old brick wall by the Statutes ground burned scarlet, spring was a very flame of green. And the steep swoop of highroad lay, in its cool morning dust, splendid with patterns of sunshine and shadow, perfectly still. The trees sloped their great green shoulders proudly; and inside the warehouse all the morning, the boy had a vision of spring outside.

When he came home at dinner-time his mother was rather excited.

"Are we going?" he asked.

"When I'm ready," she replied.

Presently he got up.

"Go and get dressed while I wash up," he said.

She did so. He washed the pots, straightened, and then took her boots. They were quite clean. Mrs. Morel was one of those naturally exquisite people who can walk in mud without dirtying their shoes. But Paul had to clean them for her. They were kid boots at eight shillings a pair. He, however, thought them the most dainty boots in the world, and he cleaned them with as much reverence as if they had been flowers.

Suddenly she appeared in the inner doorway

rather shyly. She had got a new cotton blouse on. Paul jumped up and went forward.

"Oh, my stars!" he exclaimed. "What a bobby-dazzler!"

She sniffed in a little haughty way, and put her head up.

"It's not a bobby-dazzler at all!" she replied. "It's very quiet."

She walked forward, whilst he hovered round her.

"Well," she asked, quite shy, but pretending to be high and mighty, "do you like it?"

"Awfully! You *are* a fine little woman to go jaunting out with!"

He went and surveyed her from the back.

"Well," he said, "if I was walking down the street behind you, I should say: 'Doesn't *that* little person fancy herself!' "

"Well, she doesn't," replied Mrs. Morel. "She's not sure it suits her."

"Oh no! she wants to be in dirty black, looking as if she was wrapped in burnt paper. It *does* suit you, and *I* say you look nice."

She sniffed in her little way, pleased, but pretending to know better.

"Well," she said, "it's cost me just three shillings. You couldn't have got it ready-made for that price, could you?"

"I should think you couldn't," he replied.

"And, you know, it's good stuff."

"Awfully pretty," he said.

The blouse was white, with a little sprig of heliotrope and black.

"Too young for me, though, I'm afraid," she said.

"Too young for you!" he exclaimed in disgust. "Why don't you buy some false white hair and stick it on your head."

"I s'll soon have no need," she replied. "I'm going white fast enough."

"Well, you've no business to," he said. "What do I want with a white-haired mother?"

"I'm afraid you'll have to put up with one, my lad," she said rather strangely.

They set off in great style, she carrying the umbrella William had given her, because of the sun. Paul was considerably taller than she, though he was not big. He fancied himself.

On the fallow land the young wheat shone silkily. Minton pit waved its plumes of white steam, coughed, and rattled hoarsely.

"Now look at that!" said Mrs. Morel. Mother and son stood on the road to watch. Along the ridge of the great pit-hill crawled a little group in silhouette against the sky, a horse, a small truck, and a man. They climbed the incline against the heavens. At the end the man tipped the wagon. There was an undue rattle as the waste fell down the sheer slope of the enormous bank.

"You sit a minute, mother," he said, and she took a seat on a bank, whilst he sketched rapidly. She was silent whilst he worked, looking round at the afternoon, the red cottages shining among their greenness.

"The world is a wonderful place," she said, "and wonderfully beautiful."

"And so's the pit," he said. "Look how it heaps together, like something alive almost—a big creature that you don't know."

"Yes," she said. "Perhaps!"

"And all the trucks standing waiting, like a string of beasts to be fed," he said.

"And very thankful I am they *are* standing," she said, "for that means they'll turn middling time this week."

"But I like the feel of *men* on things, while they're alive. There's a feel of men about trucks, because they've been handled with men's hands, all of them."

"Yes," said Mrs. Morel.

They went along under the trees of the highroad. He was constantly informing her, but she was interested. They passed the end of Nethermere, that was tossing its sunshine like petals lightly in its lap. Then they turned on a private road, and in some trepidation approached a big farm. A dog barked furiously. A woman came out to see.

"Is this the way to Willey Farm?" Mrs. Morel asked.

Paul hung behind in terror of being sent back. But the woman was amiable, and directed them. The mother and son went through the wheat and oats, over a little bridge into a wild meadow.

Peewits, with their white breasts glistening, wheeled and screamed about them. The lake was still and blue. High overhead a heron floated. Opposite, the wood heaped on the hill, green and still.

"It's a wild road, mother," said Paul. "Just like Canada."

"Isn't it beautiful!" said Mrs. Morel, looking round.

"See that heron—see—see her legs?"

He directed his mother, what she must see and what not. And she was quite content.

"But now," she said, "which way? He told me through the wood."

The wood, fenced and dark, lay on their left.

"I can feel a bit of a path this road," said Paul. "You've got town feet, somehow or other, you have."

They found a little gate, and soon were in a broad green alley of the wood, with a new thicket of fir and pine on one hand, an old oak glade dipping down on the other. And among the oaks the blue-bells stood in pools of azure, under the new green hazels, upon a pale fawn floor of oak-leaves. He found flowers for her.

"Here's a bit of new-mown hay," he said; then, again, he brought her forget-me-nots. And, again, his heart hurt with love, seeing her hand, used with work, holding the little bunch of flowers he gave her. She was perfectly happy.

But at the end of the riding was a fence to climb. Paul was over in a second.

"Come," he said, "let me help you."

"No, go away. I will do it in my own way."

He stood below with his hands up ready to help her. She climbed cautiously.

"What a way to climb!" he exclaimed scornfully, when she was safely to earth again.

"Hateful stiles!" she cried.

"Duffer of a little woman," he replied, "who can't get over 'em."

In front, along the edge of the wood, was a cluster of low red farm buildings. The two hastened forward. Flush with the wood was the apple orchard, where blossom was falling on the grindstone. The pond was deep under a hedge and overhanging oak trees. Some cows stood in the shade. The farm and buildings, three sides of a quadrangle, embraced the sunshine towards the wood. It was very still.

Mother and son went into the small railed garden, where was a scent of red gillivers. By the open door were some floury loaves, put out to cool. A hen was just coming to peck them. Then, in the doorway suddenly appeared a girl in a dirty apron. She was about fourteen years old, had a rosy dark face, a bunch of short black curls, very fine and free, and dark eyes; shy, questioning, a little resentful of the strangers, she disappeared. In a minute another figure appeared, a small, frail woman, rosy, with great dark brown eyes.

"Oh!" she exclaimed, smiling with a little glow, "you've come, then. I *am* glad to see you." Her voice was intimate and rather sad.

The two women shook hands.

"Now are you sure we're not a bother to you?" said Mrs. Morel. "I know what a farming life is."

"Oh no! We're only too thankful to see a new face, it's so lost up here."

"I suppose so," said Mrs. Morel.

They were taken through into the parlour—a long, low room, with a great bunch of guelder-roses in the fireplace. There the women talked, whilst Paul went out to survey the land. He was in the garden smelling the gillivers and looking at the plants, when the girl came out quickly to the heap of coal which stood by the fence.

"I suppose these are cabbage-roses?" he said to her, pointing to the bushes along the fence.

She looked at him with startled, big brown eyes.

"I suppose they are cabbage-roses when they come out?" he said.

"I don't know," she faltered. "They're white with pink middles."

"Then they're maiden-blush."

Miriam flushed. She had a beautiful warm colouring.

"I don't know," she said.

"You don't have *much* in your garden," he said.

"This is our first year here," she answered, in a distant, rather superior way, drawing back and going indoors. He did not notice, but went his round of exploration. Presently his mother came out, and they went through the buildings. Paul was hugely delighted.

"And I suppose you have the fowls and calves and pigs to look after?" said Mrs. Morel to Mrs. Leivers.

"No," replied the little woman. "I can't find time to look after cattle, and I'm not used to it. It's as much as I can do to keep going in the house."

"Well, I suppose it is," said Mrs. Morel.

Presently the girl came out.

"Tea is ready, mother," she said in a musical, quiet voice.

"Oh, thank you, Miriam, then we'll come," replied her mother, almost ingratiatingly. "Would you *care* to have tea now, Mrs. Morel?"

"Of course," said Mrs. Morel. "Whenever it's ready."

Paul and his mother and Mrs. Leivers had tea together. Then they went out into the wood that was flooded with bluebells, while fumy forget-me-nots were in the paths. The mother and son were in ecstasy together.

When they got back to the house, Mr. Leivers and Edgar, the eldest son, were in the kitchen. Edgar was about eighteen. Then Geoffrey and Maurice, big lads of twelve and thirteen, were in from school. Mr. Leivers was a good-looking man in the prime of life, with a golden-brown moustache, and blue eyes screwed up against the weather.

The boys were condescending, but Paul scarcely observed it. They went round for eggs, scrambling into all sorts of places. As they were feeding the fowls Miriam came out. The boys took no notice of

207

her. One hen, with her yellow chickens, was in a coop. Maurice took his hand full of corn and let the hen peck from it.

"Durst you do it?" he asked of Paul.

"Let's see," said Paul.

He had a small hand, warm, and rather capable-looking. Miriam watched. He held the corn to the hen. The bird eyed it with her hard, bright eye, and suddenly made a peck into his hand. He started, and laughed. "Rap, rap, rap!" went the bird's beak in his palm. He laughed again, and the other boys joined.

"She knocks you, and nips you, but she never hurts," said Paul, when the last corn had gone.

"Now, Miriam," said Maurice, "you come an' 'ave a go."

"No," she cried, shrinking back.

"Ha! baby. The mardy-kid!" said her brothers.

"It doesn't hurt a bit," said Paul. "It only just nips rather nicely."

"No," she still cried, shaking her black curls and shrinking.

"She dursn't," said Geoffrey. "She niver durst do anything except recite poitry."

"Dursn't jump off a gate, dursn't tweedle, dursn't go on a slide, dursn't stop a girl hittin' her. She can do nowt but go about thinkin' herself somebody. 'The Lady of the Lake.' Yah!" cried Maurice.

Miriam was crimson with shame and misery.

"I dare do more than you," she cried. "You're

208

never anything but cowards and bullies."

"Oh, cowards and bullies!" they repeated mincingly, mocking her speech.

> "Not such a clown shall anger me,
> A boor is answered silently,"

he quoted against her, shouting with laughter.

She went indoors. Paul went with the boys into the orchard, where they had rigged up a parallel bar. They did feats of strength. He was more agile than strong, but it served. He fingered a piece of apple-blossom that hung low on a swinging bough.

"I wouldn't get the apple-blossom," said Edgar, the eldest brother. "There'll be no apples next year."

"I wasn't going to get it," replied Paul, going away.

The boys felt hostile to him; they were more interested in their own pursuits. He wandered back to the house to look for his mother. As he went round the back, he saw Miriam kneeling in front of the hen-coop, some maize in her hand, biting her lip, and crouching in an intense attitude. The hen was eyeing her wickedly. Very gingerly she put forward her hand. The hen bobbed for her. She drew back again quickly with a cry, half of fear, half of chagrin.

"It won't hurt you," said Paul.

She flushed crimson and started up.

"I only wanted to try," she said in a low voice.

"See, it doesn't hurt," he said, and, putting only two corns in his palm, he let the hen peck, peck, peck at his bare hand. "It only makes you laugh," he said.

She put her hand forward and dragged it away, tried again, and started back with a cry. He frowned.

"Why, I'd let her take corn from my face," said Paul, "only she bumps a bit. She's ever so neat. If she wasn't, look how much ground she'd peck up every day."

He waited grimly, and watched. At last Miriam let the bird peck from her hand. She gave a little cry—fear, and pain because of fear—rather pathetic. But she had done it, and she did it again.

"There, you see," said the boy. "It doesn't hurt, does it?"

She looked at him with dilated dark eyes.

"No," she laughed, trembling.

Then she rose and went indoors. She seemed to be in some way resentful of the boy.

"He thinks I'm only a common girl," she thought, and she wanted to prove she was a grand person like the "Lady of the Lake".

Paul found his mother ready to go home. She smiled on her son. He took the great bunch of flowers. Mr. and Mrs. Leivers walked down the fields with them. The hills were golden with evening; deep in the woods showed the darkening purple of bluebells. It was everywhere perfectly still, save for the rustling of leaves and birds.

"But it is a beautiful place," said Mrs. Morel.

"Yes," answered Mr. Leivers; "it's a nice little place, if only it weren't for the rabbits. The pasture's bitten down to nothing. I dunno if ever I s'll get the rent off it."

He clapped his hands, and the field broke into motion near the woods, brown rabbits hopping everywhere.

"Would you believe it!" exclaimed Mrs. Morel.

She and Paul went on alone together.

"Wasn't it lovely, mother?" he said quietly.

A thin moon was coming out. His heart was full of happiness till it hurt. His mother had to chatter, because she, too, wanted to cry with happiness.

"Now *wouldn't* I help that man!" she said. "*Wouldn't* I see to the fowls and the young stock! And *I'd* learn to milk, and *I'd* talk with him, and *I'd* plan with him. My word, if I were his wife, the farm would be run, I know! But there, she hasn't the strength—she simply hasn't the strength. She ought never to have been burdened like it, you know. I'm sorry for her, and I'm sorry for him too. My word, if *I'd* had him, I shouldn't have thought him a bad husband! Not that she does either; and she's very lovable."

William came home again with his sweetheart at the Whitsuntide. He had one week of his holidays then. It was beautiful weather. As a rule, William and Lily and Paul went out in the morning together for a walk. William did not talk to his beloved much, except to tell her things from his boyhood. Paul talked endlessly to both of them. They lay

211

down, all three, in a meadow by Minton Church. On one side, by the Castle Farm, was a beautiful quivering screen of poplars. Hawthorn was dropping from the hedges; penny daisies and ragged robin were in the field, like laughter. William, a big fellow of twenty-three, thinner now and even a bit gaunt, lay back in the sunshine and dreamed, while she fingered with his hair. Paul went gathering the big daisies. She had taken off her hat; her hair was black as a horse's mane. Paul came back and threaded daisies in her jet-black hair—big spangles of white and yellow, and just a pink touch of ragged robin.

"Now you look like a young witch-woman," the boy said to her. "Doesn't she, William?"

Lily laughed. William opened his eyes and looked at her. In his gaze was a certain baffled look of misery and fierce appreciation.

"Has he made a sight of me?" she asked, laughing down on her lover.

"That he has!" said William, smiling.

He looked at her. Her beauty seemed to hurt him. He glanced at her flower-decked head and frowned.

"You look nice enough, if that's what you want to know," he said.

And she walked without her hat. In a little while William recovered, and was rather tender to her. Coming to a bridge, he carved her initials and his in a heart.

L. L. W.
W. M.

212

She watched his strong, nervous hand, with its glistening hairs and freckles, as he carved, and she seemed fascinated by it.

All the time there was a feeling of sadness and warmth, and a certain tenderness in the house, whilst William and Lily were at home. But often he got irritable. She had brought, for an eight-days' stay, five dresses and six blouses.

"Oh, would you mind," she said to Annie, "washing me these two blouses, and these things?"

And Annie stood washing when William and Lily went out the next morning. Mrs. Morel was furious. And sometimes the young man, catching a glimpse of his sweetheart's attitude towards his sister, hated her.

On Sunday morning she looked very beautiful in a dress of foulard, silky and sweeping, and blue as a jay-bird's feather, and in a large cream hat covered with many roses, mostly crimson. Nobody could admire her enough. But in the evening, when she was going out, she asked again:

"Chubby, have you got my gloves?"

"Which?" asked William.

"My new black *suède*."

"No."

There was a hunt. She had lost them.

"Look here, mother," said William, "that's the fourth pair she's lost since Christmas—at five shillings a pair!"

"You only gave me *two* of them," she remonstrated.

And in the evening, after supper, he stood on the hearth-rug whilst she sat on the sofa, and he seemed to hate her. In the afternoon he had left her whilst he went to see some old friend. She had sat looking at a book. After supper William wanted to write a letter.

"Here is your book, Lily," said Mrs. Morel. "Would you care to go on with it for a few minutes?"

"No, thank you," said the girl. "I will sit still."

"But it is so dull."

William scribbled irritably at a great rate. As he sealed the envelope he said:

"Read a book! Why, she's never read a book in her life."

"Oh, go along!" said Mrs. Morel, cross with the exaggeration.

"It's true, mother—she hasn't," he cried, jumping up and taking his old position on the hearth-rug. "She's never read a book in her life."

" 'Er's like me," chimed in Morel. " 'Er canna see what there is i' books, ter sit borin' your nose in 'em for, nor more can I."

"But you shouldn't say these things," said Mrs. Morel to her son.

"But it's true, mother—she *can't* read. What did you give her?"

"Well, I gave her a little thing of Annie Swan's. Nobody wants to read dry stuff on Sunday afternoon."

"Well, I'll bet she didn't read ten lines of it."

"You are mistaken," said his mother.

All the time Lily sat miserably on the sofa. He turned to her swiftly.

"*Did* you read any?" he asked.

"Yes, I did," she replied.

"How much?"

"I don't know how many pages."

"Tell me *one thing* you read."

She could not.

She never got beyond the second page. He read a great deal, and had a quick, active intelligence. She could understand nothing but love-making and chatter. He was accustomed to having all his thoughts sifted through his mother's mind; so, when he wanted companionship, and was asked in reply to be the billing and twittering lover, he hated his betrothed.

"You know, mother," he said, when he was alone with her at night, "she's no idea of money, she's so wessel-brained. When she's paid, she'll suddenly buy such rot as *marrons glacés*, and then *I* have to buy her season ticket, and her extras, even her underclothing. And she wants to get married, and I think myself we might as well get married ncxt year. But at this rate——"

"A fine mess of a marriage it would be," replied his mother. "I should consider it again, my boy."

"Oh, well, I've gone too far to break off now," he said, "and so I shall get married as soon as I can."

"Very well, my boy. If you will, you will, and

215

there's no stopping you; but I tell you, *I* can't sleep when I think about it."

"Oh, she'll be all right, mother. We shall manage."

"And she lets you buy her underclothing?" asked the mother.

"Well," he began apologetically, "she didn't ask me; but one morning—and it *was* cold—I found her on the station shivering, not able to keep still; so I asked her if she was well wrapped up. She said: 'I think so.' So I said: 'Have you got warm under-things on?' And she said: 'No, they were cotton.' I asked her why on earth she hadn't got something thicker on in weather like that, and she said because she *had* nothing. And there she is—a bronchial sub-ject! I *had* to take her and get some warm things. Well, mother, I shouldn't mind the money if we had any. And, you know, she *ought* to keep enough to pay for her season-ticket; but no, she comes to me about that, and I have to find the money."

"It's a poor lookout," said Mrs. Morel bitterly.

He was pale, and his rugged face, that used to be so perfectly careless and laughing, was stamped with conflict and despair.

"But I can't give her up now; it's gone too far," he said. "And, besides, for *some* things I couldn't do without her."

"My boy, remember you're taking your life in your hands," said Mrs. Morel. "*Nothing* is as bad as a marriage that's a hopeless failure. Mine was bad enough, God knows, and ought to teach you some-

216

thing; but it might have been worse by a long chalk."

He leaned with his back against the side of the chimney-piece, his hands in his pockets. He was a big, raw-boned man, who looked as if he would go to the world's end if he wanted to. But she saw the despair on his face.

"I couldn't give her up now," he said.

"Well," she said, "remember there are worse things than breaking off an engagement."

"I can't give her up *now*," he said.

The clock ticked on; mother and son remained in silence, a conflict between them; but he would say no more. At last she said:

"Well, go to bed, my son. You'll feel better in the morning, and perhaps you'll know better."

He kissed her, and went. She raked the fire. Her heart was heavy now as it had never been. Before, with her husband, things had seemed to be breaking down in her, but they did not destroy her power to live. Now her soul felt lamed in itself. It was her hope that was struck.

And so often William manifested the same hatred towards his betrothed. On the last evening at home he was railing against her.

"Well," he said, "if you don't believe me, what she's like, would you believe she has been confirmed three times?"

"Nonsense!" laughed Mrs. Morel.

"Nonsense or not, she *has*! That's what confirmation means for her—a bit of a theatrical show where she can cut a figure."

"I haven't, Mrs. Morel!" cried the girl—"I haven't! It is not true!"

"What!" he cried, flashing round on her. "Once in Bromley, once in Beckenham, and once somewhere else."

"Nowhere else!" she said, in tears—"nowhere else!"

"It *was*! And if it wasn't why were you confirmed *twice*?"

"Once I was only fourteen, Mrs. Morel," she pleaded, tears in her eyes.

"Yes," said Mrs. Morel; "I can quite understand it, child. Take no notice of him. You ought to be ashamed, William, saying such things."

"But it's true. She's religious—she had blue velvet Prayer-Books—and she's not as much religion, or anything else, in her than that table-leg. Gets confirmed three times for show, to show herself off, and that's how she is in *everything—everything*!"

The girl sat on the sofa, crying. She was not strong.

"As for *love*!" he cried, "you might as well ask a fly to love you! It'll love settling on you——"

"Now, say no more," commanded Mrs. Morel. "If you want to say these things, you must find another place than this. I am ashamed of you, William! Why don't you be more manly. To do nothing but find fault with a girl, and then pretend you're engaged to her!"

Mrs. Morel subsided in wrath and indignation.

William was silent, and later he repented, kissed and comforted the girl. Yet it was true, what he had said. He hated her.

When they were going away, Mrs. Morel accompanied them as far as Nottingham. It was a long way to Keston station.

"You know, mother," he said to her, "Gyp's shallow. Nothing goes deep with her."

"William, I *wish* you wouldn't say these things," said Mrs. Morel, very uncomfortable for the girl who walked beside her.

"But it doesn't, mother. She's very much in love with me now, but if I died she'd have forgotten me in three months."

Mrs. Morel was afraid. Her heart beat furiously, hearing the quiet bitterness of her son's last speech.

"How do you know?" she replied. "You *don't* know, and therefore you've no right to say such a thing."

"He's always saying these things!" cried the girl.

"In three months after I was buried you'd have somebody else, and I should be forgotten," he said. "And that's your love!"

Mrs. Morel saw them into the train in Nottingham, then she returned home.

"There's one comfort," she said to Paul—"he'll never have any money to marry on, that I *am* sure of. And so she'll save him that way."

So she took cheer. Matters were not yet very desperate. She firmly believed William would never marry his Gipsy. She waited, and she kept Paul near to her.

All summer long William's letters had a feverish tone; he seemed unnatural and intense. Sometimes he was exaggeratedly jolly, usually he was flat and bitter in his letter.

"Ah," his mother said, "I'm afraid he's ruining himself against that creature, who isn't worthy of his love—no, no more than a rag doll."

He wanted to come home. The midsummer holiday was gone; it was a long while to Christmas. He wrote in wild excitement, saying he could come for Saturday and Sunday at Goose Fair, the first week in October.

"You are not well, my boy," said his mother, when she saw him.

She was almost in tears at having him to herself again.

"No, I've not been well," he said. "I've seemed to have a dragging cold all the last month, but it's going, I think."

It was sunny October weather. He seemed wild with joy, like a schoolboy escaped; then again he was silent and reserved. He was more gaunt than ever, and there was a haggard look in his eyes.

"You are doing too much," said his mother to him.

He was doing extra work, trying to make some money to marry on, he said. He only talked to his mother once on the Saturday night; then he was sad and tender about his beloved.

"And yet, you know, mother, for all that, if I died she'd be broken-hearted for two months, and then she'd start to forget me. You'd see, she'd never come home here to look at my grave, not even once."

"Why, William," said his mother, "you're not going to die, so why talk about it?"

"But whether or not——" he replied.

"And she can't help it. She is like that, and if you choose her—well, you can't grumble," said his mother.

On the Sunday morning, as he was putting his collar on:

"Look," he said to his mother, holding up his chin, "what a rash my collar's made under my chin!"

Just at the junction of chin and throat was a big red inflamation.

"It ought not to do that," said his mother. "Here, put a bit of this soothing ointment on. You should wear different collars."

He went away on Sunday midnight, seeming better and more solid for his two days at home.

On Tuesday morning came a telegram from London that he was ill. Mrs. Morel got off her knees from washing the floor, read the telegram, called a neighbour, went to her landlady and borrowed a sovereign, put on her things, and set off. She hurried to Keston, caught an express for London in Nottingham. She had to wait in Nottingham nearly an hour. A small figure in her black bonnet, she was anxiously asking the porters if they knew how to get to Elmers End. The journey was three hours. She sat in her corner in a kind of stupor, never moving. At King's Cross still no one could tell her how to get to Elmers End. Carrying her string bag, that contained her nightdress, a comb and brush, she went from person to person. At last they sent her underground to Cannon Street.

It was six o'clock when she arrived at William's lodging. The blinds were not down.

"How is he?" she asked.

"No better," said the landlady.

She followed the woman upstairs. William lay on the bed, with bloodshot eyes, his face rather discoloured. The clothes were tossed about, there was no fire in the room, a glass of milk stood on the stand at his bedside. No one had been with him.

"Why, my son!" said the mother bravely.

He did not answer. He looked at her, but did not see her. Then he began to say, in a dull voice, as if repeating a letter from dictation: "Owing to a leakage in the hold of this vessel, the sugar had set, and become converted into rock. It needed hacking——"

He was quite unconscious. It had been his business to examine some such cargo of sugar in the Port of London.

"How long has he been like this?" the mother asked the landlady.

"He got home at six o'clock on Monday morning, and he seemed to sleep all day; then in the night we

222

heard him talking, and this morning he asked for you. So I wired, and we fetched the doctor."

"Will you have a fire made?"

Mrs. Morel tried to soothe her son, to keep him still.

The doctor came. It was pneumonia, and, he said, a peculiar erysipelas, which had started under the chin where the collar chafed, and was spreading over the face. He hoped it would not get to the brain.

Mrs. Morel settled down to nurse. She prayed for William, prayed that he would recognise her. But the young man's face grew more discoloured. In the night she struggled with him. He raved, and raved, and would not come to consciousness. At two o'clock, in a dreadful paroxysm, he died.

Mrs. Morel sat perfectly still for an hour in the lodging bedroom; then she roused the household.

At six o'clock, with the aid of the charwoman, she laid him out; then she went round the dreary London village to the registrar and the doctor.

At nine o'clock to the cottage on Scargill Street came another wire:

"William died last night. Let father come, bring money."

Annie, Paul and Arthur were at home; Mr. Morel was gone to work. The three children said not a word. Annie began to whimper with fear; Paul set off for his father.

It was a beautiful day. At Brinsley pit the white steam melted slowly in the sunshine of a soft blue sky; the wheels of the headstocks twinkled high up; the screen, shuffling its coal into the trucks, made a busy noise.

"I want my father; he's got to go to London," said the boy to the first man he met on the bank.

"Tha wants Walter Morel? Go in theer an' tell Joe Ward."

Paul went into the little top office.

"I want my father; he's got to go to London."

"Thy feyther? Is he down? What's his name?"

"Mr. Morel."

"What, Walter? Is owt amiss?"

"He's got to go to London."

The man went to the telephone and rang up the bottom office.

"Walter Morel's wanted, number 42, Hard. Summat's amiss; there's his lad here."

Then he turned round to Paul.

"He'll be up in a few minutes," he said.

Paul wandered out to the pit-top. He watched the chair come up, with its wagon of coal. The great iron cage sank back on its rest, a full carfle was hauled off, an empty tram run on to the chair, a bell ting'ed somewhere, the chair heaved, then dropped like a stone.

Paul did not realise William was dead; it was impossible, with such a bustle going on. The puller-off swung the small truck on to the turn-table, another man ran with it along the bank down the curving lines.

"And William is dead, and my mother's in Lon-

224

don, and what will she be doing?" the boy asked himself, as if it were a conundrum.

He watched chair after chair come up, and still no father. At last, standing beside a wagon, a man's form! the chair sank on its rests, Morel stepped off. He was slightly lame from an accident.

"Is it thee, Paul? Is 'e worse?"

"You've got to go to London."

The two walked off the pit-bank, where men were watching curiously. As they came out and went along the railway, with the sunny autumn field on one side and a wall of trucks on the other, Morel said in a frightened voice:

" 'E's niver gone, child?"

"Yes."

"When wor't?"

"Last night. We had a telegram from my mother."

Morel walked on a few strides, then leaned up against a truck-side, his hand over his eyes. He was not crying. Paul stood looking round, waiting. On the weighing machine a truck trundled slowly. Paul saw everything, except his father leaning against the truck as if he were tired.

Morel had only once before been to London. He set off, scared and peaked, to help his wife. That was on Tuesday. The children were left alone in the house. Paul went to work, Arthur went to school, and Annie had in a friend to be with her.

On Saturday night, as Paul was turning the corner, coming home from Keston, he saw his mother and father, who had come to Sethley Bridge Station. They were walking in silence in the dark, tired, straggling apart. The boy waited.

"Mother!" he said, in the darkness.

Mrs. Morel's small figure seemed not to observe. He spoke again.

"Paul!" she said, uninterestedly.

She let him kiss her, but she seemed unaware of him.

In the house she was the same—small, white, and mute. She noticed nothing, she said nothing, only:

"The coffin will be here tonight, Walter. You'd better see about some help." Then, turning to the children: "We're bringing him home."

Then she relapsed into the same mute looking into space, her hands folded on her lap. Paul, looking at her, felt he could not breathe. The house was dead silent.

"I went to work, mother," he said plaintively.

"Did you?" she answered, dully.

After half an hour Morel, troubled and bewildered, came in again.

"Wheer s'll we ha'e him when he *does* come?" he asked his wife.

"In the front-room."

"Then I'd better shift th' table?"

"Yes."

"An' ha'e him across th' chairs?"

"You know there—— Yes, I suppose so."

Morel and Paul went, with a candle, into the parlour. There was no gas there. The father unscrewed the top of the big mahogany oval table, and cleared the middle of the room; then he arranged six chairs opposite each other, so that the coffin could stand on their beds.

"You niver seed such a length as he is!" said the miner, and watching anxiously as he worked.

Paul went to the bay window and looked out. The ash-tree stood monstrous and black in front of the wide darkness. It was a faintly luminous night. Paul went back to his mother.

At ten o'clock Morel called:

"He's here!"

Everyone started. There was a noise of unbarring and unlocking the front door, which opened straight from the night into the room.

"Bring another candle," called Morel.

Annie and Arthur went. Paul followed with his mother. He stood with his arm round her waist in the inner doorway. Down the middle of the cleared room waited six chairs, face to face. In the window, against the lace curtains, Arthur held up one candle, and by the open door, against the night, Annie stood leaning forward, her brass candlestick glittering.

There was the noise of wheels. Outside in the darkness of the street below Paul could see horses and a black vehicle, one lamp, and a few pale faces; then some men, miners, all in their shirt-sleeves, seemed to struggle in the obscurity. Presently two men appeared, bowed beneath a great weight. It was Morel and his neighbour.

"Steady!" called Morel, out of breath.

He and his fellow mounted the steep garden step, heaved into the candlelight with their gleaming coffin-end. Limbs of other men were seen struggling behind. Morel and Burns, in front, staggered; the great dark weight swayed.

"Steady, steady!" cried Morel, as if in pain.

All the six bearers were up in the small garden, holding the great coffin aloft. There were three more steps to the door. The yellow lamp of the carriage shone alone down the black road.

"Now then!" said Morel.

The coffin swayed, the men began to mount the three steps with their load. Annie's candle flickered, and she whimpered as the first men appeared, and the limbs and bowed heads of six men struggled to climb into the room, bearing the coffin that rode like sorrow on their living flesh.

"Oh, my son—my son!" Mrs. Morel sang softly, and each time the coffin swung to the unequal climbing of the men: "Oh, my son—my son—my son!"

"Mother!" Paul whimpered, his hand round her waist.

She did not hear.

"Oh, my son—my son!" she repeated.

Paul saw drops of sweat fall from his father's brow. Six men were in the room—six coatless men, with yielding, struggling limbs, filling the room and knocking against the furniture. The coffin veered, and was gently lowered on to the chairs. The sweat fell from Morel's face on its boards.

"My word, he's a weight!" said a man, and the five miners sighed, bowed, and, trembling with the struggle, descended the steps again, closing the door behind them.

The family was alone in the parlour with the great polished box. William, when laid out, was six feet four inches long. Like a monument lay the bright brown, ponderous coffin. Paul thought it would never be got out of the room again. His mother was stroking the polished wood.

They buried him on the Monday in the little cemetery on the hillside that looks over the fields at the big church and the houses. It was sunny, and the white chrysanthemums frilled themselves in the warmth.

Mrs. Morel could not be persuaded, after this, to talk and take her old bright interest in life. She remained shut off. All the way home in the train she had said to herself: "If only it could have been me!"

When Paul came home at night he found his mother sitting, her day's work done, with hands folded in her lap upon her coarse apron. She always used to have changed her dress and put on a black apron, before. Now Annie set his supper, and his mother sat looking blankly in front of her, her mouth shut tight. Then he beat his brains for news to tell her.

"Mother, Miss Jordan was down today, and she said my sketch of a colliery at work was beautiful."

But Mrs. Morel took no notice. Night after night he forced himself to tell her things, although she did not listen. It drove him almost insane to have her thus. At last:

"What's a-matter, mother?" he asked.

She did not hear.

"What's a-matter?" he persisted. "Mother, what's a-matter?"

"You know what's the matter," she said irritably, turning away.

The lad—he was sixteen years old—went to bed drearily. He was cut off and wretched through October, November and December. His mother tried, but she could not rouse herself. She could only brood on her dead son; he had been let to die so cruelly.

At last, on December 23, with his five shillings Christmas-box in his pocket, Paul wandered blindly home. His mother looked at him, and her heart stood still.

"What's the matter?" she asked.

"I'm badly, mother!" he replied. "Mr. Jordan gave me five shillings for a Christmas-box!"

He handed it to her with trembling hands. She put it on the table.

"You aren't glad!" he reproached her; but he trembled violently.

"Where hurts you?" she said, unbuttoning his overcoat.

It was the old question.

"I feel badly, mother."

She undressed him and put him to bed. He had pneumonia dangerously, the doctor said.

"Might he never have had it if I'd kept him at home, not let him go to Nottingham?" was one of the first things she asked.

"He might not have been so bad," said the doctor.

Mrs. Morel stood condemned on her own ground.

"I should have watched the living, not the dead," she told herself.

Paul was very ill. His mother lay in bed at nights with him; they could not afford a nurse. He grew worse, and the crisis approached. One night he tossed into consciousness in the ghastly, sickly feeling of dissolution, when all the cells in the body seem in intense irritability to be breaking down, and consciousness makes a last flare of struggle, like madness.

"I s'll die, mother!" he cried, heaving for breath on the pillow.

She lifted him up, crying in a small voice:

"Oh, my son—my son!"

That brought him to. He realised her. His whole will rose up and arrested him. He put his head on her breast, and took ease of her for love.

"For some things," said his aunt, "it was a good thing Paul was ill that Christmas. I believe it saved his mother."

Paul was in bed for seven weeks. He got up white and fragile. His father had bought him a pot of scarlet and gold tulips. They used to flame in the window in the March sunshine as he sat on the sofa chattering to his mother. The two knitted together in perfect intimacy. Mrs. Morel's life now rooted itself in Paul.

William had been a prophet. Mrs. Morel had a little present and a letter from Lily at Christmas. Mrs. Morel's sister had a letter at the New Year.

"I was at a ball last night. Some delightful people were there, and I enjoyed myself thoroughly," said the letter. "I had every dance—did not sit out one."

Mrs. Morel never heard any more of her.

Morel and his wife were gentle with each other for some time after the death of their son. He would go into a kind of daze, staring wide-eyed and blank across the room. Then he got up suddenly and hurried out to the Three Spots, returning in his normal state. But never in his life would he go for a walk up Shepstone, past the office where his son had worked, and he always avoided the cemetery.

# *Part 2*

Part 2

# 7

## LAD-AND-GIRL LOVE

PAUL had been many times up to Willey Farm during the autumn. He was friends with the two youngest boys. Edgar, the eldest, would not condescend at first. And Miriam also refused to be approached. She was afraid of being set at naught, as by her own brothers. The girl was romantic in her soul. Everywhere was a Walter Scott heroine being loved by men with helmets or with plumes in their caps. She herself was something of a princess turned into a swine-girl in her own imagination. And she was afraid lest this boy, who, nevertheless, looked something like a Walter Scott hero, who could paint and speak French, and knew what algebra meant, and who went by train to Nottingham every day, might consider her simply as the swine-girl, unable to perceive the princess beneath; so she held aloof.

Her great companion was her mother. They were both brown-eyed, and inclined to be mystical, such women as treasure religion inside them, breathe it in their nostrils, and see the whole of life in a mist thereof. So to Miriam, Christ and God made one great figure, which she loved tremblingly and passionately when a tremendous sunset burned out the western sky, and Ediths, and Lucys, and Rowenas, Brian de Bois Guilberts, Rob Roys, and Guy Mannerings, rustled the sunny leaves in the morning, or sat in her bedroom aloft, alone, when it snowed. That was life to her. For the rest, she drudged in the house, which work she would not have minded had not her clean red floor been mucked up immediately by the trampling farm-boots of her brothers. She madly wanted her little brother of four to let her swathe him and stifle him in her love; she went to church reverently, with bowed head, and quivered in anguish from the vulgarity of the other choir-girls and from the common-sounding voice of the curate; she fought with her brothers, whom she considered brutal louts; and she held not her father in too high esteem because he did not carry any mystical ideals cherished in his heart, but only wanted to have as easy a time as he could, and his meals when he was ready for them.

She hated her position as swine-girl. She wanted to be considered. She wanted to learn, thinking that if she could read, as Paul said he could read, "Columba", or the "Voyage autour de ma Chambre", the world would have a different face for her and a deepened respect. She could not be princess by wealth or standing. So she was mad to have learning whereon to pride herself. For she was different from other folk, and must not be scooped up among the common fry. Learning was the only distinction to which she thought to aspire.

Her beauty—that of a shy, wild, quiveringly sensitive thing—seemed nothing to her. Even her soul, so strong for rhapsody, was not enough. She must have something to reinforce her pride, because she felt different from other people. Paul she eyed rather wistfully. On the whole, she scorned the male sex. But here was a new specimen, quick, light, graceful, who could be gentle and who could be sad, and who was clever, and who knew a lot, and who had a death in the family. The boy's poor morsel of learning exalted him almost sky-high in her esteem. Yet she tried hard to scorn him, because he would not see in her the princess but only the swine-girl. And he scarcely observed her.

Then he was so ill, and she felt he would be weak. Then she would be stronger than he. Then she could love him. If she could be mistress of him in his weakness, take care of him, if he could depend on her, if she could, as it were, have him in her arms, how she would love him!

As soon as the skies brightened and plum-blossom was out, Paul drove off in the milkman's heavy float up to Willey Farm. Mr. Leivers shouted in a kindly fashion at the boy, then clicked to the horse as they climbed the hill slowly, in the freshness of the morning. White clouds went on their way, crowding to the back of the hills that were rousing in the spring-time. The water of Nethermere lay below, very blue against the seared meadows and the thorn-trees.

It was four and a half miles drive. Tiny buds on the hedges, vivid as copper-green, were opening into rosettes; and thrushes called, and blackbirds

237

shrieked and scolded. It was a new, glamorous world.

Miriam, peeping through the kitchen window, saw the horse walk through the big white gate into the farmyard that was backed by the oak-wood, still bare. Then a youth in a heavy overcoat climbed down. He put up his hands for the whip and the rug that the good-looking, ruddy farmer handed down to him.

Miriam appeared in the doorway. She was nearly sixteen, very beautiful, with her warm colouring, her gravity, her eyes dilating suddenly like an ecstasy.

"I say," said Paul, turning shyly aside, "your daffodils are nearly out. Isn't it early? But don't they look cold?"

"Cold!" said Miriam, in her musical, caressing voice.

"The green on their buds——" and he faltered into silence timidly.

"Let me take the rug," said Miriam over-gently.

"I can carry it," he answered, rather injured. But he yielded it to her.

Then Mrs. Leivers appeared.

"I'm sure you're tired and cold," she said. "Let me take your coat. It *is* heavy. You mustn't walk far in it."

She helped him off with his coat. He was quite unused to such attention. She was almost smothered under its weight.

"Why, mother," laughed the farmer as he passed

238

through the kitchen, swinging the great milk-churns, "you've got almost more than you can manage there."

She beat up the sofa cushions for the youth.

The kitchen was very small and irregular. The farm had been originally a labourer's cottage. And the furniture was old and battered. But Paul loved it—loved the sack-bag that formed the hearthrug, and the funny little corner under the stairs, and the small window deep in the corner, through which, bending a little, he could see the plum trees in the back garden and the lovely round hills beyond.

"Won't you lie down?" said Mrs. Leivers.

"Oh no; I'm not tired," he said. "Isn't it lovely coming out, don't you think? I saw a sloe-bush in blossom and a lot of celandines. I'm glad it's sunny."

"Can I give you anything to eat or to drink?"

"No, thank you."

"How's your mother?"

"I think she's tired now. I think she's had too much to do. Perhaps in a little while she'll go to Skegness with me. Then she'll be able to rest. I s'll be glad if she can."

"Yes," replied Mrs. Leivers. "It's a wonder she isn't ill herself."

Miriam was moving about preparing dinner. Paul watched everything that happened. His face was pale and thin, but his eyes were quick and bright with life as ever. He watched the strange, almost rhapsodic way in which the girl moved about, carrying a great stew-jar to the oven, or looking in the saucepan. The atmosphere was different from that of his own home, where everything seemed so ordinary. When Mr. Leivers called loudly outside to the horse, that was reaching over to feed on the rose-bushes in the garden, the girl started, looked round with dark eyes, as if something had come breaking in on her world. There was a sense of silence inside the house and out. Miriam seemed as in some dreamy tale, a maiden in bondage, her spirit dreaming in a land far away and magical. And her discoloured, old blue frock and her broken boots seemed only like the romantic rags of King Cophetua's beggar maid.

She suddenly became aware of his keen blue eyes upon her, taking her all in. Instantly her broken boots and her frayed old frock hurt her. She resented his seeing everything. Even he knew that her stocking was not pulled up. She went into the scullery, blushing deeply. And afterwards her hands trembled slightly at her work. She nearly dropped all she handled. When her inside dream was shaken, her body quivered with trepidation. She resented that he saw so much.

Mrs. Leivers sat for some time talking to the boy, although she was needed at her work. She was too polite to leave him. Presently she excused herself and rose. After a while she looked into the tin saucepan.

"Oh *dear*, Miriam," she cried, "these potatoes have boiled dry!"

Miriam started as if she had been stung.

"*Have* they, mother?" she cried.

"I shouldn't care, Miriam," said the mother, "if I hadn't trusted them to you." She peered into the pan.

The girl stiffened as if from a blow. Her dark eyes dilated; she remained standing in the same spot.

"Well," she answered, gripped tight in self-conscious shame, "I'm sure I looked at them five minutes since."

"Yes," said the mother, "I know it's easily done."

"They're not much burned," said Paul. "It doesn't matter, does it?"

Mrs. Leivers looked at the youth with her brown, hurt eyes.

"It wouldn't matter but for the boys," she said to him. "Only Miriam knows what a trouble they make if the potatoes are 'caught'."

"Then," thought Paul to himself, "you shouldn't let them make a trouble."

After a while Edgar came in. He wore leggings, and his boots were covered with earth. He was rather small, rather formal, for a farmer. He glanced at Paul, nodded to him distantly, and said:

"Dinner ready?"

"Nearly, Edgar," replied the mother apologetically.

"I'm ready for mine," said the young man, taking up the newspaper and reading. Presently the rest of the family trooped in. Dinner was served. The meal went rather brutally. The over-gentleness and

241

apologetic tone of the mother brought out all the brutality of manners in the sons. Edgar tasted the potatoes, moved his mouth quickly like a rabbit, looked indignantly at his mother, and said:

"These potatoes are burnt, mother."

"Yes, Edgar. I forgot them for a minute. Perhaps you'll have bread if you can't eat them."

Edgar looked in anger across at Miriam.

"What was Miriam doing that she couldn't attend to them?" he said.

Miriam looked up. Her mouth opened, her dark eyes blazed and winced, but she said nothing. She swallowed her anger and her shame, bowing her dark head.

"I'm sure she was trying hard," said the mother.

"She hasn't got sense even to boil the potatoes," said Edgar. "What is she kept at home for?"

"On'y for eating everything that's left in th' pantry," said Maurice.

"They don't forget that potato-pie against our Miriam," laughed the father.

She was utterly humiliated. The mother sat in silence, suffering, like some saint out of place at the brutal board.

It puzzled Paul. He wondered vaguely why all this intense feeling went running because of a few burnt potatoes. The mother exalted everything—even a bit of housework—to the plane of a religious trust. The sons resented this; they felt themselves cut away underneath, and they answered with brutality and also with a sneering superciliousness.

242

Paul was just opening out from childhood into manhood. This atmosphere, where everything took a religious value, came with a subtle fascination to him. There was something in the air. His own mother was logical. Here there was something different, something he loved, something that at times he hated.

Miriam quarrelled with her brothers fiercely. Later in the afternoon, when they had gone away again, her mother said:

"You disappointed me at dinner-time, Miriam."

The girl dropped her head.

"They are such *brutes*!" she suddenly cried, looking up with flashing eyes.

"But hadn't you promised not to answer them?" said the mother. "And I believed in you. I *can't* stand it when you wrangle."

"But they're so hateful!" cried Miriam, "and—and *low*."

"Yes, dear. But how often have I asked you not to answer Edgar back? Can't you let him say what he likes?"

"But why should he say what he likes?"

"Aren't you strong enough to bear it, Miriam, if even for my sake? Are you so weak that you must wrangle with them?"

Mrs. Leivers stuck unflinchingly to this doctrine of "the other cheek". She could not instil it at all into the boys. With the girls she succeeded better, and Miriam was the child of her heart. The boys loathed the other cheek when it was presented to them. Miriam was often sufficiently lofty to turn it. Then they spat on her and hated her. But she walked in her proud humility, living within herself.

There was always this feeling of jangle and discord in the Leivers family. Although the boys resented so bitterly this eternal appeal to their deeper feelings of resignation and proud humility, yet it had its effect on them. They could not establish between themselves and an outsider just the ordinary human feeling and unexaggerated friendship; they were always restless for the something deeper. Ordinary folk seemed shallow to them, trivial and inconsiderable. And so they were unaccustomed, painfully uncouth in the simplest social intercourse, suffering, and yet insolent in their superiority. Then beneath was the yearning for the soul-intimacy to which they could not attain because they were too dumb, and every approach to close connection was blocked by their clumsy contempt of other people. They wanted genuine intimacy, but they could not get even normally near to anyone, because they scorned to take the first steps, they scorned the triviality which forms common human intercourse.

Paul fell under Mrs. Leivers's spell. Everything had a religious and intensified meaning when he was with her. His soul, hurt, highly developed, sought her as if for nourishment. Together they seemed to sift the vital fact from an experience.

Miriam was her mother's daughter. In the sunshine of the afternoon mother and daughter went down the fields with him. They looked for nests. There was a jenny wren's in the hedge by the orchard.

"I *do* want you to see this," said Mrs. Leivers.

He crouched down and carefully put his finger through the thorns into the round door of the nest.

"It's almost as if you were feeling inside the live body of the bird," he said, "it's so warm. They say a bird makes its nest round like a cup with pressing its breast on it. Then how did it make the ceiling round, I wonder?"

The nest seemed to start into life for the two women. After that, Miriam came to see it every day. It seemed so close to her. Again, going down the hedgeside with the girl, he noticed the celandines, scalloped splashes of gold, on the side of the ditch.

"I like them," he said, "when their petals go flat back with the sunshine. They seemed to be pressing themselves at the sun."

And then the celandines ever after drew her with a little spell. Anthropomorphic as she was, she stimulated him into appreciating things thus, and then they lived for her. She seemed to need things kindling in her imagination or in her soul before she felt she had them. And she was cut off from ordinary life by her religious intensity which made the world for her either a nunnery garden or a paradise, where sin and knowledge were not, or else an ugly, cruel thing.

So it was in this atmosphere of subtle intimacy,

this meeting in their common feeling for something in Nature, that their love started.

Personally, he was a long time before he realized her. For ten months he had to stay at home after his illness. For a while he went to Skegness with his mother, and was perfectly happy. But even from the seaside he wrote long letters to Mrs. Leivers about the shore and the sea. And he brought back his beloved sketches of the flat Lincoln coast, anxious for them to see. Almost they would interest the Leivers more than they interested his mother. It was not his art Mrs. Morel cared about; it was himself and his achievement. But Mrs. Leivers and her children were almost his disciples. They kindled him and made him glow to his work, whereas his mother's influence was to make him quietly determined, patient, dogged, unwearied.

He soon was friends with the boys, whose rudeness was only superficial. They had all, when they could trust themselves, a strange gentleness and lovableness.

"Will you come with me on to the fallow?" asked Edgar, rather hesitatingly.

Paul went joyfully, and spent the afternoon helping to hoe or to single turnips with his friend. He used to lie with the three brothers in the hay piled up in the barn and tell them about Nottingham and about Jordan's. In return, they taught him to milk, and let him do little jobs—chopping hay or pulping turnips—just as much as he liked. At midsummer he worked all through hay-harvest with them, and then he loved them. The family was so cut off from the world actually. They seemed, somehow, like *"les derniers fils d'une race épuisée"*. Though the lads were strong and healthy, yet they had all that over-sensitiveness and hanging-back which made them so lonely, yet also such close, delicate friends once their intimacy was won. Paul loved them dearly, and they him.

Miriam came later. But he had come into her life before she made any mark on his. One dull afternoon, when the men were on the land and the rest at school, only Miriam and her mother at home, the girl said to him, after having hesitated for some time:

"Have you seen the swing?"

"No," he answered. "Where?"

"In the cowshed," she replied.

She always hesitated to offer or to show him anything. Men have such different standards of worth from women, and her dear things—the valuable things to her—her brothers had so often mocked or flouted.

"Come on, then," he replied, jumping up.

There were two cowsheds, one on either side of the barn. In the lower, darker shed there was standing for four cows. Hens flew scolding over the manger-wall as the youth and girl went forward for the great thick rope which hung from the beam in the darkness overhead, and was pushed back over a peg in the wall.

"It's something like a rope!" he exclaimed appreciatively; and he sat down on it, anxious to try it. Then immediately he rose.

"Come on, then, and have first go," he said to the girl.

"See," she answered, going into the barn, "we put some bags on the seat"; and she made the swing comfortable for him. That gave her pleasure. He held the rope.

"Come on, then," he said to her.

"No, I won't go first," she answered.

She stood aside in her still, aloof fashion.

"Why?"

"You go," she pleaded.

Almost for the first time in her life she had the pleasure of giving up to a man, of spoiling him. Paul looked at her.

"All right," he said, sitting down. "Mind out!"

He set off with a spring, and in a moment was flying through the air, almost out of the door of the shed, the upper half of which was open, showing outside the drizzling rain, the filthy yard, the cattle standing disconsolate against the black cart-shed, and at the back of all the grey-green wall of the wood. She stood below in her crimson tam-o'-shanter and watched. He looked down at her, and she saw his blue eyes sparkling.

"It's a treat of a swing," he said.

"Yes."

He was swinging through the air, every bit of him swinging, like a bird that swoops for joy of movement. And he looked down at her. Her crimson cap hung over her dark curls, her beautiful warm face, so still in a kind of brooding, was lifted towards him. It was dark and rather cold in the shed. Suddenly a swallow came down from the high roof and darted out of the door.

"I didn't know a bird was watching," he called.

He swung negligently. She could feel him falling and lifting through the air, as if he were lying on some force.

"Now I'll die," he said, in a detached, dreamy voice, as though he were the dying motion of the swing. She watched him, fascinated. Suddenly he put on the brake and jumped out.

"I've had a long turn," he said. "But it's a treat of a swing—it's a real treat of a swing!"

Miriam was amused that he took a swing so seriously and felt so warmly over it.

"No; you go on," she said.

"Why, don't you want one?" he asked, astonished.

"Well, not much. I'll have just a little."

She sat down, whilst he kept the bags in place for her.

"It's so ripping!" he said, setting her in motion. "Keep your heels up, or they'll bang the manger wall."

She felt the accuracy with which he caught her, exactly at the right moment, and the exactly proportionate strength of his thrust, and she was afraid. Down to her bowels went the hot wave of fear. She was in his hands. Again, firm and inevitable came

249

the thrust at the right moment. She gripped the rope, almost swooning.

"Ha!" she laughed in fear. "No higher!"

"But you're not a *bit* high," he remonstrated.

"But no higher."

He heard the fear in her voice, and desisted. Her heart melted in hot pain when the moment came for him to thrust her forward again. But he left her alone. She began to breathe.

"Won't you really go any farther?" he asked. "Should I keep you there?"

"No; let me go by myself," she answered.

He moved aside and watched her.

"Why, you're scarcely moving," he said.

She laughed slightly with shame, and in a moment got down.

"They say if you can swing you won't be sea-sick," he said, as he mounted again. "I don't believe I should ever be sea-sick."

Away he went. There was something fascinating to her in him. For the moment he was nothing but a piece of swinging stuff; not a particle of him that did not swing. She could never lose herself so, nor could her brothers. It roused a warmth in her. It were almost as if he were a flame that had lit a warmth in her whilst he swung in the middle air.

And gradually the intimacy with the family concentrated for Paul on three persons—the mother, Edgar, and Miriam. To the mother he went for that sympathy and that appeal which seemed to draw him out. Edgar was his very close friend. And to Miriam he more or less condescended, because she seemed so humble.

But the girl gradually sought him out. If he brought up his sketch-book, it was she who pondered longest over the last picture. Then she would look up at him. Suddenly, her dark eyes alight like water that shakes with a stream of gold in the dark, she would ask:

"Why do I like this so?"

Always something in his breast shrank from these close, intimate, dazzled looks of hers.

"Why *do* you?" he asked.

"I don't know. It seems so true."

"It's because—it's because there is scarcely any shadow in it; it's more shimmery, as if I'd painted the shimmering protoplasm in the leaves and everywhere, and not the stiffness of the shape. That seems dead to me. Only this shimmeriness is the real living. The shape is a dead crust. The shimmer is inside really."

And she, with her little finger in her mouth, would ponder these sayings. They gave her a feeling of life again, and vivified things which had meant nothing to her. She managed to find some meaning in his struggling, abstract speeches. And they were the medium through which she came distinctly at her beloved objects.

Another day she sat at sunset whilst he was painting some pine-trees which caught the red glare from the west. He had been quiet.

"There you are!" he said suddenly. "I wanted that. Now, look at them and tell me, are they pine trunks or are they red coals, standing-up pieces of fire in that darkness? There's God's burning bush for you, that burned not away."

Miriam looked, and was frightened. But the pine trunks were wonderful to her, and distinct. He packed his box and rose. Suddenly he looked at her.

"Why are you always sad?" he asked her.

"Sad!" she exclaimed, looking up at him with startled, wonderful brown eyes.

"Yes," he replied. "You are always sad."

"I am not—oh, not a bit!" she cried.

"But even your joy is like a flame coming off of sadness," he persisted. "You're never jolly, or even just all right."

"No," she pondered. "I wonder—why?"

"Because you're not; because you're different inside, like a pine-tree, and then you flare up: but you're not just like an ordinary tree, with fidgety leaves and jolly——"

He got tangled up in his own speech; but she brooded on it, and he had a strange, roused sensation, as if his feelings were new. She got so near him. It was a strange stimulant.

Then sometimes he hated her. Her youngest brother was only five. He was a frail lad, with immense brown eyes in his quaint fragile face—one of Reynolds's "Choir of Angels", with a touch of elf. Often Miriam knelt to the child and drew him to her.

252

"Eh, my Hubert!" she sang, in a voice heavy and surcharged with love. "Eh, my Hubert!"

And, folding him in her arms, she swayed slightly from side to side with love, her face half lifted, her eyes half closed, her voice drenched with love.

"Don't!" said the child, uneasy—"don't, Miriam!"

"Yes; you love me, don't you?" she murmured deep in her throat, almost as if she were in a trance, and swaying also as if she were swooned in an ecstasy of love.

"Don't!" repeated the child, a frown on his clear brow.

"You love me, don't you?" she murmured.

"What do you make such a *fuss* for?" cried Paul, all in suffering because of her extreme emotion. "Why can't you be ordinary with him?"

She let the child go, and rose, and said nothing. Her intensity, which would leave no emotion on a normal plane, irritated the youth into a frenzy. And this fearful, naked contact of her on small occasions shocked him. He was used to his mother's reserve. And on such occasions he was thankful in his heart and soul that he had his mother, so sane and wholesome.

All the life of Miriam's body was in her eyes, which were usually dark as a dark church, but could flame with light like a conflagration. Her face scarcely ever altered from its look of brooding. She might have been one of the women who went with Mary when Jesus was dead. Her body was not flex-

253

ible and living. She walked with a swing, rather heavily, her head bowed forward, pondering. She was not clumsy, and yet none of her movements seemed quite *the* movement. Often, when wiping the dishes, she would stand in bewilderment and chagrin because she had pulled in two halves a cup or a tumbler. It was as if, in her fear and self-mistrust, she put too much strength into the effort. There was no looseness or abandon about her. Everything was gripped stiff with intensity, and her effort, overcharged, closed in on itself.

She rarely varied from her swinging, forward, intense walk. Occasionally she ran with Paul down the fields. Then her eyes blazed naked in a kind of ecstasy that frightened him. But she was physically afraid. If she were getting over a stile, she gripped his hands in a little hard anguish, and began to lose her presence of mind. And he could not persuade her to jump from even a small height. Her eyes dilated, became exposed and palpitating.

"No!" she cried, half laughing in terror—"no!"

"You shall!" he cried once, and, jerking her forward, he brought her falling from the fence. But her wild "Ah!" of pain, as if she were losing consciousness, cut him. She landed on her feet safely, and afterwards had courage in this respect.

She was very much dissatisfied with her lot.

"Don't you like being at home?" Paul asked her, surprised.

"Who would?" she answered, low and intense. "What is it? I'm all day cleaning what the boys make just as bad in five minutes. I don't *want* to be at home."

"What do you want, then?"

"I want to do something. I want a chance like anybody else. Why should I, because I'm a girl, be kept at home and not allowed to be anything? What chance *have* I?"

"Chance of what?"

"Of knowing anything—of learning, of doing anything. It's not fair, because I'm a woman."

She seemed very bitter. Paul wondered. In his own home Annie was almost glad to be a girl. She had not so much responsibility; things were lighter for her. She never wanted to be other than a girl. But Miriam almost fiercely wished she were a man. And yet she hated men at the same time.

"But it's as well to be a woman as a man," he said, frowning.

"Ha! Is it? Men have everything."

"I should think women ought to be as glad to be women as men are to be men," he answered.

"No!"—she shook her head—"no! Everything the men have."

"But what do you want?" he asked.

"I want to learn. Why *should* it be that I know nothing?"

"What! such as mathematics and French?"

"Why *shouldn't* I know mathematics? Yes!" she cried, her eye expanding in a kind of defiance.

"Well, you can learn as much as I know," he said. "I'll teach you, if you like."

255

Her eyes dilated. She mistrusted him as teacher. "Would you?" he asked.

Her head had dropped, and she was sucking her finger broodingly.

"Yes," she said hesitatingly.

He used to tell his mother all these things.

"I'm going to teach Miriam algebra," he said.

"Well," replied Mrs. Morel, "I hope she'll get fat on it."

When he went up to the farm on the Monday evening, it was drawing twilight. Miriam was just sweeping up the kitchen, and was kneeling at the hearth when he entered. Everyone was out but her. She looked round at him, flushed, her dark eyes shining, her fine hair falling about her face.

"Hello!" she said, soft and musical. "I knew it was you."

"How?"

"I knew your step. Nobody treads so quick and firm."

He sat down, sighing.

"Ready to do some algebra?" he asked, drawing a little book from his pocket.

"But——"

He could feel her backing away.

"You said you wanted," he insisted.

"Tonight, though?" she faltered.

"But I came on purpose. And if you want to learn it, you must begin."

She took up her ashes in the dustpan and looked at him, half tremulously, laughing.

"Yes, but tonight! You see, I haven't thought of it."

"Well, my goodness! Take the ashes and come."

He went and sat on the stone bench in the backyard, where the big milk-cans were standing, tipped up, to air. The men were in the cowsheds. He could hear the little sing-song of the milk spurting into the pails. Presently she came, bringing some big greenish apples.

"You know you like them," she said.

He took a bite.

"Sit down," he said, with his mouth full.

She was short-sighted, and peered over his shoulder. It irritated him. He gave her the book quickly.

"Here," he said. "It's only letters for figures. You put down '$a$' instead of '2' or '6'."

They worked, he talking, she with her head down on the book. He was quick and hasty. She never answered. Occasionally, when he demanded of her, "Do you see?" she looked up at him, her eyes wide with the half-laugh that comes of fear. "Don't you?" he cried.

He had been too fast. But she said nothing. He questioned her more, then got hot. It made his blood rouse to see her there, as it were, at his mercy, her mouth open, her eyes dilated with laughter that was afraid, apologetic, ashamed. Then Edgar came along with two buckets of milk.

"Hello!" he said. "What are you doing?"

"Algebra," replied Paul.

"Algebra!" repeated Edgar curiously. Then he passed on with a laugh. Paul took a bite at his forgotten apple, looked at the miserable cabbages in the garden, pecked into lace by the fowls, and he wanted to pull them up. Then he glanced at Miriam. She was poring over the book, seemed absorbed in it, yet trembling lest she could not get at it. It made him cross. She was ruddy and beautiful. Yet her soul seemed to be intensely supplicating. The algebra-book she closed, shrinking, knowing he was angered; and at the same instant he grew gentle, seeing her hurt because she did not understand.

But things came slowly to her. And when she held herself in a grip, seemed so utterly humble before the lesson, it made his blood rouse. He stormed at her, got ashamed, continued the lesson, and grew furious again, abusing her. She listened in silence. Occasionally, very rarely, she defended herself. Her liquid dark eyes blazed at him.

"You don't give me time to learn it," she said.

"All right," he answered, throwing the book on the table and lighting a cigarette. Then, after a while, he went back to her repentant. So the lessons went. He was always either in a rage or very gentle.

"What do you tremble your *soul* before it for?" he cried. "You don't learn algebra with your blessed soul. Can't you look at it with your clear simple wits?"

Often, when he went again into the kitchen, Mrs. Leivers would look at him reproachfully, saying:

"Paul, don't be so hard on Miriam. She may not be quick, but I'm sure she tries."

"I can't help it," he said rather pitiably. "I go off like it."

"You don't mind me, Miriam, do you?" he asked of the girl later.

"No," she reassured him in her beautiful deep tones—"no, I don't mind."

"Don't mind me; it's my fault."

But, in spite of himself, his blood began to boil with her. It was strange that no one else made him in such a fury. He flared against her. Once he threw the pencil in her face. There was a silence. She turned her face slightly aside.

"I didn't——" he began, but got no farther, feeling weak in all his bones. She never reproached him or was angry with him. He was often cruelly ashamed. But still again his anger burst like a bubble surcharged; and still, when he saw her eager, silent, as it were, blind face, he felt he wanted to throw the pencil in it; and still, when he saw her hand trembling and her mouth parted with suffering, his heart was scalded with pain for her. And because of the intensity to which she roused him, he sought her.

Then he often avoided her and went with Edgar. Miriam and her brother were naturally antagonistic. Edgar was a rationalist, who was curious, and had a sort of scientific interest in life. It was a great bitterness to Miriam to see herself deserted by Paul for Edgar, who seemed so much lower. But the

259

youth was very happy with her elder brother. The two men spent afternoons together on the land or in the loft doing carpentry, when it rained. And they talked together, or Paul taught Edgar the songs he himself had learned from Annie at the piano. And often all the men, Mr. Leivers as well, had bitter debates on the nationalizing of the land and similar problems. Paul had already heard his mother's views, and as these were as yet his own, he argued for her. Miriam attended and took part, but was all the time waiting until it should be over and a personal communication might begin.

"After all," she said within herself, "if the land were nationalized, Edgar and Paul and I would be just the same." So, she waited for the youth to come back to her.

He was studying for his painting. He loved to sit at home, alone with his mother, at night, working and working. She sewed or read. Then, looking up from his task, he would rest his eyes for a moment on her face, that was bright with living warmth, and he returned gladly to his work.

"I can do my best things when you sit there in your rocking-chair, mother," he said.

"I'm sure!" she exclaimed, sniffing with mock scepticism. But she felt it was so, and her heart quivered with brightness. For many hours she sat still, slightly conscious of him labouring away, whilst she worked or read her book. And he, with all his soul's intensity directing his pencil, could feel her warmth inside him like strength. They were both very happy so, and both unconscious of it. These times, that meant so much, and which were real living, they almost ignored.

He was conscious only when stimulated. A sketch finished, he always wanted to take it to Miriam. Then he was stimulated into knowledge of the work he had produced unconsciously. In contact with Miriam he gained insight; his vision went deeper. From his mother he drew the life-warmth, the strength to produce; Miriam urged this warmth into intensity like a white light.

When he returned to the factory the conditions of work were better. He had Wednesday afternoon off to go to the Art School—Miss Jordan's provision— returning in the evening. Then the factory closed at six instead of eight on Thursday and Friday evenings.

One evening in the summer Miriam and he went over the fields by Herod's Farm on their way from the library home. So it was only three miles to Willey Farm. There was a yellow glow over the mowing-grass, and the sorrel-heads burned crimson. Gradually, as they walked along the high land, the gold in the west sank down to red, the red to crimson, and then the chill blue crept up against the glow.

They came out upon the high road to Alfreton, which ran white between the darkening fields. There Paul hesitated. It was two miles home for him, one mile forward for Miriam. They both looked up the road that ran in shadow right under the glow of the north-west sky. On the crest of the hill, Selby, with its stark houses and the up-pricked headstocks of the pit, stood in black silhouette small against the sky.

He looked at his watch.

"Nine o'clock!" he said.

The pair stood, loth to part, hugging their books.

"The wood is so lovely now," she said. "I wanted you to see it."

He followed her slowly across the road to the white gate.

"They grumble so if I'm late," he said.

"But you're not doing anything wrong," she answered impatiently.

He followed her across the nibbled pasture in the dusk. There was a coolness in the wood, a scent of leaves, of honeysuckle, and a twilight. The two walked in silence. Night came wonderfully there, among the throng of dark tree-trunks. He looked round, expectant.

She wanted to show him a certain wild-rose bush she had discovered. She knew it was wonderful. And yet, till he had seen it, she felt it had not come into her soul. Only he could make it her own, immortal. She was dissatisfied.

Dew was already on the paths. In the old oakwood a mist was rising, and he hesitated, wondering whether one whiteness were a strand of fog or only campion-flowers pallid in a cloud.

By the time they came to the pine-trees Miriam was getting very eager and very tense. Her bush

262

might be gone. She might not be able to find it; and she wanted it so much. Almost passionately she wanted to be with him when he stood before the flowers. They were going to have a communion together—something that thrilled her, something holy. He was walking beside her in silence. They were very near to each other. She trembled, and he listened, vaguely anxious.

Coming to the edge of the wood, they saw the sky in front, like mother-of-pearl, and the earth growing dark. Somewhere on the outermost branches of the pine-wood the honeysuckle was streaming scent.

"Where?" he asked.

"Down the middle path," she murmured, quivering.

When they turned the corner of the path she stood still. In the wide walk between the pines, gazing rather frightened, she could distinguish nothing for some moments; the greying light robbed things of their colour. Then she saw her bush.

"Ah!" she cried, hastening forward.

It was very still. The tree was tall and straggling. It had thrown its briers over a hawthorn-bush, and its long streamers trailed thick, right down to the grass, splashing the darkness everywhere with great spilt stars, pure white. In bosses of ivory and in large splashed stars the roses gleamed on the darkness of foliage and stems and grass. Paul and Miriam stood close together, silent, and watched. Point after point the steady roses shone out to them, seeming to kindle something in their souls. The

263

dusk came like smoke around, and still did not put out the roses.

Paul looked into Miriam's eyes. She was pale and expectant with wonder, her lips were parted, and her dark eyes lay open to him. His look seemed to travel down into her. Her soul quivered. It was the communion she wanted. He turned aside, as if pained. He turned to the bush.

"They seem as if they walk like butterflies, and shake themselves," he said.

She looked at her roses. They were white, some incurved and holy, others expanded in an ecstasy. The tree was dark as a shadow. She lifted her hand impulsively to the flowers; she went forward and touched them in worship.

"Let us go," he said.

There was a cool scent of ivory roses—a white, virgin scent. Something made him feel anxious and imprisoned. The two walked in silence.

"Till Sunday," he said quietly, and left her; and she walked home slowly, feeling her soul satisfied with the holiness of the night. He stumbled down the path. And as soon as he was out of the wood, in the free open meadow, where he could breathe, he started to run as fast as he could. It was like a delicious delirium in his veins.

Always when he went with Miriam, and it grew rather late, he knew his mother was fretting and getting angry about him—why, he could not understand. As he went into the house, flinging down his cap, his mother looked up at the clock. She had

264

been sitting thinking, because a chill to her eyes prevented her reading. She could feel Paul being drawn away by this girl. And she did not care for Miriam. "She is one of those who will want to suck a man's soul out till he has none of his own left," she said to herself; "and he is just such a gaby as to let himself be absorbed. She will never let him become a man; she never will." So, while he was away with Miriam, Mrs. Morel grew more and more worked up.

She glanced at the clock and said, coldly and rather tired:

"You have been far enough tonight."

His soul, warm and exposed from contact with the girl, shrank.

"You must have been right home with her," his mother continued.

He would not answer. Mrs. Morel, looking at him quickly, saw his hair was damp on his forehead with haste, saw him frowning in his heavy fashion, resentfully.

"She must be wonderfully fascinating, that you can't get away from her, but must go trailing eight miles at this time of night."

He was hurt between the past glamour with Miriam and the knowledge that his mother fretted. He had meant not to say anything, to refuse to answer. But he could not harden his heart to ignore his mother.

"I *do* like to talk to her," he answered irritably.

"Is there nobody else to talk to?"

"You wouldn't say anything if I went with Edgar."

"You know I should. You know, whoever you went with, I should say it was too far for you to go trailing, late at night, when you've been to Nottingham. Besides"—her voice suddenly flashed into anger and contempt—"it is disgusting—bits of lads and girls courting."

"It is *not* courting," he cried.

"I don't know what else you call it."

"It's not! Do you think we *spoon* and do? We only talk."

"Till goodness knows what time and distance," was the sarcastic rejoinder.

Paul snapped at the laces of his boots angrily.

"What are you so mad about?" he asked. "Because you don't like her."

"I don't say I don't like her. But I don't hold with children keeping company, and never did."

"But you don't mind our Annie going out with Jim Inger."

"They've more sense than you two."

"Why?"

"Our Annie's not one of the deep sort."

He failed to see the meaning of this remark. But his mother looked tired. She was never so strong after William's death; and her eyes hurt her.

"Well," he said, "it's so pretty in the country. Mr. Sleath asked about you. He said he'd missed you. Are you a bit better?"

266

"I ought to have been in bed a long time ago," she replied.

"Why, mother, you know you wouldn't have gone before quarter-past ten."

"Oh, yes, I should!"

"Oh, little woman, you'd say anything now you're disagreeable with me, wouldn't you?"

He kissed her forehead that he knew so well: the deep marks between the brows, the rising of the fine hair, greying now, and the proud setting of the temples. His hand lingered on her shoulder after his kiss. Then he went slowly to bed. He had forgotten Miriam; he only saw how his mother's hair was lifted back from her warm, broad brow. And somehow, she was hurt.

Then the next time he saw Miriam he said to her:

"Don't let me be late tonight—not later than ten o'clock. My mother gets so upset."

Miriam dropped her head, brooding.

"Why does she get upset?" she asked.

"Because she says I oughtn't to be out late when I have to get up early."

"Very well!" said Miriam, rather quietly, with just a touch of a sneer.

He resented that. And he was usually late again.

That there was any love growing between him and Miriam neither of them would have acknowledged. He thought he was too sane for such sentimentality, and she thought herself too lofty. They both were late in coming to maturity, and psychical ripeness was much behind even the physical.

Miriam was exceedingly sensitive, as her mother had always been. The slightest grossness made her recoil almost in anguish. Her brothers were brutal, but never coarse in speech. The men did all the discussing of farm matters outside. But, perhaps, because of the continual business of birth and of begetting which goes on upon every farm, Miriam was the more hypersensitive to the matter, and her blood was chastened almost to disgust of the faintest suggestion of such intercourse. Paul took his pitch from her, and their intimacy went on in an utterly blanched and chaste fashion. It could never be mentioned that the mare was in foal.

When he was nineteen, he was earning only twenty shillings a week, but he was happy. His painting went well, and life went well enough. On the Good Friday he organised a walk to the Hemlock Stone. There were three lads of his own age, then Annie and Arthur, Miriam and Geoffrey. Arthur, apprenticed as an electrician in Nottingham, was home for the holiday. Morel, as usual, was up early, whistling and sawing in the yard. At seven o'clock the family heard him buy threepennyworth of hot-cross buns; he talked with gusto to the little girl who brought them, calling her "my darling"; He turned away several boys who came with more buns, telling them they had been "kested" by a little lass. Then Mrs. Morel got up, and the family straggled down. It was an immense luxury to everybody, this lying in bed just beyond the ordinary time on a weekday. And Paul and Arthur read before breakfast, and had the meal unwashed, sitting in their shirt-sleeves. This was another holiday luxury. The room was warm. Everything felt free of care and anxiety. There was a sense of plenty in the house.

While the boys were reading, Mrs. Morel went into the garden. They were now in another house, an old one, near the Scargill Street home, which had been left soon after William had died. Directly came an excited cry from the garden:

"Paul! Paul! come and look!"

It was his mother's voice. He threw down his book and went out. There was a long garden that ran to a field. It was a grey, cold day, with a sharp wind blowing out of Derbyshire. Two fields away Bestwood began, with a jumble of roofs and red house-ends, out of which rose the church tower and the spire of the Congregational Chapel. And beyond went woods and hills, right away to the pale grey heights of the Pennine Chain.

Paul looked down the garden for his mother. Her head appeared among the young currant-bushes.

"Come here!" she cried.

"What for?" he answered.

"Come and see."

She had been looking at the buds on the currant trees. Paul went up.

"To think," she said, "that here I might never have seen them!"

Her son went to her side. Under the fence, in a little bed, was a ravel of poor grassy leaves, such as come from very immature bulbs, and three scyllas in bloom. Mrs. Morel pointed to the deep blue flowers.

"Now, just see those!" she exclaimed. "I was looking at the currant bushes, when, thinks I to myself, 'There's something very blue; is it a bit of sugar-bag?' and there, behold you! Sugar-bag! Three glories of the snow, and *such* beauties! But where on earth did they come from?"

"I don't know," said Paul.

"Well, that's a marvel, now! I *thought* I knew every weed and blade in this garden. But *haven't* they done well? You see, that gooseberry-bush just shelters them. Not nipped, not touched!"

He crouched down and turned up the bells of the little blue flowers.

"They're a glorious colour!" he said.

"Aren't they!" she cried. "I guess they come from Switzerland, where they say they have such lovely things. Fancy them against the snow! But where have they come from? They can't have *blown* here, can they?"

Then he remembered having set here a lot of little trash of bulbs to mature.

"And you never told me," she said.

"No! I thought I'd leave it till they might flower."

"And now, you see! I might have missed them. And I've never had a glory of the snow in my garden in my life."

She was full of excitement and elation. The garden was an endless joy to her. Paul was thankful for her sake at last to be in a house with a long garden that went down to a field. Every morning after breakfast she went out and was happy pottering about in it. And it was true, she knew every weed and blade.

Everybody turned up for the walk. Food was packed, and they set off, a merry, delighted party. They hung over the wall of the mill-race, dropped paper in the water on one side of the tunnel and watched it shoot out on the other. They stood on the footbridge over Boathouse Station and looked at the metals gleaming coldly.

"You should see the Flying Scotsman come through at half-past six!" said Leonard, whose father was a signalman. "Lad, but she doesn't half buzz!" and the little party looked up the lines one way, to London, and the other way, to Scotland, and they felt the touch of these two magical places.

In Ilkeston the colliers were waiting in gangs for the public-houses to open. It was a town of idleness and lounging. At Stanton Gate the iron foundry blazed. Over everything there were great discussions. At Trowell they crossed again from Derbyshire into Nottinghamshire. They came to the Hemlock Stone at dinner-time. Its field was crowded with folk from Nottingham and Ilkeston.

They had expected a venerable and dignified monument. They found a little, gnarled, twisted stump of rock, something like a decayed mushroom, standing out pathetically on the side of a field. Leonard and Dick immediately proceeded to carve

271

their initials, "L. W." and "R. P.", in the old red sandstone; but Paul desisted, because he had read in the newspaper satirical remarks about initial-carvers, who could find no other road to immortality. Then all the lads climbed to the top of the rock to look round.

Everywhere in the field below, factory girls and lads were eating lunch or sporting about. Beyond was the garden of an old manor. It had yew-hedges and thick clumps and borders of yellow crocuses round the lawn.

"See," said Paul to Miriam, "what a quiet garden!"

She saw the dark yews and the golden crocuses, then she looked gratefully. He had not seemed to belong to her among all these others; he was different then—not her Paul, who understood the slightest quiver of her innermost soul, but something else, speaking another language than hers. How it hurt her, and deadened her very perceptions. Only when he came right back to her, leaving his other, his lesser self, as she thought, would she feel alive again. And now he asked her to look at this garden, wanting the contact with her again. Impatient of the set in the field, she turned to the quiet lawn, surrounded by sheaves of shut-up crocuses. A feeling of stillness, almost of ecstasy, came over her. It felt almost as if she were alone with him in this garden.

Then he left her again and joined the others. Soon they started home. Miriam loitered behind,

272

alone. She did not fit in with the others; she could very rarely get into human relations with anyone: so her friend, her companion, her lover, was Nature. She saw the sun declining wanly. In the dusky, cold hedgerows were some red leaves. She lingered to gather them, tenderly, passionately. The love in her finger-tips caressed the leaves; the passion in her heart came to a glow upon the leaves.

Suddenly she realised she was alone in a strange road, and she hurried forward. Turning a corner in the lane, she came upon Paul, who stood bent over something, his mind fixed on it, working away steadily, patiently, a little hopelessly. She hesitated in her approach, to watch.

He remained concentrated in the middle of the road. Beyond, one rift of rich gold in that colourless grey evening seemed to make him stand out in dark relief. She saw him, slender and firm, as if the setting sun had given him to her. A deep pain took hold of her, and she knew she must love him. And she had discovered him, discovered in him a rare potentiality, discovered his loneliness. Quivering as at some "annunciation", she went slowly forward.

At last he looked up.

"Why," he exclaimed gratefully, "have you waited for me!"

She saw a deep shadow in his eyes.

"What is it?" she asked.

"The spring broken here;" and he showed her where his umbrella was injured.

Instantly, with some shame, she knew he had not

273

done the damage himself, but that Geoffrey was responsible.

"It is only an old umbrella, isn't it?" she asked.

She wondered why he, who did not usually trouble over trifles, made such a mountain of this molehill.

"But it was William's an' my mother can't help but know," he said quietly, still patiently working at the umbrella.

The words went through Miriam like a blade. This, then, was the confirmation of her vision of him! She looked at him. But there was about him a certain reserve, and she dared not comfort him, not even speak softly to him.

"Come on," he said. "I can't do it;" and they went in silence along the road.

That same evening they were walking along under the trees by Nether Green. He was talking to her fretfully, seemed to be struggling to convince himself.

"You know," he said, with an effort, "if one person loves, the other does."

"Ah!" she answered. "Like mother said to me when I was little, 'Love begets love.' "

"Yes, something like that, I think it *must* be."

"I hope so, because, if it were not, love might be a very terrible thing," she said.

"Yes, but it *is*—at least with most people," he answered.

And Miriam, thinking he had assured himself, felt strong in herself. She always regarded that sudden coming upon him in the lane as a revelation.

And this conversation remained graven in her mind as one of the letters of the law.

Now she stood with him and for him. When, about this time, he outraged the family feeling at Willey Farm by some overbearing insult, she stuck to him, and believed he was right. And at this time she dreamed dreams of him, vivid, unforgettable. These dreams came again later on, developed to a more subtle psychological stage.

On the Easter Monday the same party took an excursion to Wingfield Manor. It was great excitement to Miriam to catch a train at Sethley Bridge, amid all the bustle of the Bank Holiday crowd. They left the train at Alfreton. Paul was interested in the street and in the colliers with their dogs. Here was a new race of miners. Miriam did not live till they came to the church. They were all rather timid of entering, with their bags of food, for fear of being turned out. Leonard, a comic, thin fellow, went first; Paul, who would have died rather than be sent back, went last. The place was decorated for Easter. In the font hundreds of white narcissi seemed to be growing. The air was dim and coloured from the windows and thrilled with a subtle scent of lilies and narcissi. In that atmosphere Miriam's soul came into a glow. Paul was afraid of the things he mustn't do; and he was sensitive to the feel of the place. Miriam turned to him. He answered. They were together. He would not go beyond the Communion-rail. She loved him for that. Her soul expanded into prayer beside him. He felt the strange fascination of shadowy religious places. All his latent mysticism quivered into life. She was drawn to him. He was a prayer along with her.

Miriam very rarely talked to the other lads. They at once became awkward in conversation with her. So usually she was silent.

It was past midday when they climbed the steep path to the manor. All things shone softly in the sun, which was wonderfully warm and enlivening. Celandines and violets were out. Everybody was tip-top full with happiness. The glitter of the ivy, the soft, atmospheric grey of the castle walls, the gentleness of everything near the ruin, was perfect.

The manor is of hard, pale grey stone, and the other walls are blank and calm. The young folk were in raptures. They went in trepidation, almost afraid that the delight of exploring this ruin might be denied them. In the first courtyard, within the high broken walls, were farm-carts, with their shafts lying idle on the ground, the tyres of the wheels brilliant with gold-red rust. It was very still.

All eagerly paid their sixpences, and went timidly through the fine clean arch of the inner courtyard. They were shy. Here on the pavement, where the hall had been, an old thorn tree was budding. All kinds of strange openings and broken rooms were in the shadow around them.

After lunch they set off once more to explore the ruin. This time the girls went with the boys, who could act as guides and expositors. There was one tall tower in a corner, rather tottering, where they say Mary Queen of Scots was imprisoned.

"Think of the Queen going up here!" said Miriam in a low voice, as she climbed the hollow stairs.

"If she could get up," said Paul, "for she had rheumatism like anything. I reckon they treated her rottenly."

"You don't think she deserved it?" asked Miriam.

"No, I don't. She was only lively."

They continued to mount the winding staircase. A high wind, blowing through the loopholes, went rushing up the shaft, and filled the girl's skirts like a balloon, so that she was ashamed, until he took the hem of her dress and held it down for her. He did it perfectly simply, as he would have picked up her glove. She remembered this always.

Round the broken top of the tower the ivy bushed out, old and handsome. Also, there were a few chill gillivers, in pale cold bud. Miriam wanted to lean over for some ivy, but he would not let her. Instead, she had to wait behind him, and take from him each spray as he gathered it and held it to her, each one separately, in the purest manner of chivalry. The tower seemed to rock in the wind. They looked over miles and miles of wooded country, and country with gleams of pasture.

The crypt underneath the manor was beautiful, and in perfect preservation. Paul made a drawing: Miriam stayed with him. She was thinking of Mary Queen of Scots looking with her strained, hopeless eyes, that could not understand misery, over the hills whence no help came, or sitting in this crypt, being told of a God as cold as the place she sat in.

They set off again gaily, looking round on their beloved manor that stood so clean and big on its hill.

"Supposing you could have *that* farm," said Paul to Miriam.

"Yes!"

"Wouldn't it be lovely to come and see you!"

They were now in the bare country of stone walls, which he loved, and which, though only ten miles from home, seemed so foreign to Miriam. The party was straggling. As they were crossing a large meadow that sloped away from the sun, along a path embedded with innumerable tiny glittering points, Paul, walking alongside, laced his fingers in the strings of the bag Miriam was carrying, and instantly she felt Annie behind, watchful and jealous. But the meadow was bathed in a glory of sunshine, and the path was jewelled, and it was seldom that he gave her any sign. She held her fingers very still among the strings of the bag, his fingers touching; and the place was golden as a vision.

At last they came into the straggling grey village of Crich, that lies high. Beyond the village was the famous Crich Stand that Paul could see from the garden at home. The party pushed on. Great expanse of country spread around and below. The lads were eager to get to the top of the hill. It was capped by a round knoll, half of which was by now cut away, and on the top of which stood an ancient monument, sturdy and squat, for signalling in old days far down into the level lands of Nottinghamshire and Leicestershire.

It was blowing so hard, high up there in the exposed place, that the only way to be safe was to stand nailed by the wind to the wall of the tower. At their feet fell the precipice where the limestone was quarried away. Below was a jumble of hills and tiny villages—Matlock, Ambergate, Stoney Middleton. The lads were eager to spy out the church of Bestwood, far away among the rather crowded country on the left. They were disgusted that it seemed to stand on a plain. They saw the hills of Derbyshire fall into the monotony of the Midlands that swept away South.

Miriam was somewhat scared by the wind, but the lads enjoyed it. They went on, miles and miles, to Whatstandwell. All the food was eaten, everybody was hungry, and there was very little money to get home with. But they managed to procure a loaf and a currant-loaf, which they hacked to pieces with shut-knives, and ate sitting on the wall near the bridge, watching the bright Derwent rushing by, and the brakes from Matlock pulling up at the inn.

Paul was now pale with weariness. He had been responsible for the party all day, and now he was done. Miriam understood, and kept close to him, and he left himself in her hands.

They had an hour to wait at Ambergate Station.

Trains came, crowded with excursionists returning to Manchester, Birmingham, and London.

"We might be going there—folk easily might think we're going that far," said Paul.

They got back rather late. Miriam, walking home with Geoffrey, watched the moon rise big and red and misty. She felt something was fulfilled in her.

She had an elder sister, Agatha, who was a school-teacher. Between the two girls was a feud. Miriam considered Agatha worldly. And she wanted herself to be a school-teacher.

One Saturday afternoon Agatha and Miriam were upstairs dressing. Their bedroom was over the stable. It was a low room, not very large, and bare. Miriam had nailed on the wall a reproduction of Veronese's "St. Catherine". She loved the woman who sat in the window, dreaming. Her own windows were too small to sit in. But the front one was dripped over with honeysuckle and virginia creeper, and looked upon the tree-tops of the oak-wood across the yard, while the little back window, no bigger than a handkerchief, was a loophole to the east, to the dawn beating up against the beloved round hills.

The two sisters did not talk much to each other. Agatha, who was fair and small and determined, had rebelled against the home atmosphere, against the doctrine of "the other cheek". She was out in the world now, in a fair way to be independent. And she insisted on worldly values, on appearance, on manners, on position, which Miriam would fain have ignored.

Both girls liked to be upstairs, out of the way, when Paul came. They preferred to come running down, open the stair-foot door, and see him watching, expectant of them. Miriam stood painfully pulling over her head a rosary he had given her. It caught in the fine mesh of her hair. But at last she had it on, and the red-brown wooden beads looked well against her cool brown neck. She was a well-developed girl, and very handsome. But in the little looking-glass nailed against the whitewashed wall she could only see a fragment of herself at a time. Agatha had bought a little mirror of her own, which she propped up to suit herself. Miriam was near the window. Suddenly she heard the well-known click of the chain, and she saw Paul fling open the gate, push his bicycle into the yard. She saw him look at the house, and she shrank away. He walked in a nonchalant fashion, and his bicycle went with him as if it were a live thing.

"Paul's come!" she exclaimed.

"Aren't you glad?" said Agatha cuttingly.

Miriam stood still in amazement and bewilderment.

"Well, aren't you?" she asked.

"Yes, but I'm not going to let him see it, and think I wanted him."

Miriam was startled. She heard him putting his bicycle in the stable underneath, and talking to Jimmy, who had been a pit-horse, and who was seedy.

"Well, Jimmy my lad, how are ter? Nobbut sick an' sadly, like? Why, then, it's a shame, my owd lad."

She heard the rope run through the hole as the horse lifted its head from the lad's caress. How she loved to listen when he thought only the horse could hear. But there was a serpent in her Eden. She searched earnestly in herself to see if she wanted Paul Morel. She felt there would be some disgrace in it. Full of twisted feeling, she was afraid she did want him. She stood self-convicted. Then came an agony of new shame. She shrank within herself in a coil of torture. Did she want Paul Morel, and did he know she wanted him? What a subtle infamy upon her! She felt as if her whole soul coiled into knots of shame.

Agatha was dressed first, and ran downstairs. Miriam heard her greet the lad gaily, knew exactly how brilliant her grey eyes became with that tone. She herself would have felt it bold to have greeted him in such wise. Yet there she stood under the self-accusation of wanting him, tied to that stake of torture. In bitter perplexity she kneeled down and prayed:

"O Lord, let me not love Paul Morel. Keep me from loving him, if I ought not to love him."

Something anomalous in the prayer arrested her. She lifted her head and pondered. How could it be wrong to love him? Love was God's gift. And yet it caused her shame. That was because of him, Paul Morel. But, then, it was not his affair, it was her

282

own, between herself and God. She was to be a sacrifice. But it was God's sacrifice, not Paul Morel's or her own. After a few minutes she hid her face in the pillow again, and said:

"But, Lord, if it is Thy will that I should love him, make me love him—as Christ would, who died for the souls of men. Make me love him splendidly, because he is Thy son."

She remained kneeling for some time, quite still, and deeply moved, her black hair against the red squares and the lavender-sprigged squares of the patchwork quilt. Prayer was almost essential to her. Then she fell into that rapture of self-sacrifice, identifying herself with a God who was sacrificed, which gives to so many human souls their deepest bliss.

When she went downstairs Paul was lying back in an armchair, holding forth with much vehemence to Agatha, who was scorning a little painting he had brought to show her. Miriam glanced at the two, and avoided their levity. She went into the parlour to be alone.

It was tea-time before she was able to speak to Paul, and then her manner was so distant he thought he had offended her.

Miriam discontinued her practice of going each Thursday evening to the library in Bestwood. After calling for Paul regularly during the whole spring, a number of trifling incidents and tiny insults from his family awakened her to their attitude towards her, and she decided to go no more. So she announced to Paul one evening she would not call at his house again for him on Thursday nights.

"Why?" he asked, very short.

"Nothing. Only I'd rather not."

"Very well."

"But," she faltered, "if you'd care to meet me, we could still go together."

"Meet you where?"

"Somewhere—where you like."

"I shan't meet you anywhere. I don't see why you shouldn't keep calling for me. But if you won't, I don't want to meet you."

So the Thursday evenings which had been so precious to her, and to him, were dropped. He worked instead. Mrs. Morel sniffed with satisfaction at this arrangement.

He would not have it that they were lovers. The intimacy between them had been kept so abstract, such a matter of the soul, all thought and weary struggle into consciousness, that he saw it only as a platonic friendship. He stoutly denied there was anything else between them. Miriam was silent, or else she very quietly agreed. He was a fool who did not know what was happening to himself. By tacit agreement they ignored the remarks and insinuations of their acquaintances.

"We aren't lovers, we are friends," he said to her. "*We* know it. Let them talk. What does it matter what they say."

Sometimes, as they were walking together, she slipped her arm timidly into his. But he always

284

resented it, and she knew it. It caused a violent conflict in him. With Miriam he was always on the high plane of abstraction, when his natural fire of love was transmitted into the fine stream of thought. She would have it so. If he were jolly and, as she put it, flippant, she waited till he came back to her, till the change had taken place in him again, and he was wrestling with his own soul, frowning, passionate in his desire for understanding. And in this passion for understanding her soul lay close to his; she had him all to herself. But he must be made abstract first.

Then, if she put her arm in his, it caused him almost torture. His consciousness seemed to split. The place where she was touching him ran hot with friction. He was one internecine battle, and he became cruel to her because of it.

One evening in midsummer Miriam called at the house, warm from climbing. Paul was alone in the kitchen; his mother could be heard moving about upstairs.

"Come and look at the sweet-peas," he said to the girl.

They went into the garden. The sky behind the townlet and the church was orange-red; the flower-garden was flooded with a strange warm light that lifted every leaf into significance. Paul passed along a fine row of sweet-peas, gathering a blossom here and there, all cream and pale blue. Miriam followed, breathing the fragrance. To her, flowers appealed with such strength she felt she must make them

285

part of herself. When she bent and breathed a flower, it was as if she and the flower were loving each other. Paul hated her for it. There seemed a sort of exposure about the action, something too intimate.

When he had got a fair bunch, they returned to the house. He listened for a moment to his mother's quiet movement upstairs, then he said:

"Come here, and let me pin them in for you." He arranged them two or three at a time in the bosom of her dress, stepping back now and then to see the effect. "You know," he said, taking the pin out of his mouth, "a woman ought always to arrange her flowers before her glass."

Miriam laughed. She thought flowers ought to be pinned in one's dress without any care. That Paul should take pains to fix her flowers for her was his whim.

He was rather offended at her laughter.

"Some women do—those who look decent," he said.

Miriam laughed again, but mirthlessly, to hear him thus mix her up with women in a general way. From most men she would have ignored it. But from him it hurt her.

He had nearly finished arranging the flowers when he heard his mother's footsteps on the stairs. Hurriedly he pushed in the last pin and turned away.

"Don't let mater know," he said.

Miriam picked up her books and stood in the

doorway looking with chagrin at the beautiful sunset. She would call for Paul no more, she said.

"Good-evening, Mrs. Morel," she said, in a deferential way. She sounded as if she felt she had no right to be there.

"Oh, is it you, Miriam?" replied Mrs. Morel coolly.

But Paul insisted on everybody's accepting his friendship with the girl, and Mrs. Morel was too wise to have any open rupture.

It was not till he was twenty years old that the family could ever afford to go away for a holiday. Mrs. Morel had never been away for a holiday, except to see her sister, since she had been married. Now at last Paul had saved enough money, and they were all going. There was to be a party: some of Annie's friends, one friend of Paul's, a young man in the same office where William had previously been, and Miriam.

It was great excitement writing for rooms. Paul and his mother debated it endlessly between them. They wanted a furnished cottage for two weeks. She thought one week would be enough, but he insisted on two.

At last they got an answer from Mablethorpe, a cottage such as they wished for thirty shillings a week. There was immense jubilation. Paul was wild with joy for his mother's sake. She would have a real holiday now. He and she sat at evening picturing what it would be like. Annie came in, and Leonard, and Alice, and Kitty. There was wild rejoicing and anticipation. Paul told Miriam. She seemed to brood with joy over it. But the Morels' house rang with excitement.

They were to go on Saturday morning by the seven train. Paul suggested that Miriam should sleep at his house, because it was so far for her to walk. She came down for supper. Everybody was so excited that even Miriam was accepted with warmth. But almost as soon as she entered the feeling in the family became close and tight. He had discovered a poem by Jean Ingelow which mentioned Mablethorpe, and so he must read it to Miriam. He would never have got so far in the direction of sentimentality as to read poetry to his own family. But now they condescended to listen. Miriam sat on the sofa absorbed in him. She always seemed absorbed in him, and by him, when he was present. Mrs. Morel sat jealously in her own chair. She was going to hear also. And even Annie and the father attended, Morel with his head cocked on one side, like somebody listening to a sermon and feeling conscious of the fact. Paul ducked his head over the book. He had got now all the audience he cared for. And Mrs. Morel and Annie almost contested with Miriam who should listen best and win his favour. He was in very high feather.

"But," interrupted Mrs. Morel, "what *is* the 'Bride of Enderby' that the bells are supposed to ring?"

"It's an old tune they used to play on the bells for a warning against water. I suppose the Bride of

Enderby was drowned in a flood," he replied. He had not the faintest knowledge what it really was, but he would never have sunk so low as to confess that to his womenfolk. They listened and believed him. He believed himself.

"And the people knew what that tune meant?" said his mother.

"Yes—just like the Scotch when they heard 'The Flowers o' the Forest'—and when they used to ring the bells backward for alarm."

"How?" said Annie. "A bell sounds the same whether it's rung backwards or forwards."

"But," he said, "if you start with the deep bell and ring up to the high one—der—der—der—der—der—der—der—der!"

He ran up the scale. Everybody thought it clever. He thought so too. Then, waiting a minute, he continued the poem.

"Hm!" said Mrs. Morel curiously, when he finished. "But I wish everything that's written weren't so sad."

"*I* canna see what they want drownin' theirselves for," said Morel.

There was a pause. Annie got up to clear the table.

Miriam rose to help with the pots.

"Let *me* help to wash up," she said.

"Certainly not," cried Annie. "You sit down again. There aren't many."

And Miriam, who could not be familiar and insist, sat down again to look at the book with Paul.

He was master of the party; his father was no good. And great tortures he suffered lest the tin box should be put out at Firsby instead of at Mablethorpe. And he wasn't equal to getting a carriage. His bold little mother did that.

"Here!" she cried to a man. "Here!"

Paul and Annie got behind the rest, convulsed with shamed laughter.

"How much will it be to drive to Brook Cottage?" said Mrs. Morel.

"Two shillings."

"Why, how far is it?"

"A good way."

"I don't believe it," she said.

But she scrambled in. There were eight crowded in one old seaside carriage.

"You see," said Mrs. Morel, "it's only threepence each, and if it were a tram-car——"

They drove along. Each cottage they came to, Mrs. Morel cried:

"Is it this? Now, this is it!"

Everybody sat breathless. They drove past. There was a universal sigh.

"I'm thankful it wasn't that brute," said Mrs. Morel. "I *was* frightened." They drove on and on.

At last they descended at a house that stood alone over the dyke by the highroad. There was wild excitement because they had to cross a little bridge to get into the front garden. But they loved the house that lay so solitary, with a sea-meadow on one side, and immense expanse of land patched in white

290

barley, yellow oats, red wheat, and green root-crops, flat and stretching level to the sky.

Paul kept accounts. He and his mother ran the show. The total expenses—lodging, food, every-thing—was sixteen shillings a week per person. He and Leonard went bathing in the morning. Morel was wandering abroad quite early.

"You, Paul," his mother called from the bedroom, "eat a piece of bread-and-butter."

"All right," he answered.

And when he got back he saw his mother presiding in state at the breakfast-table. The woman of the house was young. Her husband was blind, and she did laundry work. So Mrs. Morel always washed the pots in the kitchen and made the beds.

"But you said you'd have a real holiday," said Paul, "and now you work."

"Work!" she exclaimed. "What are you talking about!"

He loved to go with her across the fields to the village and the sea. She was afraid of the plank bridge, and he abused her for being a baby On the whole he stuck to her as if he were *her* man.

Miriam did not get much of him, except, perhaps, when all the others went to the "Coons". Coons were insufferably stupid to Miriam, so he thought they were to himself also, and he preached prig-gishly to Annie about the fatuity of listening to them. Yet he, too, knew all their songs, and sang them along the roads roisterously. And if he found himself listening, the stupidity pleased him very much. Yet to Annie he said:

"Such rot! There isn't a grain of intelligence in it. Nobody with more gumption than a grasshopper could go and sit and listen." And to Miriam he said, with much scorn of Annie and the others: "I suppose they're at the 'Coons'."

It was queer to see Miriam singing coon songs. She had a straight chin that went in a perpendicular line from the lower lip to the turn. She always reminded Paul of some sad Botticelli angel when she sang, even when it was:

"Come down lover's lane
For a walk with me, talk with me."

Only when he sketched, or at evening when the others were at the "Coons", she had him to herself. He talked to her endlessly about his love of horizontals: how they, the great levels of sky and land in Lincolnshire, meant to him the eternality of the will, just as the bowed Norman arches of the church, repeating themselves, meant the dogged leaping forward of the persistent human soul, on and on, nobody knows were; in contradiction to the perpendicular lines and to the Gothic arch, which, he said, leapt up at heaven and touched the ecstasy and lost itself in the divine. Himself, he said, was Norman, Miriam was Gothic. She bowed in consent even to that.

One evening he and she went up the great sweep-

292

ing shore of sand towards Theddlethorpe. The long breakers plunged and ran in a hiss of foam along the coast. It was a warm evening. There was not a figure but themselves on the far reaches of sand, no noise but the sound of the sea. Paul loved to see it clanging at the land. He loved to feel himself between the noise of it and the silence of the sandy shore. Miriam was with him. Everything grew very intense. It was quite dark when they turned again. The way home was through a gap in the sandhills, and then along a raised grass road between two dykes. The country was black and still. From behind the sandhills came the whisper of the sea. Paul and Miriam walked in silence. Suddenly he started. The whole of his blood seemed to burst into flame, and he could scarcely breathe. An enormous orange moon was staring at them from the rim of the sand-hills. He stood still, looking at it.

"Ah!" cried Miriam, when she saw it.

He remained perfectly still, staring at the immense and ruddy moon, the only thing in the far-reaching darkness of the level. His heart beat heavily, the muscles of his arms contracted.

"What is it?" murmured Miriam, waiting for him.

He turned and looked at her. She stood beside him, for ever in shadow. Her face, covered with the darkness of her hat, was watching him unseen. But she was brooding. She was slightly afraid—deeply moved and religious. That was her best state. He was impotent against it. His blood was concentrated like a flame in his chest. But he could not get across to her. There were flashes in his blood. But somehow she ignored them. She was expecting some religious state in him. Still yearning, she was half aware of his passion, and gazed at him, troubled.

"What is it?" she murmured again.

"It's the moon," he answered, frowning.

"Yes," she assented. "Isn't it wonderful?" She was curious about him. The crisis was past.

He did not know himself what was the matter. He was naturally so young, and their intimacy was so abstract, he did not know he wanted to crush her on his breast to ease the ache there. He was afraid of her. The fact that he might want her as a man wants a woman had in him been suppressed into a shame. When she shrank in her convulsed, coiled torture from the thought of such a thing, he had winced to the depths of his soul. And now this "purity" prevented even their first love-kiss. It was as if she could scarcely stand the shock of physical love, even a passionate kiss, and then he was too shrinking and sensitive to give it.

As they walked along the dark fen-meadow he watched the moon and did not speak. She plodded beside him. He hated her, for she seemed in some way to make him despise himself. Looking ahead—he saw the one light in the darkness, the window of their lamp-lit cottage.

He loved to think of his mother, and the other jolly people.

"Well, everybody else has been in long ago!" said his mother as they entered.

"What does that matter!" he cried irritably. "I can go a walk if I like, can't I?"

"And I should have thought you could get in to supper with the rest," said Mrs. Morel.

"I shall please myself," he retorted. "It's not *late*. I shall do as I like."

"Very well," said his mother cuttingly, "then *do* as you like." And she took no further notice of him that evening. Which he pretended neither to notice nor to care about, but sat reading. Miriam read also, obliterating herself. Mrs. Morel hated her for making her son like this. She watched Paul growing irritable, priggish, and melancholic. For this she put the blame on Miriam. Annie and all her friends joined against the girl. Miriam had no friend of her own, only Paul. But she did not suffer so much, because she despised the triviality of these other people.

And Paul hated her because, somehow, she spoilt his ease and naturalness. And he writhed himself with a feeling of humiliation.

# 8

## STRIFE IN LOVE

ARTHUR finished his apprenticeship, and got a job on the electrical plant at Minton Pit. He earned very little, but had a good chance of getting on. But he was wild and restless. He did not drink nor gamble. Yet he somehow contrived to get into endless scrapes, always through some hot-headed thoughtlessness. Either he went rabbiting in the woods, like a poacher, or he stayed in Nottingham all night instead of coming home, or he miscalculated his dive into the canal at Bestwood, and scored his chest into one mass of wounds on the raw stones and tins at the bottom.

He had not been at his work many months when again he did not come home one night.

"Do you know where Arthur is?" asked Paul at breakfast.

"I do not," replied his mother.

"He is a fool," said Paul. "And if he *did* anything I shouldn't mind. But no, he simply can't come away from a game of whist, or else he must see a girl home from the skating-rink—quite proprietously—and so can't get home. He's a fool."

"I don't know that it would make it any better if

296

he did something to make us all ashamed," said Mrs. Morel.

"Well, *I* should respect him more," said Paul.

"I very much doubt it," said his mother coldly.

They went on with breakfast.

"Are you fearfully fond of him?" Paul asked his mother.

"What do you ask that for?"

"Because they say a woman always likes the youngest best."

"She may do—but I don't. No, he wearies me."

"And you'd actually rather he was good?"

"I'd rather he showed some of a man's common sense."

Paul was raw and irritable. He also wearied his mother very often. She saw the sunshine going out of him, and she resented it.

As they were finishing breakfast came the postman with a letter from Derby. Mrs. Morel screwed up her eyes to look at the address.

"Give it here, blind eye!" exclaimed her son, snatching it away from her.

She started, and almost boxed his ears.

"It's from your son, Arthur," he said.

"What now——!" cried Mrs. Morel.

" 'My dearest Mother,' " Paul read, " 'I don't know what made me such a fool. I want you to come and fetch me back from here. I came with Jack Bredon yesterday, instead of going to work, and enlisted. He said he was sick of wearing the seat of a stool out, and, like the idiot you know I am, I came away with him.

" 'I have taken the King's shilling, but perhaps if you came for me they would let me go back with you. I was a fool when I did it. I don't want to be in the army. My dear mother, I am nothing but a trouble to you. But if you get me out of this, I promise I will have more sense and consideration. . . .' "

Mrs. Morel sat down in her rocking-chair.

"Well, *now*," she cried, "let him stop!"

"Yes," said Paul, "let him stop."

There was silence. The mother sat with her hands folded in her apron, her face set, thinking.

"If I'm not *sick*!" she cried suddenly. "Sick!"

"Now," said Paul, beginning to frown, "You're not going to worry your soul out about this, do you hear."

"I suppose I'm to take it as a blessing," she flashed, turning on her son.

"You're not going to mount it up to a tragedy, so there," he retorted.

"The *fool*!—the young fool!" she cried.

"He'll look well in uniform," said Paul irritatingly.

His mother turned on him like a fury.

"Oh, will he!" she cried. "Not in my eyes!"

"He should get in a cavalry regiment; he'll have the time of his life, and will look an awful swell."

"Swell!—*swell!*—a mighty swell idea indeed!—a common soldier!"

"Well," said Paul, "what am I but a common clerk?"

298

"A good deal, my boy!" cried his mother, stung. "What?"

"At any rate, a *man*, and not a thing in a red coat."

"I shouldn't mind being in a red coat—or dark blue, that would suit me better—if they didn't boss me about too much."

But his mother had ceased to listen.

"Just as he was getting on, or might have been getting on, at his job—a young nuisance—here he goes and ruins himself for life. What good will he be, do you think, after *this*?"

"It may lick him into shape beautifully," said Paul.

"Lick him into shape!—lick what marrow there *was* out of his bones. A *soldier*!—a common *soldier*!—nothing but a body that makes movements when it hears a shout! It's a fine thing!"

"I can't understand why it upsets you," said Paul.

"No, perhaps you can't. But *I* understand;" and she sat back in her chair, her chin in one hand, holding her elbow with the other, brimmed up with wrath and chagrin.

"And shall you go to Derby?" asked Paul.

"Yes."

"It's no good."

"I'll see for myself."

"And why on earth don't you let him stop. It's just what he wants."

"Of course," cried the mother, "*you* know what he wants!"

She got ready and went by the first train to Derby, where she saw her son and the sergeant. It was, however, no good.

When Morel was having his dinner in the evening, she said suddenly:

"I've had to go to Derby today."

The miner turned up his eyes, showing the whites in his black face.

"Has ter, lass. What took thee there?"

"That Arthur!"

"Oh—an' what's agate now?"

"He's only enlisted."

Morel put down his knife and leaned back in his chair.

"Nay," he said, "that he niver 'as!"

"And is going down to Aldershot tomorrow."

"Well!" exclaimed the miner. "That's a winder." He considered it a moment, said "H'm!" and proceeded with his dinner. Suddenly his face contracted with wrath. "I hope he may never set foot i' my house again," he said.

"The idea!" cried Mrs. Morel. "Saying such a thing!"

"I do," repeated Morel. "A fool as runs away for a soldier, let 'im look after 'issen; I s'll do no more for 'im."

"A fat sight you have done as it is," she said.

And Morel was almost ashamed to go to his public-house that evening.

"Well, did you go?" said Paul to his mother when he came home.

"I did."

"And could you see him?"

"Yes."

"And what did he say?"

"He blubbered when I came away."

"H'm!"

"And so did I, so you needn't 'h'm'!"

Mrs. Morel fretted after her son. She knew he would not like the army. He did not. The discipline was intolerable to him.

"But the doctor," she said with some pride to Paul, "said he was perfectly proportioned—almost exactly; all his measurements were correct. He *is* good-looking, you know."

"He's awfully nice-looking. But he doesn't fetch the girls like William, does he?"

"No; it's a different character. He's a good deal like his father, irresponsible."

To console his mother, Paul did not go much to Willey Farm at this time. And in the autumn exhibition of students' work in the Castle he had two studies, a landscape in water-colour and a still life in oil, both of which had first-prize awards. He was highly excited.

"What do you think I've got for my pictures, mother?" he asked, coming home one evening. She saw by his eyes he was glad. Her face flushed.

"Now, how should I know, my boy!"

"A first prize for those glass jars——"

"H'm!"

"And a first prize for that sketch up at Willey Farm."

"Both first?"

"Yes."

"H'm!"

There was a rosy, bright look about her, though she said nothing.

"It's nice," he said, "isn't it?"

"It is."

"Why don't you praise me up to the skies?"

She laughed.

"I should have the trouble of dragging you down again," she said.

But she was full of joy, nevertheless. William had brought her his sporting trophies. She kept them still, and she did not forgive his death. Arthur was handsome—at least, a good specimen—and warm and generous, and probably would do well in the end. But Paul was going to distinguish himself. She had a great belief in him, the more because he was unaware of his own powers. There was so much to come out of him. Life for her was rich with promise. She was to see herself fulfilled. Not for nothing had been her struggle.

Several times during the exhibition Mrs. Morel went to the Castle unknown to Paul. She wandered down the long room looking at the other exhibits. Yes, they were good. But they had not in them a certain something which she demanded for her satisfaction. Some made her jealous, they were so good. She looked at them a long time trying to find fault with them. Then suddenly she had a shock that made her heart beat. There hung Paul's picture! She knew it as if it were printed on her heart.

"Name—Paul Morel—First Prize."

It looked so strange, there in public, on the walls of the Castle gallery, where in her lifetime she had seen so many pictures. And she glanced round to see if anyone had noticed her again in front of the same sketch.

But she felt a proud woman. When she met well-dressed ladies going home to the Park, she thought to herself:

"Yes, you look very well—but I wonder if *your* son has two first prizes in the Castle."

And she walked on, as proud a little woman as any in Nottingham. And Paul felt he had done something for her, if only a trifle. All his work was hers.

One day, as he was going up Castle Gate, he met Miriam. He had seen her on the Sunday, and had not expected to meet her in town. She was walking with a rather striking woman, blonde, with a sullen expression, and a defiant carriage. It was strange how Miriam, in her bowed, meditative bearing, looked dwarfed beside this woman with the handsome shoulders. Miriam watched Paul searchingly. His gaze was on the stranger, who ignored him. The girl saw his masculine spirit rear its head.

"Hello!" he said, "you didn't tell me you were coming to town."

"No," replied Miriam, half apologetically. "I drove in to Cattle Market with father."

He looked at her companion.

"I've told you about Mrs. Dawes," said Miriam huskily; she was nervous. "Clara, do you know Paul?"

"I think I've seen him before," replied Mrs. Dawes indifferently, as she shook hands with him. She had scornful grey eyes, a skin like white honey, and a full mouth, with a slightly lifted upper lip that did not know whether it was raised in scorn of all men or out of eagerness to be kissed, but which believed the former. She carried her head back, as if she had drawn away in contempt, perhaps from men also. She wore a large, dowdy hat of black beaver, and a sort of slightly affected simple dress that made her look rather sack-like. She was evidently poor, and had not much taste. Miriam usually looked nice.

"Where have you seen me?" Paul asked of the woman.

She looked at him as if she would not trouble to answer. Then:

"Walking with Louie Travers," she said.

Louie was one of the "Spiral" girls.

"Why, do you know her?" he asked.

She did not answer. He turned to Miriam.

"Where are you going?" he asked.

"To the Castle."

"What train are you going home by?"

"I am driving with father. I wish you could come too. What time are you free?"

"You know not till eight tonight, damn it!"

And directly the two women moved on.

Paul remembered that Clara Dawes was the daughter of an old friend of Mrs. Leivers. Miriam had sought her out because she had once been Spiral overseer at Jordan's, and because her husband, Baxter Dawes, was smith for the factory, making the irons for cripple instruments, and so on. Through her Miriam felt she got into direct contact with Jordan's, and could estimate better Paul's position. But Mrs. Dawes was separated from her husband, and had taken up Women's Rights. She was supposed to be clever. It interested Paul.

Baxter Dawes he knew and disliked. The smith was a man of thirty-one or thirty-two. He came occasionally through Paul's corner—a big, well-set man, also striking to look at, and handsome. There was a peculiar similarity between himself and his wife. He had the same white skin, with a clear, golden tinge. His hair was of soft brown, his moustache was golden. And he had a similar defiance in his bearing and manner. But then came the difference. His eyes, dark brown and quick-shifting, were dissolute. They protruded very slightly, and his eyelids hung over them in a way that was half hate. His mouth, too, was sensual. His whole manner was of cowed defiance, as if he were ready to knock anybody down who disapproved of him—perhaps because he really disapproved of himself.

From the first day he had hated Paul. Finding the

lad's impersonal, deliberate gaze of an artist on his face, he got into a fury.

"What are yer lookin' at?" he sneered, bullying.

The boy glanced away. But the smith used to stand behind the counter and talk to Mr. Pappleworth. His speech was dirty, with a kind of rottenness. Again he found the youth with his cool, critical gaze fixed on his face. The smith started round as if he had been stung.

"What'r yer lookin' at, three hap'orth o' pap?" he snarled.

The boy shrugged his shoulders slightly.

"Why yer——!" shouted Dawes.

"Leave him alone," said Mr. Pappleworth, in that insinuating voice which means, "He's only one of your good little sops who can't help it."

Since that time the boy used to look at the man every time he came through with the same curious criticism, glancing away before he met the smith's eye. It made Dawes furious. They hated each other in silence.

Clara Dawes had no children. When she had left her husband the home had been broken up, and she had gone to live with her mother. Dawes lodged with his sister. In the same house was a sister-in-law, and somehow Paul knew that this girl, Louie Travers, was now Dawes's woman. She was a handsome, insolent hussy, who mocked at the youth, and yet flushed if he walked along to the station with her as she went home.

The next time he went to see Miriam it was

306

Saturday evening. She had a fire in the parlour, and was waiting for him. The others, except her father and mother and the young children, had gone out, so the two had the parlour together. It was a long, low, warm room. There were three of Paul's small sketches on the wall, and his photo was on the mantelpiece. On the table and on the high old rosewood piano were bowls of coloured leaves. He sat in the arm-chair, she crouched on the hearthrug near his feet. The glow was warm on her handsome, pensive face as she kneeled there like a devotee.

"What did you think of Mrs. Dawes?" she asked quietly.

"She doesn't look very amiable," he replied.

"No, but don't you think she's a fine woman?" she said, in a deep tone.

"Yes—in stature. But without a grain of taste. I like her for some things. *Is* she disagreeable?"

"I don't think so. I think she's dissatisfied."

"What with?"

"Well—how would *you* like to be tied for life to a man like that?"

"Why did she marry him, then, if she was to have revulsions so soon?"

"Ay, why did she!" repeated Miriam bitterly.

"And I should have thought she had enough fight in her to match him," he said.

Miriam bowed her head.

"Ay?" she queried satirically. "What makes you think so?"

"Look at her mouth—made for passion—and the

very set-back of her throat——" He threw his head back in Clara's defiant manner.

Miriam bowed a little lower.

"Yes," she said.

There was a silence for some moments, while he thought of Clara.

"And what were the things you liked about her?" she asked.

"I don't know—her skin and the texture of her—and her—I don't know—there's a sort of fierceness somewhere in her. I appreciate her as an artist, that's all."

"Yes."

He wondered why Miriam crouched there brooding in that strange way. It irritated him.

"You don't really like her, do you?" he asked the girl.

She looked at him with her great, dazzled dark eyes.

"I do," she said.

"You don't—you can't—not really."

"Then what?" she asked slowly.

"Eh, I don't know—perhaps you like her because she's got a grudge against men."

That was more probably one of his own reasons for liking Mrs. Dawes, but this did not occur to him. They were silent. There had come into his forehead a knitting of the brows which was becoming habitual with him, particularly when he was with Miriam. She longed to smooth it away, and she was afraid of it. It seemed the stamp of a man who was not her man in Paul Morel.

There were some crimson berries among the leaves in the bowl. He reached over and pulled out a bunch.

"If you put red berries in your hair," he said, "why would you look like some witch or priestess, and never like a reveller?"

She laughed with a naked, painful sound.

"I don't know," she said.

His vigorous warm hands were playing excitedly with the berries.

"Why can't you laugh?" he said. "You never laugh laughter. You only laugh when something is odd or incongruous, and then it almost seems to hurt you."

She bowed her head as if he were scolding her.

"I wish you could laugh at me just for one minute—just for one minute. I feel as if it would set something free."

"But"—and she looked up at him with eyes frightened and struggling—"I do laugh at you—I *do*."

"Never! There's always a kind of intensity. When you laugh I could always cry; it seems as if it shows up your suffering. Oh, you make me knit the brows of my very soul and cogitate."

Slowly she shook her head despairingly.

"I'm sure I don't want to," she said.

"I'm so damned spiritual with *you* always!" he cried.

She remained silent, thinking, "Then why don't you be otherwise." But he saw her crouching, brooding figure, and it seemed to tear him in two.

"But, there, it's autumn," he said, "and everybody feels like a disembodied spirit then."

There was still another silence. This peculiar sadness between them thrilled her soul. He seemed so beautiful with his eyes gone dark, and looking as if they were deep as the deepest well.

"You make me so spiritual!" he lamented. "And I don't want to be spiritual."

She took her finger from her mouth with a little pop, and looked up at him almost challenging. But still her soul was naked in her great dark eyes, and there was the same yearning appeal upon her. If he could have kissed her in abstract purity he would have done so. But he could not kiss her thus—and she seemed to leave no other way. And she yearned to him.

He gave a brief laugh.

"Well," he said, "get that French and we'll do some—some Verlaine."

"Yes," she said in a deep tone, almost of resignation. And she rose and got the books. And her rather red, nervous hands looked so pitiful, he was mad to comfort her and kiss her. But then he dared not—or could not. There was something prevented him. His kisses were wrong for her. They continued the reading till ten o'clock, when they went into the kitchen, and Paul was natural and jolly again with the father and mother. His eyes were dark and shining; there was a kind of fascination about him.

310

When he went into the barn for his bicycle he found the front wheel punctured.

"Fetch me a drop of water in a bowl," he said to her. "I shall be late, and then I s'll catch it."

He lighted the hurricane lamp, took off his coat, turned up the bicycle, and set speedily to work. Miriam came with the bowl of water and stood close to him, watching. She loved to see his hands doing things. He was slim and vigorous, with a kind of easiness even in his most hasty movements. And busy at his work he seemed to forget her. She loved him absorbedly. She wanted to run her hands down his sides. She always wanted to embrace him, so long as he did not want her.

"There!" he said, rising suddenly. "Now, could you have done it quicker?"

"No!" she laughed.

He straightened himself. His back was towards her. She put her two hands on his sides, and ran them quickly down.

"You are so *fine*!" she said.

He laughed, hating her voice, but his blood roused to a wave of flame by her hands. She did not seem to realise *him* in all this. He might have been an object. She never realised the male he was.

He lighted his bicycle-lamp, bounced the machine on the barn floor to see that the tyres were sound, and buttoned his coat.

"That's all right!" he said.

She was trying the brakes, that she knew were broken.

"Did you have them mended?" she asked.

"No!"

"But why didn't you?"

"The back one goes on a bit."

"But it's not safe."

"I can use my toe."

"I wish you'd had them mended," she murmured.

"Don't worry—come to tea tomorrow, with Edgar."

"Shall we?"

"Do—about four. I'll come to meet you."

"Very well."

She was pleased. They went across the dark yard to the gate. Looking across, he saw through the uncurtained window of the kitchen the heads of Mr. and Mrs. Leivers in the warm glow. It looked very cosy. The road, with pine trees, was quite black in front.

"Till tomorrow," he said, jumping on his bicycle.

"You'll take care, won't you?" she pleaded.

"Yes."

His voice already came out of the darkness. She stood a moment watching the light from his lamp race into obscurity along the ground. She turned very slowly indoors. Orion was wheeling up over the wood, his dog twinkling after him, half smothered. For the rest the world was full of darkness, and silent, save for the breathing of cattle in their stalls. She prayed earnestly for his safety that night. When he left her, she often lay in anxiety, wondering if he had got home safely.

312

He dropped down the hills on his bicycle. The roads were greasy, so he had to let it go. He felt a pleasure as the machine plunged over the second, steeper drop in the hill. "Here goes!" he said. It was risky, because of the curve in the darkness at the bottom, and because of the brewers' waggons with drunken waggoners asleep. His bicycle seemed to fall beneath him, and he loved it. Recklessness is almost a man's revenge on his woman. He feels he is not valued, so he will risk destroying himself to deprive her altogether.

The stars on the lake seemed to leap like grasshoppers, silver upon the blackness, as he spun past. Then there was the long climb home.

"See, mother!" he said, as he threw her the berries and leaves on to the table.

"H'm!" she said, glancing at them, then away again. She sat reading, alone, as she always did.

"Aren't they pretty?"

"Yes."

He knew she was cross with him. After a few minutes he said:

"Edgar and Miriam are coming to tea tomorrow."

She did not answer.

"You don't mind?"

Still she did not answer.

"Do you?" he asked.

"You know whether I mind or not."

"I don't see why you should. I have plenty of meals there."

"You do."

"Then why do you begrudge them tea?"

"I begrudge whom tea?"

"What are you so horrid for?"

"Oh, say no more! You've asked her to tea, it's quite sufficient. She'll come."

He was very angry with his mother. He knew it was merely Miriam she objected to. He flung off his boots and went to bed.

Paul went to meet his friends the next afternoon. He was glad to see them coming. They arrived home at about four o'clock. Everywhere was clean and still for Sunday afternoon. Mrs. Morel sat in her black dress and black apron. She rose to meet the visitors. With Edgar she was cordial, but with Miriam cold and rather grudging. Yet Paul thought the girl looked so nice in her brown cashmere frock.

He helped his mother to get the tea ready. Miriam would have gladly proffered, but was afraid. He was rather proud of his home. There was about it now, he thought, a certain distinction. The chairs were only wooden, and the sofa was old. But the hearthrug and cushions were cosy; the pictures were prints in good taste; there was a simplicity in everything, and plenty of books. He was never ashamed in the least of his home, nor was Miriam of hers, because both were what they should be, and warm. And then he was proud of the table; the china was pretty, the cloth was fine. It did not matter that the spoons were not silver nor the knives ivory-handled; everything looked nice. Mrs. Morel had managed wonderfully while her children were growing up, so that nothing was out of place.

Miriam talked books a little. That was her unfailing topic. But Mrs. Morel was not cordial, and turned soon to Edgar.

At first Edgar and Miriam used to go into Mrs. Morel's pew. Morel never went to chapel, preferring the public-house. Mrs. Morel, like a little champion, sat at the head of her pew, Paul at the other end; and at first Miriam sat next to him. Then the chapel was like home. It was a pretty place, with dark pews and slim, elegant pillars, and flowers. And the same people had sat in the same places ever since he was a boy. It was wonderfully sweet and soothing to sit there for an hour and a half, next to Miriam, and near to his mother, uniting his two loves under the spell of the place of worship. Then he felt warm and happy and religious at once. And after chapel he walked home with Miriam, whilst Mrs. Morel spent the rest of the evening with her old friend, Mrs. Burns. He was keenly alive on his walks on Sunday nights with Edgar and Miriam. He never went past the pits at night, by the lighted lamp-house, the tall black head-stocks and lines of trucks, past the fans spinning slowly like shadows, without the feeling of Miriam returning to him, keen and almost unbearable.

She did not very long occupy the Morels' pew. Her father took one for themselves once more. It was under the little gallery, opposite the Morels'. When Paul and his mother came in the chapel the

Leivers's pew was always empty. He was anxious for fear she would not come: it was so far, and there were so many rainy Sundays. Then, often very late indeed, she came in, with her long stride, her head bowed, her face hidden under her hat of dark green velvet. Her face, as she sat opposite, was always in shadow. But it gave him a very keen feeling, as if all his soul stirred within him, to see her there. It was not the same glow, happiness, and pride, that he felt in having his mother in charge: something more wonderful, less human, and tinged to intensity by a pain, as if there were something he could not get to.

At this time he was beginning to question the orthodox creed. He was twenty-one, and she was twenty. She was beginning to dread the spring: he became so wild, and hurt her so much. All the way he went cruelly smashing her beliefs. Edgar enjoyed it. He was by nature critical and rather dispassionate. But Miriam suffered exquisite pain, as, with an intellect like a knife, the man she loved examined her religion in which she lived and moved and had her being. But he did not spare her. He was cruel. And when they went alone he was even more fierce, as if he would kill her soul. He bled her beliefs till she almost lost consciousness.

"She exults—she exults as she carries him off from me," Mrs. Morel cried in her heart when Paul had gone. "She's not like an ordinary woman, who can leave me my share in him. She wants to absorb him. She wants to draw him out and absorb him till there is nothing left of him, even for himself. He will never be a man on his own feet—she will suck him up." So the mother sat, and battled and brooded bitterly.

And he, coming home from his walks with Miriam, was wild with torture. He walked biting his lips and with clenched fists, going at a great rate. Then, brought up against a stile, he stood for some minutes, and did not move. There was a great hollow of darkness fronting him, and on the black up-slopes patches of tiny lights, and in the lowest trough of the night, a flare of the pit. It was all weird and dreadful. Why was he torn so, almost bewildered and unable to move? Why did his mother sit at home and suffer? He knew she suffered badly. But why should she? And why did he hate Miriam, and feel so cruel towards her, at the thought of his mother. If Miriam caused his mother suffering, then he hated her—and he easily hated her. Why did she make him feel as if he were uncertain of himself, insecure, an indefinite thing, as if he had not sufficient sheathing to prevent the night and the space breaking into him? How he hated her! And then, what a rush of tenderness and humility!

Suddenly he plunged on again, running home. His mother saw on him the marks of some agony, and she said nothing. But he had to make her talk to him. Then she was angry with him for going so far with Miriam.

"Why don't you like her, mother?" he cried in despair.

"I don't know, my boy," she replied piteously. "I'm sure I've tried to like her. I've tried and tried, but I can't—I can't!"

And he felt dreary and hopeless between the two.

Spring was the worst time. He was changeable, and intense and cruel. So he decided to stay away from her. Then came the hours when he knew Miriam was expecting him. His mother watched him growing restless. He could not go on with his work. He could do nothing. It was as if something were drawing his soul out towards Willey Farm. Then he put on his hat and went, saying nothing. And his mother knew he was gone. And as soon as he was on the way he sighed with relief. And when he was with her he was cruel again.

One day in March he lay on the bank of Nethermere, with Miriam sitting beside him. It was a glistening, white-and-blue day. Big clouds, so brilliant, went by overhead, while shadows stole along on the water. The clear spaces in the sky were of clean, cold blue. Paul lay on his back in the old grass, looking up. He could not bear to look at Miriam. She seemed to want him, and he resisted. He resisted all the time. He wanted now to give her passion and tenderness, and he could not. He felt that she wanted the soul out of his body, and not him. All his strength and energy she drew into herself through some channel which united them. She did not want to meet him, so that there were two of them, man and woman together. She wanted to draw all of him into her. It urged him to an intensity like madness, which fascinated him, as drug-taking might.

He was discussing Michael Angelo. It felt to her as if she were fingering the very quivering tissue, the very protoplasm of life, as she heard him. It gave her deepest satisfaction. And in the end it frightened her. There he lay in the white intensity of his search, and his voice gradually filled her with fear, so level it was, almost inhuman, as if in a trance.

"Don't talk any more," she pleaded softly, laying her hand on his forehead.

He lay quite still, almost unable to move. His body was somewhere discarded.

"Why not? Are you tired?"

"Yes, and it wears you out."

He laughed shortly, realising.

"Yet you always make me like it," he said.

"I don't wish to," she said, very low.

"Not when you've gone too far, and you feel you can't bear it. But your unconscious self always asks it of me. And I suppose I want it."

He went on, in his dead fashion:

"If only you could want *me*, and not want what I can reel off for you!"

"I!" she cried bitterly—"I! Why, when would you let me take you?"

"Then it's my fault," he said, and, gathering himself together, he got up and began to talk trivialities. He felt insubstantial. In a vague way he hated her for it. And he knew he was as much to

319

blame himself. This, however, did not prevent his hating her.

One evening about this time he had walked along the home road with her. They stood by the pasture leading down to the wood, unable to part. As the stars came out the clouds closed. They had glimpses of their own constellation, Orion, towards the west. His jewels glimmered for a moment, his dog ran low, struggling with difficulty through the spume of cloud.

Orion was for them chief in significance among the constellations. They had gazed at him in their strange, surcharged hours of feeling, until they seemed themselves to live in every one of his stars. This evening Paul had been moody and perverse. Orion had seemed just an ordinary constellation to him. He had fought against his glamour and fascination. Miriam was watching her lover's mood carefully. But he said nothing that gave him away, till the moment came to part, when he stood frowning gloomily at the gathered clouds, behind which the great constellation must be striding still.

There was to be a little party at his house the next day, at which she was to attend.

"I shan't come and meet you," he said.

"Oh, very well; it's not very nice out," she replied slowly.

"It's not that—only they don't like me to. They say I care more for you than for them. And you understand, don't you? You know it's only friendship."

Miriam was astonished and hurt for him. It had cost him an effort. She left him, wanting to spare him any further humiliation. A fine rain blew in her face as she walked along the road. She was hurt deep down; and she despised him for being blown about by any wind of authority. And in her heart of hearts, unconsciously, she felt that he was trying to get away from her. This she would never have acknowledged. She pitied him.

At this time Paul became an important factor in Jordan's warehouse. Mr. Pappleworth left to set up a business of his own, and Paul remained with Mr. Jordan as Spiral overseer. His wages were to be raised to thirty shillings at the year-end, if things went well.

Still on Friday night Miriam often came down for her French lesson. Paul did not go so frequently to Willey Farm, and she grieved at the thought of her education's coming to end; moreover, they both loved to be together, in spite of discords. So they read Balzac, and did compositions, and felt highly cultured.

Friday night was reckoning night for the miners. Morel "reckoned"—shared up the money of the stall—either in the New Inn at Bretty or in his own house, according as his fellow-butties wished. Barker had turned a non-drinker, so now the men reckoned at Morel's house.

Annie, who had been teaching away, was at home again. She was still a tomboy; and she was engaged to be married. Paul was studying design.

Morel was always in good spirits on Friday evening, unless the week's earnings were small. He bustled immediately after his dinner, prepared to get washed. It was decorum for the women to absent themselves while the men reckoned. Women were not supposed to spy into such a masculine privacy as the butties' reckoning, nor were they to know the exact amount of the week's earnings. So, whilst her father was spluttering in the scullery, Annie went out to spend an hour with a neighbour. Mrs. Morel attended to her baking.

"Shut that doo-er!" bawled Morel furiously.

Annie banged it behind her, and was gone.

"If tha oppens it again while I'm weshin' me, I'll ma'e thy jaw rattle," he threatened from the midst of his soap-suds. Paul and the mother frowned to hear him.

Presently he came running out of the scullery, with the soapy water dripping from him, dithering with cold.

"Oh, my sirs!" he said. "Wheer's my towel?"

It was hung on a chair to warm before the fire, otherwise he would have bullied and blustered. He squatted on his heels before the hot baking-fire to dry himself.

"F-ff-f!" he went, pretending to shudder with cold.

"Goodness, man, don't be such a kid!" said Mrs. Morel. "It's *not* cold."

"Thee strip thysen stark nak'd to wesh thy flesh i' that scullery," said the miner, as he rubbed his hair; "nowt b'r a ice-'ouse!"

322

"And I shouldn't make that fuss," replied his wife.

"No, tha'd drop down stiff, as dead as a door-knob, wi' thy nesh sides."

"Why is a door-knob deader than anything else?" asked Paul, curious.

"Eh, I dunno; that's what they say," replied his father. "But there's that much draught i' yon scullery, as it blows through your ribs like through a five-barred gate."

"It would have some difficulty in blowing through yours," said Mrs. Morel.

Morel looked down ruefully at his sides.

"Me!" he exclaimed. "I'm nowt b'r a skinned rabbit. My bones fair juts out on me."

"I should like to know where," retorted his wife.

"Iv'ry-wheer! I'm nobbut a sack o' faggots."

Mrs. Morel laughed. He had still a wonderfully young body, muscular, without any fat. His skin was smooth and clear. It might have been the body of a man of twenty-eight, except that there were, perhaps, too many blue scars, like tattoo-marks, where the coal-dust remained under the skin, and that his chest was too hairy. But he put his hand on his side ruefully. It was his fixed belief that, because he did not get fat, he was as thin as a starved rat.

Paul looked at his father's thick, brownish hands all scarred, with broken nails, rubbing the fine smoothness of his sides, and the incongruity struck him. It seemed strange they were the same flesh.

"I suppose," he said to his father, "you had a good figure once."

"Eh!" exclaimed the miner, glancing round, startled and timid, like a child.

"He had," exclaimed Mrs. Morel, "if he didn't hurtle himself up as if he was trying to get in the smallest space he could."

"Me!" exclaimed Morel—"me a good figure! I wor niver much more n'r a skeleton."

"Man!" cried his wife, "don't be such a pulamiter!"

" 'Strewth!" he said. "Tha's niver knowed me but what I looked as if I wor goin' off in a rapid decline."

She sat and laughed.

"You've had a constitution like iron," she said; "and never a man had a better start, if it was body that counted. You should have seen him as a young man," she cried suddenly to Paul, drawing herself up to imitate her husband's once handsome bearing.

Morel watched her shyly. He saw again the passion she had had for him. It blazed upon her for a moment. He was shy, rather scared, and humble. Yet again he felt his old glow. And then immediately he felt the ruin he had made during these years. He wanted to bustle about, to run away from it.

"Gi'e my back a bit of a wesh," he asked her.

His wife brought a well-soaped flannel and clapped it on his shoulders. He gave a jump.

"Eh, tha mucky little 'ussy!" he cried. "Cowd as death!"

324

"You ought to have been a salamander," she laughed, washing his back. It was very rarely she would do anything so personal for him. The children did those things.

"The next world won't be half hot enough for you," she added.

"No," he said; "tha'lt see as it's draughty for me."

But she had finished. She wiped him in a desultory fashion, and went upstairs, returning immediately with his shifting-trousers. When he was dried he struggled into his shirt. Then, ruddy and shiny, with hair on end, and his flannelette shirt hanging over his pit-trousers, he stood warming the garments he was going to put on. He turned them, he pulled them inside out, he scorched them.

"Goodness, man!" cried Mrs. Morel, "get dressed!"

"Should thee like to clap thysen into britches as cowd as a tub o' water?" he said.

At last he took off his pit-trousers and donned decent black. He did all this on the hearth-rug, as he would have done if Annie and her familiar friends had been present.

Mrs. Morel turned the bread in the oven. Then from the red earthenware punchion of dough that stood in a corner she took another handful of paste, worked it to the proper shape, and dropped it into a tin. As she was doing so Barker knocked and entered. He was a quiet, compact little man, who looked as if he would go through a stone wall. His black hair was cropped short, his head was bony. Like most miners, he was pale, but healthy and taut.

"Evenin', missis," he nodded to Mrs. Morel, and he seated himself with a sigh.

"Good evening," she replied cordially.

"Tha's made thy heels crack," said Morel.

"I dunno as I have," said Barker.

He sat, as the men always did in Morel's kitchen, effacing himself rather.

"How's missis?" she asked of him.

He had told her some time back:

"We're expectin' us third just now, you see."

"Well," he answered, rubbing his head, "she keeps pretty middlin', I think."

"Let's see—when?" asked Mrs. Morel.

"Well, I shouldn't be surprised any time now."

"Ah! And she's kept fairly?"

"Yes, tidy."

"That's a blessing, for she's none too strong."

"No. An' I've done another silly trick."

"What's that?"

Mrs. Morel knew Barker wouldn't do anything very silly.

"I'm come be-out th' market-bag."

"You can have mine."

"Nay, you'll be wantin' that yourself."

"I shan't. I take a string bag always."

She saw the determined little collier buying in the week's groceries and meat on the Friday nights, and she admired him. "Barker's little, but he's ten times

326

the man you are," she said to her husband.

Just then Wesson entered. He was thin, rather frail-looking, with a boyish ingenuousness and a slightly foolish smile, despite his seven children. But his wife was a passionate woman.

"I see you've kested me," he said, smiling rather vapidly.

"Yes," replied Barker.

The newcomer took off his cap and his big woollen muffler. His nose was pointed and red.

"I'm afraid you're cold, Mr. Wesson," said Mrs. Morel.

"It's a bit nippy," he replied.

"Then come to the fire."

"Nay, I s'll do where I am."

Both colliers sat away back. They could not be induced to come on to the hearth. The hearth is sacred to the family.

"Go thy ways i' th' arm-chair," cried Morel cheerily.

"Nay, thank yer; I'm very nicely here."

"Yes, come, of course," insisted Mrs. Morel.

He rose and went awkwardly. He sat in Morel's arm-chair awkwardly. It was too great a familiarity. But the fire made him blissfully happy.

"And how's that chest of yours?" demanded Mrs. Morel.

He smiled again, with his blue eyes rather sunny.

"Oh, it's very middlin'," he said.

"Wi' a rattle in it like a kettle-drum," said Barker shortly.

"T-t-t-t!" went Mrs. Morel rapidly with her tongue. "Did you have that flannel singlet made?"

"Not yet," he smiled.

"Then, why didn't you?" she cried.

"It'll come," he smiled.

"Ah, an' Doomsday!" exclaimed Barker.

Barker and Morel were both impatient of Wesson. But, then, they were both as hard as nails, physically.

When Morel was nearly ready he pushed the bag of money to Paul.

"Count it, boy," he asked humbly.

Paul impatiently turned from his books and pencil, tipped the bag upside down on the table. There was a five-pound bag of silver, sovereigns and loose money. He counted quickly, referred to the checks— the written papers giving amount of coal—put the money in order. Then Barker glanced at the checks.

Mrs. Morel went upstairs, and the three men came to table. Morel, as master of the house, sat in his arm-chair, with his back to the hot fire. The two butties had cooler seats. None of them counted the money.

"What did we say Simpson's was?" asked Morel; and the butties cavilled for a minute over the dayman's earnings. Then the amount was put aside.

"An' Bill Naylor's?"

This money also was taken from the pack.

Then, because Wesson lived in one of the company's houses, and his rent had been deducted, Morel and Barker took four-and-six each. And because Morel's coals had come, and the leading was stopped, Barker and Wesson took four shillings each. Then it was plain sailing. Morel gave each of them a sovereign till there were no more sovereigns; each half a crown till there were no more half-crowns; each a shilling till there were no more shillings. If there was anything at the end that wouldn't split, Morel took it and stood drinks.

Then the three men rose and went. Morel scuttled out of the house before his wife came down. She heard the door close, and descended. She looked hastily at the bread in the oven. Then, glancing on the table, she saw her money lying. Paul had been working all the time. But now he felt his mother counting the week's money, and her wrath rising.

"T-t-t-t!" went her tongue.

He frowned. He could not work when she was cross. She counted again.

"A measly twenty-five shillings!" she exclaimed. "How much was the cheque?"

"Ten pounds eleven," said Paul irritably. He dreaded what was coming.

"And he gives me a scrattlin' twenty-five, an' his club this week! But I know him. He thinks because *you're* earning he needn't keep the house any longer. No, all he has to do with his money is to guttle it. But I'll show him!"

"Oh, mother, don't!" cried Paul.

"Don't what, I should like to know?" she exclaimed.

"Don't carry on again. I can't work."

She went very quiet.

"Yes, it's all very well," she said; "but how do you think I'm going to manage?"

"Well, it won't make it any better to whittle about it."

"I should like to know what you'd do if you had it to put up with."

"It won't be long. You can have my money. Let him go to hell."

He went back to his work, and she tied her bonnet-strings grimly. When she was fretted he could not bear it. But now he began to insist on her recognizing him.

"The two loaves at the top," she said, "will be done in twenty minutes. Don't forget them."

"All right," he answered; and she went to market.

He remained alone working. But his usual intense concentration became unsettled. He listened for the yard-gate. At a quarter-past seven came a low knock, and Miriam entered.

"All alone?" she said.

"Yes."

As if at home, she took off her tam-o'-shanter and her long coat, hanging them up. It gave him a thrill. This might be their own house, his and hers. Then she came back and peered over his work.

"What is it?" she asked.

"Still design, for decorating stuffs, and for embroidery."

She bent short-sightedly over the drawings.

330

It irritated him that she peered so into everything that was his, searching him out. He went into the parlour and returned with a bundle of brownish linen. Carefully unfolding it, he spread it on the floor. It proved to be a curtain or *portière*, beautifully stencilled with a design on roses.

"Ah, how beautiful!" she cried.

The spread cloth, with its wonderful reddish roses and dark green stems, all so simple, and somehow so wicked-looking, lay at her feet. She went on her knees before it, her dark curls dropping. He saw her crouched voluptuously before his work, and his heart beat quickly. Suddenly she looked up at him.

"Why does it seem cruel?" she asked.

"What?"

"There seems a feeling of cruelty about it," she said.

"It's jolly good, whether or not," he replied, folding up his work with a lover's hands.

She rose slowly, pondering.

"And what will you do with it?" she asked.

"Send it to Liberty's. I did it for my mother, but I think she'd rather have the money."

"Yes," said Miriam. He had spoken with a touch of bitterness, and Miriam sympathised. Money would have been nothing to *her*.

He took the cloth back into the parlour. When he returned he threw to Miriam a smaller piece. It was a cushion-cover with the same design.

"I did that for you," he said.

She fingered the work with trembling hands, and did not speak. He became embarrassed.

"By Jove, the bread!" he cried.

He took the top loaves out, tapped them vigorously. They were done. He put them on the hearth to cool. Then he went to the scullery, wetted his hands, scooped the last white dough out of the puncheon, and dropped it in a baking-tin. Miriam was still bent over her painted cloth. He stood rubbing the bits of dough from his hands.

"You do like it?" he asked.

She looked up at him, with her dark eyes one flame of love. He laughed uncomfortably. Then he began to talk about the design. There was for him the most intense pleasure in talking about his work to Miriam. All his passion, all his wild blood, went into this intercourse with her, when he talked and conceived his work. She brought forth to him his imaginations. She did not understand, any more than a woman understands when she conceives a child in her womb. But this was life for her and for him.

While they were talking, a young woman of about twenty-two, small and pale, hollow-eyed, yet with a relentless look about her, entered the room. She was a friend at the Morels'.

"Take your things off," said Paul.

"No, I'm not stopping."

She sat down in the arm-chair opposite Paul and Miriam, who were on the sofa. Miriam moved a little farther from him. The room was hot, with a

332

scent of new bread. Brown, crisp loaves stood on the hearth.

"I shouldn't have expected to see you here tonight, Miriam Leivers," said Beatrice wickedly.

"Why not?" murmured Miriam huskily.

"Why, let's look at your shoes."

Miriam remained uncomfortably still.

"If tha doesna tha durs'na," laughed Beatrice.

Miriam put her feet from under her dress. Her boots had that queer, irresolute, rather pathetic look about them, which showed how self-conscious and self-mistrustful she was. And they were covered with mud.

"Glory! You're a positive muck-heap," exclaimed Beatrice. "Who cleans your boots?"

"I clean them myself."

"Then you wanted a job," said Beatrice. "It would ha' taken a lot of men to ha' brought me down here tonight. But love laughs at sludge, doesn't it, 'Postle my duck?"

"*Inter alia*," he said.

"Oh, Lord! are you going to spout foreign languages? What does it mean, Miriam?"

There was a fine sarcasm in the last question, but Miriam did not see it.

" 'Among other things,' I believe," she said humbly.

Beatrice put her tongue between her teeth and laughed wickedly.

" 'Among other things,' 'Postle?" she repeated. "Do you mean love laughs at mothers, and fathers,

333

and sisters, and brothers, and men friends, and lady friends, and even at the b'loved himself?"

She affected a great innocence.

"In fact, it's one big smile," he replied.

"Up its sleeve, 'Postle Morel—you believe me," she said; and she went off into another burst of wicked, silent laughter.

Miriam sat silent, withdrawn into herself. Every one of Paul's friends delighted in taking sides against her, and he left her in the lurch—seemed almost to have a sort of revenge upon her then.

"Are you still at school?" asked Miriam of Beatrice.

"Yes."

"You've not had your notice, then?"

"I expect it at Easter."

"Isn't it an awful shame, to turn you off merely because you didn't pass the exam?"

"I don't know," said Beatrice coldly.

"Agatha says you're as good as any teacher anywhere. It seems to me ridiculous. I wonder why you didn't pass."

"Short of brains, eh, 'Postle?" said Beatrice briefly.

"Only brains to bite with," replied Paul, laughing.

"Nuisance!" she cried; and, springing from her seat, she rushed and boxed his ears. She had beautiful small hands. He held her wrists while she wrestled with him. At last she broke free, and seized two handfuls of his thick, dark brown hair, which she shook.

"Beat!" he said, as he pulled his hair straight with his fingers. "I hate you!"

She laughed with glee.

"Mind!" she said. "I want to sit next to you."

"I'd as lief be neighbours with a vixen," he said, nevertheless making place for her between him and Miriam.

"Did it ruffle his pretty hair, then!" she cried; and, with her hair-comb, she combed him straight. "And his nice little moustache!" she exclaimed. She tilted his head back and combed his young moustache. "It's a wicked moustache, 'Postle," she said. "It's a red for danger. Have you got any of those cigarettes?"

He pulled his cigarette-case from his pocket. Beatrice looked inside it.

"And fancy me having Connie's last cig.," said Beatrice, putting the thing between her teeth. He held a lit match to her, and she puffed daintily.

"Thanks so much, darling," she said mockingly.

It gave her a wicked delight.

"Don't you think he does it nicely, Miriam?" she asked.

"Oh, very!" said Miriam.

He took a cigarette for himself.

"Light, old boy?" said Beatrice, tilting her cigarette at him.

He bent forward to her to light his cigarette at hers. She was winking at him as he did so. Miriam saw his eyes trembling with mischief, and his full, almost sensual, mouth quivering. He was not himself, and she could not bear it. As he was now, she had no connection with him; she might as well not have existed. She saw the cigarette dancing on his full red lips. She hated his thick hair for being tumbled loose on his forehead.

"Sweet boy!" said Beatrice, tipping up his chin and giving him a little kiss on the cheek.

"I s'll kiss thee back, Beat," he said.

"Tha wunna!" she giggled, jumping up and going away. "Isn't he shameless, Miriam?"

"Quite," said Miriam. "By the way, aren't you forgetting the bread?"

"By Jove!" he cried, flinging open the oven door.

Out puffed the bluish smoke and a smell of burned bread.

"Oh, golly!" cried Beatrice, coming to his side. He crouched before the oven, she peered over his shoulder. "This is what comes of the oblivion of love, my boy."

Paul was ruefully removing the loaves. One was burnt black on the hot side; another was hard as a brick.

"Poor mater!" said Paul.

"You want to grate it," said Beatrice. "Fetch me the nutmeg-grater."

She arranged the bread in the oven. He brought the grater, and she grated the bread on to a newspaper on the table. He set the doors open to blow away the smell of burned bread. Beatrice grated away, puffing her cigarette, knocking the charcoal off the poor loaf.

336

"My word, Miriam! you're in for it this time," said Beatrice.

"I!" exclaimed Miriam in amazement.

"You'd better be gone when his mother comes in. *I* know why King Alfred burned the cakes. Now I see it! 'Postle would fix up a tale about his work making him forget, if he thought it would wash. If that old woman had come in a bit sooner, she'd have boxed the brazen thing's ears who made the oblivion, instead of poor Alfred's."

She giggled as she scraped the loaf. Even Miriam laughed in spite of herself. Paul mended the fire ruefully.

The garden gate was heard to bang.

"Quick!" cried Beatrice, giving Paul the scraped loaf. "Wrap it up in a damp towel."

Paul disappeared into the scullery. Beatrice hastily blew her scrapings into the fire, and sat down innocently. Annie came bursting in. She was an abrupt, quite smart young woman. She blinked in the strong light.

"Smell of burning!" she exclaimed.

"It's the cigarettes," replied Beatrice demurely.

"Where's Paul?"

Leonard had followed Annie. He had a long comic face and blue eyes, very sad.

"I suppose he's left you to settle it between you," he said. He nodded sympathetically to Miriam, and became gently sarcastic to Beatrice.

"No," said Beatrice, "he's gone off with number nine."

"I just met number five inquiring for him," said Leonard.

"Yes—we're going to share him up like Solomon's baby," said Beatrice.

Annie laughed.

"Oh, ay," said Leonard. "And which bit should you have?"

"I don't know," said Beatrice. "I'll let all the others pick first."

"An' you'd have the leavings, like?" said Leonard, twisting up a comic face.

Annie was looking in the oven. Miriam sat ignored. Paul entered.

"This bread's a fine sight, our Paul," said Annie.

"Then you should stop an' look after it," said Paul.

"You mean *you* should do what you're reckoning to do," replied Annie.

"He should, shouldn't he!" cried Beatrice.

"I s'd think he'd got plenty on hand," said Leonard.

"You had a nasty walk, didn't you, Miriam?" said Annie.

"Yes—but I'd been in all week——"

"And you wanted a bit of a change, like," insinuated Leonard kindly.

"Well, you can't be stuck in the house for ever," Annie agreed. She was quite amiable. Beatrice pulled on her coat, and went out with Leonard and Annie. She would meet her own boy.

"Don't forget that bread, our Paul," cried Annie.

338

"Goodnight, Miriam. I don't think it will rain."

When they had all gone, Paul fetched the swathed loaf, unwrapped it, and surveyed it sadly.

"It's a mess!" he said.

"But," answered Miriam impatiently, "what is it, after all—twopence ha'penny."

"Yes, but—it's the mater's precious baking, and she'll take it to heart. However, it's no good bothering."

He took the loaf back into the scullery. There was a little distance between him and Miriam. He stood balanced opposite her for some moments considering, thinking of his behaviour with Beatrice. He felt guilty inside himself, and yet glad. For some inscrutable reason it served Miriam right. He was not going to repent. She wondered what he was thinking of as he stood suspended. His thick hair was tumbled over his forehead. Why might she not push it back for him, and remove the marks of Beatrice's comb? Why might she not press his body with her two hands. It looked so firm, and every whit living. And he would let other girls, why not her?

Suddenly he started into life. It made her quiver almost with terror as he quickly pushed the hair off his forehead and came towards her.

"Half-past eight!" he said. "We'd better buck up. Where's your French?"

Miriam shyly and rather bitterly produced her exercise-book. Every week she wrote for him a sort of diary of her inner life, in her own French. He had found this was the only way to get her to do

339

compositions. And her diary was mostly a love-letter. He would read it now; she felt as if her soul's history were going to be desecrated by him in his present mood. He sat beside her. She watched his hand, firm and warm, rigorously scoring her work. He was reading only the French, ignoring her soul that was there. But gradually his hand forgot its work. He read in silence, motionless. She quivered.

" 'Ce matin les oiseaux m'ont éveillé,' " he read. " 'Il faisait encore un crépuscule. Mais la petite fenêtre de ma chambre était blême, et puis, jaûne, et tous les oiseaux du bois éclatèrent dans un chanson vif et résonnant. Toute l'aûbe tressaillit. J'avais rêvé de vous. Est-ce que vous voyez aussi l'aûbe? Les oiseaux m'éveillent presque tous les matins, et toujours il y a quelque chose de terreur dans le cri des grives. Il est si clair——' "

Miriam sat tremulous, half ashamed. He remained quite still, trying to understand. He only knew she loved him. He was afraid of her love for him. It was too good for him, and he was inadequate. His own love was at fault, not hers. Ashamed, he corrected her work, humbly writing above her words.

"Look," he said quietly, "the past participle conjugated with *avoir* agrees with the direct object when it precedes."

She bent forward, trying to understand. Her free, fine curls tickled his face. He started as if they had been red hot, shuddering. He saw her peering forward at the page, her red lips parted piteously, the black hair springing in fine strands across her tawny, ruddy cheek. She was coloured like a pomegranate for richness. His breath came short as he watched her. Suddenly she looked up at him. Her dark eyes were naked with their love, afraid, and yearning. His eyes, too, were dark, and they hurt her. They seemed to master her. She lost all her self-control, was exposed in fear. And he knew, before he could kiss her, he must drive something out of himself. And a touch of hate for her crept back again into his heart. He returned to her exercise.

Suddenly he flung down the pencil, and was at the oven in a leap, turning the bread. For Miriam he was too quick. She started violently, and it hurt her with real pain. Even the way he crouched before the oven hurt her. There seemed to be something cruel in it, something cruel in the swift way he pitched the bread out of the tins, caught it up again. If only he had been gentle in his movements she would have felt so rich and warm. As it was, she was hurt.

He returned and finished the exercise.

"You've done well this week," he said.

She saw he was flattered by her diary. It did not repay her entirely.

"You really do blossom out sometimes," he said. "You ought to write poetry."

She lifted her head with joy, then she shook it mistrustfully.

"I don't trust myself," she said.

"You should try!"

Again she shook her head.

341

"Shall we read, or is it too late?" he asked.

"It is late—but we can read just a little," she pleaded.

She was really getting now the food for her life during the next week. He made her copy Baudelaire's "Le Balcon". Then he read it for her. His voice was soft and caressing, but growing almost brutal. He had a way of lifting his lips and showing his teeth, passionately and bitterly, when he was much moved. This he did now. It made Miriam feel as if he were trampling on her. She dared not look at him, but sat with her head bowed. She could not understand why he got into such a tumult and fury. It made her wretched. She did not like Baudelaire, on the whole—nor Verlaine.

> "Behold her singing in the field
> Yon solitary highland lass."

That nourished her heart. So did "Fair Ines". And—

> "It was a beauteous evening, calm and pure,
> And breathing holy quiet like a nun."

These were like herself. And there was he, saying in his throat bitterly:

> "*Tu te rappelleras la beauté des caresses.*"

The poem was finished; he took the bread out of

the oven, arranging the burnt loaves at the bottom of the punchion, the good ones at the top. The desiccated loaf remained swathed up in the scullery.

"Mater needn't know till morning," he said. "It won't upset her so much then as at night."

Miriam looked in the bookcase, saw what postcards and letters he had received, saw what books were there. She took one that had interested him. Then he turned down the gas and they set off. He did not trouble to lock the door.

He was not home again until a quarter to eleven. His mother was seated in the rocking-chair. Annie, with a rope of hair hanging down her back, remained sitting on a low stool before the fire, her elbows on her knees, gloomily. On the table stood the offending loaf unswathed. Paul entered rather breathless. No one spoke. His mother was reading the little local newspaper. He took off his coat, and went to sit down on the sofa. His mother moved curtly aside to let him pass. No one spoke. He was very uncomfortable. For some minutes he sat pretending to read a piece of paper he found on the table. Then——

"I forgot that bread, mother," he said.

There was no answer from either woman.

"Well," he said, "it's only twopence ha'penny. I can pay you for that."

Being angry, he put three pennies on the table and slid them towards his mother. She turned away her head. Her mouth was shut tightly.

"Yes," said Annie, "you don't know how badly my mother is!"

The girl sat staring glumly into the fire.

"Why is she badly?" asked Paul, in his overbearing way.

"Well!" said Annie. "She could scarcely get home."

He looked closely at his mother. She looked ill.

"*Why* could you scarcely get home?" he asked her, still sharply. She would not answer.

"I found her as white as a sheet sitting here," said Annie, with a suggestion of tears in her voice.

"Well, *why*?" insisted Paul. His brows were knitting, his eyes dilating passionately.

"It was enough to upset anybody," said Mrs. Morel, "hugging those parcels—meat, and greengroceries, and a pair of curtains——"

"Well, why *did* you hug them; you needn't have done."

"Then who would?"

"Let Annie fetch the meat."

"Yes, and I *would* fetch the meat, but how was I to know. You were off with Miriam, instead of being in when my mother came."

"And what was the matter with you?" asked Paul of his mother.

"I suppose it's my heart," she replied. Certainly she looked bluish round the mouth.

"And have you felt it before?"

"Yes—often enough."

"Then why haven't you told me?—and why haven't you seen a doctor?"

Mrs. Morel shifted in her chair, angry with him for his hectoring.

"You'd never notice anything," said Annie. "You're too eager to be off with Miriam."

"Oh, am I—and any worse than you with Leonard?"

"*I* was in at a quarter to ten."

There was silence in the room for a time.

"I should have thought," said Mrs. Morel bitterly, "that she wouldn't have occupied you so entirely as to burn a whole ovenful of bread."

"Beatrice was here as well as she."

"Very likely. But we know why the bread is spoilt."

"Why?" he flashed.

"Because you were engrossed with Miriam," replied Mrs. Morel hotly.

"Oh, very well—then it was *not*!" he replied angrily.

He was distressed and wretched. Seizing a paper, he began to read. Annie, her blouse unfastened, her long ropes of hair twisted into a plait, went up to bed, bidding him a very curt goodnight.

Paul sat pretending to read. He knew his mother wanted to upbraid him. He also wanted to know what had made her ill, for he was troubled. So, instead of running away to bed, as he would have liked to do, he sat and waited. There was a tense silence. The clock ticked loudly.

"You'd better go to bed before your father comes in," said the mother harshly. "And if you're going to have anything to eat, you'd better get it."

"I don't want anything."

It was his mother's custom to bring him some trifle for supper on Friday night, the night of luxury for the colliers. He was too angry to go and find it in the pantry this night. This insulted her.

"If I *wanted* you to go to Selby on Friday night, I can imagine the scene," said Mrs. Morel. "But you're never too tired to go if *she* will come for you. Nay, you neither want to eat nor drink then."

"I can't let her go alone."

"Can't you? And why does she come?"

"Not because I ask her."

"She doesn't come without you want her——"

"Well, what if I *do* want her——" he replied.

"Why, nothing, if it was sensible or reasonable. But to go trapseing up there miles and miles in the mud, coming home at midnight, and got to go to Nottingham in the morning——"

"If I hadn't, you'd be just the same."

"Yes, I should, because there's no sense in it. Is she *so* fascinating that you must follow her all that way?" Mrs. Morel was bitterly sarcastic. She sat still, with averted face, stroking with a rhythmic, jerked movement, the black sateen of her apron. It was a movement that hurt Paul to see.

"I do like her," he said, "but——"

"*Like* her!" said Mrs. Morel, in the same biting tones. "It seems to me you like nothing and nobody

346

else. There's neither Annie, nor me, nor anyone now for you."

"What nonsense, mother—you know I don't love her—I—I tell you I *don't* love her—she doesn't even walk with my arm, because I don't want her to."

"Then why do you fly to her so often?"

"I *do* like to talk to her—I never said I didn't. But I *don't* love her."

"Is there nobody else to talk to?"

"Not about the things we talk of. There's a lot of things that you're not interested in, that——"

"What things?"

Mrs. Morel was so intense that Paul began to pant.

"Why—painting—and books. *You* don't care about Herbert Spencer."

"No," was the sad reply. "And *you* won't at my age."

"Well, but I do now—and Miriam does——"

"And how do you know," Mrs. Morel flashed defiantly, "that *I* shouldn't. Do you ever try me!"

"But you don't, mother, you know you don't care whether a picture's decorative or not; you don't care what *manner* it is in."

"How do you know I don't care? Do you ever try me? Do you ever talk to me about these things, to try?"

"But it's not that that matters to you, mother, you know it's not."

"What is it, then—what is it, then that matters to me?" she flashed. He knitted his brows with pain.

"You're old, mother, and we're young."

He only meant that the interests of *her* age were not the interests of his. But he realised the moment he had spoken that he had said the wrong thing.

"Yes, I know it well—I am old. And therefore I may stand aside; I have nothing more to do with you. You only want me to wait on you—the rest is for Miriam."

He could not bear it. Instinctively he realised that he was life to her. And, after all, she was the chief thing to him, the only supreme thing.

"You know it isn't, mother, you know it isn't!"

She was moved to pity by his cry.

"It looks a great deal like it," she said, half putting aside her despair.

"No, mother—I really *don't* love her. I talk to her, but I want to come home to you."

He had taken off his collar and tie, and rose, barethroated, to go to bed. As he stooped to kiss his mother, she threw her arms round his neck, hid her face on his shoulder, and cried, in a whimpering voice, so unlike her own that he writhed in agony:

"I can't bear it. I could let another woman—but not her. She'd leave me no room, not a bit of room——"

And immediately he hated Miriam bitterly.

"And I've never—you know, Paul—I've never had a husband—not really——"

He stroked his mother's hair, and his mouth was on her throat.

348

"And she exults so in taking you from me—she's not like ordinary girls."

"Well, I don't love her, mother," he murmured, bowing his head and hiding his eyes on her shoulder in misery. His mother kissed him a long, fervent kiss.

"My boy!" she said, in a voice trembling with passionate love.

Without knowing, he gently stroked her face.

"There," said his mother, "now go to bed. You'll be *so* tired in the morning." As she was speaking she heard her husband coming. "There's your father—now go." Suddenly she looked at him almost as if in fear. "Perhaps I'm selfish. If you want her, take her, my boy."

His mother looked so strange, Paul kissed her, trembling.

"Ha—mother!" he said softly.

Morel came in, walking unevenly. His hat was over one corner of his eye. He balanced in the doorway.

"At your mischief again?" he said venomously.

Mrs. Morel's emotion turned into sudden hate of the drunkard who had come in thus upon her.

"At any rate, it is sober," she said.

"H'm—h'm! h'm—h'm!" he sneered. He went into the passage, hung up his hat and coat. Then they heard him go down three steps to the pantry. He returned with a piece of pork-pie in his fist. It was what Mrs. Morel had bought for her son.

"Nor was that bought for you. If you can give me

no more than twenty-five shillings, I'm sure I'm not going to buy you pork-pie to stuff, after you've swilled a bellyful of beer."

"Wha-at—wha-at!" snarled Morel, toppling in his balance. "Wha-at—not for me?" He looked at the piece of meat and crust, and suddenly, in a vicious spurt of temper, flung it into the fire.

Paul started to his feet.

"Waste your own stuff!" he cried.

"What—what!" suddenly shouted Morel, jumping up and clenching his fist. "I'll show yer, yer young jockey!"

"All right!" said Paul viciously, putting his head on one side. "Show me!"

He would at that moment dearly have loved to have a smack at something. Morel was half crouching, fists up, ready to spring. The young man stood, smiling with his lips.

"Ussha!" hissed the father, swiping round with a great stroke just past his son's face. He dared not, even though so close, really touch the young man, but swerved an inch away.

"Right!" said Paul, his eyes upon the side of his father's mouth, where in another instant his fist would have hit. He ached for that stroke. But he heard a faint moan from behind. His mother was deadly pale and dark at the mouth. Morel was dancing up to deliver another blow.

"Father!" said Paul, so that the word rang.

Morel started, and stood at attention.

"Mother!" moaned the boy. "Mother!"

350

She began to struggle with herself. Her open eyes watched him, although she could not move. Gradually she was coming to herself. He laid her down on the sofa, and ran upstairs for a little whisky, which at last she could sip. The tears were hopping down his face. As he kneeled in front of her he did not cry, but the tears ran down his face quickly. Morel, on the opposite side of the room, sat with his elbows on his knees glaring across.

"What's a-matter with 'er?" he asked.

"Faint!" replied Paul.

"H'm!"

The elderly man began to unlace his boots. He stumbled off to bed. His last fight was fought in that home.

Paul kneeled there, stroking his mother's hand.

"Don't be poorly, mother—don't be poorly!" he said time after time.

"It's nothing, my boy," she murmured.

At last he rose, fetched in a large piece of coal, and raked the fire. Then he cleared the room, put everything straight, laid the things for breakfast, and brought his mother's candle.

"Can you go to bed, mother?"

"Yes, I'll come."

"Sleep with Annie, mother, not with him."

"No. I'll sleep in my own bed."

"Don't sleep with him, mother."

"I'll sleep in my own bed."

She rose, and he turned out the gas, then followed

her closely upstairs, carrying her candle. On the landing he kissed her close.

"Goodnight, mother."

"Goodnight!" she said.

He pressed his face upon the pillow in a fury of misery. And yet, somewhere in his soul, he was at peace because he still loved his mother best. It was the bitter peace of resignation.

The efforts of his father to conciliate him next day were a great humiliation to him.

Everybody tried to forget the scene.

# 9

## DEFEAT OF MIRIAM

PAUL was dissatisfied with himself and with everything. The deepest of his love belonged to his mother. When he felt he had hurt her, or wounded his love for her, he could not bear it. Now it was spring, and there was battle between him and Miriam. This year he had a good deal against her. She was vaguely aware of it. The old feeling that she was to be a sacrifice to this love, which she had had when she prayed, was mingled in all her emotions. She did not at the bottom believe she ever would have him. She did not believe in herself primarily: doubted whether she could ever be what he would demand of her. Certainly she never saw herself living happily through a lifetime with him. She saw tragedy, sorrow, and sacrifice ahead. And in sacrifice she was proud, in renunciation she was strong, for she did not trust herself to support everyday life. She was prepared for the big things and the deep things, like tragedy. It was the sufficiency of the small day-life she could not trust.

The Easter holidays began happily. Paul was his own frank self. Yet she felt it would go wrong. On the Sunday afternoon she stood at her bedroom window, looking across at the oak-trees of the wood, in whose branches a twilight was tangled, below the bright sky of the afternoon. Grey-green rosettes of honeysuckle leaves hung before the window, some already, she fancied, showing bud. It was spring, which she loved and dreaded.

Hearing the clack of the gate she stood in suspense. It was a bright grey day. Paul came into the yard with his bicycle, which glittered as he walked. Usually he rang his bell and laughed towards the house. Today he walked with shut lips and cold, cruel bearing, that had something of a slouch and a sneer in it. She knew him well by now, and could tell from that keen-looking, aloof young body of his what was happening inside him. There was a cold correctness in the way he put his bicycle in its place, that made her heart sink.

She came downstairs nervously. She was wearing a new net blouse that she thought became her. It had a high collar with a tiny ruff, reminding her of Mary, Queen of Scots, and making her, she thought, look wonderfully a woman, and dignified. At twenty she was full-breasted and luxuriously formed. Her face was still like a soft rich mask, unchangeable. But her eyes, once lifted, were wonderful. She was afraid of him. He would notice her new blouse.

He, being in a hard, ironical mood, was entertaining the family to a description of a service given in the Primitive Methodist Chapel, conducted by one of the well-known preachers of the sect. He sat at

354

the head of the table, his mobile face, with the eyes that could be so beautiful, shining with tenderness or dancing with laughter, now taking on one expression and then another, in imitation of various people he was mocking. His mockery always hurt her; it was too near the reality. He was too clever and cruel. She felt that when his eyes were like this, hard with mocking hate, he would spare neither himself nor anybody else. But Mrs. Leivers was wiping her eyes with laughter, and Mr. Leivers, just awake from his Sunday nap, was rubbing his head in amusement. The three brothers sat with ruffled, sleepy appearance in their shirt-sleeves, giving a guffaw from time to time. The whole family loved a "take-off" more than anything.

He took no notice of Miriam. Later, she saw him remark her new blouse, saw that the artist approved, but it won from him not a spark of warmth. She was nervous, could hardly reach the teacups from the shelves.

When the men went out to milk, she ventured to address him personally.

"You were late," she said.

"Was I?" he answered.

There was silence for a while.

"Was it rough riding?" she asked.

"I didn't notice it."

She continued quickly to lay the table. When she had finished——

"Tea won't be for a few minutes. Will you come and look at the daffodils?" she said.

355

He rose without answering. They went out into the back garden under the budding damson-trees. The hills and the sky were clean and cold. Everything looked washed, rather hard. Miriam glanced at Paul. He was pale and impassive. It seemed cruel to her that his eyes and brows, which she loved, could look so hurting.

"Has the wind made you tired?" she asked. She detected an underneath feeling of weariness about him.

"No, I think not," he answered.

"It must be rough on the road—the wood moans so."

"You can see by the clouds it's a south-west wind; that helps me here."

"You see, I don't cycle, so I don't understand," she murmured.

"Is there need to cycle to know that!" he said.

She thought his sarcasms were unnecessary. They went forward in silence. Round the wild, tussocky lawn at the back of the house was a thorn hedge, under which daffodils were craning forward from among their sheaves of grey-green blades. The cheeks of the flowers were greenish with cold. But still some had burst, and their gold ruffled and glowed. Miriam went on her knees before one cluster, took a wild-looking daffodil between her hands, turned up its face of gold to her, and bowed down, caressing it with her mouth and cheeks and brow. He stood aside, with his hands in his pockets, watching her. One after another she turned up to

356

him the faces of the yellow, bursten flowers appealingly, fondling them lavishly all the while.

"Aren't they magnificent?" she murmured.

"Magnificent! It's a bit thick—they're pretty!"

She bowed again to her flowers at his censure of her praise. He watched her crouching, sipping the flowers with fervid kisses.

"Why must you always be fondling things?" he said irritably.

"But I love to touch them," she replied, hurt.

"Can you never like things without clutching them as if you wanted to pull the heart out of them? Why don't you have a bit more restraint, or reserve, or something?"

She looked up at him full of pain, then continued slowly to stroke her lips against a ruffled flower. Their scent, as she smelled it, was so much kinder than he; it almost made her cry.

"You wheedle the soul out of things," he said. "I would never wheedle—at any rate, I'd go straight."

He scarcely knew what he was saying. These things came from him mechanically. She looked at him. His body seemed one weapon, firm and hard against her.

"You're always begging things to love you," he said, "as if you were a beggar for love. Even the flowers, you have to fawn on them——"

Rhythmically, Miriam was swaying and stroking the flower with her mouth, inhaling the scent which ever after made her shudder as it came to her nostrils.

357

"You don't want to love—your eternal and abnormal craving is to be loved. You aren't positive, you're negative. You absorb, absorb, as if you must fill yourself up with love, because you've got a shortage somewhere."

She was stunned by his cruelty, and did not hear. He had not the faintest notion of what he was saying. It was as if his fretted, tortured soul, run hot by thwarted passion, jetted off these sayings like sparks from electricity. She did not grasp anything he said. She only sat crouched beneath his cruelty and his hatred of her. She never realised in a flash. Over everything she brooded and brooded.

After tea he stayed with Edgar and the brothers, taking no notice of Miriam. She, extremely unhappy on this looked-for holiday, waited for him. And at last he yielded and came to her. She was determined to track this mood of his to its origin. She counted it not much more than a mood.

"Shall we go through the wood a little way?" she asked him, knowing he never refused a direct request.

They went down to the warren. On the middle path they passed a trap, a narrow horseshoe hedge of small fir-boughs, baited with the guts of a rabbit. Paul glanced at it frowning. She caught his eye.

"Isn't it dreadful?" she asked.

"I don't know! Is it worse than a weasel with its teeth in a rabbit's throat? One weasel or many rabbits? One or the other must go!"

358

He was taking the bitterness of life badly. She was rather sorry for him.

"We will go back to the house," he said. "I don't want to walk out."

They went past the lilac-tree, whose bronze leaf-buds were coming unfastened. Just a fragment remained of the haystack, a monument squared and brown, like a pillar of stone. There was a little bed of hay from the last cutting.

"Let us sit here a minute," said Miriam.

He sat down against his will, resting his back against the hard wall of hay. They faced the amphitheatre of round hills that glowed with sunset, tiny white farms standing out, the meadows golden, the woods dark and yet luminous, tree-tops folded over tree-tops, distinct in the distance. The evening had cleared, and the east was tender with a magenta flush under which the land lay still and rich.

"Isn't it beautiful?" she pleaded.

But he only scowled. He would rather have had it ugly just then.

At that moment a big bull-terrier came rushing up, open-mouthed, pranced his two paws on the youth's shoulders, licking his face. Paul drew back, laughing. Bill was a great relief to him. He pushed the dog aside, but it came leaping back.

"Get out," said the lad, "or I'll dot thee one."

But the dog was not to be pushed away. So Paul had a little battle with the creature, pitching poor Bill away from him, who, however, only floundered tumultuously back again, wild with joy. The two

359

fought together, the man laughing grudgingly, the dog grinning all over. Miriam watched them. There was something pathetic about the man. He wanted so badly to love, to be tender. The rough way he bowled the dog over was really loving. Bill got up, panting with happiness, his brown eyes rolling in his white face, and lumbered back again. He adored Paul. The lad frowned.

"Bill, I've had enough o' thee," he said.

But the dog only stood with two heavy paws, that quivered with love, upon his thigh, and flickered a red tongue at him. He drew back.

"No," he said—"no—I've had enough."

And in a minute the dog trotted off happily, to vary the fun.

He remained staring miserably across at the hills, whose still beauty he begrudged. He wanted to go and cycle with Edgar. Yet he had not the courage to leave Miriam.

"Why are you sad?" she asked humbly.

"I'm not sad; why should I be," he answered. "I'm only normal."

She wondered why he always claimed to be normal when he was disagreeable.

"But what is the matter?" she pleaded, coaxing him soothingly.

"Nothing!"

"Nay!" she murmured.

He picked up a stick and began to stab the earth with it.

"You'd far better not talk," he said.

360

"But I wish to know——" she replied.

He laughed resentfully.

"You always do," he said.

"It's not fair to me," she murmured.

He thrust, thrust, thrust at the ground with the pointed stick, digging up little clods of earth as if he were in a fever of irritation. She gently and firmly laid her hand on his wrist.

"Don't!" she said. "Put it away."

He flung the stick into the currant-bushes, and leaned back. Now he was bottled up.

"What is it?" she pleaded softly.

He lay perfectly still, only his eyes alive, and they full of torment.

"You know," he said at length, rather wearily— "you know—we'd better break off."

It was what she dreaded. Swiftly everything seemed to darken before her eyes.

"Why!" she murmured. "What has happened?"

"Nothing has happened. We only realise where we are. It's no good——"

She waited in silence, sadly, patiently. It was no good being impatient with him. At any rate, he would tell her now what ailed him.

"We agreed on friendship," he went on in a dull, monotonous voice. "How often *have* we agreed for friendship! And yet—it neither stops there, nor gets anywhere else."

He was silent again. She brooded. What did he mean? He was so wearying. There was something he would not yield. Yet she must be patient with him.

"I can only give friendship—it's all I'm capable of—it's a flaw in my make-up. The thing over-balances to one side—I hate a toppling balance. Let us have done."

There was warmth of fury in his last phrases. He meant she loved him more than he her. Perhaps he could not love her. Perhaps she had not in herself that which he wanted. It was the deepest motive of her soul, this self-mistrust. It was so deep she dared neither realise nor acknowledge. Perhaps she was deficient. Like an infinitely subtle shame, it kept her always back. If it were so, she would do without him. She would never let herself want him. She would merely see.

"But what has happened?" she said.

"Nothing—it's all in myself—it only comes out just now. We're always like this towards Easter-time."

He grovelled so helplessly, she pitied him. At least she never floundered in such a pitiable way. After all, it was he who was chiefly humiliated.

"What do you want?" she asked him.

"Why—I mustn't come often—that's all. Why should I monopolise you when I'm not—— You see, I'm deficient in something with regard to you——"

He was telling her he did not love her, and so ought to leave her a chance with another man. How foolish and blind and shamefully clumsy he was! What were other men to her! What were men to her at all! But he, ah! she loved his soul. Was *he* deficient in something? Perhaps he was.

362

"But I don't understand," she said huskily. "Yesterday——"

The night was turning jangled and hateful to him as the twilight faded. And she bowed under her suffering.

"I know," he cried, "you never will! You'll never believe that I can't—can't physically, any more than I can fly up like a skylark——"

"What?" she murmured. Now she dreaded.

"Love you."

He hated her bitterly at that moment because he made her suffer. Love her! She knew he loved her. He really belonged to her. This about not loving her, physically, bodily, was a mere perversity on his part, because he knew she loved him. He was stupid like a child. He belonged to her. His soul wanted her. She guessed somebody had been influencing him. She felt upon him the hardness, the foreignness of another influence.

"What have they been saying at home?" she asked.

"It's not that," he answered.

And then she knew it was. She despised them for their commonness, his people. They did not know what things were really worth.

He and she talked very little more that night. After all he left her to cycle with Edgar.

He had come back to his mother. Hers was the strongest tie in his life. When he thought round, Miriam shrank away. There was a vague, unreal feel about her. And nobody else mattered. There was one place in the world that stood solid and did not melt into unreality: the place where his mother was. Everybody else could grow shadowy, almost non-existent to him, but she could not. It was as if the pivot and pole of his life, from which he could not escape, was his mother.

And in the same way she waited for him. In him was established her life now. After all, the life beyond offered very little to Mrs. Morel. She saw that our chance for *doing* is here, and doing counted with her. Paul was going to prove that she had been right; he was going to make a man whom nothing should shift off his feet; he was going to alter the face of the earth in some way which mattered. Wherever he went she felt her soul went with him. Whatever he did she felt her soul stood by him, ready, as it were, to hand him his tools. She could not bear it when he was with Miriam. William was dead. She would fight to keep Paul.

And he came back to her. And in his soul was a feeling of the satisfaction of self-sacrifice because he was faithful to her. She loved him first; he loved her first. And yet it was not enough. His new young life, so strong and imperious, was urged towards something else. It made him mad with restlessness. She saw this, and wished bitterly that Miriam had been a woman who could take this new life of his, and leave her the roots. He fought against his mother almost as he fought against Miriam.

It was a week before he went again to Willey Farm. Miriam had suffered a great deal, and was afraid to see him again. Was she now to endure the ignominy of his abandoning her? That would only be superficial and temporary. He would come back. She held the keys to his soul. But meanwhile, how he would torture her with his battle against her. She shrank from it.

However, the Sunday after Easter he came to tea. Mrs. Leivers was glad to see him. She gathered something was fretting him, that he found things hard. He seemed to drift to her for comfort. And she was good to him. She did him that great kindness of treating him almost with reverence.

He met her with the young children in the front garden.

"I'm glad you've come," said the mother, looking at him with her great appealing brown eyes. "It is such a sunny day. I was just going down the fields for the first time this year."

He felt she would like him to come. That soothed him. They went, talking simply, he gentle and humble. He could have wept with gratitude that she was deferential to him. He was feeling humiliated.

At the bottom of the Mow Close they found a thrush's nest.

"Shall I show you the eggs?" he said.

"Do!" replied Mrs. Leivers. "They seem *such* a sign of spring, and so hopeful."

He put aside the thorns, and took out the eggs, holding them in the palm of his hand.

"They are quite hot—I think we frightened her off them," he said.

"Ay, poor thing!" said Mrs. Leivers.

Miriam could not help touching the eggs, and his hand which, it seemed to her, cradled them so well.

"Isn't it a strange warmth!" she murmured, to get near him.

"Blood heat," he answered.

She watched him putting them back, his body pressed against the hedge, his arm reaching slowly through the thorns, his hand folded carefully over the eggs. He was concentrated on the act. Seeing him so, she loved him; he seemed so simple and sufficient to himself. And she could not get to him.

After tea she stood hesitating at the bookshelf. He took "Tartarin de Tarascon". Again they sat on the bank of hay at the foot of the stack. He read a couple of pages, but without any heart for it. Again the dog came racing up to repeat the fun of the other day. He shoved his muzzle in the man's chest. Paul fingered his ear for a moment. Then he pushed him away.

"Go away, Bill," he said. "I don't want you."

Bill slunk off, and Miriam wondered and dreaded what was coming. There was a silence about the youth that made her still with apprehension. It was not his furies, but his quiet resolutions that she feared.

Turning his face a little to one side, so that she could not see him, he began, speaking slowly and painfully:

"Do you think—if I didn't come up so much—you might get to like somebody else—another man?"

So this was what he was still harping on.

"But I don't know any other men. Why do you ask?" she replied, in a low tone that should have been a reproach to him.

"Why," he blurted, "because they say I've no right to come up like this—without we mean to marry——"

Miriam was indignant at anybody's forcing the issues between them. She had been furious with her own father for suggesting to Paul, laughingly, that he knew why he came so much.

"Who says?" she asked, wondering if her people had anything to do with it. They had not.

"Mother—and the others. They say at this rate everybody will consider me engaged, and I ought to consider myself so, because it's not fair to you. And I've tried to find out—and I don't think I love you as a man ought to love his wife. What do *you* think about it?"

Miriam bowed her head moodily. She was angry at having this struggle. People should leave him and her alone.

"I don't know," she murmured.

"Do you think we love each other enough to marry?" he asked definitely. It made her tremble.

"No," she answered truthfully. "I don't think so—we're too young."

"I thought perhaps," he went on miserably, "that you, with your intensity in things, might have given me more—than I could ever make up to you.

367

And even now—if you think it better—we'll be engaged."

Now Miriam wanted to cry. And she was angry, too. He was always such a child for people to do as they liked with.

"No, I don't think so," she said firmly.

He pondered a minute.

"You see," he said, "with me—I don't think one person would ever monopolize me—be everything to me—I think never."

This she did not consider.

"No," she murmured. Then, after a pause, she looked at him and her dark eyes flashed.

"This is your mother," she said. "I know she never liked me."

"No, no, it isn't," he said hastily. "It was for your sake she spoke this time. She only said, if I was going on, I ought to consider myself engaged." There was a silence. "And if I ask you to come down any time, you won't stop away, will you?"

She did not answer. By this time she was very angry.

"Well, what shall we do?" she said shortly. "I suppose I'd better drop French. I was just beginning to get on with it. But I suppose I can go on alone."

"I don't see that we need," he said. "I can give you a French lesson, surely."

"Well—and there are Sunday nights. I shan't stop coming to chapel, because I enjoy it, and it's all the

368

social life I get. But you've no need to come home with me. I can go back alone."

"All right," he answered, rather taken aback. "But if I ask Edgar, he'll always come with us, and then they can say nothing."

There was silence. After all, then, she would not lose much. For all their talk down at his home there would not be much difference. She wished they would mind their own business.

"And you won't think about it, and let it trouble you, will you?" he asked.

"Oh, no," replied Miriam, without looking at him.

He was silent. She thought him unstable. He had no fixity of purpose, no anchor of righteousness that held him.

"Because," he continued, "a man gets across his bicycle—and goes to work—and does all sorts of things. But a woman broods."

"No, I shan't bother," said Miriam. And she meant it.

It had gone rather chilly. They went indoors.

"How white Paul looks!" Mrs. Leivers exclaimed. "Miriam, you shouldn't have let him sit out of doors. Do you think you've taken cold, Paul?"

"Oh, no!" he laughed.

But he felt done up. It wore him out, the conflict in himself. Miriam pitied him now. But quite early, before nine o'clock, he rose to go.

"You're not going home, are you?" asked Mrs. Leivers anxiously.

"Yes," he replied. "I said I'd be early." He was very awkward.

"But this *is* early," said Mrs. Leivers.

Miriam sat in the rocking-chair, and did not speak. He hesitated, expecting her to rise and go with him to the barn as usual for his bicycle. She remained as she was. He was at a loss.

"Well—goodnight, all!" he faltered.

She spoke her goodnight along with all the others. But as he went past the window he looked in. She saw him pale, his brows knit slightly in a way that had become constant with him, his eyes dark with pain.

She rose and went to the doorway to wave good-bye to him as he passed through the gate. He rode slowly under the pine-trees, feeling a cur and a miserable wretch. His bicycle went tilting down the hills at random. He thought it would be a relief to break one's neck.

Two days later he sent her up a book and a little note, urging her to read and be busy.

At this time he gave all his friendship to Edgar. He loved the family so much, he loved the farm so much; it was the dearest place on earth to him. His home was not so lovable. It was his mother. But then he would have been just as happy with his mother anywhere. Whereas Willey Farm he loved passionately. He loved the little pokey kitchen, where men's boots tramped, and the dog slept with one eye open for fear of being trodden on; where the lamp hung over the table at night, and everything was so silent. He loved Miriam's long, low parlour, with its atmosphere of romance, its flowers, its books, its high rosewood piano. He loved the gardens and the buildings that stood with their scarlet roofs on the naked edges of the fields, crept towards the wood as if for cosiness, the wild country scooping down a valley and up the un-cultured hills of the other side. Only to be there was an exhilaration and a joy to him. He loved Mrs. Leivers, with her unworldliness and her quaint cynicism; he loved Mr. Leivers, so warm and young and lovable; he loved Edgar, who lit up when he came, and the boys and the children and Bill—even the sow Circe and the Indian game-cock called Tippoo. All this besides Miriam. He could not give it up.

So he went as often, but he was usually with Edgar. Only all the family, including the father, joined in charades and games at evening. And later, Miriam drew them together, and they read "Macbeth" out of penny books, taking parts. It was great excitement. Miriam was glad, and Mrs. Leivers was glad, and Mr. Leivers enjoyed it. Then they all learned songs together from tonic sol-fa, singing in a circle round the fire. But now Paul was very rarely alone with Miriam. She waited. When she and Edgar and he walked home together from chapel or from the literary society in Bestwood, she knew his talk, so passionate and so unorthodox nowadays, was for her. She did envy Edgar, however, his cycling with Paul, his Friday nights, his days working in the fields. For her Friday nights and her French lessons were gone. She was nearly always alone, walking, pondering in the wood, reading, studying, dreaming, waiting. And he wrote to her frequently.

One Sunday evening they attained to their old rare harmony. Edgar had stayed to Communion—he wondered what it was like—with Mrs. Morel. So Paul came on alone with Miriam to his home. He was more or less under her spell again. As usual, they were discussing the sermon. He was setting now full sail towards Agnosticism, but such a religious Agnosticism that Miriam did not suffer so badly. They were at the Renan "Vie de Jésus" stage. Miriam was the threshing-floor on which he threshed out all his beliefs. While he trampled his ideas upon her soul, the truth came out for him. She alone was his threshing-floor. She alone helped him towards realization. Almost impassive, she submitted to his argument and expounding. And somehow, because of her, he gradually realized where he was wrong. And what he realized, she realized. She felt he could not do without her.

They came to the silent house. He took the key out of the scullery window, and they entered. All the time he went on with his discussion. He lit the gas, mended the fire, and brought her some cakes from the pantry. She sat on the sofa, quietly, with a plate on her knee. She wore a large white hat with some pinkish flowers. It was a cheap hat, but he liked it. Her face beneath was still and pensive, golden-

372

brown and ruddy. Always her ears were hid in her short curls. She watched him.

She liked him on Sundays. Then he wore a dark suit that showed the lithe movement of his body. There was a clean, clear-cut look about him. He went on with his thinking to her. Suddenly he reached for a Bible. Miriam liked the way he reached up—so sharp, straight to the mark. He turned the pages quickly, and read her a chapter of St. John. As he sat in the arm-chair reading, intent, his voice only thinking, she felt as if he were using her unconsciously as a man uses his tools at some work he is bent on. She loved it. And the wistfulness of his voice was like a reaching to something, and it was as if she were what he reached with. She sat back on the sofa away from him, and yet feeling herself the very instrument his hand grasped. It gave her great pleasure.

Then he began to falter and to get self-conscious. And when he came to the verse, "A woman, when she is in travail, hath sorrow because her hour is come", he missed it out. Miriam had felt him growing uncomfortable. She shrank when the well-known words did not follow. He went on reading, but she did not hear. A grief and shame made her bend her head. Six months ago he would have read it simply. Now there was a scotch in his running with her. Now she felt there was really something hostile between them, something of which they were ashamed.

She ate her cake mechanically. He tried to go on

with his argument, but could not get back the right note. Soon Edgar came in. Mrs. Morel had gone to her friends'. The three set off to Willey Farm.

Miriam brooded over his split with her. There was something else he wanted. He could not be satisfied; he could give her no peace. There was between them now always a ground for strife. She wanted to prove him. She believed that his chief need in life was herself. If she could prove it, both to herself and to him, the rest might go; she could simply trust to the future.

So in May she asked him to come to Willey Farm and meet Mrs. Dawes. There was something he hankered after. She saw him, whenever they spoke of Clara Dawes, rouse and get slightly angry. He said he did not like her. Yet he was keen to know about her. Well, he should put himself to the test. She believed that there were in him desires for higher things, and desires for lower, and that the desire for the higher would conquer. At any rate, he should try. She forgot that her "higher" and "lower" were arbitrary.

He was rather excited at the idea of meeting Clara at Willey Farm. Mrs. Dawes came for the day. Her heavy, dun-coloured hair was coiled on top of her head. She wore a white blouse and navy skirt, and somehow, wherever she was, seemed to make things look paltry and insignificant. When she was in the room, the kitchen seemed too small and mean altogether. Miriam's beautiful twilighty parlour looked stiff and stupid. All the Leivers were eclipsed

374

like candles. They found her rather hard to put up with. Yet she was perfectly amiable, but indifferent, and rather hard.

Paul did not come till afternoon. He was early. As he swung off his bicycle, Miriam saw him look round at the house eagerly. He would be disappointed if the visitor had not come. Miriam went out to meet him, bowing her head because of the sunshine. Nasturtiums were coming out crimson under the cool green shadow of their leaves. The girl stood, dark-haired, glad to see him.

"Hasn't Clara come?" he asked.

"Yes," replied Miriam in her musical tone. "She's reading."

He wheeled his bicycle into the barn. He had put on a handsome tie, of which he was rather proud, and socks to match.

"She came this morning?" he asked.

"Yes," replied Miriam, as she walked at his side. "You said you'd bring me that letter from the man at Liberty's. Have you remembered?"

"Oh, dash, no!" he said. "But nag at me till you get it."

"I don't like to nag at you."

"Do it whether or not. And is she any more agreeable?" he continued.

"You know I always think she is quite agreeable."

He was silent. Evidently his eagerness to be early today had been the newcomer. Miriam already began to suffer. They went together towards the

375

house. He took the clips off his trousers, but was too lazy to brush the dust from his shoes, in spite of the socks and tie.

Clara sat in the cool parlour reading. He saw the nape of her white neck, and the fine hair lifted from it. She rose, looking at him indifferently. To shake hands she lifted her arm straight, in a manner that seemed at once to keep him at a distance, and yet to fling something to him. He noticed how her breasts swelled inside her blouse, and how her shoulder curved handsomely under the thin muslin at the top of her arm.

"You have chosen a fine day," he said.

"It happens so," she said.

"Yes," he said; "I am glad."

She sat down, not thanking him for his politeness.

"What have you been doing all morning?" asked Paul of Miriam.

"Well, you see," said Miriam, coughing huskily, "Clara only came with father—and so—she's not been here very long."

Clara sat leaning on the table, holding aloof. He noticed her hands were large, but well kept. And the skin on them seemed almost coarse, opaque, and white, with fine golden hairs. She did not mind if he observed her hands. She intended to scorn him. Her heavy arm lay negligently on the table. Her mouth was closed as if she were offended, and she kept her face slightly averted.

"You were at Margaret Bonford's meeting the other evening," he said to her.

Miriam did not know this courteous Paul. Clara glanced at him.

"Yes," she said.

"Why," asked Miriam, "how do you know?"

"I went in for a few minutes before the train came," he answered.

Clara turned away again rather disdainfully.

"I think she's a lovable little woman," said Paul.

"Margaret Bonford!" exclaimed Clara. "She's a great deal cleverer than most men."

"Well, I didn't say she wasn't," he said, deprecating. "She's lovable for all that."

"And, of course, that is all that matters," said Clara witheringly.

He rubbed his head, rather perplexed, rather annoyed.

"I suppose it matters more than her cleverness," he said; "which, after all, would never get her to heaven."

"It's not heaven she wants to get—it's her fair share on earth," retorted Clara. She spoke as if he were responsible for some deprivation which Miss Bonford suffered.

"Well," he said, "I thought she was warm, and awfully nice—only too frail. I wished she was sitting comfortably in peace——"

" 'Darning her husband's stockings,' " said Clara scathingly.

"I'm sure she wouldn't mind darning even my

377

stockings," he said. "And I'm sure she'd do them well. Just as I wouldn't mind blacking her boots if she wanted me to."

But Clara refused to answer this sally of his. He talked to Miriam for a little while. The other woman held aloof.

"Well," he said, "I think I'll go and see Edgar. Is he on the land?"

"I believe," said Miriam, "he's gone for a load of coal. He should be back directly."

"Then," he said, "I'll go and meet him."

Miriam dared not propose anything for the three of them. He rose and left them.

On the top road, where the gorse was out, he saw Edgar walking lazily beside the mare, who nodded her white-starred forehead as she dragged the clanking load of coal. The young farmer's face lighted up as he saw his friend. Edgar was good-looking, with dark, warm eyes. His clothes were old and rather disreputable, and he walked with considerable pride.

"Hello!" he said, seeing Paul bareheaded. "Where are you going?"

"Came to meet you. Can't stand 'Nevermore'."

Edgar's teeth flashed in a laugh of amusement.

"Who is 'Nevermore'?" he asked.

"The lady—Mrs. Dawes—it ought to be Mrs. The Raven that quothed 'Nevermore'."

Edgar laughed with glee.

"Don't you like her?" he asked.

"Not a fat lot," said Paul. "Why, do you?"

"No!" The answer came with a deep ring of conviction. "No!" Edgar pursed up his lips. "I can't say she's much in my line." He mused a little. Then: "But why do you call her 'Nevermore'?" he asked.

"Well," said Paul, "if she looks at a man she says haughtily 'Nevermore', and if she looks at herself in the looking-glass she says disdainfully 'Nevermore', and if she thinks back she says it in disgust, and if she looks forward she says it cynically."

Edgar considered this speech, failed to make much out of it, and said, laughing:

"You think she's a man-hater?"

"*She* thinks she is," replied Paul.

"But you don't think so?"

"No," replied Paul.

"Wasn't she nice with you, then?"

"Could you imagine her *nice* with anybody?" asked the young man.

Edgar laughed. Together they unloaded the coal in the yard. Paul was rather self-conscious, because he knew Clara could see if she looked out of the window. She didn't look.

On Saturday afternoons the horses were brushed down and groomed. Paul and Edgar worked together, sneezing with the dust that came from the pelts of Jimmy and Flower.

"Do you know a new song to teach me?" said Edgar.

He continued to work all the time. The back of his neck was sun-red when he bent down, and his fingers that held the brush were thick. Paul watched him sometimes.

" 'Mary Morrison'?" suggested the younger.

Edgar agreed. He had a good tenor voice, and he loved to learn all the songs his friend could teach him, so that he could sing whilst he was carting. Paul had a very indifferent baritone voice, but a good ear. However, he sang softly, for fear of Clara. Edgar repeated the line in a clear tenor. At times they both broke off to sneeze, and first one, then the other, abused his horse.

Miriam was impatient of men. It took so little to amuse them—even Paul. She thought it anomalous in him that he could be so thoroughly absorbed in a triviality.

It was tea-time when they had finished.

"What song was that?" asked Miriam.

Edgar told her. The conversation turned to singing.

"We have such jolly times," Miriam said to Clara.

Mrs. Dawes ate her meal in a slow, dignified way. Whenever the men were present she grew distant.

"Do you like singing?" Miriam asked her.

"If it is good," she said.

Paul, of course, coloured.

"You mean if it is high-class and trained?" he said.

"I think a voice needs training before the singing is anything," she said.

"You might as well insist on having people's

380

voices trained before you allowed them to talk," he replied. "Really, people sing for their own pleasure, as a rule."

"And it may be for other people's discomfort."

"Then the other people should have flaps to their ears," he replied.

The boys laughed. There was a silence. He flushed deeply, and ate in silence.

After tea, when all the men had gone but Paul, Mrs. Leivers said to Clara:

"And you find life happier now?"

"Infinitely."

"And you are satisfied?"

"So long as I can be free and independent."

"And you don't *miss* anything in your life?" asked Mrs. Leivers gently.

"I've put all that behind me."

Paul had been feeling uncomfortable during this discourse. He got up.

"You'll find you're always tumbling over the things you've put behind you," he said. Then he took his departure to the cow-sheds. He felt he had been witty, and his manly pride was high. He whistled as he went down the brick track.

Miriam came for him a little later to know if he would go with Clara and her for a walk. They set off down to Strelley Mill Farm. As they were going beside the brook, on the Willey Water side, looking through the brake at the edge of the wood, where pink campions glowed under a few sunbeams, they saw, beyond the tree-trunks and the thin hazel

381

bushes, a man leading a great bay horse through the gullies. The big red beast seemed to dance romantically through that dimness of green hazel drift, away there where the air was shadowy, as if it were in the past, among the fading bluebells that might have bloomed for Deidre or Iseult.

The three stood charmed.

"What a treat to be a knight," he said, "and to have a pavilion here."

"And to have us shut up safely?" replied Clara.

"Yes," he answered, "singing with your maids at your broidery. I would carry your banner of white and green and heliotrope. I would have 'W.S.P.U.' emblazoned on my shield, beneath a woman rampant."

"I have no doubt," said Clara, "that you would much rather fight for a woman than let her fight for herself."

"I would. When she fights for herself she seems like a dog before a looking-glass, gone into a mad fury with its own shadow."

"And *you* are the looking-glass?" she asked, with a curl of the lip.

"Or the shadow," he replied.

"I am afraid," she said, "that you are too clever."

"Well, I leave it to you to be *good*," he retorted, laughing. "Be good, sweet maid, and just let *me* be clever."

But Clara wearied of his flippancy. Suddenly, looking at her, he saw that the upward lifting of her face was misery and not scorn. His heart grew tender for everybody. He turned and was gentle with Miriam, whom he had neglected till then.

At the wood's edge they met Limb, a thin, swarthy man of forty, tenant of Strelley Mill, which he ran as a cattle-raising farm. He held the halter of the powerful stallion indifferently, as if he were tired. The three stood to let him pass over the stepping-stones of the first brook. Paul admired that so large an animal should walk on such springy toes, with an endless excess of vigour. Limb pulled up before them.

"Tell your father, Miss Leivers," he said, in a peculiar piping voice, "that his young beas'es 'as broke that bottom fence three days an' runnin'."

"Which?" asked Miriam, tremulous.

The great horse breathed heavily, shifting round its red flanks, and looking suspiciously with its wonderful big eyes upwards from under its lowered head and falling mane.

"Come along a bit," replied Limb, "an' I'll show you."

The man and the stallion went forward. It danced sideways, shaking its white fetlocks and looking frightened, as it felt itself in the brook.

"No hanky-pankyin'," said the man affectionately to the beast.

It went up the bank in little leaps, then splashed finely through the second brook. Clara, walking with a kind of sulky abandon, watched it half-fascinated, half-contemptuous. Limb stopped and pointed to the fence under some willows.

"There, you see where they got through," he said. "My man's druv 'em back three times."

"Yes," answered Miriam, colouring as if she were at fault.

"Are you comin' in?" asked the man.

"No, thanks; but we should like to go by the pond."

"Well, just as you've a mind," he said.

The horse gave little whinneys of pleasure at being so near home.

"He is glad to be back," said Clara, who was interested in the creature.

"Yes—'e's been a tidy step today."

They went through the gate, and saw approaching them from the big farm-house a smallish, dark, excitable-looking woman of about thirty-five. Her hair was touched with grey, her dark eyes looked wild. She walked with her hands behind her back. Her brother went forward. As it saw her, the big bay stallion whinneyed again. She came up excitedly.

"Are you home again, my boy!" she said tenderly to the horse, not to the man. The great beast shifted round to her, ducking his head. She smuggled into his mouth the wrinkled yellow apple she had been hiding behind her back, then she kissed him near the eyes. He gave a big sigh of pleasure. She held his head in her arms against her breast.

"Isn't he splendid!" said Miriam to her.

Miss Limb looked up. Her dark eyes glanced straight at Paul.

384

"Oh, good evening, Miss Leivers," she said. "It's ages since you've been down."

Miriam introduced her friends.

"Your horse *is* a fine fellow!" said Clara.

"Isn't he!" Again she kissed him. "As loving as any man!"

"More loving than most men, I should think," replied Clara.

"He's a nice boy!" cried the woman, again embracing the horse.

Clara, fascinated by the big beast, went up to stroke his neck.

"He's quite gentle," said Miss Limb. "Don't you think big fellows are?"

"He's a beauty!" replied Clara.

She wanted to look in his eyes. She wanted him to look at her.

"It's a pity he can't talk," she said.

"Oh, but he can—all but," replied the other woman.

Then her brother moved on with the horse.

"Are you coming in? *Do* come in, Mr.—I didn't catch it."

"Morel," said Miriam. "No, we won't come in, but we should like to go by the mill-pond."

"Yes—yes, do. Do you fish, Mr. Morel?"

"No," said Paul.

"Because if you do you might come and fish any time," said Miss Limb. "We scarcely see a soul from week's end to week's end. I should be thankful."

"What fish are there in the pond?" he asked.

They went through the front garden, over the sluice, and up the steep bank to the pond, which lay in shadow, with its two wooded islets. Paul walked with Miss Limb.

"I shouldn't mind swimming here," he said.

"Do," she replied. "Come when you like. My brother will be awfully pleased to talk with you. He is so quiet, because there is no one to talk to. Do come and swim."

Clara came up.

"It's a fine depth," she said, "and so clear."

"Yes," said Miss Limb.

"Do you swim?" said Paul. "Miss Limb was just saying we could come when we liked."

"Of course there's the farm-hands," said Miss Limb.

They talked a few moments, then went on up the wild hill, leaving the lonely, haggard-eyed woman on the bank.

The hillside was all ripe with sunshine. It was wild and tussocky, given over to rabbits. The three walked in silence. Then:

"She makes me feel uncomfortable," said Paul.

"You mean Miss Limb?" asked Miriam. "Yes."

"What's a matter with her? Is she going dotty with being too lonely?"

"Yes," said Miriam. "It's not the right sort of life for her. I think it's cruel to bury her there. I really ought to go and see her more. But—she upsets me."

"She makes me feel sorry for her—yes, and she bothers me," he said.

"I suppose," blurted Clara suddenly, "she wants a man."

The other two were silent for a few moments.

"But it's the loneliness sends her cracked," said Paul.

Clara did not answer, but strode on uphill. She was walking with her head hanging, her legs swinging as she kicked through the dead thistles and the tussocky grass, her arms hanging loose. Rather than walking, her handsome body seemed to be blundering up the hill. A hot wave went over Paul. He was curious about her. Perhaps life had been cruel to her. He forgot Miriam, who was walking beside him talking to him. She glanced at him, finding he did not answer her. His eyes were fixed ahead on Clara.

"Do you still think she is disagreeable?" she asked.

He did not notice that the question was sudden. It ran with his thoughts.

"Something's the matter with her," he said.

"Yes," answered Miriam.

They found at the top of the hill a hidden wild field, two sides of which were backed by the wood, the other sides by high loose hedges of hawthorn and elder bushes. Between these overgrown bushes were gaps that the cattle might have walked through had there been any cattle now. There the turf was smooth as velveteen, padded and holed by the rabbits. The field itself was coarse, and crowded

387

with tall, big cowslips that had never been cut. Clusters of strong flowers rose everywhere above the coarse tussocks of bent. It was like a roadstead crowded with tall, fairy shipping.

"Ah!" cried Miriam, and she looked at Paul, her dark eyes dilating. He smiled. Together they enjoyed the field of flowers. Clara, a little way off, was looking at the cowslips disconsolately. Paul and Miriam stayed close together, talking in subdued tones. He kneeled on one knee, quickly gathering the best blossoms, moving from tuft to tuft restlessly, talking softly all the time. Miriam plucked the flowers lovingly, lingering over them. He always seemed to her too quick and almost scientific. Yet his bunches had a natural beauty more than hers. He loved them, but as if they were his and he had a right to them. She had more reverence for them: they held something she had not.

The flowers were very fresh and sweet. He wanted to drink them. As he gathered them, he ate the little yellow trumpets. Clara was still wandering about disconsolately. Going towards her, he said:

"Why don't you get some?"

"I don't believe in it. They look better growing."

"But you'd like some?"

"They want to be left."

"I don't believe they do."

"I don't want the corpses of flowers about me," she said.

"That's a stiff, artificial notion," he said. "They don't die any quicker in water than on their roots.

And besides, they *look* nice in a bowl—they look jolly. And you only call a thing a corpse because it looks corpse-like."

"Whether it is one or not?" she argued.

"It isn't one to me. A dead flower isn't a corpse of a flower."

Clara now ignored him.

"And even so—what right have you to pull them?" she asked.

"Because I like them, and want them—and there's plenty of them."

"And that is sufficient?"

"Yes. Why not? I'm sure they'd smell nice in your room in Nottingham."

"And I should have the pleasure of watching them die."

"But then—it does not matter if they do die."

Whereupon he left her, and went stooping over the clumps of tangled flowers which thickly sprinkled the field like pale, luminous foam-clots. Miriam had come close. Clara was kneeling, breathing some scent from the cowslips.

"I think," said Miriam, "if you treat them with reverence you don't do them any harm. It is the spirit you pluck them in that matters."

"Yes," he said. "But no, you get 'em because you want 'em, and that's all." He held out his bunch.

Miriam was silent. He picked some more.

"Look at these!" he continued; "sturdy and lusty like little trees and like boys with fat legs."

Clara's hat lay on the grass not far off. She was

389

kneeling, bending forward still to smell the flowers. Her neck gave him a sharp pang, such a beautiful thing, yet not proud of itself just now. Her breasts swung slightly in her blouse. The arching curve of her back was beautiful and strong; she wore no stays. Suddenly, without knowing, he was scattering a handful of cowslips over her hair and neck, saying:

"Ashes to ashes, and dust to dust,
If the Lord won't have you the devil must."

The chill flowers fell on her neck. She looked up at him, with almost pitiful, scared grey eyes, wondering what he was doing. Flowers fell on her face, and she shut her eyes.

Suddenly, standing there above her, he felt awkward.

"I thought you wanted a funeral," he said, ill at ease.

Clara laughed strangely, and rose, picking the cowslips from her hair. She took up her hat and pinned it on. One flower had remained tangled in her hair. He saw, but would not tell her. He gathered up the flowers he had sprinkled over her.

At the edge of the wood the bluebells had flowed over into the field and stood there like flood-water. But they were fading now. Clara strayed up to them. He wandered after her. The bluebells pleased him.

390

"Look how they've come out of the wood!" he said.

Then she turned with a flash of warmth and of gratitude.

"Yes," she smiled.

His blood beat up.

"It makes me think of the wild men of the woods, how terrified they would be when they got breast to breast with the open space."

"Do you think they were?" she asked.

"I wonder which was more frightened among old tribes—those bursting out of their darkness of woods upon all the space of light, or those from the open tiptoeing into the forests."

"I should think the second," she answered.

"Yes, you *do* feel like one of the open space sort, trying to force yourself into the dark, don't you?"

"How should I know?" she answered queerly.

The conversation ended there.

The evening was deepening over the earth. Already the valley was full of shadow. One tiny square of light stood opposite at Crossleigh Bank Farm. Brightness was swimming on the tops of the hills. Miriam came up slowly, her face in her big, loose bunch of flowers, walking ankle-deep through the scattered froth of the cowslips. Beyond her the trees were coming into shape, all shadow.

"Shall we go?" she asked.

And the three turned away. They were all silent. Going down the path they could see the light of home right across, and on the ridge of the hill a thin

391

dark outline with little lights, where the colliery village touched the sky.

"It has been nice, hasn't it?" he asked.

Miriam murmured assent. Clara was silent.

"Don't you think so?" he persisted.

But she walked with her head up, and still did not answer. He could tell by the way she moved, as if she didn't care, that she suffered.

At this time Paul took his mother to Lincoln. She was bright and enthusiastic as ever, but as he sat opposite her in the railway carriage, she seemed to look frail. He had a momentary sensation as if she were slipping away from him. Then he wanted to get hold of her, to fasten her, almost to chain her. He felt he must keep hold of her with his hand.

They drew near to the city. Both were at the window looking for the cathedral.

"There she is, mother!" he cried.

They saw the great cathedral lying couchant above the plain.

"Ah!" she exclaimed. "So she is!"

He looked at his mother. Her blue eyes were watching the cathedral quietly. She seemed again to be beyond him. Something in the eternal repose of the uplifted cathedral, blue and noble against the sky, was reflected in her, something of the fatality. What was, *was*. With all his young will he could not alter it. He saw her face, the skin still fresh and pink and downy, but crow's-feet near her eyes, her eyelids steady, sinking a little, her mouth always closed with disillusion; and there was on her the same eternal look, as if she knew fate at last. He beat against it with all the strength of his soul.

"Look, mother, how big she is above the town! Think, there are streets and streets below her! She looks bigger than the city altogether."

"So she does!" exclaimed his mother, breaking bright into life again. But he had seen her sitting, looking steady out of the window at the cathedral, her face and eyes fixed, reflecting the relentlessness of life. And the crow's-feet near her eyes, and her mouth shut so hard, made him feel he would go mad.

They ate a meal that she considered wildly extravagant.

"Don't imagine I like it," she said, as she ate her cutlet. "I *don't* like it, I really don't! Just *think* of your money wasted!"

"You never mind my money," he said. "You forget I'm a fellow taking his girl for an outing."

And he bought her some blue violets.

"Stop it at once, sir!" she commanded. "How can I do it?"

"You've got nothing to do. Stand still!"

And in the middle of High Street he stuck the flowers in her coat.

"An old thing like me!" she said, sniffing.

"You see," he said, "I want people to think we're awful swells. So look ikey."

"I'll jowl your head," she laughed.

"Strut!" he commanded. "Be a fantail pigeon."

It took him an hour to get her through the street.

She stood above Glory Hole, she stood before Stone Bow, she stood everywhere, and exclaimed.

A man came up, took off his hat, and bowed to her.

"Can I show you the town, madam?"

"No, thank you," she answered. "I've got my son."

Then Paul was cross with her for not answering with more dignity.

"You go away with you!" she exclaimed. "Ha! that's the Jew's House. Now, do you remember that lecture, Paul——?"

But she could scarcely climb the cathedral hill. He did not notice. Then suddenly he found her unable to speak. He took her into a little public-house, where she rested.

"It's nothing," she said. "My heart is only a bit old; one must expect it."

He did not answer, but looked at her. Again his heart was crushed in a hot grip. He wanted to cry, he wanted to smash things in fury.

They set off again, pace by pace, so slowly. And every step seemed like a weight on his chest. He felt as if his heart would burst. At last they came to the top. She stood enchanted, looking at the castle gate, looking at the cathedral front. She had quite forgotten herself.

"Now *this* is better than I thought it could be!" she cried.

But he hated it. Everywhere he followed her, brooding. They sat together in the cathedral. They

394

attended a little service in the choir. She was timid.

"I suppose it is open to anybody?" she asked him.

"Yes," he replied. "Do you think they'd have the damned cheek to send us away."

"Well, I'm sure," she exclaimed, "they would if they heard your language."

Her face seemed to shine again with joy and peace during the service. And all the time he was wanting to rage and smash things and cry.

Afterwards, when they were leaning over the wall, looking at the town below, he blurted suddenly:

"Why can't a man have a *young* mother? What is she old for?"

"Well," his mother laughed, "she can scarcely help it."

"And why wasn't I the oldest son? Look—they say the young ones have the advantage—but look, *they* had the young mother. You should have had me for your eldest son."

"*I* didn't arrange it," she remonstrated. "Come to consider, you're as much to blame as me."

He turned on her, white, his eyes furious.

"What are you old for!" he said, mad with his impotence. "*Why* can't you walk? *Why* can't you come with me to places?"

"At one time," she replied, "I could have run up that hill a good deal better than you."

"What's the good of that to *me*?" he cried, hitting his fist on the wall. Then he became plaintive. "It's too bad of you to be ill, Little, it is——"

"Ill!" she cried. "I'm a bit old, and you'll have to put up with it, that's all."

They were quiet. But it was as much as they could bear. They got jolly again over tea. As they sat by Brayford, watching the boats, he told her about Clara. His mother asked him innumerable questions.

"Then who does she live with?"

"With her mother, on Bluebell Hill."

"And have they enough to keep them?"

"I don't think so. I think they do lace work."

"And wherein lies her charm, my boy?"

"I don't know that she's charming, mother. But she's nice. And she seems straight, you know—not a bit deep, not a bit."

"But she's a good deal older than you."

"She's thirty, I'm going of twenty-three."

"You haven't told me what you like her for."

"Because I don't know—a sort of defiant way she's got—a sort of angry way."

Mrs. Morel considered. She would have been glad now for her son to fall in love with some woman who would—she did not know what. But he fretted so, got so furious suddenly, and again was melancholic. She wished he knew some nice woman—— She did not know what she wished, but left it vague. At any rate, she was not hostile to the idea of Clara.

Annie, too, was getting married. Leonard had gone away to work in Birmingham. One week-end when he was home she had said to him:

396

"You don't look very well, my lad."

"I dunno," he said. "I feel anyhow or nohow, ma."

He called her "ma" already in his boyish fashion.

"Are you sure they're good lodgings?" she asked.

"Yes—yes. Only—it's a winder when you have to pour your own tea out—an' nobody to grouse if you team it in your saucer and sup it up. It somehow takes a' the taste out of it."

Mrs. Morel laughed.

"And so it knocks you up?" she said.

"I dunno. I want to get married," he blurted, twisting his fingers and looking down at his boots. There was a silence.

"But," she exclaimed, "I thought you said you'd wait another year."

"Yes, I did say so," he replied stubbornly.

Again she considered.

"And you know," she said, "Annie's a bit of a spendthrift. She's saved no more than eleven pounds. And I know, lad, you haven't had much chance."

He coloured up to the ears.

"I've got thirty-three quid," he said.

"It doesn't go far," she answered.

He said nothing, but twisted his fingers.

"And you know," she said, "I've nothing——"

"I didn't want, ma!" he cried, very red, suffering and remonstrating.

"No, my lad, I know. I was only wishing I had. And take away five pounds for the wedding and things—and it leaves twenty-nine pounds. You won't do much on that."

He twisted still, impotent, stubborn, not looking up.

"But do you really want to get married?" she asked. "Do you feel as if you ought?"

He gave her one straight look from his blue eyes.

"Yes," he said.

"Then," she replied, "we must all do the best we can for it, lad."

The next time he looked up there were tears in his eyes.

"I don't want Annie to feel handicapped," he said, struggling.

"My lad," she said, "you're steady—you've got a decent place. If a man had *needed* me I'd have married him on his last week's wages. She may find it a bit hard to start humbly. Young girls *are* like that. They look forward to the fine home they think they'll have. But *I* had expensive furniture. It's not everything."

So the wedding took place almost immediately. Arthur came home, and was splendid in uniform. Annie looked nice in a dove-grey dress that she could take for Sundays. Morel called her a fool for getting married, and was cool with his son-in-law. Mrs. Morel had white tips in her bonnet, and some white on her blouse, and was teased by both her sons for fancying herself so grand. Leonard was jolly and cordial, and felt a fearful fool. Paul could not quite see what Annie wanted to get married for.

He was fond of her, and she of him. Still, he hoped rather lugubriously that it would turn out all right. Arthur was astonishingly handsome in his scarlet and yellow, and he knew it well, but was secretly ashamed of the uniform. Annie cried her eyes up in the kitchen, on leaving her mother. Mrs. Morel cried a little, then patted her on the back and said:

"But don't cry, child, he'll be good to you."

Morel stamped and said she was a fool to go and tie herself up. Leonard looked white and overwrought. Mrs. Morel said to him:

"I s'll trust her to you, my lad, and hold you responsible for her."

"You can," he said, nearly dead with the ordeal. And it was all over.

When Morel and Arthur were in bed, Paul sat talking, as he often did, with his mother.

"You're not sorry she's married, mother, are you?" he asked.

"I'm not sorry she's married—but—it seems strange that she should go from me. It even seems to me hard that she can prefer to go with her Leonard. That's how mothers are—I know it's silly."

"And shall you be miserable about her?"

"When I think of my own wedding day," his mother answered, "I can only hope her life will be different."

"But you can trust him to be good to her?"

"Yes, yes. They say he's not good enough for her. But I say if a man is *genuine*, as he is, and a girl is fond of him—then—it should be all right. He's as good as she."

"So you don't mind?"

"I would *never* have let a daughter of mine marry a man I didn't *feel* to be genuine through and through. And yet, there's a gap now she's gone."

They were both miserable, and wanted her back again. It seemed to Paul his mother looked lonely, in her new black silk blouse with its bit of white trimming.

"At any rate, mother, I s'll never marry," he said.

"Ay, they all say that, my lad. You've not met the one yet. Only wait a year or two."

"But I shan't marry, mother. I shall live with you, and we'll have a servant."

"Ay, my lad, it's easy to talk. We'll see when the time comes."

"What time? I'm nearly twenty-three."

"Yes, you're not one that would marry young. But in three years' time——"

"I shall be with you just the same."

"We'll see, my boy, we'll see."

"But you don't want me to marry?"

"I shouldn't like to think of you going through your life without anybody to care for you and do—no."

"And you think I ought to marry?"

"Sooner or later every man ought."

"But you'd rather it were later."

"It would be hard—and very hard. It's as they say:

" 'A son's my son till he takes him a wife,
     But my daughter's my daughter the whole of
     her life.' "

"And you think I'd let a wife take me from you?"

"Well, you wouldn't ask her to marry your mother as well as you," Mrs. Morel smiled.

"She could do what she liked; she wouldn't have to interfere."

"She wouldn't—till she'd got you—and then you'd see."

"I never will see. I'll never marry while I've got you—I won't."

"But I shouldn't like to leave you with nobody, my boy," she cried.

"You're not going to leave me. What are you? Fifty-three! I'll give you till seventy-five. There you are, I'm fat and forty-four. Then I'll marry a staid body. See!"

His mother sat and laughed.

"Go to bed," she said—"go to bed."

"And we'll have a pretty house, you and me, and a servant, and it'll be just all right. I s'll perhaps be rich with my painting."

"Will you go to bed!"

"And then you s'll have a pony-carriage. See yourself—a little Queen Victoria trotting round."

"I tell you to go to bed," she laughed.

He kissed her and went. His plans for the future were always the same.

Mrs. Morel sat brooding—about her daughter,

401

about Paul, about Arthur. She fretted at losing Annie. The family was very closely bound. And she felt she *must* live now, to be with her children. Life was so rich for her. Paul wanted her, and so did Arthur. Arthur never knew how deeply he loved her. He was a creature of the moment. Never yet had he been forced to realise himself. The army had disciplined his body, but not his soul. He was in perfect health and very handsome. His dark, vigorous hair sat close to his smallish head. There was something childish about his nose, something almost girlish about his dark blue eyes. But he had the full red mouth of a man under his brown moustache, and his jaw was strong. It was his father's mouth; it was the nose and eyes of her own mother's people—good-looking, weak-principled folk. Mrs. Morel was anxious about him. Once he had really run the rig he was safe. But how far would he go?

The army had not really done him any good. He resented bitterly the authority of the officers. He hated having to obey as if he were an animal. But he had too much sense to kick. So he turned his attention to getting the best out of it. He could sing, he was a boon-companion. Often he got into scrapes, but they were the manly scrapes that are easily condoned. So he made a good time out of it, whilst his self-respect was in suppression. He trusted to his good looks and handsome figure, his refinement, his decent education to get him most of what he wanted, and he was not disappointed. Yet he was restless. Something seemed to gnaw him inside. He was never still, he was never alone. With his mother he was rather humble. Paul he admired and loved and despised slightly. And Paul admired and loved and despised him slightly.

Mrs. Morel had had a few pounds left to her by her father, and she decided to buy her son out of the army. He was wild with joy. Now he was like a lad taking a holiday.

He had always been fond of Beatrice Wyld, and during his furlough he picked up with her again. She was stronger and better in health. The two often went long walks together, Arthur taking her arm in soldier's fashion, rather stiffly. And she came to play the piano whilst he sang. Then Arthur would unhook his tunic collar. He grew flushed, his eyes were bright, he sang in a manly tenor. Afterwards they sat together on the sofa. He seemed to flaunt his body: she was aware of him so—the strong chest, the sides, the thighs in their close-fitting trousers.

He liked to lapse into the dialect when he talked to her. She would sometimes smoke with him. Occasionally she would only take a few whiffs at his cigarette.

"Nay," he said to her one evening, when she reached for his cigarette. "Nay, tha doesna. I'll gi'e thee a smoke kiss if ter's a mind."

"I wanted a whiff, no kiss at all," she answered.

"Well, an' tha s'lt ha'e a whiff," he said, "along wi' t' kiss."

"I want a draw at thy fag," she cried, snatching for the cigarette between his lips.

He was sitting with his shoulder touching her. She was small and quick as lightning. He just escaped.

"I'll gi'e thee a smoke kiss," he said.

"Tha'rt a knivey nuisance, Arty Morel," she said, sitting back.

"Ha'e a smoke kiss?"

The soldier leaned forward to her, smiling. His face was near hers.

"Shonna!" she replied, turning away her head.

He took a draw at his cigarette, and pursed up his mouth, and put his lips close to her. His dark-brown cropped moustache stood out like a brush. She looked at the puckered crimson lips, then suddenly snatched the cigarette from his fingers and darted away. He, leaping after her, seized the comb from her back hair. She turned, threw the cigarette at him. He picked it up, put it in his mouth, and sat down.

"Nuisance!" she cried. "Give me my comb!"

She was afraid that her hair, specially done for him, would come down. She stood with her hands to her head. He hid the comb between his knees.

"I've non got it," he said.

The cigarette trembled between his lips with laughter as he spoke.

"Liar!" she said.

" 'S true as I'm here!" he laughed, showing his hands.

404

"You brazen imp!" she exclaimed, rushing and scuffling for the comb, which he had under his knees. As she wrestled with him, pulling at his smooth, tight-covered knees, he laughed till he lay back on the sofa shaking with laughter. The cigarette fell from his mouth almost singeing his throat. Under his delicate tan the blood flushed up, and he laughed till his blue eyes were blinded, his throat swollen almost to choking. Then he sat up. Beatrice was putting in her comb.

"Tha tickled me, Beat," he said thickly.

Like a flash her small white hand went out and smacked his face. He started up, glaring at her. They stared at each other. Slowly the flush mounted her cheek, she dropped her eyes, then her head. He sat down sulkily. She went into the scullery to adjust her hair. In private there she shed a few tears, she did not know what for.

When she returned she was pursed up close. But it was only a film over her fire. He, with ruffled hair, was sulking upon the sofa. She sat down opposite, in the arm-chair, and neither spoke. The clock ticked in the silence like blows.

"You are a little cat, Beat," he said at length, half apologetically.

"Well, you shouldn't be brazen," she replied.

There was again a long silence. He whistled to himself like a man much agitated but defiant. Suddenly she went across to him and kissed him.

"Did it, pore fing!" she mocked.

He lifted his face, smiling curiously.

"Kiss?" he invited her.

"Daren't I?" she asked.

"Go on!" he challenged, his mouth lifted to her. Deliberately, and with a peculiar quivering smile that seemed to overspread her whole body, she put her mouth on his. Immediately his arms folded round her. As soon as the long kiss was finished she drew back her head from him, put her delicate fingers on his neck, through the open collar. Then she closed her eyes, giving herself up again in a kiss.

She acted of her own free will. What she would do she did, and made nobody responsible.

Paul felt life changing around him. The conditions of youth were gone. Now it was a home of grown-up people. Annie was a married woman, Arthur was following his own pleasure in a way unknown to his folk. For so long they had all lived at home, and gone out to pass their time. But now, for Annie and Arthur, life lay outside their mother's house. They came home for holiday and for rest. So there was that strange, half-empty feeling about the house, as if the birds had flown. Paul became more and more unsettled. Annie and Arthur had gone. He was restless to follow. Yet home was for him beside his mother. And still there was something else, something outside, something he wanted.

He grew more and more restless. Miriam did not satisfy him. His old mad desire to be with her grew weaker. Sometimes he met Clara in Nottingham, sometimes he went to meetings with her, sometimes he saw her at Willey Farm. But on these last occasions the situation became strained. There was a triangle of antagonism between Paul and Clara and Miriam. With Clara he took on a smart, worldly, mocking tone very antagonistic to Miriam. It did not matter what went before. She might be intimate and sad with him. Then as soon as Clara appeared, it all vanished, and he played to the newcomer.

Miriam had one beautiful evening with him in the hay. He had been on the horse-rake, and having finished, came to help her to put the hay in cocks. Then he talked to her of his hopes and despairs, and his whole soul seemed to lie bare before her. She felt as if she watched the very quivering stuff of life in him. The moon came out: they walked home together: he seemed to have come to her because he needed her so badly, and she listened to him, gave him all her love and her faith. It seemed to her he brought her the best of himself to keep, and that she would guard it all her life. Nay, the sky did not cherish the stars more surely and eternally than she would guard the good in the soul of Paul Morel. She went on home alone, feeling exalted, glad in her faith.

And then, the next day, Clara came. They were to have tea in the hayfield. Miriam watched the evening drawing to gold and shadow. And all the time Paul was sporting with Clara. He made higher and higher heaps of hay that they were jumping over. Miriam did not care for the game, and stood aside. Edgar and Geoffrey and Maurice and Clara and

Paul jumped. Paul won, because he was light. Clara's blood was roused. She could run like an Amazon. Paul loved the determined way she rushed at the haycock and leaped, landed on the other side, her breasts shaken, her thick hair come undone.

"You touched!" he cried. "You touched!"

"No!" she flashed, turning to Edgar. "I didn't touch, did I? Wasn't I clear?"

"I couldn't say," laughed Edgar.

None of them could say.

"But you touched," said Paul. "You're beaten."

"I did *not* touch!" she cried.

"As plain as anything," said Paul.

"Box his ears for me!" she cried to Edgar.

"Nay," Edgar laughed. "I daren't. You must do it yourself."

"And nothing can alter the fact that you touched," laughed Paul.

She was furious with him. Her little triumph before these lads and men was gone. She had forgotten herself in the game. Now he was to humble her.

"I think you are despicable!" she said.

And again he laughed, in a way that tortured Miriam.

"And I *knew* you couldn't jump that heap," he teased.

She turned her back on him. Yet everybody could see that the only person she listened to, or was conscious of, was he, and he of her. It pleased the men to see this battle between them. But Miriam was tortured.

408

Paul could choose the lesser in place of the higher, she saw. He could be unfaithful to himself, unfaithful to the real, deep Paul Morel. There was a danger of his becoming frivolous, of his running after his satisfaction like any Arthur, or like his father. It made Miriam bitter to think that he should throw away his soul for this flippant traffic of triviality with Clara. She walked in bitterness and silence, while the other two rallied each other, and Paul sported.

And afterwards, he would not own it, but he was rather ashamed of himself, and prostrated himself before Miriam. Then again he rebelled.

"It's not religious to be religious," he said. "I reckon a crow is religious when it sails across he sky. But it only does it because it feels itself carried to where it's going, not because it thinks it is being eternal."

But Miriam knew that one should be religious in everything, have God, whatever God might be, present in everything.

"I don't believe God knows such a lot about Himself," he cried. "God doesn't *know* things, He *is* things. And I'm sure He's not soulful."

And then it seemed to her that Paul was arguing God on to his own side, because he wanted his own way and his own pleasure. There was a long battle between him and her. He was utterly unfaithful to her even in her own presence; then he was ashamed, then repentant; then he hated her, and went off again. Those were the ever-recurring conditions.

409

She fretted him to the bottom of his soul. There she remained—sad, pensive, a worshipper. And he caused her sorrow. Half the time he grieved for her, half the time he hated her. She was his conscience; and he felt, somehow, he had got a conscience that was too much for him. He could not leave her, because in one way she did hold the best of him. He could not stay with her because she did not take the rest of him, which was three-quarters. So he chafed himself into rawness over her.

When she was twenty-one he wrote her a letter which could only have been written to her.

"May I speak of our old, worn love, this last time. It, too, is changing, is it not? Say, has not the body of that love died, and left you its invulnerable soul? You see, I can give you a spirit love, I have given it you this long, long time; but not embodied passion. See, you are a nun. I have given you what I would give a holy nun—as a mystic monk to a mystic nun. Surely you esteem it best. Yet you regret—no, have regretted—the other. In all our relations no body enters. I do not talk to you through the senses—rather through the spirit. That is why we cannot love in the common sense. Ours is not an everyday affection. As yet we are mortal, and to live side by side with one another would be dreadful, for somehow with you I cannot long be trivial, and, you know, to be always beyond this mortal state would be to lose it. If people marry, they must live together as affectionate humans, who may be commonplace with each other without feeling awkward—not as two souls. So I feel it.

"Ought I to send this letter?—I doubt it. But there—it is best to understand. *Au revoir.*"

Miriam read this letter twice, after which she sealed it up. A year later she broke the seal to show her mother the letter.

"You are a nun—you are a nun." The words went into her heart again and again. Nothing he ever had said had gone into her so deeply, fixedly, like a mortal wound.

She answered him two days after the party.

" 'Our intimacy would have been all-beautiful but for one little mistake,' " she quoted. "Was the mistake mine?"

Almost immediately he replied to her from Nottingham, sending her at the same time a little "Omar Khayyám".

"I am glad you answered; you are so calm and natural you put me to shame. What a ranter I am! We are often out of sympathy. But in fundamentals we may always be together I think.

"I must thank you for your sympathy with my painting and drawing. Many a sketch is dedicated to you. I do look forward to your criticisms, which, to my shame and glory, are always grand appreciations. It is a lovely joke, that. *Au revoir.*"

This was the end of the first phase of Paul's love affair. He was now about twenty-three years old, and, though still virgin, the sex instinct that Miriam had over-refined for so long now grew particularly strong. Often, as he talked to Clara Dawes, came that thickening and quickening of his blood, that peculiar concentration in the breast, as if something were alive there, a new self or a new centre of consciousness, warning him that sooner or later he would have to ask one woman or another. But he belonged to Miriam. Of that she was so fixedly sure that he allowed her right.

# 10

## CLARA

WHEN he was twenty-three years old, Paul sent in a landscape to the winter exhibition at Nottingham Castle. Miss Jordan had taken a good deal of interest in him, and invited him to her house, where he met other artists. He was beginning to grow ambitious.

One morning the postman came just as he was washing in the scullery. Suddenly he heard a wild noise from his mother. Rushing into the kitchen, he found her standing on the hearth-rug wildly waving a letter and crying "Hurrah!" as if she had gone mad. He was shocked and frightened.

"Why, mother!" he exclaimed.

She flew to him, flung her arms round him for a moment, then waved the letter, crying:

"Hurrah, my boy! I knew we should do it!"

He was afraid of her—the small, severe woman with greying hair suddenly bursting out in such frenzy. The postman came running back, afraid something had happened. They saw his tipped cap over the short curtains. Mrs. Morel rushed to the door.

"His picture's got first prize, Fred," she cried, "and is sold for twenty guineas."

"My word, that's something like!" said the young postman, whom they had known all his life.

"And Major Moreton has bought it!" she cried.

"It looks like meanin' something, that does, Mrs. Morel," said the postman, his blue eyes bright. He was glad to have brought such a lucky letter. Mrs. Morel went indoors and sat down, trembling. Paul was afraid lest she might have misread the letter, and might be disappointed after all. He scrutinised it once, twice. Yes, he became convinced it was true. Then he sat down, his heart beating with joy.

"Mother!" he exclaimed.

"Didn't I *say* we should do it!" she said, pretending she was not crying.

He took the kettle off the fire and mashed the tea.

"You didn't think, mother——" he began tentatively.

"No, my son—not so much—but I expected a good deal."

"But not so much," he said.

"No—no—but I knew we should do it."

And then she recovered her composure, apparently at least. He sat with his shirt turned back, showing his young throat almost like a girl's, and the towel in his hand, his hair sticking up wet.

"Twenty guineas, mother! That's just what you wanted to buy Arthur out. Now you needn't borrow any. It'll just do."

"Indeed, I shan't take it all," she said.

"But why?"

"Because I shan't."

414

"Well—you have twelve pounds, I'll have nine."

They cavilled about sharing the twenty guineas. She wanted to take only the five pounds she needed. He would not hear of it. So they got over the stress of emotion by quarrelling.

Morel came home at night from the pit, saying:

"They tell me Paul's got first prize for his picture, and sold it to Lord Henry Bentley for fifty pound."

"Oh, what stories people do tell!" she cried.

"Ha!" he answered. "I said I wor sure it wor a lie. But they said tha'd told Fred Hodgkisson."

"As if I would tell him such stuff!"

"Ha!" assented the miner.

But he was disappointed nevertheless.

"It's true he has got the first prize," said Mrs. Morel.

The miner sat heavily in his chair.

"Has he, beguy!" he exclaimed.

He stared across the room fixedly.

"But as for fifty pounds—such nonsense!" She was silent awhile. "Major Moreton bought it for twenty guineas, that's true."

"Twenty guineas! Tha niver says!" exclaimed Morel.

"Yes, and it was worth it."

"Ay!" he said. "I don't misdoubt it. But twenty guineas for a bit of a paintin' as he knocked off in an hour or two!"

He was silent with conceit of his son. Mrs. Morel sniffed, as if it were nothing.

"And when does he handle th' money?" asked the collier.

"That I couldn't tell you. When the picture is sent home, I suppose."

There was silence. Morel stared at the sugar-basin instead of eating his dinner. His black arm, with the hand all gnarled with work lay on the table. His wife pretended not to see him rub the back of his hand across his eyes, nor the smear in the coal-dust on his black face.

"Yes, an' that other lad 'ud 'a done as much if they hadna ha' killed 'im," he said quietly.

The thought of William went through Mrs. Morel like a cold blade. It left her feeling she was tired, and wanted rest.

Paul was invited to dinner at Mr. Jordan's. Afterwards he said:

"Mother, I want an evening suit."

"Yes, I was afraid you would," she said. She was glad. There was a moment or two of silence. "There's that one of William's," she continued, "that I know cost four pounds ten and which he'd only worn three times."

"Should you like me to wear it, mother?" he asked.

"Yes. I think it would fit you—at least the coat. The trousers would want shortening."

He went upstairs and put on the coat and vest. Coming down, he looked strange in a flannel collar and a flannel shirt-front, with an evening coat and vest. It was rather large.

"The tailor can make it right," she said,

416

smoothing her hand over his shoulder. "It's beautiful stuff. I never could find in my heart to let your father wear the trousers, and very glad I am now."

And as she smoothed her hand over the silk collar she thought of her eldest son. But this son was living enough inside the clothes. She passed her hand down his back to feel him. He was alive and hers. The other was dead.

He went out to dinner several times in his evening suit that had been William's. Each time his mother's heart was firm with pride and joy. He was started now. The studs she and the children had bought for William were in his shirt-front; he wore one of William's dress shirts. But he had an elegant figure. His face was rough, but warm-looking and rather pleasing. He did not look particularly a gentleman, but she thought he looked quite a man.

He told her everything that took place, everything that was said. It was as if she had been there. And he was dying to introduce her to these new friends who had dinner at seven-thirty in the evening.

"Go along with you!" she said. "What do they want to know me for?"

"They do!" he cried indignantly. "If they want to know me—and they say they do—then they want to know you, because you are quite as clever as I am."

"Go along with you, child!" she laughed.

But she began to spare her hands. They, too, were work-gnarled now. The skin was shiny with so

417

much hot water, the knuckles rather swollen. But she began to be careful to keep them out of soda. She regretted what they had been—so small and exquisite. And when Annie insisted on her having more stylish blouses to suit her age, she submitted. She even went so far as to allow a black velvet bow to be placed on her hair. Then she sniffed in her sarcastic manner, and was sure she looked a sight. But she looked a lady, Paul declared, as much as Mrs. Major Moreton, and far, far nicer. The family was coming on. Only Morel remained unchanged, or rather, lapsed slowly.

Paul and his mother now had long discussions about life. Religion was fading into the background. He had shovelled away all the beliefs that would hamper him, had cleared the ground, and come more or less to the bedrock of belief that one should feel inside oneself for right and wrong, and should have the patience to gradually realise one's God. Now life interested him more.

"You know," he said to his mother, "I don't want to belong to the well-to-do middle class. I like my common people best. I belong to the common people."

"But if anyone else said so, my son, wouldn't you be in a tear. *You* know you consider yourself equal to any gentleman."

"In myself," he answered, "not in my class or my education or my manners. But in myself I am."

"Very well, then. Then why talk about the common people?"

418

"Because—the difference between people isn't in their class, but in themselves. Only from the middle classes one gets ideas, and from the common people— life itself, warmth. You feel their hates and loves."

"It's all very well, my boy. But, then, why don't you go and talk to your father's pals?"

"But they're rather different."

"Not at all. They're the common people. After all, whom do you mix with now—among the common people? Those that exchange ideas, like the middle classes. The rest don't interest you."

"But—there's the life——"

"I don't believe there's a jot more life from Miriam than you could get from any educated girl— say Miss Moreton. It is *you* who are snobbish about class."

She frankly *wanted* him to climb into the middle classes, a thing not very difficult, she knew. And she wanted him in the end to marry a lady.

Now she began to combat him in his restless fretting. He still kept up his connection with Miriam, could neither break free nor go the whole length of engagement. And this indecision seemed to bleed him of his energy. Moreover, his mother suspected him of an unrecognised leaning towards Clara, and, since the latter was a married woman, she wished he would fall in love with one of the girls in a better station of life. But he was stupid, and would refuse to love or even to admire a girl much, just because she was his social superior.

"My boy," said his mother to him, "all your

419

cleverness, your breaking away from old things, and taking life in your own hands, doesn't seem to bring you much happiness."

"What is happiness!" he cried. "It's nothing to me! How *am* I to be happy?"

The plump question disturbed her.

"That's for you to judge, my lad. But if you could meet some *good* woman who would *make* you happy—and you began to think of settling your life—when you have the means—so that you could work without all this fretting—it would be much better for you."

He frowned. His mother caught him on the raw of his wound of Miriam. He pushed the tumbled hair off his forehead, his eyes full of pain and fire.

"You mean easy, mother," he cried. "That's a woman's whole doctrine for life—ease of soul and physical comfort. And I do despise it."

"Oh, do you!" replied his mother. "And do you call yours a divine discontent?"

"Yes. I don't care about its divinity. But damn your happiness! So long as life's full, it doesn't matter whether it's happy or not. I'm afraid your happiness would bore me."

"You never give it a chance," she said. Then suddenly all her passion of grief over him broke out. "But it does matter!" she cried. "And you *ought* to be happy, you ought to try to be happy, to live to be happy. How could I bear to think your life wouldn't be a happy one!"

"Your own's been bad enough, mater, but it

420

hasn't left you so much worse off than the folk who've been happier. I reckon you've done well. And I am the same. Aren't I well enough off?"

"You're not, my son. Battle—battle—and suffer. It's about all you do, as far as I can see."

"But why not, my dear? I tell you it's the best——"

"It isn't. And one *ought* to be happy, one *ought*."

By this time Mrs. Morel was trembling violently. Struggles of this kind often took place between her and her son, when she seemed to fight for his very life against his own will to die. He took her in his arms. She was ill and pitiful.

"Never mind, Little," he murmured. "So long as you don't feel life's paltry and a miserable business, the rest doesn't matter, happiness or unhappiness."

She pressed him to her.

"But I want you to be happy," she said pathetically.

"Eh, my dear—say rather you want me to live."

Mrs. Morel felt as if her heart would break for him. At this rate she knew he would not live. He had that poignant carelessness about himself, his own suffering, his own life, which is a form of slow suicide. It almost broke her heart. With all the passion of her strong nature she hated Miriam for having in this subtle way undermined his joy. It did not matter to her that Miriam could not help it. Miriam did it, and she hated her.

She wished so much he would fall in love with a girl equal to be his mate—educated and strong. But he would not look at anybody above him in station. He seemed to like Mrs. Dawes. At any rate that feeling was wholesome. His mother prayed and prayed for him, that he might not be wasted. That was all her prayer—not for his soul or his righteousness, but that he might not be wasted. And while he slept, for hours and hours she thought and prayed for him.

He drifted away from Miriam imperceptibly, without knowing he was going. Arthur only left the army to be married. The baby was born six months after his wedding. Mrs. Morel got him a job under the firm again, at twenty-one shillings a week. She furnished for him, with the help of Beatrice's mother, a little cottage of two rooms. He was caught now. It did not matter how he kicked and struggled, he was fast. For a time he chafed, was irritable with his young wife, who loved him; he went almost distracted when the baby, which was delicate, cried or gave trouble. He grumbled for hours to his mother. She only said: "Well, my lad, you did it yourself, now you must make the best of it." And then the grit came out in him. He buckled to work, undertook his responsibilities, acknowledged that he belonged to his wife and child, and did make a good best of it. He had never been very closely inbound into the family. Now he was gone altogether.

The months went slowly along. Paul had more or less got into connection with the Socialist, Suffragette, Unitarian people in Nottingham, owing to his acquaintance with Clara. One day a friend of his and of Clara's, in Bestwood, asked him to take a message to Mrs. Dawes. He went in the evening across Sneinton Market to Bluebell Hill. He found the house in a mean little street paved with granite cobbles and having causeways of dark blue, grooved bricks. The front door went up a step from off this rough pavement, where the feet of the passers-by rasped and clattered. The brown paint on the door was so old that the naked wood showed between the rents. He stood on the street below and knocked. There came a heavy footstep; a large stout woman of about sixty towered above him. He looked up at her from the pavement. She had a rather severe face.

She admitted him into the parlour, which opened on to the street. It was a small, stuffy, defunct room, of mahogany, and deathly enlargements of photographs of departed people done in carbon. Mrs. Radford left him. She was stately, almost martial. In a moment Clara appeared. She flushed deeply, and he was covered with confusion. It seemed as if she did not like being discovered in her home circumstances.

"I thought it couldn't be your voice," she said.

But she might as well be hung for a sheep as for a lamb. She invited him out of the mausoleum of a parlour into the kitchen.

That was a little, darkish room too, but it was smothered in white lace. The mother had seated herself again by the cupboard, and was drawing thread from a vast web of lace. A clump of fluff and ravelled cotton was at her right hand, a heap of three-quarter-inch lace lay on her left, whilst in front of her was the mountain of lace web, piling the hearthrug. Threads of curly cotton, pulled out from between the lengths of lace, strewed over the fender and the fireplace. Paul dared not go forward, for fear of treading on piles of white stuff.

On the table was a jenny for carding the lace. There was a pack of brown cardboard squares, a pack of cards of lace, a little box of pins, and on the sofa lay a heap of drawn lace.

The room was all lace, and it was so dark and warm that the white, snowy stuff seemed the more distinct.

"If you're coming in you won't have to mind the work," said Mrs. Radford. "I know we're about blocked up. But sit you down."

Clara, much embarrassed, gave him a chair against the wall opposite the white heaps. Then she herself took her place on the sofa, shamedly.

"Will you drink a bottle of stout?" Mrs. Radford asked. "Clara, get him a bottle of stout."

He protested, but Mrs. Radford insisted.

"You look as if you could do with it," she said. "Haven't you never any more colour than that?"

"It's only a thick skin I've got that doesn't show the blood through," he answered.

Clara, ashamed and chagrined, brought him a bottle of stout and a glass. He poured out some of the black stuff.

"Well," he said, lifting the glass, "here's health!"

"And thank you," said Mrs. Radford.

He took a drink of stout.

"And light yourself a cigarette, so long as you don't set the house on fire," said Mrs. Radford.

"Thank you," he replied.

"Nay, you needn't thank me," she answered. "I s'll be glad to smell a bit of smoke in th' 'ouse again. A house o' women is as dead as a house wi' no fire, to my thinkin'. I'm not a spider as likes a corner to myself. I like a man about, if he's only something to snap at."

Clara began to work. Her jenny spun with a subdued buzz; the white lace hopped from between her fingers on to the card. It was filled; she snipped off the length, and pinned the end down to the banded lace. Then she put a new card in her jenny. Paul watched her. She sat square and magnificent. Her throat and arms were bare. The blood still mantled below her ears; she bent her head in shame of her humility. Her face was set on her work. Her arms were creamy and full of life beside the white lace; her large, well-kept hands worked with a balanced movement, as if nothing would hurry them. He, not knowing, watched her all the time. He saw the arch of her neck from the shoulder, as she bent her head; he saw the coil of dun hair; he watched her moving, gleaming arms.

"I've heard a bit about you from Clara," continued the mother. "You're in Jordan's, aren't you?" She drew her lace unceasing.

425

"Yes."

"Ay, well, and I can remember when Thomas Jordan used to ask *me* for one of my toffees."

"Did he?" laughed Paul. "And did he get it?"

"Sometimes he did, sometimes he didn't—which was latterly. For he's the sort that takes all and gives naught, he is—or used to be."

"I think he's very decent," said Paul.

"Yes; well, I'm glad to hear it."

Mrs. Radford looked across at him steadily. There was something determined about her that he liked. Her face was falling loose, but her eyes were calm, and there was something strong in her that made it seem she was not old; merely her wrinkles and loose cheeks were an anachronism. She had the strength and sang-froid of a woman in the prime of life. She continued drawing the lace with slow, dignified movements. The big web came up inevitably over her apron; the length of lace fell away at her side. Her arms were finely shapen, but glossy and yellow as old ivory. They had not the peculiar dull gleam that made Clara's so fascinating to him.

"And you've been going with Miriam Leivers?" the mother asked him.

"Well——" he answered.

"Yes, she's a nice girl," she continued. "She's very nice, but she's a bit too much above this world to suit my fancy."

"She is a bit like that," he agreed.

"She'll never be satisfied till she's got wings and can fly over everybody's head, she won't," she said.

426

Clara broke in, and he told her his message. spoke humbly to him. He had surprised her in drudgery. To have her humble made him feel a: he were lifting his head in expectation.

"Do you like jennying?" he asked.

"What can a woman do!" she replied bitterly.

"Is it sweated?"

"More or less. Isn't *all* woman's work? That's another trick the men have played, since we force ourselves into the labour market."

"Now then, you shut up about the men," said her mother. "If the women wasn't fools, the men wouldn't be bad uns, that's what I say. No man was ever that bad wi' me but what he got it back again. Not but what they're a lousy lot, there's no denying it."

"But they're all right really, aren't they?" he asked.

"Well, they're a bit different from women," she answered.

"Would you care to be back at Jordan's?" he asked Clara.

"I don't think so," she replied.

"Yes, she would!" cried her mother; "thank he stars if she could get back. Don't you listen to he She's for ever on that 'igh horse of hers, an' i back's that thin an' starved it'll cut her i' two one these days."

Clara suffered badly from her mother. Paul fel if his eyes were coming very wide open. Wasn' to take Clara's fulminations so seriously, after She spun steadily at her work. He experienc

thrill of joy, thinking she might need his help. She seemed denied and deprived of so much. And her arm moved mechanically, that should never have been subdued to a mechanism, and her head was bowed to the lace, that never should have been bowed. She seemed to be stranded there among the refuse that life has thrown away, doing her jennying. It was a bitter thing to her to be put aside by life, as if it had no use for her. No wonder she protested.

She came with him to the door. He stood below in the mean street, looking up at her. So fine she was in her stature and her bearing, she reminded him of Juno dethroned. As she stood in the doorway, she winced from the street, from her surroundings.

"And you will go with Mrs. Hodgkisson to Hucknall?"

He was talking quite meaninglessly, only watching her. Her grey eyes at last met his. They looked dumb with humiliation, pleading with a kind of captive misery. He was shaken and at a loss. He had thought her high and mighty.

When he left her, he wanted to run. He went to the station in a sort of dream, and was at home without realising he had moved out of her street.

He had an idea that Susan, the overseer of the Spiral girls, was about to be married. He asked her the next day.

"I say, Susan, I heard a whisper of your getting married. What about it?"

Susan flushed red.

"Who's been talking to you?" she replied.

428

"Nobody. I merely heard a whisper that you *were* thinking——"

"Well, I am, though you needn't tell anybody. What's more, I wish I wasn't!"

"Nay, Susan, you won't make me believe that."

"Shan't I? You *can* believe it, though. I'd rather stop here a thousand times."

Paul was perturbed.

"Why, Susan?"

The girl's colour was high, and her eyes flashed.

"That's why!"

"And must you?"

For answer, she looked at him. There was about him a candour and gentleness which made the women trust him. He understood.

"Ah, I'm sorry," he said.

Tears came to her eyes.

"But you'll see it'll turn out all right. You'll make the best of it," he continued rather wistfully.

"There's nothing else for it."

"Yea, there's making the worst of it. Try and make it all right."

He soon made occasion to call again on Clara.

"Would you," he said, "care to come back to Jordan's?"

She put down her work, laid her beautiful arms on the table, and looked at him for some moments without answering. Gradually the flush mounted her cheek.

"Why?" she asked.

Paul felt rather awkward.

429

"Well, because Susan is thinking of leaving," he said.

Clara went on with her jennying. The white lace leaped in little jumps and bounds on to the card. He waited for her. Without raising her head, she said at last, in a peculiar low voice:

"Have you said anything about it?"

"Except to you, not a word."

There was again a long silence.

"I will apply when the advertisement is out," she said.

"You will apply before that. I will let you know exactly when."

She went on spinning her little machine, and did not contradict him.

Clara came to Jordan's. Some of the older hands, Fanny among them, remembered her earlier rule, and cordially disliked the memory. Clara had always been "ikey", reserved, and superior. She had never mixed with the girls as one of themselves. If she had occasion to find fault, she did it coolly and with perfect politeness, which the defaulter felt to be a bigger insult than crossness. Towards Fanny, the poor, overstrung hunchback, Clara was unfailingly compassionate and gentle, as a result of which Fanny shed more bitter tears than ever the rough tongues of the other overseers had caused her.

There was something in Clara that Paul disliked, and much that piqued him. If she were about, he always watched her strong throat or her neck, upon

430

which the blonde hair grew low and fluffy. There was a fine down, almost invisible, upon the skin of her face and arms, and when once he had perceived it, he saw it always.

When he was at his work, painting in the afternoon, she would come and stand near to him, perfectly motionless. Then he felt her, though she neither spoke nor touched him. Although she stood a yard away he felt as if he were in contact with her. Then he could paint no more. He flung down the brushes, and turned to talk to her.

Sometimes she praised his work; sometimes she was critical and cold.

"You are affected in that piece," she would say; and, as there was an element of truth in her condemnation, his blood boiled with anger.

Again: "What of this?" he would ask enthusiastically.

"H'm!" She made a small doubtful sound. "It doesn't interest me much."

"Because you don't understand it," he retorted.

"Then why ask me about it?"

"Because I thought you would understand."

She would shrug her shoulders in scorn of his work. She maddened him. He was furious. Then he abused her, and went into passionate exposition of his stuff. This amused and stimulated her. But she never owned that she had been wrong.

During the ten years that she had belonged to the women's movement she had acquired a fair amount of education, and, having had some of Miriam's passion to be instructed, had taught herself French, and could read in that language with a struggle. She considered herself as a woman apart, and particularly apart, from her class. The girls in the Spiral department were all of good homes. It was a small, special industry, and had a certain distinction. There was an air of refinement in both rooms. But Clara was aloof also from her fellow-workers.

None of these things, however, did she reveal to Paul. She was not the one to give herself away. There was a sense of mystery about her. She was so reserved, he felt she had much to reserve. Her history was open on the surface, but its inner meaning was hidden from everybody. It was exciting. And then sometimes he caught her looking at him from under her brows with an almost furtive, sullen scrutiny, which made him move quickly. Often she met his eyes. But then her own were, as it were, covered over, revealing nothing. She gave him a little, lenient smile. She was to him extraordinarily provocative, because of the knowledge she seemed to possess, and gathered fruit of experience he could not attain.

One day he picked up a copy of *Lettres de mon Moulin* from her work-bench.

"You read French, do you?" he cried.

Clara glanced round negligently. She was making an elastic stocking of heliotrope silk, turning the Spiral machine with slow, balanced regularity, occasionally bending down to see her work or to adjust the needles; then her magnificent neck, with its

432

down and fine pencils of hair, shone white against the lavender, lustrous silk. She turned a few more rounds, and stopped.

"What did you say?" she asked, smiling sweetly.

Paul's eyes glittered at her insolent indifference to him.

"I did not know you read French," he said, very polite.

"Did you not?" she replied, with a faint, sarcastic smile.

"Rotten swank!" he said, but scarcely loud enough to be heard.

He shut his mouth angrily as he watched her. She seemed to scorn the work she mechanically produced; yet the hose she made were as nearly perfect as possible.

"You don't like Spiral work," he said.

"Oh, well, all work is work," she answered, as if she knew all about it.

He marvelled at her coldness. He had to do everything hotly. She must be something special.

"What would you prefer to do?" he asked.

She laughed at him indulgently, as she said:

"There is so little likelihood of my ever being given a choice, that I haven't wasted time considering."

"Pah!" he said, contemptuous on his side now. "You only say that because you're too proud to own up what you want and can't get."

"You know me very well," she replied coldly.

"I know you think you're terrific great shakes,

433

and that you live under the eternal insult of working in a factory."

He was very angry and very rude. She merely turned away from him in disdain. He walked whistling down the room, flirted and laughed with Hilda.

Later on he said to himself:

"What was I so impudent to Clara for?" He was rather annoyed with himself, at the same time glad. "Serve her right; she stinks with silent pride," he said to himself angrily.

In the afternoon he came down. There was a certain weight on his heart which he wanted to remove. He thought to do it by offering her chocolates.

"Have one?" he said. "I bought a handful to sweeten me up."

To his great relief, she accepted. He sat on the work-bench beside her machine, twisting a piece of silk round his finger. She loved him for his quick, unexpected movements, like a young animal. His feet swung as he pondered. The sweets lay strewn on the bench. She bent over her machine, grinding rhythmically, then stooping to see the stocking that hung beneath, pulled down by the weight. He watched the handsome crouching of her back, and the apron-strings curling on the floor.

"There is always about you," he said, "a sort of waiting. Whatever I see you doing, you're not really there: you are waiting—like Penelope when she did her weaving." He could not help a spurt of wickedness. "I'll call you Penelope," he said.

"Would it make any difference?" she said, carefully removing one of her needles.

"That doesn't matter, so long as it pleases me. Here, I say, you seem to forget I'm your boss. It just occurs to me."

"And what does that mean?" she asked coolly.

"It means I've got a right to boss you."

"Is there anything you want to complain about?"

"Oh, I say, you needn't be nasty," he said angrily.

"I don't know what you want," she said, continuing her task.

"I want you to treat me nicely and respectfully."

"Call you 'sir', perhaps?" she asked quietly.

"Yes, call me 'sir'. I should love it."

"Then I wish you would go upstairs, sir."

His mouth closed, and a frown came on his face. He jumped suddenly down.

"You're too blessed superior for anything," he said.

And he went away to the other girls. He felt he was being angrier than he had any need to be. In fact, he doubted slightly that he was showing off. But if he were, then he would. Clara heard him laughing, in a way she hated, with the girls down the next room.

When at evening he went through the department after the girls had gone, he saw his chocolates lying untouched in front of Clara's machine. He left them. In the morning they were still there, and Clara was at work. Later on Minnie, a little brunette they called Pussy, called to him:

435

"Hey, haven't you got a chocolate for anybody?"

"Sorry, Pussy," he replied. "I meant to have offered them; then I went and forgot 'em."

"I think you did," she answered.

"I'll bring you some this afternoon. You don't want them after they've been lying about, do you?"

"Oh, I'm not particular," smiled Pussy.

"Oh no," he said. "They'll be dusty."

He went up to Clara's bench.

"Sorry I left these things littering about," he said.

She flushed scarlet. He gathered them together in his fist.

"They'll be dirty now," he said. "You should have taken them. I wonder why you didn't. I meant to have told you I wanted you to."

He flung them out of the window into the yard below. He just glanced at her. She winced from his eyes.

In the afternoon he brought another packet.

"Will you take some?" he said, offering them first to Clara. "These are fresh."

She accepted one, and put it on to the bench.

"Oh, take several—for luck," he said.

She took a couple more, and put them on the bench also. Then she turned in confusion to her work. He went on up the room.

"Here you are, Pussy," he said. "Don't be greedy!"

"Are they all for her?" cried the others, rushing up.

"Of course they're not," he said.

The girls clamoured round. Pussy drew back from her mates.

"Come out!" she cried. "I can have first pick, can't I, Paul?"

"Be nice with 'em," he said, and went away.

"You *are* a dear," the girls cried.

"Tenpence," he answered.

He went past Clara without speaking. She felt the three chocolate creams would burn her if she touched them. It needed all her courage to slip them into the pocket of her apron.

The girls loved him and were afraid of him. He was so nice while he was nice, but if he were offended, so distant, treating them as if they scarcely existed, or not more than the bobbins of thread. And then, if they were impudent, he said quietly: "Do you mind going on with your work," and stood and watched.

When he celebrated his twenty-third birthday, the house was in trouble. Arthur was just going to be married. His mother was not well. His father, getting an old man, and lame from his accidents, was given a paltry, poor job. Miriam was an eternal reproach. He felt he owed himself to her, yet could not give himself. The house, moreover, needed his support. He was pulled in all directions. He was not glad it was his birthday. It made him bitter.

He got to work at eight o'clock. Most of the clerks had not turned up. The girls were not due till 8.30. As he was changing his coat, he heard a voice behind him say:

"Paul, Paul, I want you."

It was Fanny, the hunchback, standing at the top of her stairs, her face radiant with a secret. Paul looked at her in astonishment.

"I want you," she said.

He stood, at a loss.

"Come on," she coaxed. "Come before you begin on the letters."

He went down the half-dozen steps into her dry, narrow, "finishing-off" room. Fanny walked before him: her black bodice was short—the waist was under her armpits—and her green-black cashmere skirt seemed very long, as she strode with big strides before the young man, himself so graceful. She went to her seat at the narrow end of the room, where the window opened on to chimney-pots. Paul watched her thin hands and her flat red wrists as she excitedly twitched her white apron, which was spread on the bench in front of her. She hesitated.

"You didn't think we'd forgot you?" she asked, reproachful.

"Why?" he asked. He had forgotten his birthday himself.

" 'Why,' he says! 'Why!' Why, look here!" She pointed to the calendar, and he saw, surrounding the big black number "21", hundreds of little crosses in black-lead.

"Oh, kisses for my birthday," he laughed. "How did you know?"

"Yes, you want to know, don't you?" Fanny mocked, hugely delighted. "There's one from

438

everybody—except Lady Clara—and two from some. But I shan't tell you how many *I* put."

"Oh, I know, you're spooney," he said.

"There you *are* mistaken!" she cried, indignant. "I could never be so soft." Her voice was strong and contralto.

"You always pretend to be such a hard-hearted hussy," he laughed. "And you know you're as sentimental——"

"I'd rather be called sentimental than frozen meat," Fanny blurted. Paul knew she referred to Clara, and he smiled.

"Do you say such nasty things about me?" he laughed.

"No, my duck," the hunchback woman answered, lavishly tender. She was thirty-nine. "No, my duck, because you don't think yourself a fine figure in marble and us nothing but dirt. I'm as good as you, aren't I, Paul?" and the question delighted her.

"Why, we're not better than one another, are we?" he replied.

"But I'm as good as you, aren't I, Paul?" she persisted daringly.

"Of course you are. If it comes to goodness, you're better."

She was rather afraid of the situation. She might get hysterical.

"I thought I'd get here before the others—won't they say I'm deep! Now shut your eyes——" she said.

439

"And open your mouth, and see what God sends you," he continued, suiting action to words, and expecting a piece of chocolate. He heard the rustle of the apron, and a faint clink of metal. "I'm going to look," he said.

He opened his eyes. Fanny, her long cheeks flushed, her blue eyes shining, was gazing at him. There was a little bundle of paint-tubes on the bench before him. He turned pale.

"No, Fanny," he said quickly.

"From us all," she answered hastily.

"No, but——"

"Are they the right sort?" she asked, rocking herself with delight.

"Jove! they're the best in the catalogue."

"But they're the right sorts?" she cried.

"They're off the little list I'd made to get when my ship came in." He bit his lip.

Fanny was overcome with emotion. She must turn the conversation.

"They was all on thorns to do it; they all paid their shares, all except the Queen of Sheba."

The Queen of Sheba was Clara.

"And wouldn't she join?" Paul asked.

"She didn't get the chance; we never told her; we wasn't going to have *her* bossing *this* show. We didn't *want* her to join."

Paul laughed at the woman. He was much moved. At last he must go. She was very close to him. Suddenly she flung her arms round his neck and kissed him vehemently.

440

"I can give you a kiss today," she said apologetically. "You've looked so white, it's made my heart ache."

Paul kissed her, and left her. Her arms were so pitifully thin that his heart ached also.

That day he met Clara as he ran downstairs to wash his hands at dinner-time.

"You have stayed to dinner!" he exclaimed. It was unusual for her.

"Yes; and I seem to have dined on old surgical-appliance stock. I *must* go out now, or I shall feel stale india-rubber right through."

She lingered. He instantly caught at her wish.

"You are going anywhere?" he asked.

They went together up to the Castle. Outdoors she dressed very plainly, down to ugliness; indoors she always looked nice. She walked with hesitating steps alongside Paul, bowing and turning away from him. Dowdy in dress, and drooping, she showed to great disadvantage. He could scarcely recognise her strong form, that seemed to slumber with power. She appeared almost insignificant, drowning her stature in her stoop, as she shrank from the public gaze.

The Castle grounds were very green and fresh. Climbing the precipitous ascent, he laughed and chattered, but she was silent, seeming to brood over something. There was scarcely time to go inside the squat, square building that crowns the bluff of rock. They leaned upon the wall where the cliff runs sheer down to the Park. Below them, in their holes in the sandstone, pigeons preened themselves and cooed softly. Away down upon the boulevard at the foot of the rock, tiny trees stood in their own pools of shadow, and tiny people went scurrying about in almost ludicrous importance.

"You feel as if you could scoop up the folk like tadpoles, and have a handful of them," he said.

She laughed, answering:

"Yes; it is not necessary to get far off in order to see us proportionately. The trees are much more significant."

"Bulk only," he said.

She laughed cynically.

Away beyond the boulevard the thin stripes of the metals showed upon the railway-track, whose margin was crowded with little stacks of timber, beside which smoking toy engines fussed. Then the silver string of the canal lay at random among the black heaps. Beyond, the dwellings, very dense on the river flat, looked like black, poisonous herbage, in thick rows and crowded beds, stretching right away, broken now and then by taller plants, right to where the river glistened in a hieroglyph across the country. The steep scarp cliffs across the river looked puny. Great stretches of country darkened with trees and faintly brightened with corn-land, spread towards the haze, where the hills rose blue beyond grey.

"It is comforting," said Mrs. Dawes, "to think the town goes no further. It is only a *little* sore upon the country yet."

"A little scab," Paul said.

She shivered. She loathed the town. Looking drearily across at the country which was forbidden her, her impassive face, pale and hostile, she reminded Paul of one of the bitter, remorseful angels.

"But the town's all right," he said; "it's only temporary. This is the crude, clumsy make-shift we've practised on, till we find out what the idea is. The town will come all right."

The pigeons in the pockets of rock, among the perched bushes, cooed comfortably. To the left the large church of St. Mary rose into space, to keep close company with the Castle, above the heaped rubble of the town. Mrs. Dawes smiled brightly as she looked across the country.

"I feel better," she said.

"Thank you," he replied. "Great compliment!"

"Oh, my brother!" she laughed.

"H'm! that's snatching back with the left hand what you gave with the right, and no mistake," he said.

She laughed in amusement at him.

"But what was the matter with you?" he asked. "I know you were brooding something special. I can see the stamp of it on your face yet."

"I think I will not tell you," she said.

"All right, hug it," he answered.

She flushed and bit her lip.

"No," she said, "it was the girls."

"What about 'em?" Paul asked.

"They have been plotting something for a week now, and today they seem particularly full of it. All alike; they insult me with their secrecy."

"Do they?" he asked in concern.

"I should not mind," she went on, in the metallic, angry tone, "if they did not thrust it into my face—the fact that they have a secret."

"Just like women," said he.

"It is hateful, their mean gloating," she said intensely.

Paul was silent. He knew what the girls gloated over. He was sorry to be the cause of this new dissension.

"They can have all the secrets in the world," she went on, brooding bitterly; "but they might refrain from glorying in them, and making me feel more out of it than ever. It is—it is almost unbearable."

Paul thought for a few minutes. He was much perturbed.

"I will tell you what it's all about," he said, pale and nervous. "It's my birthday, and they've bought me a fine lot of paints, all the girls. They're jealous of you"—he felt her stiffen coldly at the word 'jealous'—"merely because I sometimes bring you a book," he added slowly. "But, you see, it's only a trifle. Don't bother about it, will you—because"—he laughed quickly—"well, what would they say if they saw us here now, in spite of their victory?"

She was angry with him for his clumsy reference to their present intimacy. It was almost insolent of

444

him. Yet he was so quiet, she forgave him, although it cost her an effort.

Their two hands lay on the rough stone parapet of the Castle wall. He had inherited from his mother a fineness of mould, so that his hands were small and vigorous. Hers were large, to match her large limbs, but white and powerful looking. As Paul looked at them he knew her. "She is wanting somebody to take her hands—for all she is so contemptuous of us," he said to himself. And she saw nothing but his two hands, so warm and alive, which seemed to live for her. He was brooding now, staring out over the country from under sullen brows. The little, interesting diversity of shapes had vanished from the scene; all that remained was a vast, dark matrix of sorrow and tragedy, the same in all the houses and the river-flats and the people and the birds; they were only shapen differently. And now that the forms seemed to have melted away, there remained the mass from which all the landscape was composed, a dark mass of struggle and pain. The factory, the girls, his mother, the large, uplifted church, the thicket of the town, merged into one atmosphere—dark, brooding, and sorrowful, every bit.

"Is that two o'clock striking?" Mrs. Dawes said in surprise.

Paul started, and everything sprang into form, regained its individuality, its forgetfulness, and its cheerfulness.

They hurried back to work.

445

When he was in the rush of preparing for the night's post, examining the work up from Fanny's room, which smelt of ironing, the evening postman came in.

" 'Mr. Paul Morel,' " he said, smiling, handing Paul a package. "A lady's handwriting! Don't let the girls see it."

The postman, himself a favourite, was pleased to make fun of the girls' affection for Paul.

It was a volume of verse with a brief note: "You will allow me to send you this, and so spare me my isolation. I also sympathise and wish you well.—C.D." Paul flushed hot.

"Good Lord! Mrs. Dawes. She can't afford it. Good Lord, who ever'd have thought it!"

He was suddenly intensely moved. He was filled with the warmth of her. In the glow he could almost feel her as if she were present—her arms, her shoulders, her bosom, see them, feel them, almost contain them.

This move on the part of Clara brought them into closer intimacy. The other girls noticed that when Paul met Mrs. Dawes his eyes lifted and gave that peculiar bright greeting which they could interpret. Knowing he was unaware, Clara made no sign, save that occasionally she turned aside her face from him when he came upon her.

They walked out together very often at dinner-time; it was quite open, quite frank. Everybody seemed to feel that he was quite unaware of the state of his own feeling, and that nothing was wrong. He

446

talked to her now with some of the old fervour with which he had talked to Miriam, but he cared less about the talk, he did not bother about his conclusions.

One day in October they went out to Lambley for tea. Suddenly they came to a halt on top of the hill. He climbed and sat on a gate, she sat on the stile. The afternoon was perfectly still, with a dim haze, and yellow sheaves glowing through. They were quiet.

"How old were you when you married?" he asked quietly.

"Twenty-two."

Her voice was subdued, almost submissive. She would tell him now.

"It is eight years ago?"

"Yes."

"And when did you leave him?"

"Three years ago."

"Five years! Did you love him when you married him?"

She was silent for some time; then she said slowly:

"I thought I did—more or less. I didn't think much about it. And he wanted me. I was very prudish then."

"And you sort of walked into it without thinking?"

"Yes. I seemed to have been asleep nearly all my life."

"Somnambule? But—when did you wake up?"

"I don't know that I ever did, or ever have—since I was a child."

447

"You went to sleep as you grew up to be a woman? How queer! And he didn't wake you?"

"No; he never got there," she replied, in a monotone.

The brown birds dashed over the hedges where the rose-hips stood naked and scarlet.

"Got where?" he asked.

"At me. He never really mattered to me."

The afternoon was so gently warm and dim. Red roofs of the cottages burned among the blue haze. He loved the day. He could feel, but he could not understand, what Clara was saying.

"But why did you leave him? Was he horrid to you?"

She shuddered lightly.

"He—he sort of degraded me. He wanted to bully me because he hadn't got me. And then I felt as if I wanted to run, as if I was fastened and bound up. And he seemed dirty."

"I see."

He did not see at all.

"And was he always dirty?" he asked.

"A bit," she replied slowly. "And then he seemed as if he couldn't get *at* me, really. And then he got brutal—he *was* brutal!"

"And why did you leave him finally?"

"Because—because he was unfaithful to me—"

They were both silent for some time. Her hand lay on the gate-post as she balanced. He put his own over it. His heart beat quickly.

448

"But did you—were you ever—did you ever give him a chance?"

"Chance? How?"

"To come near to you."

"I married him—and I was willing——"

They both strove to keep their voices steady.

"I believe he loves you," he said.

"It looks like it," she replied.

He wanted to take his hand away, and could not. She saved him by removing her own. After a silence, he began again:

"Did you leave him out of count all along?"

"He left me," she said.

"And I suppose he couldn't *make* himself mean everything to you?"

"He tried to bully me into it."

But the conversation had got them both out of their depth. Suddenly Paul jumped down.

"Come on," he said. "Let's go and get some tea."

They found a cottage, where they sat in the cold parlour. She poured out his tea. She was very quiet. He felt she had withdrawn again from him. After tea, she stared broodingly into her tea-cup, twisting her wedding ring all the time. In her abstraction she took the ring off her finger, stood it up, and spun it upon the table. The gold became a diaphanous, glittering globe. It fell, and the ring was quivering upon the table. She spun it again and again. Paul watched, fascinated.

But she was a married woman, and he believed in simple friendship. And he considered that he was

449

perfectly honourable with regard to her. It was only a friendship between man and woman, such as any civilised persons might have.

He was like so many young men of his own age. Sex had become so complicated in him that he would have denied that he ever could want Clara or Miriam or any woman whom he *knew*. Sex desire was a sort of detached thing, that did not belong to a woman. He loved Miriam with his soul. He grew warm at the thought of Clara, he battled with her, he knew the curves of her breast and shoulders, as if they had been moulded inside him; and yet he did not positively desire her. He would have denied it for ever. He believed himself really bound to Miriam. If ever he should marry, some time in the far future, it would be his duty to marry Miriam. That he gave Clara to understand, and she said nothing, but left him to his courses. He came to her, Mrs. Dawes, whenever he could. Then he wrote frequently to Miriam, and visited the girl occasionally. So he went on through the winter; but he seemed not so fretted. His mother was easier about him. She thought he was getting away from Miriam.

Miriam knew now how strong was the attraction of Clara for him; but still she was certain that the best in him would triumph. His feeling for Mrs. Dawes—who, moreover, was a married woman—was shallow and temporal, compared with his love for herself. He would come back to her, she was sure; with some of his young freshness gone, perhaps, but cured of his desire for the lesser things which other women than herself could give him. She could bear all if he were inwardly true to her and must come back.

He saw none of the anomaly of his position. Miriam was his old friend, lover, and she belonged to Bestwood and home and his youth. Clara was a newer friend, and she belonged to Nottingham, to life, to the world. It seemed to him quite plain.

Mrs. Dawes and he had many periods of coolness, when they saw little of each other; but they always came together again.

"Were you horrid with Baxter Dawes?" he asked her. It was a thing that seemed to trouble him.

"In what way?"

"Oh, I don't know. But weren't you horrid with him? Didn't you do something that knocked him to pieces?"

"What, pray?"

"Making him feel as if he were nothing—*I* know," Paul declared.

"You are so clever, my friend," she said coolly.

The conversation broke off there. But it made her cool with him for some time.

She very rarely saw Miriam now. The friendship between the two women was not broken off, but considerably weakened.

"Will you come in to the concert on Sunday afternoon?" Clara asked him just after Christmas.

"I promised to go up to Willey Farm," he replied.

"Oh, very well."

"You don't mind, do you?" he asked.

"Why should I?" she answered.

Which almost annoyed him.

"You know," he said, "Miriam and I have been a lot to each other ever since I was sixteen—that's seven years now."

"It's a long time," Clara replied.

"Yes; but somehow she—it doesn't go right——"

"How?" asked Clara.

"She seems to draw me and draw me, and she wouldn't leave a single hair of me free to fall out and blow away—she'd keep it."

"But you like to be kept."

"No," he said, "I don't. I wish it could be normal, give and take—like me and you. I want a woman to keep me, but not in her pocket."

"But if you love her, it couldn't be normal, like me and you."

"Yes; I should love her better then. She sort of wants me so much that I can't give myself."

"Wants you how?"

"Wants the soul out of my body. I can't help shrinking back from her."

"And yet you love her!"

"No, I don't love her. I never even kiss her."

"Why not?" Clara asked.

"I don't know."

"I suppose you're afraid," she said.

"I'm not. Something in me shrinks from her like hell—she so good, when I'm not good."

452

"How do you know what she is?"

"I do! I know she wants a sort of soul union."

"But how do you know what she wants?"

"I've been with her for seven years."

"And you haven't found out the very first thing about her."

"What's that?"

"That she doesn't want any of your soul communion. That's your own imagination. She wants you."

He pondered over this. Perhaps he was wrong.

"But she seems——" he began.

"You've never tried," she answered.

# 11

## THE TEST ON MIRIAM

WITH the spring came again the old madness and battle. Now he knew he would have to go to Miriam. But what was his reluctance? He told himself it was only a sort of overstrong virginity in her and him which neither could break through. He might have married her; but his circumstances at home made it difficult, and, moreover, he did not want to marry. Marriage was for life, and because they had become close companions, he and she, he did not see that it should inevitably follow they should be man and wife. He did not feel that he wanted marriage with Miriam. He wished he did. He would have given his head to have felt a joyous desire to marry her and to have her. Then why couldn't he bring it off? There was some obstacle; and what was the obstacle? It lay in the physical bondage. He shrank from the physical contact. But why? With her he felt bound up inside himself. He could not go out to her. Something struggled in him, but he could not get to her. Why? She loved him. Clara said she even wanted him; then why couldn't he go to her, make love to her, kiss her? Why, when she put her arm in his, timidly, as they walked, did he feel he would burst forth in brutality and recoil? He owed himself to her; he wanted to belong to her. Perhaps the recoil and the shrinking from her was love in its first fierce modesty. He had no aversion for her. No, it was the opposite; it was a strong desire battling with a still stronger shyness and virginity. It seemed as if virginity were a positive force, which fought and won in both of them. And with her he felt it so hard to overcome; yet he was nearest to her, and with her alone could he deliberately break through. And he owed himself to her. Then, if they could get things right, they could marry; but he would not marry unless he could feel strong in the joy of it—never. He could not have faced his mother. It seemed to him that to sacrifice himself in a marriage he did not want would be degrading, and would undo all his life, make it a nullity. He would try what he *could* do.

And he had a great tenderness for Miriam. Always, she was sad, dreaming her religion; and he was nearly a religion to her. He could not bear to fail her. It would all come right if they tried.

He looked round. A good many of the nicest men he knew were like himself, bound in by their own virginity, which they could not break out of. They were so sensitive to their women that they would go without them for ever rather than do them a hurt, an injustice. Being the sons of mothers whose husbands had blundered rather brutally through their feminine sanctities, they were themselves too diffident and shy. They could easier deny themselves than incur any reproach from a woman; for a woman was like their mother, and they were full of the sense of their mother. They preferred themselves to suffer the misery of celibacy, rather than risk the other person.

He went back to her. Something in her, when he looked at her, brought the tears almost to his eyes. One day he stood behind her as she sang. Annie was playing a song on the piano. As Miriam sang her mouth seemed hopeless. She sang like a nun singing to heaven. It reminded him so much of the mouth and eyes of one who sings beside a Botticelli Madonna, so spiritual. Again, hot as steel, came up the pain in him. Why must he ask her for the other thing? Why was there his blood battling with her? If only he could have been always gentle, tender with her, breathing with her the atmosphere of reverie and religious dreams, he would give his right hand. It was not fair to hurt her. There seemed an eternal maidenhood about her; and when he thought of her mother, he saw the great brown eyes of a maiden who was nearly scared and shocked out of her virgin maidenhood, but not quite, in spite of her seven children. They had been born almost leaving her out of count, not of her, but upon her. So she could never let them go, because she never had possessed them.

Mrs. Morel saw him going again frequently to Miriam, and was astonished. He said nothing to his mother. He did not explain nor excuse himself. If he came home late, and she reproached him, he

456

frowned and turned on her in an overbearing way:

"I shall come home when I like," he said; "I am old enough."

"Must she keep you till this time?"

"It is I who stay," he answered.

"And she lets you? But very well," she said.

And she went to bed, leaving the door unlocked for him; but she lay listening until he came, often long after. It was a great bitterness to her that he had gone back to Miriam. She recognised, however, the uselessness of any further interference. He went to Willey Farm as a man now, not as a youth. She had no right over him. There was a coldness between him and her. He hardly told her anything. Discarded, she waited on him, cooked for him still, and loved to slave for him; but her face closed again like a mask. There was nothing for her to do now but the housework; for all the rest he had gone to Miriam. She could not forgive him. Miriam killed the joy and the warmth in him. He had been such a jolly lad, and full of the warmest affection; now he grew colder, more and more irritable and gloomy. It reminded her of William; but Paul was worse. He did things with more intensity, and more realisation of what he was about. His mother knew how he was suffering for want of a woman, and she saw him going to Miriam. If he had made up his mind, nothing on earth would alter him. Mrs. Morel was tired. She began to give up at last; she had finished. She was in the way.

He went on determinedly. He realised more or

less what his mother felt. It only hardened his soul. He made himself callous towards her; but it was like being callous to his own health. It undermined him quickly; yet he persisted.

He lay back in the rocking-chair at Willey Farm one evening. He had been talking to Miriam for some weeks, but had not come to the point. Now he said suddenly:

"I am twenty-four, almost."

She had been brooding. She looked up at him suddenly in surprise.

"Yes. What makes you say it?"

There was something in the charged atmosphere that she dreaded.

"Sir Thomas More says one can marry at twenty-four."

She laughed quaintly, saying:

"Does it need Sir Thomas More's sanction?"

"No; but one ought to marry about then."

"Ay," she answered broodingly; and she waited.

"I can't marry you," he continued slowly, "not now, because we've no money, and they depend on me at home."

She sat half-guessing what was coming.

"But I want to marry now——"

"You want to marry?" she repeated.

"A woman—you know what I mean."

She was silent.

"Now, at last, I must," he said.

"Ay," she answered.

"And you love me?"

458

"Yes," she answered.

"That's all," he said, and his voice seemed sure, and his mouth was kissing her throat.

Then she raised her head and looked into his eyes with her full gaze of love. The blaze struggled, seemed to try to get away from her, and then was quenched. He turned his head quickly aside. It was a moment of anguish.

"Kiss me," she whispered.

He shut his eyes, and kissed her, and his arms folded her closer and closer.

When she walked home with him over the fields, he said:

"I am glad I came back to you. I feel so simple with you—as if there was nothing to hide. We will be happy?"

"Yes," she murmured, and the tears came to her eyes.

"Some sort of perversity in our souls," he said, "makes us not want, get away from, the very thing we want. We have to fight against that."

"Yes," she said, and she felt stunned.

As she stood under the drooping-thorn tree, in the darkness by the roadside, he kissed her, and his fingers wandered over her face. In the darkness, where he could not see her but only feel her, his passion flooded him. He clasped her very close.

"Sometime you will have me?" he murmured, hiding his face on her shoulder. It was so difficult.

"Not now," she said.

His hopes and his heart sunk. A dreariness came over him.

"No," he said.

His clasp of her slackened.

"I love to feel your arm *there*!" she said, pressing his arm against her back, where it went round her waist. "It rests me so."

He tightened the pressure of his arm upon the small of her back to rest her.

"We belong to each other," he said.

"Yes."

"Then why shouldn't we belong to each other altogether?"

"But——" she faltered.

"I know it's a lot to ask," he said; "but there's not much risk for you really—not in the Gretchen way. You can trust me there?"

"Oh, I can trust you." The answer came quick and strong. "It's not that—it's not that at all—but——"

"What?"

She hid her face in his neck with a little cry of misery.

"I don't know!" she cried.

She seemed slightly hysterical, but with a sort of horror. His heart died in him.

"You don't think it ugly?" he asked.

"No, not now. You have *taught* me it isn't."

"You are afraid?"

She calmed herself hastily.

"Yes, I am only afraid," she said.

462

He kissed her tenderly.

"Never mind," he said. "You should please yourself."

Suddenly she gripped his arms round her, and clenched her body stiff.

"You *shall* have me," she said, through her shut teeth.

His heart beat up again like fire. He folded her close, and his mouth was on her throat. She could not bear it. She drew away. He disengaged her.

"Won't you be late?" she asked gently.

He sighed, scarcely hearing what she said. She waited, wishing he would go. At last he kissed her quickly and climbed the fence. Looking round he saw the pale blotch of her face down in the darkness under the hanging tree. There was no more of her but this pale blotch.

"Goodbye!" she called softly. She had no body, only a voice and a dim face. He turned away and ran down the road, his fists clenched; and when he came to the wall over the lake he leaned there, almost stunned, looking up the black water.

Miriam plunged home over the meadows. She was not afraid of people, what they might say; but she dreaded the issue with him. Yes, she would let him have her if he insisted; and then, when she thought of it afterwards, her heart went down. He would be disappointed, he would find no satisfaction, and then he would go away. Yet he was so insistent; and over this, which did not seem so all-important to her, was their love to break down.

463

After all, he was only like other men, seeking his satisfaction. Oh, but there was something more in him, something deeper! She could trust to it, in spite of all desires. He said that possession was a great moment in life. All strong emotions concentrated there. Perhaps it was so. There was something divine in it; then she would submit, religiously, to the sacrifice. He should have her. And at the thought her whole body clenched itself involuntarily, hard, as if against something; but Life forced her through this gate of suffering, too, and she would submit. At any rate, it would give him what he wanted, which was her deepest wish. She brooded and brooded and brooded herself towards accepting him.

He courted her now like a lover. Often, when he grew hot, she put his face from her, held it between her hands, and looked in his eyes. He could not meet her gaze. Her dark eyes, full of love, earnest and searching, made him turn away. Not for an instant would she let him forget. Back again he had to torture himself into a sense of his responsibility and hers. Never any relaxing, never any leaving himself to the great hunger and impersonality of passion; he must be brought back to a deliberate, reflective creature. As if from a swoon of passion she called him back to the littleness, the personal relationship. He could not bear it. "Leave me alone—leave me alone!" he wanted to cry; but she wanted him to look at her with eyes full of love. His eyes, full of the dark, impersonal fire of desire, did not belong to her.

There was a great crop of cherries at the farm. The trees at the back of the house, very large and tall, hung thick with scarlet and crimson drops, under the dark leaves. Paul and Edgar were gathering the fruit one evening. It had been a hot day, and now the clouds were rolling in the sky, dark and warm. Paul climbed high in the tree, above the scarlet roofs of the buildings. The wind, moaning steadily, made the whole tree rock with a subtle, thrilling motion that stirred the blood. The young man, perched insecurely in the slender branches, rocked till he felt slightly drunk, reached down the boughs, where the scarlet beady cherries hung thick underneath, and tore off handful after handful of the sleek, cool-fleshed fruit. Cherries touched his ears and his neck as he stretched forward, their chill finger-tips sending a flash down his blood. All shades of red, from a golden vermilion to a rich crimson, glowed and met his eyes under a darkness of leaves.

The sun, going down, suddenly caught the broken clouds. Immense piles of gold flared out in the south-east, heaped in soft, glowing yellow right up the sky. The world, till now dusk and grey, reflected the gold glow, astonished. Everywhere the trees, and the grass, and the far-off water, seemed roused from the twilight and shining.

Miriam came out wondering.

"Oh!" Paul heard her mellow voice call, "isn't it wonderful?"

He looked down. There was a faint gold glimmer

465

on her face, that looked very soft, turned up to him.

"How high you are!" she said.

Beside her, on the rhubarb leaves, were four dead birds, thieves that had been shot. Paul saw some cherry stones hanging quite bleached, like skeletons, picked clear of flesh. He looked down again to Miriam.

"Clouds are on fire," he said.

"Beautiful!" she cried.

She seemed so small, so soft, so tender, down there. He threw a handful of cherries at her. She was startled and frightened. He laughed with a low, chuckling sound, and pelted her. She ran for shelter, picking up some cherries. Two fine red pairs she hung over her ears; then she looked up again.

"Haven't you got enough?" she asked.

"Nearly. It is like being on a ship up here."

"And how long will you stay?"

"While the sunset lasts."

She went to the fence and sat there, watching the gold clouds fall to pieces, and go in immense, rose-coloured ruin towards the darkness. Gold flamed to scarlet, like pain in its intense brightness. Then the scarlet sank to rose, and rose to crimson, and quickly the passion went out of the sky. All the world was dark grey. Paul scrambled quickly down with his basket, tearing his shirt-sleeve as he did so.

"They are lovely," said Miriam, fingering the cherries.

"I've torn my sleeve," he answered.

466

She took the three-cornered rip, saying: "I shall have to mend it." It was near the shoulder. She put her fingers through the tear. "How warm!" she said.

He laughed. There was a new, strange note in his voice, one that made her pant.

"Shall we stay out?" he said.

"Won't it rain?" she asked.

"No, let us walk a little way."

They went down the fields and into the thick plantation of fir-trees and pines.

"Shall we go in among the trees?" he asked.

"Do you want to?"

"Yes."

It was very dark among the firs, and the sharp pines pricked her face. She was afraid. Paul was silent and strange.

"I like the darkness," he said. "I wish it were thicker—good, thick darkness."

He seemed to be almost unaware of her as a person: she was only to him then a woman. She was afraid.

He stood against a pine-tree trunk and took her in his arms. She relinquished herself to him, but it was a sacrifice in which she felt something of horror. This thick-voiced, oblivious man was a stranger to her.

Later it began to rain. The pine-trees smelled very strong. Paul lay with his head on the ground, on the dead pine needles, listening to the sharp hiss of the rain—a steady, keen noise. His heart was down, very heavy. Now he realised that she had not been with him all the time, that her soul had stood apart, in a sort of horror. He was physically at rest, but no more. Very dreary at heart, very sad, and very tender, his fingers wandered over her face pitifully. Now again she loved him deeply. He was tender and beautiful.

"The rain!" he said.

"Yes—is it coming on you?"

She put her hands over him, on his hair, on his shoulders, to feel if the raindrops fell on him. She loved him dearly. He, as he lay with his face on the dead pine-leaves, felt extraordinarily quiet. He did not mind if the raindrops came on him: he would have lain and got wet through: he felt as if nothing mattered, as if his living were smeared away into the beyond, near and quite lovable. This strange, gentle reaching-out to death was new to him.

"We must go," said Miriam.

"Yes," he answered, but did not move.

To him now, life seemed a shadow, day a white shadow; night, and death, and stillness, and in-action, this seemed like *being*. To be alive, to be urgent and insistent—that was *not-to-be*. The highest of all was to melt out into the darkness and sway there, identified with the great Being.

"The rain is coming in on us," said Miriam.

He rose and assisted her.

"It is a pity," he said.

"What?"

"To have to go. I feel so still."

468

"Still!" she repeated.

"Stiller than I have ever been in my life."

He was walking with his hand in hers. She pressed his fingers, feeling a slight fear. Now he seemed beyond her; she had a fear lest she should lose him.

"The fir-trees are like presences on the darkness: each one only a presence."

She was afraid, and said nothing.

"A sort of hush: the whole night wondering and asleep: I suppose that's what we do in death—sleep in wonder."

She had been afraid before of the brute in him: now of the mystic. She trod beside him in silence. The rain fell with a heavy "Hush!" on the trees. At last they gained the cart-shed.

"Let us stay here awhile," he said.

There was a sound of rain everywhere, smothering everything.

"I feel so strange and still," he said; "along with everything."

"Ay," she answered patiently.

He seemed again unaware of her, though he held her hand close.

"To be rid of our individuality, which is our will, which is our effort—to live effortless, a kind of curious sleep—that is very beautiful, I think; that is our after-life—our immortality."

"Yes?"

"Yes—and very beautiful to have."

"You don't usually say that."

"No."

469

In a while they went indoors. Everybody looked at them curiously. He still kept the quiet, heavy look in his eyes, the stillness in his voice. Instinctively, they all left him alone.

About this time Miriam's grandmother, who lived in a tiny cottage in Woodlinton, fell ill, and the girl was sent to keep house. It was a beautiful little place. The cottage had a big garden in front, with red brick walls, against which the plum trees were nailed. At the back another garden was separated from the fields by a tall old hedge. It was very pretty. Miriam had not much to do, so she found time for her beloved reading, and for writing little introspective pieces which interested her.

At the holiday-time her grandmother, being better, was driven to Derby to stay with her daughter for a day or two. She was a crotchety old lady, and might return the second day or the third; so Miriam stayed alone in the cottage, which also pleased her.

Paul used often to cycle over, and they had as a rule peaceful and happy times. He did not embarrass her much; but then on the Monday of the holiday he was to spend a whole day with her.

It was perfect weather. He left his mother, telling her where he was going. She would be alone all day. It cast a shadow over him; but he had three days that were all his own, when he was going to do as he liked. It was sweet to rush through the morning lanes on his bicycle.

He got to the cottage at about eleven o'clock. Miriam was busy preparing dinner. She looked so

470

perfectly in keeping with the little kitchen, ruddy and busy. He kissed her and sat down to watch. The room was small and cosy. The sofa was covered all over with a sort of linen in squares of red and pale blue, old, much washed, but pretty. There was a stuffed owl in a case over a corner cupboard. The sunlight came through the leaves of the scented geraniums in the window. She was cooking a chicken in his honour. It was their cottage for the day, and they were man and wife. He beat the eggs for her and peeled the potatoes. He thought she gave a feeling of home almost like his mother; and no one could look more beautiful, with her tumbled curls, when she was flushed from the fire.

The dinner was a great success. Like a young husband, he carved. They talked all the time with unflagging zest. Then he wiped the dishes she had washed, and they went out down the fields. There was a bright little brook that ran into a bog at the foot of a very steep bank. Here they wandered, picking still a few marsh-marigolds and many big blue forget-me-nots. Then she sat on the bank with her hands full of flowers, mostly golden water-blobs. As she put her face down into the marigolds, it was all overcast with a yellow shine.

"Your face is bright," he said, "like a transfiguration."

She looked at him, questioning. He laughed pleadingly to her, laying his hands on hers. Then he kissed her fingers, then her face.

The world was all steeped in sunshine, and quite

471

still, yet not asleep, but quivering with a kind of expectancy.

"I have never seen anything more beautiful than this," he said. He held her hand fast all the time.

"And the water singing to itself as it runs—do you love it?" She looked at him full of love. His eyes were very dark, very bright.

"Don't you think it's a great day?" he asked.

She murmured her assent. She *was* happy, and he saw it.

"And our day—just between us," he said.

They lingered a little while. Then they stood up upon the sweet thyme, and he looked down at her simply.

"Will you come?" he asked.

They went back to the house, hand in hand, in silence. The chickens came scampering down the path to her. He locked the door, and they had the little house to themselves.

He never forgot seeing her as she lay on the bed, when he was unfastening his collar. First he saw only her beauty, and was blind with it. She had the most beautiful body he had ever imagined. He stood unable to move or speak, looking at her, his face half-smiling with wonder. And then he wanted her, but as he went forward to her, her hands lifted in a little pleading movement, and he looked at her face, and stopped. Her big brown eyes were watching him, still and resigned and loving; she lay as if she had given herself up to sacrifice: there was her body for him; but the look at the back of her eyes, like a creature awaiting immolation, arrested him, and all his blood fell back.

"You are sure you want me?" he asked, as if a cold shadow had come over him.

"Yes, quite sure."

She was very quiet, very calm. She only realised that she was doing something for him. He could hardly bear it. She lay to be sacrificed for him because she loved him so much. And he had to sacrifice her. For a second, he wished he were sexless or dead. Then he shut his eyes again to her, and his blood beat back again.

And afterwards he loved her—loved her to the last fibre of his being. He loved her. But he wanted, somehow, to cry. There was something he could not bear for her sake. He stayed with her till quite late at night. As he rode home he felt that he was finally initiated. He was a youth no longer. But why had he the dull pain in his soul? Why did the thought of death, the after-life, seem so sweet and consoling?

He spent the week with Miriam, and wore her out with his passion before it was gone. He had always, almost wilfully, to put her out of count, and act from the brute strength of his own feelings. And he could not do it often, and there remained afterwards always the sense of failure and of death. If he were really with her, he had to put aside himself and his desire. If he would have her, he had to put her aside.

"When I come to you," he asked her, his eyes

dark with pain and shame, "you don't really want me, do you?"

"Ah, yes!" she replied quickly.

He looked at her.

"Nay," he said.

She began to tremble.

"You see," she said, taking his face and shutting it out against her shoulder—"you see—as we are—how can I get used to you? It would come all right if we were married."

He lifted her head, and looked at her.

"You mean, now, it is always too much shock?"

"Yes—and——"

"You are always clenched against me."

She was trembling with agitation.

"You see," she said, "I'm not used to the thought——"

"You are lately," he said.

"But all my life. Mother said to me: 'There is one thing in marriage that is always dreadful, but you have to bear it.' And I believed it."

"And still believe it," he said.

"No!" she cried hastily. "I believe, as you do, that loving, even in *that* way, is the high-water mark of living."

"That doesn't alter the fact that you never *want* it."

"No," she said, taking his head in her arms and rocking in despair. "Don't say so! You don't understand." She rocked with pain. "Don't I want your children?"

474

"But not me."

"How can you say so? But we must be married to have children——"

"Shall we be married, then? *I* want you to have my children."

He kissed her hand reverently. She pondered sadly, watching him.

"We are too young," she said at length.

"Twenty-four and twenty-three——"

"Not yet," she pleaded, as she rocked herself in distress.

"When you will," he said.

She bowed her head gravely. The tone of hopelessness in which he said these things grieved her deeply. It had always been a failure between them. Tacitly, she acquiesced in what he felt.

And after a week of love he said to his mother suddenly one Sunday night, just as they were going to bed:

"I shan't go so much to Miriam's, mother."

She was surprised, but she would not ask him anything.

"You please yourself," she said.

So he went to bed. But there was a new quietness about him which she had wondered at. She almost guessed. She would leave him alone, however. Precipitation might spoil things. She watched him in his loneliness, wondering where he would end. He was sick, and much too quiet for him. There was a perpetual little knitting of his brows, such as she had seen when he was a small baby, and which had been gone for many years. Now it was the same again. And she could do nothing for him. He had to go alone, make his own way.

He continued faithful to Miriam. For one day he had loved her utterly. But it never came again. The sense of failure grew stronger. At first it was only a sadness. Then he began to feel he could not go on. He wanted to run, to go abroad, anything. Gradually, he ceased to ask her to have him. Instead of drawing them together, it put them apart. And then he realised, consciously, that it was no good. It was useless trying: it would never be a success between them.

For some months he had seen very little of Clara. They had occasionally walked out for half an hour at dinner-time. But he always reserved himself for Miriam. With Clara, however, his brow cleared, and he was gay again. She treated him indulgently, as if he were a child. He thought he did not mind. But deep below the surface it piqued him.

Sometimes Miriam said:

"What about Clara? I hear nothing of her lately."

"I walked with her about twenty minutes yesterday," he replied.

"And what did she talk about?"

"I don't know. I suppose I did all the jawing—I usually do. I think I was telling her about the strike, and how the women took it."

"Yes."

So he gave the account of himself.

But insidiously, without his knowing it, the

warmth he felt for Clara drew him away from Miriam, for whom he felt responsible, and to whom he felt he belonged. He thought he was being quite faithful to her. It was not easy to estimate exactly the strength and warmth of one's feelings for a woman till they have run away with one.

He began to give more time to his men friends. There was Jessop, at the art school; Swain, who was chemistry demonstrator at the University; Newton, who was a teacher; besides Edgar and Miriam's younger brothers. Pleading work, he sketched and studied with Jessop. He called in the University for Swain, and the two went "down town" together. Having come home in the train with Newton, he called and had a game of billiards with him in the Moon and Stars. If he gave to Miriam the excuse of his men friends, he felt quite justified. His mother began to be relieved. He always told her where he had been.

During the summer Clara wore sometimes a dress of soft cotton stuff with loose sleeves. When she lifted her hands, her sleeves fell back, and her beautiful strong arms shone out.

"Half a minute," he cried. "Hold your arm still."

He made sketches of her hand and arm, and the drawings contained some of the fascination the real thing had for him. Miriam, who always went scrupulously through his books and papers, saw the drawings.

"I think Clara has such beautiful arms," he said.

"Yes! When did you draw them?"

"On Tuesday, in the work-room. You know, I've got a corner where I can work. Often I can do every single thing they need in the department, before dinner. Then I work for myself in the afternoon, and just see to things at night."

"Yes," she said, turning the leaves of his sketch-book.

Frequently he hated Miriam. He hated her as she bent forward and pored over his things. He hated her way of patiently casting him up, as if he were an endless psychological account. When he was with her, he hated her for having got him, and yet not got him, and he tortured her. She took all and gave nothing, he said. At least, she gave no living warmth. She was never alive, and giving off life. Looking for her was like looking for something which did not exist. She was only his conscience, not his mate. He hated her violently, and was more cruel to her. They dragged on till the next summer. He saw more and more of Clara.

At last he spoke. He had been sitting working at home one evening. There was between him and his mother a peculiar condition of people frankly finding fault with each other. Mrs. Morel was strong on her feet again. He was not going to stick to Miriam. Very well; then she would stand aloof till he said something. It had been coming a long time, this bursting of the storm in him, when he would come back to her. This evening there was between them a peculiar condition of suspense. He worked feverishly and mechanically, so that he could escape from himself. It grew late. Through the open door, stealthily, came the scent of madonna lilies, almost as if it were prowling abroad. Suddenly he got up and went out of doors.

The beauty of the night made him want to shout. A half-moon, dusky gold, was sinking behind the black sycamore at the end of the garden, making the sky dull purple with its glow. Nearer, a dim white fence of lilies went across the garden, and the air all round seemed to stir with scent, as if it were alive. He went across the bed of pinks, whose keen perfume came sharply across the rocking, heavy scent of the lilies, and stood alongside the white barrier of flowers. They flagged all loose, as if they were panting. The scent made him drunk. He went down to the field to watch the moon sink under.

A corncrake in the hay-close called insistently. The moon slid quite quickly downwards, growing more flushed. Behind him the great flowers leaned as if they were calling. And then, like a shock, he caught another perfume, something raw and coarse. Hunting round, he found the purple iris, touched their fleshy throats and their dark, grasping hands. At any rate, he had found something. They stood stiff in the darkness. Their scent was brutal. The moon was melting down upon the crest of the hill. It was gone; all was dark. The corncrake called still.

Breaking off a pink, he suddenly went indoors.

"Come, my boy," said his mother. "I'm sure it's time you went to bed."

He stood with the pink against his lips.

"I shall break off with Miriam, mother," he answered calmly.

She looked up at him over her spectacles. He was staring back at her, unswerving. She met his eyes for a moment, then took off her glasses. He was white. The male was up in him, dominant. She did not want to see him too clearly.

"But I thought——" she began.

"Well," he answered, "I don't love her. I don't want to marry her—so I shall have done."

"But," exclaimed his mother, amazed, "I thought lately you had made up your mind to have her, and so I said nothing."

"I had—I wanted to—but now I don't want. It's no good. I shall break off on Sunday. I ought to, oughtn't I?"

"You know best. You know I said so long ago."

"I can't help that now. I shall break off on Sunday."

"Well," said his mother, "I think it will be best. But lately I decided you had made up your mind to have her, so I said nothing, and should have said nothing. But I say as I have always said, I *don't* think she is suited to you."

"On Sunday I break off," he said, smelling the pink. He put the flower in his mouth. Unthinking, he bared his teeth, closed them on the blossom slowly, and had a mouthful of petals. These he spat into the fire, kissed his mother, and went to bed.

On Sunday he went up to the farm in the early afternoon. He had written Miriam that they would

480

walk over the fields to Hucknall. His mother was very tender with him. He said nothing. But she saw the effort it was costing. The peculiar set look on his face stilled her.

"Never mind, my son," she said. "You will be so much better when it is all over."

Paul glanced swiftly at his mother in surprise and resentment. He did not want sympathy.

Miriam met him at the lane-end. She was wearing a new dress of figured muslin that had short sleeves. Those short sleeves, and Miriam's brown-skinned arms beneath them—such pitiful, resigned arms—gave him so much pain that they helped to make him cruel. She had made herself look so beautiful and fresh for him. She seemed to blossom for him alone. Every time he looked at her—a mature young woman now, and beautiful in her new dress—it hurt so much that his heart seemed almost to be bursting with the restraint he put on it. But he had decided, and it was irrevocable.

On the hills they sat down, and he lay with his head in her lap, whilst she fingered his hair. She knew that "he was not there," as she put it. Often, when she had him with her, she looked for him, and could not find him. But this afternoon she was not prepared.

It was nearly five o'clock when he told her. They were sitting on the bank of a stream, where the lip of turf hung over a hollow bank of yellow earth, and he was hacking away with a stick, as he did when he was perturbed and cruel.

481

"I have been thinking," he said, "we ought to break off."

"Why?" she cried in surprise.

"Because it's no good going on."

"Why is it no good?"

"It isn't. I don't want to marry. I don't want ever to marry. And if we're not going to marry, it's no good going on."

"But why do you say this now?"

"Because I've made up my mind."

"And what about these last months, and the things you told me then?"

"I can't help it! I don't want to go on."

"You don't want any more of me?"

"I want us to break off—you be free of me, I free of you."

"And what about these last months?"

"I don't know. I've not told you anything but what I thought was true."

"Then why are you different now?"

"I'm not—I'm the same—only I know it's no good going on."

"You haven't told me why it's no good."

"Because I don't want to go on—and I don't want to marry."

"How many times have you offered to marry me, and I wouldn't?"

"I know; but I want us to break off."

There was silence for a moment or two, while he dug viciously at the earth. She bent her head, pondering. He was an unreasonable child. He was

482

like an infant which, when it has drunk its fill, throws away and smashes the cup. She looked at him, feeling she could get hold of him and *wring* some consistency out of him. But she was helpless. Then she cried:

"I have said you were only fourteen—you are only *four!*"

He still dug at the earth viciously. He heard.

"You are a child of four," she repeated in her anger.

He did not answer, but said in his heart: "All right; if I'm a child of four, what do you want me for? *I* don't want another mother." But he said nothing to her, and there was silence.

"And have you told your people?" she asked.

"I have told my mother."

There was another long interval of silence.

"Then what do you *want?*" she asked.

"Why, I want us to separate. We have lived on each other all these years; now let us stop. I will go my own way without you, and you will go your way without me. You will have an independent life of your own then."

There was in it some truth that, in spite of her bitterness, she could not help registering. She knew she felt in a sort of bondage to him, which she hated because she could not control it. She hated her love for him from the moment it grew too strong for her. And, deep down, she had hated him because she loved him and he dominated her. She had resisted his domination. She had fought to keep herself free

483

of him in the last issue. And she *was* free of him, even more than he of her.

"And," he continued, "we shall always be more or less each other's work. You have done a lot for me, I for you. Now let us start and live by ourselves."

"What do you want to do?" she asked.

"Nothing—only to be free," he answered.

She, however, knew in her heart that Clara's influence was over him to liberate him. But she said nothing.

"And what have I to tell my mother?" she asked.

"I told my mother," he answered, "that I was breaking off—clean and altogether."

"I shall not tell them at home," she said.

Frowning, "You please yourself," he said.

He knew he had landed her in a nasty hole, and was leaving her in the lurch. It angered him.

"Tell them you wouldn't and won't marry me, and have broken off," he said. "It's true enough."

She bit her finger moodily. She thought over their whole affair. She had known it would come to this; she had seen it all along. It chimed with her bitter expectation.

"Always—it has always been so!" she cried. "It has been one long battle between us—you fighting away from me."

It came from her unawares, like a flash of lightning. The man's heart stood still. Was this how she saw it?

"But we've had *some* perfect hours, *some* perfect times, when we were together!" he pleaded.

484

"Never!" she cried; "never! It has always been you fighting me off."

"Not always—not at first!" he pleaded.

"Always, from the very beginning—always the same!"

She had finished, but she had done enough. He sat aghast. He had wanted to say: "It has been good, but it is at an end." And she—she whose love he had believed in when he had despised himself—denied that their love had ever been love. "He had always fought away from her?" Then it had been monstrous. There had never been anything really between them; all the time he had been imagining something where there was nothing. And she had known. She had known so much, and had told him so little. She had known all the time. All the time this was at the bottom of her!

He sat silent in bitterness. At last the whole affair appeared in a cynical aspect to him. She had really played with him, not he with her. She had hidden all her condemnation from him, had flattered him, and despised him. She despised him now. He grew intellectual and cruel.

"You ought to marry a man who worships you," he said; "then you could do as you liked with him. Plenty of men will worship you, if you get on the private side of their natures. You ought to marry one such. They would never fight you off."

"Thank you!" she said. "But don't advise me to marry someone else any more. You've done it before."

485

"Very well," he said; "I will say no more."

He sat still, feeling as if he had had a blow, instead of giving one. Their eight years of friendship and love, *the* eight years of his life, were nullified.

"When did you think of this?" she asked.

"I thought definitely on Thursday night."

"I knew it was coming," she said.

That pleased him bitterly. "Oh, very well! If she knew then it doesn't come as a surprise to her," he thought.

"And have you said anything to Clara?" she asked.

"No; but I shall tell her now."

There was a silence.

"Do you remember the things you said this time last year, in my grandmother's house—nay last month even?"

"Yes," he said; "I do! And I meant them! I can't help that it's failed."

"It has failed because you want something else."

"It would have failed whether or not. *You* never believed in me."

She laughed strangely.

He sat in silence. He was full of a feeling that she had deceived him. She had despised him when he thought she worshipped him. She had let him say wrong things, and had not contradicted him. She had let him fight alone. But it stuck in his throat that she had despised him whilst he thought she worshipped him. She should have told him when she found fault with him. She had not played fair. He hated her. All these years she had treated him as

486

if he were a hero, and thought of him secretly as an infant, a foolish child. Then why had she left the foolish child to his folly? His heart was hard against her.

She sat full of bitterness. She had known—oh, well she had known! All the time he was away from her she had summed him up, seen his littleness, his meanness, and his folly. Even she had guarded her soul against him. She was not overthrown, not prostrated, not even much hurt. She had known. Only why, as he sat there, had he still this strange dominance over her? His very movements fascinated her as if she were hypnotised by him. Yet he was despicable, false, inconsistent, and mean. Why this bondage for her? Why was it the movement of his arm stirred her as nothing else in the world could? Why was she fastened to him? Why, even now, if he looked at her and commanded her, would she have to obey? She would obey him in his trifling commands. But once he was obeyed, then she had him in her power, she knew, to lead him where she would. She was sure of herself. Only, this new influence! Ah, he was not a man! He was a baby that cries for the newest toy. And all the attachment of his soul would not keep him. Very well, he would have to go. But he would come back when he had tired of his new sensation.

He hacked at the earth till she was fretted to death. She rose. He sat flinging lumps of earth in the stream.

"We will go and have tea here?" he asked.

487

"Yes," she answered.

They chattered over irrelevant subjects during tea. He held forth on the love of ornament—the cottage parlour moved him thereto—and its connection with æsthetics. She was cold and quiet. As they walked home, she asked:

"And we shall not see each other?"

"No—or rarely," he answered.

"Nor write?" she asked, almost sarcastically.

"As you will," he answered. "We're not strangers—never should be, whatever happened. I will write to you now and again. You please yourself."

"I see!" she answered cuttingly.

But he was at that stage at which nothing else hurts. He had made a great cleavage in his life. He had had a great shock when she had told him their love had been always a conflict. Nothing more mattered. If it never had been much, there was no need to make a fuss that it was ended.

He left her at the lane-end. As she went home, solitary, in her new frock, having her people to face at the other end, he stood still with shame and pain in the highroad, thinking of the suffering he caused her.

In the reaction towards restoring his self-esteem, he went into the Willow Tree for a drink. There were four girls who had been out for the day, drinking a modest glass of port. They had some chocolates on the table. Paul sat near with his whisky. He noticed the girls whispering and nudging.

Presently one, a bonny dark hussy, leaned to him and said:

"Have a chocolate?"

The others laughed loudly at her impudence.

"All right," said Paul. "Give me a hard one—nut. I don't like creams."

"Here you are, then," said the girl; "here's an almond for you."

She held the sweet between her fingers. He opened his mouth. She popped it in, and blushed.

"You *are* nice!" he said.

"Well," she answered, "we thought you looked overcast, and they dared me offer you a chocolate."

"I don't mind if I have another—another sort," he said.

And presently they were all laughing together.

It was nine o'clock when he got home, falling dark. He entered the house in silence. His mother, who had been waiting, rose anxiously.

"I told her," he said.

"I'm glad," replied the mother, with great relief.

He hung up his cap wearily.

"I said we'd have done altogether," he said.

"That's right, my son," said the mother. "It's hard for her now, but best in the long run. I know. You weren't suited for her."

He laughed shakily as he sat down.

"I've had such a lark with some girls in a pub," he said.

His mother looked at him. He had forgotten Miriam now. He told her about the girls in the

Willow Tree. Mrs. Morel looked at him. It seemed unreal, his gaiety. At the back of it was too much horror and misery.

"Now have some supper," she said very gently. Afterwards he said wistfully:

"She never thought she'd have me, mother, not from the first, and so she's not disappointed."

"I'm afraid," said his mother, "she doesn't give up hopes of you yet."

"No," he said, "perhaps not."

"You'll find it's better to have done," she said.

"I don't know," he said desperately.

"Well, leave her alone," replied his mother.

So he left her, and she was alone. Very few people cared for her, and she for very few people. She remained alone with herself, waiting.

# 12

## PASSION

HE was gradually making it possible to earn a livelihood by his art. Liberty's had taken several of his painted designs on various stuffs, and he could sell designs for embroideries, for altar-cloths, and similar things, in one or two places. It was not very much he made at present, but he might extend it. He had also made friends with the designer for a pottery firm, and was gaining some knowledge of his new acquaintance's art. The applied arts interested him very much. At the same time he laboured slowly at his pictures. He loved to paint large figures, full of light, but not merely made up of lights and cast shadows, like the impressionists; rather definite figures that had a certain luminous quality, like some of Michael Angelo's people. And these he fitted into a landscape, in what he thought true proportion. He worked a great deal from memory, using everybody he knew. He believed firmly in his work, that it was good and valuable. In spite of fits of depression, shrinking, everything, he believed in his work.

He was twenty-four when he said his first confident thing to his mother.

"Mother," he said, "I s'll make a painter that they'll attend to."

She sniffed in her quaint fashion. It was like a half-pleased shrug of the shoulders.

"Very well, my boy, we'll see," she said.

"You shall see, my pigeon! You see if you're not swanky one of these days!"

"I'm quite content, my boy," she smiled.

"But you'll have to alter. Look at you with Minnie!"

Minnie was the small servant, a girl of fourteen.

"And what about Minnie?" asked Mrs. Morel, with dignity.

"I heard her this morning: 'Eh, Mrs. Morel! I was going to do that,' when you went out in the rain for some coal," he said. "That looks a lot like your being able to manage servants!"

"Well, it was only the child's niceness," said Mrs. Morel.

"And you apologising to her: 'You can't do two things at once, can you?' "

"She *was* busy washing up," replied Mrs. Morel.

"And what did she say? 'It could easy have waited a bit. Now look how your feet paddle!' "

"Yes—brazen young baggage!" said Mrs. Morel, smiling.

He looked at his mother, laughing. She was quite warm and rosy again with love of him. It seemed as if all the sunshine were on her for a moment. He continued his work gladly. She seemed so well when she was happy that he forgot her grey hair.

And that year she went with him to the Isle of Wight for a holiday. It was too exciting for them both, and too beautiful. Mrs. Morel was full of joy and wonder. But he would have her walk with him more than she was able. She had a bad fainting bout. So grey her face was, so blue her mouth! It was agony to him. He felt as if someone were pushing a knife in his chest. Then she was better again, and he forgot. But the anxiety remained inside him, like a wound that did not close.

After leaving Miriam he went almost straight to Clara. On the Monday following the day of the rupture he went down to the work-room. She looked up at him and smiled. They had grown very intimate unawares. She saw a new brightness about him.

"Well, Queen of Sheba!" he said, laughing.

"But why?" she asked.

"I think it suits you. You've got a new frock on."

She flushed, asking:

"And what of it?"

"Suits you—awfully! *I* could design you a dress."

"How would it be?"

He stood in front of her, his eyes glittering as he expounded. He kept her eyes fixed with his. Then suddenly he took hold of her. She half-started back. He drew the stuff of her blouse tighter, smoothed it over her breast.

"More *so*!" he explained.

But they were both of them flaming with blushes, and immediately he ran away. He had touched her. His whole body was quivering with the sensation.

There was already a sort of secret understanding between them. The next evening he went to the cinematograph with her for a few minutes before train-time. As they sat, he saw her hand lying near him. For some moments he dared not touch it. The pictures danced and dithered. Then he took her hand in his. It was large and firm; it filled his grasp. He held it fast. She neither moved nor made any sign. When they came out his train was due. He hesitated.

"Good night," she said. He darted away across the road.

The next day he came again, talking to her. She was rather superior with him.

"Shall we go a walk on Monday?" he asked.

She turned her face aside.

"Shall you tell Miriam?" she replied sarcastically.

"I have broken off with her," he said.

"When?"

"Last Sunday."

"You quarrelled?"

"No! I had made up my mind. I told her quite definitely I should consider myself free."

Clara did not answer, and he returned to his work. She was so quiet and so superb!

On the Saturday evening he asked her to come and drink coffee with him in a restaurant, meeting him after work was over. She came, looking very reserved and very distant. He had three-quarters of an hour to train-time.

"We will walk a little while," he said.

494

She agreed, and they went past the Castle into the Park. He was afraid of her. She walked moodily at his side, with a kind of resentful, reluctant, angry walk. He was afraid to take her hand.

"Which way shall we go?" he asked as they walked in darkness.

"I don't mind."

"Then we'll go up the steps."

He suddenly turned round. They had passed the Park steps. She stood still in resentment at his suddenly abandoning her. He looked for her. She stood aloof. He caught her suddenly in his arms, held her strained for a moment, kissed her. Then he let her go.

"Come along," he said, penitent.

She followed him. He took her hand and kissed her finger-tips. They went in silence. When they came to the light, he let go her hand. Neither spoke till they reached the station. Then they looked each other in the eyes.

"Good night," she said.

And he went for his train. His body acted mechanically. People talked to him. He heard faint echoes answering them. He was in a delirium. He felt that he would go mad if Monday did not come at once. On Monday he would see her again. All himself was pitched there, ahead. Sunday intervened. He could not bear it. He could not see her till Monday. And Sunday intervened—hour after hour of tension. He wanted to beat his head against the door of the carriage. But he sat still. He drank some whisky on the way home, but it only made it worse. His mother must not be upset, that was all. He dissembled, and got quickly to bed. There he sat, dressed, with his chin on his knees, staring out of the window at the far hill, with its few lights. He neither thought nor slept, but sat perfectly still, staring. And when at last he was so cold that he came to himself, he found his watch had stopped at half-past two. It was after three o'clock. He was exhausted, but still there was the torment of knowing it was only Sunday morning. He went to bed and slept. Then he cycled all day long, till he was fagged out. And he scarcely knew where he had been. But the day after was Monday. He slept till four o'clock. Then he lay and thought. He was coming nearer to himself—he could see himself, real, somewhere in front. She would go a walk with him in the afternoon. Afternoon! It seemed years ahead.

Slowly the hours crawled. His father got up; he heard him pottering about. Then the miner set off to the pit, his heavy boots scraping the yard. Cocks were still crowing. A cart went down the road. His mother got up. She knocked the fire. Presently she called him softly. He answered as if he were asleep. This shell of himself did well.

He was walking to the station—another mile! The train was near Nottingham. Would it stop before the tunnels? But it did not matter; it would get there before dinner-time. He was at Jordan's. She would come in half an hour. At any rate, she would be near. He had done the letters. She would be there. Perhaps she had not come. He ran down-stairs. Ah! he saw her through the glass door. Her shoulders stooping a little to her work made him feel he could not go forward; he could not stand. He went in. He was pale, nervous, awkward, and quite cold. Would she misunderstand him? He could not write his real self with this shell.

"And this afternoon," he struggled to say. "You will come?"

"I think so," she replied, murmuring.

He stood before her, unable to say a word. She hid her face from him. Again came over him the feeling that he would lose consciousness. He set his teeth and went upstairs. He had done everything correctly yet, and he would do so. All the morning things seemed a long way off, as they do to a man under chloroform. He himself seemed under a tight band of constraint. Then there was his other self, in the distance, doing things, entering stuff in a ledger, and he watched that far-off him carefully to see he made no mistake.

But the ache and strain of it could not go on much longer. He worked incessantly. Still it was only twelve o'clock. As if he had nailed his clothing against the desk, he stood there and worked, forcing every stroke out of himself. It was a quarter to one; he could clear away. Then he ran downstairs.

"You will meet me at the Fountain at two o'clock," he said.

"I can't be there till half-past."

"Yes!" he said.

She saw his dark, mad eyes.

"I will try at a quarter past."

And he had to be content. He went and got some dinner. All the time he was still under chloroform, and every minute was stretched out indefinitely. He walked miles of streets. Then he thought he would be late at the meeting-place. He was at the Fountain at five past two. The torture of the next quarter of an hour was refined beyond expression. It was the anguish of combining the living self with the shell. Then he saw her. She came! And he was there.

"You are late," he said.

"Only five minutes," she answered.

"I'd never have done it to you," he laughed.

She was in a dark blue costume. He looked at her beautiful figure.

"You want some flowers," he said, going to the nearest florist's.

She followed him in silence. He bought her a bunch of scarlet, brick-red carnations. She put them in her coat, flushing.

"That's a fine colour!" he said.

"I'd rather have had something softer," she said. He laughed.

"Do you feel like a blot of vermilion walking down the street?" he said.

She hung her head, afraid of the people they met. He looked sideways at her as they walked. There was a wonderful close down on her face near the ear that he wanted to touch. And a certain heaviness, the heaviness of a very full ear of corn that dips slightly in the wind, that there was about her, made his brain spin. He seemed to be spinning down the street, everything going round.

As they sat in the tramcar, she leaned her heavy shoulder against him, and he took her hand. He felt himself coming round from the anæsthetic, beginning to breathe. Her ear, half-hidden among her blonde hair, was near to him. The temptation to kiss it was almost too great. But there were other people on top of the car. It still remained to him to kiss it. After all, he was not himself, he was some attribute of hers, like the sunshine that fell on her.

He looked quickly away. It had been raining. The big bluff of the Castle rock was streaked with rain, as it reared above the flat of the town. They crossed the wide, black space of the Midland Railway, and passed the cattle enclosure that stood out white. Then they ran down sordid Wilford Road.

She rocked slightly to the tram's motion, and as she leaned against him, rocked upon him. He was a vigorous, slender man, with exhaustless energy. His face was rough, with rough-hewn features, like the common people's; but his eyes under the deep brows were so full of life that they fascinated her. They seemed to dance, and yet they were still trembling on the finest balance of laughter. His mouth the same was just going to spring into a laugh of triumph, yet did not. There was a sharp suspense about him. She bit her lip moodily. His hand was hard clenched over hers.

They paid their two halfpennies at the turnstile

499

and crossed the bridge. The Trent was very full. It swept silent and insidious under the bridge, travelling in a soft body. There had been a great deal of rain. On the river levels were flat gleams of flood water. The sky was grey, with glisten of silver here and there. In Wilford churchyard the dahlias were sodden with rain—wet black-crimson balls. No one was on the path that went along the green river meadow, along the elm-tree colonnade.

There was the faintest haze over the silvery-dark water and the green meadow-bank, and the elm-trees that were spangled with gold. The river slid by in a body, utterly silent and swift, intertwining among itself like some subtle, complex creature. Clara walked moodily beside him.

"Why," she asked at length, in rather a jarring tone, "did you leave Miriam?"

He frowned.

"Because I *wanted* to leave her," he said.

"Why?"

"Because I didn't want to go on with her. And I didn't want to marry."

She was silent for a moment. They picked their way down the muddy path. Drops of water fell from the elm-trees.

"You didn't want to marry Miriam, or you didn't want to marry at all?" she asked.

"Both," he answered—"both!"

They had to manœuvre to get to the stile, because of the pools of water.

"And what did she say?" Clara asked.

"Miriam? She said I was a baby of four, and that I always *had* battled her off."

Clara pondered over this for a time.

"But you have really been going with her for some time?" she asked.

"Yes."

"And now you don't want any more of her?"

"No. I know it's no good."

She pondered again.

"Don't you think you've treated her rather badly?" she asked.

"Yes; I ought to have dropped it years back. But it would have been no good going on. Two wrongs don't make a right."

"How old *are* you?" Clara asked.

"Twenty-five."

"And I am thirty," she said.

"I know you are."

"I shall be thirty-one—or *am* I thirty-one?"

"I neither know nor care. What does it matter!"

They were at the entrance to the Grove. The wet, red track, already sticky with fallen leaves, went up the steep bank between the grass. On either side stood the elm-trees like pillars along a great aisle, arching over and making high up a roof from which the dead leaves fell. All was empty and silent and wet. She stood on top of the stile, and he held both her hands. Laughing, she looked down into his eyes. Then she leaped. Her breast came against his; he held her, and covered her face with kisses.

They went on up the slippery, steep red path.

Presently she released his hand and put it round her waist.

"You press the vein in my arm, holding it so tightly," she said.

They walked along. His finger-tips felt the rocking of her breast. All was silent and deserted. On the left the red wet plough-land showed through the doorways between the elm-boles and their branches. On the right, looking down, they could see the tree-tops of elms growing far beneath them, hear occasionally the gurgle of the river. Sometimes there below they caught glimpses of the full, soft-sliding Trent, and of water-meadows dotted with small cattle.

"It has scarcely altered since little Kirke White used to come," he said.

But he was watching her throat below the ear, where the flush was fusing into the honey-white, and her mouth that pouted disconsolate. She stirred against him as she walked, and his body was like a taut string.

Half-way up the big colonnade of elms, where the Grove rose highest above the river, their forward movement faltered to an end. He led her across to the grass, under the trees at the edge of the path. The cliff of red earth sloped swiftly down, through trees and bushes, to the river that glimmered and was dark between the foliage. The far-below water-meadows were very green. He and she stood leaning against one another, silent, afraid, their bodies touching all along. There came a quick gurgle from the river below.

"Why," he asked at length, "did you hate Baxter Dawes?"

She turned to him with a splendid movement. Her mouth was offered him, and her throat; her eyes were half-shut; her breast was tilted as if it asked for him. He flashed with a small laugh, shut his eyes, and met her in a long, whole kiss. Her mouth fused with his; their bodies were sealed and annealed. It was some minutes before they withdrew. They were standing beside the public path.

"Will you go down to the river?" he asked.

She looked at him, leaving herself in his hands. He went over the brim of the declivity and began to climb down.

"It is slippery," he said.

"Never mind," she replied.

The red clay went down almost sheer. He slid, went from one tuft of grass to the next, hanging on to the bushes, making for a little platform at the foot of a tree. There he waited for her, laughing with excitement. Her shoes were clogged with red earth. It was hard for her. He frowned. At last he caught her hand, and she stood beside him. The cliff rose above them and fell away below. Her colour was up, her eyes flashed. He looked at the big drop below them.

"It's risky," he said; "or messy, at any rate. Shall we go back?"

"Not for my sake," she said quickly.

"All right. You see, I can't help you; I should only hinder. Give me that little parcel and your gloves. Your poor shoes!"

They stood perched on the face of the declivity, under the trees.

"Well, I'll go again," he said.

Away he went, slipping, staggering, sliding to the next tree, into which he fell with a slam that nearly shook the breath out of him. She came after cautiously, hanging on to the twigs and grasses. So they descended, stage by stage, to the river's brink. There, to his disgust, the flood had eaten away the path, and the red decline ran straight into the water. He dug in his heels and brought himself up violently. The string of the parcel broke with a snap; the brown parcel bounded down, leaped into the water, and sailed smoothly away. He hung on to his tree.

"Well, I'll be damned!" he cried crossly. Then he laughed. She was coming perilously down.

"Mind!" he warned her. He stood with his back to the tree, waiting. "Come now," he called, opening his arms.

She let herself run. He caught her, and together they stood watching the dark water scoop at the raw edge of the bank. The parcel had sailed out of sight.

"It doesn't matter," she said.

He held her close and kissed her. There was only room for their four feet.

"It's a swindle!" he said. "But there's a rut where

a man has been, so if we go on I guess we shall find the path again."

The river slid and twined its great volume. On the other bank cattle were feeding on the desolate flats. The cliff rose high above Paul and Clara on their right hand. They stood against the tree in the watery silence.

"Let us try going forward," he said; and they struggled in the red clay along the groove a man's nailed boots had made. They were hot and flushed. Their barkled shoes hung heavy on their steps. At last they found the broken path. It was littered with rubble from the water, but at any rate it was easier. They cleaned their boots with twigs. His heart was beating thick and fast.

Suddenly, coming on to the little level, he saw two figures of men standing silent at the water's edge. His heart leaped. They were fishing. He turned and put his hand up warningly to Clara. She hesitated, buttoned her coat. The two went on together.

The fishermen turned curiously to watch the two intruders on their privacy and solitude. They had had a fire, but it was nearly out. All kept perfectly still. The men turned again to their fishing, stood over the grey glinting river like statues. Clara went with bowed head, flushing; he was laughing to himself. Directly they passed out of sight behind the willows.

"Now they ought to be drowned," said Paul softly.

Clara did not answer. They toiled forward along a tiny path on the river's lip. Suddenly it vanished.

The bank was sheer red solid clay in front of them, sloping straight into the river. He stood and cursed beneath his breath, setting his teeth.

"It's impossible!" said Clara.

He stood erect, looking round. Just ahead were two islets in the stream, covered with osiers. But they were unattainable. The cliff came down like a sloping wall from far above their heads. Behind, not far back, were the fishermen. Across the river the distant cattle fed silently in the desolate afternoon. He cursed again deeply under his breath. He gazed up the great steep bank. Was there no hope but to scale back to the public path?

"Stop a minute," he said, and, digging his heels sideways into the steep bank of red clay, he began nimbly to mount. He looked across at every tree-foot. At last he found what he wanted. Two beech-trees side by side on the hill held a little level on the upper face between their roots. It was littered with damp leaves, but it would do. The fishermen were perhaps sufficiently out of sight. He threw down his rainproof and waved to her to come.

She toiled to his side. Arriving there, she looked at him heavily, dumbly, and laid her head on his shoulder. He held her fast as he looked round. They were safe enough from all but the small, lonely cows over the river. He sunk his mouth on her throat, where he felt her heavy pulse beat under his lips. Everything was perfectly still. There was nothing in the afternoon but themselves.

When she arose, he, looking on the ground all the

time, saw suddenly sprinkled on the black wet beech-roots many scarlet carnation petals, like splashed drops of blood; and red, small splashes fell from her bosom, streaming down her dress to her feet.

"Your flowers are smashed," he said.

She looked at him heavily as she put back her hair. Suddenly he put his finger-tips on her cheek.

"Why dost look so heavy?" he reproached her.

She smiled sadly, as if she felt alone in herself. He caressed her cheek with his fingers, and kissed her.

"Nay!" he said. "Never thee bother!"

She gripped his fingers tight, and laughed shakily. Then she dropped her hand. He put the hair back from her brows, stroking her temples, kissing them lightly.

"But tha shouldna worrit!" he said softly, pleading.

"No, I don't worry!" she laughed tenderly and resigned.

"Yea, tha does! Dunna thee worrit," he implored, caressing.

"No!" she consoled him, kissing him.

They had a stiff climb to get to the top again. It took them a quarter of an hour. When he got on to the level grass, he threw off his cap, wiped the sweat from his forehead, and sighed.

"Now we're back at the ordinary level," he said.

She sat down, panting, on the tussocky grass. Her cheeks were flushed pink. He kissed her, and she gave way to joy.

"And now I'll clean thy boots and make thee fit for respectable folk," he said.

He kneeled at her feet, worked away with a stick and tufts of grass. She put her fingers in his hair, drew his head to her, and kissed it.

"What am I supposed to be doing," he said, looking at her laughing; "cleaning shoes or dibbling with love? Answer me that!"

"Just whichever I please," she replied.

"I'm your boot-boy for the time being, and nothing else!" But they remained looking into each other's eyes and laughing. Then they kissed with little nibbling kisses.

"T-t-t-t!" he went with his tongue, like his mother. "I tell you, nothing gets done when there's a woman about."

And he returned to his boot-cleaning, singing softly. She touched his thick hair, and he kissed her fingers. He worked away at her shoes. At last they were quite presentable.

"There you are, you see!" he said. "Aren't I a great hand at restoring you to respectability? Stand up! There, you look as irreproachable as Britannia herself!"

He cleaned his own boots a little, washed his hands in a puddle and sang. They went on into Clifton village. He was madly in love with her; every movement she made, every crease in her garments, sent a hot flash through him and seemed adorable.

The old lady at whose house they had tea was roused into gaiety by them.

508

"I could wish you'd had something of a better day," she said, hovering round.

"Nay!" he laughed. "We've been saying how nice it is."

The old lady looked at him curiously. There was a peculiar glow and charm about him. His eyes were dark and laughing. He rubbed his moustache with a glad movement.

"Have you been saying *so*!" she exclaimed, a light rousing in her old eyes.

"Truly!" he laughed.

"Then I'm sure the day's good enough," said the old lady.

She fussed about, and did not want to leave them.

"I don't know whether you'd like some radishes as well," she said to Clara; "but I've got some in the garden—*and* a cucumber."

Clara flushed. She looked very handsome.

"I should like some radishes," she answered.

And the old lady pottered off gleefully.

"If she knew!" said Clara quietly to him.

"Well, she doesn't know; and it shows we're nice in ourselves, at any rate. You look quite enough to satisfy an archangel, and I'm sure I feel harmless—so—if it makes you look nice, and makes folk happy when they have us, and makes us happy—why, we're not cheating them out of much!"

They went on with the meal. When they were going away, the old lady came timidly with three tiny dahlias in full blow, neat as bees, and speckled scarlet and white. She stood before Clara, pleased with herself, saying:

"I don't know whether——" and holding the flowers forward in her old hand.

"Oh, how pretty!" cried Clara, accepting the flowers.

"Shall she have them all?" asked Paul reproachfully of the old woman.

"Yes, she shall have them all," she replied, beaming with joy. "You have got enough for your share."

"Ah, but I shall ask her to give me one!" he teased.

"Then she does as she pleases," said the old lady, smiling. And she bobbed a little curtsey of delight.

Clara was rather quiet and uncomfortable. As they walked along, he said:

"You don't feel criminal, do you?"

She looked at him with startled grey eyes.

"Criminal!" she said. "No."

"But you seem to feel you have done a wrong?"

"No," she said. "I only think, 'If they knew!' "

"If they knew, they'd cease to understand. As it is, they do understand, and they like it. What do they matter? Here, with only the trees and me, you don't feel not the least bit wrong, do you?"

He took her by the arm, held her facing him, holding her eyes with his. Something fretted him.

"Not sinners, are we?" he said, with an uneasy little frown.

"No," she replied.

He kissed her, laughing.

"You like your little bit of guiltiness, I believe," he said. "I believe Eve enjoyed it, when she went cowering out of Paradise."

But there was a certain glow and quietness about her that made him glad. When he was alone in the railway-carriage, he found himself tumultuously happy, and the people exceedingly nice, and the night lovely, and everything good.

Mrs. Morel was sitting reading when he got home. Her health was not good now, and there had come that ivory pallor into her face which he never noticed, and which afterwards he never forgot. She did not mention her own ill-health to him. After all, she thought, it was not much.

"You are late!" she said, looking at him.

His eyes were shining; his face seemed to glow. He smiled to her.

"Yes; I've been down Clifton Grove with Clara."

His mother looked at him again.

"But won't people talk?" she said.

"Why? They know she's a suffragette, and so on. And what if they do talk!"

"Of course, there may be nothing wrong in it," said his mother. "But you know what folks are, and if once she gets talked about——"

"Well, I can't help it. Their jaw isn't so almighty important, after all."

"I think you ought to consider *her*."

"So I *do*! What can people say?—that we take a walk together. I believe you're jealous."

"You know I should be *glad* if she weren't a married woman."

"Well, my dear, she lives separate from her husband, and talks on platforms; so she's already singled out from the sheep, and, as far as I can see, hasn't much to lose. No; her life's nothing to her, so what's the worth of nothing? She goes with me—it becomes something. Then she must pay—we both must pay! Folks are so frightened of paying; they'd rather starve and die."

"Very well, my son. We'll see how it will end."

"Very well, my mother. I'll abide by the end."

"We'll see!"

"And she's—she's *awfully* nice, mother; she is really! You don't know!"

"That's not the same as marrying her."

"It's perhaps better."

There was silence for a while. He wanted to ask his mother something, but was afraid.

"Should you like to know her?" He hesitated.

"Yes," said Mrs. Morel coolly. "I should like to know what she's like."

"But she's nice, mother, she is! And not a bit common!"

"I never suggested she was."

"But you seem to think she's—not as good as— She's better than ninety-nine folk out of a hundred, I tell you! She's *better*, she is! She's fair, she's honest, she's straight! There isn't anything underhand or superior about her. Don't be mean about her!"

512

Mrs. Morel flushed.

"I am sure I am not mean about her. She may be quite as you say, but——"

"You don't approve," he finished.

"And do you expect me to?" she answered coldly.

"Yes!—yes!—if you'd anything about you, you'd be glad! Do you *want* to see her?"

"I said I did."

"Then I'll bring her—shall I bring her here?"

"You please yourself."

"Then I *will* bring her here—one Sunday—to tea. If you think a horrid thing about her, I shan't forgive you."

His mother laughed.

"As if it would make any difference!" she said.

He knew he had won.

"Oh, but it feels so fine, when she's there! She's such a queen in her way."

Occasionally he still walked a little way from chapel with Miriam and Edgar. He did not go up to the farm. She, however, was very much the same with him, and he did not feel embarrassed in her presence. One evening she was alone when he accompanied her. They began by talking books: it was their unfailing topic. Mrs. Morel had said that his and Miriam's affair was like a fire fed on books—if there were no more volumes it would die out. Miriam, for her part, boasted that she could read him like a book, could place her finger any minute on the chapter and the line. He, easily taken in, believed that Miriam knew more about him than anyone else. So it pleased him to talk to her about himself, like the simplest egoist. Very soon the conversation drifted to his own doings. It flattered him immensely that he was of such supreme interest.

"And what have you been doing lately?"

"I—oh, not much! I made a sketch of Bestwood from the garden, that is nearly right at last. It's the hundredth try."

So they went on. Then she said:

"You've not been out, then, lately?"

"Yes; I went up Clifton Grove on Monday afternoon with Clara."

"It was not very nice weather," said Miriam, "was it?"

"But I wanted to go out, and it was all right. The Trent *is* full."

"And did you go to Barton?" she asked.

"No; we had tea in Clifton."

"*Did* you! That would be nice."

"It was! The jolliest old woman! She gave us several pompom dahlias, as pretty as you like."

Miriam bowed her head and brooded. He was quite unconscious of concealing anything from her.

"What made her give them you?" she asked.

He laughed.

"Because she liked us—because we were jolly, I should think."

Miriam put her finger in her mouth.

"Were you late home?" she asked.

At last he resented her tone.

"I caught the seven-thirty."

514

"Ha!"

They walked on in silence, and he was angry.

"And how *is* Clara?" asked Miriam.

"Quite all right, I think."

"That's good!" she said, with a tinge of irony. "By the way, what of her husband? One never hears anything of him."

"He's got some other woman, and is also quite all right," he replied. "At least, so I think."

"I see—you don't know for certain. Don't you think a position like that is hard on a woman?"

"Rottenly hard!"

"It's so unjust!" said Miriam. "The man does as he likes——"

"Then let the woman also," he said.

"How can she? And if she does, look at her position!"

"What of it?"

"Why, it's impossible! You don't understand what a woman forfeits——"

"No, I don't. But if a woman's got nothing but her fair fame to feed on, why, it's thin tack, and a donkey would die of it!"

So she understood his moral attitude, at least, and she knew he would act accordingly.

She never asked him anything direct, but she got to know enough.

Another day, when he saw Miriam, the conversation turned to marriage, then to Clara's marriage with Dawes.

"You see," he said, "she never knew the fearful

importance of marriage. She thought it was all in the day's march—it would have to come—and Dawes—well, a good many women would have given their souls to get him; so why not him? Then she developed into the *femme incomprise*, and treated him badly, I'll bet my boots."

"And she left him because he didn't understand her?"

"I suppose so. I suppose she had to. It isn't altogether a question of understanding; it's a question of living. With him, she was only half-alive; the rest was dormant, deadened. And the dormant woman was the *femme incomprise*, and she *had* to be awakened."

"And what about him."

"I don't know. I rather think he loves her as much as he can, but he's a fool."

"It was something like your mother and father," said Miriam.

"Yes; but my mother, I believe, got real joy and satisfaction out of my father at first. I believe she had a passion for him; that's why she stayed with him. After all, they were bound to each other."

"Yes," said Miriam.

"That's what one *must have*, I think," he continued—"the real, real flame of feeling through another person—once, only once, if it only lasts three months. See, my mother looks as if she'd *had* everything that was necessary for her living and developing. There's not a tiny bit of feeling of sterility about her."

516

"No," said Miriam.

"And with my father, at first, I'm sure she had the real thing. She knows; she has been there. You can feel it about her, and about him, and about hundreds of people you meet every day; and, once it has happened to you, you can go on with anything and ripen."

"What happened, exactly?" asked Miriam.

"It's so hard to say, but the something big and intense that changes you when you really come together with somebody else. It almost seems to fertilise your soul and make it that you can go on and mature."

"And you think your mother had it with your father?"

"Yes; and at the bottom she feels grateful to him for giving it her, even now, though they are miles apart."

"And you think Clara never had it?"

"I'm sure."

Miriam pondered this. She saw what he was seeking—a sort of baptism of fire in passion, it seemed to her. She realised that he would never be satisfied till he had it. Perhaps it was essential to him, as to some men, to sow wild oats; and afterwards, when he was satisfied, he would not rage with restlessness any more, but could settle down and give her his life into her hands. Well, then, if he must go, let him go and have his fill—something big and intense, he called it. At any rate, when he had got it, he would not want it—that he said himself; he

517

would want the other thing that she could give him. He would want to be owned, so that he could work. It seemed to her a bitter thing that he must go, but she could let him go into an inn for a glass of whisky, so she could let him go to Clara, so long as it was something that would satisfy a need in him, and leave him free for herself to possess.

"Have you told your mother about Clara?" she asked.

She knew this would be a test of the seriousness of his feeling for the other woman: she knew he was going to Clara for something vital, not as a man goes for pleasure to a prostitute, if he told his mother.

"Yes," he said, "and she is coming to tea on Sunday."

"To your house?"

"Yes; I want mater to see her."

"Ah!"

There was a silence. Things had gone quicker than she thought. She felt a sudden bitterness that he could leave her so soon and so entirely. And was Clara to be accepted by his people, who had been so hostile to herself?

"I may call in as I go to chapel," she said. "It is a long time since I saw Clara."

"Very well," he said, astonished, and unconsciously angry.

On the Sunday afternoon he went to Keston to meet Clara at the station. As he stood on the platform he was trying to examine in himself if he had a premonition.

"Do I *feel* as if she'd come?" he said to himself, and he tried to find out. His heart felt queer and contracted. That seemed like foreboding. Then he *had* a foreboding she would not come! Then she would not come, and instead of taking her over the fields home, as he had imagined, he would have to go alone. The train was late; the afternoon would be wasted, and the evening. He hated her for not coming. Why had she promised, then, if she could not keep her promise? Perhaps she had missed her train—he himself was always missing trains—but that was no reason why she should miss this particular one. He was angry with her; he was furious.

Suddenly he saw the train crawling, sneaking round the corner. Here, then, was the train, but of course she had not come. The green engine hissed along the platform, the row of brown carriages drew up, several doors opened. No; she had not come! No! Yes; ah, there she was! She had a big black hat on! He was at her side in a moment.

"I thought you weren't coming," he said.

She was laughing rather breathlessly as she put out her hand to him; their eyes met. He took her quickly along the platform, talking at a great rate to hide his feeling. She looked beautiful. In her hat were large silk roses, coloured like tarnished gold. Her costume of dark cloth fitted so beautifully over her breast and shoulders. His pride went up as he walked with her. He felt the station people, who

519

knew him, eyed her with awe and admiration.

"I was sure you weren't coming," he laughed shakily.

She laughed in answer, almost with a little cry.

"And I wondered, when I was in the train, what*ever* I should do if you weren't there!" she said.

He caught her hand impulsively, and they went along the narrow twitchel. They took the road into Nuttall and over the Reckoning House Farm. It was a blue, mild day. Everywhere the brown leaves lay scattered; many scarlet hips stood upon the hedge beside the wood. He gathered a few for her to wear.

"Though, really," he said, as he fitted them into the breast of her coat, "you ought to object to my getting them, because of the birds. But they don't care much for rose-hips in this part, where they can get plenty of stuff. You often find the berries going rotten in the springtime."

So he chattered, scarcely aware of what he said, only knowing he was putting berries in the bosom of her coat, while she stood patiently for him. And she watched his quick hands, so full of life, and it seemed to her she had never *seen* anything before. Till now, everything had been indistinct.

They came near to the colliery. It stood quite still and black among the corn-fields, its immense heap of slag seen rising almost from the oats.

"What a pity there is a coal-pit here where it is so pretty!" said Clara.

"Do you think so?" he answered. "You see, I am so used to it I should miss it. No; and I like the pits here and there. I like the rows of trucks, and the headstocks, and the steam in the daytime, and the lights at night. When I was a boy, I always thought a pillar of cloud by day and a pillar of fire by night was a pit, with its steam, and its lights, and the burning bank,—and I thought the Lord was always at the pit-top."

As they drew near home she walked in silence, and seemed to hang back. He pressed her fingers in his own. She flushed, but gave no response.

"Don't you want to come home?" he asked.

"Yes, I want to come," she replied.

It did not occur to him that her position in his home would be rather a peculiar and difficult one. To him it seemed just as if one of his men friends were going to be introduced to his mother, only nicer.

The Morels lived in a house in an ugly street that ran down a steep hill. The street itself was hideous. The house was rather superior to most. It was old, grimy, with a big bay window, and it was semi-detached; but it looked gloomy. Then Paul opened the door to the garden, and all was different. The sunny afternoon was there, like another land. By the path grew tansy and little trees. In front of the window was a plot of sunny grass, with old lilacs round it. And away went the garden, with heaps of dishevelled chrysanthemums in the sunshine, down to the sycamore-tree, and the field, and beyond one looked over a few red-roofed cottages to the hills with all the glow of the autumn afternoon.

Mrs. Morel sat in her rocking-chair, wearing her black silk blouse. Her grey-brown hair was taken smooth back from her brow and her high temples; her face was rather pale. Clara, suffering, followed Paul into the kitchen. Mrs. Morel rose. Clara thought her a lady, even rather stiff. The young woman was very nervous. She had almost a wistful look, almost resigned.

"Mother—Clara," said Paul.

Mrs. Morel held out her hand and smiled.

"He has told me a good deal about you," she said.

The blood flamed in Clara's cheek.

"I hope you don't mind my coming," she faltered.

"I was pleased when he said he would bring you," replied Mrs. Morel.

Paul, watching, felt his heart contract with pain. His mother looked so small, and sallow, and done-for beside the luxuriant Clara.

"It's such a pretty day, mother!" he said. "And we saw a jay."

His mother looked at him; he had turned to her. She thought what a man he seemed, in his dark, well-made clothes. He was pale and detached-looking; it would be hard for any woman to keep him. Her heart glowed; then she was sorry for Clara.

"Perhaps you'll leave your things in the parlour," said Mrs. Morel nicely to the young woman.

"Oh, thank you," she replied.

"Come on," said Paul, and he led the way into

522

the little front room, with its old piano, its mahogany furniture, its yellowing marble mantelpiece. A fire was burning; the place was littered with books and drawing-boards. "I leave my things lying about," he said. "It's so much easier."

She loved his artist's paraphernalia, and the books, and the photos of people. Soon he was telling her: this was William, this was William's young lady in the evening dress, this was Annie and her husband, this was Arthur and his wife and the baby. She felt as if she were being taken into the family. He showed her photos, books, sketches, and they talked a little while. Then they returned to the kitchen. Mrs. Morel put aside her book. Clara wore a blouse of fine silk chiffon, with narrow black-and-white stripes; her hair was done simply, coiled on top of her head. She looked rather stately and reserved.

"You have gone to live down Sneinton Boulevard?" said Mrs. Morel. "When I was a girl—girl, I say!—when I was a young woman *we* lived in Minerva Terrace."

"Oh, did you!" said Clara. "I have a friend in number 6."

And the conversation had started. They talked Nottingham and Nottingham people; it interested them both. Clara was still rather nervous; Mrs. Morel was still somewhat on her dignity. She clipped her language very clear and precise. But they were going to get on well together, Paul saw.

Mrs. Morel measured herself against the younger

woman, and found herself easily stronger. Clara was deferential. She knew Paul's surprising regard for his mother, and she had dreaded the meeting, expecting someone rather hard and cold. She was surprised to find this little interested woman chatting with such readiness; and then she felt, as she felt with Paul, that she would not care to stand in Mrs. Morel's way. There was something so hard and certain in his mother, as if she never had a misgiving in her life.

Presently Morel came down, ruffled and yawning, from his afternoon sleep. He scratched his grizzled head, he podded in his stocking feet, his waistcoat hung open over his shirt. He seemed incongruous.

"This is Mrs. Dawes, father," said Paul.

Then Morel pulled himself together. Clara saw Paul's manner of bowing and shaking hands.

"Oh, indeed!" exclaimed Morel. "I am very glad to see you—I am, I assure you. But don't disturb yourself. No, no make yourself quite comfortable, and be very welcome."

Clara was astonished at this flood of hospitality from the old collier. He was so courteous, so gallant! She thought him most delightful.

"And may you have come far?" he asked.

"Only from Nottingham," she said.

"From Nottingham! Then you have had a beautiful day for your journey."

Then he strayed into the scullery to wash his hands and face, and from force of habit came on to the hearth with the towel to dry himself.

At tea Clara felt the refinement and sang-froid of the household. Mrs. Morel was perfectly at her ease. The pouring out the tea and attending to the people went on unconsciously, without interrupting her in her talk. There was a lot of room at the oval table; the china of dark blue willow-pattern looked pretty on the glossy cloth. There was a little bowl of small, yellow chrysanthemums. Clara felt she completed the circle, and it was a pleasure to her. But she was rather afraid of the self-possession of the Morels, father and all. She took their tone; there was a feeling of balance. It was a cool, clear atmosphere, where everyone was himself, and in harmony. Clara enjoyed it, but there was a fear deep at the bottom of her.

Paul cleared the table whilst his mother and Clara talked. Clara was conscious of his quick, vigorous body as it came and went, seeming blown quickly by a wind at its work. It was almost like the hither and thither of a leaf that comes unexpected. Most of herself went with him. By the way she leaned forward, as if listening, Mrs. Morel could see she was possessed elsewhere as she talked, and again the elder woman was sorry for her.

Having finished, he strolled down the garden, leaving the two women to talk. It was a hazy, sunny afternoon, mild and soft. Clara glanced through the window after him as he loitered among the chrysanthemums. She felt as if something almost tangible fastened her to him; yet he seemed so easy in his graceful, indolent movement, so detached as he tied up the too-heavy flower branches to their stakes, that she wanted to shriek in her helplessness.

Mrs. Morel rose.

"You will let me help you wash up," said Clara.

"Eh, there are so few, it will only take a minute," said the other.

Clara, however, dried the tea-things, and was glad to be on such good terms with his mother; but it was torture not to be able to follow him down the garden. At last she allowed herself to go; she felt as if a rope were taken off her ankle.

The afternoon was golden over the hills of Derbyshire. He stood across in the other garden, beside a bush of pale Michaelmas daisies, watching the last bees crawl into the hive. Hearing her coming, he turned to her with an easy motion, saying:

"It's the end of the run with these chaps."

Clara stood near him. Over the low red wall in front was the country and the far-off hills, all golden dim.

At that moment Miriam was entering through the garden-door. She saw Clara go up to him, saw him turn, and saw them come to rest together. Something in their perfect isolation together made her know that it was accomplished between them, that they were, as she put it, married. She walked very slowly down the cinder-track of the long garden.

Clara had pulled a button from a hollyhock spire, and was breaking it to get the seeds. Above her bowed head the pink flowers stared, as if defending her. The last bees were falling down to the hive.

"Count your money," laughed Paul, as she broke the flat seeds one by one from the roll of coin. She looked at him.

"I'm well off," she said, smiling.

"How much? Pf!" He snapped his fingers. "Can I turn them into gold?"

"I'm afraid not," she laughed.

They looked into each other's eyes, laughing. At that moment they became aware of Miriam. There was a click, and everything had altered.

"Hello, Miriam!" he exclaimed. "You said you'd come!"

"Yes. Had you forgotten?"

She shook hands with Clara, saying:

"It seems strange to see you here."

"Yes," replied the other; "it seems strange to be here."

There was a hesitation.

"This is pretty, isn't it?" said Miriam.

"I like it very much," replied Clara.

Then Miriam realised that Clara was accepted as she had never been.

"Have you come down alone?" asked Paul.

"Yes; I went to Agatha's to tea. We are going to chapel. I only called in for a moment to see Clara."

"You should have come in here to tea," he said.

Miriam laughed shortly, and Clara turned impatiently aside.

"Do you like the chrysanthemums?" he asked.

"Yes; they are very fine," replied Miriam.

"Which sort do you like best?" he asked.

"I don't know. The bronze, I think."

"I don't think you've seen all the sorts. Come and look. Come and see which are *your* favourites, Clara."

He led the two women back to his own garden, where the towsled bushes of flowers of all colours stood raggedly along the path down to the field. The situation did not embarrass him, to his knowledge.

"Look, Miriam; these are the white ones that came from your garden. They aren't so fine here, are they?"

"No," said Miriam.

"But they're hardier. You're so sheltered; things grow big and tender, and then die. These little yellow ones I like. Will you have some?"

While they were out there the bells began to ring in the church, sounding loud across the town and the field. Miriam looked at the tower, proud among the clustering roofs, and remembered the sketches he had brought her. It had been different then, but he had not left her even yet. She asked him for a book to read. He ran indoors.

"What! is that Miriam?" asked his mother coldly.

"Yes; she said she'd call and see Clara."

"You told her, then?" came the sarcastic answer.

"Yes; why shouldn't I?"

"There's certainly no reason why you shouldn't," said Mrs. Morel, and she returned to her book. He

528

winced from his mother's irony, frowned irritably, thinking: "Why can't I do as I like?"

"You've not seen Mrs. Morel before?" Miriam was saying to Clara.

"No; but she's *so* nice!"

"Yes," said Miriam, dropping her head; "in some ways she's very fine."

"I should think so."

"Had Paul told you much about her?"

"He had talked a good deal."

"Ha!"

There was silence until he returned with the book.

"When will you want it back?" Miriam asked.

"When you like," he answered.

Clara turned to go indoors, whilst he accompanied Miriam to the gate.

"When will you come up to Willey Farm?" the latter asked.

"I couldn't say," replied Clara.

"Mother asked me to say she'd be pleased to see you any time, if you cared to come."

"Thank you; I should like to, but I can't say when."

"Oh, very well!" exclaimed Miriam rather bitterly, turning away.

She went down the path with her mouth to the flowers he had given her.

"You're sure you won't come in?" he said.

"No, thanks."

"We are going to chapel."

"Ah, I shall see you, then!" Miriam was very bitter.

"Yes."

They parted. He felt guilty towards her. She was bitter, and she scorned him. He still belonged to herself, she believed; yet he could have Clara, take her home, sit with her next his mother in chapel, give her the same hymn-book he had given herself years before. She heard him running quickly indoors.

But he did not go straight in. Halting on the plot of grass, he heard his mother's voice, then Clara's answer:

"What I hate is the bloodhound quality in Miriam."

"Yes," said his mother quickly, "yes; *doesn't* it make you hate her, now!"

His heart went hot, and he was angry with them for talking about the girl. What right had they to say that? Something in the speech itself stung him into a flame of hate against Miriam. Then his own heart rebelled furiously at Clara's taking the liberty of speaking so about Miriam. After all, the girl was the better woman of the two, he thought, if it came to goodness. He went indoors. His mother looked excited. She was beating with her hand rhythmically on the sofa-arm, as women do who are wearing out. He could never bear to see the movement. There was a silence. Then he began to talk.

In chapel Miriam saw him find the place in the hymn-book for Clara, in exactly the same way as he used for herself. And during the sermon he could see the girl across the chapel, her hat throwing a dark shadow over her face. What did she think, seeing Clara with him? He did not stop to consider. He felt himself cruel towards Miriam.

After chapel he went over Pentrich with Clara. It was a dark autumn night. They had said goodbye to Miriam, and his heart had smitten him as he left the girl alone. "But it serves her right," he said inside himself, and it almost gave him pleasure to go off under her eyes with this other handsome woman.

There was a scent of damp leaves in the darkness. Clara's hand lay warm and inert in his own as they walked. He was full of conflict. The battle that raged inside him made him feel desperate.

Up Pentrich Hill Clara leaned against him as he went. He slid his arm round her waist. Feeling the strong motion of her body under his arm as she walked, the tightness in his chest because of Miriam relaxed, and the hot blood bathed him. He held her closer and closer.

Then: "You still keep on with Miriam," she said quietly.

"Only talk. There never *was* a great deal more than talk between us," he said bitterly.

"Your mother doesn't care for her," said Clara.

"No, or I might have married her. But it's all up really!"

Suddenly his voice went passionate with hate.

"If I was with her now, we should be jawing about the 'Christian Mystery', or some such tack. Thank God, I'm not!"

531

They walked on in silence for some time.

"But you can't really give her up," said Clara.

"I don't give her up, because there's nothing to give," he said.

"There is for her."

"I don't know why she and I shouldn't be friends as long as we live," he said. "But it'll only be friends."

Clara drew away from him, leaning away from contact with him.

"What are you drawing away for?" he asked.

She did not answer, but drew farther from him.

"Why do you want to walk alone?" he asked.

Still there was no answer. She walked resentfully, hanging her head.

"Because I said I would be friends with Miriam!" he exclaimed.

She would not answer him anything.

"I tell you it's only words that go between us," he persisted, trying to take her again.

She resisted. Suddenly he strode across in front of her, barring her way.

"Damn it!" he said. "What do you want now?"

"You'd better run after Miriam," mocked Clara.

The blood flamed up in him. He stood showing his teeth. She drooped sulkily. The lane was dark, quite lonely. He suddenly caught her in his arms, stretched forward, and put his mouth on her face in a kiss of rage. She turned frantically to avoid him. He held her fast. Hard and relentless his mouth came for her. Her breasts hurt against the wall of

532

his chest. Helpless, she went loose in his arms, and he kissed her, and kissed her.

He heard people coming down the hill.

"Stand up! stand up!" he said thickly, gripping her arm till it hurt. If he had let go, she would have sunk to the ground.

She sighed and walked dizzily beside him. They went on in silence.

"We will go over the fields," he said; and then she woke up.

But she let herself be helped over the stile, and she walked in silence with him over the first dark field. It was the way to Nottingham and to the station, she knew. He seemed to be looking about. They came out on a bare hilltop where stood the dark figure of the ruined windmill. There he halted. They stood together high up in the darkness, looking at the lights scattered on the night before them, handfuls of glittering points, villages lying high and low on the dark, here and there.

"Like treading among the stars," he said, with a quaky laugh.

Then he took her in his arms, and held her fast. She moved aside her mouth to ask, dogged and low:

"What time is it?"

"It doesn't matter," he pleaded thickly.

"Yes it does—yes! I must go!"

"It's early yet," he said.

"What time is it?" she insisted.

All round lay the black night, speckled and spangled with lights.

"I don't know."

She put her hand on his chest, feeling for his watch. He felt the joints fuse into fire. She groped in his waistcoat pocket, while he stood panting. In the darkness she could see the round, pale face of the watch, but not the figures. She stooped over it. He was panting till he could take her in his arms again.

"I can't see," she said.

"Then don't bother."

"Yes; I'm going!" she said, turning away.

"Wait! I'll look!" But he could not see. "I'll strike a match."

He secretly hoped it was too late to catch the train. She saw the glowing lantern of his hands as he cradled the light: then his face lit up, his eyes fixed on the watch. Instantly all was dark again. All was black before her eyes; only a glowing match was red near her feet. Where was he?

"What is it?" she asked, afraid.

"You can't do it," his voice answered out of the darkness.

There was a pause. She felt in his power. She had heard the ring in his voice. It frightened her.

"What time is it?" she asked, quiet, definite, hopeless.

"Two minutes to nine," he replied, telling the truth with a struggle.

"And can I get from here to the station in fourteen minutes?"

"No. At any rate——"

She could distinguish his dark form again a yard or so away. She wanted to escape

"But can't I do it?" she pleaded.

"If you hurry," he said brusquely. "But you could easily walk it, Clara; it's only seven miles to the tram. I'll come with you."

"No; I want to catch the train."

"But why?"

"I do—I want to catch the train."

Suddenly his voice altered.

"Very well," he said, dry and hard. "Come along, then."

And he plunged ahead into the darkness. She ran after him, wanting to cry. Now he was hard and cruel to her. She ran over the rough, dark fields behind him, out of breath, ready to drop. But the double row of lights at the station drew nearer. Suddenly:

"There she is!" he cried, breaking into a run.

There was a faint rattling noise. Away to the right the train, like a luminous caterpillar, was threading across the night. The rattling ceased.

"She's over the viaduct. You'll just do it."

Clara ran, quite out of breath, and fell at last into the train. The whistle blew. He was gone. Gone!—and she was in a carriage full of people. She felt the cruelty of it.

He turned round and plunged home. Before he knew where he was he was in the kitchen at home. He was very pale. His eyes were dark and dangerous-looking, as if he were drunk. His mother looked at him.

"Well, I must say your boots are in a nice state!" she said.

He looked at his feet. Then he took off his overcoat. His mother wondered if he were drunk.

"She caught the train then?" she said.

"Yes."

"I hope *her* feet weren't so filthy. Where on earth you dragged her I don't know!"

He was silent and motionless for some time.

"Did you like her?" he asked grudgingly at last.

"Yes, I liked her. But you'll tire of her, my son; you know you will."

He did not answer. She noticed how he laboured in his breathing.

"Have you been running?" she asked.

"We had to run for the train."

"You'll go and knock yourself up. You'd better drink hot milk."

It was as good a stimulant as he could have, but he refused and went to bed. There he lay face down on the counterpane, and shed tears of rage and pain. There was a physical pain that made him bite his lips till they bled, and the chaos inside him left him unable to think, almost to feel.

"This is how she serves me, is it?" he said in his heart, over and over, pressing his face in the quilt. And he hated her. Again he went over the scene, and again he hated her.

The next day there was a new aloofness about

536

him. Clara was very gentle, almost loving. But he treated her distantly, with a touch of contempt. She sighed, continuing to be gentle. He came round.

One evening of that week Sarah Bernhardt was at the Theatre Royal in Nottingham, giving "*La Dame aux Camélias*". Paul wanted to see this old and famous actress, and he asked Clara to accompany him. He told his mother to leave the key in the window for him.

"Shall I book seats?" he asked of Clara.

"Yes. And put on an evening suit, will you? I've never seen you in it."

"But, good Lord, Clara! Think of *me* in evening suit at the theatre!" he remonstrated.

"Would you rather not?" she asked.

"I will if you *want* me to; but I s'll feel a fool."

She laughed at him.

"Then feel a fool for my sake, once, won't you?"

The request made his blood flush up.

"I suppose I s'll have to."

"What are you taking a suitcase for?" his mother asked.

He blushed furiously.

"Clara asked me," he said.

"And what seats are you going in?"

"Circle—three-and-six each!"

"Well, I'm sure!" exclaimed his mother sarcastically.

"It's only once in the bluest of blue moons," he said.

He dressed at Jordan's, put on an overcoat and a cap, and met Clara in a café. She was with one of her suffragette friends. She wore an old long coat, which did not suit her, and had a little wrap over her head, which he hated. The three went to the theatre together.

Clara took off her coat on the stairs, and he discovered she was in a sort of semi-evening dress, that left her arms and neck and part of her breast bare. Her hair was done fashionably. The dress, a simple thing of green crape, suited her. She looked quite grand, he thought. He could see her figure inside the frock, as if that were wrapped closely round her. The firmness and the softness of her upright body could almost be felt as he looked at her. He clenched his fists.

And he was to sit all the evening beside her beautiful naked arm, watching the strong throat rise from the strong chest, watching the breasts under the green stuff, the curve of her limbs in the tight dress. Something in him hated her again for submitting him to this torture of nearness. And he loved her as she balanced her head and stared straight in front of her, pouting, wistful, immobile, as if she yielded herself to her fate because it was too strong for her. She could not help herself; she was in the grip of something bigger than herself. A kind of eternal look about her, as if she were a wistful sphinx, made it necessary for him to kiss her. He dropped his programme, and crouched down on the floor to get it, so that he could kiss her hand and wrist. Her beauty was a torture to him. She sat immobile. Only, when the lights went down, she sank a little against him, and he caressed her hand and arm with his fingers. He could smell her faint perfume. All the time his blood kept sweeping up in great white-hot waves that killed his consciousness momentarily.

The drama continued. He saw it all in the distance, going on somewhere; he did not know where, but it seemed far away inside him. He was Clara's white heavy arms, her throat, her moving bosom. That seemed to be himself. Then away somewhere the play went on, and he was identified with that also. There was no himself. The grey and black eyes of Clara, her bosom coming down on him, her arm that he held gripped between his hands, were all that existed. Then he felt himself small and helpless, her towering in her force above him.

Only the intervals, when the lights came up, hurt him expressibly. He wanted to run anywhere, so long as it would be dark again. In a maze, he wandered out for a drink. Then the lights were out, and the strange, insane reality of Clara and the drama took hold of him again.

The play went on. But he was obsessed by the desire to kiss the tiny blue vein that nestled in the bend of her arm. He could feel it. His whole face seemed suspended till he had put his lips there. It must be done. And the other people! At last he bent quickly forward and touched it with his lips. His moustache brushed the sensitive flesh. Clara shivered, drew away her arm.

539

When all was over, the lights up, the people clapping, he came to himself and looked at his watch. His train was gone.

"I s'll have to walk home!" he said.

Clara looked at him.

"Is it too late?" she asked.

He nodded. Then he helped her on with her coat.

"I love you! You look beautiful in that dress," he murmured over her shoulder, among the throng of bustling people.

She remained quiet. Together they went out of the theatre. He saw the cabs waiting, the people passing. It seemed he met a pair of brown eyes which hated him. But he did not know. He and Clara turned away, mechanically taking the direction to the station.

The train had gone. He would have to walk the ten miles home.

"It doesn't matter," he said. "I shall enjoy it."

"Won't you," she said, flushing, "come home for the night? I can sleep with mother."

He looked at her. Their eyes met.

"What will your mother say?" he asked.

"She won't mind."

"You're sure?"

"Quite!"

"*Shall* I come?"

"If you will."

"Very well."

And they turned away. At the first stopping-place they took the car. The wind blew fresh in their faces. The town was dark; the tram tipped in its haste. He sat with her hand fast in his.

"Will your mother be gone to bed?" he asked.

"She may be. I hope not."

They hurried along the silent, dark little street, the only people out of doors. Clara quickly entered the house. He hesitated.

He leaped up the step and was in the room. Her mother appeared in the inner doorway, large and hostile.

"Who have you got there?" she asked.

"It's Mr. Morel; he has missed his train. I thought we might put him up for the night, and save him a ten-mile walk."

"H'm," exclaimed Mrs. Radford. "That's your look-out! If you've invited him, he's very welcome as far as I'm concerned. *You* keep the house!"

"If you don't like me, I'll go away again," he said.

"Nay, nay, you needn't! Come along in! I dunno what you'll think of the supper I'd got her."

It was a little dish of chip potatoes and a piece of bacon. The table was roughly laid for one.

"You can have some more bacon," continued Mrs. Radford. "More chips you can't have."

"It's a shame to bother you," he said.

"Oh, don't you be apologetic! It doesn't *do* wi' me! You treated her to the theatre, didn't you?" There was a sarcasm in the last question.

"Well?" laughed Paul uncomfortably.

"Well, and what's an inch of bacon! Take your coat off."

The big, straight-standing woman was trying to estimate the situation. She moved about the cupboard. Clara took his coat. The room was very warm and cosy in the lamplight.

"My sirs!" exclaimed Mrs. Radford; "but you two's a pair of bright beauties, I must say! What's all that get-up for?"

"I believe we don't know," he said, feeling a victim.

"There isn't room in *this* house for two such bobby-dazzlers, if you fly your kites *that* high!" she rallied them. It was a nasty thrust.

He in his dinner jacket, and Clara in her green dress and bare arms, were confused. They felt they must shelter each other in that little kitchen.

"And look at *that* blossom!" continued Mrs. Radford, pointing to Clara. "What does she reckon she did it for?"

Paul looked at Clara. She was rosy; her neck was warm with blushes. There was a moment of silence.

"You like to see it, don't you?" he asked.

The mother had them in her power. All the time his heart was beating hard, and he was tight with anxiety. But he would fight her.

"Me like to see it!" exclaimed the old woman. "What should I like to see her make a fool of herself for?"

"I've seen people look bigger fools," he said. Clara was under his protection now.

"Oh, ay! and when was that?" came the sarcastic rejoinder.

"When they made frights of themselves," he answered.

Mrs. Radford, large and threatening, stood suspended on the hearthrug, holding her fork.

"They're fools either road," she answered at length, turning to the Dutch oven.

"No," he said, fighting stoutly. "Folk ought to look as well as they can."

"And do you call *that* looking nice!" cried the mother, pointing a scornful fork at Clara. "That—that looks as if it wasn't properly dressed!"

"I believe you're jealous that you can't swank as well," he said laughing.

"Me! I could have worn evening dress with anybody, if I'd wanted to!" came the scornful answer.

"And why didn't you want to?" he asked pertinently. "Or *did* you wear it?"

There was a long pause. Mrs. Radford readjusted the bacon in the Dutch oven. His heart beat fast, for fear he had offended her.

"Me!" she exclaimed at last. "No, I didn't! And when I was in service, I knew as soon as one of the maids came out in bare shoulders what sort *she* was, going to her sixpenny hop!"

"Were you too good to go to a sixpenny hop?" he said.

Clara sat with bowed head. His eyes were dark and glittering. Mrs. Radford took the Dutch oven from the fire, and stood near him, putting bits of bacon on his plate.

543

"*There's* a nice crozzly bit!" she said.

"Don't give me the best!" he said.

"*She's* got what *she* wants," was the answer.

There was a sort of scornful forbearance in the woman's tone that made Paul know she was mollified.

"But *do* have some!" he said to Clara.

She looked up at him with her grey eyes, humiliated and lonely.

"No thanks!" she said.

"Why won't you?" he answered carelessly.

The blood was beating up like fire in his veins. Mrs. Radford sat down again, large and impressive and aloof. He left Clara altogether to attend to the mother.

"They say Sarah Bernhardt's fifty," he said.

"Fifty! She's turned sixty!" came the scornful answer.

"Well," he said, "you'd never think it! She made me want to howl even now."

"I should like to see myself howling at *that* bad old baggage!" said Mrs. Radford. "It's time she began to think herself a grandmother, not a shrieking catamaran——"

He laughed.

"A catamaran is a boat the Malays use," he said.

"And it's a word as *I* use," she retorted.

"My mother does sometimes, and it's no good my telling her," he said.

"I s'd think she boxes your ears," said Mrs. Radford, good-humouredly.

544

"She'd like to, and she says she will, so I give her a little stool to stand on."

"That's the worst of my mother," said Clara. "She never wants a stool for anything."

"But she often can't touch *that* lady with a long prop," retorted Mrs. Radford to Paul.

"I s'd think she doesn't want touching with a prop," he laughed. "*I* shouldn't."

"It might do the pair of you good to give you a crack on the head with one," said the mother, laughing suddenly.

"Why are you so vindictive towards me?" he said. "I've not stolen anything from you."

"No; I'll watch that," laughed the older woman.

Soon the supper was finished. Mrs. Radford sat guard in her chair. Paul lit a cigarette. Clara went upstairs, returning with a sleeping-suit, which she spread on the fender to air.

"Why, I'd forgot all about *them*!" said Mrs. Radford. "Where have they sprung from?"

"Out of my drawer."

"H'm! You bought 'em for Baxter, an' he wouldn't wear 'em, would he?"—laughing. "Said he reckoned to do wi'out trousers i' bed." She turned confidentially to Paul, saying: "He couldn't *bear* 'em, them pyjama things."

The young man sat making rings of smoke.

"Well, it's everyone to his taste," he laughed.

Then followed a little discussion of the merits of pyjamas.

545

"My mother loves me in them," he said. "She says I'm a pierrot."

"I can imagine they'd suit you," said Mrs. Radford.

After a while he glanced at the little clock that was ticking on the mantelpiece. It was half-past twelve.

"It is funny," he said, "but it takes hours to settle down to sleep after the theatre."

"It's about time you did," said Mrs. Radford, clearing the table.

"Are *you* tired?" he asked of Clara.

"Not the least bit," she answered, avoiding his eyes.

"Shall we have a game at cribbage?" he said.

"I've forgotten it."

"Well, I'll teach you again. May we play crib, Mrs. Radford?" he asked.

"You'll please yourselves," she said; "but it's pretty late."

"A game or so will make us sleepy," he answered.

Clara brought the cards, and sat spinning her wedding-ring whilst he shuffled them. Mrs. Radford was washing up in the scullery. As it grew later Paul felt the situation getting more and more tense.

"Fifteen two, fifteen four, fifteen six, and two's eight——!"

The clock struck one. Still the game continued. Mrs. Radford had done all the little jobs preparatory to going to bed, had locked the door and filled the kettle. Still Paul went on dealing and counting. He was obsessed by Clara's arms and throat. He believed he could see where the division was just beginning for her breasts. He could not leave her. She watched his hands, and felt her joints melt as they moved quickly. She was so near; it was almost as if he touched her, and yet not quite. His mettle was roused. He hated Mrs. Radford. She sat on, nearly dropping asleep, but determined and obstinate in her chair. Paul glanced at her, then at Clara. She met his eyes, that were angry, mocking, and hard as steel. Her own answered him in shame. He knew *she*, at any rate, was of his mind. He played on.

At last Mrs. Radford roused herself stiffly, and said:

"Isn't it nigh on time you two was thinking o' bed?"

Paul played on without answering. He hated her sufficiently to murder her.

"Half a minute," he said.

The elder woman rose and sailed stubbornly into the scullery, returning with his candle, which she put on the mantelpiece. Then she sat down again. The hatred of her went so hot down his veins, he dropped his cards.

"We'll stop, then," he said, but his voice was still a challenge.

Clara saw his mouth shut hard. Again he glanced at her. It seemed like an agreement. She bent over the cards, coughing, to clear her throat.

"Well, I'm glad you've finished," said Mrs. Rad-

547

ford. "Here, take your things"—she thrust the warm suit in his hand—"and this is your candle. Your room's over this; there's only two, so you can't go far wrong. Well, good night. I hope you'll rest well."

"I'm sure I shall; I always do," he said.

"Yes; and so you ought at your age," she replied.

He bade good night to Clara, and went. The twisting stairs of white, scrubbed wood creaked and clanged at every step. He went doggedly. The two doors faced each other. He went in his room, pushed the door to, without fastening the latch.

It was a small room with a large bed. Some of Clara's hair-pins were on the dressing-table—her hair-brush. Her clothes and some skirts hung under a cloth in a corner. There was actually a pair of stockings over a chair. He explored the room. Two books of his own were there on the shelf. He undressed, folded his suit, and sat on the bed, listening. Then he blew out the candle, lay down, and in two minutes was almost asleep. Then click!—he was wide awake and writhing in torment. It was as if, when he had nearly got to sleep, something had bitten him suddenly and sent him mad. He sat up and looked at the room in the darkness, his feet doubled under him, perfectly motionless, listening. He heard a cat somewhere away outside; then the heavy, poised tread of the mother; then Clara's distinct voice:

"Will you unfasten my dress?"

548

There was silence for some time. At last the mother said:

"Now then! aren't you coming up?"

"No, not yet," replied the daughter calmly.

"Oh, very well then! If it's not late enough, stop a bit longer. Only you needn't come waking me up when I've got to sleep."

"I shan't be long," said Clara.

Immediately afterwards Paul heard the mother slowly mounting the stairs. The candlelight flashed through the cracks in his door. Her dress brushed the door, and his heart jumped. Then it was dark, and he heard the clatter of her latch. She was very leisurely indeed in her preparations for sleep. After a long time it was quite still. He sat strung up on the bed, shivering slightly. His door was an inch open. As Clara came upstairs, he would intercept her. He waited. All was dead silence. The clock struck two. Then he heard a slight scrape of the fender downstairs. Now he could not help himself. His shivering was uncontrollable. He felt he must go or die.

He stepped off the bed, and stood a moment, shuddering. Then he went straight to the door. He tried to step lightly. The first stair cracked like a shot. He listened. The old woman stirred in her bed. The staircase was dark. There was a slit of light under the stair-foot door, which opened into the kitchen. He stood a moment. Then he went on, mechanically. Every step creaked, and his back was creeping, lest the old woman's door should open behind him up above. He fumbled with the door at the bottom. The latch opened with a loud clack. He went through into the kitchen, and shut the door noisily behind him. The old woman daren't come now.

Then he stood, arrested. Clara was kneeling on a pile of white underclothing on the hearth-rug, her back towards him, warming herself. She did not look round, but sat crouching on her heels, and her rounded beautiful back was towards him, and her face was hidden. She was warming her body at the fire for consolation. The glow was rosy on one side, the shadow was dark and warm on the other. Her arms hung slack.

He shuddered violently, clenching his teeth and fists hard to keep control. Then he went forward to her. He put one hand on her shoulder, the fingers of the other hand under her chin to raise her face. A convulsed shiver ran through her, once, twice, at his touch. She kept her head bent.

"Sorry!" he murmured, realising that his hands were very cold.

Then she looked up at him, frightened, like a thing that is afraid of death.

"My hands are so cold," he murmured.

"I like it," she whispered, closing her eyes.

The breath of her words were on his mouth. Her arms clasped his knees. The cord of his sleeping-suit dangled against her and made her shiver. As the warmth went into him, his shuddering became less.

At length, unable to stand so any more, he raised

her, and she buried her head on his shoulder. His hands went over her slowly with an infinite tenderness of caress. She clung close to him, trying to hide herself against him. He clasped her very fast. Then at last she looked at him, mute, imploring, looking to see if she must be ashamed.

His eyes were dark, very deep, and very quiet. It was as if her beauty and his taking it hurt him, made him sorrowful. He looked at her with a little pain, and was afraid. He was so humble before her. She kissed him fervently on the eyes, first one, then the other, and she folded herself to him. She gave herself. He held her fast. It was a moment intense almost to agony.

She stood letting him adore her and tremble with joy of her. It healed her hurt pride. It healed her; it made her glad. It made her feel erect and proud again. Her pride had been wounded inside her. She had been cheapened. Now she radiated with joy and pride again. It was her restoration and her recognition.

Then he looked at her, his face radiant. They laughed to each other, and he strained her to his chest. The seconds ticked off, the minutes passed, and still the two stood clasped rigid together, mouth to mouth, like a statue in one block.

But again his fingers went seeking over her, restless, wandering, dissatisfied. The hot blood came up wave upon wave. She laid her head on his shoulder.

"Come you to my room," he murmured.

She looked at him and shook her head, her mouth pouting disconsolately, her eyes heavy with passion. He watched her fixedly.

"Yes!" he said.

Again she shook her head.

"Why not?" he asked.

She looked at him still heavily, sorrowfully, and again she shook her head. His eyes hardened, and he gave way.

When, later on, he was back in bed, he wondered why she had refused to come to him openly, so that her mother would know. At any rate, then things would have been definite. And she could have stayed with him the night, without having to go, as she was, to her mother's bed. It was strange, and he could not understand it. And then almost immediately he fell asleep.

He awoke in the morning with someone speaking to him. Opening his eyes, he saw Mrs. Radford, big and stately, looking down on him. She held a cup of tea in her hand.

"Do you think you're going to sleep till Doomsday?" she said.

He laughed at once.

"It ought only to be about five o'clock," he said.

"Well," she answered, "it's half-past seven, whether or not. Here, I've brought you a cup of tea."

He rubbed his face, pushed the tumbled hair off his forehead, and roused himself.

"What's it so late for!" he grumbled.

He resented being wakened. It amused her. She saw his neck in the flannel sleeping-jacket, as white and round as a girl's. He rubbed his hair crossly.

"It's no good your scratching your head," she said. "It won't make it no earlier. Here, an' how long d'you think I'm going to stand waiting wi' this here cup?"

"Oh, dash the cup!" he said.

"You should go to bed earlier," said the woman.

He looked up at her, laughing with impudence.

"I went to bed before *you* did," he said.

"Yes, my Guyney, you did!" she exclaimed.

"Fancy," he said, stirring his tea, "having tea brought to bed to me! My mother'll think I'm ruined for life."

"Don't she never do it?" asked Mrs. Radford.

"She'd as leave think of flying."

"Ah, I always spoilt my lot! That's why they've turned out such bad uns," said the elderly woman.

"You'd only Clara," he said. "And Mr. Radford's in heaven. So I suppose there's only you left to be the bad un."

"I'm not bad; I'm only soft," she said, as she went out of the bedroom. "I'm only a fool, I am!"

Clara was very quiet at breakfast, but she had a sort of air of proprietorship over him that pleased him infinitely. Mrs. Radford was evidently fond of him. He began to talk of his painting.

"What's the good," exclaimed the mother, "of your whittling and worrying and twistin' and tooin' at that painting of yours? What *good* does it do

553

you, I should like to know? You'd better be enjoyin' yourself."

"Oh, but," exclaimed Paul, "I made over thirty guineas last year."

"Did you! Well, that's a consideration, but it's nothing to the time you put in."

"And I've got four pounds owing. A man said he'd give me five pounds if I'd paint him and his missis and the dog and the cottage. And I went and put the fowls in instead of the dog, and he was waxy, so I had to knock a quid off. I was sick of it, and I didn't like the dog. I made a picture of it. What shall I do when he pays me the four pounds?"

"Nay! you know your own uses for your money," said Mrs. Radford.

"But I'm going to bust this four pounds. Should we go to the seaside for a day or two?"

"Who?"

"You and Clara and me."

"What, on your money!" she exclaimed, half-wrathful.

"Why not?"

"*You* wouldn't be long in breaking your neck at a hurdle race!" she said.

"So long as I get a good run for my money! Will you?"

"Nay; you may settle that atween you."

"And you're willing?" he asked, amazed and rejoicing.

"You'll do as you like," said Mrs. Radford, "whether I'm willing or not."

# 13

## BAXTER DAWES

SOON after Paul had been to the theatre with Clara, he was drinking in the Punch Bowl with some friends of his when Dawes came in. Clara's husband was growing stout; his eyelids were getting slack over his brown eyes; he was losing his healthy firmness of flesh. He was very evidently on the downward track. Having quarrelled with his sister, he had gone into cheap lodgings. His mistress had left him for a man who would marry her. He had been in prison one night for fighting when he was drunk, and there was a shady betting episode in which he was concerned.

Paul and he were confirmed enemies, and yet there was between them that peculiar feeling of intimacy, as if they were secretly near to each other, which sometimes exists between two people, although they never speak to one another. Paul often thought of Baxter Dawes, often wanted to get at him and be friends with him. He knew that Dawes often thought about him, and that the man was drawn to him by some bond or other. And yet the two never looked at each other save in hostility.

Since he was a superior employee at Jordan's, it was the thing for Paul to offer Dawes a drink.

"What'll you have?" he asked of him.

"Nowt wi' a bleeder like you!" replied the man.

Paul turned away with a slight disdainful movement of the shoulders, very irritating.

"The aristocracy," he continued, "is really a military institution. Take Germany, now. She's got thousands of aristocrats whose only means of existence is the army. They're deadly poor, and life's deadly slow. So they hope for a war. They look for war as a chance of getting on. Till there's a war they are idle good-for-nothings. When there's a war, they are leaders and commanders. There you are, then—they *want* war!"

He was not a favourite debater in the public-house, being too quick and overbearing. He irritated the older men by his assertive manner, and his cocksureness. They listened in silence, and were not sorry when he finished.

Dawes interrupted the young man's flow of eloquence by asking, in a loud sneer:

"Did you learn all that at th' theatre th' other night?"

Paul looked at him; their eyes met. Then he knew Dawes had seen him coming out of the theatre with Clara.

"Why, what about th' theatre?" asked one of Paul's associates, glad to get a dig at the young fellow, and sniffing something tasty.

"Oh, him in a bob-tailed evening suit, on the lardy-da!" sneered Dawes, jerking his head contemptuously at Paul.

"That's comin' it strong," said the mutual friend. "Tart an' all?"

"Tart, begod!" said Dawes.

"Go on; let's have it!" cried the mutual friend.

"You've got it," said Dawes, "an' I reckon Morelly had it an' all."

"Well, I'll be jiggered!" said the mutual friend. "An' was it a proper tart?"

"Tart, God blimey—yes!"

"How do you know?"

"Oh," said Dawes, "I reckon he spent th' night——"

There was a good deal of laughter at Paul's expense.

"But who *was* she? D'you know her?" asked the mutual friend.

"I should *shay sho*," said Dawes.

This brought another burst of laughter.

"Then spit it out," said the mutual friend.

Dawes shook his head, and took a gulp of beer.

"It's a wonder he hasn't let on himself," he said. "He'll be braggin' of it in a bit."

"Come on, Paul," said the friend; "it's no good. You might just as well own up."

"Own up what? That I happened to take a friend to the theatre?"

"Oh well, if it was all right, tell us who she was, lad," said the friend.

"She *was* all right," said Dawes.

Paul was furious. Dawes wiped his golden moustache with his fingers, sneering.

"Strike me——! One o' that sort?" said the mutual friend. "Paul, boy, I'm surprised at you. And do you know her, Baxter?"

"Just a bit, like!"

He winked at the other men.

"Oh well," said Paul, "I'll be going!"

The mutual friend laid a detaining hand on his shoulder.

"Nay," he said, "you don't get off as easy as that, my lad. We've got to have a full account of this business."

"Then get it from Dawes!" he said.

"You shouldn't funk your own deeds, man," remonstrated the friend.

Then Dawes made a remark which caused Paul to throw half a glass of beer in his face.

"Oh, Mr. Morel!" cried the barmaid, and she rang the bell for the "chucker-out".

Dawes spat and rushed for the young man. At that minute a brawny fellow with his shirt-sleeves rolled up and his trousers tight over his haunches intervened.

"Now, then!" he said, pushing his chest in front of Dawes.

"Come out!" cried Dawes.

Paul was leaning, white and quivering, against the brass rail of the bar. He hated Dawes, wished something could exterminate him at that minute; and at the same time, seeing the wet hair on the man's forehead, he thought he looked pathetic. He did not move.

"Come out, you —," said Dawes.

"That's enough, Dawes," cried the barmaid.

"Come on," said the "chucker-out", with kindly insistence, "you'd better be getting on."

And, by making Dawes edge away from his own close proximity, he worked him to the door.

"*That's* the little sod as started it!" cried Dawes, half-cowed, pointing to Paul Morel.

"Why, what a story, Mr. Dawes!" said the barmaid. "You know it was you all the time."

Still the "chucker-out" kept thrusting his chest forward at him, still he kept edging back, until he was in the doorway and on the steps outside; then he turned round.

"All right," he said, nodding straight at his rival.

Paul had a curious sensation of pity, almost of affection, mingled with violent hate, for the man. The coloured door swung to; there was silence in the bar.

"Serve him jolly well right!" said the barmaid.

"But it's a nasty thing to get a glass of beer in your eyes," said the mutual friend.

"I tell you *I* was glad he did," said the barmaid. "Will you have another, Mr. Morel?"

She held up Paul's glass questioningly. He nodded.

"He's a man as doesn't care for anything, is Baxter Dawes," said one.

"Pooh! is he?" said the barmaid. "He's a loud-mouthed one, he is, and they're never much good. Give me a pleasant-spoken chap, if you want a devil!"

"Well, Paul, my lad," said the friend, "you'll have to take care of yourself now for a while."

"You won't have to give him a chance over you, that's all," said the barmaid.

"Can you box?" asked a friend.

"Not a bit," he answered, still very white.

"I might give you a turn or two," said the friend.

"Thanks, I haven't time."

And presently he took his departure.

"Go along with him, Mr. Jenkinson," whispered the barmaid, tipping Mr. Jenkinson the wink.

The man nodded, took his hat, said: "Good night all!" very heartily, and followed Paul, calling:

"Half a minute, old man. You an' me's going the same road, I believe."

"Mr. Morel doesn't like it," said the barmaid. "You'll see, we shan't have him in much more. I'm sorry; he's good company. And Baxter Dawes wants locking up, that's what he wants."

Paul would have died rather than his mother should get to know of this affair. He suffered tortures of humiliation and self-consciousness. There was now a good deal of his life of which necessarily he could not speak to his mother. He had a life apart from her—his sexual life. The rest she still kept. But he felt he had to conceal something from her, and it irked him. There was a certain silence between them, and he felt he had, in that silence, to defend himself against her; he felt condemned by her. Then sometimes he hated her, and pulled at her bondage. His life wanted to free itself of her. It

560

was like a circle where life turned back on itself, and got no farther. She bore him, loved him, kept him, and his love turned back into her, so that he could not be free to go forward with his own life, really love another woman. At this period, unknowingly, he resisted his mother's influence. He did not tell her things; there was a distance between them.

Clara was happy, almost sure of him. She felt she had at last got him for herself; and then again came the uncertainty. He told her jestingly of the affair with her husband. Her colour came up, her grey eyes flashed.

"That's him to a 'T'," she cried—"like a navvy! He's not fit for mixing with decent folk."

"Yet you married him," he said.

It made her furious that he reminded her.

"I did!" she cried. "But how was I to know?"

"I think he might have been rather nice," he said.

"You think *I* made him what he is!" she exclaimed.

"Oh no! he made himself. But there's something about him——"

Clara looked at her lover closely. There was something in him she hated, a sort of detached criticism of herself, a coldness which made her woman's soul harden against him.

"And what are you going to do?" she asked.

"How?"

"About Baxter."

"There's nothing to do, is there?" he replied.

"You can fight him if you have to, I suppose?" she said.

561

"No; I haven't the least sense of the 'fist'. It's funny. With most men there's the instinct to clench the fist and hit. It's not so with me. I should want a knife or a pistol or something to fight with."

"Then you'd better carry something," she said.

"Nay," he laughed; "I'm not a daggeroso."

"But he'll do something to you. You don't know him."

"All right," he said, "we'll see."

"And you'll let him?"

"Perhaps, if I can't help it."

"And if he kills you?" she said.

"I should be sorry, for his sake and mine."

Clara was silent for a moment.

"You *do* make me angry!" she exclaimed.

"That's nothing afresh," he laughed.

"But why are you so silly? You don't know him."

"And don't want."

"Yes, but you're not going to let a man do as he likes with you?"

"What must I do?" he replied, laughing.

"*I* should carry a revolver," she said. "I'm sure he's dangerous."

"I might blow my fingers off," he said.

"No; but won't you?" she pleaded.

"No."

"Not anything?"

"No."

"And you'll leave him to——?"

"Yes."

"You are a fool!"

562

"Fact!"

She set her teeth with anger.

"I could *shake* you!" she cried, trembling with passion.

"Why?"

"Let a man like *him* do as he likes with you."

"You can go back to him if he triumphs," he said.

"Do you want me to hate you?" she asked.

"Well, I only tell you," he said.

"And *you* say you *love* me!" she exclaimed, low and indignant.

"Ought I to slay him to please you?" he said. "But if I did, see what a hold he'd have over me."

"Do you think I'm a fool!" she exclaimed.

"Not at all. But you don't understand me, my dear."

There was a pause between them.

"But you ought *not* to expose yourself," she pleaded.

He shrugged his shoulders.

" 'The man in righteousness arrayed,
The pure and blameless liver,
Needs not the keen Toledo blade,
Nor venom-freighted quiver,' "

he quoted.

She looked at him searchingly.

"I wish I could understand you," she said.

"There's simply nothing to understand," he laughed.

563

She bowed her head, brooding.

He did not see Dawes for several days; then one morning as he ran upstairs from the Spiral room he almost collided with the burly metal-worker.

"What the——!" cried the smith.

"Sorry!" said Paul, and passed on.

"*Sorry!*" sneered Dawes.

Paul whistled lightly, "Put Me among the Girls".

"I'll stop your whistle, my jockey!" he said.

The other took no notice.

"You're goin' to answer for that job of the other night."

Paul went to his desk in his corner, and turned over the leaves of the ledger.

"Go and tell Fanny I want order 097, quick!" he said to his boy.

Dawes stood in the doorway, tall and threatening, looking at the top of the young man's head.

"Six and five's eleven and seven's one-and-six," Paul added aloud.

"An' you hear, do you!" said Dawes.

"*Five and ninepence!*" He wrote a figure. "What's that?" he said.

"I'm going to show you what it is," said the smith.

The other went on adding the figures aloud.

"Yer crawlin' little ——, yer daresn't face me proper!"

Paul quickly snatched the heavy ruler. Dawes started. The young man ruled some lines in his ledger. The elder man was infuriated.

564

"But wait till I light on you, no matter where it is, I'll settle your hash for a bit, yer little swine!"

"All right," said Paul.

At that the smith started heavily from the doorway. Just then a whistle piped shrilly. Paul went to the speaking-tube.

"Yes!" he said, and he listened. "Er—yes!" He listened, then he laughed. "I'll come down directly. I've got a visitor just now."

Dawes knew from his tone that he had been speaking to Clara. He stepped forward.

"Yer little devil!" he said. "I'll visitor you, inside of two minutes! Think I'm goin' to have *you* whipperty-snappin' round?"

The other clerks in the warehouse looked up. Paul's office-boy appeared, holding some white article.

"Fanny says you could have had it last night if you'd let her know," he said.

"All right," answered Paul, looking at the stocking. "Get it off."

Dawes stood frustrated, helpless with rage. Morel turned round.

"Excuse me a minute," he said to Dawes, and he would have run downstairs.

"By God, I'll stop your gallop!" shouted the smith, seizing him by the arm. He turned quickly.

"Hey! Hey!" cried the office-boy, alarmed.

Thomas Jordan started out of his little glass office, and came running down the room.

"What's-a-matter, what's-a-matter?" he said, in his old man's sharp voice.

565

"I'm just goin' ter settle this little ——, that's all," said Dawes desperately.

"What do you mean?" snapped Thomas Jordan.

"What I say," said Dawes, but he hung fire.

Morel was leaning against the counter, ashamed, half-grinning.

"What's it all about?" snapped Thomas Jordan.

"Couldn't say," said Paul, shaking his head and shrugging his shoulders.

"Couldn't yer, couldn't yer!" cried Dawes, thrusting forward his handsome, furious face, and squaring his fist.

"Have you finished?" cried the old man, strutting. "Get off about your business, and don't come here tipsy in the morning."

Dawes turned his big frame slowly upon him.

"Tipsy!" he said. "Who's tipsy? I'm no more tipsy than *you* are!"

"We've heard that song before," snapped the old man. "Now you get off, and don't be long about it. Comin' *here* with your rowdying."

The smith looked down contemptuously on his employer. His hands, large, and grimy, and yet well shaped for his labour, worked restlessly. Paul remembered they were the hands of Clara's husband, and a flash of hate went through him.

"Get out before you're turned out!" snapped Thomas Jordan.

"Why, who'll turn me out?" said Dawes, beginning to sneer.

Mr. Jordan started, marched up to the smith,

waving him off, thrusting his stout little figure at the man, saying:

"Get off my premises—get off!"

He seized and twitched Dawes's arm.

"Come off!" said the smith, and with a jerk of the elbow he sent the little manufacturer staggering backwards.

Before anyone could help him, Thomas Jordan had collided with the flimsy spring-door. It had given way, and let him crash down the half-dozen steps into Fanny's room. There was a second of amazement; then men and girls were running. Dawes stood a moment looking bitterly on the scene, then he took his departure.

Thomas Jordan was shaken and bruised, not otherwise hurt. He was, however, beside himself with rage. He dismissed Dawes from his employment, and summoned him for assault.

At the trial Paul Morel had to give evidence. Asked how the trouble began, he said:

"Dawes took occasion to insult Mrs. Dawes and me because I accompanied her to the theatre one evening; then I threw some beer at him, and he wanted his revenge."

"*Cherchez la femme!*" smiled the magistrate.

The case was dismissed after the magistrate had told Dawes he thought him a skunk.

"You gave the case away," snapped Mr. Jordan to Paul.

"I don't think I did," replied the latter. "Besides, you didn't really want a conviction, did you?"

"What do you think I took the case up for?"

"Well," said Paul, "I'm sorry if I said the wrong thing." Clara was also very angry.

"Why need *my* name have been dragged in?" she said.

"Better speak it openly than leave it to be whispered."

"There was no need for anything at all," she declared.

"We are none the poorer," he said indifferently.

"*You* may not be," she said.

"And you?" he asked.

"I need never have been mentioned."

"I'm sorry," he said; but he did not sound sorry. He told himself easily: "She will come round." And she did.

He told his mother about the fall of Mr. Jordan and the trial of Dawes. Mrs. Morel watched him closely.

"And what do you think of it all?" she asked him.

"I think he's a fool," he said.

But he was very uncomfortable, nevertheless.

"Have you ever considered where it will end?" his mother said.

"No," he answered; "things work out of themselves."

"They do, in a way one doesn't like, as a rule," said his mother.

"And then one has to put up with them," he said.

"You'll find you're not as good at 'putting up' as you imagine," she said.

He went on working rapidly at his design.

"Do you ever ask *her* opinion?" she said at length.

"What of?"

"Of you, and the whole thing."

"I don't care what her opinion of me is. She's fearfully in love with me, but it's not very deep."

"But quite as deep as your feeling for her."

He looked up at his mother curiously.

"Yes," he said. "You know, mother, I think there must be something the matter with me, that I *can't* love. When she's there, as a rule, I *do* love her. Sometimes, when I see her just as *the woman*, I love her, mother; but then, when she talks and criticises, I often don't listen to her."

"Yet she's as much sense as Miriam."

"Perhaps; and I love her better than Miriam. But *why* don't they hold me?"

The last question was almost a lamentation. His mother turned away her face, sat looking across the room, very quiet, grave, with something of renunciation.

"But you wouldn't want to marry Clara?" she said.

"No; at first perhaps I would. But why—why don't I want to marry her or anybody? I feel sometimes as if I wronged my women, mother."

"How wronged them, my son?"

"I don't know."

He went on painting rather despairingly; he had touched the quick of the trouble.

"And as for wanting to marry," said his mother, "there's plenty of time yet."

569

"But no, mother. I even love Clara, and I did Miriam; but to *give* myself to them in marriage I couldn't. I couldn't belong to them. They seem to want *me*, and I can't ever give it them."

"You haven't met the right woman."

"And I shall never meet the right woman while you live," he said.

She was very quiet. Now she began to feel again tired, as if she were done.

"We'll see, my son," she answered.

The feeling that things were going in a circle made him mad.

Clara was, indeed, passionately in love with him, and he with her, as far as passion went. In the daytime he forgot her a good deal. She was working in the same building, but he was not aware of it. He was busy, and her existence was of no matter to him. But all the time she was in her Spiral room she had a sense that he was upstairs, a physical sense of his person in the same building. Every second she expected him to come through the door, and when he came it was a shock to her. But he was often short and offhand with her. He gave her his directions in an official manner, keeping her at bay. With what wits she had left she listened to him. She dared not misunderstand or fail to remember, but it was a cruelty to her. She wanted to touch his chest. She knew exactly how his breast was shapen under the waistcoat, and she wanted to touch it. It maddened her to hear his mechanical voice giving orders about the work. She wanted to break through the sham of it, smash the trivial coating of business which covered him with hardness, get at the man again; but she was afraid, and before she could feel one touch of his warmth he was gone, and she ached again.

He knew that she was dreary every evening she did not see him, so he gave her a good deal of his time. The days were often a misery to her, but the evenings and the nights were usually a bliss to them both. Then they were silent. For hours they sat together, or walked together in the dark, and talked only a few, almost meaningless words. But he had her hand in his, and her bosom left its warmth in his chest, making him feel whole.

One evening they were walking down by the canal, and something was troubling him. She knew she had not got him. All the time he whistled softly and persistently to himself. She listened, feeling she could learn more from his whistling than from his speech. It was a sad dissatisfied tune—a tune that made her feel he would not stay with her. She walked on in silence. When they came to the swing bridge he sat down on the great pole, looking at the stars in the water. He was a long way from her. She had been thinking.

"Will you always stay at Jordan's?" she asked.

"No," he answered without reflecting. "No; I s'll leave Nottingham and go abroad—soon."

"Go abroad! What for?"

"I dunno! I feel restless."

"But what shall you do?"

"I shall have to get some steady designing work, and some sort of sale for my pictures first," he said. "I am gradually making my way. I know I am."

"And when do you think you'll go?"

"I don't know. I shall hardly go for long, while there's my mother."

"You couldn't leave her?"

"Not for long."

She looked at the stars in the black water. They lay very white and staring. It was an agony to know he would leave her, but it was almost an agony to have him near her.

"And if you made a nice lot of money, what would you do?" she asked.

"Go somewhere in a pretty house near London with my mother."

"I see."

There was a long pause.

"I could still come and see you," he said. "I don't know. Don't ask me what I should do; I don't know."

There was a silence. The stars shuddered and broke upon the water. There came a breath of wind. He went suddenly to her, and put his hand on her shoulder.

"Don't ask me anything about the future," he said miserably. "I don't know anything. Be with me now, will you, no matter what it is?"

And she took him in her arms. After all, she was a married woman, and she had no right even to what he gave her. He needed her badly. She had him in her arms, and he was miserable. With her warmth she folded him over, consoled him, loved him. She would let the moment stand for itself.

After a moment he lifted his head as if he wanted to speak.

"Clara," he said, struggling.

She caught him passionately to her, pressed his head down on her breast with her hand. She could not bear the suffering in his voice. She was afraid in her soul. He might have anything of her—anything; but she did not want to *know*. She felt she could not bear it. She wanted him to be soothed upon her—soothed. She stood clasping him and caressing him, and he was something unknown to her—something almost uncanny. She wanted to soothe him into forgetfulness.

And soon the struggle went down in his soul, and he forgot. But then Clara was not there for him, only a woman, warm, something he loved and almost worshipped, there in the dark. But it was not Clara, and she submitted to him. The naked hunger and inevitability of his loving her, something strong and blind and ruthless in its primitiveness, made the hour almost terrible to her. She knew how stark and alone he was, and she felt it was great that he came to her; and she took him simply because his need was bigger either than her or him, and her soul was still within her. She did this for him in his need, even if he left her, for she loved him.

All the while the peewits were screaming in the field. When he came to, he wondered what was near his eyes, curving and strong with life in the dark, and what voice it was speaking. Then he realised it was the grass, and the peewit was calling. The warmth was Clara's breathing heaving. He lifted his head, and looked into her eyes. They were dark and shining and strange, life wild at the source staring into his life, stranger to him, yet meeting him; and he put his face down on her throat, afraid. What was she? A strong, strange, wild life, that breathed with his in the darkness through this hour. It was all so much bigger than themselves that he was hushed. They had met, and included in their meeting the thrust of the manifold grass stems, the cry of the peewit, the wheel of the stars.

When they stood up they saw other lovers stealing down the opposite hedge. It seemed natural they were there; the night contained them.

After such an evening they both were very still, having known the immensity of passion. They felt small, half-afraid, childish and wondering, like Adam and Eve when they lost their innocence and realised the magnificence of the power which drove them out of Paradise and across the great night and the great day of humanity. It was for each of them an initiation and a satisfaction. To know their own nothingness, to know the tremendous living flood which carried them always, gave them rest within themselves. If so great a magnificent power could overwhelm them, identify them altogether with itself, so that they knew they were only grains in the tremendous heave that lifted every grass blade its little height, and every tree, and living thing, then why fret about themselves? They could let themselves be carried by life, and they felt a sort of peace each in the other. There was a verification which they had had together. Nothing could nullify it, nothing could take it away; it was almost their belief in life.

But Clara was not satisfied. Something great was there, she knew: something great enveloped her. But it did not keep her. In the morning it was not the same. They had *known*, but she could not keep the moment. She wanted it again; she wanted something permanent. She had not realised fully. She thought it was he whom she wanted. He was not safe to her. This that had been between them might never be again; he might leave her. She had not got him; she was not satisfied. She had been there, but she had not gripped the—the something—she knew not what—which she was mad to have.

In the morning he had considerable peace, and was happy in himself. It seemed almost as if he had known the baptism of fire in passion, and it left him at rest. But it was not Clara. It was something that happened because of her, but it was not her. They were scarcely any nearer to each other. It was as if they had been blind agents of a great force.

When she saw him that day at the factory her heart melted like a drop of fire. It was his body, his brows. The drop of fire grew more intense in her breast; she must hold him. But he, very quiet, very subdued this morning, went on giving his instruc-

575

tion. She followed him into the dark, ugly basement, and lifted her arms to him. He kissed her, and the intensity of passion began to burn him again. Somebody was at the door. He ran upstairs; she returned to her room, moving as if in a trance.

After that the fire slowly went down. He felt more and more that his experience had been impersonal, and not Clara. He loved her. There was a big tenderness, as after a strong emotion they had known together; but it was not she who could keep his soul steady. He had wanted her to be something she could not be.

And she was mad with desire of him. She could not see him without touching him. In the factory, as he talked to her about Spiral hose, she ran her hand secretly along his side. She followed him out into the basement for a quick kiss; her eyes, always mute and yearning, full of unrestrained passion, she kept fixed on his. He was afraid of her, lest she should too flagrantly give herself away before the other girls. She invariably waited for him at dinner-time for him to embrace her before she went. He felt as if she were helpless, almost a burden to him, and it irritated him.

"But what do you always want to be kissing and embracing for?" he said. "Surely there's a time for everything."

She looked up at him, and the hate came into her eyes.

"*Do* I always want to be kissing you?" she said.

"Always, even if I come to ask you about the

work. I don't want anything to do with love when I'm at work. Work's work——"

"And what is love?" she asked. "Has it to have special hours?"

"Yes; out of work hours."

"And you'll regulate it according to Mr. Jordan's closing time?"

"Yes; and according to the freedom from business of any sort."

"It is only to exist in spare time?"

"That's all, and not always then—not the kissing sort of love."

"And that's all you think of it?"

"It's quite enough."

"I'm glad you think so."

And she was cold to him for some time—she hated him; and while she was cold and contemptuous, he was uneasy till she had forgiven him again. But when they started afresh they were not any nearer. He kept her because he never satisfied her.

In the spring they went together to the seaside. They had rooms at a little cottage near Theddlethorpe, and lived as man and wife. Mrs. Radford sometimes went with them.

It was known in Nottingham that Paul Morel and Mrs. Dawes were going together, but as nothing was very obvious, and Clara always a solitary person, and he seemed so simple and innocent, it did not make much difference.

He loved the Lincolnshire coast, and she loved the sea. In the early morning they often went out together to bathe. The grey of the dawn, the far, desolate reaches of the fenland smitten with winter, the sea-meadows rank with herbage, were stark enough to rejoice his soul. As they stepped on to the high-road from their plank bridge, and looked round at the endless monotony of levels, the land a little darker than the sky, the sea sounding small beyond the sandhills, his heart filled strong with the sweeping relentlessness of life. She loved him then. He was solitary and strong, and his eyes had a beautiful light.

They shuddered with cold; then he raced her down the road to the green turf bridge. She could run well. Her colour soon came, her throat was bare, her eyes shone. He loved her for being so luxuriously heavy, and yet so quick. Himself was light; she went with a beautiful rush. They grew warm, and walked hand in hand.

A flush came into the sky, the wan moon, half-way down the west, sank into insignificance. On the shadowy land things began to take life, plants with great leaves became distinct. They came through a pass in the big, cold sandhills on to the beach. The long waste of foreshore lay moaning under the dawn and the sea; the ocean was a flat dark strip with a white edge. Over the gloomy sea the sky grew red. Quickly the fire spread among the clouds and scattered them. Crimson burned to orange, orange to dull gold, and in a golden glitter the sun came up, dribbling fierily over the waves in little splashes, as if someone had gone along and the light had spilled from her pail as she walked.

The breakers ran down the shore in long, hoarse strokes. Tiny seagulls, like specks of spray, wheeled above the line of surf. Their crying seemed larger than they. Far away the coast reached out, and melted into the morning, the tussocky sandhills seemed to sink to a level with the beach. Mablethorpe was tiny on their right. They had alone the space of all this level shore, the sea, and the up-coming sun, the faint noise of the waters, the sharp crying of the gulls.

They had a warm hollow in the sandhills where the wind did not come. He stood looking out to sea.

"It's very fine," he said.

"Now don't get sentimental," she said.

It irritated her to see him standing gazing at the sea, like a solitary and poetic person. He laughed. She quickly undressed.

"There are some fine waves this morning," she said triumphantly.

She was a better swimmer than he; he stood idly watching her.

"Aren't you coming?" she said.

"In a minute," he answered.

She was white and velvet skinned, with heavy shoulders. A little wind, coming from the sea, blew across her body and ruffled her hair.

The morning was of a lovely limpid gold colour. Veils of shadow seemed to be drifting away on the north and the south. Clara stood shrinking slightly from the touch of the wind, twisting her hair. The sea-grass rose behind the white stripped woman. She glanced at the sea, then looked at him. He was watching her with dark eyes which she loved and could not understand. She hugged her breasts between her arms, cringing, laughing:

"Oo, it will be so cold!" she said.

He bent forward and kissed her, held her suddenly close, and kissed her again. She stood waiting. He looked into her eyes, then away at the pale sands.

"Go, then!" he said quietly.

She flung her arms round his neck, drew him against her, kissed him passionately, and went, saying:

"But you'll come in?"

"In a minute."

She went plodding heavily over the sand that was soft as velvet. He, on the sandhills, watched the great pale coast envelop her. She grew smaller, lost proportion, seemed only like a large white bird toiling forward.

"Not much more than a big white pebble on the beach, not much more than a clot of foam being blown and rolled over the sand," he said to himself.

She seemed to move very slowly across the vast sounding shore. As he watched, he lost her. She was dazzled out of sight by the sunshine. Again he saw her, the merest white speck moving against the white, muttering sea-edge.

"Look how little she is!" he said to himself. "She's lost like a grain of sand in the beach—just a concentrated speck blown along, a tiny white foam-bubble, almost nothing among the morning. Why does she absorb me?"

The morning was altogether uninterrupted: she was gone in the water. Far and wide the beach, the sandhills with their blue marram, the shining water, glowed together in immense, unbroken solitude.

"What is she, after all?" he said to himself "Here's the sea-coast morning, big and permanent and beautiful; there is she, fretting, always unsatisfied, and temporary as a bubble of foam. What does she mean to me, after all? She represents something, like a bubble of foam represents the sea. But what is *she*? It's not her I care for."

Then, startled by his own unconscious thoughts, that seemed to speak so distinctly that all the morning could hear, he undressed and ran quickly down the sands. She was watching for him. Her arm flashed up to him, she heaved on a wave, subsided, her shoulders in a pool of liquid silver. He jumped through the breakers, and in a moment her hand was on his shoulder.

He was a poor swimmer, and could not stay long in the water. She played round him in triumph, sporting with her superiority, which he begrudged her. The sunshine stood deep and fine on the water. They laughed in the sea for a minute or two, then raced each other back to the sandhills.

When they were drying themselves, panting heavily, he watched her laughing, breathless face, her bright shoulders, her breasts that swayed and

581

made him frightened as she rubbed them, and he thought again:

"But she is magnificent, and even bigger than the morning and the sea. Is she——? Is she——"

She, seeing his dark eyes fixed on her, broke off from her drying with a laugh.

"What are you looking at?" she said.

"You," he answered, laughing.

Her eyes met his, and in a moment he was kissing her white "goose-fleshed" shoulder, and thinking:

"What is she? What is she?"

She loved him in the morning. There was something detached, hard, and elemental about his kisses then, as if he were only conscious of his own will, not in the least of her and her wanting him.

Later in the day he went out sketching.

"You," he said to her, "go with your mother to Sutton. I am so dull."

She stood and looked at him. He knew she wanted to come with him, but he preferred to be alone. She made him feel imprisoned when she was there, as if he could not get a free deep breath, as if there were something on top of him. She felt his desire to be free of her.

In the evening he came back to her. They walked down the shore in the darkness, then sat for awhile in the shelter of the sandhills.

"It seems," she said, as they stared over the darkness of the sea, where no light was to be seen—"it seemed as if you only loved me at night—as if you didn't love me in the daytime."

582

He ran the cold sand through his fingers, feeling guilty under the accusation.

"The night is free to you," he replied. "In the daytime I want to be by myself."

"But why?" she said. "Why, even now, when we are on this short holiday?"

"I don't know. Love-making stifles me in the daytime."

"But it needn't be always love-making," she said.

"It always is," he answered, "when you and I are together."

She sat feeling very bitter.

"Do you ever want to marry me?" he asked curiously.

"Do you me?" she replied.

"Yes, yes; I should like us to have children," he answered slowly.

She sat with her head bent, fingering the sand.

"But you don't really want a divorce from Baxter, do you?" he said.

It was some minute before she replied.

"No," she said, very deliberately; "I don't think I do."

"Why?"

"I don't know."

"Do you feel as if you belonged to him?"

"No; I don't think so."

"What, then?"

"I think he belongs to me," she replied.

He was silent for some minutes, listening to the wind blowing over the hoarse, dark sea.

583

"And you never really intended to belong to *me?*" he said.

"Yes, I do belong to you," she answered.

"No," he said; "because you don't want to be divorced."

It was a knot they could not untie, so they left it, took what they could get, and what they could not attain they ignored.

"I consider you treated Baxter rottenly," he said another time.

He half-expected Clara to answer him, as his mother would: "You consider your own affairs, and don't know so much about other people's." But she took him seriously, almost to his own surprise.

"Why?" she said.

"I suppose you thought he was a lily of the valley, and so you put him in an appropriate pot, and tended him according. You made up your mind he was a lily of the valley and it was no good his being a cow-parsnip. You wouldn't have it."

"I certainly never imagined him a lily of the valley."

"You imagined him something he wasn't. That's just what a woman is. She thinks she knows what's good for a man, and she's going to see he gets it; and no matter if he's starving, he may sit and whistle for what he needs, while she's got him, and is giving him what's good for him."

"And what are you doing?" she asked.

"I'm thinking what tune I shall whistle," he laughed.

And instead of boxing his ears, she considered him in earnest.

"You think I want to give you what's good for you?" she asked.

"I hope so; but love should give a sense of freedom, not of prison. Miriam made me feel tied up like a donkey to a stake. I must feed on her patch, and nowhere else. It's sickening!"

"And would *you* let a *woman* do as she likes?"

"Yes; I'll see that she *likes* to love me. If she doesn't—well, I don't hold her."

"If you were as wonderful as you say——," replied Clara.

"I should be the marvel I am," he laughed.

There was a silence in which they hated each other, though they laughed.

"Love's a dog in a manger," he said.

"And which of us is the dog?" she asked.

"Oh well, you, of course."

So there went on a battle between them. She knew she never fully had him. Some part, big and vital in him, she had no hold over; nor did she ever try to get it, or even to realise what it was. And he knew in some way that she held herself still as Mrs. Dawes. She did not love Dawes, never had loved him; but she believed he loved her, at least depended on her. She felt a certain surety about him that she never felt with Paul Morel. Her passion for the young man had filled her soul, given her a certain satisfaction, eased her of her self-mistrust, her doubt. Whatever else she was, she was inwardly assured. It was almost as if she had gained *herself*, and stood now distinct and complete. She had received her confirmation; but she never believed that her life belonged to Paul Morel, nor his to her. They would separate in the end, and the rest of her life would be an ache after him. But at any rate, she *knew* now, she was sure of herself. And the same could almost be said of him. Together they had received the baptism of life, each through the other; but now their missions were separate. Where he wanted to go she could not come with him. They would have to part sooner or later. Even if they married, and were faithful to each other, still he would have to leave her, go on alone, and she would only have to attend to him when he came home. But it was not possible. Each wanted a mate to go side by side with.

Clara had gone to live with her mother upon Mapperley Plains. One evening, as Paul and she were walking along Woodborough Road, they met Dawes. Morel knew something about the bearing of the man approaching, but he was absorbed in his thinking at the moment, so that only his artist's eye watched the form of the stranger. Then he suddenly turned to Clara with a laugh, and put his hand on her shoulder, saying, laughing:

"But we walk side by side, and yet I'm in London arguing with an imaginary Orpen; and where are you?"

At that instant Dawes passed, almost touching Morel. The young man glanced, saw the dark brown eyes burning, full of hate and yet tired.

"Who was that?" he asked of Clara.

"It was Baxter," she replied.

Paul took his hand from her shoulder and glanced round; then he saw again distinctly the man's form as it approached him. Dawes still walked erect, with his fine shoulders flung back, and his face lifted; but there was a furtive look in his eyes that gave one the impression he was trying to get unnoticed past every person he met, glancing suspiciously to see what they thought of him. And his hands seemed to be wanting to hide. He wore old clothes, the trousers were torn at the knee, and the handkerchief tied round his throat was dirty; but his cap was still defiantly over one eye. As she saw him, Clara felt guilty. There was a tiredness and despair on his face that made her hate him, because it hurt her.

"He looks shady," said Paul.

But the note of pity in his voice reproached her, and made her feel hard.

"His true commonness comes out," she answered.

"Do you hate him?" he asked.

"You talk," she said, "about the cruelty of women; I wish you knew the cruelty of men in their brute force. They simply don't know that the woman exists."

"Don't *I*?" he said.

"No," she answered.

"Don't I know you exist?"

"About *me* you know nothing," she said bitterly—"about *me*!"

"No more than Baxter knew?" he asked.

"Perhaps not as much."

He felt puzzled, and helpless, and angry. There she walked unknown to him, though they had been through such experiences together.

"But you know *me* pretty well," he said.

She did not answer.

"Did you know Baxter as well as you know me?" he asked.

"He wouldn't let me," she said.

"And I have let you know me?"

"It's what men *won't* let you do. They won't let you get really near to them," she said.

"And haven't I let you?"

"Yes," she answered slowly; "but you've never come near to me. You can't come out of yourself, you can't. Baxter could do that better than you."

He walked on pondering. He was angry with her for preferring Baxter to him.

"You begin to value Baxter now you've not got him," he said.

"No; I can only see where he was different from you."

But he felt she had a grudge against him.

One evening, as they were coming home over the fields, she startled him by asking:

"Do you think it's worth it—the—the sex part?"

"The act of loving, itself?"

"Yes; is it worth anything to you?"

"But how can you separate it?" he said. "It's the

588

culmination of everything. All our intimacy culminates then."

"Not for me," she said.

He was silent. A flash of hate for her came up. After all, she was dissatisfied with him, even there, where he thought they fulfilled each other. But he believed her too implicitly.

"I feel," she continued slowly, "as if I hadn't got you, as if all of you weren't there, and as if it weren't *me* you were taking——"

"Who, then?"

"Something just for yourself. It has been fine, so that I daren't think of it. But is it *me* you want, or is it *It*?"

He again felt guilty. Did he leave Clara out of count, and take simply women? But he thought that was splitting a hair.

"When I had Baxter, actually had him, then I *did* feel as if I had all of him," she said.

"And it was better?" he asked.

"Yes, yes; it was more whole. I don't say you haven't given me more than he ever gave me."

"Or could give you."

"Yes, perhaps; but you've never given me yourself."

He knitted his brows angrily.

"If I start to make love to you," he said, "I just go like a leaf down the wind."

"And leave me out of count," she said.

"And then is it nothing to you?" he asked, almost rigid with chagrin.

589

"It's something; and sometimes you have carried me away—right away—I know—and—I reverence you for it—but——"

"Don't 'but' me," he said, kissing her quickly, as a fire ran through him.

She submitted, and was silent.

It was true as he said. As a rule, when he started love-making, the emotion was strong enough to carry with it everything—reason, soul, blood—in a great sweep, like the Trent carries bodily its backswirls and intertwinings, noiselessly. Gradually the little criticisms, the little sensations, were lost, thought also went, everything borne along in one flood. He became, not a man with a mind, but a great instinct. His hands were like creatures, living; his limbs, his body, were all life and consciousness, subject to no will of his, but living in themselves. Just as he was, so it seemed the vigorous, wintry stars were strong also with life. He and they struck with the same pulse of fire, and the same joy of strength which held the bracken-frond stiff near his eyes held his own body firm. It was as if he, and the stars, and the dark herbage, and Clara were licked up in an immense tongue of flame, which tore onwards and upwards. Everything rushed along in living beside him; everything was still, perfect in itself, along with him. This wonderful stillness in each thing in itself, while it was being borne along in a very ecstasy of living, seemed the highest point of bliss.

And Clara knew this held him to her, so she

trusted altogether to the passion. It, however, failed her very often. They did not often reach again the height of that once when the peewits had called. Gradually, some mechanical effort spoilt their loving, or, when they had splendid moments, they had them separately, and not so satisfactorily. So often he seemed merely to be running on alone; often they realised it had been a failure, not what they had wanted. He left her, knowing *that* evening had only made a little split between them. Their loving grew more mechanical, without the marvellous glamour. Gradually they began to introduce novelties, to get back some of the feeling of satisfaction. They would be very near, almost dangerously near to the river, so that the black water ran not far from his face, and it gave a little thrill; or they loved sometimes in a little hollow below the fence of the path where people were passing occasionally, on the edge of the town, and they heard footsteps coming, almost felt the vibration of the tread, and they heard what the passers-by said—strange little things that were never intended to be heard. And afterwards each of them was rather ashamed, and these things caused a distance between the two of them. He began to despise her a little, as if she had merited it!

One night he left her to go to Daybrook Station over the fields. It was very dark, with an attempt at snow, although the spring was so far advanced. Morel had not much time; he plunged forward. The town ceases almost abruptly on the edge of a steep hollow; there the houses with their yellow lights stand up against the darkness. He went over the stile, and dropped quickly into the hollow of the fields. Under the orchard one warm window shone in Swineshead Farm. Paul glanced round. Behind, the houses stood on the brim of the dip, black against the sky, like wild beasts glaring curiously with yellow eyes down into the darkness. It was the town that seemed savage and uncouth, glaring on the clouds at the back of him. Some creature stirred under the willows of the farm pond. It was too dark to distinguish anything.

He was close up to the next stile before he saw a dark shape leaning against it. The man moved aside.

"Good evening!" he said.

"Good evening!" Morel answered, not noticing.

"Paul Morel?" said the man.

Then he knew it was Dawes. The man stopped his way.

"I've got yer, have I?" he said awkwardly.

"I shall miss my train," said Paul.

He could see nothing of Dawes's face. The man's teeth seemed to chatter as he talked.

"You're going to get it from me now," said Dawes.

Morel attempted to move forward; the other man stepped in front of him.

"Are yer goin' to take that top-coat off," he said, "or are you goin' to lie down to it?"

Paul was afraid the man was mad.

"But," he said, "I don't know how to fight."

"All right, then," answered Dawes, and before the younger man knew where he was, he was staggering backwards from a blow across the face.

The whole night went black. He tore off his overcoat and coat, dodging a blow, and flung the garments over Dawes. The latter swore savagely. Morel, in his shirt-sleeves, was now alert and furious. He felt his whole body unsheath itself like a claw. He could not fight, so he would use his wits. The other man became more distinct to him; he could see particularly the shirt-breast. Dawes stumbled over Paul's coats, then came rushing forward. The young man's mouth was bleeding. It was the other man's mouth he was dying to get at, and the desire was anguish in its strength. He stepped quickly through the stile, and as Dawes was coming through after him, like a flash he got a blow in over the other's mouth. He shivered with pleasure. Dawes advanced slowly, spitting. Paul was afraid; he moved round to get to the stile again. Suddenly, from out of nowhere, came a great blow against his ear, that sent him falling helpless backwards. He heard Dawes's heavy panting, like a wild beast's, then came a kick on the knee, giving him such agony that he got up and, quite blind, leapt clean under his enemy's guard. He felt blows and kicks, but they did not hurt. He hung on to the bigger man like a wild cat, till at last Dawes fell with a crash, losing his presence of mind. Paul went down with him. Pure instinct brought his hands to the

593

man's neck, and before Dawes, in frenzy and agony, could wrench him free, he had got his fists twisted in the scarf and his knuckles dug in the throat of the other man. He was a pure instinct, without reason or feeling. His body, hard and wonderful in itself, cleaved against the struggling body of the other man; not a muscle in him relaxed. He was quite unconscious, only his body had taken upon itself to kill this other man. For himself, he had neither feeling nor reason. He lay pressed hard against his adversary, his body adjusting itself to its one pure purpose of choking the other man, resisting exactly at the right moment, with exactly the right amount of strength, the struggles of the other, silent, intent, unchanging, gradually pressing its knuckles deeper, feeling the struggles of the other body become wilder and more frenzied. Tighter and tighter grew his body, like a screw that is gradually increasing in pressure, till something breaks.

Then suddenly he relaxed, full of wonder and misgiving. Dawes had been yielding. Morel felt his body flame with pain, as he realised what he was doing; he was all bewildered. Dawes's struggles suddenly renewed themselves in a furious spasm. Paul's hands were wrenched, torn out of the scarf in which they were knotted, and he was flung away, helpless. He heard the horrid sound of the other's gasping, but he lay stunned; then, still dazed, he felt the blows of the other's feet, and lost consciousness.

Dawes, grunting with pain like a beast, was kicking the prostrate body of his rival. Suddenly the

594

whistle of the train shrieked two fields away. He turned round and glared suspiciously. What was coming? He saw the lights of the train draw across his vision. It seemed to him people were approaching. He made off across the field into Nottingham, and dimly in his consciousness as he went, he felt on his foot the place where his boot had knocked against one of the lad's bones. The knock seemed to re-echo inside him; he hurried to get away from it.

Morel gradually came to himself. He knew where he was and what had happened, but he did not want to move. He lay still, with tiny bits of snow tickling his face. It was pleasant to lie quite, quite still. The time passed. It was the bits of snow that kept rousing him when he did not want to be roused. At last his will clicked into action.

"I mustn't lie here," he said; "it's silly."

But still he did not move.

"I said I was going to get up," he repeated. "Why don't I?"

And still it was some time before he had sufficiently pulled himself together to stir; then gradually he got up. Pain made him sick and dazed, but his brain was clear. Reeling, he groped for his coats and got them on, buttoning his overcoat up to his ears. It was some time before he found his cap. He did not know whether his face was still bleeding. Walking blindly, every step making him sick with pain, he went back to the pond and washed his face and hands. The icy water hurt, but helped to bring him back to himself. He crawled back up the hill to the tram. He wanted to get to his mother—he must get to his mother—that was his blind intention. He covered his face as much as he could, and struggled sickly along. Continually the ground seemed to fall away from him as he walked, and he felt himself dropping with a sickening feeling into space; so, like a nightmare, he got through with the journey home.

Everybody was in bed. He looked at himself. His face was discoloured and smeared with blood, almost like a dead man's face. He washed it, and went to bed. The night went by in delirium. In the morning he found his mother looking at him. Her blue eyes—they were all he wanted to see. She was there; he was in her hands.

"It's not much, mother," he said. "It was Baxter Dawes."

"Tell me where it hurts you," she said quietly.

"I don't know—my shoulder. Say it was a bicycle accident, mother."

He could not move his arm. Presently Minnie, the little servant, came upstairs with some tea.

"Your mother's nearly frightened me out of my wits—fainted away," she said.

He felt he could not bear it. His mother nursed him; he told her about it.

"And now I should have done with them all," she said quietly.

"I will, mother."

She covered him up.

"And don't think about it," she said—"only try to

go to sleep. The doctor won't be here till eleven."

He had a dislocated shoulder, and the second day acute bronchitis set in. His mother was pale as death now, and very thin. She would sit and look at him, then away into space. There was something between them that neither dared mention. Clara came to see him. Afterwards he said to his mother:

"She makes me tired, mother."

"Yes: I wish she wouldn't come," Mrs. Morel replied.

Another day Miriam came, but she seemed almost like a stranger to him.

"You know, I don't care about them, mother," he said.

"I'm afraid you don't, my son," she replied sadly.

It was given out everywhere that it was a bicycle accident. Soon he was able to go to work again, but now there was a constant sickness and gnawing at his heart. He went to Clara, but there seemed, as it were, nobody there. He could not work. He and his mother seemed almost to avoid each other. There was some secret between them which they could not bear. He was not aware of it. He only knew that his life seemed unbalanced, as if it were going to smash into pieces.

Clara did not know what was the matter with him. She realised that he seemed unaware of her. Even when he came to her he seemed unaware of her; always he was somewhere else. She felt she was clutching for him, and he was somewhere else. It tortured her, and so she tortured him. For a month at a time she kept him at arm's length. He almost hated her, and was driven to her in spite of himself. He went mostly into the company of men, was always at the George or the White Horse. His mother was ill, distant, quiet, shadowy. He was terrified of something; he dared not look at her. Her eyes seemed to grow darker, her face more waxen; still she dragged about at her work.

At Whitsuntide he said he would go to Blackpool for four days with his friend Newton. The latter was a big, jolly fellow, with a touch of the bounder about him. Paul said his mother must go to Sheffield to stay a week with Annie, who lived there. Perhaps the change would do her good. Mrs. Morel was attending a woman's doctor in Nottingham. He said her heart and her digestion were wrong. She consented to go to Sheffield, though she did not want to; but now she would do everything her son wished of her. Paul said he would come for her on the fifth day, and stay also in Sheffield till the holiday was up. It was agreed.

The two young men set off gaily for Blackpool. Mrs. Morel was quite lively as Paul kissed her and left her. Once at the station, he forgot everything. Four days were clear—not an anxiety, not a thought. The two young men simply enjoyed themselves. Paul was like another man. None of himself remained—no Clara, no Miriam, no mother that fretted him. He wrote to them all, and long letters to his mother; but they were jolly letters that made her laugh. He was having a good time, as young fellows will in a place like Blackpool. And underneath it all was a shadow for her.

Paul was very gay, excited at the thought of staying with his mother in Sheffield. Newton was to spend the day with them. Their train was late. Joking, laughing, with their pipes between their teeth, the young men swung their bags on to the tram-car. Paul had bought his mother a little collar of real lace that he wanted to see her wear, so that he could tease her about it.

Annie lived in a nice house, and had a little maid. Paul ran gaily up the steps. He expected his mother laughing in the hall, but it was Annie who opened to him. She seemed distant to him. He stood a second in dismay. Annie let him kiss her cheek.

"Is my mother ill?" he said.

"Yes; she's not very well. Don't upset her."

"Is she in bed?"

"Yes."

And then the queer feeling went over him, as if all the sunshine had gone out of him, and it was all shadow. He dropped the bag and ran upstairs. Hesitating, he opened the door. His mother sat up in bed, wearing a dressing-gown of old-rose colour. She looked at him almost as if she were ashamed of herself, pleading to him, humble. He saw the ashy look about her.

"Mother!" he said.

"I thought you were never coming," she answered gaily.

But he only fell on his knees at the bedside, and

buried his face in the bedclothes, crying in agony, and saying:

"Mother—mother—mother!"

She stroked his hair slowly with her thin hand.

"Don't cry," she said. "Don't cry—it's nothing."

But he felt as if his blood was melting into tears, and he cried in terror and pain.

"Don't—don't cry," his mother faltered.

Slowly she stroked his hair. Shocked out of himself, he cried, and the tears hurt in every fibre of his body. Suddenly he stopped, but he dared not lift his face out of the bedclothes.

"You *are* late. Where have you been?" his mother asked.

"The train was late," he replied, muffled in the sheet.

"Yes; that miserable Central! Is Newton come?"

"Yes."

"I'm sure you must be hungry, and they've kept dinner waiting."

With a wrench he looked up at her.

"What is it, mother?" he asked brutally.

She averted her eyes as she answered:

"Only a bit of a tumour, my boy. You needn't trouble. It's been there—the lump has—a long time."

Up came the tears again. His mind was clear and hard, but his body was crying.

"Where?" he said.

She put her hand on her side.

"Here. But you know they can't sweal a tumour away."

He stood feeling dazed and helpless, like a child. He thought perhaps it was as she said. Yes; he reassured himself it was so. But all the while his blood and his body knew definitely what it was. He sat down on the bed, and took her hand. She had never had but the one ring—her wedding-ring.

"When were you poorly?" he asked.

"It was yesterday it began," she answered submissively.

"Pains?"

"Yes; but not more than I've often had at home. I believe Dr. Ansell is an alarmist."

"You ought not to have travelled alone," he said, to himself more than to her.

"As if that had anything to do with it!" she answered quickly.

They were silent for a while.

"Now go and have your dinner," she said. "You *must* be hungry."

"Have you had yours?"

"Yes; a beautiful sole I had. Annie *is* good to me."

They talked a little while, then he went downstairs. He was very white and strained. Newton sat in miserable sympathy.

After dinner he went into the scullery to help Annie to wash up. The little maid had gone on an errand.

"Is it really a tumour?" he asked.

Annie began to cry again.

"The pain she had yesterday—I never saw anybody suffer like it!" she cried. "Leonard ran like a madman for Dr. Ansell, and when she'd got to bed she said to me: 'Annie, look at this lump on my side. I wonder what it is?' And there I looked, and I thought I should have dropped. Paul, as true as I'm here, it's a lump as big as my double fist. I said: 'Good gracious, mother, whenever did that come?' 'Why, child,' she said, 'it's been there a long time.' I thought I should have died, our Paul, I did. She's been having these pains for months at home, and nobody looking after her."

The tears came to his eyes, then dried suddenly.

"But she's been attending the doctor in Nottingham—and she never told me," he said.

"If I'd have been at home," said Annie, "I should have seen for myself."

He felt like a man walking in unrealities. In the afternoon he went to see the doctor. The latter was a shrewd, lovable man.

"But what is it?" he said.

The doctor looked at the young man, then knitted his fingers.

"It may be a large tumour which has formed in the membrane," he said slowly, "and which we *may* be able to make go away."

"Can't you operate?" asked Paul.

"Not there," replied the doctor.

"Are you sure?"

"*Quite!*"

602

Paul meditated a while.

"Are you sure it's a tumour?" he asked. "Why did Dr. Jameson in Nottingham never find out anything about it? She's been going to him for weeks, and he's treated her for heart and indigestion."

"Mrs. Morel never told Dr. Jameson about the lump," said the doctor.

"And do you *know* it's a tumour?"

"No, I am not sure."

"What else *might* it be? You asked my sister if there was cancer in the family. Might it be cancer?"

"I don't know."

"And what shall you do?"

"I should like an examination, with Dr. Jameson."

"Then have one."

"You must arrange about that. His fee wouldn't be less than ten guineas to come here from Nottingham."

"When would you like him to come?"

"I will call in this evening, and we will talk it over."

Paul went away, biting his lip.

His mother could come downstairs for tea, the doctor said. Her son went upstairs to help her. She wore the old-rose dressing-gown that Leonard had given Annie, and, with a little colour in her face, was quite young again.

"But you look quite pretty in that," he said.

"Yes; they make me so fine, I hardly know myself," she answered.

But when she stood up to walk, the colour went. Paul helped her, half-carrying her. At the top of the stairs she was gone. He lifted her up and carried her quickly downstairs; laid her on the couch. She was light and frail. Her face looked as if she were dead, with blue lips shut tight. Her eyes opened—her blue, unfailing eyes—and she looked at him pleadingly, almost wanting him to forgive her. He held brandy to her lips, but her mouth would not open. All the time she watched him lovingly. She was only sorry for him. The tears ran down his face without ceasing, but not a muscle moved. He was intent on getting a little brandy between her lips. Soon she was able to swallow a teaspoonful. She lay back, so tired. The tears continued to run down his face.

"But," she panted, "it'll go off. Don't cry!"

"I'm not doing," he said.

After a while she was better again. He was kneeling beside the couch. They looked into each other's eyes.

"I don't want you to make a trouble of it," she said.

"No, mother. You'll have to be quite still, and then you'll get better soon."

But he was white to the lips, and their eyes as they looked at each other understood. Her eyes were so blue—such a wonderful forget-me-not blue! He felt if only they had been of a different colour he could have borne it better. His heart seemed to be ripping slowly in his breast. He kneeled there, holding her hand, and neither said anything. Then Annie came in.

"Are you all right?" she murmured timidly to her mother.

"Of course," said Mrs. Morel.

Paul sat down and told her about Blackpool. She was curious.

A day or two after, he went to see Dr. Jameson in Nottingham, to arrange for a consultation. Paul had practically no money in the world. But he could borrow.

His mother had been used to go to the public consultation on Saturday morning, when she could see the doctor for only a nominal sum. Her son went on the same day. The waiting-room was full of poor women, who sat patiently on a bench around the wall. Paul thought of his mother, in her little black costume, sitting waiting likewise. The doctor was late. The women all looked rather frightened. Paul asked the nurse in attendance if he could see the doctor immediately he came. It was arranged so. The women sitting patiently round the walls of the room eyed the young man curiously.

At last the doctor came. He was about forty, good-looking, brown-skinned. His wife had died, and he, who had loved her, had specialised on women's ailments. Paul told his name and his mother's. The doctor did not remember.

"Number forty-six M.," said the nurse; and the doctor looked up the case in his book.

"There is a big lump that may be a tumour," said

605

Paul. "But Dr. Ansell was going to write you a letter."

"Ah, yes!" replied the doctor, drawing the letter from his pocket. He was very friendly, affable, busy, kind. He would come to Sheffield the next day.

"What is your father?" he asked.

"He is a coal-miner," replied Paul.

"Not very well off, I suppose?"

"This—I see after this," said Paul.

"And you?" smiled the doctor.

"I am a clerk in Jordan's Appliance Factory."

The doctor smiled at him.

"Er—to go to Sheffield!" he said, putting the tips of his fingers together, and smiling with his eyes. "Eight guineas?"

"Thank you!" said Paul, flushing and rising. "And you'll come tomorrow?"

"Tomorrow—Sunday? Yes! Can you tell me about what time there is a train in the afternoon?"

"There is a Central gets in at four-fifteen."

"And will there be any way of getting up to the house? Shall I have to walk?" The doctor smiled.

"There is the tram," said Paul; "the Western Park tram."

The doctor made a note of it.

"Thank you!" he said, and shook hands.

Then Paul went on home to see his father, who was left in the charge of Minnie. Walter Morel was getting very grey now. Paul found him digging in the garden. He had written him a letter. He shook hands with his father.

606

"Hello, son! Tha has landed, then?" said the father.

"Yes," replied the son. "But I'm going back tonight."

"Are ter, beguy!" exclaimed the collier. "An' has ter eaten owt?"

"No."

"That's just like thee," said Morel. "Come thy ways in."

The father was afraid of the mention of his wife. The two went indoors. Paul ate in silence; his father, with earthy hands, and sleeves rolled up, sat in the arm-chair opposite and looked at him.

"Well, an' how is she?" asked the miner at length, in a little voice.

"She can sit up; she can be carried down for tea," said Paul.

"That's a blessin'!" exclaimed Morel. "I hope we s'll soon be havin' her whoam, then. An' what's that Nottingham doctor say?"

"He's going tomorrow to have an examination of her."

"Is he beguy! That's a tidy penny, I'm thinkin'!"

"Eight guineas."

"Eight guineas!" the miner spoke breathlessly. "Well, we mun find it from somewhere."

"I can pay that," said Paul.

There was silence between them for some time.

"She says she hopes you're getting on all right with Minnie," Paul said.

"Yes, I'm all right, an' I wish as she was," answered Morel.

"But Minnie's a good little wench, bless 'er heart!" He sat looking dismal.

"I s'll have to be going at half-past three," said Paul.

"It's a trapse for thee, lad! Eight guineas! An' when dost think she'll be able to get as far as this?"

"We must see what the doctors say tomorrow," Paul said.

Morel sighed deeply. The house seemed strangely empty, and Paul thought his father looked lost, forlorn, and old.

"You'll have to go and see her next week, father," he said.

"I hope she'll be a-whoam by that time," said Morel.

"If she's not," said Paul, "then you must come."

"I dunno wheer I s'll find th' money," said Morel.

"And I'll write to you what the doctor says," said Paul.

"But tha writes i' such a fashion, I canna ma'e it out," said Morel.

"Well, I'll write plain."

It was no good asking Morel to answer, for he could scarcely do more than write his own name.

The doctor came. Leonard felt it his duty to meet him with a cab. The examination did not take long. Annie, Arthur, Paul, and Leonard were waiting in the parlour anxiously. The doctors came down.

608

Paul glanced at them. He had never had any hope, except when he had deceived himself.

"It *may* be a tumour; we must wait and see," said Dr. Jameson.

"And if it is," said Annie, "can you sweal it away?"

"Probably," said the doctor.

Paul put eight sovereigns and half a sovereign on the table. The doctor counted them, took a florin out of his purse, and put that down.

"Thank you!" he said. "I'm sorry Mrs. Morel is so ill. But we must see what we can do."

"There can't be an operation?" said Paul.

The doctor shook his head.

"No," he said; "and even if there could, her heart wouldn't stand it."

"Is her heart risky?" asked Paul.

"Yes; you must be careful with her."

"Very risky?"

"No—er—no, no! Just take care."

And the doctor was gone.

Then Paul carried his mother downstairs. She lay simply, like a child. But when he was on the stairs, she put her arms round his neck, clinging.

"I'm so frightened of these beastly stairs," she said.

And he was frightened, too. He would let Leonard do it another time. He felt he could not carry her.

"He thinks it's only a tumour!" cried Annie to her mother. "And he can sweal it away."

609

"I *knew* he could," protested Mrs. Morel scornfully.

She pretended not to notice that Paul had gone out of the room. He sat in the kitchen, smoking. Then he tried to brush some grey ash off his coat. He looked again. It was one of his mother's grey hairs. It was so long! He held it up, and it drifted into the chimney. He let go. The long grey hair floated and was gone in the blackness of the chimney.

The next day he kissed her before going back to work. It was very early in the morning, and they were alone.

"You won't fret, my boy!" she said.

"No, mother."

"No; it would be silly. And take care of yourself."

"Yes," he answered. Then, after a while: "And I shall come next Saturday, and shall bring my father?"

"I suppose he wants to come," she replied. "At any rate, if he does you'll have to let him."

He kissed her again, and stroked the hair from her temples, gently, tenderly, as if she were a lover.

"Shan't you be late?" she murmured.

"I'm going," he said, very low.

Still he sat a few minutes, stroking the brown and grey hair from her temples.

"And you won't be any worse, mother?"

"No, my son."

"You promise me?"

"Yes; I won't be any worse."

He kissed her, held her in his arms for a moment, and was gone. In the early sunny morning he ran to the station, crying all the way; he did not know what for. And her blue eyes were wide and staring as she thought of him.

In the afternoon he went a walk with Clara. They sat in the little wood where bluebells were standing. He took her hand.

"You'll see," he said to Clara, "she'll never be better."

"Oh, you don't know!" replied the other.

"I do," he said.

She caught him impulsively to her breast.

"Try and forget it, dear," she said; "try and forget it."

"I will," he answered.

Her breast was there, warm for him; her hands were in his hair. It was comforting, and he held his arms round her. But he did not forget. He only talked to Clara of something else. And it was always so. When she felt it coming, the agony, she cried to him:

"Don't think of it, Paul! Don't think of it, my darling!"

And she pressed him to her breast, rocked him, soothed him like a child. So he put the trouble aside for her sake, to take it up again immediately he was alone. All the time, as he went about, he cried mechanically. His mind and hands were busy. He cried, he did not know why. It was his blood weeping. He was just as much alone whether he was with

611

Clara or with the men in the White Horse. Just himself and this pressure inside him, that was all that existed. He read sometimes. He had to keep his mind occupied. And Clara was a way of occupying his mind.

On the Saturday Walter Morel went to Sheffield. He was a forlorn figure, looking rather as if nobody owned him. Paul ran upstairs.

"My father's come," he said, kissing his mother.

"Has he?" she answered weariedly.

The old collier came rather frightened into the bedroom.

"How dun I find thee, lass?" he said, going forward and kissing her in a hasty, timid fashion.

"Well, I'm middlin'," she replied.

"I see tha art," he said. He stood looking down on her. Then he wiped his eyes with his handkerchief. Helpless, and as if nobody owned him, he looked.

"Have you gone on all right?" asked the wife, rather wearily, as if it were an effort to talk to him.

"Yis," he answered. " 'Er's a bit behint-hand now and again, as yer might expect."

"Does she have your dinner ready?" asked Mrs. Morel.

"Well, I've 'ad to shout at 'er once or twice," he said.

"And you *must* shout at her if she's not ready. She *will* leave things to the last minute."

She gave him a few instructions. He sat looking at her as if she were almost a stranger to him, before whom he was awkward and humble, and also as if he had lost his presence of mind, and wanted to run. This feeling that he wanted to run away, that he was on thorns to be gone from so trying a situation, and yet must linger because it looked better, made his presence so trying. He put up his eyebrows for misery, and clenched his fists on his knees, feeling so awkward in presence of big trouble.

Mrs. Morel did not change much. She stayed in Sheffield for two months. If anything, at the end she was rather worse. But she wanted to go home. Annie had her children. Mrs. Morel wanted to go home. So they got a motor-car from Nottingham—for she was too ill to go by train—and she was driven through the sunshine. It was just August; everything was bright and warm. Under the blue sky they could all see she was dying. Yet she was jollier than she had been for weeks. They all laughed and talked.

"Annie," she exclaimed, "I saw a lizard dart on that rock!"

Her eyes were so quick; she was still so full of life.

Morel knew she was coming. He had the front door open. Everybody was on tiptoe. Half the street turned out. They heard the sound of the great motor-car. Mrs. Morel, smiling, drove home down the street.

"And just look at them all come out to see me!" she said. "But there, I suppose I should have done the same. How do you do, Mrs. Mathews? How are you, Mrs. Harrison?"

They none of them could hear, but they saw her smile and nod. And they all saw death on her face, they said. It was a great event in the street.

Morel wanted to carry her indoors, but he was too old. Arthur took her as if she were a child. They had set her a big, deep chair by the hearth where her rocking-chair used to stand. When she was unwrapped and seated, and had drunk a little brandy, she looked round the room.

"Don't think I don't like your house, Annie," she said; "but it's nice to be in my own home again."

And Morel answered huskily:

"It is, lass, it is."

And Minnie, the little quaint maid, said:

"An' we glad t' 'ave yer."

There was a lovely yellow ravel of sunflowers in the garden. She looked out of the window.

"There are my sunflowers!" she said.

# 14

## THE RELEASE

"BY the way," said Dr. Ansell one evening
when Morel was in Sheffield, "we've got a
man in the fever hospital here who comes
from Nottingham—Dawes. He doesn't seem to have
many belongings in this world."

"Baxter Dawes!" Paul exclaimed.

"That's the man—has been a fine fellow, physically, I should think. Been in a bit of a mess lately.
You know him?"

"He used to work at the place where I am."

"Did he? Do you know anything about him? He's
just sulking, or he'd be a lot better than he is by
now."

"I don't know anything of his home circumstances, except that he's separated from his
wife and has been a bit down, I believe. But tell him
about me, will you? Tell him I'll come and see
him."

The next time Morel saw the doctor he said:

"And what about Dawes?"

"I said to him," answered the other, " 'Do you
know a man from Nottingham named Morel?' and
he looked at me as if he'd jump at my throat. So I
said: 'I see you know the name; it's Paul Morel.'

Then I told him about your saying you would go and see him. 'What does he want?' he said, as if you were a policeman."

"And did he say he would see me?" asked Paul.

"He wouldn't say anything—good, bad or indifferent," replied the doctor.

"Why not?"

"That's what I want to know. There he lies and sulks, day in, day out. Can't get a word of information out of him."

"Do you think I might go?" asked Paul.

"You might."

There was a feeling of connection between the rival men, more than ever since they had fought. In a way Morel felt guilty towards the other, and more or less responsible. And being in such a state of soul himself, he felt an almost painful nearness to Dawes, who was suffering and despairing, too. Besides, they had met in a naked extremity of hate, and it was a bond. At any rate, the elemental man in each had met.

He went down to the isolation hospital, with Dr. Ansell's card. This sister, a healthy young Irishwoman, led him down the ward.

"A visitor to see you, Jim Crow," she said.

Dawes turned over suddenly with a startled grunt.

"Eh?"

"Caw!" she mocked. "He can only say 'Caw!' I have brought you a gentleman to see you. Now say 'Thank you,' and show some manners."

616

Dawes looked swiftly with his dark, startled eyes beyond the sister at Paul. His look was full of fear, mistrust, hate, and misery. Morel met the swift, dark eyes, and hesitated. The two men were afraid of the naked selves they had been.

"Dr. Ansell told me you were here," said Morel, holding out his hand.

Dawes mechanically shook hands.

"So I thought I'd come in," continued Paul.

There was no answer. Dawes lay staring at the opposite wall.

"Say 'Caw!' " mocked the nurse. "Say 'Caw!' Jim Crow."

"He is getting on all right?" said Paul to her.

"Oh yes! He lies and imagines he's going to die," said the nurse, "and it frightens every word out of his mouth."

"And you *must* have somebody to talk to," laughed Morel.

"That's it!" laughed the nurse. "Only two old men and a boy who always cries. It *is* hard lines! Here am I dying to hear Jim Crow's voice, and nothing but an odd 'Caw!' will he give!"

"So rough on you!" said Morel.

"Isn't it?" said the nurse.

"I suppose I am a godsend," he laughed.

"Oh, dropped straight from heaven!" laughed the nurse.

Presently she left the two men alone. Dawes was thinner, and handsome again, but life seemed low in him. As the doctor said, he was lying sulking,

617

and would not move forward towards convalescence. He seemed to grudge every beat of his heart.

"Have you had a bad time?" asked Paul.

Suddenly again Dawes looked at him.

"What are you doing in Sheffield?" he asked.

"My mother was taken ill at my sister's in Thurston Street. What are you doing here?"

There was no answer.

"How long have you been in?" Morel asked.

"I couldn't say for sure," Dawes answered grudgingly.

He lay staring across at the wall opposite, as if trying to believe Morel was not there. Paul felt his heart go hard and angry.

"Dr. Ansell told me you were here," he said coldly.

The other man did not answer.

"Typhoid's pretty bad, I know," Morel persisted.

Suddenly Dawes said:

"What did you come for?"

"Because Dr. Ansell said you didn't know anybody here. Do you?"

"I know nobody nowhere," said Dawes.

"Well," said Paul, "it's because you don't choose to, then."

There was another silence.

"We s'll be taking my mother home as soon as we can," said Paul.

"What's a-matter with her?" asked Dawes, with a sick man's interest in illness.

"She's got a cancer."

There was another silence.

618

"But we want to get her home," said Paul. "We s'll have to get a motor-car."

Dawes lay thinking.

"Why don't you ask Thomas Jordan to lend you his?" said Dawes.

"It's not big enough," Morel answered.

Dawes blinked his dark eyes as he lay thinking.

"Then ask Jack Pilkington; he'd lend it you. You know him."

"I think I s'll hire one," said Paul.

"You're a fool if you do," said Dawes.

The sick man was gaunt and handsome again. Paul was sorry for him because his eyes looked so tired.

"Did you get a job here?" he asked.

"I was only here a day or two before I was taken bad," Dawes replied.

"You want to get in a convalescent home," said Paul.

The other's face clouded again.

"I'm goin' in no convalescent home," he said.

"My father's been in the one at Seathorpe, an' he liked it. Dr. Ansell would get you a recommend."

Dawes lay thinking. It was evident he dared not face the world again.

"The seaside would be all right just now," Morel said. "Sun on those sandhills, and the waves not far out."

The other did not answer.

"By Gad!" Paul concluded, too miserable to bother much; "it's all right when you know you're going to walk again, and swim!"

Dawes glanced at him quickly. The man's dark eyes were afraid to meet any other eyes in the world. But the real misery and helplessness in Paul's tone gave him a feeling of relief.

"Is she far gone?" he asked.

"She's going like wax," Paul answered; "but cheerful—lively!"

He bit his lip. After a minute he rose.

"Well, I'll be going," he said. "I'll leave you this half-crown."

"I don't want it," Dawes muttered.

Morel did not answer, but left the coin on the table.

"Well," he said, "I'll try and run in when I'm back in Sheffield. Happen you might like to see my brother-in-law? He works in Pyecrofts."

"I don't know him," said Dawes.

"He's all right. Should I tell him to come? He might bring you some papers to look at."

The other man did not answer. Paul went. The strong emotion that Dawes aroused in him, repressed, made him shiver.

He did not tell his mother, but next day he spoke to Clara about this interview. It was in the dinner-hour. The two did not often go out together now, but this day he asked her to go with him to the Castle grounds. There they sat while the scarlet geraniums and the yellow calceolarias blazed in the sunlight. She was now always rather protective, and rather resentful towards him.

620

"Did you know Baxter was in Sheffield Hospital with typhoid?" he asked.

She looked at him with startled grey eyes, and her face went pale.

"No," she said, frightened.

"He's getting better. I went to see him yesterday—the doctor told me."

Clara seemed stricken by the news.

"Is he very bad?" she asked guiltily.

"He has been. He's mending now."

"What did he say to you?"

"Oh, nothing! He seems to be sulking."

There was a distance between the two of them. He gave her more information.

She went about shut up and silent. The next time they took a walk together, she disengaged herself from his arm, and walked at a distance from him. He was wanting her comfort badly.

"Won't you be nice with me?" he asked.

She did not answer.

"What's the matter?" he said, putting his arm across her shoulder.

"Don't!" she said, disengaging herself.

He left her alone, and returned to his own brooding.

"Is it Baxter that upsets you?" he asked at length.

"I *have* been *vile* to him!" she said.

"I've said many a time you haven't treated him well," he replied.

And there was a hostility between them. Each pursued his own train of thought.

"I've treated him—no, I've treated him badly," she said. "And now you treat *me* badly. It serves me right."

"How do I treat you badly?" he said.

"It serves me right," she repeated. "I never considered him worth having, and now you don't consider *me*. But it serves me right. He loved me a thousand times better than you ever did."

"He didn't!" protested Paul.

"He did! At any rate, he did respect me, and that's what you don't do."

"It looked as if he respected you!" he said.

"He did! And I *made* him horrid—I know I did! You've taught me that. And he loved me a thousand times better than ever you do."

"All right," said Paul.

He only wanted to be left alone now. He had his own trouble, which was almost too much to bear. Clara only tormented him and made him tired. He was not sorry when he left her.

She went on the first opportunity to Sheffield to see her husband. The meeting was not a success. But she left him roses and fruit and money. She wanted to make restitution. It was not that she loved him. As she looked at him lying there her heart did not warm with love. Only she wanted to humble herself to him, to kneel before him. She wanted now to be self-sacrificial. After all, she had failed to make Morel really love her. She was morally frightened. She wanted to do penance. So she kneeled to Dawes, and it gave him a subtle pleasure. But the

622

distance between them was still very great—too great. It frightened the man. It almost pleased the woman. She liked to feel she was serving him across an insuperable distance. She was proud now.

Morel went to see Dawes once or twice. There was a sort of friendship between the two men, who were all the while deadly rivals. But they never mentioned the woman who was between them.

Mrs. Morel got gradually worse. At first they used to carry her downstairs, sometimes even into the garden. She sat propped in her chair, smiling, and so pretty. The gold wedding-ring shone on her white hand; her hair was carefully brushed. And she watched the tangled sunflowers dying, the chrysanthemums coming out, and the dahlias.

Paul and she were afraid of each other. He knew, and she knew, that she was dying. But they kept up a pretence of cheerfulness. Every morning, when he got up, he went into her room in his pyjamas.

"Did you sleep, my dear?" he asked.

"Yes," she answered.

"Not very well?"

"Well, yes!"

Then he knew she had lain awake. He saw her hand under the bedclothes, pressing the place on her side where the pain was.

"Has it been bad?" he asked.

"No. It hurt a bit, but nothing to mention."

And she sniffed in her old scornful way. As she lay she looked like a girl. And all the while her blue eyes watched him. But there were the dark pain-circles beneath that made him ache again.

"It's a sunny day," he said.

"It's a beautiful day."

"Do you think you'll be carried down?"

"I shall see."

Then he went away to get her breakfast. All day long he was conscious of nothing but her. It was a long ache that made him feverish. Then, when he got home in the early evening, he glanced through the kitchen window. She was not there; she had not got up.

He ran straight upstairs and kissed her. He was almost afraid to ask:

"Didn't you get up, pigeon?"

"No," she said. "It was that morphia; it made me tired."

"I think he gives you too much," he said.

"I think he does," she answered.

He sat down by the bed, miserably. She had a way of curling and lying on her side, like a child. The grey and brown hair was loose over her ear.

"Doesn't it tickle you?" he said, gently putting it back.

"It does," she replied.

His face was near hers. Her blue eyes smiled straight into his, like a girl's—warm, laughing with tender love. It made him pant with terror, agony, and love.

"You want your hair doing in a plait," he said. "Lie still."

And going behind her, he carefully loosened her

624

hair, brushed it out. It was like fine long silk of brown and grey. Her head was snuggled between her shoulders. As he lightly brushed and plaited her hair, he bit his lip and felt dazed. It all seemed unreal, he could not understand it.

At night he often worked in her room, looking up from time to time. And so often he found her blue eyes fixed on him. And when their eyes met, she smiled. He worked away again mechanically, producing good stuff without knowing what he was doing.

Sometimes he came in, very pale and still, with watchful, sudden eyes, like a man who is drunk almost to death. They were both afraid of the veils that were ripping between them.

Then she pretended to be better, chattered to him gaily, made a great fuss over some scraps of news. For they had both come to the condition when they had to make much of the trifles, lest they should give in to the big thing, and their human independence would go smash. They were afraid, so they made light of things and were gay.

Sometimes as she lay he knew she was thinking of the past. Her mouth gradually shut hard in a line. She was holding herself rigid, so that she might die without ever uttering the great cry that was tearing from her. He never forgot that hard, utterly lonely and stubborn clenching of her mouth, which persisted for weeks. Sometimes, when it was lighter, she talked about her husband. Now she hated him. She did not forgive him. She could not bear him to be in the room. And a few things, the things that had been most bitter to her, came up again so strongly that they broke from her, and she told her son.

He felt as if his life were being destroyed, piece by piece, within him. Often the tears came suddenly. He ran to the station, the tear-drops falling on the pavement. Often he could not go on with his work. The pen stopped writing. He sat staring, quite unconscious. And when he came round again he felt sick, and trembled in his limbs. He never questioned what it was. His mind did not try to analyse or understand. He merely submitted, and kept his eyes shut; let the thing go over him.

His mother did the same. She thought of the pain, of the morphia, of the next day; hardly ever of the death. That was coming, she knew. She had to submit to it. But she would never entreat it or make friends with it. Blind, with her face shut hard and blind, she was pushed towards the door. The days passed, the weeks, the months.

Sometimes, in the sunny afternoons, she seemed almost happy.

"I try to think of the nice times—when we went to Mablethorpe, and Robin Hood's Bay, and Shanklin," she said. "After all, not everybody has seen those beautiful places. And wasn't it beautiful! I try to think of that, not of the other things."

Then, again, for a whole evening she spoke not a word; neither did he. They were together, rigid, stubborn, silent. He went into his room at last to go to bed, and leaned against the doorway as if paralysed, unable to go any farther. His consciousness went. A furious storm, he knew not what, seemed to ravage inside him. He stood leaning there, submitting, never questioning.

In the morning they were both normal again, though her face was grey with the morphia, and her body felt like ash. But they were bright again, nevertheless. Often, especially if Annie or Arthur were at home, he neglected her. He did not see much of Clara. Usually he was with men. He was quick and active and lively; but when his friends saw him go white to the gills, his eyes dark and glittering, they had a certain mistrust of him. Sometimes he went to Clara, but she was almost cold to him.

"Take me!" he said simply.

Occasionally she would. But she was afraid. When he had her then, there was something in it that made her shrink away from him—something unnatural. She grew to dread him. He was so quiet, yet so strange. She was afraid of the man who was not there with her, whom she could feel behind this make-belief lover; somebody sinister, that filled her with horror. She began to have a kind of horror of him. It was almost as if he were a criminal. He wanted her—he had her—and it made her feel as if death itself had her in its grip. She lay in horror. There was no man there loving her. She almost hated him. Then came little bouts of tenderness. But she dared not pity him.

Dawes had come to Colonel Seely's Home near Nottingham. There Paul visited him sometimes, Clara very occasionally. Between the two men the friendship developed peculiarly. Dawes, who mended very slowly and seemed very feeble, seemed to leave himself in the hands of Morel.

In the beginning of November Clara reminded Paul that it was her birthday.

"I'd nearly forgotten," he said.

"I'd thought quite," she replied.

"No. Shall we go to the seaside for the week-end?"

They went. It was cold and rather dismal. She waited for him to be warm and tender with her, instead of which he seemed hardly aware of her. He sat in the railway-carriage, looking out, and was startled when she spoke to him. He was not definitely thinking. Things seemed as if they did not exist. She went across to him.

"What is it, dear?" she asked.

"Nothing!" he said. "Don't those windmill sails look monotonous?"

He sat holding her hand. He could not talk nor think. It was a comfort, however, to sit holding her hand. She was dissatisfied and miserable. He was not with her; she was nothing.

And in the evening they sat among the sandhills, looking at the black, heavy sea.

"She will never give in," he said quietly.

Clara's heart sank.

"No," she replied.

"There are different ways of dying. My father's people are frightened, and have to be hauled out of life into death like cattle into a slaughter-house, pulled by the neck; but my mother's people are pushed from behind, inch by inch. They are stubborn people, and won't die."

"Yes," said Clara.

"And she won't die. She can't. Mr. Renshaw, the parson, was in the other day. 'Think!' he said to her; 'you will have your mother and father, and your sisters, and your son, in the Other Land.' And she said: 'I have done without them for a long time, and *can* do without them now. It is the living I want, not the dead.' She wants to live even now."

"Oh, how horrible!" said Clara, too frightened to speak.

"And she looks at me, and she wants to stay with me," he went on monotonously. "She's got such a will, it seems as if she would never go—never!"

"Don't think of it!" cried Clara.

"And she was religious—she is religious now—but it is no good. She simply won't give in. And do you know, I said to her on Thursday: 'Mother, if I had to die, I'd die. I'd *will* to die.' And she said to me, sharp: 'Do you think I haven't? Do you think you can die when you like?' "

His voice ceased. He did not cry, only went on speaking monotonously. Clara wanted to run. She looked round. There was the black, re-echoing shore, the dark sky down on her. She got up terrified. She wanted to be where there was light,

629

where there were other people. She wanted to be away from him. He sat with his head dropped, not moving a muscle.

"And I don't want her to eat," he said, "and she knows it. When I ask her: 'Shall you have anything' she's almost afraid to say 'Yes'. 'I'll have a cup of Benger's,' she says. 'It'll only keep your strength up,' I said to her. 'Yes'—and she almost cried—'but there's such a gnawing when I eat nothing, I can't bear it.' So I went and made her the food. It's the cancer that gnaws like that at her. I wish she'd die!"

"Come!" said Clara roughly. "I'm going."

He followed her down the darkness of the sands. He did not come to her. He seemed scarcely aware of her existence. And she was afraid of him, and disliked him.

In the same acute daze they went back to Nottingham. He was always busy, always doing something, always going from one to the other of his friends.

On the Monday he went to see Baxter Dawes. Listless and pale, the man rose to greet the other, clinging to his chair as he held out his hand.

"You shouldn't get up," said Paul.

Dawes sat down heavily, eyeing Morel with a sort of suspicion.

"Don't you waste your time on me," he said, "if you've owt better to do."

"I wanted to come," said Paul. "Here! I brought you some sweets."

The invalid put them aside.

630

"It's not been much of a week-end," said Morel.

"How's your mother?" asked the other.

"Hardly any different."

"I thought she was perhaps worse, being as you didn't come on Sunday."

"I was at Skegness," said Paul. "I wanted a change."

The other looked at him with dark eyes. He seemed to be waiting, not quite daring to ask, trusting to be told.

"I went with Clara," said Paul.

"I knew as much," said Dawes quietly.

"It was an old promise," said Paul.

"You have it your own way," said Dawes.

This was the first time Clara had been definitely mentioned between them.

"Nay," said Morel slowly; "she's tired of me."

Again Dawes looked at him.

"Since August she's been getting tired of me," Morel repeated.

The two men were very quiet together. Paul suggested a game of draughts. They played in silence.

"I s'll go abroad when my mother's dead," said Paul.

"Abroad!" repeated Dawes.

"Yes; I don't care what I do."

They continued the game. Dawes was winning.

"I s'll have to begin a new start of some sort," said Paul; "and you as well, I suppose."

He took one of Dawes's pieces.

"I dunno where," said the other.

631

"Things have to happen," Morel said. "It's no good doing anything—at least—no, I don't know. Give me some toffee."

The two men ate sweets, and began another game of draughts.

"What made that scar on your mouth?" asked Dawes.

Paul put his hand hastily to his lips, and looked over the garden.

"I had a bicycle accident," he said.

Dawes's hand trembled as he moved the piece.

"You shouldn't ha' laughed at me," he said, very low.

"When?"

"That night on Woodborough Road, when you and her passed me—you with your hand on her shoulder."

"I never laughed at you," said Paul.

Dawes kept his fingers on the draught-piece.

"I never knew you were there till the very second when you passed," said Morel.

"It was that as did me," Dawes said, very low.

Paul took another sweet.

"I never laughed," he said, "except as I'm always laughing."

They finished the game.

That night Morel walked home from Nottingham, in order to have something to do. The furnaces flared in a red blotch over Bulwell; the black clouds were like a low ceiling. As he went along the ten miles of highroad, he felt as if he were walking

632

out of life, between the black levels of the sky and the earth. But at the end was only the sick-room. If he walked and walked for ever, there was only that place to come to.

He was not tired when he got near home, or he did not know it. Across the field he could see the red firelight leaping in her bedroom window.

"When she's dead," he said to himself, "that fire will go out."

He took off his boots quietly and crept upstairs. His mother's door was wide open, because she slept alone still. The red firelight dashed its glow on the landing. Soft as a shadow, he peeped in her doorway.

"Paul!" she murmured.

His heart seemed to break again. He went in and sat by the bed.

"How late you are!" she murmured.

"Not very," he said.

"Why, what time is it?" The murmur came plaintive and helpless.

"It's only just gone eleven."

That was not true; it was nearly one o'clock.

"Oh!" she said; "I thought it was later."

And he knew the unutterable misery of her nights that would not go.

"Can't you sleep, my pigeon?" he said.

"No, I can't," she wailed.

"Never mind, Little!" he said crooning. "Never mind, my love. I'll stop with you half an hour, my pigeon; then perhaps it will be better."

633

And he sat by the bedside, slowly, rhythmically stroking her brows with his finger-tips, stroking her eyes shut, soothing her, holding her fingers in his free hand. They could hear the sleepers' breathing in the other rooms.

"Now go to bed," she murmured, lying quite still under his fingers and his love.

"Will you sleep?" he asked.

"Yes, I think so."

"You feel better, my Little, don't you?"

"Yes," she said, like a fretful, half-soothed child.

Still the days and the weeks went by. He hardly ever went to see Clara now. But he wandered restlessly from one person to another for some help, and there was none anywhere. Miriam had written to him tenderly. He went to see her. Her heart was very sore when she saw him, white, gaunt, with his eyes dark and bewildered. Her pity came up, hurting her till she could not bear it.

"How is she?" she asked.

"The same—the same!" he said. "The doctor says she can't last, but I know she will. She'll be here at Christmas."

Miriam shuddered. She drew him to her; she pressed him to her bosom; she kissed him and kissed him. He submitted, but it was torture. She could not kiss his agony. That remained alone and apart. She kissed his face, and roused his blood, while his soul was apart writhing with the agony of death. And she kissed him and fingered his body, till at last, feeling he would go mad, he got away from

634

her. It was not that he wanted just then—not that. And she thought she had soothed him and done him good.

December came, and some snow. He stayed at home all the while now. They could not afford a nurse. Annie came to look after her mother; the parish nurse, whom they loved, came in morning and evening. Paul shared the nursing with Annie. Often, in the evenings, when friends were in the kitchen with them, they all laughed together and shook with laughter. It was reaction. Paul was so comical, Annie was so quaint. The whole party laughed till they cried, trying to subdue the sound. And Mrs. Morel, lying alone in the darkness heard them, and among her bitterness was a feeling of relief.

Then Paul would go upstairs gingerly, guiltily, to see if she had heard.

"Shall I give you some milk?" he asked.

"A little," she replied plaintively.

And he would put some water with it, so that it should not nourish her. Yet he loved her more than his own life.

She had morphia every night, and her heart got fitful. Annie slept beside her. Paul would go in in the early morning, when his sister got up. His mother was wasted and almost ashen in the morning with the morphia. Darker and darker grew her eyes, all pupil, with the torture. In the mornings the weariness and ache was too much to bear. Yet she could not—would not—weep, or even complain much.

"You slept a bit later this morning, little one," he would say to her.

"Did I?" she answered, with fretful weariness.

"Yes; it's nearly eight o'clock."

He stood looking out of the window. The whole country was bleak and pallid under the snow. Then he felt her pulse. There was a strong stroke and a weak one, like a sound and its echo. That was supposed to betoken the end. She let him feel her wrist, knowing what he wanted.

Sometimes they looked in each other's eyes. Then they almost seemed to make an agreement. It was almost as if he were agreeing to die also. But she did not consent to die; she would not. Her body was wasted to a fragment of ash. Her eyes were dark and full of torture.

"Can't you give her something to put an end to it?" he asked the doctor at last.

But the doctor shook his head.

"She can't last many days now, Mr. Morel," he said.

Paul went indoors.

"I can't bear it much longer; we shall all go mad," said Annie.

The two sat down to breakfast.

"Go and sit with her while we have breakfast, Minnie," said Annie. But the girl was frightened.

Paul went through the country, through the woods, over the snow. He saw the marks of rabbits

636

and birds in the white snow. He wandered miles and miles. A smoky red sunset came on slowly, painfully, lingering. He thought she would die that day. There was a donkey that came up to him over the snow by the wood's edge, and put its head against him, and walked with him alongside. He put his arms round the donkey's neck, and stroked his cheeks against his ears.

His mother, silent, was still alive, with her hard mouth gripped grimly, her eyes of dark torture only living.

It was nearing Christmas; there was more snow. Annie and he felt as if they could go on no more. Still her dark eyes were alive. Morel, silent and frightened, obliterated himself. Sometimes he would go into the sick-room and look at her. Then he backed out, bewildered.

She kept her hold on life still. The miners had been out on strike, and returned a fortnight or so before Christmas. Minnie went upstairs with the feeding-cup. It was two days after the men had been in.

"Have the men been saying their hands are sore, Minnie?" she asked, in the faint, querulous voice that would not give in. Minnie stood surprised.

"Not as I know of, Mrs. Morel," she answered.

"But I'll bet they are sore," said the dying woman, as she moved her head with a sigh of weariness. "But, at any rate, there'll be something to buy in with this week."

Not a thing did she let slip.

"Your father's pit things will want well airing,

Annie," she said, when the men were going back to work.

"Don't you bother about that, my dear," said Annie.

One night Annie and Paul were alone. Nurse was upstairs.

"She'll live over Christmas," said Annie. They were both full of horror.

"She won't," he replied firmly. "I s'll give her morphia."

"Which?" said Annie.

"All that came from Sheffield," said Paul.

"Ay—do!" said Annie.

The next day he was painting in the bedroom. She seemed to be asleep. He stepped softly backwards and forwards at his painting. Suddenly her small voice wailed:

"Don't walk about, Paul."

He looked round. Her eyes, like dark bubbles in her face, were looking at him.

"No, my dear," he said gently. Another fibre seemed to snap in his heart.

That evening he got all the morphia pills there were, and took them downstairs. Carefully he crushed them to powder.

"What are you doing?" said Annie.

"I s'll put 'em in her night milk."

Then they both laughed together like two conspiring children. On top of all their horror flicked this little sanity.

Nurse did not come that night to settle Mrs.

Morel down. Paul went up with the hot milk in a feeding-cup. It was nine o'clock.

She was reared up in bed, and he put the feeding-cup between her lips that he would have died to save from any hurt. She took a sip, then put the spout of the cup away and looked at him with her dark, wondering eyes. He looked at her.

"Oh, it *is* bitter, Paul!" she said, making a little grimace.

"It's a new sleeping draught the doctor gave me for you," he said. "He thought it wouldn't leave you in such a state in the morning."

"And I hope it won't," she said, like a child.

She drank some more of the milk.

"But it *is* horrid!" she said.

He saw her frail fingers over the cup, her lips making a little move.

"I know—I tasted it," he said. "But I'll give you some clean milk afterwards."

"I think so," she said, and she went on with the draught. She was obedient to him like a child. He wondered if she knew. He saw her poor wasted throat moving as she drank with difficulty. Then he ran downstairs for more milk. There were no grains in the bottom of the cup.

"Has she had it?" whispered Annie.

"Yes—and she said it was bitter."

"Oh!" laughed Annie, putting her under lip between her teeth.

"And I told her it was a new draught. Where's that milk?"

639

They both went upstairs.

"I wonder why nurse didn't come to settle me down?" complained the mother, like a child, wistfully.

"She said she was going to a concert, my love," replied Annie.

"Did she?"

They were silent a minute. Mrs. Morel gulped the little clean milk.

"Annie, that draught *was* horrid!" she said plaintively.

"Was it, my love? Well, never mind."

The mother sighed again with weariness. Her pulse was very irregular.

"Let *us* settle you down," said Annie. "Perhaps nurse will be so late."

"Ay," said the mother—"try."

They turned the clothes back. Paul saw his mother like a girl curled up in her flannel nightdress. Quickly they made one half of the bed, moved her, made the other, straightened her nightgown over her small feet, and covered her up.

"There," said Paul, stroking her softly. "There!—now you'll sleep."

"Yes," she said. "I didn't think you could do the bed so nicely," she added, almost gaily. Then she curled up, with her cheek on her hand, her head snugged between her shoulder. Paul put the long thin plait of grey hair over her shoulder and kissed her.

"You'll sleep, my love," he said.

"Yes," she answered trustfully. "Good night."

They put out the light, and it was still.

Morel was in bed. Nurse did not come. Annie and Paul came to look at her about eleven. She seemed to be sleeping as usual after her draught. Her mouth had come a bit open.

"Shall we sit up?" said Paul.

"I s'll lie with her as I always do," said Annie. "She might wake up."

"All right. And call me if you see any difference."

"Yes."

They lingered before the bedroom fire, feeling the night big and black and snowy outside, their two selves alone in the world. At last he went into the next room and went to bed.

He slept almost immediately, but kept waking every now and again. Then he went sound asleep. He started awake at Annie's whispered, "Paul, Paul!" He saw his sister in her white nightdress, with her long plait of hair down her back, standing in the darkness.

"Yes?" he answered, sitting up.

"Come and look at her."

He slipped out of bed. A bud of gas was burning in the sick chamber. His mother lay with her cheek on her hand, curled up as she had gone to sleep. But her mouth had fallen open, and she breathed with great, hoarse breaths, like snoring, and there were long intervals between.

"She's going!" he whispered.

"Yes," said Annie.

"How long has she been like it?"

"I only just woke up."

Annie huddled into the dressing-gown, Paul wrapped himself in a brown blanket. It was three o'clock. He mended the fire. Then the two sat waiting. The great, snoring breath was taken—held awhile—then given back. There was a space—a long space. Then they started. The great, snoring breath was taken again. He bent close down and looked at her.

"Isn't it awful!" whispered Annie.

He nodded. They sat down again helplessly. Again came the great, snoring breath. Again they hung suspended. Again it was given back, long and harsh. The sound, so irregular, at such wide intervals, sounded through the house. Morel, in his room, slept on. Paul and Annie sat crouched, huddled, motionless. The great snoring sound began again—there was a painful pause while the breath was held—back came the rasping breath. Minute after minute passed. Paul looked at her again, bending low over her.

"She may last like this," he said.

They were both silent. He looked out of the window, and could faintly discern the snow on the garden.

"You go to my bed," he said to Annie. "I'll sit up."

"No," she said, "I'll stop with you."

"I'd rather you didn't," he said.

At last Annie crept out of the room, and he was

642

alone. He hugged himself in his brown blanket, crouched in front of his mother, watching. She looked dreadful, with the bottom jaw fallen back. He watched. Sometimes he thought the great breath would never begin again. He could not bear it—the waiting. Then suddenly, startling him, came the great harsh sound. He mended the fire again, noiselessly. She must not be disturbed. The minutes went by. The night was going, breath by breath. Each time the sound came he felt it wring him, till at last he could not feel so much.

His father got up. Paul heard the miner drawing his stocking on, yawning. Then Morel, in shirt and stockings, entered.

"Hush!" said Paul.

Morel stood watching. Then he looked at his son, helplessly, and in horror.

"Had I better stop a-whoam?" he whispered.

"No. Go to work. She'll last through tomorrow."

"I don't think so."

"Yes. Go to work."

The miner looked at her again, in fear, and went obediently out of the room. Paul saw the tape of his garters swinging against his legs.

After another half-hour Paul went downstairs and drank a cup of tea, then returned. Morel, dressed for the pit, came upstairs again.

"Am I to go?" he said.

"Yes."

And in a few minutes Paul heard his father's

heavy steps go thudding over the deadening snow. Miners called in the streets as they tramped in gangs to work. The terrible, long-drawn breaths continued—heave—heave—heave; then a long pause—then—ah-h-h-h-h! as it came back. Far away over the snow sounded the hooters of the iron-works. One after another they crowed and boomed, some small and far away, some near, the blowers of the collieries and the other works. Then there was silence. He mended the fire. The great breaths broke the silence—she looked just the same. He put back the blind and peered out. Still it was dark. Perhaps there was a lighter tinge. Perhaps the snow was bluer. He drew up the blind and got dressed. Then, shuddering, he drank brandy from the bottle on the wash-stand. The snow *was* growing blue. He heard a cart clanking down the street. Yes, it was seven o'clock, and it was coming a little bit light. He heard some people calling. The world was waking. A grey, deathly dawn crept over the snow. Yes, he could see the houses. He put out the gas. It seemed very dark. The breathing came still, but he was almost used to it. He could see her. She was just the same. He wondered if he piled heavy clothes on top of her it would stop. He looked at her. That was not her—not her a bit. If he piled the blanket and heavy coats on her——

Suddenly the door opened, and Annie entered. She looked at him questioningly.

"Just the same," he said calmly.

They whispered together a minute, then went

644

downstairs to get breakfast. It was twenty to eight. Soon Annie came down.

"Isn't it awful! Doesn't she look awful!" she whispered, dazed with horror.

He nodded.

"If she looks like that!" said Annie.

"Drink some tea," he said.

They went upstairs again. Soon the neighbours came with their frightened question:

"How is she?"

It went on just the same. She lay with her cheek in her hand, her mouth fallen open, and the great, ghastly snores came and went.

At ten o'clock nurse came. She looked strange and woebegone.

"Nurse," cried Paul, "she'll last like this for days?"

"She can't, Mr. Morel," said nurse. "She can't."

There was a silence.

"Isn't it dreadful!" wailed the nurse. "Who would have thought she could stand it? Go down now, Mr. Morel, go down."

At last, at about eleven o'clock, he went downstairs and sat in the neighbour's house. Annie was downstairs also. Nurse and Arthur were upstairs. Paul sat with his head in his hand. Suddenly Annie came flying across the yard crying, half mad:

"Paul—Paul—she's gone!"

In a second he was back in his own house and upstairs. She lay curled up and still, with her face on her hand, and nurse was wiping her mouth.

645

They all stood back. He kneeled down, and put his face to hers and his arms round her:

"My love—my love—oh, my love!" he whispered again and again. "My love—oh, my love!"

Then he heard the nurse behind him, crying, saying:

"She's better, Mr. Morel, she's better."

When he took his face up from his warm, dead mother he went straight downstairs and began blacking his boots.

There was a good deal to do, letters to write, and so on. The doctor came and glanced at her, and sighed.

"Ay—poor thing!" he said, then turned away. "Well, call at the surgery about six for the certificate."

The father came home from work at about four o'clock. He dragged silently into the house and sat down. Minnie bustled to give him his dinner. Tired, he laid his black arms on the table. There were swede turnips for his dinner, which he liked. Paul wondered if he knew. It was some time, and nobody had spoken. At last the son said:

"You noticed the blinds were down?"

Morel looked up.

"No," he said. "Why—has she gone?"

"Yes."

"When wor that?"

"About twelve this morning."

"H'm!"

The miner sat still for a moment, then began his

dinner. It was as if nothing had happened. He ate his turnips in silence. Afterwards he washed and went upstairs to dress. The door of her room was shut.

"Have you seen her?" Annie asked of him when he came down.

"No," he said.

In a little while he went out. Annie went away, and Paul called on the undertaker, the clergyman, the doctor, the registrar. It was a long business. He got back at nearly eight o'clock. The undertaker was coming soon to measure for the coffin. The house was empty except for her. He took a candle and went upstairs.

The room was cold, that had been warm for so long. Flowers, bottles, plates, all sick-room litter was taken away; everything was harsh and austere. She lay raised on the bed, the sweep of the sheet from the raised feet was like a clean curve of snow, so silent. She lay like a maiden asleep. With his candle in his hand, he bent over her. She lay like a girl asleep and dreaming of her love. The mouth was a little open as if wondering from the suffering, but her face was young, her brow clear and white as if life had never touched it. He looked again at the eyebrows, at the small, winsome nose a bit on one side. She was young again. Only the hair as it arched so beautifully from her temples was mixed with silver, and the two simple plaits that lay on her shoulders were filigree of silver and brown. She would wake up. She would lift her eyelids. She was with him still. He bent and kissed her passionately. But there was coldness against his mouth. He bit his lips with horror. Looking at her, he felt he could never, never let her go. No! He stroked the hair from her temples. That, too, was cold. He saw the mouth so dumb and wondering at the hurt. Then he crouched on the floor, whispering to her:

"Mother, mother!"

He was still with her when the undertakers came, young men who had been to school with him. They touched her reverently, and in a quiet, businesslike fashion. They did not look at her. He watched jealously. He and Annie guarded her fiercely. They would not let anybody come to see her, and the neighbours were offended.

After a while Paul went out of the house, and played cards at a friend's. It was midnight when he got back. His father rose from the couch as he entered, saying in a plaintive way:

"I thought tha wor niver comin', lad."

"I didn't think you'd sit up," said Paul.

His father looked so forlorn. Morel had been a man without fear—simply nothing frightened him. Paul realised with a start that he had been afraid to go to bed, alone in the house with his dead. He was sorry.

"I forgot you'd be alone, father," he said.

"Dost want owt to eat?" asked Morel.

"No."

"Sithee—I made thee a drop o' hot milk. Get it down thee; it's cold enough for owt."

Paul drank it.

After a while Morel went to bed. He hurried past the closed door, and left his own door open. Soon the son came upstairs also. He went in to kiss her good night, as usual. It was cold and dark. He wished they had kept her fire burning. Still she dreamed her young dream. But she would be cold.

"My dear!" he whispered. "My dear!"

And he did not kiss her, for fear she should be cold and strange to him. It eased him she slept so beautifully. He shut her door softly, not to wake her, and went to bed.

In the morning Morel summoned his courage, hearing Annie downstairs and Paul coughing in the room across the landing. He opened her door, and went into the darkened room. He saw the white uplifted form in the twilight, but her he dared not see. Bewildered, too frightened to possess any of his faculties, he got out of the room again and left her. He never looked at her again. He had not seen her for months, because he had not dared to look. And she looked like his young wife again.

"Have you seen her?" Annie asked of him sharply after breakfast.

"Yes," he said.

"And don't you think she looks nice?"

"Yes."

He went out of the house soon after. And all the time he seemed to be creeping aside to avoid it.

Paul went about from place to place, doing the business of the death. He met Clara in Nottingham, and they had tea together in a café, when they were quite jolly again. She was infinitely relieved to find he did not take it tragically.

Later, when the relatives began to come for the funeral, the affair became public, and the children became social beings. They put themselves aside. They buried her in a furious storm of rain and wind. The wet clay glistened, all the white flowers were soaked. Annie gripped his arm and leaned forward. Down below she saw a dark corner of William's coffin. The oak box sank steadily. She was gone. The rain poured in the grave. The procession of black, with its umbrellas glistening, turned away. The cemetery was deserted under the drenching cold rain.

Paul went home and busied himself supplying the guests with drinks. His father sat in the kitchen with Mrs. Morel's relatives, "superior" people, and wept, and said what a good lass she'd been, and how he'd tried to do everything he could for her—everything. He had striven all his life to do what he could for her, and he'd done nothing to reproach himself with. She was gone, but he'd done his best for her. He wiped his eyes with his white handkerchief. He'd nothing to reproach himself for, he repeated. All his life he'd done his best for her.

And that was how he tried to dismiss her. He never thought of her personally. Everything deep in him he denied. Paul hated his father for sitting sentimentalising over her. He knew he would do it in the public-houses. For the real tragedy went on in

Morel in spite of himself. Sometimes, later, he came down from his afternoon sleep, white and cowering.

"I *have* been dreaming of thy mother," he said in a small voice.

"Have you, father? When I dream of her it's always just as she was when she was well. I dream of her often, but it seems quite nice and natural, as if nothing had altered."

But Morel crouched in front of the fire in terror.

The weeks passed half-real, not much pain, not much of anything, perhaps a little relief, mostly a *nuit blanche*. Paul went restless from place to place. For some months, since his mother had been worse, he had not made love to Clara. She was, as it were, dumb to him, rather distant. Dawes saw her very occasionally, but the two could not get an inch across the great distance between them. The three of them were drifting forward.

Dawes mended very slowly. He was in the convalescent home at Skegness at Christmas, nearly well again. Paul went to the seaside for a few days. His father was with Annie in Sheffield. Dawes came to Paul's lodgings. His time in the home was up. The two men, between whom was such a big reserve, seemed faithful to each other. Dawes depended on Morel now. He knew Paul and Clara had practically separated.

Two days after Christmas Paul was to go back to Nottingham. The evening before he sat with Dawes smoking before the fire.

"You know Clara's coming down for the day tomorrow?" he said.

The other man glanced at him.

"Yes, you told me," he replied.

Paul drank the remainder of his glass of whisky.

"I told the landlady your wife was coming," he said.

"Did you?" said Dawes, shrinking, but almost leaving himself in the other's hands. He got up rather stiffly, and reached for Morel's glass.

"Let me fill you up," he said.

Paul jumped up.

"You sit still," he said.

But Dawes, with rather shaky hand, continued to mix the drink.

"Say when," he said.

"Thanks!" replied the other. "But you've no business to get up."

"It does me good, lad," replied Dawes. "I begin to think I'm right again, then."

"You are about right, you know."

"I am, certainly I am," said Dawes, nodding to him.

"And Len says he can get you on in Sheffield."

Dawes glanced at him again, with dark eyes that agreed with everything the other would say, perhaps a trifle dominated by him.

"It's funny," said Paul, "starting again. I feel in a lot bigger mess than you."

"In what way, lad?"

"I don't know. I don't know. It's as if I was in a

652

tangled sort of hole, rather dark and dreary, and no road anywhere."

"I know—I understand it," Dawes said, nodding. "But you'll find it'll come all right."

He spoke caressingly.

"I suppose so," said Paul.

Dawes knocked his pipe in a hopeless fashion.

"You've not done for yourself like I have," he said.

Morel saw the wrist and the white hand of the other man gripping the stem of the pipe and knocking out the ash, as if he had given up.

"How old are you?" Paul asked.

"Thirty-nine," replied Dawes, glancing at him.

Those brown eyes, full of the consciousness of failure, almost pleading for reassurance, for someone to re-establish the man in himself, to warm him, to set him up firm again, troubled Paul.

"You'll just be in your prime," said Morel. "You don't look as if much life had gone out of you."

The brown eyes of the other flashed suddenly.

"It hasn't," he said. "The go is there."

Paul looked up and laughed.

"We've both got plenty of life in us yet to make things fly," he said.

The eyes of the two men met. They exchanged one look. Having recognised the stress of passion each in the other, they both drank their whisky.

"Yes, begod!" said Dawes, breathless.

There was a pause.

"And I don't see," said Paul, "why you shouldn't go on where you left off."

"What——" said Dawes, suggestively.

"Yes—fit your old home together again."

Dawes hid his face and shook his head.

"Couldn't be done," he said, and looked up with an ironic smile.

"Why? Because you don't want?"

"Perhaps."

They smoked in silence. Dawes showed his teeth as he bit his pipe stem.

"You mean you don't want her?" asked Paul.

Dawes stared up at the picture with a caustic expression on his face.

"I hardly know," he said.

The smoke floated softly up.

"I believe she wants you," said Paul.

"Do you?" replied the other, soft, satirical, abstract.

"Yes. She never really hitched on to me—you were always there in the background. That's why she wouldn't get a divorce."

Dawes continued to stare in a satirical fashion at the picture over the mantelpiece.

"That's how women are with me," said Paul. "They want me like mad, but they don't want to belong to me. And she *belonged* to you all the time. I knew."

The triumphant male came up in Dawes. He showed his teeth more distinctly.

"Perhaps I was a fool," he said.

654

"You were a big fool," said Morel.

"But perhaps even *then* you were a bigger fool," said Dawes.

There was a touch of triumph and malice in it.

"Do you think so?" said Paul.

They were silent for some time.

"At any rate, I'm clearing out tomorrow," said Morel.

"I see," answered Dawes.

Then they did not talk any more. The instinct to murder each other had returned. They almost avoided each other.

They shared the same bedroom. When they retired Dawes seemed abstract, thinking of something. He sat on the side of the bed in his shirt, looking at his legs.

"Aren't you getting cold?" asked Morel.

"I was lookin' at these legs," replied the other.

"What's up with 'em? They look all right," replied Paul, from his bed.

"They look all right. But there's some water in 'em yet."

"And what about it?"

"Come and look."

Paul reluctantly got out of bed and went to look at the rather handsome legs of the other man that were covered with glistening, dark gold hair.

"Look here," said Dawes, pointing to his shin. "Look at the water under here."

"Where?" said Paul.

The man pressed in his finger-tips. They left little dents that filled up slowly.

"It's nothing," said Paul.

"You feel," said Dawes.

Paul tried with his fingers. It made little dents.

"H'm!" he said.

"Rotten, isn't it?" said Dawes.

"Why? It's nothing much."

"You're not much of a man with water in your legs."

"I can't see as it makes any difference," said Morel. "I've got a weak chest."

He returned to his own bed.

"I suppose the rest of me's all right," said Dawes, and he put out the light.

In the morning it was raining. Morel packed his bag. The sea was grey and shaggy and dismal. He seemed to be cutting himself off from life more and more. It gave him a wicked pleasure to do it.

The two men were at the station. Clara stepped out of the train, and came along the platform, very erect and coldly composed. She wore a long coat and a tweed hat. Both men hated her for her composure. Paul shook hands with her at the barrier. Dawes was leaning against the bookstall, watching. His black overcoat was buttoned up to the chin because of the rain. He was pale, with almost a touch of nobility in his quietness. He came forward, limping slightly.

"You ought to look better than this," she said.

"Oh, I'm all right now."

656

The three stood at a loss. She kept the two men hesitating near her.

"Shall we go to the lodging straight off," said Paul, "or somewhere else?"

"We may as well go home," said Dawes.

Paul walked on the outside of the pavement, then Dawes, then Clara. They made polite conversation. The sitting-room faced the sea, whose tide, grey and shaggy, hissed not far off.

Morel swung up the big arm-chair.

"Sit down, Jack," he said.

"I don't want that chair," said Dawes.

"Sit down!" Morel repeated.

Clara took off her things and laid them on the couch. She had a slight air of resentment. Lifting her hair with her fingers, she sat down, rather aloof and composed. Paul ran downstairs to speak to the landlady.

"I should think you're cold," said Dawes to his wife. "Come nearer to the fire."

"Thank you, I'm quite warm," she answered.

She looked out of the window at the rain and at the sea.

"When are you going back?" she asked.

"Well, the rooms are taken until tomorrow, so he wants me to stop. He's going back tonight."

"And then you're thinking of going to Sheffield?"

"Yes."

"Are you fit to start work?"

"I'm going to start."

657

"You've really got a place?"

"Yes—begin on Monday."

"You don't look fit."

"Why don't I?"

She looked again out of the window instead of answering.

"And have you got lodgings in Sheffield?"

"Yes."

Again she looked away out of the window. The panes were blurred with streaming rain.

"And can you manage all right?" she asked.

"I s'd think so. I s'll have to!"

They were silent when Morel returned.

"I shall go by the four-twenty," he said as he entered.

Nobody answered.

"I wish you'd take your boots off," he said to Clara. "There's a pair of slippers of mine."

"Thank you," she said. "They aren't wet."

He put the slippers near her feet. She left them there.

Morel sat down. Both the men seemed helpless, and each of them had a rather hunted look. But Dawes now carried himself quietly, seemed to yield himself, while Paul seemed to screw himself up. Clara thought she had never seen him look so small and mean. He was as if trying to get himself into the smallest possible compass. And as he went about arranging, and as he sat talking, there seemed something false about him and out of tune. Watching him unknown, she said to herself there was no stability about him. He was fine in his way, passionate, and able to give her drinks of pure life when he was in one mood. And now he looked paltry and insignificant. There was nothing stable about him. Her husband had more manly dignity. At any rate *he* did not waft about with any wind. There was something evanescent about Morel, she thought, something shifting and false. He would never make sure ground for any woman to stand on. She despised him rather for his shrinking together, getting smaller. Her husband at least was manly, and when he was beaten gave in. But this other would never own to being beaten. He would shift round and round, prowl, get smaller. She despised him. And yet she watched him rather than Dawes, and it seemed as if their three fates lay in his hands. She hated him for it.

She seemed to understand better now about men, and what they could or would do. She was less afraid of them, more sure of herself. That they were not the small egoists she had imagined them made her more comfortable. She had learned a good deal—almost as much as she wanted to learn. Her cup had been full. It was still as full as she could carry. On the whole, she would not be sorry when he was gone.

They had dinner, and sat eating nuts and drinking by the fire. Not a serious word had been spoken. Yet Clara realised that Morel was withdrawing from the circle, leaving her the option to stay with her husband. It angered her. He was a mean fellow, after all, to take what he wanted and then give her back. She did not remember that she herself had had what she wanted, and really, at the bottom of her heart, wished to be given back.

Paul felt crumpled up and lonely. His mother had really supported his life. He had loved her; they two had, in fact, faced the world together. Now she was gone, and for ever behind him was the gap in life, the tear in the veil, through which his life seemed to drift slowly, as if he were drawn towards death. He wanted someone of their own free initiative to help him. The lesser things he began to let go from him, for fear of this big thing, the lapse towards death, following in the wake of his beloved. Clara could not stand for him to hold on to. She wanted him, but not to understand him. He felt she wanted the man on top, not the real him that was in trouble. That would be too much trouble to her; he dared not give it her. She could not cope with him. It made him ashamed. So, secretly ashamed because he was in such a mess, because his own hold on life was so unsure, because nobody held him, feeling unsubstantial, shadowy, as if he did not count for much in this concrete world, he drew himself together smaller and smaller. He did not want to die; he would not give in. But he was not afraid of death. If nobody would help, he would go on alone.

Dawes had been driven to the extremity of life, until he was afraid. He could go to the brink of death, he could lie on the edge and look in. Then, cowed, afraid, he had to crawl back, and like a beggar take what offered. There was a certain nobility in it. As Clara saw, he owned himself beaten, and he wanted to be taken back whether or not. That she could do for him.

It was three o'clock.

"I am going by the four-twenty," said Paul again to Clara. "Are you coming then or later?"

"I don't know," she said.

"I'm meeting my father in Nottingham at seven-fifteen," he said.

"Then," she answered. "I'll come later."

Dawes jerked suddenly, as if he had been held on a strain. He looked out over the sea, but he saw nothing.

"There are one or two books in the corner," said Morel. "I've done with 'em."

At about four o'clock he went.

"I shall see you both later," he said, as he shook hands.

"I suppose so," said Dawes. "An' perhaps—one day—I s'll be able to pay you back the money as——"

"I shall come for it, you'll see," laughed Paul. "I s'll be on the rocks before I'm very much older."

"Ay—well——" said Dawes.

"Goodbye," he said to Clara.

"Goodbye," she said, giving him her hand. Then she glanced at him for the last time, dumb and humble.

He was gone. Dawes and his wife sat down again.

"It's a nasty day for travelling," said the man.

661

"Yes," she answered.

They talked in a desultory fashion until it grew dark. The landlady brought in the tea. Dawes drew up his chair to the table without being invited, like a husband. Then he sat humbly waiting for his cup. She served him as she would, like a wife, not consulting his wish.

After tea, as it drew near to six o'clock, he went to the window. All was dark outside. The sea was roaring.

"It's raining yet," he said.

"Is it?" she answered.

"You won't go tonight, shall you?" he said, hesitating.

She did not answer. He waited.

"I shouldn't go in this rain," he said.

"Do you *want* me to stay?" she asked.

His hand as he held the dark curtain trembled.

"Yes," he said.

He remained with his back to her. She rose and went slowly to him. He let go the curtain, turned, hesitating, towards her. She stood with her hands behind her back, looking up at him in a heavy, inscrutable fashion.

"Do you want me, Baxter?" she asked.

His voice was hoarse as he answered:

"Do you want to come back to me?"

She made a moaning noise, lifted her arms, and put them round his neck, drawing him to her. He hid his face on her shoulder, holding her clasped.

"Take me back!" she whispered, ecstatic. "Take

me back, take me back!" And she put her fingers through his fine, thin dark hair, as if she were only semi-conscious. He tightened his grasp on her.

"Do you want me again?" he murmured, broken.

# 15

## DERELICT

CLARA went with her husband to Sheffield, and Paul scarcely saw her again. Walter Morel seemed to have let all the trouble go over him, and there he was, crawling about on the mud of it, just the same. There was scarcely any bond between father and son, save that each felt he must not let the other go in any actual want. As there was no one to keep on the home, and as they could neither of them bear the emptiness of the house, Paul took lodgings in Nottingham, and Morel went to live with a friendly family in Bestwood.

Everything seemed to have gone smash for the young man. He could not paint. The picture he finished on the day of his mother's death—one that satisfied him—was the last thing he did. At work there was no Clara. When he came home he could not take up his brushes again. There was nothing left.

So he was always in the town at one place or another, drinking, knocking about with the men he knew. It really wearied him. He talked to barmaids, to almost any woman, but there was that dark, strained look in his eyes, as if he were hunting something.

Everything seemed so different, so unreal. There seemed no reason why people should go along the street, and houses pile up in the daylight. There seemed no reason why these things should occupy the space, instead of leaving it empty. His friends talked to him: he heard the sounds, and he answered. But why there should be the noise of speech he could not understand.

He was most himself when he was alone, or working hard and mechanically at the factory. In the latter case there was pure forgetfulness, when he lapsed from consciousness. But it had to come to an end. It hurt him so, that things had lost their reality. The first snowdrops came. He saw the tiny drop-pearls among the grey. They would have given him the liveliest emotion at one time. Now they were there, but they did not seem to mean anything. In a few moments they would cease to occupy that place, and just the space would be, where they had been. Tall, brilliant tram-cars ran along the street at night. It seemed almost a wonder they should trouble to rustle backwards and forwards. "Why trouble to go tilting down to Trent Bridges?" he asked of the big trams. It seemed they just as well might *not* be as be.

The realest thing was the thick darkness at night. That seemed to him whole and comprehensible and restful. He could leave himself to it. Suddenly a piece of paper started near his feet and blew along down the pavement. He stood still, rigid, with clenched fists, a flame of agony going over him.

And he saw again the sick-room, his mother, her eyes. Unconsciously he had been with her, in her company. The swift hop of the paper reminded him she was gone. But he had been with her. He wanted everything to stand still, so that he could be with her again.

The days passed, the weeks. But everything seemed to have fused, gone into a conglomerated mass. He could not tell one day from another, one week from another, hardly one place from another. Nothing was distinct or distinguishable. Often he lost himself for an hour at a time, could not remember what he had done.

One evening he came home late to his lodging. The fire was burning low; everybody was in bed. He threw on some more coal, glanced at the table, and decided he wanted no supper. Then he sat down in the arm-chair. It was perfectly still. He did not know anything, yet he saw the dim smoke wavering up the chimney. Presently two mice came out, cautiously, nibbling the fallen crumbs. He watched them as it were from a long way off. The church clock struck two. Far away he could hear the sharp clinking of the trucks on the railway. No, it was not they that were far away. They were there in their places. But where was he himself?

The time passed. The two mice, careering wildly, scampered cheekily over his slippers. He had not moved a muscle. He did not want to move. He was not thinking of anything. It was easier so. There was no wrench of knowing anything. Then, from

666

time to time, some other consciousness, working mechanically, flashed into sharp phrases.

"What am I doing?"

And out of the semi-intoxicated trance came the answer:

"Destroying myself."

Then a dull, live feeling, gone in an instant, told him that it was wrong. After a while, suddenly came the question:

"Why wrong?"

Again there was no answer, but a stroke of hot stubbornness inside his chest resisted his own annihilation.

There was a sound of a heavy cart clanking down the road. Suddenly the electric light went out; there was a bruising thud in the penny-in-the-slot meter. He did not stir, but sat gazing in front of him. Only the mice had scuttled, and the fire glowed red in the dark room.

Then, quite mechanically and more distinctly, the conversation began again inside him.

"She's dead. What was it all for—her struggle?"

That was his despair wanting to go after her.

"You're alive."

"She's not."

"She is—in you."

Suddenly he felt tired with the burden of it.

"You've got to keep alive for her sake," said his will in him.

Something felt sulky, as if it would not rouse.

"You've got to carry forward her living, and what she had done, go on with it."

But he did not want to. He wanted to give up.

"But you can go on with your painting," said the will in him. "Or else you can beget children. They both carry on her effort."

"Painting is not living."

"Then live."

"Marry whom?" came the sulky question.

"As best you can."

"Miriam?"

But he did not trust that.

He rose suddenly, went straight to bed. When he got inside his bedroom and closed the door, he stood with clenched fist.

"Mater, my dear——" he began, with the whole force of his soul. Then he stopped. He would not say it. He would not admit that he wanted to die, to have done. He would not own that life had beaten him, or that death had beaten him. Going straight to bed, he slept at once, abandoning himself to the sleep.

So the weeks went on. Always alone, his soul oscillated, first on the side of death, then on the side of life, doggedly. The real agony was that he had nowhere to go, nothing to do, nothing to say, and *was* nothing himself. Sometimes he ran down the streets as if he were mad: sometimes he was mad; things weren't there, things were there. It made him pant. Sometimes he stood before the bar of the public-house where he called for a drink. Everything suddenly stood back away from him. He saw the face of the barmaid, the gabbling drinkers, his own glass on the slopped, mahogany board, in the distance. There was something between him and them. He could not get into touch. He did not want them; he did not want his drink. Turning abruptly, he went out. On the threshold he stood and looked at the lighted street. But he was not of it or in it. Something separated him. Everything went on there below those lamps, shut away from him. He could not get at them. He felt he couldn't touch the lamp-posts, not if he reached. Where could he go? There was nowhere to go, neither back into the inn, or forward anywhere. He felt stifled. There was nowhere for him. The stress grew inside him; he felt he should smash.

"I mustn't," he said; and, turning blindly, he went in and drank. Sometimes the drink did him good; sometimes it made him worse. He ran down the road. For ever restless, he went here, there, everywhere. He determined to work. But when he had made six strokes, he loathed the pencil violently, got up, and went away, hurried off to a club where he could play cards or billiards, to a place where he could flirt with a barmaid who was no more to him than the brass pump-handle she drew.

He was very thin and lantern-jawed. He dared not meet his own eyes in the mirror; he never looked at himself. He wanted to get away from himself, but there was nothing to get hold of. In despair he thought of Miriam. Perhaps—perhaps——?

Then, happening to go into the Unitarian Church one Sunday evening, when they stood up to sing the second hymn he saw her before him. The light glistened on her lower lip as she sang. She looked as if she had got something, at any rate: some hope in heaven, if not in earth. Her comfort and her life seemed in the after-world. A warm, strong feeling for her came up. She seemed to yearn, as she sang, for the mystery and comfort. He put his hope in her. He longed for the sermon to be over, to speak to her.

The throng carried her out just before him. He could nearly touch her. She did not know he was there. He saw the brown, humble nape of her neck under its black curls. He would leave himself to her. She was better and bigger than he. He would depend on her.

She went wandering, in her blind way, through the little throngs of people outside the church. She always looked so lost and out of place among people. He went forward and put his hand on her arm. She started violently. Her great brown eyes dilated in fear, then went questioning at the sight of him. He shrank slightly from her.

"I didn't know——" she faltered.

"Nor I," he said.

He looked away. His sudden, flaring hope sank again.

"What are you doing in town?" he asked.

"I'm staying at Cousin Anne's."

"Ha! For long?"

670

"No; only till tomorrow."

"Must you go straight home?"

She looked at him, then hid her face under her hat-brim.

"No," she said—"no; it's not necessary."

He turned away, and she went with him. They threaded through the throng of church people. The organ was still sounding in St. Mary's. Dark figures came through the lighted doors; people were coming down the steps. The large coloured windows glowed up in the night. The church was like a great lantern suspended. They went down Hollow Stone, and he took the car for the Bridges.

"You will just have supper with me," he said: "then I'll bring you back."

"Very well," she replied, low and husky.

They scarcely spoke while they were on the car. The Trent ran dark and full under the bridge. Away towards Colwick all was black night. He lived down Holme Road, on the naked edge of the town, facing across the river meadows towards Sneinton Hermitage and the steep scarp of Colwick Wood. The floods were out. The silent water and the darkness spread away on their left. Almost afraid, they hurried along by the houses.

Supper was laid. He swung the curtain over the window. There was a bowl of freesias and scarlet anemones on the table. She bent to them. Still touching them with her finger-tips, she looked up at him, saying:

"Aren't they beautiful?"

671

"Yes," he said. "What will you drink—coffee?"

"I should like it," she said.

"Then excuse me a moment."

He went out to the kitchen.

Miriam took off her things and looked round. It was a bare, severe room. Her photo, Clara's, Annie's, were on the wall. She looked on the drawing-board to see what he was doing. There were only a few meaningless lines. She looked to see what books he was reading. Evidently just an ordinary novel. The letters in the rack she saw were from Annie, Arthur, and from some man or other she did not know. Everything he had touched, everything that was in the least personal to him, she examined with lingering absorption. He had been gone from her for so long, she wanted to rediscover him, his position, what he was now. But there was not much in the room to help her. It only made her feel rather sad, it was so hard and comfortless.

She was curiously examining a sketch-book when he returned with the coffee.

"There's nothing new in it," he said, "and nothing very interesting."

He put down the tray, and went to look over her shoulder. She turned the pages slowly, intent on examining everything.

"H'm!" he said, as she paused at a sketch. "I'd forgotten that. It's not bad, is it?"

"No," she said. "I don't quite understand it."

He took the book from her and went through it.

672

Again he made a curious sound of surprise and pleasure.

"There's some not bad stuff in there," he said.

"Not at all bad," she answered gravely.

He felt again her interest in his work. Or was it for himself? Why was she always most interested in him as he appeared in his work?

They sat down to supper.

"By the way," he said, "didn't I hear something about your earning your own living?"

"Yes," she replied, bowing her dark head over her cup.

"And what of it?"

"I'm merely going to the farming college at Broughton for three months, and I shall probably be kept on as a teacher there."

"I say—that sounds all right for you! You always wanted to be independent."

"Yes."

"Why didn't you tell me?"

"I only knew last week."

"But I heard a month ago," he said.

"Yes; but nothing was settled then."

"I should have thought," he said, "you'd have told me you were trying."

She ate her food in the deliberate, constrained way, almost as if she recoiled a little from doing anything so publicly, that he knew so well.

"I suppose you're glad," he said.

"Very glad."

"Yes—it will be something."

673

He was rather disappointed.

"I think it will be a great deal," she said, almost haughtily, resentfully.

He laughed shortly.

"Why do you think it won't?" she asked.

"Oh, I don't think it won't be a great deal. Only you'll find earning your own living isn't everything."

"No," she said, swallowing with difficulty; "I don't suppose it is."

"I suppose work *can* be nearly everything to a man," he said, "though it isn't to me. But a woman only works with a part of herself. The real and vital part is covered up."

"But a man can give *all* himself to work?" she asked.

"Yes, practically."

"And a woman only the unimportant part of herself?"

"That's it."

She looked up at him, and her eyes dilated with anger.

"Then," she said, "if it's true, it's a great shame."

"It is. But I don't know everything," he answered.

After supper they drew up to the fire. He swung her a chair facing him, and they sat down. She was wearing a dress of dark claret colour, that suited her dark complexion and her large features. Still, the curls were fine and free, but her face was much older, the brown throat much thinner. She seemed

674

old to him, older than Clara. Her bloom of youth had quickly gone. A sort of stiffness, almost of woodenness, had come upon her. She meditated a little while, then looked at him.

"And how are things with you?" she asked.

"About all right," he answered.

She looked at him, waiting.

"Nay," she said, very low.

Her brown, nervous hands were clasped over her knee. They had still the lack of confidence or repose, the almost hysterical look. He winced as he saw them. Then he laughed mirthlessly. She put her fingers between her lips. His slim, black, tortured body lay quite still in the chair. She suddenly took her finger from her mouth and looked at him.

"And you have broken off with Clara?"

"Yes."

His body lay like an abandoned thing, strewn in the chair.

"You know," she said, "I think we ought to be married."

He opened his eyes for the first time since many months, and attended to her with respect.

"Why?" he said.

"See," she said, "how you waste yourself! You might be ill, you might die, and I never know—be no more then than if I had never known you."

"And if we married?" he asked.

"At any rate, I could prevent you wasting yourself and being a prey to other women—like—like—Clara."

675

"A prey?" he repeated, smiling.

She bowed her head in silence. He lay feeling his despair come up again.

"I'm not sure," he said slowly, "that marriage would be much good."

"I only think of you," she replied.

"I know you do. But—you love me so much, you want to put me in your pocket. And I should die there smothered."

She bent her head, put her fingers between her lips, while the bitterness surged up in her heart.

"And what will you do otherwise?" she asked.

"I don't know—go on, I suppose. Perhaps I shall soon go abroad."

The despairing doggedness in his tone made her go on her knees on the rug before the fire, very near to him. There she crouched as if she were crushed by something, and could not raise her head. His hands lay quite inert on the arms of his chair. She was aware of them. She felt that now he lay at her mercy. If she could rise, take him, put her arms round him, and say, "You are mine," then he would leave himself to her. But dare she? She could easily sacrifice herself. But dare she assert herself? She was aware of his dark-clothed, slender body, that seemed one stroke of life, sprawled in the chair close to her. But no; she dared not put her arms round it, take it up, and say, "It is mine, this body. Leave it to me." And she wanted to. It called to all her woman's instinct. But she crouched, and dared not. She was afraid he would not let her. She was

676

afraid it was too much. It lay there, his body, abandoned. She knew she ought to take it up and claim it, and claim every right to it. But—could she do it? Her impotence before him, before the strong demand of some unknown thing in him, was her extremity. Her hands fluttered; she half-lifted her head. Her eyes, shuddering, appealing, gone almost distracted, pleaded to him suddenly. His heart caught with pity. He took her hands, drew her to him, and comforted her.

"Will you have me, to marry me?" he said very low.

Oh, why did not he take her? Her very soul belonged to him. Why would he not take what was his? She had borne so long the cruelty of belonging to him and not being claimed by him. Now he was straining her again. It was too much for her. She drew back her head, held his face between her hands, and looked him in the eyes. No, he was hard. He wanted something else. She pleaded to him with all her love not to make it *her* choice. She could not cope with it, with him, she knew not with what. But it strained her till she felt she would break.

"Do you want it?" she asked, very gravely.

"Not much," he replied, with pain.

She turned her face aside; then, raising herself with dignity, she took his head to her bosom, and rocked him softly. She was not to have him, then! So she could comfort him. She put her fingers through his hair. For her, the anguished sweetness of self-sacrifice. For him, the hate and misery of

677

another failure. He could not bear it—that breast which was warm and which cradled him without taking the burden of him. So much he wanted to rest on her that the feint of rest only tortured him. He drew away.

"And without marriage we can do nothing?" he asked.

His mouth was lifted from his teeth with pain. She put her little finger between her lips.

"No," she said, low and like the toll of a bell. "No, I think not."

It was the end then between them. She could not take him and relieve him of the responsibility of himself. She could only sacrifice herself to him—sacrifice herself every day, gladly. And that he did not want. He wanted her to hold him and say, with joy and authority: "Stop all this restlessness and beating against death. You are mine for a mate." She had not the strength. Or was it a mate she wanted? or did she want a Christ in him?

He felt, in leaving her, he was defrauding her of life. But he knew that, in staying, stifling the inner, desperate man, he was denying his own life. And he did not hope to give life to her by denying his own.

She sat very quiet. He lit a cigarette. The smoke went up from it, wavering. He was thinking of his mother, and had forgotten Miriam. She suddenly looked at him. Her bitterness came surging up. Her sacrifice, then, was useless. He lay there aloof, careless about her. Suddenly she saw again his lack of religion, his restless instability. He would destroy himself like a perverse child. Well, then, he would!

"I think I must go," she said softly.

By her tone he knew she was despising him. He rose quietly.

"I'll come along with you," he answered.

She stood before the mirror pinning on her hat. How bitter, how unutterably bitter, it made her that he rejected her sacrifice! Life ahead looked dead, as if the glow were gone out. She bowed her face over the flowers—the freesias so sweet and spring-like, the scarlet anemones flaunting over the table. It was like him to have those flowers.

He moved about the room with a certain sureness of touch, swift and relentless and quiet. She knew she could not cope with him. He would escape like a weasel out of her hands. Yet without him her life would trail on lifeless. Brooding, she touched the flowers.

"Have them!" he said; and he took them out of the jar, dripping as they were, and went quickly into the kitchen. She waited for him, took the flowers, and they went out together, he talking, she feeling dead.

She was going from him now. In her misery she leaned against him as they sat on the car. He was unresponsive. Where would he go? What would be the end of him? She could not bear it, the vacant feeling where he should be. He was so foolish, so wasteful, never at peace with himself. And now where would he go? And what did he care that he wasted her? He had no religion; it was all for the moment's attraction that he cared, nothing else, nothing deeper. Well, she would wait and see how it turned out with him. When he had had enough he would give in and come to her.

He shook hands and left her at the door of her cousin's house. When he turned away he felt the last hold for him had gone. The town, as he sat upon the car, stretched away over the bay of railway, a level fume of lights. Beyond the town the country, little smouldering spots for more towns—the sea—the night—on and on! And he had no place in it! Whatever spot he stood on, there he stood alone. From his breast, from his mouth, sprang the endless space, and it was there behind him, everywhere. The people hurrying along the streets offered no obstruction to the void in which he found himself. They were small shadows whose footsteps and voices could be heard, but in each of them the same night, the same silence. He got off the car. In the country all was dead still. Little stars shone high up; little stars spread far away in the flood-waters, a firmament below. Everywhere the vastness and terror of the immense night which is roused and stirred for a brief while by the day, but which returns, and will remain at last eternal, holding everything in its silence and its living gloom. There was no Time, only Space. Who could say his mother had lived, and did not live? She had been in one place, and was in another; that was all. And his soul could not leave her, wherever she was.

Now she was gone abroad into the night, and he was with her still. They were together. But yet there was his body, his chest, that leaned against the stile, his hands on the wooden bar. They seemed something. Where was he?—one tiny upright speck of flesh, less than an ear of wheat lost in the field. He could not bear it. On every side the immense dark silence seemed pressing him, so tiny a spark, into extinction, and yet, almost nothing, he could not be extinct. Night, in which everything was lost, went reaching out, beyond stars and sun. Stars and sun, a few bright grains, went spinning round for terror, and holding each other in embrace, there in a darkness that outpassed them all, and left them tiny and daunted. So much, and himself, in-finitesimal, at the core a nothingness, and yet not nothing.

"Mother!" he whispered—"mother!"

She was the only thing that held him up, himself, amid all this. And she was gone, intermingled herself. He wanted her to touch him, have him alongside with her.

But no, he would not give in. Turning sharply, he walked towards the city's gold phosphorescence. His fists were shut, his mouth set fast. He would not take that direction, to the darkness, to follow her. He walked towards the faintly humming, glow-ing town, quickly.

# EINSTEIN

# RONALD W. CLARK

---

# EINSTEIN

## THE LIFE AND TIMES

HODDER AND STOUGHTON

LONDON SYDNEY AUCKLAND TORONTO

*"I have little patience with scientists who take a board of wood, look for its thinnest part, and drill a great number of holes where drilling is easy."*

Albert Einstein (quoted by Philipp Frank
in "Einstein's Philosophy of Science",
*Reviews of Modern Physics, Vol. 21,*
№ 3, July 1949)

This edition of *Einstein: The Life and Times* contains material not available when the American edition was published. Copyright restrictions have also produced other differences between the American and the British edition. However, detailed references to material both quoted and unquoted will be found in full on pp 611—648.

# *Foreword*

THE STORY OF ALBERT EINSTEIN, SCIENTIST, PHILOSOPHER AND contemporary conscience, with all its impact and influence, would fit better within the walls of a library than between the covers of a single book. For Einstein was far more than the scientist who confidently claimed that space and time were not what everybody thought, including the most sophisticated heirs of Newton, and who shrugged it off when he was found to be right. In his technical language, the universe was four-dimensional, while fallible human beings thought they had a right to no more than three. He passionately indulged in pacifism, and as passionately qualified it when Hitler began to show that he really meant what he said about the Jews and the master-race. Throughout it all he stuck to the job in hand, determined to squeeze the next secret from Nature.

The different facets of Einstein's life and work will long continue to be explored. Deeper and deeper theses on ever smaller aspects of his science will continue to be written. The impact of his support for pacifism between the two world wars will one day get the detailed and possibly disillusioning analysis it warrants; so will the result of that honest enthusiasm for Zionism which for long led him to believe that the promised land could be reached without force of arms. In theology he is likely to remain something of an enigma, even among those who do not take his cosmic religion too seriously. As a peg on which to hang an argument on science and government, he is less useful than might be expected; even so, the real relevance of his famous letter to Roosevelt in 1939, and of his lesser-known actions in the winter of 1944, provide the substance of more than one might-have-been which could be explored in detail. Einstein the philosopher is certain to get even more critical study as the deeper implications of his work continue to be investigated. And few can read his correspondence — whose publication is long overdue — without feeling that Einstein's wit is worth a slim volume on its own. All this will come one day.

But something more than these specialist portraits, each with

Einstein at the centre of a technical argument, emerges from digging hard into the documents, and from a critical appraisal of the myth and reminiscence which have grown around his memory in the last two or three decades. It is the picture of a man who can, without exaggeration, be called one of the great tragic figures of our time. It is the picture of a man who while still young abandoned, with all the passion of the convinced monastic, much of what life had to offer — and who was shot back into the struggle by the unobliging stumble of history. Thus the youth who relinquished his nationality at the age of sixteen returned to the fold later; opted out of German nationality a second time in middle life; and even in old age, when reconciliation had become respectable, refused to return to "the land of the mass murderers". The dedicated pacifist, who after his change of stance was reviled for his apostasy, believed himself to be among those who pressed the buttons which destroyed Hiroshima and Nagasaki. The Zionist who put peace with the Arabs as a first essential was forced finally to agree that it was necessary to fight. In science the greatest physicist in three centuries, or possibly of all time, found himself after middle age pushed by the advance of quantum theory into a backwater, "a genuine old museumpiece" as he described himself.

These ironies not only gave Einstein's life a great personal poignancy; they also combined to keep him in the glare of the public limelight, first switched on with such spectacular results in 1919 when, in Whitehead's words, "a great adventure in thought had at length come safe to shore." In this glare, the human figure has tended to be enlarged into the Delphic oracle. The aureole of white hair helped. So did the great luminous eyes. So did the brave stand which Einstein made for civic and academic freedoms. After his death, all this encouraged a biographical molly-coddling which was less than his genius deserved. It also tended to encourage the belief that, as he once put it, all men dance to the tune of an invisible piper. This is not so. "Wherever a system is really complicated, as in the brain or in an organized community," Sir George Thomson has said, "indeterminacy comes in, not necessarily because of $h$ [Planck's constant] but because to make a prediction so *many* things must be known that the stray consequences of studying them will disturb the *status quo*, which can never therefore be discovered. History is not and cannot be determinate. The supposed causes only *may* produce the consequences we expect."*

* From a letter to the author from Sir George Thomson, February 16, 1970.

This has rarely been more true than of Albert Einstein, whose thought and action in science and life became interrelated in a way no dramatist would dare to conceive. His extraordinary story has itself some quality of the indeterminacy which in physics he was so reluctant to accept. He would not have liked it. But he would have appreciated the situation. He might even have laughed about it.

RONALD W. CLARK

# *Acknowledgments*

I AM GRATEFUL FOR PERMISSION TO CONSULT THE EINSTEIN ARCHIVE in Princeton. In addition I wish to thank: Dr. Jagdish Mehra of the University of Texas at Austin, Texas, for reading the manuscript; and Professor Norman Bentwich, Josef Fraenkel, Professor N. Kemmer, Professor Sir Bernard Lovell, Dr. R. E. W. Maddison, Professor C. W. McCombie, Dr. David Mitrany, Heinz Norden, Dr. Peter Plesch, Sir George Thomson, and Lancelot Law Whyte for reading portions of the manuscript. A very large number of people in the United States, Europe, and the Middle East have been generous in providing documents and reminiscences. It is unfortunately impossible to name them all, but I would practically like to thank the following, while stressing that, throughout the book, any opinions expressed, and the responsibility for the facts given, are entirely my own:

Sir Walter Adams, Director, The London School of Economics and Political Science; Professor Aage Bohr; Dr. Vannevar Bush; Dr. C. H. Collie; Professor A. Vibert Douglas; Eidg. Amt für geistiges Eigentum, Berne; Dr. H. A. Einstein; Churchill Eisenhart; Dr. Elizabeth Eppler, Institute of Jewish Affairs; Professor I. Estermann; Mme. M. Fawtier, UNESCO; Frau Kate Freundlich; Professor Dennis Gabor; Mrs. Barbara Gamow; Dr. Judith R. Goodstein, California Institute of Technology; Dr. Max Gottschalk; Kurt R. Grossmann; Sir Roy Harrod; Drs. J. van Herwaarden, Rijksuniversiteit te Utrecht, Universiteitsmuseum, Utrecht; Dr. Max J. Herzberger; Richard G. Hewlett, Chief Historian, U.S. Atomic Energy Commission; Professor Banesh Hoffmann; Alvin E. Jaeggli, Eidg. Technische Hochschule Bibliothek, Zurich; Bernard Jaffe; Miss Suzanne Christine Kennedy, Nuffield College, Oxford; Oscar Kocherthaler; Professor C. Lanczos, Dublin Institute for Advanced Studies; Dr. W. Lanzer, Verein für Geschichte der Arbeiterbewegung Vienna; Colonel Charles A. Lindbergh; Dr. Jacob R. Marcus, American Jewish Archives; Julian L. Meltzer, the Weizmann Archives; Professor Ashley Montagu; Mrs. B. Mulholland; Dr. John N. Nagy; Professor Linus Pauling; Professor J. Pelseneer, Université Libre de

Bruxelles; Y. Perotin, League of Nations Archives, Geneva; Dr. Peter Plesch; Professor William Ready, McMaster University, Hamilton, Ontario; Professor Nathan Rosen; Professor Leonora Cohen Rosenfield; Professor J. Rotblat; Dr. Alexander Sachs; Mrs. Esther Salaman; Mrs. Alice Kimball Smith; Dr. P. van der Star, Rijksmuseum voor de Geschiedenis der Natuurwetenschappen, Leiden; Dr. Gertrud Weiss Szilard; U. S. Department of the Navy; U. S. National Archives and Records Service; E. Vandewoude, Cabinet du Roi, Bruxelles; Dr. Charles Weiner and Mrs. Joan Warnow of the American Institute of Physics, for their help and guidance in the use of materials in the Niels Bohr Library for History and Philosophy of Physics; Jeremy Weston, The Royal Institution; Dr. G. J. Whitrow; Professor Eugene P. Wigner; E. T. Williams, The Rhodes Trust.

Finally, I wish to thank the large number of Jewish organisations in the United States, Britain, Israel, and elsewhere who have helped to resolve specific problems; the numerous German bodies who have supplied information on the question of Einstein's nationality; the librarians and archivists of the universities and other sources listed in the section on references who have helped to make my work less arduous; and the following for permission to quote copyrighted material:

Algemeen Rijksarchief, The Hague (H. A. Lorentz correspondence); *American Journal of Physics* (R. S. Shankland's "Conversations with Albert Einstein"); His Majesty King Baudouin of the Belgians (letter to Einstein from His Majesty King Albert of the Belgians); Professor Aage Bohr (letters of Professor Niels Bohr); Burndy Library (Ehrenhaft manuscript); The California Institute of Technology Archives, Pasadena (quotations from the Hale and Millikan Papers); Cambridge University Press (Lord Rayleigh's *The Life of Sir J. J. Thomson;* Einstein and Infeld's *The Evolution of Physics;* Hermann Bondi's *Assumption and Myth in Physical Theory;* Sir James Jeans' *The New Background of Science*); Jonathan Cape Ltd. and Alfred Knopf (Philipp Frank's *Einstein*); Columbia University (1912 correspondence with Einstein); Thomas Y. Crowell Co. (*The Questioners*, by Barbara Lovett Cline); Deutsche Verlags-amstalt Stuttgart, and Dr. H. Tramer (Blumenfeld's *Erlebte Judenfrage*); Eyre & Spottiswoode (Publishers) Ltd. (Anton Reiser's *Albert Einstein: A Biographical Portrait*); Frau Kate Freundlich (Freundlich correspondence); Victor Gollancz Ltd. (Leopold Infeld's *Quest: The Evolution of a Scientist*); Institute for Advanced Study, Princeton (letters of Dr. Frank Aydelotte and Dr. Abraham Flexner); Lady

Jeans (Sir James Jeans' letter); Martin J. Klein (*Paul Ehrenfest*); Mrs. Henry R. Labouisse (correspondence of Madame Curie); Dr. Wanda Lanzer (Adler correspondence); the executors of the late Lord Cherwell (Lord Cherwell's correspondence); McGraw-Hill Book Company (Max Talmey's *The Relativity Theory Simplified*); Mrs. B. Mulholland (Commander Locker-Lampson's letters); North Holland Publishing Company and Dr. Abraham Pais (*Niels Bohr*, ed L. Rosenfeld); North Holland Publishing Company (*Niels Bohr: An Essay*, by L. Rosenfeld); Oxford University Press (Robert Oppenhemier's *The Flying Trapeze: Three Crises for Physicists*, the Whidden Lectures, 1962); Dr. Peter Plesch (*Janos*, by Janos Plesch); *Punch* (for poem, "Einstein and Epstein Are Wonderful Men..."); Dr. Nesca Robb (Dr. A. A. Robb's poem); Mme Romain Rolland and Editions Albin Michel (Romain Rolland's *Journal des Années de Guerre 1914-1918*); Professor Peggie Sampson (R. A. Sampson's letter); The Hon. Godfrey Samuel and The House of Lords (Samuel material); Charles Scribner's Sons (Harlow Shapley's *Through Rugged Ways to the Stars*); *The Scientific American* ("An Interview with Albert Einstein," by I. Bernard Cohen); Raglan Squire (Sir John Squire's answer to Pope's epitaph on Sir Isaac Newton); Staples Press and Miss Joyce Weiner (Carl Seelig's *Albert Einstein*); Dr. Gertrud Weiss Szilard (Dr. Leo Szilard's letters and *Reminiscences*); The Master and Fellows of Trinity College, Cambridge (the writings of Sir Arthur Eddington); United Nations (League of Nations archival material); University Museum, Utrecht (Professor Julius correspondence); Mrs. G. W. Watters (writings of Dr. Leon L. Watters); George Weidenfield & Nicholson Ltd. (Antonina Vallentin's *Einstein*); the Trustees of the Weizmann Archives (letters written by Chaim Weizmann).

R.W.C.

# Contents

PART FOUR   THE EINSTEIN AGE

PART FIVE   *THE ILLUSTRIOUS IMMIGRANT*

# *Illustrations*

Einstein at the commencement of his work for the U. S. Navy's
Bureau of Ordnance
Einstein entertains a group of young displaced persons, 1949
Einstein with Irene Joliot-Curie
Einstein in his Princeton study
Einstein's desk at the Institute for Advanced Study, Princeton
Einstein, a portrait by Robert M. Gottschalk

# PART ONE

# The Making of a Mission

# 1

## *GERMAN BOY*

THE LIFE OF ALBERT EINSTEIN HAS A DRAMATIC QUALITY THAT DOES not rest exclusively on his theory of relativity. For the extravagant timing of history linked him with three shattering developments of the twentieth century: the rise of modern Germany, the birth of nuclear weapons, and the growth of Zionism. Their impact on his simple genius combined to drive him into a contact with the affairs of the world for which he had little taste. The result would have made him a unique historical figure even had he not radically altered man's ideas of the physical world. Yet Einstein was also something more, something very different from the Delphic, hair-haloed oracle of his later years. To the end he retained a touch of clowning humour as well as a resigned and understanding amusement at the follies of the human race. Behind the great man there lurked a perpetual glint in the eye, a fundamental irreverence for authority, and an unexpected sense of the ridiculous that could unlatch a deep belly-laugh that shook the windows; together with decent moral purpose it combined to make him a character rich in his own non-scientific right.

German by nationality, Jewish by origin, dissenting in spirit, Einstein reacted ambivalently against these three birthday gifts. He threw his German nationality overboard at the age of fifteen but twenty years later, after becoming Swiss, settled in Berlin where he remained throughout the First World War; after Germany's defeat in 1918 he took up German civic rights again, one of the follies of his life as he later called it, only to renounce his country a second time when Hitler came to power. His position as a Jew was buttressed by his support of Zionism, yet he offended more than once by insistence that Jews were, more importantly, members of the human species. Moreover his Zionism conflicted at times with his pacifism; and to his old friend, Lord Samuel, he commented that he was, despite anti-Semitic attacks, "pas très Juif". The free-thinking ideals of his youth continued into old age; yet these included a belief in the ordered and orderly nature of the universe which was by no means in conflict with the idea of a God — even though what Einstein meant by the word was peculiar to himself and a small number of others. In these and other ways, in his private and his professional life, Einstein became the great contradiction; the German who detested the Germans; the pacifist who encouraged men to arms and played a significant part in the birth of nuclear weapons; the Zionist who wished to placate the Arabs; the physicist who with his "heuristic viewpoint" of 1905 suggested that light could be both wave and particle, and who was ultimately to agree that all matter presented the same enigma. Yet Einstein himself supplied part of the answer to his own riddle. In ordinary life, as well as in the splendid mysteries of physics, absolutes were to be distrusted; events were often relative to circumstance.

He was born in Ulm, an old city on the Danube with narrow winding streets and the great cathedral on which workmen were then building the tallest spire in Europe. Lying in the foothills of the Swabian Alps, where the Blau and the Iller join the Danube, the city had in 1805 been the scene of the Austrians' defeat by Napoleon. Four years later it was ceded to Württemberg under the Treaty of Vienna. In 1842 the old fortifications were restored by German engineers, and with the creation of the new German Empire in the Hall of Mirrors in 1870, Prussian discipline began to reach down from the north German plains towards the free-and-easy Swabians of which the Einsteins were commonplace examples.

They came from Buchau, a small town between Lake Constance and Ulm, comfortable and complacent on the Federnsee, a minor marsh of prehistoric interest whose story is admirably told in the fine new Federnsee Museum and whose shores are today thronged with weekend tourists. Since 1577 the Jews had formed a distinguished and respectable community in the area. They prospered down the centuries; they hung on, despite the burning of the synagogue in 1938 and all that followed it, until 1968. Only then could the local papers report: "Death of the Last Jew in Buchau". His name was Siegbert Einstein, a relative, many times removed, of the most famous Jew in modern history.

Industrious and mildly prosperous, the Einsteins had lived in Buchau at least since the 1750s according to the six family registers kept by the Jewish authorities. By the middle of the nineteenth century they were numerous, and eleven of that name are shown on the

roll of those who subscribed to the new synagogue in 1839. Albert
Einstein's great-grandfather had been born in the town in 1759
and the Jewish registers record his marriage to Rebekka Obernauer;
the birth of their son Abraham in 1808; and Abraham's marriage
to Helene Moos. Their son Hermann, father of Albert, was born in
Buchau on August 30th, 1847. Nineteen years later Abraham and his
family moved to Ulm, thirty miles to the north, and in 1876 Hermann married Pauline Koch, born in Cannstadt, only a few miles
away, and eleven years his junior.

Like the Einsteins, the Kochs had been part of the Württemberg
Jewish community for more than a century, a family with roots
rather more to the north — in Goppingen, Jebenhausen and Cannstadt. Like her husband, Pauline Koch spoke the soft Swabian
dialect, hallmark of an ancient duchy that had once spread from
Franconia to Switzerland, from Burgundy to Bavaria, and whose
inhabitants lacked both the discipline of Prussia and the coarseness
of Bavaria.

Although Einstein was not of peasant stock, he came from people
almost as close to the earth, and his reactions were often those of the
man tied to the hard facts of life by the seasons. His second wife's
scathing: "My husband mystical!" may not be literally justified,
but it illustrates the difference which has grown through the years
between the unreservedly philosophical Einstein whom many of his
admirers would like him to have been and the more practical man
he very often was. Absent-minded scientist, of course; that was real
and not sham. Einstein never played to the gallery, although more
aware of its existence than is sometimes imagined; but, more than
most men, he was usually absent-minded about things that didn't
matter; or when he knew there was someone to remember for him.

The differences between his parents, a devoted, cheerful couple
who faced the results of the husband's happy-go-lucky character
with resignation, were largely those of emphasis. The picture of the
father that comes through, second-hand, from a grandson he never
knew, is of a jovial hopeful man — fond of beer and good food,
of Schiller and Heine. This fits the description which Einstein
himself presented to his friend Philipp Frank, who wrote of Hermann: "His mode of life and his *Weltanschauung* differed in no
respect from those of the average citizen in that locality. When his
work was done, he liked to go on outings with his family into the
beautiful country round Munich, to the romantic lakes and mountains, and he was fond of stopping at the pleasant, comfortable
Bavarian taverns, with their good beer, radishes and sausages." More

than half a century later Albert Einstein remembered those Sunday
excursions with enjoyment, the discussions between his father and his
mother as to which way they should go, and the husband's careful
selection of a route which would end up where his wife wanted.
"Exceedingly friendly, mild and wise", was how he spoke of his
father as he approached the age of seventy. Easy-going and unruffle-
able, a large optimistic man with thick moustache who looks out
from his portraits through rimmed pince-nez with all the quiet certitude of the nineteenth century, Hermann Einstein would have
thought it slightly presumptuous to have fathered a genius.

To the union Pauline Koch, with even features and mass of dark
hair piled high above broad forehead, brought more than the comparative affluence of a woman whose father was a Stuttgart grain
merchant and Court Purveyor. She brought also a breath of genuine
culture, a love of music which was to be inextricably entwined with
her son's work and, in the pursuit of her ambition for him, a touch
of the ruthlessness with which he followed his star. She appears to
have had a wider grasp than her husband of German literature and
while for him Schiller and Heine were an end in themselves, for her
they were only a beginning. To Pauline Koch, it might well be
thought, Einstein would attribute the imaginative genius which was
to make him so much more than a mere scientist. He took a different
view.

For a year the young Einsteins lived in Buchau. Then in 1877
they moved back to Ulm where Hermann set up, in a building on
the south side of the Cathedral Square which later became the
"Englander" wine tavern, a small electrical and engineering workshop financed by his more prosperous in-laws. He and his wife lived
a few hundred yards away in an apartment at No. 135, city-division
B, an undistinguished four-storey building re-numbered 20 Bahnhof-
strasse in 1880 and destroyed in an Allied air raid sixty-four years
later. Below it, one of the tributaries of the river Blau flowed in a
cutting beside the street, past the over-jutting windows of houses that
had not changed much since the fifteenth century, turning before it
reached the cathedral and entered the Danube. Here, in the town
whose inhabitants proudly claimed that *"Ulmense sunt mathematici"*
(the people of Ulm are mathematicians), Albert Einstein was born
on March 14th, 1879.

Within a year of the birth, Hermann's small business had collapsed, a victim of his own perpetual good nature and high hopes. He
now moved to Munich and with his brother Jakob opened a small
electro-chemical works. Thus for Einstein Ulm was merely a vestigial

memory, a town from whose winding medieval streets the open
country could still be seen, a town where the Jews retained their own
identity yet lived at ease with the rest of the community; a smallish
place through whose squares the cows with their great clanging bells
were driven, and into which there drifted, on summer evenings, the
scent of the forests and the surrounding hills.

The move to Munich brought the Einstein family from an almost
rural environment into the capital of Bavaria, already more than a
quarter of a million strong, still fresh from the architectural adorn-
ments added to it by the mad King Ludwig at a cost of 7,000,000
thalers. Overwhelmingly Catholic, its air was heavy with the sound
of bells from numerous churches: the cathedral of the archbishopric
of Munich-Freising, with its unfinished towers; the Jesuit St. Michael's; the Louis, with Cornelius' fresco of the Last Judgement; and
St. Mariahilf with its gorgeous glass and fine woodwork. The city
was rich in art galleries, proud of its seven bridges across the Isar,
and of the Konigsbau built in the style of the Pitti Palace in Florence;
a city still epitomising the baroquerie of southern Germany before it
bowed knee to the Prussians from the north. From its narrow alley-
ways and its fine arcades there was carried on one of the great art
trades of Europe; and from its breweries there came, each year, no
less than 49,000,000 gallons, of which 37,000,000 were drunk in the
city itself.

In the University of Munich there had begun to work in 1880
a man whose influence on Einstein was to be continuous, critical
and, in the final assessment, enigmatic. This was Max Karl Ernst
Ludwig Planck, then aged twenty-two, the latest in a long line of
"excellent, reliable, incorruptible, idealistic and generous men devoted to the service of Church and State". Born in Kiel while the
port was still part of Danish Schleswig-Holstein, aged eight at the
time of Prussia's conquest of the province, Max Planck was born
into a professional German family which had moved south to
Munich the following year. Later he studied at the University before
going north to Berlin. Then, dedicated to the task of discovering
how nature worked, Planck returned to Munich where he served as
a *privatdozent* for five years; as he walked daily to the University
the young private tutor may have brushed shoulders with a boy
whose life was to be intimately linked with his own. For two
decades later Einstein was to provide a revolutionary development
to Planck's own quantum theory. Another decade on, and Planck
was to attract Einstein from the Switzerland he loved to the Germany which he detested. Planck was to encourage him into becoming

a German citizen for the second time, and, more than once during the 1920s, to dissuade him from leaving the Fatherland. In these, and in other ways, the two men's lives were to be ironically linked in a way which reads like nature aping art.

The first Einstein home in Munich was a small rented house. After five years the family business had prospered sufficiently for a move to be made to a larger home in the suburb of Sendling. This was surrounded by big trees and a rambling garden, usually unkempt, which separated it from the main road. Only a short distance away were buildings soon converted into a small factory for manufacture of electrical equipment. Here Hermann attended to the business while brother Jakob, with more technical knowledge, ran the works.

A year after the family's arrival in Munich, Albert's sister Maja was born. Only two years younger, she was to become constant companion and unfailing confidant. Himself unconcerned with death, he faced the loss of two wives with equanimity; but the death of his sister, at the age of seventy, dented the hard defensive shell he had built round his personal feelings.

In one way the Einsteins failed to fit any of the convenient slots of their history and environment. In a predominantly Catholic community — eighty-four per cent in Munich — they were not merely Jews, but Jews who had fallen away. Many deep-grained Jewish characteristics remained, it is true. The tradition of the close-knit intermarrying community is well brought out in the family trees, and Einstein himself was to add to it when, after divorce, he married a double cousin. The deep respect for learning which the Jew shares with the Celt ran in the very marrow of the family. And Einstein was to become but one more witness to the prominent part that Jews have played in the revolutionary developments of science — from Jacques Loeb in physiology to Levi-Civita and Minkowski in mathematics, Paul Ehrenfest in the quantum theory, Haber in chemistry, and Lise Meitner, Leo Szilard and many others in nuclear physics. Thus he belonged to a group whose loyalties crossed frontiers and oceans, known by its members to be steadfastly self-succouring and claimed by its enemies to operate an international conspiracy.

Despite this, the essential Jewish root of the matter was lacking: the family did not attend the local synagogue. It did not deny itself bacon or ham, nor certain sea foods. It did not demand that animals must be slaughtered according to ritual and did not forbid the eating of meat and dairy products together. All this was to Hermann Einstein but "an ancient superstition" and equally so were the other customs and traditions of the Jewish faith. There was also in the family one particularly hard-bitten agnostic uncle, and Einstein used him as peg for the old Jewish joke. He would always describe with relish how he had surprised him one day in full formal dress preparing to go to the synagogue. The uncle had responded to the nephew's astonishment with the warning: "Ah, but you never know."

Thus Einstein was nourished on a family tradition which had broken with authority; which disagreed, sought independence, had deliberately trodden out of line. This also, as surely as the humanitarian tradition of Jewish self-help, was to pull him the way he went, so that at times he closely resembled J. B. S. Haldane who came to believe that authority and government itself must be bad — any government and any authority. Sent first to a Catholic elementary school apparently on the grounds that it was convenient, he was there a Jew among Christians; among Jews he was, like the members of his family, an outsider. The pattern was to repeat itself through much of his life.

The bare facts of his early years are well-enough known, but an aura of mythology surrounds much of the detail. This would suggest caution; but there is also Einstein's own admission that his evidence could be faulty. The admission, which is substantiated by Einstein's son, was made in old age after Dr. Janos Plesch, who had known Einstein at least since 1919 when he attended Pauline Einstein on her deathbed, sent him for comment the material he was incorporating in his own autobiography. "It has always struck me as singular," this went, "that the marvellous memory of Einstein for scientific matters does not extend to other fields. I don't believe that Einstein could forget anything that interested him scientifically, but matters relating to his childhood, his scientific beginnings and his development are in a different category, and he rarely talks about them — not because they don't interest him but simply because he doesn't remember them well enough." Einstein agreed. Many of the reported details of his very early years must therefore be believed in more as an act of faith than as the result of reliable evidence — a situation true to a lesser extent of his later life when there grew up round his activities a thick jungle of distortions, misconceptions, inventions and simple lies. A biography with frontispiece drawing showing "Einstein at the first test of the atomic bomb" — a test of which he knew nothing at the time — is illustration rather than exception.

Nothing in Einstein's early history suggests dormant genius. Quite the contrary. The one feature of his childhood about which there appears no doubt is the lateness with which he learned to speak. Even at the age of nine he was not fluent, while reminiscences of his youth stress hesitancies and the fact that he would reply to questions only after consideration and reflection. His parents feared that he might be subnormal, and it has even been suggested that in his infancy he may have suffered from a form of dyslexia. "Leonardo da Vinci, Hans Christian Anderson, Einstein and Niels Bohr," it is claimed by the Dyslexic Society — with understandable special pleading — "are super-men who have survived the handicap of dyslexia." Far more plausible is the simpler situation suggested by Einstein's son Hans Albert when interviewed by Bela Kornitzer for his study of *Fathers and Sons:* "My father ... was shy, lonely and withdrawn from the world even then. He was even considered backward by his teachers. He told me that his teachers reported to his father that he was mentally slow, unsociable and adrift forever in his foolish dreams." This is in line with the family legend that when Hermann Einstein asked his son's headmaster what profession his son should adopt, the answer was simply: "It doesn't matter; he'll never make a success of anything."

His boyhood was straightforward enough. From the age of five until the age of ten he attended a Catholic school near his home, and at ten was transferred to the Luitpold Gymnasium, where the children of the middle classes had drummed into them the rudiments of Latin and Greek, of history and geography, as well as of simple mathematics. The choice of a Catholic school was not as curious as it seems. Elementary education in Bavaria was run on a denominational basis. The nearest Jewish school was some distance from the Einstein home and its fees were high. To a family of little religious feeling the dangers of Catholic orientation were outweighed by the sound general instruction which the school gave.

According to some sources he was here confronted for the first time with his Jewishness. For as an object lesson a teacher one day produced a large nail with the words: "The nails with which Christ was nailed to the cross looked like this." Almost sixty years later Einstein gave his seal to the tale: "A true story." But Frank, to whom he appears to have told it, comments that the teacher "did not add, as sometimes happens, that the Crucifixion was the work of the Jews. Nor did the idea enter the minds of the students that because of this they must change their relations with their classmate Albert." It seems likely, despite the highlight sometimes given to the incident, that none of the boys took much notice of the nail from the Crucifixion. And in later life Einstein was to repeat more

than once that the fact of his Jewishness was only brought home
when he arrived in Berlin a few months before the start of the First
World War.

Before Einstein left his Catholic elementary school for the
sterner Luitpold Gymnasium he received what appears to have been
the first genuine shock to his intellectual system. The "appears" is
necessary. For this was the famous incident of the pocket compass
and while he confirmed that it actually happened he was also to
put a gloss on its significance.

The story is simply that when the boy was five, ill in bed, his
father showed him a pocket compass. What impressed the child was
that since the iron needle always pointed in the same direction,
whichever way the case was turned, it must be acted upon by something that existed in space — the space that had always been
considered empty. The incident, so redolent of "famous childhoods",
is reported persistently in the accounts of Einstein's youth that began
to be printed after he achieved popular fame at the end of the First
World War. Whether it always had its later significance is another
matter. Einstein himself, answering questions in 1953 at the time
of his seventy-fourth birthday, seemed uncertain.

Soon afterwards another influence entered Einstein's life. From
the age of six he began to learn the violin. The enthusiasm this
evoked did not come quickly. He was taught by rote rather than
inspiration, and seven years passed before he was aroused by Mozart
into an awareness of the mathematical structure of music. Yet his
delight in the instrument grew steadily and became a psychological
safety-valve; it was never quite matched by performance. In later
years the violin became the hallmark of the world's most famous
scientist; but it was Einstein's supreme and obvious enjoyment in
performance which was the thing. Amateur, gifted or not, remained
amateur.

Hermann Einstein with his compass and Pauline Einstein with
her insistence on music lessons brought two influences to bear on
their son. A third was provided by his uncle Jakob, the sound
engineer without whom Hermann would have foundered even faster
in the sea of good intentions. Jakob Einstein is a relatively shadowy
figure, and his memorial is a single anecdote, remembered over more
than thirty years and recalled by Einstein to his early biographers.
"Algebra is a merry science," Uncle Jakob would say. "We go hunting for a little animal whose name we don't know, so we call it x.
When we bag our game we pounce on it and give it its right name."
Uncle Jakob may or may not have played a significant part in

making mathematics appear attractive, but his influence seems to have been long-lasting. In many of Einstein's later attempts to present the theory of relativity to non-mathematicians, there is recourse to something not so very different; to analogies with lifts, trains and ships, that suggest a memory of the stone house at Sendling and Uncle Jakob's "little animal whose name we don't know".

However, the Einstein family included an in-law more important than father, mother or Uncle Jakob. This was Cäsar Koch, Pauline Koch's brother who lived in Stuttgart and whose visits to the Einstein family were long remembered. In January, 1885 Cäsar Koch returned to Germany from Russia, where part of his family was living. With him he brought as a present for Albert a model steam engine, handed over during a visit to Munich that year, and drawn from memory by his nephew thirty years later. Soon afterwards Cäsar married and moved to Antwerp — where the young Albert was subsequently taken on a conducted tour of the Bourse. A well-to-do grain merchant, Cäsar Koch appears to have had few intellectual pretensions. But some confidence was sparked up between uncle and nephew and it was to Cäsar that Einstein was to send, as a boy of sixteen, an outline of the imaginative ideas which foreshadowed the Special Theory of Relativity.

However, nothing so precocious appeared likely when Einstein in 1889 made his first appearance at the Luitpold Gymnasium. Still slightly backward, introspective, keeping to himself the vague stirrings of interest which he felt for the world about him, he had so far given no indication that he was in any way different from the common run of children. The next six years at the Gymnasium were to alter that, although hardly in the way his parents can have hoped.

Within the climate of the time, the Luitpold Gymnasium seems to have been no better and no worse than most establishments of its kind. It is true that it put as great a premium on a thick skin as any British public school but there is no reason to suppose that it was particularly ogreish. Behind what might be regarded as no more than normal discipline it held, in reserve, the ultimate weapon of appeal to the unquestionable Prussian god of authority. Yet boys, and even sensitive boys, have survived as much; some have even survived Eton.

The Gymnasium was to have a critical effect on Einstein in separate ways. The first was that its discipline created in him a deep suspicion of authority in general and of educational authority in particular. This feeling lasted all his life, without qualification. The Gymnasium also taught him the virtues of scepticism. It encouraged

him to question and to doubt, always valuable qualities in a scientist
and particularly so at this period in the history of physics. Here
the advance of technology was bringing to light curious new phenomena which, however hard men might try, could not be fitted
into the existing order of things. Yet innate conservatism presented
a formidable barrier to discussion, let alone acceptance, of new
ideas. If Einstein had not been pushed by the Luitpold Gymnasium
into the stance of opposition he was to retain all his life, then he
might not have questioned so quickly so many assumptions that most
men took for granted, nor have arrived at such an early age at the
Special Theory of Relativity.

A third effect was of a very different kind. There is no doubt
that he despised educational discipline and that this in turn nourished the radical enquiring attitude that is essential to the scientist.
Yet it was only years later, as he looked back from middle life to
childhood, that he expressed his dislike of the Gymnasium so vehemently. Until then, according to one percipient biographer who
came to know him well, "he could not even say that he hated it.
According to family legend, this taciturn child, who was not given
to complaining, did not even seem very miserable. Only long afterwards did he identify the tone and atmosphere of his schooldays
with that of barracks, the negation, in his opinion, of the human
being."

Yet by the end of the First World War this school environment
had become a symbol in an equation whose validity Einstein never
doubted. The Luitpold Gymnasium as he looked back on it equalled
ruthless discipline, and the Luitpold Gymnasium was German. Thus
the boyhood hardships became transformed into the symbol of all
that was worst in the German character — a transformation that
was to produce dire and ironic consequences. With the stench of
Belsen still in the nostrils after twenty-five years, it is easy enough
to understand the near-paranoia that affected Einstein when in later
life he regarded his own countrymen. It is easy enough to understand
his reply when, at the age of sixty-nine he was asked: "Is there any
German person towards whom you feel an estimation and who was
your very personal friend among the German born?" "Respect for
Planck," Einstein had replied. "No friendship for any real German.
Max von Laue was the closest to me." All this is understandable.
Yet Germans were among the first to die in the concentration camps,
and it is remarkable to find in Einstein, normally the most com-
passionate of men, what must reluctantly be identified as a trace of
Vansittartism. Thus the Luitpold Gymnasium, transmogrified by

memory, has a lot to answer for; it convinced Einstein that the Prussians had been handed out a double dose of original sin. Later experiences tended to confirm the belief.

At the Gymnasium there appears to have been, as there frequently is in such schools, one master who stood apart, the odd man out going his nonconformist way. His name was Reuss. He tried to make his pupils think for themselves while most of his colleagues did little more — in Einstein's later opinion — than encourage an academic *Kadavergehorsamkeit* "the obedience of the corpse" that was required among troops of the Imperial Prussian Army. In later life Einstein would recall how Reuss had tried to spark alive a real interest in ancient civilisations and their influences which still could be seen in the contemporary life of southern Germany.

There was to be an unexpected footnote to Einstein's memory. For after his first work had begun to pass a disturbing electric shock through the framework of science, he himself visited Munich and called on his old teacher, then living in retirement. But the worn suit and baggy trousers which had already become the Einstein hallmark among his colleagues, merely suggested poverty. Reuss had no recollection of Einstein's name and it became clear that he thought his caller was on a begging errand. Einstein left hurriedly.

The influence that initially led Einstein on to his chosen path did not come from the Luitpold Gymnasium but from Max Talmey, a young Jewish medical student who in 1889 matriculated at Munich University. Talmey's elder brother, a practising doctor, already knew the Einstein family, and quickly introduced him to what Max called "the happy, comfortable and cheerful Einstein home, where I received the same generous consideration as he did." In later life Talmey was seized with the idea for a universal language, an Esperanto which he felt would be particularly valuable for science. He tried to enlist Einstein's support, became interested in relativity, and then, like so many others, attempted to explain the theory. More important, he included in his little-known book on the subject his own impressions of Einstein at the age of twelve, the only reliable first-hand account that exists.

> He was a pretty, dark-haired boy ... a good illustration ... against the theory of Houston Stewart Chamberlain and others who try to prove that only the blond races produce geniuses, (Talmey wrote). He showed a particular inclination toward physics and took pleasure in conversing on physical phenomena. I gave him therefore as reading matter A. Bernstein's *Popular Books on Physical Science* and L. Buchner's *Force and Matter,* two works that were then quite popular in Germany. The

boy was profoundly impressed by them. Bernstein's work especially, which describes physical phenomena lucidly and engagingly, had a great influence on Albert, and enhanced considerably his interest in physical science.

Soon afterwards he began to show keenness for mathematics, and Talmey gave him a copy of Spieker's *Lehrbuch der ebenen Geometrie*, a popular textbook. Thereafter, whenever the young medical student arrived for the midday meal on Thursdays, he would be shown the problems solved by Einstein during the previous week.

After a short time, a few months, he had worked through the whole book of Spieker. He thereupon devoted himself to higher mathematics, studying all by himself Lubsen's excellent works on the subject. These, too, I had recommended to him if memory serves me right. Soon the flight of his mathematical genius was so high that I could no longer follow. Thereafter philosophy was often a subject of our conversations. I recommended to him the reading of Kant.

He also read Darwin — at least according to the more reliable of his stepsons-in-law. There is no evidence that he was particularly moved. One reason was that the battle for evolution had by this time been fought and won. Yet even in his youth Einstein may have believed, as he was to write years later, that living matter and clarity were opposites. The same feeling that "biological procedures cannot be expressed in mathematical formulae," gave him a life-long scepticism of medicine according to his friend Gustav Bucky, and it certainly tended to concentrate Einstein's interests on non-biological subjects. This attitude, a sense almost of annoyance with the Creator at having produced things which could not be quantified, explains at least something of the invisible barrier which so often rises to separate Einstein, the intuitively understanding and kind human being, from Einstein ordering his daily life. The bugle-calls of science were always sounding and he could rarely devote much time to individual men and women. His reaction to the living world was illustrated one day as he stood with a friend watching flocks of emigrating birds flying overhead: "I think it is easily possible that they follow beams which are so far unknown to us".

Discovering the nature of the physical world was certainly task enough for one man. Nevertheless, it is interesting to speculate on what might have happened to biology in the twentieth century had Einstein decided to turn his genius towards the animate rather than the inanimate world.

The decision appears to have been made soon after the age of twelve. It is not too definite a word although details and date must be inferred rather than demonstrated, deduced from circumstantial evidence rather than illustrated by the hard fact and undeniable statement that form part and parcel of more extrovert and better-documented childhoods. By the time he was twelve, Einstein had attained, in his own words, a deep religiosity. His approval of this translation of the original German in his autobiographical notes is significant; for religiosity, the "affected or excessive religiousness" of the dictionary, appears to describe accurately the results of his education so far. Always sensitive to beauty, abnormally sensitive to music, Einstein had no doubt been deeply impressed by the splendid trappings which decked out the Bavarian Catholicism of those days. But if his emotions were won over, his mind remained free — with considerable results, for through the reading of popular scentific books he soon reached the conviction that much of the stories in the Bible could not be true.

The resulting change of heart was important not because the change of heart itself was unusual but because of Einstein's future history. For centuries children have abandoned revealed religion at the impressionable age and turned to the laws of nature as a substitute. The process is hardly one for wide-eyed wonder. What was different with Einstein was that the common act should have such uncommon results.

His need of something to fill the void, the desperate need to find order in a chaotic world, may possibly have been a particularly Jewish need. Certainly Abba Eban, former Israeli Ambassador to the United States, noted after Einstein's death how "the Hebrew mind has been obsessed for centuries by a concept of order and harmony in the universal design. The search for laws hitherto unknown which govern cosmic forces; the doctrine of a relative harmony in nature; the idea of a calculable relationship between matter and energy — these are all more likely to emerge from a basic Hebrew philosophy and turn of mind than from many others." This may sound like hindsight plus special pleading; yet the long line of Jewish physicists from the nineteenth century, and the even longer list of those who later sought the underlying unifications of the subatomic world, give it a plausibility which cannot easily be contested.

If there were no order or logic in the man-made conceptions of the world based on revealed religion, surely order and logic could be discovered in the external world. The young Einstein, like the Victorian ecclesiastic who wished "to penetrate into the *arcana* of nature, so as to discern 'the law within the law'," picked up science where religion appeared to leave off. Later he was to see both as different sides of the same coin, as complementary as the wave and corpuscle conceptions of light, and both just as necessary if one were to see reality in the round. All this, however, developed in the decades after conversion.

Conversion did not come in a day. Common sense, together with what little evidence exists, suggests that Einstein's determination to probe the secrets of the physical world did not appear like a Pauline vision on the Damascus road but crystallised over a period. Nevertheless, it was a conversion which began in early youth, quickly hardened, and set fast for the rest of his life.

Brooding on the "lies" he had been told in the Luitpold Gymnasium, Einstein decided on the work to which he would be willing to devote everything and sacrifice anything with a steely determination which separated him from other men. On two occasions he put down in simple words what that work was. The first came during an hour's meeting with the Jewish philosopher Martin Buber who pressed him hard "with a concealed question about his faith". Finally, in Buber's words, Einstein "burst forth", revealingly. "'What we (and by this 'we' he meant we physicists) strive for', he cried, 'is just to draw His lines after Him'. To draw after - as one retraces a geometrical figure." And years later, walking with a young woman physicist to his Berlin University office, Einstein spelt out the same task in more detail. He had no interest in learning a new language, nor in food nor in new clothes. "I'm not much with people", he continued, "and I'm not a family man. I want my peace. I want to know how God created this world. I am not interested in this or that phenomenon, in the spectrum of this or that element. I want to know His thoughts, the rest are details."

This aim was matched by a belief: "God is subtle but he is not malicious." With these words he was to crystallise his view that complex though the laws of nature might be, difficult though they were to understand, they were yet understandable by human reason. If a man worried away at the law behind the law — if, in Rutherford's words, he knew what questions to ask nature — then the answers could be discovered. God might pose difficult problems but He never broke the rules by posing unanswerable ones. What is more, He never left the answers to blind chance — "God does not play dice with the world."

However, Einstein's God was not the God of most other men. When he wrote of religion, as he often did in middle and later life, he tended to adopt the belief of Alice's Red Queen that "words mean what you want them to mean", and to clothe with different names what to more ordinary mortals — and to most Jews — looked like a variant of simple agnosticism. Yet years later, asked by Ben Gurion whether he believed in God, "even he, with his great formula about energy and mass, agreed that there must be something behind the energy." No doubt. But much of Einstein's writing gives the impression of belief in a God even more intangible and impersonal than a celestial machine-minder, running the universe with undisputable authority and expert touch. Instead, Einstein's God appears as the physical world itself, with its infinitely marvellous structure operating at atomic level with the beauty of a craftsman's wristwatch, and at stellar level with the majesty of a massive cyclotron. This was belief enough. It grew early and rooted deep. Only later was it dignified by the title of cosmic religion, a phrase which gave plausible respectability to the views of a man who did not believe in a life after death and who felt that if virtue paid off in the earthly one, then this was the result of cause and effect rather than celestial reward. Einstein's God thus stood for an orderly system obeying rules which could be discovered by those who had the courage, the imagination and the persistence to go on searching for them. And it was to this task which he began to turn his mind soon after the age of twelve. For the rest of his life everything else was to seem almost trivial by comparison.

Einstein had three more years at the Gymnasium, uninterested in the classics, increasingly able at mathematics, precocious in philosophical matters which one can assume he discussed only rarely with his masters and not at all with his fellow pupils. This time in Munich would have been longer still had not the family business failed again. For now the Einsteins decided to cross the Alps to Milan. The reason why is obscure, but it seems that the Kochs came to the rescue once more. A wealthy branch of the family lived in Genoa, and it may well have been their stipulation that the new business enterprise should start where they could keep a watchful eye on the happy-go-lucky optimism of Hermann Einstein.

The family moved from Munich in 1894, taking their daughter Maja with them and leaving Albert in a boarding-house under the care of a distant relative. It was anticipated that he would in due time finish his course, acquire the diploma which would ensure entry to a university, and would then enter the profession of electrical engineering which his father had vaguely chosen for him. The son had other views and within six months had followed his family across the Alps.

The details of Einstein's departure from the Gymnasium come in various forms, at second remove, from his own comments in middle and old age. What is certain is that he left before acquiring the necessary diploma. It has been stated that he first obtained a doctor's certificate saying that because of a nervous breakdown he should join his parents in Italy, plus a statement from his mathematics master testifying to his ability; before the medical certificate could be presented Einstein was summarily expelled on the grounds that: "Your presence in the class is disruptive and affects the other students." This should be taken with caution but the general lines of the incident have the ring of truth. For the kindly, gentle Einstein who is remembered today, the friend of all mankind (except the Prussians), a saint insulated from the rest of the world, is largely a figure of his later years; it is a figure very different from the precocious, half-cocksure, almost insolent Einstein of youth and early manhood. Einstein was the boy who knew not merely which spanner to throw in the works, but also how best to throw it. This may well explain why the Gymnasium was glad to send him packing. And the ignominy of being sacked before going could explain much of his later dislike of the place.

He was by now heartily glad to see the last of the Luitpold Gymnasium. The feeling was reciprocated. Yet the years there had left their mark in a way which neither his masters nor even he can fully have appreciated. They had made him detest discipline; but, under his guard, they had taught him the virtues of self-discipline, of concentration, of dedication to an ideal, of an attitude which can be described as firm or as relentless according to taste. Years later, when colleagues were discussing the single-minded determination with which he had followed his star without regard for others, one listener noted: "You must not forget. He was a German."

Little is known about the period which the young Einstein spent in Italy, but he looked back on it as extremely happy. "I was so surprised, when I crossed the Alps to Italy, to see how the ordinary Italian, the ordinary man and woman, uses words and expressions of a high level of thought and cultural content, so different from the ordinary Germans," he remembered nearly forty years later. "This is due to their long cultural history. The people of northern Italy are the most civilised people I have ever met."

It may not have been literally true that "he went into galleries and wherever he found a Michelangelo he remained the longest," as was claimed by one of his step sons-in-law in a book which Einstein smartly repudiated. But there is little doubt that he enjoyed the

people and the air of freedom, both very different from what he
had known in the Munich Gymnasium. When his father's business
failed yet again, almost as expected, and was restarted in Pavia,
his own travels began to take him farther afield to Padua, Pisa,
Siena and Perugia.

His education appears to have been halted in mid-stream and
the Swiss School in Milan, at which he is sometimes reported to
have studied — in those days the International School of the Protestant Families in Milan — have no record of him. His sister Maja
and his cousin Robert were on the rolls but Einstein was aged fifteen
when he arrived in the city and the Swiss School took children only
to the age of thirteen.

However, this freedom could not last, since the continuing pre-
cariousness of the family finances made it necessary to prepare for a
career. The only record of how he was prodded into this comes
secondhand from his son: "At the age of sixteen," he has said, "his
father urged him to forget his 'philosophical nonsense', and apply
himself to the 'sensible trade' of electrical engineering." The lack of
a necessary Gymnasium certificate at once made itself felt, since
entry to a University was barred without it.

There was one possible way out. Conveniently over the Alps
from Milan, there existed in Zurich the Swiss Federal Polytechnic
School,* outside Germany the best technical school in central Europe.
The Polytechnic demanded no Gymnasium diploma and all a candidate had to do was pass the necessary examination. There was one
difficulty, however. In the spring of 1895 Einstein was only sixteen,
at least two years younger than most scholars when they joined the
E.T.H. However, it was decided that the risk should be taken, and
in the autumn he was despatched over the Alps.

Before he went — probably a few weeks or months earlier,
although the date is uncertain — he sent to his Uncle Cäsar in
Stuttgart a "paper", an augury of things to come, in which he
proposed tackling one of the most hotly disputed scientific subjects,
the relationship between electricity, magnetism and the ether, that
hypothetical non-material entity which was presumed to fill all space
and to transmit electro-magnetic waves.

Neither letter nor paper are dated, but in 1950 Einstein recalled
that they were written in 1894 or 1895, while the internal reference

* The organisation is known variously by its German, French, Italian and
English titles: Eidg. Technische Hochschule (E. T. H.); École Polytechnique
Fédérale (E. P. F.); Svizzera Polytechnik Federale (S. P. F.); and Swiss
Federal Institute of Technology (F. I. T.).

to the E.T.H. in Zurich suggests that the latter was the more likely year.

The accompanying essay, written in sloping and spidery Gothic script on five pages of lined paper, was headed: "Concerning the Investigation State of Aether in Magnetic Fields" and began by outlining the nature of electro-magnetic phenomena and stressing the little that was known concerning their relationship with the ether, a situation which, it was suggested, could be remedied by experiment.

It was a remarkable paper for a boy of sixteen and if it is straining too far to see in it the seeds of the Special Theory, it gives a firm enough pointer to the subject which was to remain constantly at the back of his mind for a decade. As he wrote in old age, at the age of sixteen he had discovered a paradox by considering what would happen if one could follow a beam of light at the speed of light. He did not put it quite like that to Uncle Cäsar; but it was no doubt still in his mind as he arrived in Zurich, carrying the high hopes of the family and, judging from the odd hint, a firm determination that he would not become an electrical engineer.

# 2

# STATELESS PERSON

EINSTEIN ARRIVED IN ZURICH, THE BUSTLING MERCANTILE CAPITAL of Switzerland, in the autumn of 1895. Set on its long finger of lake between among the foothills of the Alps, the city was half cultural remnant from the Middle Ages, half commercial metropolis, a centre whose nonconformist devotees were within the next few years to include Lenin, Rosa Luxembourg and James Joyce. Einstein, for whom the attractions of Zurich never palled, was to be another.

During this first visit as a youth of sixteen and a half he stayed with the family of Gustav Meier, an old friend of his father and a former inhabitant of Ulm. He may have been accompanied by his mother, and it is certain that Mrs. Einstein approached a Zurich councillor on her son's behalf, asking "whether he could use his influence to let Albert jump a class in view of his unusual talent and the fact that owing to the movement of his family, his schooling had been a little erratic". Einstein did, in fact, take the normal entrance examination for the E. T. H. shortly afterwards. He did not pass. The accepted reason for his failure is that although his knowledge of mathematics was exceptional he did not reach the necessary standard in modern languages or in zoology and botany.

This is less than the whole truth. So is the statement that while the exam was usually taken at the age of eighteen, Einstein was two years younger. More significantly, his father's decision that he should follow a technical occupation was one which the young Einstein would have found it difficult to evade directly. Subsequently, he admitted that failure in Zurich "was entirely his own fault because he had made no attempt whatever to prepare himself"; and, asked in later life whether he might have been forced into choosing a "profitable profession" rather than becoming a scientist, he bluntly replied "I was supposed to choose a practical profession, but this was simply unbearable to me." Although the horse had been brought to the water in Zurich nothing could make it drink. But the principal of the E. T. H., Albin Herzog, had been impressed by Einstein's mathematical ability. Reading between the lines, he had also been impressed by his character. With the support of Meier, it was arranged that the boy should attend the cantonal school at Aarau, twenty miles to the west, where a year's study might enable him to pass the E. T. H. entrance exam.

A small picturesque town on the Aare, from whose banks the vineyards climb the slopes of the Jura, Aarau could justifiably boast of its cantonal school run by Professor Winteler. But wherever Einstein had been sent in Switzerland, he would have been impressed by the contrast with the Munich Gymnasium. For in spite of the Swiss tradition under which every man appears eager to spring to arms, and has his rifle on the wall, the spirit of militarism is singularly absent. Contrariwise, the practice of democracy, about which Einstein early showed what was to be a lifelong enthusiasm, had for centuries been an ingrained feature of the country. Even so, he was lucky with Aarau and with Winteler, with whose family he lived during his stay at the school.

A slightly casual teacher, as ready to discuss work or politics with his pupils as with his fellow teachers, Winteler was friendly and liberal-minded, an ornithologist never happier than when taking his students and his own children for walks in the nearby mountains. Teaching resembled university lectures rather than high school instruction. There was a room for each subject rather than for each class, and in one of them Einstein was introduced to the outer mysteries of physics by a first-class teacher, August Tuchschmid. More than half a century later he remembered the school as a pleasant place. Instruction was good, authority was exercised with a light hand, and it is clear that in this friendly climate Einstein began to open out, even though the details that have survived are scanty and tantalising. On a three-day school outing during which pupils climbed the 8,000-foot Santis above Feldkirch, he slipped on a steep slope and was saved from destruction only by the prompt move of a colleague who stretched out his alpenstock for the boy to grasp, a quick action that helped change the course of history. When, on another school outing, a master asked: "Now Einstein, how do the strata run here? From below upwards or vice versa?" the reply was unexpected: "It is pretty much the same to me whichever way they run, Professor."

The story may well have been embroidered by recollection. But it reflects an attitude that juts out during Einstein's youth from beneath the layers of adulation which increased with the years. The description of "impudent Swabian", given by his fellow-pupil Hans Byland, belongs to this period. "Sure of himself, his grey felt hat pushed back on his thick, black hair, he strode energetically up and down in a rapid, I might almost say crazy, tempo of a restless spirit which carries a whole world in itself," Byland has said. These rougher corners eventually became smoothed off so that he would bite back the comment he might consider natural and others might consider bitter; but the essential attitude remained, an intellectual disinclination to give a damn for anybody. As a rock never very far below the surface it was as likely to capsize Einstein as anyone else.

This prickly arrogance appears increasingly throughout his student years. The gentle philosopher, benignly asking questions of the universe, was always to be one part of the complete Einstein. But there was another part during youth. He knew not only the clanging existence of metropolitan Munich but the delights of northern Italy. He was, judged by the experience of his contemporaries, a young man of the world, well filled with his own opinions, careless of expressing them without reserve, regarding the passing scene with a sometimes slightly contemptuous smile. Had it not been for his deep underlying sense of the mystery of things, a humility that at this age he was apt to conceal, he would have been the model iconoclast.

Einstein enjoyed Aarau. He enjoyed not only the business of learning, an unexpected revelation after the Munich experience, but also the Swiss with their mixture of serious responsibility and easy-going democracy, their refusal to be drawn into the power game already dividing Europe, their devotion to a neutrality which was personal as well as political. The effect remained. Even in his last decades, dazzled by the American future, Einstein still showed a homesickness for Europe that was epitomised by Zurich or Leiden; in the late 1940s, as the liberal image faded in the United States, the feeling was reinforced, and he tended to look back to a golden age that centred on pre-war Switzerland.

Life in Aarau was to have one specific and far-reaching result. For the antagonism to all things German which had been burning away in Einstein for years now came to the surface in what was, for a boy, a remarkable explosion. He refused to continue being German. The usual story is that on arriving in Milan from Munich the youthful Einstein told his father that he no longer wished to be German and at the same time announced that he was severing all formal connection with the Jewish faith. In general it is the second half of the story, which would have caused his religiously happy-go-lucky family little worry, which is given most credence; the first has been considered a later magnification of youthful disenchantment and wishful thinking. In fact, the reverse is true.

As far as the Jewish faith is concerned, the boy had as little to renounce as the grown man. While Einstein the Zionist speaker of adult life had an intense feeling for Jewish culture, a dedication to preservation of the people, and a deep respect for the Jewish intellectual tradition, his feelings for the faith itself rarely went beyond kindly tolerance and the belief that it did no more harm than other revealed religions.

The question of German nationality was different. At first, the idea of a sixteen-year-old renouncing his country appears slightly bizarre, while in the modern world the mechanics of the operation would be complicated. So much so that the story has been taken rather lightly and André Mercier, head of the Department of Theoretical Physics in the University of Berne, and Secretary General of the International Committee on General Relativity, has gone on record as saying that when Einstein arrived in Switzerland "he was by nationality a German and remained so until he became of age". It has also been pointed out that if the young Einstein did "give up his passport at the age of fifteen", as has been claimed by Dr. Walter Jens of the University of Tubingen, then this act would have been of no legal consequence.

In fact, no passport was involved. On birth, Einstein had become a citizen of the state of Württemburg and, as a result, a German national. According to a letter in the Princeton archives he had pleaded with his father, even before the latter had crossed the Alps to Milan, to renounce this nationality on his behalf. Nothing appears to have been done. But the boy returned home from Switzerland to Milan to spend the Christmas of 1895 with his parents. And soon after his return to Aarau early in 1896 Hermann Einstein, presumably yielding at last to his son's renewed badgerings, wrote to the Württemburg authorities. They acknowledged the application, and on January 28th, 1896 formally ended Einstein's German nationality. Two memoranda sent by them to Ulm on January 30th and February 5th confirmed this with various departments in the city. Thus he completed his education in Switzerland and obtained his degree in Zurich as a stateless person, merely "the son of German parents" as he put it on official forms.

The dislike of Germany revealed by this precocious move may

genuinely have sprung from stern discipline and it is quite possible
that Einstein was seriously contemplating this move before his arrival
in Milan. His feelings may well have been increased by the contemptuous way in which he was expelled from the school before
he could resign. Northern Italy in the mid-1890s provided one
contrast with a Germany already flexing its muscles, and the sober
Swiss provided another. Whatever the relative importance of these
different motivations, the net result was an attitude that later developed into an anti-Germanism that had a trace of paranoia, an
emotional fissure which split Einstein's character from end to end
like a geological fault.

During those first weeks of 1896 in Aarau none of these
dark overtones could be discerned. He was now free of Germany.
He would, in due course and with good luck, acquire the Swiss
nationality on which he had set his heart. What is more, he had
by now succeeded in switching academic horses in mid-stream:
despite the family decision that he should become an electrical
engineer, it was now agreed that he should study for a teacher's
degree. The details can only be inferred. But it is significant that
it was his mother's comparatively well-to-do family which was to
underwrite his student days; and it is not difficult to envisage the
fond mother being won over by her son's arguments and then persuading her relatives that they would be investing in the future.
There is little doubt that in his younger days he had a way with
women.

Einstein sat for his examination at the E. T. H. in the summer
of 1896. He passed, returned to his parents in Italy, and in October
left them for Switzerland, now dedicated to a four-year course
which would, if he were successful, qualify him for a post on the
lowest rung of the professional teacher's ladder.

On October 29th, 1896, he settled down in Zurich, first in the
lodgings of Frau Kagi at 4 Unionstrasse. There he was to remain
for two years before moving to Frau Markwalder in 87 Klosbach
and then, after twelve months, returning to Frau Kagi at a new
address. At the end of each term he visited his family in Milan or,
later, Pavia, while in Zurich he was under the watchful but discreet
eye of the Karr Family, moderately well-to-do people distantly
related to Einstein's mother, whose relatives now provided the 100
francs a month on which he lived.

His fellow-students came mainly from the families of minor
professional people or small businessmen, typified by Marcel Grossmann whose father owned a factory making agricultural machinery

at Hongg, a few miles from Zurich. There was Louis Kollross from the watchmaking centre of Chaux-de-Fonds in the Jura, Jakob Ehrat from Schaffhausen with its Rhine falls, and a group of young girls from Hungary of whom one joined the class of '96 with Einstein. This was Mileva Maric, born in 1875 and like the rest of the class a few years older than Einstein, daughter of a Serbian peasant from Titel in southern Hungary, who had laboured her way to Zurich by dogged determination, handicapped by a limp, anxious to succeed.

Superficially, the picture of Einstein's student days was conventional enough. There was the fairly frequent change of "digs"; the frugal diet of restaurants and cafés, supplemented by snacks from the nearby bakery or tit-bits provided by kind Swiss landladies. There was the weekend outing to one or more of the minor summits surrounding the Zurichsee, the Swiss version of the reading parties in the Lakes or North Wales which were a feature of the Victorian scene in Britain. And there were frequent visits back to Aarau where his sister Maja was now spending the first of three years in the Aargau teachers' seminary.

Einstein was casual of dress, unconventional of habit, with the happy-go-lucky absentmindedness of a man concentrating on other things which he was to retain all his life. "When I was a very young man," he once confided to an old friend, "I visited overnight at the home of friends. In the morning I left, forgetting my valise. My host said to my parents: 'That young man will never amount to anything because he can't remember anything'." And he would often forget his key and have to knock up his landlady late at night, calling: "It's Einstein — I've forgotten my key again."

He followed the normal student pursuits, picking up on the Zurichsee a passion for sailing that never deserted him, taking occasional walks among the mountains even though, in the later words of his eldest son, "he did not care for large, impressive mountains, but . . . liked surroundings that were gentle and colourful and gave one lightness of spirit." On the water he would invariably have a small notebook. Fräulein Markwalder, who sometimes accompanied him, remembered years later how when the breeze died and the sails dropped, out would come the notebook, and he would be scribbling away. "But as soon as there was a breath of wind he was immediately ready to start sailing again."

The picture is almost prosaic. Yet a hint of something to come is suggested by the barely concealed arrogant impatience that showed itself even during the musical evenings to which he was often invited by the parents of his Swiss friends. If attention to his performance was not adequate he would stop, sometimes with a remark that verged on boorishness. To a group of elderly ladies who continued knitting while he played, and who then asked why he was closing his score and putting his violin back in its case, he explained: "We would not dream of disturbing your work." And when, politely asked on one occasion: "Do you count the beat?" he quickly replied, "Heavens, no. It's in my blood." Perhaps there was always something a little risky in questioning Einstein. The "not much with people" as he later put it, was true despite his personality, not because of it. Even as a youth, moodily aloof at times from his companions, he had a quality that attracted as certainly as it could rebuff. As a man, he was the kind who made heads turn when he entered the room, and not merely because the founder of relativity had come in. If the word charisma has a modern meaning outside the public relations trade, Einstein had it.

It is noticeable that he appears to have been particularly happy in the company of women. The feelings were often mutual. The well set-up young man with his shock of jet-black wavy hair, his huge luminous eyes and his casual air, was distinctly attractive. More than one young Zurich girl, more than one Swiss matron, was delighted that the young Herr Einstein was such an excellent performer on the violin and was agreeable to accompany them at evening parties. And he was a frequent visitor to the house of Frau Bachtold where several of the women students lodged, sitting in the living-room and attentively listening as Mileva Maric played the piano. At Aarau he had been the confidant of one young woman who played Schubert with him and asked his advice when proposed to by a much older man, and at Zurich he appears to have exercised a similar influence. Years later Antonina Vallentin, a great friend of Einstein's second wife, said significantly that "as a young man and even in middle age, Einstein had regular features, plump cheeks, a round chin — masculine good looks of the type that played havoc at the turn of the century."

Einstein's pleasure in the company of women lasted all his life. But there was little more to it than that. Like most famous men he attracted the hangers-on, the adorers and the semi-charlatans. On at least two occasions women claimed him as the father of their children. In one instance the claimant was insane; the case of the other appears to have been equally groundless. His doctor-friend, Janos Plesch, suggested in a letter after Einstein's death that he may have formed a liaison during the First World War when he had been left by one wife and had not yet acquired another. Other comparably vague suggestions have been handed down from the early Berlin days. While they cannot be ignored, it would be wrong to give them more weight than unsubstantiated observations deserve — suggestions which tended to be kept afloat by Einstein's own personal attitude. According to Vera Weizmann, wife of the Jewish leader Chaim Weizmann, Einstein's second wife did not mind him flirting with her since "intellectual women did not attract him; out of pity he was attracted to women who did physical work." The same comment has been made in strikingly similar terms by more than one of his friends, who have drawn attention to the fact that he preferred to have women rather than men around him. All this is true. Yet the implications remain unsubstantiated. As a young man he tended to keep his women friends at arm's-length since he wished to devote the maximum energy and resource to the one great game; later on, as youth merged first into middle and later into old age, he still tended to like having women around, but in an almost old-maidish way. He had, after all, resigned himself to the necessary priorities; first research, second Einstein. This was an order of duties which at first makes it easy to be sorry for him — the man who had apparently cut himself off from so many of the things that make life worth living. The feeling is misplaced. Einstein himself was, as he acknowledged to his friend Michelangelo Besso, somewhat cold and something of a tough nut. Monks and nuns, spinsters and dedicated military men, manage to live happily and quite a few live usefully; Einstein, answering a call quite as compelling, enjoyed a satisfaction from his work as great as most men enjoy from anything else.

This life-long dedication set him apart in a number of ways. As Bertrand Russell once wrote, "Personal matters never occupied more than odd nooks and crannies in his thoughts." Other men allowed themselves to become implicated in the human predicament, on one level willingly dealing with the trivia of life and on another being swept off course by the normal passions. Einstein avoided such energy-wasting complications at all levels. To this extent his self-imposed task, the determination to keep first things first, forced him into abdicating his human position. He felt an intuitive sympathy with human beings in the mass and many of his letters — notably those to his friends Max and Hedi Born — reveal a deeply compassionate nature. Yet throughout much of his life he could find little time to express this, while his own isolation from the normal run of human feelings did not make its expression any easier or any more frequent. For many of the things that moved most men failed to move Albert Einstein. "He was devoid of the human feelings that can cause trouble and misery," wrote the son of Dr. Bucky, whom Einstein knew for almost a quarter of a century. "In the twenty-three years of our friendship I never saw him show jealousy, vanity, bitterness, anger, resentment, or personal ambition. He seemed to be immune to these emotions." This fact of nature certainly lightened his personal burden; it also created a gulf which he had to leap before he could fully understand the emotions of others.

Einstein's obsession with exploring and understanding the physical world caught him early. He followed it, as André Mercier has noted, as the result of a double experience, "the experience of the exterior world, revealing material facts, numberless and numerical; and the revelation of an interior or spiritual world which showed him the path he should follow". But there was another dichotomy about the early years. A good deal of his genius lay in the imagination which gave him courage to challenge accepted beliefs. This quality has been rightly stressed and his old friend Morris Cohen went so far as to claim that "like so many of the very young men who have revolutionised physics in our day [Einstein] has not been embarrassed by too much learning about the past or by what the Germans call the literature of the subject." Yet the "too much" is relative. Einstein's ability to soar up from the nineteenth century basis of physics, and his own dislike of the routine involved in understanding that basis, has tended to undervalue the four-year slog of routine which he went through at the E. T. H. Yet this routine was demanding enough.

Working to become a teacher in mathematical physics, he had to devote himself to both mathematics and the natural sciences. Under six professors — notably Hermann Minkowski, who was to play such an important part in giving mathematical formality to Special Relativity — he studied mathematical subjects that included the differential and integral calculus, descriptive and analytical geometry, the geometry of numbers and the theory of the definite integral. Two professors, Weber and Pernet, dealt with physics, while Professor Wolfer lectured on astro-physics and astronomy. The theory of scientific thought and Kantian philosophy was studied under Professor Stadler. To these compulsory subjects Einstein added an odd rag-bag of optionals which included not only gnomic projection and exterior ballistics, both of which might have been expected, but also anthropology and the geology of mountains under the famous Albert Heim; banking and Stock Exchange business; Swiss politics; and under a *privatdozent,* Goethe's works and philosophy.

Despite the emphasis on mathematics, Einstein himself was more drawn towards the natural sciences, one reason being that he saw mathematics as being split up into numerous specialities, any of which could take up a whole lifetime. One result of his choice was the difficulty that faced him when, between 1905 and 1915, he struggled to extend the Special Theory of Relativity, and it dawned on him that more mathematics was required.

Thus it was physics to which he turned, working most of the time in the physical laboratory. This was in strange contrast with the period when he would answer a question about his laboratory by pointing to his head and a question about his tools by pointing to his fountain pen. Yet despite this he never ceased to emphasise that the bulk of his work sprang directly and naturally from observed facts; the co-ordinating theory explaining them might arise from an inspired gleam of intuition, but the need for it arose only after observation.

In June 1899 Einstein seriously injured a hand in the Zurich laboratories — typically enough after tearing up a chit of paper telling him how to do an experiment one way and then attempting to do it another. And it is significant that a biography by one of his stepsons-in-law, whose facts were described by Einstein himself as "duly accurate" should contain the following sentences:

> He wanted to construct an apparatus which would accurately measure the earth's movement against the ether... He wanted to proceed quite empirically, to suit his scientific feeling of the time, and believed that an apparatus such as he sought would lead him to the solution of a problem of far-reaching perspectives of which he already sensed. But there was no chance to build this apparatus. The scepticism of his teachers was too great, the spirit of enterprise too small.

Without Einstein's imprimatur this would sound unlikely. With it, the story provides an interesting gloss.

From the first, however, it was theoretical physics which attracted him, and here he was unlucky. Subsequently he was to write of the excellent teachers of these Zurich days. But it is significant that he omitted all reference to Heinrich Weber, who held the physics course. According to Einstein's fellow-student, Louis Kollross, this course was designed primarily for engineers. Certainly it taught nothing of Maxwell, whose theory of electromagnetism was already changing not only men's ideas of the physical world, but the practical applications of physics to that world. Of the two sets of notes made by Einstein at Weber's own lectures, one dealt with heat and dynamics, the other with technical problems and with electricity from Coulomb's law to induction; yet Maxwell's work was not touched upon. This was not as startling as it sounds. For Maxwell's theory was symptomatic of the radically new ideas which were about to transform the face of physics.

Only a few years earlier, as the nineteenth century moved towards its close, the empire of the physical sciences had appeared to be on the edge of the millennium. Just as there seemed no possible limit to the industrial development of the United States, to the political advances in Europe, over much of which the Liberal spirit still reigned, or to the technological progress which could be achieved in the world's workshops so did physical science seem to be moving towards a solution of its final problems. Almost a century earlier Laplace had made his fine boast: "An intelligence knowing, at a given instance of time, all forces acting in nature, as well as the momentary position of all things of which the universe consists, would be able to comprehend the motions of the largest bodies of the world and those of the lightest atoms in one single formula, provided his intellect were sufficiently powerful to subject all data to analysis; to him nothing would be uncertain, both past and future would be present in his eyes."

This prophecy from the Newton of France had been in some ways an extrapolation from the spectacular success of Newton's own celestial mechanics with whose help the motions of moon, comets, asteroids and satellites could be computed with splendid accuracy. The confidence appeared to be justified, not only by the advances made throughout the nineteenth century but by the ease with which these could be seen as intelligible parts of one vast but finite *corpus* of knowledge whose final understanding must be only a few years away. Mechanics, acoustics and optics were all set on firm foundations during this heroic age of classical physics. Faraday's work on electro-magnetism from 1831 onwards produced the dynamo and the first shoots of what was to become the great electrical industry. The first scientific knowledge of electricity led to the electric telegraph. And to crown the fine structure there came Maxwell in the 1860s with the synthesis of his electro-magnetic equations, giving the answer to so many natural phenomena and forecasting the radio waves to be discovered by Heinrich Hertz twenty-five years later. "In their various branches the explanations of new discoveries fitted together, giving confidence in the whole," says Sir William Dampier, "and it came to be believed that the main lines of scientific theory had been laid down once and for all, and that it only remained to carry measurements to the higher degree of accuracy represented by another decimal place, and to frame some reasonably credible theory of the structure of the luminiferous ether."

It was the problem of this luminiferous ether, through which Maxwell's electro-magnetic waves appeared to be transmitted like shakings in an invisible jelly, which had during the last decades of the century begun to sap the foundations of classical science, and to reveal the electro-magnetic theory as the revolutionary theory it was. Yet this was not the only worm in the apple. The imposing structure which had been built on Newtonian mechanics, the solid edifice of knowledge utilised by so many of the sciences to which it had seemed that man was now putting the finishing touches, had in fact been undermined by a score of experimental physicists tunnelling along their own separate routes from a dozen different directions. Their work was continuing and the repercussions from it were beginning to be felt.

In the world of Newtonian physics, an obstinate planet had failed to conform to the calculations, for it had been confirmed that the motion of the perihelion of Mercury's orbit was advancing by a small but regular amount for which the Newtonian hypothesis could provide no explanation. From Vienna there came the heresy of Ernst Mach who was sceptical of the very foundations of Newton's universe, absolute space and absolute time. In the United States Albert Michelson and Edward Morley had performed an experiment which confronted scientists with an appalling choice. Designed to show the existence of the ether, at that time considered essential, it had yielded a null result, leaving science with the alternatives of tossing aside the key which had helped to explain the phenomena of electricity, magnetism and light, or of deciding that the earth was not in fact moving at all. Wien, in Berlin, was investigating discrepancies in the phenomena of heat and radiation which stubbornly refused to be explained by the concepts of classical physics. In Leiden the great Dutch physicist, Hendrik Lorentz, had formed a new theory of matter in which atoms — still regarded as John Dalton's solid billiard balls of matter when their existence was credited at all — contained electrically-charged particles. In the Cavendish Laboratory, Cambridge, J. J. Thomson — about to be joined by a young New Zealand graduate, Ernest Rutherford — was showing that these extraordinary bits of electricity, or electrons, not only had an existence of their own but a mass and an electric charge which could be measured. If this were not enough to strike at the very vitals of accepted ideas, Becquerel in Paris had found that at least one element, the metal uranium, was giving off streams of radiation and matter, an awkward fact which appeared to make nonsense of contemporary ideas. These were only the more important of a disturbing new group of discoveries made possible as much by technological advance as by exceptionally nimble minds, which were about to destroy the comfortable complacency into which physics had worked itself. It is hardly surprising that in this climate, "Maxwell's theory of the electro-magnetic field was ... not a part of the ordinary syllabus of a provincial German university," as Max Born has pointed out. The reluctance of the more conservative men of science to acknowledge this revolutionary concept — marking a change from Newton's idea of forces operating at a distance to that of fields of force as fundamental variables — was no more surprising than any other human weakness for things as they are. For the embrace of Newtonian mechanics had continued for so long, and was still so firm, that those who either saw or suspected the fundamental incompatibility of Maxwell's theory with these long-accepted ideas tended to look the other way and, above all, to avoid discussion of such a potentially disturbing subject. This was physics as presented to Einstein and his fellow-students, and accepted by all except the few contemporaries fortunate enough to fall under the influence of a few questioning minds in Berlin, in Leiden, in Paris or in Cambridge.

Einstein thus comes on to the scene as a student at a moment when physics was about to be revolutionised but when few students were encouraged to be revolutionaries. Without his own basically dissenting spirit he would have got nowhere. With it, the almost inevitable consequence was that he rubbed along with his formal work just as much as he had to and found his real education elsewhere, in his own time. Military parallels are naturally obnoxious to civilian minds, but just as insistence on cavalry between the two World Wars forced creative military minds such as Liddell Hart, de Gaulle and Guderian to think for themselves, so the plodding insistence of Weber and his colleagues drove Einstein into reading and studying for himself. The human comparison is distressing, the professional one unavoidable. Einstein would have developed his original mind whatever happened; but the conformity of Weber, the pervasive air of a science learned for examination rather than for probing into the natural world, speeded up the process.

In his spare time, at home, Einstein studied the works of Kirchhoff, Helmholtz and Hertz. Maxwell was another of the scientific revolutionaries whose works he read in his lodgings, or on the banks of the Zurichsee while his friend Marcel Grossmann attended lectures on his behalf, took notes, and later passed these on so that when examination questions had to be faced Einstein was adequately briefed.

There was also Henri Poincaré, "the last man to take practically all mathematics, both pure and applied, as his province". Poincaré's influence on Einstein has sometimes been exaggerated. However, it has rarely been noted that the first International Congress of Mathematicians was held in Zurich at the end of Einstein's first year as a student there; that Poincaré was due to attend; and that while he was prevented from doing so, there was read at the conference his famous paper containing the prophecy: "Absolute space, absolute time, even Euclidean geometry, are not conditions to be imposed on mechanics; one can express the fact connecting them in terms of non-Euclidean space." There is no evidence that Einstein attended the conference; but it seems unlikely that news of such an expression, so in tune with the freedom of his own way of thinking, should entirely have passed him by.

Whatever the exact weight of Poincaré's influence on Einstein, at Zurich or after, there is no doubt about the significance of Ernst Mach, that disappointed man who ran a close second to Maxwell himself in Einstein's estimation. The philosopher-scientist whose fortunes slowly sank before his death in 1916, and who is now mainly remembered for the eponymous Mach Number of supersonic flight, had been born in 1838 in Turas, Moravia. He was in succession Professor of Mathematics at Graz and Prague, and Professor of Physics at Vienna where he expounded his ideas in books, papers and lectures. He had been strongly influenced by Gustav Fechner, the physicist turned philosopher who had unsuccessfully tried to found the "science of psycho-physics", and the basis of Mach's outlook was simple: that all knowledge is a matter of sensations and that what men delude themselves into calling "laws of nature" are merely summaries of experiences provided by their own — fallible — senses. "Colours, space, tones, etc. These are the only realities. Others do not exist," he had written in his daybook.

Einstein's views on the importance of such purely observational factors in discovering the way in which the world is built changed considerably throughout the years. His formulation of the Special

Theory of Relativity, he was never tired of emphasising "was not speculative in origin; it owes its invention entirely to the desire to make physical theory fit observed facts as well as possible." Yet as the years passed, the value of pure thought, objective and dissociated from exterior circumstance, appeared to increase.

However, the renunciation of almost all that Mach stood for began only in Einstein's mid-life, the final stage in a long philosophical pilgrimage. During the first or second year of his studies in Zurich there was nothing but awed enthusiasm when his attention was drawn to Mach's *Science of Mechanics* by Michelangelo Besso, an Italian engineering student six years older than Einstein who had come to the E. T. H. from Rome. One expression of Mach's independence lay in his analysis of Newtonian mechanics and his conclusion that it contained no principle that was self-evident to the human mind. The nub of this criticism was that Newton had used expressions which were impossible of definition in terms of observable quantities or processes — expressions such as "absolute space" and "absolute time", which to Mach were thus quite meaningless. One result was that in Mach's view the Newtonian laws would have to be rewritten in more comprehensible terms, substituting in the law of inertia, for instance, "relative to the fixed stars" for "relative to absolute space". This critical attitude to the whole Newtonian framework as it had been utilised for more than two centuries helped to prepare Einstein's mind for things to come; for if Mach could claim, with at least a measure of plausibility, that men had been misled about the definition of the material world, then a similarly audacious venture was not beyond Einstein. Realisation that accepted views could be so readily challenged came as a revelation to the student who intuitively felt that the world of degree courses was at the best incomplete and at the worst wrong. If he were really to discover how God had made the world he could take nothing for granted: not even Newton.

This scepticism was a useful scientific qualification, but one side-effect was inevitable: Einstein became, as far as the professorial staff of the E. T. H. was concerned, one of the awkward scholars who might or might not graduate but who in either case was a great deal of trouble. In such a situation it was natural that he should be asked by Professor Pernet, responsible for practical physics, why did he not study medicine, law or philology rather than physics. It was natural that Pernet, faced with the young man's assertion that he felt he had a natural talent for physics, should reply: "You can do what you like: I only wish to warn you in your own interest."

And it was natural that Weber, who disliked the young man addressing him as "Herr Weber" instead of "Herr Professor", should add, after admitting Einstein's cleverness: "But you have one fault: one can't tell you anything."

The situation throughout his four academic years at the E. T. H. from 1896 until 1900 was not improved by his own attitude towards examinations. After passing his finals he was put off scientific work for a whole year. For graduate he did, in August 1900, receiving an overall mark of 4.91 out of 6.00; celebrating with his particular friends, of whom all except Mileva Maric had been successful; and expecting that he would now be offered, as was the custom of the time, a place on the lowest rung of the academic ladder, an appointment in the physics department of the E. T. H. However, the laws of human nature worked as rigorously for Albert Einstein as for others. Kollross was given a post under Hurwitz. Marcel Grossmann went to Fiedler, Ehrat to Rudio. Weber the physicist took on two mechanical engineers but overlooked the physicist Einstein. For the difficult fellow, no opening could be found.

The refusal of the E.T.H. to employ him was a blow not only to his prospects but to his pride and the contrast with his colleagues bit deep. Yet it cannot have been entirely unexpected and it was certainly not unnatural. For the trappings of the grand old man of science have tended to obscure the reality of the self-willed youth from which he developed; the floating aureole of white hair has evolved not from the dedicated student but from the rebel. In the autumn of 1900 Albert Einstein was the graduate who denied rather than defied authority, the perverse young man for whom "you must" was the father of "I won't"; the keen seeker-out of heresies to support; a young man who was written off as virtually unemployable by many self-respecting citizens.

These awkward facts became apparent throughout the next few months. One of the first results of Einstein's failure to gain a post in the E. T. H. was the summary ending of his allowance from the Koch relations in Genoa. Having come of age he would have to stand on his own feet. He crossed the Alps once more to join his parents in Milan, and from here, in September 1900, wrote the first of numerous letters asking for work. It went to Adolf Hurwitz, the Zurich professor under whom he had read differential and integral calculus, and asked whether there was any chance of becoming his assistant. Shortly afterwards, a further letter followed; but the post went elsewhere.

Later that autumn Einstein was back in Zurich, working with

Professor Alfred Wolfer under whom he had studied astrophysics and astronomy and who was now a director of the Swiss Federal Observatory. The work, though temporary, served its purpose, as shown in Einstein's first letter to Hurwitz. In this he revealed that he was applying for Zurich citizenship, but for this he had to have a job.

Citizenship — in effect, Swiss nationality — had been one of Einstein's objectives since the first weeks of 1896. Almost half a century later he remembered how he had been "happy in Switzerland because there men are left to themselves and privacy is respected", and throughout his student days he regularly set aside twenty francs a month towards the cost of obtaining Swiss naturalisation. Now at last he had the necessary cash, the necessary residential qualifications, and the necessary job. He had made his formal application to the Zurich authorities the previous autumn, on October 19th, 1899, enclosing a testimonial of good character and proof of unbroken residence in the city since October 29th, 1896. But the wheels of the Zurich authorities ground as slowly as God's and it was the following summer before the necessary declaration was demanded of his father. It was given on July 4th, Hermann Einstein formally stating that he was "perfectly in agreement with the request of his son, Albert Einstein regarding immigration to Switzerland and [the granting of] civic rights of the city of Zurich."

Einstein made only passing references to the formalities in later years. But the "duly accurate" biography by his stepson-in-law, Anton Reiser, contained details which can only have come from himself. Even though they came thirty years later they have an interest in showing Einstein as seen by Einstein.

> The process had not been simple [Reiser wrote]. The Zurich city fathers definitely mistrusted the unwordly dreamy young scholar of German descent who was so bound [sic] to become a citizen of Switzerland. They could not be too sure that he was not engaged in dangerous practices. They decided to examine the young man in person and to question him rigorously. Was he inclined to drink, had his grandfather been syphilitic, did he himself lead a proper life? Young Einstein had to give information on all these questions. He had hardly expected that the acquisition of Swiss naturalisation papers was so morally involved a matter. Finally, the authorities observed how harmless and how innocent of the world the young man was. They laughed at him, teased him about his ignorance of the world, and finally honoured him by recognising his right to Swiss citizenship.

The tests do not seem exacting, even for 1900, but they lodged in his memory firmly enough.

On February 21st, 1901 he was granted the three-fold citizen rights of the Swiss — of the city, of the canton and of the Swiss confederation. As such he became due for his three-month military service like all other young Swiss men. Thirty years later he was to be among those who signed a protest against this system but in 1901 he felt differently, dutifully presenting himself to the authorities who rejected him for military service because of flat feet and varicose veins. According to contemporaries he was shocked and distressed. He certainly kept his *Dienstbüchlein*, or Service book, for many years, at least until the 1930s.

The formality over, Einstein was now a fully fledged Swiss, a status he was to retain all his life and of which he was always proud. There is little doubt that his chances of permanent employment were now greater than they had been as a German Jew. Yet his move had been far from merely utilitarian. He felt a basic attachment to Switzerland and the Swiss which continued throughout the years and grew with self-imposed exile in the United States into reminiscent affection. The reasons for it are revealing.

The people were humane and there was also their pacific political record. As Einstein's old friend Morris Cohen has stressed, "Like other opponents of military imperialism, Einstein [was] inclined to look upon the smaller European nations as on the right path" — while tending to ignore the fact that "their present attitude is in part at least due to the fact that the path of military aggrandisement is no longer open to them." Quite apart from this record, which on the political plane gave Switzerland an honourable place among nations, the country had physical and psychological characteristics which helped to make it a national example of all that Einstein felt the world might be if only men behaved sanely. Thus within its frontiers were French and Italian-speaking peoples as well as German-speaking, and within these boundaries the rough corners of national attitudes tended to be smoothed off by mutual contact. The Swiss therefore tended to be tolerant of national idiosyncracies and of personal ones as well. In the early years of the century, moreover, before the country had become the home of international agencies, before the reputation of Swiss bank accounts and of Swiss bankers gave it an aura of power, Switzerland existed in a European backwater that was particularly satisfying to Einstein, a man anxious only to be left to his work. Here, safe in the Swiss cocoon, he could carry on with minimum interruption. This was the prospect although it was not to be enjoyed immediately. His expectations of quickly getting a permanent job were still not justified and in March he was back with his parents in Milan.

However, his hopes were rising. In 1901, as much as today, publication produced the rungs of the ladder up which scientists climbed to fame and in December of the previous year Einstein set up the first rung. This was *"Folgerungen aus der Kapillaritatser- scheinungen"* ("Deductions from the Phenomena of Capillarity") which appeared on December 13th, 1900 in the *Annalen der Physik*. Shortly after the issue appeared he sent a copy to Wilhelm Ostwald, the German physical chemist who was carrying out his pioneer work on the principles of catalysis. The paper had been inspired by Ost- wald's own work, and Einstein enquired whether there was a job in Ostwald's laboratory. He appears to have received no reply, either to this first letter, or to a second which was, unknown to Einstein himself, supported by an appeal from his father. Certainly he got no job.

Before sending the second letter he also wrote to Kamerlingh Onnes, the Dutch physicist, who in Leiden was already probing down towards the depths of ultimate cold. He had heard through a student friend, he wrote on a simple reply-paid card, that there was a vacancy for a University assistant. He outlined his quali- fications and added that he was putting in the same post a copy of his treatise published in the *Annalen der Physik*. This card, now in the Leiden Museum for the History of Science, was the first link between Einstein and the Dutch university city, dreaming away among its canals and its great past, most of its honest burghers unaware that Kamerlingh Onnes was founding under their patronage the science of cryogenics and that Lorentz was dramatically intro- ducing atomic ideas into Maxwell's electro-magnetic theory. Two decades later Einstein was to become an honoured visiting professor to the University. In its great hall he was to give some of his first lectures on the General Theory of Relativity. But his first contact with Leiden was of a different kind. Kamerlingh Onnes did not even answer, and the reply-paid second half of the card, self- addressed to "A. Einstein, Via Bigli 21, Milano", remains blank in the Museum's archives.

But rescue was at hand, and on May 3rd he wrote from Milan to Professor Alfred Stern of Zurich, who had taught him history in the E. T. H., telling him that from mid-May to mid-July he would be teaching mathematics in a technical school at Winterthur, while the regular professor did national service.

A few days later he was off, crossing the Alps and walking on down through the valleys of the Grisons to Coire and eastern Switzerland.

Einstein's stand-in for Professor Gasser at the Winterthur Technical School was uneventful. But no cause was found for keeping his services after Gasser's return and once again he found himself back in Zurich, looking for work.

He was now saved by a combination of persistence and personal wire-pulling. In a Zurich newspaper he read that a teacher was required in a boarding school run by a Dr. Jakob Nuesch of Schaffhausen, the little town on the Swiss frontier, famous alike for its Rhine falls and its position astride the narrow neck of land joining the main body of Switzerland to its "island" on the right bank of the Rhine. In Schaffhausen there lived Conrad Habicht, a former fellow-student from the E. T. H. and a young man able to drop the right word in the right place. With Habicht's help, Einstein was given the post which turned out to be, for the most part, coaching a young English boy, Louis Cohen. He held it for only a few months.

Just what happened is difficult to discover but easy to imagine. Einstein's detestation of the rigid discipline and the methods of the Gymnasium had in a way been compounded by his experiences in Zurich where he considered the routine teachings of the professors an unmitigated evil and the helpful notes of Marcel Grossmann a satisfactory method of evading them. Schaffhausen was not Munich and the methods of Switzerland were not those of the Fatherland. But Einstein's ideas of minimum routine and minimum discipline were very different from those of his employer, Jakob Nuesch. By the end of the year he was back once more in his old Zurich "digs", out of work again.

By this time, however, there were two gleams of light on the horizon. Before he left Schaffhausen he had completed a thesis on the kinetic theory of gases for his Ph. D. and sent it to the University of Zurich. He had also made formal application for the post in the Swiss Patent Office which was to be his first regular job.

The Office had been founded only in 1888 and still went its official if individual way under the control of its original Director, Herr Friedrich Haller. A large, friendly, rough diamond, Haller was an engineer who had won his professional spurs during the seventies and eighties when the Swiss were establishing their reputation for driving railways through mountains, across mountains and, if really necessary, up the near-vertical sides of mountains.

Success was the yardstick and if success were attained by a leavening of by-guess-and-by-God to formal scientific work, Haller saw little harm in that. He ran the Patent Office on his own unconventional lines, "with a whip in one hand and a bun in the other" according to a much later Patent Office official, and it was largely his own idiosyncratic rule which appears eventually to have brought Einstein to the Swiss capital as a minor civil servant.

Among Haller's personal friends was Herr Grossmann, father of Marcel Grossmann of the E. T. H. The Grossmanns' intervention on Einstein's behalf is certain, although the details are not clear; yet it seems likely that a casual talk between the two older men brought a generous promise that when a vacancy arose Marcel's friend would be favourably considered. Einstein learned of such an opening in December 1901 and a few months after applying was among those selected for interview.

Shortly afterwards, he travelled from Milan to Berne for the all-important personal meeting with Haller. The Director has left no account of what must have been, for Einstein, a troublesome event. The only evidence that remains consists of a brief paragraph in Reiser. "Albert was examined for two full hours" this says. "The Director placed before him literature on new patents about which he was required to form an immediate opinion. The examination unfortunately disclosed his obvious lack of technical training." However, this minor detail was no embarrassment to a man such as Haller, intent on helping an old friend. On June 16th Einstein was formally appointed, together with a J. Heinrich Schenk, as Technical Expert, at a salary of 3,500 francs a year. But Haller's goodwill could stretch only so far. The post for which Einstein had applied was Technical Expert (Second Class). He was made Technical Expert (Third Class).

Two legends have grown up around the appointment. One is that Einstein was employed because a knowledge of Maxwell's equations was considered essential and he was the only applicant who had it. The second is that the authorities in Zurich had already noted Einstein as a genius and passed on the good news to Haller, who had then seized the chance of bringing on to his staff a young man whose fame and fortune would all come in good time.

The first of these legends is easily disposed of. The vacancy officially advertised in the Swiss *Gazette* listed the qualifications for the Patent Office Post merely as follows: *Gründliche Hochschulbildung in mechanischtechnischer oder speciell physikalischer Richtung, Beherrschung der deutschen und Kenntnis der französischen*

*Sprache oder Beherrschung der Französischen und Kenntnis der deutschen Sprache, eventuell auch Kenntnis der italienischen Sprache.* ("Thorough academic education in technical mechanics, or special leaning towards physics, a mastery of German and knowledge of French, or mastery of French and knowledge of German and possibly knowledge of Italian.") The *"speciell physikalischer Richtung"* is the nearest that the requirement comes to a knowledge of Maxwell's laws and it is unlikely that Haller would — as is sometimes suggested — have pulled them into his interviews of candidates to eliminate everyone but Einstein.

It is easy to see the way in which the second legend, of long-standing in the Patent Office, quietly grew throughout the years. For in retrospect it must have been maddening for the authorities to reflect that they had taken an ordinary, if not an ugly, duckling under their wing without realising that he would develop into the most amazing swan of the scientific world. What more natural than that a legend of prescience, of inner awareness of the young man's potential genius, should steadily grow? The picture of Haller, nodding sagely in his retirement whenever the name of Einstein arose, is a picture which one hardly likes to shatter. Yet there appears not the slightest evidence for it. Neither Zurich nor any other Swiss university would have passed Einstein over, and on to others, had they seen in him anything more than an awkward, slightly lazy and certainly intractable young man who thought he knew more than his elders and betters. He had in fact been set on his path to the future by an act of no more intellectual judgment than a good turn for an old friend.

But it was to be a future very different from what must have been anticipated. The Grossmanns, father and son, no doubt felt that they had shovelled a good companion into a safe job for life. Einstein saw it mainly as a useful base from which he could begin his self-imposed task of exploring the nature of the physical world.

A week after being formally appointed, he took up his post in the Patent Office.

# 3

# *SWISS CIVIL SERVANT*

THE CITY TO WHICH EINSTEIN MOVED IN THE SUMMER OF 1902 WAS
very different in character from Zurich. Standing on its high sandstone ridge, three parts encircled by the swift waters of the Aare,
looking towards the fine prospect of the Oberland, Berne was less
tied to technology and industry, more tuned to the arts, than the
city to the east. Embassies and legations occupied many of the fine
houses to the south of the river across the Kirchenfeld Bridge.
Summer tourists came to gaze at the famous clocktower with its
midday procession of model bears which was the pride not only of
the city but of all Switzerland. The British had already begun to
make the huge main hotel, standing cheek by jowl with the Swiss
Parliament house, a base from which they moved into the mountains for the fashionable sport of skiing which they had introduced.
In Berne the wrappings of the Swiss cocoon, which tended to shelter
the country from the brute buffets of a Europe already being
polarised towards Paris or Berlin, were slightly less protective. Here
Einstein was to spend the first creative years of his life, transforming
the face of physics from the small back room of an apartment
behind the arcades of Kramgasse into which there vibrated the
chimes of the city clock-tower.

His work as a technical officer in the Swiss Patent Office,
then housed in the upper stories of the Federal Telegraph offices in
Speichergasse, began on June 23rd, 1902. The details of his seven-
year career there are simple enough. The initial appointment was
provisional and it was agreed that when this was confirmed his
salary should be "regularised to suit that of his work at the time".
Confirmation did not come until September 5th, 1904 when Haller
wrote to the Federal Council, noting that Einstein had "proved
himself very useful" and proposing that his salary should be raised
from 3,500 to 3,900 francs. He should, however, remain Class III

rather than be promoted to Class II since "he is not yet fully accustomed to matters of mechanical engineering (he is actually a physicist)."

Upgrading to a higher class followed in 1906 when his salary was increased by another 600 francs. Since the autumn of 1904, Haller then wrote, Einstein had "continued to familiarise himself with the work, so that he now handles very difficult patent applications with the greatest success and is one of the most valued experts in the Office." The Director went on to note that his young technical officer had "acquired the title of Dr. Phil. from the University of Zurich this winter, and the loss of this man, who is still young, would be much regretted by the administration of the Office."

Three points are of interest. The first is that Einstein had won his academic spurs in 1905. They had come after his presentation to the University of Zurich of a twenty-one-page paper on "A New Definition of Molecular Dimensions", dedicated to his friend Marcel Grossmann. Judging by the records, it was touch and go whether he got his doctorate. Professor Alfred Kleiner, Director of the Zurich Physics Institute, recommended acceptance of the dissertation. But "as the principal achievement of Einstein's work consists of the treatment of differential equations, it is thus of a mathematical nature and belongs to analytical mechanics..." and Kleiner recommended two more opinions. That of Professor Burckhardt appears to have been decisive; despite "crudeness in style and slips of the pen in the formulae which can, and must, be overlooked," he noted that Einstein's paper showed "thorough mastery of mathematical methods".

Director Haller's remark about his young technical officer not only notes his academic advance but also implies that Einstein was by this time already searching around for another post and had not concealed the fact from his employers. Circumstantial evidence — casual references to teaching posts in Einstein's correspondence of this period — confirms that this was so. Thirdly it is significant that the Director of the Patent Office, writing about his employee's progress in the spring of 1906, did not even comment on the three papers that the young man had by this time contributed to a single issue of the *Annalen der Physik* — one important enough to take him into the history books, one which helped to bring him the Nobel Prize sixteen years later, and a third containing the outline of the Special Theory of Relativity.

Einstein's first home in Berne was one small room in Gerechtigkeitsgasse and from this he walked every morning the few hundred yards to the building in whose third-floor office he learned his routine duties. One of his early visitors was the Max Talmey who had introduced him to science a decade earlier and who had recently called on his parents in Milan. They were "rather reticent" about their son, noted Talmey, and in Berne the reason became obvious. "I found my friend there and spent a day with him," he wrote. "His environment betrayed a good deal of poverty. He lived in a small, poorly furnished room. I learned that he had a hard life struggle with the scant salary of an official at the Patent Office. His hardships were aggravated through obstacles laid in his way by people who were jealous of him." The "obstacles" should not be taken too seriously. Einstein, the potential schoolmaster, with one paper already to his credit in the *Annalen der Physik*, increasingly sure of himself, was an intellectual cut above his colleagues. He still had the confident brashness that seeps out from some of his early letters and it is inconceivable that he should not have been put in his place from time to time by more pedestrian companions.

The work of the Patent Office at the turn of the century was strikingly different from what it later became. The difference is illustrated by one fact: until 1907 patents were granted only for inventions which could be represented by a model. The model, it is difficult not to feel, may have been as important as the specification which described, in words which ideally should allow of no dispute, the duties which the device was intended to perform. These inventions, ideas and proposals which were directed to the Office consisted largely of suggestions for practical, utilitarian, basically simple and often homely applications of technology to the mundane affairs of everyday life. At first glance, all this appears to be singularly unrelated to Einstein's special genius. Yet despite the apparently esoteric quality of the theories on which his fame was founded, these theories sprang, as he was never tired of stressing, from observation of facts and from deductions which would account for these facts. This demanded an intuitive discernment of essentials, and it was just this which was sharpened during his days at the Patent Office. For the work frequently involved rewriting inventors' vague applications to give them legal protection; this in turn required an ability to see, among sometimes tortuous descriptions, the basic idea or ideas on which an application rested. The demand was not so much for the routine application of a routine mind to routine documents, as for perceptive intuition. "It is no exaggeration", says a member of the Patent Office staff, "to say that Einstein's activity was, at least in the first few months, literally an apprenticeship in the critical reading of technical specifications and in understanding the drawings that went with them."

Observation and analysis were therefore brought to a sharper edge, as from the summer of 1902 onwards Einstein sat in the long narrow room of the government office with his fellow technical officers sorting, reading, and putting into intelligible German the specifications for typewriters and cameras, engineering devices and the hundred and one curious appliances for which inventors wished to claim legal protection. He himself was in no doubt of what he learned at the Patent Office. "More severe than my father," was how he described the Director to his colleague Joseph Sauter. "He taught me to express myself correctly."

But there was more to it than that. It was the opportunity to think about physics that mattered. For while the Patent Office work helped to tickle into first-class condition Einstein's ability to discern the essentials of a scientific statement, it acted also as an undemanding occupation which released his mind for creative work at a different level. The process is not uncommon, and there had been an example in the very city in which he worked — that of Albrecht Haller, the scientist who as Secretary of the Berne City Council had in the 1700s kept the council minutes. Reprimanded one day by the Council Chairman for writing a scientific treatise as a meeting proceeded, Haller was able to read out the detailed minutes that he had, simultaneously, been correctly keeping. Many men of genius need an occupation which keeps the wolf from the door while their intellectual work thus continues undisturbed. Trollope working in the Post Office while concentrating on the Barchester novels; Maurice Baring helping Trenchard plan the bombing offensive of 1918 while continuing his work as man of letters, Churchill politicking away through the inter-war years while producing *Marlborough* — these are examples of great men immersing part of themselves in a routine that helped to release their creative genius. In Berne, Einstein was another, unobtrusively trotting from Gerechtigkeitsgasse to the Patent Office each morning, usually lunching at his desk, returning to his lodgings each evening with the orthodoxy of the city clerk, then setting himself down in a quiet corner to discover the laws of nature.

His first original papers had no connection with the theory of relativity which was to make him world famous. They concerned, instead, the nature of the forces which hold together the molecules of a liquid. A number of eminent scientists — notably Mach and Ostwald — did not believe in the physical existence of atoms as such; for them it was almost as if Dalton had lived in vain. It was typical that Einstein, still in his early twenties, should set about educating them.

The first five papers in which he started to do this were published between 1901 and 1904. They were followed by a sixth
which come in his *annus mirabilis* of 1905 and which applied several
of his earlier results in a dramatically conclusive way.* The first two
papers dealt with capillarity and potential differences. Neither was
particularly successful, but the attraction of their subject for Einstein,
dealing as it did with the links between intermolecular and other
forces, was made clear in a letter he wrote to Marcel Grossmann in
April 1901. Even at this early stage, when dealing with a subject
far removed from his shattering new concept of space and time
to be embodied in relativity, Einstein revealed two aspects of his
approach to science which became the keys to his work: the search
for a unity behind disparate phenomena, and the acceptance of a
reality distinct from what could be seen.

The subject-matter of this early work was the immense numbers
of particles which made up the liquids or the gases being considered.
It is not possible to deal with the movements of individual particles
and therefore statistical methods, which could handle the averaged-
out movements of vast numbers, had to be used. If man had time
enough, and equipment sensitive enough, it would be possible to
calculate the movement of each molecule and each atom, since these
movements were the result of cause and effect. But statistics, as in
life insurance, provided a handy short cut. As yet they provided no
more.

His methods in the first two papers were those of thermodynamics. When he had completed them, he turned to the statistical
foundations of the subject, attempting in three more papers to derive
the laws describing equilibrium and irreversibility from the general
equations of mechanics and the theory of probability. He believed
his methods to be new, although they had, unknown to him, already
been used by the American, Josiah Willard Gibbs;† however it can
be claimed that this work was in some ways more profound than
that of Gibbs.

Between the first of these early papers, written in Zurich, and
the last of them, written in Berne, Einstein's circumstances changed.
He became the centre of a small coterie of young students who were

---

* The part played by thermodynamics in Einstein's search for a unified basis
for physics is analysed by Martin J. Klein in "Thermodynamics in Einstein's Thought", *Science,* Vol. 157 (August 4, 1967) pp. 509-16.

† Gibbs's main papers were written between 1876 and 1878 and published
in the *Transactions of the Connecticut Academy of Sciences.* Only in 1892
were they translated into German.

to remain his friends for life; and, soon after this was formed, he married the friend of his Zurich days, Mileva Maric.

The group came into being shortly after Einstein moved to Berne. He had arrived a few weeks before taking up his Patent Office appointment and he was doubtful whether his funds would last until the first pay-day. What he really loved and really understood was physics. Berne was a university city and it was thus the most natural thing in the world that he should set up shop as a private tutor, offering to teach physics at so much an hour.

His first pupil was Maurice Solovine, a young Rumanian studying at Berne University a rag-bag of subjects that included literature, philosophy, Greek, mathematics and geology. "Walking in the streets of Berne one day during the Easter holidays of 1902, and having bought a newspaper, I noticed an advertisement saying that Albert Einstein, former pupil of the École Polytechnique of Zurich, gave lessons in physics at three francs an hour," he has written. Solovine sought out the house, climbed the stairs to the first storey, and rang the bell.

The second visit was followed by a third, and on Solovine's suggestion it was agreed that they should read some of the standard works and discuss the problems they presented. Einstein proposed starting with Karl Pearson's *The Grammar of Science* and this was soon followed by Mill, Hume, Spinoza, Mach, Henri Poincaré and the Riemann whose non-Euclidean geometry was utilised in Einstein's development of the General Theory of Relativity a decade later.

The two men were soon joined by Conrad Habicht, Einstein's former friend from Zurich who had now arrived in Berne to continue his mathematical studies. The faint line between teacher and taught, between the twenty-three-year-old Einstein and his companions of twenty, soon disappeared and the lessons dissolved into discussions that were continued week by week and month by month.

At times they would top off their argument with a long walk. Sometimes a Sunday would be enlivened by an eighteen-mile tramp to the Lake of Thun, by whose side they would camp for the day before returning to Berne on the evening train.

Einstein himself was the natural leader, and not only by virtue of the elder-statesman advantage which a year or two's seniority gave him. Even in his early twenties the force of character which was so to impress observers later on, made itself felt. Something of this shows through even in the factual description given by Lucien Chavan, a young electrical engineer in the Federal Post and Telegraph Administration who was an occasional member of what became the self-styled "Olympia Academy". "Einstein is 1.76 metres tall," he wrote beneath a picture of Einstein which was given to the Swiss postal Library after Chavan's death, "broadshouldered, with a slight stoop. His short skull seems remarkably broad. His complexion is swarthy. He has a narrow moustache above a large sensitive mouth, an acquiline nose. His brown eyes have a deep benign lustre. He has a fine voice, like the vibrant tones of a cello. Einstein speaks a good French with a slight foreign accent."

Discussion was the magnet which held the group together and when it was in full swing little else mattered. Solovine has recorded how shortly before Einstein's birthday he saw caviare displayed in a shop window in the city. Knowing it from his earlier days in Rumania, he decided with Habicht to buy some as an expensive birthday treat. When it was put on the table Einstein was talking about the problems of Galilean inertia. He went on talking, eating the caviare without comment.

What mattered was the talk. It went on intermittently until 1905 when Solovine left the country for the University of Lyons, and Habicht moved to another part of Switzerland.

The impact of mind on mind, the cut and thrust of argument, did much to sharpen the intellectual rapier with which Einstein was preparing to attack the body of classical physics. Even so, the Olympia Academy should be viewed in perspective. It was not a group of young men living in the academic stratosphere. The faces which look out from the contemporary photograph above wing collars and bow ties have a smile in the eyes, and if the attitude of Einstein implies a deep earnestness, he suggests also an air of half-amused human tolerance which not even seventy years was to remove. During the Academy's night-long discussions of physics and philosophy, their walks through the solitary Berne streets or on the hills, Einstein certainly clarified his own thoughts and began to see more plainly the special problems to which he must devote himself. But if this was a debating society of a particularly high order it was also something more normal: a group of high-spirited young men, active and contentious, lively-legged as well as lively-minded and as anxious as most others to pursue their discussions in the Café Bollwerk, a few steps from the Patent Office, as they were to pursue them in the quiet of their own rooms. It is history which has isolated the group; to most of the inhabitants of Berne — as well as to its members — the Olympia Academy might have been duplicated in a hundred towns and cities across Europe.

This carefree, almost undergraduate existence, was drastically changed when in January 1903 Einstein married Mileva Maric. The daughter of a Slav peasant, four years his senior, Mileva was to remain his wife until, early in 1919, a divorce was agreed on when the prospects of a Nobel Prize, whose 30,000 kroner he promised to pass on to her if he won it, seemed likely to secure her own future and that of their two sons. She had left him in the summer of 1914; but she was wife and companion during the decade which brought him from the anonymity of the Patent Office to a secure position in international science and to the threshold of world-wide fame. Thus the part that Mileva played in helping him up the ladder of success, or in holding him back, is important in Einstein's own story; it has remained untold partly because of his reluctance to reveal details of his personal affairs — "after 300 years a man's private life should still remain private," he once said of Newton; partly because Mileva lived on, despite crippling illness, until 1948; partly because legal problems have prevented publication of a long series of letters between the couple. Yet the story, also told in many dozens of letters which Einstein wrote to his colleague and confidant Michelangelo Besso, is a story of incompatibility rather than conflict; of a couple who respected one another as long as they did not have to live together. And it is a story which makes all the more remarkable the intellectual accomplishment of a man who, as he wrote on one occasion, would have become mentally and physically exhausted if he had not been able to keep his wife at a distance.

This confidence to Besso was made in 1916, when relations between Einstein and Mileva were at their worst, but it illustrates the role of friend and father-confessor which the Italian engineer was to play in Einstein's life. Besso, six years older, had come from Rome to study in the E. T. H. engineering department, but his real link with Einstein was stronger; while Maja Einstein, who had studied at Aarau, was to marry Paul Winteler, the son of the town's schoolmaster, Besso married Paul's sister Anna. In 1904, a year after he married Mileva, Einstein helped Besso into a position as examiner at the Berne Patent Office. The two men walked the same way home. Their confidences were professional — with the result that Besso was to become the only man thanked for help in the famous relativity paper — but they were also personal, and after Einstein moved to Zurich in 1909 his letters to Besso reveal the deteriorating stages of his marriage.

According to some accounts the couple had become engaged while still students, an event frowned upon by Hermann Einstein who had apparently never met Mileva when he died in Italy in 1902. Certainly

Einstein crossed the Alps to be present at his father's deathbed and certainly he married Mileva a few months after his return to Berne. The photographs which survive show her as a not unattractive woman of pleasant features, broadish nose above a good sensual mouth, and with an aura of thick dark hair. She had a limp, but this was not serious; and judging by the generally unkind descriptions of her, her deficiencies, such as they were, lay elsewhere. "A modest, unassuming creature" was the best that Fraulein Markwalder, daughter of Einstein's landlady, could muster. Carl Seelig, who like Mileva lived in Zurich for the greater part of his life, comments that "her dreamy, ponderous nature often curdled her life and her studies. Her contemporaries found Mileva a gloomy, laconic and distrustful character. Whoever got to know her better began to appreciate her Slav openmindedness and the simple modesty with which she often followed the liveliest debates from the background." He notes in addition that she was "hardly the typical Swiss-German house-sprite, the height of whose ambition is a constant war against dust, moths and dirt". There is more than a touch of race-bias in some of this, and it is fair to assume that to many Teutons Mileva had the unpardonable Slav tendency of letting things slip. There was one compensation. Einstein, hearing a friend comment, "I should never have the courage to marry a woman unless she were absolutely sound," replied, "But she has such a lovely voice."

Einstein himself has given various accounts of why he did in fact marry her. One old friend to whom he confided his own account, says, "How it came about he doesn't seem to know himself," and to another he said that he married despite his parents' determined opposition but out of a feeling of duty. In old age he also tried to rationalise his action claiming that what he called this tragedy in his life probably explained his immersion in serious work. However, whether the emotional crises of an unhappy marriage are likely to affect the work of the theoretical physicist in the same beneficent way that they can affect the artist is a moot point; certainly Einstein, writing not years later but as the rift with Mileva developed, gives little sign of it.

In many ways Einstein would have been happier in 1903 with a dedicated housekeeper; instead, he tumbled into marriage, almost by accident, possibly while thinking of more important things. But even in those days, before pacifism, before Zionism, before the anti-bomb movement, he was a decent man beneath the determination of his scientific exterior. Just as, even then, he felt a responsibility towards the human race, so did he feel a responsibility towards those with whom circumstance had joined him. He hardly had time or inclination to be a family man, but he did his best.

Relations worsened as the years passed, particularly after 1905 when the Special Theory of Relativity began to make him famous. His acquaintances, the men and women against whom he was brushed by the chances of everyday life, were only too ready to admit that relativity was beyond them; his second wife was to say so with an air of relief. With Mileva the situation was different, for was she not a physicist like her husband? Had she not, in fact, got just enough "little learning" to enter the new world he had created, if only he would spare time to explain things? The answer was "no", but she would never believe it.

Another factor was quite as important. When Einstein married, he expected to win more time for work; he expected to shuffle off the domestic detail which hangs round bachelor necks. The physicist who in later life was to discard socks as unnecessary complications and who insisted that washing and shaving with the same soap made life that much simpler, had one basic desire, even in the early 1900s: to transfer to other shoulders the tiresome tasks which diverted time from more important things. Many men have married for worse reasons; and many have found that, failing the grand passion, such mundane considerations have enabled a couple to rub along happily enough.

It is true Einstein could always isolate himself from surrounding trivia with an enviable ease. In a mob, at a concert, listening to speeches, he could follow the exterior pattern of events while an essential part of his mind worked away at the problem of the moment. But it would, even so, be useful if marriage removed the clutter of workaday duties and diversions. That it failed to do so, that it merely exchanged the preoccupations of bachelordom for those of a family man, is clear from the pictures of his early family life that have survived.

"He was sitting in his study in front of a heap of papers covered with mathematical formulae," says one student who visited him a few years after his marriage. "Writing with his right hand and holding his younger son in his left, he kept replying to questions from his elder son Albert who was playing with his bricks. With the words, 'Wait a minute, I've nearly finished,' he gave me the children to look after for a few moments and went on working." A similar picture is painted by David Reichinstein, one of the Zurich professors. "The door of the flat was open to allow the floor which had just been scrubbed, as well as the washing hung up in the hall, to dry," he says. "I entered Einstein's room. He was calmly philosophic, with one hand rocking the bassinet in which there was a child. In his mouth Einstein had a bad, a very bad, cigar, and in the other hand an open book. The stove was smoking horribly. How in the world could he bear it?"

The home life of a poorly paid academic in Switzerland in the first decade of the century must be kept in perspective. All the same, a colleague felt it necessary to ask: "How could he bear it?" The answer is that he had to.

Einstein married Mileva Maric in Berne on Tuesday, January 6th, 1903. The two witnesses at the quiet wedding were the original members of the Olympia Academy, Maurice Solovine and Conrad Habicht. There was no honeymoon, and after a celebratory meal in a local restaurant the couple returned to their new home, a small flat in 49 Kramgasse only a hundred yards from Berne's famous clock-tower. Here there was a minor incident. Many stories were to arise, or to be invented, of the absentminded professor; but here, on his wedding day, Einstein did find on arriving back home that he had forgotten the key to his flat.

Superficially, he now slipped down into one of the innumer-able ruts occupied by minor members of the Swiss civil service. His rise in salary eighteen months after marriage did little more than compensate for the additional expenses of a son, Hans Albert, who was born towards the end of 1903. The distant goal of First-Grade Technical Assistant must have seemed at first glance to be the ulti-mate end of all human hope and ambition for the aloof young man who walked to work every day from his apartment, its entrance protected by stone arcades supported on stout stone pillars. On one of them, there rests today a plaque: *In Diesem Haus*, it records, *schuf Albert Einstein in den Jahren 1903—5 seine Grundlegendeab-handlung über die Relativitätstheorie* ("In this house between 1903 and 1905 Albert Einstein created his basic paper on the theory of relativity").

In March, 1905, Einstein was twenty-six. Only his papers on intermolecular forces distinguished him from hundreds of other young men serving their time in Government offices, and they did not distinguish him all that much. When, early in 1905, he rounded off the series in an inaugural dissertation for Zurich University, he had a total of six papers to show for the five years that had passed since his graduation.

Up to now, Einstein had no academic status. He had the run of the Patent Office Library, strong on engineering but weak on physics, and he read the leading physics journals published in German. But he had access to little else. Neither did he work, nor could he talk and debate even on social occasions, inside a university environment with its incessant point counter-point of argument, its constant cross-fertilisation of ideas and its stimulating climate of enquiry. The Olympia Academy, lively as it was, was no substitute for this. He corresponded with his former student friends in Zurich and he occasionally visited them. But that was all. Thus from 1902 until 1905 Einstein worked on his own, an outsider of outsiders, scientifically provincial and having few links with the main body of contemporary physics. This isolation accounts for his broad view of specific scientific problems — he ignored the detailed arguments of others because he was unaware of them. It also shows a courage beyond the call of scientific duty, submission to the inner compulsion which was to drive him on throughout life and for which he was willing to sacrifice everything.

Any one of the main papers which he published in 1905 would alone have assured him a place in the textbooks. Three were published in the single famous Volume 17 of *Annalen der Physik* — today a bibliographical rarity which changes hands at more than £ 1,000 — and the fourth was published in Volume 18. All were comparatively short, and all contained the foundations for new theories even though they did not elaborate on them — "blazing rockets which in the dark of the night suddenly cast a brief but powerful illumination over an immense unknown region" as they have been described by Louis de Broglie.

In one way it was the wide variety of ground illuminated which made this achievement of 1905 so remarkable. It was as if a young explorer had in one dazzling year of travel shown himself to be master navigator, a good man in tropical jungle, and at the same time a first-rate mountaineer. Yet in science there had been one burst of genius strikingly similar to Einstein's. Almost two and a half centuries earlier Newton had been driven by the plague at Cambridge to the quiet of Woolsthorpe and had there produced the calculus, an explanation of the spectral nature of white light, and the law of gravitation.

In the spring of 1905, Einstein gave a résumé of things to come in a letter to his friend Conrad Habicht. He would soon, he said, be able to let him see four different papers, the first of which was very revolutionary and dealt with radiation and the energy of light. The next discussed different ways of discovering the real dimensions of atoms. The third dealt with the Brownian movement, discovered earlier in the century by a Scottish biologist, while the fourth was based on concepts of the electrodynamics of moving bodies and modified current ideas of time and space.

The promised papers were a peculiar mixture — as though a competently executed water-colour from the local art society had been thrown in with three Rembrandts. For the "second work" was merely Einstein's inaugural dissertation for Zurich University which he was having printed in Berne, interesting enough in its own way, but a minnow among the whales of the other three papers. Of these, that dealing with Brownian motion sprang most obviously from earlier work. For his doctoral dissertation had discussed various methods of statistical thermodynamics and it was these tools that he used to predict not only that in certain circumstances the results of molecular movement could actually be seen under the microscope, but also the mass and the numbers of molecules in any particular volume.

This motion had been reported some seventy years earlier by Robert Brown, the Scottish naturalist, who had discovered that when pollen dust was suspended in water and studied under the microscope the individual particles exhibited a continuous, zigzag, and apparently random motion. "These motions", he wrote, "were such as to satisfy me, after frequently repeated observation, that they arose neither from current in the fluid nor from its gradual evaporation, but belonged to the particle itself." Brown repeated his experiments with pollen from a number of plants. He observed a similar "swarming" motion in all of them and at first believed he had discovered the "primitive molecule". Then he found the same effect when the dusty particles of inorganic matter were treated in the same way. Many men discovered more about the Brownian motion in the years that followed. M. Gouy saw that as the viscosity of the liquid increased, so did the sluggishness of the movements; Franz Exner noted that speed of movement increased with a rise in temperature but decreased if bigger particles were used.

When Einstein later observed this never-diminishing motion through the microscope for himself he was fascinated since it seemed to him contrary to all experience. It was the explanation of this "contrary" experience that Einstein now gave in his paper "On the Motion of Small Particles Suspended in a Stationary Liquid According to the Molecular Kinetic Theory of Heat". The random motion of the individual particles was due to the kinetic energy of the invisible molecules with which they were constantly colliding. From this point he went on to use his new statistical machinery to predict the mass and numbers of molecules involved. It was the essence of his theory that the mean kinetic energy of agitation of the particles would be exactly the same as the roughly-known energy of agitation in a gas molecule, and this was in fact shown experimentally only a few years later — by Jean Perrin in Paris in 1908 and by Fletcher and Millikan four years later in Chicago.

"To appreciate the importance of this step," Max Born has written of Einstein's successful attempt to quantify the Brownian motion, "one has to remember that at that time [about 1900] atoms and molecules were still far from being as real as they are today — there were still physicists who did not believe in them." The latter included both Mach and "the old fighter against atomistics, Wilhelm Ostwald" who, Arnold Sommerfeld has stated, "told me once that he had been converted to atomistics by the complete explanation of the Brownian motion." Thus Einstein's figures for the invisible molecules had something in common with the Hertzian sparks which showed the existence of the radio waves postulated by Maxwell two decades earlier.

But Einstein's paper was also to have an important consequence for scientific methodology in general.

The accuracy of measurement depends [as Max Born has pointed out] on the sensitivity of the instruments, and this again on the size and weight of the mobile parts, and the restoring forces acting on them. Before Einstein's work it was tacitly assumed that progress in this direction was limited only by experimental technique. Now it became obvious that this was not so. If an indicator, like the needle of a galvanometer, became too small or the suspending fibre too thin, it would never be at rest but perform a kind of Brownian movement. This has in fact been observed. Similar phenomena play a large part in modern electronic technique, where the limit of observation is given by irregular observations which can be heard as a "noise" in a loud-speaker. There is a limit of observability given by the laws of nature themselves.

Einstein's virtual proof of the existence of molecules, invisible to the human eye, postulated by theory rather than produced by experimental evidence, was symptomatic of the line which he was to take throughout the career on which he was now embarking. He believed that theories into which facts were later seen to fit were more likely to stand the test of time than theories constructed entirely from experimental evidence. This was certainly the case with the first paper which he had described in his letter to Habicht, a paper which "fell like a bolt from the blue, so much so that the crisis which it ushered in some fifty years ago is not yet passed today", as Louis de Broglie described it in 1955. It was to help bring Einstein the Nobel Prize for Physics sixteen years later. It was to play a key part in the development of modern technology, since the photo-electric effect whose law it propounded was to become a cornerstone of television. It contained Einstein's first implied admission of the duality of nature which was to haunt his life and an early hint of the indeterminacy problem which drove him, as de Broglie has put it "to end his scientific life in sad isolation and — paradoxically enough — apparently far behind the ideas of his time". Moreover, with the sense of theatre which chance was to utilise so often in Einstein's life, it linked his scientific work at the age of twenty-six with two men whose non-scientific beliefs and attitudes were to influence him, and on some occasions to dominate him, for more than forty years — Max Planck, that devoted upholder of the German State who was also the founder of the quantum theory, and Philipp Lenard, composed in almost equal parts of Nobel Prize winner and Jew-baiter.

This famous paper, "On a Heuristic Viewpoint Concerning the Production and Transformation of Light", explained one particular phenomenon, the photo-electric effect, which had been puzzling scientists for years, and it suggested answers to a number of other less important scientific riddles. But it did a great deal more and while it is usually known as Einstein's "photo-electric paper" it did not spring from consideration of this specific problem but from something far more fundamental. For Einstein, mulling over his previous work on thermodynamics and statistical mechanics, noted a discrepancy in current scientific beliefs and wondered how it could be removed: the photo-electric riddle was merely a particularly convenient one which could apparently be resolved by applying a revolutionary explanation of the discrepancy. To understand its importance it is necessary to consider briefly how the nature of light was regarded at the start of the twentieth century.

To the Greeks, the idea that light consisted of minute grains in rapid movement appeared to be borne out by the fact that it travelled in straight lines and bounced off mirrors in the same way that balls bounce off walls. Only in the early 1600s was there made the first of a series of discoveries which culminated, in the last third of the century, in the theory put forward by Huygens: that light was composed of waves propagated through a medium which he called the ether and which permeated all space. Newton, in his *Opticks*,

apparently favoured the corpuscular theory, although he also outlined a scheme in which corpuscles of light were associated with
waves which influenced them — an idea revived some two and a half
centuries later in the form of wave mechanics to explain the nature
of matter. Not until the nineteenth century did the work first of
Fresnel and then of Maxwell provide a wave explanation of light
which appeared — at least for a few years — to deal satisfactorily
with all the experimental evidence.

It was Hertz who raised one of the first questions which were
to bring this comfortable state of affairs to an end. What he found
was that when a sheet of glass was put between his wave-transmitter
and his receiver, the sparks produced in the transmitter failed to
produce as large a group of sparks in the receiver. He decided,
naturally enough, that the receiving loop must be affected by the
sparks' ultra-violet light, which does not penetrate glass, and that in
some inexplicable way this light was thus increasing the electrical
discharge from his metal receiver. Other scientists discovered that
this photo-electric effect, as it came to be known, could be produced
by visible as well as by ultraviolet light; that it was produced with
some metals more easily than with others; and that the receiving
metal acquired a small positive electrical charge.

Now elucidation of the nature of light by Maxwell's electro-
magnetic equations, had been paralleled by another, and apparently
contradictory, development. For while it had been found that light
was radiated as electro-magnetic waves, other physicists — Hendrik
Lorentz in Leiden and J. J. Thomson in Cambridge among them —
had been discovering that what could only be considered particles,
the negatively-charged electrons, played an important part in the
constitution of electrified matter. It is at this stage that Lenard comes
on the scene. A scientist of great skill, Lenard was a German whose
desperation at his country's defeat in 1918 quickly led him into the
welcoming arms of the Nazi party; in addition his paranoic hatred
of the Jews brought him, after 1919, into the movement which
attempted to discredit both Einstein's honesty and his work. At the
turn of the century Lenard put forward a simple explanation of the
photo-electric effect; it was that photo-electrons, or negative charges,
were knocked out of the metal by the light which hit it. Soon, however, he reported another less easily explicable phenomenon. Since
electrons were ejected from the sensitive metal solely as a result of
light falling upon it, then it might surely be assumed that an increase
in light would produce an increase in the speed at which the electrons
were thrown from the metal? However, this was not the case. If the

intensity of the light was increased, then a greater number of electrons would be ejected from the metal, but they would continue to be ejected at the same speed. But — and this appeared even more inexplicable — if there was a change in the colour of the light, or in other words in its frequency, then there would be a change in the speeds at which the electrons were thrown out; and the higher the frequency, the higher the speed of ejection.

While Lenard was thus occupied in the familiar scientific operation of answering one riddle and creating another in the process Max Planck, by this time Professor of Theoretical Physics in the University of Berlin, was grappling with a problem which at first glance seemed to be only indirectly concerned with the photo-electric effect. Planck had taken the chair after the death of Kirchhoff in 1887, and it was from a continuation of Kirchhoff's work that he produced the theory which was to alter man's idea of energy as drastically as Einstein's theory of relativity was to alter ideas of time and space.

Kirchhoff had been interested, like many of his contemporaries, in discovering more about the mechanism by which radiant energy was emitted by electro-magnetic waves, already known to include not only the spectrum of visible light but the infra-red and ultra-violet rays either side of them, as well as the newly-discovered radio waves. It was known that as a body was heated its maximum energy was produced at shorter and shorter wavelengths, and its colour passed from red to yellow and then to bluish-white. But all experiments appeared to be affected by the nature of the emitting body, only overcome by Kirchhoff's ingenious method of using "black body radiation" which utilised a closed container with blackened inner walls and one tiny pinhole. When the container was heated to incandescence, genuinely pure light of all the visible wavelengths could, in theory at least, be observed coming from the pinhole. This primitive equipment was supplemented in 1881 by the bolometer, invented by Samuel Langley, whose aerodynamic work led on to the Wright brothers and Kittyhawk. With Langley's bolometer, which depended on the electrical measurement of minute quantities of heat set up in a blackened platinum wire, it was possible to record temperature changes as little as one millionth of a degree under the impact of specific wavelengths; thus there was now, it appeared, a route to an adequate description of the way that energy was radiated.

During the 1890s, Planck found that this was far from being the case. Despite the efforts of physicists throughout Europe it became clear that while one set of distribution formulas, produced by Wilhelm Wien, served well enough to explain radiation at low wavelengths, those at high wavelengths demanded the different mathematical explanation produced by Lord Rayleigh — as though nature had changed the rules of the game at half-time. No one could explain it. "The discrepancy," Sir Basil Schonland has stated "suggested that something fundamental had been missed by both. The affair, which was extremely closely examined by the best minds of the time, presented something like a scientific scandal."

It was to this discrepancy that Planck turned during the latter half of the 1890s. In the autumn of 1900 he thought he had solved the problem and on October 14th read a paper to the Berlin Physical Society which proposed a single neat expression to explain how radiation worked. This satisfied the Wien distribution formula at low wavelengths and Rayleigh's distribution formula at high ones; in fact it fitted experimental observations between infra-red measurements towards one end of the spectrum and ultra-violet measurements towards the other so well that some men working on ultra-violet found it necessary to repeat their experiments and amend their figures.

For Planck, this was not enough. Intuitively, he felt that something more and something different was required. "After some weeks of the most intense work of my life, clearness began to dawn upon me, and an unexpected view revealed itself in the distance," he later said.

Some weeks after his October address, Planck found the explanation. Walking in the Grunewald woods in Berlin, he turned to his son. "Today," he said, "I have made a discovery as important as that of Newton."

On December 14th, 1900, he appeared again before the Physical Society. This time he announced that his earlier expression could best be derived from an entirely new hypothesis. It was not only new but startling. For Planck now stated that his whole theory was based on one assumption: that energy was emitted not in the continuous flow that everyday common sense suggested but as discrete bursts for which he used the Latin "how much", or quanta. The size of quanta was, moreover, directly related to the frequency of the electromagnetic wave with which they are associated; violet light, which has twice the frequency of red light, having associated quanta twice as large as those associated with red light. Linking the frequency of the radiation and the size of the quantum there was, in the units current in Planck's time which are still widely but not exclusively used, the magic quantity of $h = 6.6 \times 10^{-27}$, erg. sec., quickly known as Planck's constant and soon recognised as one of the fundamental constants of nature.

At first sight this revolutionary idea appeared to stick a dagger between the ribs of the accepted view that light consisted of waves rather than particles. But not even Planck could go as far as that. His theory, he stressed, was concerned with the relationship between radiation and matter, not with the nature of radiation on its journey between emission and reception; thus he allowed the discontinuous bursts of energy to join up in some inexplicable way and produce waves which dissolved into particulate entities as they were absorbed. Thus the "scientific scandal", as Schonland was later to describe it, had been removed only by creating a fresh one.

In 1903 J. J. Thomson, giving the Silliman Lectures at Yale University, appears to have been on the verge of dissipating it when he suggested that some form of localised radiant energy might account for a number of unexplained experimental facts, including the manner in which ultraviolet light ejected electrons from a metal surface. But the idea was taken no further. This preserved the wave-nature of light; it also left the way open for Einstein. For just as Niels Bohr was later to use the quantum theory to explain the structure of the atom, so did Einstein now use it to justify the idea that light could have characteristics of both wave and particle.

Until 1905 his published papers had dealt almost exclusively with thermodynamics and statistical mechanics; they were essentially studies in which the laws of nature were considered by reference to the random movements of vast numbers of individual particles which obeyed Newton's laws as obediently as the planets. But there were also Einstein's unpublished thoughts; and these were obsessed with the reality of light and its associated electro-magnetic waves, a reality conceived not in terms of Newtonian particles but of the field which had been proposed by Faraday and developed by Maxwell. No one had up till now thought of asking the awkward questions which the contradiction begged; or if they had thought of it they had not dared. Einstein both thought and dared.

The formal difference between the theoretical ideas that physicists had formed about gases and other ponderable bodies, and Maxwell's theory of electro-magnetic processes in so-called empty space, could be resolved, he suggested, if for some purposes light could be considered as a collection of independent particles which behaved like the particles of a gas — the "heuristic viewpoint" of his title. When Einstein began to consider this new concept in the light of his earlier work, he found that it provided some startlingly useful results. The photo-electric explanation was one of them.

For the size of Planck's quanta depended on the frequency of the light concerned, and the small quanta of a low-frequency light would, if they were considered as discrete packages of particulate energy, therefore eject the electrons they hit with a comparatively low speed; the bigger "packets of energy", as the quanta making up the higher-frequency colours could be considered, would of course eject at higher speeds the electrons they hit. This explanation would also account for what happened when the intensity of the light of any specific colour was decreased. Each individual quantum which went to make it up would have the same power to eject an electron which it hit. But there would be fewer quanta, fewer "hits", and fewer electrons ejected. As Sir James Jeans said in describing the photochemical law that Einstein produced, his explanation of the photo-electric effect "not only prohibits the killing of two birds by one stone, but also the killing of one bird with two stones".

In his paper Einstein did more than put forward a theory which was, as he said, "in perfect agreement with observation" — and which was later to be confirmed experimentally, by Millikan for visible light, by de Broglie for X rays and by Jean Thibaud and Ellis for gamma rays. In addition, he calculated the maximum kinetic energy of the electron which was emitted, giving this by the use of the formula $hv-e$ where $h$ is Planck's constant, $v$ is the frequency of the light, and $e$ is the energy lost by the electron in its escape from the metal surface, called the work function. Thus Einstein's conception of light as being formed of light quanta — or photons as they were later christened — in itself involved a paradoxical contradiction from which a man of lesser mental stature might have edged away. For while light consisting of discrete packets of energy as indivisible as the atom was still thought to be, conformed — if it conformed to anything — to the corpuscular theory of Newton's day, the idea also utilised frequency, a vital feature of the wave theory. Thus, as Bohr was later to write, physics was "confronted with a novel kind of complementary relationship between the applications of different fundamental concepts of classical physics". Physicists began to study more closely these contradictory ideas which alone seemed to explain verifiable facts, and eventually, in the 1920s, they began to see the limitations of deterministic description. At the level of simple atomic processes, nature could be described in terms of statistical chance — the case of "God playing dice with the world" that Einstein would never accept. Yet he had pushed the stone that started the avalanche.

This was not clear in 1905. Even so, Einstein had to face the embarrassing contradiction that Planck had tried to avoid: for some purposes light must be regarded as a stream of particles, as Newton had regarded it; for others, it must be considered in terms of wave motion. But he believed that eventually, if men were only persistent enough, a satisfactory explanation for the contradiction would emerge. This was in fact to be the case some two decades later when de Broglie and Schrödinger, Born and Heisenberg, were to produce a conception of the physical world that could be regarded in terms either of waves or of particles — or, as one humorist called it, of "wavicles".

Planck himself was reluctant to accept Einstein's development of his theory, and as late as 1912 was rejecting, in Berlin lectures, the idea that light travelled through space as bunches of localised energy. "I think it is correct to say," writes Robert Millikan, who was to win the Nobel Prize for demonstrating the corpuscular nature of electricity with his work on the electron, "that the Einstein view of light quanta, shooting through space in the form of localised light pulses, or, as we now call them, photons, had practically no convinced adherents prior to about 1915, by which time convincing experimental proof had been found."

Einstein's record was thus an unusual one. He had applied Planck's revolutionary theory with apparent success to a physical phenomenon that classical physics could not explain. He had been more revolutionary than his elders and they would not credit him with what he had done. It needed courage; but this was to be expected from the man who could, in the same volume of the *Annalen der Physik*, explode the bomb which was his new theory of relativity.

# PART TWO

# The Voyage of Discovery

# 4

# *EINSTEIN'S RELATIVITY*

THE SPECIAL THEORY OF RELATIVITY WHICH WAS TO GIVE EINSTEIN his unique position in history was outlined in the third paper which he wrote for the *Annalen der Physik* in the summer of 1905. Entitled simply "On the Electrodynamics of Moving Bodies", it was in many ways one of the most remarkable scientific papers that had ever been written. Even in form and style it was unusual, lacking the notes and references which give weight to most serious expositions and merely noting, in its closing paragraph, that the author was indebted for a number of valuable suggestions to his friend and colleague, M. Besso. Yet this dissertation of some nine thousand words overturned man's accepted ideas of time and space in a way which was, as *The Times* once put it, "an affront to common sense" and drastically altered the classical concepts of physics still held by the overwhelming majority of scientists. In addition it provided such an accurate blueprint for the way in which the physical world was built that within a generation men could no more ignore relativity in the teaching of physics than they could ignore grammar in the teaching of language.

During the sixty-odd years that have passed since Einstein tossed this rock into the pool an immense literature and exegesis has spread out round the paper, the theory, and its history. This literature does more than describe, explain and criticise what Einstein wrote, and attempt with varying degrees of success to outline his theory to the layman. It also gives differing assessments of Einstein's debt to his predecessors, and shows scientific historians to be as practised as their less specialised colleagues in the gentle art of blacking an opponent's eye. This is natural enough. Most revolutionary theories — scientific as well as political — have roots deep in the past; about

the exact direction of such roots, historians argue and scholars write
theses. As time blurs details, as old men "remember with advantages",
as rumour is transformed first into myth and then into fact, the
genesis of scientific theory becomes increasingly difficult to describe
with more than scholarly plausibility. Darwin's theory of evolution,
so long worked over yet springing to the surface almost simultaneously with that of Wallace, is an example from one other field: the
conscription of Hertz's radio waves into the utilitarian strait-jacket
of radar, long possible in many countries and then, within a few
months, suddenly crystallising in Britain, the United States and
Germany, is an example from another.

Relativity is no exception to the rule. Today, two thirds of a
century after Einstein posted the manuscript of his paper to *Annalen
der Physik*, the dust is still stirred by discussion of what inspired him.
The controversy about how much he owed to his predecessors com-
plicates still further the problem of explaining a complicated subject
to a lay public. However, it is not insuperable and is best tackled by
outlining briefly the background against which his paper was written;
by describing first the daring propositions he put forward and then
their implications; and by surveying the sometimes contradictory
evidence of the paper's genesis.

Over the background of the scientific world as it existed in the
first years of the twentieth century there still towered, as central
ornament, the bold figure of Sir Isaac Newton. Driven in 1666 from
Cambridge to his Lincolnshire home by the plague when only twenty-
four, he had been almost of an age with Einstein; and, like Einstein,
he had in a single summer delivered three hammer-blows at the
foundations of contemporary science. The formulation of the law of
gravity was the greatest of the three, showing that the fall of the
apple and the passage of the moon in its orbit were governed by the
same natural laws. For, starting with an explanation of the forces
which kept the planets on their tracks, Newton constructed the first
modern synthesis of the physical world, a logical explanation of the
universe. Judged by contemporary standards, his universe was a
simple and comforting place through which planets and stars, men
and animals, the smallest particles of matter, and even the particles
of which light was deemed to consist, moved in accordance with the
same mathematical laws.

From the time of Newton up to the end of the last century, [Robert
Oppenheimer has noted] physicists built, on the basis of these laws,
a magnificently precise and beautiful science involving the celestial

mechanics of the solar system, involving incredible problems in the Cambridge Tripos, involving the theory of gases, involving the behaviour of fluids, of elastic vibrations, of sound — indeed, a comprehensive system so robust and varied and apparently all-powerful that what was in store for it could hardly be imagined.

In the first pages of his *Philosophiae Naturalis Principia Mathematica* which enshrined these laws, Newton used two words whose definitions formed the basis not only of his whole system but of everything which had been constructed as a by-product of it — two words which between them formed the bottom layer of the house which science had been building for two and a half centuries. One of them was "time", the other was "space". "Absolute, true and mathematical time," as Newton put it, "of itself and from its own nature, flows equably, without relation to anything external, and by another name is called duration." Space could be "absolute space, in its own nature, without relation to anything external" which "remains always similar and immovable"; or relative space, which was "some movable dimensions or measure of the absolute spaces".

From these definitions Newton went on to illustrate the principle of the addition of velocities, a principle so obvious that at first there seems little point in repeating it. Yet it was to be radically amended by Einstein's Special Theory, and it is salutary to consider how Newton expressed it.

Absolute motion, [he wrote] is the translation of a body from one relative place into another. Thus in a ship under sail the relative place of a body is that part of the ship which the body possesses; or that part of the cavity which the body fills, and which therefore moves together with the ship; and relative rest is the continuance of the body in the same part of that immovable space, in which the ship itself, its cavity, and all that it contains, is moved. Wherefore, if the earth is really at rest, the body which relatively rests in the ship, will really and absolutely move with the same velocity which the ship has on the earth. But if the earth also moves, the true and absolute motion of the body will arise, partly from the true motion of the earth, in immovable space, partly from the relative motion of the ship on the earth; and if the body moves also relatively in the ship, its true motion will arise, partly from the true motion of the earth, in immovable space, and partly from the relative motions as well of the ship on the earth, as of the body in the ship; and from these relative motions will arise the relative motion of the body on the earth. As if that part of the earth, where the ship is, was truly moved towards the east, with a velocity of 10,010 parts; while the ship itself, with a fresh gale, and full sails, is carried towards the west, with a velocity expressed by 10 of those parts; but a sailor walks in the ship towards the east, with 1 part of the said velocity; then the sailor will be moved truly in immovable space towards the east, with a velocity of 10,001 parts, and relatively on the earth towards the west, with a velocity of 9 of those parts . . .

Newton's sailor — pacing 3 miles an hour east on the deck of his ship while the ship sails past the coast at 12 miles an hour in the same direction and therefore moving past the land at 15 miles an hour — has his modern counterpart: the train passenger travelling at 40 miles an hour whose carriage is passed by a second train travelling at 50 miles an hour, to whom a passenger in the faster train is moving at only 10 miles an hour. In both cases it is possible to describe the movement of a person — or a particle — in one frame of reference (the sailor relative to the ship) and then to describe it in a second frame of reference (the sailor relative to the land) by the simple addition of velocities.

Newton's sailor and the train movements of the twentieth century have one other important thing in common. Newton himself gives a clue to it when he writes: "The motions of bodies included in a given space are the same among themselves, whether that space is at rest or moves uniformly forward in a straight line." In other words, the mechanical laws which are applicable in a ship — or a train — when at rest are also applicable when it is moving uniformly. Nature does not give special preference to one situation or the other, and any measurements or experiments made on a vehicle in uniform motion will produce the same results as when it is at rest.

During the second half of the nineteenth century, attacks began to be made on this mechanical view of the universe. From one side came those prepared to strike at its epistemological roots and those who sought to deny that the apparently sound mechanical structure was anything more than a convenient illusion. Gustav Kirchhoff, whose work prepared the way for the quantum revolution, looked on Newtonian concepts merely as convenient explanations for various unrelated phenomena which had been noted, and which did not demand the creation of a single comprehensive explanation of the physical world. Ernst Mach, the physicist turned philosopher whose influence on Einstein was so great and who had for the hard currency of observable sensations much the same respect that Soames Forsyte had for property, went further in the same direction. In *The Science of Mechanics: A Critical and Historical Account of its Development*, Mach boldly challenged Newton's assumptions of absolute space and absolute time, claiming that he had "acted contrary to his expressed intention only to investigate *actual facts*. No one is competent to predicate things about absolute space and absolute motion; they are pure things of thought, pure mental constructs, that cannot be produced in experience." And Henri Poincaré, "the last man to take practically all mathematics, both pure and applied, as his province", went even further, not only throwing overboard in lordly manner absolute time and absolute space but insisting that even the laws of nature, the simple ways of tabulating and ordering the sensations of life which Mach allowed, were merely the free creations of the human mind.

But if such men were able to cast doubt on Newton's absolute space and time, an equally dangerous attack was to come from a different quarter, as confusing, and sometimes conflicting evidence on the nature and behaviour of light accumulated during the nineteenth century. To Newton, light was a stream of particles moving according to mechanical laws, although his contemporary, Christiaan Huygens, thought it might be instead a vibration in an unspecified medium, much as sound was a vibration in the air. The problem looked as if it had been solved in mid-century when the French physicists Dominique Arago, followed by Jean Foucault, produced evidence supporting the wave theory. If any doubt remained it appeared to be dispelled during the next few decades. Maxwell's theoretical calculations showed that the vibrations associated with light were due to very rapid oscillations of electric and magnetic fields; twenty years later Hertz, with his demonstration of electromagnetic radio waves, seemed to put this beyond question.

But there was one particular way in which Maxwell's electro magnetism operated in a manner totally different from Newtonian mechanics. In the first place Newton had built his law of gravitation on the idea of action-at-a-distance, believing that the pull of gravity between the apple and the ground, the moon and the earth, the earth and the sun, in fact between all the components of the universe, operated as a mysterious and instantaneous force across empty space. Maxwell utilised instead the idea of "the field" which had been conceived by Faraday: a region of space in which certain physical conditions were created and through which forces were transmitted; somewhat like ripples through an invisible jelly, the electromagnetic waves of light being propagated through the field in straight lines at a finite speed, and the pull of the magnet for iron filings being a property of the field which the magnet had itself created.

Largely due to the concept of the field, it was believed during the last decades of the nineteenth century that electromagnetic waves

required a medium through which they could travel, just as sound
needs the molecules of air before it can be heard and seismic waves
require the medium of the earth before they can be recorded. Scientists decided that this medium was the ether, vaguely postulated since
the time of the Greeks. But the presence of the ether had never been
confirmed and there was a doubt about its existence, like the pea
under the princess's mattress — minute, yet sufficient to prevent
peace of mind. It was to resolve this doubt that the famous — indeed,
almost legendary — Michelson-Morley experiment was designed in
1887. How much Einstein knew of this before 1905 is questionable,
and even more so is the importance to his thinking of what he did
know. The awkward results of the experiment permeated the scientific climate of the 1890s and its implications must even have been
noted by Einstein in the Berne Patent Office. Later, moreover, it
could be seen as a linch-pin of the whole theory of relativity. As
Einstein said years later, talking to Sir Herbert Samuel in the
grounds of Government House, Jerusalem, "If Michelson-Morley is
wrong, then relativity is wrong."

By the time that Einstein came on the scene other experiments
had been carried out in an effort to show the existence of the ether
by recording the effects of the earth's passage through it. Trouton
and Noble had tried to discover experimentally the torque which
should, in theory, have been shown by the charging of a condenser
hung from a fine filament with its plates inclined to the ether drift.
Both Lord Rayleigh and Brace had looked for double refraction in a
transparent body produced by the passage of the ether through it.
All these experiments had failed to produce any evidence for the
existence of the ether. It was, however, the Michelson-Morley experiment which lodged in the scientific gullet, partly because it seemed
impossible to escape from its implications, partly on account of its
basic simplicity.

What Michelson and Morley set out to discover was the effect
of the earth's passage through the postulated ether on the speed of
light. Long known to be roughly 186,000 miles per second, it was so
great as to present technical problems which would have ruled out
the experiment before the last decades of the nineteenth century. On
the other hand, the experiment's basic mathematics are quite simple.

To understand them one has merely to consider the case of two
oarsmen rowing respectively across a river 400 yards wide and 400
yards up and down the same stream of water, an analogy which is
one of many littering the pages explaining Einstein's work. Both
oarsmen have the same speed — which can be arbitrarily given as

500 yards a minute, with the stream running at an equally arbitrary rate of 300 yards a minute. The first oarsman starts from one bank, aiming to arrive at a point on the far bank directly opposite — in other words 400 yards away. If there were no current he would reach it in four-fifths of a minute. But since there is a current he must point his boat upstream. Now an observer starting at the same point as the oarsman but allowing himself merely to float downstream will see the "aiming-point" on the far bank moving "back" at a rate of 300 yards a minute (the rate of the stream's movement), while the oarsman is moving away from him at a rate of 500 yards a minute (the speed at which he is rowing). The construction of a simple right-angled triangle using this information, plus an equally simple use of Pythagoras, will show that the oarsman will have travelled 500 yards before he reaches the far bank and that the time he takes will be one minute for the single journey or two minutes there and back.

Now what of the oarsman given the comparable task of rowing 400 yards upstream and returning to the same point? During the first minute he will have covered 500 minus 300 yards, which is 200 yards. So he will take two minutes for the journey against the stream. On his return, his speed of 500 yards a minute will be aided by the 300-yard-a-minute stream so that the 400 yards will take him only half a minute. That is, the time for the double journey measured up and down the stream is more than the double journey measured across the stream and it always will be more except in a currentless river. And by measuring the times both oarsmen take it is possible to calculate both the speed at which they row and also the speed of the river. Similarly, Michelson and Morley proposed, it should be possible to confirm the existence of the ether.

In their experiment the ether, presumably streaming past the earth at 20 miles a second as the earth moved in its orbit round the sun, would represent the current. A ray of light, split into two, would represent the two oarsmen. These two rays would be directed along two paths identical in length but at right-angles to one another; then they would be reflected back to the "test-bed" of the experiment — after having made journeys which would be respectively "across", and "up" and then "down", the presumed flow of the ether. If the "ether flow" had an effect on light comparable to the normal mechanical effects, the two returning rays would be out of phase. The result would be interference-fringes, or bands of alternately light and dark colour, and from these it would be possible to calculate the speed of the ether wind relative to the movement of the earth.

Nearly forty years later Edward Appleton used a comparable technique with radio waves to pinpoint the height of the ionosphere from which such waves are reflected back to the earth.

The huge difference between the speed of light and the mere 20 miles per second of the earth's orbit round the sun presented considerable problems and an earlier experiment carried out in 1881 by Michelson alone had failed. Now these inherent problems had been solved and "pure" science was able to move forward once again on the vehicle provided by technology. This has happened frequently. From the days of William Herschel, whose discovery of infra-red rays in 1800 was aided by sensitive thermometers, through the work of Oersted, von Fraunhofer, Wheatstone and Joule, knowledge of the physical world has marched steadily forward on the achievements of the craftsmen. Maxwell, on arriving at Aberdeen had stated significantly: "I am happy in the knowledge of a good instrument maker, in addition to a smith, an optician and a carpenter." In another field, accurate gravimetric analysis was made possible by improvements in the chemical balance. Hermann Bondi has emphasised that "the enormous stream of discoveries at the end of the nineteenth century that gave us such insight as the discovery of X-rays, working with radioactivity, and all that, is entirely due to the fact that the technologists developed decent vacuum pumps."

The process of pure science moving forward with the pack-horses of technology was now illustrated by Michelson and Morley who set up their apparatus in the Case Institute of Technology in Cleveland, Ohio. The massive stone test-bed, nearly five feet square, was floated in a bowl of mercury to obviate vibrations. The light rays used were ingeniously lengthened by a system of mirrors. The experiments were carried out at various times of day to lessen the chances of experimental error. Yet the results, however they were considered, told one incontrovertible story: light which travelled back and forth across the ether stream did the journey in exactly the same time as light travelling the same distance up and down the ether stream.

The problem which now faced science was considerable. For there seemed to be only three alternatives. The first was that the earth was standing still, a scuttling of the whole Copernican theory which was unthinkable. The second was that the ether was carried along by the earth in its passage through space, a possibility which had already been ruled out to the satisfaction of the scientific community by a number of experiments, notably those of the English astronomer, James Bradley. The third solution was that the ether just did not exist, which to many nineteenth century scientists was equivalent to scrapping current views of light, electricity and magnetism and starting again.

The only other explanation must surely lie in some perverse feature of the physical world which scientists had not yet suspected and during the next few years this was sought by three men in particular — George Fitzgerald, Professor of Natural and Experimental Philosophy at Trinity College, Dublin; Hendrik Lorentz of Leiden, the kindly humanitarian physicist whose lifetime spanned the closing days of Newtonian cosmology and the splitting of the atom — the man who, wrote Einstein within a few weeks of his own death, "for me personally . . . meant more than all the others I have met on my life's journey"; and the French mathematician, Henri Poincaré.

The Fitzgerald explanation came first. To many it must have seemed that he had strained at a gnat and swallowed an elephant. For while Fitzgerald was unwilling to believe that the velocity of light could remain unaffected by the velocity of its source, he suggested instead that all moving objects were shortened along the axis of their movement. A foot-rule moving end forwards would be slightly shorter than a stationary foot-rule, and the faster it moved the shorter it would be. The speed of the earth's movement was all that was involved, so the contraction would be extremely small, and it would only rise to appreciable amounts as the speed involved rose to a sizeable proportion of the speed of light itself. But it was not this alone that made the proposal apparently incapable of proof or disproof. Any test instruments would adjust themselves in the same way, shortening themselves as they were turned into the direction of the earth's movement through the ether. For some years this explanation appeared to be little more than a plausible trick — "I have been rather laughed at for my view over here," Fitzgerald wrote to Lorentz from Dublin in 1894 — and it was only transformed into something more when Lorentz turned his mind to the question.*

Lorentz had been among the first to postulate the electron, the negatively-charged particle whose existence had finally been proved

* The history of the Fitzgerald-Lorentz contraction has striking resemblances with the story of Wallace and Darwin's concurrent work on evolution. Fitzgerald was the first to publish the contraction hypothesis, doing so in a letter to *Science;* but not even Fitzgerald himself, let alone Lorentz, knew that the letter had appeared. For details see "The 'Fitzgerald' Contraction" by Alfred M. Brok, *Isis,* № 57 (1966) pp. 199—207, and "Note on the History of the Fitzgerald-Lorentz Contraction" by Stephen G. Brush, *Isis,* № 58 (1967) pp. 231—232.

by J. J. Thomson at Cambridge. It now seemed to him that such a contraction could well be a direct result of electro-magnetic forces produced when a body with its electrical charges was moved through the ether. These would disturb the equilibrium of the body, and its particles would assume new relative distances from one another. The result would be a change in the shape of the body, which would become flattened in the direction of its movement. The contraction could thus be explained, as Philipp Frank has put it, as "a logical consequence of several simultaneous hypotheses, namely the validity of the electro-magnetic field equations and laws of force and the hypothesis that all bodies are built up of electric charges".

Lorentz' invocation of electro-magnetism thus brought a whiff of sanity into the game. Here at least was a credible explanation of how a foot-rule in motion could be of a different length from the foot-rule at rest. However, if this solved one problem it created others; and it played havoc with the simple transformation which had hitherto been used to describe events taking place in one frame of reference in terms of a different one. This had served well enough throughout the centuries for sailors on ships, for men on horseback and for the early railways. It serves well enough for flight and even for contemporary space travel. Yet if Lorentz' hypothesis was correct the simple addition of velocities could no longer hold water. For if distances contract with relative speed then the yards paced out on th deck by Newton's sailor will be slightly shorter than the relatively stationary yards on the shore which his ship has sailed past. The smallness of the difference, so minute that it can be disregarded for practical purposes, can be gauged by even a non-mathematician's comparison of the simple equations, or "transformations", of the Newtonian world with those which Fitzgerald had provided and which were given a fresh significance by Lorentz. In the old Galilean transformation, the new place of the sailor on his deck is given by his old position plus or minus the speed of his walking multiplied by the time he has been on the move — in other words his old position $x$, plus or minus $vt$. But using the new set of equations which Lorentz now developed — and which soon became known as the Lorentz transformations — the sailor's new position is represented by this $x \pm vt$ divided by $\sqrt{1 - (v^2/c^2)}$. In the case of the sailor walking at 3 miles an hour, $v^2$ will be 9, and in most examples from everyday life it will be a similarly humble figure; but $c$ is the speed of light in miles per second, and $c^2$ is many millions of millions miles per hour. Once this is realised, two things become immediately clear: that the sailor need not be worried by the Lorentz transformations and that these will, as Fitzgerald had forecast, begin to have significant applications only when the speeds concerned are a significant percentage of the speed of light.

While Fitzgerald and Lorentz were struggling to produce these explanations for physical experiments, Henri Poincaré was making a different approach. He was concerned not so much with the awkward specific problem of the speed of light as with the conglomeration of problems being presented to physicists at the turn of the century. He was, moreover, tackling them from an angle more philosophical than that of Fitzgerald and Lorentz. "Suppose," he argued, "that in one night all the dimensions of the universe became a thousand times larger. The world will remain *similar* to itself if we give the word *similitude* the meaning it has in the third book of Euclid . . . Have we any right, therefore, to say that we know the distance between two points?" Poincaré's answer was "No" — the concept of space being relative to the frame of reference within which its distances were measured.

Poincaré reached the climax of his reputation in the 1900s, and in 1904 he was among those invited to a Congress of Arts and Sciences at the Universal Exposition, St. Louis, 1904, held to commemorate the Louisiana Purchase a century earlier. Here he dealt, in a speech which was part of a symposium surveying human thought in the nineteenth century, with the contemporary crisis in physics. "Perhaps," he said, "we should construct a whole new mechanics, of which we only succeed in catching a glimpse, where, inertia increasing with the velocity, the velocity of light would become an impassable limit." The Lorentz transformation would no doubt be included in the new structure and it might well form part of a new principle of relativity which would replace, or supplement, the restricted principle which was epitomised by the Galilean transformation. Yet Poincaré was, as he stressed, doing his best to fit such new ideas as were required into the existing classical principles — "and as yet," he concluded at St. Louis "nothing proves that the principles will not come forth from the combat victorious and intact."

His speech was an indication of the scientific unrest and philosophical distrust created not only by the Michelson-Morley experiment but by others made during the preceding two decades in Cambridge and Berlin, in Leiden and Paris. But there was no hint of the Special Theory, created by Einstein for different reasons after an approach across different territory.

While Fitzgerald, Lorentz and Poincaré were trying to rescue

physics from the cul-de-sac into which it appeared to have been led
by the Michelson-Morely experiment, Einstein was wondering about
the world in general, gaining a basic grounding in physics at the
E.T.H. and giving special attention to what he realised, early on,
were the revolutionary implications of Maxwell's electro-magnetic
theory, based on continuous fields. This was a basically new idea
of the way in which the world had been made, and it continued to
exercise Einstein for a decade, working away like a fermenting yeast
in contrast to the boring material with which the Zurich masters
tried to fill the stock-pot of his mind.

As early as the age of sixteen, he had considered what he would
see were he able to follow a beam of light at its own velocity
through space. Here is a problem-picture as graphic as any of the
number with which he was to explain his ideas. What, in fact, would
be seen by anyone who could travel as fast as the oscillating electro-
magnetic waves which by the turn of the century were known to
cause the phenomenon of light? The answer, believed Einstein, was a
spatially oscillatory electro-magnetic field at rest. But this was a
contradiction in terms of which Maxwell's equations gave no hint.
Quite as important, if such a conception were feasible, it would mean
that the laws of electro-magnetism would be different for observers
at rest and for those on the move — at least for those moving at the
speed of light. But it seemed soundly established that the mechanical
laws of the Newtonian universe were the same for all observers and
Einstein saw no reason for thinking that the laws of electro-magnetism would be any different. Thus it looked as certain as the Q.E.D.
at the end of a theorem that the laws of nature would prevent anyone
or anything moving at the speed of light. But this idea, in turn,
raised its own problems. For in the mechanical Newtonian world it
was always possible to add a little more force and thus make the
billiard ball, or the cannon ball, go a little faster. What was there
to prevent addition plus addition pushing up speeds above that of
light?

This was one of the problems which worried Einstein persistently during his studies at the E.T.H. and during his early years
at the Patent Office, a constant background to his other work and
a hobbyhorse he could pull down from the shelf of his mind when
more pressing work gave him a moment to spare.

Einstein himself has given more than a hint of how he worked
away at it. "I must confess," he told Alexander Moszkowski in
Berlin in 1915, "that at the very beginning, when the Special Theory
of Relativity began to germinate in me, I was visited by all sorts of

nervous conflicts. When young, I used to go away for weeks in a state of confusion, as one who at that time had yet to overcome the stage of stupefaction in his first encounter with such questions." To R. S. Shankland, professor at the Case Institute of Technology, Cleveland, Ohio, he said in old age that he had "worked for ten years; first as a student when, of course, he could only spend part-time on it, but the problem was always with him. He abandoned many fruitless attempts, 'until at last it came to me that time was suspect.'" And to Carl Seelig he wrote on March 11th, 1952 saying that while only five or six weeks separated the conception of Special Relativity and the completion of his paper, preparatory thought and arguments had been going on for years.

He worked alone, or almost alone. His earlier papers had brought him into the physicists' world — or, more accurately, into contact with it by correspondence. But he had none of the stimulus of university life, he played no part in any scientific group or society. For all practical purposes he was a scientific loner, trying out his ideas not on sharp minds of professional equals but on the blunt edges of the Swiss civil service. His only two confidants were two colleagues, Josef Sauter and the Michelangelo Besso whom he had eased into the Patent Office the previous year.

Sauter, eight years older than Einstein, was given the young man's notes to criticise after they had walked home from the office one evening and Einstein had outlined his ideas. "I pestered him for a whole month with every possible objection without managing to make him in the least impatient, until I was finally convinced that my objections were no more than the usual judgments of contemporary physics" Sauter has written. "I cannot forget the patience and good temper with which he listened, agreeing or disagreeing with my objections. He went over it again and again until he saw that I had understood his ideas. 'You are the second to whom I have told my discovery', he said."

Sauter believes that Einstein's first confidant was Maurice Solovine. More probably it was Besso, with whom Einstein certainly discussed his ideas and whom he described as the best sounding-board in all Europe. Besso's version of events was: "Einstein the eagle took Besso the sparrow under his wing. Then the sparrow fluttered a little higher." Certainly Besso was the only person given a niche in history in the famous paper outlining the Special Theory.

This was possibly the most important scientific paper written in the twentieth century, in some ways a custom-built example of those described by Hermann Bondi. Their aim, he has said, "is to leave as disembodied, as impersonalised a piece of writing as anybody might be willing to read, knowing that others have to read it if they wish to know what has been achieved. The paper is very likely to tell the reader almost nothing about how the result was found." Yet if in outlining the Special Theory it thus conformed in one respect, it was an exception in other ways. Supporting evidence was not called upon at all; in fact the paper which was to set the scientific world by the ears contained not a single footnote or reference, those stigmata of scholarly respectability, and as acknowledgement only a casual reference to Michelangelo Besso, thrown off almost as an afterthought.

Einstein began by doing exactly what he had done when dealing with the photo-electric effect: he noted a contradiction in contemporary scientific beliefs apparent for years but conveniently ignored. In the first case it was the contradiction between the Newtonian world of corpuscles and the Maxwellian world of fields. Here it was something perhaps even more fundamental: the contradiction implicit in Faraday's law of induction. This had for years been one of the accepted facts of life and to raise awkward questions about it was to spit in a sacred place. Yet, Einstein pointed out, the current induced between a magnet and a conductor depends according to observation only on the relative motion of the conducting wire and the magnet "whereas the customary view", in other words the accepted theory of currents, drew a distinction according to which of the two bodies was in motion. Faraday had discovered the induction law in 1834 but, as Born has put it, "everybody had known all along that the effect depended only on relative motion, but nobody had taken offence at the theory not accounting for this circumstance." Even had they done so, few would have had the temerity to pass on, in Einstein's grand style, to what he saw as the inevitable consequences: the destruction of the idea of absolute rest and the proposal that the same laws of electrodynamics and optics would be valid for all frames of reference for which the equations of mechanics held good.

This linking of electrodynamics and mechanics was the crux of the matter. In the world of electromagnetism, governed by the field-laws of Faraday and Maxwell, light was propagated at a constant speed which could not be surpassed; but there seemed to be little connection here with Newtonian mechanics which made it possible to increase the speed of an object indefinitely by adding more energy to it. What Einstein now proposed was that the velocity of light was a constant and a maximum in the electro-magnetic and the mechanical worlds and that light would thus travel with a constant velocity that was independent of the bodies emitting or receiving it.

This would explain the failure to discover the movement of the earth through the ether and it would also answer Einstein's boyhood riddle of how a beam of light would look if you travelled at its own speed. The answer to the riddle was that this would be impossible since only light could reach the speed of light.

Yet the inclusion of Newton's mechanical world within that of Maxwell's electro-magnetism is difficult to conceive. For what it says is this: that while a cricket ball thrown forward at $x$ miles an hour from a train travelling at $y$ miles an hour will apparently be travelling at $x$ plus $y$ miles an hour, something very different happens with light. Whatever the speed of the train from which it is being emitted, light will travel at the same constant speed of some 186,000 miles a second. Furthermore, it will be received at this same constant speed, whatever the speed of the vehicle that receives it — as though the cricket ball thrown from the speeding train would arrive at the fielder on the ground with the same speed whether he was standing still, running in the direction of the train or running towards it.

This of course appeared to be ridiculous. As Bertrand Russell has said, "Everybody knows that if you are on an escalator you reach the top sooner if you walk up than if you stand still. But if the escalator moved with the velocity of light you would reach the top at exactly the same moment whether you walked up or stood still." But Einstein went on to link this assumption with his initial idea — that all the laws of nature are identical to all observers moving uniformly relative to one another. It required more than vision and audacity — qualities demanded of Blondin crossing the Falls, of Whymper nonchalantly tackling the unclimbed Matterhorn, of Whittle, confident that the jet would work. It required also the quality of intuition, a feel for nature as indefinable as a poet's sense of words or the artist's knowledge of what his last dab of materialistic paint can unlock in the human mind.

Einstein once wrote with his collaborator, Leopold Infeld, of "the eternal struggle of the inventive human mind for a fuller understanding of the law governing physical phenomena." Sir Basil Schonland, writing of Maxwell — whose relaxation was writing verse — has no hesitation in describing him as "fey", a word not commonly used to describe scientific genius. Einstein himself was always ready to agree that inventiveness, imagination, the intuitive approach — the very stuff of which artists rather than scientists are usually thought to be made — played a serious part in his work. And when his friend Janos Plesch commented years later that there seemed to be some connenction between mathematics and fiction, a field in which the writer made a world out of invented characters and situations and then compared it with the existing world, Einstein replied that there might be something in this idea.

The problems created by linking Einstein's two assumptions — the similarity of all natural laws for all observers and the constancy of the speed of light in both the electro-magnetic and the mechanical worlds — become evident when one reconsiders Newton's handy sailor. Consider him standing on deck as his ship sails parallel to a long jetty. At each end of the jetty there stands a signal lamp and mid-way between the two lamps there stands an observer. As the sailor passes the observer, flashes of light are sent out by the two lamps. They are sent out, so far as the stationary observer on the jetty is concerned, at exactly the same time. The light rays coming from each end of the jetty have to travel the same distance to reach him, and they will reach him simultaneously. So far, so good. But what about the sailor on the ship — who will have been at an equal distance from both lamps as each sent out its light signal? He knows that both flashes travel with the same speed. Although this speed is very great it is finite, and since he is moving away from one lamp and towards the other he will receive the light signals at different times. As far as he is concerned, they will not have been switched on simultaneously.

Here is the first extraordinary result of linking Einstein's two assumptions. If they are correct — and there is now no doubt about this — the old idea of simultaneity is dethroned; for events which are simultaneous to the observer on the jetty are not simultaneous to the sailor on deck. If the nub of Einstein's Special Relativity can be considered as resting within any one sentence it rests in this realisation that one man's "now" is another man's "then"; that "now" itself is a subjective conception, valid only for an observer within one specific frame of reference.

Yet despite the apparent chaos that this appears to cause, there is one stable factor which it is possible to grasp as thankfully as a rock-climber grasps a jug-handle hold in a dangerous place. That factor is the constancy of the speed of light, and with its aid all natural phenomena can be described in terms which are correct for all frames of reference in constant relative motion with each other. All that was needed, Einstein went on to demonstrate, were the Lorentz transformation equations. Using these instead of the earlier and simpler Newtonian transformations, it was still possible to connect events in any two frames of reference, whether the difference in their relative speeds was that between a sailor and the deck, between a ship and the coast or between a physicist in the laboratory and the electrons of atomic experiments which were already known to move at a sizeable proportion of the speed of light.

But a price had to be paid for resolving this difference between two conceptions of simultaneity; or, put more accurately, it had to be admitted that if the constancy of the speed of light was allowed to restore order from chaos, then not one but two factors in the equations were different from the simple stable things that man had always imagined. For velocity is provided by distance divided by time, and if velocity was invariant in the Lorentz Transformations, not only distance but time itself could be variable. If the Newtonian world of mechanics as well as the Maxwellian world of electromagnetism were subject to the invariant velocity of light both distance — or space — and time were no longer absolute.

It is at this point that the difference between the ideas of Fitzgerald, Lorentz and even Poincaré, and the ideas of Einstein, begin to appear. For Einstein's predecessors, the Lorentz transformation was merely a useful tool for linking objects in relative motion. For him it was not a mathematical tool so much as a revelation about nature itself.

The difference between the earlier view and that of Einstein was exemplified by what Max Born, one of the first expositors of relativity, called "the notorious controversy as to whether the contraction is 'real' or only 'apparent'." Lorentz had one view. "Asked if I consider this contraction as a real one, I should answer 'Yes'," he said. "It is as real as anything we can observe." Sir Arthur Eddington, the later great exponent of Einstein, held a rather different view. "When a rod is started from rest into uniform motion, nothing whatever happens to the rod," he has written. "We say that it contracts; but length is not a property of the rod; it is a relation between the rod and the observer. *Until the observer is specified the length of the rod is quite indeterminate.*"

But it was not only distance but also time which was now seen to be relative. The idea was not entirely new. Voigt had suggested in 1887 that it might be mathematically convenient to use a local time in moving reference systems. But just as Einstein transformed earlier ideas of the curious 'contraction' by showing that it was space itself which was altered by relative speed, so was his concept of relative time far more than a mathematical convenience. It was, in fact, more than a concept in the proper meaning of the word. For with his Special Theory Einstein was not so much propounding an idea as revealing a truth of nature that had previously been overlooked. And as far as time was concerned the truth was that a clock attached to any moving system in relative movement ran more slowly than a clock that was stationary. This was not in any sense a mechanical phenomena; it was not in any way connected with the physical properties of the clock and — as was to be shown less than half a century later — it was as true of clocks operated by atomic vibrations as of those operated by other methods; it was a property of the way in which God had made the world.

Once it is accepted, as it was during the years that followed 1905, that space and time are relatively different in moving and in stationary systems, and that both can be linked by the Lorentz transformations, the position of the velocity of light as the limiting velocity of the universe becomes clear. For the stationary measuring rod which shrinks at an ever-faster rate as its speed increases, and reaches half its original length at nine-tenths the speed of light, would shrink to nothing as it reached ten-tenths. Similarly, the recordings on a clock would slow to a standstill as it reached the same speed.

Three questions arise. One is the question of which is the "real" dimension and which the "real" time. Another is the riddle of why the extraordinary characteristic of the universe revealed by the Special Theory had escaped man's notice for so long. The third is the question of what difference the Special Theory could make to the world. The answer to the first is simple. The "real" dimension and the "real" time is that of the observer, and the stationary and the moving observers are each concerned with their own reality. Just as beauty lies in the eye of the beholder, so does each man carry with him his own space and his own time. But there is one rider to this, a restriction put even on relativity. For while the time at which something happens is indeed a relative matter there is a limitation. For if two events happen at different places in such a way that a light signal starting at the first event could reach the second before it took place, then no use of the Lorentz transformations will make the first event take place after the second one. In other words, relativity does not claim that if a man is hit by a bullet, then it is possible for an observer somewhere else in the universe to have seen the gun being fired after the bullet landed. This, however, does not invalidate the famous thought-experiment — an experiment possible in theory but ruled out by experimental difficulties — concerning the alleged twin-paradox. Here, two twins, one of whom "stays at home" while the other travels through the universe at great speed, age differently — an outcome still disputed by a few who refuse to accept the restrictions on "common sense" that Einstein showed to be necessary.*

The answer to the second question is that the human physiological apparatus is too insensitive to record the extremely minute changes in space and time which are produced by anything less than exceptionally high speeds. In other, and better known ways, the five senses have their limitations. The unreliability of touch is exemplified by the "burn" which cold metal can give. Taste is not only notoriously subjective — "one man's meat, another man's poison" — but is also governed, to an extent not yet fully known, by genetic inheritance. So, too, smell is an indicator whose gross incapacity in humans is thrown into relief by insects who can identify members of their species at ranges of up to a mile. Sound is hardly better. The pattern of "reality" heard by the human is different from that heard by the dog — witness the "soundless" dog-whistles of trainers; while the "real" world of the near-sightless bat is one in which "real" objects are "seen" — and avoided — by ultra-sonic waves which play no part in the construction of the external human world.

And sight, a stimulation of the human retina by certain electro -magnetic waves, is perhaps the most illusory of all senses. "Seeing is believing," and so it is difficult to appreciate that the light of common day — all that unaided human physiology allows in the visual search for the world around — comes through only a narrow slit in a broad curtain. At one end of this curtain there exist the cosmic rays, a trillionth of a centimetre in wavelength; at the other, the infra-red, heat radiations, and the even longer wavelengths used for radar, radio and television. In between lies the narrow band of the visible

---

* Although novelists have often played tricks with time, one of the most extravagant examples was provided, some years before Einstein, by Camille Flammarion, the French astronomer. This was *Lummen*, published in 1873, the story of an adventurer who travelled back through time at 250,000 miles a second to witness, among other things, the end of the battle of Waterloo before the beginning. "You only comprehend things which you perceive," Lumen told the reader. "And as you persist in regarding your ideas of time and space as *absolute*, although they are only *relative*, and thence form a judgment on truths which are quite beyond your sphere, and which are imperceptible to your terrestrial organism and faculties, I should not do you a true service, my friend, in giving you fuller details of my ultra-terrestrial observations . . ."
   The weakness was, of course, shown years later by Einstein's revelation that c was the limiting speed in the universe since at the speed of light a body's mass would become infinitely great. Flammarion — in whose honour the 141st of the minor planets was named Lumen — believed in vegetation on the moon and in advanced and intelligent life on Mars, wrote many books of popular astronomy, including *The Plurality of Inhabited Worlds* which went through thirty editions, and late in life turned to psychic research.

spectrum, for long the only source of man's incomplete visual picture, supplemented but slowly as he used instruments to increase his own limited powers. The landscape seen with human eyes is dramatically different, yet no more "real", than the scene captured on the infra-red plate and showing a mass of detail beyond human vision; the "real" world of the partially colour-blind is the same "real" world seen more colourfully by most humans and both worlds are composed of the same objects which make up the "real" but again different world of totally colour-blind animals.

Thus the human species is unconsciously and inevitably selective in describing the nature of the physical world in which it lives and moves. Once this is appreciated, the implications of Einstein's Special Theory begin to take on a more respectable air. For his achievement showed beyond all reasonable doubt that there existed a further limitation, so far unnoticed, produced by man's lack of experience of speeds comparable to that of light. Until such speeds were reached the variability of space and time which was a product of relative motion was so small as to be unobservable. Thus it was, as Professor Lindemann was later to point out in an article which foreshadowed his power to explain complicated scientific matters to Winston Churchill, "precisely because the old conceptions are so nearly right, because we have no personal experience of their being inaccurate in everyday life, that our so-called common sense revolts when we are asked to give them up, and that we tend to attribute to them a significance infinitely beyond their deserts." In fact the human concepts of absolute space and time, which Einstein appeared to have violated so brusquely, had been produced simply by the rough-and-ready observation of countless generations of men using a physiological apparatus too coarse-grained to supply any better approximation of reality. As Bertrand Russell once wrote in describing the speeds at which relativity is significant, "since every-day life does not confront us with such swiftly moving bodies, Nature, always economical, had educated common sense only up to the level of everyday life."

Thus Special Relativity did not so much "overthrow Newton" as show that Newtonian ideas were valid only in circumstances which were restricted even though they did appear to permeate everyday life. As Oppenheimer has written, the apparent paradoxes of relativity

> do not involve any contradictions on the part of nature; what they
> do involve is a gross change, a rather sharp change, from what learned
> people and ordinary people thought throughout the past centuries,

thought as long as they had thought about things at all. The simple facts, namely that light travels with a velocity that cannot be added to or subtracted from by moving a source of light, the simple fact that objects do contract when they are in motion, the simple fact that processes are slowed down when they take place in motion, and very much so if they move with velocities comparable to the speed of light — these are new elements of the natural world and what the theory of relativity has done is to give coherence and meaning to the connection between them.

But Einstein's revelation was one which only a very few could ever hope to prove by experiment in the laboratory and which would remain forever outside the experience of most people. Thus to the non-scientist — as well as to some physicists — Einstein had really offended against common sense, the limited yardstick with which men measure the exterior world. In addition, the mental effort required before the theory could be fully grasped turned it for the general public, when they were eventually forced to notice it, into a fantasy which further separated the world of science from the world of ordinary men and women. Only Einstein could have transformed amused scepticism of the theory into a veneration for its author which no one deplored more than Einstein himself.

Yet even when it is accepted that the theory of special relativity is not a metaphysical concept but, as Einstein was never tired of pointing out, an explanation of certain observable features of the universe, even when it is appreciated how this explanation had hitherto slipped through the net of human understanding, the third question remains. For at first glance the Special Theory appears to deal with matters that are outside the range of human experience. Nevertheless, there are two answers, one general and the other specific, to the question of what difference the Special Theory was to make to the world.

The general answer has been concisely given by Eddington, the British astronomer who was to play an important role in Einstein's later life.

Distance and duration are the most fundamental terms in physics; velocity, acceleration, force, energy, and so on, all depend of them; and we can scarcely make any statement in physics without direct or indirect reference to them. Surely then we can best indicate the revolutionary consequences of [relativity] by the statement that distance and duration, and all the physical quantities derived from them, do not as hitherto supposed refer to anything absolute in the external world, but are relative quantities which alter when we pass from one observer to another with different motion. The consequence in physics of the discovery that a yard is not an absolute chunk of space, and that what is a yard for one observer may be eighteen inches for another observer, may be compared with the consequences in economics of the discovery that a pound sterling is not an absolute quantity of wealth, and in certain circumstances may "really" be seven and sixpence.

However, the differences in these varying values of time and space were so small as to become significant only when the speeds involved were far beyond the range of human experience. How, then, could they really affect the world? It is here that one comes to the more specialised answer, and to what, in the light of history, can be considered as either an extraordinary coincidence or as part of the natural evolution of science.

For Einstein's Special Theory was evolved just as the investigations of physicists were reaching into the sub-atomic world of the nucleus, and as astronomers were for the first time peering out beyond the confines of the galaxy in which the earth is a minute speck towards the immensities of outer space. In the atomic world there were already known to be particles such as the electron which moved at speeds which were a sizeable percentage of the speed of light; and in outer space, beyond our own galaxy, it was soon to be discovered that there were others which were moving at similar speeds. Thus in both of the fresh fields which were opening up during the first decades of the twentieth century, the microscopically small and the macroscopically large, the revelations of relativity were to have a significant place.

But there was another, and in some ways more important, result which flowed directly from the acceptance of Einstein's theory which during the next decade was seen as inevitable. For the absolute quality of space and time had not only been generally accepted up to now but had been confirmed by the overwhelming bulk of observational evidence. Now it was realised that the conventional belief, so soundly induced from observation, was gravely lacking, a circumstance with important philosophical implications. For it underlined, more strongly than had previously been the case, that science might really be a search not for absolute truth but for a succession of theories that would progressively approach the truth. It suggested, furthermore, that the best path to be followed might not be that of observation followed by the induction of general laws, but the totally different process of postulating a theory and then discovering whether or not the facts fitted it. Thus a theory should start with more scientific and philosophical assumptions than the facts alone warranted. A decade later the method was to provide the startling results of the General Theory.

How much, it is now necessary to ask, did these revelations owe to Einstein's predecessors? It should be clear by this time that the problem he tackled was different from that faced by Fitzgerald and Lorentz who were mainly concerned with explaining the awkward result of an important experiment, and different in many ways from that faced by Poincaré, whose problem was largely a philosophical one. Einstein, not over-concerned with specific experiments, or with philosophy, had a grander aim: to penetrate the fog and discern more clearly the principles on which the material world had been built. "The theory of relativity", he once said, "was nothing more than a further consequential development of the field theory." Asked by Hans Reichenbach, later a Berlin colleague and later still a professor of philosophy at the University of California, how the theory of relativity had been arrived at, he "replied that he had discovered it because he was so firmly convinced of the harmony of the universe".

Yet in science as elsewhere, "no man is an Island, entire of itself". Einstein himself spoke repeatedly in later life of his debt to Lorentz — "the four men who laid the foundations of physics on which I have been able to construct my theory are Galileo, Newton, Maxell and Lorentz" he said during his visit to the United States in 1921. In more general terms he emphasised that "in science... the work of the individual is so bound up with that of his scientific predecessors and contemporaries that it appears almost as an impersonal product of his generation." Thus the problem resolves itself into that of deciding the extent of Einstein's knowledge of specific papers and of the Michelson-Morley experiment.*

Einstein himself made a number of statements on the subject. At first, when he spoke of relativity in Berlin, in the United States and in London, he was apt to stress, as in London in 1921, merely "that this theory is not speculative in origin; it owes its invention entirely to the desire to make physical theory fit observed fact as well as possible." At Columbia University, the same year, he noted that "to start with, it disturbed me that electrodynamics should pick out *one* state of motion in preference to others, without any experi-

---

* The most detailed analysis of the situation has been by Gerald Holton in a number of papers. See in particular "On the Origins of the Special Theory of Relativity," *American Journal of Physics*, Vol. 28 (1960) pp. 627—636 and "Einstein, Michelson and the 'Crucial' Experiment", *Isis* Vol. 60. Part 2, № 202, (Summer, 1969) pp. 133—197.

mental justification for this preferential treatment. Thus arose the
Special Theory of Relativity . . ." Both statements tended by implication to sustain the idea that the Michelson-Morley experiment had
played a part in his thinking.

Later evidence provided by Einstein is contradictory and is
probably influenced by the fact that, as Maitland put it, "events now
long in the past were once in the future". "When I asked him how he
had learned of the Michelson-Morley experiment", says R. S. Shankland, who visited Einstein on February 4th, 1950, from the Case
Institute of Technology, while preparing a historical account of the
work, "he told me he had become aware of it through the writings
of H. A. Lorentz, but *only after 1905* had it come to his attention.
'Otherwise,' he said, 'I would have mentioned it in my paper.' He
continued to say that the experimental results which had influenced
him most were the observations of stellar aberration and Fizeau's
measurements of the speed of light in moving water. 'They were
enough,' he said." Yet when Shankland again visited Princeton on
October 24th, 1952, Einstein was not so certain. "This is not so
easy," Shankland quotes him as saying.

> "I am not sure when I first heard of the Michelson experiment. I was
> not conscious that it had influenced me directly during the seven
> years that relativity had been my life. I guess I just took it for granted
> that it was true." However, Einstein said that in the years 1905 to
> 1909, he thought a great deal about Michelson's result, in his discus-
> sions with Lorentz and others in his thinking about general relativity.
> He then realised (so he told me) that he had also been conscious of
> Michelson's result before 1905 partly through his reading of the papers
> of Lorentz and more because he had assumed this result of Michelson
> to be true.

In 1954, for Michael Polanyi's *The Art of Knowing*, Einstein
personally approved the statement that "the Michelson-Morley experiment had a negligible effect on the discovery of relativity". Furthermore, a supplementary note from Dr. N. Balazs, who was working
with Einstein in Princeton in the summer of 1953, and who
questioned him on the subject for Polanyi, runs as follows:

> The Michelson-Morley experiment had no role in the foundation of
> the theory. He got acquainted with it while reading Lorentz' paper
> about the theory of this experiment (he of course does not remember
> exactly when, though prior to his paper), but it had no further influ-
> ence on Einstein's consideration and the theory of relativity was not
> founded to explain its outcome at all.

To David Ben-Gurion, who asked whether the theory of relativity was the result of thought only, Einstein confirmed that this was so but added: "I naturally had before me the experimental works of those preceding me. These served as material for my thoughts and studies." And finally there is a letter from Einstein to Carl Seelig, published in the *Technische Rundschau* № 20, 47, Jahrgang, Berne on May 6th, 1955, two months after Einstein's death, in which he stresses that the Special Theory of Relativity was ripe for discovery in 1905.

From this not entirely satisfactory evidence two general conclusions have been drawn. One is the view of the popular eulogy, in which Einstein is seen as the inspired genius, working in an intellectual vacuum and drawing the Special Theory from his brain like the conjuror producing the rabbit from the hat. The other is typified by Sir Edmund Whittaker, the notable British physicist who in Einstein's biographical memoir for the Royal Society wrote that he had "adopted Poincaré's Principle of Relativity (using Poincaré's name for it) as a new basis of physics", a view which tends to produce enraged speechlessness in some scientists.

The truth appears to be different from both tidy black-and-white versions. It is rather that Einstein, travelling from his own starting point to his own lonely destination, noted Lorentz' work as bearing on his own, different, problems. When light dawned, during that creative fortnight in 1905, what Einstein had already heard of the Michelson-Morley experiment fell into place. But it was no more than an interesting piece of evidence which gave comforting confirmation of the theory which he had already decided could provide a more accurate picture of the material world than that provided by Newtonian mechanics alone. What he had produced was, as he wrote in *The Times* in 1919, "simply a systematic extension of the electrodynamics of Clerk-Maxwell and Lorentz". Certainly Lorentz himself had no doubt about whose theory it was. "To discuss Einstein's Principle of Relativity here in Gottingen . . ." he said when he spoke there in 1910, "appears to be a particularly welcome task."

If there are any missing acknowledgments in Einstein's work, they belong not to Michelson-Morley, to Lorentz, Fitzgerald or Poincaré but to August Föppl, a German administrator and teacher whose *Introduction to Maxwell's Theory of Electricity* was almost certainly studied by Einstein. The famous relativity paper has similarities in style and argument with Föppl's treatment of "relative and absolute motion in space"; and Föppl himself writes of "a deep-going revision of that conception of space which has been impressed upon human thinking in its previous period of development" as presenting "perhaps the most important problem of science of our time".

Thus Föppl, like the Lorentz equations, can justifiably be considered as another of the useful instruments lying to hand which Einstein was able to utilise. As *The Times* was later to say of Einstein's General Theory, there is no need to defend his originality. "The genius of Einstein consists in taking up the uninterpreted experiments and scattered suggestions of his predecessors, and welding them into a comprehensive scheme that wins universal admiration by its simplicity and beauty."

The "comprehensive scheme" of 1905 had shown that space and time, previously thought to be absolute, in fact depended on relative motion. Yet these are but two of the three yardsticks used to measure the nature of the physical world. The third is mass. Was this, also, linked in some hitherto unexpected way with the speed of light? Einstein considered the question.

The result was a brief paper which appeared in the *"Annalen der Physik"* later in 1905 almost as a footnote to his earlier relativity paper It asked whether the inertia of a body depended on its energy content, and concluded with the comment that the theory might be put to the test by the use of such materials as radium salts whose energy content was very variable, and that radiation appeared to convey inertia between emitting and absorbing bodies. Yet the immediately important conclusion was that mass increased with relative speed. There had already been laboratory examples of this awkward process. Both J. J. Thomson in Cambridge and subsequently W. Kauffmann in Göttingen, had investigated the ways in which fast cathode rays, the steams of electrons whose existence had been postulated by Lorentz and confirmed by Thomson, could be electromagnetically deflected; both had found that mass of the particle appeared to depend on velocity. Some years later F. Hasenöhrl had shown that light radiation enclosed in a vessel increased that vessel's resistance to acceleration — and that its mass was altered in the process. Finally, in 1900, Poincaré had suggested that this inertia or resistance to acceleration was a property of all energy and not merely of electromagnetic energy.

Now Einstein leap-frogged one jump ahead, ignoring the separate experimental results which had been puzzling individual workers and coming up with a simple overall explanation which, almost staring them in the face, had appeared too simple to be true. All mass was merely congealed energy; all energy merely liberated matter. Thus the photons or light quanta of the photo-electric effect were just particles which had shed their mass and were travelling with the speed of light in the form of energy; while energy below the speed of light had been transformed by its slowing down, a transformation which had had the effect of congealing it into matter. There had been a whiff of this very idea from Newton, who in his *Opticks* had asked: "Are not gross Bodies and Light convertible into one another, and may not Bodies receive much of their Activity from the Particles of Light which enter their Composition?" The apparent rightness of this was underlined by his comment, a few lines lower, that "the changing of Bodies into Light, and Light into Bodies, is very conformable to the Course of Nature, which seems delighted with Transmutations."

The nub of this revelation — which involved two separate things, the difference between the mass of a body at rest and its mass in motion, and the transformation of a material body into energy — linked the previously separate concepts of conservation of energy and conservation of matter, and was embodied in two equations. One showed that the mass of a body moving at any particular velocity was its mass at rest divided by $\sqrt{1 - v^2/c^2}$. This quickly provides a clue to man's long ignorance of the difference between the mass of a body at rest and in movement; for the difference will be very small indeed until the velocity concerned leaves the speeds of ordinary life and begins to approach the velocity of light. As with space and time, the changes are too small to be noted by man's inadequate senses. The second equation follows on from the fact that the motion whose increase raises the mass of a body is a form of energy. This is the famous $E - mc^2$ which states, in the shorthand of science, that the energy contained in matter is equal in ergs to its mass in grammes multiplied by the square of the velocity of light in centimetres per second. Here again, one needed no mathematical expertise to see the essence of the argument: the velocity of light being what it is, a very small amount of mass is equivalent to a vast amount of energy.

Einstein's "follow-through" from his Special Theory of Relativity thus explained how electrons weighed more when moving than when at rest, since this was the natural result of their speed. It helped to explain how materials such as radium, whose radioactivity still puzzled the men experimenting with them, were able to eject particles at great speeds and to go on doing so for long periods, since creation of the comparatively large amounts of energy involved could be attained by the loss of a minute amount of mass. It helped to explain, furthermore, the ability of the sun — and of the stars — to continue radiating a large amount of light and heat by losing only a small amount of mass.

Forty years on, the facts of nature as revealed by Einstein's equation were to be demonstrated in another way. For by then it had been discovered that if the nucleus of a heavy atom could be split into two parts, the mass of its two fragments would be less than that of the original nucleus. The difference in mass would have been transformed into energy; its amount would be minute, but the energy released would be this minute mass multiplied by the square of the speed of light — the energy which, released from vast numbers of nuclei by the fission process, destroyed Hiroshima and Nagasaki.

The chances of splitting the atom appeared insoluble in 1905. But the equation was there. And for writers and cranks, for visionaries and men who lived on the borderland of the mind, a new pipedream became possible. A few scientists thought along similar lines, and in 1921 Hans Thirring commented: "... it takes one's breath away to think of what might happen in a town, if the dormant energy of a single brick were to be set free, say in the form of an explosion. It would suffice to raze a city with a million inhabitants to the ground." Most of his professional colleagues did not speculate thus far. Rutherford maintained almost to the end of his life, in 1937, that the use of the energy locked within the atom was "moonshine". And when a young man approached Einstein in Prague in 1921, wanting to produce a weapon from nuclear energy based on $E = mc^2$, he was told to calm himself. "You haven't lost anything if I don't discuss your work with you in detail," Einstein said. "Its foolishness is evident at first glance. You cannot learn anything more from a longer discussion."

The demonstration of Einstein's mass-energy equation in the destruction of Hiroshima and Nagasaki has naturally given this by-product of his Special Theory a popular predominance over all others. But it should be emphasised that nuclear fission, whose utilisation made nuclear weapons possible, was "discovered" by other men moving along very different paths. Fission illustrated — dramatically in the case of the atomic bombs — Einstein's mass-energy equation rather than being based on it.

But the atomic bomb came forty years after Einstein had cut at the foundation of classical physics, and the effects of relativity during these four decades were to be all-pervasive. So much so that while the immense effects of evolution and communism, those two other revolutionary ideas of the last hundred years, are as toughly debated as they are freely admitted, a different attitude exists about relativity. So much has it been assimilated into human knowledge that it is sometimes overlooked altogether.

Yet there are three ways in which man's relationship with his physical world has been changed by relativity. The first, and possibly the least important, is that it has helped him to understand some phenomena which would otherwise have been incomprehensible. The behaviour of nuclear particles discovered during the last half-century is only the most obvious example. "We use it," Oppenheimer has said of Special Relativity, "literally in almost every branch of nuclear physics and many branches of atomic physics, and in all branches of physics dealing with the fundamental particles. It has been checked and cross-checked and counter-checked in the most numerous ways and it is a very rich part of our heritage."

In addition to supplying this very practical tool, relativity has enabled man to give more accurate, more descriptive accounts of the world of which he is a part. As Philipp Frank has pointed out, the plain statement that a table is three feet long is not only incomplete but meaningless when compared with the statement that it is three feet long relative to the room in which it stands. "Relativism," he says, "means the introduction of a richer language which allows us to meet adequately the requirements of the enriched experience. We are now able to cover these new facts by plain and direct words and to come one step nearer to what one may call the 'plain truth about the universe'."

It is this "plain truth about the universe" which suggests the third and most important change that relativity has produced. Its epistemological implications are still hotly debated. Nevertheless, it is indisputable that while the theory has enabled man to describe his position in the universe with greater accuracy it has also thrown into higher relief the limitations of his own personal experiences.

> Physical science [Sir James Jeans has emphasised] does not of course suggest that we must abandon the intuitive concepts of space and time which we derive from individual experience. These may mean nothing to nature, but they still mean a good deal to us. Whatever conclusions the mathematicians may reach, it is certain that our newspapers, our historians and story-tellers will still place their truths and fictions in a framework of space and time; they will continue to say — this event happened at such an instant in the course of the ever-flowing stream of time, this other event at another instant lower down the stream, and so on.
>
> Such a scheme is perfectly satisfactory for any single individual, or for any group of individuals whose experiences keep them fairly close together in space and time — and, compared with the vast ranges of nature, all the inhabitants of the earth form such a group. The

theory of relativity merely suggests that such a scheme is private to single individuals or to small colonies of individuals; it is a parochial method of measuring, and so is not suited for nature as a whole. It can represent all the facts and phenomena of nature, but only by attaching a subjective taint to them all; it does not represent nature so much as what the inhabitants of one rocket, or of one planet, or better still an individual pair of human eyes, see of nature. Nothing in our experiences or experiments justifies us in extending either this or any other parochial scheme to the whole of nature, on the supposition that it represent any sort of objective reality.

Relativity has thus helped human beings to appreciate their place in the physical world just as T.H. Huxley's *Man's Place in Nature* gave them context in the biological world. It is significant that one of the most hard-headed remarks on relativity made after Einstein's death should come from a religious journal. His theory has shown, remarked *The Tablet*, that "space and time for the physicist are defined by the operations used to measure them, and that any theory in which they appear must implicitly take these operations into account. Thus modern science looks at nature from the viewpoint of a man, not from that of an angel."

# 5

# *FRUITS OF SUCCESS*

EINSTEIN'S PAPERS OF 1905 REVEALED TO THE SMALL HANDFUL OF leading European physicists that they had a potential leader in their midst; only the next decade would show whether that potential was to be realised. Other men, in the arts as well as in science, in politics and in war, had sent up sparks of genius during their early years yet failed to set the world ablaze. And even if Einstein did have the qualities needed to carry through and exploit his early promise, there were still a dozen ways in which chance might circumscribe or cut short his future — the Great War, taking Hasenöhrl on the German side and Moseley on Britain's, was only one pitfall lying ahead.

However, Einstein's statistical work which led to his paper on the Brownian motion, his conception of photons, and his adventurous theory of relativity, were all soon seen as more than isolated efforts. Instead, it became clear that they were logically consequential operations, each of which could be further developed to throw fresh light on the current problems of physics. In this development he was to be helped by the climate of the times. From 1905 until 1914 he was able to think and read and move in a truly international scientific society that was shattered with the outbreak of the Great War and was not fully restored for almost half a century. Travelling from Berne or Zurich to Leiden or Salzburg, to Brussels or Vienna, he crossed frontiers that were political but not cultural. Talking with Lorentz in Holland, with Mach in Austria, and in Belgium with Rutherford from England, Madame Curie and Langevin from France, Planck and Nernst from Berlin, he was embraced as a full member of that small truly international group whose work was concentrated on the single task of discovering the nature of the physical world. For a short while, it was a scientific world without politics, an unusual state of affairs to which Einstein always looked back as though it were the norm rather than an exception which occurred as science prepared to tackle the riddles of the atom. Among these colleagues he moved with a calm assurance and a quizzical smile; for all his innate humbleness, both came from an inner certainty of being right. Thus he looked ahead from 1905, untroubled by the Jewish problem which was later to engage his energies, unworried by thoughts of war in a Europe which had surely given up such a recklessly wasteful occupation, totally unaware that his work with brain, pen and paper would have any impact beyond the circumscribed scientific field in which he moved.

The story of his life for the next decade is therefore first of scientific consolidation and then of scientific exploration, of increasing contact with the men and women who produced the twentieth century's scientific revolution. In it there appear rarely, and as if by accident, the figures of his family and the everyday emotions which move most ordinary men. He was kind, but in a slightly casual way; amiable as long as people allowed him to get on with his work, and totally uninterested in what he regarded as the superficialities of life. Thus when his wife returned from Serbia, where she had been on holiday, with his two sons, and announced that she had become a Catholic, the news left him unmoved, as he made startlingly clear in a comment to Professor Hurwitz. He did not care.

In the summer of 1905 he visited Belgrade with Mileva. They stayed with her relatives and friends, spending a week in the lakeside holiday resort of Kijevo, and then travelling on to Novi Sad where he met his wife's parents for the first time. It was one of numerous holiday journeys to what is now Yugoslavia but was then part of the Austro-Hungarian Empire, holidays which are remembered today by his eldest son Hans as pleasant rambling interludes during which the odd character of a father amiably visits his in-laws from another world, accompanied first by his small son and, later, by a baby second son as well. Einstein never forgot his Serbian hosts and kept up an intermittent correspondence with them for nearly half a century — mentioning only casually, they recounted after his death, that he had been awarded a Nobel Prize.

Other holidays were spent in the nearby Oberland, sometimes in Murren, not yet over-fashionable, quiet holidays of a minor civil servant who superficially seemed likely to spend the rest of his life on much the same local round. He would occasionally visit Cäsar Koch in Antwerp. He kept in touch with his former colleagues of Aarau or Zurich, and to friends and relations he jotted off the postcards with their spidery writing that were later to become collector's items. It was all rather low key. Yet it was this that still seemed to

be the genuine Einstein. Surely the real person was the slightly
shabby, poor man's Bohemian of the rather broken-down apartment
in Märktgasse. Surely the potential genius of which whispers began
to come from Planck and the great names in Berlin was merely a
dream-figure which had stepped down from one of Paul Klee's early
landscapes.

The only hint that the potential genius might be the real Einstein came from his ferocious concentration on the task to be done
and his determination that nothing should be allowed to divert him
from it. A few years earlier it might have been only a hangover from
graduate enthusiasm; now it began to look as though it was part and
parcel of the mature man. Here there is a similarity — first pointed
out by C. P. Snow — between Einstein and Churchill. The comparison
is not surprising once the picture-book image of both scientist and
statesman is scraped away to reveal the machinery beneath. Of
Churchill it has been written that almost obsessional concentration
"was one of the keys to his character. It was not always obvious,
but he never really thought of anything but the job in hand. He was
not a fast worker, especially when dealing with papers, but he was
essentially a non-stop worker." Einstein, with the black notebook in
his pocket, handy for the moment when the sails began to hang limp,
reading while he rocked the cradle in his Berne apartment, was much
the same.

He had his music. But this, as he would explain on occasions,
was in some ways an extension of his thinking processes, a method
of allowing the subconscious to solve particularly tricky problems.
"Whenever he felt that he had come to the end of the road or into a
difficult situation in his work," his eldest son has said, "he would
take refuge in music, and that would usually resolve all his difficulties."

There was also his sailing, and here a remark by his second wife
is pertinent — "He is so much on the water that people cannot easily
reach him." On the Zurichsee, on the Lake of Thun or on any of
Switzerland's myriad of small lakes, where the hand responded instinctively to the demands of the breeze and an able man could let a
boat sail itself, the mind could get on with the job without fear of
interruption. What is more, the surroundings helped. "He needed
this kind of relaxation from his intense work," says his eldest son.
And with relaxation there would often come the solution. For his
work needed neither laboratory nor equipment.

During the years that immediately followed 1905 Einstein is
thus outwardly the minor Jewish civil servant of slightly radical

ideas, the professional odd man out, with a Slav wife and illusions of grandeur that had actually gained him a doctorate of philosophy. But slowly, and as surely as the tide comes in, the other image began to harden, the picture of the man who for some inexplicable reason really was being sought out by those who had made their way in the world. This metamorphosis was nothing to do with the popular acclaim which brought Einstein international renown after the First World War. As far as the outside world was concerned he remained totally unknown until 1912, when some aspects of relativity became headline news in Austria, and almost totally unknown until 1919. But in the academic world the significance of the relativity papers soon began to be appreciated.

First off the mark seems to have been Wilhelm Wien who as editor of the *Annalen der Physik* had accepted the papers.

In Berlin, Planck was equally quick. This is confirmed by Max von Laue, the young son of an army officer whose path was to cross and recross Einstein's for half a century. Von Laue had been born in Coblenz within a few months of Einstein and had gained his doctorate at Strasbourg before starting the work on X-rays for which he later won a Nobel Prize. When he came to Berlin in the autumn of 1905 as assistant to Planck, he has written, the first lecture which he heard in the physics colloquium of the University was one by Planck on Einstein's work, "On the Electro-Dynamics of Moving Bodies," which had appeared in September. It described the beginnings of the theory of relativity. This theory immediately made the greatest impression on him, although he needed years to understand it thoroughly. But he used the next summer holidays to make a tour through the Swiss mountains in order to visit Albert Einstein in Berne.

Another man who quickly realised the significance of his work was the Pole, Professor Witkowski, who after reading the famous Volume 17 of *Annalen der Physik* exclaimed to his friend, Professor Loria in Cracow, "A new Copernicus is born! Read Einstein's paper." But there was a sequel — apparently in 1907 — according to Einstein's future collaborator, Leopold Infeld. "Later, when Professor Loria met Professor Max Born at a physics meeting, he told him about Einstein and asked Born if he had read the paper," writes Infeld. "It turned out that neither Born nor anyone else there had heard about Einstein." They went to the library, took from the bookshelves the seventeenth volume of *Annalen der Physik,* and started to read the articles. "Although I was quite familiar with the relativistic idea and the Lorentz transformations," Born has said of the incident, "Einstein's reasoning was a revelation to me." Elsewhere he has said that the paper "had a stronger influence on my thinking than any other scientific experience."

It is clear that during the years immediately following 1905 the concept of relativity percolated slowly through accepted ideas like rain through limestone rather than breaking them down like the weight of water cracking a dam. But as water slowly penetrates the myriad channels, so did the Special Theory begin to affect the whole body of physics. There were some setbacks, and one early reaction to the theory was of unqualified rejection. It came as a paper by W. Kaufmann on the constitution of the electron, and it included the following blunt statement: "I anticipate right away the general result of the measurements to be described in the following: *the results are not compatible with the Lorentz-Einsteinian fundamental assumptions.*" The results had been obtained experimentally in Kaufmann's laboratory and were in line with other theories which had given plausible accounts of the electron's characteristics without invoking relativity. But neither Einstein nor anyone else fully realised that the technology of the times was incapable of delivering results accurate enough to support or refute the theory of relativity.

The scientific world awaited Einstein's reply with some interest — much as Central Europe held its breath after Tetzel had committed Luther's theses to the flames. It came the following year in the first of two articles in the *Jahrbuch der Radioaktivität und Elektronik.* Taking the theory of relativity a number of important steps further forward, the articles were to be of great importance for other reasons. Here it is only necessary to note the startling way, suggesting assurance or arrogance according to point of view, with which Einstein handled Kaufmann. For while he agreed that Kaufmann's results could not apparently be faulted, he refused to take this too seriously. The great scientific theories that mattered, he inferred, explained a blueprint of nature as revealed in general terms; only then was a search made to see whether minor details supported it. Einstein's attitude was not that of *tant pis pour les faits;* but to some sceptics it must have looked dangerously like it.

His attitude was all the more surprising in that it was taken by a young man who lacked academic status. Einstein was still a humble Patent Office employee, even though he was beginning to be sought out, personally or through correspondence, by young physicists who wished to discuss the vital affairs of theoretical physics.

The theory of relativity remained the central scientific problem with which he concerned himself. He saw it, rightly most scientists feel today, as one of the vital factors in man's understanding of the natural world, a factor whose omission had distorted ideas across the whole spectrum of physical knowledge. But there was another of equal importance; this was the conception of quanta which Planck had seen as accounting for certain characteristics of radiation and which Einstein with his light quanta or photons had adventurously developed. The subject, which seemed to present numerous and almost insuperable problems, continued to exercise him. For while the theory of the photon helped to clarify heat, radiation and the photo-electric effect, it totally failed to explain interference, the diffraction of light, or other phenomena. There was something, if not wrong, then at least incomplete about the explanations that had so far been put forward, and during these years in Berne Einstein worked hard to lessen this.

One of his confidants was young Laub, who during his degree examination had mentioned relativity. Wien disagreed with certain of his statements and advised him to talk with Einstein. Early in 1907 Laub therefore travelled to Berne and was drawn, like everyone else who met Einstein on a professional basis, into an obsessional discussion that soon rose and swamped everything else. Their interchange of letters gives a good deal of insight into Einstein's preoccupations and into the conditions under which he worked during these years. "He found Einstein kneeling in front of the oven, poking the fire, quite alone in his flat . . ." says Seelig. "They found so much to discuss that for several weeks at midday, and during the evening, Laub fetched his new sparring partner from the Patent Office, and he visited him again the following year." Their intellectual collaboration produced three joint works dealing with the basic equations of electro-magnetism and the pondero-motive force of the electro-magnetic field. As the well-trained mathematician, Laub naturally took over the complicated mathematical tasks, while Einstein concentrated on their physical implications.

In the letters between them there is constant reference to the radiation problem, which continued to absorb Einstein. The need for solving it seemed pressing enough, for both Lorentz and Planck continued to stress that the purely corpuscular theory of light which it appeared to postulate failed to account for many observable phenomena. However, Einstein struggled on, as intrigued as his contemporaries at the dual qualities of light which neither he nor any of them could as yet resolve. What he did succeed in doing during this period was to apply Planck's quantum formula to the vibrations of atoms, molecules and solids, thereby explaining the deviations of the specific heat of solids from the classical laws. The fact that different amounts of heat were needed to raise different solids the same number of degrees had so far been difficult to explain satisfactorily. But in "Planck's Theory of Radiation and the Theory of Specific Heat" Einstein opened the door to a solution. This decisive step led to a good deal of fresh experimental research, to the investigations by Nernst and his followers on specific heat at very low temperatures, and to the solution of subsequent problems by such men as Lindemann, Debye and Born.

Meanwhile his thoughts were increasingly preoccupied with another subject, linked as closely to philosophy as to physics, more nebulous yet even more fundamental. This was the looming problem of causality, taken for granted in one shape or form for centuries by the majority of scientists who believed that the explanation of every event could be found in its antecedent conditions. The billiard balls on the green baize tables moved along paths that could be predicted once the vectors imposed on them were known; and if the equations involved had for strict accuracy to be those of the Special Theory rather than of Newtonian mechanics, effect yet followed cause in exactly the same way. Surely the motions of the atoms, and of their components, infinitely small though they were, could be comparably predicted once it became possible to quantify the forces imposed upon them?

This was not to be so. Doubts had been raised with the discovery of radioactivity and of the way in which the atoms comprising an element distintegrated — apparently without reason and in a pattern which enabled the statistician to forecast the future of a collection of atoms but not of an individual atom. At first it had appeared that this statistical forecast might be similar to the prediction of how a tossed coin would fall — used only because sufficient factors were not known with enough accuracy to allow the use of anything better. Once enough was known, it would surely be possible not merely to predict statistically the outcome of a series of coin-tossings, but to predict in terms of cause and effect the result of each particular toss. Surely, it was argued, the grand designs of nature operated along similar causal lines, with all that was required being merely sufficient information on the causes.

On this question, which grew steadily in importance as the century advanced, Einstein became increasingly separated from the bulk of his colleagues. While they moved on, he remained faithful to the attitude he had adopted as early as 1907 and which he revealed in a letter of that year to Philipp Frank, a young Austrian who had just taken his doctorate at the University of Vienna. In a paper

entitled "Causality and Knowledge" Frank had set out to show that
the law of causality "can be neither confirmed nor disproved by
experience; not, however, because it is a truth known *a priori* but
because it is a purely conventional definition". Einstein, who developed a rich correspondence with any scientist who had similar interests, wrote to Frank.

> He approved the logic of my argument [Frank has said] but he
> objected that it demonstrates only that there is a conventional element
> in the law of causality and not that there is merely a convention or
> definition. He agreed with me that, whatever may happen in nature,
> one can never prove that a violation of the law of causality has taken
> place. One can always introduce by convention a terminology by
> which this law is saved. But it could happen that in this way our
> language and terminology might become highly complicated and
> cumbersome.

What Einstein was saying was this: if all the details of a coin's
velocity, mass, moment of inertia, and other relevant factors were
known as soon as it was in the air, and if it was still impossible to
tell only by statistics which way it would fall, this was due not to a
failure of causality. There was simply another causative factor which
had not been considered. So with the laws of nature. Current ability
to understand events in the atomic world only in statistical terms
sprang from the limitations imposed by ignorance. In due course
scientists might learn all the necessary facts, and the mysteries
would then be removed. In 1907 it was difficult to dispute that this
would eventually be so. The arguments were not developed until
more than a decade later when the progress of physics slowly revealed that at the atomic level the laws of cause and effect give way to
the laws of chance. Einstein remained unmoved, acknowledging that
the work of his earlier years had led to the new situation, confident
that "God did not play dice with the world."

All this lay two decades away as Einstein the scientist built up
his connections with Europe's leading physicists and Einstein the
Patent Office employee played the role of minor civil servant. The
situation was growing more incongruous. But the reflection was not
on Einstein so much as on a system which could apparently find no
place for him in the academic world. The first steps to remedy this
were taken in 1907 — mainly at the instigation of Professor Kleiner
who in 1905 had helped to push through Einstein's Ph. D. in Zurich.
Kleiner wanted Einstein on his staff. But during the early years of
the century it was impossible for a man to be appointed professor in
Switzerland — or in most other Continental countries — before serv-

ing a spell as *privatdozent*. The holders of such posts, which have no equivalent in Britain or the United States, lecture as much or as little as they like and normally receive only nominal sums from the students whom they serve.

In 1907 Kleiner proposed that Einstein should apply for a post as *privatdozent* in the University of Berne, a post in which the looseness of obligations would enable him to combine it easily with his Patent Office job. Einstein applied for entry to the Faculty of Theoretical Physics, submitting as proof of his ability the printed version of the paper which had won him his Zurich doctorate. With his usual mixture of impatience and optimism he did not wait for the outcome before writing to the Dean and suggesting what he might do. However, he was to receive a shock. His application was rejected; partly because it was too short, an example of academic red tape, as he later noted; partly because Professor Aimé Forster did not want a *privatdozent* on his staff. There were probably other reasons. The aura of the great man that has surrounded Einstein's name since 1919, when his work on the General Theory suddenly became well known, has overshadowed his position and his nature, during the years before the First World War. The Einstein of the early 1900s was not only a scientist of minor academic qualifications who had launched an obscure theory on the world. He was also the man who failed to fit in or to conform, the non-respecter of professors, the dropper of conversational bricks, the awkward Jewish customer, the man who although approaching the age of thirty still seemed to prefer the company of students. However, help was at hand. Shortly afterwards the decision was revised and Einstein appointed.

Thus he started on his academic career at the age of twenty-nine. His first lectures as a *privatdozent* in Berne were delivered in the winter term of 1908—9. The subject was "The Theory of Radiation". He had only four students and during the following term the numbers shrank to a single man. Formality was abandoned and the session continued in Einstein's own rooms. The contradictions of his life still obstinately continued. The genius who had at first been rejected by the E. T. H. had been succeeded by the minor Patent Office official who in a single issue of the *Annalen der Physik* had delivered three major blows at the accepted body of physics. Now this picture was succeeded by that of the apparently unsuccessful university part-timer. But once again the situation was on the point of being transformed.

The events which combined to give Einstein a new status were his formulation of the Principle of Equivalence, the cornerstone of the Theory of General Relativity, and the arrival of two papers from Hermann Minkowski, who had left Zurich in 1902 for Göttingen, which gave mathematical formality to Special Relativity.

The Principle of Equivalence, which first saw the light of day in *"Relativitatsprinzip und die aus demselben gezogenen Folgerungen"* ("The Principle of Relativity and the Inferences to be Drawn from it"), published in two issues of the *Jahrbuch der Radioaktivität und Elektronik* in 1907 and 1908, emerged from a problem that had been worrying Einstein since his formulation of the Special Theory in 1905. This theory had been complete in itself. But it was a characteristic of Einstein's whole scientific life that most of his main achievements sprang directly from their predecessors. Each advance was first consolidated and then used as base for a fresh move into unexplored territory.

In the Special Theory he had shown that there was no place for the word "absolute" when motion was considered. Movement was relative, whether it was the movement of the stars in their courses or of the electrons in the physicist's laboratory. Yet the motion concerned was of a very limited variety — hence the "special" in the description of the theory. For he had dealt only with motion in a straight line at a constant velocity. In the world of everyday life, to which he clung with such determination, this was exemplified by the train moving at constant speed, from which it was impossible to discover the existence of motion except by looking out of the window and relating the train to another frame of reference. But this situation altered radically if there was a change in the speed of the train. Then acceleration thrust a passenger back into a forward-facing seat, or deceleration slumped him forward, while the movement of inanimate objects in the train — a glass of water, for instance — would clearly show that a change of movement was taking place. Similarly, if constant motion were maintained in a circular motion — as in a car on a merry-go-round — then the outward pull on the body (or on the glass of water) would once again provide a yardstick for the movement involved. "Because of this," said Einstein in describing how his argument had progressed from Special to General Relativity, "we feel compelled at the present juncture to grant a kind of absolute physical reality to non-uniform motion . . ."

This discrepancy between the relativity of uniform motion and the apparent non-relativity of non-uniform motion, between the fact that the first has no meaning unless it is compared to something else, while the second is self-evident within its own frame of reference, greatly worried him. As it has been put by Dr. Sciama, "This was

displeasing to Einstein, who felt that the harmony of his theory of
relativity required that all motion should be equally relative." He
had come to it by considering the empirical equivalence of all inertial
systems in regard to light. But he now raised the purely epistemological question: "Why should relativity concern only uniform motion?"

As he sat at his desk on the third floor of the Post and Telegraph
building; walked down towards the Kirchenfeld Bridge in the evening, only half-seeing the splendid vision of the Oberland spread
out before him; and as he casually rocked Hans Albert in his cradle,
Einstein refused to let the discrepancy remain unexplained. What
was it, he wondered, that lay at the heart of inertia, that tendency
of a body to resist acceleration?

At first he thought back to Ernst Mach, now in his mid-sixties,
still deeply sceptical of the atomic theory, already becoming out-of-
touch, by-passed, and half-forgotten. Mach, who attributed the movement of earthly bodies to the influence of the stars — it "savours
of astrology and is scientifically incredible" was Bertrand Russell's
opinion — had revived Bishop Berkeley's notion that centrifugal
forces were governed by the same thing. Einstein arrived at a somewhat similar conclusion by a very different route. But first he had
begun to reflect on one force which had always been taken for
granted, the force of gravity.

He began by returning to Newton's conception of inertia which
triggers the senses into knowing when the train has jerked forward
or a body is being pulled out of a straight line in a swing or on a
merry go round. First, "every body continues in its state of rest, or
of uniform motion in a straight line, unless it is compelled to change
that state by forces impressed thereon"; and, secondly, the greater
the mass of the body, the greater the force needed to accelerate it
or to change its course. These formal statements were the quint-
essence of everyday experience, the scientists' explanation of the fact
that it is easier to throw a tennis ball than a cannonball and less
difficult to get a small barrow on the move than a large one. But
there was one exception to this otherwise unfailing rule that different
forces were necessary to move objects of different masses. That
exception was gravity, the mysterious force which appeared to
pervade space and which tended to draw all objects to the ground.
More than three centuries earlier Simon Stevenus, quarter-master of
the Dutch Army, had shown that different weights — reputedly
cannonballs of different sizes — fell to the ground at the same speed.
Some years later, Galileo repeated and refined the experiment to

produce his revolutionary conclusion: that the force of gravity had the same effect on all objects regardless of their size or mass. Air resistance prevented cannonballs and feathers from falling at similar speeds but if this resistance were eliminated, by the use of a perfect vacuum for instance, then cannonballs and feathers would reach the ground at the same time if dropped from equal heights — a proposition subsequently found to be correct.

The explanation proposed by Newton for this curious exception to his laws of inertia was ingenious; to Einstein it was too ingenious. The explanation was that gravity, reaching up into the heavens to attract material objects down to earth, exercised its power precisely in proportion to the mass concerned. On objects of small mass, the "pull" was relatively small; on those of greater mass, the "pull" was increased — to just the extent needed to bring them all down towards the ground at the accelerating speed of 32 feet per second per second. Thus the force of gravity operated so that it always counterbalanced inertia — a proposition which Einstein found it very hard to take for granted.

But there was another aspect of Newton's explanation which he found it difficult to accept. For the effect of gravitiy was in Newtonian terms transmitted through space instantaneously, a proposition which conflicted harshly with Einstein's assumption in the Special Theory that the speed of light is a limiting speed in the universe. The more he contemplated this instantaneous and apparently fortuitous balancing of the effect of gravity and the effect of inertia, the less he liked it. It was an accident of nature that he considered too odd to be truly accidental, a lucky chance which he felt must be the result of something more than luck.

This was a repetition of the situation which had led to the photo-electric paper and to the theory of Special Relativity. In the first Einstein had started by drawing attention to the contradictions between the corpuscular and the field theories which science had been content to leave rubbing up against one another with little more than an occasional comment. And the famous relativity paper had begun by drawing attention to the discrepancy between the observational and the theoretical aspects of Faraday's law of induction. Now here, once more, was a curious state of affairs which science had either not noticed or had thought it better to leave alone.

Einstein's reaction was typical. He visualised the situation in concrete terms, in the "man in a box" problem which appears in different guises in most discussions of General Relativity. Einstein's illustration was basically simple — although it appears more so now, when men have been shot out of the earth's gravitational field, than it did some half-century ago when space travel was only a theoretical fancy.

In the first place Einstein envisaged a box falling freely down a suitably long shaft. Inside it, an occupant who took his money and keys from his pocket would find that they did not fall to the floor. Man, box and objects were all falling freely in a gravitational field; but, and this was the important point, their temporary physical situation was identical to what it would have been in space, far beyond any gravitational field. With this in mind, Einstein then mentally transported both box and occupant to such a point in space beyond the pull of gravity. Here, all would have been as before. But he then envisaged the box being accelerated. The means were immaterial, since it was the result that mattered. Money and keys now fell to the bottom of the box. But the same thing would have happened had the box been at rest in a gravitational field. So the effect of gravity on the box at rest was identical with the effect of acceleration beyond the pull of gravity. What is more, it was clearly apparent that if a centrifugal force replaced acceleration the results would be the same. As it was later described by Professor Lindemann, a friend of Einstein for more than forty years, it would be as impossible for the man in the box "to tell whether he was in a gravitational field or subject to uniform acceleration, as it is for an aeroplane pilot in a cloud to tell whether he is flying straight or executing a properly banked turn."

Thus logical reasoning showed that the effects of gravitation were equivalent to those of inertia, and that there was no way of distinguishing acceleration or centrifugal force from gravity. At least, this appeared to be so with money and keys and other material objects. But what would happen if one thought, instead, in terms of light? Here it was necessary to change the "thought-experiment". Once again there was the closed box. But this time, instead of dropped keys and money it was necessary to envisage a ray of light crossing the box from one side to the other while the box was being accelerated. The far side of the box would have moved upwards before the ray of light reached it; the wall would be hit by the light ray nearer the floor than the point at which it set out. In other words, to the man in the box there would have apparently been a bend in a horizontal ray of light.

But it was the very substance of Einstein's conception that the two situations — one produced by non-uniform motion and the other produced by gravity — were indistinguishable whether one used merely mechanical tricks or those of electro-dynamics. Thus the ray of light, seen as bent by the man in the box when the box was subject to acceleration, would surely be seen in the same way if gravity were involved when the box was at rest. From one point of view this was not as outrageous as it sounded. In 1905 Einstein had given fresh support to the idea that light consisted not of waves but of a stream of minute machine-gun bullets, the light quanta which were later christened photons. Why, after all, should not these light quanta be affected by gravity in the same way as everything else?

But even as the idea was contemplated its implications began to grow like the genie from the lamp. For a straight line is the path of a ray of light, while the basis of time measurement is the interval taken by light to pass from one point to another. Thus if light were affected by gravity, time and space would have two different configurations — one when viewed from within the gravitational field and one when viewed from without. In the absence of gravitation the shortest distance between $A$ and $B$ — the path along which a light ray would travel from $A$ to $B$ — is a straight line. But when gravitation is present the line travelled by light is not the straight line of ordinary geometry. Nevertheless, there is no way of getting from $A$ to $B$ faster than light gets along this path. The "light-line" then *is* the straight line. This might not matter very much in the mundane affairs of the terrestrial world, where the earth's gravity was for all practical purposes a constant that was a part of life. But for those looking out from the earth to the solar system and the worlds beyond, the Principle of Equivalence suggested that they might have been looking out through distorting spectacles. Einstein's new idea appeared to have slipped a disc in the backbone of the universe.

Yet he still did not know what gravity was. He still did not know the characteristics of the gravitational field in the way that one could know the characteristics of the electro-magnetic field by referring to Maxwell's equations. Only two things seemed clear. One was that gravity did not operate as Newton had said it operated. The second was that a reasonable theory of gravitation might be obtained by generalising the principle of relativity. Just as "Special" Relativity could produce an accurate account of events in a frame of reference which was moving uniformly in relation to the observer, so could a more general version of the theory do the same thing when the frame of reference was moving at accelerating speeds — and then the theory should automatically be able to describe motion in a gravitational field as well.

Therefore Einstein now began to look out towards the problems beyond the earth just as he had earlier looked in towards the problems of molecules and atoms. The work took time, and another eight years passed before he produced the General Theory, described in 1919 by J. J. Thomson, the President of the Royal Society, as "one of the most momentous pronouncements of human thought" that the world had known. The delay was due not to Einstein's commitment to other research but to the complexity of the problems involved. Their solution came with the aid of other men, among them Hermann Minkowski who in 1909 transformed Einstein's earlier Special Theory into a convenient mathematical tool.

While Einstein had been at work in his Berne apartment, as unaware of his coming influence as Marx in the Reading Room of the British Museum, important events had been taking place in Göttingen. Standing on the outliers of the Harz mountains, its ancient ramparts planted with lindens, proud of its university and its splendid botanic garden laid out by Albrecht von Haller, the little town still retained a whiff of the Middle Ages. The later memories of Gauss and Riemann were still fresh as there began the "great and brilliant period which mathematics experienced during the first decade of the century . . . unforgettable to those who lived through it". Among its heroes was Hermann Minkowski, the man who at the E. T. H. had taught Einstein, the "lazy dog" who "never bothered about mathematics at all", as Minkowski described him to Max Born.

Minkowski, Russian by birth, had been in his early thirties when lecturing in Zurich. He had been only a middling teacher but earlier, as a boy of eighteen had won the Paris Prize for Mathematics. It was natural that he should have been drawn to Göttingen in 1902, much as physicists were drawn to the Cavendish at Cambridge during its heyday under Thomson and Rutherford. Minkowski was the most recent of the Jews who since the early 1800s had been helping to develop mathematics. Karl Jacobi had discovered elliptic functions and been followed by Johann Rosenheim who proved the existence of Jacobi's Abel functions. He in turn had been followed by George Cantor who developed the theory of transfinite numbers.

Minkowski's contribution to the development of Special Relativity was in effect a single paper, "Basic Equations for the Electromagnetic Phenomena in Moving Bodies", published in the *Göttinger Nachrichten* in 1907; and, more far-reaching in its effects, "Space and Time," a popular lecture which he read to the Gesellschaft Deutscher Naturforscher in Cologne on September 2nd, 1908. The combined effect of the two was to be immense. For Minkowski not only gave a new mathematical formalism to the special theory but also, in some opinions, enabled Einstein to solve the problems of gravitation by means of the General Theory — "whether he would ever have done it without the genius of Minkowski we cannot tell", says E. Cunningham. Yet, contrariwise, Minkowski introduced fresh specialised meanings to old familiar words which brought a new and confusingly esoteric element to an already difficult subject.

Einstein himself described Minkowski's contribution as the provision of equations in which "the natural laws satisfying the demands of the [special] theory of relativity assume mathematical forms, in which the time co-ordinate plays exactly the same role as the three space co-ordinates". To understand the importance of this it is necessary to reconsider exactly what it was that Einstein had already achieved. He had shown that an accurate description of mechanical and optical phenomena is linked with the movement of the observer relative to the phenomena observed. And he had, with his use of the Lorentz equations, been able to demonstrate the mathematical relationship between such observations made by observers moving at different relative speeds. What Minkowski now demonstrated was that a limitless number of different descriptions of the same phenomenon could be provided by a single equation through the introduction, in a certain way, of time as a fourth variable. In this the three space co-ordinates were used as in the Lorentz transformation; the time variable, however, was no longer represented by $t$ but by $\sqrt{-1}\,ct$. The result was an equation which dealt with the "real" world, of which the differing descriptions as seen from differently moving bodies were but partial and incomplete expressions; moreover the curve produced from plotting a series of such equations representing phenomena contiguous in time would represent nothing less than a continuum of the real world — much as to the wolf and the dog of George Lewes, "the external world seems a continuum of scents".

Minkowski thus gave a mathematical formalism to what had been the purely physical conception of Special Relativity. But more important in some ways was the language in which he clothed his work — essential in the mathematical context where it was used, but misleading outside it unless sufficient explanation were given. Thus an event which takes place in three-dimensional space at a specific time is described as a "world-point", while a series of consecutive events — the movement of a rocket, of a man or of an electron — is described as a "world-line". More significantly, and confusingly, time is described as "the fourth dimension".

Einstein was well aware of the bewilderment which such language created. "The non-mathematician," he wrote, "is seized by a mysterious shuddering when he hears of 'four-dimensional' things, by a feeling not unlike that awakened by thoughts of the occult. And yet there is no more commonplace statement than that the world in which we live is a four-dimensional space-time continuum." Here even Einstein, whose scientific explanations have at times a breath-taking simplicity, does not go quite far enough. For he does not explain that while for the layman the world "dimension" signifies one of the three measurements of a body represented by length, breadth or thickness, for the mathematician it means a fourth variable which must, naturally enough, be inserted into any equation concerning events, since these occur not only in space but at a certain instant in time.

The change produced by Minkowski was clear enough — "from a 'happening' in three-dimensional space, physics becomes, as it were, an 'existence' in the four-dimensional 'world'," as Einstein said. Or, as Jeans had written of Einstein's original paper, "the study of the inner workings of nature passed from the engineer-scientist to the mathematician." Einstein was in no doubt about the difficulties that might ensue in the non-mathematical world. "Since the mathematicians have attacked the relativity theory, I myself no longer understand it any more," he claimed, tongue-in-cheek. "The people in Göttingen sometimes strike me," he said on another occasion, "not as if they wanted to help one formulate something clearly, but as if they wanted only to show us physicists how much brighter they are than we."

However, all this was merely the ripple of his exterior amusement. He knew, and he was subsequently to stress the fact, that it was Minkowski who not only transformed the Special Theory but who brought it to the attention of men outside the comparatively small world of theoretical physics.

The paper in the *Göttinger Nachrichten* had been important but was of limited influence. Something more significant was involved when in September, 1908 the Versammlung Deutscher Naturforscher und Ärtzte, a body rather like the British Association, used by scientists to help spread the knowledge of their individual disciplines among a wider audience, met in Cologne. Here Minkowski delivered his semi-popular lecture on "Space and Time", and after half a century his opening words still have a fine ring:

Gentlemen! The ideas on space and time which I wish to develop before you grew from the soil of experimental physics. Therein lies their strength. Their tendency is radical. From now on, space by itself and time by itself must sink into the shadows, while only a union of the two preserves independence.

For Minkowski, relativity had become a central fact of life. After he and David Hilbert had visited an art exhibition at Kassel, Hilbert's wife asked what they thought of the pictures. "I do not know," was the reply. "We were so busy discussing relativity that we never really saw the art." He was among the most austere and dedicated of mathematicians. He was the last man to popularise, to play to the gallery. Yet he had sounded the trumpet for relativity in no uncertain fashion. He was still only forty-four and in the early winter of 1908 it would not have been too outrageous to speculate on the prospects of future long-term collaboration between Minkowski in Göttingen and Einstein in Berne. Then, towards the end of the year he fell ill. He was taken to hospital and died of peritonitis on January 12th, 1909 — regretting on his deathbed, according to a legend which has more than a touch of plausibility: "What a pity that I have to die in the age of relativity's development."

The increased fame which Minkowski brought Einstein among a larger circle of German scientists looks less surprising today than it did in 1908. In retrospect it is possible to see Einstein's papers of 1905, the almost equally dramatic paper of 1907, and Minkowski's denouement of 1908, as parts of a steady increase of reputation which in the end would inevitably be too great to be contained by the four walls of the Patent Office.

The break came the following year. So did Einstein's first honorary doctorate, his first professional appointment, and his first major invited paper, read to the annual meeting of the same Naturforscherversammlung whose members had twelve months earlier listened to Minkowski. In fact 1909 was the year when the chrysalis opened and the professor of theoretical physics emerged, fully formed, equipped at all points, an independent animal whose eccentricities, once regarded as the irresponsibilities of a too casual youth, were now seen as the stigmata of genius.

The first important event in this year which marked a watershed in Einstein's life was an invitation to Geneva, where the University was celebrating the 350th anniversary of its foundation by Calvin. Einstein, it had been decided, should be awarded an honorary doctorate. Almost forty years afterwards, he recalled that he thought the letter from Geneva was merely a circular and had tossed it into a wastepaper basket; only when Geneva enquired why there had been no reply, was the crumpled invitation retrieved and accepted.

Einstein travelled to Geneva early in July and was duly

honoured together with Marie Curie, steely and determined, the woman who "felt herself at every moment to be a servant of society"; Ernest Solvay, the Belgian whose chemical profits endowed his eponymous congresses; and Wilhelm Ostwald who a few months later won the Nobel Prize in chemistry for his work on catalysis.

No first-hand record of Einstein's visit to Geneva appears to have survived, but the second-hand stories are in character if not entirely free from an air of mythology. Certainly he seems to have arrived at the various ceremonies in informal dress, possibly in the straw hat with which legend credits him. And it was in the true Einstein tradition that he should turn to a neighbour at the sumptuous university banquet with the remark: "Do you know what Calvin would have done had he been here? He would have erected an enormous stake and had all of us burnt for sinful extravagance."

Two months after the Geneva visit came something more important. The previous summer Einstein had been visited in Berne by Rudolf Ladenburg, a physicist from Berlin who was also an official of the Gesellschaft Deutscher Naturforscher. The result was an invitation to lecture at the organisation's 1909 conference, and in September Einstein left Berne for Salzburg where this was to be held. The next few days were significant; before he was thirty, he told a colleague of this occasion, he had never met a real physicist.

At Salzburg Einstein gave his first major "invited paper", thus exhibiting himself before an informed and critical audience. He thus came under the close-range scrutiny of the pillars of the scientific establishment. But he in turn was able to scrutinise them. Those he met included Planck, Wien, Rubens, Sommerfeld, young Ludwig Hopf, who was to become his assistant in Zurich and Prague, and Max Born from Breslau, the physicist who had listened entranced to Minkowski's "Space and Time" in Cologne and had then joined him in Göttingen.

Judging by what was to follow, it was Planck whom Einstein might have singled out for special mention; for it was he for whom Einstein was to have a near-reverence which Planck noted and turned to Germany's benefit when he could. The two men had been in correspondence, at first desultory, since 1900, but Planck was increasingly impressed by the young man who had boldly taken his quantum theory into fresh fields. In 1908 Planck, an ardent mountaineer — climbing the 12,000-foot Ortler when well into his sixties — had been staying at Axalp in the Bernese Oberland and he and Einstein were to have met there; but the plan fell through. Only now, at Salzburg, did the two men come face to face. Einstein's lasting attitude was illustrated twenty years later. Asked to contribute a preface to Planck's *Where is Science Going?*, "he said that it would be presumptuous on his part to introduce Max Planck to the public, for the discoverer of the quantum theory did not need the reflected light of any lesser luminary to show him off. That was Einstein's attitude towards Planck, expressed with genuine and naïve emphasis."

At Salzburg, relativity as such was dealt with by Max Born, three years younger than Einstein and still with his name to make. "This seems to be rather amusing," Born wrote subsequently. "Einstein had already proceeded beyond Special Relativity which he left to minor prophets, while he himself pondered about the new riddles arising from the quantum structure of light, and of course about gravitation and general relativity which at that time was not ripe for general discussion."

Einstein was still only thirty. He had already shaken the scientific world with an esoteric theory about which some of his elders still retained doubts. It would not have been surprising if he had chosen a comparatively "safe" subject on which to discourse before such a high-powered audience. But that was not the Einstein way. His paper was entitled "The Development of our Views on the Nature and Constitution of Radiation". It was subsequently described by Wolfgang Pauli as "one of the landmarks in the development of theoretical physics", and its challenge came quickly.

Einstein began by pointing out that some facts about radiation were more easily explained in terms of Newton's corpuscular theory of light than in terms of the current wave theory. What was therefore necessary, he went on, was a profound change in contemporary views of the nature of light — one which would tend to fuse the two ideas.

So the young man — still a mere "doctor" with not a professorship to his name — was to make the members of his audience profoundly change their views about light and to suggest that it was both particle and wave as well! Planck, rising first when the discussion was opened, probably spoke for the majority: "That seems to me," he said, "to be a step that, in my opinion, is not yet called for."

Einstein's paper lived up to its promise. For he invoked the $E = mc^2$ of his second relativity paper of 1905 which showed that the emission of energy in the form of light caused a change of mass and therefore supported the corpuscular theory. And he went on to argue that the elementary process of emission took place not as a spherical wave which classical theory demanded but as directed, or needle, radiation. This was grasping Planck's nettle with a vengeance.

With the benefit of hindsight, it is clear that only Einstein would have dared to do it.

In the audience was Lise Meitner, a young woman of thirty-one studying under Planck in Berlin.

> At that time I certainly did not yet realise the full implications of his theory of relativity, [she wrote more than half a century later] and the way in which it would contribute to a revolutionary transformation of our concepts of time and space. In the course of this lecture he did, however, take the theory of relativity and from it derive the equation: energy = mass times the square of the velocity of light, and showed that to every radiation must be attributed an inert mass. These two facts were so overwhelmingly new and surprising that, to this day, I remember the lecture very well.

Almost exactly three decades later, walking at Christmas with her nephew Otto Frisch in the Stockholm woods, Lise Meitner hit upon the explanation of what Otto Hahn, one of Planck's successors, had just discovered in Berlin: nuclear fission, which was the key to nuclear weapons.

Einstein left Salzburg after the conference of 1909 for a short holiday in the surrounding country and then returned to Berne. But this time it was a return with a difference. For now, at the age of thirty, he was at last to part company with the Patent Office and to take up his first full-time academic post.

In 1908 it had been decided to establish a chair of theoretical physics in the University of Zurich and Professor Kleiner, who had helped Einstein into the post of *privatdozent* in Berne, chose him for the post. However, Kleiner's early enthusiasm had waned, due partly it appears to Einstein's facility for being his own worst enemy. According to Philipp Frank, the professor had attended one of Einstein's lectures in Berne and concluded that it did not seem to be at the right level for students. "I don't demand to be appointed a professor at Zurich," Einstein retorted. Here it may not have been only his brusque honesty coming to the surface. He may have had his sights on something higher than the university. For while this was merely a cantonal institution, the E.T.H. where Einstein had graduated, and for which he always kept a soft spot in his heart, was a Federal organisation, standing on the higher educational ground and with the reputation that went with the situation.

Whatever Kleiner's personal feelings, something else was involved. His assistant was Friedrich Adler, the son of Viktor Adler who had founded the Austrian Social Democratic Party and a former fellow-student with Einstein at the E.T.H. The father had sent the son to study physics in Switzerland in the hope that he would be kept from politics. Yet it was politics which now stretched out to touch him in the academic world. For the members of the Zurich Board of Education had the final say in the appointment to the newly created chair, and a majority of the board were Social Democrats. In an ideal world this would have been irrelevant; nevertheless, the chair was offered to Adler.

This fact does not appear to have worried Einstein. However, the affair of the professorship had not yet ended. The young Adler was a man of integrity, and of a nature which was to bring him to the gate of the execution yard a few years later. Once he learned that Einstein would have accepted the post had it been offered, he reported to the Board of Education in no uncertain words: "If it is possible to obtain a man like Einstein for our university, it would be absurd to appoint me. I must quite frankly say that my ability as a research physicist does not bear even the slightest comparison to Einstein's. Such an opportunity to obtain a man who can benefit us so much by raising the general level of the university should not be lost because of political sympathies."

To his father in Vienna, Adler wrote in much the same style. On November 28th he reported that he had again spoken with Kleiner, urging him to end the protracted argument by making a firm recommendation about Einstein, and adding: "I hope to have achieved this by Christmas."

During this period Einstein himself appears to have been searching around for another non-university appointment. He wrote to Marcel Grossmann, asking whether he should apply for a post in the Technical College at Winterthur; applied to the Gymnasium of the Zurich Kantonsschule for details of a vacancy for a mathematical master; and discussed in more than one letter to Laub the prospects for what appear to be non-university posts.

However, while he was still searching around, Adler's honest argument had its effect. Early in the New Year Einstein was called to Zurich to see Kleiner. But the following April he was still waiting. "Would you believe," Adler wrote to his father on April 16th, apparently after a fresh series of appointments had been announced, "Einstein was not mentioned, and I'm glad that I did not wait any longer but began my holiday." Then, in the early summer, Einstein's appointment was formally announced.

On July 6th, 1909 he handed in his resignation to the Federal Department of Justice and Police by whom he was formally employed. According to Patent Office legend, Haller at first refused to take the resignation seriously. When forced to realise that Einstein really was intent on leaving, he wrote to the Federal Council, officially making a request for his employee's release. "The departure means a loss for the office," he wrote. "However, Herr Einstein feels that teaching and scientific research are his proper calling, and thus the Director of the Office has refrained from tempting him to remain at the Office by offers of financial improvement."

Einstein, returning to Switzerland from the Salzburg meeting, first supervised the change of home from Berne to Zurich and then, in October, took up his post in the university. Two days later he realised he had forgotten to report his move to the authorities and wrote to his friend Chavan, still in Berne, sending his *Dienstbüchlein* and asking his friend to report his departure to the Police and the Army's District Command.

# 6

## *MOVES UP THE LADDER*

EINSTEIN'S APPOINTMENT IN ZURICH WAS THAT OF ASSOCIATE PROFESSOR, not full professor, and his salary was only the 4,500 francs a year he had been receiving at the Patent Office. It was augmented by lecture fees, and was raised by 1,000 francs in 1910, but these additions did not compensate for the increased outgoings of a university professor and the higher cost of living in Zurich. By contrast with his position little more than a decade later, when he could have commanded whatever salary he wished, Einstein still lived and worked among the poorly paid, overworked lower professional classes and, to make ends meet, Mileva took in student lodgers. "In my relativity theory," he once said to Frank, "I set up a clock at every point in space, but in reality I find it difficult to provide even one clock in my room."

Even so, Einstein had at last officially broken through into the academic world and the future seemed plain sailing. The prospect was of a placid life at one or possibly two Swiss universities, of responsibility increasing steadily through the years, life in an ivory tower safe within the citadel. In fact the future was to be dramatically different. Within five years Einstein was to have served three universities in three countries as well as the Zurich E.T.H., a more than usually peripatetic record for a scientist of those times. Within a few more years he was to become involved in the battles of pacifism, the struggle for Zionism, and the expanding role of scientists in world affairs. And in 1939 he was to help unleash nuclear weapons on the world. But there was no hint of this in 1909 when he expected, as he was to say after another twenty years, "to spend all his time in more solitary pursuits".

If there was any suggestion of a coming change in his life it concerned his private affairs. The mutual patience of Einstein and his wife with each other was already wearing thin, and he made this clear to Besso to whom he wrote a few weeks after settling into Zurich. This situation had a bearing on his movement during the next few years, from Zurich to Prague, back to Zurich and then on to Berlin. But the restlessness of his wife, who acquiesced in his move to Prague yet whose dislike of the ferment in the Bohemian capital was partly responsible for his return to Switzerland, was only one factor.

There was also his own personal ambition. It is fashionable to think of Einstein as a man insulated from the problems of real life, never worrying about money, scornful of honours and careless of the position which the world accorded him. Later on, as the most famous scientist in the world, he could afford to be casual. But earlier when he was, as T. H. Huxley once said of himself, only "at the edge of the crush at the pit-door of this great fools' theatre", he had perfectly valid reasons for wishing to press on for recognition. With his ill-organised wife, a certain minimum of money was required to cope with the day-to-day routines of life and provide peace and leisure for his work. Apart from this financial need, which justified a circumspect move from one appointment to the next, there was one other, dominating, reason for his shuttlings back and forth across Europe during these years before the First World War. He was, as he often said, the kind of man who did not work well in a team. Furthermore, his mental stature was such that he needed little stimulation from other workers in his own field. At the same time he preferred to work in a congenial intellectual climate. It is no coincidence that in Prague he was directed by Georg Pick towards the mathematical apparatus which he needed for his General Theory of Relativity, and that he completed this work in a wartime Germany amid a galaxy of talent which included such men as Sommerfeld, von Laue, Planck and Weyl.

Little of this could have been forecast as he turned to the business of academic life for the first time in the autumn of 1909. With his wife and his son Hans Albert he moved into an apartment in Moussonstrasse at the bottom of the Zurichberg, and here his second son, Eduard, was born in July 1910.

The Adlers also lived in the same building. Friedrich Adler wrote to his parents on October 28th:

We are on extremely good terms with the Einsteins, who live above us, and as things turned out I have become closer to him than to any of the other academics. The Einsteins live the same Bohemian life as ourselves. They have a son the same age as Annika who spends a lot of time with us ... The more I speak with Einstein, and this happens often, the more convinced do I become that I was right in my opinion of him. Among contemporary physicists he is not only the clearest but the one who has the most independent of brains, and it is true that the majority of physicists don't even understand his approach. Apart from that, he is a pure physicist, which means that he is interested in theoretical problems which unfortunately is not the case with me.

In addition, Einstein was popular as a lecturer. This was due partly to his lack of convention, partly to his humour, partly to memories of the Munich Gymnasium which made it impossible for him to fit into the usual professorial mould. "He went to a great deal of trouble over his first lecture, in order to help students," recalled his old friend from Aarau, Dr. Adolf Fisch. "He kept stopping and asking whether he was understood. In the pauses he was surrounded by students who wanted to ask questions which he answered in a most patient and friendly way. This contact between lecturer and student was not at all usual at the time."

He lectured in Zurich regularly throughout term-time; on an "Introduction to Mechanics", on thermodynamics, the kinetic theory of heat, on electricity and magnetism, and on selected topics from theoretical physics. The number of students was usually in single figures — more the result of the tepid interest in physics than of any lack of ability in the master. Adler neatly sums up the situation after Einstein had taken up his appointment. "My mathematics lecture had an audience of only four, which is as good as can be expected in a small university such as this. But people must go and listen to Einstein, as they have to take their examinations with him, and after seven hours they have had more than enough."

He was precise and clear, he rarely used notes, yet he never floundered as even the best extempore lecturer can. His humour was of the quiet, throwaway kind which illustrated points in his thesis, a sometimes quixotic, frequently irreverent humour which delighted his students. He was, moreover, one of the few lecturers who openly invited his listeners to interrupt him if they failed to understand a point, and it was obvious that the memory of the Luitpold Gymnasium was still in his mind. He also cultivated a casual friendship with his students, unusual at that time. Taking them to the Terrasse Café after the weekly physics colloquium, bringing them home to discuss the riddle of the universe over coffee in the manner of the Olympia Academy little more than a decade before, Einstein appeared a happy man, outwardly satisfied with his financial status and content with the fame he had already achieved.

The niche in which circumstance had placed him seemed a satisfactory one. He was sixteen and a half when he had arrived in Switzerland. Now he was thirty-one, a whole impressionable lifetime away, a Swiss citizen bound to the country by the strong bonds of all converts, blind to its defects and soberly convinced that in their system of government the Swiss had found the democratic key to the political millennium. He occasionally travelled outside the frontiers and brushed shoulders with other members of the international physicists' community — Planck from Berlin, Rutherford from England, Poincaré from Paris — the scientific revolutionaries who were already overturning man's idea of the place he lived in. Yet their more rumbustious world — the world of the Berlin laboratories, of the Collège de France and of the Cavendish, all places against which Zurich had a faintly provincial air — had little attraction for Einstein. He needed no more than pencil, paper and pipe, peace for relaxation with his violin, a nearby lake to sail on, the opportunity for an occasional not-too-strenuous stroll in pleasant scenery. Switzerland, that happy, happy land, offered it all.

This was outwardly the situation at the end of 1910, when he had been teaching in Zurich for little more than a year. Yet during the first months of 1911 his colleagues heard astounding news: Einstein was about to leave Switzerland for Prague. This was, as his Swiss biographer has noted, "a grievous blow for Swiss science". It would have seemed even more grievous had it been known that Einstein had been considering the move within a few months of coming to the city in October 1909.

So much, and a good deal more, is clear from the correspondence between Friedrich Adler and Adler's father in Vienna, to whom the son described in blow-by-blow detail the moves which preceded Einstein's next step up the ladder. Although Adler had refused the chair in Zurich eventually taken by Einstein he had continued to hold a post in the university. "I am still after all a physicist and this has its drawbacks because when Einstein leaves people will look upon it as a tragedy if I am not his successor, which I do not want," he wrote on January 23rd, 1910. This was no boasting letter from son to father. Adler had in fact been offered the chief editorship of the Social Democrat *Volksrecht* and was at first unable to understand why Einstein was, as he put it on February 15th, "so upset that I am not remaining a scientist".

The reason became clear the following month.

Einstein remonstrated most strongly with me about joining the *Volks-*

*recht*, [he wrote to his father] asking me at least to cancel my holiday
for this term. And at last something has come out which *no one* knows;
he has received the offer of a post at another university. He has told me
this in confidence, so please *do not* repeat it. His argument is that he
can then propose me for his post with added confidence, which he
wants to do not from feelings of personal friendship but from impartial
conviction. This is nice of him but does not alter the situation.

Exactly a month later Einstein revealed to his colleague that the
mysterious offer was from the German University in Prague, where
the Faculty had unanimously put forward his name. "No one knows
of this other than myself, and I ask you not to mention it," Adler
wrote to his father.

For Einstein there was more than one attraction in an appointment to the capital of Bohemia, third city of Austria-Hungary, a
splendid assembly of noble palaces, royal parks and lavishly decorated churches. The first Rector of the University had been Ernst
Mach. And at Benetek, a few miles outside Prague, Tycho Brahe, the
Swede who had ushered in a great age of astronomy, had employed
the young Kepler. These were associations which could not be ignored
by a man of Einstein's background. He would not have ignored them
even had he been aware of the complex emotional, racial and political situation which was already beginning to develop in Prague. But
in 1910 Einstein was not very aware; he was then even less of a
political animal than he became in later life; most of what went on
outside his own world he considered irrelevant and much of it he
considered unpleasant. Thus he was barely awake to the fact that in
Prague the struggle between the indigenous population and their
German masters was already bitter if concealed, or that the existence
of two universities in the city, German and Czech, created as a compromise solution in 1888, was only one indication of this. In addition,
but apparently unknown to him, a large Jewish community had for
years added an important racial element to what was essentially a
political situation.

As in Zurich two years previously, two main names were put
forward for the Prague appointment. But whereas in Zurich the
initial solution had been simple, hacked out by the chopper of political loyalties, the complications in Prague were numerous enough to
add an air of farce. On the one hand there was Einstein. On the
other there was Gustav Jaumann, professor at the Technical Institute
in Brno. The choice between them rested on the recommendation of
Anton Lampa, head of the physics faculty, and exercised formally by
the Emperor through the Ministry of Education. Lampa favoured

Einstein, influenced as he himself was by the belief that the latter was still an unequivocal Machist — and no doubt by Planck's words of advice: "If Einstein's theory should prove correct, as I suspect it will, he will be considered the Copernicus of the twentieth century." The Ministry preferred Jaumann not only because he was a Machist; in addition he had the virtue of Austrian birth.

The situation was further complicated by university regulations, which laid down that the importance of candidates' publications should govern their positions on the entry list. Einstein's papers from 1902 onwards brought him to the top. But this was too much for Jaumann, a self-styled unrecognised genius who now withdrew from the race protesting: "If Einstein has been proposed as first choice because of the belief that he has greater achievements to his credit, then I will have nothing to do with a university that chases after modernity and does not appreciate merit." The move appeared to leave the field open for Einstein.

But now another impediment arose. While the Emperor Franz-Joseph had no direct role in the appointment, he could exercise an overriding veto; and it was known that the Emperor would confirm university appointments only of confessing members of a recognised church, a state of grace from which Einstein was self-excluded. This local difficulty became clear soon, and on the 23rd Adler wrote to his father telling him that his friend's Prague appointment might not be definite. For although Einstein had never officially renounced his faith, and was therefore technically a Jew, it was well known in Zurich that for all practical purposes he was an "unbeliever".

The position was made clearer in a letter — undated but apparently also written on June 23rd — which Adler's wife, Katya, sent to her father-in-law.

On Sunday Einstein came and told us that the offer from Prague was not going to materialise [this went.] There was a second problem: they did not want "a foreigner". However, [Adler] maintains that the trouble is not that Einstein is a "foreigner" but that he is an unbeliever. The University found this out and this is the inevitable result. . . Now Einstein is as unpractical as a child in cases like this, and [Adler] finally got out of him the fact that on the application form he put down that he was an unbeliever but did not say that he had not left the Church. As Einstein very much wants the Prague post, and as the first hurdle would be the question of his religion, [Adler] suggested to him at the time that he should pass the whole thing over to Lampa in Prague so that should the question arise in discussion, Lampa would be briefed. Einstein did not do this; and now, following the letter from Lampa, he can hardly do so. Einstein is naturally disappointed that the appointment is rejected since this means that the same thing will happen with any other position for which he applies.

But all was not yet lost. "The affair is under way again," Adler wrote to his father on September 23rd; Einstein had received a request to call on the Minister of Education in Vienna, and was leaving Zurich for the city that morning. "Perhaps," Fritz added, "it would be useful for him to see you and discuss things while he is there ... In all practical things he is absolutely impractical."

This time there was no hitch. Imperial doubts were circumvented and Einstein's appointment to the chair was at last confirmed. Only, however, after he had reluctantly agreed to take Austro-Hungarian nationality, a necessity since the appointment would make him a civil servant. As a consolation he was allowed to remain a Swiss so that now, for the first but not the last time, he was able to claim the privileges of dual nationality.

According to Katya, Einstein wanted this Prague appointment "very much", and for several reasons. In Prague he would be a full rather than an associate professor; his salary, moreover, would be higher, and friends who later met him in Prague commented on his improved standard of living. In Berne the Einstein home had been lit by oil lamps. In Zurich there had been gas. In Prague it was electricity. This was more than an index of technological advance; in Prague, the Einsteins for the first time had a maid living in.

But the clue to the real attraction of this capital where the swords of German-Czech animosity were already being sharpened, is to be found in a letter from Einstein to Lucien Chavan written a few months after his arrival. He was having a good time in Prague although not so pleasant a time as in Switzerland. He liked Zurich and the Swiss, but what was that against "a fine Institute and a magnificent library".

The move to Prague took place in March 1911, and Einstein quickly settled down in his new post, considerably helped by Ludwig Hopf, his young assistant in Zurich who had moved east with him. He was to stay in the city less than eighteen months yet the experience was to be important. Here he was forced to note, however much he tried to push out of his mind all except his work, the ambiguous position of the Jews in a community already divided against itself. He was forced to notice the emotions aroused in many Jewish friends by the very mention of the Zionist cause, as well as the Pan-German feelings which were already moving the Central Powers towards the precipice of the First World War. In Prague he had as pupil Otto Stern, the Silesian physicist who was to follow him to Zurich in

1912, hold a succession of posts in Germany, cross the Atlantic in the great refugee wave of the 1930s, and dramatically re-enter Einstein's life during the final months of the Second World War. And in Prague Einstein was introduced to the mathematical machinery which helped him solve the problems of general relativity.

This extension of his powers came through Georg Pick, once an assistant of Ernst Mach and twenty years older than Einstein. Pick and Einstein had a mutual interest in music. They struck up a strong friendship and when Einstein spoke of the difficulties he was having Pick proposed that he consider using the absolute differential calculus of Ricci and Levi-Civita. The two men remained in touch long after Einstein had left Prague and in June 1939, with the Germans already in occupation of the city, Pick, then aged eighty, sent a long letter to Einstein in Princeton reminiscently discussing the past. He died, a few years later, in Theresienstadt concentration camp.

Comparatively little is known of Einstein's life in the Bohemian capital, and the fullest account is given by Philipp Frank, the Austrian physicist with whom he had corresponded about causality in 1907. Frank had become a leading member of the Vienna Circle, a group including Carnap, Neurath and Moritz Schlick, which formed the hard core of the logical positivists who stressed "Mach's requirement" that worthwhile statements had to be capable of test by physical experiment. Einstein's Machist beliefs were still strong. Frank was a young physicist of great promise. And when Einstein left Prague in the summer of 1912 Frank, only just twenty-eight, was appointed in his place.

One thing is quite clear both from Frank's account and from the stray reminiscences which Einstein himself passed on to his friends over the years. This is that he responded to "the political air in which the town was steeped" and to the situation in which the Jews of Prague found themselves. For here Czech and Germans lived in their own closed worlds. The professors of the two universities rarely met and the Germans isolated themselves from the Czech majority within their own cultural ring of concerts and lectures and theatres. Yet half the Germans were Jews, a fact which tended to drive them towards a mutually supporting alliance.

> On the other hand, [Frank points out] the relation of the Jews to the other Germans had already begun to assume a problematical character. Formerly the German minority in Prague had befriended the Jews as allies against the upward-striving Czechs, but these good relations were breaking down at the time when Einstein was in Prague. When the racial theories and tendencies that later came to be known there as

Nazi creed were still almost unknown in Germany itself, they had already an important influence on the Sudeten Germans. Hence a somewhat paradoxical situation existed for the Germans in Prague. They tried to live on good terms with the Jews so as to have an ally against the Czechs. But they also wanted to be regarded as thoroughly German by the Sudeten Germans, and therefore manifested hostility against the Jews. This peculiar situation was characterised outwardly by the fact that the Jews and their worst enemies met in the same cafés and had a common social circle.

All this presented a particularly piquant state of affairs for Einstein — a reneged German, Swiss by choice, who by accepting a post at the German University had been forced to take Austro-Hungarian nationality against his own wishes. It was the first of many non-scientific problems that the pursuit of physics was to pose. He resolved it by openly becoming a member of the Jewish community although tending to ignore his German origin.

The Prague community included Franz Kafka, Hugo Bergmann and the writer Max Brod. Much of its activity centred on the home of Bertha Fanta, an ardent Zionist and, while its sphere of influence was intellectual and artistic rather than political, the ultimate triumph of Zionism was accepted almost as a fact of nature. Einstein could not be troubled with such an idea. It was one thing to be concerned with the affairs of fellow-Jews in a foreign capital; it was quite another to consider Jewry and its problems on a world basis. For, in the words of Philipp Frank, "The problems of nationality and of the relations of the Jews with the rest of the world appeared to him only as a matter of petty significance."

His aloofness from what many fellow-Jews regarded as the great cause no doubt affected the interpretation of Einstein which Brod introduced into his novel *The Redemption of Tycho Brahe*.

Here the portrait of the young Kepler has many of the characteristics of Einstein. Frank claims that Walther Nernst, professor of physical chemistry in Berlin with whom Einstein was to be closely associated, told Einstein on reading the book: "You are this man Kepler." This is significant as suggesting how not only Brod in Prague, but Nernst at a later period, considered the Einstein whom they saw at close quarters and whom both felt they must understand. For the figure of Kepler-Einstein is that of the scientist at the height of his intellectual powers; fully stretched in this case on the generalisation of relativity; not concerned with the rest of the human race; only distantly aware of the surrounding turmoil, and regarding the responsibility of science as a responsibility confined to the scientific arena.

Some phrases in Brod's book epitomise Albert Einstein at this central period of his life; others give a clue to his failure as from the 1920s onwards he became the supporter of every good cause that could gain his ear. Thus the young Kepler-Einstein begins to inspire the old Tycho Brahe with a feeling of awe.

> The tranquillity with which he applied himself to his labours and entirely ignored the warblings of flatterers was to Tycho almost super-human. There was something incomprehensible in its absence of emotion, like a breath from a distant region of ice... He had no heart and therefore had nothing to fear from the world. He was not capable of emotion or love. And for that reason he was naturally also secure against the aberrations of feelings.

It would have been easy to consider such a man as an intriguer whose continuing success was due to cunning, but it was clear to Brahe "that Kepler was the very opposite of an intriguer; he never pursued a definite aim and in fact transacted all affairs lying outside the bounds of his science in a sort of dream." The picture of a Kepler working with the instinct of genius within his own scientific shell, but all at sea when he left it, is a not too inaccurate picture of Einstein in his later years, of the man with two Achilles heels: a too-trusting belief in the goodness of people and a desperately held and innocent belief that the grand investigations of science not only should but could be insulated from the worlds of politics and power. Strangely, the belief survived even Haber and the First World War. It did not survive his desire to beat the Germans twenty-five years later.

But all this was to come. In Prague there was merely the faintest glimmer of awakening in his Jewish consciousness, an awareness which he himself did not recognise until he arrived in Berlin in 1914. This is clear not only from Frank but from the testimony of Dmitri Marianoff, one of Einstein's two stepsons-in-law. Einstein himself protested strongly against Marianoff's biography — as he was to protest against almost any public mention of his private life and tastes — but there is little reason to dispute the non-scientific details of the book which have obviously come from Einstein in reminiscent family mood, barriers down.

Marianoff makes a point of the way in which Einstein was thrown up against his inner Jewishness by the daily circumstances of Prague life.

Once in his strolls through the city he stumbled on a short alley that

10

led to an old high-walled Jewish cemetery, preserved there since the fifth century, [he wrote.] The story of his race for a thousand years was told before him on the tombstones. On them were inscriptions in Hebrew with symbolic records of a tribe or a name. A fish for Fisher, a stag for Hirsch, two hands for the tribe of Aaron. Here he found the battered, chipped and crumbling slab of the tomb of Rabbi Loeue, the friend of Tycho Brahe, the sixteenth-century astronomer whose statue with the globe and compass in his hands Einstein had just passed in front of the Svato-Tynsky-Chram.

What Einstein also tended to remember from Prague, according to Marianoff, was "the solemn sounds of the organ in Catholic cathedrals, the chorales in Protestant churches, the mournful Jewish melodies, the resonant Hussite hymns, folk music and the works of Czech, Russian and German composers". This was the world in which he sought relaxation, moving in "a sort of dream" while his mind concentrated on the work that mattered.

Most important within this work was the continuing riddle of gravity. Throughout the whole of his stay in Prague he worked steadily towards a solution of the problems it presented, returning to the Principle of Equivalence and the "thought-experiment" with light that he had devised to test its validity. The result was another paper for the *Annalen der Physik,* in which he brought forward his ideas of how gravity affected the matter of the physical world. Matter, as he had already shown, was really congealed energy, while light quanta, or photons, consisted of particles which had changed their mass in the process of reaching the speed of light. Viewed thus it seemed plausible, even without Einstein's logical structure of argument, that light itself should be affected by the tug of gravity as certainly as the cannonball. In fact Newton had asked in his *Opticks:* "Do not bodies act upon Light at a distance and by their action bend its Rays; and is not this action *(coeteris paribus)* strongest at the least distance?" And the German astronomer Soldner had used Newton's corpuscular theory of light for predicting a similar deviation although his figure was only half that demanded by Einstein's eventual theory of 1916.

But there was another consequence which Einstein now brought forward for the first time. If light is produced in a star or in the sun, an area of strong gravity, and then streams down on the earth, an area of weak gravity, then its energy will not be dissipated by a reduction of speed, since this is impossible, light always having the same constant speed.

What would happen, Einstein postulated, was something very

different: the wavelength of the light would be changed. This "Einstein shift", the assumption that "the spectral lines of sunlight, as compared with the corresponding spectral lines of terrestrial sources of light, must be somewhat displaced toward the red" was spelt out in some detail. However, he was careful to add the qualification that in view of other influences it might be difficult to isolate the effect he was now describing. In fact the Doppler shift, produced by the motion of the stars relative to the solar system, was to provide an additional and even more important complication. What he concentrated on instead was the deflection of light by the sun, and his paper ended with the proposal that astronomers should try to record this deflection.

The paper had one major limitation. For what it considered was one, and only one, special case of the effects of gravity: that in which gravity had the same force and direction throughout the entire space that was being considered. This was a simplification that helped Einstein to move the theory forward, but it worried him, partly because of its artificiality and partly because he realised that its removal — and the consequent creation of a theory more in accord with reality — would demand a mathematical expertise that was still beyond him.

Despite this limitation, which was eventually to lead him deeper into the mathematicians' world, and which was in some ways to blunt the intuitive feel for physics which was his real genius, the paper of 1911 was important for one special reason. In it, Einstein threw down the gauntlet to the experimentalists. Was light bent by gravity as it passed near the sun? Surely this was a question to which it should be possible to provide a clear-cut yes-or-no answer? It was not to be quite as simple as that; but from 1911 onwards he pointed out with increasing persistence that here was one way of proving or disproving experimentally a theory which had been built up logically but which had as its foundation little more than an intuitive hunch.

Meanwhile he worked on in Prague. And meanwhile the new status he was acquiring began to bring lecture invitations in increasing numbers. In January 1911, he was invited to Leiden by Lorentz, and he and Mileva stayed with the Lorentz family the following month. Shortly afterwards he was formally invited to a major scientific conference, the first Solvay Congress,* held in Brussels between

* The Conseil de Physique Solvay is usually translated into English as the Solvay Congress. However, Jean Pelseneer, Professeur Extraordinaire, Brussels University and the author of an unpublished "Historique aes Instituts Internationaux de Physique de Chimie Solvay depuis leur fondation", points out that while a "Congress" involves a large number of scientists or others, Solvay's scheme was almost the reverse — the invitation of a small number

October 30th and November 3rd, 1911. Einstein, the ex-German Swiss, attended it as an Austro-Hungarian.

The Solvay Congress, the first of many, was organised by the Belgian chemist and industrialist, Ernest Solvay, at the instigation of Walther Nernst, a leading figure in the German scientific hierarchy. Solvay was an able man, already in his seventies, who had patented his own soda process and whose companies were reported to be making nine-tenths of the world's supply. He had for long been in close contact with Nernst to whom he proposed the idea of using part of his great wealth for the good of science. Solvay's own hobby was the development of a new physical theory and Nernst pointed out that if he called a conference of Europe's leading physicists he would then be able to outline the theory to them. Subsequently they could discuss among themselves, in a series of invited papers, the crisis in physics which had been introduced during the past decade by the quantum theory, the discovery of radioactivity, and the investigation of the atom. Solvay responded, and in the autumn of 1911 a score of Europe's leading physicists arrived in Brussels. Their fares had been paid, accommodation was provided in the Hotel Metropole, where two rooms had been set aside for the Congress, and each was given an honorarium of 1,000 francs for attendance.

It was not these lavish trappings but the standing of those who came to Brussels which made the Congress more important for Einstein than any other he had attended. Planck, Nernst and Rubens were among those from Germany; Poincaré, Madame Curie and Langevin among those from France. James Jeans and Rutherford came from England while from Austria-Hungary came Einstein and Franz Hasenöhrl, later to be spuriously credited with Einstein's mass-energy equation. Lorentz himself presided over the Congress which was also attended by Kamerlingh Onnes from Leiden. Maurice de Broglie from Paris, Goldschmidt from Brussels, and Frederick Lindemann, then studying under Nernst in Berlin, acted as secretaries. It was very different from the Salzburg meeting. In Brussels Einstein was brought in to an "experts only" conference whose quality can be gauged from the studied photograph which survived in the Metropole through two German occupations. It shows a striking group of men — and one woman — the real revolutionaries of the twentieth century.

Einstein now met Planck, Nernst, and Lorentz on equal terms for the first time. He also met Madame Curie, then at the height of

of men representing the cream of European physicists. "Council" or "Conference" is suggested — but "Congress" is by this time probably too well used to be changed.

her fame, and Ernest Rutherford, the epitome of the huge New
Zealand farmer looking round for new land to bring into cultivation
— but this time the unexplored territory of physics. "Einstein all
calculation, Rutherford all experiment," was the verdict of Chaim
Weizmann, the man as close to Rutherford scientifically in the coming war as he was close to Einstein in the post-war Zionist movement. There were other contrasts between the two men, highlighted
by the fact that Rutherford never entirely lost a trace of scepticism
when dealing with foreigners. Thus when Wien claimed that no
Anglo-Saxon could understand relativity, Rutherford had a ready
answer: "No, they have too much sense."

   In Brussels there also met for the first time the two men
who occupied such ironically contrasted positions during the Second
World War: Einstein popularly credited with the most important
influence on the creation of nuclear weapons, and Lindemann, later
Lord Cherwell, more correctly credited, as Churchill's *eminence grise,*
with a comparable influence on Britain's wartime science. Lindemann, only twenty-five at the time of the Solvay Conference, facing
a distinguished and disgruntled future, as different from Einstein as
man-of-the-world from provincial recluse, was to become firm friend
and devoted admirer. "I well remember my co-secretary, M. de
Broglie, saying that of all those present Einstein and Poincaré moved
in a class by themselves," he wrote almost half a century later. His
first reaction was given in a letter to his father. "I got on very well
with Einstein who made the most impression on me except perhaps
Lorentz. He looks rather like Fritz Fleischer 'en mal', but has not
got a Jewish nose. He asked me to come and stay with him if I came
to Prague and I nearly asked him to come and see us at Sinholme* . . .
He says he knows very little mathematics, but he seems to have had
a great success with them . . ."

   Lindemann's biographer notes that:

Observing this shy genius at close quarters, [he] formed an opinion
of Einstein's character which he never revised. He saw there the
towering intellect which made him for Lindemann the greatest genius
of the century, but he saw also a pathetic naïveté in the ordinary
affairs of life. Einstein appeared to him to be living in a universe of
his own creation, and almost to need protection when he touched the
mundane sphere. In all matters of politics he was a guileless child, and
would lend his great name to worthless causes which he did not
understand, signing any ridiculous political or other manifestos put
before him by designing people.

* The Lindemann home in south Devon.

Yet the two men were united by one thing: the view that human beings counted for little when weighed against the splendid problems of physics. Lindemann, according to one colleague, "had time for a few dukes and a few physicists, but regarded most of the rest of mankind as furry little animals". Substituting "pacifists" for "dukes", much the same was true of Einstein.

The theme of the Congress was radiation and quanta, and Einstein contributed a paper, "The Actual State of the Problems of Specific Heats" which dealt with the fundamental arguments he had used to explain the anomalies of specific heat at low temperatures. Madame Curie's reaction was typical. She "appreciated the clearness of his mind, the shrewdness with which he marshalled his facts, and the depth of his knowledge". Most of those attending felt much the same.

While the Congress was in progress, Einstein was involved in a typically Einsteinian imbroglio. It arose from his readiness to leave the chair in Prague to which he had been appointed only some eight months previously. Mileva's attitude played a part. Although she had enjoyed life in Switzerland it is clear from her letters to the Adlers that she approved the move to Prague; thus the readiness to uproot herself again, and so quickly, at first seems surprising. Frank, who was to succeed Einstein in the German University, has given one explanation. To some degree, he has said, it was certainly the wish of his first wife who was accustomed to Zurich. She had found it very difficult to adapt herself to the life in Prague. This was strange since she was by birth a Yugoslav woman. But she had come to Switzerland as a student and was not able to perform a second assimilation. However, Einstein was not a man to be unduly swayed by his wife's feelings. And whatever Mileva may have thought about Switzerland, it was to yet another country that Einstein's eyes now turned. The reason, as so often with Einstein, can be found in the answer to one question: "What would be the effect of the move on his scientific work?"

In Prague there was the fine library, there was contact with such minds as Georg Pick. But the enthusiasm of the first few weeks soon evaporated. One reason is supplied by his eldest son, only six at the time but vividly remembering how his father later explained the situation. "He had," he says, "to lecture on experimental physics. And he was always happy when something went right." This was not at all what Einstein had bargained for. He liked contact with young students. He was always happy explaining the excitements of physics. But he liked to do this when he wished, not when he had to, and he liked to keep clear of routine experimental work. In fact he was not really cut out for a normal university chair, and if he had to occupy one he wanted the terms to be more flexible than they were at Prague. "I want my peace", he was to explain a decade later. He wanted it even in 1911, peace in which to think and reach out to touch the stars. At Prague it was difficult to get. Within a few months of arrival, he was preparing to move.

The circumstances are described in a long series of letters between Einstein, Lorentz, and Professor Julius of Utrecht University, the solar physicist whom Einstein respected as a "clear-sighted, artistically fine-spirited man". It is not easy to acquit Einstein of some deviousness in the situation which they reveal. However, the evidence is circumstantial and can possibly be explained by the muddled simplicity with which he handled most affairs outside physics; in this case it was, for him, a singularly fortunate muddle.

On August 20th, 1911, some two months before the first Solvay Congress, Professor Julius informed Einstein that Professor Windt, the university's professor of physics, had died earlier in the month. "Our university and the interests of physics would best be served if it were possible for you to take over the professorship," he wrote. But several members of the faculty would be against the appointment of a foreigner and his letter should therefore be regarded only as an unofficial feeler. Einstein replied by return, pointing out that he had been in Prague for only four months, had acclimatised himself there, and must ask Julius to consider someone else.

However, he was by this time an important enough scientific fish to be worth angling for carefully. The following month Julius tried again after the members of the faculty had met. "It was simply unthinkable at our meeting not to mention your name," he wrote. "Everyone was in full agreement that your reasons for refusing were not decisive and that I should make a further attempt at convincing you." Einstein's reply suggested that perhaps the attractions of Prague were not really so great after all. He recalled his lectures at Leiden the previous spring and noted how everyone there had charmed him, quite apart from the incomparable Lorentz. And he was, he added, seriously thinking of accepting the Utrecht offer. But there was one point that Julius might well have taken as a warning. Before he had left Zurich for Prague, he had promised to let the E.T.H. know if he were offered another post. The implications of this might have been clear to Julius who had just received a letter from Lorentz saying: "Einstein only prefers Prague because there is little hope of going to the Polytechnic." But he still pressed on, writing on September 27th that he hoped Einstein would be "more impressed with the prospects at Utrecht than at Zurich" and following it up with a further letter on October 11th, saying that he was still waiting for Einstein's answer.

Einstein finally replied on October 18th. He apologised for the long delay and explained that he had been away for three weeks, first to the Naturforscherversammlung in Karlsruhe. Then he had gone to Zurich to take part in a vacation course. And at Zurich he had learned that the Polytechnic might wish to offer him a post. He had to consider it, partly because he was himself a citizen of Zurich.

This was the position when he went to Brussels at the end of October for the Solvay Congress. Just what was said there about the Utrecht appointment is not certain. But it is clear that Lorentz, having been asked by his Dutch colleagues to use his influence with Einstein, bungled the mission; also that Einstein backed the choice of Peter Debye, the Dutch physicist who had taken his chair at the University of Zurich the previous year. He also pushed Debye's claims when he went on from Brussels to meet Julius in Utrecht before returning to Prague; and from Prague, on November 15th, he wrote to Julius finally turning down the Utrecht post.

In this reply Einstein thanked Julius for his friendly welcome in Utrecht. But he had, he said, finally decided to stay in Prague. He had written to Debye, received his reply, and was very pleased that Debye would be going to Utrecht.

There is no doubt that he was, indeed, very pleased. For the offer from Zurich, casually mentioned to Julius some weeks earlier, had been hardening. The authorities had already written to Madame Curie and Henri Poincaré about Einstein's suitability for the post and a letter now arrived in Prague from Marcel Grossmann telling him what was going on. In reply, Einstein said that he was delighted by the prospect of returning to Zurich. The possibility had in fact, he went on, induced him to refuse an offer from Utrecht. This was not quite the story he had given to Julius.

Einstein's correspondence with Lorentz hints at a twinge of misgiving.

> You have gathered by now, despite my long silence to your last letter, that not the slightest shadow is cast on our relationship through the Utrecht affair, [Lorentz wrote to him on December 6th.] I would like to stress once more that there is no question of your having hurt my feelings, and am convinced that you have taken the course that you think right. This does not deny that I am very depressed about the

result of your discussion with the Utrecht Faculty, but that is not your fault; only that of fate which did not wish to treat us favourably this time. If only I had written to you at the start. But it was not possible as one is very reserved in Utrecht, and rightly so. In the meantime I guessed, but did not know, that you had been contacted. Because I suspected as much, I mentioned to Julius the day before I left for Brussels that you and I would meet (I saw him at the Academy Conference). I had hoped in this way to be able to speak to you about the offer from Utrecht, and immediately received permission to do so, as well as being asked to try to persuade you to accept. If only I had succeeded in expressing myself better or, before it was too late, known about your scruples; I could perhaps have removed any obstacles. But I will not continue with this 'if only . . .'; it does not help us. I will console myself with the fact that after all you will be achieving great things in Zurich too.

Lorentz concluded with the best of wishes, hoped that they would meet again soon, noted that if Einstein was able "to open up fresh vistas in physics, that will be one of my greatest joys", and ended with a postscript: "I have caught you out in a mathematical error: Namely, 25 francs = 12 Fl. Dutch, and you sent me Fl. 15.09. I therefore return Fl. 3."

The convoluted negotiations for the Utrecht Chair, reminiscent of C. P. Snow at his best, were now followed by a further misunderstanding, surprising to find among grown men. For two days later Lorentz wrote again, asking whether Einstein's decision to go to Zurich was final. Einstein, not knowing that Lorentz had decided to retire from his chair at Leiden, thought that he still had the Utrecht chair in mind. His ignorance saved him from making an awkward choice. He would have found it difficult to refuse Lorentz, yet he preferred Zurich to Leiden — and was by this time justifiably confident that it would formally be offered to him. He had accepted before Lorentz brought the real situation to his notice.

Einstein had been given outstanding references for what it had now been decided should be a new chair of Mathematical Physics at the E. T. H. One was from Madame Curie.

I much admire the work which M. Einstein has published on matters concerning modern theoretical physics, [she wrote from Paris on November 17th.] I think, moreover, that mathematical physicists are at one in considering his work as being in the first rank. At Brussels, where I took part in a scientific conference attended by M. Einstein, I was able to appreciate the clearness of his mind, the shrewdness with which he marshalled his facts and the depth of his knowledge. If one takes into consideration the fact that M. Einstein is still very young, one is justified in basing great hopes on him and in seeing in him one of the leading theoreticians of the future. I think that a scientific institution which gave M. Einstein the means of work which he wants, by appointing him to a chair in the conditions he merits, could only be greatly honoured by such a decision and would certainly render a great service to science.

Henri Poincaré wrote in similar vein, stressing Einstein's youth and the vistas which his ideas had opened out. "The role of mathematical physics," he concluded, "is to ask questions; it is only experience that can answer them. The future will show, more and more, the worth of Einstein, and the University which is able to capture this young master is certain of gaining much honour from the operation."

Some news of the situation seems to have seeped through from Zurich to Prague, probably via Marcel Grossmann, and by the end of 1911 Einstein knew that his star was rising rapidly. In addition to the aborted offer from Lorentz, there had come others from Vienna and from the Reichsanstalt in Berlin. Both had been turned down and he now looked hopefully forward to a return to Zurich. By now, moreover, his fame had spread to the United States and during the first days of 1912 he received an invitation from New York's Columbia University. Would he consider coming for four to six weeks as a special lecturer in physics during the autumn, or the spring of 1913?

> While I am not authorised to make you any definite proposition, I wish if possible to open the way for one, [wrote George Pegram.] We have in times past been honoured by the presence here of such men as Professors Larmor, Planck, Lorentz and others on the basis of such a lectureship ... I can assure you that your coming would be welcomed, not only by the men at Columbia, but by many from neighbouring institutions who have been interested in watching, even if not contributing to, the development of the Relativity Theory ...
>
> Personally I have been very much interested in the Relativity Theory since my attention was first directed to it by Professor Lorentz, and I should be glad to see greater appreciation of it in America, where I confess our physicists have been rather slow to take it up.

Einstein declined on January 29th.

His spare time was now filled with thoughts of a return to Zurich.

But before he left Prague, he had one visitor whose impact was to be considerable. This was Paul Ehrenfest, a man ill-starred for a tragic life whose work in physics was perpetually to hover round the borders of genius. Ehrenfest had been born in Vienna and had studied and graduated there before obtaining a special professorship at the St. Petersburg Polytechnic. But his position as an Austrian barred the way ahead; so did the fact that he was a Jew, even though he declared himself as without religion. In addition, Ehrenfest's gay unconventionality, which so mirrored Einstein's, hardly helped him in the clamber up the academic ladder. He was, it has been written, bored by lectures at which the audience was not expected to interrupt, and especially so if he was the lecturer.

> In contrast to the usual educational principles, he infected his students with his own enthusiasm and rushed with them to the outposts of the empire of physics, where the fighting against the great unknowns — relativity and quantum theory — was going on. But at the same time, he did not forget to take them to an occasional tower from which he could show and explain to them in his masterly way the domains already conquered.

In the autumn of 1912 Ehrenfest decided to tour German-speaking Europe in search of a better post, and almost automatically found his way to Einstein in Prague. The two men had been in professional touch a few years earlier, and by 1912 each admired the other's work.

Ehrenfest arrived on February 23rd and stayed with Einstein for a week. They talked only a little about the search for a new appointment. As Einstein wrote later, it was the state of science that took up almost all their time.

Martin Klein, whose first volume of Ehrenfest's biography, *The Making of a Theoretical Physicist*, gives such a splendid portrait of the man, has described that first week's encounter in some detail.

Ehrenfest stuck to his non-religious guns and was not offered the Prague chair. But before the end of the year he had been appointed to Leiden as successor to Lorentz. Soon afterwards Einstein made the first of many journeys to stay with the Ehrenfests, as happy with their children as when he accompanied their parents in playing Bach. What he had found was another man to whom physics was the whole of life and who put everything else firmly in its right place.

Einstein and his family left Prague for Switzerland in August 1912. His appointment at the E.T.H. was for ten years, and as he moved into his fifth home in Zurich he may well have looked forward to settling down at last.

In the autumn of 1912 he began holding weekly afternoon colloquia at which new work was discussed. By now his reception was very different from what it had been in the university only three years earlier, and it was not only members of the E.T.H. who attended. Students at the university, and their professors, found ways and means of joining in, and the meetings were usually crowded, Einstein affably discussing the latest developments with anyone who could contrive to be present. He remained unchanged. The meetings over, he would do as he had done years previously, carrying on the discussion outside the building with those who accompanied him to his favourite café. He found it difficult to relinquish his grasp on the problem in hand. Years afterwards his students recalled him standing in a snowstorm under a lamp at the foot of the Zurichberg, handing his umbrella to a companion and jotting down formulae for ten minutes as the snowflakes fell on his notebook.

Von Laue now crossed his path again, coming to speak on interference of X-rays, an occasion which was followed by Einstein opening the discussion and extemporising "on the most intricate problems of physics with as much ease as if he were talking about the weather". Many scientists came to Zurich specifically to see him and von Laue recalls one particular visit. "I can still see Einstein and Ehrenfest striding along in front of a great swarm of physicists as they climbed the Zurichberg, and Ehrenfest bursting out in a jubilant cry: 'I have understood it.'" Von Laue's words echo the same air of nuclear innocence that then permeated the Cavendish Laboratory where Andrade could offer a toast to: "the useless electron, and long may it remain so".

Another visitor was Madame Curie with whom Einstein and his wife stayed in Paris late in March, 1913 when he addressed the Société Française de Physique. It is clear from Madame Curie's correspondence, and from Einstein and Mileva's "thank you" letters, that she had shepherded an unsophisticated pair through the rigours of a hurried and demanding visit. In return, Einstein hoped that she would allow him to worry her about a trip to the Alps later in the year. Typically, he ended the invitation with a brief postscript which dealt only with physics.

The Curies — mother and two daughters — arrived in Zurich in July for a fortnight in the Bregaglia Alps and the Engadine with Einstein, his wife and his eldest son. The holiday was a great success. Years later Hans Einstein remembered how they had crossed the Maloja Pass on foot; how his father and Madame Curie had inspected the glacier mills, Einstein cogitating on the forces which had carved these deep vertical wells; and how Madame Curie, recalling the fact that Einstein was technically a Swiss, demanded that he name every peak on the horizon.

There was ample reason for her to seek out Einstein and to mull over with him, during the informal talks of a walking holiday, the implications of the new ferment in physics on her own specialised field of radioactivity. Fresh radioactive substances were being discovered, and the key to their characteristics and behaviour obviously had to be sought within Rutherford's new concept of the atom, now known to consist of a positively-charged central nucleus surrounded, at a comparatively great distance, by one, by a few, or by a cloud of orbiting electrons. Einstein, with his instinctive feel for the nature of things, would obviously have worthwhile views — while it was already clear that sub-nuclear particles moved at speeds fast enough to make relativistic effects important.

However, it was so far only physicists who were brought into intimate day-to-day contact with the implications of relativity. Many other technical men found it difficult to see that "the new physics" formed part of their world, as was evident when Einstein spoke on the subject during a visit to Göttingen.

> I remember watching the engineering professors who were present and who were, of course, horrified by his approach, because to them reality was the wheels in machinery — really solid entities, [says Professor Hyman Levy, then a research student at the university.] And here was this man talking in abstract terms about space-time and the geometry of space-time, not the geometry of a surface which you can think of as a physical surface, but the geometry of space-time, and the curvature of space-time; and showing how you could explain gravitation by the way in which a body moves in space-time along a geodesic — namely the shortest curve in space-time. This was all so abstract that it became unreal to them. I remember seeing one of the professors getting up and walking out in a rage, and as he went out I heard him say, "*Das ist absolut Bloedsinn*" ("That is absolute nonsense").

Whatever arguments there might be among engineers, physicists realised that a new star had risen in the scientific firmament and was still rising fast. Einstein was now among the "European professors distinguished in philosophy and science", and as such he supported in the summer of 1912 the foundation of a scientific association "quite indifferent to metaphysical speculation and so-called critical, transcendental doctrines" and "opposed to all metaphysical undertakings". The idea started in Berlin and foundered with the outbreak of war two years later. But its manifesto was the first such collective statement to be signed by Einstein and it underlines his frequent statements that Special Relativity was the outcome not of metaphysical speculation but of considering scientifically the results of experimental evidence.

Einstein signed the document while still trying to generalise his theory of relativity so that it would apply not only to the special case where gravity operated as a force of constant intensity and direction but in all the multiplicity of special cases which existed throughout the universe. In this he was aided by his old friend Marcel Grossmann, the former colleague of a dozen years before, whose notes during student days had enabled him to skip mathematics and concentrate on physics. This particular chicken was coming home to roost and it was on Grossmann that Einstein now leaned heavily for the mathematical support which he needed. Even so, it was hard going.

There was an ironic outcome of the work. In 1913 Einstein and Grossmann published jointly a paper which came much nearer to the theory of gravity for which Einstein was still groping. This was *"Entwurf einer Verallgemeinerten Relativitätstheorie und eine Theorie der Gravitation"*, to which Einstein contributed the physical sections and Grossmann the mathematical. Einstein was dissatisfied with the paper, for its equations appeared to show that instead of a single solution to any particular set of gravitational circumstances there was an infinitude of solutions. He believed "that they were not compatible with experience". This, together with the conclusion that the results would not agree with the principle of causality, led him to believe that the theory was untenable. Yet the 1913 paper contained the clue to its own apparent discrepancy: what appeared to be an infinitely large number of solutions to one problem was really a single solution applicable to each of an infinitely large number of different frames of reference. Thus the cards of the General Theory of Relativity had been laid face upwards on the table in 1913. They were picked up again by Einstein himself in 1915. But they had lain there unnoticed for two years.

By 1913 Einstein had thus reached a temporary impasse. But his views on the need for generalising the Special Theory aroused great interest, and in September he put them before the eighty-fifth Deutscher Naturforscherversammlung, held in Vienna. The auditorium was packed with scientists anxious to hear about a theory even more outlandish than Special Relativity. In some ways they were disappointed. Instead of the esoteric explanations they had expected, there came one of Einstein's minor masterpieces of simple statement, an account in which he compared the development of the various theories of gravitation with the development of successive concepts of electricity. As one of his Zionist friends was later to comment, when he wished, he could "speak of basic metaphysical concepts such as time or space as matter-of-factly as others speak of sandwiches or potatoes".

The lecture was remarkable, however, not only for the clear exposition which foreshadowed some of Einstein's later scientific writings, so much more understandable than many of his interpreters, but for an incident which well illustrates his character. In his recent work he had used a generally covariant form of the electromagnetic equation first given the previous year by a young Viennese physicist, Friedrich Kottler. In their paper Einstein and Grossmann had acknowledged their indebtedness, but Einstein had never met Kottler personally. On the spur of the moment he asked whether Kottler was in the audience. A young man rose. Einstein asked him to remain standing — so that all could see the man whose help had been so useful.

Although Special Relativity had by this time become incorporated into the new framework of physics with little more than a disapproving grunt from its more conservative critics, the situation was very different with Einstein's still tentative generalised theory. "It was clear in the discussion that followed that many German-speaking men of science were not yet converted to his ideas," says Robert Lawson, a young English physicist then working in the city's Radium Institute, and the man who later translated into English Einstein's first book on relativity. "Doubts were expressed on the validity of his velocity of propagation of gravitational processes, on the possibility of ever being able to detect the deflection of light rays in a gravitational field or the predicted red shift of spectral lines in such a field." At one point the debate grew quite heated, with Felix Ehrenhaft, for long a colleague and later an opponent of Einstein, arguing at length with two of the critics. To relieve the tension, someone pressed the button that automatically shifted the blackboard from one part of the platform to another — calling out as he did so: "Look. The blackboard moves against the lecture hall and not the lecture hall against the blackboard". Einstein remained unperturbed, smiling and noting only that he was prepared to stand or fall by experimental results.

During this visit to Vienna Einstein heard dramatic news of the theory put forward by the Danish physicist Niels Bohr which united Rutherford's concept of the nuclear atom with the Planck-Einstein quantum theory. Bohr was still only twenty-eight, but already as deeply concerned as Einstein not only with the upheaval in physics through which they were living, but with its underlying philosophical implications. The two were to be friends for nearly forty years, but the matters on which they agreed were more than balanced by those in which each unsuccessfully struggled to convert the other. Both at first failed to appreciate the practical results which would flow from their work; both, when nuclear weapons arrived, appreciated more quickly than many of their fellow-scientists the political and moral implications; both, in many ways epitomising the stock character of absentminded scientist, were anxious to direct nations into decent ways. These motives united them as much as the argument for and against determinacy divided them, an argument which was to lead Einstein into scientific isolation for the later years of his life.

Bohr had been educated as a physicist in Copenhagen and had come under the special influence of Max Planck. But he had also studied and worked in England, first under J. J. Thomson at the Cavendish and then under Rutherford at Manchester. Long afterwards, reminiscing on his past, he reflected on his good luck that Denmark had been politically free until the German invasion of 1940, thus allowing him to maintain contacts with both the German and the British schools of thought. One result of these contrasted contacts was the theory, whose confirmation Einstein now heard in 1913, which successfully accounted for some puzzling features of Rutherford's nuclear atom by invoking the idea of Planck's quanta.

According to classical physics the electrons orbiting the nucleus of Rutherford's atom would lose energy by radiation and inevitably spiral into the nucleus itself, giving out as they did so a continuous spectrum of radiation. But this did not happen; instead, free atoms radiated certain specific and discrete frequencies that were characteristic of the atom concerned. Bohr explained this behaviour with two suppositions. The first was that atoms exist only at well defined stationary states or levels, and that at each of these states the electrons circle the nucleus in specific "allowed" orbits. While this continues the atom emits no radiation. Bohr's second supposition was that when an electron jumped — for whatever reason — from one of its "allowed" orbits to another "allowed" orbit nearer the nucleus, then radiation was emitted; by contrast, when an atom absorbed radiation one or more of its orbiting electrons jumped from its "allowed" orbit to another farther from the nucleus. Both emission of radiation and its absorption took place in discrete units — the light quanta of the Planck-Einstein quantum theory of 1905.

Thus Bohr had shown that electro-magnetic radiation was produced not by the oscillation or acceleration of subatomic particles but by changes in their "energy levels" — and had done so by making use both of Planck's conception of radiation by discontinuous surges of energy and Rutherford's idea of the atom as a miniature solar system with electrons orbiting a central nucleus.

He had, moreover, gone further than disembodied theory. He had applied this to the hydrogen atom and, "leaning directly on Einstein's treatment of the photo-electric effect" as he himself wrote, had proposed to Rutherford that the theory was now susceptible to spectroscopic proof. Such proof was provided in Cambridge in the autumn of 1913 and Rutherford passed it on to George de Hevesy, the Hungarian-Danish chemist from the Cavendish who was attending the conference in Vienna. Hevesy in turn told Einstein, and on October 14th wrote to Rutherford describing the occassion.

"Speaking with Einstein on different topics we came to speak on Bohr's theorie [sic]," he wrote from Budapest. "He told me that he had once similar ideas but he did not dare to publish them. 'Should Bohr's theories be right, so it is from the greatest importance.' When I told him about the Fowler Spectrum the big eyes of Einstein looked still bigger and he told: 'Then it is one of the greatest discoveries.' I felt very happy hearing Einstein saying so." Hevesy's statement that Einstein "had once similar ideas" about this crucial problem was supported years later by Bohr himself, speaking in Moscow at the Institute of Physical Problems. Einstein's reaction, as apparently explained to Bohr himself was: "I could probably have arrived at something like this myself but if all this is true then it means the end of physics."

The result of Bohr's work was, as Planck put it in 1920 when he received the Nobel Prize, that "a stream of knowledge poured in a sudden flood, not only over this entire field but into the adjacent territories of physics and chemistry". But there was one other result which increasingly affected Einstein over the years. When the new picture of the atom was outlined — the Rutherford-Bohr model as it was called — it was appreciated that the causes lying behind the movements of individual sub-nuclear particles were not known. But causes were nevertheless believed to exist. Only during the next few years did it become more and more apparent that this was not always so: that whatever happened at other levels, individual events at the level of the sub-atomic world were unpredictable and could only be described statistically. But Einstein would never agree.

This great schism which the apparent indeterminacy of the sub-nuclear world was to create still lay in the future as Einstein listened to Hevesy in Vienna and lectured to the slightly dubious

11

audience on his theory of General Relativity. In the city he had earlier met Ernst Mach, whose writings a decade and a half earlier had buttressed his doubts about Newton's absolute time and absolute space. The meeting took place in 1911, possibly while Einstein was travelling to or from the Solvay Congress, an encounter between the young man on the crest of the wave, and the elderly Mach, crippled in physical health and bypassed intellectually by the swift stream of science. Mach was now in his seventies. Half-paralysed, he had retired from the University of Vienna a number of years previously and lived in semi-seclusion in the suburbs of the city, half-forgotten and seeing few visitors. "On entering his room," says Frank, "one saw a man with a grey, unkempt beard and a half-good-natured, half-cunning expression on his face, who looked like a Slav peasant and said: 'Please speak loudly to me; in addition to my other unpleasant characteristics I am also almost stone-deaf'."

Einstein had not yet noticeably fallen away from Mach's basic beliefs, even though it seems likely that his acceptance of them was weakening. Similarly Mach, while strongly opposed to what he considered merely the assumptions of relativity, had so far kept the fact to himself. Thus the two men were still openly united on many scientific matters. One of their comparatively few differences was their attitude to atomic theory. Einstein accepting it freely while Mach did so only grudgingly and with considerable philosophical reservation.

Few details of the encounter have survived but Bernard Cohen, interviewing Einstein shortly before his death, says he recalled one thing:

Einstein asked Mach what his position would be if it proved possible to predict a property of a gas by assuming the existence of atoms — some property that could not be predicted without the assumption of atoms and yet one that could be observed. Einstein said he had always believed that the invention of scientific concepts and the building of theories upon them was one of the great creative properties of the human mind. His own view was thus opposed to Mach's, because Mach assumed that the laws of science were only an economical way of describing a large collection of facts. Could Mach accept the hypothesis of atoms under the circumstances Einstein had stated, even if it meant very complicated computations? Einstein told me how delighted he was when Mach replied affirmatively. If an atomic hypothesis would make it possible to connect by logic some observable properties which would remain unconnected without this hypothesis, then, Mach said, he would have to accept it. Under these circumstances it would be "economical" to assume that atoms may exist because then one could derive relations between observations. Einstein had been satisfied: indeed more than a little pleased. With a serious expression on his face, he told me the story all over again to be sure that I understood it fully. Wholly apart from the philosophical victory over what Einstein had conceived Mach's philosophy to have been, he had been very gratified because he had admitted that there might, after all, be some use to the atomistic philosophy to which Einstein had been so strongly committed.

The two men parted on the best of terms and when Mach died in 1916 Einstein's tributes were eulogistic and unqualified. Yet before his death Mach had reneged, although Einstein knew nothing of this when he wrote a laudatory obituary notice.

In the summer of 1913, Mach signed the Preface of *The Principles of Physical Optics* which did not appear until 1921. In this — "what may be the last opportunity" as he put it — he reversed his views on relativity.

I gather from the publications which have reached me [he wrote,] and especially from my correspondence, that I am gradually being regarded as the forerunner of relativity. I am able even now to picture approximately what new expositions and interpretations many of the ideas expressed in my book on Mechanics will receive in the future from the point of view of relativity.

It was to be expected that philosophers and physicists should carry on a crusade against me, for, as I have repeatedly observed, I was merely an unprejudiced rambler, endowed with original ideas, in varied fields of knowledge. I must, however, as assuredly disclaim to be a forerunner of the relativists as I withhold from the atomistic belief of the present day.

The reason why, and the extent to which, I discredit the present-day relativity theory, which I find to be growing more and more dogmatical, together with the particular reasons which have led me to such a view — the considerations based on the physiology of the senses, the theoretical ideas, and above all the conceptions resulting from my experiments — must remain to be treated in the sequel.

There was no sequel. But the voice from the grave shocked Einstein and deepened the differences which were soon separating his epistemology from that of Mach. Speaking in Paris in 1922, he went on record as describing Mach in terms which would have sounded strange only a short while earlier — "*un bon mécanicien*" ... but "*deplorable philosophe*".

The date at which Mach changed his views is not known. But his Preface was dated, and therefore probably concluded, within a few weeks of his receiving a significant letter which Einstein wrote to him on June 25th, 1913. In this he revealed that the following year it should be possible to discover whether light was, in fact, bent by the gravitational pull of the sun. For in the late summer of 1914 an expedition would be travelling from Berlin to southern Russia where the necessary observations could be made during an eclipse.

The leader of the expedition was to be Erwin Finlay-Freundlich, an astronomer of mixed German and Scottish descent and at this time the youngest assistant at the Berlin University Observatory. Einstein's friendship with Freundlich is interesting and revealing. It had begun in the summer of 1911 when Professor L. W. Pollak, then a student at Prague University, had visited the Berlin Observatory. He recalled that Einstein had concluded his recent paper by suggesting that the new theory might be tested astronomically, and he mentioned Einstein's passing regret that no one seemed interested.

It is not clear whether Freundlich had actually read Einstein's latest paper. But something in its ideas as he heard them from Pollak sparked his imagination. From then onward he showed a constant, if sometimes critical, interest in the development of relativity, carrying out measurements for Einstein during the next few years, working with him during the war, producing the first book on what became the General Theory of Relativity, and acting as interpreter and shock-absorber during Einstein's first visit to Britain in 1921.

Shortly after Pollak's visit, Freundlich wrote to Einstein in Prague, offering to search for any deflection of light near Jupiter, an ambitious idea that must have been doomed from the start. Einstein welcomed the help but nothing came of these first efforts, nor of Freundlich's subsequent inspections of old photographic plates which he described in the *Astronomische Nachrichten*. When that failed, he went on to the study of double stars. Einstein still had doubts, saying that if the speed of light was affected by the speed of the light source, then his theory of relativity and of gravity would be false.

When the eclipse of 1914 offered a definite chance of providing experimental proof or disproof, the next step was obvious. The Berlin Observatory was unenthusiastic, but willing to let Freundlich visit the Crimea — at his own expense and in his own time. This was the situation in the summer of 1913. Freundlich, who had not yet met Einstein, was preparing to marry and to spend his honeymoon in the Alps. On August 26th he was delighted to receive a letter from Switzerland. "This morning," he wrote to his fiancée, "I had a nice letter from Einstein in Zurich in which he asked me to meet him in Switzerland between September 9th and 15th. This is wonderful because it fits in with our plans."

A fortnight later, as the train pulled into Zurich, Freundlich and his bride saw waiting for them the short figure of Fritz Haber, Director of the Kaiser Wilhelm Institute for Chemistry which had been opened in Berlin two years earlier. Beside him stood an untidy figure in almost sporting clothes, wearing what Frau Freundlich remembers after half a century as a very conspicuous straw hat: Einstein, the maker of new worlds.

Einstein was delighted to meet his friends, and insisted that they accompany him to Frauenfeld, a few miles from Zurich, where he was to speak to the Swiss Society of Natural Sciences. Then he invited them to lunch with himself and Otto Stern, now working in Zurich as his assistant. Only at the end of the meal did he discover that he had no money. The situation was saved by Stern who passed him a 100-franc note under the table.

At Frauenfeld, where both he and Grossmann spoke on the new theory, Einstein announced, to the embarrassment of Freundlich, that the company had among them "the man who will be testing the theory next year". From Frauenfeld they all travelled for the Society's outing to Ermatingen on the shores of Lake Constance, Einstein later insisting that he and the Freundlichs return alone to Zurich. Throughout the entire journey the two men discussed the problems of gravitation while the young bride studied the scenery of a Switzerland she had never before seen.

The Zurich meeting settled details of what Freundlich would do in the Crimea the following summer. Soon afterwards, Einstein invoked the aid of Professor George Ellery Hale of the Mount Wilson Observatory, Pasadena, California, a man whose similarity of outlook with Einstein's is shown by an early passage in his autobiography — "Naturally I do not share the common fallacy of an antagonism between science, literature and art, which appeals to me in much the same way. Creative imagination is the vital factor in all of them, and I was fortunate to learn this at an early age." Hale passed on Einstein's letter to Professor Campbell of the Lick Observatory.

He writes to me, [Hale replied to Einstein on November 8th] that he has undertaken to secure eclipse photographs of stars near the sun for Doctor Freundlich of the Berlin Observatory, who will measure them in the hope of detecting differential deflections. Doubtless he will send you further particulars, as I requested him to communicate directly with you.

I fear there is no possibility of detecting the effect in full sunlight . . .
The eclipse method, on the contrary, appears to be very promising,
as it eliminates all . . . difficulties, and the use of photography would
allow a large number of stars to be measured. I therefore strongly recommend that plan.

Einstein also recommended it. So did Freundlich. But the problem of money still remained, as Freundlich pointed out in December.
Einstein himself was willing to contribute up to 2,000 marks, but in
the end he did not have to dig into his own pocket. During the first
months of 1914 help came from unexpected sources. The money was
provided by Krupp von Bohlen und Halbach and by the chemist
Emil Fischer.

Thus Einstein, firmly settled in Zurich, would await the results
of a German expedition which in the late summer of 1914 would
provide proof or disproof of a theory on whose development he was
still hard at work. He had at last achieved full professional status in
the establishment which had grudgingly accepted him as a student of
sixteen, in a country whose atmosphere and environment he enjoyed.
His sister Maja had now settled in Lucerne with her husband, Paul
Winteler. To the same city, only thirty miles away from Zurich
across the intervening hills, his mother also came. For Mileva, Switzerland seemed the only country in which it was possible to live and
thus family feelings appeared to chime in which professional success.
It must have seemed that now, at last, he might finally settle down.

Yet Einstein was not the kind of man for whom family feelings
weighed very heavily. And although he felt a compelling need for
the intellectual climate of Europe, he did not quickly throw down
deep roots. Links provided by sentiment or the emotions were gossa-
mer-thick. Thus it is less surprising than it seems that by the autumn
of 1913 he was preparing to move to Berlin, capital of a German
Empire whose policies he detested and whose inner spirit he deeply
distrusted.

# 7

# A JEW IN BERLIN

EINSTEIN'S ATTENDANCE AT THE SOLVAY CONGRESS OF 1911 HAD repercussions which decisively affected the rest of his life. For among those in Brussels most deeply impressed by his ability were Max Planck and Walther Nernst, twin pillars of the Prussian scientific establishment. Following their return to Berlin both men became engaged in a difficult and delicate task which exercised their scientific enthusiasm and their patriotic instincts.

The task was recruitment of staff for the new and ambitious series of research institutes which the Emperor had graciously allowed to be called the Kaiser Wilhelm Gesellschaft. These institutes were not only to investigate pure science; they would also, it was intended, help increase Germany's lead in the application of scientific discoveries made during the previous half-century. In this field the country was now technologically supreme in Europe, providing much of the continent with dye-stuffs, with the tungsten needed for steel-making, with magnetos for the petrol-engines which were revolutionising land transport and were soon to bring a new dimension to warfare, and providing also the best scientific instruments. Significantly, when war broke out in 1914, the British found much of their artillery using gun-sights exclusively made by Goerz of Berlin.

Yet the Germans were well aware that applied technology demands a constant diet of pure research. They were aware that in the United States the General Electric Company had invited Charles Steinmetz, the electrophysicist, to head their laboratories and to do what work he pleased. They knew that in Britain Lord Haldane, Secretary of State for War until 1912, had seen the country to be "at a profound disadvantage with the Germans, who were building up their Air Service on a foundation of science" and had, as a result, laid the foundations at Farnborough of what was to become the Royal Aircraft Establishment. All this constituted a warning that

was heeded by Friedrich Althoff, the permanent Secretary in the
Prussian Ministry of Education. Althoff "knew the weakness of
human beings for decorations and titles, and he exploited it as
another man would exploit a gold mine. The 'voluntary subscriptions'
he obtained in this way went to further his great plans. Among other
things he reorganised the whole system of higher education and
brought the main body of scientific research into special research
institutes." Then came his crowning achievement, the Kaiser Wilhelm
Gesellschaft, the ambitious plans for which were approved by the
Emperor himself. They were in the true Althoff tradition. The institutes were to be financed by bankers and industrialists who were to
be rewarded not merely by a flush of patriotism but by the title of
"Senator", the right to wear handsome gowns, and the honour of an
occasional breakfast with the Emperor.

The scheme was announced in the autumn of 1911 and during
the following summer work began at Dahlem, on a site near the end
of the new underground from Berlin, on buildings for the Institute
for Physical Chemistry and Electrochemistry which was to be run by
Haber. The Physics Institute was to follow, and as little difficulty
was expected in staffing it as there had been in attracting men to
work under Haber. Indeed, as far as physics was concerned, the
scientific atmosphere of the German capital was almost magnet
enough. Only the Cavendish Laboratory at Cambridge, forging
ahead into the nuclear world under the command of J. J. Thomson,
could compare with the physics faculty of the University of Berlin.

Therefore, it was felt in the Prussian capital, there would be
little difficulty in attracting Einstein. It was perhaps strange that a
theoretical physicist should be considered the best man to run such an
institute; and Einstein himself was the most unlikely of men to
grapple successfully with the practical problems of any major organisation. However, that was not really the point, since the actual
creation of the Institute was known to be some way off in the
future; what mattered was getting this unconventional Swiss to
Berlin for the ideas he might produce.

One possible impediment lay concealed in the word "Swiss",
for Einstein had reneged on his German nationality more than a
decade and a half previously. And even if the authorities could be
induced to accept him, for the sake of German progress if not for the
sake of science alone, there was always the chance that Einstein
might not accept Berlin. There is little evidence that up to this date
he had openly voiced the criticism of the Prussian regime and of the
German mentality which later so obsessed him; but such views as he

had were almost certainly known, implicitly if not explicitly, to
Planck and Nernst. But both were determined men, and in the
summer of 1913 they decided to visit Einstein in Zurich.

Some of the preliminaries appear to have been dealt with by
this time. In the spring of 1912, while still in Prague Einstein had
gone to Berlin for appointments with Nernst, Planck, Rubens, Warburg, Haber ... Later, when his German nationality became an issue
on his winning the Nobel Prize, he officially wrote that this question
of nationality had been discussed with Haber when his appointment
was being considered. It seems likely, therefore, that Planck and
Nernst, the subject having already been raised, were visiting Zurich
to make sure that if a formal offer were made then it would be
accepted.

The high drama of these two major figures in German science
travelling south from Berlin to tempt the young Einstein back into
the Prussian orbit was equalled by the incongruity of the men themselves — Planck aloof and superbly professional, always master of
the situation, the tall trimmed figure from whom his country could
never demand too much; Nernst the businesslike genius, a jolly
plump little man against whom Planck appeared as the epitome of
discipline. Both were excellent as fishers for Einstein who had a
respect for Planck only just this side idolatry. For Nernst there was
even some warmth.

Planck and Nernst met Einstein in his rooms at the E.T.H.
and pleaded their case with him at some length. He was unwilling to
give a decision then and there, and the two professors decided to
ascend the Rigi, the most famous of nineteenth-century Swiss view-
points, while he was making up his mind. After their excursion by
train and funicular railway they would return to Zurich for their
answer. Einstein, exhibiting the quirkish humour with which he often
tweaked authority's tail, announced that they would know the verdict as soon as they saw him. If he was carrying a white rose the
answer would be "No"; if the rose was red, then he would accept
the offer from Berlin if it were formally made.

When the two men later stepped down from their carriage they
were relieved to see Einstein trotting up the platform carrying a red
rose.

The proposal had been that Einstein should become director of
the Kaiser Wilhelm Institute for Physics when it was set up, and
would meanwhile give advice on research in the subject carried out
in other parts of the organisation. However, had this been the sum
total of the offer it seems probable that he would have been carrying

white rose rather than red. But the Kaiser Wilhelm appointment was only one part of an attractive package deal.

Almost exactly three years earlier, Jacobus Hendrikus van't Hoff, the originator of the theory of the spatial structure of molecules, had died at the age of fifty-nine. He had been a member of the Prussian Academy of Sciences, the oldest scientific institution in Germany, planned by Liebnitz and established by Frederick the First as the "Society of Sciences", and his chair remained empty. Planck and Nernst were confident that with the help of their colleagues they could persuade the Prussian Ministry of Education to approve Einstein's appointment to the chair — a necessary move since the Academy existed under the umbrella of the Prussian civil service. Most members occupied only honorary and unpaid positions. A few, however, were endowed from one of various funds, and it was part of the plan that, with such help, Einstein should be offered a salary much in excess of what he was receiving in Zurich. If this were not attraction enough, there was a third item in the offer which Einstein agreed to accept if it were officially made. This was a nominal professorship in the University of Berlin, nominal since under the proposed special arrangements Einstein would be able to lecture as much or as little as he wished and would have none of the normal duties concerned with university administration. To sum up, he would be left free to devote himself, exactly as he wished, to the business of pure research. He would, moreover, be able to do so in the best possible place — to the remark that only a dozen men in the world really understood relativity, Nernst once replied: "Eight of them live in Berlin."

On their return to Berlin, Planck and Nernst, supported by Heinrich Rubens and Emil Warburg, the founder of modern photochemistry, prepared their draft notice for presentation to the Ministry of Education. The original proposed Einstein "for full membership of the Academy with special personal salary of 6,000 marks", but the figure was subsequently doubled to "12,000", an indication that the Germans were anxious that this particular catch should not slip through their fingers. The draft — in which the German birth and education of this apparently Swiss professor was inserted almost as an afterthought — described Einstein's early years, and the publication of his first relativity paper.

"This new interpretation of the time concept has had sweeping repercussions on the whole of physics, especially mechanics and even epistemology", it went on. "The mathematician Minkowski subsequently formulated it in terms which unify the whole system of

physics inasmuch as time enters the stage as a dimension on completely equal terms with the three conventional dimensions." It then,
somewhat surprisingly in the light of later events, turned to what
were considered more relevant matters.

> Although this idea of Einstein's has proved itself so fundamental for
> the development of physical principles, its application still lies for the
> moment on the frontier of the measurable. Far more important for
> practical physics is his penetration of other questions on which, for
> the moment, interest is focused. Thus he was the first man to show
> the importance of the quantum theory for the energy of atomic and
> molecular movements, and from this he produced a formula for the
> specific heat of solids which, although not yet entirely proved in
> detail, has become a basis for further development of the newer atomic
> kinetics. He has also linked the quantum hypothesis with photo-electric
> and photo-chemical effects by the discovery of interesting new rela-
> tionships capable of being checked by measurement, and he was one
> of the first to point out the close relationship between the constant
> of elasticity and those in the optical vibrations of crystals.
>
> All in all, one can say that among the great problems, so abundant
> in modern physics, there is hardly one to which Einstein has not
> brought some outstanding contribution. That he may sometimes have
> missed the target in his speculations, as, for example in his theory
> of light quanta, cannot really be held against him. For in the most
> exact of natural sciences every innovation entails risk. At the moment
> he is working intensively on a new theory of gravitation, with what
> success only the future will tell. Apart from his own productivity,
> Einstein has a special talent for probing peculiar original views and
> premises, and estimating their inter-relationship with uncanny certainty
> from his own experience.
>
> In his treatment and investigation of classical theory, even in the
> earliest of his publications, as well as in his demonstration and cri-
> ticism of new hypotheses, Einstein must rank as a master.

The interest in this account, which was to open the gates to
Berlin, lies in the way in which it glosses over Einstein's work on
relativity and quickly dismisses the "heuristic viewpoint" of the
photo-electric paper for which he was to be awarded the Nobel Prize
for Physics nine years later. Nernst and Planck, who presumably
drew up the document, took into account not only the conservative
views of their colleagues but also the character of the Minister. And
Planck, reluctant to admit that his quanta did not somehow take on
wave characteristics during the journey from here to there, still felt
it necessary to insist that when it came to photons Einstein had
"missed the target".

Having been approved by the Academy, the proposal was submitted to the Government on July 28th, 1913. It was nearly four months later before the reply came. On November 20th the Minister stated that the Kaiser had approved the appointment, that the Minister of Finance had agreed to grant Dr. Einstein travelling expenses, and that he now wished to be informed if "Professor Einstein actually accepts his new post". Long before this, Nernst took the matter as settled. "At Easter, Einstein will move to Berlin," he wrote to Lindemann on August 18th, 1913: "Planck and I were in Zurich to see him the other day and the Academy has already elected him. We have great expectations of him."

Einstein formally accepted on December 7th, having by this time asked for his release from the post he had taken up only eighteen months earlier. His acceptance was significant in a number of ways. The most obvious was later stressed by Sommerfeld who wrote that "We owe the completion of his general theory of relativity to his leisure while in Berlin." But there is more to it than that. Had Einstein remained in Zurich until the outbreak of war in August 1914 it is almost inconceivable that he would have returned to Germany. The anti-Semites in that country would have been deprived both in the post-war chaos of the early 1920s and in the preparations for the Nazi take-over, of a ready-made target on which to concentrate their fire. It is almost equally unlikely that Einstein would have moved to the United States in 1933 — and thus been available on Long Island in the summer of 1939 to prod America into research which gave them nuclear weapons before the end of the war in the Pacific.

For these reasons, if no other, it is worth considering the pros and cons of what must for Einstein have been a difficult decision. On the credit side there was the enormous attraction of the intellectual climate into which he would be moving. There was also the attraction of the salary. Einstein was never a man to care about money but he was the father of two growing sons and he felt responsible for them if not extravagantly affectionate.

"In addition," says one of his generally more reliable biographers, Philipp Frank, "there were also personal factors that entered into the decision. Einstein had an uncle in Berlin, a fairly successful businessman, whose daughter, Elsa, was now a widow. Einstein remembered that his cousin Elsa as a young girl had often been in Munich and had impressed him as a friendly, happy person. The prospects of being able to enjoy the pleasant company of this cousin in Berlin made him think of the Prussian capital more favourably."

This statement must be taken with some caution. Frank, who wrote his book in 1947, more than thirty years later, was an intimate of Einstein, and it is difficult not to believe that the source of the comment was Einstein himself. Yet if this is so, and if the comment is correct, it implies considerable guile. It is true that Albert eventually married Elsa Einstein; but when he moved to Berlin in April 1914, he moved with Mileva and their two sons. The marriage had not yet broken up; and while there are indications that it was almost on the rocks, it seems over-harsh to suggest that he accepted the Berlin appointment in the hope that it would eventually bring his marriage to an end. However, that is what happened.

Mileva Einstein's reaction to Berlin, very largely Slav dislike for all things Teuton, which for her contrasted so strongly with the casual happy atmosphere of Switzerland, had a counterpart in Einstein's own feelings. Seventeen years previously he had renounced not only German nationality but what he considered the essential Germanism: reverence for obedience, regimentation of the body, and a rigidity of the spirit which forced minds narrowly upwards like the pinetrunks of the dark German forests. Now, as a man, he would be walking back into the environment from which he had escaped as a boy. Yet throwing down an intellectual gauntlet, taking a calculated risk, were actions which not only had led to Einstein's fame but were typical of his mental make-up; accepting a post in the Kaiser Wilhelm would enable him to do both things. There was also one other factor which mattered more than anything else. Einstein's friend Reichinstein put it clearly after he had talked with him in Berlin about the work that led to the General Theory. "To be able to work when a great idea is at stake," he wrote, "[an idea] which has to be nursed to maturity during a longer period of time, a scientist must be unencumbered by cares, must avoid all disturbing conflicts of life, must bear with all humiliations from his opponents in order to safeguard that precious something which he bears in his soul." In Berlin, under the conditions provided by Planck and Nernst, Einstein would be unencumbered by money worries, would avoid the disturbing conflicts of a teaching routine. More than one friend, more than one colleague, has stressed how he was in some ways more of an artist than a scientist — or at least "an artist in science". And "the true artist will let his wife starve, his children go barefoot, his mother drudge for his living at seventy, sooner than work at anything but his art." Einstein would even put himself in pawn to the Prussians.

The problem of nationality, raised when the question of going to Berlin had first been discussed, at last appeared settled. Haber had pointed out that membership of the Prussian Academy of Sciences would automatically make Einstein a Prussian citizen — and two decades later Professor Dr. Ernst Heyman, Perpetual Secretary of the Academy, wrote of Einstein's "Prussian nationality which he acquired in 1913 simply by becoming a full member of the Academy". Einstein's version was that he made acceptance of a possible appointment dependent on there being no change in his nationality, and that this was agreed to. Exactly what was finally done is not clear even today. But there had been a Professor Haguenin, a Frenchman in the Academy's Faculty of Letters, who had insisted on remaining French. The position was no doubt different in the case of a German who had renounced his German nationality, but Einstein was left with the impression that in Berlin he would not only retain his Swiss nationality but would avoid becoming a German once again. The Government, but not the Academy, later denied that this was so. If the Government was right, this did not necessarily mean that Planck and Nernst had failed to keep their promise. The "agreement" may have first been discussed early in the summer. And it was only on July 13th, 1913 that a new Nationality Law provided in its Section 14 that state employment in the service of the Reich, or in one of the federal states, gave German citizenship to the respective foreign employee, official or civil servant.

Certainly for a good deal of his life Einstein believed that he, as a Swiss, had gained professorial status in Berlin only by diplomatic sleight-of-hand. But it is typical of what his elder son has called his delight in making up good stories for good listeners that he should later give a different version. To Dr. Max Gottschalk, a prominent Belgian Jewish scholar and good friend, who asked how a Swiss had become a full German professor, Einstein explained that the Kaiser had visited the University one day. "He asked to be introduced to Professor Einstein and I was brought forward," he said. "After that, as the Kaiser had called me a professor I had to be a full professor."*

Details were settled before the end of 1913, and it was arranged that he should take up his duties in Berlin on April 1st, 1914. It had been a remarkable triumph for a man not yet thirty-five, so much so that even Einstein himself, confident as he usually was of Einstein,

* His close friend Leon Watters later quoted him as saying: "Though I lived in Germany for many years, I never became a German citizen. I made this a condition of my going there. I never met the Kaiser, probably on that account."

mentally kept his fingers crossed. In the circumstances this was natural enough. He was still stuck on the General Theory, even with Marcel Grossmann's aid. He was still in the middle of "errors of thinking which caused me two years of hard work", as he described them, and to Besso he wrote deploring the fact that German theorists were not receptive to general discussion based on fundamental principles. He was, he added, somewhat uneasy as he saw the Berlin adventure approaching.

In Zurich, Louis Kollros, his old colleague of E. T. H. days, organised a farewell supper for him in the Kronenhalle. "We all regretted his departure," Kollros has said. "He himself was delighted at the prospect of being able to devote all his time to research ... delighted and a little anxious nevertheless; he did not know what the future held in store for him. When I accompanied him home that evening he turned to me and said: 'The gentlemen in Berlin are gambling on me as if I were a prize hen. As for myself I don't even know whether I'm going to lay another egg'."*

Einstein moved with his family from Zurich to Berlin on April 6th, 1914. Haber had helped him find and lease a flat in Berlin-Dahlem and here he spent the early part of the summer settling in.

While events moved on towards Freundlich's expedition to the Crimea, Einstein travelled each morning to his office in the Academy, then housed in the Prussian State Library on Unter den Linden. Here he arranged with his new colleagues from the University how, when and about what, he would lecture during the coming autumn term. And here he was visited by officials of the Kaiser Wilhelm Gesellschaft with whom he arranged details of the new institute. He has denied that when asked to outline his needs he said that these consisted only of pencils and paper which he would supply himself. However, it is quite clear that he was determined to keep himself as clear as possible of the German bureaucratic machinery.

In Berlin Einstein was to see for the first time how the ramifications of science spread out not only into philosophy and metaphysics, but into politics and power and how they penetrated, like the metal rods in a ferro-concrete building, organisations on which the equilibrium of European peace still rested. At first, he was barely distressed by the new climate, while there were compensations. His

---

* Einstein was apparently fond of the simile. Talking after dinner in Göttingen one evening with Paul Hertz, who taught theoretical physics there, he compared the whole concept of new ideas to that of a chicken laying an egg: "*Kieks — auf einmal ist es da.*" ("Cheep — suddenly there it is").

status had been raised not merely in scientific esteem and financial reward, but in the eyes of his relatives, particularly those of his mother. In his youth they had tended to write him off. Now, "they felt honoured to receive him in their homes and to be mentioned as his relatives."

There was above all, the new freedom to devote himself almost entirely to his work. The most urgent thing now was the expedition to Southern Russia to observe the eclipse in August, and from April onwards Einstein and his family were in regular and close contact with the Freundlichs. As the date of the expedition's departure approached, Einstein withdrew more and more into his own scientific carapace; more frequently, he became the Einstein of the later newspaper caricatures, insulated from the normal contacts of life by his own interior problems. Thus there was the occasion when he pushed back the plates at the end of a meal with the Freundlichs. Before a word could be said he began to cover a much-prized "party" table-cloth with equations as he talked with his host. "Had I kept it unwashed as my husband told me," says Frau Freundlich half a century afterwards, "it would be worth a fortune." But this was typical. "I have seen him in his keenness," Lord Samuel once wrote, "when no table was handy, kneel down on the floor and scribble diagrams and equations on a scrap of paper on a chair."

There was also the complementary occasion when the Freundlichs arrived to dine with the Einsteins. After a long wait without their host, Mileva answered the telephone to discover her husband was ringing from Dahlem. He had, he said, been waiting more than an hour at the underground station for Freundlich. As agreed Freundlich had kept the rendezvous at the Einstein apartment.

By this time Einstein was not only engrossed. He was also confident. Earlier doubts had been swept away and even before coming to Berlin in the spring he had written in high spirits to Besso, saying he was confident of the theory whatever the results of the eclipse expedition might be. This is revealing. For Einstein was saying that if a man stood fast by his intuition, if he hung on in the face of difficulties, if he really felt from an inner sense of conviction that he were right, then an explanation for discrepancies would arrive; inconsistencies in the evidence would become explicable. It was, although he does not seem to have realised it himself, a final farewell to Mach and his deification of the sensations. It was also indulgence in an act of faith. Only Einstein the philosopher, could have convinced Einstein the scientist that if the evidence did not agree with the theory then the evidence must be faulty.

All these hopes were wrecked by Germany's declaration of war on Russia on August 1st, 1914, her declaration of war on France two days later, and her invasion of Belgium which brought Britain into the war on August 4th. But Freundlich and the members of his team in Southern Russia were luckier than they might have been, although their equipment was impounded and they themselves were arrested and taken to Odessa. By the end of the month their exchange for a number of highranking Russian officers had been arranged and by September 2nd Freundlich was back in Berlin. Here he spent the rest of the war, mainly at the Observatory but giving part-time assistance to Einstein.

Thus the war delayed the testing of the General Theory for five years. But it was to affect Einstein decisively in one other way. For it was the instrument which finally brought his first marriage to an end.

His relations with Mileva had become increasingly fragile. Years later he complained that in Switzerland she had been jealous of all his friends, with the solitary exception of Solovine, and inferred that her disposition had made life together impossible. But he looked back more in sorrow than in pain, accepting with resignation the fact that nothing could have made the marriage work properly and acquitting both his wife and himself of anything worse than bad luck. In 1914 he was far less equable about the matter.

It was at least reasonable that Mileva should return to Zurich with the two sons in the summer of 1914; it was even more reasonable that she should stay with them there when war broke out in August — at least until the immediate prospects had become clearer. But by Christmas it was plain that something more was involved. Mileva remained in Switzerland with the children. Einstein, still a Swiss citizen, remained in Berlin, spending the holiday with Professor and Frau Nernst, a lonely but perhaps not entirely unhappy figure playing his violin to them on Christmas Eve.

Mileva did not return. Einstein did not care. In fact there is a good deal of circumstantial evidence to suggest that he was heartily glad to remain on his own while he got down to the hard work of completing the General Theory. Not all his friends felt this was a satisfactory situation, and Haber in particular began a long series of kindly but unsuccessful attemps to bring the two together again. The slender hope of this is shown by a letter that Einstein wrote to Besso, some months after the famous General Theory paper had been published and after he had experienced a stormy meeting with his wife in Switzerland. If he had not had the strength of mind

12

to keep her at a distance, he would, he said, have been worn out.

Even by Christmas, 1914, one problem was evident — how to provide for Mileva and the two sons, one aged ten, the other four. Einstein had a qualified affection for the boys, as long as it did not take up too much of his time, and he was anxious that they should not suffer from the break-up of their parents' marriage. For the next few years, therefore, money — and the difficulty of getting it without loss from wartime Germany to neutral Switzerland — became one of Einstein's preoccupations.

If the First World War quickly put a temporary spoke in one of Einstein's scientific wheels and brought his private life to a climax, it also did something far more important: it brought him face to face, for the first time, with the inter-relationships between science and world affairs. Until now he had looked on science as a vocation to be followed only by men of intelligence and moral integrity, occupying positions not higher than, but usually cut off from, most other people. They were not necessarily better but they were certainly different. Surely the appalling business of international politics, of war and all that went with it, was something in which they, last of all people, should be involved?

This belief was ingenuous. Newton himself had been an adviser to the British Admiralty. Michael Faraday and Sir Frederick Abel were advisers to the British War Office. Dewar and Abel produced cordite, Nobel invented dynamite, and the studies on the Stassfurt carried out by Van't Hoff whose chair Einstein now filled were of great use to Germany's wartime industry. Science had in fact been one of war's handmaidens since bronze replaced stone in prehistoric times. Yet the nature of Einstein's work on the fundamental problems of physics had tended to quarantine him away from this fact and his self-imposed dedication to the task had aided the process. He was, therefore, shocked at what he witnessed in Berlin. For now his colleagues leapt to arms unbidden, as certain as Rupert Brooke where duty lay. His former assistant, Ludwig Hopf, joined the German Air Ministry and helped to develop military aircraft. Otto Stern was soon serving with the forces on the eastern front from which he maintained contact with Einstein by a series of brief letters and field postcards. The young Max Born, brought to the University of Berlin from Göttingen when Planck persuaded the Prussian Ministry of Education that he needed help, worked first for the German air force and then for a military board investigating the physics of sound-ranging. Schwarzchild the astronomer, whose calculations were to support the first confirmation of Einstein's General Theory, served as a mathematical expert with the German armies on the eastern front. Nernst became first a War Ministry consultant, advising on chemical agents for shells and subsequently accepted a commission.

Above all there was Fritz Haber who had at once volunteered for service but been rejected on medical grounds. "His resulting depression," says his biographer, "disappeared when he received a problem from the Ordnance Department. Request was made for gasoline with a low freezing point, since the army expected to fight through a Russian winter." Furthermore it was not long before Haber was in uniform, and telling his wife that a scientist belonged to the world during times of peace but to his country during times of war. It had quickly become clear that his revolutionary method for producing ammonia — for which he was later awarded the Nobel Prize for Chemistry — was essential to the stockpiling of explosives and fertiliser without which the German war effort could hardly have continued. First he was consulted on how this process could best be utilised. Next he was brought in to advise on the practicability of gas warfare, first as a sergeant. "One of [his] great disappointments was lack of a higher military title", says his biographer. "As a full professor at a university, he had the feeling he was equivalent to a general; academy members had a comparable uniform for court occasions." Later he was commissioned as a captain — but not before he compelled his hesitating colleague Richard Willstatter to join in gas mask research: "I am a sergeant" he said. "I command you to the task." Haber soon joined forces with Nernst, and within a few months was supervising production of enough chlorine for the first German gas attack in the spring of 1915. By the following year he had become the head of Germany's chemical warfare service and, after experimenting with hundreds of substances, achieved a major technological success by introducing mustard gas in 1917. Einstein had no illusions. Reading a report of the Allied use of gas-bombs, he remarked to his colleagues: "This is supposed to say that they stunk first, but we know better how to do it."

Even Einstein, critical of his own country since youth, had expected something different from what he now witnessed. "One imagines that at least a few educated Germans had private moments of horror at the slaughter which was about to commence," says Fritz Ringer. "In public, however, German academics of all political persuasions spoke almost exclusively of their optimism and enthusiasm. Indeed, they greeted the war with a sense of relief. Party differences and class antagonisms seemed to evaporate at the call of national duty. Social Democrats marched singing to the front in the

company of their betters, and the mandarin intellectuals rejoiced at
the apparent rebirth of 'idealism' in Germany."

Reaction from the universities reinforced all Einstein's distaste
for what he saw as the exclusively German characteristic of marching to the band. He looked askance at his own colleagues and he
later tended to overlook the fact that Lindemann risked his life testing service aircraft, that Madame Curie drove Red Cross ambulances
and that both Rutherford and Langevin worked as scientists on the
inter-Allied anti-submarine committee which produced the first
Asdic detectors. It might be wrong for Allied scientists to prostitute
science; but, by Einstein's implication, it was worse for German
scientists to do the same thing since Germany had been the aggressor.
It was a plausible argument; but it should have destroyed any vestigial illusion that scientists could remain outside the battle.

The sight of the Berlin scientific establishment devoting itself to
war with hardly a murmur of dissent drove Einstein towards a treble
commitment to internationalism, pacifism and socialism. These were
all fine ideals and all appealed to the best in him. Yet although there
is little evidence that his support had any effect on the course of
history, that support, the direct result of his wartime experiences in
Berlin, led him after the war into waters where he was dangerously
out of his depth. By that time, he was a world figure. All his public
actions were followed — either with reverence or amusement. The
upshot was a worldwide belief that Einstein was fired by an almost
saintly honesty of purpose and a less justifiable feeling that scientists
almost inevitably lost their way in the corridors of power.

The war thus revolutionised Einstein's attitude to the world
about him. He could no longer remain isolated. He had to play his
part on the side of the angels. But physics still came first. It held
him to Berlin, despite the fact that while he apparently hoped for
an Allied victory he was forced to turn a Nelsonian blind eye not
only to the work of his colleagues but even to the sources of some of
his own money. For this came, at least in part, from Leopold Koppel
who in 1916 created the Kaiser Wilhelm Foundation for Military
Technical Sciences. The full details of Einstein's links with Koppel
are not known, but in a letter to Freundlich in December, 1913,
Einstein named Koppel as the man providing his Academy salary.
According to the Max Planck Gesellschaft into which the Kaiser
Wilhelm Institute was transformed in 1946, Einstein's Institute for
Physics received regular sums — 25,000 marks from October 1st,
1917 to March 31st, 1918 — from the Koppel donation which set up
the military foundation. Einstein himself wrote to Born in 1919

saying that his academic pay depended on Herr Koppel, while Professor Jens of Tübingen University has stated that Einstein "was first given the opportunity for undisturbed research by a Prussian banker who undertook to pay Einstein a supplementary salary of 4,000 Reichsmarks from April 1st, 1914 onwards for a period of twelve years", and names the banker as Koppel. "Einstein," he sums up, "knew that the sumptuous bed in which he lay swarmed with bugs."

Whatever the exact figures, it is clear that Einstein at the height of his powers was being supported by the very people he was soon condemning, and exibiting a surprising ability to prevent his left hand know what his right hand was doing. But physics came first; so much so that even had he troubled to think about the matter there would have been no contradiction in declaiming against the war while using for science the money of those who supported the war. Like Major Barbara, Einstein would no doubt have reflected that the money was better in his hands than theirs.

Einstein's ingrained distrust of all things military and of all things Prussian was first revealed clearly by his reaction to the "Manifesto to the Civilized World". This manifesto was a fulsome and pained expression of surprise that the world should have objected to the German invasion of Belgium. Issued early in October 1914, it disclaimed Germany's war guilt, justified the violation of Belgium on the grounds that it would have been suicide to have done anything else, spoke of "Russian hordes . . . unleashed against the white race" in the tones of Dr. Goebbels twenty years on, and claimed that "were it not for German militarism, German culture would have been wiped off the face of the earth". The Manifesto gained ninety-three supporters from the upper echelons of the intellectual world where it was circulated. Wilhelm Röntgen, the discoverer of X-rays, signed it. So did Ernst Haeckel the evolutionist. So did Paul Ehrlich, the biologist. And so did Max Planck.

A reaction to "The Manifesto of the 93" as it became known came within days from George Nicolai, Professor of Physiology in the University of Berlin, soon to be the author of *The Biology of War,* and the conscript-turned-pacifist who during the closing months of the war made a sensational escape from Germany by plane. The exact part that Einstein played in Nicolai's "Manifesto to Europeans" is not clear, but Nicolai himself gives him credit for being co-author. Even though the counter-manifesto was a joint effort, its wording is extraordinarily reminiscent of the statements, announcements, messages and exhortations for international co-operation which were to come in a stream from Einstein throughout the next forty years.

Drawn up in the University of Berlin, it was circulated among the professors. It was signed by Nicolai and by Einstein. It was signed by Wilhelm Forster, the eighty-year-old head of the Berlin Observatory who had already signed the Manifesto of the 93, and by Otto Buek. That was all.

Einstein no doubt felt its ineffectiveness, and a month later was drawn for the first time into membership of a political party. This was the Bund Neues Vaterland, established on November 16th, 1914 and including among its founder-members the banker Hugo Simon who in 1919 became Prussian Minister of Finance, and Ernst Reuter who became a famous burgomaster of Berlin after the Second World War. The main object of the group was to bring about an early peace. The second was the creation of an international body that would make future wars impossible. Both were aims with which Einstein wholeheartedly sympathised and he is reported to have been "very active, attending meetings and delivering speeches". The Bund, struggling for existence in a nation not only at war but enthusiastically supporting the war, was obviously doomed to an early death. However, Einstein's support was open, something very different from the support which he was to give, through connections in Holland and Switzerland, to the forces striving for an early end to the war even if this involved Germany's defeat.

It has been said with some justice that "to work in any open way for peace under the Kaiser's regime in 1914 was equivalent to treason" and if Einstein is taken to be a German some of his actions have more than a touch of it. Had all of them been publicly known in the immediate aftermath of the Armistice, his trials and tribulations during the early 1920s would have been that much greater. For he appears to have hoped not only for an end to the war but, more specifically, for German defeat. The attitude linked him loosely with at least part of the "German resistance" of thirty years later, although with one difference. In the Europe of 1914–1918 he was not only able to continue his life's work from his priviliged position in Berlin; he was also able to carry on his "resistance" work of pleading peace in both Holland and Switzerland with the minimum of personal risk since in any trouble he could always claim the protection of his Swiss passport. There is nothing shameful in the fact that circumstance thus enabled him to have the best of both worlds; yet it tended to widen the gap that already separated him from most other men.

Einstein's first wartime contacts outside Germany — with the exception of personal letters to his wife — were with Ehrenfest and Lorentz in Holland. To both he wrote with a mixture of resignation, pity and disgust. How was it possible for sane men to behave like this? Especially, how was it possible for some of the great men of science to support war, doing in the name of the State what had once been done in the name of religion? Surely something could be done to unite men of science in the various "Fatherlands"? Surely scholars and intellectuals were not helpless? This was the tenor of his writings for the first year of the war. He seems, despite everything, to have gone on hoping that peace would break out.

Then, in September 1915, he left Berlin for Switzerland. With his Swiss passport, his wife still living in Zurich, and his numerous friends in both Zurich and Berne, this was on the face of it an acceptable journey to make. Its main object, however, was to visit Romain Rolland, the famous author and pacifist then living in Vevey on the shores of Lake Geneva. Einstein had written to Rolland in March, telling him that he had heard through the Bund Neues Vaterland of Rolland's efforts to remove the differences between the French and the German people. He was, he went on, anxious to help in any way possible.

It is not quite clear how he thought he could help, but Rolland in neutral Switzerland subsequently received a letter from Berlin saying that there was much good news about their work which could be given by a man close to them — the scholar Einstein who would be visiting him shortly.

Now, in mid-September, Einstein arrived at Vevey from Zurich, accompanied by Dr. Zangger from the E.T.H., who had helped get him back there in 1912. Rolland's long diary entry of September 16th, 1915 is extraordinarily revealing.

> Professor Einstein, the brilliant physicist and mathematician of the University of Berlin, who wrote to me last winter, came to see me from Zurich, where he is staying, with his friend, Professor Dr. Zangger, [this reads.] We spent the whole of the afternoon on the terrace of the Hotel Mooser, at the bottom of the garden, amid swarms of bees who were plundering the ivy, which was in flower. Einstein is still young, not very tall, with an ample figure, great mane of hair a little frizzled and dry, very black but sprinkled with grey, which rises from a high forehead, with nose fleshy and prominent, small mouth, full lips, a small moustache cut short, full cheeks and rounded chin. He speaks French with difficulty and mixes it with German. He is very lively and gay; and he finds no difficulty in giving an amusing twist to the most serious of subjects. He is Swiss by origin, born in Germany, a naturalised German and then, as far as I can understand, re-naturalised Swiss two or three years before the war. I admire the Swiss German's brilliant vitality. Two or three small

cantons have given Germany her greatest modern painter, Boecklin;
her greatest novelist, Keller; her greatest poet, Spitteler; her greatest
physicist, Einstein. And what others are there that I fail to mention?
And, in all, this common quality as much in Einstein as in Spitteler;
absolute independence of the spirit, solitary and happy. Einstein is
unbelievably free in his judgements on Germany where he lives. No
German has such a liberty. Anyone other than he would suffer by
being so isolated in his thoughts during this terrible year. Not he,
however. He laughs. And he has even been able, during the war, to
write his most important scientific work. I asked him if he expressed
his views to his German friends and talked about them. He said no.
He contents himself with asking a series of Socratic questions in order
to disturb their complacency. And he says that "people don't like
that much". What he says is hardly encouraging; for it shows the
impossibility of concluding a peace with Germany before one has
crushed her. Einstein says that the situation seems to him far less
favourable than it was a few months ago. The victories on the Russian
front have revived the pride and the appetite of the Germans. "Hungry" seems to Einstein to be the word which best characterises the
Germans. Above all one sees the will for power, the admiration for
force and their exclusive decision for conquests and annexations. The
Government is more moderate than the nation. It wishes to evacuate
Belgium but is unable to do so. The officers threatened revolt. The big
bankers, the industrialists, big business, is all-powerful; they expect
to be paid for the sacrifices they have made, the Emperor is only a tool
in their hands and in those of the officers; he is good, feeble, hopeless
about the war that he has never wanted, but into which he was forced
because he is so easy to manipulate. All his unpredictable actions of the
last few years, and his disconcerting brusquenesses, were carefully prepared by pan-German groups who used him without his knowing it.
Tirpitz and Falkenhayn are the protagonists of the most bloody
action. Falkenhayn seems the most dangerous; Tirpitz is above all a
powerful impersonal machine. As to the intellectuals in the universities,
Einstein divides them into two very clear classes; the mathematicians,
doctors and the exact sciences who are tolerant; and the historians and
the arts faculties which stir up the nationalist passions. The mass of
the nation is immensely submissive, "domesticated" (Einstein approves
of this description by Spitteler). Einstein blames above all else the
education which is aimed at national pride and blind submission to
the state. He does not think that race is responsible since French Hu-
guenots, refugees for two centuries, have the same characteristics. The
socialists are the only independent element (to some extent); however,
they form only a minority of the party grouped round Bernstein. The
Bund Neues Vaterland goes ahead only slowly and does not grow
much. Einstein does not expect any salvation of Germany by herself;
she has neither the energy nor the audacity to make such an initiative.

He hopes for a victory by the Allies which will ruin the power of Prussia and of the dynasty. When I asked whether this would not rally the nation around its unfortunate masters, Einstein the sceptic said that faithfulness was not a part of its nature; for her masters she has the admiration of fear and the respect for force, but no affection; if this force is smashed Germany will become like a country of savages who having adored their idol, throw it into the flames when they realise that they have been defeated. Einstein and Zangger dream of a partitioned Germany; on one hand southern Germany and Austria, on the other Prussia. But such a break-up of the Empire is more than doubtful. In Germany, everyone is convinced of victory; and one hears officially that the war will continue only for another six months or even less. However, Einstein says that those who know realise that the situation is grave and that it will become worse if the war goes on. It is not food which they will feel the most need of but certain chemical products necessary for the war. It is true that the ingenuity, truly admirable, of the German professors, supplies the necessary products in the form of substitutes. All the professors at the universities have been put at the head of military services or commissions. Alone, Einstein has refused to take part. Whatever the outcome of the war the main victim will be France. All Germans know this; and for this reason Germany has a pitying sympathy. When I said that this sympathy from the Germans always has, for us, a disdainful character, Einstein and Zangger strongly protested. The political interest of England grows all the time in their eyes. Zangger, like all the German Swiss, speaks of it with antipathy. He is well-informed and gives little-known proofs of British speculation. England has decided that France should hold at Marseilles (as well as at Genoa) goods destined for Switzerland. After that she sells them at double or treble the price to the Swiss. The war is really a battle between two worlds. France and Europe are crushed between them. Einstein, in spite of his lack of sympathy for England, prefers her victory to that of Germany because she will be more able to bring the world back to life.

We speak of the voluntary blindness and the lack of psychology on the part of the Germans. Einstein describes, laughing as he does so, how at each meeting of the Council of the University of Berlin, all the professors meet after the session in a café and there *each time,* the conversation opens with the same question: "Why does the world hate us?" Then everyone talks, everyone gives his own reply and everyone takes care not to say the truth. He spoke of one general meeting of the universities which was held in secret last July; there it was discussed whether the German universities should break all their links with the rest of the world's universities and academies. The motion was turned down by the universities of Southern Germany which formed the majority. But the University of Berlin supported it. She is the most official and the most imperialist of them all; her professors are specially chosen with this in mind.

It is clear that Einstein, in the hatred of his fellow-countrymen that Rolland's entry indicates, forgot that they, as well as the English, heard "bugles calling for them from sad shires"; for once his humanity escaped him. Another significant point in Rolland's account is the exculpation of the Kaiser. It seems unlikely that Einstein was swayed by personal sympathies, and all accounts of a meeting between the two men appear to be apocryphal. But he clung to the Emperor's good intentions. "The Kaiser meant well," he said in an interview a decade after the end of the war. "He often had the right instinct. His intuitions were frequently more inspired than the laboured reasons of his Foreign Office. Unfortunately, the Kaiser was always surrounded by poor advisers." And, asked whether the Kaiser or the Jews were responsible for the debacle of 1918, he replied: "Both are largely guiltless. The German debacle was due to the fact that the German people, especially the upper classes, failed to produce men of character strong enough to take hold of the reins of government and to tell the truth to the Kaiser."

With Rolland, Einstein laid the blame unequivocally on what he saw as the essential German spirit, but the intensity of his feeling shocked Rolland. The two men exchanged a few more words, standing on the station platform at Vevey as the train prepared to leave for Berne. "In looking at Einstein," wrote Rolland, "I noted how he, one of the very few men whose spirit had remained free among the general servility, had been led, as a reaction, to see the worst side of his own nation and to judge her almost with the severity of her enemies. I known certain men in the French camp who, for the same reason, would shake hands with him. (Incidentally, Einstein is a Jew which explains his international outlook and the mocking character of his criticism)." The strength of Einstein's feeling was remarkable; and he must have questioned even the scientific benefits of life in Berlin when he considered that his patrons included the creator and financial supporter of the Kaiser Wilhelm Foundation for Military Technical Sciences.

In neutral Switzerland his views could be declared without fear of serious contradiction. In Germany, he put a slightly different emphasis on reasons for the war. Asked by the Berlin Goethe Association a few months after his return for a short article outlining his feelings, he made no mention of the German guilt he had stressed so strongly to Rolland, but bluntly laid the cause of war on the aggresive nature of *homo sapiens*.

This was a good deal more cautious than the opinions he had voiced to Rolland. But by the end of 1915, prospects of a quick victory had faded and with them went the comparative freedom of the first year of war. Not even Einstein would have survived expression of open hope "for a victory by the Allies which will ruin the power of Prussia and the dynasty". Indeed, he seems to have compartmentalised his feelings with surprising ease. He remained on the friendliest terms with Haber, the poison gas expert, and with his help was able to squeeze from the German General Staff a travel permit for a colleague. He was also, according to Max Born, one of the Berlin intellectuals who in midwar met high officials in the German Foreign Office to dissuade them from starting unrestricted U-boat warfare "as it would be bound to bring the United States into the war and thus lead to final defeat."

However, it can be claimed that Einstein was supporting such humanitarian pleas on moral grounds under the cover of expediency. For as hopes of a quick victory faded, any suggestions of limiting operations had a defeatist ring that could no longer be tolerated. The Bund Neues Vaterland was outlawed, and while hints of a negotiated peace might be made privately, they produced in public the same vilification that comparable ideas produced in Britain. There is little evidence that this tightening of the official attitude had much effect on Einstein's privately-expressed views, and his correspondence with Lorentz, largely concerned with scientific work, continued to be sprinkled with the strongest pacifist sentiments which could have been noted by the censor. Luckily he was not involved in work where indiscretion would have been more dangerous to friends than to foes.

He retained the privileged position of a critic whose presence would be tolerated although his views were disliked. This position was the result partly of the renown which the General Theory had brought him in 1915, partly of his legal status as a Swiss. It nevertheless rankled with more than one Allied scientist when the war was over. They would have been even more rankled had they known that on one occasion he had discussed proposals for an improved airfoil with the Luftverkehrsgesellschaft in Berlin-Johannistal.

The story was brought to light in September 1955 when the international journal *Interavia* published the facsimile of a letter written by Einstein on September 7th, 1954 to the German pilot Paul G. Erhardt.* The previous month Erhardt had written to Einstein

---

* My attention was drawn to the *Interavia* material after publication of *Einstein* in the United States by Professor Squire of the West Virginia University's Department of Aerospace Engineering.

recalling that in 1917 he, Erhardt, had taken over technical management of the experimental section of the Luftverkehrsgesellschaft in
Berlin-Johannistal. "My duties", he wrote, "included the thankless
task of dealing with offers from inventors ... I was therefore not
exactly enthusiastic when one day I found on my desk a several-page
document of this kind, written by hand to make matters worse...
However, my first glance through the weighty manuscript showed
me that the writer had far greater knowledge of theoretical physics
than I had."

Einstein's proposal was for an airfoil which he believed would
provide maximum lift with minimum drag. Within a few weeks an
experimental version of the new airfoil had been fitted to the fuse-
lage of an LVG biplane which was then test-flown from Adlershof
airfield. First one pilot tried it, then another. But, as Ehrhardt had
feared, the new wing failed to come up to Einstein's expectations. The
experiment was called off — and Ehrhardt recalled how at the concluding meeting with the head of the LVG Einstein read them all a
short paper on relativity.

Replying in 1954 to Ehrhardt's letter, Einstein said that he
clearly recalled the event and, after describing the theory on which
his proposals had been made, said that he had not worked it out in
full. "I have to admit," he concluded, "that I have often been
ashamed of my folly of those days, but got a great deal of pleasure
from your good-natured letter."

The "folly" appears to have been scientific folly, and Einstein's
letter does not imply that he regretted his meeting with Ehrhardt,
the date of which is not certain. His proposal might have led to an
improved aircraft, although not necessarily to an improved military
aircraft, since most German firms kept alive an interest in civilian
planes. Furthermore, Einstein's idea appears to have been for a foil
which would provide more lift at low speeds, not high speeds, and
would therefore be of limited value — but one possibly comparable
to that used on the British DH 6, built mainly for primary training
of service pilots. Nevertheless there is something incongruous in the
idea of Einstein hob-nobbing with German aircraft designers either
during the war or after it.

As a Swiss, Einstein retained advantages in Berlin, not the least
being freedom to visit neutral countries with less bureaucratic interference than most Germans, and he made use of this at Easter 1916
to visit his wife in Zurich. The meeting was disastrous. Einstein,
according to his correspondence with Besso, made an irrevocable
decision not to see Mileva again. Hans stopped writing to his father

when Einstein returned to Berlin. And when, Mileva being ill, the question of another visit to Zurich was raised in the summer, Einstein poured out his troubles in a long letter to Besso who henceforth was to act as honest broker between the couple. If he came to Zurich, he said, Mileva would demand to see him and he would have to refuse, partly because of his earlier decision, partly to avoid emotional scenes. If his wife had to go to hospital that would be different. Then he would visit her — and see the children on neutral ground. Otherwise, "no".

From now onwards Besso — or "Uncle Toby" as Einstein, remembering *Tristram Shandy*, sometimes called him — acted as a regular go-between, helping to arrange schools for the boys, working out expenses, and advising him of the current Mileva situation in Zurich in a long series of letters that were divided between scientific gossip and domestic detail.

With the worsening war situation, even travel abroad became complicated. In the autumn of 1916 Einstein visited Holland, but was able to do so only after Lorentz had sent him an official invitation and he had obtained his original Swiss naturalisation papers from Zurich.

Soon after his return from Leiden to Berlin, Einstein discovered that his old friend Friedrich Adler not only thought along anti-war lines similar to his own but had taken up arms to reinforce them. In 1912 Adler had left Switzerland for Austria and here, desperate at the Government's refusal to convene Parliament and thus put its action to the test of public debate, he took what seemed to be the most reasonable logical action. In October 1916, he walked into the fashionable Hotel Meissel and Schadn and at point-blank range shot dead the Prime Minister, Count Stürgkh.

When Adler was put on trial Einstein wrote offering to give evidence as a character witness, an offer which Adler, in keeping with his subsequent actions, appears to have loftily declined as being unnecessary. Awaiting trial, he settled down into a succession of prisons and military fortresses to write a long thesis on relativity, "Local Time, System Time, Zone Time".

On July 14th, 1917, Adler wrote to Einstein asking for advice on his work. Einstein replied cordially, and a typewritten draft of the manuscript soon arrived in Berlin. Meanwhile, other copies were being sent to psychiatrists and physicists who were asked whether Adler was mentally deranged. "The experts, especially the physicists, were placed in a very difficult situation," says Philipp Frank, who himself received a copy. "Adler's father and family desired that this work should be made the basis for the opinion that Adler was mentally deranged. But this would necessarily be highly insulting to the author, since he believed that he had produced an excellent scientific achievement. Moreover, speaking objectively, there was nothing in any way abnormal about it except that his arguments were wrong." Einstein held much the same views, noting that it was based on "very shaky foundations".

Whether or not Adler's critical study of relativity influenced his fate is unclear. But although he was condemned to death, this sentence was commuted to eighteen months, probably the most lenient punishment in history for assassination of a Prime Minister. The eighteen months do not seem to have been notably rigorous; and a letter to Einstein, written from the military fortress of Stein-an-Donau in July 1918, reveals a prisoner happily immersed in the problems of science who could end his letter with the comment that in these difficult times conditions were much better inside prison walls than outside them.

Einstein's correspondence with Adler was carried on as he struggled to counteract a serious breakdown, partly nervous collapse, partly long standing stomach upset, the latter no doubt exacerbated by the trials of wartime Berlin and a bachelor existence. At first he thought he had cancer and confided the fact to Freundlich, adding that it was unimportant whether or not he died, since his theory of General Relativity had been published* and that was what really mattered. Freundlich induced him to visit a relative of his wife, a Dr. Rosenheim, who quickly diagnosed the stomach trouble which was to worry him for the rest of his life.

The illness was hardly surprising. For years he had been deeply immersed in scientific work which has been described as the greatest intellectual effort of any single human brain. His views on the war were different from those of the men and women around him. In addition, he was living a makeshift existence which gave full rein to the inclination summed up by his doctor friend Janos Plesch. "As his mind knows no limits, so his body follows no set rules," he wrote; "he sleeps until he is wakened; he stays awake until he is told to go to bed; he will go hungry until he is given something to eat; and then he eats until he is stopped." That Einstein, mentally hard-pressed and physically underorganised, should experience a breakdown in wartime Berlin is not to be wondered at; the surprise is that he avoided one so long.

During the first two months he lost four stone in weight.

* See p. 198

Although he wrote to Lorentz in April that he was getting better, it was summer before he was out and about, and August before he was able to recuperate in Switzerland.

While he was ill Hedwig Born, the young wife of Max Born, became a frequent visitor. "His utter independence and objectivity, and his serene outlook, enabled me to ride up over the awful darkness of those days and to look far beyond the desperate day-to-day conditions," she has said of the years in the German capital.

Independence from the hopes and fears of ordinary men included independence from the fear of death itself. "No," Einstein told Frau Born when on one visit during his illness she asked whether he was afraid of dying. "I feel myself so much a part of all life that I am not in the least concerned with the beginning or the end of the concrete existence of any particular person in this unending stream." This, she says, was typical of the unity which he looked for in all nature.

> It is probably not surprising that it was he who helped me to be an objective scientist, and to avoid feeling that the whole thing was impersonal. Modern physics left me standing. Here was only objective truth, which unhappily meant nothing to me, and perhaps the possibility that in the future everything would be expressed scientifically. So I asked Einstein one day "Do you believe that absolutely everything can be expressed scientifically?" "Yes," he replied, "it would be possible, but it would make no sense. It would be description without meaning — as if you described a Beethoven symphony as a variation of wave pressure." This was a great solace to me.

There was certainly a flaw in this attempt to regard all human life — even one's own — as merely a bubble on the cosmic stream. To Freundlich, Einstein once confided that there was no one in the world whose death would worry him. "I thought how terrible it was for a man with a wife and two children to believe and say such a thing," says Frau Freundlich. "Then, a year or so afterwards, Einstein's mother died in Berlin, where she had come to spend the last few months of her life with him. In a way I was glad. For Einstein wept, like other men, and I knew that he could really care for someone." And many years later his friend Gustav Bucky wrote: "He believed that nothing really touched him inwardly. But this man who never wanted to show emotion wrote just one sentence to me after my bad illness: 'From now on, I will be thankful every hour of my life that we are left together'." Always, despite himself, humanity kept breaking in.

Einstein's illness of 1917 had a more important result than stomach trouble. For it at last brought him under the wing, first mothering and eventually matrimonial, of his cousin Elsa. At what point they renewed their youthful acquaintance is vague but it was almost inevitable that he should meet, if only on a family basis, the cousin he remembered from his childhood days in Munich.

Elsa's mother was the sister of Pauline Koch, which meant that both Elsa and Albert could claim Cäsar Koch as an uncle, while both were also related farther back along the family tree. By 1917 Elsa had become Elsa Lowenthal, a pleasant widow with two daughters, Ilse aged twenty and Margot aged eighteen. In appearance she was comfortable rather than beautiful and she lacked the curiosity which had at times made Mileva so mentally importunate. "I'm glad my wife doesn't know any science," Einstein later said to a colleague. "My first wife did."

Near-sighted and slightly provincial, Elsa was an easy butt during her husband's triumphal progress through the world for the enemies which her protectiveness easily made. But she was careful, conscientious, undemanding, and suitably awed by fame — in many ways the ideal wife for the absentminded genius of which Einstein was the epitome. Her character was unconsciously described by Einstein himself when he made a remark to his friend Philipp Frank "based," as Frank says, "on many years of experience". Said Einstein: "When women are in their homes, they are attached to their furniture. They run round it all day long and are always fussing over it. But when I am with a woman on a journey, I am the only piece of furniture that she has available, and she cannot refrain from moving round me all day long and improving something about me."

It is not true that from 1917 onwards Einstein allowed Elsa to make up his mind for him on everything except science, pacifism and politics. Even outside the three interests of his life, only Einstein made up Einstein's mind. But when he had done so he allowed Elsa to organise details, to implement decisions, to handle the minutiae and thus allow him to get on with his work. Field Marshal Montgomery once wrote in a privately produced booklet for his troops that "the wise commander... will be well advised to withdraw to his tent or caravan after dinner at night and have time for quiet thoughts and reflection." Montgomery had no wish to be worried by unnecessary detail. Neither had Einstein.

During his illness Elsa, not surprisingly, looked after him. In the later stages of his convalescence he was taken to the Haberlandstrasse apartment. Given the context, it was a not unexpected outcome that in 1919, after finally obtaining a divorce from Mileva, he should marry cousin Elsa.

As he slowly recovered in 1917 he decided to finish his recuperation in Switzerland; the Swiss citizen thus exchanged the growing austerity of wartime Berlin for the comparative luxury of a neutral country. He had intended to take the cure at Tarasp in the Lower Engadine but, as he explained to Besso, lack of funds forced him to content himself with a rest at his mother's in Lucerne.

In Switzerland he had hoped to meet Rolland again. When this proved impossible, he wrote instead. His letter was long and pessimistic, although he claimed that he was not more depressed than he had been two years previously. He criticised Germany's religion of power, stressed that it would be dangerous to come to terms with her, and emphasised that she must be made to realise that neither force nor treachery would work any longer.

The vigour of the anti-German sentiments which Einstein expressed struck Rolland forcefully. In his diary he pointed out that the policy of crushing Germany had no greater supporters than some prominent Germans. "I note once again," he added, "the extreme injustice, through an excess of justice, to which the most liberal spirits come, vis-à-vis their own country . . ."

Bearing all this in mind it is at first strange that Einstein should have returned to Berlin as quickly as he did. Zangger wrote to Rolland urging him to induce the visitor to remain in Switzerland. Other friends did the same. But after spending a week with his two sons in Arosa, he returned from the country which he loved to the country he detested.

The unfortunate meeting with Mileva at Easter, 1916, had not been repeated. He had no intention that it should be, and any hint that he was making more than a brief visit to Switzerland might well have brought his wife to his door. He had continued to support her; but now more than ever he had no wish to be brought personally into the negotiations, so far mainly conducted through Besso, the ever-faithful go-between. In a letter written to him on May 15th, he confided that he was increasingly hard-pressed financially. Of his total income of about 13,000 marks a year, roughly 7,000 was being sent regularly for the upkeep of his wife and children. Another 600 marks a year went to his mother in Lucerne, and some of his customary additional fees were now disappearing. He had perilously little left to maintain the status of a professor, let alone anything for luxuries or reserves. He had, after all, been obliged to abandon fashionable Tarasp for homely Lucerne.

Soon, however, there was hope of a change. Shortly after his return to Berlin, he told Besso that his address would in future be

Haberlandstrasse 5, adding that his move seemed to have taken place already — a turn of phrase which suggests that Elsa was the initiator of the marriage which was to take place in eighteen months' time.

This was to have little effect on the course of Einstein's purely scientific career which had reached its climax before 1919. It did, however, affect crucially his impact on the world, as father-figure, as oracle, as the man whose support was for years a useful weapon in the hands of any group ingenious enough to win it. For without the care and protecting intervention of this kindly figure, placid and housewifely, of no intellectual pretensions but with a practised mothering ability which made her the ideal organiser of genius, two things would almost certainly have happened: he would have cracked under the strain of unrelenting publicity and public demands, and withdrawn from pacifism, Zionism and socialism, into the shell where he carried on his scientific work. He would also have made a fool of himself more often than he did, have issued more statements that he had to retract, signed more documents without reading them properly, and been used more frequently by men of ill-will.

From the first, Elsa knew the part that had been cut out for her. "All I can do is to look after his outside affairs, take business matters off his shoulders, and take care that he is not interrupted in his work," she said during his visit to England in 1921. "It is enough to be a means of communication between him and all sorts of human beings." And a decade later, describing her role to Dr. Chaim Tschernowitz, the Jewish scholar who was visiting their house outside Berlin, she said: "When the Americans come to my house they carry away details about Einstein and his life, and about me they say incidentally: he has a good wife, who is very hospitable, and offers a fine table." The point of her remark was not to be missed, says Dr. Tschernowitz. "Einstein might be the lion among thinkers, but this good woman felt, and rightly so, that to a large extent the world owed him to her, who watched over him as one might over a child." Einstein was aware of these possibilities. Thus in the summer of 1917 he willingly became the Bohemian setpiece of a bourgeois household.

It was part of his genius that he could isolate himself from his surroundings, and this was never more necessary than in the apartment of № 5, Haberlandstrasse. On the dark green wallpaper of the main sitting-room there hung the expected portrait of Frederick the Great, looking down without a smile on the heavy immobility of the Biedermeier furniture, on the corner cabinets stocked with porcelain, on the huge round central table with the starched white tablecloth edged with crochet, on Schiller and Goethe, the white eyes of their white busts firmly fixed on each other from opposite sides of the room. Beyond lay the library, its walls soon to be ornamented by a large framed picture of Michael Faraday. Into this epitome of all things that were proper came Albert Einstein, unchangeable by the pleas of Elsa, happy to be shepherded by her through the mundane necessities of everyday life, grateful for the protecting shield which she was to interpose between himself and the over-curious world, yet quite determined to go his own way in the things that mattered.

Before the situation could be regularised, however, Mileva had to agree to a divorce. This she did within less than a year. Negotiations were under way by the early summer of 1918 when Einstein sent through Besso details of how he would be prepared to support her and the children. During these negotiations the question of the Nobel Prize was raised. It is not quite certain who first suggested that the interest from the Prize, then some 30,000 Swedish kroner, would be sufficient to keep Einstein's family in at least modest circumstances, but it appears to have been Mileva. If so, it is a striking tribute to her faith in him.

Early in July, Einstein received the first divorce papers. Then he had to give evidence before a tribunal in Berlin. And after that an ever-growing dossier had to be returned to Zurich. All this he took lightly enough, acknowledging receipt of the first papers with the exclamation "Till Eulenspiegel!" and later noting to Besso that the divorce was entertaining all those in Berlin who were in the know.

As the legal moves continued and as Einstein heard from friends in Holland that the British were planning to carry out a test of his theory during the eclipse of 1919, the war situation began to change dramatically. After the failure of the great German offensive in the spring, the influence of the United States began decisively to affect the balance of forces. On the Western Front preparations continued for the Allied offensive which in August 1918 ruptured the German front for the first time in four years. In September the Allied Expeditionary Force at Salonika broke through the Bulgarian lines and the following month British forces gained a decisive victory over the Turks, those redoubtable German allies in the Middle East. On November 9th, the Kaiser abdicated. Karl Ebert, the staunch imperturbable saddler's son was handed the Chancellorship and at 2 p. m. the Republic was proclaimed from the steps of the Reichstag.

For Einstein, as for other Germans of like mind, the Republic and the Armistice were twin trumpets heralding the millenium. Now, they fondly imagined, they would have help in the task of leading their misguided countrymen back into the peaceful ways from which they had been diverted half a century earlier. Perhaps so. But even Einstein, optimistic as ever, might have thought twice as he considered his old friend Planck. A few weeks before the fall of the Kaiser, the Bund Neues Vaterland, which had continued an underground existence since being banned by the authorities in February 1916, came into the open once more. Einstein sent Planck a copy of the opening declaration and asked for his support. But this would mean a demand for the Kaiser's abdication; Planck replied that his oath to the Emperor made support impossible. No such problems worried Albert Einstein who threw himself wholeheartedly on the side of the Republic.

With the formation of workers' and soldiers' councils which followed the disintegration of law and order on November 11th, there had come a similar move in the University of Berlin. Here one of the first actions of the student council was to depose and lock up the Rector and other members of the staff. The remaining members of the administration knew Einstein's left-wing views and turned to him for help. Would he intervene on their behalf with the students?

Einstein telephoned Max Born and another colleague, the psychologist Max Wertheimer. The three men made their way to the Reichstag where the student council was meeting.

As soon as Einstein was recognised, all doors were opened, and the trio was escorted to a room where the student council was in session. The chairman, before dealing with their business, asked Einstein what he thought of the new regulations for students. He did not think very much of them, a reaction which caused the council to decide that the problem presented by the three professors was not one for them but, instead, for the new government.

In the Reich Chancellor's Palace, amid a contradiction of Imperial footmen and delegations from the new workers' and soldiers' councils, the three men were received by President Ebert. The fate of the Reich itself still hung in the balance and he could spare them little time. But he wrote for them a few words to the appropriate minister.

At the time, November 1918, Einstein was, within the comparatively small world of physicists, a creature of extraordinary power and imagination. Outside it, he was still unknown. This situation was to be dramatically altered within a year.

# 8

## *THE SENSORIUM OF GOD*

THE AUTUMN OF 1918 WHICH BROUGHT GERMANY BITTER AND apparently irretrievable defeat also brought the Republic. To Einstein this was a gleam of hope in the darkness, the only one which held out a promise for the future as the Empire dissolved between the hammer of the Allied armies on the west and the anvil of emergent communism to the east. Just as he now believed there was political hope for a country he had so long considered beyond hope, so was there at last the prospect of proof or disproof for the General Theory of Relativity over whose difficulties he had triumphed while the war went on.

In Berlin, four years earlier, he had settled down to work in earnest. First he had expectantly looked forward to the results which Freundlich and his party would bring back from the Crimea. Yet even had their efforts not been snuffed out by the war, they would have provided experimental confirmation only for a theory which was incomplete. For while Einstein was now convinced of the revolutionary idea that gravity was not force but a property of space itself he had not yet been able to construct the mathematical framework within which it could be described. He continued to wrestle with this task as his colleagues went to war, Haber struggled with his poison-gas production and his English friend Lindemann reported at the Royal Aircraft Factory, Farnborough, as a temporary technical assistant at £3 a week.

After the failure of the Russian expedition to the Crimea and Freundlich's return to Berlin, he pressed on with the theoretical work for every available minute, letting slide everything that would slide. During this period Freundlich, entering Einstein's study, saw hanging from the ceiling a large meat-hook end bearing a thick sheaf of letters. These, Einstein explained, he had no time to answer. Freundlich, asking what he did when the hook was filled up, was answered by two words: "Burn them."

The agony continued into the summer of 1915 and into the autumn. In November 1915, he wrote to Sommerfeld saying that he had lived through the most exacting and the most fruitful period of his life. He had at last realised what was wrong with his field equations for gravitation. He had tackled the problem from a different point and had finally succeeded. Sommerfeld was not impressed at first — causing Einstein to send him a postcard saying that he would be convinced once he had studied the General Theory which was about to be published.

Sommerfeld did not have long to wait. There soon appeared Volume 49 of the *Annalen der Physik*. It contained, on pages 769 to 822, *"Grundlage der Allgemeinen Relativitätstheorie"* (The Foundation of the General Theory of Relativity). "The theory appeared to me then, and it still does", said Born, "the greatest feat of human thinking about Nature, the most amazing combination of philosophical penetration, physical intuition and mathematical skill. But its connections with experience were slender. It appealed to me like a great work of art, to be enjoyed and admired from a distance."

The General Theory which brought the first realisation "that space is not merely a background for events, but possesses an autonomous structure," was to be the starting point for an even larger collection of papers and developments than the Special Theory. Einstein wrote some of them, and for another forty years he was, necessarily, deeply involved in the arguments about the universe that the General Theory unleashed. Yet in some ways he saw this as the cornerstone of the arch he had started to build more than a decade previously and he himself as now free for other things. From now onwards, according to Wolfgang Pauli — aged only sixteen in 1916 but within five years to be writing one of the classic expositions of the General Theory — Einstein was often to comment: "For the rest of my life I want to reflect on what light is."

Whereas Special Relativity had brought under one set of laws the electro-magnetic world of Maxwell and Newtonian mechanics as far as they applied to bodies in uniform relative motion, the General Theory did the same thing for bodies with the accelerated relative motion epitomised in the acceleration of gravity. But first it had been necessary for Einstein to develop the true nature of gravity from his Principle of Equivalence. Newton had seen it as a force operating instantaneously over limitless distances; Einstein's conception was very different, even though in practice most of his results approximated very closely to those of Newton. Basically, he proposed that gravity was a function of matter itself and that its effects were transmitted between contiguous portions of space-time, rather as the effects of a shunting engine are transmitted down a line of stationary railway waggons. Where matter exists, so does energy; the greater the mass of matter involved, the greater the effect of the energy which can be transmitted.

In addition gravity, as he had postulated as far back as 1911, affected light — the arbiter of straight lines and the wave-emanation whose passage over a unit of distance gives a unit of time — exactly as it affected material particles. Thus the universe which Newton had seen, and for which he had constructed his apparently impeccable mechanical laws, was not the real universe but only what he had seen through the misleading spectacles produced by gravity. The law which appeared to have worked out so well had been drawn up for a universe that did not exist, as through a tailor had made a suit for a man he had seen only in a distorting mirror. This was the logical follow-on from the Principle of Equivalence and from Einstein's assumption that gravity was basically a field-characteristic of matter. That Newton's suit fitted the real man tolerably well was hardly the point.

Einstein's paper gave not only a corrected picture of the universe but also a fresh set of mathematical laws by which its details could be described. These were of two kinds. There were the structural laws which dealt with the relationships between the mass of a gravitating body and the gravitational field which the very existence of the mass automatically created; and there were the laws of motion which could be used to describe the paths taken by moving bodies in gravitational fields. These laws utilised Riemannian geometry, the need for which had been the direct result of the assumption that light would be deflected by a gravitational field and that the shortest distance between two points in such a field would not, when viewed from outside it, be coincident with a straight line. For there were certain consequences of assuming that what appeared as a straight line-of-sight to anywhere in the universe, as ramrod true as any sergeant-major could wish, was in fact as curved as the route followed by a ship steaming round the world on the shortest path from $A$ to $B$ — and that the exact curvature would depend on the gravitational field, and therefore the mass of matter, which was involved.

One consequence is evident from the simple consideration of a globe. It is that Euclidean geometry, in which the angles in a triangle always add up to two right angles, is not relevant for a triangle formed by the Equator and two lines of longitude. Those running from the Equator to the North Pole through Greenwich and New Orleans, for instance, enclose with the Equator not two but three right-angles — even though Equator and lines of longitude follow the shortest route from point to point. As Einstein allegedly explained to his younger son, Edouard: "When the blind beetle crawls over the surface of a globe, he doesn't notice that the track he has covered is curved. I was lucky enough to have spotted it."

Einstein had seen that his assumption of a curvature of light in a gravitational field meant that Euclidean geometry, satisfactory enough when coping with the small distances of everyday life, had to be replaced by something more sophisticated when dealing with the universe. The geographer and the surveyor have a comparable problem, selecting one projection which is satisfactory for the small areas of topographical maps and another projection for the vastly larger areas of regional or national maps. Einstein searched about for some while before he found what he wanted. In Prague, on George Pick's advice, he had studied the work of Ricci and Levi-Civita. Back in Zurich he had worked with Marcel Grossmann to make the preliminary sketch of the General Theory which appeared in 1913. But it was only when he turned back to Riemann, the young German who had died almost half a century earlier, that he found what he wanted.

Riemann was the mathematician whose masterpiece, *"On the Hypotheses which determine the Foundations of Geometry" (Über die Hypotheseen, welche der Geometrie zu Grunde liegen)* Einstein had studied a decade earlier with his companions of the Olympia Academy in Berne. Handicapped by a shy character, dogged by bad luck and the bad health which killed him at forty, Riemann had been a brilliant product of nineteeth century Göttingen who at the age of twenty-four had speculated that "a complete, well-rounded mathematical theory can be established which progresses from the elementary laws for individual points to the processes given to us in the plenum ('continuously filled space') of reality, without distinction between gravitation, electricity, magnetism, or thermostatics." This apparent rejection of "action at a distance" in favour of the field theory was dramatically in advance of its time. Yet it was merely a prelude to the construction of a non-Euclidean geometry which, in the words of the late E. T. Bell "taught mathematicians to disbelive in *any* geometry, or in *any* space, as a *necessary* mode of human perception. It was the last nail in the coffin of absolute space, and the first in that of the 'absolutes' of nineteenth-century physics."

In Riemann's geometry, parallel lines do not exist, the angles of a triangle do not add up to 180°, and perpendiculars to the same line converge, a conception which is easier to understand in an age of worldwide air travel than when the University of Göttingen was the intellectual pride of the Kingdom of Hanover. In Riemann's world the shortest lines joining any two points are not straight lines but geodesics and, a corollary self-evident even to non-mathematicians, the length of the shortest distance between any two points on such a curved surface is determined by a formula different from that determining the length of a line on a plane surface.

Einstein used Riemannian geometry to create equations by which the movements of the stars in their courses and the structure of the universe itself could be described. But this was followed by the introduction of a phrase well enough understood by mathematicians but almost as confusing to the layman as the definition of time as the fourth "dimension". This was "curvature of space", part of that terminology which Sir Edmund Whittaker later described as "so well established that we can never hope to change it, regrettable though it is, and which has been responsible for a great deal of popular misconception". Mathematicians apply the word "curved" to any space whose geometry was not Euclidean.

> It is an unfortunate custom (Whittaker went on) because curvature, in the sense of bending, is a meaningless term except when the space is immersed in another space, whereas the property of being non-Euclidean is an intrinsic property which has nothing to do with immersion. However, nothing can be done but to utter a warning that what mathematicians understand by the term "curvature" is not what the word connotes in ordinary speech; what the mathematician means is simply that the relations between the mutual distances of the points are different from the relations which obtain in Euclidean geometry. Curvature (in the mathematical sense) has nothing to do with the *shape* of the space — whether it is bent or not — but is defined solely by the metric, that is to say, the way in which "distance" is defined. It is not the space that is curved, but the geometry of the space.

All this, as pointed out by Max Talmey the Jewish student who had first introduced the young Einstein to the physical sciences in Munich, could be attributed not only to lack of communication between mathematicians and non-mathematicians, but also to imperfections in translation from the language in which all Einstein's original papers, as well as a great number of others on general relativity, have been written. In German, as Talmey says, one cannot form from the adjective *uneuklidisch,* a noun corresponding to the English substantive non-Euclideanism formable from the adjective non-Euclidean. *Nichteuklidisch* is used, but many German authors, in Talmey's words, used the expression *Raum-Krummung,* "space-curvature", to denote that quality which, in the end, is due to a straight line being interminable in a gravitational field. English writers followed their example although they did not need to do this.

"Space-curvature", the renewed claim that light did not go straight, the idea that the universe could only be viewed from the earth through the distorting spectacles of gravity, would all have combined to create an immediate sensation had Europe been at peace. As it was, only a narrow path led through the minefields of the war from Einstein in the Berlin of 1916 to the shattering first proof of the theory in 1919.

Einstein himself was well aware that proof would not be easy. Two and a half centuries earlier Newton, pressed on the question of whether gravity was or was not exercised instantaneously, admitted that he could see no way of experimentally solving the problem. To do so would require, he commented, "the sensorium of God". Einstein, if challenged, would no doubt have been torn between modesty and a full awareness of what he was accomplishing. For despite the fundamentally different concepts of gravity put forward by Newton and himself, the differences in experimental results would in most cases be slight and thus difficult to detect.

One prospect seemed to be offered by the planet Mercury. In the two hundred years which had followed Newton, the discoveries of science had revealed a succession of facts which had each fallen into place in his grand design. Not only the passage of the moon round the earth and the curving flight of the cricket ball, but the flow of the tides and the fiery trails of the comets were shown to follow the orderly paths which his universal scheme demanded. One feature of this had been the repetition of the planetary circuits round the sun; Venus and Mercury, Mars, Jupiter and Uranus, together with their orbiting colleagues, followed their same elliptical paths with only insignificant change, tracing out through the heavens circuits that appeared to remain the same throughout the centuries.

The first man to suspect that this might not be so was Dominique Arago, the fiery French republican from whom not even Louis Napoleon could extract an oath of allegiance. In the early 1840s Arago proposed to Urbain Jean Joseph Leverrier, a young French astronomer, that he should carefully analyse the motions of Mercury. The result was surprising. For Leverrier's figures showed clearly that the perihelion of Mercury — the point on its elliptical path which is nearest to the sun — advanced by a specific amount each year. The rate was extremely small, but even after the effects of the other planets had been taken into account the advance remained about forty-three seconds of arc each century. Thus the path of Mercury round the sun was not a static closed ellipse, but a nearly-closed circuit, slowly gyrating and coming back to its original position once every 3,000,000 years.

This lack of coincidence with the path planned out for it by Newton in his grand scheme profoundly distressed astronomers, and some desperate expedients were put forward in an effort to correlate fact and theory. Leverrier himself decided that the anomaly would be accounted for if there existed an as yet unseen planet, only 1,000 miles across and circling the sun at a distance of 19,000,000 miles. In anticipation of discovery, this was named Vulcan; but despite careful searching of the skies at each subsequent eclipse no such planet could be located. From Asaph Hall, the discoverer of the satellites of Mars, there came an even more ingenious proposal: that in the Newtonian formula concerned the exponent 2 might be altered to 2,0000001612. The suggested trick had something in common with that of the "scientist", armed with chisel and tape-measure, who was found by Flinders Petrie to be "adjusting" a side of the Great Pyramid "which did not quite conform to the length required by his theory". As Einstein was to comment, the discrepancy in Mercury's orbit "could be explained by means of classical mechanics only on the assumption of hypotheses which have little probability, and which were devised solely for this purpose". So much was true even after fullest consideration had been given to the various influences which the planets as a group exercised on each individual in the group, the astronomical problem of "perturbations", as it was called.

The discrepancy had worried Einstein as far back as 1907 when he had told his colleague Conrad Habicht that he was working on a theory which he hoped would account for the changes in the perihelion movement of Mercury. Now with Riemannian geometry the perihelion of a planet moving round a central attracting body in a nearly circular orbit would advance. The amount would not be great, but Mercury's enormous speed, comparatively small size, and closeness to the intense gravitational field of the sun might yield a significant figure. Einstein applied the equations from the General Theory to the motion of Mercury. The results showed that the perihelion should advance about 0.1" for each complete orbital revolution of the pla-

net. Roughly 420 such revolutions were made in a century. Thus the
secular advance of Mercury's perihelion each century as deduced
from the General Theory was some 42″ — almost exactly the figure
provided by Leverrier's observations. The theory thus, as Einstein
said to the daughter of Simon Newcomb, who spent much of his life
in producing more accurate orbital tables for the moon and the planets, brought about a full agreement between theory and experience.

Einstein announced this result before he had completed his General Theory, reading two papers on it to the Prussian Academy of
Sciences in the autumn of 1915. He was immensely excited with his
success but it was not the excitement of surprise. Asked whether he
had been worried about the outcome of the calculations, he replied:
"Such questions did not lie in my path. The result could not be otherwise than correct. I was only concerned with putting the answer into
a lucid form. I did not for one second doubt that it would agree with
observation. There was no sense in getting excited about what was
self-evident." However confident he may have been, he was delighted when shortly after the publication of his own Mercury paper the
astronomer K. Schwarzschild published a description of how to obtain the same results in a far more elegant manner.

The use of the field equations of the General Theory to supply
figures which were unlikely to be coincidental, and which solved one
of the most stubborn riddles of astronomy, was cited by Einstein in
his paper of 1916. The figures certainly supported his theory but they
did not exactly give proof; the Mercury anomaly had been known
for years, the General Theory had merely provided one satisfactory
explanation and there might be others. The two remaining possibilities for a test put forward by Einstein in 1911 both concerned the
behaviour of light in a gravitational field and both had one thing in
common. They concerned phenomena which had never been either
known or suspected; and if they could be shown to exist, they would
therefore be in a totally different class. They would in fact be comparable to the prediction of a new planet in the sky just where Nep-
tune was later discovered, or to Mendeleyev's forcast of the undisco-
vered elements in the Periodic Table. They would by implication
give substantial proof that in the General Theory there was to be
found a more accurate description of the universe.

The more esoteric of the two tests concerned the effect of gravity on the frequency of light. The mathematical route followed by
Einstein led him to assume that an atom radiating in a strong gravitational field would vibrate more slowly than in a weak gravitational field. For if time as well as space was inevitably altered by the

deflection of gravity then the vibration of atoms, those impeccable timepieces of the universe, would also be affected. But the frequency of vibration governs the colour of light radiated and an atom radiating in a strong gravitational field would emit light a little closer to the red end of the spectrum than when it was radiating a weaker gravitational field. Such displacements had already been noted by L. F. Jewell in 1897 and by other workers early in the twentieth century, but they had been explained as entirely due to "pressure effects". These did indeed exist, and their presence increased the difficulty of isolating as a separate characteristic "the Einstein shift" as it was unlikely to be observed even if the gravitational field of the sun were used as a test-bench. However, there are bodies in the universe producing immensely stronger fields than the sun, and a decade after Einstein's prediction the huge gravitational field of the "white dwarf" star near Sirius — so dense that a cubic inch of it would weigh more than half a ton on earth — was utilised.* And almost half a century after Einstein's paper, Robert Oppenheimer was able to write of the Einstein shift: "The most precise and, I think, by far the most beautiful example of this is a recent experiment conducted at Harvard in which light was simply allowed to fall down from the third floor to the basement of the Physics Building. One could see how much bluer it had become; one part in $10^{14}$; not very much."

No such possibilities existed in 1916, and readers of Einstein's paper turned naturally to the other proposed method of testing the theory. This was the method which Freundlich had been going to adopt in the Crimea in August 1914: the observation of light from the stars during an eclipse to discover whether it was deflected when passing through the gravitational field of the sun.

The summer of 1916 was hardly a propitious period for devoting men, money, materials and thought to any scientific subject unless it seemed likely to help the war effort. Britain and Germany were locked in a struggle whose outcome no one could yet foresee, and American entry into the war was still nearly a year away. All effort was harnessed to the task of winning; in Germany the Kaiser Wilhelm Institutes and the University of Berlin were on national service, and elsewhere the situation was similar. Rutherford from Britain and Langevin from France were deeply engaged on anti-submarine work. Pure science, it seemed, must await the coming of peace.

In these circumstances, one of Einstein's acts was to be of crucial importance. On receiving copies of *Annalen der Physik* con-

* See page 316

taining his paper on the General Theory he sent one to Willem de Sitter, professor of Astronomy in the University of Leiden and a foreign correspondent of the Royal Astronomical Society in London. De Sitter passed on his copy to the Society's secretary, Arthur Eddington, who was now drawn into a developing drama. Only a few years later Rutherford was to apologise for non-appearance at a Service meeting with the explanation that he had apparently accomplished something "of far greater importance than the war", the disintegration of the atomic nucleus. In much the same way, the long train of events set in motion by de Sitter and continued by Eddington was to have repercussions quite as formidable in their own way as the bloody battles being waged on the Western Front.

Arthur Eddington was in 1916 Plumian Professor of Astronomy at Cambridge, and director of the university observatory. A Quaker, with the Friends' typical mixture of bold humanity and mystic faith, he had been a Senior Wrangler, and his *Stellar Movements and the Structure of the Universe,* published in 1914, had created the new subject of stellar dynamics. He was still only thirty-four and it was confidently predicted of him that great promise would be followed by even greater performance. As Secretary of the Royal Astronomical Society, Eddington had the task of producing the Society's *Monthly Notices* and this involved close scrutiny of Einstein's paper which arrived from Holland, a scrutiny which soon convinced him of its importance to his own cosmological investigations.

The important factor in 1916 was Eddington's superb mathematical ability which "enabled him not only to grasp the argument, but very soon to master the absolute differential calculus of Ricci and Levi-Civita, and to use tensors as a tool in developing contributions of his own". One result was that Eddington asked de Sitter to write for the Royal Astronomical Society's *Monthly Notices* three long articles explaining the General Theory. These articles, the second produced after Einstein had held several conversations with de Sitter in Leiden, introduced Einstein's new theory to the non-German-speaking world. Their importance in what was to follow cannot be overestimated.

> Even if Einstein has not explained the origin of inertia, [concluded the second article] his theory represents an enormous progress over the physics of yesterday. Perceiving the irrelevance of the representation by co-ordinates in which our science is clothed, he has penetrated to the deeper realities which lay hidden behind it and not only has he entirely explained the exception and universal nature of gravitation by the principle of the identity of gravitation and inertia, but he has laid

bare intimate connections between branches of science which up to now were considered as entirely independent from each other, and has thus made an important step towards the unity of nature. Finally his theory not only explains all that the old theory of relativity could explain (experiment of Michelson, etc), but *without any new hypothesis or empirical constant*, it explains the anomalous motion of the perihelion of Mercury, and it predicts a number of phenomenon which have not yet been observed. It has thus at once proved to be a very powerful instrument of discovery.

Even in the gloomy concentration of the war, scientists were soon speculating on how to investigate the "number of phenomena which have not yet been observed". Sir Frank Dyson, the Astronomer Royal, ordered a study to be made of photographs taken during the eclipse of 1905 in the hope that something might be discovered from them, but the search was unsuccessful. Lindemann and his father contributed a paper to the *Monthly Notices* on the daylight photography of stars and concluded: "It is suggested that experiments . . . be undertaken by some observatory possessing a suitable instrument, and enjoying a fine climate, with a view to testing Einstein's theory". The possibility had been rejected as impracticable by Hale before the 1914 eclipse, and even if a suitable observatory could have been found and persuaded to do the work it seems unlikely that current technology could have produced useful results. There were other suggestions, but none which seemed likely to be successful.

However, help was at hand. Another solar eclipse would take place on a day when the stellar background would be ideal. If the problem of testing the General Theory "had been put forward at some other period of history", as Eddington later pointed out, "it might have been necessary to wait some thousands of years for a total eclipse of the sun to happen on the lucky date". The wait was only three years.

That this opportunity was seized by the British was due not only to Eddington's personal enthusiasm for relativity but to his influence on Dyson. Sir Frank was to become a firm friend of Einstein, and the latter's portrait by Rothenstein for long hung in a place of honour in Flamsteed House, the Astronomer Royal's official home at Greenwich. Throughout his career he had shown a special interest in solar eclipses, and despite the uncertainties of war he was anxious to make full use of the opportunities provided by 1919. But it was nevertheless largely due to Eddington's influence that Dyson so quickly emphasised the opportunities for testing the General Theory that the eclipse would offer. De Sitter's articles, which had whetted the scientific appetite, had been published largely as a result of his, Eddington's, initiative, and soon afterwards he was commissioned by the Physical Society to prepare his own account of what the General Theory was and signified. The *Report on the Relativity Theory of Gravitation* that followed was published in 1918 and later expanded as *The Mathematical Theory of Relativity*. Long before this, however, Dyson had moved into action.

On May 29th, 1919, the sun would be seen in a field of stars of quite exceptional brightness, part of the Hyades group which lies at the head of the Taurus constellation. In a note from Greenwich dated March 2nd, 1917, and printed in the *Monthly Notices*, Dyson drew attention to "the unique opportunities" which this would offer. "There are an unusual number of bright stars, and with weather conditions as good as those at Sfax in 1905 — which were by no means perfect — no less than thirteen stars might be obtained", he wrote, adding that these "should serve for an ample verification, or the contrary", of Einstein's theory. The track of the eclipse would unfortunately cross the Atlantic, but he had been in touch with the Secretary of the Royal Geographical Society, who would tell him how many observing stations might be used, and he had "brought the matter forward so that arrangements for observing at as many stations as possible may be made at the earliest possible moment".

These plans were made as the U-boat blockade was tightening on Britain and the Russian front collapsing, as American entry into the war was still problematical, and peace remained below any visible horizon. Yet they typified not so much British isolation from reality as a somewhat lofty confidence equalled a quarter of a century later when, with the Germans hammering at the gates of Stalingrad and the Eighth Army with its backs to the Nile, the Allied Ministers of Education in exile met in London to plan what eventually became UNESCO.

During 1917, as British plans for the eclipse expeditions went ahead, Einstein published two more important papers. In one of them he returned to the radiation problem which had occupied him intermittently since 1905; in the other he used the General Theory to give a picture of the universe which was not only important in its own scientific right, but added a spectacular significance to the theory itself.

In the radiation paper, in which he derived Planck's original quantum law from a different starting point, he suggested that as well as spontaneous emission and absorption there could also take place the process of stimulated emission. In 1917 this seemed mainly of theoretical interest; forty years later it was utilised to provide the maser and laser of modern technology. In addition to postulating this fresh process, Einstein also stressed that the momentum transfer which took place with emission was directional. The importance of this, as far as Einstein was concerned, lay in the admission that had to be made at the same time — that the direction was "in the present state of the theory . . . determined only by 'chance'". It is significant that Einstein put quotation marks round "chance". He still believed that what had to be attributed to chance in the current state of knowledge would one day be explicable on causal grounds. How strongly he continued to feel about this was shown when he wrote to Born seven years later, saying how intolerable he found the idea of an electron, exposed to radiation, being able to choose, of its own free will, not only the moment at which it jumped off but also its direction. Yet it was his paper of 1917 which provided chapter and verse for just such an idea.

Meanwhile, his development of the General Theory continued. Just how great were the demands made on him is indicated in a letter to Ehrenfest in February in which he jokingly complained that his work was producing the risk of his being placed in a madhouse.

The paper which occasioned this outburst was shorter than the final outline of the General Theory but was in some ways almost as important. For while the details of the General Theory were to remain in dispute over the years, and the first rapture created by the results of the British expeditions was to be qualified by later observations, the importance of Einstein's potentially explosive paper of 1917 was to remain undisputed — even though its suppositions were to be questioned with a brusqueness which has not affected the General Theory itself. The paper was called, quite simply, "Cosmological Considerations on the General Theory of Relativity". What it did was to utilise the equations of the General Theory to speculate on the physical extent of the universe; and in so doing, it is generally accepted, to found the study of modern cosmology. Even for Einstein, this was playing for high stakes.

His reason for starting on this controversial game was a very practical one. The idea that the system of fixed stars should ultimately determine the existence of centrifugal force was an important part of the conceptual background to the Theory of General Relativity. This was not a new idea and had been put forward in general terms by both Berkeley and Mach. However, with his field equations Einstein had given a numerical quantity to account for this action of the surrounding stars.

14

He had linked the distant twinkle of the night sky with the homely gravity of everyday life and one question quickly followed: were there enough stars in the universe to produce the centrifugal force which could be observed and recorded? The need to answer this question inexorably drew Einstein into thinking about a specific extension of the question to which he was devoting his life. He now needed to know not merely how God had made the world but also about its actual extent. Thus the relativistic cosmology which Einstein now initiated was, as Hubble later described it, a natural off-shoot of the General Theory, a "superstructure including other principles". If it was subsequently found to be wanting, it did not necessarily invalidate the General Theory itself.

The comfortable idea of a finite universe with the earth at its centre had been suspect from the beginning of the scientific renaissance and had finally been abandoned with the coming of Newton. For with Newton it had seemed clear that a finite material universe would tend to collapse in upon itself much as it had been suspected, before Bohr's prescribed electron orbits, that particles circling an atomic nucleus would inevitably be drawn down towards it. The new universe of Newton's day was something nobler if more impersonal, an infinitude of stars scattered through infinite Euclidean space, an idea that survived against only sporadic objections, usually overcome by special pleading. With the nineteenth century, and the growing interest in astronomy, an alternative was put forward: a finite universe which existed, island-like, in the immensities of infinite and "empty" space. But all such blueprints had one thing in common; each represented a static universe whose size and contents remained unchanging in quantity throughout the endless passage of time.

As Einstein wrestled with the cosmological implications of the General Theory, the first of these alternatives, the world-centred universe of the Middle Ages, was effectively ruled out; but both the others were considered. Both were rejected. The reasons for rejecting the Newtonian universe can be simply understood, although in the light of current knowledge about the recession of the galaxies they appear rather dated. For it seemed mathematically clear that the effect of an infinite number of stars would, even at infinite distances, produce an infinitely strong force whose effect would be to give the stars a high velocity through the universe. But observation indicated that compared with the speed of light the velocities of stars were small. Thus it was essential that the stars should be finite in number.

The possibility of a finite "island-universe" in an infinitude of empty space was ruled out for slightly more complex reasons. One was based on a theory of the way in which particles — or stars — would distribute themselves in random movement, and which appeared to make an "island-universe" impossible. Another reason sprang from the fact that since the curvature of space was dependent on the distribution of matter, space would be curved in the vicinity of the island-universe but Euclidean in the empty space of infinity beyond. This in turn meant that bodies beyond the island-universe would move in straight lines, according to Newton's law of inertia, since inertia was itself equivalent to gravitational force, which would not be present.

Einstein was therefore forced to consider whether it was possible to conceive of a universe that would contain a finite number of stars distributed equally through unbounded space. His answer to the apparent contradiction lay in the idea that matter itself produced the curvature of space. For in the "Einstein world", as it soon became known, the curvature produced by matter turned space back on itself so that a ray of light, moving in a straight line in terrestrial terms, would return to its starting point after circling the universe: a universe whose three dimensions contained as finite a number of stars as the number of names on the two-dimensional surface of a globe, but whose surface was itself as unbounded as that of the same globe. These stars were, moreover, distributed equally, as though the names were spread out equally across the surface of a globe. This was an essential if the "Einstein world" was to conform to Einstein's own inner intuition that just as the laws of nature must be the same for all observers, so must the view of the universe. "There must be no favoured location in the universe, no centre, no boundary; all must see the universe alike", as Hubble put it. "And, in order to ensure this situation, the cosmologist postulates spatial isotropy and spatial homogeneity, which is his way of saying that the universe must be pretty much alike everywhere and in all directions". This universe included local irregularities of curvature, comparable to the hills and valleys on a world globe built in relief; yet it also had an overall curvature, like the overall curvature of the earth itself which produces a terrestrial world with a radius of some four thousand miles.

With the help of the General Theory, two equations could be obtained which included only two unknowns — the curvature of space and the total mass of the particles making up the universe. It was a relatively simple matter to provide estimates from these for-the mass; thus the universe of the "Cosmological Considerations" of 1917 was a universe to which a size might be given, however rough an estimate this was.

> The whole universe, [Einstein said to his friend Alexander Moskowski in Berlin] has a diameter of about 100 million light years, in round numbers. That amounts to about 700 trillion miles. It follows from the mathematical calculations which I have presented in "Cosmological Considerations arising from the General Theory of Relativity", in which the figure I have just quoted is not given. The exact figure is a minor question. What is important is to recognise that the universe may be regarded as a closed continuum as far as distance-measurements are concerned.

Einstein had achieved a plausible result. But he had done so only by a piece of mathematical juggling which was to have an interesting history. This was the introduction of a fresh term into the field equations of the General Theory, the "cosmological constant" which represents a repulsive force which, contrary to ordinary gravitational attraction, increases with the distance between objects. The value given to this term determines the character of the universe which is produced, and from the first it was a matter of controversy. Einstein justified its use when he gave "the theoretical view of the actual universe" at the end of his 1917 paper.

The Einstein world with its "quasi-static distribution of matter" was quickly challenged by de Sitter who maintained that while the General Theory indicated a curved space, this curvature was continually decreasing. Thus the de Sitter world built on the General Theory was steadily increasing in size; space was constantly straightening itself out, becoming less curved and more Euclidean. This idea of an expanding universe had as yet no observational support, and for some while the ideas of both Einstein and de Sitter on the structure of the universe were considered as equally comparable possibilities between which it was difficult to make a choice. Only in the 1920s, as the work of Hubble and others at Mount Wilson verified the recession of the galaxies and the continual expansion of the universe, was the position drastically altered. And only in 1930 did Einstein withdraw the "cosmological constant".

Long before this, however, the term had come under attack for totally different reasons from Professor Friedmann, a Russian astronomer who had begun to study Einstein's publications from a purely mathematical standpoint. George Gamow, who was working under Friedmann at the time, has described what happened.

Friedmann noticed that Einstein had made a mistake in his alleged proof that the universe must necessarily be stable and unchangeable in time [he says.] It is well known to students of high-school algebra that it is permissable to divide both sides of an equation by any quantity, provided that this quantity is not zero. However, in the course of his proof, Einstein had divided both sides of one of his intermediate equations by a complicated expression which, in certain circumstances, could become zero.

In the case, however, when this expression becomes equal to zero, Einstein's proof does not hold, and Friedmann realised that this opened an entire new world of time-dependent universes: expanding, collapsing and pulsating ones. Thus Einstein's original gravity equation was correct, and changing it was a mistake. Much later, when I was discussing cosmological problems with Einstein, he remarked that the introduction of the cosmological term was the biggest blunder he ever made in his life. But the "blunder", rejected by Einstein, and the cosmological constant denoted by the Greek letter $\lambda$, rears its ugly head again and again.

Despite Gamow's well-justified comments, Einstein's entry into the cosmological arena was important both for science and for Einstein.

This suggestion of a finite, but unbounded space is one of the greatest ideas about the nature of the world which ever has been conceived, [as Max Born put it.] It solved the mysterious fact why the system of stars did not disperse and thin out which it would do if space were infinite; it gave a physical meaning to Mach's principle which postulated that the law of inertia should not be regarded as a property of empty space but as an effect of the total system of stars, and it opened the way to the modern concept of the expanding universe.

Furthermore, the idea was put forward at a significant moment, just as observational astronomy was preparing to give practical muscle to the theoretical flesh.

At a different level, Einstein's direct use of the General Theory to present a picture of the universe gave him an almost mystic significance for the layman. A scientist who could give a fresh, and apparently more reliable, explanation for the movements of the stars in their courses was an important enough figure. A physicist who could apparently show that light did not always run straight had at his command an almost conjuring-trick attraction. But a man who could talk in familiar terms of curved space, and with a friendly gesture from the blackboard explain how the universe was both finite and boundless, had stretched out to touch untouchable things in a way that made him part magician and part messiah.

That is, if the General Theory were right. As Einstein, Born and Wertheimer intervened with the students in Berlin in November 1918, as the Empire went down in defeat and de Sitter in Holland constructed his own blueprint of the universe, final plans were being made in Britain to discover whether this was so.

# 9

# *THE FABRIC OF THE UNIVERSE*

THE FIRST TURNING POINT IN EINSTEIN'S LIFE HAD COME WITH publication of his paper on the electrodynamics of moving bodies, an event whose significance, like the thunder of the guns at Valmy, was recognised at first by only a few. The second was of a totally different order — and not only because the implications of the General Theory were more important. This of itself would have ended his normal life as a Berlin professor, well enough known in his own field but still comparatively obscure outside it. But the circumstances in which the General Theory was tested brought Einstein a worldwide scientific fame which arrived almost literally overnight and swept him away from his scientific moorings into the stream of public events. Between the Armistice of November 1918 and the end of the following year he became the most famous scientist in the world.

This was not all. Scientific renown came just as events in Germany and elsewhere pushed him into a political activity for which he had little aptitude. He instinctively supported the left-wing movements set free by defeat and became a devoted if muddled supporter both of pacifism and of a world government which could only be maintained by force. He revealed his zealous and perhaps ingenuous belief that Germany's good name would be restored if her war crimes were publicly investigated and, if necessary, admitted. And he became emotionally committed to the cause of Zionism. These actions were enough to make his name disliked by German nationalists while he remained obscure, and detested once he became famous. As a result, his scientific fame became during 1919 inextricably entangled with political controversies. All this was further complicated at a personal level by his divorce from Mileva, his marriage to Elsa, and the death of his mother who spent her final days with him in a Berlin threatened equally by starvation, inflation and revolution.

Within a few months of Germany's defeat Einstein's opinion of his own countrymen had begun to change. Up until now he had tended to forget — or to try to forget — that he himself was a German, and to submerge what remained of the thought in the reality of his Swiss passport. He had looked upon the majority of his compatriots with almost unqualified distaste, regarding them as the people who supported an aggressive war with only minor protest and condoned barbarous activities which he did not shrink from calling war crimes. But as the defeat of November 1918 merged into the starvation of 1919, so the differences between the Germans he had detested and the Allies whom he had so hoped would win tended to disappear. During the war he had thought that an Allied victory would be a lesser evil than a German victory. Now he believed that the difference was not as great as he had imagined. In a similar way he now began to feel that, in general, mankind's moral qualities were the same in most countries. He held these opinions for little more than a decade between the anti-Prussian hatred of his youth and the more understandable anti-German paranoia of his later years. But during this decade Einstein's native Germanism rose to the surface once again and he was no longer so worried about being what he was.

Einstein's attempt to exculpate the German academics, much as the "stab-in-the-back" theory attempted to exculpate the German armed forces, was partly the result of his being knocked off balance during the immediate post-war months. For Einstein, and others, trustingly expected that they would have Allied co-operation in rebuilding a new and democratic Germany; that they would now be helped in the task of putting their house in order. The fact that the Reichswehr could boast of a formidable army still in being, that there remained a considerable danger that the Armistice would not easily be enforced, did not damp their hopes. But instead of the hand stretched out, in co-operation if not in friendship, they met the rigour of the Allied blockade whose only effect, other than the starvation of civilians, was to make the task of the Republican Government even more difficult.

All this quickly prodded Einstein into the political activity for which he had little liking and less competence and when the Bund

Neues Vaterland, illegally revived in September, was formally re-
founded on November 10th, 1918, after an open-air meeting at the
foot of Bismarck's statue in front of the Reichstag, Professor Albert
Einstein appeared not only as a member but among those who sat
on the Working Committee. He was one of the hundred intellectuals
from Europe and the United States who in December signed the
Petition du Comité de la Fédération des Peuples, addressed to the
heads of state about to meet in Versailles for the Peace Conference
and prophetically asking them to "make a peace that does not conceal a future war". And in December 1918, he hoped that he would
shortly be visiting Paris to plead with the Allies for food for the
German population.

Einstein's changed attitude cannot be accounted for entirely by
bitterness at the Allied blockade. With the exception of pacifism —
for which he had an honourable blind spot and on whose behalf
he would usually sign the most specious of propaganda manifestos
— he was not abnormally gullible. His enthusiasms were rarely of the
ephemeral sort which justified the claim made of Lloyd George that
he was a pillow, always bearing the imprint of the last head which
had rested on it. His changing and sometimes contradictory views
on the Germans, and on the need for political action, often sprang
from his belief that different situations demanded different attitudes.
Circumstances, he felt, really did alter cases, and in fields other than
science. Just as there were no absolutes in time and space, so was
there nothing immutable about the attitudes that men should take
up when dealing with the kalaedoscopic, irrational and infinitely
complicated actions of their fellow-men. The point of view was
logical enough. But it gave his enemies useful weapons.

Einstein did not go to Paris at the turn of the year. Instead
he went to Zurich, where he had some months earlier been offered
a Chair to be held jointly at the University and the E. T. H. He
had turned down the offer but had agreed, instead, to visit the
city for a month or six weeks, twice a year, and give on each occasion a series of a dozen conferences. Explaining to Besso his reactions
at the offer, he said that he would demand from Zurich nothing
more than his expenses and would thus free himself of painful feelings while at the same time acting in a correct manner in the eyes
of his friends and his Berlin patrons.

The arrangement was convenient for another reason. His
divorce was at last in its final stages. The thing would be settled
within the first few weeks of 1919 and it would be useful, if not
essential, for him to be in Switzerland.

He left Berlin during the last week of January 1919, arrived in Zurich on the 27th, and stayed at the Sternwarte boarding house in Hochstrasse. The General Theory of Relativity had in academic circles become as great a subject of discussion as the Special Theory, but it was still a subject for specialists alone and its author was known in Zurich as a former professor rather than as a man about to shake the world. This is illustrated by an incident recalled by Hermann Weyl. Due to the coal shortage which was an aftermath of the European war, the authorities had to "ration" entry to the lectures, which could only be attended by those who bought an invitation card for a few francs. On this occasion Einstein appeared with Professor Weyl and the latter's wife. But Frau Weyl had forgotten her invitation card, and a steward stopped her. Einstein became as angry as Einstein ever could become and said that if Frau Weyl was not allowed in, then there would be no lecture. The steward gave way, under protest. But shortly afterwards Einstein received a letter from the rector in which he was politely but firmly asked not to interfere with the authorities' regulations.

His divorce was settled in Zurich on February 14th, 1919. Simultaneously, he awarded to Mileva any money that might come from a Nobel Prize. When it came, three years later, the cash was passed on from Sweden, via Berlin, to Zurich. Some was lost in movement through the foreign exchanges and more by bad management. With what was left Mileva bought a pleasant house on the Zurichberg. The following year she formally obtained permission to retain the name of Einstein; and, as Mileva Einstein, she lived for another quarter of a century, overshadowed by illness and the worry of a schizophrenic younger son.

Einstein did not lose touch with her. Once the final break had been agreed upon mutual animosities loosened and dislike dissolved, if not into affection at least into mutual understanding. Even before the divorce had gone through Mileva was advising him on his projected marriage to Elsa; what it was can be inferred from his reply — that if he ever wished to leave his second wife no power on earth would stop him.

As soon as his lecture series in Zurich was completed in the spring of 1919, Einstein returned to Berlin. And here, on June 2nd, he married Elsa in the registry office at Berlin-Wilimersdorf, travelling back to Zurich shortly afterwards, apparently to discuss the future of his sons with Mileva. He remained in Zurich until June 25th when he appeared again in Berlin, leaving for Zurich once more on the 28th and remaining in Switzerland for another three months until, on September 21st he returned to Berlin again.

While thus settling his personal affairs, Einstein was also being swept up by the rising tide of Zionism. Here it is only necessary to note that during his Berlin visits of the spring and summer of 1919 he was approached by the Zionists and won over to their cause. They were gratified. But as they saw it, their "catch" was merely that of a prominent Jewish scientist. Before the year was out their minnow was to grow into Leviathan.

Espousal of the Zionist cause greatly affected Einstein's position in Germany during the next decade and increased his non-scientific notoriety. This was augmented by the fervour with which he now began to discuss German war crimes. He had first raised the subject with Lorentz in 1915 and he returned to it now in the hope that investigation would help to create an understanding among the Germans of how non-Germans felt.

It is doubtful whether the crimes that most countries commit in the heat of war can satisfactorily be examined afterwards either by their own nationals or by the victors — let alone on the instigation of anyone who had hated his own country from his youth. Even among those who believe that the Nuremburg trials were not only necessary but just, many would have preferred to see the work carried out with the visible impartiality of neutrals. In this light, Einstein's revival of the subject was well-intentioned but unfortunate. It was doubly so since he was still apparently a renegade German who preferred to travel on a Swiss passport, and whose ignorance of international machinery was equalled by his lack of any personal contact with the machinery of war.

This much was clear to Lorentz, to whom Einstein wrote on April 26th, 1919, saying that with five other private citizens he had formed a commission to examine the charges which were considered as proven. Would Lorentz join the commission as one of the neutrals who would help to get documentary evidence?

Lorentz' reply was a cautious masterpiece of tact. He was an internationalist. He was visibly a man of goodwill. More than most, he understood Einstein, and a few months earlier he had written to Ernest Solvay, when future congresses were being discussed, noting that "a man such as Einstein, that great physicist, is in no way 'German' in the way that one often uses the word nowadays; his opinion of events in recent years is no different from yours and mine." But Lorentz had also a far clearer idea of the possible, and of the likely reactions of fallible men. While willing to help Einstein through second parties, he himself deftly sidestepped the invitation to serve on the proposed commission. "You must not deceive yourself that your task will be an easy one," he replied. "The main difficulty, of course, is that this first step has only just been taken; it would have been more successful if it had been taken when Germany was still winning." Moreover, he pointed out, it was extremely urgent that the Germans officially supported the move. "You must be absolutely certain," he went on, "that the Government will allow you full discussion and publication and not put obstacles in your way. It seems to me that you must obtain this assurance before you make any contact with the Belgians or the French because if they discover, after they have heard of your intentions, that you are not completely free to speak out, then you will have lost more than you have won." However, Lorentz was about to visit Paris and Brussels. He would make what enquiries he could. And he arranged with a colleague in Holland to pass on news from Einstein while he, Lorentz, was travelling. The results were hardly satisfactory. Lorentz, willing to help, was obliged to inform Einstein of the detestation felt for Germans "good" and "bad" alike, inside the countries which had been occupied.

This was underlined shortly afterwards when he discussed prospects for the next Solvay Congress. "It is clear that at the moment Germans will not be invited (there is difficulty in their coming to Brussels)," he said, "even though there is no mention of their formal exclusion; the door will be held open to you, so that in future it will be possible for everybody to work together again. Unfortunately, however, this will have to wait for many years." There was, in fact, some doubt whether the door would be held open even for Einstein. M. Tassel, the Congress Secretary, had to deal particularly with Professor Brillouin, who had attended the 1911 Congress and who on June 1st, 1919, wrote from the Collège de France about "the pro-German neutrals, whatever their scientific value," as well as about the problem of Germans. "I am thinking, for example," he went on, "of Debye, the Dutchman of great merit, who spent all the war as a professor in Göttingen. Naturally, also of Einstein who, whatever his genius, however great his anti-militarist sentiments, nevertheless spent the whole war in Berlin and is in the same position. It is only afterwards, that they have made the necessary political effort to throw light on their German colleagues and dispute the abominable and lying Manifesto of the 93."

Einstein's relations with the Congress were to complement his weathercock attitude to his own countrymen. He had attended the Second Congress in 1913, although he read no paper there and, as forecast by Lorentz, he was invited in the summer of 1920 to the

Third Congress, to be held the following April. Germans as such were still not to be invited. But as the Secretary wrote, "an exception [had] been made for Einstein, of ill-defined nationality, Swiss I believe, who was roundly abused in Berlin during the war because of his pacifist sentiments which have never varied for a moment." Rutherford put it slightly differently. "The only German invited is Einstein who is considered for this purpose to be international," he wrote. Einstein accepted with great pleasure and later in the year Lorentz informed Rutherford that he would be speaking at the April 1921 Congress on "L'Électron et la Magnétisme; effets gyroscopiques". Only in February, two months before the Congress was to be held, was he told that Einstein would not be present. The reason was the request for him to speak for the Zionists in the United States in March and April. Nevertheless, Einstein wished the Congress every success.

Two years later, when the Fourth Congress was being planned for 1924, the situation was different. Once again Einstein was to be invited. But on August 16th he wrote to Lorentz from Lautrach in southern Germany. He was staying with Sommerfeld, who said that it would not be right for Einstein to take part in the Solvay Congress if his German colleagues were excluded. And Einstein himself felt that politics should not have come into the matter at all, and that if he went to Brussels he would be condoning a situation which he believed was wrong.

Only in 1926, after Germany had joined the League of Nations and the international relations of science were returning to normal, did the position alter. "Now," Lorentz noted on the telegram which told him of the new situation, "I am able to write to Einstein." But in 1926 there was still one more formality to be observed — and in view of Einstein's subsequent links with the Royal Palace in Brussels it has some significance. It was thought proper that the approval of King Albert of the Belgians should be sought, and on April 2nd, 1926 Lorentz was given an audience at which His Majesty specifically approved the nomination of Einstein to the scientific committee of the coming Congress, and the proposal to invite Planck and other ex-enemy scientists. "His Majesty," Lorentz subsequently reported, "expressed the opinion that, seven years after the war, the feelings which they aroused should be gradually damped down, that a better understanding between peoples was absolutely necessary for the future, and that science could help to bring this about. He also felt it necessary to stress that in view of all that the Germans had done for physics, it would be very difficult to pass them over." This sweet reasonableness was just as well. By 1926 physics was in the ferment of the new quantum mechanics, and the 1927 Congress would have been meaningless without the presence of Heisenberg, Born, Planck and Einstein from the former enemy countries.

Eight years earlier, as in the summer of 1919 Einstein tried to conscript Lorentz into an investigation of German war crimes, things were not like that. Just what degree of help Lorentz finally gave is not clear, either from the correspondence in the Algemeen Rijksarchief in The Hague or from the complementary letters in the Museum of Science in Leiden. But at the end of the summer the commission on whose behalf Einstein was working produced its first publication. This was a small booklet dealing with alleged atrocities in Lille which startled Einstein when he saw it. The preface was "tactless" and — partly at Einstein's instigation one suspects — the whole edition was eventually withdrawn for correction, amendment, and reissue early in 1920.

It is at this point in 1919 that Einstein, facing what seemed to be the Allied condemnation of a whole nation, further qualified his previous rabid anti-Germanism and rejected an extraordinarily tempting offer from Leiden. The reason may have been partly a wish to give "the new Germany" a chance to pull herself up by her moral boot-straps, partly the fear that a "thirst for power" might be growing up in an "elsewhere" that Einstein — like many other Germans — identified with France.

The offer came from Ehrenfest. He had not yet got the approval of the authorities, but there seemed little doubt that he would get it — even for the terms which he outlined on September 2nd, 1919. What he suggested was that Einstein should come to Leiden University, where the normal maximum salary of 7,500 guilders would be Einstein's minimum. There would be no lecturing duties and the only obligation would be for him to make his base in or near the city.

To Einstein it was most tempting — an offer whose acceptance would bring him close to the orbit of Lorentz in Haarlem and of de Sitter, and which would strengthen his ties with Ehrenfest. The terms of his rejection are revealing. He made it clear when he replied on September 12th that he himself was greatly attracted by the offer. He liked Leiden, he liked the people there and he liked the working environment. But he had obligations as well as inclinations.

Planck had written while he was in Zurich, and he enclosed the letter. It was a revealing document. For Planck, the man of honour who had yet signed the Manifesto of the 93 was now, for the first but not the last time, doing as much to keep Einstein in

Berlin as he had done to bring him there in the first place. His letter, which now induced Einstein not to turn his back on Berlin, was written on July 20th, 1919 and began by explaining how he, Planck, had contrived to get equipment funds for Freundlich by an ingenious slight-of-finance. Then he went on to explain his deeper and more important reason for writing. Rumours were circulating that the Zurich authorities were trying to induce Einstein to remain in Switzerland. Planck felt sure, he went on, that Einstein would not make up his mind before he had consulted his friends in Berlin. But he wanted to stress one thing: that a matter as important as Einstein's future, important both for the Academy and for German science as a whole, should not be settled entirely in terms of money. The letter worked. It would be wrong, Einstein pointed out to Ehrenfest, for him to desert Berlin.

Planck was not merely a good German — in both senses of the phrase — but also an imaginative scientist with a keen sense of things to come. And it cannot have been wholly coincidence that his plea for Einstein to remain within the German fold was stressed now. As he must have guessed, a transformation was coming.

A fortnight after Einstein replied to Ehrenfest, turning down the Leiden offer, he received an historic telegram sent by Lorentz from Leiden five days earlier. It was dated September 27th, 1919 and ran: "Eddington found star displacement at rim of sun, preliminary measurement between nine-tenths of a second and twice that value." The words were to mark a turning point in the life of Einstein and in the history of science.

In Britain the Royal Astronomical Society had noted of the Special Theory in 1917 that "experimental confirmation has been ample, and no serious doubt of its truth is entertained, criticism being confined to questions of its exact scope and philosophical implications." But confirmation was the result of physicists labouring in their laboratories, almost in the normal course of their work; something on a different scale was required to test the General Theory, and it says much for Sir Frank Dyson that in March 1917 he had drawn "attention to the unique opportunities afforded by the eclipse of 1919" to test Einstein's theory. "It was not without international significance, for it opportunely put an end to wild talk of boycotting German science," Eddington later wrote of the decision. "By standing foremost in testing, and ultimately verifying the 'enemy' theory, our national Observatory kept alive the finest traditions of science; and the lesson is perhaps still needed in the world today."

In March 1917, Britain's darkest weeks of the war still lay
ahead, and the prospect of sending expeditions to South America
and to Africa, where the eclipse could best be seen, could not be
viewed without misgiving. Despite this, Dyson was given £1,000
from the Government, and a Joint Permanent Eclipse Committee of
the Royal Society and the Royal Astronomical Society was set up
under his chairmanship. In the spring of 1918, as the Germans broke
through to the Marne and once again brought the issue of the war
into doubt, plans went steadily ahead for British expeditions to Sobral in Northern Brazil and to Principe on the Gulf of Guinea.

Early the following year, in January 1919, a series of test photographs, showing the Hyades against a reference frame of other
stars, was taken at Greenwich Observatory. Two months later Eddington and E. T. Cottingham, who were to make the eclipse observations in Principe, and C. D. Crommelin and C. R. Davidson who
were to do the same at Sobral, met for a final briefing in Flamsteed
House, Greenwich. Eddington's enthusiasm for the General Theory
was illustrated when Cottingham asked, in Dyson's study: "What will
it mean if we get double the Einstein deflection?" "Then," said Dyson,
"Eddington will go mad and you will have to come home alone."

Next morning both parties left for Funchal, Crommelin and Davidson travelling on to Brazil, while Eddington and Cottingham
sailed to Principe, where they arrived on April 23rd. One month of
hard work followed, setting up instruments, taking test photographs, and making final preparations for the great day.

May 29th began with heavy rain which stopped only about
noon. Not until 1.30 p. m., when the eclipse had already begun, did
the party get its first glimpse of the sun.

> We had to carry out our programme of photographs on faith, [wrote
> Eddington in his diary.] I did not see the eclipse, being too busy
> changing plates, except for one glance to make sure it had begun and
> another half-way through to see how much cloud there was. We took
> sixteen photographs. They are all good of the sun, showing a very
> remarkable prominence; but the cloud has interfered with the star
> images. The last six photographs show a few images which I hope will
> give us what we need...

It looked as though the effort, so far as the Principe expedition was concerned, might have been abortive. Only on June 3rd
was the issue settled. "We developed the photographs, two each
night for six nights after the eclipse," Eddington wrote, "and I
spent the whole day measuring. The cloudy weather upset my plans
and I had to treat the measures in a different way from what I

intended, consequently I have not been able to make any preliminary announcement of the result. But one plate that I measured gave a result agreeing with Einstein."

"This," says Eddington's biographer, "was a moment which Eddington never forgot. On one occasion in later years he referred to it as the greatest moment of his life." Turning to his companion he said, remembering the evening in Dyson's study nearly three months previously: "Cottingham, you won't have to go home alone."

At a dinner of the Royal Astronomical society following Eddington's return to Britain, he described the trials and tribulations of Principe in a parody of the *Rubaiyat* whose final verses went thus:

The Clock no question makes of Fasts or Slows,
But steadily and with a constant Rate it goes.
And Lo! the clouds are parting and the Sun
A crescent glimmering on the screen — It shows! — It shows!!

Five minutes, not a moment left to waste,
Five minutes, for the picture to be traced —
The Stars are shining, and coronal light
Streams from the Orb of Darkness — Oh make haste!

For in and out, above, about, below
'Tis nothing but a magic *Shadow* show
Played in a Box, whose Candle is the Sun
Round which we phantom figures come and go

Oh leave the Wise our measures to collate.
One thing at least is certain, LIGHT has WEIGHT
One thing is certain, and the rest debate —
Light-rays, when near the Sun, DO NOT GO STRAIGHT.

Despite Eddington's moment of drama at Principe, full confirmation did not come all at once. While the Principe photographs had been developed and measured in West Africa, those of the Sobral expedition were brought to Britain before being processed. The first were disappointing. Then came the main set of seven. "They gave a final verdict," wrote Eddington, "definitely confirming Einstein's value of the deflection, in agreement with the results obtained at Principe."

But the news had not yet percolated beyond the small circle of those connected with the expeditions. Einstein knew through his friends in Holland that the expeditions had been in progress, but he had known little more. On September 2nd he wrote to Dr. E.

Hartmann of Fulda noting that he knew nothing about the expeditions' measurements, and in rejecting Ehrenfest's proposals for a Leiden post ten days later, he asked whether there was news about the British eclipse expedition.

Ehrenfest passed on Einstein's message to Lorentz, who with his more numerous contacts abroad was able to discover what was happening. And on September 27th, 1919 there came Lorentz' telegram: "Eddington found star displacement at rim of sun ..."

Einstein's first reaction was to pass on the good news to his mother in Lucerne.

Looking back, both Einstein and his colleagues were apt to harp on his inner certainty. But this was not the certainty of hindsight; all along he had believed that the theory would be confirmed. Nevertheless, he was glad enough to begin preparations for a trip to Holland.

First he had to obtain the necessary travel documents. On October 5th he wrote to Ehrenfest, explaining that he had been to the Dutch Embassy in Berlin and asking his friends in Holland to help. Kamerlingh Onnes now used his influence as the head of Leiden's world-famous Cryogenic Laboratory to intercede on Einstein's behalf. Within a few days he had a Dutch entry permit.

Before he left Berlin he received further news from Lorentz. "I have not yet written to you about the observation of the rays glancing off the edge of the sun, as I thought that one of the English journals, *Nature* for instance, would have written fully about it," Lorentz explained on October 7th.

> This has not yet happened so I do not wish to wait any longer. I have heard of Eddington's results through Mr. Van der Pohl, the conservator of this laboratory. He visited the British Association meeting at Bournemouth and told me on his return what Eddington spoke about. As the plates are still being measured he cannot give exact values, but according to Eddington's opinion the thing is certain and one can say with certainty that the deflection (at the edge of the sun) lies between 0.87" and 1'74". Van der Pohl also told me that there was a discussion about it (I wish I had been there) and that Sir Oliver Lodge wished you and Eddington the best of luck with the figures when they came.

He went on to describe some of his own work and then returned to the Eddington results. "They are certainly," he noted, "some of the most beautiful results that science has produced and we should indeed rejoice."

So far, the warnings that a major change in man's ideas of the physical world was at hand had seeped out only gradually. No results had been publicly available when the British expeditions had returned to London. The accounts given at the British Association meeting had stressed that vital measurements and comparisons still had to be completed. Even Lorentz' telegram to Einstein had given a general rather than a specific indication of success. Thus the reports had hardened up slowly, over the weeks, lacking the suddenness which alone could give headline quality in a Europe grappling with the problems of post-war chaos. There was, moreover, to be a final twist before the news finally broke on the world.

This was given in Leiden where Einstein arrived in the latter half of October. The vital results of the British expeditions were known here, privately at least, by October 23rd. But even now only a small handful of professors were in the know. Two days later, on the evening of Saturday, October 25th, the situation changed dramatically. The Dutch Royal Academy met in Amsterdam. Einstein was there. So was Lorentz and so was Ehrenfest. First the routine business was disposed of. Next, Einstein was formally welcomed. Then, in the words of the Academy's official report, "Mr. H. A. Lorentz communicated the most recent confirmation of Professor Einstein's General Theory of Relativity." But, as the agenda put it, the communication would "not be printed in the report". No Press representatives appear to have been present. For another ten days the rest of the world remained in ignorance of the fact that Newton's view of the universe had received an amendment from which it would never totally recover.

It was not until the afternoon of Thursday, November 6th, 1919, that the Fellows of the Royal and the Royal Astronomical Societies met in Burlington House to hear the official results of the two eclipse expeditions. Dyson read the reports on behalf of himself, Eddington and Davidson. He had devoted a good deal of his professional life to the study of solar eclipses and had personally observed no less than three. This time it was different. The aim of the operation had been to test Einstein's theory, and unofficial news of the results had been rumbling round the scientific world for weeks. Here, if nowhere else, men were aware that an age was ending, and the main hall of the Society was crowded. J. J. Thomson, now President of the Royal Society, James Jeans, and Lindemann were present. So were Sir Oliver Lodge and the mathematician and philosopher Alfred Whitehead. All were agitated by the same question. Were the ideas upon which they had relied for so long at last to be found wanting?

The whole atmosphere of tense interest was exactly that of the Greek drama [wrote Whitehead later]. We were the chorus commenting on the decree of destiny as disclosed in the development of a supreme incident. There was dramatic quality in the very staging — the traditional ceremonial, and in the background the picture of Newton to remind us that the greatest of scientific generalisations was now, after more than two centuries, to receive its first modification. Nor was the personal interest wanting; a great adventure in thought had at length come safe to shore.

Thomson rose to address the meeting, speaking of Einstein's theory as "one of the greatest achievements in the history of human thought" and then pushing home the full measure of what relativity meant. "It is not the discovery of an outlying island but of a whole continent of new scientific ideas," he said. "It is the greatest discovery in connection with gravitation since Newton enunciated his principles." As *The Times* put it, Einstein's Theory dealt with the fabric of the universe.

Then Dyson read the body of his report, giving the figures provided by the photographs and describing their significance. "Thus the results of the expeditions to Sobral and Principe," he concluded, "leave little doubt that a deflection of light takes place in the neighbourhood of the sun and that it is of the amount demanded by Einstein's generalised theory of relativity as attributable to the sun's gravitational field."

The discussion that followed brought out one thing: that while the results of the eclipse expedition had yielded a convincing key piece of evidence, the new theory was acceptable on entirely different grounds. Eddington was to emphasise the point nearly twenty years later when there had been further astronomical support. The theory, he said, was primarily concerned with phenomena which, without it, might have seemed mildly puzzling.

But we do not need to observe an eclipse of the sun to ascertain whether a man is talking coherently or incoherently. The Newtonian framework, as was natural after 250 years, had been found too crude to accommodate the new observational knowledge which was being acquired. In default of a better framework, it was still used, but definitions were strained to purposes for which they were never intended. We were in the position of a librarian whose books were still being arranged according to a subject-scheme drawn up a hundred years ago, trying to find the right place for books on Hollywood, the Air Force, and detective novels.

Einstein had altered all that.

# PART THREE

# The Hinge of Fate

# 10

## THE NEW MESSIAH

EINSTEIN AWOKE IN BERLIN ON THE MORNING OF NOVEMBER 7TH, 1919, to find himself famous. It was an awkward morning for fame, with the Wilhelmstrasse barricaded, all traffic stopped on the orders of Gustav Noske, the Republican Minister of Defence, and warning leaflets from the Citizens Defence Force being handed out to passers-by. On the second anniversary of the Russian Revolution it seemed that Berlin was to be torn apart by a struggle between the workers who believed that the German Government had not moved far enough to the Left and the army who believed that it had moved too far.

Einstein was of course already known to the equivalent of today's science correspondents. In addition, the esoteric quality of his work had combined with his own individuality to produce a local notoriety. Now, on the morning of November 7th, the situation was dramatically changed. Even a month later he could write to Born that the publicity was so bad that he could hardly get down to work. Any journalist who felt that the newsworthiness of the British expeditions had ended with their safe return to England learned better as accounts of the previous afternoon's meeting in Burlington House, and the subsequent leading article in *The Times*, arrived in the German capital. Under "The Fabric of the Universe", *The Times* stated that "the scientific conception of the fabric of the Universe must be changed". And after an account of the British expeditions and their purpose, it concluded thus: "But it is confidently believed by the greatest experts that enough has been done to overthrow the certainty of ages, and to require a new philosophy of the universe, a philosophy that will sweep away nearly all that has hitherto been accepted as the axiomatic basis of physical thought."

This was strong meat. Its effect was not lessened by accounts in other papers, which with few exceptions agreed that the world

would never be the same again. Attention turned to the man responsible. Little was known about him except that in 1914 he had
not signed the notorious Manifesto of the 93. Whether he was Swiss
or German was uncertain, but *The Times* described him as an ardent
Zionist and added that when the Armistice had been announced the
previous year, he "signed an appeal in favour of the German revolution" — probably a reference to his support of the re-formed Bund
Neues Vaterland.

Throughout the day Einstein was visited by an almost continuous stream of reporters. He genuinely did not like it. But he
soon realised that there is a time for compromise as well as a time
for standing firm. There was, moreover, one way in which the dis-
tasteful interest could be turned to good use. So there were no free
photographs of Einstein; as one reporter later noted, "these, his wife
told me, are sold for the benefit of the starving children of Vienna".
It was not only photographs which could coax money into the
channels through which he thought it should flow. There was also a
demand for simple explanations of relativity for which the newspapers of the world would pay large sums. Einstein never succumbed to the temptation of writing articles galore. But before the end
of the month he was in touch with a young correspondent for
*Nature* and had agreed to contribute an article to *The Times*.

The *Nature* correspondent was Robert Lawson, the young physicist who had attended his lecture in Vienna six years previously.
Interned at the outbreak of war, but nevertheless allowed to continue his scientific work at the Radium Institute, Lawson returned
to the University of Sheffield at the end of 1919, and now, as well
as writing to Einstein himself, gave Arnold Berliner, the editor of
*Naturwissenschaften*, an account of the situation in Britain.

> The talk here is of almost nothing but Einstein, [he said] and if he
> were to come here now I think he would be welcomed like a victorious
> general. The fact that a theory formulated by a German has been
> confirmed by observations on the part of Englishmen has brought the
> possibility of co-operation between these two scientifically-minded
> nations much closer. Quite apart from the great scientific value of his
> brilliant theory, Einstein has done mankind an incalculable service.

Berliner passed on the letter to Einstein who in acknowledging
Lawson's direct request for material for *Nature* mentioned the
article he was writing for *The Times*. This appeared on the 28th, but
the paper had already renewed its efforts to explain to readers how
important the confirmation of the General Theory really was. For

it was becoming clear that the announcement at the Burlington House meeting was not just a nine-days' wonder. Although some scientists were reluctant to accept all that Einstein had claimed, and although others, like Sir Oliver Lodge, were still gruffly sceptical, the ablest minds in science realised, and publicly acknowledged, that this was not an end but a beginning. On November 15th *The Times* added its weight in a leading article headed "The Revolution in Science".

> The ideals of Aristotle and Euclid and Newton which are the basis of all our present conceptions prove in fact not to correspond with what can be observed in the fabric of the universe, [it concluded.] Space is merely a relation between two sets of data, and an infinite number of times may co-exist. Here and there, past and present, are relative, not absolute, and change according to the ordinates and co-ordinates selected. Observational science has in fact led back to the purest subjective idealism, if without Berkley's major premise, itself an abstraction of Aristotelian notions of infinity, to take it out of chaos.

A fortnight later came Einstein's own article. Using the opportunity to deplore the war, he began with a typical Einsteinian flourish by saying: "After the lamentable breach in the former international relations existing among men of science, it is with joy and gratefulness that I accept this opportunity of communication with English astronomers and physicists." He went on to outline the basic principles of relativity, special and general, displaying in what was his first popular exposition all those abilities which still make Einstein on relativity a good deal clearer than most other writers.

At the end of the same article he lightly commented on the status that the English had given him, tossing a joke into the future that was to be thrust back in his face within a decade. "The description of me and my circumstances in *The Times* show an amusing feat of imagination on the part of the writer," he said. "By an application of the theory of relativity to the taste of readers, today in Germany I am called a German man of science and in England I am represented as a Swiss Jew. If I come to be regarded as a 'bête noire' the description will be reversed, and I shall become a Swiss Jew for the Germans and a German man of science for the English." Unwilling to censor the comment, *The Times* was equally unwilling to let it pass. "We conceded him his little jest", an editorial admitted. "But we note that, in accordance with the general tenor of his theory, Dr. Einstein does not supply any absolute description of himself."

The comment was indicative of an undertow of feeling in some conservative circles, both scientific and lay. Thomson, Eddington, Jeans, and many other bright Fellows of the Royal Society, appeared to have accepted the extraordinary ideas of this Jew of whose nationality no one appeared to be certain. But could the thing really be true? Was there not somewhere, in some fashion, a more reasonable explanation to which sane men would wake up one morning? Some distinguished men thought so. Among them was Sir Oliver Lodge, who had left before the end of the famous meeting of November 6th, even though expected to speak in the discussion — and who later explained this on the grounds of a previous engagement and the need to catch the six o'clock train. On the 24th, Lodge, whose *The Ether of Space* well qualified him for leading the sceptics, addressed an impressive if polyglot company which included the Bishop of London, Lord Lytton, Lord Haldane, Sir Francis Younghusband, H. A. L. Fischer and Sir Martin Conway. Newton, Lodge affirmed, had not understood what gravitation was. "We do not understand it now," he went on. "Einstein's theory would not help us to understand it. If Einstein's third prediction were verified, Einstein's theory would dominate all physics and the next generation of mathematical physicists would have a terrible time." Indeed, they did.

This third prediction, the Einstein shift, still exercised Einstein himself, as he revealed in a letter to Eddington which shows vestigial doubt as well as gratitude, courtesy and humility. He congratulated Eddington on his work and said how amazed he was at the English interest in the theory.

Einstein was not alone. In addition to the doubters headed by Lodge — and Sir Joseph Larmor, who had been among the first to describe matter as consisting of electrified particles — there were others who feared that relativity might be beyond them, or who had doubts as to whether the results of the eclipse expeditions were, scientifically speaking, a good thing.

The archives reveal some surprising names in both camps. In the first there is Dyson, who wrote to Hale at the Mount Wilson Observatory on December 29th. "I was myself a sceptic, and expected a different result," he said. "Now I am trying to understand the principle of relativity and am gradually getting to think I do." Hale was less optimistic. "I congratulate you again on the splendid results you have obtained" he wrote to Dyson on February 9th, 1920, "though I confess that the complications of the theory of relativity are altogether too much for my comprehension. If I were a good mathematician I might have some hope of forming a feeble conception of the principle, but as it is I fear it will always remain beyond my grasp. However, this does not decrease my interest in the problem, to which we will try to contribute to the best of our ability." His doubts were repeated to Rutherford to whom he wrote that relativity seemed "to complicate matters a good deal".

Rutherford's own qualifications and doubts were unlike those of Dyson and Hale. He noted that the interest of the general public was very remarkable and almost without precedent, the reason being, he felt, that no one was able to give an intelligent explanation of relativity to the average man. He himself did not have much doubt about the accuracy of Einstein's conclusions and considered it a great bit of work. However, he feared that it might tend to draw scientific men away from experiments towards broad metaphysical conceptions. There were already many like that in Britain, he went on, and no more were needed if science was to continue advancing.

This was a typical Rutherford attitude, illustrating his built-in belief that the only worthwhile experiments were those whose results he could personally repeat and check. So far as the work of Einstein was relative to Newton, he said in 1923, it was simply "a generalisation and broadening of its basis, in fact a typical case of mathematical and physical development". But nine years later the balance had altered. "The theory of relativity by Einstein, quite apart from any question of its validity," he agreed, "cannot but be regarded as a magnificent work of art." This qualification, however deeply rooted in scientific intuition, may have reflected the slight allergy to Einstein himself which comes out at times in Rutherford's comments. Certainly he showed no wish to have him in Cambridge when the idea was mooted in 1920, or even when Einstein was a refugee from Germany in 1933.

Much the same lukewarm view appears beneath the surface in J. J. Thomson. "[He] accepted these results (1919) and the interpretation put upon them, but he never seemed particularly enthusiastic on the subject nor did he attempt to develop it, either theoretically or by experiment," said his biographer, Lord Rayleigh, some years later. "I believe, from a conversation which I can recall, that he thought attention was being too much concentrated on it by ordinary scientific workers, with the neglect of other subjects to which they were more likely to be able to make a useful contribution. His attitude to relativity was that of a looker-on. Probably the same was true of nearly all his contemporaries. It was the creation of a younger generation." And when it came to cosmology, Thomson's patience ran out. "We have Einstein's space, de Sitter's space, expanding universes, contracting universes, vibrating universes, mysterious universes," he noted in his memoirs. "In fact the pure mathematician may create universes just by writing down an equation, and indeed if he is an individualist he can have a universe of his own."

The semi-quizzical note can be heard in many of the repercussions which followed the November meeting at Burlington House. Eddington, speaking in support of relativity in Trinity College, Cambridge, early in December, said that although six feet tall he would, if moving vertically at 161,000 miles a second, shrink to a height of only three feet. J. J. Thomson, adopting the same line, remarked that "the tutor who preferred rooms on the ground floor to the attic would hardly be consoled to know that the higher he was up, the more Euclidean his space became because it was further from the effects of gravitation." A good deal of the light-headedness which took hold of so many serious men when they began to discuss relativity no doubt sprang from Eddington's example. As his biographer has said in writing of *Space, Time and Gravitation*, the relativist could, like the Mad Hatter, experience time standing still. In later books Alice herself moved mystifyingly across his stage, the living embodiment of the Fitzgerald contraction; and the Red Queen, "that ardent relativist", proclaimed the relativity even of nonsense.

The trend was spurred on by the simultaneous fame of Epstein and produced the following verse.

> Einstein and Epstein are wonderful men,
>> Bringing new miracles into our ken.
> Einstein upset the Newtonian rule;
>> Epstein demolished the Pheidian School.
> Einstein gave fits to the Royal Society
>> Epstein delighted in loud notoreity.
> Einstein made parallels meet in infinity
>> Epstein remodelled the form of divinity.

Anti-Germanism, understandably enough after the long haul that victory had demanded, also showed itself in divers reactions, and from Rutherford's Cavendish Laboratory there came a typical poem from A. A Robb. One of the few English physicists who had given more than passing attention to the Special Theory, Robb had written as early as 1914 that "although generally associated with the names of Einstein and Minkowski, the really essential physical considerations underlying the theories are due to Larmor and Lorentz." His allergy to Einstein was increased by General Relativity and in the introduction to *The Absolute Relations of Time and Space,* he caustically wrote of Einstein's theory of simultaneity that "this seemed to destroy all sense of the reality of the external world and to leave the physical universe no better than a dream, or rather a nightmare."

The acclaim which surged up at the end of 1919 naturally presented too good an opportunity to miss; the result was Robb's "Hymn to Einstein", to be sung to the tune of "Deutschland Über Alles":

> Scientists so unbelieving
>> Have completely changed their ways;
> Now they humbly sing to Einstein
>> Everlasting hymns of praise.
> Journalists in search of copy
>> First request an interview;
> Then they boost him, boost him, boost him;
>> Boost him until all is blue.
>
> He the universe created;
>> Spoke the word and it was there.
> Now he reigns in radiant glory
>> On his professorial chair.
> Editions of daily papers,
>> Yellow red and every hue
> Boost him, boost him, boost him, boost him;
>> Boost him until all is blue.
>
> Philosophic speculators
>> Stand in awe around his throne.
> University professors
>> Blow upon his loud trombone.
> Praise him on the Riemann symbols
>> On Christoffel symbols too
> They boost him, boost him, boost him;
>> Boost him until all is blue.
>
> Other scientists neglected
>> May be feeling somewhat sick;
> And imagine that the butter
>> Is laid on a trifle thick.
> Heed not such considerations
>> Be they false, or be they true;

Boost him, boost him, boost him, boost him;
Boost him until all is blue.

Einstein himself also seems to have been affected. Thus he started, early in December, one hare that was to run through decades of
books about relativity, naturally enough ignored by science but enjoyed by many simple souls. Interviewed by the *New York Times*,
he was asked how he had come to start work on the General Theory.
He had been triggered off, he replied, by seeing a man falling from
a Berlin roof. The man had survived with little injury. Einstein had
run from his house. The man said that he had not felt the effects of
gravity — a pronouncement that had led to a new view of the universe. Here is perhaps a link with Planck's illustration of energy — his
story of a workman, carrying bricks to the top of a house and piling
up energy which remained there until the bricks slipped and fell on
his head weeks later. Here, too, is another illustration of Hans Einstein's statement that his father was always willing to exaggerate in
order to explain, and would at times delight in making up a story
to please an audience.

All this, however, was froth on the top of the argument. Beneath
the humour, the Alice in Wonderland analogies, the limericks concerning the young lady called Bright, whose speed was much faster
than light,* there lay an almost universal agreement that Einstein's
view of gravitation was more consistent with the available facts
than Newton's. There might be debate over details, the third proof
had not yet been obtained, and there were to be several attempts —
all either unsuccessful or inconclusive — to show that the outcome of
the Michelson-Morley experiment itself could be faulted. But the
band of responsible critics was comparatively small, and it was clear
that Einstein had in fact cast fresh light not only on the subject of
gravitation but on the whole question of how scientific knowledge
might be acquired. For Newton's theory had been founded on the
most detailed observational evidence; each twinkling pinpoint in the
heavens appeared to support the belief that the accumulation of evidence, and the induction from it of general laws, could lead to the
ultimate truth. Now it had been shown that by starting with a
purely speculative idea, it was possible to construct a theory which
would not only be supported by the mass of observational evidence
with which Newton had worked, but which would also explain evi-

---

* The most respectable is Arthur Butler's: "There was a young lady called
Bright/Whose speed was much faster than light/She went out one day/In
a relative way/And came back the previous night."

dence which Newton could not explain. By the opening weeks of 1920 it was clear that Einstein held the field.

But to some people he had yet to live down his presence in Berlin throughout the war, however pacifist his sentiments might be. M. Brouillon had his counterparts in England as Eddington was forced to make clear early in the New Year.

As keen as Einstein himself for the restoration of scientific cooperation between the belligerent countries, Eddington had stressed this point in his first letter when on December 1st, 1919, he had written to Einstein from Cambridge saying that since November 6th "all England has been talking about your theory.... It is the best possible thing that could have happened for scientific relations between England and Germany", he went on. "I do not anticipate rapid progress towards official reunion, but there is a big advance towards a more reasonable frame of mind among scientific men, and that is even more important than the renewal of formal associations.... Although it seems unfair that Dr. Freundlich, who was first in the field, should not have had the satisfaction of accomplishing the experimental test of your theory, one feels that things have turned out very fortunately in giving this object lesson of the solidarity of German and British science even in time of war".

So far so good. Eddington's liberal sentiments were held by many men of science, possibly a majority. When, later in December, three names were proposed for the Royal Astronomical Society's Gold Medal, Einstein was voted for the award by an overwhelming majority. He was duly informed and writing to Born on January 27th about the Peace Treaty noted that he would be going to England in the spring to receive it.

A few days later he received an apologetic letter from Eddington and was disabused. Eddington said that the officials of the Royal Astronomical Society had met to vote on the Gold Medal award. But a purely chauvinistic lobby had been mustered at the last minute and had successfully stopped its being made to Einstein. For the first time in thirty years, no Gold Medal would be awarded. "I am sure," wrote Eddington, "that your disappointment will not be in any way personal and that you will share with me the regret that this promising opening of a better international spirit has had a rebuff from reaction. Nevertheless, I am sure the better spirit is making progress."

As with Solvay, Einstein had to wait for a change in the political climate. Then, at last allowed to join in the game, he scooped the pool. In 1925 he was awarded the Royal Society's Copley Medal;

and, the following year, the Royal Astronomical Society's Gold Medal.

Whatever the difficulties in making formal British awards to a German, Einstein had by the first months of 1920 gained not only success but notoriety.

The speed with which his fame spread across the world, down through the intellectual layers to the man-in-the-street, the mixture of semi-religious awe and near-hysteria which his figure aroused, created a startling phenomenon which has never been fully explained, but is well described by Alexander Moszkowski, a Berlin literateur and critic who moved on the fringe of the Einstein circle. Moszcowski's book, *Einstein the Searcher*, caused Einstein's friends a great deal of misgiving, and the Borns felt so strongly about it that they persuaded him to try and stop publication. The outcome of a long series of conversations during which Einstein had spoken about his work quite freely and in simple terms, the book was an overpopularisation of science more unusual then than it would be today. It also had considerable, and somewhat dramatic pre-publication publicity, and it was this, more than the substance of the book itself, which angered Einstein's would-be protectors. He himself appears to have cared very little about the temporary furore that the book created.*

> Everything sank away in the face of this universal theme which had taken possession of humanity [Moszkowski wrote of the huge public interest in relativity.] The converse of educated people circled about this pole, and could not escape from it, continually reverted to the same theme pressed aside by necessity or accident. Newspapers entered on a chase for contributors who could furnish them with short or long, technical or non-technical, notices about Einstein's theory. In all nooks and corners, social evenings of instruction sprang up, and wondering universities appeared with errant professors that led people out of the three-dimensional misery of daily life into the more hospitable Elysian fields of four-dimensionality. Women lost sight of domestic worries and discussed co-ordinate systems, the principle of simultaneity, and negatively-charged electrons. All contemporary questions had gained a fixed centre from which threads could be spun to each. Relativity had become the sovereign password.

* From the correspondence published in the Born-Einstein letters it seems that Einstein gave permission for publication of Moszkowski's book: on the advice of his friends, informed Moszkowski that his "splendid work" must not appear; but on the advice of Lorentz and others did not start the legal proceedings that alone might have stopped publication. Whether or not he was fully aware, when he initially gave the interviews, of the furore they would cause, is certainly not clear.

Exaggerated as it sounds, this account is more than the truth, even if the truth in fancy dress. The attitude was, moreover, not confined to the uninitiated.

To those who have the vision, the world of physics will take on a new and wonderful life, [wrote the reviewer in *Nature* of Einstein's own book on relativity.] The commonest phenomena become organic parts of the great plan. The rationality of the universe becomes an exciting romance, not a cold dogma. The thrill of a comprehensive understanding runs through us, and yet we find ourselves on the shores of the unknown. For this new doctrine, after all, is but a touchstone of truth. We must submit all our theories to the test of it; we must allow our deepest thoughts to be gauged by it. The metaphysician and he who speculates over the meaning of life cannot be indifferent.

It was therefore predictable that learned societies should hold many meetings at which the special and the general theories were discussed; that *The Times Educational Supplement* should devote three full-page articles to interpretations of relativity by Professor Lindemann, Dr. Herbert Carr, and Alfred Whitehead, and that an Einstein Society should be started in the House of Commons in 1920. "Its formation was due more to the curiosity of those of us who had unexpectedly survived the First World War than to any profound scientific search," says one of its members, Colin Coote.

It was understandable that within a year there should be more than a hundred books on the subject, and that intellectual interest should be shown not only in the world's capitals but in the provinces. "At this time," writes Infeld, later to become one of Einstein's collaborators, "I was a school teacher in a small Polish town, and I did what hundreds of others did all over the world. I gave a public lecture on the Relativity Theory, and the crowd that queued up on a cold winter's night was so great that it could not be accommodated in the largest hall in the town." When Eddington had lectured in Cambridge on a similar night in December, in his own words, "hundreds were turned away, unable to get the room". In Paris the American Eugene Higgins presented 5,000 dollars through the *Scientific American* for the best 3,000-word exposition of relativity. "I am the only one in my entire circle of friends who is not entering"," observed Einstein "I don't believe I could do it." The prize, fittingly enough in view of Einstein's Berne background, was won by Lyndon Bolton a senior examiner of the British Patent Office.

If all this was explicable in terms of an important new scientific theory which had become the common coin of intelligent conversation, Einstein was also raised to the far less comprehensible position of a popular celebrity. From London, the Palladium music hall asked whether he would appear, virtually at his own figure, for a three week "performance". The "Einstein cigar" appeared on the market. Children were blessed, or otherwise, with his name. The cartoonists took him to their hearts. In Germany, he was shown in company with the French President Mitterand who was advocating the heaviest possible reparations from the country. "Can't you persuade the simpleminded Bôche that even with an absolute deficit of 67,000,000,000 marks he is still *relatively* well off?" In Britain, a detective shown catching a bank thief with the help of a torch whose light rays turned corners, laconically remarked: "Elementary, my dear Einstein." He had in fact been hoisted into position by the same mob which hoists film stars. Reason had little to do with the matter. But in one way the treatment of Einstein was different in its results. Film stars pontificating on the future of the world, boxers dogmatising on politics, can be good entertainment and few people take them more seriously than this. Einstein was in another category. His theory might not be understandable to most men but it was clear that he had an intellect of unique proportions. Surely his brain could be turned to illuminate, with good effect, some of the problems that worried ordinary mortals? It was easy to answer "yes".

All this was only a prelude to a long series of invitations to lecture in foreign countries; to bags of letters and pleas for money which come to famous men and, in Einstein's case, were brought up the stairs by the sack-load. It was a prelude to determined appeals from more substantial causes, above all from the Zionists and the pacifists, both quick to realise that in Einstein they might be able to secure a unique totem-figure.

The photogenic white-haired Messiah to which the world later became accustomed cannot be invoked to explain the extraordinary and world-wide phenomenon. The picture of Einstein as he toured the world in the early 1920s, well-booted and accoutred, broad-brimmed hat giving a touch of mystery, is quite the reverse: a picture of the distinguished man of the times, possibly aloof, but certainly established. The sheer audacity of his theory helped. "Light caught bending" was an affront to common sense that few could in their heart of hearts take seriously; there was, if nothing else, a curiosity value about the man who had apparently shown that it did.

Yet to attribute Einstein's popularity to this alone is to rate the inner awareness of the common people too low. Some weight must be given to Infeld's view.

It was just after the end of the war. People were weary of hatred, of killing and international intrigues. The trenches, bombs and murder had left a bitter taste. Books about war did not sell. Everyone looked for a new era of peace, and wanted to forget the war. Here was something which captured the imagination; human eyes looking from an earth covered with graves and blood to the heavens covered with the stars. Abstract thought carrying the human mind far away from the sad and disappointing reality. The mystery of the sun's eclipse and of the penetrating power of the human mind. Romantic scenery, a strange glimpse of the eclipsed sun, an imaginary picture of bending light rays, all removed from the oppressive reality of life. One further reason, perhaps even more important; a new event was predicted by a *German* scientist Einstein, and confirmed by *English* astronomers. Scientists belonging to two warring nations had collaborated again. It seemed the beginning of a new era.

Even this was only part of the story. Quite as important was the intuitive realisation that the new light cast on the physical world struck at the very vitals of what they had always believed. Few could understand the implications, let alone the complex intellectual structure from which these implications sprang; even so, deep within there lay a sensitive sounding-board, developed since the days when man had first stood up on two feet out of four. Erwin Schrödinger, who six years later was to become a standard-bearer in the new cause of wave mechanics, hinted at the underlying reason for the Einstein phenomenon in his Tarner Lectures of 1956.

I have sometimes wondered why they made such a great stir both among the general public and among philosophers, [he said of the transformations of time and space produced by relativity.] I suppose it is this, that it meant the dethronement of time as a rigid tyrant imposed on us from outside, a liberation from the unbreakable rule of "before and after". For indeed time is our most severe master by ostensibly restricting the existence of each of us to narrow limits - seventy or eighty years, as the Pentateuch has it. To be allowed to play about with such a master's programme believed unassailable until then, to play about with it albeit in a small way, seems to be a great relief, it seems to encourage the thought that the whole "timetable" is probably not quite as serious as it appears at first sight. And this thought is a religious thought, nay I should call it *the* religious thought.

With the "great stir" there started the Einstein mythology, the complex structure of story and half-story, half-truth, quarter-truth, adorned exaggeration and plain lie, which from now onwards increasingly surrounded his activities. All men caught in the white-hot glare of public interest discover, sometimes with amusement, sometimes with resignation, often with resentment, that their smallest doings are memorialised, embroidered and explained away in a continuous flow of anecdote whose connection with the truth is frequently marginal. Einstein was to suffer more than most from such attentions and soon learned to regard them with amusement — as must any biographer who meets the same quasi-documented story appearing in different decades, from different continents, and being retailed in all good faith, to illustrate one or more of Einstein's extraordinary, endearing, or unconventional attitudes.

There were many reasons for the mythology which developed from 1920 onwards. One was that inventions had good ground to grow in. Immersed in his work in Berlin, Einstein did on one occasion use a cheque as a book-mark; it was therefore pardonable that the story should surface as the account of how he had placed a 1,500-dollar cheque into a book and then lost the book. His character was kindly and gentle, and he was at least once asked by a neighbour's small girl to help with her sums; after that, small girls all over the world had Einstein doing their homework — despite the fact that he had refused the request on the grounds that it would not be fair. The legends themselves, melting in the harsh light of investigation, show not so much what sort of man he really was as what kind of man the world thought him. Behind his confidence, Einstein was genuinely humble — and legend made him forbear comment when a girl graduate, failing to recognise him, voiced surprise that he should still be studying physics with the words: "I finished physics when I was twenty-five." Only Einstein, out of time with his fellow-musicians at an amateur gathering recital, would receive the criticism: "Einstein, can't you count?" Only Einstein, unable to find his glasses and asking the dining-car attendant to read the menu, would be met with the comment: "Sorry sir, I ain't had education either." And only Einstein, looking like an untidy middle-class nonentity, could go unrecognised by officialdom in a score of stories, pottering his way through the crowd, a Chaplinesque figure somehow embodying all the human virtues of "us" against "them". Thus he became, as the forces of Left and Right jockeyed for position in the post-war Germany of the Weimar Republic, a new sort of international image, the scientist with the touch of a saint, a man from whom an awed public expected not only research but revelation.

From outside Germany there came adulation — and in 1921 the much-prized Foreign Fellowship of the Royal Society. Inside, opinion was mixed. Planck and Sommerfeld, von Laue and Rubens, Nernst and Haber, were among those who knew what Einstein had accomplished, while some Weimar politicians mentally seized upon him as typifying the new Germany which they hoped could now be presented to the world. Yet there were many others to whom his success was deeply offensive, uniting in one man all that they detested — the success of an intellectual left-wing pacifist Jew.

This feeling counterbalanced the adulation in many ways. In Ulm, for instance, the authorities at first intended to make him a freeman of the city. "But before I approach our collegium," wrote Herr Dr. Schemberger, Stadtvorstand, to the Faculty of Philosophy in Tübingen University, "I would like to find out whether it is true that Einstein's work is really of such outstanding merit." The answer was an unqualified "yes" which concluded: "What Newton did for mechanics, Einstein has done for physics." But when Dr. Schemberger wrote to Einstein on March 22nd, it was not the freedom of the city which was offered, but merely congratulations and the assurance that the town was glad to have him as one of its sons. Einstein's thanks were read out at the next council meeting. Two years later, when the award of the Nobel Prize for Physics put the seal on his work, the authorities settled for a street to be named after him. Perhaps it was only coincidence that it lay on the outskirts of the city and in a poorish area. More than a quarter of a century later, in 1949, he was asked to become an honorary citizen. He refused.

The honours from outside Germany increased throughout 1920. The first came from Leiden. Lorentz had telegraphed him as soon as he had heard of the Royal Society's meeting in November, 1919, and there soon followed the proposal of Kamerlingh Onnes that he be appointed *byzondere Hoogleerarden,* or Special Professor, for three years at an annual salary of 2,000 guilders. The duties would involve only one or two visits a year, each of a few weeks, and there would be no need to interrupt his Berlin work. Einstein accepted, after receiving a plea to do so from Ehrenfest, and having been told by Lorentz that Kamerlingh Onnes, who just twenty years earlier had ignored Einstein's appeal for work, "would regard it as a high honour if you would discuss with him the researches being carried out in his cryogenic laboratory".

There were numerous delays, and although Einstein visited his friends in Leiden in May 1920, it was not until five months later that he made his first formal visit as a Special Professor. Between these two visits, he met Niels Bohr for the first time. Bohr, who had just started the Institute of Theoretical Physics in Copenhagen, made possible by an endowment from the Carlsberg organisation, had been invited by Planck to lecture to the Physikalische Gesellschaft and on his arrival both Planck and Einstein came forward to meet him. So similar in work and outlook, few men were more dissimilar in appearance; Planck formal and precise behind his rimless glasses, immaculately dressed, the German professor down the ages; Einstein still dark-haired, still rather splendid in a leonine way, but already beginning to foreshadow the familiar figure of untidy genius which became the hallmark of his later years.

Something was sparked off between Bohr and Einstein at this meeting, the first of a long series of mental collisions whose succession through the years was to have a quality quite separate from the impact of genius on genius. For it was Einstein who, fifteen years earlier, had first brought an air of unexpected respectability to the idea that light might conceivably consist both of wave and of particle and to the implication that Planck's quantum theory might be applied not only to radiation but to matter itself. It was Bohr who was to bring scientific plausibility to the first of these ideas with his principle of complementarity and substance for the second with his explanation of Rutherford's nuclear atom. Yet these very ideas were to create not a unity between the two men but a chasm. From the early 1920s, as Bohr and those of like mind followed them on to what they saw as inevitable conclusions, Einstein drew back in steadily growing disagreement, withdrawing himself from the main stream of physics and giving to his later years a tragic air which not even the staunchest of his friends could argue away.

Immediately after this first meeting with Bohr, Einstein wrote to Ehrenfest saying how much he had enjoyed it. Bohr was quite as impressed with Einstein. "The discussions, to which I have often reverted in my thoughts," he later wrote, "added to all my admiration for Einstein a deep impression of his detached attitude. Certainly his favoured use of such picturesque phrases as 'ghost waves [*Gespensterfelder*] guiding the photons' implied no tendency to mysticism but illuminated a rather profound humour belind his piercing remarks." And on July 27th he wrote to Rutherford, saying that his visit had been "a very interesting experience, it being the first time I had the opportunity of meeting Planck and Einstein personally, and I spend [sic] the days discussing theoretical problems from morning till night."

Later he gave some details of these discussions. "What do you hope to achieve," he had asked, when Einstein had doubted whether it was necessary to give up causality and continuity? "You, the man who introduced the idea of light as particles! If you are so concerned with the situation in physics in which the nature of light allows for a dual interpretation, then ask the German Government to ban the use of photo-electric cells if you think that light is waves, or the use of diffraction gratings if light is corpuscular."

Einstein remarked: "There you are: a man like you comes and one would expect that two like-minded persons had met, yet we are unable to find a common language. Maybe we physicists ought to agree on certain general fundamentals, on certain general propositions which we would regard as positive before embarking on discussions."

But Bohr objected: "No, never! I would regard it as the greatest treachery on my part if, in embarking on a new domain of knowledge, I accepted any foregone conclusions." This "certain difference in attitude and outlook" between the two men, as Bohr described it, was clear from the first day. It was sharpened and increased during long discussions over more than three decades. But it was the difference between the sides in a great game in which both men strove "To set the cause beyond renown / To love the game beyond the prize / To honour, while you strike him down, / The foe that comes with fearless eyes."

Something of their mutual admiration shines out from their first letters.

> For me, [wrote Bohr as he learned that Einstein would be visiting Copenhagen] it is one of the great experiences of life that I can be near you and talk to you, and I cannot say how grateful I am for all the friendliness which you showed to me on my visit to Berlin, and for your letter which I am ashamed not to have answered before. You do not know how great a stimulus it was for me to have the long-awaited opportunity of hearing from you personally your views on the very question with which I myself have been busy. I will never forget our conversation on the way from Dahlem to your house, and I very much hope that during your visit here an opportunity will arise of continuing it.

Einstein was by the mid- summer of 1920 making numerous lecture-visits of the sort that Bohr referred to. After each he returned to Berlin, and after each he found opposition to himself, and to all that he stood for, ominously growing. And now he decided to straighten out the anomalous question of his nationality. He had renounced his German citizenship and as far as he knew was merely a German-born Swiss, an awkward situation which made him a sitting target for his enemies. There was one simple way of coming into the body of the Kirk: he could take up German civic rights again, an action that might underline his support for the Republic but would at least suggest that he was no longer ashamed of his country.

On July 1st, 1920, Einstein was sworn into the Weimar constitution and some nine months later, on March 15th, 1921, into the Prussian constitution.

If Einstein hated Germany, a portion of Germany certainly hated him. The reasons for this, given the situation in the country July and August, 1920, are simple to explain, if difficult to excuse. In countries which had won the war only at desperate cost, Einstein polarised a longing for co-operation and reconstruction, for an end to the anarchy and for the rational use of scientific knowledge for the common good. In Germany it was otherwise. Here patriotic passion, born of defeat, distrusted pacifist leanings and international connections; and if anti-Semitism was a convenient though dishonourable weapon, desperate times demanded desperate measures. Such feelings were epitomised by the new symbol of General von Luttwitz' Erhardt Brigade which had marched into Berlin from the Baltic to support the abortive Kapp Putsch a few months earlier. On their helmets they wore a reverse of the swastika, a religious symbol usually associated with the worship of the Aryan sun-gods Apollo and Odin.

In the ferment of post-war Germany, where internal divisions were lessened by what appeared to be the vindictive brutality of the Allied blockade, there was more than one group willing to direct rising passions against Einstein, a ready-made target for hatred. There were those scientists who genuinely did not believe in the theories which had brought him a fame unique in their scientific experience. There were others who, whatever they believed, could not bear the thought of such acclaim being lavished on a man who had spent the hard-fought war burrowing away in the University of Berlin. It was bad enough that an unknown professor should have declaimed against the war, held out a welcoming hand to the enemy across the French frontier, and failed even to bend his energies to the commonweal like other scientists such as Haber and Nernst; it was intolerable that the same line should be followed by the man now that he had been jerked to fame overnight. Thus the renown which was to take Einstein round the world in the first half of the 1920s acted as an irritant to the anti-Semitism which burgeoned with the coming of Hitler a decade later. Its roots were bedded deep down in the immediate post-war period and as the years passed it became more firmly established, so that it later proved a weapon which the Nazis could wield. They would have utilised something, of course. But the steady growth of anti-Semitism during the inter-war years was at least partly due to the ease with which its supporters could concentrate their attacks on Einstein and the "new physics".

The attacks started before the end of 1919. In December, while Einstein was still half-submerged by the first tidal wave of publicity which followed the Royal Society meeting in London, he had written to Ehrenfest noting that anti-Semitism was strong in Berlin. In March, Wolfgang Kapp seized Berlin but failed to hold it in the face of a general strike called by the Weimar Government. Internal evidence suggests that the same right-wing forces which subsidised the Kapp Putsch — claimed by Kurt Grossman to include "secret groups round Krupp" — played at least some part in the growing anti-Einstein movement. Finally they created the "Study group of German Natural Philosophers", the Arbeitsgemeinschaft Deutscher Naturforscher, which had at its disposal large sums of money, offered fees to those who would write or speak against Einstein, and advertised its meetings by large posters as though they were announcing public concerts. Leader of this so-called study group was Paul Weyland, a man entirely unknown in scientific circles and of whom, over the years, nothing was discovered. Much of his support came from assorted riffraff; some of it came from more scientifically respectable sources. The physicist Ernst Gehrcke joined the association and so did a number of other men who could genuinely claim to be classed as *bona fide* even if undistinguished scientists.

Above all there was Philip Lenard, whose work on the photoelectric effect had been the forerunner of Einstein's and whose achievements had been stressed by Einstein in his letters to Laub. Lenard had been considered something of an oddity by many of his colleagues at Heidelberg, but before the war he had not been an anti-Semite. He read the ultra-respectable *Frankfurter Zeitung* and, according to Laub, held a high opinion of Einstein's photo-electric paper. One thing that did rankle was Einstein's implied dismissal of the ether as an unnecessary complication in the universe; this in turn, although rather irrelevantly, led him to denigrate the theory of relativity. His views no doubt hardened during the war. They certainly became fixed by the torrent of praise which poured over Einstein from November 1919 onwards. And in 1920 Lenard reappears as the Nobel Prize Winner enthusiastically providing scientific respectability for the Weyland organisation which described relativity as part of a vast Semitic plot to corrupt the world in general and Germany in particular. Its attacks avoided scientific argument; instead, they concentrated on the "Jewish nature" of

relativity, and on the personal character of Einstein. This made them
an embarrassment to the scientific community. But to the uninform-
ed public the news that the Study Group was supported by a Nobel
Prize winner gave the organisation a backbone of pseudo-respect-
ability it would otherwise have lacked.

In August the "Anti-Relativity Company" as Einstein called it
announced twenty meetings to be held in Germany's biggest towns.
Berlin was its headquarters and it hired the Berlin Philharmonic
Hall for a setpiece demonstration against both relativity and Einstein to be held on August 27th.

In some ways the packed meeting had an air of farce as much
as of high drama. On to the stage came Weyland, apparently the
"handsome dark-haired man of about thirty who wore a frockcoat
and spoke with enthusiasm about interesting things" later described
by Einstein's colleague Leopold Infeld. "He said that uproar about
the theory of relativity was hostile to the German spirit. Then there
came a university lecturer who had a little beard, was small, who
also wore a frockcoat, and who read out his speech from a brochure
which had been sold before the lecture. He raised objections about
understanding the theory of relativity."

This second spokesman seems to have been Gehrcke, and as he
dived into some rudimentary technicalities there was a murmur of
"Einstein, Einstein" in the audience. For Einstein had arrived to see
what it was all about. There he was, sitting in a box, obviously
enjoying himself. As the speakers went on, attacking relativity, omitting, distorting, unbalancing, appealing to the good Aryan common
sense of their audience and invoking its members not to take such
stuff seriously, the clown that lies not far below genius began to
show itself. At the more absurd statements about relativity Einstein
could be seen bursting into laughter and clapping his hands in mock-
applause. When the meeting had ended he greeted his friends: "That
was most amusing."

However, the so-called Study Group was a symptom of something more sinister than scientific absurdity, and Einstein replied
in the columns of the *Berliner Tageblatt*, the first time that he had
come down into the marketplace to face his accusers. His statement
was headed: "My Answer to the Anti-Relativity Theory Company
Ltd." Opponents, he said, had relied on such devices as quoting
results from one British eclipse station, already known to be incorrect
due to a technical defect, and omitting all reference to the British
announcement that the theory had been proved. Thus his demolition
task was easy.

Fifty years ago it was almost unknown for a scientist to use the columns of the daily press in this way. Even Einstein's friends were shocked. Sommerfeld described the letter as "not very happy" while Hedwig Born wrote that he must have suffered very much — "for otherwise you would not have allowed yourself to be goaded in to that rather unfortunate reply . . ." Ehrenfest was even more condemnatory. But Einstein had felt that he had to reply to the charges of charlatanism, self-advertisement and plagiarism if the wanted to remain in Berlin. That the result was yet further publicity was unfortunate yet inevitable.

Second only to the sense of shock that a scientist should defend himself in this way was astonishment that a member of the scientific fraternity should need to do so. "The incredible thing", von Laue wrote to Sommerfeld, "is that men such as Lenard and Wolf of Heidelberg, who have a reputation as scholars, actually lecture to such an association. Yesterday Gehrcke spoke after Weyland, and although he stoked up the old fires, his quiet manner of speaking was a relief after Weyland, who can compete with the most unscrupulous demagogue. It is a disgrace that such a thing can happen."

Von Laue went on to say that he, Rubens and Nernst had sent their own short letter of protest against the activities of the association to the leading Berlin newspapers. This, published in the *Berliner Tageblatt*, read as follows:

> We cannot presume in this place to utter our opinion on the profound, exemplary intellectual work which Einstein has brought to his relativity theory. Surprising successes have already been achieved, and further proof must naturally lie in future research. On the other hand, we must stress that apart from Einstein's researches into relativity, his work has assured him a permanent place in the history of science. In this respect his influence on the scientific life not only of Berlin but of the whole of Germany can hardly be over-estimated. Whoever is fortunate enough to be close to Einstein knows that he will never be surpassed in his respect for the cultural values of others, in personal modesty and dislike of all publicity.

Sommerfeld himself had been deeply aroused, particularly in view of fresh rumours that Einstein was planning to leave Germany. As President of the German Physics Society he felt it necessary to come to the rescue.

Dear Einstein, [he wrote on September 3rd.]
With real fury I have, as man and as President, followed the Berlin hunt against you. A word of warning to Wolf of Heidelberg was unne-

cessary. His name, as he has meanwhile written to you, has simply been misused. I feel sure it will be the same with Lenard. A fine type, this Weyland-Gehrcke!

Today I have conferred with Planck about what has to be done about the Association of Scientists [Naturforscher Gesellschaft]. We would like to put to the President, my colleague von Müller, a sharp protest against "scientific" demagogy and a vote of confidence in you. This would not be formally voted upon but would only be raised as an expression of the scientific conscience.

You must not leave Germany! Your whole work is rooted in German (and Dutch) science; nowhere will you find so much understanding as in Germany. It is not in your character to leave Germany now, when she is being so dreadfully misinterpreted by everyone. Just one more point: had you, with your views, lived during the war in France, England or America, you would certainly have been locked up, had you turned your back on the Entente and its false system as I do not doubt you would have done (as were Jaurés, Russell, Caillaus, etc.)

That you, even you, have to defend yourself seriously is a mockery and — although criticism shrinks from saying so — really an insult to justice and intelligence.

The South German monthlies have asked you for an article and are anxious to have your answer. You can, if you prefer, send it to me. But we must have it as soon as possible because of distribution. The South German monthlies are much read and of high repute; incidentally, you can make clear in your article your attitude against the "bugs". I have not read your explanation in the *Berliner Tageblatt;* it is judged by others as not very happy and not quite like you. However, it dealt well with the "bugs". The *Berliner Tageblatt* seems to me hardly the right place in which to get your own back on the anti-Semitic hulla-baloo. It would make us very happy if you would collaborate with the South Germans.

I hope that you have, in the meantime, regained your philosophical laughter and sympathy with Germany whose trials are everywhere obvious. But no more of desertion.

Affectionately yours, A. Sommerfeld

P. S.   I have asked Grebe to demonstrate his survey in Nauheim. He will do it. This question seems to me most important for the discussion. You will, of course come to Nauheim?

In emphasising that Einstein should stand his ground he was appealing, ironically enough, to Einstein's feelings for Germany, the nation cast off in 1896 whose actions he had bitterly criticised throughout the war. To retire to Holland, or even Switzerland, would be desertion, desertion not only of his scientific colleagues but of that Germany "whose trials are everywhere so apparent".

At the end of August, 1920, Einstein was therefore once again being pulled in two directions — away from Berlin by the threat of anti-Semitism and the friendships of Lorentz and Ehrenfest; towards Berlin by his loyalty to University colleagues and his new-found hope for a Republican Germany. He knew that a permanent post at Leiden University could be his for the asking and the same was no doubt still true of Zurich. His thoughts were already turning to England, and to a young British visitor who called on him to discuss German requests for periodicals from British universities, he "referred to his lecturing at Oxford and expressed the pleasure that it would be for him to do so some time". Lindemann, recently made head of the Clarendon Laboratory, Oxford, had also called on him in Berlin. They had recalled their last meeting at the Solvay Congress, agreed to exchange future papers, and it is more than likely — especially in the light of future events — that Lindemann put the idea of an Oxford visit into Einstein's head. Something more substantial had already been suggested to Rutherford, who had taken J. J. Thomson's place at the Cavendish the previous year. For on September 1st, Jeans had written to him from Zermatt, sending what was probably a report of Einstein's statement in the *Berliner Tageblatt*.

My dear Rutherford, [he said] you spoke of the need of a first-class applied mathematician or math [ematica]l physicist for Cambridge. I have been wondering what you would think of Albert Einstein. From the enclosed it seems quite likely that he will be leaving Berlin very soon— there has been a good deal of disturbance over him there, as you have probably seen, and he would probably consider an English offer I should think.

In my opinion he is just the man needed, in conjunction with yourself, to re-establish a school of mathematical physics in Cambridge. The only serious drawback I think of is that he does not, or did not, speak English, but I imagine he would soon learn. His age is forty-two, nearly forty-three, and I imagine he has still plenty of creative power left.

There is no record of Rutherford's reply, but it seems likely that he was still slightly allergic to Einstein. Nevertheless, for a man of such unique reputation almost all options were open and it would not have been surprising had Einstein now left Germany for a permanent post outside the Reich. But by the time he replied to Sommerfeld on September 6th, he had decided otherwise.

For a couple of days he had really thought of leaving Berlin. But then he realised that he had taken the attacks too seriously —

and that it would, in any case, be wrong to leave his friends. But he had felt it impossible to say nothing in his own defence as the attacks had continued. Nevertheless, it was clear that he had turned the corner once again and would be staying with the Academy.

A few days after writing to Sommerfeld he said much the same thing to the Borns. If they had any doubts they might have been reassured by the news that he was now thinking of buying a sailing boat and a country cottage near one of the lakes which reach out from Berlin into the open country.

Yet if he had agreed not to leave Germany, the decision could easily be changed. The agents of the German Republic now acted to prevent such a catastrophe. One was Planck, the other was Haenisch, the German Minister for Education; both were determined that for the sake of German science Einstein should be discouraged from having second thoughts.

Planck wrote to Einstein on September 5th, from Gmund am Tegernsee in the South Tyrol. He could scarcely believe reports of the meeting in the Berlin Philharmonic and found it impossible to understand what was going on. But one thing was very much more important. He was, he went on, tormented by the thought that Einstein might eventually lose patience and take a step which would punish both German science and his friends. He was able to write not only from his Olympian height but also from a position of long friendship.

He was, moreover, now supported by the Minister, Haenisch. "Most respected professor", Haenisch wrote to Einstein, "with sorrow and shame I see by the Press that the theory represented by you has become a public object of spiteful attacks which go far beyond the limits of pertinent criticism, and that even your own scientific personality has not been spared from defamation and slanders.

> It is of special satisfaction to me to know in connection with this affair that scholars of recognised repute, among whom are prominent representatives of the University of Berlin, are supporting you, are denouncing the contemptible attacks upon your person, and are drawing attention to the fact that your scientific work has assured you a unique place in the history of science. Where the best people are defending you, it will be the easier for you to pay no further attention to such ugly actions. Therefore, I may well allow myself to express the definite hope that there is no truth in the rumours that, because of these vicious attacks, you wished to leave Berlin which always was, and always will be, proud to count you, most respected professor, among the first ornaments of the scientific world.

Einstein appears to have delayed his reply, although he no doubt acknowledged the Minister's appeal. He had good reason to be cautious, for it seemed possible that the "Anti-Relativity Company" might muster considerable support, from rabblerousers if not from scientists. "The first anti-Einstein lecture," the *New York Times* had reported, "had a decided anti-Semitic complexion, which applied equally to the lecture and to a large part of the audience." And in the volatile atmosphere of early Weimar Germany there was a genuine danger of violence at Bad Nauheim where the meeting of the Naturforscher Gesellschaft was to start on September 25th. It seemed likely that there would at the least be a dramatic confrontation comparable to that between Bishop Wilberforce and T. H. Huxley at the British Association in Oxford sixty years earlier.

Bad Nauheim is only some twenty miles from Frankfurt, where Born had recently been appointed professor, and Einstein stayed with the Borns for the duration of the meeting, travelling into the small town each day with his friends. The spa is a leisurely place in the foothills of the Taunus, lying among the pines, accustomed to conferences and old people, and on the morning of September 25th its inhabitants were surprised to find the Badehaus guarded by armed police with fixed bayonets: an indication both of the extent to which anti-Semitism had already been aroused and of Weimar's wish to avoid trouble. The opposition to Einstein had been fully organised. "I had previously received a letter, signed by Weyland, in which I was guaranteed a very large sum (I forget the details) if I would side with them," Ehrenhaft has written. Instead, he passed on the letter to Einstein.

The Badehalle was packed for the discussion on relativity. "When Lenard began," says Dr. Friedrich Dessauer, who was sitting on Einstein's left, "Einstein wanted to make notes but, as one would expect, he had no pencil. He asked to borrow mine in order to reply clearly and convincingly to Lenard's objections. . . As a minor joke, Einstein has my pencil to this day. At least, he never returned it to me, so that what has come from it is probably more intelligent than it would have been if I had got it back."

Lenard's style can be judged from his opening words: "I have much pleasure in today taking part in a discussion on the gravitation theory of the ether. But I must say that as soon as one passes from the theory of gravitation to those of the powers of mass-proportion, the simple understanding of the scientist must take exception to the theory." One could, he went on, express the result of observations through equations; or one could explain equations in terms of observations. "I would very much favour the second idea whereas Einstein favours the first."

Einstein now rose to reply. No verbatim account appears to have survived. Dr. Dessauer says that the argument was not quite as grim as was feared, and the report in the *Physikalische Zeitschrift* gives the impression of a decorous exchange and counter-exchange. However, Born later commented that Einstein "was provoked into making a caustic reply", while Einstein himself later wrote to Born saying that he would not allow himself to get excited again, as he had in Nauheim. According to Felix Ehrenhaft, he was "interrupted repeatedly by exclamations and uproar. It was obviously an organised interruption. Planck understood this and was pale as death as he raised his voice and told those making the row to be quiet."

When Einstein had finished, Lenard rose to say that he had not heard anything new. "I believe," he added, "that the fields of gravitation which have been spoken of must correspond to examples, and such examples have not yet appeared in practice". Instead of the obvious retort that the British expeditions had provided them, Einstein replied more soothingly: "I would like to say that what seems obvious to people and what does not seem obvious, has changed. Opinions about obviousness are to a certain extent a function of time. I believe that physics is abstract and not obvious, and as an example of the changing views of what is clear, and what is not, I recommend you to consider the clarity with which Galilean mechanics has been interpreted at different times."

The argument was continued at this level. A Professor Rudolph claimed that proof of the General Theory was no argument against the ether. A Professor Palagyi looked on the difference of opinion as merely an example of "the old historical opposition between the experimentalist and the mathematical physicist, such as existed for example, between Faraday and Maxwell". Max Born weighed in with a brief comment in favour of Einstein, and before much more could be said it was discovered, no doubt to Planck's relief, that time was up. "Since the relativity theory unfortunately has not yet made it possible to extend the absolute time interval that is available for the meeting," he announced, "our session must be adjourned."

The dangerous corner had been turned. Einstein went home to Berlin, comforted. Early in October it was formally announced that he would be remaining there.

If this decision had been made solely on the same grounds as

# Table of Ancestors of Albert Einstein

**Professor Dr. Albert Einstein**
Born March 14, 1879 Ulm
Died April 18, 1955 Princeton, N.J.

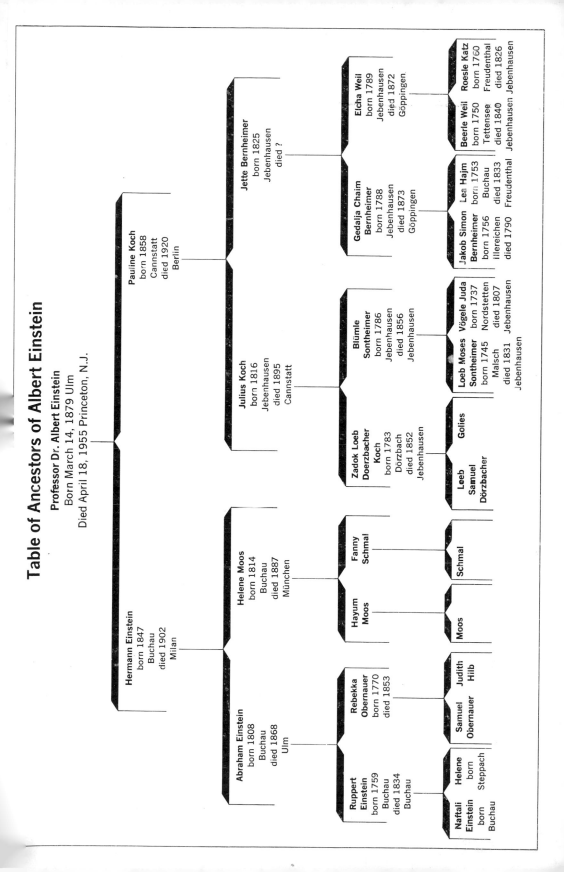

**Hermann Einstein**
born 1847
Buchau
died 1902
Milan

**Pauline Koch**
born 1858
Cannstatt
died 1920
Berlin

**Abraham Einstein**
born 1808
Buchau
died 1868
Ulm

**Helene Moos**
born 1814
Buchau
died 1887
München

**Julius Koch**
born 1816
Jebenhausen
died 1895
Cannstatt

**Jette Bernheimer**
born 1825
Jebenhausen
died ?

**Ruppert Einstein**
born 1759
Buchau
died 1834
Buchau

**Rebekka Obernauer**
born 1770
died 1853

**Hayum Moos**

**Fanny Schmal**

**Zadok Loeb Doerzbacher Koch**
born 1783
Dörzbach
died 1852
Jebenhausen

**Blümle Sontheimer**
born 1786
Jebenhausen
died 1856
Jebenhausen

**Gedalja Chaim Bernheimer**
born 1788
Jebenhausen
died 1873
Göppingen

**Elcha Weil**
born 1789
Jebenhausen
died 1872
Göppingen

**Naftali Einstein**
born
Buchau

**Helene**
born
Steppach

**Samuel Obernauer**

**Judith Hilb**

**Moos**

**Schmal**

**Leeb Samuel Dörzbacher**

**Golies**

**Loeb Moses Sontheimer**
born 1745
Malsch
died 1831
Jebenhausen

**Vögele Juda**
born 1737
Nordstetten
died 1807
Jebenhausen

**Jakob Simon Bernheimer**
born 1756
Illereichen
died 1790

**Lea Hajm**
born 1753
Buchau
died 1833
Freudenthal

**Beerle Weil**
born 1750
Tettensee
died 1840
Jebenhausen

**Roesle Katz**
born 1760
Freudenthal
died 1826
Jebenhausen

*Einstein, third from right, front row,*
*seen with his Munich schoolfellows.*
*Undated photograph believed*
*to have been taken in the early*
*1890s. (Stadtarchiv, Ulm)*

*Einstein's mother, Pauline Koch.*
*Photograph of unknown date,*
*probably taken at the turn*
*of the century. (E.T.H., Zurich)*

*Einstein in his early twenties.
Undated photograph, believed to have
been taken in Zurich or Berne,
shortly before Einstein joined
the Swiss Patent Office. (E.T.H., Zurich)*

*Einstein and
his first wife, Mileva Maric,
taken in 1911 when both were in
their early thirties. (E.T.H., Zurich)*

*The first Solvay Congress, 1911. A unique photograph, taken in the Hotel Metropole, Brussels, and showing the cream of European physicists in the early years of the century. Seated, left to right: Nernst, Brillouin, Solvay, Lorentz, Warburg, Perrin, Wien, Madame Curie, Poincaré. Standing: Goldschmidt, Planck, Rubens, Sommerfeld, Lindemann, de Broglie, Knudsen, Hasenöhrl, Hostelet, Herzen, Jeans, Rutherford, Kamerlingh Onnes, Einstein, Langevin. (Institut International de Physique, Solvay)*

Einstein and Lorentz.
Undated photograph believed to have
been taken in Leiden shortly after
the end of the First World War.
(Rijksmuseum voor de Geschiedenis
der Natuurwetenschappen, Leiden)

Einstein and President Harding,
taken during Einstein's first visit to
the United States in 1921. (U.P.I.)

*Einstein and Chaim Weizmann arriving in the United States
aboard the S. S. Rotterdam, April 2nd, 1921. Left to right:  Menachem Mendel Ussishkin;
Professor Chaim Weizmann; unidentified woman; Einstein;
unidentified woman—almost certainly Elsa Einstein; Ben Zien Messensohn. (U.P.I.)*

*Ehrenfest, Ehrenfest's son, and Einstein, taken in Ehrenfest's home in Leiden,
June, 1920. (Rijksmuseum voor de Geschiedenis der Natuurwetenschappen, Leiden)*

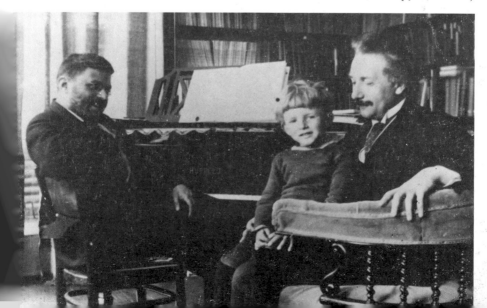

*Einstein at the age of 50,
shown in his Berlin home
with his second wife, Elsa Einstein,
and his stepdaughter, Margot.
(Ullstein)*

*Einstein at a reception held by
Reich Chancellor Dr. Heinrich Bruning
in Berlin, August 1931.
Left to right: Max Planck;
Ramsay MacDonald; Einstein;
Dr. Dietrich, German Finance
Minister (foreground);
and Geheimrat Schmitz, of
I. G. Farben. (Salamon)*

his original decision to join the Kaiser Wilhelm Institute — the wish to remain in closest possible contact with the men who were investigating the nature of the physical world — this would have been understandable enough. But by 1920 it was no longer necessary for Einstein to move towards the centre of interest; by now, the mountain would come to Mahomet. Einstein thus stayed on in Berlin for a tangle of motives almost as complex as those which had brought him there six years earlier. According to Frank, his reassuring letter to Haenisch, saying that he would not be leaving, had stated: "Berlin is the place to which I am bound by the closest human and scientific ties." But there was more to it than that. He believed that the Weimar Republic held out a new hope for Europe in general as well as for Germany in particular; and also, according to Frank, he felt that "it was now important for all progressively-minded elements to do everything possible to increase the prestige of the German Republic."

His multiple commitments left little time for active work in the revived Bund Neues Vaterland that in 1920 became the German League for Human Rights, but he was a co-operating well-wisher and, says one of its supporters was "such a celebrity that we took him to one of the large 'no more war' mass demonstrations in the Berlin Lustgarten and presented him to the fifty or sixty thousand people there gathered." It was also significant that early in 1921 he should become a founder member of the Republican League, one of whose principal tasks it was "to enlighten German youth on the causes of the Empire's collapse and to propagate the conviction that Germany's resuscitation is possible solely on the basis of a Republican form of Government". The Republican League was, for better or for worse, of no particular importance. But Einstein was not lapsing from his wartime Socialism into his former contempt for all political action. His founder-membership of the League was a straw which showed which way the gale of events was blowing him.

Quite apart from human and scientific ties there was another reason for his staying in Berlin. Lenard and his supporters, aiming to discredit all for which Einstein was the symbol, were to have greater effects than they can ever have imagined. For he responded to a challenge with what was at times an almost stubborn pig-headedness. They had provided one.

Basically, he still wanted a quiet life. He still half-believed, as he had hopefully said to Elsa towards the end of December 1919, that "it will soon all die down". But Lenard and the "Anti-Relativity Company" had kicked him into full awareness of what anti-

17

Semitism could really be like. Thus there was a compensation for the objectionable limelight that now burned down on him. If he had to live within its glare, he would at least make use of it, he would use the ridiculous acclaim that he was now being given to good, non-ridiculous purpose. He would ensure that his fellow-Jews were given all possible support in their efforts to preserve their culture, in a homeland of their own if necessary. He would fight the good fight against militarism and nationalism with all the logic and reason which he still expected other men to appreciate. And Berlin was a better place for that task than Leiden or Cambridge or Zurich.

In almost any other circumstances the Berlin professor of 1918 who had become a world figure by 1920 would have passed by with contempt the door on to the political world which the transformation had swung open for him. Now he passed through, anxious to do what he could with his influence in the German capital, sensing that his esoteric work had given him "That power which erring men call Chance", but still totally ignorant of the ways in which the machinery of power could be used to produce results.

# 11

# *AMBASSADOR*
# *- AT - LARGE*

BY THE TIME THE BERLIN CHURCH BELLS WERE RINGING IN 1921, IT
was clear that Einstein had weathered the first of the nationalist,
anti-Jewish storms for which he was to act as lightning-conducor. It
was also clear that his fame was to be neither nine-days' nor nine-
months' wonder; the blaze of public interest that had flared up
throughout the world showed every sign of continuing into the foreseeable future.

He therefore faced a series of foreign engagements and tours
which he could hardly avoid. He faced them with mixed feelings,
well aware that in spite of what he had done he was in some ways
like the men on Everest, metaphorically standing on the shoulders
of predecessors. "I've had good ideas", he would say, "and so have
other men. But it's been my good fortune that my ideas have been
accepted." He was never in any doubt about his own worth, it is
true; he had no cause to be. But in general he hated the hubbub
created around him by those ignorant of the very language of science
which he spoke.

Nevertheless, there were compensations; for Einstein could now
dispense his favours much as he had signed photographs during the
first flush of fame at the end of 1919. Then the publicity had been
made bearable by contributions which he exacted for the poor. Now
the rigmarole of tours and public lectures was counterbalanced in
the United States by aid to the Zionist cause, in Britain and France
by the help he could bring to the forces which wanted to rebuild a
new Europe, including Germany, on a basis of mutual trust. In
science he had achieved almost transcendental success by paring problems down to their simplest terms. Surely the same process would

work in national politics and international affairs? Einstein walked
into the lion's den devoutly believing this was so.

The first of his major tours — the thorns in the side of his colleagues at the Academy as he called them — was to the United States,
primarily in support of the Zionist cause, even though he also lectured at Columbia and Princeton Universities. Before this, however,
early in 1921, he visited both Prague and Vienna, returning to the
former city's University as the man who had unexpectedly become
its most famous professor.

In Prague he stayed with his old friend Philipp Frank who has
left a vivid account of how Einstein spoke to a crowded audience,
explaining relativity in far more homely terms that had been expected. When the clapping and cheering had died down, he said simply:
"It will perhaps be pleasanter and more understandable if instead
of making a speech I play a piece for you on the violin."

In two curious ways, shadows from the future temporarily
darkened this visit to the city where he had first sensed both the
undercurrent of European anti-Semitism and the growl that he always
believed to be the voice of pan-Germanism. For despite his personal
feelings he was now, for those Germans who found it convenient, a
German hero. Thus a Sudeten paper could claim, on his arrival in
the Czech capital, that "the whole world will now see that a race
that has produced a man like Einstein, the Sudeten German race,
will never be suppressed." Here in Prague all his fears for the future,
all the suspicions that the war had nurtured and that the Weimar
Government had only partially subdued, rose to the surface once
again. To Frank he confided one thing: his fear that he would be
forced to leave Germany within ten years. From a man who had so
recently sworn allegiance to Weimar and to Prussia, the forecast at
first seems puzzling. It was wrong by only two years.

In Prague, also, a young man insisted on speaking to Einstein
after his lecture. He had considered Einstein's mass-energy equation,
and on its basis concluded it would be possible to use the energy
locked within the atom for production of a new and immensely
powerful explosive; furthermore, he had invented a machine which
he claimed could help make such an explosive. It would be interesting to know more of the youth, and it is tantalising to speculate on
what might have happened had Einstein been other than what he
was. All we have is Frank's version of his reaction. "Calm yourself.
You haven't lost anything if I don't discuss your work with you
in detail. Its foolishness is evident at first glance. You cannot learn
more from a longer discussion."

Einstein no doubt meant what he said. But one wonders whether the "Foolishness" which he saw was purely technological, or whether his mind might not have harked back to the example of John Napier, the discoverer of logarithms, for whose work he had a profound respect. During Elizabethan times Napier invented a "tank" and the "burning mirrors" with which he hoped to destroy the Armada; but before his death he burned all records of his allegedly most deadly weapon — a device reputed to have wiped out a flock of Pentland sheep. One wonders, also, whether eighteen years later, writing his plea to Roosevelt that the Americans should investigate nuclear weapons, Einstein remembered Prague.

In Vienna, soon afterwards, he spoke in the University Physics Institute and also gave his first big public lecture, being sketched while he was lecturing by a young English artist, Edmond Kapp, and refusing to sign one of the sketches "because it makes me look too Chinese". The lecture was given to an audience of 3,000 in one of the city's largest concert halls, and on realising its size Einstein experienced a minor fit of agoraphobia, insisting that his host Felix Ehrenhaft walk with him to the hall and then sit near him. In 1921 Ehrenhaft held the chair of experimental physics in the University of Vienna, and he and Einstein were still good friends. Later he developed an obsessional idea that Einstein had plagiarised his work.

> Einstein stayed in my house, [Ehrenhaft recalled.] He came to Vienna with two coats, two pairs of trousers, two white shirts, but only one white collar. When my wife asked him if there was not something that he had left at home he answered "No". However, she found neither slippers nor toilet articles. She supplied everything including the necessary collars. However, when she met him in the hall in the morning he was barefooted, and she asked him if he didn't need slippers. He answered, "No. They are unnecessary ballast." Since his trousers were terribly crumpled, my wife pressed the second pair and put them in order so that he would be neat for the second lecture. When he stepped on to the stage she saw to her horror that he was wearing the unpressed pair.

This was the familiar Einstein *en voyage*, travelling with the minimum of baggage, forgetful of the mechanics of everyday life, and a constant worry to Elsa who on occasion would pack a suitcase for his journeys only to find on his return that it had not been opened. The trait worried his hosts. It never worried Einstein, with his mind tied to the essentials. If the rest of the world wanted to fuss about such trivia as trousers and ties and toothbrushes, so much for the world.

From Vienna he returned to Germany. And here, during the next few months, he agreed to make a propaganda tour of the United States during which he would speak specifically to raise money for the Hebrew University, already being built in Jerusalem.

Shortly after the trip had been settled, he received a letter from which great consequences were to flow. Dated February 14th, 1921, it came from Sir Henry Miers, Vice-Chancellor of Manchester University, and invited Einstein to give the Adamson Lecture there at some date convenient to himself. Professor Sherrington, the President of the Royal Society, and his predecessor J. J. — by this time Sir Joseph — Thomson, had both been Adamson Lecturers, but it was an imaginative stroke of Sir Henry's to invite Einstein so soon after the end of the war, while many Englishmen were still allergic to the idea of meeting Germans either socially or professionally.

Einstein accepted the invitation, but implied that he would have to speak in German since his English was practically non-existent and his French was imperfect. He could not settle a date, as he was already irrevocably committed to an American tour in March but there was no doubt about his reason for acceptance: it was clear that he looked upon the invitation as evidence of a move to re-establish international links among scholars. A month later Sir Henry confirmed acceptance, adding that the lecture should be the first that Einstein delivered in England even though there was little doubt that he would receive other invitations. This was to be the case. Soon after, Lindemann wrote to Sir Henry from Oxford to ask how much Einstein was being paid for the lecture and added: "I should like to arrange one here but there seems to be a difficulty about funds." London University's King's College went farther, inviting Einstein to speak after he left Manchester — "what Manchester thinks today London thinks tomorrow."

Einstein left Germany for the United States at the end of March 1921.* Meanwhile Lindemann was involved in arrangements for the visit to England. He had received a letter from Freundlich and as a result wrote to Sir Henry: "Einstein would like [Freundlich] to be with him in England, if possible, to help him avoid any incidents when travelling. Freundlich's mother was English, in fact he proposes to stay with an aunt in Manchester, so that he should be able to look after the courier part of the visit." A special request to Lord Curzon, then Foreign Secretary, expedited the necessary visa and

* See page 365

Freundlich was waiting when the White Star liner *Celtic* docked at Liverpool on June 8th. On board was Einstein, with his wife, somewhat exhausted after a marathon three-month tour but quite confident that he had helped Zionism towards a promising future.

In the United States he had learnt to be cautious of interviews, and he now refused to comment on relativity, noting that "quite apart from the sensational aspect, there was a deeper scientific aspect, and he had to distinguish between those who really understood the subject and those who did not." In addition he may have wondered what his reception would be in a country where the Gold Medal of a learned society could be given with one hand and snatched back with the other.

The following day he began by addressing the members of the University Jewish Students Society on the needs of the Hebrew University, explaining what had made him "an international man", underlining the current anti-Semitism in German universities, and speaking of the Jerusalem plans as "not a question of taste but of necessity".

Later, in the main hall of the University, he came to the subject of relativity. He spoke in German throughout this first public apearance in Britain but, reported the *Manchester Guardian* — in the words of David Mitrany, a young Rumanian political scientist later to become Einstein's colleague and close personal friend at Princeton — "the excellence of his diction, together with the kindly twinkle which never ceased to shine in his eye even through the sternest run of the argument, did not fail to make their impression upon the audience." Subsequently he was created a Doctor of Science, the first such honour to be bestowed upon a German in England since the outbreak of war seven years previously.

After half a century — and after a war with Germany that was waged almost as much on idealogical as on national lines — it is difficult to appreciate the psychological barrier which Einstein, and men like him, had to overcome. But the idiocy which had brought death in Britain to dachshunds on account of their ancestry was still plastering London with warnings that "Every Performance of a German Play is a Vote for German 'Culture'." It was not only the Germans who could illustrate nationalism run mad, and even when the objectivity of Einstein's work and nature is allowed for, his success in Britain is something of an achievement. The *Manchester Guardian* helped in its leading article on June 10th to explain how this came about, and to indicate what it was that raised Einstein to his unique position.

The man in the street, a traveller between life and death, is compact of all elements, and is neither devoid of science nor of poetry, [it said.] He may have few ideas in either, but he probably cherishes what he has, and whatever touches them nearly is of moment to him. Professor Einstein's Theory of Relativity, however vaguely he may comprehend it, disturbs fundamentally his basic conceptions of the universe and even of his own mind. It challenges somehow the absolute nature of his thought. The very idea that he can use his mind in a disinterested way is assailed by a conception which gives partiality to every perception. And with his keen thrust at personal things, the idea of Relativity stretches out to the very conceptions of the universe as can be seen from the mere titles of the closing chapters of Professor Einstein's little book on the subject.

From Manchester, Einstein moved south to London, where Sir John Squire had added to Pope's epitaph on Newton, so that it now ran:

> Nature and Nature's law lay hid in night.
> God said "Let Newton be" and all was light.
> It did not last: the Devil howling "Ho!
> Let Einstein be!" restored the status quo.

There had been more than one change of plan in his departure from the United States and in the date of his arrival in London. "I recall . . . I had invitations to meet him in London and Manchester on the same night," Eddington wrote to Lindemann when he was due to see Einstein again a decade later. "This is doubtless explicable by the Principle of Indeterminacy; still I hope on this occasion you will have a more condensed distribution" — an Eddintgon remark comparable to his comment that Einstein had "taken Newton's plant, which had outgrown its pot, and transplanted it to a more open field".

In London, the Einsteins' host was Viscount Haldane of Cloan, former Secretary of State for War and former Lord Chancellor. Haldane had a special link both with Germany and with Einstein's philosophical outlook. He had studied at Göttingen before Einstein was born, and had often returned to renew his friendships in the town; he had been sent by the British Government on an abortive mission to Germany in 1912 and had subsequently, almost on the outbreak of war, been unwise enough to speak of Germany as his "spiritual home". Not unexpectedly, he had been hounded from office in 1915 after a propaganda campaign which alleged, among other things that he was an illegitimate brother of the Kaiser, had a German wife — he was in fact a life-long bachelor — and had delayed the mobilisation of the British Expeditionary Force in 1914. In a post-war Britain drained of most things except bitterness, Haldane was therefore in a delicate position vis-à-vis the Germans. It was certainly courageous of Einstein to have come so willingly to London; it was equally courageous of Haldane to be his host.

The former Minister "had much admiration for the power of systematic reflection which distinguished the German people", and his interest in Einstein lay in a genuine and dogged preoccupation with epistemology, a preoccupation which had just produced *The Reign of Relativity*. This dealt only in passing with Einstein's theories, and was more concerned with "Knowledge itself and the relativity of reality to the character of Knowledge" — "Haldane is doing for Einstein what Herbert Spencer did for Darwin," said Sir Oliver Lodge. "To say that he understood [relativity] better than any other British pure philosopher at that time would, I am afraid, be a poor compliment," was Eddington's reaction. "For what it is worth, it is undoubtedly true. . ." And Asquith's account of Haldane explaining relativity at a dinner party is significant: "Gradually a cloud descended until, at last, even the candles lost their lighting power in the complexities of Haldane's explanations." Nevertheless, the 1st Viscount felt a respect for Einstein verging on veneration, and for years only two pictures hung in the study at Cloan, his Scottish home: one of his mother, the other of Albert Einstein.

In 1921 Haldane also had a less scientific interest in the visit. "Einstein arrives here in the early days of June", he wrote on May 12th to John Murray, his publisher, "and his advent will make a market for us which we must not lose". His foresight was well justified. In mid-June he was able to inform his mother that '*The Reign of Relativity*', which was to go into three editions in six weeks, was "being sold with Einstein's books in the bookshops". He had in fact written to Einstein from his home in Queen Anne's Gate as soon as news of the proposed visit to England leaked out. "Will you do me the honour of being my guest at the above address during your London stay?" he asked. "I do not know whether you are coming alone or whether your wife will be with you. But it does not matter because the house is large enough." He followed the letter with a telegram, and the small *Absagen*, written on it suggests that Einstein had at first declined. If so, he changed his mind — a wise course since there were few men better qualified than Haldane to convoy him through a Britain which was still uncertain whether it much wished to honour any German scientist, relativity or not.

In spite of this, "there was," Haldane wrote to his mother in Scotland on May 26th "much interest in the Einstein visit. Lord Stamfordham [private secretary to King George V] talked to me of it last night." Four days later he told her: "The social world is beginning to worry for invitations to meet Einstein, and I am sternly refusing two smart ladies — which I have no doubt they think rather brutal." Two days later, he wrote to his sister, "I have repelled Lady Cunard, who wanted to get up a party for Einstein."

It was not only fashionable London that was anxious to meet this mystery man who had emerged from the shambles of a defeated Germany. From St. Pancras, where Haldane met the Einsteins at 2 o'clock on Friday the 10th, the visitors were taken direct to a meeting of the Royal Astronomical Society in Burlington House.

Here Eddington, recently elected President, recalled how the first printed references to the General Theory had been published in England in the Society's *Monthly Notices*. He described the preliminaries to the two eclipse expeditions, and he indicated how one man's imaginative concept had changed the traditional view of the universe. Einstein, modestly smiling, accepted it all with the self-assured charm of a very bright boy.

Then the visitors were taken to Queen Anne's Gate where a dinner party of quite exceptional nature was to be held for them that evening. Earlier, Haldane had planned a reception at which the Prime Minister was to be present. But Lloyd George had failed to follow in President Harding's footsteps and meet Einstein.

The private dinner party which did duty for the reception was a glittering enough occasion. Heading the list of guests was the Archbishop of Canterbury. His apprehensions about the evening can be judged by a letter written to J. J. Thomson a few weeks earlier by Lord Sanderson, for many years a high Foreign Office official.

The Archbishop ... can make neither head nor tail of Einstein, and protests that the more he listens to Haldane, and the more newspaper articles he reads on the subject, the less he understands, [Sanderson confided]. I am, or believe myself to be, in an intermediate stage, roaming the lawns and meadow leazes half way down. I therefore offered to write for the Archbishop a short sketch of what I imagined to be the pith of the theory in its more elementary form. I enclose it with his comment. It is of course very inadequate, but I fancy that as far as it goes it is not entirely at variance with Einstein's argument — some of his followers' critics seem to me to go further. But I should have been sorry to have misled the Archbishop. Do you think you could glance through it, or ask some expert to do so, and write a short note of any grosser errors?

Thomson obliged, thus helping to brief Archbishop Davidson for what seemed likely to be an intellectual tournament on the heroic scale. For also present in Queen Anne's Gate on the evening of the 10th were Eddington and Alfred Whitehead who had been among the "chorus" at the Burlington House meeting two years earlier. Dr. Inge, the "gloomy Dean" of St. Paul's, was present with his wife. So was Bernard Shaw, Professor Harold Laski of the London School of Economics, and General Sir Ian Hamilton, the ill-starred leader from Gallipoli who had been a close friend of Haldane since the latter's days as Secretary of State for War. Over this formidable brains trust, a regiment which could have laid down an intellectual barrage sufficient to overcome most men, there presided Haldane and his sister Elizabeth, a distinguished woman in her own right and the translator of Descartes and Hegel.

The main outcome of the evening, disappointing to Haldane in some respects, must have been reassuring to the Archbishop. "I have never seen a more typical scientific lion in appearance — he might have been prepared for the role on the stage", he later wrote percipiently, "— a mass of long black hair tossed back, and a general appearance of scientific untidiness, but he was modest and quiet to talk to, and disclaimed a great deal of what is attributed to him".

Choosing his moment carefully, Davidson turned to Einstein and queried: "Lord Haldane tells us that your theory ought to make a great difference to our morale." But Einstein modestly replied: "Do not believe a word of it. It makes no difference. It is purely abstract science." This was only a brief version of his reply to an interviewer a few years later. "The meaning of relativity has been widely misunderstood," he said. "Philosophers play with the word, like a child with a doll. Relativity, as I see it, merely denotes that certain physical and mechanical facts which have been regarded as positive and permanent, are relative with regard to certain other facts in the sphere of physics and mechanics." However he took the Archbishop's interest as natural, and noted later that more clergymen than physicists were interested in relativity. "Because," he explained when asked the reason, "clergymen are intersted in the general laws of nature and physicists, very often, are not."

The Archbishop's wife fared little better than her husband. When, after dinner, she explained to Elsa how a friend had been talking about Professor Einstein's theory "especially in its mystical aspect", Mrs. Einstein broke into laughter with the words: "Mystical!

Mystical! My husband mystical!" echoing his own reply to a Dutch lady who in the German Embassy in The Hague said that she liked his mysticism. "Mysticism is in fact the only reproach that people cannot level at my theory," he had replied.

Mrs. Einstein's reply was not what was expected. But it was part of the defence which the Einsteins erected around themselves, Elsa unconsciously no doubt, but her husband after due thought. "I can well understand [him] hastily shearing off the subject," Eddington later noted of the remark to Davidson; "in those days one had to become an expert in dodging persons who mixed up the fourth dimension with spiritualism. But surely the answer need not be preserved as though it were one of Einstein's more perspicacious utterances. The non-sequitur is obvious." What might also have been obvious by this time was a certain flagging in the guest of honour who had been spared Lady Cunard but after a long morning's journey from Manchester had been whisked to the Royal Astronomical Society, taken from Burlington House through a quick-change into formal clothes, and then presented on a plate as the main dish of a testing evening.

Saturday was a day of comparative rest during which Einstein, sitting on a simple kitchen chair at the back of Haldane's house, was informally photographed. And, apparently at the same time, "Einstein . . . had one done of myself to hang in his study in Berlin," Haldane proudly informed his mother. The following day the guests were taken to lunch with the Rothschilds where they met Lord Crewe and Lord Rayleigh who had first seen Einstein at the Solvay Congress a decade earlier. According to Sir Almeric Fitzroy, the Clerk of the Privy Council, Rayleigh listened to Einstein's explanation of relativity, then commented: "If your theories are sound, I understand it is open to us to affirm that the events, say, of the Norman Conquest have not yet occurred". Afterwards, Haldane related to his mother in one of the long accounts which he wrote to her almost daily, Lord Rothschild drove the party to a Jewish meeting, through the City to the Tower, and back along the Embankment. "In the evening we dined at the Harmers where Einstein played the violin. . ."

Then they returned to the row of fashionable but modest town houses where Einstein was introduced to London life. Some of the later second- and third-hand accounts of the visit appear not only to have been overimpressed with Haldane's "Lordship", but also to have confused Queen Anne's Gate with Haldane's Scottish estate which Einstein never visited. Thus in some stories they moved in an atmosphere of deferential butlers, vast Tudor beds, and the exaggerations of a Hollywood spectacular.

Boris Kutnetzov is typical. "Their room in his palatial residence was bigger than the whole of their Berlin apartment," he says. "Einstein's embarrassment turned into dismay when he found that a footman had been assigned to him. When he saw the liveried monument he whispered to his wife: 'Elsa, do you think they will let us out if we try to run away?' They slept in a spacious bedroom with heavily curtained windows. Next morning Einstein rose early, as was his custom, and tried in vain to open the curtains. Behind him his wife asked laughingly: 'Albertle, why didn't you call the footman to do it?' 'Oh, no,' he replied, 'he frightens me'." No doubt they were impressed, after Berlin, with the wealth that still remained in Britain at the end of a long war; but, equally without doubt, they took it in their stride.

On Monday morning Einstein was taken by Haldane to Westminster Abbey where he placed a wreath on Newton's grave before being handed over to the Dean. After lunch he prepared for his first public appearance in London. It was to be made at King's College in the Strand and the Principal, Ernest (later Sir Ernest) Barker, had some misgiving about his guest's reception. "Feeling against Germany was very much stronger after that War of 1914–1918 than it has been since the War of 1939–45" he later wrote, "and there were fears that the lecture might be disturbed or even prevented." All the tickets, sold in aid of charity for distressed European students, were taken up well in advance and when Haldane led Einstein on to the platform even the gangways were filled with students. Among those in the audience were Whitehead, James Jeans, Professor Lindemann – and William Rothenstein, making notes for his remarkable portrait of Einstein who is presented as a Struwelpeter character, smiling from an aureole of almost electrified hair.

He had insisted on speaking in German – partly because of his almost non-existent English; partly, it was reported, because "he had complete confidence in English broadmindedness". Thus the hall was filled by those who, as Barker said, "would probably understand nothing, being ignorant alike of German and of relativity, but would none the less be eager to listen". There had been no applause when the two men had walked on to the platform. The meeting could easily swing either way.

"Einstein had no notes, no hesitations and no repetitions," wrote the anonymous commentator of *The Nation* "and the logical order in which he expounded his ideas was masterly beyond praise. One sat wondering how much of this exquisite performance was being wasted upon the audience; to how many was this carefully precise German an unintelligible noise?" As on other occasions, the objectivity of Einstein's demeanour, the other-worldliness of his dreamy eyes and his shock of flowing hair, disarmed potential critics. He talked for an hour, without interruption, somehow evoking an interest even among those who could understand little more than the occasional phrase. The he paused and, still speaking in German, announced: "My lecture is already a little long." There was an unexpected storm of encouraging applause. "I shall take that as an invitation," he said. "But my further remarks will not be so easy to follow." Finally, he sat down. Then someone started clapping. The applause grew and whole rows of men stood up, a spontaneous acclamation of courage as much as of relativity.

One interesting point in the lecture was Einstein's statement on the ancestry of Relativity. "I am anxious to draw attention to the fact that this theory is not speculative in origin," he said. "It owes its invention entirely to the desire to make physical theory fit observed facts as well as possible. We have here no revolutionary act, but the natural combination of a line that can be traced through centuries. The abandonment of certain notions connected with space, time, and motion, hitherto treated as fundamentals, must not be regarded as arbitrary, but only as conditioned by observed facts." Emphasis on observational experience compared with the exterior flash of intuition was really more true of the General than of the Special Theory. But it was more revealingly true of the earlier, "pro-Machian" philosophy that had so far supported Einstein than of the newer outlook which was already taking its place as his faith in sensation as the real yardstick of the physical world began to falter. When, later in life, he was asked by Hans Reichenbach, professor of philosophy in the University of California, how he had arrived at the theory of relativity, Einstein no longer mentioned observed facts. On that occasion his explanation was of a totally different kind: he had come to it, he said, because he had been "so firmly convinced of the harmony of the Universe".

In Britain, men of goodwill were well aware of Einstein's potential influence in bringing a new attitude of reconciliation into the relationship between wartime enemies, and many said as much during his visit. Thus Haldane had introduced the King's College lecture with the statement that Britain was grateful to Germany for giving the world the genius of Einstein just as Germany has been grateful to Britain for giving the world the genius of Newton. That evening when Einstein was entertained in King's College, Sir Ernest Barker opened his after-dinner speech by comparing the two "observers" of the theory of relativity, and then suggested that his listeners should substitute two nations for them. "Each of these two nations has its own way of life, its own space, its own ethics and character. If it were possible to find some means by which these two nations could have the same view of life, then there would be new possibilities, whether by leagues of nations, or other ways, to arrive at better understanding with each other." Then Barker turned to Einstein. "If at your command, the straight lines have been banished from the universe, there is yet one straight line that will always remain — the straight line of right and justice. May both our nations follow this straight line side by side in a parallel movement which, in spite of Euclid, will yet bring them together in friendship with one another and with the other nations of the world."

The words were significant, not only of the attitude of men like Barker in Britain but of others in France, in the United States and elsewhere. A few months later, when Australian universities invited Einstein to visit their country, *The Times* noted that "it is considered that as Australia is resuming trade with Germany, no better start can be made than by extending an invitation to one of the world's greatest scientists." On this occasion pressure of engagements forced Einstein to refuse. But from the time of this first visit to Britain he was even more eager to play the role of reconciliator.

On the morning following the King's College lecture, Lindemann collected Einstein from Queen Anne's Gate and drove him to Oxford, where the two men spent the day. Two months earlier, when he had first heard of Einstein's coming visit, Lindemann had invited him to stay at his father's home in Sidmouth, Devon. Einstein had declined and Lindemann had to be content with showing him the Clarendon Laboratory where he had recently taken up the chair of Experimental Philosophy.

There was no doubt about the success of the visit to England. As *The Nation* noted in a leader headed "The Entente of the Intellectuals", the reception of the King's College lecture had marked "a definite turning-point in the post-war feeling" of Britain; the general welcome given to Einstein had gone "some way to restore the pre-war unity of culture for Europe and the civilised world". And, Haldane later wrote to Lindemann: "I think the German Ambassador was right when he told me on Monday evening that the reception of Einstein in England would do something towards making the way smoother for the approach to better international relations." Thus a main aim of the visit, a loosening of the pack-ice which kept Britain and Germany apart, had been achieved.

As Einstein returned across the North Sea a few days later, Haldane wrote in his diary; "Professor Whitehead, the mathematician, dined with me alone, to compare notes." There was much to compare. British scientists had been immensely impressed by Einstein, but some of them still thought that the extraneous metaphysical overtones were part of the man himself and of his theory. This was well illustrated by R. A. Sampson, the Astronomer Royal for Scotland who was present at the London lecture and who wrote to Lindemann three days later.

> I would say at once, [he wrote] that there is no room for question that Einstein "explained" gravitation, and as it seems to me, said absolutely the last word upon it. Beyond this I prefer to keep reserve on certain points, as thinking them unproved and the attempt to prove them misdirected.
>
> One of them is the retranslation into spatial terms of the formula to which gravitation has been reduced. That formula is so general that it transcends any "meaning", and to give it one is gratuitous.
>
> Next I reject the philosophical implication that all that we know is equally relative and intangible or else unreal.
>
> As regards reality if we admit that our existence is real, though presumbly relative to some more comprehensive existence, and we can explain neither our own nor the other, then it is evidently not a condition of reality that we should be able to explain what we mean. Hence I have no difficulty in admitting absolute rotation even though I do not know what I mean.
>
> Nor for that matter absolute translation, (but Einstein has proved this an uncalled for idea in gravitation).
>
> It appears to me that Einstein's argument regarding rotation proves that we do not know that the earth rotates. Yet I assert that we do know that it rotates, though the argument is mathematically correct. You ask, with respect to what does it rotate? I have no final answer, but I don't think you will say it is open to a rational man to hold that it does not rotate . . .

Einstein returned to Berlin as the first post-war German to be lionised in the United States and Britain. The word "German" is important. For, whatever his previous feelings, the German defeat of 1918 had induced him to slough off the hard skin of bitter distaste for his compatriots which had first formed in Munich. In this he was illogical. Whatever inner spirit may drive a nation on towards its destiny, for better or worse, it is unlikely to be altered within a few years by the tribulations of defeat or the triumphs of victory. If the Germany of 1921 held high hopes, then these lay within its marrow in 1890; and if the Germany of the Luitpold Gymnasium was more than a local nightmare then there was little hope for her in 1921. Einstein did not see it that way. Weimar had changed everything, and if he still held reservations about the treatment that the Jews could expect, he yet hoped that Germany was now freely walking back into the European body politic.

Certainly he now had confident hopes for her future. It is not clear whether he believed that his earlier feelings had been unbalanced, or whether the whole German nation had undergone a Pauline conversion on the road to Versailles. But although he was still using a Swiss passport he now had no inhibitions about travelling as an unofficial German ambassador.

Einstein's genuine attempts to create a climate of reconciliation — so strikingly in contrast to his attitude after the Second World War — and the power which his position gave him to push forward this cause, were not lost on his compatriots. In Berlin, on July 1st., 1921, he was the guest of honour at a party given by Herr von Winterfeldt, President of the German Red Cross, and attended by President Ebert, many members of the German Cabinet, and the Chief Burgomaster of Berlin. Here, his remarks were to be the subject of criticism.

> In America, [he told those present] there undeniably predominated a markedly unfriendly feeling towards everything German. American public opinion was so excited that even the use of the German language was suppressed. At present a noticeable change is taking place. I was received heartily by America's learned men and learned corporations. They gladly spoke German, and everywhere were mindful with genuine sympathy of the German scientists and institutes with which they maintained so close a friendship before the war. In England the impression forced itself upon me that the English statesmen and scholars had it in mind again to bring about friendly relations with Germany. The heartiness of the speeches in England could hardly be surpassed. Better times appear to be coming.

That Einstein should not only make such a judgment between the attitudes of his two hosts — strongly in contrast with the general opinion of most other people — but that he should openly announce it, indicates a double lack of judgment. The *New York Times* was quick to jump on his words, noting that "Perhaps . . . in spite of his wonderful mind [he] is as much mistaken, and in about the same way, when he says that 'England' is warmly pro-German as he is when he said that 'America' is warmly anti-German."

18

This was not quite the case. The trouble was that Einstein learn-ed only tardily that the casual statements of famous men, perhaps tossed off rather lightheartedly, look very different when presented under black headlines. And it was typical that he should conclude a letter to Sommerfeld, protesting against a *Figaro* article by a corres-pondent with whom he had talked, by saying that the writer had no right to reproduce what he had said, even though there were no lies in the article but only a wrong emphasis.

Einstein's weakness for making unguarded statements that could easily be used against him was shown in one incident, trivial in itself, which had important repercussions on the way he later allowed him-self to be presented to the world. This started with a report from Cyril Brown, a *New York Times* correspondent in Berlin. The report quoted an account of Einstein's views on the United States, given to a "sympathetic-looking Hollander". The statements were distinctly unflattering. After admitting that American men worked hard, Ein-stein was quoted as saying: "For the rest, they are the toy dogs of the women, who spend the money in a most unmeasurable, illimi-table way and wrap themselves in a fog of extravagance." Later, the genesis of the *New York Times* story became known. Einstein had spoken in German to the reporter of the *Nieuwe Rotterdamsche Courant* which had printed its story in Dutch; the *Berliner Tage-blatt* had taken parts of the Dutch story and printed it in German; the *Times* correspondent had then taken parts of the *Berliner Tage-blatt* story and cabled this in English to New York. With the best will in the world, excluding any assumption that the Berlin paper would wish to make Einstein look ridiculous, or that the *Times* man overemphasised any anti-Americanism, these choppings, subbings and translations inevitably did more than alter the balance of the ori-ginal. Few readers, even in the more sophisticated present, would be expected to allow for all this; half a century ago the "toy dogs" remark — apparently quoted elsewhere as "lap-dogs" — had the effect of a match to gunpowder.

It was followed by a leading article in the *New York Times*. After claiming that the report appeared to be correct even though the writer wished it were not, it put forward as possible causes of Einstein's irritation "the failure of himself and his companion to make more than a partial success of the special mission on which they came to the U. S., and the antagonism they aroused where they had expected to win full approval and co-operation." Further cri-ticism followed; so did letters to the editor; and, on the 11th, a se-cond leader, presumably written after the paper had been in touch with its Berlin correspondent. "Dr. Einstein," it said, "will not be forgiven and should not be, for his boorish ridicule of hospitable hosts who honoured him because they believed the guarantors of his greatness in his own domain. That he is small out of that domain is a matter of no great consequence, however, for it is a peculiarity shared by many other specialists of like eminence, and in no degree reduces their value to the world."

Einstein was also bearded by the correspondent of the New--York *World* to whom he said that "the Amsterdam interview in no way expressed my sentiment. I never made unfavourable comments on the American people and their mode of life." This attempt by a rival to undercut the *Times'* own story failed to impress that paper which rather loftily replied that it was easy to get the impression that Einstein had now "explained rather than denied the essential part of the *Courant's* article". However, the *Times* had second thoughts; and after another two and a half weeks it admitted in a long report from Berlin that Einstein's remarks did not, after all, "turn out to be as harsh as they appear in the cabled reports".

The effect of this storm in a teacup was considerable. Years later Einstein was still refusing interviews on the grounds that he had been misquoted as calling American men lap-dogs of their women; and it says much for the tact and tenacity of the *New York Times* chief correspondent in Berlin that his paper became one of the few to which Einstein was eventually willing to speak freely. Nevertheless, the memory of the incident remained. It had come just as he was on the crest of popularity's wave and it reinforced his natural dislike of sharing his non-scientific thoughts and emotions with a public for whom he had become a compound of guru, film star, oracle and saint. Thus the dichotomy which marked so much of his life began to appear here as well. For his views on Zionism and pacifism, for his explanations of what the grand structure of science could mean, he needed the large public which only the popular press could provide; he was usually unwilling to pay the price, to subject himself to what even in the best-run world must be a fair percentage of distortion and invention. When he was willing to take the risk, he usually gained the symphathy of all but the most bloody-minded opponents. When he was not being his own enemy he could get a "good Press" that was the despairing envy of experienced publicists; too often, he mentally muttered "lap-dogs" and was content to let his case go by default.

One result of his journey to the United States and Britain was that Einstein now felt there was a genuine hope of re-opening scientific relations between these countries and Germany. It could be argued that the German aggression of 1914, and the excesses to which it led, had cleared the disease from a body politic which could now, more mature, more internationally-orientated, play its part in creating a new and better Europe. Einstein, the new citizen of the Weimar Republic, sincerely hoped so.

France was a different proposition, as he realised when, early in 1922, he was invited to lecture in Paris. The invitation had first been made in 1913 when those administering the Michonis Fund in the Collège de France asked him to succeed Lorentz as visiting lecturer the following year. Einstein accepted, but the visit had been cancelled with the outbreak of war. Now his old friend Langevin revived the idea. One impediment immediately arose. Many French scientists felt that such an invitation would imply that their hatred of the Germans was diminishing. They protested, and their protests might have succeeded had it not been for the support which Langevin obtained from Paul Painlevé. Powerful Minister of War a few years earlier, and now Premier and President of the Chamber of Deputies, Painlevé was a mathematician by profession, an amateur enthusiast of relativity, and he gladly gave unofficial blessing to Langevin's proposal.

In Berlin, Einstein was at first dubious. The idea chimed in with his wish to reforge the links between German scientists and those in other countries, but he had no illusion about the deep and bitter feelings that outside the limited scientific, artistic and professional circles — and sometimes inside them — still divided the peoples of France and Germany. At first, he tentatively refused the invitation. Then he mentioned it in passing to Walther Rathenau, the German Minister of Reconstruction.

Rathenau was in many ways the antithesis of all that Einstein stood for. A German-Jewish industrialist, he had inherited control of the great Allgemeine Elektrizität-Gesellschaft and twice during the war had striven hard to save the Empire: first in 1916 when he had reorganised German economy to counter the effects of the British blockade; secondly in 1918 when, almost alone among responsible officials, he had proposed a *levée en masse* to meet the advancing Allies. With the coming of the Weimar Republic, Rathenau founded the new "Democratic Party" and rose swiftly to ministerial status. He first met Einstein in the house of a mutual friend, and Einstein invited him to the Haberlandstrasse home. The friendship ripened. Einstein was concerned by the effect which Rathenau's acceptance of a ministry might have on the position of the Jews in Germany;

Rathenau, in his turn, was interested in Einstein as a unique un-official ambassador. There was no doubt about the advice he now gave. Einstein accepted.

In Paris there were fears that the visit would bring protests from French nationalists, and as arrangements for the occasion were completed, Langevin was careful to secure an apartment to which his guest could be taken in secret. Langevin himself remained uncertain of the reception to be expected and on the afternoon of March 28th, 1922, travelled out from Paris to Juemont on the Belgian frontier. With him went Charles Nordmann, the Astronomer of the Paris Observatory whose *Einstein and the Universe,* published in France the previous year, was a minor classic of popular description and interpretation.

Nordmann has left, in the *Revue des Deux Mondes* and *L'Illu-stration,* two graphic accounts of the visit. At the frontier station they found their guest unassumingly sitting in the corner of a second-class apartment. Nordmann had never met him and it is clear from his account that he was vastly impressed — not so much by the "creator of worlds", which would have been natural enough, as by the physical presence of the man. Einstein's sense of command was later to become so overlaid with the image of the seemingly frail, white-haired saint, "Charlie Chaplin with the brow of Shakespeare" as the *New Statesman* once put it, that it is well to be reminded of what he was like in his prime.

> The first impression that one gets is of astonishing youth, [Nordmann wrote.] Einstein is big (he is about 1 m 76), with large shoulders and the back only very slightly bent. His head, the head where the world of science has been re-created, immediately attracts and fixes the attention. His skull is clearly, and to an extraordinary degree, brachycephalic, great in breadth and receding towards the nape of the neck without exceeding the vertical. Above all, the impression is one of disconcerting youth, strongly romantic, and at certain moments evoking in me the irrepressible idea of a young Beethoven, on which meditation had already left its mark, and who had once been beautiful. And then, suddenly, laughter breaks out and one sees a student. Thus appeared to us the man who has plumbed with his mind, deeper than any before him, the astonishing depths of the mysterious universe.

The three men faced a four-hour journey, from which Nord-mann remembered some revealing remarks. When they began to talk of quantum problems, Einstein noted, significantly: "That is a wall before which one is stopped. The difficulties are terrible; for me, the theory of relativity was only a sort of respite which I gave myself during their examination." And, remarking that there was something crazy about it, he went on: "But there, physicists are all a bit crazy, aren't they. But it's just the same with racehorses: what one buys one has to sell!"

When they discussed the world-wide interest that his ideas had aroused, Einstein noted, as he repeatedly did with undisguised amazement: "It's unbelievable." Of the opposition to him and his ideas in Germany he commented, putting his hands on his chest: "So long as they don't get violent, I want to let everyone say what they wish, for I myself have always said exactly what pleased me." And, asked about the left-wing parties, he said, with a broad smile: "I don't know what to say about that since I believe that the Left is 'une chose polydimensionelle'."

It was midnight by the time they arrived at the Gare du Nord. Here there was a reception party of journalists and photographers. Einstein had no wish to meet them; Langevin was still worried about nationalist protests. Thus one plan suited both men. Together with Nordmann, they left the train by dropping from the coach on the side away from the platform, crossed the railway lines, and disappeared into a side door on the farther platform. Then, unnoticed, they vanished into the Métro. Einstein enjoyed the operation — particularly as the Métro train moved off below the spot where the crowds were still waiting.

On the afternoon of Friday, March 31st, he was driven to the Collège de France. Here, in the main hall, where Ernest Renan, Henri Bergson, and other giants of the French establishment had lectured, he explained the conflict between classical relativity and electro-dynamics in a slow French to which his slight accent added a touch of mystery. Langevin sat immediately behind, ready to prompt him with the occasional word if he hesitated. Madame Curie was among the audience. So was Bergson. But the room was not packed as some had expected. Tickets had been sent only to a restricted number of scientists and students with a special interest in the subject. Paul Painlevé himself stood by the door, checking the formal invitations.

Einstein spoke to other selected audiences during the next few days, to the College's philosophical and mathematical sections and, on April 6th, to a session of the French Philosophical Society at the Sorbonne. Langevin was again present, as well as Bergson and Painlevé. His reception was kind if questioning, an attitude less critical than that of Emile Picard, permanent secretary of the French Academy of Sciences, who was quoted as saying: "On the subject of relativity I see red." Einstein was closely questioned about the philosophical implications of his theory. And here, answering a question from Emile Mayerson, he appeared finally to cut the strings which had held him to Mach. "Mach's system studied the relationships which exist between the data of experience," he said. "For Mach, science is the sum total of these relationships. It is a bad point of view; in short, what Mach created was a catalogue and not a system. To the extent that Mach was a good mechanic he was a deplorable philosopher."

Some gaps in the French welcome were the result of politics as much as science, and the Société Francaise de Physique, strongly nationalist in outlook, virtually refused to accept his presence in the capital. Opinion was more evenly divided in the Academy where a number of friends argued strongly that he should address "the immortals". But the fact that Germany was not yet a member of the League of Nations was raised as a barrier. The argument was finally settled when thirty members announced they would leave in a body as soon as Einstein entered the room.

As well as the French people, the French press was in two minds about the problem of how to regard members of the nation they had fought for more than four long years. "If a German were to discover a remedy for cancer or tuberculosis," asked one paper, "would these thirty academicians have to wait for the application of the remedy until Germany joined the League?" Among others which tried to edge their readers towards conciliation was the paper with the large headline: "Einstein in Paris! It is the victory of the archangel over the demon of the abyss." Yet the verdict of the Academy, essentially a verdict on Germany, would probably have been endorsed by the majority of Frenchmen. Einstein would have sympathised, even had he not agreed. For there were occasions when his perceptions about the human race equalled his intuitive genius in science. He knew that in France he was suspect three times over. He was the man who had upset the scientific applecart — or at least appeared to have done so — and thus he naturally aroused the resentment of those who believed in things-as-they-are. He was not only a scientific iconoclast but German as well. To compound the crime he was not only German but a German Jew. It is not surprising that he received only a qualified welcome in a country which had recently lost more than 1,350,000 men dead and missing at German hands and which still argued over the rights and wrongs of the Dreyfus case.

However, it was not only in France that Einstein's new popularity was less than wholehearted. England had welcomed him the previous year, but now *The Times*, a fair enough reflection of informed opinion, produced an enigmatic leading article. It began by quoting a remark of Painlevé in Paris: "A sustained effort of the brain is necessary to penetrate the thought of the great German savant and to follow his logic. Thus the craze of society to discuss Einstein between two rubbers of bridge appears to be one of the funniest things in the world." In a mild attempt to cut both Einstein and relativity down to size, the paper then continued: "Relativity is an interesting word in itself and it expresses just what a number of people are always doing, namely thinking of everything in terms of something else." Mathematical theories, it continued, "never make much practical difference, and perhaps it is as well that they should not; for if, owing to the theory of relativity, the apple no longer fell to the ground, a number of other things might happen, some of them dangerous, and Einstein might become as unpopular as he is now popular." This may have been no more than *The Times* on an off morning, but it is easy to see it as a mild reproof to the scientist who was already revealing, now that people were taking notice of him, an interest in public affairs that was unexpected, unwelcome, and slightly irregular.

Before he left France Einstein was to demonstrate this interest in a highly delicate way. During the journey into Paris he had confided to Nordmann that he would like to see the battlefields and on the last day of his visit he was collected from his apartment at 6.30 in the morning by Nordmann, Solovine and Langevin.

Einstein brought the single small travelling bag that was his entire luggage, and the party drove off north-eastwards along the line of the German advance in 1914. They were quickly among the ruins of war, a landscape of flattened villages, mouldering trench-systems and entire forests levelled by artillery barrage. Frequently they stopped and dismounted. Einstein visibly shaken, bewildered and almost uncomprehending that war could really have been like this, even worse than the propagandists claimed. At one point, among devastated farms and beside trees withered by gas, he turned to his friends. "All the students of Germany must be brought here," he said, "all the students of the world, so that they can see how ugly war really is. People often have a wrong idea because it comes from books. Thus most Germans have an image of Frenchmen that is purely literary; and many men have an equally literary idea of war and the ruins that it creates. How necessary it is that they should come and *see*."

They went on through St. Quentin, where the Americans had first gone into action in strength, and then into the ruins of Rheims, Einstein stopping from time to time with the single word "Terrible". In Rheims they had lunch, and here an extraordinary incident occurred.

At a nearby table sat two senior French officers, immaculate in full dress, and a fashionably accoutred woman. Nordmann noticed that they first appeared to recognise Einstein and then confirmed his identity by sending a waiter to Nordmann's chauffeur. As the Einstein party later rose to leave the restaurant, the French officers and their companion stood up, turned to Einstein and, without saying a word, politely bowed.

From Rheims they drove north across fifty miles of devastation and Einstein was put on the train to Cologne. As it prepared to move off, he waved his broad-brimmed hat towards the German frontier: "I will describe all I have seen to the people over there."

He arrived back in Berlin to find that during his absence an exhibition of the first "relativity film" had taken place. Made by a Professor Nicolai and a Herr Kornbaum, it consisted of four parts. The first showed the familiar experiment of an object falling first from a car in motion and then from a car at rest; the second, the contradictions met with in the accepted theory of light. The third part tried to show how relativity solved these problems in terms of space and time, while the last dealt with the deflection of starlight revealed by the British expedition of 1919. The film was ingenious, but it took for granted that the audience had a working knowledge of physics, and thus failed to achieve complete success in a complicated problem. Strangely enough, it was only after a lapse of almost two months that Einstein wrote to the German papers saying that he had had no hand in the film's production and had in fact asked its makers to use a different title. But it crossed the Atlantic and was reviewed in *Vanity Fair* for a fee of 100 dollars by Morris Raphael Cohen who had translated Einstein's lectures in New York. "It was the only movie I had ever gone to," he later wrote. "I have often expressed a willingness to go to another movie on the same terms but have found no takers."

Einstein was still concentrating on reconciliation. Some Frenchmen, it had been clear from his experiences in Paris, were ready to stretch out their hands in a gesture of reconciliation. And it was with this fact very much in mind that on June 11th he addressed a meeting of the German Peace Federation on the floor of the Reichstag. He made a plea for European unity, deplored the differences created by language, and said that in future men of goodwill should ask, not "What can be done for my country?" but rather "What must my country do to make it possible for the greater entity to exist?" And he went on to express the beliefs he was to hold for another decade — until the rise of Hitler made him abandon them in despair: "I hold it to be of extreme consequence that wherever the possibility arises men of different languages, of different political and cultural ideas, should get in touch with one another across their frontiers — not with the feeling that something might be squeezed out of the other for their and their country's benefit, but with a spirit of good will to bridge the gap between the spiritual groups in comparatively independent spheres."

Perhaps there was at last a chance to build a new world from the post-war chaos. Perhaps there was more than a glimmer of hope for Europe. Einstein thought so, and when he was invited by Sir Eric Drummond, Secretary-General of the League of Nations, to join the newly-formed International Committee on Intellectual Co-operation, he quickly agreed. The Weimar Republic was still threatened from within, a prickly bitterness still hampered Franco-German relations and a sense of imminent chaos suffused Berlin itself. Even so, it did appear that the forces which stood for international reconstruction, for the slow painful business of recasting Germany in a less military mould so that she could live with her continental neighbours, were at last gaining strength.

Then, on June 24th, 1922, Walther Rathenau was assassinated by right-wing extremists as he left his home in the Berlin Grunewald.

The murder was part of a pattern. Earlier in the month two Nationalists had only just failed to kill Herr Scheidemann, the former Prime Minister, and a few days after Rathenau's death attackers seriously wounded another prominent Jew, the publicist Maximilian Harden.

Einstein saw Rathenau's murder as symbolic of a rising tide of anti-Semitism which would soon be lapping round his own feet. It pushed him into temporary resignation from the League Committee and it drove him to the edge of leaving Germany — for the second time in less than two years. This time, moreover, he took the decision, planned his withdrawal, and was dissuaded only by pleas from the League to change his mind and remain in Berlin.

Rathenau had become Foreign Minister in February. By April, he had successfully concluded the Treaty of Rapallo under which Germany and Russia re-established diplomatic relations, renounced financial claims on each other, and pledged themselves to economic co-operation. Engineered without the knowledge of America, Britain or France, it had been an omen of things to come; to many in Germany it had seemed yet another sign that the Weimar Republic in general and Jews in particular were tarred with the same red brush of Communism.

Thus Rathenau's murder tended to polarise the two forces already jockeying for influence within the Republic. The day of his burial was proclaimed an official day of mourning, and all schools, universities and theatres were ordered to close. But in Heidelberg Philipp Lenard ostentatiously gave his lectures as usual. And in Berlin it was rumoured that Einstein, the Jewish scientific equivalent of the Jewish Foreign Minister, was next on the assassins' list.

The rumours had some foundation. While Einstein had been in the United States the previous year a young German, Rudolph Leibus, had been charged in Berlin with offering a reward for the murder of Einstein, of Professor Foerster and of Harden, on the grounds that "it was a patriotic duty to shoot these leaders of pacifist sentiment". Found guilty, Herr Leibus was fined the equivalent of three pounds. It seems unlikely that the rate for provocation to murder had risen since then.

Einstein himself was under no illusions. On July 4th he wrote to Geneva resigning from the newly-formed commission.* At the same time he explained to Madame Curie, whom he had only recently recommended to accept, that he was doing so not only because of Rathenau's assassination but because of anti-Semitism among the people he was supposed to represent.

However, this was only a beginning, and two days later he cancelled a lecture which he had planned to give to the Natural Science Society in Berlin.

Madame Curie now wrote pleading with him to stay on the League Commission, saying that this would have been Rathenau's reaction. Einstein replied on July 11th that she did not understand the situation in Germany, and added that it was quite impossible for a Jew to serve both the German and an international intelligentsia.

By mid-July, 1922, he was thus yet again resigned to being driven from the country. He had lived there eight years, longer than he had lived anywhere since his youth. Now, once more, it seemed that he would be moving on. And now, as in 1919 and 1920, he was dissuaded from going at the last moment: from going possibly

* See page 339

to Holland, possibly to Switzerland. This time he was dissuaded by Pierre Comert of the League of Nations who appealed to him* on much the same grounds as Madame Curie: to leave Germany now would be to abandon ship. Einstein decided to stay, for the moment, both in Germany and on the League Committee.

Some grounds for confidence were indeed provided the following month at the centennial meeting of the Gesellschaft Deutscher Naturforscher, held in Leipzig. Einstein, still anxious not to provide too easy a target for the anti-Semites, had refused to attend as a key speaker. But the authorities had insisted on making relativity an important feature, and lectures on it were planned by von Laue and others. As soon as this became known the former members of the "Anti-Relativity Society" went into action, preparing a broadsheet which was sent to the papers and distributed in Leipzig as the conference opened. "The undersigned," it said, "consider it irreconcilable with the seriousness and dignity of German science that a theory, much open to attack, is prematurely and vulgarly broadcast to the lay world and that the Society of German-Scientists and Physicists is used to support such attempts." But "the undersigned" was an even less impressive group than had been mustered at Bad Nauheim the previous year. It looked as through the anti-relativity plank in the anti-Semites' platform was cracking.

However, Einstein was by this time alert enough to realise that the situation might change once again, just as significantly and just as quickly. Doubts remained beneath the brave front which he put on affairs — even though in the autumn of 1922 he was given one recognition which many felt he should have received earlier: the Nobel Prize for Physics.

However, it is possibly truer in the case of physics than in the other subjects for which the Prize is awarded — chemistry, physiology or medicine, literature, and peace — that considerable time must pass before achievements can be properly evaluated. Thus only in 1947 did Appleton receive the Prize for his investigations of the ionosphere carried out in 1924 and 1925 and it was not until 1951 that Cockcroft and Walton were awarded the Prize for their artificial disintegration of the nucleus in 1932. In the case of Einstein, other factors were at work. Whether the argument still raging over General Relativity was one of them is a question whose answer will forever be locked within the bosom of the Swedish Academy of Science. However, there was no need to invoke the General Theory,

* See page 340

since Einstein's earlier work was available. But here the members of
the Academy were baulked by a wording of their brief which might
have worried them even more had they decided to consider relativity
as the basis of the award. For when Alfred Nobel laid down the
lines on which the Physics Prize was to be given, he stipulated that
is should be for a "discovery"; furthermore, it should be one from
which mankind had derived great use. Now it was questionable
whether the Special Theory was, strictly speaking, a "discovery" at
all; even if it were, it was still difficult to claim that by the early
1920s mankind had derived any great use from it. Relativity was
already a commonplace tool in the laboratory when subatomic
particles were being investigated, but this was not what Nobel had
meant. However, during the autumn of 1922 the Academy decided
that it could make the award and yet dodge the difficult relativity
issues. The prize was awarded "independently of such value as may
be ultimately attached to his theories of relativity and gravity, if
these are confirmed, for his services to the theory of physics, and
especially for discovery of the law of the photo-electric effect".
Here they were on safe ground; for the photo-electric law was not
only a discovery revealing the quantatitive relationship between
light and the emission of electrons, but was even by the early 1920s
being utilised in practical ways.

The announcement produced one reaction that was hardly unexpected: Lenard wrote bitterly to the Swedish Academy accusing it
of trying to restore Einstein's prestige without committing itself to
the support of relativity. But the award also produced something of
greater significance. This was an anguished enquiry from the Swiss
and German Ambassadors in Stockholm both of whom wanted to
claim Einstein as their own. The result was a mixture of pathos and
farce which was not without international interest; for on the answer
to the question depended the country whose ambassador could support Einstein at the elaborate Nobel Prize ceremony and at the state
banquet given by the King of Sweden every year in honour of the
Prizewinners.

Einstein was travelling on a Swiss passport, a fact which the
German Foreign Office immediately passed on to the German
Ambassador, Herr Nadolny, but which Nadolny, in the professional
nature of things, was reluctant to take at its face value. He appears
to have been justified. For when he telegraphed an enquiry to the
Berlin Academy of Sciences at the beginning of December he imme-
diately received the reply: *"Einstein ist Reichsdeutscher."* "The Swiss
Ambassador was surprised when I told him this," Nadolny later

wrote. "However, when I described the telegram to him he calmed down and accepted the situation with the comment that Einstein was generally looked upon as a German and probably now wished to be considered as a German." Nadolny, on his part, was equally gracious, suggesting to Berlin that Switzerland's part in Einstein's life and work should be stressed in any announcement to the papers and later proposing that the Swiss Ambassador might, "as a worthwhile courtesy", be invited to the Nobel Lecture which Einstein was to give in Stockholm. The outcome was in fact a compromise. Einstein himself was unable to accept the award personally, being out of Europe on December 11th, the anniversary of Nobel's death on which the prizes are awarded. This lucky chance enabled both the Germans and the Swiss to play parts in the act. For in Stockholm the award was received by the German Ambassador on Einstein's behalf, but in Berlin it was handed over to him, at his own request, not by the Swedish Ambassador to Germany but by the Swiss. But in the Nobel records Einstein was recorded as "German".

One result of the imbroglio was that the Berlin Academy was instructed by the German Minister of Science, Art and Popular Education to elucidate once and for all the riddle of Einstein's nationality. Its report, made on January 13th, 1923, merely stated that since all civil servants must be Germans and Einstein had in 1914 become a civil servant "it must be inferred" that he was German, "even if he did not possess it [German nationality] from birth." The earlier Swiss nationality was not involved, it concluded, and the Academy therefore considered their man "chiefly Reichsdeutscher", the "chiefly" being a qualification which may have crept into the argument due either to caution or an inability to find the vital documents.

This, however, was not the end of the matter. When Einstein returned to Germany early in 1923 he was asked by the Academy to put forward his own views. He gave them on March 24th, 1923, reiterating that when he had accepted the Berlin appointments in 1914 he had stipulated that he must be able to retain his Swiss nationality. In one way this was irrelevant. At issue was not his retention of Swiss nationality but whether he had, on moving to the University, automatically become German as well.

The German civil service would not easily let go — and it was supported by the German Consul-General in Barcelona who reported to Berlin after Einstein's visit to Spain in 1923: "On the whole the local visit of Einstein, who, however, always appears as German not as Swiss, is reckoned a complete success, as much for himself and for

German science as for German—Spanish cultural relations."

On May 14th, 1923, the Minister wrote to Einstein stating that there was nothing in the records concerning his nationality and advising that if he wished the matter to be finally settled he should get in touch with a senior civil servant, Dr. von Rothenburg. The interview took place six months later. Its result was a statement by Einstein, dated February 7th, 1924, in which he accepted the situation. There the affair rested until, nine years later, Einstein gave up his passport in the German Embassy in Brussels and walked off German soil for the last time.

Documents may have been destroyed. The officials of 1923 may have been unduly anxious to claim that Einstein had been a German since 1914. But it seems curious that the swearing-in to Weimar in 1920 and to Prussia in 1921, should not have been mentioned during this dispute. Yet no one can doubt either Einstein's passionate dislike of becoming a German again in 1913, or his equally passionate change of heart which followed the birth of the Republic.

There is one explanation which fits the known facts. It is conceivable that Planck and Nernst, despite their friendly intentions in 1914, were unable to prevent Einstein's automatic re-enrolment as a fully-fledged German. He was also a Swiss; he had his Swiss passport. Why should they trouble him by telling him the technical truth that he was also, inevitably under the law of June 1913, a son of the Fatherland once again? When, in the euphoria of Weimar, he wished to become a German, Planck and Nernst could hardly dissuade him on the grounds that he already was a German, and in the circumstances it would have been natural for them to encourage the purely formal act which did not in fact alter his status but which he later remembered as one of the follies of his life. Planck and Nernst could then let their consciences rest happy: if it was not exactly true that two wrongs had in this case produced a right, at least two misunderstandings had combined to bring about the desired result and Einstein could move about the world as an unofficial German ambassador, which appeared to satisfy all parties.

The Nobel Prize money went to Mileva. Even Einstein's closest friends did not know this, and Lorentz wrote happily that, quite apart from the honour, there was "a material side to the Nobel Prize and I trust that this will ease the cares of your daily life." By this time his financial position was in fact more reassuring. Requests to lecture came thick and fast, and it was the acceptance of one of these, arranged by a Japanese publisher, which had taken him from the country during the Nobel ceremonies. Acceptance of the Japanese invitation was very much a leap in the dark and both his brief diary notes and the oblique references in several newspaper interviews suggest that in practice it turned out to be a disillusioning experience, even though he liked what he considered to be the simple, gentle Japanese. Little more might have been expected. He had been invited to lecture from one end of the country to the other, all expenses paid; he should not have been surprised if he was to be milked hard in the process.

He and Elsa arrived in Japan in mid-November. He held a press conference at the Imperial Hotel in Tokyo and then prepared for his first lecture. This was to be given in the main hall of Keio University and by the time that he was due, the *Japan Weekly Chronicle* recorded, "the hall was filled with scholars, teachers and students. Some women were present, too." There was also Mr. Yamamoto Sanehiko, the proprietor of *Kaizosha*. Einstein began speaking at 1.30 p. m. and continued for three hours, a formidable effort even allowing time for translation. After this there was an hour's break, presumably for what might be called light refreshments. At 5.30 he was back at the rostrum once more. He started where he had left off, apparently delighted at having such attentive listeners and continuing for another three hours. "The audience," it was reported, "were astonished at his staying power."

It was an auspicious start to what was on the whole an unsatisfactory tour. The Einsteins were introduced to the Emperor and the Empress, a singular honour, and Einstein later recorded how he had spoken with the Empress in French. They attended the Feast of Chrysanthemums in the Imperial Gardens and there were a number of other formal receptions before the start of the month-long tour. The audiences to which he now spoke were less serious than those in Tokyo, being attracted by his name as much as by the almost mystic significance which relativity had assumed for the Japanese. Not everyone welcomed its new status. "The excessive reliance on science and the contempt for faith have made a failure of the last century or so," noted the *Japan Weekly Chronicle*. "It is sad to reflect that the Japanese should nevertheless be so elated over a new scientific theory."

To Einstein, "elated" would have seemed an understatement as he was paraded through Japan, a scientific curiosity to be gazed at as well as listened to. In view of the time taken for translation he cut his original lecture, only to restore its former length after being told he had gravely offended his hosts by giving them less than Tokyo. His reactions can be gauged by a report in the *Japan Weekly Chro-*

*nicle* whose correspondent noted that the tour was "weighing on him rather heavily". Einstein had also shown, it went on, "a strong distaste for the popular style of lecture, boosted and crowded with people who are simply curious to pay the fee to see the latest lion. He had expected that his audience would consist only of curious students of physics."

His impact can be estimated not only by the reception but by the levels at which relativity appears to have been discussed. One account, published in the *Mainichi* and reprinted in English in the *Japan Weekly Chronicle* need not be credited with literal accuracy; but it does indicate the national importance which was accorded in Japan to a theory which only a minute proportion of the population could understand.

The report described a discussion "of quite unusual nature" by the Cabinet Council:

One of the Ministers asked whether ordinary people would understand Professor Einstein's lectures on the theory of relativity. Mr. Kamada, Minister of Education, rather rashly said of course they would. Dr. Okano, Minister of Justice, contradicted Mr. Kamada, saying that they would never understand. Mr. Arai, Minister of Agriculture and Commerce, was rather sorry for Mr. Kamada, so he said that they would perhaps understand vaguely. The headstrong Minister of Justice insisted that there could be no midway between understanding and not understanding. If they understood, they understood clearly. If they did not understand, they did not understand at all. A chill fell on the company. Mr. Baba, the tactful director of the Legislation Bureau, said that they could understand if they made efforts. Their efforts would be useless, persisted the Minister of Justice. He had himself ordered a book on the theory of relativity when the theory was first introduced into Japan last year and tried to study it. On the first page he found higher mathematics, and he had to shut the book for the present. When the members of the Imperial Academy were invited to dinner at the Hama detached palace, he had mentioned the problem to Dr. Tanakadate Aikitsu, who was seated next to him. Dr. Fujisawa Rikitaio (an authority on mathematics) overhearing their discussion, said that in America they were collecting popular explanations of the theory, offering an enormous prize. Such being the case, Dr. Fujisawa said, it was wiser not to begin the study at once. He supported Dr. Okano's opinion. Hearing this elaborate explanation, Mr. Baba, director of the Legislation Bureau, decided to eschew Einstein for the time being.

The rest of the population behaved otherwise and by the end of December Einstein was thankful to board ship for Europe. Even so, he had a high opinion of the people themselves. On the way home he visited Palastine* formally opening there the Hebrew University whose foundation stone had been laid on Mount Scopus some five years earlier. Then he and his wife sailed on to Marseilles, travelling from the port to Madrid where, during his absence from Europe, arrangements had been completed for what was to be another triumphal tour.

The lecture which Einstein gave to the Academy of Sciences in Madrid, before being elected a member, was attended by King Alphonso XIII. The Rector of Madrid University proposed that not only Professor, but also Mrs. Einstein should be granted the Diploma of Doctor Honoris Causa. And the Spanish Minister of Education offered him a home, in the name of the Spanish nation, should conditions in Germany "impede the tranquil continuation of his intellectual studies". Opinion there continued divided; the anti-Semite lobby continued to make itself heard, but in Ulm the city councillors decided on March 20th that a new street should be named Einstein-strasse. In Spain, there was only one hint of trouble. Before reaching Madrid, Einstein lectured in Barcelona and here he attended a meeting of the local Syndicalists, workers dedicated to obtaining control of industry by direct action. Exactly what he said to them is not clear, but *The Times,* not notably inaccurate in such matters, quoted him addressing them with the words: "I also am a revolutionary, though only a scientific one. The persecutions you tell me of seem to have been more stupid than wicked. You see only the bad side of things. There is also a good side." This seems harmless enough, but the left-wing Spanish newspapers may have embroidered their stories, and Einstein was obliged to state that reports of this meeting did "not correctly convey what he said" — an elegant phrase which, as *The Times* reported, from Madrid, "thus dissipated a rather painful impression which was made in some circles here by the words attributed to him".

Einstein arrived back in Berlin only a few weeks before an announcement in Washington gave further support to the General Theory. The previous September there had been another total eclipse of the sun, visible throughout a narrow belt stretching from Somaliland across the Indian Ocean to Australia, and a number of expeditions had been sent out to gather further evidence for or against the theory. A party from the Greenwich Observatory and a Dutch-German expedition — the German contingent led by Freundlich with special equipment prepared in the Postdam Observatory — had gone

* See page 373

to Christmas Island. From Sydney a photo-telescope had been taken to Cunnamulla in Queensland, and the government of New South Wales had sent a party to Cordillo Downs, deep in the Australian interior, to which a dismantled telescope had been carried more than a hundred miles from the railhead on the backs of camels. In addition, Australian, Canadian and American astronomers had set up their instruments near Broome on the north-west coast of Australia, the American expedition being led by Professor W. W. Campbell of the Lick Observatory.

As in 1919, the observers were at the mercy of the weather. This time, however, one minor source of possible error had been eliminated. In 1919 the light from the sun and its nearby stars had been collected by mirrors whose small distortions complicated the resulting calculations; in most of the instruments now being used, the light was directly collected by the telescopes' object glasses. Other refinements had been incorporated in the equipment and it was generally accepted, as *The Times* wrote on September 21st, 1922, that "if the expected verification has been made this morning it will have to be admitted that human observations of the universe can be reconciled with a theory from which absolute space and absolute time have been excluded, although at present they are not reconcilable with a theory based on these Newtonian conceptions."

Seven months later it was revealed that the verification had been made. Some teams had been frustrated by bad weather, but Professor Campbell's party had met with almost perfect conditions. Hundreds of star images were recorded on their four special photo-telescopes and some scores of these, shown on ten plates, had been selected for calculation and checking. Now, on April 12th, 1923, Campbell reported that the prints taken on September 21st and compared with those taken at Tahiti three months before the eclipse, showed agreement with Einstein's prediction "as close as the most ardent proponent of the relativity theory could hope for". The following evening, Eddington reported the results of the Lick expedition to his fellow-astronomers in Burlington House, recalling the two expeditions of 1919 and adding: "I think it was the Bellman in *The Hunting of the Snark* who laid down the rule: 'When I say it three times, it is right.' The stars have now said it three times to three separate expeditions, and I am convinced that their answer is right."

Not everyone was pleased. "It is an interesting commentary on the reluctance of many leading men of science to accept the relativity theory," says Eddington's biographer, "that when Campbell was asked what he anticipated from the eclipse plates, he replied: 'I hoped it would not be true.' Undoubtedly some Fellows of the Royal Society and even a few in the Royal Astronomical Society felt the same way."

Even though the Lick expedition provided the third proof "that light does not go straight" when affected by gravity, conservative doubts were to some extent justified by later events. For as technological advance made more accurate results possible, speculation continued about the amount of deflection involved; and thirty years later it could be claimed that this was "still controversial, at least in regard to magnitude".

Back in Germany, Einstein must have felt that his travels were over, for the time being. His fears of the previous summer were evaporating and he now looked forward to an untroubled continuation of work in Berlin. He might well have been warned by the extraordinary story of his alleged "trip to Russia". In the *Deutsche Allgemeine Zeitung* of September 15th, 1923, there appeared the report that Einstein was expected in Moscow at the end of the month. On October 6th the *Berliner Tageblatt* took up the story with an announcement that he had left for the Russian capital, while on October 27th, the nationalist *Berliner Borsenzeitung* quoted Russian reports that Einstein would be "arriving in Petersburg on October 28th and will speak on the relativity theory to a group of trained scientific workers". Not to be outdone, the *Kieler Zeitung* reported on November 2nd that: "Einstein is staying in Petersburg for three days." With such a wealth of circumstantial report, his fellow-countrymen could be justified in thinking that he had visited Russia, even though dates and details might not be correct. In fact he was never in the country — the story was merely another item in the anti-Jewish, anti-relativity campaign which was always anxious to tar its enemies with the Communist brush.

Yet the *canard,* damaging to Einstein at a time when many still considered Weimar's resumption of relations with Russia to be a betrayal, was given a plausibility by his own actions. For he was not only on comparatively friendly terms with Georg Tschisherrin, the Russian People's Commissar for Foreign Affairs in Berlin, but was on at least one occasion used as an intermediary by the Zionist leader, Kurt Blumenfeld, in an effort to ease the conditions of the Jews in Russia.

Blumenfeld has himself told the story, revealing how he one day met an East European Jew who had been closely following Zionist activities. "You have won Einstein for the Zionist cause," said this man. "Tschisherrin has the greatest respect for Einstein, with whom he has often spoken. Get him to introduce you to Tschisherrin; if you meet him alone with Einstein then something can come of it." Blumenfeld recalls how he mentioned the matter to Einstein who immediately went to the telephone, saying: "This conversation can be really interesting." A few days later, the two men visited the Soviet Embassy, the Ambassador saying a few minutes after their meeting: "I know what is in your mind." The interview was long and inconclusive. Tschisherrin was prepared to admit that the movement of small groups of Russian Jews to Palestine might be allowed but that "mass emigration is out of the question: it conflicts with the Soviet system." Einstein was certainly willing to intervene with the Russians if this was likely to help the cause of Zionism. He would just as willingly have intervened with the devil had he seen any hope of success. But he was not used to supping with long spoons.

Early in November he was suddenly jerked awake again to his position in Germany, and to the dangerous situation of anyone who fraternised with Communists. During the first days of the month he was visited by a prominent Jewish leader who appears to have advised him that his life was in danger. Just how serious the warning was is not known. But on November 7th Einstein wrote Planck a letter — no copy of which appears to have survived — saying that he was leaving the country for a few days and cancelling a dinner date with Planck at Haberlandstrasse for the evening of the 9th.

Planck failed to receive the letter and arrived at the Einstein home on the 9th, only to be received by Elsa with news of her husband's sudden departure for Leiden. Both had good cause for alarm. For between the writing of Einstein's letter on the 7th and Planck's arrival in the Haberlandstrasse, the National Socialists, led by Hitler and supported by General Ludendorff, had begun their attempt to take over the Bavarian Government in Munich as prelude to a march on Berlin. There had been fighting during the day and what was to happen next was still uncertain.

Einstein's flight was not, in fact, linked with the Munich *putsch*. It was, rather, an indication of the anti-Semitic climate of the times; but on the night of the 9th it can hardly have looked fortuitous. But the rising was put down, and on November 10th Planck wrote to Einstein in Leiden, pleading with him yet again not to accept any of the offers which would no doubt be made to him.

There is no evidence whatever that Einstein suffered from personal fear; rather the reverse. But he wanted to get on with his work, he knew that there would be little chance of that under a

National Socialist government, and it was in character that until he learned that the *putsch* had been crushed he should seek the security of Leiden. It was equally in character that Planck should write to him in the name of German science and implore him to come back. He came.

He did not return solely in reply to Planck's appeal; much as he respected the older man's scientific genius, Einstein always went his own way. He did not return because of Elsa and the comfort of the Haberlandstrasse home. In 1923, as in 1914, Berlin still provided — as long as Weimar remained — the intellectual climate in which he could best get on with his work.

PART
FOUR

# The Einstein Age

# 12

## *UNTER DEN LINDEN*

EINSTEIN RETURNED FROM HOLLAND TO BERLIN TOWARDS THE END
of November 1923. For the next decade the city was his base for
a central, consolidating period of his life. But what consolidated
was not only the physicist with the international reputation, the man
who had shown the universe to be built differently from accepted
ideas. This absentminded scientist turning his huge, luminous and
enquiring eyes on visitors, behaving at times with an almost studied
childlike simplicity, more an actor playing Einstein than the man
himself, was only one facet. It was matched by another, by the man
whom the President of the United States and the Emperor of Japan
had been honoured to meet, the Nobel Prize winner coaxed into
helping the League of Nations, the physicist whose advice was constantly sought by the more formidable of the Jewish leaders. Moreover this Swabian, whose triumphs in the realm of abstract thought
had brought him the fame of an oracle and the veneration that goes
with it, had during the transformation decided to use the reputation
that chance had unexpectedly tossed him. He would campaign with
the Zionists for a Jewish homeland in Palestine and he would help
build a new Europe — although whether it should be built on unarmed pacifist goodwill or beneath the umbrella of international
arms was something which he found it difficult to decide.

With these political ambitions, it would have been natural
enough if Einstein had exercised considerable influence outside his
specialist field during the decade which began in 1924. Many physicists did so. The British Government was apt to consult Rutherford
as a matter of course on any question affecting science. There was
Madame Curie and Professor Langevin in France, Lorentz in Holland. Edward Appleton, pioneer of the ionosphere, had a finger in
innumerable government pies. Lindemann later became, as Lord
Cherwell, one of the most influential, and controversial, politico-

scientific figures of his time. Yet Einstein operated throughout this period at a very different level and with very different results. His name was invaluable for transferring cash from wealthy Jews into Zionist funds. His name on pacifist manifestos was always a sign of honest intent, and of considerable publicity value until the law of diminishing returns came into action. But during the years between the two world wars the effect of his efforts in these fields was in many ways as counterproductive as his enthusiasm was unlimited. The reasons do not lie entirely in the fact that, operating as a Jew in Germany, he was something of a fish out of water; other Jews in other spheres helped to drive opinion the way they wanted it until the Nazis chopped them down.

He was handicapped in all his efforts to implement his good intentions by the very qualities that made him the genius he was. First, and of overwhelming importance, was his determination to devote as much time as possible to discovering how the physical world was built. He wanted to aid the Jews and he wanted to help keep the peace of the world. But whenever he was in danger of becoming too deeply implicated there was some new riddle of the universe that demanded attention. Kurt Blumenfeld, who recruited Einstein into the Zionist cause, shrewdly noted of him to Weizmann that "Zionism and Palestine were only peripheral concerns"; and in 1923 Einstein himself revealed his own view of the priorities when he told Weizmann that he would give his name and talk to people in Berlin but would not "travel around or visit congresses". His dedication to the pacifist cause was equally unquestioned between 1919 and 1933. But his enthusiasm had perpetually to contend with the fact that there were scientific papers to be written or read, and men like Planck or Sommerfeld or von Laue to discuss them with. Thus he was forced to overlook his homework, to skimp his practice in a game where there is always a watcher in the slips waiting to catch a man out.

With this tendency to give less attention to non-scientific matters than enthusiasm required, there went a dislike for the formalities demanded of those who try to influence others, and a contempt for the sleight-of-mind that is often called for. Einstein despised the careful cultivation of men or women for particular ends, the balancing of interest against interest, the bland statement that conceals truth rather than illuminates it, and the ability to judge the right moment for dropping the right hint into the right ear.

Finally there was his sense of the ridiculous. He did not mind what he looked like and he often did not mind what he said. He was, quite simply, too unconcerned to worry about trifles, even when circumstances began to push him more frequently than his scientific colleagues on to the public stage where trifles matter more frequently. But they managed to look like figures from the great drama of public affairs; he too often evoked something less serious. Thus it was inevitable that he should occupy a large place in human hearts and a small one in the corridors of power.

The Berlin into which Einstein settled back in 1924 has a special niche in history. This was the Berlin whose fortunes changed as Germany struggled up from the post-war economic morass and was then pushed back into it by the world depression of 1929, a city which had done with the soldiers' councils of the revolution, and the troops of the Kapp Putsch, but was soon to be beguiled by the presidency of Hindenburg; and, eventually, by Hindenburg's candidate for the chancellorship, Adolf Hitler.

In the capital, Einstein not only occupied a unique position but lived under conditions more favourable than those he had previously been used to. For the first time in his life he had one home for more than a few years. To counteract the undertow of anti-Semitic nationalism, quiescent for a while but never very far below the surface, there was the respect of the university and the Kaiser Wilhelm Institute which he knew was his due. In Leiden, where he delighted to stay with the Ehrenfests on his visits as professor extraordinary, he was enormously popular. Royalties from his book on relativity and his fees from Leiden helped to raise him from the rut of most professors; he had always been careless of money but now he could almost afford to be. He had his music and he had his sailing — on a fine choice of lakes which ringed Berlin with the circlet of watery fingers that were to be marker-points for the bombers in the Second World War whatever the camouflage experts could do. He had, moreover, an entrée into the polyglot world of educated industrialists and civilised financiers, of artists and actors and designers who during the first years of Weimar appeared to have taken over the privileged position in the state so long occupied by the military. Thus he was a close friend of Willy Meinhardt, the head of the Osram Company, at whose house in the Engadine he began to stay. He was a friend of Slevogt the painter, of Emil Orlik the designer. A typical stag-party organised by his doctor-friend, Janos Plesch, consisted of Einstein and Haber, Slevogt and Orlik, Fritz Kreisler, Arthur Schnabel and the German Foreign Minister, Count Rantzau. Just as in his student days Einstein had at times been more than the retiring contemplative physicist, so now, on the crest of the wave, he became for a while almost as human as other men, expanding in the Weimar renaissance.

It was during this period that he walked one evening, as described by Plesch, to a favourite restaurant with the Russian physicist Joffé, with Plesch, and with a third companion. Einstein and Joffé, walking behind the other couple, were talking loudly and Einstein burst out in a roar of enjoyment. When they caught up with their friends, Einstein explained: "Poor old Joffé can't make up his mind through which hole an electron will go if he fires it through a lead obstacle with a number of holes. An electron is indivisible, and therefore it must go through one hole only. But which hole? And the solution" — with a gust of Einstein laughter — "is really very simple; it goes through the fifth dimension." Physics was still, as yet, too important to be taken too seriously.

Einstein's base for operations was of course No. 5 Haberlandstrasse, where his wife quietly helped to organise his life and where his stepdaughter Ilse often acted as secretary. The most important room in the apartment was Einstein's study in a corner turret of the block, reached by a small staircase and with a view only of rooftops and the sky. Here were the expected books, a round table in the small window alcove stacked with papers, notes, references, and an assortment of pamphlets. Here also, almost hidden on top of a bookcase, was the cigar-box surreptitiously filled from time to time by Einstein's friends who knew how Elsa tried to ration him to one a day for the sake of his health. The study was Einstein's absolute preserve. No cleaner was allowed in. Neither was Elsa. "It was here that his work was done and his friends received to discuss problems without interference," Plesch has written. "It was always a matter of regret to his wife (he always referred to her as 'my old lady' that she was unable to look after him and his things in that room as everywhere else, but Einstein was adamant; never mind the dust and disorder; it was the independence that mattered."

Here he spent most of his mornings and many of the afternoons when not engaged on university business or lectures, filling sheet after sheet of paper with calculations; immersed in the implications and development of the General Theory; and, from 1920 onwards, struggling to find the mathematical framework which would include both the phenomena of electro-magnetism and those of gravity, the unified field theory which would encompass, as the New York Times put it, "the wheeling of the planets, the speeding of light on its course, the attraction of earth for a falling stone, the lustre of the diamond, the instability of radium, the lightness of hydrogen and the heaviness of lead, the flow of electricity through a wire, millions of manifestations of matter, energy, time, space".

The academic situation in Germany can be judged from an appeal for money which he made early in April, 1924. Before the war, the income of the Kaiser Wilhelm Institute for Physics had been 75,000 marks, worth £3,750; now it was 22,000 marks, worth £225. In real terms the salaries of scholars and teachers, Einstein had estimated in a British journal the previous year, were only a fifth of what they had been before the war; in many cases they were much less. Fewer scientific meetings were taking place, and one reason was that many who would have attended lacked the tram fares to take them across Berlin. Einstein himself was in a different category. He wanted to pay for his own assistants, as was then customary. But his rich industrial friends would have none of this in the straightened circumstances of post-war Berlin, and put a lump sum into a special bank account on which he could draw as and when he wished. However much he drew, the account was always made up to the original sum.

That his appeal was not special pleading is borne out by a young Oxford man, Edward Skillings, who some while earlier had visited Berlin and eight other University centres to assess German requests for English books and periodicals. "It is plain to see that large sections of the professors are suffering from grievous privations both physical and mental," he reported. In Hallé the wife of one of them explained that her husband would not be able to work without the "fearfully humiliating" help from England. In Göttingen the professor Skillings hoped to see had recently died of undernourishment. These were of course only details in the larger picture of gloom and depression which was already beginning to lower the confidence of the Germans in the ability of their new Republican Government — a foreseeable result which can be attributed to a casual lack of Allied interest or to a Machiavellian method of sapping the authority of a left-wing government. Einstein had no doubt about which alternative was the more likely.

Against this dull and depressing background, the phenomenon of relativity, embodied in the photogenic figure of Einstein himself, was a colourful exception, an example which the nationalists could have used, had they only wished, to illustrate the genius of German science. Part of the phenomenon was the "relativity industry" which by the early 1920s was flooding the Continent, as well as Britain and the United States, with explanations that ranged from the erudite to the simple-minded. "The stream continues," wrote E. Cunning-

ham in *Nature* in June, 1922. "Here are seven more books on relativity." The previous year a bibliography prepared by the director
of the International Catalogue of Scientific Literature included
nearly 650 papers, articles and books dealing with the subject, and
many score more had been added by the time that Dr. Cunningham
settled down to his reviewing.

Von Laue in Germany had been the first to write a fullscale
book explaining special relativity — *Das Relativitätsprinzip* — which
appeared in Brunswick in 1911. Five years later Freundlich did much
the same for the General Theory. Eddington's *Report on the Relativity Theory of Gravitation* for the Physical Society of London had
quickly gone into a second edition, and his *Space, Time and Gravitation* which appeared in 1920 had, like the *Report* "awakened English-speaking physicists and astronomers to the importance of the
new theory. They began to bestir themselves for there was 'the sound
of a going in the tops of the mulberry trees'; old ideas were in the
melting pot; an exciting spirit of adventure was vaguely felt even
by those not mathematically equipped to read the book critically."

Einstein's major paper on the General Theory had been reprinted in book form in Leipzig in 1916, and his *Relativity: The Special
and the General Theory* appeared the following year. By 1920 it had
run through fourteen German editions totalling 65,000 copies. The
English edition, translated by Robert Lawson and published in 1920,
ran through seven editions in nineteen months. In addition, the lectures which Einstein gave in Princeton in the spring of 1921 were
quickly reprinted and a number of his original papers on relativity,
together with others by Lorentz and Minkowski, were reprinted as
a book two years later in Germany and Britain.

Lorentz, Planck, Born and Weyl were among Einstein's colleagues who wrote books on the subject, and even Lenard was represented with his strongly critical *Über Relativitätsprinzip, Aether,
Gravitation*. In Paris, Charles Nordmann had written *Einstein and
the Universe: A Popular Exposition of the Famous Theory* in which
razor-sharp French logic cut through to reveal the simplicity of
Einstein's ideas with an effectiveness that not even Einstein could
better. More remarkable than any of these was the massive encyclopaedia article which Sommerfeld had commissioned from Wolfgang Pauli for the *Encyclopädie der Mathematischen Wissenschaft*.
Aged only twenty, Pauli was one of Sommerfeld's students who had
attended the famous Bad Nauheim meeting; his account of relativity
for the encyclopaedia was quickly reprinted in book form, "in view
of the apparently insatiable demand ... for accounts of the theory

of relativity" as Sommerfeld said in the Preface. Reprinted forty years later, it was then described by Niels Bohr as "still one of the most valuable expositions of the basis and scope of Einstein's original conceptions".

Just over the horizon, and to appear in 1925, was Bertrand Russell's *The ABC of Relativity*, a book almost as important for the friendship which it was to encourage between Einstein and Russell as for its extraordinarily clear presentation of the subject. Russell, who in the columns of the *Athenaeum* had been among the first to describe the implications of the 1919 eclipse expeditions, was in the next third of a century to show remarkable similarities with Einstein. Like Einstein he was basically pacifist. Like Einstein he supported the Second World War as certainly as he opposed the First. Both men were frequently, and unjustifiably, tarred with the Communist brush, and both were concerned with the fundamental problem of the human predicament. But two main differences kept them apart. Einstein was proud of his similarities with his fellow-men, Russell proud of those things which made him different and while Einstein only left his study against his better judgment, Russell was always up front in the political battle.

The study did not only see Einstein at work on those problems of the natural world that obsessed all physicists. Here he dealt also as best he could with the torrent of appeals and begging letters, and requests for advice that poured down on him during these years of fame and notoriety. If Einstein could prove that light did not go straight then he could do anything, however impossible it sounded. Such was a common belief.

Rudolph Kayser who married Einstein's older stepdaughter Ilse has a picture which may not be literally true but at least gives a good impression of what had to be dealt with:

> Poor people beg for money, for clothing, and jobs. A young man has taken the notion to become an explorer; won't Einstein help him to go to India or Africa? A woman telegraphs — would the professor please obtain a visa. Actors ask for engagements, young people in small towns who have hardly attended high school would like to come to Berlin and become his disciples. Einstein reads all these requests with kindliness and understanding, and also with a sense of humour. These are obligations of fame which one must bear with a smile, but this fame has consequences, frequently responsible for bitterness. There are letters and magazine articles filled with hatred, malice, envy and vulgarity. And since Einstein is a Jew and an opponent of all nationalistic pride, all the garbage of political strife is also cast at him. In addition, there

come the fools and the prophets, who sprout, like mushrooms, especially in the years of insecurity and anarchy. This one writes that he has finally discovered the essence of sleep. That one writes that he has found the only correct way to lower the price of coal. Another one has invented new senses, since the old five senses are no longer sufficient for man's use. Technicians report on their new inventions. They send blueprints of new contraptions and flying machines. Still another is engaged in overthrowing the traditional astronomy and building up a new one. Still another believes that he has found new mathematical formulae, and everything was at least glanced at.

He was much tried in other ways. The flat-earthers, the spiritualists, the inveterate believers, all latched on to the apparent enigma of relativity to bolster their own ideas. Sometimes they rolled many of them into one packet like the author of *Spiritism: The Hidden Secret in Einstein's Theory of Relativity* for whom Hebrew words, the "uranium cubic diatonal" and mystic numbers all contributed to the secret. So, almost inevitably, did another old standby. "This wonderful portrayal of the earth and the heavens as interlocked bodies of darkness and light is involved" readers were informed, "in the dimensions of the Great Pyramid of Egypt whose missing top expresses the space area of the 'time' of the day and of the night, of the universal 'unit space of division'." Einstein might well have murmured, with some of the internationalists who looked askance at his statements on their affairs, "God save me from my friends."

To those in his own line of country he was always generous of time, money and effort, a fact which quickly permeated the academic world. Thus the young foreign student who wished to study chemistry in Bonn, had been rejected by the Prussian Ministry of Education and who knew it was against the law to make a second application, wrote as a matter of course to Einstein. He sent his entire biography, with every detail. "When you are twenty, he wrote years later, you feel as important as I did. You are certain that the whole world appreciates this importance. Einstein did." For he not only recommended a second, albeit unlawful, application but produced for enclosure a letter from himself supporting the application and denouncing the injustice.

A clear picture of this Einstein, always anxious to help lame scientific dogs over bureaucratic stiles, is given by Leopold Infeld, a young Pole studying at the University of Cracow who was later to collaborate with him in the United States. Infeld wished to complete his studies in Berlin but found that Poles were unwelcome there and Polish Jews more so. Finally, in desperation, he telephoned Einstein and was given a time to call.

Einstein listened to what Infeld had to say, claimed that his signature did not carry very much weight — "because I have given very many recommendations and they are anti-Semites" — and then wrote a few helpful words to Planck. "Instead of thinking about his genius, about his achievements in physics," Infeld wrote, "I thought then, and later, about his great kindness, about his loud laugh, about the gentle way he talked, about the brilliance of his eyes, about the clumsiness with which he looked about for a piece of paper on a desk full of paper, about the queer mixture of great warmth and great aloofness."

The incident was significant both of Einstein's perpetual kindness and of his Achilles heel; for he wrote, says Infeld, "without knowing whether I had the slightest idea of physics". The practice continued — so much so that refugee scientists, arriving in Oxford in 1933 and proudly showing a testimonial from Einstein, were often advised to keep quiet about it.

The combination of prodigious intellect and human vulnerability which made him such a contradictory human being became more obvious during these early 1920s as the image of the tousle-headed eccentric began to form and harden round the central character of the man. At one level, the physicist who technically headed the Kaiser Wilhelm Institute for Physics, still being developed, was the remote genius who had changed the human picture of the universe, a being so divorced from other men that his *obiter dicta* had the authority of the Delphic oracle. At another level he was the Einstein who delighted in taking control of the lift in his Haberlandstrasse block and manipulating the buttons so that guests were whisked up, back, then up and down again past the floor at which they wished to alight. This was the Einstein who when nagged about well-worn dress clothes would say: "I will simply fasten a notice to it saying: 'This suit has just been cleaned'." He retained the mixture of clown and small boy delighted with simple jokes, engrossed by absurdities. He was always ready to respond to the ridiculous challenge, and when a group of eminent friends called for him one evening, he accepted a bet to take off his waistcoat without first removing his coat. He was wearing his only dress suit, but immediately began a series of elaborate contortions. These continued for some while. It seemed he would have to pay up. Then, with a final tortuous twist he did the trick, triumphantly waving his crumpled waistcoat and exploding into his long deep belly-laugh. This was

not at all the thing for the quieter waters of Berlin academic society.
It was not even the thing for some of Einstein's friends such as
Haber with his perfectly-run home. Ehrenhaft recalls how on one
occasion he and his wife arrived at the Habers together with Einstein
and Elsa, both men properly dinner-jacketed. As they sat down in
the drawing-room Elsa exclaimed: "But Albert, you haven't put your
socks on." "Yes, yes," he replied, unblinkingly. "I have already
disclosed the secret to Frau Ehrenhaft."

But Einstein's idiosyncracies were accepted. And his friend,
Willy Meinhardt, President of the Osram concern, helping his guest
find his overcoat, could without offence produce it with the words:
"This must be Einstein's: it's made by Peek & Kloppenburg" — at
that time the cut-price tailors of Berlin.

The stories of Einstein's reluctance to attend formal functions,
to play the social lion in the expected way, are still numerous and
must have been more so in the Berlin of half a century ago. Many
are certainly apocryphal but some ring true, as when he replied
to a Berlin hostess who had described her list of guests: "So you
would like me to serve as a table centre?" His frequent description
of the more formal social functions was "Feeding time at the Zoo",
while of academic dinners he confessed to one of his sons-in-law:
"On occasions like this I retire to the back of my mind and there
I am happy."

He genuinely hated it all — announcing to a companion as he
joined one dinner party: "Now I go on the trapeze." Antonina
Vallentin, who knew him well during the Berlin days, says that it
was in vain that "one would explain to him the customary formalities, and those who had not known him long would explain patiently, as to a backward child. They would repeat: This is done . . .
Why is it done? he would ask. Until you noticed his smile, he seemed
like a malicious child. Tails? Why tails? I never had any and never
missed them. Once his wife employed all her powers of persuasion,
her charm and humour, to make him order an evening suit for a
solemn occasion, and after violent resistance from him a compromise
was eventually reached: a dinner jacket instead of tails. Afterwards
he merely said, yes, he did have a dinner jacket in his cupboard
which he was even ready to exhibit, until the day when 'the fine
thing', as he called it, had grown too small and was no longer
presentable".

He tried to please, and years later arrived at the wedding in
the New York Plaza of a friend who knew that he hated formal
occasions and wanted to spare him the discomfort of a white tie

occasions. "He showed up, without being invited", he wrote later. "He was dressed in a dark suit, with white shirt and tie — the perfect attire for the proceedings, according to his standards. He also wore an overcoat that bore the NRA label of the 1930s and a navy blue wool seaman's cap".

Even here, Einstein could not bear to waste time. He found some hotel stationery and during the lulls in the wedding could be noted writing equation after equation of small neat figures and symbols.

If a streak of bloody-mindedness, a reluctance to be pushed along paths down which he did not wish to go, tended to buttress his non-conformity, the deep feeling behind it was genuine enough: the feeling that pretentiousness and hypocrisy were among the ingredients of the 'dressing-up' on which so much of the world insisted. Behind this gentle charade there was also an urgency which for Einstein had a particular poignancy. All those buttons; all those tails; all that putting on and taking off, wasting valuable minutes and hours while in the distance he could hear, with Marvell, "Time's winged chariot hurrying near". What a waste it all was. And so with shoes which could be replaced by sandals, and socks that could be dispensed with altogether. How he would have sympathised with his near-contemporary J. B. S. Haldane who rejoiced on his emigration to India that he would now be able to go foot-free and added, "Sixty years in socks is enough." Einstein, for his part, was delighted that he could turn to a companion at a formal dinner where his own merits were being lauded and whisper: "But the man doesn't wear socks!"

These newsworthy stigmata of the *enfant terrible*, like his frequent avowals of humility, sprang from deeply-rooted convictions. And what often appeared to be awkwardness for awkwardness' sake was the natural action of a natural man. "I am happy because I want nothing from anyone," he once told an American correspondent. "I do not care for money. Decorations, titles, or distinctions mean nothing to me. I do not crave praise. The only thing that gives me pleasure, apart from my work, my violin and my sailboat, is the appreciation of my fellow-workers." Here is a hint of the bridge between the skylarking clown, the eccentric who at times gives the impression of acting with one eye on posterity, and the dedicated scientist. As his son says, he was always "a great ham". He enjoyed sending people away with the answers they expected to get. But for most of the time his air of wandering aberration from the normal standards of life was genuine enough. He was just too occupied with more important matters to worry.

It was this fierce dedication, as much as the revelations of the
eclipse expeditions, which helped to set him apart from other scientists. At the lower levels, men said that only three physicists understood the riddles of the world — Einstein, Planck and Lorentz. More
to the point was Planck's reply to Freundlich, who one day presented him with a problem and hoped for an answer off the cuff.
Freundlich's widow still recalls how her husband repeated to her
what Planck had said: "I shall have to think about it and then I
will write down the answer. I cannot provide it at once, just like
that. Einstein could do so. I cannot." It is unlikely that the exact
words are remembered correctly over half a century; but their significance was unforgettable.

The same attitude is shown in an incident recalled by Ehrenfest's widow. This involved Einstein, Nernst and Lorentz at a meeting of the Berlin Physical Society. After Nernst had made a statement, Einstein said: "You know, I don't think that reference is ad-
missable." Whereupon Nernst replied: "But Herr Colleague, it is the
very reference which you yourself used in your last publication."
To Einstein, this presented no difficulty. "How can I help it if the
dear God will not take account of what I said in my last publication?" he asked. This was no more than permitted by-play. Something more was contributed by Lorentz who did not laugh with the
rest of the assembly. Instead, he remained silent for a moment. Then
he spoke:

"Ah, yes. Anything is allowed to Einstein."

Einstein was lucky in having at least some support from industry. The prediction that light reaching the earth from the stars
would be altered in frequency by the gravitational field through
which it passed had interested Freundlich since his first contacts with
Einstein. He had close connections with German business, and soon
after the war persuaded a number of industrialists, notably Dr.
Bosch, a director of I. G. Farben, to finance an institute which could
investigate the phenomenon. This was the Einstein Institute in Potsdam, later to be amalgamated with the Royal Observatory there as
the Institute for Solar Research. Throughout the 1920s a long series
of observations was made from it. The results were inconclusive, a
fact which may have played its part in the gradual estrangement
between Einstein and Freundlich. Certainly Planck took it that there
had been a definite rupture in their relations — so much so that he
wrote to Freundlich offering to intervene. Memories must be taken
with caution; but Freundlich, with his Scots ancestry, was remarkably British in looks, sympathies, and demeanour. Einstein, in the

early 1920s, had great hopes for Germany. "It was almost," says Frau Freundlich, thinking back with a pin-sharp perception that cannot be discounted, "as though my husband was too British, not Jewish enough."

The heart of the Institute was a long-focus telescope accommodated in a sixty-foot tower, surrounded by a second tower, built of stone and the sunlight reflected down this was turned through 90 degrees and taken along a forty-foot room, partly sunk in the ground. The demands made on the architect, Erich Mendelsohn, were considerable, and he satisfied them by designing a building in marked contrast to those standing nearby in the grounds of the Astro-Physical Observatory. They, built at the end of the previous century, were in the sober traditional Prussian style and utilised the red bricks of the Mark Brandenburg. Mendelsohn's "Einstein Tower", as it was soon known, was a concrete construction whose flowing white outlines were in some ways symbolic of the artistic renaissance already sweeping the Weimar Republic. It was even suggested that while the older buildings with their separate bricks epitomised the Euclidean concept of mathematics and atomic structure as understood at the turn of the century, Mendelsohn's long elegant curves epitomised post-Einsteinian physics. Certainly the building became one of the things to be seen in Potsdam, and more than one tourist agency added the Einstein Tower to its tour of the Potsdam palaces.

Not everyone liked the new building. Photographs were taken to illustrate its slightly bizarre outline, and among the German papers which described it there was one which called it "a cross between a New York skyscraper and an Egyptian pyramid."

The architecture of the Institute was in fact to play its own small part in the anti-Einstein campaign which grew with the rise of the National Socialist party in the 1930s. For, it was asked, was it not in keeping that investigation of the absurd relativity theory should be carried out in a grotesque building which had no roots in German traditions? Was it not typical that the theory of the Jew Einstein should be investigated by the half-Jew Freundlich from a building which offended so deeply the decent nationalist traditions? A small point, but one not to be ignored by any competent rabble-rouser.

Einstein's observations with Freundlich were fitted into gaps between many other duties. He had an office in the Academy of Sciences and his work at the Kaiser Wilhelm Institute took a good deal of time. Under his agreement with the university he did not have to lecture, but he nevertheless did so fairly frequently. On these occasions, as at most other continental universities, attendance was not restricted to students taking specific courses. Some came more out of curiosity than scientific interest and it was easy even for non-students to slip in as long as they did not cause trouble. On more than one occasion a ripple of anticipation passed through the listeners as a prostitute in full war-paint came in, sat in one of the back rows to see for herself what the great man was like, and then left as silently as she had come. Einstein would continue unchecked; but it was clear from his quizzical half-smile that he noticed.

Every Thursday afternoon he attended the special students' physics seminar, watching for talent, listening to ideas, quite happy if even the youngest member of the group could suggest a line of thought worth following.

> When my turn came to give a talk, I was terribly nervous, [says Esther Salaman, then a young student in Berlin.] Einstein was in the front row, with his pipe; beside him was von Laue. Turning round after I had pointed to my slides, I saw in the semi-darkness Einstein looking at me as if to say "Don't worry". I was talking about some work on radioactivity done at the Cavendish Laboratory at Cambridge, which raised a difficult problem. A young lecturer got up and suggested a solution in a long statement, but I could not follow. Einstein came to my rescue. "Clever, but not true," he said ("*Schlau, aber nicht wahr*"), and he restated the problem, and said what we knew and did not know about it so clearly and simply that everyone was satisfied.

There were also the seminars organised by von Laue at which the latest scientific papers would be discussed by Planck, Nernst, Haber, Lise Meitner or Einstein. These members of the university staff would occupy the front row of the old university building in which the meetings were held. Behind them there often sat physicists from the larger German industrial firms, invited men whose presence in the rarified upper atmosphere of the academic world was a sign of the co-operation which had strengthened the country's industrial sinews since the start of the century.

Then the talking started. "Sometimes he would step up to the blackboard," says Professor Cornelius Lanczos who was his assistant for a while. "Then, all at once, what had seemed complicated seemed simple." The transformation was stimulating. In these early 1920s Einstein was at the height of his powers as a creative physicist, confident of his own abilities, still believing that just one more heave on the intellectual rope would bring victory and an explanation of the mysteries which clouded the quantum theory. His position was very comparable to that of the assured company who half a century earlier believed that the natural world by that time contained few secrets. Before them, only just over the horizon, had lain Rutherford's nuclear atom; before Einstein lay the indeterminacy in physics which would end the world he knew.

Before him also lay a fresh and daunting experience: investigation of the unified field problem, a problem with which he knew that he was making little or no progress despite the recurrent but illusory signs of success. The reason was not merely that the 1920s were Einstein's forties, and that as they ran out he drew farther away from the magic age at which the creative scientist — in contrast to the artist who utilises experience as well as logic — is usually admitted to have shot his bolt. Einstein was genius enough to have broken this "finished at forty" convention as he broke many others. But after 1920 something more was involved. As he turned to the unified field, his work became increasingly that of the mathematician rather than the physicist. It was no longer so much the investigation of the natural world which presented difficulties as the presentation of known facts within an adequate mathematical structure. This change of emphasis came at an unfortunate moment. For the mathematical stockpile of the preceding century was now almost exhausted and few mathematicians had been building a new one. Einstein, moving ever more deeply into the subject, was for the first time in his life handicapped by a lack of instruments, of the mathematical tools which he knew to be essential if the job were to be tackled properly. Thus in the speciality to which he increasingly devoted his energies Einstein found himself blocked in a way he had not previously experienced. Yet even this was only half the story. For as he turned to mathematics his old intuitive sense of physics began to fall away. Like an artist turning to sculpture after a lifetime of painting, he began to lose the "feel" of the medium he knew so well. He was still Einstein. He was still head and shoulders above the rest. But it was to be a shorter head and shoulders, and in the battle royal over quantum mechanics that lay only a decade ahead his view was to be that much more restricted.

Something of this shows in the photographs. He was always the introvert Einstein compared with the extrovert Rutherford. Nevertheless, until he began to tackle the unified field seriously — and until he found himself foxed by the developments of quantum mechanics — he had much the same confidence as Rutherford, accused of being on the crest of the wave and answering: "Well, I made the wave, didn't I — at least to some extent." The transformation was noticeable from the mid-1920s onwards and it was not entirely age or the deepening tones of the international situation that created it. For the first time in his life Einstein was getting out of his depth in scientific waters.

All this was as yet no more than the smallest cloud on the horizon. He was still the supreme master rather than the old master. This comes through clearly in memories of a seminar on statistical mechanics held for graduate students, in the winter of 1921–22.

> I was finishing my doctor's thesis in mathematics and was probably the only mathematician in the group, [says Max Herzburger, later one of the world's greatest instrumental opticians.] Each student who had to give one of the talks was attached to a professor who helped him prepare his remarks, and I had the great fortune to be attached to Dr. Einstein. I frequently visited him and went with him for walks in the nearby park to discuss the problems of my lecture. The discussions were unforgettable. He took nothing as certain truth merely because it was written in books, and he was always asking questions which led to a deeper understanding of the problem.

The impression on Denis Gabor, then another young student, is as vivid now as half a century ago.

> I can still hear his voice, [he writes] and I could repeat some of his sayings verbatim. On some occasions he took the floor, and one was particularly unforgettable. One doctor, who later became very famous as the theoretician of electrical circuits, but who at that time was a very shy young man, made rather a bad job of Einstein's famous elucidation of Planck's law of radiation. Einstein went to the blackboard and started by saying that the job was to reconcile Wien's Law with Rayleigh's so that they would contradict one another as little as possible. By the way, he went on, Wien found his law by noticing how similar the radiation curves are to Maxwell's law. "You see," he continued, "that the saying of Oxenstiern — 'with how little wisdom the world is governed' — is true also in science. What the individual contributes to it is very little. The whole is of course admirable." He then went on to give with enormous gusto his dissertation which is found in all books on physics. I have never known anybody who enjoyed science so sensuously as Einstein. Physics melted in his mouth!

Also present on this occasion was the young Hungarian who became the *deus ex machina* of Einstein's later years, an extraordinary character well meriting his soubriquet of "the grey eminence of physics". This was Leo Szilard, the man who on March 12th, 1934 — more than four years before Otto Hahn split the uranium atom, more than five years before Einstein's famous letter to Roosevelt — applied for a patent covering the laws of a nuclear chain reaction and later filed it as a secret Admiralty patent because of his "conviction that if a nuclear chain reaction can be made to work it can be used to set up violent explosions". In 1922 Szilard was only twenty-four. But he was a student in whom Einstein quickly saw one of those men, rich in ideas, who create intellectual and spiritual life wherever they are. He soon became a regular visitor to the Haberlandstrasse home.

Both Szilard and Einstein were theoreticians; but both had a complementary side to their interests, as though a miniature-painter were to take up carpentry as a hobby. Thus Szilard had a practical inventive flair that tied in with Einstein's long experience in the Berne Patent Office. One result was a series of joint patents, lodged in Britain and the United States as well as in Germany, for what was then a revolutionary form of heat exchange refrigerator. Some recollections claim that Elsa expected Einstein to make a fortune from the patents; others, more plausibly, claim that the hopes were Szilard's. Little came of the scheme although the Einstein-Szilard heat-pump, which provides its essential mechanism, has become a feature of many post-war nuclear power stations.

Einstein's self-imposed duties at the university, his collaboration with Freundlich at the Potsdam Observatory and his work at the Kaiser Wilhelm Institute would have been enough to occupy the mental energies of a normal man; to him, it was the background to more important things. What still concerned him most was any indication that he, or physicists elsewhere in the world, were touching things nearer the heart of nature. Thus he was a familiar figure at conferences, picking out the men he wanted to meet but dodging the social round. He conferred with Bohr in Denmark, and was a frequent visitor to Holland where he never missed a chance of seeing Lorentz.

In Leiden he usually stayed with the Ehrenfests, writing his name on the huge white wall of the study that did duty for a visitors' book and relaxing as he did in few other places.

In Berlin he would take time off with Max Planck, carrying his violin round on informal social visits — as far as anything could be informal with Planck — and after dinner enjoying duets with his host as pianist. His small circle of artists, industrialists and literary people could almost be considered "cronies". In his own mild way, he enjoyed good food and drink with a peasant heartiness and years later looked in astonishment at a colleague who turned down a glass of wine. "One should not neglect the pleasures that nature provides," was his comment. Yet Berlin, with its undercurrent of anti-Semitism,

with its sense of still being the centre of a struggle for power between
two diametrically opposed forces, had a near-the-brink atmosphere
that was lacking in Holland. In Leiden Einstein could not only talk
physics as easily as draw breath; here he could still find something
of the non-political atmosphere he had known before his Berlin days.
Here he could be quite uninhibited, quite relaxed — and when he
allowed himself to be, Einstein was a good and total relaxer.

He also wanted the company of children, although it was not
in his nature to admit it. Therefore he was a happy man when he
took Ehrenfest's small children and their companions down to the
sea-coast dunes a few miles away and let them bury him up to the
neck in the sands without a trace of concern. He was happy when he
stood at the open windows of Ehrenfest's study on a summer evening,
playing the violin in his shirtsleeves while Ehrenfest accompanied him
on the grand piano in the book-lined room. How often he must have
thought back a decade to the rejected chance of spending a life in the
comparable quiet of Utrecht, only a few miles away. And yet
how often, being Einstein, did he not congratulate himself on keeping
his priorities right, on following his star to Berlin where a combination of free time and intellectual stimulus had enabled him to crack
the nut of the General Theory.

Even in Leiden, he could be plucked out of his freedom. Thus
there is a record of one uproarious occasion on which Einstein and
Ehrenfest were awakened by the telephone from an after-lunch siesta.
Queen Wilhelmina, the Prince Regent, and Emma the Queen Mother,
were visiting the Marine School in Leiden. They had heard that Einstein was "in residence", and they requested that he and his host
should attend the reception being held later that same day.

No question or answer was needed to pose the first problem.
Einstein knew that his nearest black suit was five hundred miles
away in Berlin. Ehrenfest knew that his solitary specimen was lying
in a mothproofed trunk in the attic. Frau Ehrenfest rose to the occasion by telephoning several professors of Einstein's build and begging
them to have their suits delivered as soon as possible. A few hours
later the two men presented themselves to their Majesties, Einstein in
a suit that fitted where it touched, Ehrenfest smelling strongly of
mothballs.

This was only the beginning of a difficult evening. After a
formal shaking of hands by the Queen, the two men tried to disappear in the crowd, duty done, honour satisfied — and now to get
out of those clothes. They had not gone far when they were cut off
by the Queen Mother's adjutant and asked to return. "I noticed that

you tried to escape me, but I managed to catch you," she said according to the story that Einstein and his friend told their neighbour. "Surely you could offer your hand to an old lady too."

Einstein's regular visits to Leiden, the amiable round of work in Berlin, his interest in the affairs of Zionism in general and of the Hebrew University in particular, as well as a steadily increasing involvement in the problem of world peace, were all interrupted in 1925 by a lecture tour to South America. In itself, this was of little importance in his life. Indirectly, it was of great significance since it caused him to turn down an invitation to the California Institute of Technology later in the same year. Had he accepted, it is unlikely that he would have spent the last two decades of his life in Princeton.

There were many reasons why Einstein would have enjoyed a visit to the United States in 1925, not the least being that two quite separate but equally important confirmations of his "heuristic viewpoint" of 1905 had come from American scientists. The first was given by Robert Millikan who as a professor at the University of Chicago had in 1915 determined the size of the charge on a single electron. But he had also done something more. "I spent ten years of my life testing that 1905 equation of Einstein's", he wrote, "and contrary to all my expectations, I was compelled in 1915 to assert its unambiguous experimental verification in spite of its unreasonableness, since it seemed to violate everything that we knew about the interference of light."

Eight years later Arthur Compton found that when X-rays were scattered by matter the wavelength of some was lengthened; in other words, their energy was decreased. The unequivocal way in which this confirmed Einstein's ideas of two decades previously is made clear in a key paragraph of the paper describing what soon came to be known as the Compton effect.

> We find [Compton wrote] that the wavelength and the intensity of the scattered rays are what they should be if a quantum of radiation bounced from an electron, just as one billiard ball bounces from another. Not only this, but we actually observe the recoiling billiard ball, or electron, from which the quantum has bounced, and we find that it moves with just the speed it should if a quantum had bumped into it. The obvious conclusion would be that X rays, and so also light, consist of discrete units, proceeding in definite directions, each unit possessing the energy $h\upsilon$ and the corresponding momentum $h\lambda$. So in a recent letter to me Sommerfeld has expressed the opinion that this discovery of the change of wavelength of radiation, due to scattering, sounds the death-knell of the wave theory of radiation.

It was not to be quite that. But it was to lead on, easily enough, to the idea that was to develop during the next few years: that not only radiation but matter itself might be both corpuscle and wave.

Millikan had met Einstein briefly during 1921 in Chicago. Later in the year he moved to California as head of the Troop College of Technology at Pasadena, renamed the California Institute of Technology, and by 1925 he was attracting to it not only a galaxy of brilliant staff but also as many distinguished visitors as could be encouraged into his orbit. There was one particular reason for thinking that Einstein might soon be among them, quite apart from any general desire to discuss physics at first hand with his American counterparts.

For it was at Mount Wilson Observatory, high in the Sierra above Pasadena, that Dayton Miller had for years been carrying out a complex repetition of the Michelson-Morley experiment whose verdict he still hoped to alter. In the spring of 1921 he announced results which at first glance appeared to do this. They broke down on investigation, but four years later he issued further figures. Einstein's reaction to the second announcement was shown by a letter to Millikan in June in which he inferred that if Miller's figures were correct, then the whole theory would collapse. Other scientists, to whom Miller announced his results at a special meeting, lacked Einstein's qualifications. "Not one of them thought for a moment of abandoning relativity," Michael Polanyi has commented. "Instead — as Sir Charles Darwin once described it — they sent Miller home to get his results right." Einstein later came round to much the same view. He would have been further persuaded by his friend Max Born, who visited Mount Wilson in the winter of 1925–26 and operated Miller's interferometer. "I found it very shaky and unreliable," Born later wrote; "a tiny movement of one's hand, or a slight cough, made the interference-fringes so unstable that no readings were possible. From then onwards I completely lost faith in Miller's results."

At Mount Wilson there was also Walter S. Adams, who had shown some years earlier that the Companion to Sirius — the star later known as Sirius B — must be of the phenomenal density of about one ton to the cubic inch. At the beginning of the century this would have been considered impossible. But Rutherford, showing that the atom consisted largely of empty space, had thereby opened up the possibility of superdense stars in which sub-atomic particles were squeezed together in a concentration unknown on earth. Eddington pointed out soon after the success of the 1919 eclipse expeditions that such stars must have extremely intense gravitational fields. If

Adams were correct, the "Einstein shift" exercised by Sirius B should be thirty times that exercised by the sun, and this would bring it well within the range of experimental test. Adams took up the challenge and by the beginning of 1925 was planning experiments which did eventually show a shift towards the red. Results were not precisely those predicted by the General Theory but they were near enough to be considered as additional confirmation. If the presence of Millikan as head of Caltech and of Adams at Mount Wilson was not in itself enough to attract Einstein to Pasadena, there was also Edwin Hubble, now using the observatory's 100-inch telescope to open up the study of the universe beyond the galaxy and raise fresh questions about the "Einstein world" of general relativity.

The new institute thus had a general leaning towards the cosmology that Einstein had forced science to consider. Eddington had been a visitor in 1924, and it was at a dinner held in his honour that Professor W. H. Williams, himself a specialist in relativity, had produced "The Einstein and the Eddington", a parody of "The Walrus and the Carpenter", following a round of golf with Eddington. Recited at a Faculty Club dinner, it went as follows:

> The Einstein and the Eddington
>     Were counting up their score;
> The Einstein's card showed ninety-eight
>     And Eddington's was more,
> And both lay bunkered in the trap
>     And both stood up and swore.
>
> I hate to see, the Einstein said
>     Such quantities of sand;
> Just why they placed a bunker here
>     I cannot understand;
> If one could smooth this landscape out,
>     I think it would be grand.
>
> If seven maids with seven mops
>     Would sweep the fairway clean
> I'm sure that I could make this hole
>     In less than seventeen.
> I doubt it, said the Eddington,
>     Your slice is pretty mean.
>
> The time has come, said Eddington,
>     To talk of many things;

Of cubes and clocks and meter-sticks,
    And why a pendulum swings,
And how far space is out of plumb,
    And whether time has wings.

I learned at school the apple's fall
    To gravity was due,
But now you tell me that the cause
    Is merely G mu nu.
I cannot bring myself to think
    That this is really true.

And space, it has dimensions four,
    Instead of only three.
The square on the hypotenuse
    Ain't what it used to be.
It grieves me sore, the things you've done
    To plane geometry.

You hold that time is badly warped,
    That even light is bent;
I think I get the idea there,
    If this is what you meant;
The mail the postman brings today,
    Tomorrow will be sent.

The shortest line, Einstein replied,
    Is not the one that's straight;
It curves around upon itself,
    Much like a figure eight,
And if you go too rapidly
    You will arrive too late.

But Easter day is Christmas time
    And far away is near,
And two and two is more than four
    And over there is here.
You may be right, said Eddington,
    It seems a trifle queer.

Pasadena's concern with relativity was certainly strong enough
to augment Einstein's general interest in the work of American phy-

sicists, and early in 1925 he tentatively agreed to visit the institute later in the year. However, he had previously arranged to visit South America — partly to lecture at the Argentine State University, partly in the hope of coaxing money into Zionist funds from wealthy Jews. He loved South America but was slightly embarrassed by the fulsome welcome of the German colony whose members metaphorically clasped him to their Teutonic bosom. As usual, he did not spare himself, and was forced to cancel the proposed visit to Pasadena.

In 1927 and in 1929 Millikan renewed the invitation. Again Einstein was forced to decline.

Thus the link with California — and with the work of Hubble and Hale at Mount Wilson which was dramatically to affect Einstein's cosmological outlook — did not begin until 1930, and was to last a mere three years. Then he was swept into the arms of Abraham Flexner and the Institute for Advanced Study at Princeton, a development which would probably not have taken place had his links with Pasadena been more permanent by that time. The result was that throughout the later 1920s Einstein remained in Europe, and for most of the time in Germany, ever more deeply involved in two major dramas. The first* concerned post-war Germany's struggle first to pull herself back into European political respectability and then to hold her position, a struggle closely linked with her attitude to rearmament. It was a drama which for Einstein rose to its climax in 1933 with his decision to remain outside Germany for ever and his breathtaking apostasy of pacifism that for many disciples had all the horror of a good man suddenly cutting his throat.

Yet this story of Germany between the wars was in some ways less important for Einstein than the scientific drama which from now onwards increasingly overshadowed his life. This concerned the riddle of the dual nature of things, by this time being extended from radiation to matter itself, and its solution by a method which led on to the dethronement of causality, up to now a cornerstone of physics. For as the physicists of the post-war world began to explain the duality of nature inherent in Einstein's conception of the photon, it eventually became difficult to fault one uncomfortable conclusion: that in the sub-atomic world, probabilities, rather than events, were all that could be forecast from any particular set of circumstances.

This was a conclusion against which Einstein battled with conservative determination, fighting a stubborn rearguard action and then, when all appeared lost, taking up a stance which his friend Max Born described as aloof and sceptical — "a tragedy, for him, as he gropes his way in loneliness, and for us who miss our leader and standard-bearer".

The story began during the early 1920s as it became evident that the great advances in physics started in the first decade of the century were losing their head of steam. They had solved individual problems, but they had done nothing to replace the all-embracing pattern of classical physics which they had first questioned, then shattered. Planck's quantum theory, and Einstein's photons; Rutherford's first ground-plan of the nuclear atom and Bohr's disturbing explanation of it — these had each provided isolated answers to isolated problems. Yet in the process they seemed to have produced more riddles than they had solved. Thus Wolfgang Pauli, one of the most outspoken of the younger theorists, could write to a friend: "Physics is very muddled again at the moment; it is much too hard for me anyway, and I wish I were a movie comedian or something like that and had never heard anything about physics."

Yet within a few years the confusions of this situation had been drastically altered by a fresh picture of the sub-atomic world. This new conception which came into being during the 1920s has been considerably modified during the last forty years. Yet its fundamentals have stood the test and have tended to show it as a natural evolution from the ideas which started with the electron of Lorentz and J. J. Thomson and were altered and expanded by Planck, Einstein, Rutherford and Bohr.

A fundamental premise of classical physics was that events followed each other in succession on a basis which could be predicted if only one understood the laws of nature and had sufficient facts. Laplace's belief that the positions and the velocities of all the objects of the universe would provide sufficient data for a prediction of the future might be an extravagant illustration of the idea. Yet this was little more than a grand if fantastic extrapolation of the idea that events could be determined not only in the laboratory but throughout the whole range of human experience. Certain factors in the quantum theory had first cast a ray of doubt upon this comfortable assumption; the electron in the Bohr atom, jumping from one orbit to another without obvious cause, tended to increase this doubt. Was there, perhaps, no real "cause" for such movements. Though they could be "predicted" in one sense of the word, must this forever be merely a statistical prediction, possible only because of the vast numbers involved? And if there were no identifiable "cause", if events at the sub-atomic level were governed solely by chance, might this not also be true at other levels? Might not the whole conception of causality in the universe be merely an illusion?

This possibility had already gravely disturbed Einstein. It had disturbed not only the remnants of his belief in classical physics but his sense of rightness in an ordered and orderly world, and as early as January 1920 he had voiced his doubts to Max Born,* saying how very loath he would be to abandon complete causality.

Thus the new concept of the sub-atomic world was even by 1924 beginning to produce a gulf. Bohr, Born, and a number of Einstein's other contemporaries, as well as many of the younger men who were in great part responsible for the new idea, readily jumped the gap. Einstein stayed where he was. Therefore the scene in many ways paralleled that into which he had launched his theory of relativity two decades earlier. But then he had been in the iconoclastic vanguard; now he took up station with the small conservative rearguard.

A chronological account of the story shows revealingly how the different groups of thinkers, starting to clear the confusion of the early 1920s from different points of attack, produced two different concepts of nature which were quickly synthesised into one, a process which transformed the newly-conceived wave mechanics into the more embracing quantum mechanics.**

The first move came in 1923, and it was more directly linked with Einstein himself than is commonly realised. It was made by Louis de Broglie, younger brother of Maurice de Broglie who had been co-secretary of the first Solvay Congress, a French physicist who had begun by studying medieval history, changed to physics in midstream, and worked on radio during the war. During his early studies before 1914 de Broglie had been captivated by relativity. "When, after a long absence, I returned to my studies with greater maturity at the end of World War I," he has written, "it was again the ideas of Einstein" which guided him. "I had a sudden inspiration," he says. "Einstein's wave particle dualism was an absolutely general phenomenon extending to all physical nature, and, that being the case, the motion of all particles, photons, electrons, protons, or any others, must be associated with the propagation of a wave."

---

* Einstein's preoccupation with this theme from 1920 until the end of his life is referred to regularly throughout the long series of letters published in *Briefwechsel 1916-1955 Albert Einstein/Max Born* (Nymphenbuger, München, 1969; Macmillan, London, 1970).

** Twenty-one of the key letters by Einstein, Schrödinger, Planck and Lorentz which deal with this period, together with an illuminating introduction by Martin J. Klein are published in *Letters on Wave Mechanics* (Philosophical Library, New York, 1967; Vision Press, London, 1967).

De Broglie outlined this unconventional proposal — "the suggestion made... purely on grounds of intellectual beauty, to ascribe wave nature to ponderable particles" as it has been described — in three papers published in the Academie des Sciences' *Comptes Rendus in* 1923.

> In the months that followed [he says] I did my utmost to develop and extend my ideas still further in preparation of my doctoral thesis. Before doing so, I asked Paul Langevin, who was so well versed in the theory of relativity and in quantum theory, to examine my conclusions, and he saw fit to ask me for a second copy which he proposed to send to Einstein. Einstein quickly realised that my generalisation of his theory of light quanta was bound to open entirely new horizons to atomic physics, and wrote back to Langevin saying that I had lifted a corner of the great veil.

What was revealed behind the veil was more startling than the earlier idea that light might be considered as a collection of particles at one moment and as a series of waves at another. De Broglie's idea was not of the either/or variety; instead, he postulated that particles such as electrons were guided by what were soon to be called "de Broglie waves" or "matter waves". These waves produced the interference effects that were familiar to scientists in their studies of light. Where the interference effects added up, they produced the "preferred orbits" which Bohr had already postulated, and within these the movements of the particles were governed by the laws of wave-propagation.

While de Broglie was developing this revolutionary idea for his doctoral thesis, Einstein again came into the picture. In the summer of 1924 he received from S. N. Bose, an Indian physicist of Dacca University, a short paper on "Planck's Law and the Hypothesis of Light Quanta", which considered radiation as a form of gas consisting of photons. Einstein was so impressed by the paper that he himself translated it into German and sent it to the editor of the *Zeitschrift für Physik* who published it in July. The reason for his interest was simple. He had seen immediately that it was possible to extend Bose's statistical methods to ordinary atoms — "Bose-Einstein statistics" as they became known — if it were assumed, as de Broglie was assuming, that material particles had the simultaneous wave and particulate properties he himself had assumed for radiation two decades earlier. "His quick and immediate response... proved ultimately to be the turning point in my career as a scientist," says Bose. Einstein developed this theme in two papers for the Prussian

Academy. Before he read the second he had received from his friend Langevin a draft of de Broglie's doctoral thesis, and he stressed in his paper how useful he had found de Broglie's ideas. "The scientific world of the time hung on every one of Einstein's words," de Broglie has written, "for he was then at the peak of his fame. By stressing the importance of wave-mechanics, the illustrious scientist had done a great deal to hasten its development. Without his paper my thesis might not have been appreciated until very much later."

This was indeed so. But Einstein's comment on de Broglie's dissertation had also been noted by Erwin Schrödinger, a thirty-seven-year-old Viennese who was later to show a remarkable facility for riding across the frontiers between science and the humanities without noticing their existence, a man of two cultures who could claim ironically of later cosmic ray studies that they promised "the stepped-up realisation of the plan to exterminate mankind which is close to all our hearts". Schrödinger, in no doubt about the debt he owed to Einstein, now exhibited one of those brief spurts of concentrated genius which have more than once changed the face of physics. Within four months he erected the basic structure of what became known as wave mechanics. In this, the emphasis of the de Broglie waves on the electron particle was taken a step farther. The particle itself now gave way to what was, in effect, a standing electron wave; instead of being a wave-controlled corpuscle it became a corpuscular wave.

What had thus occurred within a very few years was a steady merging of the particle and wave concepts. The electron — and possibly the other particles about which physicists were still comparatively ignorant — had changed from being either a particle or a wave to being one under certain circumstances and the other under different circumstances. Now it appeared that it was both at the same time. Here it seemed that science had run up not only against "common sense", which was already suspect when it began to deal with events in the sub-atomic world, but with rational logic. For could anything really be one thing and its opposite at one and the same time?

Waiting to provide the answer was Niels Bohr. His answer was an unqualified "Yes". He said so in the "principle of complementarity", which proposed that whether light or electrons were waves or moving particles depended entirely on the specific properties which were being investigated; the subject under study had dual characteristics, and whether it conformed to those we knew as wave-like properties or to those we knew as particulate depended solely on how we studied it. Bohr had his own characteristic way of explaining what he called the poetry of complementarity, and his disciple L. Rosenfeld describes how Bohr used a scene in Japan to illustrate it.

> At sunset the top of Fujiyama disappeared behind a curtain of gold-fringed clouds: the black mass of the mountain, surmounted by this fulgent crown, conveyed an impression of awe and majesty. On the next morning, it offered an entirely different spectacle: the pointed summit alone, covered with shining snow, emerged from the dense mist filling the valley; the landscape was radiating gladness and joy. So, Bohr mused, the two half-mountains together are not simply equal to a mountain: to each belongs a peculiar, individual impression, and the two are complementary.

Schrödinger's wave mechanics, which were quickly seen to provide a plausible explanation for much that had not previously been explicable, was thus credible on the grounds that reality is what you make it. This was disturbing enough to those who believed that all ignorance in science could be removed by an addition of knowledge. But more was to follow.

Even before de Broglie and Schrödinger had begun to explain the inner workings of the atom by what was essentially a physicist's combination of wave and particle ideas, a totally different approach was being made by Werner Heisenberg, a young German in his early twenties. Heisenberg started from Mach's assumption that theories should be based on physically verifiable phenomena, and in trying to discover the structure of the atom he seized upon the spectral lines that were the individual fingerprints of each element's atoms. The wave lengths for these could be determined by using a mathematical system called matrix mechanics or quantum mechanics. Thus by 1927 the de Broglie–Schrödinger picture of the electron was being matched by a purely mathematical explanation of the atom which used the spectral lines as a starting point but soon abandoned discrete pictorial representation for a discrete set of numbers.

These two advances had in fact been along parallel paths. And they were now brought together by arguments which effectively showed that both explanations were saying the same thing in different languages. Schrödinger made the first move in uniting the two ideas and Born carried it further by providing a statistical interpretation of Schrödinger's wave conception; but he did so only by admitting that he was dealing with large numbers of random events and that his results dealt solely with their probability. The suggestion that a satisfactory picture of the physical world could consist not of a description of events but of their probabilities had already been made in Heisenberg's famous "uncertainty principle". This showed convincingly that at the subatomic level the mere act of observation affected what one was observing, and that the nearer one reached an accurate figure for either the position or the momentum of a particle, the less accurate became the figure for the other. Moreover the uncertainty in the two factors was found to be linked, as though by a master craftsman, with a figure which had by this time become familiar: the Planck's constant of the quantum theory, discovered a quarter of a century earlier.

At this point, a stage in one of the great dramas of physics was brought to a satisfactory conclusion. De Broglie had played his part with Heisenberg. Schrödinger and Born had contributed in equal measure to the new conception, and both, forced to leave Germany a few years later, were to disagree on its implications. Planck with the magician's wand of his universal constant and Einstein with his power to influence men's minds by example, had played significant parts. Together they had produced "the new physics". Now they had to lie on the bed they had made.

The significant outcome of these events was, as de Broglie put it many years later, that quantum physics now appeared to be

> governed by statistical laws and not by any causal mechanisms, hidden or otherwise. The "wave" of wave mechanics ceased to be a physical reality and became a solution of partial differential equations of the classical type, and thus the means of representing the probability of phenomena taking place. The corpuscle, too, was turned into a mere phantom — we can no longer say "at such an instant a corpuscle will be found in such a place with such an energy or momentum", but only "at such an instant there will be such a probability that a corpuscle will be found at such and such a place". In other words, while a given experiment can either localise a corpuscle or ascertain its momentum, it cannot do both.

There were subtle differences in the manner in which the physicists involved regarded this central feature of indeterminacy which occupied a key position in the new picture of the subatomic world. While Born, Heisenberg and Bohr accepted it without qualification, Einstein and Planck accepted it only with the strongest qualifications. Yet these two were the very men who a quarter of a century earlier had pulled into physics the very ideas which they now thought of as its Trojan horse.

The break with the old world which this new concept epitomises can be illustrated by two statements. One is by Sir Basil Schonland, who describes the new world in *The Atomists.*

> It appeared experimentally proven [he says] that at the bottom of all phenomena there were to be discerned laws of chance which made it impossible to think of an ordered deterministic world; the basic laws of nature appeared to be fundamentally statistical and indeterminate, governed by the purest chance. On a large scale they could appear exactly the reverse but this was only because they involved such a vast number of events. They had the monumental stability of an enormous life insurance company though, like it, they rested on individual uncertainty.

This was the world now presented, as Max Born put it, to the generation to which Einstein, Bohr and he belonged. It was a generation which had been

> taught that there exists an objective physical world, which unfolds itself according to immutable laws independent of us; we are watching this process like the audience watching a play in a theatre. Einstein still believes that this should be the relation between the scientific observer and his subject. Quantum mechanics, however, interprets the experience gained in atomic physics in a different way. We may compare the observer of a physical phenomenon not with the audience of a theatrical performance, but with that of a football game where the act of watching, accompanied by applauding or hissing, has a marked influence on the speed and concentration of the players, and thus on what is watched. In fact, a better simile is life itself, where audience and actors are the same persons. It is the action of the experimentalist who designs the apparatus, which determines essential features of the observations. Hence there is no objectively existing situation, as was supposed to exist in classical physics.

The distressing position in which Einstein now found himself was not unique. Robert Oppenheimer has pointed out how "many of the men who have contributed to the great changes in science have really been very unhappy over what they have been forced to do" and cites not only Planck and Einstein but Kepler and de Broglie. The process is not restricted to physics. Lord Conway, bemoaning the *vulgarisation des Alpes* which his own guidebooks had done so much to bring about, has pointed out that "each generation makes of the world more or less the kind of place they dream it should be, and each when its day is done is often in a mood to regret the work of its own hands and to praise the conditions that obtained when it was young."

So with Einstein. At times he was wryly humorous about his inability to accept the new world which his colleagues had created. Phillip Frank visited him in Berlin, apparently in 1932, and they began to talk of the new physics. Then, says Frank,

> Einstein said, partly as a joke, something like this: "A new fashion has now arisen in physics. By means of ingeniously formulated theoretical experiments it is proved that certain physical magnitudes cannot be measured, or, to put it more precisely, that according to accepted natural laws the investigated bodies behave in such a way as to baffle all attempts at measurement. From this the conclusion is drawn that it is completely meaningless to retain these magnitudes in the language of physics. To speak about them is pure metaphysics."

And when Frank pointed out to Einstein that he had invented the fashion in 1905, Einstein answered: "A good joke should not be repeated too often." More cogently, he explained to Infeld — the Pole who had visited him in Berlin and who was later to join him in the United States — "Yes, I may have started it, but I regarded these ideas as temporary. I never thought that others would take them so much more seriously than I did."

His feelings went deep, and were epitomised in the famous phrase — linked with his name as firmly as the equation $E = mc^2$ — which he used in a letter to Max Born in December 1926. Quantum mechanics was very imposing, he said, but he was convinced that God did not throw dice. That remark was altered, repeated, paraphrased, and was to go round the world second and third-hand. But the central meaning was clear and unqualified — that, in its usually repeated form, "God does not play dice with the world."

Thus he regarded the statistical laws necessary to explain the subatomic world as merely second-best; he could not accept them as the fundamental laws of physical reality — these, he believed, should determine events themselves rather than their probabilities. In time, when much more had been learned, it would be possible to throw overboard the current, purely statistical, explanations and replace them with something better. More satisfactory laws would be discovered. Eventually men would find out how a non-dice-throwing God had made the world. This was the stance which he took up in the late 1920s. He retained it, almost unchanged, to the end of his life.

The formulation of this new idea of the subatomic world took place between the publication of de Broglie's papers in 1924, and the summer and autumn of 1927 which saw the publication of Heisenberg's Uncertainty Principle and the exposition of Bohr's complementarity principle. But most physicists still retained qualifications. Most realised that in matters of this sort there is no finality and that the solution of one set of problems usually produces another; most realised that it would be unwise to take up too dogmatic a stance. Then, in October, they were forced out of their corners, compelled to stand up and be counted, to state their loyalties. The occasion was the Fifth Solvay Congress in 1927. Together with the Sixth which was held three years later in 1930, it marked a notable change in Einstein's position in the scientific world.

The general subject of discussion at the Fifth Congress was "Electrons and Photons" and the list of speakers and papers made it clear that differing views of the wave-like or corpuscular nature of matter would be hammered out energetically; so, it was equally clear, would the underlying riddle of causality versus indeterminacy, that ghost which European physicists had raised and which now looked over their shoulders wherever they went. Lorentz came from Holland, Sir William Bragg with his son Lawrence from England, Arthur Compton from the United States, Born and Heisenberg from Göttingen, Einstein from Berlin, Schrödinger from Stuttgart and de Broglie from Paris. And from Copenhagen there came Bohr, anxious to explain his complementarity principle, strongly supported by Heisenberg. "At the Solvay meetings," he later wrote, "Einstein had from their beginning been a most prominent figure, and several of us came to the conference with great anticipation to learn his reactions to the latest stage of the development which, to our view, went far in clarifying the problems which he had himself from the outset elicited so ingeniously."

At the start of the conference, Bohr threw down the gauntlet with an account of the epistemological problems presented by the latest developments in physics. He agreed that certainty had been removed from the subatomic world, that there was now, as he put it elsewhere, "the impossibility of any sharp separation between the behaviour of atomic objects and the interaction with the measuring instruments which serve to define the conditions under which the phenomena appear". This meant that the wave or particle concept was determined by the type of experiment. Yet even when it had been decided to study the wave or the particle characteristics, Heisenberg's uncertainty principle still masked an exact picture of what nature was like. The trapdoor of indeterminacy had been opened and those involved would have to make the best they could of it.

Einstein made very little. Strangely perhaps, he read no paper at the Fifth Congress — in fact it is often overlooked that his account of specific heats in 1911 is the only Solvay paper he ever did read. But when those attending the Congress met after the sessions in the Fondation Universitaire — the university club founded after the First World War with the residue of the Hoover Fund — Einstein came out into the open. He still disliked uncertainty, and Bohr's complementarity, and he bluntly said so.

Then the discussion opened out. Lorentz did his best to give the floor to only one speaker at a time. But everyone felt strongly. Everyone wanted to put his own view. There was the nearest thing to an uproar that could occur in such distinguished company, and in the near-confusion Ehrenfest moved up to the blackboard which successive speakers had used and wrote on it: "The Lord did there confound the language of all the earth."

On that and following evenings, Bohr made abortive attempts to convince Einstein of his views. Ingenious experiments were postulated by Einstein in which it was sought to show that with the right equipment all the characteristics of an electron could theoretically be discovered. Each time Bohr proved that this was not so. Both sides stuck to their guns. Einstein maintained that the statistical nature of the quantum theory and the apparent impossibility of discovering all the characteristics of physical reality that sprang from it was merely the result of ignorance. In due course physicists would be able not merely to estimate the probability of an event happening but to discover whether it would happen. Bohr, and the many who supported him, claimed that indeterminacy was here a part of nature itself.

Strong passions and strong loyalties were aroused even though "a most humorous spirit animated the discussions", according to Bohr.

> On his side, Einstein mockingly asked us whether we could really believe that the providential authorities took recourse to dice-playing ("... *ob der liebe Gott würfelt*"), to which I replied by pointing at the great caution, already called for by ancient thinkers, in ascribing attributes to Providence in everyday language. I remember, also how at the peak of the discussion Ehrenfest, in his affectionate manner of teasing his friends, jokingly hinted at the apparent similarity between Einstein's attitude and that of the opponents of relativity theory; but instantly Ehrenfest added that he would not be able to find relief in his own mind before concord with Einstein was reached.

Schrödinger attempted to provide a causal interpretation for wave mechanics and de Broglie proposed what he described as a "double solution" which some felt tried to make the best of both worlds. But at the end of the day the field was occupied by Born, Bohr, Heisenberg, and by Paul Dirac whose statistical interpretations fitted in with the new uncertainty principle and all that went with it, and who was later to tower over the scene.

Throughout all this Einstein remained Einstein.

> During a fairly long walk, he made a profound impression on me and fully confirmed my faith in him, [writes de Broglie whose papers had started the avalanche.] I was particularly won over by his sweet disposition, by his general kindness, by his simplicity and his friendliness. Occasionally, gaiety would gain the upper hand and he would strike a more personal note and even disclose some detail of his day-to-day life. Then again, reverting to his characteristic mood of reflection and meditation, he would launch into a profound and original discussion of a variety of scientific and other problems.

To de Broglie, Einstein revealed an instinctive reason for his inability to accept the purely statistical interpretation of wave mechanics. It was a reason which linked him with Rutherford who used to state that "it should be possible to explain the laws of physics to a barmaid". Einstein, having a final discussion with de Broglie on the platform of the Gare du Nord in Paris, where they had travelled from Brussels to attend the Fresnel centenary celebrations, said "that all physical theories, their mathematical expressions apart, ought to lend themselves to so simple a description 'that even a child could understand them'." And what could be less simple than the statistical interpretations of wave mechanics?

None of the protagonists was willing to let go this particular argument and it was taken up with renewed vigour when the next Solvay Congress was held in 1930. The central problem still revolved round the one question: was it, or was it not, theoretically possible to ascertain the position of a particle and also its momentum at one specific moment?

In 1930 Einstein proposed a "thought-experiment", one that was theoretically possible even if ruled out by experimental limitations. The proposal was to enclose light within a mirror-lined box which was weighed. One photon would then be automatically released by a time-control mechanism within the box which would then be weighed again. From the change in mass it would be possible, using Einstein's equation, to calculate the energy or momentum of the photon which was released at one specific moment. At first, and even at second glance, Einstein appeared to have an unbreakable case. Only the following day did Bohr realise that Einstein had overlooked one thing: the effect of the weighing on the clock.

There have been many explanations of the results of this exchange but none clearer than that given by Barbara Cline, and it is worth quoting in full.

> Bohr's reasoning applied to any method of weighing, but to illustrate that reasoning most clearly he chose to imagine that Einstein's box of light was hung on a spring from a rigid scale. Thus when a photon was released the box would move in recoil. Its vertical position in relation to the earth's surface would change and therefore its position within the earth's gravitational field. According to the General Theory of Relativity, this change in spatial position would mean a change in the rate of the clock, preset and attached to the box. The change would be extremely small but in this case crucial. For, due to a chain of inevitable uncertainties: the uncertainty of the escaping photon's direction, therefore of the box's recoil, therefore of its position within the earth's gravitational field, the precise time when the photon was released from the box could *not* be determined. It was indeed indeterminable to the extent given by Heisenberg's law — the cornerstone of the Copenhagen interpretation. This was the way Bohr answered the serious challenge of Einstein, who had forgotten to apply his own General Theory of Relativity.

The argument, which had really started seven years earlier and had changed the face of physics, involved two separate but linked questions: was matter as well as radiation wave-like and yet corpuscular as well, depending only on how it was considered; and were the laws of the subatomic world the indeterminate laws of statistics. The first of these problems had the greater practical effect on the scientific world, and Sir William Bragg, the Director of the Royal Institution who had been present at the 1927 Congress, had once commented: "On Mondays, Wednesdays and Fridays we teach the wave theory and on Tuesdays and Saturdays the corpuscular theory." Forty years on, the synthesis had been made. "Everything that has already happened is particles, everything in the future is waves," states Sir Lawrence Bragg, Sir William's son and in turn the Director of the same Institution. "The advancing sieve of time coagulates waves into particles at the moment 'now'." On this Einstein had moved in step, seeing the contradiction as one with which he could cope, a contradiction of common sense no less amenable to reason than the apparent contradictions of relativity.

Indeterminacy was a riddle at a different level, more fundamental and, as far as Einstein was concerned, more important. Here his discomfiture — and it cannot be called less, however much his colleagues tried to soften the blow — ended the first series of battles in the long campaign he was to wage. They had altered his status in a small but certain way. To amend Snow's judgment that Einstein always remained in the Bradman class, he now appeared to have become a W. G. Grace in the Bradman era. His touch was as sure as ever, but it belonged to a previous age.

The gap remained throughout the years. At the height of the initial debate, early in 1927, Einstein showed his feelings at the end of a message to the Newton celebrations in England, concluding with the hope: "May the spirit of Newton's method give us the power to restore unison between physical reality and the profoundest characteristic of Newton's teaching — strict causality." Years afterwards he was just as hopeful.

He hoped on to the end. Just how little his hopes were justified is shown by Max Born, speaking three months after Einstein's death, at the conference held in Berne to celebrate the fiftieth anniversary of the Special Theory.

> A man of Einstein's greatness, who has achieved so much by thinking, has the right to go to the limit of the *a priori* method. Current physics has not followed him; it has continued to accumulate empirical facts, and to interpret them in a way which Einstein thoroughly disliked. For him a potential or a field component was a real natural object which changed according to definite deterministic laws. Modern physics operates with wave functions which, in their mathematical behaviour, are very similar to classical potentials, but do not represent real objects. They serve for determining the *probability* of finding real objects, whether these are particles, or electro-magnetic potentials, or other physical quantities.

A number of reasons can be adduced for the way in which Einstein thus began to slip from the mainstream of physics during the later 1920s. It can be claimed that the gem-like flame burned a little less gem-like as he diverted his energies into pacifism, the needs of the Hebrew University in Jerusalem, or the requirements of the Jewish Agency. Just as tenably, it can be argued that he spent more time in such pursuits because he felt his powers diminishing. More plausibly, it can be attributed to concentration on mathematics, so essential to his work on the unified field theory.

Yet the opposition which he maintained so stubbornly towards the indeterminacy of quantum mechanics was not based entirely on his inability to "see" it as he had "seen" many other innovations in physics. It was based on something more fundamental, upon an interior assumption about the world that had much more resemblance to religious faith than to the ever-questioning scepticism of science. Einstein believed that the universe had been designed so that its workings could be comprehensible; therefore these workings must conform to discoverable laws; thus there was no room for chance and indeterminacy — God, after, all, did not play the game that way. At a different level he stressed these beliefs in an interview in October, 1929, when the argument about quantum mechanics was at its height. "I claim credit for nothing," he said, at a mention of his modesty. "Everything is determined, the beginning as well as the end, by forces over which we have no control. It is determined for the insect as well as for the star. Human beings, vegetables or cosmic dust, we all dance to a mysterious tune, intoned in the distance by an invisible piper."

Although he felt so strongly about the problem which was to cut him off from his colleagues, Einstein still laid the cards fairly on the table, sometimes with an objectivity that tended to mask his feelings. This was shown when, early in 1928, he lectured at Davos in Switzerland. He was very vulnerable to any call from that country and responded to an appeal that was to have important repercussions. The first was a serious breakdown in health. Then, as a result of this, there came the employment of Helen Dukas, a young German woman who for the next quarter of a century was to be his secretary, general factotum and, after the death of Elsa, dedicated watch-dog.

The appeal came from the Davoser Hochschule which was starting university courses for young men and women in the surrounding sanatoria. Treatment in these meant a break from regular studies, usually for months and often for years; but special courses could alter all that, and the Davos authorities appealed for specialist teachers to give their services for a few weeks late in March. Einstein responded readily. The opening ceremonies on March 23rd were followed by a series of study groups held in the Kurhaus; by discussions, and by a concert of chamber music given for the benefit of the school. He enthusiastically took part in everything, willingly agreeing to play the violin in an *ad hoc* trio with cellist and pianist, and on the night of the concert was one of the star turns. Not least enjoyed by the audience was the sight of Einstein himself, refusing to bow but taking the music score, then bending it forward so that it was Schubert who acknowledged the applause.

His lecture was on "Fundamental Concepts of Physics and their Most recent Changes", and there was no doubt as to what he considered these were. "Today faith in unbroken causality is threatened precisely by those whose path it had illumined as their chief and unrestricted leader at the front, namely, by the representatives of physics," he noted. He went on to outline Newtonian mechanics and to describe how relativity had welded together both Newton's ideas and the more recent ideas of the field theory and had shaken the fundamental concepts of time and space. But now doubt had been thrown on the theory of strict causality which had previously remained untouched. "We reach here," he went on, "a complication of questions with which the modern generation of physicists is struggling in a gigantic display of intellectual power."

With the Hochschule course behind him, Einstein accepted an invitation to stay at Zuoz, in the neighbouring Lower Engadine, with Willy Meinhardt, the head of the Osram company in whose fortunes his colleague Fritz Haber had played a large part. During the visit he was called to Leipzig to give evidence as an expert witness in a patent dispute between the Siemens company and the A. E. G., whose former President had been his friend Walther Rathenau.

He returned from Leipzig to Zuoz unexpectedly. Typically, he refused to let a porter carry his heavy suitcase. The result of the walk over slippery snow was an unexpected collapse which revealed a delicate heart.

> The P. T. adepts have declared that it wouldn't have happened if Einstein had kept himself in constant trim by regular exercises, [Dr. Plesch has written.] Up to a point no doubt there is something in what they say. Einstein never took any exercise beyond a short walk when he felt like it (which wasn't often, because he has no sense of direction, and therefore would seldom venture very far afield), and whatever he got sailing his boat, though that was sometimes quite arduous — not the sailing exactly, but the rowing home of a heavy yacht in the evening calm when there wasn't a breath of air to stretch the sails. The Zuoz incident was therefore, as Einstein freely admits, perhaps the last of quite a series of overexertions.

Einstein himself thought that the main cause of the trouble had sprung from rowing in a sailing boat during an evening calm.

The results were serious enough. He was moved back to Berlin in easy stages. The details of the heart trouble remained unclear. Numerous remedies were sought. All were unsuccessful. Finally Janos Plesch tried his hand.

Dr. Plesch was four years older than Einstein, a wealthy Hungarian who had built up in Berlin a successful and fashionable medical practice. With a fine town house in Berlin and an equally fine

country estate at Gatow, with an intimate circle of acquaintances in
the diplomatic and theatrical world, Plesch was in character the
complete opposite of Einstein. What united the two men was not
only Plesch's diagnostic success, which dented Einstein's built-in scepticism of doctors; there was also his interest in the world of art and
letters and his love for splendid living that had already touched Einstein's innate, if usually suppressed, love of good food and drink.

Plesch quickly diagnosed inflammation of the walls of the heart,
put his patient on a salt-free diet and eventually packed him off
with Elsa and her two daughters, Ilse and Margot, to a small seaside
resort on the Baltic coast north of Hamburg. Here he recuperated.
But it was a slow business, not helped by the fact that he continued
sailing until Plesch put a stop to it.

As a result of the illness he was deprived of his normal secret-
arial help at the Kaiser Wilhelm Institute and the University, and
before he left Berlin to recuperate was obliged to engage a secretary
for work at home. Newspaper advertisements were ruled out since
they would produce a glut of useless replies. Elsa mentioned the problem to Rosa Dukas, executive secretary of the Jewish Orphan Organisation of which she was the honorary president; Miss Dukas
proposed her sister Helen, who had recently left a publisher.

Helen Dukas, who presented herself at No. 5, Haberlandstrasse
on Friday, April 13th, was competent and diffident in almost equal
parts. She had at first rejected her sister's suggestion. She knew nothing of physics; she felt it would all be beyond her; but she was persuaded to give the work a chance.

Her first task was to find a substitute for him at the coming
meeting in Geneva of the International Commission on Intellectual
Co-operation. For his work on this, like his work for the pacifist
causes which he supported, and for the Zionists, was now to suffer
a temporary interruption. He had already achieved mixed results in
these fields when he began his fiftieth year — and as Germany moved on toward the time, little more than a year away, when rising
unemployment, the support of industrialists who feared Communism, and the creation of a scapegoat in the shape of the Jews, would
together transform Hitler's National Socialists into the second
largest party in the country.

# 13

## THE CALL OF PEACE

EINSTEIN'S BREAKDOWN OF 1928 PUT A REIN ON HIS ACTIVITIES FOR a time. But he was not a man to spare himself longer than necessary and as soon as possible he was working once more in the pacifist cause which he had vigorously supported since 1914. He had long been a staunch upholder of the German League for Human Rights which the Bund Neues Vaterland had become, and from his sickbed was soon sending regular notes to its Secretary-General, Kurt Grossmann, asking for information or giving advice. And shortly after his recovery he was persuaded to make for the League a gramophone record of "My Credo" in which his soft kindly voice outlined his pacifist beliefs as though they were something that any sensible man must agree with.

Before the war Einstein took no part in the pacifist movements centred on Switzerland. His interests were strictly circumscribed by physics in those days and he concerned himself as little with the problems of politics and power as with Zionism until he saw, from Berlin, the convulsions that war produced, the eagerness with which his colleagues leapt to service, and the disruption that war caused to the grand international machinery of science. Then, like thousands of others, he was swept up emotionally, without giving much thought to the practical results of what he was doing. "My pacifism is an instinctive feeling, a feeling that possesses me because the murder of men is disgusting," he once explained to Paul Hutchinson, editor of the *Christian Century*. "My attitude is not derived from any intellectual theory but is based on my deepest antipathy to every kind of cruelty and hatred... I am an absolute pacifist." In an introduction to a handbook on pacifism, *Die Friedensbewegung*, he declared that any human being who considered spiritual values as supreme must be a pacifist. More poignantly in the light of future events, he later told *Die Wahrheit* of Prague that if another war broke out he would refuse to do war service. Not long after-wards he was persuading his friends to do the reverse.

During the first post-war years pacifists had strong popular support, not only in Germany, but throughout a continent exhaus-ted by four years of blood-letting. Thus Einstein for once marched with the crowd rather than against it. But national ambitions and strengths returned. As the price of war became blurred by time and by the jollifications of regimental reunions, so did support for the martyrdom of pacifism ebb away. By contrast, Einstein's beliefs, explained whenever he found the opportunity in a plethora of in-terviews, statements and articles remained rock-hard through the 1920s.

Mingled with these pacifist appeals were calls first for European government and later for world government. Implicit in most of them was the presumption of force or the threat of force if such governments were to survive, but Einstein came only reluctantly and slowly to the point where he would admit that this was the case. In the early 1920s it was a natural enough evolution for those so removed from affairs that they genuinely believed an appeal to in-ternational goodwill would work. But the reluctance to admit that to "fight for peace" was in pacifist terms more than a contradiction of words, helped to keep the League disarmed and impotent, handed the best cards to the potential aggressor and paved the way for Hit-ler. Einstein himself eventually saw as much.

However, in the immediate post-war years, it was the League on which the hopes of peace rested. Einstein therefore supported the League. Or, more accurately, he supported it until experience rubbed him up against it at close quarters. Then disillusion quickly set in. He was surprised that miracles were not worked overnight and shocked that when human beings began to manage great affairs of state they still behaved like human beings. After that, his support of the League had increasingly to be propped up by his friends.

He had returned to Berlin from the Collège de France only a few weeks when, on May 17th, 1922, he was invited by Sir Eric Drummond, Secretary General of the League, to become a member of the International Committee on Intellectual Co-operation* then being formed. The Committee was the brainchild of Henri Bergson and was to represent, said Gilbert Murray, a subsequent chairman,

---

* The English title was International Committee on Intellectual Co-opera-tion, the French was Commission Internationale de Co-operation Intellec-tuelle. Both sides often swopped "Committee" and "Commission" as the spirit moved them — and in even official letters dropped the "intellectual".

"the deeper spirit of the League". In many ways it was an ancestor of UNESCO, which sprang from the United Nations after the Second World War, and its members were appointed, in the words of the Under-Secretary General, "not as representatives of their respective countries but on account of their personal achievements. At the same time, the Council endeavoured as far as possible to give representation on the Committee to the big cultural groups of the world. In this sense, therefore, each member may be said to represent a certain culture, though he does not sit in the Committee as the official representative of any country in particular." This ingenious explanation, given in 1924 in reply to an enquirer who asked whether Einstein represented Germany on the Committee, covered a delicate point, since Germany had not then joined the League. Einstein was, in fact, brought on to the Committee "as a representative of German science", although it is not clear whether he himself really appreciated the fact.

The invitation to serve was the final move in a long series of negotiations. Some French officials objected to having a German on the Committee: the Germans who clung to the periphery of the League claimed brusquely Einstein was not a German but merely a Swiss Jew. A subsequent difficulty, Gilbert Murray has stated, was provided by Einstein's own mistrust of the Committee as a body formed by the victors. But "a conversation with leading members very soon satisfied him as to our real international and peaceful spirit."

Einstein therefore accepted Drummond's invitations by return, although he was not clear as to the kind of work to be done. No one, he felt, should refuse to encourage international co-operation. Shortly afterwards he wrote to Madame Curie, who had also been asked to serve, suggesting that she also accept. Einstein's attitude gave the officials of the League much satisfaction. For while Madame Curie, Lorentz, Paul Painlevé and Gilbert Murray were to be members, Einstein was the cornerstone to the arch.

However, the League was to pay a price for its acquisition. Einstein's "purity of heart", as Murray described it, the fact that he was so "very reluctant to believe evil", his inability or unwillingness to admit that whatever the fine intentions of the League, it had to operate in the world of fallible men, combined to limit his usefulness. This much is clear from the files. It should not create surprise. One of Einstein's sincerest admirers, the late Morris Raphael Cohen, made the point when he reviewed Einstein's *The World As I See It* in the *Menorah Journal:*

The example of the incomparable Newton, as well as of contemporaries like Millikan and Eddington, should warn us against assuming that those who achieve great things in physical science will necessarily display unusual wisdom in politics and religion. It is not merely that devotion to science leaves little time to acquire comparable knowledge on these more complicated subjects. When Harvey suggested that Newton pay less attention to his theosophic and theologic speculations, the latter proudly rebuked him: "Sir, I have given these subjects prolonged study." But the result of this study, as seen in Newton's commentary on the Book of Daniel and on the Apocalypse, is a striking indication of how highly specialised is human genius.

Perhaps, more accurately, how specialised it can be. At least two of the geniuses on the Committee on Intellectual Co-operation, Lorentz and Madame Curie, showed no trace of the vacillations and contradictions with which Einstein was to spread alarm and despondency among his colleagues.

The first of these came less than two months after his acceptance. In July Einstein wrote a brief letter to Pierre Comert, head of the Information Secretariat at the League, brusquely stating that he felt it necessary to resign from the Committee whose first meeting was to be held later in the summer. No reason was given, although in an accompanying note Einstein expressed concern that the situation in Berlin was such that a Jew was well advised to exercise restraint about taking part in politics. In addition he added, somewhat irrelevantly since his appointment was still on an international rather than a national basis, that he had no desire to represent people who would not have chosen him as their representative.

To Madame Curie Einstein wrote in more detail, explaining that he was resigning not only because of the murder of Rathenau* but because of anti-Semitism in Berlin and his feeling that he was no longer the right person for the job. The reply was both to the point and rather tart.

Dear Mr. Einstein, [she said] I have received your letter which has caused me a great disappointment. It seems to me that the reason you give for your abstention is not convincing. It is precisely because dangerous and prejudicial currents of opinion do exist that it is necessary to fight them and you are able to exercise, to this extent, an excellent influence, if only by your personal reputation which enables you to fight for toleration. I think that your friend Rathenau, whom I judge to have been an honest man, would have encouraged you to make at least an effort at peaceful, intellectual, international collaboration. Surely you can change your mind. Your friends here have kind memories of you.

While Madame Curie was writing to Einstein on a personal basis the officials of the League had been thrown into despair, and desperate efforts to retrieve the situation were being made by the Secretary of the Committee. This was Nitobe, a Japanese Samurai, born with the right to wear two swords, whose philosophic journey was to lead him into the ranks of the Quakers. On receiving Einstein's resignation Nitobe had cabled to Murray: "Einstein resigns giving no reasons stop important to have him stop fear his resignation will have bad effect stop grateful if you can use your influence." He also appealed to Bergson who said that he had no personal contacts with Einstein but made an ingenious suggestion. "It is my belief that since the Committee of Intellectual Co-operation is now properly constituted, the resignation of one of its members cannot become definitive until the Committee has accepted it. Therefore, before we meet you can ask Einstein to reconsider his decision." The League officials clutched gratefully at this straw and Comert was despatched to Berlin where he met Einstein on July 27th and 28th. His account of the interviews is revealing.

I explained to you, [he subsequently wrote to Einstein] that your sudden and motiveless retreat would gravely prejudice the Committee of Intellectual Co-operation since the public would be able to put a bad interpretation on your sudden decision to withdraw your collaboration.

With great sincerity, and in all confidence, you then told me of the particular distressing reasons which induced you to consider your resignation.

I was very impressed by them. We will ignore entirely these circumstances. I told you that the difficulties of your personal position in Germany appeared to me so considerable that the members of the Council of the League of Nations would never, in my opinion, have dared to appeal to you if they had suspected that this appointment would make your position in Berlin even more critical.

Then we examined together, in complete confidence, if it would be advisable in these conditions — new to me — to confirm your resignation. Although very anxious to assure your collaboration with the Committee of Intellectual Co-operation, I do not think that I put any excessive insistence on your rejoining us. I understand very well that the Committee could not lightly assume the responsibility of hindering the work of a man such as yourself by attracting to him personally serious sources of irritation.

However, before my departure from Berlin, and with a spirit which

I sincerely admire, you told me that you were giving up all thought of resignation. The work of the League of Nations, you told me, was so dear to your heart that for it you were ready to accept certain risks rather than compromise, by an inexplicable resignation, the task of the Committee. At one point during our interview I recall that concerning this you alluded to the eventuality, on your return from Japan, of a change in your domicile in order to ensure the peace and security of your work.

At the end of our conversations you wrote anew, on the 29th July, to the Secretary General. Your preparations for leaving for Japan prevented you from attending the first meeting of the Committee of Intellectual Co-operation but you declared that upon your return your collaboration would be even more zealous, thus making up, in some fashion, for the loss of time occasioned by your absence. It was with this friendly letter that you left us for the Far East.

The Committee held its first session in Geneva in August, and the official report explained that "Professor A. Einstein was prevented from assisting in the work of the Committee owing to his absence on a scientific mission to Japan."

In fact Einstein did not leave for Japan until some months later and at the end of August he was writing to Lord Haldane from Berlin in support of a solution to the reparations problem put forward in the *Berliner Tageblatt*.

He sailed for Japan with his wife in October, 1922, having failed to obtain a substitute to serve on the Committee until his return. To Geneva he explained that one professor had waited until it was too late before accepting and that another had been on holiday. Most professors who could honestly be said to represent German science were obviously reluctant to aid a League from which Germany was still excluded.

Einstein's absence, extended by a visit to Palestine and a return to Germany by way of Madrid, continued until February 1923, and it was only late in March that he returned to Berlin. He had not been in touch with the League. But, hearing indirectly that he was on his way home, its officials now expected that he would make preparations as promised for attending the session of the Committee due to start in July. They were to be startlingly disappointed.

On his way to Berlin, Einstein broke his journey in Zurich. And here, on March 21st, he wrote to the League resigning from the Committee yet again. A copy of his letter was, moreover, immediately made available to the *Nouvelle Gazette de Zurich*, in whose columns the League officials were able to read it the following morning —

while the letter itself was presumably still passing through their administrative machine.

"I have recently become convinced that the League of Nations has neither the force nor the goodwill [la bonne volonté] necessary for the accomplishment of its task", it said. "As a convinced pacifist it does not seem to me to be a good thing to have any relations whatsoever with it. I ask you to strike my name from the list of committee members."

This was his second resignation from a Committee whose meetings he had not yet attended. The reaction in Geneva can be gauged from the letter sent by Comert to Einstein the following month.

> Abruptly, on March 21st, without any preliminary notice, you sent us your resignation from Zurich, where we did not even know that you had arrived.
>
> Your letter announces only your resignation from the Committee of Intellectual Co-operation. It is a condemnation, without appeal, of the League of Nations which, you say, possesses neither the force nor the goodwill to carry out its task and with which you refuse, in your capacity as convinced pacifist, to have any connection.
>
> This judgment, my dear Professor Einstein, without having followed the work of your commission, without having attended a single one of its meetings, on your return from a voyage during which it was perhaps not easy to follow European affairs.
>
> Before this letter was able to reach Geneva, it was given to the Zurich papers, published, and thus communicated to the whole world.
>
> This sudden *volte-face*, with all its repercussions, strikes an unhappy blow at those who, like us, looking towards a realisable and human ideal, follow humbly and obstinately, in a devastated Europe, the work of international peace which symbolises for us the League of Nations. They had hoped that your collaboration would help to guide the work of the Committee of Intellectual Co-operation in the most useful way. Knowing that the task of the League of Nations cannot be carried out without the support of all men of goodwill, they were particularly happy at the help of an authority as eminent as yourself. Today their hope is disappointed. But their faith in this great work has been sufficiently hardened by the daily battle to resist the shock without being shattered. They will go on, dear Professor Einstein, with the work they have begun and with the sincere hope, I dare to say the conviction, that the road which separates you from us today will one day lead you back to us.

Einstein's action — produced, he later admitted, "more by a passing mood of despondency than by mature reflection" — had been caused by the French occupation of the Ruhr. Inflation in Germany had become unbearable, and at the end of 1922 the Weimar Government suspended payment of the German reparations agreed upon in April 1921. The French, tried beyond endurance, in January, 1923, occupied the small oval heartland of industrial Germany in an effort to squeeze blood from a stone. The result was to bring Einstein in line with the protesting German nationalists, although for reasons very different from theirs. They felt that the League, and all it stood for, was too strong; Einstein's objections were the complete reverse, as he made clear in a letter to Madame Curie, written to her nine months later when the twenty-fifth anniversary of the discovery of radium was being celebrated in Paris.

Both the British and the Americans condemned the occupation of the Ruhr. So did many Frenchmen. While there was therefore widespread regret within the League at the way in which Einstein had demonstrated his attitude, it was submerged in the belief that he must be encouraged back into the fold once more. There appeared to be a chance of this in the spring of 1924 when, on April 17th, the Acting Secretary of the Commission received a confidential note reporting that Einstein had told a friend in Berlin "how he profoundly regretted the precipitate gesture of his resignation". Would it not be possible to tempt him back?

Gilbert Murray was conscripted for the task and on May 16th wrote to Einstein telling him that if he was ready to reconsider his position, then the committee "would unanimously welcome your presence". Einstein's reply was in his usual honest and outspoken fashion. He would like to rejoin the Committee because he felt its work might aid the improvement of Franco-German relations. And he concluded on a typically humble note. If he were not elected he would still be glad to do any work for the Committee.

His return was discussed at the twenty-ninth session of the Council of the League on June 16th, and Henri Bergson "could see nothing but advantage in Professor Einstein again taking a seat on the committee". The Council agreed. But whereas all members had so far been elected "not as representatives of their respective countries but on account of their personal achievements", it was decided "that Professor Einstein should sit on the Committee as representative of German science". The formal offer was now made, and Einstein wrote his acceptance to Sir Eric Drummond on the 25th, agreeing that in view of his past attitude the offer was magnanimous.

There is one interesting point about his letter of acceptance. Attached to it in the League files there is a note: "Not to be roneographed. The S. G. [Secretary General] says that Council members should each have a copy sent privately." There is also a note which says: "As the Einstein letter is private, I do not think it should be printed in the *Official Journal.*" The League was anxious that no undue attention should be paid to Einstein's "past attitude" and that no one should be led on to disinter the reasons for which he had resigned little more than a year previously.

When Einstein was formally introduced to the Committee together with a second new member at the start of the fourth session on Friday July 25th, 1924 the statement by Henri Bergson was equally circumspect, not to say smooth. "The chairman also welcomed M. Einstein, both as an old and a new colleague," says the official report. "He had been appointed a member of the Committee, just as the other members had been, without requesting the appointment. He had returned to the Committee at his own request, having wished to become a member of it. He therefore doubly belonged to it." Bergson went on to recapitulate Einstein's achievements and concluded with the assurance that "if by his presence on a committee of the League of Nations he succeeds in attracting to this ideal all those who have been interested in his lofty speculation, he will have rendered a new and very great service to humanity."

Einstein did not succeed in doing as much as this. The results of his somewhat intermittent attendance at the Committee's sessions until his final resignation in the spring of 1932 were a good deal less important than he can have expected or many of his colleagues can have hoped. This was not entirely, or perhaps even mainly, the fault of Einstein. The disparate forces brought together in the Committee were almost equally suspicious of the France who had become the most powerful force on the continent and had every intention of remaining so, and of the German Republic which was working its passage back into respectability.

These stresses showed in the academic world as clearly as elsewhere — "it must be admitted", Einstein said on January 16th, 1926, "that scientists and artists, at least in the countries with which I am familiar, are guided by narrow nationalism to a much greater extent than are public men." This was not true of him. He was handicapped certainly, but rather by his temperamental inability to make the compromises and accommodations demanded by committee work. Furthermore, his earlier resignation in protest against the French occupation of the Ruhr now made it necessary for him to stress that he was no chauvinist; and his international status, German-born, Swiss by adoption, then full German again, made him particularly vulnerable to attack. All this tended to counterbalance the prestige of his name, which the League had been so eager to utilise but which was a somewhat doubtful asset in the work of the next few years.

One of the first developments after Einstein had at last joined the Committee was the establishment of the International Institute of Intellectual Co-operation, in effect its executive organ. It was to be financed by the French Government and set up in Paris, and there was an unwritten agreement that its head should always be a Frenchman. After initially welcoming the idea, Einstein grew suspicious of possible French domination. He himself was unable to oppose the details due to absence in South America, but he tried to persuade Lorentz to protest in his name. Lorentz declined.

The meetings of the Comittee continued to be held in Geneva, and here Einstein played his part in discussing the various proposals put forward for co-operation. "We had no funds but we could often help a man whose books or scientific instruments had been destroyed by getting him admitted to a laboratory or a library, and sometimes got men restored to lost positions," Gilbert Murray has written "I remember one case where we failed, but the man in question wrote me a letter explaining what a comfort it had been to him in his loneliness, to know that scientists like Einstein and Lorentz and Madame Curie had at least been thinking about him."

At a different level, Einstein sat on sub-committees dealing with bibliography and with a proposed international meteorological bureau. He gave personal advice on the allocation among Russian emigré intellectuals of money donated by the Red Cross and he spent much time discussing how the prospects of peace in the future might be increased by means of school education in the present. All were low-key affairs. They had their place on the outer periphery of international relations but even here their prospects depended very much on the extent to which co-operation could be forced through on the more crucial issues of armaments and trade. Thus the straight fact that the Committee achieved comparatively little during its existence is largely a measure of the status, or lack of it, which it was accorded. At the level where real decisions were made, no one took culture very seriously.

Gilbert Murray was the committee member brought most intimately into contact with Einstein.

One had the feeling that all of us were capable of understanding what each one said and meant, a feeling by no means always present to international committees, [he has written]. One felt also in the mass of one's colleagues a sense of what I would venture to call by the rather bold name of purity of heart. Einstein was one clear case —

immense intellectual power, perfect good will, and simplicity ... What struck me most about [him], apart from his mathematics and his music, which were both beyond my range, was his gaiety and instinctive kindliness ... Bergson once said of him that he had made discoveries at a greater distance from the ordinary organs of human knowledge than any other man in history ...

And to Bertrand Russell, Murray wrote, after Einstein's death: "Of course he was perfectly simple and unassuming. But once I saw him sitting by the lake and went up to speak to him and saw that he was lost in thought and didn't see anything. He was very reluctant to believe evil ... one felt a sort of confidence that he would quite simply take the right view about everything."

Einstein's main interest was the effect of education in removing the misunderstandings and hatreds which help to make war not only possible but popular, an interest closely linked with the pacifist activities which were taking up an increasing amount of his time. "To my mind the main task", he said when addressing the committee informally on one occasion, "is how generally to improve the education of the young. The League can do no greater work than help make better the elementary school system throughout the world." And it is a tribute to the extraordinary weight of his name that this informal and slightly obvious statement, thrown off in a Geneva conference room, should have been worth a leading article in the *New York Times*, which noted this was an Einstein statement which "even the least learned in mathematics and physics can understand".

Einstein's interest in education led to one of the few concrete results of his co-operation with the League. Soon after its formation, the Commission was asked "to encourage an exchange of letters between leaders of thought, on the lines of those which have always taken place at the great epochs of European history; to select subjects best calculated to serve the common interest of the League of Nations and of the intellectual life of mankind; and to publish this correspondence from time to time." The first volume, entitled *A League of Minds*, contained letters from M. Henri Focillon, Señor Salvador de Madariaga, Gilbert Murray, Paul Valéry and others. And in the autumn of 1931, M. Steinig, a League official, travelled to Berlin with the aim of securing Einstein's co-operation on a second volume. Just what it would deal with was relatively immaterial, although certain possibilities had been discussed in Geneva; what was required was a long original letter from Einstein which could be published under the League's auspices.

The idea strongly attracted Einstein who had, Steinig later reported to M. Bonnet, director of the Institute in Paris, "a horror of platonic declarations which did not look forward to an immediately realisable end".

> After M. Einstein had underlined his interest in education as a means of ensuring peace, we decided [M. Steinig went on], that he would accept in principle the idea of writing two letters to two different people on this question: one of these letters would probably be address-ed to M. Langevin, and M. Einstein proposed here to deal with an exchange of views between representatives of French and German organisations on the means of influencing the content of history books in the two countries, for instance. One could, M. Einstein considered, progressively correct the historical accuracy of such books by removing "tendentious errors" on the one hand and, on the other, the errors which provoked and nourished the feelings of national hostility.
>
> "Another letter, which would be produced in the form of a questionnaire, would be addressed to M. Freud of Vienna. M. Einstein will probably ask him to explain how an education inspired by the new principles of psychoanalysis would be able to contribute in guiding the ideas of children towards peace and in diminishing the aggressive impulses which are the foundation of all war."

The choice of Langevin, an old personal friend across the German frontier, was reasonable enough but at first it seems strange that Freud should have been mentioned. While Einstein had a firm respect for Freud's personal stature and integrity he had at this time little use for his theories and had met him only once. But it seems likely that this idea had been planted earlier, after a meeting of the Committee when Einstein and a number of colleagues had dined with Dr. Ernst Jackh, a former director of the Hochschule für Politik in Berlin, at the house of the German under-Secretary General of the League in Geneva.

> As we were going into dinner, [Jackh has written], I asked Professor Einstein: "Would you agree that it is no mere chance that your theory of relativity, and Professor Freud's psychoanalyses, the League of Nations and its World Court, and other phenomena of our time, have developed together: that they are all an expression of the same revolutionary phase through which the contemporary world is passing?"
>
> Professor Einstein looked at me, said nothing for a moment, and then: "This synthetic vision is new to me. Let me think it over."
>
> During dinner I watched him, and I noticed that he was eating and drinking nothing, but was staring in front of him and meditating. After dinner, he came up to me and said, "You are quite right: I endorse your Holism."

Einstein proposed to Steinig that he himself should write to Langevin while Steinig made first contact with Freud in Vienna. A subsequent note from Bonnet to Einstein tactfully suggested that as Langevin was already in China on a mission for the Committee and as Bonnet himself would soon be leaving for China, it might be best for Einstein to omit the first personal contact. Here it is not over-suspicious to recall Einstein's original feelings about the French and the siting of the Institute in Paris, run by a French director. The Langevin project never matured; the reasons are not clear; but the problem of reconciling the French and the German views of history given in the textbooks never had to be argued out in public.

Meanwhile, Einstein's proposals were discussed in Paris and in due course Steinig met Freud.

Freud was not optimistic. "All my life I have had to tell people truths that were difficult to swallow", he said, according to Steinig. "Now that I am old I certainly do not want to fool them." But he would answer Einstein's open letter as best he could.

This letter, dated July 30th, 1932, posed one simple question: "Is there any way of delivering mankind from the menace of war?" Having asked the question, Einstein then continued to give his own answer — the creation of an international authority, whose non-existence he put down simply to the fault of the "governing class", to those "whose aspirations are on purely mercenary, economic lines", and to the additional fact that "the ruling class at present has the schools and press, usually the Church as well, under its thumb." Yet war only appeared to be possible, he admitted, because "man has within him a lust for hatred and destruction". And here, of course, the psychoanalyst might be able to help.

Freud's long discursive answer was in some ways self-contra-dictory. He wrote of "pacifists like us"; yet while he agreed with Einstein that an international court of authority was essential to peace, he noted the need for "its investment with adequate executive force". He agreed with Einstein on man's instinct for hatred and destruction, and then continued:

The upshot of these observations, as bearing on the subject in hand, is that there is no likelihood of our being able to suppress humanity's aggressive tendencies. In some happy corners of the earth, they say, where nature brings forth abundantly whatever man desires, there flourish races whose lives go gently by, unknowing of aggression or constraint. This I can hardly credit; I would like further details about these happy folk. The Bolshevists, too, aspire to do away with human aggressiveness by insuring the satisfaction of material needs and enforcing equality between man and man. To me this hope seems vain. Meanwhile they busily perfect their armaments, and their hatred of outsiders is not the least of the factors of cohesion among themselves.

Freud concluded this depressing prognostication with one faint hope: that it was not too chimerical to believe that war might one day be ended through a combination of two factors. One of these was man's cultural disposition and the other was "a well-founded dread of the form that future wars will take". The idea of peace by the threat of terror was not one which Einstein welcomed. Yet a mere seven years later he was, by signing a letter to Roosevelt, to prod research along the road to the ultimate weapon.

The Einstein-Freud correspondence was published the following year in Paris, after lengthy discussion about what the booklet should be called. *Law and Violence*, much favoured for a while, was finally rejected for *Why War?* Translations appeared in French and in German — although *Warum Krieg?* was banned in Germany where not even advertisements for it were allowed.

*Why War?* — the one permanent memorial to Einstein's membership of the Committee — appeared only after he had finally severed all connection with the League and had made a public and ill-judged protest against the disarmament conference being held under the League's auspices in Geneva.

The reasons for this change of stance were two-fold and complementary. First in importance was his increasing involvement in the plethora of pacifist movements which grew up during the 1920s. His own personal attitude to pacifism remained unaltered; nevertheless, the framework within which it could be expressed changed substantially between 1920 and 1930. For the first few years after the Armistice another world war was so unthinkable that no argument against one was necessary. But slowly the situation began to deteriorate. As it did so, there arose the prospect of the League, certainly a potential keeper of the peace but a policeman without even a baton in his hand.

Einstein, like most other men, was at times self-contradictory. But a great deal of the confusion which surrounds his pacifist attitude disappears once it is considered dispassionately and historically and once his somewhat tortuous self-justifications are ignored. The truth is that in 1920 he was an unqualified pacifist; that the logic of events added first one qualification and then another; and that with the coming to power of Hitler even Einstein was forced to realise that pacifism would not work. The evolution took place gradually but unevenly; at times it slipped back, and at times he himself does not seem to be clear what he really wanted to say. Furthermore, he continued to call himself a pacifist even while agreeing that the dictators could only be stopped by force of arms, an attitude which spread dismay through the pacifist camp.

But as late as 1928 his attitude was still uncomplicated and was underlined in many letters, messages and appeals that he wrote or issued to such organisations as the Women's International League for Peace and Freedom and the British No More War Movement. It was useless to discuss rules of war, or methods of war. Absolute refusal of military service was the only way. Thus Einstein was still holding out against the various ifs, buts, and compromises which were being put forward; the proposals which, in whatever form they were made, suggested that conscientious objectors might work their passage in society by carrying out alternative civilian duties in lieu of military service.

Yet within little more than a year he was writing to the Finnish Minister of Defence, applauding the fact that his country allowed conscientious objectors to be employed, without penalty, for non-military work under civilian control. "It is evident", says Harold Bing, the British pacifist leader, "that Einstein considered that governments were justified in requiring of conscientious objectors to military service, some kind of civilian alternative. He had not grasped the logical position of the absolutist who refused all service under a system of military conscription." More surprisingly, even after his experiences in wartime Berlin, he had failed to grasp that service in a nation at war is indivisible, that the peaceful ploughman ploughs to feed the civilians who make the guns which serve the forces.

Einstein's apparent ambiguity deeply disturbed pacifists who believed that they had his unequivocal support.

On August 30th, 1930, [writes Bing], I was taken by Martha Steinitz [sometime Secretary of the Bund der Kriegdienstgegener and later Joint Secretary of the W. R. I.] to meet Einstein at his lakeside summer house near Potsdam* . . . and, in reply to his questions, explained why I and others had refused alternative service because to accept such service was to recognise the state's right of conscription and to acquiesce in the conscription of others and because any work imposed upon us by the state in wartime would be intended to assist the war effort. At the end of our conversation he declared that he now understood the absolutist position.

Understood maybe. But only three months later he gave little

* See page 389

evidence of this in one of his most famous pacifist speeches. This was made in the Ritz-Carlton Hotel in New York on December 14th, after he had broken his journey en route to Pasadena. There was the usual injunction on pacifists to replace words with deeds, and a demand for refusal to be conscripted. "Even if only two per cent of those assigned to perform military service should announce their refusal to fight", he said, ". . . governments would be powerless, they would not dare send such a large number of people to jail." However, this phrase, which was to produce a rash of button-badges with the words "Two per cent" on them, was followed by a plea to countries which operate conscription to bring in laws "permitting pacifists in place of military service to do some strenuous or dangerous work, in the interest of their country or of mankind as a whole . . ." It is possible to claim that Einstein had, in fact, not "understood the absolutist position". It is possible to claim that he did understand it, but rejected it and felt happy about objectors carrying out work which would in fact assist a war effort. A third possibility is that in the press of preparations for his American visit,* amid the work which had to be finished before he left Berlin, he had not thought out to a conclusion the implications of what at first seemed a satisfactory solution to a tough moral problem.

There is another explanation of his evolving pacifist attitudes. Perhaps in pacifism, as in space, there should be no absolutes, a standpoint which makes more comprehensible his attitude of 1931, evolved from that of the "two per cent" of a few months previously. "As he sees the problem, there are two ways of resisting war", wrote the chairman of War Resisters International, Fenner (now Lord) Brockway after he had visited Einstein at the head of a W. R. I. delegation, "the legal way and the revolutionary way. The legal way involves the offer of alternative service, not as a privilege for a few, but as a right for all. The revolutionary way involves uncompromising resistance, with a view to breaking the power of militarism in time of peace or the resources of the State in time of war. The general conclusion of Professor Einstein was that both tendencies are valuable, and that certain circumstances justify the one and certain circumstances the other." All was as relative here as it was in physics.

His dedication to the pacifist movement tended increasingly to tug Einstein away from the over-cosy international atmosphere of the League. Always an instinctive outsider, he felt unhappy in the role of insider automatically conferred by membership of the Committee. In addition, there were problems within the organisation

* See page 402

itself. "National Committees" had been created which by 1930 were acting as liaison groups between the central body in Geneva and the intellectual committees of individual countries. Einstein was a member of the German committee, created after Germany had joined the League in 1926, but his opinions were given only qualified support by fellow-members, and their recommendations led him to criticise the system of national committees as such.

Then, in the Spring of 1932, he wrote to M. Montenach, the Swiss secretary of the main Committee, suggesting that he should be replaced on it. The proposal was quickly followed in the League by an internal memorandum outlining various steps which it was hoped would stave off Einstein's resignation. Gilbert Murray was again asked to intercede. M. Dufour-Feronce, who had once worked in the German Foreign Office and who knew Einstein personally, was to do the same. "You might", Dufour-Feronce was instructed by Montenach, "insist on his making a special effort to come to Geneva for six days to attend the session of the Committee beginning on July 18th. You could say that the other members of the Committee who have been for nearly ten years his colleagues and have much affection and admiration for him, would greatly appreciate such a gesture of sympathy and interest which would be made by his attending the session before the expiration of his term of office."

All these blandishments failed. And Einstein, who found it "difficult to find the time" to attend Geneva for the July meeting, arrived there instead in May, and in circumstances which would certainly have made impossible any further connection with the League.

So far, despite his support for the militant pacifists, he had clung to the hope that the League, however greatly its operations might fall below his own standards, offered a genuine promise for the future. Now — and for the next eighteen months — he put more faith in the belief that "if the workers of this world, men and women, decide not to manufacture and transport ammunition, it would stop war for all time". And he also, increasingly, voiced an open distrust of what the League was doing, unconsciously echoing Wells' gibe about "this little corner of Balfourian jobs and gentility".

Einstein's distrust exploded in reaction to the Disarmament Conference which opened in Geneva in February, 1932. It was a reaction which illustrated his bigness of heart but revealed the immense gap which divided the real world of nation-states and politicians from the world which Einstein felt must exist because it should exist. It was a reaction which undermined those who believed he might be a useful ally in a practical struggle to avert war, and it was one which offered a useful weapon to those only waiting to claim that outside his own field Einstein was something between crank and buffoon. In almost every way it was one at his most disastrous interventions in public affairs.

The Disarmament Conference which sat in Geneva between 1932 and 1934 was attended by representatives of sixty nations — including non-members of the League such as Russia and the United States — and was an effort to reduce armaments within the framework of the League Covenant. At first Einstein had welcomed the idea of such a conference even if only as a last hope. "I believe [it] should take place in any event; at the very least, it will help to clarify the situation and focus attention on this important problem," he told the editor of the French journal *Paix Mondiale*. However, it must have been obvious to any knowledgeable observer that if the conference was to have the slightest chance of success, it would involve months'-long wrangling, a balancing of weapon against weapon, a long delicate series of negotiations in which a choice between comparable evils was taken only after much discussion. The reaction of Einstein, with his simple belief that all countries must abolish arms and subjugate their future to an international organisation, was easy enough to forecast. It came in May, 1932 when the conference had been meeting for only three months and its committees were deep in intricate argument.

Earlier in the year he had been asked by the Rev. J. B. Th. Hugenholz, a Dutch delegate to the Joint Peace Council of the International Union of Anti-militarist Ministers and Clergymen, to attend a meeting of the Council in Geneva in May. He declined. But towards the end of that month, following a visit to Oxford, he decided to visit Geneva after all — "because," he said, "some friends convinced me that it was my duty to do so." On Sunday May 22nd, he left London for Geneva with Lord Ponsonby, not only a leading pacifist but an old friend. Ponsonby was also an intimate of Arthur Henderson, the former British Foreign Minister now presiding over the Disarmament Conference. Under Henderson, Ponsonby had carried out much of the detailed negotiation which had preceded the trade agreement between Britain and Russia. They were men of somewhat similar outlook and it has even been suggested that Henderson "engineered" Einstein's appearance at Geneva. There is no evidence of this, and if Henderson played any part at all, which seems unlikely, even he must have been surprised at the genie which he found he had encouraged out of the bottle.

23

On the morning of Monday, May 23rd, Einstein visited the League headquarters. As he entered the public gallery, the Japanese and Russian delegates of the Air Commission were arguing that the mobility of aircraft-carriers increased the offensiveness of the planes they carried; for the United States Allen Dulles and for Britain Captain J. T. Babington — who had won a hard-earned D. S. O. for the wartime bombing of the Friedrichshafen Airship Factory — were arguing the reverse. The speaker stopped for a moment, then continued, according to Konrad Bercovici, a young Rumanian-American journalist. "That brief second, however, was an acknowledgment, a more marked acknowledgment, of the greatness the man radiated than if all had stopped everything they were doing and applauded him," he wrote. "All eyes were turned towards Einstein. Where he was, the world was."

But Einstein had not come just to watch. That afternoon he held a press conference at the Bregues Hotel attended by about sixty correspondents. What he said, both here and elsewhere in Geneva, has been variously reported. The editors of *Einstein on Peace* print one account which appears to be a cut version while noting that the War Resisters International had another transcript which Einstein "rather freely revised . . . insofar as it deals with me". But there is no doubt about the tenor of his statement, whose main points are given in a few key sentences in the "official" version: "One does not make wars less likely to occur by formulating rules of warfare." "War cannot be humanised. It can only be abolished." "People must be persuaded to refuse all military service." These seem reasonable propositions, even if they can be challenged, and at first Romain Rolland's comment quoted in *Einstein on Peace* — that Einstein's "constant about-faces, hesitations and contradictions are worse than the inexorable tenacity of a declared enemy"— seems a little harsh.

However, it was not what he said but the context of his opinions which tended to destroy his credibility for all except those who had already been converted to the conspiracy theory of war. This is made clear by Bercovici's account of the Geneva visit and of an interview with Einstein which he succeeded in obtaining before the press conference started. According to the editors of *Einstein on Peace* — naturally anxious to present their subject in the best light — this account "while possibly exaggerated, suggests, nonetheless, the universal and instinctive appreciation of Einstein's personality". Its essential content consists of a long quoted statement, triggered off when Bercovici said that he had come to the city to watch the comedy of peace.

"This is not a comedy", Einstein replied, "it is a tragedy. The greatest tragedy of modern times, despite the cap and bells and buffoonery. No one has any right to treat this tragedy lightly or to laugh when one should cry. We should be standing on rooftops, all of us, and denouncing this conference as a travesty!' . . ."

> If you want peace in America then you must join us in Europe, and together we shall ask the workers to refuse to manufacture and transport any military weapons, and also to refuse to serve any military organisation. Then we will have no more conscriptions; we will have no more war! Governments could go on talking from now to doomsday. The militarists could lay any plans they wish.

> If the workers of this world, men and women, decide not to manufacture and transport ammunition, it would end war for all time. We must do that. Dedicate our lives to drying up the source of war: ammunition factories.

> I have absolute information that if a war should break out today anywhere in Europe so many conscientious objectors would throw away or refuse to shoulder arms that one-half of every army would be busy putting down the revolt of the other half before going to fight the enemy. The trouble with the delegates here and with most people ruling over nations today is that they don't know what their peoples think and how their peoples feel about war.

> The trouble with most of these delegates is that they are unintelligent and insincere and are but puppets moved by strings in the hands of politicians at home — politicians and ammunition manufacturers. Any declaration of war would be followed by world-wide revolutions. We must prevent that, prevent the destruction of Western civilisation by the uncivilised governments of the world.

No one would claim that this is necessarily an accurate sentence by sentence verbatim account of what Einstein said. But from all available evidence it would seem to reflect his excited — and, as Bercovici puts it at one point, "almost hysterical" — attitude. Yet Germany had not yet walked out of the conference, and was not to do so for another eighteen months. The French, who were to insist that some system of general security should precede disarmament, were still trying. Hope still existed.

Against this background, Einstein's attitude marks the high tide of his pacifism which had been rising since the First World War. And with the reflection that within fourteen months he was to be encouraging men to take up arms, the only other non-scientific pre-occupation of his life must now be considered: the support of Zionism, for which he showed the same white-hot idealism, a quality often producing results which, here also, counterbalanced the value of his name.

# 14

# *THE CALL OF ZION*

IT IS DEMONSTRABLY UNFAIR YET STILL PERFECTLY TRUE, TO CLAIM
that the Zionists seized upon Einstein's fame from 1919 onwards
and exploited it to their advantage. No movement dedicated
to so difficult a mission can let its tactics be too closely controlled by the principles of a gentlefolks' aid society; and with a
genius of Weizmann's calibre in control it was inevitable that the
magnetism of Einstein, the incorruptible man of science, should be
conscripted to the general task of implementing the Balfour Declaration, and to the special one of coaxing money from the pockets of
American Jewry. The Zionists should not be criticised for this. If
criticism is warranted it springs, rather, from their failure to bring
Einstein unconditionally within their fold; to capture him so completely that his statements of support would never contain the
irritating qualifications which he saw as essential to honesty but
which could be a niggling hindrance to men fighting for their ideals.
One should have sympathy for both sides. How difficult it must have
been for Einstein to move from the world of physics into the passionate turmoil of creating the new Jerusalem! How tantalising it must
have been for the Zionists to have captured the most famous living
Jew for the cause — and then find that he was a bad speaker who
often said things out of naïveté which caused them trouble!

Einstein himself has stated that he did not become aware of his
own Jewishness until after he went to Berlin in the spring of 1914.
This is not as surprising as it sounds. The modern Zionist movement
did not come into existence until 1897. The current for assimilation
still continued to run swiftly through the Jewish community. Thus,
despite the "nail from the Crucifix" brought into the Munich school-
room, Einstein appears to have remembered no anti-Semitism from
his student days, from his work in the Berne Patent Office, or from
his years as a young professor in Zurich. "Different but equal" was

the attitude of the liberal Swiss; so much so that the correspondence of Einstein's student days, of his early married life, and of his gradual integration into the scientific world, contains comparatively few comments on his race or of the religion into which he had been born.

In Prague, the Jewish community provided a power-block in the struggle between the Czechs and the Germans into whose Austro-Hungarian Empire they had been brought. And here for the first time, it appears, Einstein became a member although certainly not a committed one, of a Jewish group. It met every Tuesday evening in the home of Bertha Fanta; but while almost every other member was an ardent Zionist, Einstein was completely uninterested.

The reason is not difficult to see once the viability of Zionism as a practical proposition in 1910 is soberly considered. Herzl had launched the movement little more than a decade previously, convening in 1897 the first Zionist Congress at Basle where it resolved "to secure for the Jewish people a home in Palestine guaranteed by public law". Led from Vienna until Herzl's death in 1904, the movement had been transferred to Germany, first to Cologne and then in 1911 to Berlin. The idea that the national home might be founded elsewhere than in Palestine, mooted more than once, was finally rejected in Basle at the Seventh Congress in 1905. Here the tentative offer made two years earlier by the British Government, under which the Zionist organisation was provisionally to be granted 6,000 square miles of East Africa, was firmly turned down: Zionists were concerned only with Palestine. But Palestine had for centuries been part of the Turkish Empire and when, even after the Revolution of 1908, it became clear that the Turks had no intention of granting the Zionists a charter, "the movement, as Herzl had conceived it, came to a standstill."

To some Jews this was not altogether unwelcome. For while many saw their people as a potential nation, others saw them only as a group held together by theological beliefs and a personal code of behaviour.

Thus, [says Leonard Stein in his history of Zionism] while there was one school of thought which stoutly denied that the Jews were a nation at all, there was another which held that the Jews were a nation and nothing else — a nation precisely like any other, except that it happened to have been temporarily deprived of its national territory. Both sets of extremists oversimplified the Jewish problem, because both of them could only conceive of nationhood in terms of the nation-state. In calling upon the Jews to be fearlessly themselves, in reminding them that, for all their differences, they had precious possessions in common,

in warning them that those possessions would be jeopardised if they
failed to maintain and to enrich their corporate life, the nationalists
performed a valuable and indeed an indispensable function. In suggesting, on the other hand, that the Jewish problem would be solved if
the Jews would only imagine themselves to be something they were not,
they were playing with fanciful analogies and using language which
was sometimes least carefully thought out by those who used it most
freely.

Einstein had no wish to be ground between these two millstones.
In 1911 his common sense estimated Zionist prospects more as a
chimera than a practical possibility. He was, moreover, already intellectually at odds with any movement which buttressed nationalism
however honourable its motives, and this intuitive feeling was to be
strengthened by the experiences of the war years. Yet in 1920 Einstein emerges as the dedicated, though sometimes qualified Zionist,
adding the lustre of his name to a cause still in need of lustre despite
its greatly improved prospects; speaking on platforms; warily putting a foot into the deep waters of Zionist politics and making an
exhausting tour of the United States for the cause. Something more
than the magic of Weizmann's personality had been needed to bring
this about.

One factor which influenced him was the transformation of
Zionism from a pious hope to a practical possibility by the Balfour
Declaration of 1917, the statement by the British Foreign Minister
that "His Majesty's Government view with favour the establishment in Palestine of a national home for the Jewish people, and will
use their best endeavours to facilitate the achievement of this object..." It was true that the Declaration was issued at a fortuitous
moment and that, as H. A. L. Fisher has sagely noted, it "rallied to
the Allied cause, at a time when money was urgently needed, the
powerful and cosmopolitan community which, not from New York
only, controls the loan market of the world". But it was also true
that the ancient plain of Philistia, after almost 1,300 years of Persian
and Turkish rule, was now being conquered by Allenby's armies.
The hopes of the Jews looked high.

Einstein's recruitment into the Zionist cause has been described
by the man who carried it out, Kurt Blumenfeld. Two things are
clear. First, that "until 1919 Einstein had no association with Zionism
and Zionist ways of thought." Second, that the method of Einstein's
recruitment was important not only in itself but by its example. "The
method," says Blumenfeld, "found effective with him brought [other]
friends and followers to Zionism: that is to say, the drawing out

from a man of what is within him rather than the forcing from him of what is not truly within his nature."

Blumenfeld's account of his meetings with Einstein in February 1919 is revealing both of Einstein and of the Zionist cause as it struggled into practical existence:

> Felix Rosenblueth [today Minister of Justice Pinhas Rosen] had prepared a list of Jewish scholars whom we wished to interest in Zionism. Einstein was among them. Scientists had known his importance for years but when we called upon him we did not know that his name would soon be resounding across the world. The abundance of interviews and photographs which later surrounded him had not yet started.
>
> I began to talk about the Jewish question. "What has that to do with Zionism?" Einstein asked. "The Zionism idea will give the Jew inner security. It will remove discord. Openness and inner freedom will be the result."
>
> These were the thoughts which interested Einstein. With extreme naïveté he asked questions, and his comments on the answers were simple and unconventional. "Is it a good idea to eliminate the Jews from the spiritual calling to which they were born? Is it not a retrograde step to put manual capabilities, and above all agriculture, at the centre of everything Zionism does?"
>
> So far Einstein had avoided giving any specific opinions. Now opposition showed itself. "Are not the Jews, through a religious tradition which has evolved outside Palestine, too much estranged from the country and country life? Are not the talents which they have exploited with such scientific accomplishment perhaps the result of an innate spirituality; is it necessary to create a Jewish national movement which is circumscribed by the Jewish question?"
>
> We felt during our talk that we were dealing with a man of unusual gifts. There was nothing very surprising in his words, but I could see the thoughts of the man in the flash of his eyes and the look told me more than the words.

A few days later Einstein and Blumenfeld met again. "On this occasion," writes Blumenfeld, "he told me that Hermann Struck, the etcher, had tried to interest him in the Bible and the Jewish religion, but that he had refused to be drawn. 'I really don't know enough about my religious feelings', he had said . . . 'I have always known exactly what I should do, and I feel satisfied with that'."

Shortly afterwards, Blumenfeld noticed a change in Einstein's attitude. "I am against nationalism but in favour of Zionism," he said. "The reason has become clear to me today. When a man has both arms and he is always saying I have a right arm, then he is a Chauvinist. However, when the right arm is missing, then he must do something to make up for the missing limb. Therefore I am, as a human being, an opponent of nationalism. But as a Jew I am from today a supporter of the Jewish Zionist efforts."

Einstein's attitude was to be complicated by the general situation in Germany. Support for assimilation was possibly even stronger among Jews there than it had previously been, partly as a result of the forces unleashed by the war, which tended to draw together all those living within the German Empire, partly as a reaction to what was considered the Jewish influence behind the Russian revolution. Few wished to carry the policy as far as Einstein's colleague Haber, who had taken himself and his family into the Christian Church. Yet there were many for whom the possibilities of Zionism had a double danger. It made more difficult their own attempts to become assimilated into the non-Jewish German community and it provided a weapon for those endemic anti-Semites whose attitude had helped to produce Zionism. Thus for every man who welcomed Einstein's espousal of the Zionist cause there was another among his friends who would warn that this was not really the way to further the cause of Jews in Germany; that pressure on them would be increased; and that if there were too much talk of a National Home outside Europe there would be increasing demands for Jews to be sent there.

The forces supporting assimilation were certainly strong, but so too were Einstein's contrary feelings once he had become seized of the Zionist cause, even though for him Zionism and Palestine were only peripheral concerns. Utilising him for publicity purposes was thus a delicate matter and, said Blumenfeld, "was only successful if I was able to get under his skin in such a way that eventually he believed that words had not been put into his mouth but had come forth from him spontaneously".

If Einstein the Zionist thus found himself at odds with much of the Jewish community on matters of practical politics, he also had reservations about the character and methods of the key man in the Zionist movement. This was Chaim Weizmann, subsequently a good friend of Einstein but diametrically opposed to him in many ways. Weizmann was a Russian Jew who had emigrated to England before the war, became naturalised, and quickly achieved a position in the scientific world that owed nothing to his work as a propagandist for Zionism. In an ironic way Weizmann was the Allied counterpart of Fritz Haber. For while Haber found a method of supplying a blockaded Germany with unlimited explosives, Weizmann was a biochemist who discovered how one particular strain of bacterium could synthesise acetone, essential for the manufacture of cordite. On the outbreak of war he moved from Manchester University to government service. Subsequently he became Director of Admiralty Laboratories under A. J. Balfour, First Lord of the Admiralty.

Thus Weizmann soon found himself well placed for staking the Zionist claim to Palestine. His connections with Whitehall increased still further as the naval war moved towards its crisis and as Balfour left the Admiralty for the Foreign Office in 1916. By September 1917 his influence was such that the Prime Minister, "on Weizmann's representation of urgency, told Sutherland [one of Lloyd George's private secretaries] to put down 'Palestine' for the next War Cabinet". The Balfour Declaration followed on November 2nd. Thus it was in the accepted order of things that Weizmann represented the Zionist Organisation when this was given a hearing by the Council of Ten at the Peace Conference on February 27th, 1919.

Positions of power are rarely gained or held by those who believe that all men are not only brothers but innocent ones. A good deal of ruthless wire-pulling is required, a good deal of balancing and counterbalancing and not occasionally the bland reassurance on facts which are not facts at all. All these, the common coin of getting things done, are required even of a statesman with the moral integrity of Weizmann. But to a man of Einstein's temperament this element of wheeling and dealing was repugnant. Thus, as Isaiah Berlin has noted,

> Weizmann's relationship with Einstein, despite their deep mutual admiration for each other, remained ambivalent; Weizmann was inclined to regard Einstein as an impractical idealist inclined to utopian attitudes in politics. Einstein, in his turn, looked on Weizmann as too much of a *Realpolitiker*, and was irritated by his failure to press for reforms in the [Hebrew] university away from what he regarded as an undesirable American collegiate pattern. Nevertheless, they remained allies and friends to the ends of their lives.

As well as these feelings which tended to qualify Einstein's enthusiasm for Zionism there was the essentially pacifist nature of his approach to the problems of the world. Even when it came to Zionism, a subject as emotionally close to his heart as anything ever was, he could never look on his opponents, in this case the Arabs, as the deep-dyed villains which the sentiments of the case demanded. He was all for the policy of live and let live. While many Zionists — possibly the majority of them — saw a Jewish National Home essentially as a political state created for political purposes, Einstein saw it rather as a cultural centre. Many Zionists called for mass emigration to the Promised Land, but Einstein foresaw the way in which Arab opposition would be intensified. Thus the dichotomy which runs through so much of his life showed itself here also. To the demands of *Realpolitik* he would oppose the need for idealism; when force was demanded he would respond that pacifism was essential. Despite these qualifications, he was drawn into the Zionist maelstrom by the climate of post-Armistice Germany, by the humiliations which the Jews from the East were suffering at the hands of Berliners and by the impassioned advocacy of such German Zionists as Kurt Blumenfeld. His support had hardly been secured when a good chance of utilising it arose.

Late in 1920 Weizmann decided to visit the United States to raise funds for the Keren Hayesod, to be formed in March 1921 to take over from the Palestine Restoration Fund the main financial burden of constructive work. He quickly picked a strong party to accompany him. "I also approached Professor Albert Einstein, with special reference to the Hebrew University," he later wrote, "and to my great delight found him ready to help." It is clear from Blumenfeld's account and from Einstein's private correspondence that this was a description of his reaction more enthusiastic than accurate.

Blumenfeld had received a detailed telegraphed directive from Weizmann.

> I was to stir up Einstein, [he says] go with him to America, and there join in the propaganda for the Keren Hayesod. Einstein must be interested, above everything else, in the idea of the Hebrew University in Jerusalem.
>
> When I appeared before Einstein with this telegram he at first said No: "Do you think so much of the idea of a Hebrew University in Jerusalem?" It was unfortunate that I, for different reasons, was a bad advocate of the idea, and Einstein therefore said: "How is it that you are asking me to publicise an idea that you yourself do not wholeheartedly support? Besides, I consider that the role which is expected of me is an unworthy one. I am not an orator. I can contribute nothing convincing, and they only need my name which is now in the public eye."
>
> I did not reply, but read Weizmann's telegram aloud again. "It is irrelevant that we know what is necessary for Zionism today," I said. "We both know too little of all the factors involved. Weizmann represents Zionism. He alone can make decisions. He is the President of our organisation, and if you take your conversion to Zionism seriously, then I have the right to ask you, in Dr. Weizmann's name, to go

with him to the United States and to do what he at the moment thinks is necessary."

Einstein had already begun to interest himself in politics and had joined the Republican League only a few days previously. But his concern with the peripheral left wing was parochial compared with the prospect that was now dangled before him. Did he really want to enter the dubious world of power politics which even he must have realised was the only world in which the great expectations of Zionism could be translated into reality? Surely his interrogation of the physical world would suffer? Surely it was all rather demeaning?

No doubt he pondered over these questions. If they had been asked two years previously he would almost certainly have given different answers. But he had emerged in the autumn of 1920 a different man from the almost lighthearted professor who only 24 months earlier had talked the Berlin students into common sense while Born and Wertheimer had looked on. Now he saw himself not only as a scientist but as one who might genuinely be able to influence world affairs. And by now he had watched the tide of anti-Semitism begin to rise again, had felt it lapping round his own feet in Berlin and Nauheim. It seems more than likely that Lenard and the Anti-Relativity Company were in his mind as he listened to Weizmann's telegram.

There was also another factor. "I learned later," Weizmann has written, "that Haber had done all he could to prevent Einstein from joining me; he said, among other things, that Einstein would be doing untold harm to his career, and to the name of the Institute of which he was a distinguished member, if he threw in his lot with the Zionists, and particularly with such a pronounced Zionist as myself." In Einstein's then state of mind, an appeal from a lapsed Jew who had helped the Germans so much in the war, could have swung him in only one direction.

"To my boundless astonishment," Blumenfeld writes, "Einstein answered: 'What you say now is right and convincing. With argument and counter-argument we get no further. To you Weizmann's telegram is a command. I realise that I myself am now part of the situation and that I must accept the invitation. Telegram Weizmann that I agree." Thus he prepared to take a major step towards the consolidation of his fame in America and of his notoriety in Germany as the focus of anti-Semitism.

Shortly after this meeting with Blumenfeld, Einstein wrote to

Maurice Solovine with whom he had kept up a desultory correspondence since the break-up of the Olympia Academy fifteen years
earlier: saying that he was going to the United States only in the
interests of the Zionists. And to the same correspondent, shortly before he set off from Berlin, he expressed the hope that the Jews in
Palestine would be immune from the folly of power.

As news of Einstein's acceptance leaked out, invitations from
the United States began to arrive in the Haberlandstrasse — not only
from Zionist organisations but from universities and other learned
bodies anxious to get the renowned Albert Einstein to explain his
theories. By mid-March it must have been satisfactorily clear to
Weizmann that whatever publicity would be coming to the Zionist
cause would be doubled by the presence of Einstein.

However, all would not be plain sailing, and some of the problems are detailed in a letter which Blumenfeld wrote to Weizmann
on March 15th, 1921. This is extraordinarily revealing, showing as
it does the way in which Einstein's enthusiasm for the Jewish cause
was being manipulated, and highlighting his own ingenuous outlook,
a characteristic which, it was clear, had to be put in the balance
against the advantages of his name.

Einstein, Blumenfeld said, was no Zionist but he would always
be willing to help at specific tasks so he should not be induced to join
the organisation. His interest arose from his aversion to assimilated
Jewry. He had doubts about some of the Jewish leaders but there
were none about the help which he would give to the efforts to be
made in the United States. Already, at Elsa's request, 10,000 marks
had been put at his disposal, and it was recommended that Weizmann should let him have further funds on the voyage. Einstein
himself was worried about running up too many expenses, had
seriously told his wife that he wanted to travel steerage, and had
insisted that detailed accounts should be kept of all that was spent.

Then Blumenfeld gave a warning. Weizmann had been expecting Einstein to prepare speeches. But he was told to be particularly
careful about this since Einstein was a bad speaker and often said
things out of naïveté that caused trouble. In spite of this there was
no doubt about his value, and Blumenfeld ended by saying how
happy he was that he had aided the cause by winning over a man
who would help to settle the American issue in their favour.

This issue was the difference in opinion between Weizmann and
many leading Zionists as to how Zionist aims might best be pushed
forward. On the question of tactics, many American Zionists, notably those led by Justice Brandeis, believed that the existing Zionist

organisation was adequate. Weizmann believed that in the long struggle ahead something more ambitious would be needed, and was already throwing his efforts into the creation of an enlarged Jewish Agency which would include not only Zionists but other Jews. Springing almost directly from this, was the great contrast in the amount of cash which each group believed would be necessary. Brandeis and his supporters talked of raising £100,000 a year; Weizmann thought of £2,000,000. These divergent views might have been resolved more easily had it not been for the character of Weizmann, "overbearing and politically ruthless", according to one version of Brandeis' opinion. To many Americans he may well have looked like an embryonic dictator, carving out his own empire; to many European Jews who knew how close to the problems he had been, neither his ambition nor his ruthlessness seemed greater than was necessary.

The journey began on March 21st, 1921, when the Einsteins left Berlin for Holland, where they were to embark on the *Rotterdam*. They were joined on board by the Weizmanns. "Einstein was young, gay and flirtatious," says Mrs. Weizmann. "His wife, I recall, told me that she did not mind her husband's flirting with me as 'intellectual women' did not attract him; out of pity he was attracted to women who did physical work" — a remark substantiated by more than one of his intimate friends. During the voyage across the Atlantic, says Weizmann, Einstein "explained his theory to me every day and on my arrival I was fully convinced that he understood it". Weizmann utilised the journey to plan the tactics of his campaign.

From the comparative security of his home in Berlin, Einstein had already felt the hot wind of publicity, but only on arrival in New York did he meet its full blast. The effect was to last a lifetime and to give him a distrust of most newspapers, even though he retained an unexpected and masterly ease at handling a press conference when he wished. First, he had to face the cameramen who came aboard with reporters as the ship docked, all of them anxious to forestall the official reception committee, which included New York's Mayor Hylan; Alfred E. Smith, soon to be elected Governor of New York State; and Fiorello La Guardia, president of the City Council. "I feel like a prima donna," said Einstein as he at last turned to the reporters and prepared for the worst.

One of the first questions had been a constant companion since November 1919: "Can you explain relativity in a few sentences?" Ever anxious not to disappoint, and in this case doubly so out of loyalty to Weizmann, Einstein had an answer that became a classic. "If you will not take the answer too seriously, and consider it only as a kind of joke, then I can explain it as follows," he said. "It was formerly believed that if all material things disappeared out of the universe, time and space would be left. According to the relativity theory, however, time and space disappear together with the things."

From then on he had their confidence, a smiling, touslehaired figure in his high wing collar and knitted tie, anxious to assure them that his theory would not change the ideas of the man in the street, claiming that every physicist who studied relativity could easily understand it, and as confounded as were his interrogators by the extraordinary interest which his work had aroused. "Well, gentlemen," he concluded, "I hope I have passed my examination."

There was the inevitable demand to know whether Mrs. Einstein understood the theory. "Oh, no," was the philosophical reply "although he has explained it to me so many times — but it is not necessary to my happiness." She wished to protect him from the adulatory mob. "He does not like to be what you call a showcase," she explained. "He would rather work and play his violin and walk in the woods." And when he was deep into a problem, she added, "there is no day and no night".

The ordeal over, they went ashore. Awaiting them was more than the official reception committee. The Jewish areas of New York were gaily decorated, while Jewish Legionnaires who had fought with the British to liberate Palestine from the Turks were present in strength. Some of the crowds wore buttons with Zionist slogans, others waved the Jewish flag, then merely white and blue, without the Star of David that it bears today.

What the crowds saw at the top of the gangway was Weizmann, smiling but stiff, almost a model for Lenin in physical features as in singlemindedness, and beside him the shorter figure of Einstein. He wore a faded grey overcoat, by no means new, and a black hat. In one hand he carried a briar pipe and in the other his violin. "He looked like an artist, a musician," wrote one reporter. "He is of medium height with strongly-built shoulders, but an air of fragility and self-effacement." Under a broad high forehead were the large and luminous eyes, almost childlike in their simplicity and unworldliness. "Great men, a very small family on earth, can unfortunately find nobody but themselves to imitate," Chateaubriand commented in his *Memoirs*. "At once a model and a copy, a real person and an actor playing that person, Napoleon was his own mime." In much the same way Einstein, the public figure now emerged from the chrysalis of the professor, unconsciously dropped into the role of Einstein playing Einstein.

The two men and their wives were driven between a police escort to the City Hall whose piazza was filled with more than 5,000 Zionists. Here they were formally received by New York, where there lived a third of all the Jews in the United States. And here, it had been tacitly arranged, Weizmann and Einstein would be given the freedom of the city.

At this point an unexpected hitch occurred. When the aldermen retired to vote the freedom to their visitors, an Alderman Bruce Falconer objected. A dozen years previously, he pointed out, New York had granted its Freedom to Dr. Cook, a gentleman whose claim to have reached the North Pole was as fraudulent as his earlier claim to have made the first ascent of Mount McKinley. How did they know that Einstein had really discovered relativity? Furthermore, while Weizmann was a British subject, Einstein was a German, a former enemy alien. Falconer successfully obstructed various attempts to push through the measure but his move was counterproductive. The following day the New York Senate in Albany gave Weizmann and Einstein the freedom of the State, without opposition. New York City eventually followed suit, while the Owasco Club, the democratic organisation of the Seventeenth Assembly District, passed a resolution noting that "the conduct of Alderman Falconer manifests a spirit of bigotry, narrowmindedness and intolerance, and displays him as a champion of anti-Semitism, which is only a stepchild of anti-Americanism." Yet it is interesting to note that the resolution which gave Einstein the freedom of the State began — "... Albert Einstein of Switzerland", a statement that conveniently ignored both his German birth and the fact that though he was a naturalised Swiss he was now also a German again.

As far as Einstein was concerned, there were three aspects to the tour that now followed. There was his involvement, inevitable although as slight as he could make it, in fund-raising and inter-Zionist argument. There was his own series of appeals for the Hebrew University, obviously closely linked with Weizmann's but launched at a slightly different level to a slightly different public. Thirdly there were his lectures on relativity, and the impression that they made on the American academic world.

From the first, it was clear that Weizmann's decision to invite Einstein had been more than justified. His appeals to the Jews of America struck deep down — even though many of them had radically different ideas on the financing of the Jewish Home. For he added more than the box-office draw of an international name and a mysterious theory. There was something romantic not only about his air of innocence but about the journey which had brought him from his study half-way round the world to what less than three years previously had been an enemy capital.

"To every person in America," says Frank, "it recalled the Holy Land and the legend of the Wandering Jew, thus striking a strongly responsive chord and evoking profound sympathies in many Christians." It needed no great stretch of the imagination to see in Einstein, trotting down the gangway with a pipe in one hand and a violin case in the other, the apotheosis of all that Jewry stood for. To the Americans, a nation of refugees, the figure had a double attraction.

As a member of the Weizmann party, Einstein could not stand aside entirely from the arguments about Jewish development in Palestine. But Weizmann had not ignored Blumenfeld's warning about Einstein's propensity for saying "things out of naïveté which cause us trouble". He had given his colleague broad hints about when to stay quiet. Einstein, for his part, kept himself well in hand — although his feelings were shown privately during a big meeting in Madison Square Garden. While one Zionist orator was speaking with great heat, Einstein turned to the man next to him on the platform and whispered in German: "What an ass!"

The classic example of his will to be good came on the evening of April 12th, after Weizmann has spoken to 8,000 Jews at the 69th Regiment Armoury.

Einstein then rose. "Your leader, Dr. Weizmann, has spoken, and he has spoken very well for us all," he said. "Follow him and you will do well. That is all I have to say."

From the controversies that followed Weizmann's first public appeal for funds on April 17th Einstein remained as aloof as possible. An open breach with the Brandeis party followed the next day. This was to be healed only after considerable wrangling, and it is difficult to estimate its effect on Weizmann's appeal. At a single meeting on April 20th, 26,000 dollars was donated and a total of 100,000 dollars pledged. Next day a Keren Hayesod Bureau opened in Union Square, to be visited by a constant stream of Jews giving cash — one man unrolling a thousand dollars worth of small notes and handing them over with the comment that he had saved them for his old age. However it was not until years later that the larger contributions which were hoped for were extracted from American pockets, and it is clear both from the Einstein-Weizmann correspondence, and from the recollections of Zionist historians, that the results of the visit, though necessarily presented as successful, fell considerably short of what had been expected.

Meanwhile Einstein was addressing Jewish audiences on the needs of the Hebrew University, "the greatest thing in Palestine since the destruction of the Temple of Jerusalem", as he called it. The man who in Berlin had experienced the plight of Jews "knocking vainly at the doors of the universities of Eastern and Central Europe" was an ideal spokesman. "Others who have gained access to the areas of free research only did so by undergoing a painful, and even dishonouring process of assimilation which robbed them again and again of their cultural leaders," he said with feeling. "The time has now come for our spiritual life to find a home of its own." Here, speaking on his own ground, he could do no harm and much good, and after his first appeal Stephen Wise, rabbi of the Free Synagogue in New York who was later to become a close friend, pledged 10,000 dollars for the university.

Einstein's lectures on relativity, which were to broaden the knowledge of his work in the United States, began on April 15th at Columbia University, which had awarded him the Barnard Medal the previous year. It was the first time he had spoken on relativity — or on anything else it appears — to an English-speaking audience. He showed the same assured naturalness he used with allies and enemies, presidents and crossing-sweepers, kings, queens and charwomen. "He several times brought chuckles and laughs from his audience by his references to the 'idiot' behaviour of certain bodies in accelerated systems," the *New York Times* noted. "Also he caused much amusement when he wished to erase some diagrams he had drawn on the blackboard and made futile motions in the air with his hand until Professor Pupin came to his rescue."

At the City College of New York, where he lectured the following week, the lectures were translated. "I happened to be the most readily available person who understood both his language and his mathematics," writes Morris Raphael Cohen, "and so I was asked to translate his lectures. This gave rise to the altogether undeserved popular legend that I was one of the unbelievably few people in the world who understood the Einstein theory."

In Washington, where Einstein and Weizmann arrived soon afterwards, an unsuccessful attempt was made to read "a popular presentation of the relativity theory" into the Congressional Record. Here also they visited President Harding with a group from the National Academy of Sciences at whose annual dinner Einstein spoke. The formal speeches went on and on, and as one scientist after another accepted the Academy's annual awards Einstein turned to his neighbour, the secretary of the Netherlands Embassy who was representing the physicist, Pieter Zeeman: "I have just got a new theory of Eternity," he confided.

Another visit was to Princeton where on Monday, May 9th an honorary degree was conferred and where he gave a lecture a day for the rest of the week. It was after one of these, during an evening discussion, that he heard of D. C. Miller's first announcement which appeared to refute the Michelson-Morley experiment. And here, believing that the truth did not lie in the convolutions demanded by Miller's results, he observed: "God is subtle but he is not malicious" ("*Raffiniert ist der Herrgot, aber boshaft ist er nicht*"). In Chicago, the next port of call, he made one contact which was greatly to affect his future. This was with Robert Millikan who a few years previously had provided experimental evidence for Einstein's photo-electric equation. While Elsa was driven around the sights of Chicago with Mrs. Millikan, Einstein discussed the future of science with her husband.

Then, a few days before he was due sail for Europe, leaving Weizmann to continue his Zionist work alone, the two men visited Cleveland. Most of the Jewish shops were closed for the occasion and the party was met at the Union Station by a 200-car parade headed by the band of the Third Regiment of the National Guard. "Only the strenuous efforts of a squad of Jewish war veterans, who fought off the people in their mad attempts to see them," the *New York Times* reported, "saved them from possible injury."

The near-hysteria which had marked more than one phase of the visit was not entirely the result of the new-felt longing to be free which surged through the Jewish world with the hopes of a National home raised by the Balfour Declaration, or of the intellectual cataclysm made by relativity. Both played their part. But both were reinforced by the extraordinary impact made by Einstein himself during what was for most practical purposes his first journey outside the academic world into the realm of the uninitiated. The curtains had parted and behind them there was seen not the austere and aloof leader of science, but an untidy figure carrying his violin, the epitome of the world's little man immortalised in different ways by Chaplin, Hans Fallada and H. G. Wells' Kipps. Astonishment increased as it became clear that however steely-keen Einstein's relentless dedication to science might be — and within the inner circle there was no doubt of that — here was the real article, genuinely humble, honestly surprised that so much fuss should be made of him. In Boston, where he was asked as part of a current "quiz" to give

the speed of sound, he admitted he was sorry but he didn't know —
and why should he, since it was a simple fact that could be looked
up in a reference book? Speaking to the National Academy of
Science, he said that "when a man after long years of searching
chances upon a thought which discloses something of the beauty of
this mysterious universe he should not therefore be personally
celebrated. He is already sufficiently paid by his experience of
seeking and finding."

For the Zionists the transparent sincerity of such remarks had
turned out to be an invaluable asset, and as the Einsteins returned
to Germany, breaking their journey in England, Weizmann had good
reason to be satisfied. For Einstein, and his reputation, the results
were more qualified. "Thank heaven, Yale did not give Einstein a
degree", went a letter to Rutherford from Bertram Boltwood, then
at the peak of his reputation. "We escaped that by a narrow margin.
If he had been over here as a scientist and not as a Zionist it would
have been entirely appropriate, but under the circumstances I think
it would have been a mistake."

Back in Berlin, Einstein reflected on his experiences. There is
no doubt that the Jews of America had given him a concept of
Jewry quite different from the one he had grown up with in Europe.

His optimism was shown when he spoke in Berlin's Bluthner
Hall on work in Palestine a few days after his return. Shortly afterwards he wrote to Ehrenfest saying that work on the important
medical buildings at the Hebrew University could now be started
soon, this having been made possible by the middle class Jews of
America, and in particular by Jewish doctors. The activities of
Weizmann and himself, he clearly felt for at least a short while
after his return to Germany, had been a distinct success. This mood
soon passed and the Zionist leader Selig Brodetsky, reporting on
his visit to Einstein in Berlin shortly afterwards, related that he was
told of the failure of his mission to the United States. Three months
later Weizmann was writing almost plaintively asking Einstein to
sign a letter to the Boston New Century Club where they had drummed up considerable support — "the Club has made difficulties regarding the handing over of the money collected; of the 20,000
dollars promised, we have actually so far collected 4,000 dollars"
he noted. The different views are not contradictory. Like the my-
thical bottle of whisky, half-full or half-empty, Weizmann's tour
could be considered either failure or success according to expectations. But as the enthusiasm engendered by the visit began to slip

away, the facts began to look less rosy. It was some years before the Hebrew University pulled in the really large contributions hoped for in 1921.

Einstein's already slightly jaundiced view of the tour was increased when he saw the price to be paid for the support gained. Forever the idealist, he could not stomach the shifts, the horse-trading and the accommodations necessary in an imperfect world. Above all, he could never reconcile himself to the fact that whoever pays the piper calls the tune; that the American Jews who provided most of the finance for the Hebrew University would in practice have a hand in the way it was run almost as powerful as the Board of Governors.

In 1921 this was still a small cloud on the horizon. Einstein remained the great Zionist capture; it followed therefore that he should be asked to visit Palestine on his return from the Far East early in 1923 and to give the inaugural address at the university. For Einstein himself the visit was a deeply emotional experience, doubly important to a man who had excluded emotion from his life whenever possible.

The Palestine Mandate, under which the former Turkish territory was administered by the British with the ultimate aim of creating a Jewish National Home, had been approved by the Council of the League of Nations only six months previously, and was not to become operative until the end of September 1923. But the British High Commissioner had already been appointed, and Jewish immigration and reconstruction was being pushed ahead. The High Commissioner, with whom the Einsteins were to stay, was Sir Herbert, later Lord, Samuel. Like Lord Haldane, he was both philosopher and statesman, a man who had been deeply moved by the implications of relativity, and one of the few outside the field of science to become a comparatively close friend. Samuel was not only a first-class administrator. He was also a Jew, and while his appointment had been intended to show the British Government's favourable attitude towards Jewish aspirations, there were repercussions which only the most Machiavellian foresight could have predicted. For Sir Herbert was also a British official whose neutrality must be above suspicion. It was therefore almost inevitable that in the Jewish-Arab disputes that spattered the unhappy history of the country during the years of his appointment, the High Commissioner should stress his impartiality by giving utmost consideration to the Arabs. In this he was no more than just; but among Jews it was often felt, as it was later to be felt of Sir Stafford Cripps in another context, that he was so busy returning good for evil that he had little time to return good for good. Therefore his long friendship with Einstein, begun in the first months of 1923, was to be marked more than once by differences as to what should be done for Palestine.

Einstein arrived with his wife at Tel Aviv on February 2nd, 1923, and was greeted by Colonel Frederick Kisch, who had retired from the British Army with a fine war record to join the Zionist Executive. "Found him rather tired as he had sat up all night", Kisch recorded in his diary, "but I later learned that this was his own fault, as he had insisted on travelling second-class in spite of every effort to persuade him to go into a *wagon-lit* which had been reserved for him." Three days later he was formally received by the Palestine Zionist Executive. "He made," Kisch recorded, "a little speech explaining the nature of his brain which he said was such that he was afraid it would be unproductive work for him to attempt to learn Hebrew."

But there was no doubt about Einstein's almost embarrassing enthusiasm for Palestine — or of Palestine for him. This was shown the following day. That the most famous scientist in the world — if the most controversial one — should give such unqualified support to their efforts, genuinely roused the inhabitants and emboldened them to think that the reward would be equally unqualified. Einstein responded with an answering enthusiasm. The interaction was shown when on February 6th he drove through streets lined with crowds of waving schoolchildren to a reception at the Lemel School organised by the Palestine Zionist Executive and the Jewish National Council. After he entered there was, the *Palestine Weekly* reported, "no holding back the crowd who had assembled outside. The outer gates were stormed, and the crowd burst into the courtyard, and tried to force the inner gates which were stoutly held by three or four stalwarts."

Inside, Einstein was baring his soul. "I consider this the greatest day of my life", he said. "Hitherto I have always found something to regret in the Jewish soul, and that is the forgetfulness of his own people — forgetfulness of its being almost. Today I have been made happy by the sight of the Jewish people learning to recognise themselves and to make themselves recognised as a force in the world. This is a great age, the age of the liberation of the Jewish soul; and it has been accomplished through the Zionist movement, so that no one in the world will be able to destroy it."

The following day he was to perform his main task in Palestine: delivery of the inaugural address at the Hebrew University, which had been founded five years earlier as the British and Turkish guns still faintly boomed away fifteen miles to the north. Before the ceremony he had a long talk with Kisch which reveals the state of his mind.

"Interview with Deedes," Kisch recorded; "then a walk back from Mount Scopus to the city with Einstein to whom I explained the political situation and some of the intricacies of the Arab question. Einstein spoke of Ussishkin's* attempt to persuade him to settle in Jerusalem. He has no intention of doing so, not because he would sever himself from his work and friends, but because in Europe he is free and here he would always be a prisoner. He is not prepared to be merely an ornament in Jerusalem."

At 4.30 the same afternoon some hundreds of men and women, including members of the Consular Corps and the newly-created Palestine Government and their wives, packed into the temporary building of the Hebrew University on Mount Scopus. "Many ... like myself ... could have no claim to understand his theory," wrote Helen Bentwich, wife of Norman Bentwich, Attorney General to the Government. "But we all wanted to hear and meet this great man, probably to be able to say in the years to come that not only had we heard Einstein lecture about his theory, but that we had attended the first lecture given at the Hebrew University of Jerusalem." The hall was hung with Zionist flags and the insignia of the twelve tribes. Above the platform hung the Union Jack with a portrait of the High Commissioner and a Zionist flag with a portrait of Dr. Herzl, while from the ceiling descended a banner bearing the words *Orah ve Torah* (Light and Learning).

Ussishkin introduced Einstein with the announcement that two thousand years ago Titus and his avenging armies had stood where they now stood. But today they were inaugurating a temple of science. "Mount the platform which has been waiting for you for two thousand years," he concluded grandly.

Einstein did so, delighting those present by giving what Samuel called "an opening sentence *pro forma* in a Hebrew that was evidently unfamiliar". Then he continued in French; and, at the end of the comparatively short address, repeated it in German. Nevertheless, the first official words spoken from the University had been in Hebrew.

During the next few days Einstein toured the country, planting a tree in the garden on Mount Carmel outside Haifa and visiting the

---

* Ussishkin was president of the Zionist Executive and had been a member of the party which visited America in 1921.

city's high school and technical college. He was impressed by what he saw, and said so to Weizmann on a leaf torn from his notebook. In Tel Aviv he was created a free citizen and at a banquet held in his honour he spoke with honesty that tact might have blue-pencilled: "I have already had the privilege of receiving the honorary citizenship of the City of New York, but I am tenfold happier to be a citizen of this beautiful Jewish town." At Rishow Le Zion, which he visited from Jaffa, he promised to "rouse the Jewish world and tell them of the strength that has been invested here", adding that until his last hour he would "work for our settlement and for our country".

His enthusiasm for the opportunities which Palestine would now be able to offer was stressed as he walked on the Mount of Olives with the Attorney General. "The Jews had produced no genius of rank in the nineteenth century save a mathematician — Jacobi — and Heine," he said, according to Bentwich.

> The National Home in Palestine could release and foster their genius. For two thousand years their common bond had been the past, the carefully guarded tradition. Now they had a new bond, the active co-operation in building up a country. Then he went on to talk of other things. He delighted in the beauty of the Arab peasant dress and the Arab village growing out of the rock, and equally in the beauty of life in Japan and in their sense of corporate union. The Japanese dinner made you understand the meaning of eternity . . . On the journey from Japan, he had been thinking out a new theory of the relation of light to gravity. The ship gave the best conditions for thought; a regular life and no disturbing influence.

And then, a decade before the same thought was to be awakened by solitude in England, Einstein commented that for similar reasons he found light-houses attractive; a man could be alone there.

Palestine strengthened his Zionist sinews, and the memory of it helped him during the difficult decade that lay ahead. When he dined with the Attorney General and his wife, borrowing a violin and making up a quartet with Bentwich and his two sisters, he not only played remarkably well, but "looked so happy while he was playing that I enjoyed watching as much as listening," Mrs. Bentwich remembered. "We talked of books, and of one he said, with a happy twinkle in his eye: 'It's not worth reading. The author writes just like a professor'."

This was but one side of the coin. The other was represented by the formality of Government House, by the mounted troops that accompanied the High Commissioner as he travelled with his guests, and by the boom of the cannon which echoed every time he left the official residence. All this worried him. He had already perfected a technique of behaving as if formality did not exist — a technique which was perfectly sincere but which at times gave a misleading impression of playing to the gallery or of being eccentric for eccentricity's sake. Elsa was also uncomfortable, but for her own reason. "I am a simple German housewife," she told Philipp Frank. "I like things to be cosy and comfortable and I feel unhappy in such a formal atmosphere. For my husband it is a different matter; he is a famous man. When he commits a breach of etiquette, it is said that he does so because he is a man of genius. In my case, however, it is attributed to a lack of culture."

Despite the contrasts between Samuel, the shrewd able statesman, and the less worldly Einstein, the two men were attracted to one another, and talking in the grounds of Government House, their conversation ranged across the future not only of Israel but of relativity. Here Samuel quoted T. H. Huxley's famous remark: "Herbert Spencer's idea of a tragedy is a deduction killed by fact." Einstein's reply was recorded by Samuel: "Every theory is killed sooner or later in that way. But if the theory has good in it, that good is embodied and continued in the next theory."

Einstein and his wife left Palestine for Europe in mid-February. His parting advice was severely practical. Kisch records that as he said goodbye to his visitor in Jerusalem, he asked Einstein "to let us know if during his tour he had observed that we were doing anything which in his opinion we should not do, or if we were leaving undone things which should be done. He answered: 'Ramassez plus d'argent.'"

The journey to Palestine consolidated Einstein's feelings for Zionism and these remained strong — despite its nationalism, which he mistrusted as he mistrusted all nationalisms, despite its foundation-stone of a religion which he could take no more seriously than he could take any other revealed religion. But there was a definite limit to the aid that he was prepared to give, and this was illustrated following his return to Europe. Later Weizmann tried to coax him to London for a major Zionist meeting but was met with the plea that attendance at the League's Commission of Intellectual Co-operation's meetings in Geneva would rule this out.

Early in 1924, he refused to make a second journey to the United States. Emotionally, he was being tempted outside. But, instinctively, he wanted to stick to his physics.

There were two other things which tended to make him qualify his support of Zionism. One was his belief that a first priority should be agreement with the Arabs. He was not alone in this opinion. "A few Jewish leaders, particularly Magnes, Hugo Bergmann, Ruppin and Calvaresci, were convinced that the first political aim should be, not maximum immigration, but understanding with the Arabs", Norman Bentwich has written. "That conviction was expressed emphatically by Albert Einstein when I visited him in his cottage during my stay in Berlin in 1930. He would not remain associated, he said, with the Zionist movement unless it tried to make peace with the Arabs in deed as well as in word. The Jews should form committees with the Arab peasants and workers, and not try to negotiate only with the leaders." As Arab feelings hardened, as Mandate policy appeared to be increasingly swayed by pro-Arab sentiment, and as practical Zionist aims were narrowed to nation-state or nothing, such internationalist and pacifist leanings began to make Einstein's position within the Zionist movement frequently difficult and sometimes anomalous.

There was also his guerilla battle with the management of the Hebrew University which continued from the University's formal opening in 1925 until the summer of 1934, a battle fought largely against the influence of Judah Magnes, the virtual ruler of the University who exercised his power in line with the U. S. interests which had so largely financed it.

Some months after Einstein gave his inaugural address early in 1923 the Institute of Chemistry was set up. The Institute for Microbiology followed in 1924. Early in April 1925 the University was formally inaugurated by Lord Balfour and its property, until then vested in the Zionist organisation, was subsequently transferred to a nine-man board of governors which met in Tel Aviv.

Einstein was elected one of the governors and the board met under his chairmanship in Munich in September 1925. Here it was enlarged. An academic council was set up, and a "Palestine Executive" was created so that in future the University could almost be said to have two masters, one in London under the stern eye of Weizmann who was to be chairman of the board for the rest of his life, the second in Jerusalem under the chancellor who as the man on the spot always had the option of acting first and asking afterwards. The chancellor was Judah Magnes.

Magnes exercised considerable influence in the Jewish community in New York, where he had been a rabbi before the First World War. He had been an uncompromising pacifist, critical both of Weizmann's work for the British Admiralty and of his willingness to base

Zionist hopes on the promises of an imperial power. Thus it would
not have been surprising if he and Einstein had been drawn together,
two birds of the same feather. Yet during the decade between 1925
and 1935 the cards fell otherwise. Weizmann supported the choice
of Magnes as chancellor; Einstein opposed it.

The battle was fought on gentlemanly lines, but with a good
deal of hard hitting, and has the fascination of all battles which are
struggles not of right against wrong but of right against right. The
issue, which Weizmann was to admit to Einstein with astonishing
frankness, was a simple one. For all practical purposes it was the
Americans who had financed the Hebrew University. Magnes was
their "nominee", and it was useless to complain about his performance in office. Einstein did complain — in general about Magnes'
lack of academic experience and in particular about the way in
which, from 1925 onwards, he ran the University.

The trouble started at the Munich meeting. Magnes later
claimed that "when Einstein entered he said: 'I find myself here
among many financiers from America.' They were in fact myself,
Judge Mack and Schloessinger. It was on this occasion that difficulties were created with me at the beginning."

There were many difficulties, not the least delicate of which
concerned the minutes of the Munich meeting. Einstein pointed out
to Magnes on December 29th, 1925, that he held the minutes and
asked for the withdrawal of a second set which Magnes had circulated. Magnes declined. He remained in possession of the field and
the best that Einstein could do was to write to him despairingly and
admit that further correspondence between them was useless.

However, he still continued to work for the good of the University, visiting Paris in January 1926 to lecture on it before the
Franco-Palestine Society and sparing for Zionist activities whatever
time he could squeeze from his work. But a man in Einstein's position, brought on to committees and governing boards for the prestige
of his name rather than for what he was expected to do, could always threaten to play the strong card of resignation. This he now
did, in the first of a series of actions that strangely mirrors his inde-
cisive turnabout with the League Committee.

Early in the summer of 1926 Weizmann visited Berlin to discuss
the unhappy University situation. Any ambiguity in Einstein's attitude was removed by a letter he wrote to Weizmann on July 6th.

You will understand [Weizmann replied immediately], that my colleagues and I who discussed the situation with you in Berlin were

most upset about its contents. Only a few days ago we discussed within the circle of the Zionist Executive that whatever it may cost we must, above all, avoid your resignation. A few days ago I wrote to Dr. Magnes and made it clear that under no circumstances will the Board of Governors allow you to resign because of him. I pointed out to him — without going into the details of your circulated address at the Munich Conference — that he cannot continue to act in this high-handed fashion with his continuous harking on the American money-bags, and that he would be more useful to the University were he not continuously dependent on the moods and threats of the donors. I think he will understand my hints, and I feel it is quite possible that when he receives your letter as well as mine he will feel it necessary to resign. I am quite determined, as I mentioned to you in Berlin, to stand behind you in this, even though your reasons, mentioned verbally in Berlin — may be somewhat inconvenient to me. But I am prepared to do this as I am fully convinced that your diagnosis of the situation is correct and that sooner or later Dr. M. will have to be got rid of.

Weizmann concluded by reiterating his appeal that Einstein should not resign, an act which would only leave Magnes in undisputed control. Einstein acquiesced, at least for the time being. But eighteen months later, on January 8th, 1928, he felt it necessary to complain in stronger terms.

As chairman of the board Weizmann, had mixed feelings. "Our income," he later stressed to Einstein, "is entirely from voluntary subscribers, and we had to depend on Magnes — as you yourself have admitted — because Magnes could secure at any rate a considerable proportion of the budget. The same argument covered even the choice of professors by the board of governors, who had to adopt the suggestions of those who controlled the purse of the University." To Weizmann, half a university was better than none. Einstein disagreed, and in his letter of January threatened to resign from the board unless action was taken within a year, since he felt it was better to delay the founding of a Hebrew University rather than create a second-class institution at once.

These were tough words. They were implemented a few months later, although Einstein's concern for the university forced him to conceal this from the world at large. Weizmann wrote in midsummer, proposing what Einstein subsequently described as compromises. He did not agree with them. And on June 14th, 1928, he wrote that in the circumstances he had decided to retire completely from the University's affairs, although he would not officially resign. But six days later he decided to go.

Einstein's genuine concern for the University was a measure of his own, individualistic, Zionism. However much he might disagree on tactics, he kept in mind the same fine end. Thus he was among those invited to attend, and to speak at, the crucial Sixteenth Zionist Congress held in Zurich in August 1929. In the words of Weizmann's invitation, the congress would "be of an unusually momentous character in view of the fact that it will be called upon to ratify the measures taken by the Zionist Executive for the enlargement of the Jewish Agency, so that it may be possible for the first meeting of the Council of the Agency to be held immediately after the Congress."

Einstein was, as always, only too happy to visit Zurich. He took the opportunity of visiting his children, telling Eduard, who asked why he had come, that he was attending a Jewish conference and adding: "I am the Jewish Saint." He visited Mileva and, although he appears to have put up at the Grand Dolder Hotel on the Zurichberg, was glad to shock Sir John and Lady Simon by telling them: "I am staying with my first wife." He visited the shop where he had bought "penny cigars" as a student. And he took the tram to visit his old landlady, Frau Markwalder, insisting that she should not be told of his coming since he "did not want to play the great man".

He had been invited to the congress because, as Weizmann assured him, he would "greatly enhance the importance of the proceedings and afford considerable gratification to all supporters". This was so, although he also gave great support to Weizmann whose name he quite justifiably linked with that of Herzl himself, and whose past work, he said, gave him a moral right to influence their future.

There had been bitter talk of "abdication" to the Jewish Agency, and it was claimed that the influential half of the new organisation was concerned only with a much watered-down version of real Zionism. Little of this argument came through at the congress, although it is significant that in his speech Einstein, after speaking of "the brave and dedicated minority who call themselves Zionists", went on to say "we others...."

The Zurich meeting marked a climax in Zionist endeavour and, for overlapping reasons, the end of one phase of Einstein's support. The enlarged Jewish Agency with Weizmann at its head had barely come into existence when serious anti-Jewish riots broke out in Palestine. On September 11th, Louis Marshall, who had been a mainstay of the non-Zionist section of the Agency, died after an operation. The following month the Wall Street Crash cut the hopes of major U. S. support and at the same time, by triggering off the great depression in Europe, provided the cue for the nationalist, and largely anti-Semitic forces, waiting in the wings of the Weimar Republic.

None of these developments directly affected Einstein, although they increasingly put him at odds with many orthodox Zionists. The complexities of the position were emphasised by Brodetsky who spoke in Berlin in 1929. "Einstein was present," he said, "but I am afraid that what I said was not well received. I told them in the best German I could manage what we demanded of the Mandatory Government, and I said that Arabs who had murdered Jews must be dealt with according to the law. The audience was shocked. Einstein complained to me afterwards that I had spoken like Mussolini. I had shown no spirit of conciliation; I had demanded that Arab murders should be punished. Most German Zionists agreed with Einstein."

Einstein's own reaction was given in further letters to Weizmann on November 25th, 1929. In them he criticised Brodetsky's Berlin speech, warned against the Jews depending too heavily on the British, and underlined once again that unless they were willing to find some ways of co-operating with the Arabs they would deserve all that would be coming to them.

The extent to which he was not only willing but apparently anxious to conciliate the Arabs, whatever provocation they might offer, was based not only on the expediency of working with the British but on a belief that turning the other cheek was morally right and practically workable. This tended to alienate him from at least a section of the Zionist movement. Yet in other ways events pushed him more firmly into the movement. From 1930 onwards, as he saw the growth of anti-Semitism in Europe and as his hopes of European peace began to fade, a sharper edge was given to the Zionist question by his own personal experiences. He now began to take a new pride in his background, and on the evening of January 29th, 1930, actually appeared in a Berlin synagogue, playing his violin in black skull-cap with the augmented choir of the new synagogue, to raise contributions for a Jewish community welfare centre. He had once looked on assimilation as a mistake; now he began to think of it as an impossibility.

# 15

## PREPARING
## FOR THE STORM

BY THE EARLY MONTHS OF 1929, EINSTEIN WAS RECOVERING FROM HIS collapse of the previous spring. He had, says his son-in-law, Rudolf Kayser, "been very patient in his suffering. He never complained about the tediousness of his rest cure. Sometimes, indeed, he seemed to enjoy the atmosphere of the sick room, since it permitted him to work undisturbed." Of his long convalescence Einstein himself said in March 1929: "Illness has its advantage; one learns to think. I have only just begun to think." He was still weak, his face drained of colour so that he looked very different from the normally almost boisterous Einstein. Nevertheless it was clear that he was recovering. The man responsible was Janos Plesch whose quick diagnosis and simple remedy had done the trick.

Plesch, who was to dedicate his *Physiology and Pathology of the Heart and Blood Vessels* to Einstein, was volatile and high-spirited, ambitious and successful. In some ways he was the complete contrast to Einstein. Yet for more than a quarter of a century the two men remained firm and mutually critical friends, a contrast in opposites in some way reminiscent of the friendship between Churchill and Lindemann.

When Einstein began to grow strong once more, he was past the age at which a scientist might be expected to produce original work; it was almost time to think of the administrative "plums" that academic life offered. After all, he was a European before he was a German, a man whose friendships, private and professional, linked him with the neighbouring countries of Holland, Switzerland and France; if he feared that the breeze of anti-Semitism blowing across Germany might soon rise to gale force, he could take any of the appointments in Leiden, Zurich or Paris that would be offered at the drop of a hint. He did nothing of the sort. He not only continued the good fight against indeterminacy in physics where Born and Heisenberg could already claim substantial victories, but pressed vigorously on with what had for almost a decade been his main preoccupation, the construction of a field theory uniting the forces of electro-magnetism and gravity.

And while he kept his European friendships in good repair he stretched out to make fresh and important contacts in both Britain and the United States. He wanted to get on with his work. He wanted to help push Europe away from the precipice of war. But as his fiftieth birthday came and went he seems to have felt the future, to have sensed that the Wehrmacht would one day reach the Channel and Atlantic coasts and that in Europe the best he could hope for would be a place behind the wire. His work continued in Berlin but from 1929 onwards there were increasing glances over the shoulder to countries not only beyond the Reich but beyond the continent itself.

The most important item in this work was his search for a unified field theory. He had studied the forces of electro-magnetism and produced the Special Theory, a new and more accurate yardstick for measuring the characteristics of the physical world. He had studied the force of gravity, found it to be not quite what men had believed it to be, and had produced the General Theory. Now he asked whether it would be possible to unite them.

Some men answered this question with an unqualified "no". Wolfgang Pauli, who believed that such a marriage of the laws of electro-magnetism and of gravitation was impossible, summed it up: "What God hath put asunder no man shall ever join." Others were more optimistic, notably Hermann Weyl and Eddington, both of whom produced plausible but by no means satisfactory theories which attempted to unify the two fields. One thing appeared certain: the scale of the task being attempted. "If the unification of physical theories was finally possible," said André Mercier years later, when such a prospect still looked remote, "its possession would put the human spirit in possession of an ideal instrument for making it master of the intellectual world. The scholar would find himself both powerful and bored, like an absolute monarch whose ideas could not be undone by human stupidity."

Einstein set out on the formidable venture soon after he had completed the General Theory and his correspondence of the immediate post-war years is spattered with references to it. In 1923 he

published a preliminary paper on the subject based on an idea
already put forward by Eddington; then, settling down after the
return from his travels, gave the problem increasing attention. His
efforts were soon given a further spur by the birth of quantum mechanics; for it was part of his life-long, but unfilled hope that a unified
field theory would help to remove the new, and for him uncon-
genial, statistical element which formed part of the new physics.

In some ways he was embarking on a search for the physicists'
Hesperides, a scientific suicide mission on which even an Einstein
might fail. This is perhaps more certainly the view today, when it is
generally felt that the structure of the universe cannot be described
by using a single set of equations. Yet even in the 1920s the prospects
looked poor. Einstein himself knew this and the explanation he gave
late in life for devotion to this particular task was as relevant in 1929
as in 1949. "He agreed that the chance of success was very small,"
he told a colleague, Professor Taub of Berkeley, "but that the attempt
must be made. He himself had established his name; his position was
assured, and so he could afford to take the risk of failure. A young
man with his way to make in the world could not afford to take a
risk by which he might lose a great career, and so Einstein felt that
in this matter he had a duty."

One paper giving the outline of a unified field was published in
the *Proceedings* of the Prussian Academy of Sciences in 1928 — probably the paper which caused Elsa to write of her husband to a
friend: "He has solved the problem whose solution was the dream
of his life." Then, on January 10th, 1929, the Academy announced
that Einstein had submitted a new paper on a unified field theory
which was being examined. This immediately aroused the interest
of the world, and not only because the Academy appeared to be
suggesting that something important was coming. Einstein was by
this time approaching his fiftieth birthday and the world was tickled
by the fact that towards the end of his fiftieth year the man who
had "caught light bending" might have perfected a set of equations
which would, in the popular phrase, "solve the riddle of the universe".

It was announced that the paper would be published at the end
of the month and extensive, ingenious, but unsuccessful efforts were
made by many of the world's newspapers to secure an advance copy.
In an age when liaison between newspapers and leading scientists
was less happy than today, distortions and absurdities were more apt
to creep in, and these were particularly irksome to Einstein who
knew that a real understanding of his work was beyond most laymen

and many scientists. It was left to the chief Berlin correspondent of the *New York Times*, for which Einstein had developed a particular fondness, to explain that the spate of telephone calls and requests, were solely the result of the theory whose publication was to be completed within a few days. Einstein could only murmur: "My God."

He was, however, persuaded to give an interview to the *Daily Chronicle*. The result was a non-mathematical explanation of what the theory was trying to do and a striking example of Einstein's ability to give explanations "so simple that a child could understand them."

The *Daily Chronicle* interview appeared on January 26th. The unified field paper was to be published four days later and it now dawned on some newspapermen that its transmission by telephone or cable to staff who were as innocent of science as many scientists were innocent of newspapers, would present abnormal difficulties. It had dawned slightly earlier to John Elliott, head of the *New York Herald Tribune's* Berlin office. On his advice, a number of physicists from Columbia University were brought into New York for the occasion. Meanwhile, Elliott in Berlin sent a code to New York, explaining that "raised" meant that the letter or number following that word should be upper index, that "sub" meant it should be lower index, and that various scientific symbols should be represented by specific words. All went as planned on the 30th. When the Einstein paper arrived Elliott himself began the cabling, with the Columbia men in the New York office carrying out decipherment as the cable-copy arrived.

The paper for which the press had been waiting consisted of six pages covered by fairly large print and including thirty-three equations. "To the layman," commented *The Times'* correspondent, "the paper conveys next to nothing." This was not surprising since, as Eddington noted, "for the present, at any rate, a non-mathematical explanation is out of the question, and in any case would miss the main purpose of the theory, which is to weld a number of laws into a mathematical expression of formal simplicity." Einstein himself did the next best thing. He wrote a 3,000-word two-part article which was published in both the *New York Times* and *The Times*, and which outlined "the chain of discovery". The most important feature of the new theory was its hypothesis that the structure of four dimensional space could be described in terms of a synthesis of Riemannian and Euclidean geometry. On this rested the erection of unitary field laws for gravitation and electro-magnetism. It was new, it was interesting, but during the next few years informed opinion tended to support the view of Eddington:

> For my part, I cannot readily give up the affine picture, where gravitational and electrical quantities supplement one another as belonging respectively to the symmetrical and antisymmetrical features of world measurement; it is difficult to imagine a neater dovetailing. Perhaps one who believes that Weyl's theory and its affine generalisation afford considerable enlightenment, may be excused for doubting whether the new theory offers sufficient inducement to make an exchange.

Einstein himself was soon dissatisfied and within a year was working on a fresh theory with a new assistant, Dr. Walther Mayer, an Austrian brought to see him in Berlin after publication of a book which Einstein greatly admired — *Lehrbuch der Differentialgeometrie*. There was at first some difficulty in getting money for Mayer — possibly an indication of the Kaiser Wilhelm's long memory of Einstein's attitude during the war — but eventually money for him was found by the Josiah Macy (Junior) Foundation of New York. He then moved from Vienna to Berlin for what was to be more than three years of collaboration.

The new attempt was announced when in October the Macy Foundation issued details of the new unified field theory from Einstein and Mayer. This too was eventually abandoned, as were the other attempts which Einstein continued to make for the rest of his life — most of them produced, as he wrote to an old friend, "in an agony of mathematical torment from which I am unable to escape".

The 1929 theory was published only a few weeks before his fiftieth birthday. This was to see the publication — although not in Germany — of what can almost be described as an authorised biography. The circumstances of publication were unusual. One of Einstein's two stepsons-in-law, Rudolf Kayser, was author as well as journalist and had a deep interest in philosophy. He got on well with his stepfather - in - law and as the fiftieth birthday approached Kayser asked if the could write Einstein's life. Einstein consented. But it was clearly a reluctant consent which he gave. For his wish to help his stepson-in-law had to struggle with his strong distaste for personal publicity. The result was a compromise that misled the reader. The author of the biography was disguised under the pseudonym of "Anton Reiser", and only the slightest hint of his identity was given in Einstein's foreword. This said that the author of the book knew the subject well, had got his facts right and was as accurate in his characterisation as could be expected.

This was fair enough, as far as it went, but it gave no indication that, as Reiser subsequently said, its factual contents rested entirely on personal information from Einstein himself. Thus the reader was being presented not with an impartial biography but with one written by Einstein's stepson-in-law from material supplied by Einstein himself. Furthermore, Einstein forbade publication of the book in German, a decision which, whether by intent or not, made any challenging of its facts distinctly less likely.

Einstein's ambivalence to the Germans was equalled by their ambivalence to him, a fact illustrated by the experiences of his fiftieth birthday. On the one hand there was such international fame that he was driven to the refuge of Janos Plesch's house at Gatow by journalists who wanted a birthday interview. The German Chancellor described him as "Germany's great savant". The University of Paris conferred an honorary degree which he received later in the year, staying in the German Embassy and meeting Briand with whom he discussed the need for Franco-German friendship. The Zionists announced that they were to plant an "Einstein wood" near Jerusalem. To the flat in Haberlandstrasse there came presents from great men and small men alike — the first which Einstein acknowledged being an ounce of tobacco, sent by a German labourer with the apology that it was "a relatively small amount but gathered in a good field".

Yet these birthday celebrations took place beneath the shadow of a significant tragi-comedy. Some of those who played important roles in it are unidentified although the events in which they took part were a warning not lost on Einstein of things to come.

Early in 1929 Dr. Plesch approached the Berlin authorities, whom he describes as being in the hands of the typical middle and lower middle class.

> I had to explain to Boess, the Mayor of Berlin, who and what Einstein was before I could convince him that his city numbered a really great man amongst its inhabitants and that it was his Council's obvious duty to show some recognition of the fact, [he has written]. I am sure the worthy Boess was not entirely satisfied with what I told him, and pursued his enquiries further as to who this Einstein was. Apparently the result was satisfactory, for he finally agreed with me that it would be a good idea to acknowledge Einstein's birthday by presenting him with a house and garden as a mark of the deep esteem in which he was held by the Berlin Municipality.

This appears to be pitching the intellectual level of Berlin disparagingly low. The outcome suggests that the judgment was justified.

Einstein's love of small boats had remained from the days when he had sailed the Zurichsee, tacking back and forth with the splendid panorama of the Alps before him. What better, the Berlin Municipal Council therefore decided, than to choose for him a country villa on one of the Berlin lakes. He was known to enjoy the Havel River and it was announced that as a birthday gift he would be presented with a fine house on its banks, a little way up stream from its junction with the Wannsee. Illustrated Berlin magazines quickly printed photographs of the "Einstein House" set among pines. Only when Elsa visited the site to make domestic enquiries did she learn that the house was already occupied. The inhabitants furthermore had no intention of leaving, even for a successor as illustrious as Einstein.

The Berlin Council certainly owned the property they had presented; but they had already let it on an inalienable lease. Realising this, they changed their plans and hastily announced that a nearby plot would be presented to Einstein. Significantly, the gift was now to consist only of the land; Einstein would have to build his own house at his own expense. To this he readily agreed — only to be faced with another difficulty. For when other property on the estate had been leased, it had been agreed by the Council that no further building would be allowed to disturb the amenities or the view. Einstein might get his land; he would not be allowed to build on it.

At this point, doubts as to Berlin efficiency became mixed with darker suspicions. These were increased when the Council selected yet a third plot, only to discover after the bequest was announced that the property was not theirs to present. German humour is not always of its legendary stodginess and the Council was quickly made a laughing-stock. To resolve the problem, Einstein was asked to select his own site; the Council would pay for it. Elsa was not long in choosing a site in the village of Caputh, a few miles from Potsdam. The Council agreed to the choice and a motion for the purchase of the land was moved at the next session. At last all seemed to be settled. But now a member of a leading nationalist party came into the open. Did Einstein deserve this municipal gift, he demanded? The Council, forced to the vote, did not know. The subject was moved forward for further discussion at the next meeting.

It is difficult to disentangle the varying parts played in the sorry business by muddle, red tape and the internal politics of the Berlin authorities. "The decisive power", says Frank "lay in the hands of persons who sabotaged the work of the apparent rulers. The officials of the city of Berlin carried out the orders of the Municipal Council in such a way as to result in failure and to make the republican administration look ridiculous." This may well have been so. But there was also the ever-present ground-swell of anti-Semitism, which like any other racial prejudice is likely to win support in a society where ballots govern by quantity rather than quality.

Einstein now acted with desperation but dignity, writing to the Mayor, thanking him for the Council's friendly intentions, noting that his birthday was now past. He declined the gift. By this time, however, he and Elsa had become fond of the plot they had chosen. So they bought it, and built their own house on it. "In this way, without wanting it, we have acquired a beautiful home of our own situated in the woods near the water," Elsa told Professor Frank. "But we have spent most of our savings. Now we have no money, but we have our land and property. This gives one a much greater sense of security." Einstein, unworldlywise in so many things, knew better. He had once warned Frank that no more than ten years might be left to him in Germany. Eight had already passed.

The new home had all the qualities of genuinely rural surroundings even though it lay only a few miles from the centre of Berlin. Beyond Potsdam, on the road that led to Werder-on-the-Havel, Caputh was at that time little more than one straggling street, and was rarely visited by the weekend crowds from the capital. North of it stretched the sandy heaths and pine forests, interspersed by lakes and streams, which continue for mile after mile to the Baltic. Just outside the village the ground rises to the edge of the trees and here, only a few minutes from the Havelsee, on which white sails could usually be seen, the Einsteins built what was to be for a few years a good deal more than a weekend cottage.

The young architect ingeniously combined sophistication with a simple style that fitted the surroundings. From the exterior the impression was almost that of a log-built cabin; inside, the half-timbered construction concealed a comfortable roominess increased by smooth brown panelling and large windows giving on to the distant prospect of red Caputh roofs, the Havelsee, and the enclosing forest. This was also the view from the long first-floor room which Einstein used as combined study and bedroom. Books lined the walls, the bed filled a recess, while in front of the tall French windows which opened on to a balcony there stood the large paper-cluttered desk at which he worked. And on the Havelsee there was berthed the *Tummler*, the small boat given him as a fiftieth birthday present by friends. It was a fine scene. Had he known his Bishop Heber, he might have considered it as another Ceylon, where "every prospect pleases and only man is vile".

While the argument over his birthday present had been going on, the theory of relativity had been used to pull him into a religious controversy from which there emerged one of his much-quoted statements of faith. It began when Cardinal O'Connell of Boston, who had attacked Einstein's General Theory on previous occasions, told a group of Catholics that it "cloaked the ghastly apparition of atheism" and "befogged speculation, producing universal doubt about God and His Creation". Einstein, who had often reiterated his remark of 1921 to Archbishop Davidson — "It makes no difference. It is purely abstract science" — was at first uninterested. Then, on April 24th, Rabbi Herbert Goldstein of the Institutional Synagogue, New York, faced Einstein with the simple five-word radiogram: "Do you believe in God?"

His reply, that he believed in Spinoza's God, was enough for Goldstein, who pointed out that "Spinoza, who is called the God-intoxicated man, and who saw God manifest in all nature, certainly could not be called an atheist." "Furthermore", he went on, "Einstein points to a unity. Einstein's theory if carried out to its logical conclusion would bring to mankind a scientific formula for monotheism. He does away with all thought of dualism or pluralism. There can be no room for any aspect of polytheism. This latter thought may have caused the Cardinal to speak out. Let us call a spade a spade."

On this occasion Einstein was merely hinting tentatively at the belief which he held in common with many scientists who distrusted revealed religions and did not see that a future life was an essential for ethical behaviour in this one: the belief that much if not all of both science and religion concerned complementary but separate aspects of human affairs. Like T. H. Huxley, he was aware that great though science was, it "could never lay its hands, could never touch, even with the tip of its finger, that dream with which our little life is rounded".

At Caputh, where he settled in during 1929, Einstein tried to isolate himself from unwanted visitors, newspaper correspondents, and the uncategorisable cranks who sought a few words with him. As there was no telephone, visitors took the train to Potsdam, the local bus to Caputh, then continued on foot, often arriving unannounced. Here came the group of Americans who wanted Einstein's advice on the organisation of a Kellogg League that would appeal to all people opposed to war. Here came Otto Hahn from the Kaiser Wilhelm Institute to discuss the work which a few years later unlocked the door to nuclear fission. And here, in the summer of 1930, came Rabindranath Tagore, the Indian philosopher and mystic.

Einstein and Tagore talked for the afternoon in the grounds, and what was described as the "authorised version" of their conversation subsequently appeared in the *American Hebrew*. In view of Einstein's statement that the report should never have been published too much faith should not be put in the account, which was headed "The Nature of Reality". Nevertheless, it rings true, and there are exchanges which have the authentic Einstein touch as when, after Tagore had denied that truth or beauty was independent of man, his companion asked: "If there would be no human beings any more, the Apollo of Belvedere would no longer be beautiful?" To Tagore's "No", Einstein noted that he agreed "with regard to this conception of Beauty, but not with regard to Truth", adding: "I cannot prove that my conception is right, but that is my religion."

Contemplation of first principles progressively occupied Einstein's attention. One visitor, Dr. Chaim Tschernowitz, has given a vivid account of a summer trip with him on the Havelsee during which their discussions were often metaphysical. "The conversation drifted back and forth from profundities about the nature of God, the universe and man to questions of a lighter and more vivacious nature . . ." he has written. "Suddenly [Einstein] lifted his head, looked upward at the clear skies, and said: 'We know nothing about it all. All our knowledge is but the knowledge of schoolchildren.' 'Do you think,' I asked, 'that we shall ever probe the secret?' 'Possibly,' he said with a movement of his shoulders, 'we shall know a little more than we do now. But the real nature of things, that we shall never know, never.'" As Born said of Einstein after his death, "he knew, as did Socrates, that we know nothing".

Meanwhile he worked on, at the unified field theory, at the problems posed by quantum mechanics, intrigued by the prospects being opened up in cosmology by the new telescopes of California, and in nuclear physics by the accumulating knowledge of the atom. In his own speciality he was lucky; in the days before computers he demanded no equipment, and as for helpers Dr. Mayer sufficed. "The kind of work I do can be done anywhere," he said when his friend Philipp Frank apologised that he might be late for a rendezvous near the Astrophysical Observatory. "Why should I be less capable of reflecting about my problems on the Potsdam bridge than at home?"

When the demon was with him nothing else mattered. Joffé, the Russian physicist, recalls how while staying in Berlin he visited Einstein to describe his recent work on the mechanical and electrical properties of crystals:

He asked me to explain in detail. I remember that I arrived at his house about three o'clock and began the account of my work. After about an hour his wife came in and asked Einstein to see, about five o'clock, someone who had come from Hamburg to make the acquaintance of the great man. Einstein hated this sort of thing, but he obviously got little support from his family. He therefore led me into a nearby park where we were able to continue the conversation undisturbed. As soon as the danger of a meeting had passed we returned to his study. In two hours I had explained all the essentials to him; and now Einstein began the process of turning the information to his own use. One can describe this process as the organic absorption of new information into an already existing uniform picture of Nature.

After the return, and a meal at eight o'clock, the discussion continued. Midnight came and went — and so did the last train for Werder where Joffé was living. He tentatively remarked that the talk could be continued at some other time, but the idea made no impression on Einstein. "Finally, at two in the morning", says Joffé, "the discussion ended; everything was settled, all doubts had been cleared up. Once again, a piece had been fitted into the contradictory jigsaw which was Einstein's picture of the world. Neither I nor many other scholars would have been capable of so long and so systematic an intellectual exercise. But for Einstein it was obviously commonplace."

It was natural that Joffé should go out of his way to consult the scientist who had by this time become, despite the reputation of Planck, Born and von Laue, and the potential fame of Heisenberg, the man physicists most wished to see when they visited Berlin. And it was natural that after mathematicians and scientists throughout the world had contributed to a special award that was to bear Max Planck's name, Einstein should be the first to receive it.

The presentation was to take place at five in the afternoon and after a morning's work Einstein visited Plesch for a lunch over which they discussed the crisis in the theory of causality. Then Einstein lay down on a couch and went to sleep. He woke at four, said: "They'll expect me to say something or the other," sat down at the doctor's writing desk, took a bootmaker's bill which was the nearest piece of paper to hand, and scribbled away for twenty minutes. Half an hour later, in the packed hall of the Institute of Physics, Planck took the platform and after a conventional speech handed over the medal.

"Then Einstein spoke," writes Plesch: " 'I knew that an honour of this sort would move me deeply' he began, 'and therefore I have put down on paper what I would like to say to you as thanks. I will read it.' And out of his waistcoat pocket came my bootmaker's bill with the scribble on the back, and he read out what he had written about the principle of causality. And because, as he said, no reasoning being could get on at all without causality he established the principle of super-causality. The atmosphere was tense and most moving." Afterwards Plesch claimed his bootmaker's bill. Einstein also handed him the medal, of solid gold and with a bust relief of Planck. "It was still in the case," Plesch noted. "He never took it out or looked at it again."

This award and the stream of comparable honours and invitations from abroad (a sign that Einstein's reputation was still uneroded despite his growing isolation in the crisis over indeterminacy) were fair indications of the German position he still held in the scientific community. Outside the situation was very different. In 1920 when he had been a convenient focus of attack for the Nationalists and the anti-Semites, the battle had been fought on the extremist fringe, in an atmosphere exacerbated both by the humiliations of the German defeat and the aggravations aroused by Einstein's own wartime record and his left-wing pacifist beliefs. A decade later it was not merely the extremists who were involved. Now it was necessary to attract a larger audience and it was here that Einstein was such a useful weapon in the hands of those already optimistic of ending the Republic. For to the less discriminating and more credulous it was comparatively easy to portray the complexities of relativity as the culminating confidence-trick of a Jewish conspiracy. Not everyone would believe this, of course. But Einstein as a symbol was far more vulnerable to attack than a hero of the medical sciences, a popular Jewish author or a leader in any of the professions whose achievements were easy to understand and difficult to deride.

The dangers of the situation were increased by Einstein's own naïveté. This has been emphasised by Lancelot Law Whyte, a young British physicist studying in Berlin at the time. Whyte had met Einstein, greatly admired him, and had so gained the master's confidence as to become translator of the 3,000-word article on the unified field which Einstein wrote for *The Times* early in 1929. Whyte has put down what many were no doubt thinking. "Late in 1928," he says, "it seemed to me, that by giving favours to Jews and foreign visitors which he was not giving to German colleagues and students, Einstein was in a sense helping to produce anti-Semitism. I

was disturbed by this; it did not correspond with my image of him
as a noble and wise person, and it made me uncomfortable that he
had been so kind to me."

Shorty afterwards Whyte consulted "a senior figure".

You do not understand [said this colleague.] There is already so much
anti-Semitism and jealousy of Einstein on the part of duller German
scholars and such a gulf between the German and Modern sides of
the university, that it is impossible for Einstein to be above the battle,
the same to all men. He is a Jew, he inevitably dislikes much that is
going on, and he is already for many a hated symbol. A German
teacher or student from some other German university could not
approach him as you have done. The universities reflect a chasm in
Germany; on the one side intellect and internationalism, and on the
other the re-creation of something peculiarly German after the disaster
of 1918.

From this situation it was possible to draw only one conclusion.

After this talk in 1929 [Whyte says,] I had an uncomfortable feeling that since Einstein could not escape his outstanding responsibility
as a symbol, he should not remain for longer than he could help in a
university where he could not treat all alike. The fact was that his
presence in Germany was acting as a focus and stimulant for anti-
Semitism. He was the hero compelled by fate to become an instrument
of evil, as again later in relation to nuclear energy."

Shortly afterwards Norman Bentwich, who as Attorney General in Palestine had walked on Mount Scopus with Einstein seven
years earlier, visited Berlin with his wife. "I was disturbed by grim
signs of the rising anti-Semitic flood and the growing strength of
the Nazi political party", he has written. "When we had spent a
week there the previous year, on our tour through Europe, all
seemed serene and hopeful. Now many Jewish shops had been
sacked, and the Jews, who in 1929 were almost derisive about Hitler,
were seriously alarmed. I visited Einstein in his sailing retreat on
one of the lakes; and for all his serenity he was anxious." Soon he
was more so. A few months later he was seriously advising a young
correspondent not to become a maths master because of the bad prospects and the difficulty bound up with the "jüdischen Nationalität".

Good enough reason for his worry arrived soon afterwards, with
the publication in Leipzig of an ill-tempered little book called *100
Authors Against Einstein (Hundert Autoren Gegen Einstein)*. With
the exception of Lenard and Stark, few scientists of even middling
reputation could be induced to condemn relativity, a fact which,

clearly made the Leipzig publication part of a careful propaganda drive. Some of the contents could be plausibly claimed as respectable, but the promoters had to scrape the bottom of the scientific barrel to find their quota of contributors. Professor Mellin of Helsingfors wrote on "The Untenability of the Relativity Theory" (*"Die Unhaltbarkeit der Relativitätstheorie"*); Professor Dr. Hans Driesch of Leipzig on "My Chief Objections to Relativity Theory" (*"Meine Haupteinwands Gegen der Relativitätstheorie"*); and Professor Dr. le Roux of Rennes on "The Bankruptcy of the Relativity Theory" (*"Die Bankrott der Relativitätstheorie"*). Dr. Arvid Reuterdahl of Minnesota contributed a long disquisition on "Einsteinism: His Deceitful Conclusions and Frauds" in which he not only attacked the alleged priority of Einstein's theory but claimed that the bombastic manner of his story had turned him into "the Barnum of science" *(den Barnum der Wissenschaft).*

He was well aware that this was merely the tip of the anti-Semitic iceberg. More than once he spoke to his wife of taking a post abroad, of renouncing German nationality for the second time, and of holding up for public examination the attitude of Germany towards the Jews. Perhaps it would have been better for the Jews had he done so. But he hesitated. The magnet provided by the society of the Berlin physicists proved too powerful.

On July 17th, 1931 he went so far as to draft a letter to Max Planck saying that he wished to give up his German citizenship. The letter was never posted and was still in its original envelope when in 1933, after Einstein's refusal to return to Germany following the rise of Hitler, his papers were retrieved from Germany by diplomatic bag through the French Embassy.

It is easy to infer what happened. With his built-in wish to cause the minimum trouble to everyone, Einstein would decide to have a private word with Planck before anything was put on record. And Planck, that figure of quintessential German loyalty, would have little difficulty in persuading his colleague, once again, where duty lay. He did not have to parade his national loyalty, nor his inner conviction that civil servants did not desert their posts in the hour of need. He had merely, from the scientific pedestal on which Einstein rightly placed him, to note that if a man genuinely wished to probe the secrets of nature there was no place better fitted for the work than Berlin.

Einstein genuinely agreed. Since 1923 he had, it is true, been a visiting lecturer at Leiden, and gladly given his services in Switzerland when required. But in spite of his feelings about Germans and Germany, he remained faithful to the Kaiser Wilhelm Institute.

Yet now, as the 1930s started their disastrous course downhill, Einstein's faith in the future of Europe in general and of Germany in particular began to wane. This was revealed not only by his increasingly pessimistic utterances, publicly on platforms and privately to friends, in magazine and newspaper articles, but also in the new pattern of life soon produced by acceptance of two different sets of engagements. One was with the California Institute of Technology which he agreed to visit for a few weeks early in 1931 on what was mutually if loosely expected to be the start of a long-term regular engagement. The other was at Christ Church, Oxford, where he accepted a research fellowship which allowed him to spend one term a year in the university. His work in Berlin would of course continue as before; but it would dovetail conveniently into an annual programme which would involve departure from Germany for the United States in December, return during the late winter or early spring, then summer in Oxford before a return to Berlin in the early autumn. This plan had the advantage of retaining his links with Planck, von Laue, and his other colleagues while providing two alternative refuges against the rise of anti-Semitism or the outbreak of war. Meanwhile, adding to the lustre of German science, he continued to feed the hand that bit him.

Before the start of these series of visits to California and to Oxford, which developed under the increasingly sinister pressure of events in Germany, Einstein made three other significant journeys abroad, one to Holland and Belgium, two to Britain. The first was the most important. It led to one meeting which helped to topple him from his pacifist stance in the summer of 1933, but it was also a journey important to the world in general and to Japan in particular. In Belgium, Einstein forged a link which ran directly from the Belgian royal family to a study in Princeton, to the fear that Belgian uranium might come under German control, and thence to a letter alerting President Roosevelt to the possibilities of nuclear weapons.

In 1929 he made one of his regular trips to Leiden. He called as usual on his Uncle Cäsar in Antwerp, just across the frontier. And here he received an invitation to visit the Queen of the Belgians at Laeken on Monday, May 20th. King Albert, epitome of the liberal-minded constitutional monarch, still a symbolic figure from the First World War, a trenchcoated king defying the German invaders in Flanders fields, had a genuine interest in science and was absent only because of an appointment in Switzerland. Queen Elizabeth, formerly Princess Elizabeth of Bavaria, was unconventional and artistic, and on May 20th Einstein and his violin spent the first of many musical afternoons at the Palace, Her Majesty "playing second fiddle". There followed, according to the Queen's own notes in her agenda book, tea under the chestnuts and a walk in the grounds, followed by dinner at 7.30. A few days later she sent him prints of the photographs she had taken, hoping he would come again soon, passing on the King's regrets that he had been away, and adding, according to her draft reply: "It was unforgettable for me when you came down from your peak of knowledge and gave me a tiny glimpse into your ingenious theory."

The meeting marked the start of an unusual friendship. During the next four years — as long as Einstein remained in Europe — he would rarely visit Belgium without being invited to the Palace at Laeken. He was the usual Einstein, being missed at the railway station by the Royal chauffeur who failed to recognise the drably-dressed figure with violin case; alarming a small café by requesting the use of a telephone and then asking direct for the Queen, and generally behaving in the simple unpremeditated way of a man with his mind on other things.

A full description of every visit went back to Elsa. In recounting one meeting he recorded that Her Majesty, an English guest, a lady-in-waiting and he had played trios and quartets for several hours after which he had sat down with the royal family to a frugal dinner. This casualness has been described by Antonina Vallentin who records how one day at Caputh Einstein was searching for a piece of paper:

> With impatient gestures he was emptying the contents of his pockets on the table. They were the pockets of a schoolboy; penknife, pieces of string, bits of biscuits, chits, bus tickets, change, tobacco dropped out of his pipe. At last, with a rustle of parchment, a large sheet of paper fell out. It was a poem that the Queen of the Belgians had dedicated to him. At the bottom of the large ivory-coloured page there were a few words and a few figures in Einstein's small, regular handwriting. I bent over the table. Immortal calculations side by side with the royal signature that cut across the page, I read: "Autobus 50 pfennig, newspaper, stationery, etc." Daily expenses, noted with care, entangled side by side with the loop of the regal "E".

King Albert died in a climbing accident in 1934. Queen Elizabeth lived on, and the quarter-century that followed her first meeting with Einstein was marked by a long series of letters. Einstein's were extremely outspoken — as though Her Majesty lived at such a far-removed level that he could write with a familiarity unusual in corespondence between royalty and commoner. Perhaps their common links with southern Germany — or the similarity of their experiences, Einstein rejecting the Fatherland and Her Majesty having her adopted country invaded by it — aroused a common sympathy. Whatever the particular fuel which kept the friendship alight, there were to be repercussions, unsuspected in 1929, of that first invitation and walk under the chestnut trees.

The following year Einstein made two visits to England. Before he left Berlin for the first, he received a request from Professor Veblen whom he had met in Princeton nine years previously. A new faculty lounge was being built in the university for the mathematics and physics department. Could they have permission to use on it his phrase which had lodged in Veblen's memory — "God is subtle but he is not malicious"? Einstein consented, adding that what he had meant was that nature concealed her mysteries by means of her essential grandeur, not by her cunning, and the original phrase was carved on the room's marble fireplace.

Shortly afterwards he left for England, going first to Nottingham where he gave to the university a general survey of relativity and the unified field theory. Then he travelled on to Cambridge to accept an honorary degree, a happy occasion since it enabled him to meet Eddington whose knighthood was announced in the King's Birthday Honours during the visit. Einstein had been invited to stay at the Cambridge Observatory with Eddington and his sister in 1920, 1925, and 1926, but had been unable to accept due to pressure of work and official engagements. He wanted to come, and in 1926 had told Eddington that it would be worth learning the English language just for the pleasure of talking with him. Now the opportunity had arrived, and the two men spent a week together.

In the autumn he came to London for a special dinner of the O. R. T. — an organisation for helping Jews in Eastern Europe — staying with Lord Samuel in Porchester Terrace where, as he later described it, he played a "star-guest role". But he skilfully evaded a further invitation "to meet... many prominent men", pleading that he had a prior appointment in Switzerland where he was anxious to discuss the health of his younger son.

Samuel's notes of Einstein's visit, written a few hours after his guest's departure, cast some interesting sidelights on Einstein at the age of fifty. At luncheon one day the two men were joined by Edmond Kapp, who a decade previously had sketched Einstein lecturing in Vienna. By now a well-known portraitist, Kapp made roughs of Einstein's head, later marrying them with his action sketches of Vienna to produce one of his best studies. By this time Einstein was an habitual "subject". When Samuel remarked that he must be constantly troubled by painters or sculptors Einstein agreed; during his journey to England, he told them, he had got into conversation with a man who asked him his occupation. "*Je suis modele,*" he replied. During the meal he mentioned that he was still frequently being attacked in Germany — "*parce que je suis Rouge et Juif.*" Samuel, knowing that Einstein's politics were pink rather than red, commented: "*Mais pas très Rouge.*" "*Et pas très Juif,*" added Einstein.

After the O. R. T. banquet — where in his speech he paid tribute to his fellow-guests, Bernard Shaw and H. G. Wells, "for whose conceptions of life I have a special sympathy" — he remarked on the difference in the way in which people had shaken hands with him. Some were nervous, some curious, some proud. The men were *fier* on account of their positions, the women on account of their beauty. "He said to me on the way to the station," Samuel continues, "that never in his early years had he imagined for a moment that he would take part in affairs of a public character such as this, which had brought him on this journey, or which arose from his interest in Palestine. He had expected that he should spend all his life in more solitary pursuits. He added that he did not really feel himself fitted for these tasks. '*Je suis pas 'praktisch'!*'" The following day he "dropped in" on the Weizmanns. "He was much amused at the O. R. T. dinner, where he says, people made the impression of a monkeys' assembly," says Mrs. Weizmann. "They were mostly concerned over whom to shake hands with first — Lord Rothschild or Einstein himself."

Soon after he arrived back in Berlin, he was visited by Arthur Fleming, the chairman of the Board of Trustees of the Californian Institute of Technology. The visit appears to have been made on the suggestion of Richard Chase Tolman, the Institute's Professor of Physical Chemistry and Mathematical Physics, for reasons which were soon to be self-evident. "The result was better than Tolman expected", Fleming wrote to a colleague "so that when I first met Einstein at his home in the country, and invited him to come to us with the money provided by Mr. Thomas Cochran, his first question was, 'You have a man named Tolman at your institution?' I said we had, and he then asked if Tolman were a visitor or one of our men. I informed him that he was one of ours."

Tolman was handling much of the theoretical work at Mount Wilson Observatory concerning the nature and size of the universe.

Einstein was anxious to discuss this first-hand with the men concerned, and he quickly agreed to visit the Institute as a research
associate early in 1931.

When the news was announced he was soon brought up once
more against the interest of the United States in all he said and did.
By now he was well aware of the power of his name; but nearly
a decade had passed since his first visit to America and his
recollection of the unrelenting eagerness with which the inhabitants
seized their enthusiasms had faded. Before the end of the week, fifty
cables a day were arriving from across the Atlantic. U. S. mail began
to outnumber German letters. Elsa, who was left to handle the wel-
ter of invitations, stated firmly that the professor would be travelling purely on holiday; that he wished to be left alone: and, finally,
that she would not allow him to land in New York, but would insist
that he remained on board while their Belgian ship continued its
journey south, through the Panama Canal, and up to California.

Despite these efforts at non-engagement, Einstein agreed to one
proposal which contributed an *hors d'oeuvres* of controversy before the start of his visit. This was a request to write for the *New
York Times* an article on religion and science, a perennial subject
on which the views of a non-practising Jew who had given a fresh
description of the universe were particularly pertinent. Ever since he
had been thrust into the limelight his religious views had been sought
not only by the press but by friends, colleagues, and acquaintances. Ernest Strauss, who worked with him in Princeton, quoted
him in the Encyclopaedia Americana as describing religious thought
as "an attempt to find an out where there is no door". His friend
Max Born observed that "he had no belief in the Church, but did
not think that religious faith was a sign of stupidity, nor unbelief
a sign of intelligence." There was a whiff of wishful thinking in
some of the views credited to him. Thus Ben Gurion, asked if he
believed in God, replied: "I once talked to Einstein. Even he, with
his great formula about energy and mass, agreed that there must be
something behind the energy." And Prince Hubertus of Lowenstein
reports him as saying, in the United States, before the Second World
War: "In view of such harmony in the cosmos which I, with my
limited human mind, am able to recognise, there are yet people who
say there is no God. But what really makes me angry is that they
quote me for the support of such views."

Maybe. To some extent the differences between Einstein and
more conventional believers were semantic, a point brought out in
his "Religion and Science" which on Sunday November 9th occupied

the entire front page of the *New York Times Magazine.* "Everything that men do or think," it began, "concerns the satisfaction of the needs they feel or the escape from pain." Einstein then went on to outline three states of religious development, starting with the religion of fear that moved primitive peoples, and which in due course became the moral religions whose driving force was social feelings. This in turn could become the "cosmic religious sense ... which recognises neither dogmas nor God made in man's image."

A leading article in the *New York Times* the following day was mildly noncommittal, a reasonable enough attitude in view of the obvious fact that the word "religion" had a different meaning for Einstein than for most people. By contrast, at opposite ends of the range, were Dr. Nathan Krass and Dr. Fulton Sheen. Dr. Krass, rabbi of the Temple Emmanuel of 64th Street and Fifth Avenue, took it favourably: "The religion of Albert Einstein will not be approved by certain sectarians but it must and will be approved by the Jews." Dr. Sheen, on the other hand, told 1,200 members of the Catholic Teachers Association the *Times* had "degraded itself" by publishing Einstein's article, which he described as "the sheerest kind of stupidity and nonsense". He asked whether anyone would be willing to lay down their life for the Milky Way, and concluded: "There is only one fault with his cosmical religion: he put an extra letter in the word — the letter 's'."

Einstein's use of the usual word 'religion' to cover his own non-usual ethical attitudes was only one example of the way in which his outlook was contrary to that of the country he was now to visit for the second time: "An impersonal God, a deterministic universe, a churchless religion, disregard of money and material gains, world government, pacifism and socialism — all of these are pretty generally thought to be un-American and more or less subversive." Einstein believed in the lot. In addition, he despised the wrong sort of publicity. To the American journalist he agreed to see on November 22nd, shortly before leaving for the United States, he deplored the letters which had been arriving at the Haberlandstrasse house from manufacturers of disinfectants, toilet waters, musical instruments and clothes — offering thousands of dollars for permission to say that Einstein had found their goods satisfactory. "Is it not a sad commentary on the commercialism and, I must add, the corruption of our time that business firms make these offers with no thought of wanting to insult me?" he asked. "It evidently means that this form of corruption — for corruption it is — is widespread." He was still unable to realise that the enthusiasm for his presence which was so frequently exploited to aid the causes of Zionism or of peace, could not be switched on or off at will. Much as he wished to utilise mass psychology in the battle for good causes, he yet deplored it. "My own case is, alas, an illustration," he said. "Why popular fancy should seize me, a scientist dealing in abstract things and happy if left alone, is one of those manifestations of mass psychology that are beyond me. I think it is terrible that this should be so and I suffer more than anybody can imagine." This may very well have been true, but if so it was ingenuous.

At Antwerp, where he and Elsa embarked on the *Belgenland* on December 2nd, 1930, he repeated that this was merely a holiday trip, although agreeing that he would be visiting El Paso Observatory and would discuss with his American friends questions in which they were mutually interested. "If you really want to send a message to the press", he told reporters, "let it be that I want to be left alone. Personally I consider it indecent to delve into people's private affairs, and the world would certainly fare better if newspapers cared more for things that really matter instead of dealing with trifles." And to the news that he would be able to speak to his friends by radio-telephone he replied: "I hope these journalists are not going to call me up in the middle of the ocean and ask me how I slept the night before." At Southampton, which according to a diary impressed him with England's might, the press appears to have been less importunate.

As the liner pulled out into the Atlantic, Einstein was left comparatively at peace in the three flower-filled staterooms which had been allotted him. Here he was to work throughout much of the voyage with Dr. Mayer, permanently guarded from intrusion by a member of the crew stationed outside the door to his suite.

But the radio-telephone continued to bring news: of the *Völkischer Beobachter*, which was violently attacking him for travelling on a Belgian ship instead of the German *Europa*, due to arrive in New York the same day (but not sailing on to the West Coast); and of the National German Jewish Union, taking up the old stick that Einstein was using his scientific fame to propagate Zionism, a charge which it would have been difficult to deny. Before the end of the voyage there came a further report from Berlin, quoting a Dr. Boris Brutzkus who recounted how Einstein had told him that he would settle in a quiet resort in the South of France if Hitler ever came to power.

On this final point, Einstein felt forced to comment. "One should not speak publicly about conditions which one hopes will not come to pass," he said. "Still less should one under such circumstances make any decision in advance or even make public such decisions." He refused to be drawn. But it seemed clear to others, if not to him, that he must be summing up the prospects in America should he be forced from Germany. There, after all, he could hope to continue his work in peace.

During the voyage, a working one for Einstein and Dr. Mayer, Elsa was persuaded that it would, after all, be better for them to go ashore in New York. Einstein himself agreed that it would be simpler for him to meet the press when the ship came into harbour. As the *New York Times* had already noted, "It is probably accurate for the Berlin paper to advise him that he cannot hope to keep his features out of the New York press unless he locks himself in the purser's safe. And even then there will be pictures taken of the safe."

The occasion, when it came, had an air of comedy. Fifty reporters and fifty photographers swooped on their victim. Einstein, good-natured but bewildered, was called upon "within the brief quarter of an hour to define the fourth dimension in one word, state his theory of relativity in one sentence, give his views on prohibition, comment on politics and religion, and discuss the virtues of his violin". The German consul, Paul Schwarz, helped interpret; Elsa did her best to stage-manage the occasion, mothering her husband away from the trick-questions, explaining, protecting, and sympathising with those who wanted the theory of relativity described in a few one-syllable words.

He proved remarkably adroit at handling his questioners, answering the scientific conundrums so that the replies were comprehensible, sidestepping the more irrelevant demands, and interspersing his remarks with the occasional debating point or colourful phrase. Asked whether there was any relation between science and metaphysics, he declared that science itself was metaphysics. And asked what he thought of Hitler, he replied: "I do not enjoy Mr. Hitler's acquaintance. Hitler is living on the empty stomach of Germany. As soon as economic conditions in Germany improve he will cease to be important."

He also broadcast from the ship, not once but twice, thus satisfying two companies and earning 1,000 dollars for his welfare fund for the Berlin poor.

After the broadcasts Einstein went ashore, for five crowded days of speechmaking and sightseeing, returning every night to the *Belgenland* where he could be protected from the hundreds of visitors who wished to invoke his personal aid. He received the keys of New York at a ceremony attended by Mayor Walker and President Butler of Columbia University. He saw his statue adorning Riverside Church overlooking the Hudson River — the only statue of a living man among the thinkers who had changed the world from the days of Socrates and Plato. He celebrated the Jewish festival of Hanukkah at a crowded meeting in Madison Square Garden, and on the 14th he gave his famous "two percent" pacifist speech to the New History Society at the Ritz-Carlton Hotel. He visited the *New York Times* and he visited the Metropolitan Opera, where he was spontaneously cheered when the audience noticed him sitting quietly in a box. Here he was handed a slip of paper on which the Metropolitan's publicity director had written: "Relativity: There is no hitching post in the universe — so far as we know." Einstein studied it carefully, added "Read, and found correct", and then signed it. And here, spying the press photographers who were awaiting him, he nimbly about-turned and escaped from them — a Marx Brothers incident in which the publicity director was seen running after the world's most famous scientist plaintively calling: "Mr. Einstein, Mr. Einstein."

The dislike of publicity was usually genuine, even if it at times gave the impression of a Lawrence of Arabia backing into the limelight. But once the cordon had been broken through Einstein could be amiable enough. Thus a young Berliner, refused permission to sketch him when he returned on board, merely sat in the *Belgenland's* restaurant and sketched while Einstein ate. The great man was amused, signed the sketch and added: *"Dieses fette satte Schwein / Soll Professor Einstein sein"* ("This fat, well-sated pig you see / Professor Einstein purports to be"). He continued to evade the trail of autograph-hunters, although those who wrote got strictly business treatment. "If the autograph is wanted very badly, if the letter brings, say, three dollars for the Berlin poor," Elsa said, "the doctor will be happy. And with pictures for autograph with, say, five dollars, the doctor will be happy." The little account book which she showed, containing the details of what Einstein sent to the Berlin poor was, she claimed, his favourite reading.

The Einsteins sailed from New York on December 16th, touched at Havana three days later, then passed through the Panama Canal before turning northwards up the coast of California. As they neared their destination the other passengers made the most of the last opportunities of being photographed with Einstein. So much so that resignation at last gave place to annoyance. But there was of course one consolation. The autograph business was flourishing. He was reported to be charging a dollar a time for charity.

At the end of the month, the *Belgenland* reached San Diego. Einstein gave a New Year broadcast over the local radio, attended local festivities including one public reception at which local Jews presented him with an inscribed gold *Mezuzah* containing a Hebrew prayer and another at which he was given a floral float. "However crazy such things may look from the outside," Hedwig Born wrote to him after watching the scene on a newsreel, "I always have the feeling that the dear Lord knows very well what he is up to. In the same way as Gretchen sensed the Devil in Faust, so he makes people sense in you — well, just the Einstein."

From San Diego the Einsteins were driven to Pasadena. Here they soon chose a small bungalow, the "shingled gingerbread house" as Einstein called it, where they were to live for their two-month stay at the Institute. As a celebrity Einstein was much sought after even in a land of celebrities. Upton Sinclair, who took him to see Eisenstein's famous film about life in Mexico, later claimed a local millionairess had contributed 10,000 dollars to Caltech on the promise of meeting him. He and Elsa dined with Charlie Chaplin "as a result of expressions of mutual desire on the part of himself and the professor to meet each other". And during a visit to Hollywood he was given a special showing of Remarque's *All Quiet on the Western Front,* already banned in Germany. "I thank you for all the things you have said of me," he said at the special dinner which followed. "If I believed them I would not be sane, and since I know I am sane, I do not believe them." Adulation was not unqualified, and Sinclair recalls a brief exchange when the Einsteins visited Professor Graham Laing and his wife. Mrs. Laing had queried Einstein's views on God, which had brought Elsa out of her corner with the declaration: "My husband has the greatest mind in the world." "Yes," came the reply, "but he doesn't know everything", a statement with which Einstein himself would have heartily agreed.

All this, however, was the froth on an important working tour. The purpose of Einstein's visit, he announced on arriving, "would be to fit into the life of the California Institute of Technology and discuss problems with noted scientists more intimately than is possible by correspondence". The day after his arrival he gave a further clue to the reason for his visit. "New observations by Hubble and Humason" — both workers at the Mount Wilson Observatory above Pasadena — "concerning the red shift of light in distant nebulae make it appear likely that the general structure of the universe is not static," he said. "Theoretical investigations made by Lemaître and Tolman fit well into the General Theory of Relativity." Einstein had in fact travelled half-way round the world to see whether it was really necessary to revise the picture of the universe with which he had virtually founded modern cosmology in 1917; and, if so, in what way.

Only thirteen years separated his "Cosmological Implications" from 1930, but within that period a revolution had taken place in cosmology quite as shattering as the revolution in physics which separated the work of Lorentz and J. J. Thomson in the last years of the nineteenth century from that of Planck and Einstein in the first years of the twentieth. In 1917 the mathematical projections of the universe provided by Einstein and de Sitter were given due consideration, even though astronomers had not entirely abandoned a belief that the Milky Way, the galaxy which contains the sun and its solar system amongst millions of other stars, formed the entire universe. However, it was not denied that some of the faint mysterious patches of light scattered across the night sky might be other galaxies lying unimagined distances away. V. M. Slipher at Lowell Observatory certainly thought so and suggested that at least some of them were receding from the Milky Way.

After the end of the war, evidence began to accumulate. Like evidence for the sub-nuclear world of the atom, it came with the advance of technology, in this case with the use of ever more powerful telescopes, notably the 100-inch instrument on Mount Wilson above Pasadena. Here Edwin Hubble had from 1920 been probing into Jeans' "mysterious universe". It seemed clear to him that some of the light patches in the sky were merely clouds of gas illuminated from stars that lay within the galaxy of the Milky Way. But about others there was doubt that slowly began to be removed. In 1924 he was able to observe individual stars within the Andromeda M 31 nebula. Shortly afterwards it became evident that such stars were some 800,000 light-years away — eight times the distance of the farthest star in the Milky Way. Thus the galaxy of which the solar system formed part was but a portion of the universe; how small a portion became more and more obvious within the next few years as improvements in techniques and equipment revealed the existence of other galaxies millions and even billions of light-years away.

These discoveries were dramatically supported within two years, by both theoretical cosmology and observational astronomy. The story is chronologically tangled and has some similarity with the simultaneous but independent work on evolution by Darwin and Wallace and the near-simultaneous but independent development of radar in Britain, the United States and Germany.

Listening to Hubble's account of his Andromeda discoveries at a meeting of the National Academy of Sciences in Washington had been a young Belgian priest who after studying astrophysics in Cambridge had moved to the Massachusetts Institute of Technology. He was Abbé Lemaître, "the mathematician for whom symmetry was nearly as important as truth". Shortly afterwards, Lemaître returned to Belgium, and in a paper published in 1927 showed not only that the Einstein world would have to be unstable, but that it would in fact expand along the lines of de Sitter's world. A unique and startling feature of Lemaître's cosmology was that his pre-supposed world had started as a "primeval atom" or "cosmic egg" which had initially contained all the matter in the universe and whose disintegration had marked the beginning of time and space. Thus the contemporary universe was merely one phase in an evolving universe. This could have started as a greatly modified "Einstein world" before turning into a continuously expanding de Sitter world in which the galaxies were moving ever farther away from one another and in which the density of matter was becoming less while its amount remained static. Lemaître's paper passed virtually unnoticed at the time. But two years later Hubble at Mount Wilson made the sensational announcement that the galaxies were receding at a speed proportional to their distance — receding not only from the Milky Way but also from each other. All inter-galactic distances were in fact increasing simultaneously, and the entire universe was expanding at a rate which doubled its dimensions roughly every 1,300 million years.

Spurred on by these revelations, Eddington began an enquiry with one of his research students into whether or not the "Einstein world" was stable. They soon received a copy of Lemaître's paper. This helped to convince them that the answer was "no". Thus by the middle of 1930 Hubble the astronomer, Lemaître the unknown theoretician, and Eddington the astrophysist, agreed that Einstein's formula for a stable universe could not be valid.

But there was an ironic corollary to this. The "Einstein world" had been produced with the aid of the cosmological constant and this had been necessary, in Einstein's own words, "only for the purpose of making possible a quasi-static distribution of matter, as required by the fact of the small velocities of the stars". But now Hubble's discoveries were revealing that some at least of the galaxies, and of course the stars within them, were moving at speeds which were sizable proportions of the speed of light. Thus there had been no need for the cosmological constant in the first place.

One other point was that Lemaître had included in his paper an equation which gave a term for the rate of recession of the galaxies. Hubble had put a figure to this term and with its aid the Lemaître equation could be used to provide a radius for the initial Einstein world. This given, Einstein's original work could still give a figure for the total mass of the universe. What it could no longer do was give a picture of what was happening to that mass, for this depended on the character of the cosmical constant. If this were zero it was possible to postulate a universe which had begun some 10,000 million years ago with a "big bang" and which had been expanding uniformly ever since. If it were positive, as Lemaître had envisaged, then his primeval atom had begun to disintegrate some 60,000 million years ago and the result had begun to stabilise itself after some 50,000 million, the contemporary expansion being caused by an upsetting of that stabilisation and not by the initial "big bang". While both these theories envisage the evolution of the universe as arising from a unique situation, use of a negative value for the cosmic constant provides a third blueprint: that of the alternately expanding and contracting universe. These possibilities — to which that of a universe constantly expanding, but kept in a steady state by the continuous creation of fresh matter, had not yet been added — formed the highlights of a development which had been going on since 1920. They were still under constant and sometimes acrimonious discussion in the scientific world when Einstein arrived in Pasadena.

He remained based there throughout January and February, meeting the aged Dr. Michelson of the Michelson-Morley experiment at a dinner given in honour of them both.* He was taken for short "rest" visits to a number of Californian ranches — sending back from them a delighted card to Queen Elizabeth of the Belgians

---

* It was for long accepted that at this dinner Einstein directly attributed to the work of Michelson, since a widespread version of his speech has him saying: "You uncovered an insidious defect in the ether theory of light, as it then existed, and stimulated the ideas of H. A. Lorentz and Fritzgerald, out of which the Special Theory of Relativity developed. Without your work this theory would today be scarcely more than an interesting speculation..." Gerald Holton has by careful detective work (see ISIS, Vol. 60, pt. 2, No. 202, Summer, 1969) discovered that Einstein in fact put a third sentence between these two — "These in turn led the way to the General Theory of Relativity and to the theory of gravitation" — thus putting a rather different gloss on the occasion.

who had visited one of them during a state visit to America in 1919 — and he cruised off Long Beach with Millikan.

Real work started when he met Tolman and Dr. Paul Epstein, the Professor of Theoretical Physics. Following this, he was driven up the long circuitous road which winds out above Pasadena and then back to the top of the Sierra Madre, from one of whose summits the Mount Wilson Observatory looks down upon the town. Here Elsa, when told that the giant telescope was required for establishing the structure of the universe, is claimed to have made a reply that may be apocryphal but is in true Elsa style: "Well, well, my husband does that on the back of an old envelope." Here Einstein conferred with Hubble. And here, early in February, he officially announced that he had abandoned the idea of a closed spherical universe. Later he was to agree with the more complex theory of an alternately expanding and contracting universe, a decision which comforted Dean Inge, who noted that this was a "revolutionary change, for it means a return to the old theory of cosmic cycles" which had always attracted him. "Jeans and Eddington say that it is utterly impossible," he went on, "but if I may take refuge behind Einstein I am content." Early in 1930 Einstein did no more than agree that his initial idea had to be given up, and it is typical that he did so only after he had personally met Hubble and peered with him through the magnifiers at the revealing pictures of galaxies from what was then the largest telescope in the world.

In mid-February, a fortnight before he was to leave Pasadena, Einstein addressed several hundred students. His speech must have been startling to many members of the faculty, particularly to Millikan, whose natural inclination was to believe that all was for the best in the best of all possible worlds. For instead of singing the praises of scientific progress, Einstein asked why it had brought such little happiness. In war it had enabled men to mutilate one another more efficiently and in peace it had enslaved man to the machine.

Millikan, who was to receive angry protests about the "two per cent" speech which Einstein had made in New York on his way to Pasadena, was worried about what would happen during his guest's overland return to the East Coast. But nothing sensational did happen. On March 3rd Einstein broke his journey in Chicago, where he was welcomed by a peace group and spoke from the rear platform of his train. In New York he found a waiting delegation from the War Resisters League, but the chance of an explosive after-dinner speech whose sentiments might brush off on to Caltech and discourage its wealthy supporters — and which would in any case have offended Millikan's conservative soul — was fortuitously removed by Weizmann.

The Jewish leader had cabled an urgent appeal for help which Einstein received before he left Pasadena:

> Financial position movement and work Palestine extremely difficult in danger of immediate collapse especially harmful now that political situation much improved through satisfactory conclusion negotiations Government. We are making all efforts here but as you know resources Europe limited. I am urged come America help drive. Serious work here and necessity going Palestine for negotiations with Arab friends prevents my undertaking trip now must be postponed till April. You are the only man to render real assistance this critical moment by responding invitation our American friends and attending very few banquets in States. I know this imposes heavy burden but having done so much for Palestine I hope you won't refuse come to its assistance at this anxious time.

Einstein did not refuse. He rarely did. And the whole of his evening in New York was spent in preparation for, and at, a fund-raising dinner organised by the American Palestine Campaign at the Astor Hotel.

When he returned to the docks he found banner-bearing pacifist groups awaiting him and he subsequently cabled the leaders a message of goodwill. Two years later he was urging that only resistance to the pacifist movement would bring success against Hitler.

In mid-March he arrived back in Berlin. Less than two months later he left Germany again, this time for Oxford to receive an honorary degree and give the Rhodes Lectures.

The Rhodes Trust had been set up only in 1926, and in 1927 Einstein had been asked to become the second lecturer. This was a singular honour and his efforts to dodge its acceptance have an almost contrived air. The first approach was made by Lindemann, on the urging of H. A. L. Fisher, Warden of New College and a Rhodes Trustee. In his letter to Berlin, Lindemann noted that acceptance would be "of great political significance" and "a conciliatory international gesture". If Einstein wished to "try the cloistered life", he could have rooms and service in college; if he wished to bring his wife, then an hotel would be found. The point that "even London and Cambridge" were within reach was added as a final inducement. Sir Otto Beit, one of the Rhodes Trustees, was conscripted to invoke the help of Lord Haldane, who supported the invitation, while the German Ambassador in London, Count Bernstorff, wrote to "the competent authorities in Berlin and [had] asked them to urge Professor Einstein to accept the invitation".

However, this was rejected, partly because it had been proposed that the visit should be for a complete term of eight weeks, partly on account of health. Einstein therefore asked to be excused, stressing that this was not due to any lack of sympathy for Britain. To Lindemann he replied in similar terms. But he did not want to disappoint him. Perhaps a four-week visit in the summer would do. By this time, however, other arrangements had been put in hand and the Trustees were, as Fisher wrote to Einstein, "put in the difficult position, which they understand has already been explained to you through Professor Lindemann, of having to wait till their offer elsewhere was refused or accepted, before they could write definitely to you."

However, although this first approach came to nothing, the Trust had the tenacious quality of its founder, and in 1930 its secretary, Philip Kerr, asked Lindemann whether he could induce Einstein to come in 1931, giving a single lecture if he felt unable to do more. At first Einstein accepted. Then, after arriving back in Berlin from Cambridge, he had second thoughts.

However, Lindemann was not the man to give up easily. In October 1930 he was in Berlin. He saw Einstein. Almost as important, he saw Mrs. Einstein. And from the Adlon he wrote to Kerr — by now Lord Lothian. "I am glad to say that his health seems quite restored, and that he is in very good form," he said. "...He told me that he could understand English quite well now and although he does not speak it he had found no difficulty in discussions in America as he speaks very slowly and almost everybody knows either French or German..." And he added later that he would like to arrange for Einstein to have rooms in Christ Church, "which he told me he would like and which I think would be eminently conducive to obtain the object you have in view".

It seems clear that the visit was not yet finally settled, but Lindemann now turned on Elsa the considerable charm he could exercise when he wished. Drawing Einstein to Oxford was worth an effort, and in February 1931 he learned that he had done the trick. On the 24th he wrote to Elsa saying how delighted he was that Einstein had finally agreed to come. "I will take every care that he has all he wants and will use my best endeavours to prevent his being bothered and troubled in any way," he went on. "He can of course have as many meals as he likes alone in his rooms and I will endeavour to preserve him as much as possible from importunate invitations.

"I am taking steps to see that he can get some sailing, so that

I hope he will not feel that he is wasting his time here altogether."

There was little danger of that. But even before his departure from Berlin Einstein was trying to refuse engagements. The Oxford Luncheon Club had written to him, he told Lindemann, and had not only invited him to eat but also to make a speech. Could this please be avoided? Lindemann seems to have intervened successfully and there does not appear to have been a Luncheon Club address.

On arrival in Oxford Einstein was taken under Lindemann's wing and given the services of the latter's indefatigable servant and general factotum, James Harvey. In addition, Lindemann acted as his mentor and guide, showing him the sights, and introducing him to his various friends and acquaintances. Among these were John Scott Haldane the physiologist, and his wife Kathleen, parents of J. B. S. Haldane, *enfant terrible* among the geneticists. "We were such good friends that my husband took a great deal of trouble to ensure that the professor should have an appreciative audience . . ." Mrs. Haldane has said. Efforts were necessary, since although the Milner Hall of the new Rhodes House was full at the inaugural lecture, many of the audience slipped away while it was still on. "I don't blame them," J. S. Haldane commented. "If their maths are good enough to follow him their German certainly is not." By the end, only a small audience was left and Einstein promised that the next time "the discourse should be in English delivered". Haldane was heard to murmur *"Bewahr"*.

The first lecture was on relativity, the second on cosmological theory and the third on the unified field theory. While the first and last were largely syntheses of views which Einstein had already expounded at length, the second dealt with his recent abandoning of the cosmological constant. He admitted that this presented two problems. It would be difficult to know from what the expansion of the universe had started: and while its age worked out at about $10^{10}$ years, there was already considerable evidence that the earth itself was older than this. Another point was that his theory now limited the radius of the universe to $10^8$ light-years, a distance to which the Mount Wilson telescope had already almost penetrated. As he said, if they went further, this would "put the varnish on" his theory.

Even in Oxford, where eccentrics are the rule rather than the exception, Einstein made his mark. The undergraduates loved him and Mrs. Haldane has recalled how a group of them helped him down from the pony trap into which he had been hurried when the Haldanes feared he would miss an important appointment. As he descended from the trap at Tom Gate a big button from his Ulster was torn off in the basket-work of the vehicle. The young girl driving him disentangled it and ran after him. "I wouldn't worry miss" said the college porter. "The gentleman will never miss it. He has one odd button on his coat already."

It was in Tom Quad that Einstein was discovered one day by Gilbert Murray with, as Arnold Toynbee describes it, a faraway look on his face. "The faraway thought behind that faraway look was evidently a happy one for, at that moment, the exile's countenance was serene and smiling," Toynbee has written. "Dr. Einstein, do tell me what you are thinking," Murray asked. 'I am thinking,' Einstein answered, 'that, after all, this is a very small star.' All the universe's eggs were not in this basket that was now infested by the Nazis; and, for a cosmogoner, this thought was convincingly consoling."

In Oxford he saw an England very different from the formality of Lord Haldane's London residence, an England where his Jewishness, his German ancestry, and his stature as a scientist all tended to be taken for granted and then passed over so that he could be weighed and considered as a human being. He liked the experience; he enjoyed Lindemann's friends, he soaked up the atmosphere of an Oxford that has largely disappeared in the last forty years; and whenever he wished he broke through the screens raised to ensure him privacy.

One typical picture has been drawn by Margaret Deneke, a leading figure at Oxford whose house was a mecca for music-lovers:

> We knew of his great interest in music [she says of Einstein] and we had great artists playing quartets and enjoying music in our house. They were people whose names were known to him and he was delighted to be invited to join. So he came to us. Afterwards we discovered that outsiders were not supposed to invite him, but he had found his way here and he chose to go on coming. We used to borrow instruments for him. He did not bring his violin. He played trios and quartets. He did not lead, and he always preferred to be the second violin. Now and again he would lose place or they had to repeat something so that he came in at the right moment.

On May 23rd he received an honorary doctorate of science. He spent a few days making final courtesy calls. Then he left for home, arriving in Berlin during the first days of June, and immediately giving Lindemann a graphic and pessimistic account of the developing situation in Germany.

His warning, written in a thank-you letter, may well have had its impact on Lindemann who during the next few years was to be the saviour of so many German Jews. Touring Germany in his chauffeur-driven Mercedes, one of the few physicists whom the head waiters of Europe's grand hotels would automatically bow to the best table, Lindemann did a great deal to extricate the cream of the country's scientists from the Reich as Hitler rose to power. Some at least of this was foreshadowed as he wrote to Lord Lothian in June, commenting on the success of Einstein in Oxford. "He threw himself into all the activities of Oxford science, attended the Colloquiums and meetings for discussion and proved so stimulating and thought-provoking that I am sure his visit will leave a permanent mark on the progress of our subject," he noted. " . . . I have hopes that this period as Rhodes Lecturer may initiate more permanent connections with this university which can only prove fertile and advantageous in every respect."

The first move came quickly. It was proposed that Einstein should be made a "Research Student", the most honorific post to which the college could elect him. This was a personal triumph for Einstein on more than one count. Inside Christ Church a considerable internal fight was being carried on about endowing research at all; on one side was the party mobilised by Lindemann and the Senior Censor, Roy (now Sir Roy) Harrod, the economist; against them was ranged a body of opinion which insisted that research men were unclubbable and would completely upset common-room life. The latter party was supported by one college official who stated strongly that the college endowments had not been given to subsidise "some German Jew".

Then, without obvious reason, it became clear that Einstein's candidacy was being favoured. The reason for the change of balance is interesting. Einstein had in Christ Church used the rooms of R. H. Dundas, who was travelling. On his return Dundas opened his Visitors' Book to find that Einstein had thanked him in doggerel for the hospitality.

Dundas was charmed with the verses. So much so that he became a keen supporter of Einstein's research fellowship. All at once everyone remembered how they had taken to Einstein, what good company he had been. Einstein had unwittingly ensured that the Dean was able formally to make the proposal with no chance of it being rejected. In fact, there was only one protestor — a former student who wrote to say that such appointments endangered his pension rights. The letter was ill received.

News of the offer came on June 29th through Lindemann, who pointed out that Einstein would be able to stay in Oxford for one term a year without giving up his Berlin appointments. The appointment as a senior member of Christ Church — "Called 'Fellows' (Socii) in most Colleges, 'Students' at Christ Church (not in the sense of Studiosum)" as Lindemann explained — would be for five years at a stipend of £400 per year with the use of a set of rooms in college and dinner allowance when he dined in hall: and it was hoped that he "would be able to visit Oxford for something like a month during term time in the course of the year at such periods as may be convenient". Einstein accepted without delay, delighted at being able to keep in touch with Oxford and with Lindemann. As events turned out, he was to appear as a Student at Christ Church during only two years of his appointment. To what must have been the chagrin of some men in Oxford, the outstanding £1,200 of his stipend went to help other German Jews.

The Christ Church offer had formally come as Einstein was completing arrangements for a second visit to the California Institute of Technology. Earlier in the year Fleming had proposed that he should come to Pasadena on a regular basis and Einstein had tentatively accepted. Fleming appears to have acted largely on his own initiative, a circumstance common to his later years and one which added an air of chaos to some of the Institute's proceedings, and details of the offer are not clear. However, he gave his own version at a meeting called to consider the proposed appointment in the early autumn of 1931, and this was described in a long letter to Hale from A. A. Noyes, director of chemical research at Caltech.

Fleming read *not* his own letters to Einstein, but two replies he had received from Einstein, the second one written in July stating that he (Einstein) had definitely accepted the permanent appointment, with $5,000 annually plus $15,000 in any year when he comes for ten weeks to the Institute, plus a $3,000 annuity to his widow. Einstein himself proposed reducing the annual payment from the $25,000 proposed by Fleming to $20,000, and the proposed annuity from some larger sum to $3,000. Fleming said that Einstein cabled him in August asking to know whether the arrangement was definite, as his plans for the present year must be consummated, but we have never been able to get out of Fleming just what reply he made to that last cablegram of Einstein, though I made two attempts. It seems *probable*, however, that Fleming told Einstein that the arrangement was definite for this year, but that the permanent plan must await action by the trustees.

This was in fact what happened. Millikan, who would shortly be in Europe, was given the job of ensuring that the Institute netted Einstein for the coming season but that any offer of a permanent post was evaded for the time being. In addition, he was given an even more delicate task. "Board is of opinion commitment of $20,000 all inclusive has been made for coming year", he was informed soon after reaching Europe by E. C. Barrett, the Institute Secretary. "If Einstein thinks so, board will carry out this commitment. If Einstein does not feel we have such commitment board voted that you offer $15,000 or thereabouts all inclusive."

However, Millikan the faithful servant of the Institute, took a worldly view of Einstein's vagueness about money.

> Now the $7,000 figure which we talked about for a ten or twelve weeks' annual stay in Pasadena [he wrote on October 11th] was one which I had already suggested to some of my financial friends as a dignified and suitable one for such a service as Professor Einstein would there render, and I hope soon to be in a position to suggest such an arrangement as a continuing one — and that too without putting a strain upon the finances of the Institute . . . For the present year, in view of some previous correspondence which I believe has already been had, I am sure the Trustees expect us to decide upon a considerably larger figure and they are prepared to meet it whatever it is that we have determined upon. In other words, they want you, and we all want you very much to come.

Despite Einstein's apparent otherworldliness, despite the fact that he once used a cheque as a book-marker instead of paying it into the bank, his character yet contained a strong streak of peasant awareness that quickly noted any attempt at financial sleight-of-hand.

His reply to Millikan, written from Caputh on October 19th, 1931, was not, therefore, as surprising as it probably appeared to Millikan. Einstein thanked his American friend but said that he had decided to remain in Germany for the winter. He had told Fleming so, and for Millikan's information he enclosed a copy of his letter to Fleming.

So far so good. But this was not the end of the encounter. What happened next is not entirely clear. But the outcome was revealed when Elsa wrote to Millikan about a month later, enclosing the contract, signed by her husband.

The sudden change on Einstein's part may well have been due to a further appeal on the part of Fleming. It is certainly true that when the Einsteins arrived in Pasadena at the end of 1931 they were accommodated not in private quarters but in the splendid premises of the Athenaeum, the Faculty Club where Fleming had given up his own apartment for the occasion.

Einstein's second journey to Pasadena was thus made in the same one-visit circumstances as the first. But the question of a journey each year had now been raised. He had been led by Millikan to assume that this was still a distinct possibility if not a likelihood, and with this in his mind he arrived in Pasadena for the second time, a significant situation in view of one meeting which was shortly to come.

This was with Abraham Flexner, the American educationalist then preparing to set up a new kind of educational institute, made possible when Mr. Louis Bamberger and Mrs. Felix Fulds had two years previously provided five million dollars for what Flexner called a "haven where scholars and scientists may regard the world and its phenomena as their laboratory without being carried off in the maelstrom of the immediate". Its small number of selected staff would have no duties in the usual sense of the word and the Institute for Advanced Study, as it was to become, thus offered something comparable to the conditions which had drawn Einstein to Berlin two decades previously: no routine and a lot of time to think.

It had been agreed that the Institute, whose location had not yet been decided, would first concentrate on mathematical studies and early in 1932 Flexner visited Pasadena to get the advice of Millikan. There was one obvious suggestion — why not have a word with Einstein? "I drove over to the Athenaeum where he and Mrs. Einstein were staying and met him for the first time," Flexner has written. "I was fascinated by his noble bearing, his simple charming manner and his genuine humility. We walked up and down the corridors of the Athenaeum for upwards of an hour, I explaining, he questioning. Shortly after twelve, Mrs. Einstein appeared to remind him that he had a luncheon engagement. 'Very well', he said in his kindly way, 'we have time for that. Let us talk a little while longer.'"

Before they parted, Flexner said that he would be in Europe later in the year. Einstein would be spending the spring term at Oxford with Lindemann and it was agreed that they would meet again. "I had no idea", Flexner later recorded, "that he would be interested in being concerned with the Institute, but he gave me the best of reasons for thinking that an informal organisation such as I had in mind would be much more important at this stage of our development and at the stage of the world's development than another organised university." This then was Flexner's story: that at this point he entertained no idea of attracting Einstein from Caltech to his new institute. Nevertheless, he left Pasadena having carefully made his arrangements for a further meeting.

27

During this visit to Pasadena Einstein lectured on space curvature and in a joint statement issued with de Sitter, also visiting the Institute, said that recent studies further strengthened the idea of an expanding universe. Hand in hand with his scientific work went a long series of pacifist statements which gravely worried Millikan and which were to have their effect on Einstein's visit the following year. To a mass disarmament meeting in the high school at Whittier he spoke of the grave danger of militarism, and pinned his hopes on the disarmament conference, due to start soon in Geneva. At a meeting on world affairs sponsored by the Los Angles University of International Relations held in Pasadena, in February, he claimed that "disarmament cannot take place by easy stages but must come in one swoop *or not at all.*" The following day he told a mass meeting in Santa Barbara that renunciation of at least some political sovereignty was essential to peace, while at the end of the month he recommended to listeners in the Pasadena Civic Auditorium that the decisions of an international court should "be enforced by all the nations acting in common". Here, although his pacifist friends may not have noticed it, were indications that Einstein's renunciation of force had a qualification: that it should be outlawed for national but not necessarily for international ends.

He returned to Berlin in the spring, and early in May set out for England once again, first to deliver the Rouse Ball Lecture on Mathematics in Cambridge and then to make his first visit to Oxford as a Research Student. He was given rooms in Christ Church and dined at High Table most evenings.

> He was a charming person, [says Sir Roy Harrod] and we entered into relations of easy intimacy with him. He divided his time between his mathematics and playing the violin; as one crossed the quad, one was privileged to hear the strains coming from his rooms. In our Governing Body I sat next to him; we had a green baize tablecloth; under cover of this he held a wad of paper on his knee, and I observed that all through our meetings his pencil was in incessant progress, covering sheet after sheet with equations. His general conversation was not stimulating, like that of the Prof. I am afraid I did not have the sense that, so far as human affairs were concerned, I was in the presence of a wise man or a deep thinker. Rather I had the idea that he was a very good man, a simple soul and rather naive about wordly matters...

On one occasion Lindemann was able to shine before his guest. "Einstein happened to mention at High Table some mathematical proposition which he took to be well established but for which he had never been able to furnish himself with the proof," says Harrod.

"The Prof returned the next day, claiming to have thought of the proof in his bath; Einstein was satisfied with it." What is more, Einstein remained satisfied. Twelve years later, writing to Lindemann, by this time Lord Cherwell and Churchill's personal scientific adviser, he asked in a P. S. to his letter whether Lindemann remembered the proof about prime factors he had found while sitting in his bath.

It appears to have been on this visit that Einstein was finally conscripted by Lindemann into the forces fighting for the site of the new Radcliffe Observatory, which it was claimed should be situated in Oxford rather than in South Africa. This bitter contest of university politics was being fought on grounds which were more parochial than scientific, and it is difficult not to believe that Einstein's involvement was a tribute to his innocence rather than to deep convictions. As Lindemann's biographer says, "the Prof must have felt a glow of triumph when he induced the great Einstein to testify emphatically upon the University side." Einstein's testimony was certainly unqualified. "I have examined the affidavits of Professors Lindemann, Milne and Plaskett and am in complete agreement with the arguments and views expressed therein," it ran.

However, not even this was enough. When Lindemann and others took the issue to court, they lost their case. The telescope was built near Pretoria.

Before Einstein left Oxford, Flexner arrived. They met in Christ Church and on a fine morning began pacing the lawn of the quadrangle, coming closer and closer to grips with the problem of the new Institute. "As it dawned on me during our conversation", Flexner has written, "that perhaps he might be interested in attaching himself to an institute of the proposed kind, before we parted I said to him: 'Professor Einstein, I would not presume to offer you a post in this new institute, but if on reflection you decide that it would afford you the opportunities which you value, you would be welcome on your own terms.'" Einstein was apparently non-committal; but he agreed that as Flexner was visiting Berlin later in the year they could well meet again.

He returned from England at the end of May 1932. Berlin was already ominously different from the city of even a few months previously. In April there had taken place what was, on the face of it, an encouraging presidental election. For the octogenarian Field-Marshal Hindenburg, representing the Democrats and Socialists, had been re-elected, defeating the leader of the National Socialist Party, Adolf Hitler. However, the President soon showed where his sympathies lay. In May he forced Brüning, the Reich Chancellor, on whose support he had largely won the election, to give way to von Papen, a man determined to end the Weimar Republic. Papen's ostensibly non-party but in fact ultra-right-wing, cabinet was formed a few days later. It quickly expelled the Socialist-Centre Prussian cabinet under a form of martial law and dissolved the Reichstag. Rule by bayonet had arrived.

What this landslide to the Right meant to Jews in general and Einstein in particular was indicated when on June 2nd Deputy Kube announced to the Prussian Diet that "when we clean house the exodus of the Children of Israel will be a child's game in comparison". To leave no doubt of his meaning, he added that "a people that possesses a Kant will not permit an Einstein to be tacked on to it." Human wisdom, noted Edgar Mowrer, "whispered that a people that refused an Einstein would be unworthy of a Kant".

Many in Germany still hoped that a quasi-military government with strong monarchist leanings would keep the Nazi Party in its place. Einstein had no such illusions. Frank records that when a professor expressed the hope one evening at Caputh during this summer of 1932, Einstein replied: "I am convinced that a military regime will not prevent the imminent National Socialist revolution. The military dictatorship will suppress the popular will and the people will seek protection against the rule of the Junkers and the officers in a right-radical revolution."

It was against this background that Abraham Flexner made his promised visit to Berlin.

> It was a cold day [he has written]. I was still wearing my winter clothes and heavy overcoat. Arriving at Einstein's country home, beautiful and commodious, I found him seated on the veranda wearing summer flannels. He asked me to sit down. I asked whether I might wear my overcoat. "Oh, yes," he replied. "Aren't you chilly?" I asked surveying his costume. "No," he replied, "my dress is according to the season, not according to the weather, it is summer!"
>
> We sat then on the veranda and talked until evening, when Einstein invited me to stay to supper. After supper we talked until almost eleven. By that time it was perfectly clear that Einstein and his wife were prepared to come to America. I told him to name his own terms and he promised me to write within a few days.

Einstein accompanied his guest back to the bus for Berlin, walking through the rain hatless and in an old sweater. "I am full of enthusiasm" ("*Ich bin Feuer und Flamme darüf*"), he said as they parted.

The following Monday Flexner prepared a memorandum covering the details of what was to become Einstein's official appointment for virtually the rest of his life. These included, in Flexner's words, location of the new Institute "contiguous to Princeton University, residence from autumn until about the middle of April, salary, pension, etc. and an independent appointment for Professor Mayer".

When the question of salary had first been raised Einstein said that he wanted 3,000 dollars a year. "Could I live on less?" he asked, according to Flexner's later recollections. "You couldn't live on that," he had replied. "Let Mrs. Einstein and me arrange it." The result was a salary of 16,000 dollars a year, to be continued after retirement.

Einstein had been careful to explain two things: that he would once again be spending the winter months in Pasadena, and that he still had his obligations both to the Prussian Academy of Sciences and to Christ Church, Oxford. Judging by the memories of Hermann Weyl, who was to join him in the Institute, there were other reservations. Recalling a meeting between Einstein and himself, Flexner, and Dr. Frank Aydelotte, a Trustee of the new Institute and later successor to Flexner, Weyl declared: "Whatever doubts and thoughts we had about turning our backs on Germany to join Flexner's new Institute, were soon dispelled by Hitler's rise to power."

It is clear that acceptance of Flexner's offer was a significant change of emphasis from West Coast to East, from the old Caltech to the new Institute. That Millikan himself saw it in this light is obvious from the disgruntled letter which he wrote to Flexner. With an air of surprise — that ignored his introduction of Flexner to Einstein the previous year — he noted that he had "just had a letter from Dr. Einstein saying that you are establishing in Princeton a theoretical research institute and that he has accepted some sort of a permanent part-time annual commitment to participate in the work of this institute beginning in the fall of 1933, and that this is likely to make his continued association with the corresponding institute which has been laborously [sic] built up during the past ten years impossible."

Millikan was not, he implied, thinking of his own Institute, but of more important things. "Whether the progress of science in the United States would be advanced by such a move, or whether Professor Einstein's productivity will be increased by such a transfer, is at least debatable", he went on. "The work in which his interest and his activity lies is certainly much more strongly developed here than it is at Princeton, and I am inclined to think that with the astrophysical advances that are in prospect here this will continue to be the case." He concluded with the hope that Flexner might still collaborate with his own Institute in some joint venture and that, even if this were not possible, Einstein might be able to "spend half the time which he would normally be in this country in Princeton and half the time here . . ."

Flexner, with the Einstein contract safely in his pocket, could afford the lofty reply. After noting that "altogether by accident" he had been in Oxford at the same time as Einstein, he defended himself in slightly injured terms. "I cannot believe that annual residence for brief periods at several places is sound or wholesome. Looking at the entire matter from Professor Einstein's point of view, I believe that you and all his friends will rejoice that it has been possible to create for him a permanent post of the character above indicated."

The question of the coming autumn visit was soon resolved: Millikan would be as glad as ever to see Einstein — not least, one must feel, because this would strengthen his hand against whatever blandishments Flexner was offering. What was to happen after Einstein had begun to visit Princeton — "maybe a solution will be found so that he can from time to time come to Pasadena," Elsa wrote to Millikan on August 13th — was left in the air. But Einstein never visited Pasadena after the winter of 1932–33.

Some comment must be made on this battle for Einstein's last years. The first is that vacillation over Fleming's initial offer, and then its supersession by Millikan's, left a nasty taste in the mouth for Einstein. Had he known the truth about Flexner's cutting-out operation against Caltech, he might have had much the same feeling about the offer from Princeton. In any case, he was shrewd enough to see how the land lay and will have had no qualms against playing off such opponents against each other. With Einstein, getting the best conditions for his work justified anything. He was certainly anxious to take Mayer with him wherever he went, and this was a useful point for Elsa to make. Just how she made it was immaterial, for once he had come to a decision, Einstein left the details to her, not worrying overmuch how his decision was implemented.

The appointment was, moreover, still only a part-time winter affair. This feature of the contract was made clear in a statement Einstein issued in Berlin. "I have received leave of absence from the Prussian Academy for five months of the year for five years," this explained. "Those five months I expect to spend at Princeton. I am not abandoning Germany. My permanent home will still be in Berlin."

And now, prepared for the worst as he continued to hope for the best, he began to get ready for his third trip to Pasadena.

Then, unexpectedly, he received news from Weizmann about the Hebrew University. There had been a meeting between Magnes and Weizmann. The details were not passed on but the upshot was that an impartial Structure Committee was to investigate the whole situation. From this fact, Weizmann went confidently on:

"Now I come to a request for you to rejoin the Board of Governors, a request which I know would be backed by everyone who really has the University at heart. I remind you of a promise you gave me, that you would do so under my leadership. All those who have fought for reforms, which now look like being successfully carried through, would see a great moral boost in your return, quite apart from the other good it would do. We cannot lose you, although we cannot offer you a "scientific home" as Princeton can. But who knows! Now that I shall be spending a longer time in Jerusalem I have every intention of improving the Physics, and Chemistry, and perhaps you will then visit us."

Einstein replied that he was delighted to hear the news. He added that he would be glad to rejoin the Board if there were university reforms but he made it clear that he did not take Weizmann's assurances entirely at their face value.

Weizmann, as well as Flexner and Millikan and Lindemann, was shopping for Einstein as events in Germany made it less and less likely that he would be able to remain in the country much longer. Einstein measured all the offers and hints by the usual yardstick: the extent to which they would enable him to get on with his work.

Now, in the late autumn, he prepared for Pasadena again. For a short while it looked as though there might not be any need. For while anti-Semitic opposition to Einstein was increasing in Germany, a groundswell of protest was building up in the United States. The board of the National Patriotic Council issued a statement describing him as a German Bolshevist and adding that his theory "was of no scientific value or purpose, not understandable because there is nothing to understand", an assessment that brought an immediate response from Einstein: "Wouldn't it be funny if they didn't let me in." The possibility was less ludicrous than it sounded, for the American Women's League now issued a formal statement protesting that the U. S. State Department should not grant an entry visa to a man such as Einstein, a member of the War Resisters International whom they described as a Communist.

As far as pacifism was concerned the protests from America were sound enough. But they were wildly out regarding Einstein's attitude to Communism and to Soviet Russia. Only a few months previously he had refused to sign an appeal from Henri Barbusse, a man with whose pacifist views he greatly sympathised, solely on account of its glorification of Soviet Russia. But these views were unknown. What was known was Einstein's belief that the Russia of the inter-war years had no aggressive intentions. More than once he said that he believed Lenin was a great man; and a decade earlier he had tried to intercede in the cause of Zionism with the Russians in Berlin. But he would have been as ready to intercede with the devil had he thought that good would come of it. His view of the Revolution was a complex if balanced one in which he weighed the bad against the good with considerable judgment; but the balance was concealed by his own default and if he was wrongly accused he had no one to blame but himself.

The visa was finally granted, and early in December he and Elsa completed their preparations. Despite the earlier statement that he intended to keep a permanent home in Berlin, despite his un-wavering hope and brave front he was under no illusions as he spent the final days of November in the house at Caputh that he had come to love. As he left it for Berlin and the train to Antwerp where he and his wife were to board ship for the States he turned to her with the warning: "Before you leave our villa this time, take a good look at it." When she asked why, he replied: "You will never see it again." Elsa, says Philipp Frank, thought he was being rather foolish.

# 16

# *GOODBYE TO BERLIN*

EINSTEIN AND ELSA ARRIVED IN CALIFORNIA EARLY IN JANUARY 1933. It was the third time he had visited Caltech in three successive years and it now looked as though this might be a regular thing, even though the summer months were securely earmarked for Princeton and commitments in Berlin would further limit his free time. Millikan certainly hoped so, and had gone to great lengths to land his catch for the third visit at a time when it seemed that the Institute might not find the necessary money.

Salvation eventually came from the Oberlaender Trust of Philadelphia, set up "to enable American men and women without regard to race, creed or color, who are actively engaged in work that affects the public welfare, to become better acquainted with similar activities in German-speaking countries". In 1931 Millikan had been given an Oberlaender grant "to contact German scholars, lecturers and universities". The following year, after further contacts with Millikan, the Trust voted "to appropriate the sum of $7,000 to cover the expenses of Professor Einstein in America some time during the academic year 1932-33. The money to be forwarded through Professor Millikan as a grant to Professor Einstein, exclusively for scientific work." However, there was a rider to the exclusivity. For while Millikan was completing arrangements with Einstein, he wrote to the Trust agreeing that his guest should make "one broadcast which will be helpful to German-American relations". This was the fee which was to be paid by Einstein for the support which made possible his third visit to Pasadena. Whether he fully appreciated this before setting out is not recorded. But Millikan's wish to keep faith with the Trust certainly increased anxiety that Einstein might queer the pitch for what was to be in many ways a propaganda broadcast.

Dourly conservative, faintly militarist, and with more than

a touch of right-wing enthusiasm, Millikan had cause for worry. Einstein's persistence in advocating his pacifist ideals during earlier visits had done much to foster the undercurrent of objection which flowed through the American scene and which not even the general adulation could entirely conceal. And it had already caused more than one of his scientific colleagues to perform verbal gymnastics in his defence. Thus Millikan himself, a man who lacked pacifist leanings as much as Einstein lacked the aggressive instinct, had been forced to reply to an impassioned appeal from Major-General Amos A. Fried who wrote to him to "protest against Americans who, in the name of science, are aiding and abetting the teaching of treason to the youth of this country by being hosts to Dr. Albert Einstein". Fried went on to say that when he had last talked with Millikan 100,000 dollars' worth of radium was being presented to Madame Curie who was, he said, in his opinion, worth a million Albert Einsteins.

The answer to General Fried throws interesting light on Einstein and also helps to explain Millikan's somewhat panic-stricken efforts to prevent him from speaking on non-scientific matters. He replied on March 8th.

It is quite true that Einstein has been exploited by all sorts of agencies that had their special axes to grind. Part of these have been of the Charlie Chaplin type and part of the Upton Sinclair type. The latter in particular have misquoted him to such an extent that I am not very much surprised that a man like yourself should have been misinformed by the flood of literature of this type.

I am not saying that Einstein has not made blunders of his own, for he has. He is an exceedingly straightforward, honest, and childlike sort, and has only recently, through rather bitter experience, been learning the lesson of the danger of trusting everybody who pretends to be actuated by high motives. Even more than that, he has not always been wise in his utterances, and in one or two instances has made very bad slips which I think he now realises himself, and I think in practically all the speeches and interviews which he has made out here he has been often times extraordinarily profound, penetrating and wise. But when he went east last year he is reported by the papers to have said a number of things which I would condemn as unsound as hard as you do — for example the two per cent comment, if he ever made it, is one which no experienced man could possibly have made. It takes all of us some time to learn wisdom.

Of course I am only writing to you now to let you know that I think you have fallen into the same error that Einstein has fallen into, and have trusted to reports of designing people who are not trustworthy, and because of that trust have made a fundamental error in your estimate of the man. I should not have confidence in my own judgment alone, but it is that he is a man of the finest qualities and character, who has made errors, indeed, but not so many as most of us have.

Millikan did what he could. He stood up in honourable fashion to defend what he had no particular wish to defend. But underneath his confident exterior he was seriously worried that his guest might make another "two per cent" speech that would invalidate the coming broadcast or affect the flow of money into the Institute from rich patrons. This much is clear from his private comments to the Trust after Einstein had met reporters on arrival in Pasadena. He "handled himself," wrote Millikan, "with a skill which, I am sure if your trustees had seen, would help to relieve their minds as to any possible adverse influence which he might exert in the way of furnishing additional ammunition to those who have been spreading these grotesquely foolish reports about his connection with influences aimed at the undermining of American Institutions and ideals . . ."

The broadcast to "help German-American relations" was to be made on January 23rd and until then Millikan's security measures worked, although only at the cost of revealing to Einstein how limited his freedom of action really was. He had agreed to make no public appearances except those personally arranged by Millikan "under dignified auspices".

> But even after this conversation, [Millikan informed the Trust] I suddenly found that some wholly non-representative group of so-called "War Resisters" at the University of California at Los Angeles had come over to see him, representing that it was just a private gathering of no public significance, and he had been unwise enough to believe them and agree to say something. I then found that this group had issued handbills which they had spread all over the institutions of Southern California that he was to appear last Sunday and speak. I saw at once that this situation was full of dynamite, and went straight to him and told him that he would have to cancel the engagement, and he then saw the necessity and authorised me to cancel it for him. I accordingly telephoned UCLA and got the whole thing eliminated, with the Los Angeles press explaining the cancellation in a way which was really helpful, I think. The form in which it went in was, as a matter of fact, prepared in our office . . .

Einstein appears to have acquiesced without protest at this adroit piece of manipulation. Millikan, had he remembered his guest's reaction to the Institute's sleight of financial hand the previous year, might have felt some qualms about the future. However, the present had been saved and Einstein's broadcast "On German-American Agreement" was the one-shot success which everyone had hoped it would be.

The broadcast was preceded by a full-dress dinner at the Athenaeum and here Einstein first met Leon Watters, a wealthy Jewish bio-chemist who was to become an intimate friend for the last two decades of his life. Watters, a New Yorker, had the previous month begun to finance work at the Institute and as a result found himself and his wife placed by Millikan at the top table, separated from Einstein only by a woman of considerable wealth who was also supporting the Institute financially.

I soon noted, [Watters later wrote] that, while the lady was doing considerable talking, Einstein was only nodding. He seemed somewhat ill at ease. I leaned over and offered him a cigarette from my case. He hesitated, then smiled, took one, lighted it, and consumed it in three strong puffs. While the coffee was being served I took a cigar from my pocket and wrote the following verse on a card which I attached to the cigar and proffered it to him. He shook his head and said: "No thanks: I prefer my pipe." But he noticed the card, read it, and burst out laughing. On the card I had written a verse from a poem by Bert Leston Taylor, reading: "When men are calling one another names and making faces / And all the world's a jangle and a jar / I mediate (sic) on interstellar space / And smoke a mild segar."

That seemed to loosen his tongue. He asked me to spell out my name for him and I showed him my place card. He asked me if I were teaching at California Institute of Technology and I explained that I was not and that I was only a visitor. Was I alone?

In some ways Watters, with his chauffeur-driven car and his apartment on Fifth Avenue, with his dilettante approach to science, was the antithesis of all that Einstein believed in. Yet an interior practical kindness was enough to bind him both to Einstein and to Elsa as the long and deeply personal correspondence between them was later to show. The foundations for it were laid that evening as Watters and the rest of the carefully-picked guests followed Einstein to the Pasadena Civic Auditorium. Here the programme, entitled "Symposium on America and the World", sponsored by the Southern California College Student Body President's Association, was to be broadcast by the National Broadcasting Company.

Einstein began by speaking of two obstacles. "The first of these", he said, "is the obstacle of the black dress suit. When men come together on ceremonial occasions attired in their dress clothes, they create about themselves as a matter of routine an atmosphere from which the realities of life with their severity are excluded. There is an atmosphere of well-sounding oratory that likes to attach itself to dress clothes. Away with it." After this typical Einsteinian opening he discussed the emotion-laden content of some words — "heretic" in relation to the Inquisition, "Communist" in the United States, "Jew" among the reactionary group in Germany, and "bourgeois" in Russia. "I should like to call it the obstacle of the tabu" he said of this feature of human relationships. He then went on, in mild and rational words to speak of the prospects for American-German relations, and of the economic situation. "It was," the *New York Times* noted in a leading article "exactly the same kind of thing that we had got hundreds of times from other people. The spirit of the Einstein address was fine, even lofty; but it cast not a single fresh ray of light upon a dark situation." Meanwhile, in Germany, Hitler was preparing to accept the call of the Germans.

Einstein remained in Pasadena for another seven weeks, obeying Millikan's injunction to hold his tongue and paying occasional rest-visits to places such as the Rayben Farm Hope Ranch, from which he sent a brief poem on a card to the Queen of the Belgians, who had visited it during a tour of the United States.

However humiliating his enforced silence may have been, he could be grateful to Millikan for extricating him from one embarrassing situation. For it was on his host's instructions that he finally declined to be guest of honour at a banquet of the Arts, Literature and Science National Convention. Earl C. Bloss, the Convention's First Vice-President, had written to Millikan explaining that many of the invited guests were withholding acceptance and adding that it had recently been "unanimously decided that the success of our banquet would be unquestioned if we were to replace Professor Einstein's presence with some other outstanding gentleman". A suitably high-ranking naval officer was finally obtained. Millikan was duly informed that the Convention more than appreciated "what you have done by witholding the presence of Professor Einstein".

Such exhibitions of the anger and distrust which Einstein's pacifist and left-wing statements aroused in Americans did much to explain Millikan's apprehension as the time for his visitor's departure approached. Earlier he had written to the Oberlaender Trust saying that he feared "the possible efforts of all kinds of radical groups to exploit him when he gets away from Pasadena, especially if he goes east — as I think perhaps he plans to do — by train instead of by boat". Early in February his worst fears were realised. Einstein was to return east by train. Moreover, he was to make one address in Chicago and another in New York. In view "of the near slips which we have been fortunate enough to avoid making", Millikan wondered what the Trust in Philadelphia could do.

The answer was that it could do very little. The Secretary, Mr. Thomas, wrote from the Trust to Einstein, noting that he had had no reply to earlier letters, stating that he had heard of plans to make addresses, and saying rather plaintively that he would like to know about them as soon as possible.

The scanty evidence suggests that if Einstein gave Mr. Thomas's letters any attention at all he stuffed them into his pocket determined that on leaving Pasadena he would make up for the silence so far forced upon him. As it turned out, other events were to dominate his thoughts. Looking back, the reasons are self-evident. For while Einstein was again discussing the riddle of the universe with Hubble and Tolman at Mount Wilson, lecturing to students, and generally acting as a scientific liaison officer between Caltech and the Berlin of the Kaiser Wilhelm Institute, events in Germany had rolled forward with ominous inevitability. During the last month of 1932 Kurt von Schleicher had become Chancellor; for some weeks he had desperately tried to form a stable Government. He failed, the third man to do so in as many years. On January 30th, President Hindenburg turned to the one leader he felt might at last square the circle — Adolf Hitler.

The effect on Einstein was immediate and unqualified, perhaps surprisingly so for a man so mild-mannered, so disinterested in the balances and counterbalances of politics, so eternally hopeful that with goodwill the worst might be avoided. But now he knew that his "Never see it again" prophecy on leaving Caputh was more likely to be borne out than the return to Germany foreshadowed in his October statement. His first action was to cancel the lecture due to be given at the Prussian Academy on his return to Berlin. A few hours later the Reichstag was in flames, set alight by the sub-normal Dutchman van der Lubbe. Within a few days the incident had been exploited by the new Nazi government to rush through emergency decrees which gave them totalitarian powers. And on March 2nd any remaining doubts that Einstein's unique position might guard him from the government's growing anti-Jewish wrath were dispelled by a leading article in the *Völkischer*

*Beobachter* on "cultural internationalism", "international treason" and "pacifist excesses". In it, Einstein was singled out for attack, together with Heinrich and Thomas Mann, Arnold Zweig, and a short list of Germany's leading intellectuals, academics and artists.

On March 10th, Einstein made his decision public. In a long interview with Evelyn Seeley of the *New York World Telegram* on the eve of his departure from Pasadena he said: "As long as I have any choice in the matter, I shall live only in a country where civil liberty, tolerance and equality of all citizens before the law prevail. Civil liberty implies freedom to express one's political convictions, in speech and in writing; tolerance implies respect for the convictions of others whatever they may be. These conditions do not exist in Germany at the present time."

Concluding the interview, Einstein said that he would probably settle in Switzerland. He then rose to attend a final seminar at the Institute. As he left the room, Los Angeles, a score of miles away, was shaken by the worst earthquake in its history. Symbolically, the reporter was able to note that "as he left for the seminar, walking across the campus, Dr. Einstein felt the ground shaking under his feet".

Thus in mid-March, 1933, Einstein arrived at the position he had correctly forecast to Infeld little more than a decade previously. He was no longer able to live in what was both the country of his birth and, since 1919, the country of his voluntary adoption. As in 1920, there were no doubt elements in Germany which were rational, civilised, and libertarian; as in 1920, they formed a minority, helpless and silent. Einstein's disillusion was thus compounded. For the rest of his life he felt a double grudge against Germany: first that he had been born there and, worse still, that he had been misguided enough to take German nationality again when he might easily have remained simply a Swiss.

Even so, it is clear that he had not even begun to comprehend the nature of the revolution that was sweeping Germany. Had he done so he would not have written to Planck as he wrote on March 9th — not only suggesting that specialists might leave Germany to work on an international scientific committee, but asking whether Planck would put up the idea to the Academy.

The answer, in the negative, arrived towards the end of April, and Einstein sent it off without delay to Hale from the Belgian resort where he had temporarily made his home.

He and Elsa had left Pasadena on March 11th, travelling overland to New York by way of Chicago, as expected. The repercussions were less than Millikan had feared, partly because he had agreed to attend a birthday luncheon arranged by a local committee in aid of the Hebrew University and his time for other matters was therefore limited. But he did what he could, and finally agreed to attend a pacifist meeting on the morning of the 14th. "After he came and found us interested in serious discussions he would not leave us even when eleven o'clock came, the hour for the luncheon to claim him," according to a report by Mrs. Lloyd, one of the organisers. "At eleven fifteen Mrs. Einstein rose and reminded him of the committee. He asked her to sit down and said he wanted another quarter of an hour with us. So we enjoyed a full hour of his valuable discussion on international, political and psychological subjects."

Thus far there appears to have been no crack in his pacifist armour. "His firm faith in the decent impulses of the human heart is evident and inspiring," wrote Mrs. Lloyd. "The peace campaign must go on. Let the Youth Peace Council whose representatives sit with us note his plain teaching. Let all pacifists take courage and be as extreme as they like. Einstein will never abandon the peace movement because it is too bold." Only thirteen weeks later the plain teaching was to be different. Were he a Belgian, Einstein then declared, he would give military service cheerfully, in the belief that he would be helping to save European civilisation.

From the pacifist meeting he went on to the luncheon, attended by, among others, Arthur Compton of the University of Chicago, and the Governor of Illinois. He spoke of the problem of "finding a method of distribution which would work as well as that of production" and he spoke of organising international affairs so that war could be abolished. But this was subdued stuff, very different from the "two per cent" speech of 1931. It was, already, almost as if Einstein was beginning to doubt his own pacifism.

The following day he travelled on to New York where he arrived shortly after Weizmann had left for Palestine — one of those missed meetings which might have altered history. In New York he spoke at a function to be held for the joint good of the Jewish Telegraph Agency and the Hebrew University. Dr. Rosenbach, the noted American bibliophile, was in charge and had organised a dinner for more than six hundred at the Commodore Hotel.

He wrote to Dr. Karl Compton of the Massachusetts Institute of Technology and Dr. Harlow Shapley of Harvard asking them to speak on the program [says Rosenbach's biographer]. He sent out invitations, and in his name a barrage of promotional publicity went out to the press. Both the eminent American scientists accepted the

invitation, but Shapley was concerned about the position of the micro-
phone (he could not have picked a worse person to whom to mention
details of that kind), was worried lest 'the publicity submerge the
spirit', was upset by rumours that Einstein's genial gullibility had been
taken advantage of by high-pressure fund-raisers; in fact, he wanted
detailed assurance that the whole program would be on a dignified
level. Dr. Rosenbach gave him that assurance.

It was on a dignified level; Einstein's Zionism was quickly
submerged in physics and Rosenbach's lost in the world of books.
Congressman Sol Bloom had given up his seat beside Einstein to
Harlow Shapley, and the two scientists were soon absorbed in the
universe, Einstein using his body to illustrate a point, the ribs being
the heavens and his backbone the Milky Way. Soon afterwards
he made a sketch for his dinner companion on the back of a place
card only to find it snatched away as a souvenir by an onlooker.
Rosenbach was not long in reaching his true love and, after mentioning the two good causes for which the dinner was being held,
presented Einstein with a first edition of Napier's *Rabdologiae*.

The following day Einstein squeezed in a visit to Princeton,
conferred there with Oswald Veblen, and went on a preliminary
round of house-hunting in preparation for his return in the autumn.
Back in New York he was driven with his wife to the Boulevard
synagogue where the eight-day-old son of the Jewish Telegraphic
Agency's managing director became their godchild, and where
Einstein wrote on the back of a photograph of himself a poem
"To little Albert Landau on the occasion of his entering the
world".

That duty performed, Einstein had but a few more hours
in New York. So far, his only public reaction to the news from
Germany had been his measured statement that he would not be
returning. This was reasonable enough; and it gave no weapons to
his enemies. Now, with only a few hours to go before sailing for
Europe, he attended a reception at the Waldorf-Astoria to launch
*The Fight Against War*, an anthology of his pacifist writings to
be published later in the year. So far, he had spoken openly only
of his own personal position in relation to the new German government; he had given the world no other reaction of the world's
most famous Jew to the rise of the world's most famous Jew-baiter.
That was the way he wanted it.

Now, at the Waldorf-Astoria, he stepped into the ring, attacking the German Academy of Arts, pointing out that in Germany
pacifists were considered enemies of the state, and saying that

the world should be made aware of the dangers of Hitlerism. All this made it easier for the German authorities to attack him. They would of course have done so anyway. But his honesty in speaking out, without reserve and while on a "mission of moulding public opinion to better German-American relations" as Millikan had put it in one letter to the Oberlaender Trust — made their task that much simpler. He issued no plea for U.S. intervention, and he was not atrocity-mongering; but by the time reports reached Germany via the New York correspondents his action could easily enough be distorted into such, and it was fuel for the virulent anti-Einstein campaign exemplified by the *Berliner Lokal-Anzeiger*. "Good news from Einstein — he's not coming back," this said. "... Relativity is in little demand by us now. On the contrary. The ideals of national honour and love of country which Herr Einstein wanted to abolish, have become absolute values to us. So the outlook for Einstein here is very bad."

It was in this atmosphere that he and his wife left for Europe. It appears that they had been given a final warning by the German Consul in New York, Dr. Paul Schwarz, whom Einstein had known in Berlin. Details of the meeting are vague, and the second-hand accounts contradictory. But the truth seems to be that Schwarz formally told Einstein that it would be safe for him to return to Germany but informally warned him against it. His warning may not have been as blunt as one reported version: "If you go to Germany, Albert, they'll drag you through the streets by the hair," but it was strong enough to convince him that his decision had been not only ethical but wise.

As the *Belgenland* crossed the Atlantic, Einstein playing the violin at benefit concerts for refugee musicians, there came more news from Germany. Bruno Walter, the Jewish conductor, had fled to Austria. The offices of the Zionist Federation of Germany had been searched. In Ulm, the State Commissioner for the city's administration had ordered that Einsteinstrasse, named eleven years previously, should in future be known as Fichestrasse after the German nationalist philosopher. Preparations were being made for the purge of the civil service which was soon to remove everyone of even partial Jewish descent, and for control of the universities by Bernard Rust, Minister for Education, who was to oust more than 1,600 Jewish lecturers and professors from their jobs. The time was coming when all books by Jews would have to be marked "Translated from the Hebrew" — and when only a greatly-daring professor would declare: "It is a mistake to believe that Einstein's original papers were translated from the Hebrew."

In mid-ocean, news came that the Einsteins' home in Caputh had been searched, the pretext being that an arms cache might be found there. "The raid ... by an armed crowd is but one example of the arbitrary acts of violence now taking place throughout Germany," said Einstein in a statement issued on the ship. "These acts are the result of the government's overnight transfer of police powers to a raw and rabid mob of the Nazi militia. My summer home has often in the past been honoured by the presence of guests. They were always welcome. No one had any reason to break in."

The *Belgenland* docked on March 28th at Antwerp, where the Einsteins were welcomed by the mayor, Camille Huysmans, and a group of professors from Ghent University. The latter was headed by Professor A. de Groodt,* and Einstein and his wife gratefully accepted the offer of a temporary refuge at "Cantecroy", an historic manor house outside Antwerp which was the de Groodt's family home. Their next move had now to be decided.

* Frans G. L. A. de Groodt, Professor de Groodt's eldest son, says that his parents, in consultation with a number of friends, had telegraphed to Einstein on the *Belgenland*, begging him not to sail on to Hamburg but to come ashore in Antwerp. "I remember that it needed some insistence to persuade Einstein not to return to his country," he says.

# 17

## SHOPPING
## FOR EINSTEIN

BETWEEN THE SPRING AND THE AUTUMN OF 1933 EINSTEIN WAS DRIVEN
to action in three different fields. Virtually barred from Germany,
he had to decide where to settle. Faced with a Third Reich under
Hitler, he had to reconsider his pacifist beliefs. And as the future
of the Jewish scholars driven from Germany grew into a major issue
he felt forced to bring into the open his long-standing argument
with the Hebrew University. These climaxes in his life, all the
direct result of Hitler's rise to the Chancellorship, developed simultaneously as he continued with his work, amiably agreed to lecture
to all and sundry, and was reluctantly transformed into a symbol of
the anti-Nazi forces which began to form throughout the Continent. They give to his life a muddled and incoherent pattern
paralleled by Europe as it reacted in its own way to the rise of
the National Socialist Party.

One of Einstein's first actions after reaching Antwerp revealed
how the events of the previous few weeks had hardened his opinions. In Pasadena, talking to Miss Seeley of the *New York World
Telegram,* he had remarked that his citizenship (of Germany) was
"a strange affair" but had gone on to say that "for an interna-
tionally-minded man, citizenship of a specific country is not
important. Humanity is more important than national citizenship."

Now he was convinced that the Nazi actions satisfied some
urge in the Prussian character. He remembered his youth in
Munich and he remembered what he had done then. How right
he had been years ago! How wrong he had been to believe that
Weimar had changed everything! Once again, he decided to
renounce his German citizenship.

He was driven to Brussels and there in the German embassy

he formally surrendered the rights of full German citizenship he had taken with such determination after the war. He retained his Swiss nationality so he could hand in his German passport. Descending the steps of the German embassy, Albert Einstein, the Swabian from Ulm, left German territory for the last time.

At the same time he unknowingly set a riddle for the German authorities. For without their consent a German continued to remain a German whatever he said or did; and within a few months, as Einstein's formal withdrawal from Prussian nationality was being considered, the authorities began to ask whether it might not be better for them to refuse his renunciation, and then themselves take away his nationality.

Two points of view emerged at a meeting held at the Ministry of the Interior in Berlin on the morning of August 16th, when officials met to discuss the first list of men whose citizenship, it was proposed, should be taken away under new regulations passed the previous month. There were seven of them: George Bernhardt, Rudolf Breitscheid, Albert Einstein, Lion Feuchtwanger, Heinrich Mann, the Communist leader Munzenberg and Philipp Scheidemann. Of Einstein it was proposed, in the words of the minutes, that "in view of the world position which he holds, the withdrawal of his citizenship rights should not be announced, at least not immediately, even though he could be accused of the same crimes as the others; instead, his application for the ending of his Prussian citizenship should be accepted. Reasons for this are: the prejudicial reaction of other countries towards Germany, particularly England, which has made provision for giving him English nationality should he be expelled." The Gestapo representative was among those who objected, especially as Einstein's possessions had already been confiscated. "As Einstein allows his world-famous name to be used as the cover for lying propaganda, his omission from the first list would not be understood and would be sharply criticized in Germany," ran this argument. One compromise suggested by the Foreign Office was that he should be deprived of his citizenship but that his scientific equipment should be freed. Finally the meeting ended without a decision being taken, the Gestapo representative repeating his concern "that the postponement should not take too long, in case Einstein's actions made it impossible to put him in the first list that was to be issued." Einstein was of course to know nothing of this, now or in the future. His immediate problem was to decide where to go. A return to Switzerland seemed likely. His personal feeling for the country and its people remained strong and

Zurich would have welcomed him back. Yet he had firm links with
Holland, where Lorentz had died only five years previously and
the ties with Switzerland were tangled by the fact that Mileva
was still living in Zurich. For the moment therefore he remained
in Belgium.

Here, in the last days of March, he received a letter which was
to have considerable repercussions later in the year. It came from
one of the more colourful, if more enigmatic, characters who was
to cross Einstein's path. This was Commander Locker-Lampson,
English barrister and journalist. Member of Parliament for the
Handsworth Division of Birmingham, he was the younger son of
Frederick Locker, the Victorian poet, and in the First World War
had pursued an adventurous career, first in the Royal Naval Air
Service and then in armoured cars, which he commanded in Belgium, Lapland, Prussia, Austrian Galacia and Russia. It was in
character that Locker-Lampson should have served under the
Grand Duke Nicholas and later been invited to murder Rasputin
by one of the men who eventually carried out the assassination.

On the face of it, the mutual attraction of Einstein, the
natural-born pacifist, and Locker-Lampson, the natural-born
fighter who had "Combative" as the first word of his telegraphic
address, seems almost absurd. On the face of it, their only similarity was that both were "outsiders" in the same way that Churchill
and Lloyd George — both of whom were introduced to Einstein
by the politician — were "outsiders" who hunted without the pack.
The simplest explanation of their friendship is probably the most
accurate: mutal support for the underdog which had produced in
Locker-Lampson a hatred of the Nazi government equalled only
by his hatred of the Communists. In addition the Commander
must fully have appreciated that association with Einstein would
bring his name into the news where he was not averse to seeing it.
This fact, though too plain in the record to be smudged, should not
hide the genuine feeling with which he acted.

Locker-Lampson, writing from the House of Commons, began
by recalling a chance meeting with Einstein at Oxford a few years
previously.

> This letter [he continued] is first of all to assure you, my dear pro-
> fessor, of how sincerely a great number of my people sympathise with
> you and your German fellow-believers in your sufferings. That even
> Einstein should be without a home has moved me deeply and perhaps
> this justifies me, a modest M.P., in approaching you, the greatest
> scientist of our age. I hope, my dear Professor, that you will therefore

see nothing more in my humble offer than a simple tribute of my boundless respect and the wish to be allowed to serve you in my way. And so, my dear professor, would you do me the great happiness — I venture to ask simply this — of you, and your wife, taking over my small house in London, such as it is, for about a year, whenever it is convenient to you. It consists of a hall, a dining-room, a sitting-room and drawing-room, two or three bedrooms, three staff bedrooms as well as well-appointed kitchens. It goes without saying that you would live in the house as my guest, that is, there would be no cost and the service would be at my expense. My house would naturally not be as comfortabe as your own, but who knows whether England's own "ether" with its atmosphere of Fair Play might not help you to explore still more deeply the mysteries of Relativity. With sincere regards, Yours truly, Oliver Locker-Lampson.

Einstein politely declined the offer and moved with his wife to Le Coq-sur-Mer, a small resort near Ostend built, like the other beads on the long chain of Belgian coast villages, between the sand-dunes and the network of streams and irrigation channels that stretches north-eastwards towards the Leopold Canal and the Dutch frontier. Here he made a base for his last six months in Europe. And from here he severed his link with the Prussian Academy, the magnet whose distinguished company had first drawn him to Berlin almost exactly two decades earlier.

For although German nationality had been discarded, membership of the Prussian Academy of Sciences — that "greatest benefit . . . which you can confer on me" as he described it when first addressing his fellow-members — still remained. He might indeed be expelled in due course. But it was not only to avoid this that he now, on March 28th, wrote to Berlin formally announcing his resignation on the grounds that he was no longer able to serve the Prussian state. A more important reason was the embarrassing position into which he feared that his old friends Nernst and Planck would be thrust. If he were expelled they would find it dangerous to protest yet disloyal not to.

Not all of Einstein's confidence was justified. Nernst, it is true, declared that the Academy was proud of such non-German members as Voltaire, d'Alembert and Maupertius and need not, under all circumstances, demand service to the Prussian state. Yet Planck's reply which reached Einstein early in April, was of a rather different character. He felt that Einstein's resignation was the only way of resolving the situation "honourably", and that this "spared Einstein's friends immeasurable grief", a clear enough indication that not all these friends were willing to stand up and be counted.

This was only the first disillusion. Early in April Einstein learned how the Academy was dealing with the situation. On the first of the month one of its permanent secretaries, Dr. Ernst Neymann, issued the following statement:

> The Prussian Academy of Sciences heard with indignation from the newspapers of Albert Einstein's participation in atrocity-mongering in France and America. It immediately demanded an explanation. In the meantime Einstein has announced his withdrawal from the Academy, giving as his reason that he cannot continue to serve the Prussian state under its present government. Being a Swiss citizen, he also, it seems, intends to resign the Prussian nationality which he acquired in 1913 simply by becoming a full member of the Academy.
>
> The Prussian Academy of Sciences is particularly distressed by Einstein's activities as an agitator in foreign countries, as it and its members have always felt themselves bound by the closest ties to the Prussian state and, while abstaining strictly from all political partisanship, have always stressed and remained faithful to the national idea. It has, therefore. no reason to regret Einstein's withdrawal.

Anyone who doubted what the coming of the Nazis meant might have been warned by this miserable fudge of the facts, perpetrated by what had once been a proud institution. Einstein was the last man to shrink from trying to put the record straight, and he now wrote to the Academy the first of a series of crossing letters which passed between Le Coq and Berlin. He denied atrocity-mongering, while admitting to what, in the newly-created hysteria of the German times, would be considered little else.

But before the Academy could deal with this letter, H. von Ficker, its senior permanent secretary, had already replied officially to Einstein's resignation, which had been accepted on March 30th. His letter deplored Einstein's action in "disseminating erroneous views and unfounded rumours".

> We had confidently expected that one who had belonged to our Academy for so long would have ranged himself, irrespective of his own political sympathies, on the side of the defenders of our nation against the flood of lies which has been let loose upon it [it concluded]. In these days of mud-slinging, some of it vile, some of it ridiculous, a good word for the German people from you in particular might have produced a great effect, especially abroad. Instead of which your testimony has served as a handle to the enemies not merely of the present Government but of the German people. This has come as a bitter and grievous disappointment to us, which would no doubt have led inevitably to a parting of the ways even if we had not received your resignation.

This exchange — closely followed by his expulsion from the Bavarian Academy of Science — drew a sharp line across his life. While the Berlin of 1933 could hardly have been foreseen from the Berlin of 1913, the rallying of the Academy behind the new German government reinforced the question mark which had hung over the offer from Nernst and Planck two decades previously. It suggested, by implication, that his acceptance had been wrong, and that his original suspicions of the Prussian spirit had been right. Moreover it sharpened and deepened his feelings about the German people as a whole, so that from now onwards he would find it less easy to look on them as did the easy-going British or the even more easy-going Americans. From now onwards the words "German menace" had for Einstein a significance more readily understood by the French and by the Russians. From now onwards, moreover, there could be no doubt about his public position as a martyr. As his old friend Rabbi Wise wrote from the United States on May 9th, "We are all very proud of the part you have played and, above all, the distinction which has been yours in being expelled from the (Nazified) Prussian Academy."

Yet even Einstein, percipient though he was about the future, can have had little idea of the wrath to come. Hitler's purge of the civil service — whose laws automatically applied to the universities — began on April 1st with the removal from office of those of Jewish descent. Bernard Rust, the Minister of Education in Prussia who was soon to be given control by Hitler over all education in Germany, had no remorse about the scores of professors and lecturers who were summarily sacked. "It is less important that a professor make discoveries," he noted, "than that he train assistants and students in the proper views of the world."

These measures went virtually unopposed. Thirteen years earlier, the anti-Jewish movement of which Einstein became the focal point had brought nodding acquiescence, if not downright approval, from a sizeable percentage of the German people. They had not changed. And on May 10th in Berlin — even Berlin, where cosmopolitanism and culture have always been a little higher up the scale than elsewhere in Germany — here in Berlin 40,000 inhabitants watched and cheered what William Shirer has called "a scene which had not been witnessed in the Western world since the late Middle Ages": the sight of 5,000 swastika-bearing students burning in a massive pile before the Opera House 2,000 volumes that included the works of Einstein and Freud, Thomas Mann, Remarque and Stefan Zweig, and of Americans such as Helen Keller and Upton Sinclair. After the flames had leapt upwards, wrote one observer later, there was a sudden silence. Perhaps it was not only conscience. Perhaps some among the crowd caught a psychic glimpse of the flames that exactly a decade later would be sweeping through far larger parts of Berlin.

However, it was not only the mob that acquiesced. Thirteen days later, on May 23rd, Professor Ernst Krieck asserted during his investiture as the new rector of the University of Frankfurt, that the German universities could never have struggled from their paralysis without a folk renascence. "The chief characteristic of this renascence is the replacement of the humanistic ideal by the national and political," he said. "Nowadays the task of the universities is not to cultivate objective science but soldierlike militant science, and their foremost task is to form the will and character of their students."

Nor was Krieck alone among the academics in such sentiments. On the day that he spoke in Frankfurt, the twenty-second annual meeting of the Kaiser Wilhelm Society was held in Berlin. Planck presided. No one in Germany could be permitted to stand aside, "rifle at rest", he said. There should be only one ideal — "the consolidation of all available forces for the reconstruction of the Fatherland". And he then read the following message sent by the Society to Chancellor Hitler: "The Kaiser Wilhelm Society for the Advancement of the Sciences begs leave to tender reverential greetings to the Chancellor, and its solemn pledge that German science is also ready to co-operate joyously in the reconstruction of the new national state."

Although a shock to Einstein, it was perhaps hardly surprising that Planck should have stood firm for his country, and seen Einstein's resignation from the Academy as the only honourable solution to a problem which Einstein had apparently created for himself. Even Max von Laue had written to him stating that the scientist should keep silent on political matters.

It was in this climate that between April 4th and May 15th no less than 164 German professors had resigned or were dismissed — 25 from Berlin; 23 from Frankfurt; six including Max Born and James Franck from Göttingen, seven from Hamburg; and others from Heidelberg, Bonn, Jena, Leipzig and Kiel. And it was in this climate that the Nazi attack on Einstein gathered weight.

On April 2nd his Berlin bank account was taken over by the authorities and cash and securities totalling 30,000 marks were confiscated on the grounds that they would otherwise be used for treasonable purposes. His Haberlandstrasse apartment was formally closed and a lock put on the door. Shortly afterwards his summer house at Caputh was seized. On April 12th his two step-daughters left Germany for France and on the same day Dr. Walther Mayer arrived at Le Coq. Dr. Plesch, the man who had discovered the real cause of Einstein's heart-trouble a few years earlier, also left. And in Le Coq there arrived a special album published in Germany and containing photographs of leading opponents of the Nazi government. On the first page was a portrait of Einstein. Underneath it were the words: "Discovered a much-contested theory of relativity. Was greatly honoured by the Jewish Press and the unsuspecting German people. Showed his gratitude by lying atrocity propaganda against Adolf Hitler abroad." And then, in brackets, there were the words *"Noch ungehangt"* — "not yet hanged".

As with the more general attack on science, so with the specific attack on Einstein: a German Nobel Prize winner supported the case.

The most important example of the dangerous influence of Jewish circles on the study of nature has been provided by Herr Einstein with his mathematically botched-up theories consisting of some ancient knowledge and a few arbitrary additions, [Lenard asserted in the *Völkischer Beobachter.*] This theory now gradually falls to pieces, as is the fate of all ideas that are estranged from nature. Even scientists who have otherwise done solid work cannot escape the reproach that they have allowed the theory of relativity to get a foothold in Germany because they did not see, or did not want to see, how wrong it is, quite apart from the field of science itself, to regard this Jew as a good German.

Throughout all this, and the worse that was to come, despite his strong feelings and his personal involvement, Einstein continued to keep part of himself outside the battle, interestedly looking on. He was still, in some ways, the man of 1920 in the Berlin opera box, loudly applauding the anti-Einstein tirades on the stage. The external, impersonal attitude remained. There still exists one of the hideously anti-Semitic cartoons then published in Germany which shows Einstein as a Jewish vulture; across the bottom of it is Einstein's autograph, superimposed possibly for a friend, possibly for a collector, a signature without comment, inscription or emotion. He felt deeply about the irrationality of anti-Semitism, he deplored its cruelties and its humiliations long before the extermination programmes of the Final Solution got under way.

But his reaction was disdainful. As with so many other human problems, he was the outsider looking in. He could afford to be dispassionate; so long, that is, as he was able to get on with his work.

As he sat on the Belgian dunes with Dr. Mayer in the spring of 1933, doggedly searching for an answer to the riddle of a unified field theory the question of where he was to work in future was still the one that mattered most. There were many ways of answering it, since the news that Einstein would not be returning to Germany had been quickly followed by a flood of academic offers. He accepted them somewhat indiscriminately, without much thought, and to the eventual embarrassment both of himself and of those who made the offers.

He agreed to lecture to the Fondation Universitaire in Brussels, a week later accepted the offer of a chair at the University of Madrid and agreed to move to Spain in April, 1934 — an acceptance from which he withdrew following an attack by the Spanish Catholic Press. Meanwhile his friends in France had been active, and on April 14th the government started to rush through a special bill to create a new chair of mathematical physics for him at the Collège de France. In its preamble, the bill noted that in 1840 the chair of Slavonic literature had been founded for Adam Mieckie- wicz, and it was recommended that the Third Republic should not be less liberal than the July Monarchy. However, the Paris appoint- ment fell through; partly, it appears, due to Einstein's commit- ments elsewhere.

Both his perplexity with the present, and his plans for the future, were expressed in a letter to his old friend Solovine, in which he deplored the hatred spreading across Germany and revealed that he wanted to start a refugee university for Jewish professors, possibly in England. Two days later, he put down his ideas for this "intellectual refuge" in a letter to Leo Szilard, his former student-colleague from Berlin, who was himself organising help from England for the wave of Jewish intellectuals moving from Germany. Szilard was a man of almost infinite imagination and panache, packed with ideas for the salvation of the world and equally at home in science, technology or international morality. A few years earlier he had tried to launch a scheme for "Twelve Just Men" who by the wisdom of their arguments would bring peace to a world reluctant to receive it. Szilard put up the scheme to H. N. Brailsford, the British Socialist leader with whom Einstein had been in contact in 1919, and Brailsford in turn asked Einstein's opinion. He gave cautious approval but noted that Szilard might "exaggerate the significance of reason in human affairs".

Einstein was not enthusiastic about an idea for a university which Szilard now put forward, but the following month Szilard crossed the Channel to Belgium where he saw Einstein on May 14th. "Though he is still at some sympathy for his original plan," he wrote on the same day to an unidentified correspondent, "he is perfectly willing to co-operate in view of the fact that our plan is further advanced than the other one. I shall stay in touch with him and will ask for his help in such a way as I think fit." He did stay in touch even though Einstein's own interest in founding a "Jewish Refugee University" in England soon evaporated. There were many reasons for this, including pressure of other work and, probably more influential, the fact that in both England and the United States academic aid organisations sprang up and showed every sign of being able to handle the worst of the problem.

Perhaps the winds which shifted Einstein out of this particular field as quickly as they had blown him in, were really favourable, for he was singularly ill-equipped to handle the complicated task involved in the resettlement of refugee academics. He himself quickly appreciated this, for by mid-July he was stating the position accurately enough to his friend Dr. Gustav Bucky, a Leipzig radiologist who had been the physician to Einstein's two step-daughters in Berlin, and who had already moved to New York. Einstein lacked, he himself admitted, both the necessary talent for organisation and the right contacts with the right people. As his friend Philipp Frank has said: "[He] might have done more for the refugees if he had undertaken to study the situation at various universities and to take advantage of the personal, economic and political factors involved, but such action was not possible for him. The people who are the most outstanding intellectually and also the kindest are not always very practical."

He might also have done more had his guerilla war with the administration of the Hebrew University not suddenly erupted into a major engagement. For now, as the situation in Germany made it essential for the Jews to form a united front, he brought his breach with the University into the open with an unthinking timing that had the quality of Greek drama.

In August 1932, the board of governors, meeting in London, had elected the committee for the purpose, in Weizmann's words, "of drawing up a constitution for the University, and of introducing into that constitution as many practical reforms as possible,

with a view to making the young and struggling university into
an institution rather more worthy of the name". Sir Herbert
Samuel, Professor Norman Bentwich — who a decade earlier had
seen much of Einstein during his visit to Palestine — Sir Philip
Hartog and Weizmann himself were members. Despite the cautious
description by Weizmann, the committee represented a first step
towards dealing with Einstein's criticism of the way Magnes was
running the University; and when Weizmann met Einstein in
Berlin in the autumn of 1932, shortly before he was to leave for the
United States, Einstein tentatively agreed that on certain conditions
he might rejoin the board of governors. But these had not yet been
brought about.

This was the situation when, soon after his arrival in Belgium
in the spring of 1933, Einstein received a cable from Weizmann in
Jerusalem which invited him to join the University. Weizmann
had received no reply when he left Palestine on April 19th. "But
on my arrival in Cairo the following day," he wrote to Einstein
on reaching London, "I was met by a statement in the press to the
effect that you had considered this invitation and had refused it
because you were dissatisfied with the management of the University." Only half-believing, Weizmann telephoned Dr. Magnes in
Jerusalem. "He read out to me, over the telephone", Weizmann
continued, "the letter just received from you in which you state
that you are refusing our invitation because you have been informed
from four different and independent sources that the position of
the University is so deplorable that it is undesirable for you to
allow your name to be associated with it."

Weizmann's shock would have been all the greater had he
known that Einstein had already unburdened himself to Samuel,
who had recently invited him to a banquet to be held in London
in support of the University. In his refusal Einstein made the same
points he was to make to Weizmann.

The private attack in his letter to Samuel was supported
in public by interviews which were a good deal more damaging than the statements Weizmann had heard in Cairo. Einstein had
told the Jewish Telegraph Agency that he had turned down the
Jerusalem offer in view of his "long-standing differences with the
University management," and had then added: "I declined in
strong terms to accept this invitation because I feel that the
conditions prevailing at the University are such as to make fruitful
work impossible until some radical improvement in the management
is introduced.

To the representative of the *Jewish Chronicle* he had been even more outspoken, declaring that "it was deplorable that this university on which such great hopes had been based, was not in a position to play the role and to cater for spiritual needs in the way that might have been expected of it at this critical time." He spoke of deficiences of the administrative and directing boards. "It really depends on those professors who have been driven out of Germany, whether they would care to associate themselves with the Hebrew University," he concluded. As far as he was concerned, he had resigned five years ago and he did not wish to be "responsible" for it any longer.

Such statements, awaiting Weizmann in London, were almost certainly justified by conditions in Jerusalem. But they were doubly damning at a time when the Jews in general and the Jerusalem authorities in particular were being overwhelmed by the refugee tide from Germany. But for Einstein's indisputably open character, it would be easy to assume that he had merely got his blow in first, that his denunciations were a clever move by a master of tactics. This was not so. He had acted with innocent intent, repeating the unthinking carelessness of his resignation from the League's Commission when news of his about-turn had come second-hand to those most concerned. As then, his attitude arose merely from the combination of thoughtlessness and innocence that so often satisfied Einstein even though it spread dismay among his friends.

Weizmann's immediate response to the news that he had made his criticisms so public, was a bitter four and a half page letter in which he recapitulated the details of what Einstein had said and done.

> In commenting on them, [he continued] I feel that I must begin by saying quite frankly that the action you have thus taken seems to me to be so surprising, and so unjust even, in substance and in manner, alike towards the University and towards me personally that the only thing I can do is to ask you to explain it, and, if you are satisfied (as I hope you will be) that it is unjust, to withdraw it. You are the bearer of a great name, and so the injustice cuts more deeply, especially as I am so entirely at a loss to account for it.

Years earlier, Max Brod had in his novel made Tycho Brahe confront Kepler/Einstein: "You are no serpent, you never lie or constrain yourself," he says. "Thus you really serve, not truth, but only yourself; that is to say, your own purity and inviolateness. But I see not only myself, I see also my relations with those among whom I must live in the determination to serve truth with the aid of adroitness and every shrewd device." One can almost hear Weizmann speaking.

Einstein did not withdraw. Neither did he back up his charges in detail; the only informant he named was Professor Yahuda, the scholar who had brought the Spanish offer from Madrid, who had been refused a chair at the Hebrew University by Magnes, and who can hardly be considered an impartial witness. Furthermore, in his reply to Weizmann on May 7th, he reaffirmed his action. For good measure he suggested that Weizmann had committed a breach of faith by not resigning from the university board when he himself had done so.

The cat had now been firmly put among the pigeons. Samuel and Hartog, who had planned a dinner to raise funds for German Jewish refugees already at the University, had to call it off. From Jerusalem, Magnes wrote to Weizmann and to Einstein saying to both that an enquiry should be set up and that he was willing to withdraw from the University if any charges against him were proven.

Throughout this imbroglio, which was to continue unabated in one form or another until he finally left Europe for the United States in the autumn, Einstein moved as though not fully aware of the turmoil he had created. He had simply done and said what he thought was right. That completed, he got on with the things that mattered to him; detached and, if not exactly serene, at least a good deal less worried than most of those around him.

As Weizmann grappled with realities, as the Jewish exodus continued to France and the temporary security of Austria and Czechoslovakia, and as Hitler prepared the Third Reich for its thousand years of power, Einstein, his future still undecided, began to get ready for his visit as a Research Student to Christ Church.

He had already suggested to Lindemann that he might come in June, overlooking the fact that the Oxford term ended in the middle of the month, and saying that he would be happy to have a less grand room than he had had on previous visits. He added that he had worked out two new mathematical-physical results with Mayer. He noted that Lindemann had probably heard of his battle with the Prussian Academy — and he concluded, with an early touch of homesickness, that he would never again see the land of his birth.

Lindemann replied by return, hoping that Einstein would be able to come at the beginning of June.

I was in Berlin for four or five weeks at Easter, [he went on] and saw

Einstein and relatives leaving Europe for the United States, December 9th, 1930. The photograph includes (extreme left) Frau Dmitri Marianoff, Einstein's stepdaughter; her husband, Dr. Marianoff; Einstein; and, extreme right, Frau Einstein. (U.P.I.)

Einstein and his friend Dr. Plesch; taken, probably in the early 1930s, in the grounds of Dr. Plesch's house outside Berlin. (U.P.I.)

The blackboard used by Einstein when he lectured at Nottingham University on June 6th, 1930. (Nottingham University)

*Einstein playing the violin. Undated photograph, stated to have been taken on board ship while travelling to the United States in 1930. (U.P.I.)*

*Five Nobel Prize winners, showing from left to right, Nernst, Einstein, Planck, Millikan, and von Laue. (Rijksmuseum voor de Geschiedenis der Natuurwetenschappen, Leiden)*

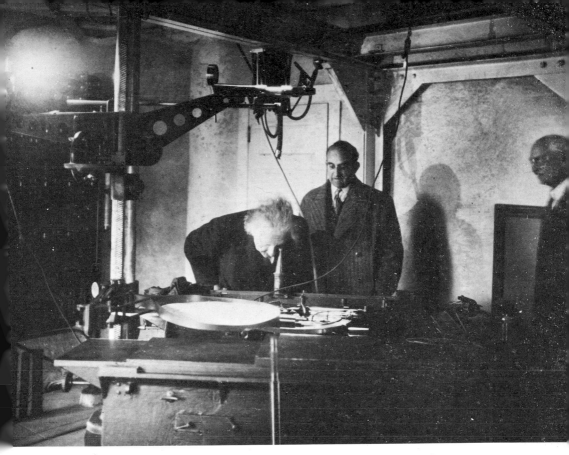

*Einstein in the 150-foot solar tower telescope at the Mount Wilson Observatory, Pasadena, California, in 1930. On the extreme right is Dr. St. John of the Mount Wilson Observatory Staff. The figure at centre, stated to be Einstein's interpreter, is believed to be his assistant, Dr. Meyer. (Hale Observatories, Pasadena)*

*Einstein "in hiding" on Roughton, Heath, near Cromer, Norfolk, in September, 1933, shortly after the publication of* The Brown Book of the Hitler Terror *and fears for his life. On horseback is his host, Commander Oliver Locker-Lampson. (U.P.I.)*

Helen Dukas (Einstein's secretary),
Einstein, and his stepdaughter,
Margot, being sworn in
as U. S. citizens. (U.P.I.)

Einstein at Oxford in 1931
when on May 23rd he was made an
honorary doctor of science. (U.P.I.)

Einstein with Ben-Gurion
on the porch of his home
at 112 Mercer Street, Princeton.
(King Features)

Einstein in his study at Princeton
on July 24th, 1943, at the commencement of his work for the U. S.
Navy's Bureau of Ordnance. With
him are Captain Geoffrey E. Sage,
U.S.N., and Lt. Cdr. Frederick L.
Douthit, U.S.N.R.

*In his Princeton home, Einstein holds Leonora Aragones, 5, on his lap, as he and the dog Chico entertain a group of recently arrived young displaced persons who visited him in honour of his 70th birthday on March 14th, 1949. Accompanying the children is William Rosenwald, National Chairman of the United Jewish Appeal. (Acme)*

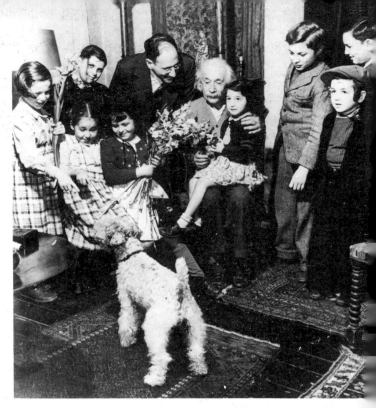

*Einstein with Irene Joliot-Curie, daughter of Madame Curie. (U.P.I.)*

*Einstein in his Princeton study. (Camera Press)*

*Einstein's desk and chair
at the Institute for Advanced Study,
Princeton, after his death. (U.P.I.)*

*Overleaf: Einstein,
a portrait by Robert M. Gottschalk.*

a great many of your colleagues. The general feeling was much against the action taken by the Academy, which was the responsibility of one of the secretaries without consultation with the members. I can tell you more about it when you come. Everybody sent you their kind regards, more especially Schrödinger, but it was felt that it would be damaging to all concerned to write to you, especially as the letter would almost certainly not be forwarded. Conditions there were extremely curious. It seems, however, that the Nazis have got their hands on the machine and they will probably be there for a long time.

Lindemann concluded with an outline of what was to became a scheme greatly affecting not only Oxford but Britain's scientific effort in the Second World War:

It appears to me that the present circumstances in Germany might provide us with an opportunity to get one or two good theoretical physicists to Oxford, at any rate for two or three years. Professor Sommerfeld told me that many of the *privatdozenten* of Jewish origin would be deprived of their positions and in the circumstances would be ready to come here at a very small salary. I need scarcely say that very little money is available and that it would cause a lot of feeling, even if it were possible to place them in positions normally occupied by Englishmen. The only chance is to get extra supernumerary jobs. These may be feasible and it occurred to me that if the unmarried were given rooms and food in college, only a very small amount of actual cash would be required for them to be reasonably comfortable for the time being. Sommerfeld suggested Bethe and London as possible men. I wonder whether you think well of them and whether you would be prepared to support their candidature. If so, a line from you would be invaluable in persuading colleges to make the offer.

The offer was a generous one, genuinely made. But the unnamed Berlin scientist quoted by Frank was also right. "What we are now doing in Germany is organising a bargain sale of good merchandise at reduced prices," he had said of the Nazis' summer purges. "Shrewd persons will certainly seize this opportunity to buy something from us."

Einstein replied non-commitally and agreed to come to England as soon as his three lectures were given in Brussels. A fortnight later he left Le Coq and its sand-dunes for Brussels, speaking on three separate evenings to invited audiences at the Fondation Universitaire. After the first packed lecture, he was asked whether he thought he had been understood by everyone. "By Professor D., perhaps," he replied, "certainly by Le Chanoine Lemaître, but as for the rest — I don't think so." He was right. The second lecture was given in a half-empty room, the third to a mere handful of listeners.

He had planned to travel direct from Brussels to Oxford but a few days before leaving Le Coq learned that his younger son Eduard was ill in Zurich and arranged to visit him. On June 1st he arrived in Oxford. Despite the disagreement which had prefaced his election to the Research Fellowship he was extremely popular and an ambitious programme had been prepared for him. The first day after his arrival he attended the Boyle Memorial Lecture, given to the Junior Scientific Society in the University Museum by Rutherford, and proposed the vote of thanks. It was an impressive occasion, Rutherford the big booming extrovert who had searched the interior of the atom contrasting once again with the smaller figure of Einstein whose mind had grappled with the immensities of space.

> I can almost see Einstein now, [writes one of the undergraduates who attended the meeting] a poor forlorn little figure, obviously disappointed at the way in which he had just been expelled from Germany by the Nazis. As he delivered his speech, it seemed to me that he was more than a little doubtful about the way in which he would be received in a British University. However, the moment he sat down he was greeted by a thunderous outburst of applause from us all. Never in all my life shall I forget the wonderful change which took place in Einstein's face at that moment. The light came back into his eyes, and his whole face seemed transfigured with joy and delight when it came home to him in this way that, no matter how badly he had been treated by the Nazis, both he himself and his undoubted genius were at any rate greatly appreciated at Oxford.

Three days later he received a letter from Weizmann, about to leave Britain for an important visit to the United States but suggesting that Einstein and he should meet. Einstein, preparing the Herbert Spencer Lecture, the Deneke Lecture which was to follow, and the first George Gibson Lecture which he was to give in Glasgow on the 20th, replied that he could not spare the time. He did not wish to be wooed away from his better judgment by oratory and personal pleas.

Weizmann replied with a three-page letter that is a minor masterpiece. He repeated his amazement at the stories of maladministration at the Hebrew University, while admitting that many things there were "far from satisfactory". He admitted that the University was dependent on Magnes since he alone could secure the hard cash necessary to keep it afloat. "The same argument covered even the choice of professors by the board of governors, who had to adopt the suggestions of those who controlled the purse of the University," he went on. Having thus presumably drawn Einstein into his line of argument, he came out with two propositions. The first was simple. "Would you", he asked, "support a proposal to dismiss some of the Jerusalem people whom we have now an opportunity of substituting by much more distinguished people?"

The second proposal was more subtle. Weizmann himself was "trying to create a completely independent institute in Rehovot, which will be able to make a fresh start, and will not be involved in the past of the Jerusalem University". Then he dangled what he hoped was the bait.

> "What I hope and believe is this, that this Institute will definitely replace, and within a relatively short period of time, the chemistry department of the University in Jerusalem. If you would undertake to do something on the same lines for physics and mathematics... what could we not do for the University? And physics would, in a way, be easier because physics does not yet exist in Jerusalem. Two great Faculties would do much to raise the status of the University."

He concluded by rounding up the arguments, pleading forgiveness for inflicting such a long letter on his friend, and finally made a moving appeal for Einstein's co-operation.

The letter exhibits all the skill of the master political advocate. If anything could have drawn Einstein to Palestine it was probably this. Yet its failure was inevitable. The Hebrew University was important; but to Einstein it was less important than physics. And as far as physics was concerned, his present arrangements with Flexner had two great advantages over anything dangled by Weizmann. Einstein was not a political animal, and he had no wish to become entangled in the skein of diplomatic manoeuvres which would inevitably hamper the scientific work of a man building a new department in such conditions. Secondly, he was not by nature the team-worker, the man who excelled in directing the energies of younger men. He did not want to direct; he wanted to get on with his thinks.

He replied by return, firmly standing his ground. The letter was as decisive as Einstein could make it. Weizmann realised this. He realised also that the outspoken refusal gave him an opportunity that could be exploited by a series of Byzantine manoeuvres.

Shortly afterwards, he left for the United States. One of his first engagements was at a dinner of the American Jewish Physicians Committee founded by Einstein and himself in 1921. He addressed its 500 members on June 29th and for the first time he brought the argument fully into the open in the United States. One of the speakers proposed — as one of them was almost certain to propose — that Einstein should join the Hebrew University. This was the opportunity for which Weizmann was waiting. Einstein, he said, had refused. "Without wishing to enter on a controversy", he went on, "I must say that unfortunately, Professor Einstein has severely criticised the University recently. The criticism was provoked by the invitiation of Chancellor Judah Leon Magnes and myself, sent to him from Jerusalem. He had been offered a chair in Madrid (which he has since accepted), a chair in the Collège de France, a chair in Leiden, a chair in Oxford; and we did not want to compete with those four distinguished universities; yet we thought Jerusalem, although it cannot offer him the same facilities, has certainly a claim on him — particularly since he does not need any special equipment but only a pencil and a piece of paper — and that we could afford him in Jerusalem." He concluded with the hope that they would still be able to draw him to Jerusalem — and with the brusque comment that Einstein's idea of founding a refugee university was "a fantastic project... [that] would mean the creation of a Jewish intellectual concentration camp".

Einstein responded immediately through the Jewish Telegraphic Agency and in what he no doubt thought were uncompromising terms. "Dr. Weizmann knows very well that, by his declaration, he has misled public opinion," he replied from Belgium. "He knows only too well the reasons for my refusal, and he has repeatedly recognised them to be justified in our private conversations. He knows, too, under what circumstances I would be prepared to undertake work for the Hebrew University."

Weizmann's ingenuity in interpreting this statement was shown three days later when, at the annual convention of the Zionist Organisation of America, he blandly announced that Einstein had "made peace with the Hebrew University in Jerusalem and agreed to accept a chair at that Institution". This was stretching interpretation a little far. His only justification for the statement appears to have been a further promise of investigation into the University which Weizmann now made, and his extrapolated assumption that this would satisfy Einstein.

But the upshot was as anticipated. With Einstein's attitude

openly criticised by Weizmann, an investigation would now be favoured. Later in the month Sir Philip Hartog wrote that he was willing to chair a committee or commission which would specifically enquire into conditions in the University. Weizmann agreed, and the tactfully-named Survey Committee was set up in the autumn. Its members visited Jerusalem at the end of 1933 to investigate "with a view as to such reform as may be found desirable, and to the framing of plans for the development of the University". In the words of Magnes' biographer, Norman Bentwich, the Committee "proposed radical changes in the administration and in his position. Action was shelved for a year; but things could never be the same to him thereafter, and he accepted a change in his functions".

On September 23rd, 1935, Rabbi Stephen Wise, returning from Palestine, reported to Einstein the outcome of the crucial meeting of the University's board of governors. "It retired Magnes from the academic direction of things and made him the President, which means that he becomes a more or less decorative figure," he said. In his place there was appointed as Rector Professor Hugo Bergmann whom Einstein had, quite coincidentally, known in Prague two decades earlier. Doing a vice-chancellor's job, Magnes had been known as Chancellor; now, ostensibly up-graded to a presidency, he was to have powers comparable to a chancellor at a British university. These powers were in some ways considerable, and he remained a trusted link with the British administration; yet effectively the move gave game, set and match to Einstein who had proposed almost this very thing a decade previously.

From the evidence that remains — the extensive Weizmann correspondence, the Report of the Survey Committee with Magnes' replies to its conclusions, and the reminiscences of those who still survive — it is clear that throughout the whole episode, spread across the decade from 1925 to 1935, Einstein made the worst of a good case. His motives were impeccable. But vacillating over his membership of the board of governors, changing and then detonating his own charges in the spring of 1933, he substantiated Magnes' claim that the Survey Committee was appointed almost solely because of Einstein's complaints. "Even the events in Germany, which required united Jewish action to make the University worthy of its mission as a sanctuary for Jewish scholars, scientists and students from Germany, did not cause Professor Einstein to abate his public and private attacks," Magnes noted. "On the contrary he was persuaded to make them even more bitter".

The result was that Weizmann, coping with the day-by-day practical problems of leading the Zionist cause, was able to bring in the reforms he wanted only after a good deal of unnecessary negotiating, subterfuge and delay. Throughout it all, Einstein's integrity could not be faulted, but it was not enough. "[His] faith has the stirring and driving quality of all truly spiritual leaders who are in the world but not of it," his friend Morris Raphael Cohen concluded in reviewing *The World As I see It.* "It needs to be supplemented by a more realistic vision of the brute actualities of our existence." Einstein's outspoken honesty could be a formidable weapon; but it was double-edged and during the argument with Magnes it was sometimes wielded to the danger of friend and foe alike.

# 18

## *OF NO ADDRESS*

THE END OF THE LONG DISAGREEMENT ABOUT THE HEBREW UNIVERSITY still lay two years ahead as Einstein dissuaded Weizmann from visiting him at Oxford and prepared to put the finishing touches to his Herbert Spencer Lecture.

He spoke in Rhodes House, "On the Method of Theoretical Physics", from an English translation, and he surprised many of the audience with his opening sentence. "If you want to find out anything from the theoretical physicists about the methods they use, I advise you to stick closely to one principle," he said. "Don't listen to their words, fix your attention on their deeds."

Two days later he gave the Deneke Lecture to a packed audience in Lady Margaret Hall, dealing with the inner meaning of physics and apparently concluding with the comment: "The deeper we search, the more we find there is to know, and as long as human life exists I believe it will always be so." The qualification is necessary. On this occasion Einstein spoke only from notes and no script of the lecture survives despite the efforts made at the time to coax some form of written version from him.

From Oxford he travelled north to Glasgow to give the first George Gibson Lecture. He arrived in the city unexpectedly and found himself, apparently unrecognised, in the centre of a huge crowd which had gathered to welcome the film star Thelma Todd. Luckily, he was soon seen by a local reporter who telephoned the University. A rescue operation soon brought Einstein safely home to port. Miss Todd, speaking of the incident later, was contrite: "I wish I had known," she said. "I'd have lent Einstein some of my crowd."

That afternoon he spoke for twenty minutes in the University's Bute Hall, addressing the attentive audience in English on "The Origins of the General Theory of Relativity". His exposition was one of the clearest ever given of the process which led from the Special to the General Theory and which, after numerous errors, led Einstein "penitently to the Riemann curvature, which enabled [him] to find the relation to the empirical facts of astronomy."

A few days later, after receiving the by now customary honorary degree, he returned to Belgium, apparently turning down the offer of a stay in Canterbury which had come from Hewlett Johnson, the "Red Dean" who recalled that twelve years earlier he had listened to Einstein's lecture in Manchester. "This is a large, quiet and very beautiful Deanery," Johnson wrote, "and nothing would please me more than that you should come here for a month or more and work in undisturbed surroundings. You could have your own rooms and see me, or anybody else, just as often or as seldom as you liked."

Einstein's refusal is significant. In his invitation, Johnson stressed Einstein's "Labours for Peace", a hint of his own long-term efforts for the Communist version of pacifism. But at this particular moment in his life, Einstein was both anxious to dissociate himself from the smear of Communism and worried about his own pacifism.

Both points were crystallised soon after his return to Le Coq. In Britain and the United States it was frequently claimed that he was a member of the Communist International and how he himself tended thoughtlessly to give support to the charge is described by Dr. Max Gottschalk, a Belgian Jewish scholar who recalled that Einstein now decided to give his patronage to the Peace Congress in Amsterdam. "When we pointed out that it was really a Communist Congress," he says, "Einstein replied: 'I saw that it was a peace congress and I didn't concern myself with the organiser.' He also signed during these same months a protest organised by Flemish youth. We told him about the subversive character of the group. He said that he had only seen in the protest a claim for equality before the law and in the light of the facts as he understood them [that] was justified."

But now the weapon that he so generously presented to his enemies was being wielded against him. He had to do something about it and on July 7th wrote to *The Times* and to the *New York Times* disclaiming any connection with the Third Communist International.

While he thus became the centre of one storm, he was busy creating a second, struggling with his own conscience and finally confirming one of the most agonising decisions of his life. For now, to the alarm of his friends and the dismay of his supporters, he crossed the great divide between pacifism and non-pacifism, renouncing his earlier conviction that the use of force was never justified; implying in the words of his former colleagues, that he lined himself up with those who would "save European civilisation by means of fire bombs, poison gas and bacteria"; announcing without a flicker, like the cool customer he was, that the change was not in himself but in the European situation, and that non-violence was no longer enough.

Einstein's rejection of the pacifist cause did not come suddenly. The blunt statement which he issued in the late summer of 1933 may give this impression, but the truth is more complex. The first hint of a change in his all-out pacifist beliefs came in November, 1932, when, shortly before leaving Berlin for the United States, he issued a statement on certain disarmament proposals put forward by Edouard Herriot, the French Premier. Included in these was one for an international police force, and Einstein agreed that this should be armed with — and would presumably be allowed to use — "truly effective weapons". The idea appears to have become even less objectionable during the next few months, and while in America he even raised it with the War Resisters International.

The genuine pacifist reaction was summed up by Lord Ponsonby in a letter to the secretary of the International. "I am quite sure we should avoid advocating anything like new forms of military organisation," he said. "Professor Einstein's mention of the fusing of small professional armies and the eventual establishment of an international police force reminds me of the French proposals and is a policy advocated here by Lord Davies and others. I personally have always strongly opposed it for two main reasons." It would be an admission that force could help solve international disputes; and it would not work. A copy of Ponsonby's letter had little effect on Einstein, whose doubts about the current practicality of pacifism were further increased during his visit to Britain in June. For in Glasgow he met Lord Davies, head of the New Commonwealth Society whose books on an international force he later praised.

Thus Einstein was already moving away from his unqualified pacifism when he returned to Le Coq from Britain late in June. This is apparent in a letter he wrote on July 1st to the Rev. J. B. Th. Hugenholtz who had visited him the previous summer at Caputh, and who now revived his idea of an International Peace House in The Hague. He felt that the times were out of joint for the further advocacy of certain pacifist ideas, he said. And he asked whether one was justified in advising Frenchmen or Belgians to refuse military service in view of the German policy for rearmament. His answer was "No". Instead, what was required was a supranational force rather than the end of all armed forces.

He sent a statement along the same lines to the *Biosophical Review* in New York, but this was not published until the autumn. Outwardly, therefore, the attitude of Albert Einstein, the most famous of those who had expelled themselves from Germany on the rise of Hitler, was still that of the confirmed pacifist. The revelation came before the end of the month.

While he had been lecturing in Oxford, two Belgians had been arrested for refusing to undertake military service. Their case had been taken up by Alfred Nahon, a young French pacifist living in Belgium who now appealed to Einstein to appear for the defence.

Before Einstein had time to reply, intervention came from an unexpected quarter. "The husband of the second fiddler," said a letter delivered to Einstein at Le Coq, "would like to see you on an urgent matter." The second fiddler was Queen Elizabeth, with whom Einstein had been playing quartets on at least three occasions during May; her husband had faced a German invasion twenty years previously and had every reason to fear the power of a Germany led by the National Socialist Party.

Einstein travelled to Brussels and met King Albert in the Palace at Laeken. The audience was handled circumspectly, and for good reason. For in some quarters Einstein's continued presence in Belgium was regarded as a distinctly mixed blessing. It would be unfair to suggest that the country harboured any sizeable pro-German party, yet there existed — as indeed there existed in England — an overall wish to mollify rather than to criticise dictators. Nowhere in Belgium was much more than three hours' drive from the German frontier, and if threats that Einstein might be kidnapped or assassinated were exaggerated, this was not certain at the time. International incidents should be avoided, and it is significant that no offers of a permanent appointment appear to have been made to Einstein from any Belgian university.

In this climate, intervention by a constitutional monarch in a matter involving military service had to be handled with care, and the King appears to have kept no record of the views which he put to Einstein, or of Einstein's reaction. These are, however, clearly implied in the exchange of letters that followed the audience. The comment of the editors of *Einstein on Peace*, that "the discussion with the King apparently helped Einstein to come to a decision on the crucial matter of war resistance", seems justified. If so, the Queen's invitation that Einstein should bring his violin to Laeken four years earlier had produced its first ripple on public affairs.

On July 14th Einstein wrote to the King. The crux of his letter was that he had decided not to intervene as Nahon had proposed. It was a letter typical of Einstein; humane and courteous, thoughtful of the wider services which men might render to one another. Yet it was still a letter written on the brink of decision; it burked the entire issue of whether mine labour, stoking furnaces aboard ships, and such services, might not be quite as essential to a country's war effort as service in the Armed Forces.

The King's reply, dated from Ostend on the 24th, was friendly but non-committal and to avoid the accusation of being unconstitutional he was careful to speak of anonymous "Belgian Governments" rather than the specific current administration.

> My dear Professor, I have received with great pleasure the letter you have so kindly written me, and I send you my warmest thanks. I am most responsive to what you say about Belgium and the sincerity of its foreign policy.
>
> Belgian Governments intend to stay out of the conflicts that are taking place in or among its neighbour countries; under no circumstances will they consent to discriminatory practices which the great majority of Belgians consider unacceptable. As you have said it so well, our army is defensive in character. To serve in it means to serve the will of a free people intent on maintaining the place which is legitimately theirs in the society of nations.
>
> We are delighted that you have set foot on our soil. There are men who by their work and intellectual stature belong to mankind rather than to any one country, yet the country they choose as their asylum takes keen pride in that fact.
>
> The Queen joins me in sending you best wishes for a pleasant stay in Belgium. Please accept my expression of high esteem. Albert.

There is an air of fencing about the exchange and it seems likely that the King was still not certain of what Einstein would do next. Judging by past record, he had every reason to keep his fingers crossed.

However, Einstein's mind had already been made up. On July 20th he wrote to Nahon. He asked that the contents of his letter should be publicised — a letter in which Albert Einstein, who had once declared that he "would rather be hacked in pieces than take part in such an abominable business as war", said that if he were now a Belgian he would cheerfully accept military service.

At first the news was passed round only in pacifist circulars, but on August 18th Einstein's letter was published in *La Patrie Humaine*. Protests were pained and vociferous. Three days later, Lord Ponsonby wrote expressing his "deep disappointment". H. Runham Brown, secretary of the War Resisters International, declared Einstein's letter to be "a great blow to our cause", while the Press Service of the International Antimilitaristic Commission claimed that "The apostasy of Einstein is a great victory for German National Socialism", a statement whose line of reasoning is perverse rather than obscure. Romain Rolland bitterly remarked in his diary that Einstein was now failing the very objectors whom he had encouraged only two years previously. The International League for Fighters for Peace, the Belgian War Resisters Committee, and many other organisations felt than Einstein's disavowal of all they stood for had the sniff of treason. To all, he replied in much the same terms: Germany was now a threat to the peace of Europe and could only be resisted by force. Circumstances altered cases.

As the protests continued to arrive, Einstein felt forced to issue a general statement.

My ideal remains the settlement of all international disputes by arbitration, [he proclaimed]. Until a year and a half ago, I considered refusal to do military service one of the most effective steps to the achievement of that goal. At that time, throughout the civilised world there was not a single nation which actually intended to overwhelm any other nation by force. I remain wholeheartedly devoted to the idea that belligerent actions must be avoided and improved relations among nations must be accomplished. For that very reason I believe nothing should be done that is likely to weaken the organised power of those European countries which today represent the best hope of realising that idea.

Years later he admitted that England, France and the United States, had by remaining more or less unarmed from 1925 to 1935, encouraged the arrogance of the Germans. For long he also had encouraged them. Now he decided, as H. G. Wells had decided in the First World War, that "every sword that is drawn against Germany is now a sword of peace".

The justification that Einstein gives for his *bouleversement* is valid as far as it goes. The European situation of the 1920s was indeed very different from the situation a decade later, when for the first time since 1919 a European country was deliberately turning to the threat of war to achieve its aims. Decent men did reluctantly admit that pacifism had to be abandoned. Circumstances did alter cases. But there is an important rider to the situation, and it lies in the contradiction between Einstein's admission that comparative disarmament had encouraged the Germans — a polite euphemism for muddled good intentions helping to bring about the very situation it was hoped to avoid — and his hope that "refusal of military service" would "once again be effective". For the essence of his argument was that after pacifism had been tucked away for a while in order to deal with an aggressive Germany, it could be pulled from the drawer and worn once again, a garment for fine days when all was set fair.

There are two other significant points that should not be smudged. Despite his readiness to abandon pacifism at the very point when it was put to the test, and despite his support for an international force, Einstein continued to regard himself as a pacifist, an attitude to which many of his former friends not unnaturally took exception. In addition it is notable that he concentrated his new-found belief in military defence against Germany in particular rather than against dictators in general. Certainly it was Germany which in 1933 represented the major threat to the peace of the world. Yet even in later years his admission that tyranny must be met by force only rarely flowed over to deal with the cases of Italy or Japan, let alone Russia. His vigour was concentrated to the exclusion of almost all else against the Germany whose evils he saw as a natural extension of his experiences at the Luitpold Gymnasium. His honesty, his international standing, his Jewishness, all helped to reinforce the anti-Nazi figurehead into which this vigour had turned him. As such he had his uses. But after 1933 not only Zionists and members of the League but also pacifists could plainly see his limitations as well. And after 1933 Wilfred Trotter's warning became even more self-evident. "It is necessary," he once said, "to guard ourselves from thinking that the practice of the scientific method enlarges the powers of the human mind. Nothing is more flatly contradiced by experience than the belief that a man, distinguished in one or even more departments of science, is more likely to think sensibly about ordinary affairs than anyone else."

Einstein's position as a symbol of the anti-German forces now beginning to coalesce was emphasised while the affair of the two Belgian conscripts was still under way. For during the second half of July he became the centre-piece of what was essentially a political operation. The prime instigator is not known, but on July

20th the indefatigable Locker-Lampson wrote to Lindemann, whom he had first met during his time as Private Secretary to Winston Churchill. "My dear Prof," he said, "someone has seen Einstein and is bringing him to England and has asked me to put him up at my cottage this weekend. I have therefore arranged to do this and am taking him to Winston's on Saturday. I do hope you are likely to be there."

Einstein arrived a few days later and was taken first to Locker-Lampson's house at Esher, Surrey, a few miles from London. From here he was escorted not to one interview but to a trio. First he met Churchill, with whom he was photographed in the gardens of Chartwell. Next he had lunch with Sir Austen Chamberlain, whom Locker-Lampson had accompanied to the Peace Conference in Paris fourteen years earlier. Finally he was taken to Lloyd George's country home at Churt, and it was here that Einstein, signing the visitor's book in the rambling Surrey house before meeting the former Prime Minister, paused for a moment when he came to the column "Address". Then he wrote "Ohne" — "without any".

The following day Locker-Lampson made the most of the incident when he spoke in the House of Commons, seeking leave to introduce a Bill "to promote and extend opportunities of citizenship for Jews resident outside the British Empire". Einstein, grave and silent in white linen suit, looked on from the Distinguished Visitors' gallery. It was a moving incident, taking place at a time when Europe had reached a watershed of history, and oddly reflecting both the best and the worst in contemporary England — the eccentric outsider taking up arms for the downtrodden, and the House which agreed in principle, but quickly moved on to other things.

"I do not happen to possess a drop, as far as I know, of Jewish blood in my veins," Locker-Lampson began. He had, he pointed out, spoken up for the Germans after the war but he thanked God that they had not won — "they might have treated England as they have treated the Jews today." Then he came to Einstein "the man without a home". "The Huns have stolen his savings. The road-hog and the racketeer of Europe have plundered his place. They have even taken away his violin." It was not very eloquent. But what it lacked in finesse it made up for in sincerity — which no doubt encouraged the *Völkischer Beobachter* to describe the incident a few days later as an "Einsteinian Jew Show in the House of Commons".

Locker-Lampson's private bill was the victim partly of apathy, partly of the British parliamentary system, since there was no chance of a second reading before the session ended on November 17th. This, in turn, meant the automatic lapsing of the bill.

There is no doubt of Locker-Lampson's sympathy for Einstein. Yet it would be ingenuous to believe that the invitation to Britain and the attempted introduction of the citizenship bill were the result only of disinterested goodwill. In the Britain of July, 1933, only a few keen-sighted men, anti-Fascists before their time, sensed the dangers to come; among them were Churchill, Lindemann, and Locker-Lampson. To them, Einstein was not only a man deserving of honest support but, as so often, a pawn in their great game.

Now he returned to Belgium, apparently accepting an open invitation from Locker-Lampson to visit him again before leaving Europe for his winter visit to Princeton. He had only a short time to wait before being thrust into a more glaring limelight.

On August 31st, *The Brown Book of the Hitler Terror* was published by the World Committee for the Victims of German Fascism — by coincidence on the same day that Professor Theodor Lessing, a German who had fled to Czechoslovakia, was tracked down by Nazi thugs and murdered in Marienbad. The central core of the book was the allegation that the Nazis had themselves instigated the burning of the Reichstag, a claim which looked plausible enough in 1933 whatever doubts can be thrown on it today. Einstein had given his name as head of the committee in his usual generous way. Now he found himself saddled with part-authorship and was forced to issue a retraction. "My name appeared in the French and English editions as if I had written it," he said. "That is not true. I did not write a word of it. The fact that I did not write it does not matter, and [sic] the truth has a certain importance. I was on the committee which authorised the book, but I certainly did not write any of it although I agree with the spirit of it. The cause of all this is that the regime in Germany is one of revenge; and I happen to be chosen as one of the victimised."

Naturally enough, this disclaimer had little effect on those who were baying for blood. "Einstein's Newest Infamy", a German newspaper banner underlined in red, was typical, and early in September it was reported that "Fehme", the extreme German nationalist organisation, had earmarked £1,000 for the man who would kill Einstein. The news that this sum had been "put on his head" caused him to touch his white hair and remark smilingly: "I did not know it was worth so much."

Ellen Wilkinson, the British Labour M.P. who was a member of the committee which had published the book, travelled to Le Coq where she met Einstein on September 2nd. "I implored him to resign, to let us take his name off our notepaper," she said. "'No,' he said quietly. 'They shall not force me to do that. The work your committee has done is good.'"

All this provided a dramatic context for the events of the next few weeks. For Einstein was now to return to England, and to remain there as Locker-Lampson's guest until, a month later, he spoke at a packed meeting in the Royal Albert Hall before leaving Britain and Europe — for the last time. Sensational overtones were given to the story. Thus it was subsequently claimed that Einstein had fled from the Continent on hearing of the assassination of Lessing; that he had been brought to England secretly in Locker-Lampson's yacht; that an armed guard had constantly kept watch over him in England; and, inevitably, that special police protection was given in England after warnings of assassination attempts. The truth is that when he left England for Belgium in July Einstein had said that he expected to be returning in September; that Locker-Lampson never had a yacht; that the "armed guards" consisted of Locker-Lampson's two girl secretaries and a farm-hand who were given sporting rifles partly as a joke, partly as local colour for photographers; and that neither Scotland Yard nor the Special Branch were warned of any murder threats. The assassination story was, in fact, made up by Locker-Lampson and "leaked" to a London evening paper when the sale of tickets for the "Einstein meeting" at the Royal Albert Hall was flagging.

Bearing all this in mind, the seriousness of any personal threat to Einstein in the late summer of 1933 appears questionable. With the final solution so well documented, there is no need to believe that this particular assassination would have been beyond the infamy of the Nazis, and their record suggests that it would not have been beyond their stupidity. But Einstein himself had the most common-sense comment. "When a bandit is going to commit a crime he keeps it a secret," he remarked on first hearing of the threats. The Belgian police had much the same attitude and their chief, quoted by the Jewish Telegraphic Agency, gives an impression of what is usually regarded as British phlegm: "The professor is taking everything quietly. When he was told that there was reputed to be a price upon his head he was only mildly surprised. He knows he is being guarded by police, but he gives me to understand that he does not wish to discuss the measures that are being taken. He told me that he is not afraid. I went this morning to ask him if he thought any further measures were required for his protection. He replied they were not needed."

This lofty disregard for his own safety was in the marrow of the man. All that worried him was the interference with his work that police surveillance often caused. Elsa was another matter and it was Elsa who on Friday September 8th asked a visiting reporter from England — Patrick Murphy of the *Sunday Express* — to telephone Locker-Lampson and ask whether Einstein could come back as a guest without delay. Locker-Lampson swung into action, eager to be host once more, especially in such dramatic circumstances, and on Saturday Einstein was driven with Murphy to Ostend. In the cabin of the Channel boat he soon had out his notebook and was hard at work.

Arrived in London, he was taken for the night to a small boarding-house in Earl's Court run by Locker-Lampson's former housekeeper, thankful that for once the hurried departure had enabled him to travel light. "If I travelled with two huge trunks my wife would still have a little paper parcel with excess luggage," he confided to Murphy.

The following morning, he was driven by the Commander's two girl secretaries north-east from London, through Newmarket where the three lunched, Einstein making himself understood as well as he could with his slight conversational English, and then on to Cromer on the East Coast. Here Locker-Lampson ran a holiday hotel in which a room had been reserved. But Einstein was taken instead to Roughton Heath, a sandy stretch of moorland three miles from the town where the Commander owned a stretch of land. Here he was installed in one of the holiday chalets. His stay was surrounded by a grotesque mixture of pseudo-secrecy and publicity. "If any unauthorised person comes near they will get a charge of buckshot," threatened the Commander. But the local Cromer photographer was allowed up to take pictures of Einstein in his sweater and sandals, while the girl "guards", carrying sporting guns, posed for the agencies whose pictures went round the world. Here Einstein stated significantly to a reporter: "I shall become a naturalised Englishman as soon as it is possible for my papers to go through. Commander Locker-Lampson has already suggested to your Parliament that England should adopt me immediately instead of my having to wait the usual five years. Parliament will give us the answer when it reassembles. I cannot tell you yet whether I shall make England my home. I do not know where my future lies. I

30

shall be here for a month, and then cross to America to fulfil engagements for a lecture tour.

"Professor Millikan the great American research worker, has invited me to make Pasadena University, in California, my home. They have there the finest observatory in the world. That is a temptation. But, although I try to be universal in thought, I am European by instinct and inclination. I shall want to return here."

Einstein spent about a month on Roughton Heath, living and eating in the small wooden building allocated to him, working with Dr. Mayer who soon joined him from Belgium, and sometimes walking for an hour or more over the rough heathlands, "talking to the goats" as he told one of the Commander's secretaries.

His presence outside Cromer had become an open secret and there were many visitors to the Locker-Lampson "encampment". One was Sir Samuel Hoare, the former British Foreign Minister. With Hoare, Einstein discussed the European situation; and, invigorated by the comparative solitude of Roughton Heath, he brought up again the idea that he had made to Norman Bentwich in Jerusalem a decade ago — that lighthouses would be good places in which young scientists could carry out routine work because the loneliness encouraged them to think.

Another visitor was Einstein's stepson-in-law Dmitri Marianoff, commissioned by a French paper to produce a popular article on relativity and a little uncertain of what his father-in-law's reaction would be to yet another request for potted relativity.

To Roughton Heath there also came Jacob Epstein who was able to obtain three sittings for a bust. These were the only meetings of sculptor and scientist and recall one of the more famous pieces of doggerel which grew in such profusion round Einstein:

Three wonderful people called Stein;
There's Gert and there's Ep and there's Ein.
Gert writes in blank verse,
Ep's sculptures are worse
And nobody understands Ein.

"Ein" appeared in a pullover with his wild hair floating in the wind, Epstein remembered in his autobiography. "His glance contained a mixture of the humane, the humorous and the profound. This was a combination which delighted me. He resembled," he added in a phrase which was later to be echoed elsewhere, "the ageing Rembrandt."

The sittings took place in Einstein's small hut which already contained a piano and was hardly the best place for the job. "I asked the girl attendants, of which there were several, secretaries of Commander Lampson, to remove the door, which they did," writes Epstein. "But they facetiously asked whether I would like the roof off next. I thought I should have liked that too, but I did not demand it, as the attendant angels seemed to resent a little my intrusion into the retreat of their professor. After the third day they thawed and I was offered beer at the end of the sitting."

Each session lasted two hours. At the first Einstein was so surrounded with smoke that work was almost impossible. "At the second I asked him to smoke in the interval," says Epstein. His manner was full of charm and *bonhomie*. He enjoyed a joke and had many a jibe at the Nazi professors, one hundred of whom in a book had condemned his theory. 'Were I wrong,' he said, 'one professor would have been quite enough.'"

When the sittings were over he would relax at the piano. On one occasion, he took out his violin and scraped away happily. "He looked altogether like a wandering gypsy, but the sea air was damp and the violin execrable and he gave up," Epstein wrote.

If these were the days of men who were anti-Nazi before their time, there were others who were still rabidly anti-Jewish. Briefly left unattended while on exhibition in London a few weeks later, the bust of the world's greatest scientist by the world's greatest sculptor — both Jews — was discovered on the floor of the gallery. Fortunately, the damage was easily repaired.

The vandalism was explicable. For while Einstein was thus living in isolation, a transformation had been taking place comparable to that which fourteen years earlier had lifted him from the obscurity of erudite science to the centre of the world stage. For more than a decade he had symbolised the other-worldliness of the theoretical physicist, a figure whose sometimes comic appearance was redeemed and made real by the transparent honesty of his beliefs, the depth of his humanity and the earthiness of his humour which touched a chord of sympathy in ordinary men. Now, as Hitler proclaimed that the Third Reich would last for a thousand years, and the lamps really began to go out in Europe, the image changed once again. Now, despite himself, he became the symbol of men who had at last, reluctantly, been forced to take up arms. But not all felt that it was right to fight against Hitler and the Nazi threat. Just as there were those in Britain, in France, and even in the Reich, who felt that the time had arrived to make a stand against the growing rearmament of Germany, so did others believe that the new German government must be built up as a bulwark against the Russian threat from the East. Thus in Europe, more poignantly than in the United States, Einstein became a symbol of that ideological schism that three years later, with the outbreak of the Spanish Civil War, was to split Britain down the mental middle.

The position was neatly summarised by the *New Statesman*.

> To our generation Einstein has been made to become a double symbol, [it stated in Miscellany] . . . a symbol of the mind travelling in the cold regions of space, and a symbol of the brave and generous outcast, pure in heart and cheerful in spirit . . . See him as he squats on Cromer beach doing sums, Charlie Chaplin with the brow of Shakespeare, whilst yet another schoolboy, Locker-Lampson, mounts guard against the bullies. So it is not accident that the Nazi lads vent a particular fury against him. He does truly stand for what they most dislike, the opposition of the blond beast — intellectualist, individualist, super-nationalist, pacifist, inky, plump. It is unthinkable that the nasty lads should not kick Albert.

But it was not only the nasty lads. Some of the comparatively nice ones, the pacifists who considered themselves dishonourably betrayed, by this time regarded Einstein as an evil renegade.

During the golden month of September 1933 Einstein was thus a man beset from all sides: by the German establishment, by the "Hands off Hitler" movement in Britain, and by his former pacifist friends with their accusations of betrayal. And now there came a more bitter personal blow; the news from Leiden that Paul Ehrenfest, perhaps after Lorentz the man for whom he felt the deepest affection and respect, had committed suicide. The circumstances were tragic. He had first shot his young son, whom he only blinded, and then himself.

The message from Holland snapped one of Einstein's links with the days before the First World War and with his crucial move to Berlin in the spring of 1914. Before he left Europe he received other news which in the most ironic of ways concerned another friend of the same period. Earlier in the summer he had received a note from Haber, who had saved Germany on two counts during the First World War. In spite of being the blondest and least distinguishable of Jews, in spite of having had himself and his family brought into the Christian faith, he was not to be spared. On April 30th he was forced to resign from the Kaiser Wilhelm Institute. One report — from the Jewish Telegraphic Agency — said that he appealed to the authorities to let him retire on pension in five months' time. If this was the case, the appeal failed. "For more than forty years", said his letter to the authorities, "I have select-ed my collaborators on the basis of their intelligence and their character and not on the basis of their grandmothers, and I am not willing to change, for the rest of my life, this method which I have found so good." In his farewell letter to the staff he stressed that for twenty-two years the Institute had striven under his leadership to serve mankind in peace and the Fatherland in war. "So far as I can judge the result, it has been favourable and has brought things of value both to science and the defence of our land."

Now the man who had helped the Fatherland in its hour of need turned to his fellow-member of the Kaiser Wilhelm who had wished only for the Fatherland's downfall. "He informs me of his intention to apply for a position at the Hebrew University in Je-rusalem," Einstein told Philipp Frank. "There you have it, the whole world is topsy-turvy."

But Einstein, who had been warned by Haber against support-ing the Zionists in 1921, now warned Haber against going to Pale-stine. His reason was simple. While Weizmann was trying to induce well-known men such as Weyl, James Frank and Einstein himself to the University, Einstein believed that the young and potentially brilliant among the flood of refugees had first call on any posts which the University had to offer. Older men, whose names were already made, should be farther down the queue.

Einstein's discouragement was effective and Haber came to England. But here his past caught up with him and, settling in Cambridge, he found that England liked him as little as he liked England. "Lord Rutherford," says Max Born, himself a refugee in Cambridge by this time, "declined an invitation to my house when Haber would also be there, because he did not want to shake hands with the inventor of chemical warfare." Haber moved to Switzerland and in the late summer he travelled up the Visp valley to meet Weizmann in Zermatt. Here the Zionist leader persuaded him to take a post in the Seiff Institute in Palestine. "The climate will be good for you," he said. "You will find a modern laboratory, able assistants. You will work in peace and honour. It will be a return home for you — your journey's end." Now Weizmann pass-ed the news to Einstein.

There was a postcript of which Einstein heard only in the United States. Early in 1934 Haber set out on the first leg of his journey to the promised land. He reached Basle. And there he died,

alone, and still incredulous that his services to the Fatherland did
not give him a privileged shelter from the gale which was sweeping
Europe.

Haber was still preparing for the move to Palestine when
Einstein left Roughton Heath during the first days of October. He
was bound for London, as star speaker at a mass meeting in
the Royal Albert Hall, organised with typical thrust by Locker-
Lampson. The initiative had come from the Academic Assistance
Council, the prototype of so many rescue organisations which
the Hitler purge brought into existence. As the *Belgenland*
with Einstein on board was docking in Antwerp six months earlier,
William (later Lord) Beveridge, Director of the London School of
Economics, had been sitting in a Vienna café reading the long list
of German professors already being dismissed from their posts
under the new Nazi statutes. He wished to help them and he was
encouraged during a meeting with Leo Szilard who had arrived
in the city one step ahead of the German authorities.

> It was agreed [Szilard has written] that Beveridge, when he got back
> to England, and when he got the most important things he had on the
> docket out of the way, would try to form a committee which would
> set itself the task of finding places for those who have to leave German
> universities. He suggested that I come to London and that I occasionally
> prod him on this, and that if I were to prod him long enough and
> frequently enough, he thought he would do it. Soon thereafter he left,
> and soon after he left I left and went to London.

Arrived back in England, Beveridge formed the Academic Freedom Fund to which members of the L.S.E. could contribute.
In May, staying with George Trevelyan, Master of Trinity, he had
discovered that Rutherford was ready to head an organisation to
help refugees from German universities. When he had first heard
of Einstein's exchange with the Prussian Academy, Rutherford's
reaction had perhaps lacked the indignation that might have been
expected, and he had written to de Hevesy: "I see that Einstein
has resigned his Berlin post but I presume he is financially well
fixed in the U.S.A. due to the special endowment there." Now,
however, he swung his energies unreservedly behind the Academic
Assistance Council — the forerunner of similar organisations in
France, Switzerland and Holland, and of the Emergency Committee
for Aid to Displaced German Scholars in the United States.

The council met in June, but the Albert Hall meeting of
October 3rd was its first major attempt to reveal to the non-

academic public the size and scope of the purge now thrusting from Germany so many of the men who might have saved her in the war that lay only six years away. A meeting of some sort had been the idea of the Council's secretary, Walter Adams, then a lecturer in history at University College, London, and later Director of the London School of Economics.

Adams drove out to Cromer a few days after Einstein had arrived. "First we were confronted by one beautiful girl with a gun," he says. "Then there was a second one, also with a gun. Finally we saw Einstein who was walking round inside what seemed to be a little hedged compound."

He quickly came to the point. Einstein as quickly agreed to speak on behalf of the Council. But it appears that neither then, nor for some while, did he fully appreciate what was involved. As he understood it, there would be a smallish meeting at which a number of well-known people would be asked to speak and would appeal for funds. But, in Adams' words, "once he had agreed Locker went away, picked up the telephone and hired the Albert Hall". Organisation was then prodded forward by the Commander and carried out by the Refugee Assistance Fund, an amalgamation of the Academic Assistance Council, the International Students Service, the Refugee Professionals Committee and the German Emergency Committee of the Society of Friends.

On the evening of the 3rd Lord Rutherford was in the chair; others on the platform included not only Einstein but also Sir James Jeans, now at the height of his fame; Sir William Beveridge; and Sir Austen Chamberlain. The hall was packed; its 10,000 seats were all taken and the overflow of hundreds sat or stood in the gangways. It was not only the famous names that had brought them; Locker-Lampson's carefully-leaked story that an attempt might be made on Einstein's life had drawn those in search of drama. For some there was the spicy attraction of a declaration on the back of each ticket, which had to be signed before its holder was allowed in: "I hereby undertake not to create any disturbance or in any way impede the progress and proper conduct of the meeting."

The danger of trouble, if only local trouble, was real enough, and large numbers of police were stationed outside the hall to deal with protests from the British Union of Fascists. More than a thousand students, many from the University of London, acted as stewards — largely to handle the expected protests from Nazi sympathisers inside the Hall. There were none.

Despite the big names on the platform, it was Einstein most of them wanted to hear. There is some disagreement about what he said and the published versions differ considerably. A truncated text appears in Einstein's own *Out of My Later Years,* and the version printed in *Einstein on Peace,* revised by the editors from the German manuscript in Einstein's papers, omits the famous "scientists and lighthouse-keepers" statement which he interpolated apparently on the spur of the moment.

He spoke in English and all versions agree that he succeeded in outlining the German menace without mentioning Germany. This was largely at the instigation of the Council itself, whose manifesto noted that "the issue raised at the moment is not a Jewish one alone; many who have suffered or are threatened have no Jewish connection. The issue, though raised acutely at the moment in Germany, is not confined to that country." Einstein thought it wrong, he later noted, specifically to condemn the country of which he had until recently been considered a national and he spoke, therefore, "as a man, as a good European, and as a Jew". He omitted a reference in his prepared notes to "the seizure of power, which results from preaching doctrines of hate and vengeance in a great country" and he also omitted a reference to "stories of clandestine German rearmament".

These reasons for describing the German purge without mentioning Germany were supported by those who did not wish to anger if it were still possible to appease — i.e. to "pacify by satisfying demands". Thus Sir William Bragg, by this time one of the key figures in the scientific establishment, noted to Rutherford on being asked to become treasurer of the Academic Assistance Council that "it is possible, I suppose, to do more harm than good by angering the people in power in Germany". Sir Austen Chamberlain felt even more strongly that while it might be right to protest it was wrong to protest too definitely. He was, Rutherford was informed, "particularly anxious that there should be no implication in the speeches of hostility to Germany and would prefer that the word 'Germany' should not occur".

Towards the end of his speech Einstein extemporised, remembering back to his recent days in Norfolk. "I lived in solitude in the country and noticed how the monotony of a quiet life stimulates the creative mind," he said. "There are certain callings in our modern organisation which entail such an isolated life without making a great claim on bodily and intellectual effort.

I think of such occupations as services in lighthouses and light-
ships. Would it not be possible to fill such places with young people
who wish to think out scientific problems especially of a mathematical or philosophical nature? In this way, perhaps, a greater
number of creative individuals could be given an opportunity for
mental development than is possible at present. In these times of
economic depression and political upheaval such considerations
seem to be worth attention."

Einstein's performance was direct, simple, and moving. He
radiated the personal magnetism that typified the born actor and
the natural politician. Like them, he believed what he said at the
moment he said it, and he gained by contrast with the platitudinous
comments of the other speakers. Only Sir James Jeans pushed
through to the uncomfortable truth — that men such as Einstein
— comparable to those whom the Council might help — "do not
labour for private gain, neither for themselves, nor for their family,
nor for their tribe, nor for their country". The meeting certainly
consolidated the position of those seeking help for academic refugees, and it brought in not only hard cash but offers of aid from
universities throughout the country. Yet Britain's sneaking feeling
that a strong Germany would be a bulwark against Russia, and the
strong business, political and traditional links which since Victorian
times had stretched into Germany, combined with an innocent trust
in the English Channel to limit the impact of such appeals on the
general public.

There were certainly those for whom Einstein was now, even
more than before, a symbol of intellectual freedom. But there were
others in Britain who would have agreed with Einstein's old colleague
Dufour-Feronce, former German secretary of the League to whom
he had explained his resignation in 1932. "I am convinced that in
time things will right themselves and meetings such as the Albert
Hall meeting for Einstein will only tend to inflame the situation and
not improve it . . ." he wrote to Lloyd George's secretary. "It is a
pity that so great a scientist should lend his name for propaganda
against the country of his birth. But although born in Bavaria, he
was never really a German in sentiment."

The meeting over, Einstein completed his preparations for
leaving Europe, apparently unaware that one of the figures from his
Zurich days was in Britain — the Friedrich Adler whose flat had
once been above his own, who had helped push him into the
Zurich chair, and whose anti-war feelings had culminated in 1916
in his assassination of the Austrian Prime Minister. After being

released from prison, Adler had quickly been elected to the Austrian National Assembly. And while Einstein had been preparing his Albert Hall speech, Adler had been addressing the British Socialist Party conference at Hastings, as secretary of the Labour and Socialist International, defending his assassination of Stürgkh on the grounds that it offered the best chance of ending the war. An exchange of views between the two former colleagues would have been interesting.

One of Einstein's last meetings in England was with the Rabbi M. L. Perizweig, chairman of the World Union of Jewish Students of which Einstein was honorary president. After the meeting, Einstein issued a statement that had a slightly ominous ring.

> The value of Judaism [this went] lies exclusively in its spiritual and ethical content, and in the way in which it has found expression in the lives of individual Jews. Study has therefore always rightly been regarded among us as a sacred activity. That, however, does not mean to say that we ought to strive to earn a livelihood through the learned professions, as is now unfortunately too often the case. In these difficult times we must explore every possibility of adjusting ourselves to practical needs, without thereby surrendering our love for the things of the spirit or the right to pursue our studies.

To make not too fine a point, he was indicating that not all refugees from Germany would be able to follow the academic lives they planned.

Before Einstein sailed from England another meeting failed to materialise. It is tantalising to speculate on what might have happened had it done so. On October 4th Lindemann drove to London from Oxford, telephoned Locker-Lampson, and made it clear that he hoped to meet Einstein the following day. With his firm intention of building up Oxford science in general and the Clarendon in particular with the help of refugee scientists it is inconceivable that he was not now hopeful of strengthening the existing links with Einstein.

What happened next is not clear. But on the 5th Einstein wrote to Lindemann saying he had learned of the attempt to speak to him on the telephone, but had heard nothing more. He looked forward to their next meeting, and certainly implied that he expected to return to Oxford, as scheduled, in the summer of 1934.

On the 7th he emphasised to reporters that he was only going to the United States for six months although he did not know what he would do when he returned. Only a couple of months earlier he had prefaced his Herbert Spencer Lecture with the assurance that the links between himself and Oxford University were "becoming progressively stronger" amd many at Oxford expected that he would soon be added to the select band already settling there under Lindemann's auspices. Lindemann himself, according to Christ Church legend, claimed for years afterwards that "Locker-Lampson frightened Einstein from Europe".

Einstein left Southampton for New York on the evening of the 7th, joining the *Westernland* on which Elsa had already embarked at Antwerp. As the liner made its way down Southampton Water, past the clustered lights of the Isle of Wight, he apparently still believed that in due course he might be offered British nationality.

The voyage was uneventful. During its later stages plans were completed for disembarkation. In the months that had elapsed since the *Belgenland* sailed from New York Einstein had learned a lot about avoiding publicity — both the personal kind which genuinely irked him and the even less pleasant publicity of the pro-Nazi and anti-Nazi groups whose attentions he was already beginning to attract. There would be no repetition of the earlier occasions on which he had been cornered; this time he was determined to avoid those interviews which had, as *The Times* said, "in 1930 made relativity seem even less comprehensible than it is".

As the *Westernland* sailed up the approaches to New York Harbour Einstein and his wife, Dr. Mayer and Miss Dukas, completed their preparations. At the Battery a tugboat came alongside. In it were two trustees of the Institute for Advanced Study, who now helped their visitor aboard. The *Westernland* continued on its way and long before it docked Einstein and his party had been transferred to a car and were being driven to Princeton, unknown to those awaiting him at the 23rd Street pier in Manhattan.

He was taken to the temporary home rented for him. He changed into casual clothes and walked out alone to explore his new environment.

On Nassau Street, which runs the length of the town, there stood the Baltimore, an ice-cream shop selling "The Balt", a special ice-cream cone which was a favourite among students. "Einstein's boat was not yet at the pier in New York," says the Rev. John Lampe, then a divinity student at Princeton Seminary, who had just entered the Balt.

> Yet Einstein walked through the doorway just as the waitress behind the counter handed me my special ice-cream cone! The great man looked at the cone, smiled at me, turned to the girl, and pointed his thumb first at the cone and then at himself.

I wish I could say that I had the generosity or presence of mind to pay for Einstein's first typically American treat. But that would not be the truth. When the waitress handed his cone over the counter, Einstein gave her a coin and she made change, muttering something like, "This one goes in my memory book."

Einstein and I stood there together, then, nibbling our ice-cream cones and looking out the window into Nassau Street. Neither of us said anything. We finished the cones about the same instant and I think I held the door for him as he stepped out.

Einstein had arrived in the United States for good.

PART
FIVE

---

*The Illustrious Immigrant*

# 19

## *LIVING WITH THE LEGEND*

WHEN EINSTEIN CAME TO PRINCETON HE WAS STILL A RESEARCH student of Christ Church, due to visit Oxford for some weeks during 1934, 1935 and 1936. A Private Member's Bill still lay on the table of the House of Commons which would have made it possible for him to be granted British nationality. The attractions of Europe were still great and nothing could quite replace the intellectual climate of the Berlin he had known, the closeness to Bohr in Copenhagen, the ease with which he could visit Leiden, Zurich or Oxford. Years previously, Rutherford had told a friend that leaving England for Canada, after three years with J. J. Thomson at the Cavendish, had been leaving "the Physical World", meaning the world of physics. And when Einstein had first confided to Janos Plesch his plans to go to Princeton, the latter had asked: "Do you want to commit suicide?" Einstein always remembered the remark.

At first the settling-in was not necessarily permanent. Not much was absolutely certain during the autumn of 1933. He might still return to Europe for visits, long or short, even if he did not live there regularly for a part of the year. Gradually this prospect faded, eventually merging into an unspoken acceptance that he would never again see Europe.

That he should finally have decided to settle permanently in New Jersey says much for the treatment he was accorded in Princeton, and for the quality of life there in the 1930s. Set conveniently midway between New York and Philadelphia, the town meanders along its one main street much as it did when Washington dated his farewell address to the army from the town. White-painted wooden-frame houses stretch into undulating country that is not offensively North American. The nostalgic pseudo-English buildings of the University, in one respect a monument to architectural poverty, provide some solace to those who have crossed the Atlantic from necessity rather than choice. Einstein, never particularly partial to humans, had some feeling for places, preferring the quieter demonstrations of nature, the hills rather than the heights, the areas where the formal transition from winter through spring to summer, and from the blaze of the dying fall to winter came regularly and without commotion. Princeton satisfied these comparatively simple yearnings, and he settled down to the winter months as content as any refugee could expect to be.

He was helped by one other accident of circumstance. Princeton was then, even more than today, surrounded by a "green belt" of estates owned by former university alumni. These in turn created the atmosphere which permeated the town, one of rich, conservative-Republican businessmen, variedly anti-Semitic. As a group they were rather displeased with the sudden descent on their town of distinguished refugees whose intellectual eminence tended to overshadow their own social position. With a few exceptions they made no attempt to establish contact with the newcomers. That suited Einstein.

The upheaval from Europe was not as great as it would have been for most people. "I have never known a place that to me was a homeland", he regretted a few years later to his friend Leon Watters. "No country, no city has such a hold on me". Even Zurich, even Berlin, did not have quite that. Later, when he had lived in Princeton for two decades, as long as he had lived anywhere, he found that its tree-lined streets and quiet houses, each a comfortable island in its own garden, had almost begun to have the quality of home.

In addition, the atmosphere of the Institute itself had its attractions. There were no undergraduates, no fraternities, no football teams, no grants, no degrees. Instead there was an intellectual monasticism which allowed him and other scholars — who already included among refugees from Germany Erwin Panofsky, Ernst Herzfeld and Dr. Otto Nathan who became Einstein's friend and literary executor — to get on with their thoughts without interruption. There was another side to the coin, however. In Berlin Einstein had enjoyed the best of both worlds with his freedom from responsibilities and his equal freedom also to hold seminars when he wished and to put the impress of his ideas wherever he thought the results might justify the trouble. In Princeton, where the only "students" were men who had already acquired their doctorates, he tended to regret the lack of contact with younger minds batting about ideas with the uninhibited pleasure of inexperience. He thus had some mixed feelings, quite in accord, as his friend Frank put it, "with his divided attitude towards contact with his fellow-men in general".

In the winter of 1933 the Institute was the work-place for eighteen academics whose only obligation was the nominal one of being in residence from October until the end of April. Fuld Hall, the elegant building which eventually housed the Institute on the outskirts of the town, was not started until 1938 and the new organisation was divided between the big frame house on Alexander Street, near the centre of the town, and the university buildings where Einstein was given quarters.

He and Elsa were soon established nearby, in 2 Library Place, a small rented house only a few hundred yards from the university campus. Around it, and the tousled head of Einstein, already haloed by the saintly white aureole that was to become his hallmark. there began to evolve a new set of legends. Within a few months he had been given a special place in American mythology, a place occupied not by the master of incomprehensible relativity but by the valiant David shaking his fist at Goliath-Hitler. When the young political scientist David Mitrany arrived in the United States to join the Institute the questioning of the customs officer ended as he explained his destination. "Oh, you mean the *Einstein* Institute," said the officer, and, pointing to his package of books, "That's all right, brother, take them away."

As Einstein became a part of the Princeton scene, he became also the great man to whom the small girl down the street was claimed to bring her "sums" regularly. He was the man to whom the local bus driver said in desperation as the stranger fumbled with his new money: "Bad at arithmetic." With his reputation for having changed man's ideas of the universe, his pervasive humility and his built-in ability to let the world make a fool of itself, he was tailor-made for apocrypha, and from the winter of 1933 onwards this grew round him just as it had grown in Berlin in the 1920s. The stories are illuminating, not for their truth but for what Einstein was expected to be and to do. His kindliness was as well established as his physical presence and if the small girl with her sums had not existed she would have been invented. He was a genuinely humble man, and it was natural that the earlier "Can't you count" story, almost certainly starting as a chance aside before being

embroidered into a score of variations which travelled wherever
he played his violin, should be transferred from Europe across the
Atlantic.

Sometimes nature apes art, sometimes the real man is more
than any legend would dare claim. Churchill Eisenhart, son of the
former Dean of Princeton University's Graduate School, tells how
a telephone call was taken in the Dean's office shortly after Einstein's arrival. "May I speak with Dean Eisenhart, please?" the
speaker asked. On being told that the Dean was out, the caller said:
"Perhaps *you* can tell me where Dr. Einstein lives." But it had
been agreed that everything should be done to protect him from
inquisitive callers, so the request was politely refused. "The voice
on the telephone dropped to a near whisper," writes Eisenhart,
"and continued: 'Please do not tell anybody, but I *am* Dr. Einstein. I am on my way home and have forgotten where my house
is'."

The absentmindedness was no more assumed than the untidiness.
It did not have to be. What looked like caricature was the man himself, merely amused as the Princeton students, puzzled as well as
honoured by the settler in their midst, chanted: "The bright boys, they
all study maths / And Albie Einstein points the paths. / Although
he seldom takes the air / We wish to God he'd cut his hair." For
Einstein was the practical Bohemian, the man who genuinely acted
the way he did because his mind and his time were devoted to
essentials. "We are slaves of bathrooms, frigidaires, cars, radios and
millions of other things," said Infeld, who joined Einstein in Princeton in 1936 and soon became an intimate. "Einstein tried to
reduce them to the absolute minimum. Long hair minimises the
need for the barber. Socks can be done without. One leather jacket
solves the coat problem for many years. Suspenders are superfluous,
as are night-shirts and pyjamas. It is a minimum problem which
Einstein has solved, and shoes, trousers, shirt, jacket are the very
necessary things; it would be difficult to reduce them further."

This was the Einstein, sockless and suspenderless, who soon
settled in, protected by the agreement that he should be left in
peace to acclimatise. Both he and Elsa gradually became accepted,
not least because he was always good company while Elsa, despite
her obvious enjoyment of Princeton's "high society", had a naturalness that soon won confidence. Thus Einstein, asked at a dinner
given by Dean Eisenhart which historical person he would most like
to meet, was expected to choose Newton or Archimedes. But his
choice was Moses — "I would like to ask him if he ever thought

that his people would obey his law so long." And Elsa, invited to tea by the wife of the President of the University, took a long time to speak on finding that she was the guest of honour. But at last she was coaxed into a conversation with a group of faculty wives who were liberally quoting their husbands: "Well," said Elsa, "*my husband always says . . . he's a physicist . . . and he always says . . .*"

A hint of this new status they were being given in the United States came at the beginning of November when Roosevelt invited him to dine at the White House. The way this was handled by the Institute was a warning of things to come, and of the battle with Abraham Flexner that was only to end when the Director was eased from office by the Board and replaced by Dr. Frank Aydelotte.

Early in November, Colonel MacIntyre, President Roosevelt's secretary, telephoned the Institute, where Einstein's secretary accepted the President's invitation on his behalf. Shortly afterwards, MacIntyre was surprised to receive a telephone call from Flexner. In the words of a memorandum from the White House Social Bureau, he "stated very strongly that appointments could not be made for Professor Einstein except through him". Lest there should be any doubt about the implication, Flexner followed up the call with a letter to the President.

> With genuine and profound reluctance I felt myself compelled this afternoon to explain to your secretary, Mr. [sic] MacIntyre that Professor Einstein had come to Princeton for the purpose of carrying on his scientific work in seclusion and that it was absolutely impossible to make any exception which would inevitably bring him into public notice.
>
> You are aware of the fact that there exists in New York an irresponsible group of Nazis. In addition, if the newspapers had access to him or if he accepted a single engagement or invitation that could possibly become public, it would be practically impossible for him to remain in the post which he has accepted in this Institute or in America at all. With his consent and at his desire I have declined on his behalf invitations from high officials and from scientific societies in whose work he is really interested.

This was not good enough. Far from failing to accept "a single engagement", Einstein made his American debut as a violinist at a public concert, attended as guest of honour a dinner given by Governor Lehmann, was officially welcomed as a resident of New Jersey and attended public celebrations to set the first type for an enlarged edition of the *Jewish Daily Bulletin,* all within a few months of his arrival. But it gives some idea of Flexner's proprietorial attitude towards the scholars and scientists he had bought up, and it suggests that the "irresponsible group of Nazis" was an excuse for keeping Einstein from a President who might expect him to spread his energies across the United States — possibly even to the California Institute of Technology. Certainly the implication of Flexner's letter was that Einstein had personally agreed to refuse the President's invitation.

Roosevelt himself might have continued to think this, had not Henry Morgenthau, then Under-Secretary of the Treasury, written casually to Einstein mentioning the invitation that had been refused. Einstein, in reply, said he had not received it. A second invitation to the White House quickly followed Einstein's letter, and he and Elsa arrived in Washington on January 24th. They dined with the President and Mrs. Roosevelt and stayed the night, their long after-dinner conversations being in German which, Einstein later recalled, the President spoke very well. There is no direct record of what they talked about. But there is indirect evidence in eight lines of doggerel which Einstein wrote before leaving, a copy of which is preserved in the White House archives. This says that there were cordial thoughts of an unidentified "you" — the identification being revealed by the fact that the original of the doggerel was written on a postcard addressed to Her Majesty the Queen of the Belgians. It lies today in the royal library in Brussels.

The situation in Europe — and presumably Belgium's position next to a swiftly rearming Germany — is unlikely to have been the only subject discussed that evening and the question of U.S. nationality appears to have been raised. This may well have been so since only a few weeks earlier Roosevelt had received a letter from Representative F. H. Shoemaker suggesting that he should "by Executive Order extend to Professor Einstein citizenship in the United States, thus making it possible for Professor Einstein to continue his scientific work and research, thus extending the helping hand, instead of perhaps the reproachful word". Roosevelt's secretary replied that Congress had never provided for U. S. citizenship to be given by Executive Order, but that no doubt the Secretary of Labor would write to Einstein telling him how to take out naturalisation papers if he wished to do so. However, Einstein was at this date quite satisfied to hold only Swiss nationality — and until the summer of 1936 continued to live in the United States only on a temporary visitor's visa.

The question of nationality was publicly raised two months later. On Wednesday, March 28th, Congressman Kenney of New

Jersey proposed a Joint Resolution in the House of Representatives
to admit Einstein to U.S. citizenship. It went as follows:

> Whereas Professor Albert Einstein has been accepted by the
> scientific world as a savant and a genius; and
> Whereas his activities as a humanitarian have placed him high
> in the regard of countless of his fellowmen; and
> Whereas he has publicly declared on many occasions to be a lover
> of the United States and an admirer of its Constitution; and
> Whereas the United States is known in the world as a haven of
> liberty and true civilisation: Therefore be it

1. Resolved by the Senate and House of Representatives
2. of the United States of America in Congress assembled,
3. That Albert Einstein is hereby unconditionally admitted to
4. the character and privileges of a citizen of the United States.

The following day, presumably by coincidence, it was officially announced in Berlin that Einstein had been formally deprived
of German citizenship by an order promulgated by Wilhelm Frick,
Minister of the Interior. By this time the list of the previous summer
had lengthened. When Einstein's name had been put on the first
list of men who might be deprived of their nationality there had
been only six more. Now his name appeared with those of 36 others.

Einstein made no public comment although his feeling was
made plain to his friends: he was quite satisfied with his Swiss citizenship — a point which he made to Kenney on April 11th in a letter
asking him to drop the motion.

This move came as Einstein's plans for the immediate future
were, according to his own evidence written at the time, still in
the balance. On Friday, March 30th, he and Elsa went to New York
and met a number of Elsa's relatives arriving from Europe on the
S.S. *Albert Ballin*. On the Sunday he attended a Carnegie Hall
concert at which he was presented with a scroll of honour before
going on to a dinner of the National Labor Committee for the
Jewish Worker in Palestine. Both were announced as farewell occasions, and Einstein was reported to be sailing for Antwerp on
Tuesday, April 3rd. But on Monday the 2nd the Jewish Telegraphic Agency — always among the best-informed sources on Einstein's
activities — announced that he had changed his plans and would
be staying indefinitely in the United States. The New York papers
announced that he had been about to leave for a visit to France
and Belgium, and the Agency quoted a statement from his secretary saying: "Many different circumstances had entered into his
decision."

In fact Einstein had been hovering for some months. Plans for his visit to Oxford, due in the spring or summer of 1934, had been discussed with Lindemann from November 1933 onwards. But he was increasingly anxious to cancel it and on December 17th wrote saying that conditions in the United States were so favourable that he was able to forego the £400 from Christ Church. Could it not be used elsewhere, he asked; a suggestion that was finally to harden into the proposal that it should support Jewish refugees from Germany. However, Lindemann was a determined fighter and early in 1934 Einstein received an invitation from Locker-Lampson almost certainly written at Lindemann's instigation, urging him to come to England.

He was still reluctant to leave America. But he had written to Mrs. Roosevelt earlier on, inferring that he would be in Princeton only until the end of March 1934. And in a letter to Max Born on March 22nd he made it clear that his mind had not yet been made up. Judging by a letter to Lindemann written by Erwin Shrödinger his final decision was made on the 28th.

Schrödinger had by this time been awarded a Fellowship at Magdalen. But he was visiting America and had called on Einstein partly out of friendship, partly as an emissary from Lindemann. Now, on March 29th, he reported back:

> Dear Lindemann, I suppose you are waiting for news from me concerning our friend A. E. and his coming to Oxford. I did not want to write to you before I had the feeling that his answer was really definitive — and of couse I did not wish to urge him, because I feared that might still reduce the likeliness of a positive answer. But now I asked him once more, adding that it would of course be wishable for you to know as soon as possible. Well, I am sorry to say, that he asked me to write to you a definite *no*. I really wanted to cable but unfortunately I said so and he had objections to it. The reason for his decision is really, that he is frightened of all the ado and the fuss and the consequent duties, that would be laid upon him, if he came to Europe at all. He considers the only way of escaping is, to stay in America this summer — I also told him that his idea of so to speak transferring the grant, that was at disposition for this purpose, on another or some other refugees, who need it, was not feasible. He understands this of course, though he regrets it.

Einstein not only regretted it. He refused to take no for an answer. He himself now wrote to Christ Church stating that he did not propose to visit Oxford that year. He did not therefore consider himself entitled to the £400 that went with his Studentship, but hoped that the governing body would apply all or part of this to help scientific refugees. The governing body considered his request which was repeated in 1935 and 1936 since he feared that if he went to Oxford he would also have to visit Paris and Madrid.

In the spring of 1934 Einstein would have been involved at two levels had he returned to Europe. As a public symbol of opposition to Hitler he would have had to speak, to lobby, to steep himself in the political ferment, an occupation for which he had no liking, even when deeply committed to a cause. Further, there were personal involvements which would inevitably take up his time and his energies. His first wife and his two sons were safe in Switzerland; his eldest stepdaughter, Ilse, had gone to Amsterdam with her husband while Margot had remained in Belgium. There were other relatives, his own and Elsa's, scattered across Europe. If he crossed the Atlantic he would inevitably be drawn more directly into discussion about their future.

With the decision, in Schrödinger's words, "to stay in America this summer" there came the search for a cottage away from Princeton, preferably where he could sail. Elsa handled the search, turning for help to Leon Watters, whom they had first met at Pasadena in January 1933. Like Dr. Bucky, the radiologist from Leipzig with whom the Einsteins also struck up a strong friendship during their first months in the United States, Watters left a large collection of letters and reminiscences which throw valuable light on the last two decades of Einstein's life. Early in 1934 plans were being made to celebrate the fiftieth anniversary of the Hebrew Technical Institute for Boys which Watters ran in New York, and he hoped that Einstein might be induced to attend.

In considering how I might approach him, [Watters later wrote] I recalled that in the course of my conversation with him at Pasadena I had mentioned a somewhat rare book which I had acquired. Its title was *Memorabila Mathematica* and it contained interesting anecdotes concerning famous mathematicians and physicists. Einstein had expressed a desire to see it and I thought that presenting it to him might afford an excuse for calling on him.

Arriving at Einstein's house in Princeton I asked my chauffeur, Martin Flattery, to go to the door, ring the bell and ask if I might see the professor. He came back to the car promptly and reported that a lady had told him that the Einsteins were not at home. I wrote a short note and asked the chauffeur to leave it at the house with the book I had brought. While thus engaged, I thought I discerned someone looking through the curtained window of the house and motioning to Martin. He went to the door again and came running back with a broad grin on his face, saying I was to come in. As I crossed the threshold Mrs. Einstein grasped my hand warmly and was most abject in apologising for having sent out word that they were not at home. She said that she had not recognised the name and explained that she had to resort to subterfuge to shield themselves from incessant annoyance by visitors. I apologised on my part for coming unannounced. After a short chat she called out "Albert!" and in a moment Einstein came down the stairs. He had on a worn grey sweater, a pair of baggy trousers and slippers, holding a pipe in his hand, and greeted me warmly. I continued to stand till he invited me to sit down, he taking a chair opposite me while fondling the book I had brought him.

Einstein was by now being deluged by demands to speak for charity, to attend dinners for charity, to give his name to a multitude of good causes. He usually declined; the exceptions were to help either the growing stream of Jewish refugees from Europe or the Jews in Palestine. "For a cause like yours I will gladly come," he told Watters.

The meeting sealed a friendship which quickly developed. Within three weeks the Einsteins had visited Watters' Institute, spent some time with him at his New York home, and accepted his offer of help in their search for a country cottage.

They met again, and often, and in April 1934 there began a long and revealing correspondence between Elsa — always anxious to push her husband into what she thought of as "society" — and the rich biochemist. Einstein wrote too, but it is his wife's letters which paint the homely picture of the great man, anxious to avoid public appearances, intent on getting on with his work, being coaxed into a synagogue for "the first time in his adult life", and relaxing only in the small boat which he would sail with a ferocious intensity that drew admiration from the experts and fear from his friends.

Watters himself is for a few years a minor Boswell in his recording of the extrovert Einstein. This is the Einstein arriving with his friend at what turned out to be a New York charity party and remarking of his host's floral exhibition: "One flower is beautiful, a surfeit of flowers is vulgar." It is the Einstein stopping Watters' chauffeur-driven car, jumping out to post his own letters, and replying to the obvious question with the answer that he "didn't wish to incommode us". It is also the Einstein who cannot or will not see that his own idea of equality can be embarrassing. "Just as we were all seated at the table", writes Watters in describing how they arrived back at the Einstein home after one Sunday drive, "Einstein rose from his chair, went outside, came back with my chauffeur and seated him at the table next to himself. Flattery, a decidedly modest person, felt ill at ease, and just as soon as the meal was finished, he made the excuse that he had to do some work on the car and thus escaped. This was the second time that he had been an unwilling guest at their table."

Watters also records an incident which casts light on the aloofness which permeated so many of Einstein's personal relationships. One evening he said, with a sense of regret and longing, that he had never put down roots. "As a youth", Watters says "he had never enjoyed the companionship of other youths, as a student he had never become intimate with his fellow students and took no part in their activities; as a noted scientist people did him homage; he never met them on a scale of equality that leads to lasting friendship. From all this I realised his craving for someone in whom he could confide." The statement does little justice to Einstein's close personal friendship with Ehrenfest that continued for more than twenty years or that with Besso which went on for more than twice as long. It reflects the lonely exile in his fifties rather than the younger man at the centre of things, dashing off his friendly postcards to all and sundry. Yet it also indicates that Einstein knew what he had lost through a combination of temperament and determination to plough his own furrow.

Such confidences came only some years after the meeting between Einstein and Watters in 1934. During the first months of their acquaintanceship, Elsa conscripted Watters' help in the choice of a summer sailing retreat. First she picked Maine. A few weeks later, there was a new plan, which followed the recommendation of Greenport which was ideal for sailing.

Before the matter could be finally decided there came news from Europe that Ilse was seriously ill in Paris. Elsa announced that she must go at once to her daughter.

What would happen to Einstein? For seventeen years, broken only by short unaccompanied journeys abroad, he had been guided and cosseted by Elsa through the minefields of everyday life. Now he was to be left, if not on his own — for there was always the incomparable Miss Dukas — at least without Elsa, in a country where he was still something of a stranger. He had no wish to stay in Princeton, and it was finally arranged that he should go after his wife's departure to "The Studio" at Watch Hill, Rhode Island, standing on the Sound just where it meets the sea. Here he would share their rented cottage for the early summer with Dr. and Mrs.

Bucky, their two sons, and Miss Dukas, who would keep house and deal with correspondence that would not wait.

At noon on May 19th Elsa sailed from New York on the French liner *Paris*. Her husband. having seen her off, was taken by Watters to his apartment and instructed to lie down before lunch. "I am not tired but I will not be insubordinate," he said. relaxing while Liszt's "Lorelei" was played on the Ampico. "Was it restful?" Watters asked as they went into lunch. "The sofa yes, the music not much — too sugary," Einstein replied. He was driven to a brief interview with his old friend Dr. Schwarz, the former German consul who had by this time been dismissed; then back to Princeton to prepare for his move to Watch Hill with the Buckys.

While Einstein's friendship with Watters reflects his unwavering interest in Jewish causes, and the determined fight that American Zionists carried on for the use of his name, that with Bucky shows something different. The doctor was not only a radiologist and physician but also an inventor, and the correspondence shows that Einstein's intuition for seeing the strengths and weaknesses of a good idea, developed in the Patent Office thirty years earlier, had not left him. The two men patented a camera, discussed means of using gravitation to measure altitudes, and also of "obtaining a proportional description of sound waves by magnetic means".

Some of the father's ingenuity seems to have been shown by the Bucky boys. At "The Studio" they had, says Watters, "set up an excellent short-wave radio set with a directional antenna. On the porch was a signboard showing at what time each country would broadcast: England, France, Holland, Germany, etc. This was during the period when Hitler was occupying the centre of the world stage. When we heard his turgid, shrieking voice come over the air, we all agreed that his antics, had they not had tragic consequences, could have been rightly designated as comic."

Watters visited the Rhode Island ménage early in July. He learned much about Einstein's habits. "When no visitors were present, he was served first and alone. The Buckys dined by themselves later. Miss Dukas did most of the cooking which consisted usually of macaroni, noodles, other soft foods and little meat.

At Watch Hill, Einstein spent most of his available time in the 17-foot boat which he kept at a small quay within walking distance of the cottage. His boat on the Havelsee outside Berlin had been, wrote Plesch, "perhaps the one thing that it hurt him to have to leave behind when the time came to shake the dust of

Germany from his feet"; and until old age joined forces with ill-health he continued to sail, not only on Princeton's Carnegie Lake but throughout the summer vacation. Sometimes his choice would be a hamlet on the eastern coast, sometimes it was one of the seaboard's inland lakes. Once he was persuaded by his friend to go to Florida instead. They had a hard time. Florida, as far as Einstein was concerned, was "too snobbish".

Sailing, like music, was with Einstein not so much a hobby as an extension of himself in which the essentials of his character and temperament were revealed. Thus it was inevitable that he should politely return an outboard motor which had been presented to him. He never drove a car — "the Herr Professor does not drive. It is too complicated," Elsa explained to one visitor — was over fifty when he handled a camera for the first time and barely learned to use a typewriter. A motor of any sort was a mechanical barrier. "The natural counterplay of wind and water delighted him most," says Bucky, who often sailed with him. "Speed, records, and above all competition were against his nature. He had a childlike delight when there was a calm and the boat came to a standstill, or when the boat ran aground."

He carried his passion for bare essentials to the point of refusing to have life-jackets or belts on board — even though he never learned to swim.

He would have liked gliding, he would have loved skiing and it was possibly only a lack of facilities which kept him from the first and a built-in physical laziness — "I like sailing," he said, "because it is the sport which demands the least energy" — which kept him from the second. He never studied navigation and never looked at a compass when in a boat, making up for this with a good sense of direction — which he rarely showed on land — and what Watters called "the ability to forecast a storm with uncanny accuracy". Wind and weather had an obvious link with stress and strain, action and reaction, and the basis of physics and his long theoretical experience clearly gave him an intuitive knowledge of how to handle a boat. This was appreciated by the designer, W. Sterling Burgess, who some years later, when Einstein was on holiday at Newport, came to confer with him. "Burgess had made a number of drawings from which to determine the best configuration of the hull of the new American yacht, and he had several pages of computations and equations," says Watters. "Einstein patiently listened while Burgess read his notes; then he sat for a few minutes in thought, and taking pencil and paper, gave Burgess his answer."

Two other traits were revealed to friends who sailed with him. One was his indifference to danger or death, reflected in such fearlessness of rough weather that more than once he had to be towed in after his mast had been blown down. Another was his perverse delight in doing the unexpected. "Once when out sailing with him", writes Watters, "and while we were engaged in an interesting conversation, I suddenly cried out 'Achtung' for we were almost upon another boat. He veered away with excellent control and when I remarked what a close call we had had, he started to laugh and sailed directly toward one boat after another, much to my horror; but he always veered off in time, and then laughed like a naughty boy." On another occasion Watters pointed out that they had sailed too close to a group of projecting reefs. Einstein replied by skimming the boat across barely submerged rock. In his boat, as in physics, he sailed close to the wind.

At Watch Hill, as well as at other sailing resorts in later years, the Bucky boys were Einstein's regular companions and as one of them has written, "While I never completely lost my awe of Einstein, he was never anything but natural and unpretentious with me. When together we simply were a man and a boy . . . During the summers we tramped together along the beaches of Rhode Island, Long Island, and Florida and the shore of Saranac Lake, New York. Often he stopped to gaze for many minutes at the sea, which held an endless fascination for him. Whenever in my private explorations I found an interesting inlet inhabited by crabs, starfish, and fish, or used by waterfowl, I reported my find to him, and we trudged to the spot to share the view in silence. We talked about geology, nature, my school studies."

Einstein enjoyed his first summer in America, even though the news, both from his wife in France and from friends who had succeeded in leaving Germany, grew steadily worse. Elsa arrived in Paris to find her younger daughter, Margot, caring for a sister who was dying. Within a few weeks she was returning across the Atlantic with her daughter's ashes, kept in a casket in the Einstein home until it disappeared after her own death two years later.

Ilse's husband was Rudolf Kayser who after the Nazis' rise to power had emigrated to Holland where he edited his stepfather-in-law's miscellaneous writings, published as *Mein Weltbild*. Kayser now crossed the Atlantic and in due course joined the Einsteins in Princeton before taking up the Chair of German Philosophy at Brandeis University. Margot also came with her husband, from whom she subsequently obtained a divorce. Eventually they too were joined by Hans Albert, Einstein's elder son who left Mileva in Zurich to care for his younger brother, already diagnosed as a schizophrenic for whom there was in those days little hope of cure. Two years later, only a few months before the outbreak of the Second World War, Einstein was reunited with his sister Maja who arrived in America from Italy. Of the relatives who remained in Europe the closest were Uncle Cäsar and his two children with whom Einstein kept up a lively correspondence that continued into the first years of the war.

The emigrants typified the growing stream of Jews from Germany — and later from Austria and Czechoslovakia — who crossed the Atlantic during the second half of the 1930s. Einstein could not isolate himself from their fortunes — the personal fortunes of his own family or the fate of refugee Jewry in general — however much the voice of physics encouraged him to do so.

From his arrival in the United States until her entry into the war with Germany in 1941 his research in Princeton was therefore carried on against a background of extra-curricular work. This ranged from fund-raising to giving confidential advice on posts into which particular men might be fitted. He wrote letters, pulled strings, and unashamedly used all the considerable force of the small tidy "A. Einstein" at the foot of the page.

Einstein disliked all that this work involved, and for several reasons. For instance he disliked flannelling, epitomised when he pleaded with a friend to speak in his place. "You know I can't make speeches. I can't lie." But this did not mean that his colleague could do so. "Oh, no. You know how to be gracious." He disliked wasting his time, and in addition his health limited what he could do, so that in 1937 he had to reject an invitation to visit London.

He was now satisfied with the post-Magnes Hebrew University — but there were still occasions when his view failed to chime in with official Zionist policy. Thus in 1930 some of his comments about narrow nationalism in Palestine brought forth a letter from Weizmann. He politely assumed that Einstein's "thoughts were being misrepresented"; but used nearly 2,000 words in an attempt to put the matter straight. Nevertheless, Einstein did what he could, and from 1934 his speeches, appeals and letter-signings multiply. During the first half of the 1930s he had pleaded that England and France should remain unarmed. Now he helped cope with the results.

In addition he was increasingly worried by the absurd idealogical division of physics into Aryan right and Jewish wrong. The first attempts at this, made in the backwash of the 1918 defeat, had been deepened by political propaganda during the decade that followed. But the straight condemnation of relativity as a Jewish theory seemed almost sane compared with the huge edifice of mumbo-jumbo being created as Einstein settled into Princeton.

At one end of the German academic spectrum stood Professor Mueller of the Technical College of Aachen, seeing Einstein and his work as part of a Jewish plot to pollute science. "The theory was", he stated in *Jewry and Science*, "directed from beginning to end towards the goal of transforming the living — that is, the non-Jewish — world of living essence, born from a mother earth and bound up with blood, and bewitching it into a spectral abstraction in which all individual differences of people and nations, and all inner limits of the races, are lost in unreality, and in which only an unsubstantial diversity of geometric dimensions survives which produces all events out of the compulsion of its godless subjection to laws."

At much the same level was Professor Tomaschek, director of the Institute of Physics at Dresden. "Modern Physics", he claimed, "is an instrument of [world] Jewry for the destruction of Nordic science. True physics is the creation of the German spirit ... In fact, all European science is the fruit of Aryan, or, better, German thought." Presumably this sounded like common sense to a writer who could claim that "statistical laws in physics must be recially understood".

At a higher level were the men whose reputation automatically gave them a hearing. Not all had the comparative harmlessness of Professor Stark, who had been forced to retire from his chair in the University of Wurzburg in 1922 because of his polemics against Einstein, but who now bounced back with the claim that "the founders of research in physics, and the great discoverers from Galileo to Newton to the physical pioneers of our time, were almost exclusively of Aryan, predominantly of the Nordic, race." There was also the irrepressible Lenard who had ordered that the word "ampere", commemorating the French physicist in the unit of electrical current, should be replaced by the German "weber" after Wilhelm Weber on the instruments in his Heidelberg laboratory. His four-volume *Deutsche Physik*, printed in Gothic type to epitomise "the German spirit", illustrated his paranoia. "Jewish science soon found many industrious interpreters of non-Jewish or practically non-Jewish blood," he said. "One may summarise them all by calling to mind the probably pure-minded Jew, Albert

Einstein. His 'theories of relativity' seek to revolutionise and dominate the whole of physics. In fact these theories are now down and out *(ausgespielt)*. They were never even intended to be true."

This line of attack was epitomised by the opening words of Lenard's fourth volume. "German physics? one asks. I might rather have said Aryan Physics or the Physics of the Nordic Species of Man. The Physics of those who have fathomed the depths of Reality, seekers after Truth, the Physics of the very founders of Science. But, I shall be answered, 'Science is and remains international.' It is false. Science, like every other human product, is racial, and conditioned by blood." Bruno Thurring, lecturing to the Heidelberg Association of Students of Science on September 4th, 1936, pointed up the same argument. Einstein, he claimed, was not the pupil of Copernicus, Galileo, Kepler and Newton, but their determined opponent. "His theory is not the keystone of a development, but a declaration of total war," he went on, "waged with the purpose of destroying what lies at the basis of this development, namely, the world view of German man."

If this negation of scientific enquiry had been confined to the lunatic fringe of the universities fewer men would have decided to pull up their emotional roots and leave quietly in the night for an unknown future wherever fortune provided it. But its implications stretched out wider, corrupting all they touched. Some did decide to fight on within Germany itself. Von Laue, visiting Einstein in Princeton shortly before the outbreak of war, explained why he had to return: "I hate them so much I must be close to them. I have to go back." Some concluded that it was their duty to acquiesce, others remained enigmatic, while yet others decided it was their duty to pack their bags and go.

Among those who had been Einstein's colleagues, the most notable to leave Germany with honest speed was Max Born, as unyielding in his opposition to Hitler as he later was to nuclear weapons, coming first to Cambridge and then to Edinburgh. In Hamburg, Einstein's old colleague Otto Stern declared on Hitler's accession to power that he would resign from his chair. He was dissuaded by his staff, but reiterated that he would leave at the first hint of intereference with his department. It came in June. Stern walked from his laboratory, never to return. Shortly afterwards he left Germany for the United States where, at the Carnegie Institute of Technology, he was awarded the Nobel Prize, acted as adviser to the Manhattan Project which built the first nuclear

weapons and later helped awaken Einstein to the problems they
posed for the post-war world. Erwin Freundlich left the Einstein
Tower at Potsdam — going first to Istanbul, where a brave but
unsuccessful effort was made to create a new centre of western
learning; than to Prague; and, after the débâcle of the Munich
Agreement, to St. Andrews, Scotland, where he was offered a post
on the initiative of Eddington and spent the rest of his working
life. Schrödinger went to Oxford and, subsequently, to Belgium and
Dublin. Leo Szilard, one of the first Hungarians to see the implications of Hitler's conquest of the Chancellory, came to England
via Austria and subsequently, for lack of support in Britain, crossed
the Atlantic.

Szilard highlights the most momentous result of the year
which brought Hitler to power, Einstein to Princeton, and drove no
less than six Nobel Prize winners from Germany; a result which can
be seen in any story of the world's first nuclear weapons. Einstein,
Szilard, Teller, Wigner, Peierls and Frisch, Otto Stern, Hans Bethe
and Victor Weisskopf — these are only a few of the men who left
Europe under attack, or threat of attack, from the Nazi government; who played their part in the work which led to Hiroshima
and Nagasaki; and who might, but for the policy of the National
Socialist Party, have written a very different opening chapter to
the story of the nuclear age.

The grotesque Nazi interpretation of the new physical theories
produced during the first third of the century, the expulsion of the
Jews and the effect of this on the situation in Palestine, together
with what seemed to be the inevitable approach of a new world
war, formed the background against which Einstein settled into
his work at the Institute for Advanced study. He was much sought
after. The prospect of a musical evening or of some new development in science were baits most commonly used to draw him from
the relative seclusion of Princeton. But he was not in demand
solely because he was the most famous scientist in the world. He
was in his mid-fifties, unsociable rather than the reverse, a dropper
of bricks as much by intent as by accident. Yet in the true dictionary definition of "a favour specially vouchsafed by God", a
charisma did not only set him apart but made almost any meeting
with him a memorable occasion. There would invariably be some
attitude, some phrase, that would be remembered long afterwards
and which could be attached to him alone.

When Harvard wanted to confer an honorary degree on him,
he was coaxed to the occasion by Harlow Shapley, who at Mount

Wilson had laid the foundations for galactic astronomy, offering a private evening of chamber music at his house. Elsa, unable to come, gave her usual list of instructions. "He is a sensitive plant," she wrote. "He should smoke no cigar. He can have coffee for break-fast, but in the evening he must have Sanka; otherwise he will not sleep well." Einstein followed his instructions, says Shapley. "When we rose from the dinner table and the men went into the library, he said 'no' to the proffered cigar. Sadly he got out his pipe. Later I tempted him again. This time he took a cigar, saying softly, 'Ach, mein Weib'."

At the end of the evening the guests began to go, but not rapidly.

> Who would want to go away hastily from an Einstein evening? [says Shapley.] He might say something — and indeed he did. He whispered it to me as I was sending the fiddlers along. "They remind me of time," he said.
> "But it is only eleven o'clock. The time is not late: they will be gone in a few minutes."
> "But they remind me of time," he persisted.
> "How so?"
> "Always going — but never gone."

Once he was induced to visit the Rockefeller Medical Centre in New York, then run by Abraham Flexner's brother. Here Dr. Alexis Carrel, whose extra-curricular interests were spiritualism and extra-sensory perception, was working with Lindbergh on an apparatus for the perfusion of human organs, a device which helped open the way to the modern heart transplant. Carrel had invited Einstein to inspect the apparatus with its pulsating exhibits. Thirty years later Lindbergh still remembers Einstein coming into the room with Carrel. The latter, expounding his spiritualism, was saying: "But doctor, what would you say if you observed this phenomenon yourself?"

"I still would not believe it," Einstein replied.

By the start of 1935 he had become reconciled to the fact that Europe would never again be his home; even a sentimental visit would present problems. Three months later he arrived in Hamilton, Bermuda, with his family and Miss Dukas. He played the usual hide-and-seek with reporters, stayed long enough to make formal visa applications to the U.S. consul necessary under U.S. law, since they still held only visitors' permits, and returned to Princeton at the end of a week. Now they were able to take out the papers which eventually meant naturalisation.

32

Long before this, Einstein had put down his first real roots in the United States. In August 1935 he bought 112 Mercer Street, the comfortable two-storey house in its own piece of ground that was to become in time one of the most famous houses in the world — the "very old and beautiful house with a long garden" as Elsa described it in a letter to Uncle Cäsar in Belgium. Mercer Street is a rib which runs from the university site on Princeton's main backbone, a broad tree-lined avenue making for open parklike country in which the Institute for Advanced Study was built. № 112, 120 years old, quiet and comfortable behind its verandah and green shutters, had little to distinguish it from many similar white-painted houses. Tidy hedge, neat lawn, five-stepped approach to the porch, broad interior stairs leading up to the bedrooms — all these were the hallmarks of anonymity as were the trees back and front which enclosed the house in its own personal countryside.

The first change in the house came with the creation of Einstein's study, a first-floor room overlooking the back garden. Half the wall was replaced with a huge window which seemed to bring the trees into the room, so that Einstein could say it was hardly like being indoors. Two of the remaining walls were transformed into floor-to-ceiling bookshelves. The centre of the room was almost filled with a large low table, usually covered with a debris of pencils, pads and pipes. In front of the window stood his desk. For ornaments there were portraits of Faraday, Clerk-Maxwell and, soon afterwards, of Ghandi. On the walls hung a simple diploma: that of his honorary membership of the Berne Naturforschende Gesellschaft. In the rooms below, contrasting grotesquely with the colonial-style surroundings, was the bulky and outmoded furniture from 5, Haberlandstrasse, surprisingly released by the Nazis and finally brought to the United States on Elsa's instructions.* It seems that Einstein hated it.

With this home as headquarters, he became a feature of the Princeton scene. The early frigidity between him and the inhabitants of the small New Jersey township had been easy to understand. Never the most gregarious of men, he felt a shy European reserve among this nation of extroverts; on their side, even the most friendly were slightly put off by an isolating whiff of genius as they consi-

---

* Einstein's scientific papers were taken from the Haberlandstrasse apartment to Rudolf Kayser's flat, and from there to the French Embassy. They then left Germany in the diplomatic bag. But treatment of refugees was still haphazard, and one Jewish physicist who left Germany in 1933 — and who was to play a key role in the Allies' nuclear war effort — was followed by his scientific equipment some months afterwards.

dered this quiet eccentric-looking fellow who had in some mysterious fashion convinced the experts that neither space nor time was
what they thought it was.

The phase passed. Long before the outbreak of war, Einstein
had been accorded his own niche inside the Princeton community.
They still felt that he was uncomfortably unique. A good many
held reservations about his uncompromising views on politics and
his unconventional views on religion. But it was tacitly agreed that
these matters could be ignored, that Einstein could be accepted in
spite of them. His greatness would be overlooked as a pardonable
eccentricity. They would pass the time of day with him, allow their
children to make friends and would generally agree that however
outrageous his views, however shy and retiring he might be, he was
yet a decent neighbour. As opinion softened, they began to regard
their genius as after all a man of flesh and blood, tortured by the
usual human anxieties and fears. They were almost right.

The tragedy which began as he and Elsa were settling into the
new home was a human enough link with other men's lives. Only
a few months after they had moved in, Elsa was affected by a
swelling of the eye. Specialists confirmed that this, as she had feared,
was a symptom of heart and kidney troubles. Hospital treatment in
New York was proposed. But she soon came back to Mercer Street,
to a drastic cure which involved complete immobilisation.

Einstein's devotion to physics throughout the months that
followed was not a sign of callousness. With dedicated men —
whether their interests be politics or science or art — the normal
emotions take their turn. Compared with the problems of the
universe, family duties were small beer, a priority that was reinforced as he grew older. Talking late one evening with Watters,
Einstein looked intently at a picture of Watters' recently dead
wife. "The individual," he reflected, "counts for little; man's individual troubles are insignificant; we place too much importance on
the trivialities of living." Yet despite this there was still a subtle
difference between the first wife with whom he had lived for a
decade and the second with whom he lived for nearly two. Elsa
herself sensed it, observing after Einstein had boasted to Watters
that he wore the same clothes all the year round: "For his first
wife he dressed up; for me, he will not." But beneath this, she
enjoyed his genius, despite the hardship that went with it.

At the start of their twenty years together, they had achieved
a working arrangement. While he devoted himself to discovering
how God had made the world, she reduced to an absolute minimum

the mundane problems of life. To an extent which offended the matriarchal society of the United States, he thought while she toiled, a division illustrated by a homely incident when they dined outdoors with two friends one summer night. As the air freshened, the hostess asked her husband to fetch her coat. Elsa was horrified: "I would never ask the professor to do that."

For his part the professor supported the family and irradiated genius from his own private world. "Your wife," Mrs. Eisenhart, wife of the Dean of Princeton University Graduate School said to him soon after his arrival, "seems to do absolutely everything for you. Just exactly what do you do for her?" Einstein replied: "I give her my understanding."

The understanding was tested in 1936. At first Elsa seemed to recover. When the summer came they both travelled to Saranac Lake, 300 miles north of New York and high in the Adirondacks. But her condition failed to improve. To Watters, she confided a great deal, as was clear from his later comments. "Einstein," he wrote, "absorbed in his intellectual pursuits, found little time to fulfil the duties expected of a husband." It was true, he went on, that Elsa "enjoyed the sharing of the many honours which were bestowed on him, and the many travels with him, but she missed the sympathy and tenderness which she craved, and found herself much alone in these respects". And writing to Watters from Saranac Lake she made it clear that Einstein could well have taken lessons from him. But, dear God, it was too late now.

Back in Princeton, her condition continued to deteriorate. The ground floor of the Mercer Street home began to resemble a hospital ward. Einstein, forsaking the Institute, worked on in his first-floor study. No more could be done and Elsa died late in December, still grieving for the daughter she had lost in Paris two years previously, still proud of what Albert was accomplishing.

After her death he got down to it with even more self-centred concentration. From the beginning of 1937 he once more, and without distraction, devoted himself to the Institute. His absorption had been intense since his first days at Princeton. Asked by the Buckys to pass a long weekend with them, he had replied that he could not, because he did not want to interrupt the work at the Institute. Offered a brief break by Leon Watters, he rejected it on similar grounds. And even in the summer of 1935 when he was working hard during the August holidays at Old Lyme, Connecticut, he refused an invitation for the same reason.

He had plunged into pacifist waters and plunged out when he

found they were taking him the wrong way. He was still a Zionist at heart and as far as the Hebrew University was concerned he was about to win a considerable victory at considerable cost. He still hoped to do good although by slightly more judicious means. But now, thank God, he would for most practical purposes concentrate on his cobbler's last, a physicist devoting himself to physics in a new world which might in due course, with only passing help from him, help to redress the balance of the old.

Thus he was always anxious to get back — even from his beloved sailboat — to the intellectual workshop of Princeton. He could of course work anywhere — "as well on a Potsdam bridge as at my home". Nevertheless his room in the Institute or his study in Mercer Street was his natural habitat. It was here that he could best carry on his main work and continue his stubborn rearguard battle against the new movements in physics which he himself had started nearly a third of a century before.

Einstein's attitude to quantum mechanics drew him further and further from the mainstream of theoretical physics. He himself was well aware of this. He told his old friend Infeld, who arrived in the United States in 1935, that "in Princeton they regard me as an old fool." Infeld, at first incredulous, later agreed. "Einstein, during my stay in Princeton, was regarded by most of the professors here more like a historic relic than as an active scientist," he wrote. The Princeton professors were not alone, and Max Born, noting that Einstein was unable to get him an invitation to the Institute, saw one obvious explanation: "Probably I was regarded there as a fossil, as he was himself, and two such relics from times past were too much for the modern masters of Princeton."

This view was widespread throughout physics and was summed up after Einstein's death by Robert Oppenheimer who became Director of the Institute in 1947. His judgment is that during the last twenty-five years of Einstein's life his tradition in a certain sense failed him.

> They were the years he spent at Princeton and this, though a source of sorrow, should not be concealed, [he said.] He had a right to that failure... He spent those years first in trying to prove that the quantum theory had inconsistencies in it. No one could have been more ingenious in thinking up unexpected and clever examples, but it turned out that the inconsistencies were not there: and often their resolution could be found in earlier work of Einstein himself. When that did not work, after repeated efforts, Einstein had simply to say that he did not like the theory. He did not like the elements of

indeterminacy. He did not like the abandonment of continuity or of causality. These were things that he had grown up with, saved by him, and enormously enlarged; and to see them lost, even though he had put the dagger in the hand of their assassin by his own work, was very hard on him. He fought with Bohr in a noble and furious way, and he fought with the theory which he had fathered but which he hated. It was not the first time that this has happened in science.

Thus Einstein's scientific position in Princeton, the aura of greatness which he radiated and the extraordinary influence of his personality on the minds of his assistants and collaborators, continued in spite of his contemporary standing in theoretical physics rather than because of it. A decade and a half earlier, when he was at the height of his powers in Berlin, his idea of how scientific problems should be tackled, his facility for "making physics melt in his mouth", had created an overwhelming impression on his listeners. Now, even though many of his firmly-held beliefs were fighting for their lives, the magic still remained.

> As I look back to our work [says Professor Nathan Rosen, who succeeded Mayer as Einstein's assistant] I think that the things which impressed me most were the simplicity of his thinking and his faith in the ability of the human mind to understand the workings of nature. Throughout his life, Einstein believed that human reason was capable of leading to theories that would provide correct descriptions of physical phenomena. In building a theory, his approach had something in common with that of an artist; he would aim for simplicity and beauty (and beauty for him was, after all, essentially simplicity). The crucial question that he would ask, when weighing an element of a theory, was: Is it reasonable? No matter how successful a theory appeared to be, if it seemed to him, not to be reasonable (the German word that he used was *vernunftig*), he was convinced that the theory could not provide a really fundamental understanding of nature.

A strikingly similar picture of Einstein during the later 1930s, as one part of him remained above the contemporary scientific battle, is given by another assistant, Banesh Hoffmann, who stressed that Einstein's method, though based on a profound knowledge of physics, "was essentially aesthetic and intuitive. Watching him, and talking with him," he says, "I came to understand the nature of science in a way that I could not possibly have understood it merely from reading his writings or the writings of other great physicists or of philosophers and historians of science. Except for the fact that he was the greatest physicist since Newton, one might almost say that he was not so much a scientist as an artist of science."

When Elsa died, Einstein was only a few months from his fifty-eighth birthday. By all the rules of the game his creative life was finished. He had what lesser men could have regarded as a well-paid sinecure, beyond students, beyond competition, beyond the need to struggle upward. Yet the extraordinary thing was that now, at a time when most scientists were ready to drop into administration, and those with a dislike for it were happy enough to potter on, Einstein stuck to his last with the fierce determination of a master-craftsman determined not to waste a minute of the waking day.

At the Institute until his retirement in 1945, and at Mercer Street until his death a decade later, he worked with a succession of colleagues and assistants on three different but closely inter-locked areas of research. First, and certainly the most important in his own view, was his persistent search for a unified field theory. He never found it. He worked on a variety of solutions; each seemed to offer hope; each had eventually to be discarded. As he himself has said, only a man with his name already made could afford to do the job. Only a man with Einstein's deep vision would have found satisfaction in it.

His attitude to what even the comprehending scientist tended to see as a thankless task is highlighted by two stories. One day his accountant and friend, Leo Mattersdorf, asked whether he felt he was nearing his goal. "He replied 'No'," says Mattersdorf, "and he added: 'God never tells us in advance whether the course we are to follow is the correct one.' He had tried at least 99 solutions and none worked but he had learned a lot. 'At least,' he said, 'I know 99 ways that won't work'."

There was also his statement to David Mitrany, one of the few people in Princeton who became a genuine confidant. The friendship had started after Mitrany, walking to the Institute one morning, gave a friendly wave to Einstein on the other side of the street. The same thing happened the following morning, and the next. "After that," says Mitrany, "we decided to walk together." To this figure from the older happier Europe — who as a young journalist had in 1921 reported Einstein's first speech in England for the *Manchester Guardian* — Einstein confided a great deal. He even talked about his work, which he did not usually discuss with men outside the subject. One day he thought he was at last on the track of a satisfactory unified field theory. Six months later he mentioned, almost casually, that the path led into a dead end; but he would, he threw off, be publishing it soon. Mitrany asked why.

"To save another fool from wasting six months on the same idea."

Second only to the problems of a unified field was development of the General Theory of Relativity, particularly so that it could accommodate the new discoveries and speculations of cosmology. Here Einstein was moving from the fringes of his own field into an area already being transformed by technological advance. Here, with his conception of the universe as he had first described it in 1917 and as he had later amended it, Einstein had much to offer. But he was now one man among many.

The third subject was the quantum theory as it had been developed a decade earlier, a theory which now seemed to satisfy the apparent duality of nature, but which in the process allowed indeterminacy to lord it over the universe. Here Einstein obstinately stuck. He refused to accept the possibility that the new order was satisfactory, and over the years made successive efforts to demolish it.

One of the most important of these efforts came when, together with two colleagues, B. Podolsky and N. Rosen, he at first appeared to have struck a mortal blow at Heisenberg's Uncertainty Principle, the idea that had become if not the backbone at least an important item in the body of quantum mechanics. The paper which Einstein produced with his two fellow-workers asked "Can Quantum-Mechanical Description of Physical Reality be Considered Complete?" When the article is stripped of its essential mathematics, it is easy to see how its simple statements constituted a major attack on the new ideas which had almost displaced those of Einstein's youth.

Heisenberg had claimed that in the study of very small objects, such as sub-atomic particles, their systems were inevitably disturbed in such a way that it was impossible to measure at the same time with equal accuracy two associated quantities. As measurement of position increased in accuracy, measurement of momentum became more uncertain; increasing certainty about the time of a subatomic event would inevitably be matched by increasing uncertainty about the energy involved.

Einstein and his colleagues began by pointing out that in judging the merits of any theory one had to consider both its agreement with human experience and the completeness which the description gave of the physical world. After this preliminary statement they went on to what was the nub of their ingenious exposition. They took a situation which could arise in quantum mechanics of two interacting systems, called for convenience system *A* and system *B*. After a while the interaction was allowed to stop.

But by taking a measurement of one quantity in system *A*, it was still possible to get its value in system *B;* and by measuring an associated quantity in system *A* it was possible to get its value in system *B*. But according to Heisenberg's Uncertainty Principle this was not possible; therefore, it was concluded, the description provided by quantum mechanics was incomplete.

The new physics had an answer to this. "I have used this opportunity to take up my old discussions with Einstein in the hope that we once may reach to an understanding regarding the actual position in atomic theory, which to my mind he does not quite realise," Bohr wrote to Rutherford. This attempt appeared in the next issue of the *Physical Review*, Bohr asking the same question as Einstein and providing the answer "Yes". Einstein refused to be convinced, clinging to the attitude which he maintained to the end of his life: that the description of nature provided by quantum mechanics was not incorrect but incomplete, a temporary makeshift which would eventually be superseded.

The problems took up most of Einstein's working days at the Institute. But he was as much on the lookout for fresh ideas and bright young people as he had been in Berlin. The Institute was until 1940 virtually a part of the University, and Einstein would often sit in on student seminars. Sometimes he learned with surprise how his own theoretical work of the pre-war years had been absorbed into common practice. This was the case even with his famous $E = mc^2$. In his original paper he had noted that it was "not impossible that with bodies whose energy content is variable to a high degree (e. g. with radium salts) the theory may be successfully put to the test". He had sown the seed and left it at that. And he was hardly aware that by the 1930s many physicists were making such tests.

One of my most vivid memories, [writes Professor A. E. Condon] is of a seminar at Princeton (1934) when a graduate student was reporting on researches of this kind and Einstein was in the audience. Einstein had been so preoccupied with other studies that he had not realised that such confirmation of his early theories had become an everyday affair in the physical laboratory. He grinned like a small boy and kept saying over and over, *"Ist das wirklich so?"* (Is it really true) as more and more specific evidence of his $E = mc^2$ relation was being presented.

In addition to listening he sometimes lectured, and it was clear that he still enjoyed displaying his mastery of the subject. One instance is recalled by Churchill Einsenhart.

When he had finished, one of the other mathematicians present proceeded to deduce Professor Einstein's principal result in short order from certain results of other authors in the then available scientific literature. The audience waited breathlessly for Professor Einstein's response. He rose, thanked his colleague for this very concise and elegant derivation of his own principal result, reminded all present that the assumptions underlying the results upon which the discussant's short proof had been based were somewhat different from those from which he himself had started, and concluded by thanking his colleague for thus revealing that his result had a somewhat broader base of validity than he himself had appreciated. The approving buzz of the audience testified to the fact that Albert Einstein had clearly not lost but gained from the intended criticism.

His ability as a lecturer, together with his reputation as the most famous scientist of the century, made him a natural choice as guest speaker when the American Association for the Advancement of Science held its annual meeting at Pittsburgh, even though he was still dubious about addressing large public audiences in English. Leon Watters stage-managed the occasion, organising Einstein's stay with mutual friends in the city, taking him there by train and later recording how Einstein, sitting in one train and watching another on a neighbouring track, said that he had never before had the chance of watching how connecting rods worked.

The meeting was remembered for Einstein's Willard Gibbs Lecture on "Elementary Derivation of the Equivalence of Mass and Energy", given in English after a great deal of persuasion had been brought to bear. Legend claims that on the morning of the great day a notice appeared in the Personal Columns of the local paper, inserted by a well-wisher and reading: "Don't be afraid, Albert, I am sure you can do it." Einstein did do it, speaking before two long blackboards which filled most of the stage. Watters and a colleague sat in the front row, ready to prompt if he stumbled over his English. It was not necessary. The only hitch came when he remarked that his line of reasoning was simple. He was greeted by shouts of "No."

Before the lecture there was the press conference. Between thirty and forty correspondents were invited and it was agreed that none of them should try to get an exclusive statement. One girl reporter, ignoring this, succeeded in getting Einstein alone and asked whether he ever conversed about subjects other than physics. He gave her a quick comprehending look and replied: "Yes, but not with you."

The conference, with reporters providing the usual barrage of questions, was to produce one historic reply, repeated with *ad variorum* renderings over the years, and much quoted a decade later. "Do you think that it will be possible to release the enormous amount of energy shown by your equation, by bombardment of the atom?" he was asked. "I feel that it will not be possible for practical purposes," he replied. "Splitting the atom by bombardment is like shooting at birds in the dark in a region where there are few birds."

Most physicists agreed, although one of the few who did not was Leo Szilard, Einstein's former collaborator in Berlin who had already lodged his secret patent with the British Admirality. But most still held the view of Lord Rutherford, given at the Leicester meeting of the British Association for the Advancement of Science in 1933 where he issued a word of warning " . . . to those who look for sources of power in atomic transmutations — such expectations are merest moonshine."

Einstein's ability to think simply about physics and describe its essentials in terms that ordinary men and women could understand was further deployed in *The Evolution of Physics* which he wrote in 1937 with Leo Infeld. During 1935, towards the end of the one-year appointment of his assistant Nathan Rosen, he received a letter from Infeld, by this time a lecturer in the Polish university of Lvov. Poland's recent Non-Aggression Pact with Germany augured ill for men of left-wing opinions and Infeld feared that he might soon be forced to leave. On Einstein's instigation he was given a small grant which enabled him to work at Princeton, where he arrived early in 1936.

Infeld's grant at the Institute was for one year: it was not renewed, even though Einstein intervened on his friend's behalf. Having burned his boats in Europe, Infeld was thus in danger of being left financially high and dry. He realised that there was one way out of his problem. He had been working for a year with Einstein. Why should they not collaborate in writing a popular book on science? There would obviously be no difficulty in finding a publisher, half of the advance might cover another year's stay in the United States, and who knew what might not turn up during that time? With a great deal of hesitation he put forward the idea, adding that it might possibly be a stupid proposition. Einstein knew that his colleague was desperate. "This is not at all a stupid idea. Not stupid at all," he replied. Then he got up, stretched out his hand to Infeld and said: "We shall do it."

Between them, the two men produced what they modestly called "a simple chat between you and me". Yet the book, describing the rise and fall of the mechanical view of the natural world, the concept of field, the idea of relativity and the development of the quantum theory, is far more than a survey of physics as the subject was understood in the 1930s. Just as Einstein discerned a link between the values of science and the values of art, just as he thought a simple theory was better than a complicated one, and just as he would have appreciated the later use of the word "elegant" to describe an experiment, so did he and Infeld describe the "connection between the world of ideas and the world of phenomena". They had, they wrote, "tried to show the active forces which compel science to invent ideas corresponding to the reality of our world . . . to give some idea of the eternal struggle of the inventive human mind for a fuller understanding of the laws governing physical phenomena."

The success of *The Evolution of Physics* in 1938 was a bright spot in a grim period. Einstein still had his science, but even a man bound up as tightly to his work as Einstein was to be until his last moments, could not isolate himself entirely from the march of events in the outside world — particularly if he happened to be a German Jew. In March, 1938, Austria found herself nipped between Nazi Germany on the north and Fascist Italy on the south, and the German army was ordered in — to the cheers of what was probably a majority of the population, ignorant of what was being prepared for them. In October, Czechoslovakia was offered up to the same occupiers, a democratic passenger thrown to the pursuing wolves in an effort to gain time for the building of fighter forces and the erection of the vital radar chain.

For Einstein, ignorant of the arguments which might justify appeasement — but, arguably, did not — this mounting record of capitulation, followed in March, 1939, by the abandonment of Prague itself, was particularly painful. He, after all, had learned his lesson even if he had learned it late. But while he had learned that pacifism was no answer to the dictators, Britain and France still appeared to be beating the retreat as unashamedly as ever.

To the sense of coming doom there was added, as his sixtieth birthday came and went, a feeling of personal limitation. This he confided to Watters, as he confided much else. After an introspective evening, his host jotted down what he remembered of their conversation. "I find my physical powers decreasing as I grow older," he remembers Einstein saying. "I find that I require more sleep now. I doubt if my mental capacity has diminished. I grasp things as quickly as I did when I was younger. My power, my particular ability, lies in visualising the effects, consequences, and possibilities, and the bearings on present thought of the discoveries of others. I grasp things in a broad way easily. I cannot do mathematical calculations easily. I do them not willingly and not readily. Others perform these details better . . ."

He would go on with his work, of course. He would continue to help all and sundry, unknown Jewish refugees, disestablished professors whom he could guide into temporary positions, relatives such as his sister Maja who arrived in the United States from Florence, fearing the future too much to continue living under Mussolini. There seemed to be prospects of little else as the summer of 1939 approached.

# 20

---

# EINSTEIN, THE BOMB, AND THE BOARD OF ORDNANCE

BY THE START OF 1939 EINSTEIN HAD SPENT MORE THAN FIVE YEARS in the United States. He had settled in satisfactorily, a self-styled bird of passage which had at last come to rest. He was a part of the Princeton scene, a landmark figure whose world-wide fame was ignored by the local inhabitants partly for decency's sake, partly because of the genuine affection in which many of them had come to hold him. At times the man who was essentially European missed the familiar sights and sound of Leiden, the Kaiser Wilhelm Institute, and the grey buildings of the E. T. H. in Zurich where so many corners reminded him of his earlier days. Nevertheless, Einstein liked America. He liked the openness and the natural generosity of the people. He liked their willingness to be lavish about research. At times he almost felt comfortable, a refugee in a nation of refugees.

But in Europe, as the Germans prepared to follow-up the Munich victory, things went from bad to worse. One consequence was that Einstein now found himself permanently joined in America by his old friend and colleague from Prague, Philipp Frank. Late in 1938 Frank had been invited to Harvard as visiting lecturer, and by the time the Germans had marched into what was left of Czechoslovakia he had begun a series of lectures on the quantum theory and the philosophical foundations of modern physics. He was to remain in the United States for the rest of his life.

Meanwhile, the Wehrmacht prepared for the late summer's campaign across the plains of Poland. And meanwhile scientists throughout the world debated the implications of an event which had taken place in the Kaiser Wilhelm during the last weeks of 1938. For here Einstein's old friend Otto Hahn had split in two the nucleus of the uranium atom. The event not only ushered in the nuclear age and ended the age of innocence in physics; it also drew Einstein into the mainstream of world events with sombre inevitability — and in circumstances still shrouded by a good deal of mythology, ignorance and special pleading.

The importance of Hahn's discovery of nuclear fission in the long trail of events which led to atomic weapons is well known. So is Einstein's later involvement in that trail, even though its significance is often misunderstood. Less appreciated is the ironic way in which theoretical research produced the prospect of an ultimate weapon just as the world was preparing for war. No dramatist would have dared to arrange such fortuitous events in such apparently contrived order.

If one is to appreciate where Einstein stands, and to assess what he did during the crucial periods of 1939-41 and 1944-45, as well as what he did not, it is necessary to recapitulate these events and to explain their significance. The interpretation of Hahn's experiments early in 1939 by Lise Meitner and her nephew Otto Frisch led on to applications far more important than any others which sprang from that generation of investigators which included the Curies and J. J. Thomson, Planck, Rutherford, Bohr and Einstein. It is true that their work had already changed the world in many ways which it would have been difficult to forecast at the start of the century. The electron of Lorentz and Thompson was already becoming the basis of great industries. The electro-magnetic waves forecast by Maxwell and discovered by Hertz, had already made near-instantaneous communication practicable across the globe. The X-rays discovered by Röntgen were giving advance warning of disease where none would have before been possible. The effect of the radium so laboriously purified and investigated by the Curies was giving the hope of life to patients who before had no hope. Einstein's explanation of the photo-electric effect had already helped to prod forward television from experiment to reality. The revolutionaries who had gathered in Brussels for the first Solvay Congress less than three decades earlier already had ample practical results to show for what had seemed, so recently, to be largely theoretical.

Yet it was only now that physics began to touch with the tips of its fingers that most stupendous of possibilities: the use of the energy locked within the nucleus of the atom. It was not that this awesome prospect had lain beyond the imagination. As early as 1903 Rutherford had made what a correspondent, Sir William Dampier-Whetham, called his "playful suggestion that, could a proper detonator be found, it was just conceivable that a wave of atomic disintegration might be started through matter, which would indeed make this old world vanish in smoke". Planck, mulling over Einstein's $E=mc^2$, declared in 1908 of the atom's "latent energy" that "though the actual production of such a 'radical' process might have appeared extremely small only a decade ago, it is now in the range of the possible..." They thought about the possibility often enough. Yet throughout the first part of the century, ignorance of the sub-nuclear world was a barrier stout enough to keep such projects within the realm of science fiction, or of those apparently impractical optimists who declared that a lump of fuel no bigger than a man's hand might one day drive a liner across the Atlantic.

The problem was transformed as knowledge increased: from being a theoretical conundrum it became a problem of practical technology. How would it be possible to penetrate the heart of the atomic nucleus with a bullet which would split the nucleus apart and release the energy which bound it together as one piece? How, moreover, could this be done not once or twice but on a vast multiplicity of occasions so that the immense number of atoms comprising the material under attack would release their energy in the minimum of time? The great steps forward in experimental physics made by Rutherford at Manchester in 1919 and by Cockcroft and Walton in 1932 had little direct effect on this central and tantalising problem. Rutherford bombarded nitrogen with the particles which were constantly being naturally ejected by radium. About one in every million of the ejected particles penetrated a nitrogen nucleus and transmuted it into the nucleus of an oxygen atom. But although the energy released by this transformation was greater than that of the bullet-particle, most particles missed the target and passed between the clouds of electrons encircling the nucleus. Much the same happened in Cambridge when Cockcroft and Walton used streams of hydrogen protons, artificially speeded up by the use of high voltages, to bombard targets of lithium. The "bullets" were not natural but artificially produced, and the "hits" were far more numerous than those which Rutherford had obtained; but the result still remained a net loss of energy. It was still true that more had to be put into the nuclear stockpot than could be obtained from it. Einstein's comment on the problem still held — "something like shooting birds in the dark in a country where there are only a few birds".

In public, Rutherford held much the same view, dismissing the use of nuclear energy as "moonshine" almost until his death in 1937. In private, he had doubts, warning Lord Hankey, then secretary of Britain's Committee of Imperial Defence, that the work of the Cavendish on nuclear transformations might one day have an important impact on defence and that someone should "keep an eye on the matter".*

Rutherford's scepticism had something in common with Einstein's views on indeterminacy, and his reluctance to admit that God might "play dice with the world". Both men, investigating nature as they found it, had pushed science along particular paths; with the years, both became increasingly reluctant to follow that path to the end.

Yet by the later 1930s, events were slowly moving towards the situation in which men like Einstein were to be faced with an agonising choice. Only a few days before Cockcroft and Walton's experiments in Cambridge, the first performance of *Wings Over Europe* had taken place in London. Writing of the play — which asks but does not answer the questions posed by nuclear weapons — Desmond McCarthy set the scene for the main involvement of Einstein's later years. "The destiny of man", he said, "has slipped (we are all aware of it) from the hands of politicians into the hands of scientists, who know not what they do, but pass responsibility for results on to those whose sense of proportion and knowledge are inadequate to the situations created by science."

Not yet, maybe. But the following year of 1933, which was to mark a crisis in human affairs with the coming of Hitler, and in Einstein's with his final departure from Europe, was also to see a new turn given to physics by Leo Szilard. In England he noted a newspaper account of Rutherford's "moonshine" description of

* It is generally believed that Rutherford publicly maintained his "moonshine" attitude to the use of atomic energy to the end of his life. This is not entirely true. Giving the Watt Anniversary Lecture in Greenock in January, 1936, he noted that "the recent discovery of the neutron, the proof of its extraordinary effectiveness in producing transformations at very low velocities, opens up new possibilities if only a method could be found of producing slow neutrons in quantity with little expenditure of energy." He went on to point out that "at the moment" natural radioactive bodies were the only known sources of getting useful energy from atoms and that this was too small a scale to be of more than scientific interest. But he was obviously already thinking about the "new possibilities".

the prospects of liberating atomic energy. A few days later, he says, "It suddenly occurred to me that if we could find an element which is split by neutrons and which would emit *two* neutrons when it absorbed *one* neutron, such an element, if assembled in sufficiently large mass, could sustain a nuclear chain reaction."

Szilard's flash of inspiration was to have its consequences. One was the filing in the spring of 1934 of a patent which described the laws governing such a chain reaction. "I assigned this patent to the British Admiralty because in England a patent could at that time be kept secret only if it was assigned to the Government," he has said. "The reason for secrecy was my conviction that if a nuclear reaction can be made to work it can be used to set up violent explosions." With this in mind he had previously approached the British War Office. But the War Office was not interested. Neither, for that matter, was the Admiralty. More important than the patent itself was the conviction behind it, a conviction which was to produce its own chain reaction six years later.

As important as Szilard among the figures now gathering in the wings was Enrico Fermi, a refugee from Fascist Italy. While Szilard had postulated the splitting of the nucleus but had failed to find experimental facilities in Britain for seeing if this could be done, Fermi had gone through a similar experience. In Italy he had used the chargeless neutrons discovered by Chadwick to bombard the heaviest known element, the metal uranium. The result had been a transformation of the uranium; but it was a transformation which took place in only a minute percentage of the atoms involved, and its true nature was missed by Fermi. What had happened, he believed, was the creation of a few atoms not found naturally on earth, the first of what came to be known as the trans-uranic elements.

Among those physicists not so sure about this was Lise Meitner, the young Austrian who had listened in rapt attention to Einstein in Salzburg almost three decades earlier, and Otto Hahn and Fritz Strassman, the two German chemists with whom she worked in the Kaiser Wilhelm Institute. All three began to repeat the Fermi experiments, which had also been carried out by Irene and Frédéric Joliot-Curie in Paris with what appeared to be comparable results. Grotesquely, the operation was disturbed by the German invasion of Austria; for the Anschluss automatically brought Fräulein Meitner German citizenship. Since she was a Jewess it also brought the threat of the concentration camp. She moved on, first to Holland and then to Sweden.

Meanwhile the work continued in Berlin under Hahn and Strassman. It finished a few days before Christmas, 1938, and Hahn immediately sent to Lise Meitner a copy of his paper describing the findings. By the first of a long series of coincidences which mark the release of nuclear energy, Lise Meitner's nephew, Otto Frisch, a worker in Niels Bohr's Copenhagen Institute, was spending the Christmas with her in Sweden.

Aunt and nephew discussed Hahn's paper during a long walk in the snow-covered woods outside Stockholm, a walk that was to help shape the future of the human race.

For Lise Meitner and her nephew discerned what Hahn had done: split the nucleus of the uranium atom into two roughly equal parts, with the release of a staggering amount of energy. "The picture," Frisch says, "was that of two fairly large nuclei flying apart with an energy of nearly two hundred million electron volts, more than ten times the energy involved in any other nuclear reaction." Bohr, about to leave Europe for the Fifth Washington Conference on Theoretical Physics, was immediately telephoned the news, which he took across the Atlantic. Within a few hours of his statement at the conference, Hahn's experiments were being repeated, notably by Szilard and by Fermi who had both arrived in the United States by this time.

But an important uncertainty remained. The fission of a uranium nucleus in a microscopic specimen certainly released an immense amount of energy. But for the process to be developed into a weapon such fissions would have to be repeated through a block of the metal. They had been produced in the Kaiser Wilhelm Institute by neutrons, and the crucial question was whether the fission process released other neutrons which would, in their turn, produce further fissions. Would the flicker of nuclear fire act as a detonator or would it merely peter harmlessly out?

Only a few weeks after Bohr had spoken to the packed and excited meeting in Washington this question was answered in Paris by a Collège de France team led by Joliot-Curie. For in Paris it was confirmed that the fission of the uranium nucleus with the resulting immense release of energy did unloose neutrons hitherto locked inside the nucleus. The number was not yet certain; but it appeared obvious that in the right conditions it would be sufficient to cause yet further fissions. These, in turn, would create still more, feeding the nuclear fire until in a minute fraction of a second the release of energy would be indescribably more damaging than that of a chemical explosion.

Thus it seemed, in the early spring of 1939, as though the world might at last be at the start of a nuclear arms race. In the United States George B. Pegram, Dean of Graduate Faculties at Columbia University, urged on by Szilard and Fermi, wrote to Admiral Hooper of the U. S. Navy, warning him of "the possibility that uranium might be used as an explosive that would liberate a million times as much energy per pound as any known explosive". In France, the members of the Collège de France team filed five patents covering the use of nuclear energy, number three being for the construction of a uranium bomb. In Holland the physicist Uhlenbeck informed his government of the situation and the Minister of Finance ordered fifty tons of uranium ore from Belgium's Union Minière, remarking: "Clever, these physicists." And in Britain, where in April research into the possibility of a nuclear weapon was officially brought under the charge of Sir Henry Tizard, both the Treasury and the Foreign Office were approached by the Committee of Imperial Defence with one object in mind: to secure the necessary uranium for research and to ensure that, as far as was possible, stocks were kept from the Germans. In 1939 the greatest known supply lay in the Belgian Congo where it was mined as ore by the Union Minière, and on May 10th, 1939, Tizard met the company's president, M. Edgar Sengier, from whom he obtained certain assurances.

In Germany Dr. Siegfried Flugge, one of Hahn's co-workers, produced a paper for *Naturwissenschaften* in which the building of a "uranium device" was considered. "Available quantitative calculations have too great a margin of error to allow us to raise this possibility into a certainty," he concluded. "Be this as it may, it is nevertheless a remarkable advance that such possibilities can be considered at all, an advance sufficient to justify thorough discussion in this paper, even if our hopes should not be fulfilled." And on April 24th Paul Harteck in Hamburg wrote with his colleague, W. Groth, to the German War Office, proposing that nuclear explosives should be investigated. Shortly afterwards, two separate groups, neither of whom acknowledged the existence of the other, began work in Germany on "the uranium problem". One was headed by Professor Erich Schumann, director of the research section of the German army's Ordnance Department, the other by Professor Abraham Esau, the official in charge of physics in the German Ministry of Education.

All this — the French patent, British earmarking of uranium stocks and German preparations — took place months before Einstein signed the famous letter to Roosevelt. Vannevar Bush, Director of the U. S. Office of Scientific Research and Development, and later the key man in America's wartime defence science, has summed up the situation neatly: "The show was going before that letter was even written." Nevertheless, Einstein's intervention was to be significant for reasons that have nothing to do with the chauvinism of priorities.

The role which Einstein was to play was singularly dramatic. For fate now compounded the joke it had perpetrated in 1919. Then the introverted scientist, only too anxious to keep to his study, had been propelled into the centre of public affairs. Now Einstein, until recently the dedicated pacifist and still a man who detested the use of force, was to help launch the weapons which killed more than 120,000 men, women and children in a few seconds. However, this is only part of the story. The truth, more complicated and more ironic, has been obscured for a quarter of a century by romantic misconceptions, failure to examine the documents and a good deal of special pleading and dodgery.

New material, including the extensive Szilard archives in San Diego, and fresh papers unearthed in Washington and elsewhere, shows that Einstein's initial letter to Roosevelt was written when he believed the prospect of nuclear weapons to be slight — but when the first moves towards them had already been taken elsewhere. It shows that Charles Lindbergh was the first choice of intermediary with the President. It shows that Einstein signed not one letter but three, of which the third, which helped to spark off the creation of the Manhattan Project, was arguably the most important. It shows that he produced a theoretical study for gaseous diffusion, later an important process in the Manhattan Project — although it is not certain that he fully realised what the study was for — and that he would have been more deeply involved had Washington suspicions of his history not made this "utterly impossible". Moreover it shows that by December 1944 he was almost certainly aware in general tems of the progress that had been made in the Manhattan Project and that he was stopped only by Niels Bohr from what might have been a disastrous political step. As final irony, a second memorandum which he tried to bring to Roosevelt's notice in March 1945 included not only the suggestion that a bomb should not be dropped on Japan, but also the idea that the United Sates might build up an "overwhelming superiority" vis-à-vis the Russians. All these were milestones on a road opened in July 1939 by Leo Szilard who comprehensively stagemanaged Einstein, not only in 1939 but in 1945.

Following Bohr's initial description of fission in January, Szilard had been almost continuously at work in Columbia and had become even more convinced that a nuclear chain reaction was possible. Like Tizard in Britain, he appreciated the danger of Germany acquiring stocks of uranium, and like Tizard he knew that the Union Minière controlled virtually the world stocks of uranium ore. At this point he discussed the situation with Eugene Wigner of Princeton University, also a physicist of note, also a refugee from Hungary.

> Both Wigner and I began to worry about what would happen if the Germans got hold of some of the vast quantities of the uranium which the Belgians had in the Congo, [Szilard has written.] So we began to think, through what channels we could approach the Belgian government and warn them against selling any uranium to Germany.
>
> It occurred to me that Einstein knew the Queen of the Belgians, [by now the Queen Mother] and I suggested to Wigner that we visit Einstein, tell him about the situation, and ask him whether he might not write to the Queen. We knew that Einstein was somewhere on Long Island but we didn't know precisely where, so I phoned his Princeton office and I was told he was staying at Dr. Moore's cabin at Peconic, Long Island. Wigner had a car and we drove out to Peconic and tried to find Dr. Moore's cabin. We drove around for about half an hour. We asked a number of people, but no one knew where Dr. Moore's cabin was. We were on the point of giving up and about to return to New York when I saw a boy of about seven or eight years of age standing at the curb. I leaned out of the window and I asked, "Say, do you by any chance know where Professor Einstein lives?" The boy knew and he offered to take us there, though he had never heard of Dr. Moore's cabin.

It is typical that Szilard, the skilled operator-by-unconventional-means, should feel that a quiet private note from Einstein to Queen Elizabeth might help prevent Germany from acquiring raw materials for the most violent explosive in the world.

Once in Dr. Moore's house, the two visitors explained their fears and their hopes, and Szilard described what Einstein later called "a specific system he (had) devised and which he thought would make it possible to set up a chain reaction". According to a letter written by Szilard to Carl Seelig in 1952 Einstein said that he "had not been aware of the possibility of a chain reaction in uranium". A few years later Einstein's statement was given by Szilard as "That never occurred to me" (*Daran habe ich gar nicht gedacht*).

Eugene Wigner, the only member of the trio still alive, does not in fact recollect Einstein's remark, although he does have a feeling that he had discussed chain reactions with Einstein some weeks earlier. These had been a major subject of debate among physicists since Bohr's dramatic announcement at the end of January. Bohr himself had spoken with Einstein in Princeton and it might seem unlikely that chain reactions were not talked about. In addition many articles, comments, and papers on the subject had by July 1939 appeared in scientific journals, more than twenty in *Nature* alone. Furthermore, Einstein's old friend Rudolf Ladenburg, who had invited him to the Salzburg meeting just thirty years previously, was himself carrying out work on fission problems in Princeton University's Palmer Laboratory only a few hundred yards from Einstein's home.

Bearing all this in mind, Einstein's remark seems at first glance to have been an extraordinary one. Is it really possible that in the summer of 1939 he should never have considered the possibility of a chain reaction, even though the subject had been the nub of controversy in the physicists' world? The answer is that it is not only possible but likely. To think otherwise is to misjudge the extent to which Einstein had by this time isolated himself from the main stream of physics. The weekly copies of *Nature* and of *Science* arrived regularly at 112 Mercer Street but they were usually filed away without Einstein glancing at them unless they contained some paper he had been specially recommended to read. He no longer joined in the seminars and discussions that his colleagues held. In some ways he was comparable to the Berne Patent Office clerk of 1905 whose strength lay partly in his isolation from the detail of current developments. His continuing preoccupation with the unified field theory made him once again the man whose life demanded, above all, "time for quiet thoughts and reflection". Professor Aage Bohr, Niels Bohr's son and today head of his father's Institute in Copenhagen, says that Einstein "was deeply involved in his own work and I hardly think that he was following the current developments in nuclear physics". Furthermore, Professor Rosenfeld, working with Bohr in Princeton in the spring of 1939, believes that "during that visit Bohr and Einstein hardly discussed the matter of possible military implications of the nuclear developments".

Even had they done so, Einstein might still have been extremely sceptical about the practicability of nuclear weapons. For as early as February 15th, Bohr had put forward in the *Physical Review* the sobering proposal that only the U-235 nuclei could

easily be split; and that the nuclei of the U-238, — which compris-
ed the overwhelming bulk of the element — would usually absorb
any neutrons which hit them. Experimental proof of this theory
was not to be given for another year. It was, Frisch has said, "a
surprising conclusion based on rather subtle arguments". Not all
scientists agreed with it, and even those who did so included many
who still believed that it would be possible to make a nuclear
explosion by using a block of the element which contained the
different isotopes in their naturally-occurring proportions. But if
Bohr were right it would be necessary to separate a substantial
quantity of U-235 before a "nuclear fire" could be produced. This
problem of isotope-separation — comparable to sorting a vast number of particular sand grains from their identical companions on
the seashore — looked totally insoluble in 1939. Indeed, it looked
totally insoluble four years later, even to Bohr. When, in the spring
of 1943, he was invited to England from German-occupied Denmark by James Chadwick, Bohr sent back a secret message through
Intelligence channels: "I have, to the best of my judgment, convinced myself that in spite of all future prospects any immediate
use of the latest marvellous discoveries of atomic physics is impracticable." He thought at the time, says his son, "that isotope
separation on the needed scale was beyond industrial potentialities
and it was a surprise for him on his arrival in England in October
1943 to learn how far the project had advanced".

The exact depth of Einstein's scepticism as he sat in his Long
Island cottage with Szilard and Wigner on that summer afternoon is
unknown. Yet he himself has gone on the record with one revealing statement about nuclear energy: "I did not, in fact, foresee that
it would be released in my time. I only believed that it was theoretically possible." Scientific scepticism, however great or little it
was, may well have been boosted by wishful thinking. Einstein's old
friend Lindemann was so repelled by the idea of such destructive
power being available to human hands that "he could scarcely
believe that the universe was constructed in this way". Sir Henry
Tizard, who had launched precautionary measures in England, had
asked the same question to a colleague in surprisingly similar terms:
"Do you really think that the universe was made in this way?"

There is no evidence to suggest that Einstein was any less sceptical about the chance of nuclear weapons in the summer of 1939
than Bohr was to be four years later; but if he could not genuinely
share his visitors' scientific views, he could share their fears.

There was always the one-in-a-million chance that a bomb

would prove feasible. Since nuclear fission had been discovered in the Kaiser Wilhelm Institute, it was wise to take precautions. If there were even a bare chance that nuclear weapons were possible, then the Americans should not lag behind the Germans.

Here Einstein parted company with his old friend Max Born who worked in Edinburgh throughout the war and took no part in the Allied nuclear effort since, as he has said, "my colleagues knew that I was opposed to taking part in war work of this character which seemed so horrible." Had his attitude convinced his colleagues, post-war history might have been different. For one day a young German working in his laboratory was asked to join the British nuclear team. "He was inclined to accept," Born has said. "I told him of my attitude to such kind of work, and tried to warn him not to involve himself in these things. But he was filled with tremendous hatred of the Nazis, and accepted." Thus Klaus Fuchs, who was to provide Russia, — and possibly Britain, — with details of the H-bomb left Edinburgh for Birmingham and Los Alamos.

In retrospect, too late, Einstein agreed with Born. "I made one great mistake in my life — when I signed the letter to President Roosevelt recommending that atom bombs be made," he said in old age to Linus Pauling, "but there was some justification — the danger that the Germans would make them." The mistake was in fact a double one. The danger from the Germans never materialised; but in America an almost superhuman technological effort gave the lie to Bohr's "impracticable".

At this first meeting with Szilard and Wigner in July 1939, Einstein agreed that Belgian stocks of uranium should not be allowed to fall into German hands. But the situation was delicate even for native-born Americans, let alone for two Hungarians and a German-born Swiss who had relinquished his first nationality but had not yet become American. Szilard therefore proposed a transitional step. "Before contacting the Belgian Government," he said, "it seemed desirable to advise the State Department of the step we proposed to take. Wigner suggested that we draft a letter to the Belgian government, send a copy to the State Department, and give the State Department two weeks in which to object if they are opposed to Professor Einstein's sending such a letter." Thus, as a first step, the Queen Mother was bypassed. Instead, Einstein dictated, a letter to a Belgian Cabinet Minister, mentioning "the danger to the Belgian State" that seemed to be apparent, and it was agreed that a copy should be sent to the Belgian ambassador in Washington.

On his return to Columbia University, Szilard typed out a draft and put it in the post to Einstein, together with the letter which he felt should be sent to the State Department.

Here the process might have stuck. But now history nudged the project back on course: ironically using for its *deus ex machina* Dr. Gustav Stolper, not only a German refugee but a former member of the Reichstag.

> Somehow, [says Szilard, referring to what had been arranged before he left Einstein's house] this procedure seemed to be an awkward one and so I decided to consult friends with more experience in things practical than we were. I went to see in New York Dr. Gustav Stolper and told him of our need to establish contact in this matter with the U.S. government. He recommended that I talk with Dr. Alexander Sachs. Dr. Sachs seemed very much interested and said that he would be willing to take a letter in person to President Roosevelt if Professor Einstein were willing to write such a letter.

It is probable that Alexander Sachs, a well-known economist and an intimate of the President, did not at the time know much of Einstein's earlier history, since he has gone on record as saying that he has "always been of the view that the real warmongering, combined with defeatism, is done by the pacifists". However, Sachs was helpful. Szilard recognised a useful contact and on July 19th wrote again to Einstein saying that Sachs had recommended a direct approach to Roosevelt and that he himself would be willing to help. Enclosed, Szilard added, was a draft of the letter he felt should be sent to the White House. Would Einstein make any proposed corrections over the telephone or did he think that a second meeting was necessary?

Einstein favoured a meeting, and a few days later Szilard was at Peconic once again. This time, Wigner having left for the West Coast, his companion was Edward Teller of George Washington University, another of the brilliant Hungarians who had found refuge in the United States, and one later to become famous, or notorious, as "the father of the H-bomb".

There is, understandably enough, some difference in recollection about the details of this second meeting. According to Teller, "at the time [of the visit] Szilard had a final formulation of the letter with him. We had tea with Einstein. Einstein read the letter, made very little comment and signed it." Later Szilard wrote: "As I remember, Einstein dictated a letter in German which Teller took down and I used this German text as a guide in preparing two drafts of a letter to the President, a shorter one and a longer one, and left it up to Einstein to choose which he liked best. I wondered how many words we could expect the President to read. How many words does the fission of uranium rate?"

As far as they go, Szilard's recollections appear accurate on this point. But his papers reveal more. For when he sent the short and the long versions to Einstein on August 2nd — the date he put on both — he accompanied them with a note saying that Sachs now thought Bernard Baruch or Karl Compton might be the best man to get the letter to Roosevelt, but that he personally favoured Colonel Lindbergh.

The last suggestion was unexpected, since it was felt in some quarters that Lindbergh was not particularly allergic to the Nazis. However, Einstein dutifully complied. He returned to Szilard not only his own choice of letters, but both of them signed. Szilard could make up his own mind which one to send, but Einstein's accompanying note urged him to curb his inner resistance and not "be too clever" — another indication that Einstein's views about the practicability of a bomb were different from Szilard's. At the same time he wrote, as requested, a note to Lindbergh, whom he had last met at the Rockefeller Centre.

Szilard acknowledged Einstein's letters on August 9th saying he would note the "admonition" about not being too clever. Five days later he wrote to Lindbergh, enclosing Einstein's letter of introduction and suggesting that Lindbergh might approach Roosevelt. At the same time he sent to Sachs the longer of the two letters which Einstein had signed.

This was the famous and repeatedly-quoted letter warning the President that a single bomb of the new type that might now be possible would be able to destroy a whole port together with some of the surrounding country. What was needed, Einstein stressed, was some contact between the U.S. administration and the physicists who were working on chain-reaction problems in America.

Whatever the details of how it was written, it is clear that this letter was the work of Szilard. Making "the greatest mistake" of his life, Einstein signed it on the dotted line.

Szilard now had two irons in the fire — the potential introduction to Lindbergh and the letter which reposed in Sach's office. Neither appeared to be getting hot. Lindbergh does not today recall the letter from Einstein. "If such a note was written and forwarded it may have been lost in the heavy mail that came in that year," he says. The same presumably happened to the reminder which Szilard sent him on September 13th. No record remains of what happened next, but on September 27th, Szilard wrote to Einstein saying: "Lindbergh is not our man." By this time the Germans had not only invaded Poland but had effectively conquered most of it, and Szilard. gloomily added that as Belgium would eventually be overrun the Americans should try to buy fifty tons of uranium as soon as possible.

Six days later he wrote with equal gloom that "Sachs confessed that he is still sitting on the letter," and that it was "possible that Sachs was useless".

However, this was far from so. Sachs knew the way official machinery works and was merely biding his time. "Our system is such that national public figures ... are, so to speak, punch-drunk with printer's ink," he has said. "So I thought there was no point in transmitting material which would be passed on to someone lower down." The outbreak of war, with Roosevelt's resulting involvement in the neutrality laws, caused initial delay and it was not until October 11th that Sachs saw Roosevelt and handed over the Einstein letter with a memorandum prepared by Szilard. This memorandum, rather oddly in view of all that preceded it, mentioned first the possibility that nuclear fission might be used to provide power; went on to suggest potential uses in medicine; and only then that it might be utilised in a weapon. It mentioned also that in the previous March an unsuccessful attempt had been made to hold up publication of information on fission — an attempt frustrated by the French — and that a further attempt might now be made.

At the meeting with Roosevelt, Sachs, according to the official American history of events, "read aloud his covering letter, which emphasised the same ideas as the Einstein communication but was more pointed on the need for funds. As the interview drew to a close, Roosevelt remarked, 'Alex, what you are after is to see that the Nazis don't blow us up.' Then he called in Pa Watson" — General Edwin M. Watson, the President's secretary — "and announced 'This requires action'." Sachs left the room with Watson and by evening the Briggs Committee had been set up, a small group of men presided over by Dr. Lyman J. Briggs, Director of the U. S. Bureau of Standards, charged with investigating the potentialities of nuclear fission.

The first meeting of the Committee was held ten days later and was attended by Szilard, Teller and Wigner. A conspicuous absentee was Einstein. The official history of the U. S. bomb project implies that he had been invited but had declined to come; but it seems clear from Szilard's paper that no invitation had been issued. At the meeting it was decided to set up an expanded group to co-ordinate the research being carried out in American universities. Einstein was formally invited to become a member of this group. He as formally declined.

However, any assumption that Einstein, having started the official machinery, was willing to let it move at its own leisurely pace, is contradicted by the events of the next few months. For Einstein, far from writing only the first letter to Roosevelt and then letting affairs take their course, did very much more.

In the New Year there was, as Sachs stated in his post-war evidence to the Senate, "pressure — by Einstein and the speaker — for a new framework and an accelerated tempo for the project... Dr. Einstein and myself were dissatisfied with the scope and the pace of the work and its progress." The pressure began after Sachs visited Einstein at Princeton in February. Here they discussed, among other things, the report in a current issue of *Science* of the latest work by Joliot-Curie's team at the Collège de France in Paris. "While we felt that it was very important that ... this exchange of ideas among free scientists should be carried on because they served as links and as stimuli to future work," says Sachs, "their accessibility through publications to Germany constituted an important problem."

However, the most important outcome of this meeting was the further nudge which it gave to the U. S. work. "Dr. Einstein said that he thought the work at Columbia was the more important," says Sachs. "He further said that conditions should be created for its extension and acceleration." There were further meetings between the two men within the next few weeks and Einstein then agreed to write another letter outlining the current situation. "I had felt", says Sachs, "that Dr. Einstein's authority was such that, combined with his insight and concern, it would affect the tempo of the work".

The letter, written to Sachs for transmission to Roosevelt, and quoted by Sachs in hearings before the U. S. Senate Special Committee on Atomic Energy, was dated March 7th, 1940 and reported increased work on nuclear research in Germany. It added that Szilard was about to publish fresh work in the "Physics Review", and it is clear that the whole purpose of the letter was to give the administration a further prod.

The letter emphasises, once again, how fear of a German atomic bomb was the main spur to the early nuclear work, American as well as British. And it also — no doubt at Szilard's instigation —

recommends by implication the censorship of scientific discovery in the nuclear field, a proposal which had been put by Szilard to the French team in the Collège de France almost exactly a year earlier and had been curtly turned down. In fact, as Sachs later said, "Dr. Szilard, Dr. Wigner and Dr. Einstein, were all of the same view, that there had to be secrecy against leaks to the enemy."

From the Szilard papers one gets the impression that Sachs' comment was a polite gloss on the situation. What Szilard and Einstein were saying was obvious: either "the uranium question" was of importance, in which case the government should take it more seriously; alternatively, it was of little importance, in which case Szilard would publish information that could be of considerable consequence to the future. It is inconceivable that Szilard, who knew what he was doing, would implement such a threat; nevertheless, arm-twisting sometimes works. It worked in this case.

Even so, the first reaction to the Einstein letter of March 7th was tepid. The Briggs Committee recommended that until a report of the work going on at Columbia University had been received, "the matter should rest in abeyance". Sachs disagreed, and finally persuaded Roosevelt to call another meeting between Briggs and army and navy representatives at which the question of enlarging the project should be thrashed out. Roosevelt, writing to Sachs on April 5th and noting that Watson would fix "a time convenient to you and Dr. Einstein", took it for granted that Einstein was part of the organisation. Watson himself, who noted that "perhaps Dr. Einstein would have some suggestions to offer as to the attendance of the other professors", apparently thought so as well.

Sachs again visited Einstein at Princeton. "It became clear", he subsequently told the Senate, "that indisposition on account of a cold, and the great shyness and humility of that really saintly scientist would make Dr. Einstein recoil from participating in large groups and would prevent his attendance. So he delegated me to report for him, too."

Precisely. As usual, Szilard had the situation well in hand. "In case you wish to decline," he had written to Einstein on April 19th, "we shall prepare a polite letter of regret in English which you can use if you think it advisable." Here, as at more than one other point during the prologue to the Manhattan Project, Szilard emerges as a combination of stage-manager and producer, organising into their correct places not only Sachs, Briggs and Watson, but also Albert Einstein.

In the letter, the third that Einstein had signed in his efforts to get the U.S. nuclear effort under way, Einstein proposed the setting-up of a board of trustees for a non-profit organisation which would be able to secure the necessary funds. It was to be implemented less than two months later. For then the drastically reorganised Briggs Committee was brought under the wing of the National Defence Research Committee which Roosevelt created, and a special committee of the National Academy of Sciences set up to inform the government of any developments in nuclear fission that might affect defence.

Two points should be made. The first is that Einstein's demand — for "large-scale experiments and exploration of practical applications" — does not mean that he necessarily thought the bomb was now a likely proposition. What he was after was the facts. If a self-sustaining chain reaction proved impossible then, as he had said when publishing his own negative results on the unified field theory, "at least it will prevent other people from making the same mistakes".

The second point is that this letter, foreshadowing the setting up of the Manhattan Project in 1942 — the "non-profit organisation which ... could secure ... the necessary funds for carrying out the work" — was perhaps even more important than the initial letter to Roosevelt. And like the rest of the pressure that Einstein had exercised since the summer of 1939 it contrasts strongly with his later claim: that his participation in the production of the atomic bomb consists only of his letter to President Roosevelt.

The initial approach to Roosevelt produced the Briggs Committee which in turn produced the new organisation under the National Defence Research Committee; this led to the Manhattan Project and the bombs on Japan. With this in mind, what is the meaning of the statement by Oppenheimer, scientific head of the project, that Einstein's letter "had very little effect"; of the evaluation of Arthur Compton, a key worker in the field, that the result of the government committee set up following Einstein's letter "was to retard rather than to advance the development of American uranium research"?

The explanation lies partly in the momentum which research into nuclear fission had already gained throughout the world, partly in the results of research carried out in Britain by workers who convincingly showed that a nuclear weapon was possible even if their own country was unable to make it. By the summer of 1940, when the Briggs Committee was transformed, Halban and Kowarski, two important members of the French team which a year prev-

iously had shown a chain reaction to be possible, reached England
and were contemplating going to America. In the United States
itself Szilard and Fermi were only two of the workers at the head
of research teams which owed comparatively little to official help.
In Germany research was known to be going ahead. In Britain,
where Frisch and Peierls had made the astounding discovery that
the separated uranium required for a bomb was measured in pounds
rather than tons, numbers of physicists were at work on detailed
studies of the time, money, labour and raw materials required to
make a specific nuclear weapon. All this would have carried the
world into the nuclear age whether or not Einstein had signed a
letter to Roosevelt.

There was also the specific impact of the Maud Report, the
account of Britain's plans for building a bomb which was completed in the summer of 1941. On October 3rd, copies were handed
to Dr. Vannevar Bush. On the 9th, according to James Baxter,
official historian of the Office of Scientific Research and Development, Bush "had a long conversation with the President and the
Vice-President in which he reported the British view that a bomb
could be constructed from U-235 produced by a diffusion plant".
And two days later Roosevelt wrote to Churchill proposing that
the British and the U.S. should work together. It would appear
chauvinistic for a British writer to assess the significance of these
dates. But two Americans may be allowed to speak: "Though the
Americans were aware of this weapon as a possibility," Arthur
Compton has written, "it was more than a year later that it became
for us the focus of attention. In 1940 it was still difficult for us in
America to concentrate our thoughts on war, while for the British
it was their prime concern." And the official historians of the American effort, writing in *The New World* have this to say of the
Maud Report: "[It] gave Bush and Dr. James Conant what they
had been looking for: a promise that there was a reasonable chance
for something militarily useful during the war in progress. The
British did more than promise; they outlined a concrete programme. None of the recommendations Briggs had made and neither
of the two National Academy reports had done as much."

All this fills out Bush's bare statement that "the show had
been going long before Einstein's letter." But it does not relegate
the letter to a place of no importance. Donald Fleming, writing in
*An American Primer* of the British scientists who sat on the Maud
Committee, and of the visit to England of Pegram and Urey in
the autumn of 1941, puts the situation in perspective. "Their opti-

mistic report of July, 1941, and the detailed case they made to
American scientists who visited England in the fall, played a major,
perhaps critical, part in the American decision to make a big push
on the eve of Pearl Harbour rather than later. It does not follow
that Einstein's letter of August, 1939, served no purpose. The
decision of December 6th, 1941 would have been comparatively
empty if the Americans had no base to build upon." In other words,
America would have built the bomb without Einstein. But they
might not have had it ready for the war against Japan. Instead, the
bomb would have been ready for Korea; by which time, without
much doubt, the Russians would have had one too.

Einstein's letter of April 1940, setting the U. S. administration
along the road towards the Manhattan Project, ended the first
phase of his wartime involvement with nuclear weapons. The
second, which came a year and a half later, is one of extraordinary
irony. For it shows Einstein anxious to help the war effort
— but kept from it as a security risk by men unaware that Einstein
himself had set the whole U. S. machine moving two years earlier.

On December 6th, 1941, a few hours before the Japanese
attack on Pearl Harbour, the Office of Scientific Research and
Development began a greatly expanded programme of research into
nuclear weapons. A key technological problem was the separation
of U-235 from its chemically-identical isotopes. One likely method
was gaseous diffusion in which uranium in gaseous form is passed
through an immense number of barriers pierced with extremely
small holes. The U-235, with three fewer neutrons than the almost
ubiquitous U-238, passes through more quickly and the lighter
isotope can eventually be concentrated. Many purely theoretical
problems are associated with the barriers. They had to be solved
without delay and early in December Bush turned to Einstein for
help.

The request was made through Dr. Frank Aydelotte, by this
time in Dr. Flexner's shoes as Director of the Institute for Advanced Study. Einstein worked at the problem which Bush gave
him and on December 19th, 1941, Aydelotte sent the handwritten
solution to Bush at the Office of Scientific Research and Development in Washington.

> As I told you over the telephone, [he said in his covering letter]
> Einstein was very much interested in your problem, has worked at it
> for a couple of days and produced the solution, which I enclose
> herewith. Einstein asks me to say that if there are other angles of the
> problem that you want him to develop or if you wish any parts of

this amplified, you need only let him know and he will be glad to do anything in his power. I very much hope that you will make use of him in any way that occurs to you, because I know how deep is his satisfaction at doing anything which might be useful in the national effort.

I hope you can read his handwriting. Neither he nor I felt free, in view of the necessary secrecy, to give the manuscript to anyone to copy. In this, as in all other respects, we shall be glad to do anything that will facilitate your work.

Bush passed on Einstein's calculations to Dr. Harold Urey, head of the American gaseous-diffusion project, and Urey in due course discussed them with Bush. One thing quickly became clear: if Einstein's work was to be really useful, the problem would have to be presented to him in much more detail. But this was impossible. And it was impossible for reasons which Bush gave Aydelotte in a letter on December 30th:

I am not going to tell him any more than I have told him already, for a number of reasons. If my statement of the problem is not sufficient to make it clear, I will of course be very glad to make the statement as precise as possible, but I really believe that my statement placed the problem in its exact form. The reason that I am not going farther is that I am not at all sure that if I place Einstein in entire contact with his subject he would not discuss it in a way that it should not be discussed, and with this doubt in my mind I do not feel that I ought to take him into confidence on the subject to the extent of showing just where this thing fits into the defence picture, and what the military aspects of the matter might be. If I were to explain more than I already have, I feel sure that the rest of the story would immediately follow. I wish very much that I could place the whole thing before him and take him fully into confidence, but this is utterly impossible in view of the attitude of people here in Washington who have studied into his whole history.

So Einstein, who had put his name to a letter warning that a single nuclear weapon might destroy a whole port, was to be kept from knowing "where this thing fits into the defence picture"! The extraordinary contradiction is in fact simply explained. For as Bush has written of Einstein's letter, "in my many discussions with President Roosevelt on the subject he did not mention it".

Trying to get an answer from Einstein without telling him too much, unaware of his earlier involvement, Bush asked for help on a subject that was academic — even though it was clearly so secret that Einstein thought it unwise to have the answer copied. Thus it is not absolutely certain that when he produced the solution, and showed his "deep . . . satisfaction at doing anything which might be useful in the national effort", Einstein knew that he was working towards a nuclear weapon. But it is a strong assumption. He would, after all, have been "glad to do anything in his power" now that the United States was at last at war with Germany.

The exclusion of Einstein from the inner counsels of the scientists who drove the Manhattan Project to its conclusion was to have one important result in 1945. For it effectively prevented him from using his enormous prestige when the future of the bomb was being discussed. By that time he was the outsider, unable even to declare openly that he knew of the bomb's existence without betraying what his friends and acquaintances had let him know, consciously or unconsciously. Thus the prophet of $E = mc^2$ did not, in theory, know of the bomb's existence until it was dropped in anger. Sometimes this has been too much for history to bear. One account mentions "Dr. Einstein" at Los Alamos — which Einstein never visited — without spoiling the story by adding that the name was a local soubriquet for someone else. And one biography has not only a drawn frontispiece showing Einstein "at the first test of the atomic bomb" but soberly has him speaking a farrago of nonsense there. In fact, Einstein remained officially — although not unofficially — unaware of America's nuclear effort until, on August 6th, 1945, he heard at Saranac Lake the radio announcement of the Hiroshima bombing.

This period of Einstein's connection with nuclear weapons runs from July 1939 until, very approximately, the American entry into the war in December 1941. Before the end of it he had taken U. S. citizenship, together with his stepdaughter Margot and Miss Dukas. Not every American was pleased. A letter in *The Tablet* complained of "Einstein the refugee Jewish Communist taking an oath of allegiance to the U. S. government", while a long article in *The Fifth Column in Our Schools* attacked Einstein's right to become a U. S. citizen at all. "If Albert Einstein is right and there is no personal God, then America is founded on fable and falsehood," this went. "If there is no God then the citizen has no God-given rights. Then all the rights set forth in the Constitution are sham and delusion. If man has no Creator, then our fathers fought for a lie; then the rights of citizenship are based on a lie. Then Professor Einstein has subscribed to a lie, in the very act of pledging allegiance to a form of government which — according to his philosophy — is founded on a lie."

The reasoning was tortuous; it was not uncommon, and fuel was added to the criticism with Einstein's support for Bertrand Russell who was first appointed to, and then sacked from, a professorship at the City College of New York. Russell's *Marriage and Morals* was used as the cudgel to belabour him in a savage attack which described the distinguished philosopher as "lecherous, libidinous, lustful, venerous, erotmaniac, aphrodisiac, irreverent, narrowminded, untruthful and bereft of moral fibre". Einstein was no longer surprised by this attitude of the Christian mob. The imbroglio brought Russell many invitations and he spent some time at Princeton where he strengthened his friendship with Einstein, with what were to be important results a decade later.

The Institute buildings were finally completed in 1940 and before the end of the year Einstein moved from his rooms in the University to the new and rather splendid quarters in their park-like setting on the outskirts of the town. Here he was allocated an imposing room with leaded windows, long curtains and even an oriental rug on the floor.

In Princeton, where familiarity had bred acceptance, his presence was taken for granted. Everywhere else in the United States Einstein was still a name which made news, and in 1944 there was a flurry of excitement when there appeared a biography written by his former stepson-in-law, Dmitri Marianoff, with the aid of another professional writer. Marianoff had separated from Margot in the summer of 1935, soon after arriving in America. Now he was cashing in on the Berlin days. "He is said to have lived with the Einstein family for eight years," Einstein said in a public denunciation of the book. "He never lived at my house for even a year, only for a few months at a time." The book was popularly written and harmless enough. But it was, Einstein stated, "generally unreliable" and the bits which he had read were "not true at all".

He was naturally enough sensitive about his name. After all, it was often his name which did the trick; as, for instance, in prising a message from Roosevelt for the American Fund for Palestinian Institutions when it held a dinner in his honour at the Waldorf-Astoria in the summer of 1944. Roosevelt declined a first request to send a message stressing the important work of the beneficiary institutions in contemporary life and in the war effort of Palestine". But a second appeal produced a Roosevelt message extending "hearty greetings to all who gather at the dinner in honour of Professor Albert Einstein". This, in the words of a memorandum from the White House, was "a compromise — a little compliment to Professor Einstein — silence about the fund-raising".

He was, inevitably, the much-sought-after distinguished guest for all manner of scientific gatherings, and he was drawn from the oasis of Princeton to attend the Carnegie Hall meeting celebrating the 400th anniversary of Copernicus' death. Since Copernicus was a revolutionary, a number of modern revolutionaries were invited. They included Einstein, T. H. Morgan the geneticist, Igor Sikorsky the helicopter designer and Henry Ford. Einstein was one of the two who made brief speeches.

> It was in broken English, and Einstein's English had been pretty badly broken, [says Harlow Shapley, who helped to organise the occasion.] He pointed out that it was not inappropriate for him to appear "because Copernicus was the great leader of scientists and he was our teacher" — or some such connection. It was a modest talk in pidgin English and the audience just roared. Carnegie Hall rattled with applause. In the front row were some of my friends from the Century Club. I had sent them tickets so they could come, and they did and applauded wildly. They are of course good Republicans and careful clubmen; that they would applaud this relativity man and his doings was a little surprising. That night I asked some of them about it and was told: "Well, I think the reason we applauded was that we'd always insisted that we couldn't understand one damn word of this relativity nonsense. And here we hear Relativity himself talking about it and still we couldn't understand it."

The members of the Century Club may have shown little logic. They accurately reflected lay opinion in mid-war — Einstein was still "Relativity himself". He was also the most famous living Jew, and it is a revelation of his attitude to non-scientific affairs that during the early years of the war his letters to relatives in German-occupied Belgium exposed them to considerable risk. They exist today, full of local gossip and still in the envelopes that had been twice slit open for the contents to be approved first by the American and then by the German censors. To conceal who they came from, the sender was given as Marianoff, Margot's married name; but the address was "112 Mercer Street, Princeton", a straight pointer to the Koch family's kinship with Hitler's *bête Juive*.

During these wartime years, Einstein was to many scientists the ultimate court of appeal and this fact drew him, the most amiable of men, into some cantankerous disputes. One was with the supporters of Felix Ehrenhaft who had been turned out of Vienna after the Nazis came to power and forced to abandon the great electro-magnet whose construction had been the light of his work. The experience may have pushed him beyond reason. Certainly his power of rational argument decreased and his insistence that the electronic charge was not constant was maintained against all comers. Einstein thought that some of Ehrenhaft's claims were nonsense, and openly said so. This brought down on his head requests to "repair the great injustice done to Felix Ehrenhaft by your attitude towards him and through the unfounded and defaming report about his discoveries which you spread not only among his colleagues but also in financial circles, among bankers who wanted to help him carry on with his research". Einstein had little time for such complaints. As far as he could, he ignored them.

He also tried to ignore his involvement with Wilhelm Reich. This eccentric distraught figure seems already to have slipped down the slope towards charlatanry or madness by the time he asked Einstein to investigate his discovery of "a specific biologically effective energy which behaves in many respects differently to all that is known about electromagnetic energy". Reich first wrote to Einstein on December 30th, 1940 informing him that he had been Freud's assistant at the Polyclinic in Vienna from 1922 until 1930, and was now teaching "experimental and clinical bio-psychology" in New York. Anyone other than Einstein would have been warned by the letter, which carried on with the admission that he had not reported his discovery to the Academy of Physics because of "extremely bad experience". But Reich added that it might possibly "be used in the fight against the Fascist pestilence". Einstein, who had encouraged the country forward in what still seemed to be the one in a million chance of using nuclear fission for this very purpose, was the last man to resist such a bait.

Reich called on Einstein in his Mercer Street home on January 13th, 1941. "He told me", his wife wrote later, "that the conversation with Einstein had been extremely friendly and cordial, that Einstein was easy to talk to, that their conversation had lasted almost five hours. Einstein was willing to investigate the phenomena that Reich had described to him, and a special little accumulator would have to be built and taken to him." Certainly there was a further visit, and certainly Einstein tested the apparatus. But his query: "What else do you do?" when told by Reich that he was not a physicist but a psychiatrist, probably contained an unnoticed hint of scepticism.

Einstein found a commonplace explanation of the phenomena which Reich had noted, and said so in polite terms. The postscript — contained in "The Einstein Affair", a privately-printed booklet from Reich's own press — was spread across the following three years of their correspondence. Reich disputed Einstein's findings and Einstein was dismayed that his name might be wrongly used to support Reich's theory. Reich took the easy way out and blamed the Communists.

Anything that would aid the "fight against the Fascist pestilence" drew his immediate support. In 1943 he was asked by the Book and Author Committee of the Fourth War Loan drive to donate his original paper of 1905 for sale. Like many others, it had been destroyed when he received printed copies. However, he agreed to write it out once more in longhand, adding above it: "The following pages are a copy of my first paper concerning the theory of relativity. I made this copy in November 1943. The original manuscript not [sic] longer exists having been discarded by me after its publication. The publication bears the title 'Elektrodynamic bewegter Körper' (Annalen der Physik; vierte Folge, Vol. 17, 1905). A. Einstein 21. XI. 1943." Miss Dukas dictated it to him from his published paper. "I could have said this more simply," he said more than once.

He also handed over an unpublished manuscript on "The Bi-Vector Field" and the two manuscripts were auctioned in Kansas City on February 4th, 1944, the Kansas City Insurance Company investing six and a half million dollars in War Bonds for the relativity paper — and subsequently presenting it to the Library of Congress — while W. T. Kemper, Jr., a custodian of insurance funds, invested five million dollars of impounded funds to obtain the second paper.

By this time Einstein had again become directly involved in defence work and by August 1943 had links with the Navy and Office of Scientific Research and Development in Washington. Vannevar Bush, the organisation's director, writes: "Some friends of Einstein visited me and told me that he was disturbed because he was not active in the war effort. I accordingly appointed him a member of a committee where it seemed to me his particular skills would be most likely to be of service." What the committee was has never been discovered, but from internal evidence it is unlikely to have been concerned with nuclear research.

No such question mark hangs over Einstein's engagement with

the U. S. Navy's Bureau of Ordnance. An announcement from Washington on June 24th, 1943, stated that "his naval assignment will be on a part-time contractual basis and he will continue his association with the Institute for Advanced Study, Princeton, N. J., where most of his studies on behalf of the Bureau of Ordnance will be undertaken". Records of the General Services Administration, St. Louis, Missouri, show that Einstein "was intermittently employed in Special Service Contract of the Department of the Navy, Washington, D. C., as a Scientist from May 31st, 1943, to June 30th, 1944. As a Technicist from July 1st, 1944, to June 30th, 1945, and also as a Consultant for Research on Explosives from July 1st, 1945, to June 30th, 1946." *Star Shell*, the Bureau of Ordnance publication, later stated that his work concerned "the theory of explosion, seeking to determine what laws govern the more obscure waves of detonation, why certain explosives have marked directional effect and other highly technical theories," while the St. Louis records further add that Einstein's service "was performed in the development of bombs and underwater weapons".

His duties were on a personal services basis, which according to Admiral Furer's official history, "allowed the Bureau to secure the services of persons which it would not otherwise have attracted". Among the eminent scientists thus employed were Dr. von Neumann, who furnished the theoretical foundation for the airburst principle used in the atomic bomb attack on Hiroshima; Dr. John Kirkwood, who developed theoretical methods for determining the relative effectiveness of explosives; and Dr. George Gamow, who worked on the theory of initiation and detonation of explosives.

Einstein said, on accepting the consultantship, that he would be unable to travel to Washington regularly and that someone must come to him at Princeton.

Since I happened to have known Einstein earlier, on nonmilitary grounds, I was selected to carry out this job, [writes George Gamow.] Thus on every other Friday I took a morning train to Princeton, carrying a briefcase tightly packed with confidential and secret navy projects. There was a great variety of proposals, such as exploding a series of underwater mines placed along a parabolic path that would lead to the entrance of a Japanese naval base with follow-up aerial bombs to be dropped on the flight decks of Japanese aircraft carriers. Einstein would meet me in his study at home, wearing one of his famous soft sweaters, and we would go through all the proposals, one by one. He approved practically all of them, saying, "Oh yes, very interesting, very, very ingenious"; and the next day the admiral in charge of the bureau was very happy whèn I reported to him Einstein's comments.

One other idea was that of producing a certain effect by using a convergent detonation wave formed by combining two explosives with different propagation velocities. After Einstein had approved it, plans were made for a model test at Indian Head, the navy proving grounds on the Potomac River. But then, recalls Gamow, the high-explosives factory in Pittsburgh which was to make the device shied away from it. "On the next day my project was moved from the top of the priority list to the bottom," he says, "and I suddenly realised what was being worked on at a mysterious place in New Mexico with the address: P. O. Box 1663, Santa Fé. Years later, when I was fully cleared for work on the A-bomb and went to Los Alamos, I learned that my guess had been correct." Gamow gives no indication of whether he mentioned the incident, or passed on his guess, to Einstein. It seems likely.

Only part of his time was devoted to the navy but there is no indication that he shirked it or shrank from that part. Indeed, there was no reason why he should. Events had taught him, in the words of his friend Max Born, "that the ultimate ethical values, on which all human existence is based, must, as a last resort, be defended even by force and with the sacrifice of human lives". Once that had been admitted, much followed, and any belief that Einstein deliberately tried to hold himself aloof from Service matters has only the shakiest foundation in fact. Thomas Lee Bucky, one of the sons of his radiologist friend recalls, for instance, how "during the early part of World War II when the Luftwaffe was bombing cities, Einstein and (his) father became engrossed in a discussion about a more accurate means of anti-aircraft fire. After toying with various ideas, they reached one possibility for a new method of fire that excited them." The writer later found them so full of enthusiasm for their new idea that they told him about it. Nothing came of the idea, but the fact that Einstein himself was so apparently eager to turn his mind to such matters emphasises his change of stance from only a decade earlier. The reluctant admission that force was sometimes ethically respectable had first been made in the summer of 1933. Now "his satisfaction at doing anything which might be useful in the national effort" pressed his actions yet further against the grain of his normal inclinations. Circumstances altered cases; even in pacifism there were no absolutes. The war had to be won. All this was common sense enough.

Many decent men did what they did in wartime only with reluctance, admitting ruefully that at times life offers only a choice between evils.

Yet the real tragedy of Einstein's situation can be judged not by the record of the war years, when his work for the Services was openly acknowledged, but by the postwar period when he banished the thought of what he had done as though it were a nightmare rather than the reality. For after the war he disclaimed that he had been involved with applied science, or worked with the military.

Were Einstein different from the man who emerges both from the archives and from reminiscences, the discrepancy between wha he did and what he later said he had done would be simple to explain; he would simply have been lying; had these matters not concerned the birth of the nuclear world it would be just as simple to claim that he had been merely forgetful. But neither explanation will do. The answer, so far as it is explicable in rational terms at all, is that he was human enough to push to the back of his mind the unpleasant facts he did not wish to acknowledge. Just as many years earlier he had been able to go to the aircraft builders with what he thought was a wonderful idea for making aircraft more efficient, so in the later 1940s did he become oblivious to what he had done a few years before; not 'conveniently', as might have been the case with other men but because that was the way he was built.

His reluctance in the later 1940s to think back to the war must also be seen in association with two other things. One was his natural, and later almost paranoic, distrust of the Germans, a distrust which he finally appreciated had paved the road to Hiroshima and which, when he considered the Japanese holocaust, must have filled him with mixed emotions. The other was his decision in December 1944, when he had learned of the peril of nuclear weapons, to "abstain from any action" which might "complicate the delicate task of the statesmen".

For as the war rose to its climax with the Allied invasion of Europe and the prospect of the Wehrmacht being driven back to Germany in defeat, the consequences of his action in July 1939, became even more difficult to ignore. It is generally believed that Einstein was totally ignorant of the progress made by the Manhattan Project until the announcement that the first bomb had been dropped on Hiroshima. He himself never pushed such a claim — a fact adequately explained by the evidence now available.

He cannot have failed to note the disappearance from the academic scene of such men as Szilard, Fermi, Compton, Teller, Wigner, and a host of others who had been involved in uranium research during 1939 and 1940. He cannot fail to have noted the sudden dropping from academic discussion of all news about nuclear fission. And if he took more than a cursory interest in the subject of uranium itself — the very nub of his initial worry — he may even have noted the reference on page 828 of the *U. S. Minerals Yearbook* of 1943 which said: "The uranium industry in 1943 was greatly stimulated by a government programme having materials priority over all other mineral procurement, but most of the facts were buried in War Department secrecy."

In addition, there was the case of his own Danish *alter ego*. In October 1943, Neils Bohr had made one of the most spectacular escapes of the war, sailing with his son across the Kattegat to Sweden in a small boat and being taken first to England in a high-flying Mosquito and then to the United States. Bohr spent most of the summer of 1944 at Los Alamos, where he "instigated some of the most important experiments on the velocity selector . . . enlivened discussions on bomb assembly, and . . . participated very actively in the design of the initiator".

Bohr also visited Einstein in Princeton. He arrived while other friends were there, and only as these friends were leaving did Einstein hurry downstairs and warn them that on no account must they mention that Bohr was in the United States. His presence in America was officially secret since he was travelling in the name of John Baker, and had even been given a British passport for the purpose — reportedly the only foreigner ever to have been granted one.

Bohr was a man of honour. He kept confidences. He no doubt denied himself the pleasure of describing to Einstein the technological successes with which he had been brought face to face at Los Alamos. But he now knew that two years previously Fermi had succeeded in producing the first self-sustaining chain reaction in the famous Fives Court in Chicago. He knew that the forecast he had made in his secret message to Chadwick a year earlier was incorrect. And it is clear from subsequent correspondence that he discussed with Einstein the postwar control of new and vastly more destructive weapons — which, in the context of their talks, can only have been atomic bombs.

It is unlikely that Einstein knew much of the technological details involved in the Manhattan Project. For one thing, General

Groves' policy of compartmentalisation made it difficult for any one man to know more than the necessary minimum — or to impart it, even if he wished to do so. More important, Einstein would not have been interested in purely technological detail. However, by the winter of 1944 he had talked on many occasions with an adviser to the Manhattan Project, had discussed with him the need to prevent a post-war arms race for weapons, and had desperately written to Bohr invoking his aid. The evidence is not that Einstein knew how, or even if, the new weapons were to be used to finish the war; but it implies beyond all reasonable doubt that by the end of 1944 he knew that they were nearing completion.

The adviser was Otto Stern, Einstein's old colleague from the Prague days who had crossed the Atlantic in 1934. Soon after America entered the war, Stern had served as consultant to one of the early radar schemes. Then, following the start of the Manhattan Project, he had become a consultant assigned to the Metallurgical Laboratory at the University of Chicago where the first nuclear pile went into operation in 1942. He continued to live in Pittsburgh, working as adviser to the other Manhattan Project consultants at the Carnegie Institute of Technology. Perhaps more important, he travelled to Chicago for the information meetings held there about every six weeks. Exactly how much he knew about the detailed progress of the bomb is not certain; there is every indication that it was considerable.

Stern paid a number of visits to Einstein, who after one of them said how terribly worried he was about the development of new weapons after the end of the war. No record of their discussions is likely to have been made, but their nature can be inferred from the climax which they produced.

This came in mid-December, 1944. Stern visited Einstein on Monday, December 11th. Once again they discussed weapons. This time Einstein appears to have become gravely alarmed. The following day he sat down and wrote to Bohr. He wrote to him at the Danish Legation in Washington, and he appears to have dropped the "John Baker" pseudonym and addressed him plainly as Professor Niels Bohr.

Writing of the news which so greatly disturbed him, he urged that influential scientists such as Compton in America, Lindemann in England and Kapitza and Joffé in Russia should bring pressure on the politicians to internationalise military power.

This letter could hardly have been more fortuitously ill-timed; the names it mentioned could hardly have been more fortuitously ill-chosen. In April, Bohr had received in London a letter from Kapitza which had invited him and his family to settle in Russia. He had shown it to the British Intelligence authorities, who had vetted his warm but innocuous reply. In May he had secured a meeting with Churchill in London, largely through Lindemann's intervention, and had tried to impress on the British Prime Minister the need for bringing the Russians into a scheme for postwar control of nuclear energy. The interview was a tragic failure; Bohr was unable to explain and Churchill was unwilling to listen. In August Bohr was better received by Roosevelt who listened sympathetically for an hour, agreed that an approach should be made to Russia, and promised to raise the matter direct with Churchill whom he was due to meet at Hyde Park the following month. But in September Roosevelt and Churchill did more than rule out any idea of an approach to the Russians. They also initialled an *aide-mémoire* the last clause of which said: "Enquiries should be made regarding the activities of Professor Bohr and steps taken to ensure that he is responsible for no leakage of information to the Russians." Bohr's friends loyally rallied to his support but he was "distressed that the whole business had now become enmeshed in the interstices of American politics..." He had moved, both in Britain and the United States, among the men who pulled the levers of power and he had put up to them proposals that were well thought out and practical where Einstein's were by comparison unreal. Nevertheless, he had been brusquely brushed off.

Bohr was in an awkward situation. He knew his Einstein. He knew that to a man of such trusting idealism the niceties of diplomatic protocol meant little. Whether he feared that Einstein might himself try to write to Kapitza or Joffé is not certain, but if he did the fear — with all his knowledge of how "the secret" of the bomb was being kept from the Russians — must have haunted him. What is beyond doubt is that when Bohr received Einstein's letter from the Embassy he hastened to Princeton, that in a long interview he persuaded Einstein to keep quiet; and that he reported in an official capacity on the incident to Washington in a private note that must have done much to vindicate the attitude of the "people... in Washington" who three years earlier decided to restrict Einstein's knowledge of the Manhattan Project.

He arrived at Mercer Street on Friday, December 22nd, and his report of what happened, dated merely "December 1944", was typed on quarto paper, apparently by Bohr himself and certainly in his own brand of English, with himself referred to as "B" and

Einstein referred to as "X". It began by stating that he had visited Einstein to whom he had explained that it "would be quite illegiti-mate [sic] and might have the most deplorable consequences if anyone who was brought into confidence about the matter con-cerned, on his own hands should take steps of the kind suggested".

The note then continued as follows:

> Confidentially B could, however, inform X that the responsible states-men in America and England were fully aware of the scope of the technical development, and that their attention had been called to the dangers to world security as well as to the unique opportunity for furthering a harmonious relationship between nations, which the great scientific advance involves. In response X assured B that he quite realised the situation and would not only abstain from any action himself, but would also — without any reference to his confidential conversation with B — impress on the friends with whom he had talked about the matter, the undesirability of all discussions which might complicate the delicate task of the statesmen.

There is no reason to doubt the accuracy of Bohr's note. There is no reason to doubt that Einstein was here, as elsewhere, a man of his word. And the inevitable conclusion is that from December 1944 until the dropping of the bombs on Japan eight months later Einstein not only knew far more of the developing nuclear situation than any of his scientist friends realised but that he used his confidential and undisclosable information from Bohr to impress on them "the undesirability of all discussions which might compli-cate the delicate task of the statesmen".

First he had to deal with Otto Stern. He waited until Christmas was half over. Then, on December 26th, he sat down and wrote what must have been, even for Einstein, an extraordinarily difficult letter — one that prevented Stern from making any ill-advised move yet did not reveal the visit from Bohr; a letter, moreover, that would have been innocuous had it fallen into the wrong hands.

Here, as on previous occasions, Einstein had stepped into a dark arena and been tripped by his own ignorance of what was going on. Furthermore his freedom of action, already limited by lack of official knowledge about the Manhattan Project, was now further hampered by what he had been told only in confidence. This was to be important in more ways than one. These arguments, and the earlier exchanges between Otto Stern and Einstein, were concerned with what was to happen after the war. Yet for practical purposes they also made it more difficult for Einstein to make his voice heard in any discussion which might be raised about use of the bomb in the Pacific or even in Europe where a week before Bohr's visit the Germans had launched the Ardennes offensive, a salutary reminder that they were not yet beaten.

First questions about the actual use of the bomb were raised in March 1945 by Leo Szilard, who since February 1942 had been chief physicist at the Metallurgical Laboratory in Chicago. Germany was now seen to be within a few weeks of defeat, while it was already known to a few men, almost certainly including Szilard, that the Third Reich was nowhere near producing a nuclear weapon.

The story there had been strange. In the United States Einstein had been kept virtually outside the nuclear effort once he had started it; in Germany there had been, by contrast, a movement which tended to rehabilitate the much-condemend "Jewish physics" which he represented. Certainly a number of German physicists, fearful that the current denigration of theoretical physics would seriously hamper their country, held a meeting in Munich in November 1940 and officially agreed that:

> 1. Theoretical physics is an indispensable part of all physics. 2. The Special Theory of Relativity belongs to the experimentally verified facts of physics. Its application to cosmic problems, however, is still uncertain. 3. The theory of relativity has nothing to do with a general relativistic philosophy. No new concepts of time and space have been introduced and 4. Modern quantum theory is the only method known to describe quantitatively the properties of the atom. As yet, no one has been able to go beyond this mathematical formalism to obtain a deeper understanding of the atomic structure.

Two years later another meeting was held, this time in Seefeld, in the Austrian Tyrol. Here a somewhat similar compromise was achieved, softening the decision that relativity had to be accepted with the consolation that "before Einstein, Aryan scientists like Lorentz, Hasenöhrl, Poincaré, etc. had created the foundations of the theory of relativity and Einstein merely followed up the already existing ideas consistently and added the cornerstone."

The need to cloak relativity in particular and "Jewish physics" in general with a respectability enabling them to be used without reproach by German physicists was part and parcel of the nuclear research which in Germany paralleled the work being carried out in the United States and Britain. In all three countries the crucial decision whether to follow up laboratory work with industrial exploitation had to be taken in 1942. In Britain it was decided that industrial resources were inadequate, and the British effort was

moved across the Atlantic. In the United States, America embarked on the multi-million-dollar Manhattan Project. In Germany,
where the theoretical results were discussed at a high-level Berlin
conference on June 4th, 1942, the decision was the reverse. For a
variety of reasons, Heisenberg and his colleagues had not been as
successful in their theoretical work as the Allies. But they had
achieved quite a lot: they had demonstrated the theoretical possibility of a weapon. Yet no serious attempt to move on to the
higher ground of industrial production was now made. This was
sensible enough. During the first two years of the war the
Germans had been so militarily successful that no need for nuclear
weapons was foreseen. But now the balance had swung too much
the other way.

> At the time [says Heisenberg of the 1942 meeting] the war situation
> was already too tense for long-term technical projects. An order is
> supposed to have been issued prohibiting technical developments which
> would require more than half a year for completion. The situation
> spared the German physicists the decision whether to plead for an
> attempt to produce atom bombs; they knew, on the basis of their
> technical experience, that such an attempt could not lead to success
> in less than three or four years. An attempt of this sort would have
> undoubtedly hastened German defeat, because the extensive manpower
> and materials necessary for it would have to be borrowed from other
> sources, thereby lessening the production of tanks and aeroplanes.

In addition there were two other reasons: Hitler could not
be interested in nuclear fission; and the anti-Jewish purges of the
previous decade had skimmed off from Germany too much of the
country's scientific cream.

Heisenberg and his colleagues carried on. During the last
months of the war he and the Kaiser Wilhelm Institute for Physics
of which he had been made Director in 1941 were evacuated to
Hechingen, bringing the end of Germany's wartime nuclear fission
story back to the little village where Elsa Einstein had been born.
But they were still only at the stage of academic research — a fact
which had become plain to an American mission in December
1944. Code-named "Alsos" — a curious choice since "groves", its
translation from the Greek, was a clear lead to General Groves
of the Manhattan Project — it had followed up the Allied advance
across Europe. With the capture of von Weizsäcker's papers in
Strasbourg, it discovered that the Allies need fear no nuclear weapons from Germany. As Heisenberg himself said later, "Whatever
one may think about the motives, it remains a fact that a serious

attempt to produce atom bombs in Germany was not undertaken, although in principle — but perhaps not in practice — the path to it had been open since 1942." 

It seems that this was the case. But clinching evidence, fortuitously provided, has been as fortuitously withheld. After the collapse of Germany in May 1945, the leading German physicists who had been involved on nuclear research — Heisenberg, Hahn and about a dozen others — were taken to France, and then unexpectedly brought to a house on the outskirts of Cambridge by Professor R. V. Jones, then Director of Scientific Intelligence in the British Air Ministry. "I had them brought to Farm Hall" he has written, "to save them from a threat they never knew — for I had been told that an American general proposed to solve the problem of nuclear energy in post-war Germany by having them shot while they were still in 'Dustbin', the Special Transit Camp in France." In England their rooms were fitted with secret microphones. Their conversations were recorded and their reactions to the news of Hiroshima, provided by the radio, were taken down in detail. Small sections of the transcripts have been printed in English in General Groves' reminiscences; but the Germans have maintained that these are mistranslations. The original texts have not been made available — due largely, it appears, to British reluctance to admit that the incident ever took place.

During the closing months of 1944 information on the position of German nuclear research was made available in Washington to a few members of the Manhattan Project. It is most unlikely, says Goudsmidt, the Alsos leader, that Einstein was aware of it until well after the war. But Szilard was no doubt informed. And in the spring of 1945, Szilard began to ask himself, he records: "What is the purpose of continuing the development of the bomb, and how would the bomb be used if the war with Japan has not ended by the time we have the first bomb?" As in 1939, he wished to bring the matter to the notice of the President. As in 1939, he approached Einstein, visiting him in Princeton — and presumably being trailed by the Manhattan Project's intelligence agents who followed him as they followed other leading members of the nuclear project.

In Princeton, Einstein gladly wrote another letter of introduction to the President.

Just how much additional information he had by this time gained either from Stern or from others is not clear. But there is a significant statement given in the June, 1945, edition of the

35

*Contemporary Jewish Record.* This contains an interview with Einstein which took place "shortly before" he retired from the Institute in April 1945, four months before the bombs on Japan. The interviewer asked "whether the disintegration of atoms would not be able to release the tremendous atomic energies for warfare". "Unhappily," Einstein replied, "such a possibility is not entirely in the Utopian domain. When military art is able to utilise nuclear atomic energies it will not be houses or blocks of houses that will be destroyed in a few seconds — it will be entire cities." Taken with the correspondence of the previous December, this suggests that Einstein's assumed ignorance of what Szilard's memorandum concerned was no more than a euphemism to protect the author.

However, this does not mean that Einstein knew the details of Szilard's proposals. It is unlikely that he did. And this was probably just as well. For while the memorandum did question the use of the bomb in the war against Japan, it did so for reasons with which Einstein would not necessarily have sympathised. The consequence of its use, Szilard warned, might be that in the ensuing arms race the United States would lose its initial advantage. And he asked whether the chances of eventual international control of nuclear weapons might not be obtained "by developing in the next two years modern methods of production which would give us an overwhelming superiority in this field at the time when Russia might be approached".

Four months later Szilard was to be one of those who went clearly and unmistakably on record in opposition on moral grounds to the use of these bombs "in the present phase of the war". But the memorandum that Einstein supported was something different. "Scrambling his technology to cloak references to the hydrogen bomb," say the official U. S. historians, "Szilard divided atomic development into two stages.* The first was reaching fruition. If the United States were well along on the second when it approached Russia, the better the chances of success. If international control proved a vain hope, the worst possible course would be to delay developing the second stage." This, one feels, was not exactly what Einstein had in mind as Szilard left Mercer Street in March with his letter to the President.

However, the effort was to be abortive as far as Roosevelt was concerned. Einstein's letter was dated March 25th. "I decided to transmit the memorandum and the letter to the President

---

* Dr. Gertrud Weiss Szilard, Leo Szilard's widow, questions the view that he was in fact referring to the hydrogen bomb.

through Mrs. Roosevelt, who once before had channelled communications from the Project to the President," Szilard has written. "I have forgotten now precisely what I wrote to Mrs. Roosevelt. I suppose that I sent her a copy of Einstein's letter — but not the memorandum. This I could not do. The memorandum I couldn't send her, because the memorandum would have been considered secret."

Mrs. Roosevelt gave Szilard an appointment for May 8th. Shortly afterwards Szilard showed his memorandum to A. H. Compton, Director of the Metallurgical Laboratory. "I hope you will get the President to read this," he said. "Elated by finding no resistance where I expected resistance, I went back to my office," he goes on. "I hadn't been in my office for five minutes when there was a knock on the door and Compton's assistant came in, telling me that he had just heard over the radio that President Roosevelt had died."

Some weeks later, Szilard took his memorandum to President Truman. Einstein's letter went too, but there is no evidence that it had any influence on Truman, who read Szilard's document and said: "I see now this is a serious matter." He then referred it to Byrnes, the new Secretary of State.

> President Truman asked me to see Szilard, who came down to Spartanburg, (South Carolina, Byrne's home) bringing with him Dr. H. C. Urey and another scientist, [Byrnes has written.] As the Einstein letter had indicated he would, Szilard complained that he and some of his associates did not know enough about the policy of the government with regard to the use of the bomb. He felt that scientists, including himself, should discuss the matter with the Cabinet, which I did not feel desirable. His general demeanour and his desire to participate in policy-making made an unfavourable impression on me, but his associates were neither as aggressive nor apparently as dissatisfied.

Szilard, like many other scientists who attempted to influence U. S. policy during the next few months, failed in his purpose. In the words of the Frank Memorandum, signed by many of the Manhattan Project scientists, and as summarised in the official U. S. history, "statesmen who did not realise that the atom had changed the world were laying futile plans for peace while scientists who knew the facts stood helplessly by." And after July 16th, when the weapon was successfully tested in the New Mexico desert, the statesmen went ahead with plans for its use over Japan.

Einstein left Princeton for his usual summer holiday. At Saranac on August 6th he heard on the radio the news that his earlier views had, indeed, been a mistake: a chain reaction had given a proof of his $E = mc^2$ far more spectacular than any given in the laboratory. To a *New York Times* reporter who visited Einstein's house to tell him the news he said: "The world is not yet ready for it." It is also claimed by the editors of *Einstein on Peace* that he exclaimed: "Oh, weh!" At first he refused to make any public comment. Instead, Miss Dukas made a statement on his behalf. "Although it can be said that the professor thoroughly understands the fundamental science of the atomic bomb," this went, "military expediency demands that he remain uncommunicative on the subject until the authorities release details."

On August 11th, he made his first public comment on the bomb, during a half-hour interview with Richard Lewis, an *Albany Times-Union* staff writer. He began by trying to damp down the hysteria which had swept the world. "In developing atomic or nuclear energy, science did not draw upon supernatural strength, but merely imitated the actions of the sun's rays," he said. "Atomic power is no more unnatural than when I sail a boat on Saranac Lake." He was asked about reports of secondary radiation which might cause sterilisation or leukaemia and answered: "I will not discuss that." He continued: "I have done no work on the subject, no work at all. I am interested in the bomb the same as any other person; perhaps a little more interested. However, I do not feel justified to say anything about it." He added that he thought it would be many years before atomic energy could be used for commercial purposes, but that substances other than uranium-235 might be found "and probably would be found" to accelerate its commercial use, an indication that he knew of the great U. S. achievement in manufacturing, on a commercial scale, the plutonium which had been used in the test-bomb and in the second of those dropped on Japan. "You will do everyone a favour by not writing any story. I don't believe anyone will be interested," he concluded.

With this exhortation and belief he faced the future, unaware that within a few days the Smyth Report, issued in Washington, would describe the genesis of the American nuclear effort and reveal to the world at least some of the part he had played in it.

Einstein's wartime attitude towards the bomb has sometimes been described as muddled and ambivalent. It was, on the contrary, quite logical; once he had reluctantly agreed that force could only be met by force, as he had agreed in 1933, all the rest followed. When there seemed a chance that the Germans might be able to utilise a new weapon of frightening proportions it followed that he should encourage the United States to counter it — even though he personally rated the danger very slight. When, in the summer of 1940, the nuclear project seemed likely to be still-born, it was natural that he should further urge the authorities into the action that produced the Manhattan Project. When he learned in the winter of 1944 that the new weapon was in fact a practical proposition, this must have seemed to justify his earlier action: what was possible in the United States might well be possible in the Third Reich. When the war had been won, postwar control would be essential.

Later, as the background to the bombing of Hiroshima and Nagasaki began to be known, Einstein supported those scientists who claimed that the bombs should not have been used. This also followed. He agreed that force had to be met by force, and he supported the Allied bombing of German civilians as morally justified, yet he believed that justification could be stretched only to cover the minimum force necessary to achieve desired moral ends. On the facts available this did not include the Japanese bombings.

However, Einstein himself would have been the last to wriggle. The available facts do not make it absolutely certain that he would have agreed, even reluctantly, with the use of nuclear weapons against Germany if only this could have prevented her conquest of the world. But it is a strong assumption.

# 21

# *THE CONSCIENCE OF THE WORLD*

WHEN THE WAR WITH JAPAN ENDED IN AUGUST 1945 WITH THE destruction of Hiroshima and Nagasaki by atomic bombs — and the threat of more to come although no more were yet ready — Einstein was sixty-six. He had officially retired from the Institute for Advanced Study in April, but the change in status was more formal than real. He still retained his study there. He still worked on, as he had for more than twenty years, his search for the elusive field theory always a step ahead of him like a scientific will-o'-the-wisp. In some ways he appeared to have shrunk back into the Einstein of pre-1914 days, an almost quaint survival of the day before yesterday, smiling to the Princeton children from his own private world, occupied only with his science and the ways in which the laws of nature were ordered.

He was still the symbol of relativity, but that was an old song, as distant from the world of the United Nations and postwar problems as Queen Victoria or the Louisiana Purchase. In 1933 he had been a symbol of the world's distaste for what was happening in Germany; a rallying point for Jewish efforts to deal with the practical problems of the refugees. But all that, too, was now part of the past. The world had eventually taken up arms, fought the good fight, and was now faced with the problem of clearing up the mess. A defeated Germany and a defeated Japan had to be dealt with; an Italy whose status was what you liked to make it had to be encouraged to work her passage back into the council of nations. In Palestine it was becoming more and more clear that the British would be unable to hold Arabs and Jews apart much longer, and a question mark hung over what was to follow the Mandate. Dominating all, there loomed the riddle of Russia's intentions and the grim thought that the worst of American and British suspicions might be justified. None of this seemed to belong to the world of Albert Einstein, a combination of the century's greatest brain and dear old gentleman.

The situation was transformed by the publication on August 11th of the Smyth Report — *Atomic Energy for Military Purposes.* The quiet recluse of Mercer Street suddenly became the man who had revolutionised modern warfare and upset both the apple-cart of military power and the accepted morality of war. What is more, the $E = mc^2$ of 1905 and the 1939 letter to President Roosevelt came from the man whose reputation in science had been equalled only by his position as a vociferous pacifist. This was some consolation to scientists who did not really like responsibility for the death of 120,000 civilians, even in the best of causes, and to the non-scientific population, most of whom were glad that the decision to drop the bombs was no business of theirs. The outcome was inevitable. Almost overnight Einstein became the conscience of the world.

As such he wrote, spoke, and broadcast throughout the ten years that remained to him. His attitude to all that had gone before August 6th, 1945, was virtually limited to two points: the claim that his only action had been to sign a single letter to Roosevelt, and his statement that had he known about the Frank Memorandum, pleading that the bomb should not be used on Japan without warning, then he would have supported it. Instead of holding an inquest on the past he looked to the future.

Towards the end of August 1945, he had written a laudatory letter to Raymond Gram Swing of the American Broadcasting Company. This brought about a meeting between the two men. The result was Einstein's first major public statement on nuclear affairs, "Atomic War or Peace, by Albert Einstein as told to Raymond Swing". Although the "as told to" formula is often open to suspicion there is no reason to doubt the accuracy of this example; Einstein's views as outlined to Swing were those which he held for the rest of his life. They are extremely revealing, not least in the parallel they show between his attitude to the United Nations and to the League twenty years earlier.

Everything was in clear black and white. "I do not believe that the secret of the bomb should be given to the Soviet Union... The secret of the bomb should be committed to a world government, and the United States should immediately announce its readiness to do so. Such a world government should be established by the United States, the Soviet Union and Great Britain, the only three powers which possess great military strength." All the rest sprang from this: the invitation to the Russians to present the first draft of a world government, "since the United States and Great Britain have the secret of the atomic bomb and the Soviet Union does not"; and the power of the world government "to interfere in countries where a minority is oppressing the majority and, therefore, is creating the kind of instability that leads to war".

Einstein himself admitted in the same article that the current advantage of the United States and Britain was a wasting asset since "we shall not have the secret of the bomb for very long". And he admitted that conditions in Spain and the Argentine "should be dealt with since the abandonment of non-intervention in certain circumstances is part of keeping the peace". Each of these two qualifications drove a coach and horses through his main argument. If Russia would soon have "the secret" there would be no incentive for her to surrender her hard-earned sovereignty to a world government whose two other members she had every reason to distrust. And "dealing with" Spain — or with the Argentine — would mean an aggressive war which would have been given little support by any world government.

Here, as on other occasions, Einstein handed a weapon to his enemies. Shortly before publication of the *Atlantic Monthly* article, Congressman John Rankin, a Mississippi politician of ultraconservative views, strongly attacked Einstein in the House of Representatives for allegedly supporting an anti-Franco organisation. "This foreign-born agitator would have us plunge into another European war in order to further the spread of Communism throughout the world," he claimed . . . "It is about time the American people got wise to Einstein." The slightly hysterical attack was off target since Einstein had made every effort to prevent the organisation concerned from using his name. A few weeks later Rankin could more reasonably have asked how Spain could be "dealt with" without war.

However, this was a minor point when compared with Einstein's assumption that Russia would be willing to co-operate in the creation of a world government. In the prewar years, he had certainly condemned a Russia which denied the freedoms taken for granted in a democracy. But now the story was changed; now the heroic actions of the Red Army without which even the power of America might have been overstretched in the struggle against the Axis nations, blinded him to the facts of political life. Russia had supported the League of Nations. He complained that the United States, on the question of supranational control of atomic energy, had offered only terms which the Soviet Union was determined not to accept. And when the defection of Igor Gouzenko laid bare the scope of Russian espionage in North America he complained, almost with an air of surprise, that this seemed to have adversely affected U. S.-Russian relations. He still criticised the Soviet Union, he still deplored her denial of academic and scientific freedom. But in his reactions to the grave nuclear problems of the immediate postwar years, he was unwilling to face the unpleasant truth: that Russia, far from being amenable to join any supranational organisation that genuinely wielded nuclear power, was determined to go it alone and get the bomb as well.

Not all physicists were so remote from real life. Szilard had revealed in his March 1945 letter to Roosevelt that he had a keen awareness of practicalities; even Bohr, in many ways the epitome of the idealist with his head in the clouds, had been brushed by circumstances into hard contact with the reality of what could, and could not, be accomplished in the immediate postwar world. And Einstein's friend Bertrand Russell also shared the vision he lacked. "I have no hope of reasonableness in the Soviet Government," Russell wrote to him on November 24th, 1947, after Einstein had suggested alterations in a statement on nuclear weapons that Russell was preparing.

> I think the only hope of peace (and that a slender one) lies in frightening Russia. I favoured appeasement before 1939, wrongly, as I now think; I do not want to repeat the same mistake ... Generally, I think it useless to make any attempt whatever to conciliate Russia. The hope of achieving anything by this method seems to me "wishful thinking". I came to my present view of Soviet government when I went to Russia in 1920; all that has happened since has made me feel more certain that I was right.

Einstein's attitude was very different. Just how different, was revealed by an interview which he gave in the summer of 1946 to Norman Thomas, the veteran socialist leader. Einstein personally approved a record of the interview which shows that in discussion of an international security force he "suggested that it might be well to have Russians in the service of the world organisation stationed in America, and Americans stationed in Russia". An analogy was given of "the way in which the old Austro-Hungarian empire allocated the troops of the different nationalities comprising it".

It is difficult to know whether public raising of the idea would have done world government more harm in the United States or in the Soviet Union.

Einstein's implied confidence that the Russians would co-operate is doubly surprising since he had only recently been given a good illustration of the reverse. He had agreed, together with a number of other scientists and intellectuals, to contribute to *One World or None*, a book designed to inform the American public of the new situation created by the bomb, and a message asking for Russian scientists to do so was sent over his name to the President of the Academy of Sciences in Moscow. After considerable delay, and apparently much lobbying, the request was refused. President Vavilov, replying for those who had been asked, noted that "because of technical difficulties they are deprived of the possibility to express their concrete opinion with respect to the facts proposed for publication".

Any doubts about the Russian attitude were dispelled in November 1947 after Einstein had written an "Open Letter to the General Assembly of the United Nations" for *United Nations World*. This called for a strengthening of the United Nations, criticised the veto with which the Russians were hamstringing operations and made a further plea for world government. Russian reaction came the following month in an Open Letter on "Dr. Einstein's Mistaken Notions...", signed by four leading Russian scientists including Vavilov and A. F. Joffé, Einstein's old friend of Berlin days. There was fulsome praise for Einstein followed by a recapitulation of Russia's struggle against Allied intervention after the First World War, and of her fight against Germany in the Second. "And now", the letter continued "the proponents of a 'world super-state' are asking us voluntarily to surrender this independence for the sake of a 'world government' which is nothing but a flamboyant signboard for the world supremacy of the capitalist monopolies."

The reply — regarded even by Einstein as a "semi-official statement" would have been enough to knock most men from the argument. Einstein hung on. But it is significant that when in April 1948, the Emergency Committee of Atomic Scientists endorsed the idea of world government in a major policy statement it noted that "this cannot be achieved overnight". Einstein had argued that something almost as instant was essential.

The Emergency Committee, the most prestigious of the early postwar bodies which attempted to guide the public into the nuclear age, was one over whose activities Einstein at first appears to have exercised considerable influence. He had been an early member of the National Committee on Atomic Information, formed to represent more than fifty educational, religious and civic organisations. In 1946 this took on the job of satisfying the ever-growing demand for information about the real implications of the bomb. It was soon clear that this was a professional task demanding a new organisation headed by an impressive name to give it moral and scientific standing. Harold Oram, a New York fund-raiser, believed that 20,000 dollars a month might be raised, and was soon in Princeton visiting Einstein. "What happened next is not entirely clear," says Alice Kimball Smith in her detailed analysis of the scientists' movement in America, *A Peril and a Hope*. "Perhaps Oram and Einstein together proposed an 'emergency committee', though one observer suspects that the vagueness of the original proposals left Einstein somewhat out on a limb from which Szilard, Urey and others united to rescue him." Whatever the details, the outcome was the Emergency Committee of Atomic Scientists with Einstein as president and chairman of trustees, Harold Urey as vice-president and vice-chairman, and Szilard, Weisskopf, Linus Pauling and Hans Bethe among the other trustees.

With headquarters in Princeton and offices in Chicago and Madison Avenue — the latter soon graced by the Epstein bust of Einstein — the Committee went into action. On May 23rd, 1946, an appeal went out over Einstein's signature for 200,000 dollars to be spent on "a nationwide campaign to inform the American people that a new type of thinking is essential if mankind is to survive and move toward higher levels", and less than a fortnight later he recorded a similar appeal for the newsreels. Later in June, his views were given in a long interview with Michael Amrine published in the *New York Times*. It stressed the need for a "great chain reaction of awareness and communication", and made the point that to "maintain the threat of military power" was to "cling to old methods in a world which is changed forever". Soon afterwards came formal incorporation of the Emergency Committee in the State of New Jersey, followed by a conference in Princeton in November; and, early in 1947, another appeal over Einstein's name, this time for 1,000,000 dollars to enable the trustees "to carry to our fellow citizens an understanding of the simple facts of atomic energy and its implications for society". But the appeal also noted that "this basic power of the universe cannot be fitted into the outmoded concept of narrow nationalism." Whether true or

not, this immediately added political overtones to what was basically an appeal for educational funds, and produced a critical reaction from those who did not believe that peace would be made
more secure by appeals to world government. Not all protests
came from the backwoodsmen. Thus Dr. Charles G. Abbot of the
Smithsonian Institution wrote to Einstein saying:

> A long life has satisfied me that pledged word of treaties, public
> opinion, and confederations, are all powerless to prevent unscrupulous
> leaders from aggressive measures. As for world government, I regard
> the very idea as chimerical for centuries to come. Also one country,
> now and for many years, has been at war with us by spying methods.
> Recognising fully the truth of your two propositions (a) no secret
> (b) no defence (that is materially), I feel that our only chance lies in
> T. Roosevelt's famous saying "Walk softly but carry a big stick."
> That has a psychological power...
> With these convictions, I think the Emergency Committee will be
> doing a disservice to this nation. For they will tend to cause people
> to rely on agreements, which will be broken reeds, no better.

Another correspondent, arguing that the Russians would "continue to bicker and refuse to submit to any kind of disarmament
and [would] insist on impossible demands from the Western world
only to gain time to perfect their own weapons," claimed that the
time to press demands for a genuinely free world had been when
the Russians were hard put to it at Stalingrad.

Despite criticism which made the most of the Emergency Committee's tendency, difficult to avoid, of mixing straight nuclear
education with political implications, the work went on successfully
until the immediate post-war need for it ended. The Committee
gave widespread support to educational work and kept the incomparable *Bulletin of the Atomic Scientists* afloat through a stormy
financial period. As its chairman, Einstein, in November 1947,
received the annual award of the Foreign Press Association "in
recognition of his valiant efforts to make the world's nations
understand the need of outlawing atomic energy as a means of
war, and of developing it as an instrument of peace". He wrote,
spoke, gave interviews, and drew on his often scanty reserves of
health and energy to an extent which went beyond the call of
duty. His output, always well-intentioned and sometimes extremely percipient, if inevitably repetitious and usually unavailing, is
well chronicled in *Einstein on Peace*.

Yet is is clear from the papers of the Committee, as from the
detailed analysis of the scientists' movement in America given by

Alice Kimball Smith, that the effect of what Einstein said and did during this period was extremely limited. After the great wash of words subsided, the breakwaters still remained. Weisskopf, a member of the Committee, puts it this way: "I do not remember that Einstein ever had any influence on our discussions. He very rarely took part in them. His only help was the influence of his name. He was not much informed about the details of the problems and tried to stay away from any decision-making discussions."

As far as the U. S. manufacture of the hydrogen bomb was concerned, Einstein's honesty combined with his common sense to limit his effectiveness. He was of course against it. But when asked to use his influence to delay the decision he replied that such an idea seemed quite impracticable. As with immediate post-war control of atomic bombs, he saw the issue in all-or-nothing terms; and it was even more difficult to dissuade the authorities now than it had been to encourage them to carry out work "with greater speed and on a larger scale" in the spring of 1940.

Apart from this — and from his obsession for getting back to the scientific work forever playing round in his brain, as dominant now as it had been when in a letter to Weizmann he had qualified the help he could give Zionism — Einstein's personal role was circumscribed by two other factors. One was his ignorance of the scientifico-military machinery that had been built as the Manhattan Project grew from 1942 onwards. Szilard and Weisskopf and Bethe, as well as Compton and many others, knew how the machine worked. Einstein hardly knew what its parts were. This ignorance was compounded by his instinctive dislike of mixing with the men in command. As Robert Oppenheimer once put it, "he did not have that convenient and natural converse with statesmen and men of power that was quite appropriate to Rutherford and Bohr, perhaps the two physicists of this century who most nearly rivalled him in eminence".

Einstein's strength lay less in diplomatic haggling and compromising, than in the bold imaginative gesture outside the normal round. Thus it is doubly galling that he should have missed by a hair's breadth one great chance of making a decisive impact on the postwar nuclear debate. The chance was all but presented by Weizmann, who in December 1945 conceived an ambitious idea for bringing Einstein to what was still Palestine. He planned to utilise Alexander Sachs, who had been brought in by Szilard six years previously, and if it was probably bad tactics to remind Einstein of the part he had played in prodding forward nuclear

weapons, this is the only flaw in the scheme outlined in Weizmann's "Suggested Draft Letter to Professor Einstein". "Reflecting upon the impetus that you gave in 1939 to an enterprise that
telescoped in a few years what otherwise might have taken a generation to accomplish," this went, "I have been moved to ask our
good friend Alex to play once more an intermediary role and to
submit to you some thoughts of mine regarding a unique service
that I fervently hope you will find yourself in a position to render
to the *Yishur* [general settlement] in Palestine and to the further-
ance of science." The service consisted of a visit to the country in
the spring of 1946, and Weizmann quickly tried to deal with the
obvious objections.

> Such a visit can be arranged to conform to the every requirement of
> your personal physician by assuring that the travel is direct from
> here to Haifa, that is, without any change, under the most comfortable
> accommodation available for yourself together with medical and other
> aides, not only for the journey but also in Palestine. For this we would
> consult with and be guided by what your physician recommends.
> Indeed, a stay of a month to six weeks in Palestine — say from the
> middle of April to the end of May — could be made to be beneficial
> for your health, as it would certainly tone up the body and the spirit
> of Jewry.

However, this was not all. The cornerstone of a new Institute
of Science was to be laid that spring.

> In connection with the inauguration of this Institute, [he went on] it
> has occurred to me that a select number of those who had contributed
> importantly to the telescoped fruition of atomic research and its
> application could be invited for the occasion, jointly by the Hebrew
> University and the Institute, and to contribute to a symposium on the
> import of that research for human progress and peace. Such a group —
> to be selected, with your aid, as representative of the oecumenical order
> of science instead of only the nations involved in the atomic bomb
> production — might thus issue from Palestine not only a synthesis of
> the current scientific views but a message for the healing of the nations
> and humanity.

This was the grand scheme which Weizmann conceived. He
finally wrote on December 28th, and shortly afterwards the letter
was in Sachs' hands. Sachs drove to Princeton, handed it over and
then took a short stroll with Einstein. During the walk they discussed the proposal and on their return to Mercer Street Einstein
said he would consider making the journey if Sachs would come too.

"But then," says Sachs, "some twinge experienced by him and re-flected in his face led him to say: 'But my poor health doesn't per-mit.' The letter was handed back to me . . ."

But the rejected invitation contained only the first half of Weizmann's initial idea, the visit to Palestine. There was no men-tion of atomic research, of a symposium on the importance of nuclear research for human progress and peace, or of a message "for the healing of the nations and humanity". What Einstein rejected was the idea of a simple visit — thinking, no doubt, of "the ado and the fuss and the consequent duties" which he had spoken of to Schrödinger in 1934. Whether he would have rejected the more significant appeal is another matter.

Einstein's influence on the development of postwar nuclear at-titudes was thus at first glance a good deal less than mythology sug-gests. His ideas for world government in which he wrapped up so tightly the solution of the nuclear dilemma were considered wildly impractical by those with experience of day-to-day international relations; those who favoured them rarely appreciated that they rested on force as surely as the policies of the Pentagon or the Kremlin. The hamstringing of the May-Johnson Bill which would have put nuclear energy in the hands of the military and which Einstein disliked, was largely the work of men from the Manhattan Project, spurred on by Szilard. And it is difficult to point to any one act of Government, any decisive swing of public opinion, and unhesitatingly declare: "Without Einstein, things would have been different."

Yet Einstein was, to most, the one figure inextricably linked with the bomb, the man who sincerely regretted the way in which it had been used. His name still caught the eye. Even without the resplendent halo of hair which made him a photographer's delight, he retained more than a touch of the guru. Ordinary people listened to him. So, to varying extents, did the men who were in the front line of the postwar battle to control nuclear energy. It was not a popular battle to fight and it was one in which their opponents could summon up — with different degrees of justification — patrio-tism, common sense, and the will of the people. It was fortifying, therefore, that they could count on the moral support of a man like Einstein; however woolly his proposals for action might be, he was a man whom most people felt, and usually with good reason, sensed right from wrong with almost uncanny intuition. Therefore it would not be right to underrate the unrecorded influence that Einstein may well have had on others: although he can be credited with no great victory, his mere presence added to the moral muscle of those who claimed that the great issues of nuclear weapons should be argued out with reason rather than emotion. Thus there are two perfectly defendable views of Einstein's influence on nuclear thinking during the postwar decade. He did more than his adversaries claimed even if he did less than his well-wishers sometimes imagine.

Einstein's concern with the nuclear debate logically drew him out into two other discussions which spread across America as scientists discovered themselves unexpectedly in the corridors of power and as the nation began to argue about the new situation which had been created. One dealt with the social responsibilities of science and scientists; the other with civil liberties and academic freedom, a subject which grew in importance as the rights and wrongs of nuclear rearmament became inextricably entangled with both national and international politics.

As far as science was concerned, the nature of Einstein's work had from the early days tended to shield him from the ways in which science could be exploited for good or evil. For him science was an investigation of the laws of nature. Certainly his old friend Haber exploited these laws in the cause of gas warfare, but that was surely only a temporary aberration? Surely the "small group of scholars and intellectuals" whom he had described to Ehrenfest in 1915 as forming "the only 'fatherland' which is worthy of serious concern to people like ourselves", was a group which must be above the battle?

This attitude had begun to change in the years that immediately followed the First World War. The movement was speeded up by the coming of the Nazis, and when even his good friend von Laue told him in 1933 that "the scientist should observe silence in political matters, i. e., human affairs in the broader sense," he had been forced to reply that he did not share the view. The evolution continued. From regarding scientists as a group almost aloof from the rest of the world, he began to consider them first as having responsibilities and rights on a level with the rest of men, and finally as a group whose exceptional position demanded the exercise of exceptional responsibilities.

"The bomb" lay at the heart of the problem. But Einstein well knew that the position of the scientist in society had been radically altered by other developments and that in many fields other than nuclear physics new guidelines had to be drawn. Here his views were realistic rather than starry-eyed. Just as he saw science and religion as complementary, one searching for the "whats" while the other sought the "whys", so did he look upon an understanding of science as necessary to good government. But he was willing to render unto Caesar only those things which were Caesar's; and he would have experienced little of the fashionable shock at the view that scientists should be "on tap but not on top".

Yet he himself provides no guide to the place that scientists should or should not occupy outside their own fields. Einstein was, even more obviously than most human beings, a one-off model. His genius was linked with attributes not only of the saint but also of the rogue elephant, and scientists in government, at whatever level they operate or advise, must be counter-balanced by the more humdrum qualities. As Rutherford showed, they need not lack the sparks of the great imaginative mind; as Szilard showed, they can retain a quirkiness fringing on eccentricity. But if they are to serve without disaster they must have something less than Einstein's white-hot fanaticism and must devote more time than he did to ordinary men and women.

On academic freedom, the right of minorities to disagree, on what he considered the almost sacred duty of dissent, emotion tied in with intellect, for his life had been marked by a long series of rearguard actions in support of temporarily retreating causes. In Germany, between the wars, his attitude was epitomised by the Gumbel case in which he publicly supported the pacifist professor of Heidelberg University's Department of Philosophy, almost harried from his post by nationalist attacks. In the United States, after 1945, he threw his support wholeheartedly behind those who defied the draft law on grounds of conscience and, later, those who refused to incriminate themselves before the Un-American Activities Committee. But the editors of *Einstein on Peace* have stressed that "Einstein, who passionately defended the intellectual and moral freedom of the individual, frequently emphasised with equal conviction the obligations which a truly free individual must assume toward the community of which he is an integral part." Thus the long list of cases and letters which they quote exhibits a splendid reserve. Einstein is as careful to be fair, to hold the balance between individual and public interest, as he had been almost forty years earlier when helping to draw up the "Manifesto to Europeans".

Not until 1953 did he at last boil over. The case was that of William Frauenglass, a Brooklyn teacher called to give evidence before one of the Congressional committees investigating political beliefs and associations. Frauenglass approached Einstein and Einstein replied with a letter in which he stated his belief that intellectuals should refuse to testify before such committees.

This claim that it was wrong to obey the law when one believed it to be a bad one brought down on Einstein's head the anticipated bucket-load of hot coals. The *New York Times* which had
published Einstein's letter — he had told Frauenglass that it need
not be considered confidential — said in an editorial that "To employ the unnatural and illegal forces of civil disobedience, as Professor Einstein advices, is in this case to attack one evil with another." A majority of papers followed suit, while in academic circles
support was less than Einstein might have expected.

Just where some of the intellectuals stood was not quite clear
and earlier in the year there had been an incident whose significance was not appreciated at the time.

On March 13th, 1954, some 200 educators, clergymen and
authors met in Princeton for a conference on "The Meaning of
Academic Freedom", held by the Emergency Civil Liberties Committee in observance of Einstein's seventy-fifth birthday the following day. He answered, in writting, a number of questions which
had been put to him. But he did not attend the conference, held in
the Nassau Inn only a few hundred yards from Mercer Street.
Norman Thomas, the veteran socialist leader, has given a clue to
the reason. Thomas had intervened in the celebrations, he has written, at the request both of the American Committee for Cultural
Freedom and the American Jewish Committee, and with the approval of Robert Oppenheimer, the Director of the Institute for Advanced Study. At that juncture in American affairs, he has said,
there was worry that Dr. Einstein's name would be exploited, not
for the defence of civil liberties, but for the aggrandisement of a
committee, "some of whose members and spokesmen were stated to
have been at least pretty indiscriminate apologists for communism".
Almost to the end Einstein remained the object of manipulation and
counter-manipulation.

Thus on the central problem of the bomb, which had transformed the world even though the world was reluctant to admit
it, on the responsibilities of science and the academic freedom to
discuss what should be done about them, his attitude was forecastable and clear-cut. As the conscience of the world he might
be naive but he was morally impregnable. But Einstein was also
the German who had turned from his country twice, the German
Jew who was appalled at the way the Germans had treated the
Jews. Here, if anywhere, was the touchstone of how he really felt

about the human race. And here, impulse was stronger than judgment. Here Einstein, as though reflecting the dichotomy that so often
marks his life, succeeded in matching white with black. His first impulse, conditioned by the Luitpold Gymnasium if not entirely
governed by it, and certainly remembered with disadvantages
through the years, had been to detest the Prussians and the Prussian spirit, an attitude which during the First World War had sub-
stituted "German" for "Prussian". A transformation had been
worked by Weimar and reinforced by the events of the immediate
postwar year. Soon he was subordinating early impulse to fresh
judgment, stressing how wrong it was to categorise men by the
places in which they had been born. "Nationalism is an infantile
disease," he told one interviewer. "It is the measles of mankind."
And throughout the 1920s, shunning Solvay because Germans
were excluded as Germans, happy to be fêted in Berlin as the
Republic's unofficial ambassador returned from America and Britain, innocently thinking that bygones were bygones, Einstein became a symbol of the international man for whom condemnation
of a nation as a nation was a mistake as much as a crime.

The coming of Hitler brought impulse to the fore again. With
the fervour of all lapsed converts, Einstein once more began to see
the problem in terms of unshaded black and white. "The Germans,"
he told one visitor seeking his views in 1935, "are cruel. No people
in the world take such delight in cruelty as they do. I thought I
knew Germans, but during the past two years I have learned to
know better the cruelty of which they are capable." Later, as Hitler marched from one conquest to the next, Einstein appeared to
forget his own reactions to Weimar and, year by year, issued statements which condemned not only Hitler and his followers but,
for practical purposes, the whole German people. Asked what educational measures should be taken in Germany after the war, he
had a simple reply: "The Germans can be killed or constrained,
but they cannot be re-educated to a democratic way of thinking
and acting within a foreseeable period of time."

All this was understandable, even if it was not rational. In
wartime it had a stern plausibility and the horrors of the concentration camps revealed by the defeat of Germany did not make
it less so. Yet if the catalogue of war and recrimination was not to
continue for ever, generation by generation, someone had to stretch
a hand across the gap that appeared to separate two different kinds of
human and discover what was reality and what mirage. Two decades
back Einstein had not looked on "reconciliation" as a dirty word.

Yet now, with the peace, his black detestation of all things German reasserted itself. It was not only the rearming of Germany as a providentially supplied weapon against Russia that he detested. That was enough to stick in the gullets of many decent men. Einstein's detestation went deeper, was more irrational, ignored the forgiveness of both Jews and Germans who had suffered far more than he. At heart, perhaps he could never forgive the fact that he himself had been born a German. The result looks today like a deep chink in his humanity.

He thought it was essential to prevent Germans from obtaining great political power. And the Einstein who had resigned from the League Committee when the French marched into the Ruhr, now believed that if the Ruhr were left to the Germans the war would have been in vain. Einstein, with Morgenthau, would have been happy to see the Reich transformed from an industrial nation into an agricultural country, and his old friend James Franck, appealing for a relaxation of postwar restraints in Germany, was firmly told that Einstein would oppose any such move. The merest hint that Churchill, not notably soft on the Germans, might let them work their passage back to respectability, brought a brusque reprimand to Janos Plesch.

His attitude towards Germany at the personal level was even more revealing than his views on the position that the country should occupy in the postwar world. Its tone was set in his uncompromising reply to Arnold Sommerfeld, who in October 1946 invited him to rejoin the Bavarian Academy. Einstein had no wish to have any dealings with the Germans or even with the Academy. The only exceptions were men like Sommerfeld, and a few others.

These others presumably included von Laue and Planck, as well as Hahn and Heisenberg, by now President and Director respectively of the Max Planck Gesellschaft with which the Allied occupation authorities had replaced the Kaiser Wilhelm Gesellschaft.

Otto Hahn himself asked whether Einstein would become a Foreign Member of the new organisation. He was met with a firm "no". Einstein refused to become an honorary member of a society much after his own heart, the German Association of World Government. He refused to become an honorary citizen of Ulm, or of West Berlin. And when President Heuss told him of plans to reform the Peace Section of the former Prussian order, *Pour le Merite*, he was told by Einstein that because of the Germans' mass murder of the Jews he had no interest in re-joining.

The same spirit was shown in letters to his old friend Born in September 1950. When Born retired from his post at Edinburgh in 1952 and moved to Bad Pyrmont in Northern Germany he was taken to task for returning to a land of mass-murderers. Born, noting that the German Quakers had their headquarters in Bad Pyrmont, replied in a letter that contained two barbs. "They are no mass-murderers," he said, and "many of our friends there suffered far worse things under the Nazis than you or I." And then, no doubt remembering his own refusal to work on nuclear weapons and Einstein's letter to Roosevelt, he went on: "The Americans have demonstrated in Dresden, Hiroshima and Nagasaki, that in sheer speed of extermination they surpass even the Nazis."

This was perhaps a failure to compare like with like; and Einstein's feelings, like Born's, were those of the now-distant 1950s. Memories of the gas chambers, and of Dresden and Hiroshima, were stronger then than they are today. Some of Einstein's friends, putting in a plea of mitigation for his attitude, believe that a few more years would have made a difference. Maybe. Later events might, just possibly, have discouraged what was dangerously near an inverted *Herrenvolk* doctrine that appealed to race as much as to the history of the last 100 years. In particular, Einstein might have been swayed — irrationally, but swayed nevertheless — by the eventual succession of the Social Democrats. He had been swung round full circle in 1919 and although he did not now feel that the postwar democratic constitution of the Weimar Republic fitted the German people, he might well have admitted that Brandt's Germany could turn over a new leaf, a concession he would never give to Adenauer's or to Ulbricht's.

This is possible; but it looks unlikely. By the end of the Second World War Einstein was refusing to see Hitler as the scapegoat of the popular papers; what was wrong was not a madman but that such a figure could express the will of the thousands burning deep. What he had experienced at the Luitpold Gymnasium was not the exception but the norm. If he thought back seriously to the halcyon days of Weimar when for a few years it seemed that a new Germany was rising from the old, he thought also of the old saying, "once bitten, twice shy". Even had he experienced a twinge of doubt, even had he started to be influenced by Born's arguments, by the dictates of common sense or by the growing evidence of a postwar German spirit which was different from the old, he might have thought it wrong to change his stance. By now he was too much a symbol of all that Jewry had suffered at

Germany's hands; by now, for Einstein, reason would have been treason.

It was in this frame of mind that in the autumn of 1947 he heard of the death of Max Planck, that servant of the state whose first son had been killed at Verdun and whose second had been executed by his own countrymen after the attempt to kill Hitler in 1944. Einstein's attitude was curiously in contrast to that of Born. The physicist who had returned to live in "the land of mass-murderers" wrote somewhat critically of Planck as the man in whom "the Prussian tradition of service to the state and allegiance to the government was deeply rooted... I think he trusted that violence and oppression would subside in time and everything return to normal. He did not see that an irreversible process was going on." Einstein remembered another side to Planck. He had, significantly enough, not written to him since the end of the war. Now the man who hated the Prussian spirit wrote to the widow of the man who typified at least some elements of that spirit.

Yet he wrote consolingly and without bitterness, recalling the fruitful period of physics through which both he and Planck had lived, stressing that Planck had been one of those rare men who had concentrated on the great truths of life but had yet remained human. When it came to Planck, and to the scientific spirit that he stood for, it was as if the years between 1913 and 1947 had not existed. Even so, it was a generous letter.

Yet Einstein, who ruled out any reconciliation between Germany and the rest of the world in general, let alone between Germany and the Jews, still hoped for something similar between Jews and Arabs. For this reason he had campaigned against the creation of yet another nation-state. But in the postwar world other ethnic and religious groups were trying to give themselves the covering of political independence. It was certain that a Jewish state would arise from the ruins of the Mandate.

Nor was this all. With the British desperately trying to restrict immigration during the last months of their control, extremists increasingly took the law into their own hands. It was not only the rise of Hitler that justified the use of force; in Palestine the situation quickly degenerated into guerrilla warfare. And now Einstein decided to swallow his pacifism once again.

In the spring of 1948 Lina Kocherthaler, Einstein's cousin in Montevideo, was approached by those wishing to raise funds for the Haganah, the Jewish resistance movement in Palestine. Would Einstein send them a letter which could be sold by auction? Einstein not only replied by return, on May 4th, 1948, ten days before the end of the Palestine Mandate, but enclosed a declaration headed: "To my Jewish brothers in Montevideo". On the letter's arrival in Montevideo it was decided to form a committee of Jewish academics, and to hold a banquet at which it could be auctioned. The banquet was on July 17th, and most of the money raised — roughly 5,000 dollars — came from the sale of the Einstein letter.

Thus the instinctive pacifist was once more driven into admitting that force was necessary. Further, the arms which he detested were now to create a nation-state which he believed to be contrary to genuine Jewish needs. Einstein's regret at this, mixed with perplexity at the juxtaposition of good ends and evil means, remained with him for the rest of his life. With his failure to move opinion along the road to nuclear control through world government, and refusal to budge from an almost Vansittartite approach to Germany, it completes a trilogy. Only science mitigated these tragedies, a field in which he was both humble enough to see his life as a link in a long chain, and confident enough to know that he had been essential.

# 22

## *TWO STARS AT THE END OF THE ROCKET*

EINSTEIN'S NON-SCIENTIFIC INTERESTS AFTER THE SECOND WORLD War were parallel to those which followed the war of 1914–1918. Then he had wanted to abolish all weapons, to bring Germany back into the comity of Europe and help create a Jewish homeland that would not be a nation-state; now his aims were control of nuclear weapons, a Germany safe within an economic strait-jacket, and the survival of Israel. There were other comparisons which suggest that outside science as well as inside it Einstein would always be cast as the same lonely and tragic figure. Not least was the feeling that America of the later 1940s was tying him with the bonds he had first felt in the Germany of the 1920s. The country of his adoption seemed to be going the same way as the country of his birth.

Pessimism about America, an intuitive fear for its future, developed in Einstein long before it was felt by most of his American colleagues. There was reason enough for this. He worked on at the Institute as he had worked on at the Kaiser Wilhelm. He listened to the distortions of his own stand on nuclear weapons much as he had listened to descriptions of the General Theory as part of an international Jewish conspiracy. And as Senator Joseph McCarthy swam into power, kept afloat on a sea of ignorance, he no doubt remembered that "the great masses of the people... will more easily fall victim to a great lie than to a small one". The whole scene began to look uncomfortably familiar.

His natural reaction to the pressures which built up as the Cold War grew in intensity made him again the target for attack. In Germany he had thought of emigration many times before he had been forced to go. Now, according to his relatives in South

America, to whom he confided his feelings and fears in a long series of intimate letters, he considered leaving the United States.

He finally decided to stay, and one cannot be sure just how serious was his thought of uprooting himself once again. But however deep his misgivings about America, however strongly he at times felt that the lunatic fringe was in control, he retained some faith that the country would eventually solve its dilemmas without the episodes of self-destruction which seemed such a recurrent feature of German history. He got over the hump. He was determined to stick it out in Princeton and a note of resignation began to creep into his correspondence.

Attempts were made to coax him to Israel. "He said he was too old," reports Brodetsky, who visited him in 1948. "I told him that according to Jewish tradition, as he was only sixty-nine, he had another fifty-one years to live to reach the age of Moses. He repeated that he was too old. But I could see that he had many other claims at Princeton."

Quite apart from claims — notably those of people with whom he still worked at the Institute — there were ties, the most important being his own poor health. Since the breakdown of 1928, when he was approaching his fiftieth birthday, he had been forced to take life more easily. His smoking, which had always been strictly rationed by Elsa, was now more drastically cut. He compromised by keeping a tiny pipe and tobacco hidden in his desk, and would occasionally be tempted to half-fill it. Then he would go outside and borrow a match — not a box, for that would be too tempting and sinful, but a single match with which he might or might not get the pipe going. He had also been put on first a fat-free and later a salt-free diet by Dr. Ehrmann, his regular Berlin doctor who had emigrated to New York before the war. Einstein hated it all, but he was never one to kick against the pricks, and his good-humoured resignation comes out in two incidents.

When a box of sweets was being passed round after dinner at Mercer Street one night he took merely a deep sniff. "You see, that's all my doctor allows me to do," he said. "The devil has put a penalty on all things we enjoy in life. Either we suffer in our health, or we suffer in our soul, or we get fat." A friend asked him why it was the devil and not God who had imposed the penalty. "What's the difference?" he answered. "One has a plus in front, the other a minus." On another occasion Ehrmann came to Mercer Street with medicine in the form of both pills and drops, not knowing which his patient would prefer. He chose the drops.

"I still remember him standing there, counting the drops into a water glass and handing it over to Einstein," says a colleague. "He swallowed the whole thing down, then turned a little green in the face, and started to throw up. After that he turned to Ehrmann and asked him: 'Do you feel better now?'"

Until 1945 his poor health was inconvenient rather than crippling. But ever since his illness in 1917 he had suffered periodically from stomach-cramp, nausea, and vomiting, and in 1945 it was decided that an operation was necessary. He recovered normally but was much weakened and even by the end of the following year still found it necessary to take a rest after lunch. In 1948 a second operation in the Brooklyn Jewish Hospital revealed an aneurysm in the main artery and two years later an examination showed that the condition had worsened. From 1950 Einstein knew that time was running out.

The threat made little difference. He was as careless of himself now as he had been as a youth or in the hungry days of the First World War. As long as he could get on with his work nothing else mattered. He got on with it relentlessly and with an inner determination which contrasted strongly with the outer picture of a frail old man. Those who saw him in his working habitat were impressed.

> One unforgettable memory [says a visitor during these last years] is of Einstein slightly ill and forced to keep to his bed. "It occupied almost the entire room. The blinds were drawn. The light attached to the head of the bed lit up the back of his head and the board on which were the sheets of paper which he covered with lines of regular writing. He was covered with an eiderdown from which his naked body emerged at one end and his feet at the other. The picture was that of an impressive Rembrandt.

The slow but steady deterioration in his condition would alone have tied him to Princeton. But there was also his work. Here his principal worry was still the removal of determinancy from physics which had been the main epistemological result of quantum mechanics, a result which to the end of his life he continued to regard as merely transitory. He suffered from no illusions. He knew that he was fighting a rearguard action against his colleagues, and he had no doubts about how they regarded him as a physicist whom physics had passed by.

With Max Born he continued to discuss, in the greatest detail, and with an almost pathetic attempt to reconcile the irreconcilable, the chasm which had opened up between him and so many of his contemporaries. The two men had been intimates since 1916. They had agreed to differ in the twenties; unknown to both, their paths had diverged when Einstein had helped launch the U.S. nuclear weapons project and Born had refused to join the British enterprise. They differed over the Germans. Yet they remained mutual fathers-confessor for their hopes and fears in physics, and it was to Born that Einstein gave the fullest explanation of how he saw the situation during the last decade of his life.

He did not attempt to put forward a logical defence of his attitude in physics. What he did was to assert his belief, his "hunch", almost his faith, that physicists would eventually, and in all probability long after his death, provide a theory which would restore the balance to which he had been accustomed in the past: a theory in which law connected in a causal way not merely probabilities but facts. This stubborn belief continued to keep him the outsider, the old man mirroring the young rebel who had dared claim that light could be both wave and corpuscle and that time and space were not what they seemed to be.

There were occasions when he was humorously sceptical of what was going on in science. Thus at his birthday celebrations he sat all day in the lecture hall of the Institute listening to a series of invited papers, and at the end was asked if he had found them tiring. "They would have been tiring if I had understood them," he replied.

Yet it was accepted that few men knew as much as Einstein about the nature of the physical world. Few were to have one of the new artificially-created elements named after them, the einsteinium which as the ninety-ninth was added to laurencium, mendelevium, fermium, and curium — and was later joined by rutherfordium and hahnium. Even fewer knew as much about the spurs to creative scientific activity, and it followed as a matter of course that when Aydelotte retired from the Directorship of the Institute in 1947 Lewis Strauss, one of the trustees, should seek his advice on a successor. Einstein would neither comment on the names put forward nor himself suggest any candidates. "I besought him to tell me, at the very least, what ideal qualities the trustees should seek in a director of the Institute," Strauss has written. " 'Ah, that I can do easily,' he replied with a smile. 'You should look for a very quiet man who will not disturb people who are trying to think'."

He might succeed in recommending a quiet man — it turned out to be Robert Oppenheimer — but his powers failed when it came to persuading the Institute to invite Max Born to Princeton. And Born, however hard he tried, could never coax Einstein back across the Atlantic. Thus their basic disagreements had to be shuttled back and forth through the post. It was different with Einstein and Bohr, since Bohr, a non-resident member of the Institute, could visit Princeton whenever he wished. He came once in 1946, for the bicentennial celebrations of Princeton University, and again in 1948 for the spring semester at the Institute. On both occasions he had long exchanges with Einstein, carrying on the argument which had started at the Solvay Congresses two decades previously. They were not particularly happy exchanges and Abraham Pais, then a temporary member of the Institute, has described how one day Bohr came into his room "in a state of angry despair", saying "I am sick of myself." Pais asked what was wrong. "He told me", he has written, "he had just been downstairs to see Einstein. As always, they had got into an argument about the meaning of quantum mechanics. And, as remained true to the end, Bohr had been unable to convince Einstein of his views. There can be no doubt that Einstein's lack of assent was a very deep frustration to Bohr."

Those lucky enough to be present at the meetings watched an interplay between master and master that had an heroic quality quite distinct from its relevance to physics. Both the 1946 and the 1948 visits also produced those dramatic highlights which seemed inseparable from contact between the two men, as though their mere presence in a room together was enough to strike flint against iron and make the sparks fly.

One such engagement occurred when Einstein attended a major address by Bohr in the Institute's main mathematics building. He was collected from Mercer Street by Dr. Mitrany who, accustomed to his friend's sweatered informality was surprised to see him in dark suit, collar and tie. They took their places in the lecture hall amongst an august company. Everyone settled down for a highly technical two-hour lecture which only Einstein and a handful of others could follow with more than polite interest. Bohr progressed towards the heart of the epistemological and scientific argument. Einstein listened, attentive from the start, then more than attentive, then with obviously mounting impatience. Finally the strain was too much. He rose from his seat and walked to the platform in front of the long roller-blackboard that covered the entire wall. Then, chalk in hand, he interrupted the lecturer. What had been a monologue became a dialogue. Bohr understood. He, like Einstein, knew this was not arrogance but submission to fate.

Only Einstein could adequately contradict what he believed was wrong even if he could not prove it was wrong. Not to do so would be dereliction of duty.

During the 1946 visit Bohr had been asked to contribute to *Albert Einstein — Philosopher-Scientist*, a volume being prepared in honour of Einstein's seventieth birthday three years later. He agreed to write a history of their epistemological arguments and completed it during his stay at the Institute in 1949. While at work on the article he invited Pais to his office.

> We went there [says Pais] ... After we had entered, Bohr asked me to sit down ("I always need an origin for the co-ordinate system") and soon started to pace furiously around the oblong table in the centre of the room. He then asked me if I could put down a few sentences as they would emerge during his pacing. It should be explained that, at such sessions, Bohr never had a full sentence ready. He would often dwell on one word, coax it, implore it, to find the continuation. This could go on for many minutes. At that moment the word was "Einstein". There Bohr was, almost running around the table and repeating: "Einstein ... Einstein ..." It would have been a curious sight for someone not familiar with Bohr. After a little while he walked to the window, gazed out, repeating every now and then: "Einstein ... Einstein ..."
>
> At that moment the door opened very softly and Einstein tiptoed in.
>
> He beckoned to me with a finger on his lips to be very quiet, his urchin smile on his face. He was to explain a few minutes later the reason for his behaviour. Einstein was not allowed by his doctor to buy any tobacco. However, the doctor had not forbidden him to steal tobacco, and this was precisely what he set out to do now. Always on tiptoe he made a bee-line for Bohr's tobacco pot which stood on the table at which I was sitting. Meanwile Bohr, unaware, was standing at the window, muttering "Einstein ... Einstein ..." I was at a loss what to do, especially because I had at that moment not the faintest idea what Einstein was up to.
>
> Then Bohr, with a firm "Einstein", turned around. There they were face to face, as if Bohr had summoned him forth. It is an understatement to say that for a moment Bohr was speechless. I myself, who had seen it coming, had distinctly felt uncanny for a moment, so I could well understand Bohr's own reaction. A moment later the spell was broken when Einstein explained his mission and soon we were all bursting with laughter.

Bohr and Einstein continued their argument. They agreed to go on differing; Bohr confident that he had reached bedrock, Einstein as confident that they were still dealing with the lower subsoil of physics. Below, he continued to believe, lay the ideas which would bring back the world he had known half a century ago. If it were based on anything more than elderly optimism, the hope of restoring the images he had helped destroy during an iconoclastic youth was based on that old panacea for a fragmented physics, a satisfactory unified field theory. He still intuitively believed that this would allow the laws of quantum mechanics to be derived from non-statistical laws governing not probabilities but facts and he had pressed on relentlessly during his early years at the Institute, throughout the war and into the peace, still in hot pursuit of the set of equations which would show that God did not really play dice with the world.

He never completely despaired. He worked on, past his seventieth birthday, and at last began to see what he thought was light at the end of the tunnel. By the autumn he was ready with "A Generalised Theory of Gravitation". A typewritten copy of the manuscript was exhibited at the Christmas meeting of the American Association for the Advancement of Science and the theory, with its twenty-eight mathematical formulae appeared two months later as a fourteen-page appendix to the fourth edition of *The Meaning of Relativity*.

A new theory from Einstein, offering at the age of seventy a key to the riddle of the universe to replace the one he had provided at the age of fifty, caused a major stir in the scientific world and its ground-swell reached out to the man in the street. Low drew a cartoon which quickly became famous showing Einstein bringing a giant key on New Year's day to a Father Time exclaiming: "About time, too!" There were large and numerous headlines; phrases such as "master theory" were freely bandied about. Some of the more weighty journals began to outline what Einstein's thirty years of thought had yielded, a new and more convenient tool with which it was hoped that the laws of nature could be described.

What no one attempted to explain was how the tool could be used. The reason was simple. Infeld considered that he would need a year to understand it and added: "Like Chinese, you have to study it first." Harold Urey had not read it. "If I had", he said, "I would probably not have understood it."

However, it was not only the remoteness of the theory from even most scientific minds that was a stumbling-block to acceptance. Unlike the General Theory of 1915, it could not apparently be tested. He knew the limitations of what had been half a lifetime's work; typically, he made light of them, replying to an enquiry about the chances of experimental evidence: "Come back in twenty years' time."

Almost two decades on, Einstein's theory of a unified field remains unsubstantiated and current thought veers away from the idea of the Universe being built in this way. Tough realist that he was, Einstein would be only moderately put out by this view. He knew that at the least he was clearing a good deal of scientific scrub. He might be regarded as a scientific curiosity; nevertheless, he was spending his last years doing a job which could be attempted by only a handful of men in the world. Therefore Einstein, a familiar figure on the tree-lined streets of Princeton in his shabby coat, old muffler and black knitted cap, was still fired by an inner certitude no less invincible than in the days of Berne and Zurich. Then he had been the silent dark horse, content to work on alone, confident of Albert Einstein. Now the older version of the man was quite as sure of the work needing to be done, happy to ignore how the rest of the world regarded him. For half a century he had stuck to his last, a Mr. Standfast of physics. He had no cause to regret the decision now.

His routine was simple. He would breakfast between 9 and 10, at the same time taking his "adrenalin cure" — reading the current political situation in the daily papers. In the winter he would be picked up from Mercer Street at about 10.30 by the green station-wagon from the Institute. He would usually walk home. In the summer he would walk to work and ride back in the early afternoon heat. On the way to the Institute, says Ernst Strauss, his assistant from 1944 until 1947, who accompanied him on occasions, a stranger would sometimes waylay him, and say how much he had wanted to meet him. "Einstein would pose with the waylayer's wife, children or grandchildren as desired and exchange a few goodhumoured words. Then he would go on, shaking his head, saying: 'Well, the old elephant has gone through his tricks again.'"

At the Institute, he would work until one o'clock, sometimes alone, sometimes with his assistant, soaring up into the mathematical stratosphere where the battle had to be fought, always with his forces well-disposed, always optimistic of eventual success, even optimistic about failures which he would face with: "Well, we've learned something." Soon after one o'clock he would put his notes into a thin worn briefcase and make for Mercer Street, sometimes stopping to chat with the two Oppenheimer children, occasionally accompanied by one of the younger faculty members or by one of the visiting professors. More frequently he walked alone. He did not like keeping good men from their duty and Miss Dukas, asking him on one occasion whether she should bring home a brilliant young mathematician just appointed to the Institute, was told: "No: let him get on with his work."

At 1.30 he would eat, then rest until the late afternoon when after a cup of tea he would work, see visitors, or more frequently deal with the correspondence which had been sorted by Miss Dukas earlier in the day. Supper came soon after 6.30 and then there would be another bout of work or more letters. Sometimes he would listen to the radio, and occasionally there were private visitors. He had by this time given up his violin, saying that he was not good enough, but continued to play Bach or Mozart each day on his Bechstein grand.

On Sundays, friends would collect him for a drive into the country or to the coast which was only an hour away. He still hated to be seen in public, and he often repeated his old claim that like Midas he changed everything he touched — but in his case it turned not into gold but into a circus.

Such was the life that went on behind the barrier raised against inquisitive callers, visitors who wanted only a glimpse of the great man or of the place where he worked and lived, and correspondents who produced an echo of the crankeries with which he had had to deal during his first days of fame in Berlin.

But there were sometimes unexpected repercussions. Thus when the IBM Corporation invited him to the unveiling of a new computer they failed to receive an answer. Dean Eisenhart of the Graduate School, Princeton University, was asked to investigate when a follow-up invitation, immaculately typed like the first one on an IBM executive machine, also failed to produce a reply.

> He explained, [says his son, Churchill Eisenhart] that something must be amiss, because Dr. Einstein was scrupulous about replying to all such invitations. He walked over to Dr. Einstein's house and explained the situation. Dr. Einstein dumped the contents of a very large wastebasket on the floor and examined an item here and there. Finally his face lighted up. He handed one of the invitational letters to my father, saying: "It looks as if it were printed. I never read printed circulars."

Life at Mercer Street was quiet and unpretentious, homely and unaffected, not blatantly the life of a genius — in fact a life in surroundings which were sometimes unexpected. "My eye", said one visitor, "was immediately caught by two inlaid cabinets containing various objects of religious art. On a canopied central shelf of one was a rather beautiful Madonna and Child; on a side-table was a statuette of a Chinese philosopher beggarman; on the wall hung a picture of the period of early Italian Christian painting."

In this house, more home of artist or polymath than theoretical physicist, Einstein was the centre-piece of a trio of women. Dominating it was Miss Dukas, since Elsa's death the person on which the main burden of the household had fallen — the housekeeper and shopper, the cook and secretary, the organiser of peace and quiet, the filer of correspondence who for lack of space was forced to store boxes of letters in the cellar and who often wished that Gutenberg had never lived. Only after Einstein's death was the priceless collection taken to the Institute to be housed in the room-safe, guarded with entry door and combination lock, that had once held the miscellaneous nuclear secrets of the former director, Robert Oppenheimer.

Also at Mercer Street there was Margot, the stepdaughter who had grown so like Einstein in attitude and outlook that it was difficult to think of them as linked only by collateral lines on the family tree. Thirdly there was Maja, two years younger than her brother, for whom he possibly felt more affection than for anyone. "Her manner of speaking and the sound of her voice, as well as the childlike and yet sceptical formulation of every statement, are unusually similar to her brother's mode of expression," Frank noted, "it is amazing to listen to her; it arouses a sense of uneasiness to find a replica of even the minor traits of a genius."

Brother and sister read much together. From 1946, when she began to be crippled by arterio-sclerosis, he would read to her every evening and he continued to do so as, from the end of 1950, her condition became more critical. Margot nursed her. But, with intelligence scarcely impaired by advancing illness, Maja died in 1951.

Since the start of the century, Einstein's life had presented a series of unexpected contradictions. The Patent Office official had been hoisted into academic life. The hater of all things German had been tempted to Berlin. The man who wanted only a quiet life had in 1919 become the most famous scientist in the world. The pacifist had been forced to support armed resistance, and the man who regarded all war as murder had helped push the buttons that killed 120,000. Now there was to come a final twist. In 1952 the image of the old eccentric, pottering along in his seventies, was to be brusquely shattered. Albert Einstein, the man who had always decried force, was invited to become President of Israel, that realisation of Zionist hopes, the state which had successfully staked out its frontiers by force of arms and was defending them against all-comers.

The proposal, practical, outrageous or pathetic according to viewpoint, splendid in its audacity if grotesque in its implications, followed the death of Chaim Weizmann, who had become first President soon after declaration of the State of Israel in May 1948. Weizmann died on Sunday November 9th, 1952, and a few days later Einstein was mooted as a successor in the Tel Aviv newspaper *Maariv*. It seems likely that this was a kite to discover public reaction. If so, it was flown by the Prime Minister, David Ben-Gurion.

> The Presidency in Israel is a symbol [he said later]. It carries with it no power. I thought to myself: if we are looking for a symbol, why not have the most illustrious Jew in the world, and possibly the greatest man alive — Einstein? That's all there was to it. Had he accepted, I would have submitted his name to the Knesset — in Israel the Knesset elects the President — and I am quite sure that the motion for his election would have been carried by acclamation.

Einstein, like most of his friends, refused to take the idea seriously and when the *New York Times* asked for his reaction on the evening of Sunday the 16th, he refused to comment. Shortly afterwards, the telephone in Mercer Street rang again and the operator said that Washington was on the line. "Herr Gott," exclaimed Miss Dukas, who had answered: "Washington. What is wrong now?" This time it was Abba Eban, the Israeli Ambassador to the United States who was making an informal enquiry. Would Einstein accept the Presidency if it were offered by a vote of the Knesset?

His reply was in keeping with his reputation. "His main and urgent thought," says Professor Mitrany who was with him when the call came through, "was how to spare the ambassador the embarrassment of his inevitable refusal."

To Eban the situation was equally clear: "Einstein was visibly moved by the splendour and audacity of the thought," he has said, "but his rejection was firm and vehement: 'I know a little about nature', he said, 'and hardly anything about men.' He implored me to accept his negative decision as final and do everything possible to divert and banish the press whose representatives were laying siege to his house in Mercer Street."

But Eban's instructions had come direct from the Prime Minister. He finally convinced Einstein that it would be improper for him to reject the proposal on the telephone, and the following day made a formal telegraphed request that he should receive his deputy to seek his "reaction on a matter of the utmost urgency and importance".

Einstein telephoned Eban, again declining the invitation. However, on Tuesday the 18th a formal letter was brought to Princeton by the Israeli minister, David Goiten. "Acceptance would entail moving to Israel and taking its citizenship," said the letter. "The Prime Minister assures me that in such circumstances complete facility and freedom to pursue your great scientific work would be afforded by the government and people who are fully conscious of the supreme significance of your labours."

It was a persuasive appeal to a man for whom the creation of Israel was a political act of an essentially moral quality. Nevertheless, Einstein felt bound to refuse. Thus the matter ended — after the editor-in-chief of *Maariv* had made an impassioned entreaty for reconsideration of the idea, and after Einstein had pointed out that however formal his functions, as President he would be responsible for the country's actions and these might conflict with his conscience.

Einstein as President was a prospect which aroused diverse emotions among those who knew him best. Weizmann had been a biochemist by profession and it might therefore be claimed that the idea of a theoretical physicist holding such a post was nothing to startle the world. Yet their links with learning and their support for Zionism were the only things which the two men had in common; in many ways their qualities were diametrically contrasted. Certainly the very characteristics of steely determination and ruthlessness which had enabled Weizmann to bring Zionism safely home to port were, except when applied to science, not in Einstein's make-up. It is possible to claim that such a world figure, transparently remote from the petty squabbles of nationalism, would never be suspected of ulterior motives, that he would be listened to where other men would be ignored. It is more likely that his innocence of public affairs would have made him easy meat for the predators of the international scene, however symbolic his appointment. The proposal was, in any case, still-born. Thirty years previously Einstein had stressed to Weizmann that his Zionist activities must be circumscribed by his need to keep quiet and get on with his work. That still held. He still put science first, second and third.

As his seventy-fifth birthday approached there were still many ways in which it seemed that while age had matured him it had hardly changed him basically. It was more than sixty years since he had decided to devote his life to a single quest, to order his days to an almost inhuman sense of priorities; nearly forty since he had reluctantly been drawn out into contact with the world of politics and power by the demands of Zionism and European peace. Yet what Einstein now stood for echoes his earlier beliefs in remarkable fashion, so that the *obiter dicta* of his last years ring like crystallised and polished examples of the casual ideas he had tossed off to fellow-students at the E.T.H. or to colleagues who broke in on his thoughts while he was remaking man's picture of the universe. He had tossed Mach overboard after long and careful thought, but most of the rest remained. About the problem of force, the dichotomy of ends and means, he appears to have returned to his instinctive pacifism, looking on the need to oppose Hitler and to sustain Israel by arms as exceptions which proved the rule. But they were, of course, the only two cases with which he had personally to deal.

As far as his own life was concerned, one thing seemed quite clear. "I made one great mistake in my life," he said to Linus Pauling, who spent an hour with him on the morning of November 11th, 1954, "... when I signed the letter to President Roosevelt recommending that atom bombs be made; but there was some justification — the danger that the Germans would make them." In a message to the American Friends of the Hebrew University, he stressed the Jewish ideal of the person who enriched the spiritual life of his people and who repudiated materialism. It was a temptation to which he had never succumbed; enjoyment of "the pleasures that nature provides", was the nearest he came to it. So too with the more insidious temptations of great success. "The only way to escape the personal corruption of praise is to go on working," he said. "One is tempted to stop and listen to it. The only thing is to turn away and go on working. Work. There is nothing else."

Some of his last scientific judgments have been put on record by the Canadian astronomer, Dr. A. Vibert Douglas, Eddington's biographer who travelled to Princeton in January 1954. Einstein began by paying a striking tribute to Eddington, whose *The Mathematical Theory of Relativity* he considered the finest presentation of the subject in any language.

> He spoke, [says Dr. Douglas] of the literary value, the beauty and brilliance of Eddington's writing in those books aimed at giving to the intelligent lay reader at least some understanding, some insight into the significance of the new scientific ideas — but with a smile he added that a scientist is mistaken if he thinks he is making the layman understand: a scientist should not attempt to popularise his

theories, if he does "he is a fakir — it is the duty of a scientist to remain obscure."

This point, which Einstein also made in other places during his later years, was in strong contrast to his earlier attempts to explain relativity in simple language. It is difficult not to see here a reflection of the disillusion with the masses which surfaced during the latter part of his life.

In regard to the developments in the early years made by Weyl and Eddington, the later theories of the expanding universe of Friedmann, Lemaître and Eddington, the still later kinematic relativity of E. A. Milne, and the yet more recent theories of continuous creation of matter of Jordan, Bondi and Hoyle, the comments of Dr. Einstein were brief and critical, [says Dr. Douglas]. He definitely disliked the hypothesis of continuous creation, he felt the necessity for a "beginning"; he regarded Milne's brilliant mathematical mind as lacking in critical judgment; he was not attracted by the idea of Lemaître's primeval atom; and he concluded by saying of his own and all the others: "Every man has his own cosmology and who can say that his own theory is right."

Thus, after two decades, what Thomson had said as a joke was repeated by Einstein in earnest.

Dr. Douglas knew that in Einstein's Berlin study there had once hung portraits of Newton and of Clerk Maxwell. Now all she saw was a portrait of Gandhi and another of a German musician. "The greatest man of our age", was how Einstein now described Gandhi; and, of Dr. Schweitzer, whose name was mentioned: "Yes, he too is a very great man."

"There remained one special thing I wanted to ask him — Who were the greatest men, the most powerful thinkers, whom he had known?" writes Dr. Douglas. "The answer came without hesitation, 'Lorentz'." None of the other theoretical physicists and cosmologists named were on the same level. "No, this one was too uncritical, that one was uneven, another was of a lesser stature... but, he added, 'I never met Willard Gibbs; perhaps, had I done so, I might have placed him beside Lorentz'." There was one other name in Dr. Douglas' thoughts: Minkowski, whose work almost half a century earlier had lifted the Special Theory of Relativity from a physical to a mathematical concept. Where would Einstein place him? "He was my very great teacher in Zurich," he said, "but I am not a good enough mathematician to know where to place him."

Just as he dotted the i's and crossed the t's of his scientific beliefs during the last year or so of his life, so did he recapitulate his religious convictions. To Dr. Douglas he stated: "If I were not a Jew I would be a Quaker." And in an interview with Professor William Hermanns he said: "I cannot accept any concept of God based on the fear of life or the fear of death or blind faith. I cannot prove to you that there is no personal God, but if I were to speak of him I would be a liar."

As to what one could believe in, the answer was simple enough. "I believe in the brotherhood of man and the uniqueness of the individual. But if you ask me to prove what I believe, I can't. You know them to be true but you could spend a whole lifetime without being able to prove them. The mind can proceed only so far upon what it knows and can prove. There comes a point where the mind takes a higher plane of knowledge, but can never prove how it got there. All great discoveries have involved such a leap." Thus, fifty years on from the papers of 1905, there came the unequivocal renunciation of Mach and his concept of divination through sensation alone.

As to the spur which pricked all men onwards, that too was simple enough to explain. "The important thing is not to stop questioning," he said. "Curiosity has its own reason for existence. One cannot help but be in awe when [one] contemplates the mysteries of eternity, of life, of the marvellous structure of reality. It is enough if one tries merely to comprehend a little of this mystery each day. Never lose a holy curiosity."

Einstein had tried to comprehend. Looking back from the vantage point of 1954 he could rightly claim to have played a major part in two achievements as great as man had ever accomplished. He had helped show that time and space were not the inelastic things which they were thought to be, but were relative to the sum total of circumstances in which they were considered. Thus he had changed the meaning attached to the word "reality". He had also encouraged physicists into accepting the dual nature of matter, that matter which had, as Sir Lawrence Bragg so percipiently stated, the perverse characteristic of being "coagulated from waves into particles by the advancing sieve of time".

These were important achievements at an intellectual level where few dared tread. Einstein had reached that level carrying little of the emotional baggage that lumbers most men. In some ways, of course, it made his task easier. He travels fastest who travels not only alone, but light; yet even in science this had brought items on the debit side. His inability to feel the human tragedy emotionally as well as intellectually had helped to disrupt his first marriage, a troublesome vexatious mistake which seems at times to have driven him to the point of desperation just when he wished to concentrate on the job in hand. These personal troubles had been overcome with his marriage to Elsa, who from 1919 helped to clear the path of greatness without complaint. To this extent the disabilities produced by his emotional isolation — by being, as he had described it to Besso as a young man, "rather cool and a bit of a hard nut" — had been overcome. He could get on with his work without worrying too much about anyone else. Outside that work, however, the aloofness which he did little to discourage brought its own reward: a man genuinely anxious to do good, he found the best of his intentions frustrated with maddening regularity.

Early in 1955 he was invited to conferences in Berne and Berlin to celebrate the fiftieth anniversary of his most famous paper. He declined. His excuses were in character: old age, poor health, and distrust of anything resembling a personality cult.

He would have enjoyed the Berne meeting, even though its appraisal of the General Theory lacked the initial scientific rapture of 1919. For the unqualified acceptance and the experimental verification that had long ago put the Special Theory beyond all dispute were still lacking here. While there was no doubt that gravity did affect light, the extent of its effect had become increasingly questioned as experimental methods improved. "A lot of work will have to be done before the astronomers really can say what is the value of the observed light deflection and whether the red shift is in existence at all," noted Freundlich at the Conference. Some of this work now has been done. But Born, to whom the General Theory continued to remain "the greatest feat of human thinking about nature", voiced qualifications which still hold. "Of the three observable consequences of the theory only the purely macroscopic one, the anomaly of the perihelion of the orbit of Mercury, is explained by Einstein's theory without doubt; the other two effects, the deflection of light-rays by the sun and the red shift of spectral lines (which are micro-phenomena), are still controversial, at least in regard to magnitude. I think that general relativity as we know it may be invalid in this domain."

Einstein would have accepted the point. More than thirty years before, walking in the grounds of the Governor's House in Jerusalem, he had remarked of Herbert Spencer's idea of tragedy — "a deduction killed by a fact" — "Every theory is killed sooner or

later in that way. But if the theory has good in it, that good is
embodied and continued in the next theory."

The jubilee meetings could carry on well enough without him.
Others could glitter in the scientific limelight while he, the man
who had started it all, wound quietly towards the end of his life
without fuss, an onlooker more than ever removed from the affairs
of the world. At least, that was the way it looked. Yet now, at
almost the last minute of the last hour, Einstein was again to be
drawn into the whirlpool of public affairs, willingly and almost
excitedly, as though determined to refute the idea that his life
would end not with a bang but a whimper.

The offer of the Presidency of Israel had come unexpectedly,
a star blazing out through the twilight at the end of a long life.
Now another arrived, and one which lit up a possible road to peace
in a way that even now is not fully appreciated.

In mid-February he received a letter from Bertrand Russell.
Both men had, in Russell's words, "opposed the First World War but
considered the Second unavoidable". Both distrusted orthodoxy and
both had been appalled by the destructive possibilities of the hydrogen bomb. Yet if both had in general sought the same objectives,
their methods had been as diametrically opposed as their characters. While Einstein had been content to continue with his work
under the aegis of the Kaiser Wilhelm, Russell had gone to prison.
While Einstein had aloofly despaired of the intelligence of mankind, Russell had protested by sitting on pavements. Einstein, for all
his genuine feelings, had rarely stepped from behind the protection
of his own interior world; Russell had insisted that he too should
be heard, tormented, anguished, and combative.

But now Russell turned to Einstein for help. He was, he wrote
on February 11th, profoundly disquieted by the nuclear arms race.
"I think that eminent men of science ought to do something dramatic to bring home to the public and governments the disasters that
may occur. Do you think it would be possible to get say, six men
of the very highest scientific repute, headed by yourself, to make
a very solemn statement about the imperative necessity of avoiding war?" The statement would best be signed by men of opposing
political creeds, and should deal not merely with the dangers of
the hydrogen bomb but with those of bacteriological warfare, thus
emphasising "the general proposition that war and science can no
longer co-exist". The letter added that the statement might
appeal to neutral countries to set up commissions of their own nationals to investigate the effect, on them, of a third world war.

Einstein replied on February 16th, 1955, with a letter which took Russell's proposal one step further. What he suggested was a public declaration, signed by a small number of scientists of international stature. Such men might even include Joliot-Curie, a leading Communist, provided they were counterbalanced by others of different views. Bohr was an obvious candidate from the uncommitted countries which Einstein hoped would supply half the signatures.

There followed another letter from Russell and a further reply from Einstein who had by this time written to Bohr. Thus Russell's initial idea was considerably influenced by Einstein and the outcome was quite rightly known as the Russell-Einstein Declaration. This was sent to Einstein by Russell on April 5th; it recapitulated the dangers of contemporary war, with special emphasis on hydrogen bombs. And it ended with the following resolution, to be put to a world convention of scientists.

In view of the fact that in any future world war nuclear weapons will certainly be employed, and that such weapons threaten the continued existence of mankind, we urge the governments of the world to realise, and to acknowledge publicly, that their purposes cannot be furthered by a world war, and we urge them, consequently, to find peaceful means for the settlement of all matters of dispute between them.

While Russell's declaration was still in the post with its accompanying letter, Einstein struck out on his own, writing to Nehru and in effect asking for his intervention in the area where an East-West war seemed most likely. This was in China where the Nationalist government's toe-hold on the offshore islands of Quemoy and Matsu threatened to lead the United States into an Asiatic quagmire. He enclosed with his letters a plan, prepared by Szilard, for the evacuation of the two islands for a definite period. Superficially this appeared the most obvious of non-starters but Einstein presumably felt that nothing but good would come of Nehru's intervention, whatever form it might take.

Three officers of the Society for Social Responsibility in Science now fortuitously called on him with a proposal for an open letter which they hoped he might sign. He explained that something similar was already afoot, that Russell was behind the move, and that he had written to Russell saying: "You understand such things. You are the general. I am just a foot soldier; give the command and I will follow." But he seems to have known that he had little time left. "He was on the porch of his house as he spoke," writes one of his visitors. "Though it was not cold he was wrapped in a blanket. And somehow the air of parting was around."

Russell's letter had stirred Einstein in a way which few things had stirred him during recent years, and he now decided that the time had come to make a major statement on the position of Israel, whose Independence Day in May was to be held in circumstances even more ominous than usual. The threats from her ring of Arab neighbours were growing while the announcement that Czechoslovakia and Russia were both to supply Egypt with arms added a new and more dangerous menace. Counter-measures were in fact already under way and Mr. Dulles had agreed to release to the Israelis a dozen Mystère fighters from the U. S. contingent to NATO as well as twenty-four Sabre jets from another source. But these measures were still unknown to the general public; this included Einstein — who only a few weeks earlier had claimed that the current Eisenhower administration was seeking "to win the sympathy of the Arab nations by sacrificing Israel".

He was therefore particularly receptive when, early in April, the Israeli authorities in Washington asked if he would make an Independence Day statement dealing with the country's scientific and cultural activities and stressing the peaceful uses of atomic energy. He would like to help, he replied on April 4th. But, in the present circumstances, cultural and scientific developments were hardly relevant. What Einstein thought might be most effective was an analysis of western policies with regard to Israel and the Arab states.

Here was a unique opportunity. The Israeli Ambassador, Abba Eban, seized it with both hands and on April 11th arrived at Mercer Street with the Israeli consul, Reuven Dafni.

Professor Einstein told me [he later wrote] that he saw the rebirth of Israel as one of the few political acts in his lifetime which had an essential moral quality. He believed that the conscience of the world should, therefore, be involved in Israel's preservation. He had always refused the requests of television and radio networks to project his views to public opinion. This issue, however, seemed to him to be of such importance that he was actually taking the initiative, through me, of seeking the opportunity to address the American people and the world. He showed me the draft which he had begun to prepare. He had reached the end of a long preamble on the Cold War and wished to hear my views at greater length before discussing the political aspects of the Middle Eastern situation.

Eban and his colleague talked with Einstein for some while and it was agreed that Dafni should return in a few days when Einstein had put the draft of his proposed address into more finished form.

On the same day, the 11th, he received the expected statement from Russell, and an accompanying list of scientists who would be asked to sign it. He agreed with the choice of names. And he signed the document. Thus he helped launch the manifesto, calling for a conference to appraise the perils of war and leading directly to the long series of influential Pugwash Conferences attended by prominent scientists from the United States, Britain and Russia among more than a dozen countries.*

The following day Einstein was in pain. But he refused to allow the doctor to be called and it was without his knowledge that Miss Dukas telephoned Margot, then ill in the local hospital, and said that Einstein's personal doctor should be told.

Despite pain, Einstein worked on his Independence Day broadcast, to be further discussed with the Israeli consul the next day.

On the 13th, he was still in pain. But in the morning he received both the Israeli consul and Janos Plesch who had come from New York. He went over his draft with Dafni. He also made additional notes. Some mystery surrounds their fate. The editors of *Einstein on Peace*, one of whom was Einstein's literary executor, describe them as "not available"; but they could find nothing to support a later rumour that the notes had been stolen from the Princeton hospital. And they criticise a "reconstruction" of Einstein's planned address, based on information provided by Dafni, subsequently published in the *New York Times*. The most likely conclusion is that the notes, whatever happened to them, were too critical of "East", of "West", or of both sides in the power-game, to be openly admitted as coming from Einstein.

Dafni left Mercer Street by midday. Soon afterwards, Einstein complained of extreme tiredness and lack of appetite. After a light meal he lay down to rest: in mid-afternoon he collapsed. Miss Dukas, managing the situation singlehanded, called the doctor who soon arrived with two colleagues, helped as an electro-cardiagram was taken, fixed up a bed in the study, and prepared for a long vigil. The patient, given morphia injections, passed a quiet night.

* Full details of the course and influence of the Pugwash Conferences are given in *Pugwash: A History of the Conferences on Science and World Affairs* by J. Rotblat (Prague, Czechoslovak Academy of Sciences, 1967).

Dr. Dean, who found Einstein "very stoical" and "his usual kind shy self", had diagnosed a small leakage of blood from a hardened aorta, and on the morning of Thursday the 14th Dr. Frank Glenn, the cardiac and aortic surgeon, arrived from New York. So did Dr. Ehrmann and Dr. Bucky. One question had to be settled quickly; whether or not to operate. By 1955 this was possible, although the chances of survival during such an operation were still low — some experts put it at fifty per cent; without it they were minimal.

Years earlier, when Einstein had first learned of his condition and been told that his aorta might burst unless he took care, he had brusquely replied: "Let it burst." Now he was similarly uncompromising. He asked Dean how long death would take and was told that it might come in a moment, might take hours, or might take days. He was, his doctor said, "violently opposed" to surgery. To Miss Dukas, he later protested: "The end comes some time: does it matter when?" Just as in physics he had developed into the conservative revolutionary, so in medicine he tended to distrust what he thought of as radical innovations; it had once been impossible to operate on a man in his condition, and he would have none of it now.

Friday night passed quietly and on Saturday morning he seemed to be better. Then, once again, there was intense pain and he was unable to move. On the arrival of the doctor, hastily called by Miss Dukas, he at first refused to budge. Most patients would have been quickly overruled; but even now it was not easy to overrule Einstein. Finally, he was persuaded that hospital was best; characteristically, the argument which counted was that the nursing was too much for Miss Dukas.

On the way to the hospital he talked animatedly to one of the volunteer ambulance men. After arrival he began to feel better and he soon telephoned Mercer Street. First he wanted his spectacles; then he wanted writing material. If there was still time left it should not be wasted.

On Sunday Margot was wheeled in to see him, but almost failed to recognise him. He would go in his own time, and insisted on one thing: "Do not let the house become a museum." He had already asked that his office at the Institute should not be preserved as he had used it, but passed on for the use of others. He did not want Mercer Street turned into a place of pilgrimage and he would have had little sympathy for those who in later years called at No. 112 asking to see his study; for those who were to write to the Institute for mementoes; or for the correspondents who from as far away as

India wrote to his son Hans Albert pleading for a piece of anything that Albert Einstein had touched. He would have been surprised that an opera based on his life should be written for presentation in East Berlin, astonished at the million words that were cabled out of Princeton as the Press moved in after his death. He would have exploded in one of his hearty gusts of laughter at the value of his signature and the hundreds of pounds which was soon to be the market price of his letters. He had wanted all this to die with him.

He had insisted that his brain should be used for research and that he be cremated; but his ashes were to be scattered at an undisclosed place. Again, no point of pilgrimage. He would have agreed with his literary executor, Otto Nathan, who was to write that the less published about Einstein's illness and the developments that led to his death, the better; Nathan did not see why the public should have an interest in the details, or why he and others should satisfy it if they had.

Hans Albert and Nathan arrived in Princeton on Sunday. With the first, Einstein discussed science; with the latter, politics and the danger of German rearmament. He was equable now, and late in the afternoon Dr. Dean even felt that the aneurysm might be repairing itself. With a recurrence of pain in the evening Einstein was given another injection; but he was sleeping peacefully when Dean took a final look at 11 p. m.

In the small hours, soon after midnight, nurse Alberta Roszel, noticed a difference in his breathing. Becoming alarmed, she called for assistance, and with the aid of another nurse cranked up the head of the bed.

He was muttering in German, the language of his despised compatriots, still the only tongue with which he felt comfortable. It was with Germans that he had first won his spurs and in Berlin that he had first become world-famous. It was only in German that he could contemplate the course of his life: his dedication to science and the subjugation of everything else; the self-imposed emotional asceticism; his belief that the human race was naturally aggressive and Germans more aggressive than the rest. It was in German that the last thoughts of one of the greatest brains since Newton's came to the surface through the unconscious mind.

Perhaps he should not have been so bearish about people? Perhaps he should never have gone to Berlin, made the way that much easier for the aggressors with his pacifism, or hated the Germans so much that he encouraged Roosevelt into the nuclear age? Perhaps he should not always have put science first? But on this there

was of course no room for doubt, no cause for regret. As he took
two deep breaths and died, it is unlikely that Einstein regretted very
much, if he regretted anything at all. But Mrs. Roszel did not understand his German. And anyway, as Elsa had felt nearly twenty
years before, dear God it was too late now.

# Sources and Bibliography

# SOURCES
# AND BIBLIOGRAPHY

The original material for a life of Albert Einstein is scattered throughout the libraries and archives of Europe, the United States and the Middle East. The largest single collections are the Einstein Archives in Princeton, currently housed at the Institute for Advanced Study, and the Einstein-Sammlung der E.T.H. Bibliothek in Zurich. The Princeton collection is particularly rich in records of Einstein's later years, but as his executor, Dr. Otto Nathan, has written: "Einstein himself was not greatly concerned with a systematic collection of his papers and correspondence; only in the last few decades of his life was sufficient attention paid to the preservation of the many important documents and letters that crossed his desk." The collection in the Eidgenossische Technische Hochschule, Zurich (E.T.H.), where Einstein both studied and taught, is naturally strong in the records of his years in Switzerland. These however are only two of the sources of original material.

Much of Einstein's long correspondence with Lorentz is divided between the Algemeen Rijksarchiv in The Hague and the Rijksmuseum voor de Geschiedenis der Natuurwetenschappen in Leiden. His meeting and early relationship with Erwin Freundlich is dealt with in the correspondence held until recently by Frau Freundlich. His friendship with Professor Lindemann — later Lord Cherwell — which began at the Solvay Congress in 1911 and continued to within a few years of his death, is covered by the Cherwell Papers in Nuffield College, Oxford. Light is thrown on his connections with the Solvay Institute by the papers at present being used by Doctor Jagdish Mehra for a history of the Congress, and on his move to Prague by the Adler Archives in Vienna. The Hale Papers and the Millikan Papers are among important material in the California Institute of Technology dealing with Einstein's early visits to the United States.

The archives of the League of Nations Library in Geneva contain much new information on Einstein's membership of the International Committee for Intellectual Co-operation, while the Royal

Library in Brussels contains his correspondence with H. M. Queen
Elizabeth of the Belgians and details of his early visits to the Royal
Palace at Laeken. The 190 pages of correspondence in the Weizmann
Archives, Rehovot, and the Samuel Papers in the House of Lords
Record Office, London, deal with Einstein's connections with Zion-
ism from 1918 until the year of his death. And the Stadtarchiv,
Ulm; the Israelitische Kultusvereinigung Württemberg und Hohen-
zollern; the Geheimes Staatsarchiv, Berlin; and many other German
sources provide the documentary evidence for his birth, background,
and citizenship.

The Rutherford Papers in the University of Cambridge; the
Haldane Papers in the National Library of Scotland; the Bibliothèque Nationale, Paris; the Curie Laboratory Archives, Paris; the Russell Archives, McMaster University, Hamilton, Ontario; the Roosevelt Library, Hyde Park, N. Y.; and the archives of the University of
Utrecht all provide material dealing with his life and work. Two
important unpublished manuscripts are Ehrenhaft's "My Experiences with Einstein" held by the Burndy Library, Norwalk, Connecticut; and "Comments on the letters of Professor and Mrs. Albert Einstein to Dr. Leon L. Watters", copies of which are held by the American Jewish Archives and by the California Institute of Technology.

Useful collections of private letters include the correspondence
of Professor and Mrs. Einstein with Leon L. Watters held by the
American Jewish Archives; the Bucky letters held by the University
of Texas; the Koch letters written by Einstein to his relatives in
Belgium, held by the Université Libre, Brussels; the Kocherthaler
letters, writen to relatives in South America, in private hands in Montevideo; the correspondence with Dr. Janos Plesch, held by the Plesch
family. In some ways the most important of all is Einstein's long
correspondence with Michelangelo Besso, continuing for almost half
a century, the various biographical aspects of which have been
pointed out to me by Professor Jagdish Mehra of the University
of Texas.

The Szilard Archives in San Diego contain much valuable background to the famous letter to Roosevelt, while the U. S. Atomic
Energy Commission, the Office of the Chief of Naval Operations,
and the National Archives and Records Service are among the official sources which hold material dealing with Einstein's work during
the Second World War.

All these sources have been drawn upon, as well as the following:

Allgemeines Staatsarchiv, Munich; American Institute of Physics; Auswärtiges, Amt, Bonn; Bureau Fédéral de la Propriété Intellectuelle, Berne; University of Chicago; Christ Church Library, Oxford; Library of Congress, Washington, D. C.; Deutsche Staatsbibliothek, Berlin; Deutsches Zentralarchiv, Potsdam; Perkins Library, Duke University, Durham, North Carolina; University of Edinburgh; Geheimes Staatsarchiv, Berlin; University of Göttingen; Landesarchiv, Berlin; MacArthur Memorial Archives, Norfolk, Virginia; University of Manchester; Max Planck - Gesellschaft, Berlin and Munich; John Murray Archives, London; National Personnel Records Centre, St. Louis, Missouri; Rhodes Trust, Oxford; Royal Netherlands Academy of Sciences and Letters, Amsterdam; Schweizer Schuler, Milan; Senatsverwaltung der Stadt, Berlin; University of Sheffield; Staatsbibliothek der Stiftung Preussischer Kulturbesitz, Berlin; Stanford University, Palo Alto, California; Records of Swiss Federal Council, Berne; Swiss National Library, Berne; University of Syracuse; UNESCO Archives, Paris.

Printed Material

The bulk of Einstein's scientific work is contained in the papers listed in *Albert Einstein. A Bibliography of his Scientific Papers, 1901–1930* by E. Weil (London, 1937). Later bibliographies include that given in *Albert Einstein: Philosopher-Scientist* edited by Paul A. Schlipp (Evanston, Ill., 1949) and *A Bibliographical Checklist and Index to the Collected Writings of Albert Einstein*, Readex Microprint edition compiled by Nell Boni, Monique Russ and Dan H. Laurence (New York, 1960); both include Einstein's non-scientific writings and bibliographical details of many interviews.

Einstein's key papers on relativity are printed, together with other relevant papers by H. A. Lorentz, H. Minkowski and H. Weyl, in *The Principle of Relativity,* (Methuen, London 1923 and Dover, New York, 1952) while his own *Relativity: The Special and the General Theory* is available in a succession of editions and translations from 1920 onwards. His major papers on the Brownian Movement are contained in *Investigations on the Theory of the Brownian Movement*, edited by R. Furth, (London, 1926). Important material dealing with the birth of quantum mechanics is contained in *Letters on Wave Mechanics — Schrödinger, Planck, Einstein, and Lorentz,* edited by K. Przibram (Philosophical Library, New York and Vision Press, London, 1967), while Einstein letters dealing with science in general and with non-scientific subjects are contained in *Briefwechsel — Albert Einstein / Arnold Sommerfeld,* edited and with commentary by Armin Hermann (Schwabe, Basel and Stuttgart, 1968) and in *Briefwechsel 1916—1955 — Albert Einstein / Max Born* (Nymphenburger, 2 March, 1969; *Born-Einstein Letters*, London, 1971).

Books explaining relativity and putting Einstein's work in the larger context of science are as numerous as their quality is varied. Among the best are *Relativity Theory: Its Origins and Impact on Modern Thought* edited by L. Pearce Williams (New York, 1968); Max Born's *Einstein's Theory of Relativity* (London, 1924); Pauli's *Theory of Relativity* (New York, 1958); Clement V. Durell's *Readable Relativity* (London, 1966); Lincoln Barnett's *The Universe and Dr. Einstein* (London, 1949); Freundlich's *The Foundations of Einstein's Theory of Gravitation* (Cambridge, 1920); Russell's *The A. B. C. of Relativity* (London, 1925); Bondi's *Relativity and Commonsense* (London, 1964); Charles Nordmann's *Einstein and the Universe* (London, 1922); and Cornelius Lanczos' *Albert Einstein and the Cosmic World Order* (London, 1965).

A number of Einstein's miscellaneous writings are contained in *The World As I see It*, (London, 1935) and *Out of My Later Years* (London, 1950), and a selection of speeches and letters in *About Zionism* (London, 1930). Many of his early pacifist writings are included in *The Fight Against War* edited by Alfred Lief (New York, 1933) and the bulk of them in *Einstein on Peace* edited by Otto Nathan and Heinz Norden (London, 1963).

Einstein's autobiographical writings are limited to the — exclusively scientific — account of his development in Schilpp's *Albert Einstein: Philosopher-Scientist* (Evanston, Ill., 1949), and the brief notes in *Helle Zeit: Dunkle Zeit* (Zurich, 1956), a volume of reminiscences edited by Carl Seelig. The first attempt to give him a biographical background was made by Alexander Moszkowski in *Einstein the Searcher: His Work Explained from Dialogues with Einstein* (Berlin, 1921), a book which Einstein's friends ineffectively urged him to suppress. It was the first of the many. The husband of one stepdaughter produced a pseudonymous biography — *Albert Einstein* by A. Reiser (London, 1931) — to which Einstein gave his cachet; the husband of another produced, together with a journalist colleague, a book — *Einstein* (New York, 1944) — which he repudiated. His doctor friend, Janos Plesch, devoted two chapters of his autobiographical *Janos* (London, 1947) to Albert Einstein; a writer-friend of his second wife, Antonina Vallentin, wrote a personal account of his life; while a Berlin acquaintance, David Reichinstein, wrote an *Albert Einstein* which its subject unsuccessfully tried to suppress. Three lives written with varying degrees of blessing from their subject are: Philipp Frank's *Einstein: His Life and Times* (London, 1948), Carl Seelig's *Albert Einstein* (London, 1956), and Leopold Infeld's *Albert Einstein* (London, 1950).

The files of *Annalen der Physik, Nature, Science, The Times* and the *New York Times* have been used extensively, as have many other journals, magazines and papers to which individual reference is made in the details of sources on pp 611—648. The following is a select bibliography of the books and journal articles which have been found useful or to which specific reference is made below. For convenience, the bibliographical details of Einstein's main papers are given here; but the full list of his scientific publications runs to nearly forty pages and should be consulted, if required, in one of the bibliographies referred to above.

# Bibliography

ADAMS, Walter S., "George Ellery Hale", reprinted from *Astrophysical Journal* Vol. 87, 1938.

BADASH, L. (ed.), *Rutherford and Boltwood: Letters on Radioactivity*, New Haven, 1969.
BARKER, Sir Ernest, *Age and Youth*, Oxford, 1953.
BARNETT, Lincoln, *The Universe and Dr. Einstein*, London, 1949.
BAXTER, James Phinney, *Scientists Against Time*, Boston, 1946.
BELL, E. T., *Men of Mathematics*, London, 1965.
BELL, G. K. A., *Randall Davidson, Archbishop of Canterbury*, London, 1935.
BEN-GURION, David, *Ben-Gurion Looks Back in Talks with Moshe Pearlman*, London, 1965.
BENTWICH, Norman, *The Hebrew University of Jerusalem 1918—60*, London, 1961.
BENTWICH, Norman, *Judah L. Magnes*, Philadelphia, 1954.
BENTWICH, Norman, *My Seventy-Seven Years: An Account of My Life and Times 1881—1960*, London, 1962.
BENTWICH, Norman, *The Rescue and Achievement of Refugee Scholars*, The Hague, 1953.
BENTWICH, Norman, *Wanderer Between Two Worlds*, London, 1941.
BENTWICH, Norman and Helen, *Mandate Memories 1918—1948*, London, 1965.
BIRKENHEAD, The Earl of, *The Prof in Two Worlds*, London, 1961.
BLUMENFELD, Kurt, *Erlebte Judenfrage*, Stuttgart, 1962.
BOHR, Niels, *Essays 1958—1962 on Atomic Physics and Human Knowledge*, New York, 1963.
BONDI, Hermann, *Assumption and Myth in Physical Theory*, Cambridge, 1965.
BONDI, Hermann, *Relativity and Commonsense*, London, 1964.
BOORSTIN, Daniel (ed.), *An American Primer*, Chicago, 1966.
BORK, Alfred H., "The Fitzgerald Contraction", *Isis*, Vol. 57 (1966), pp. 199—207.

BORN, Max, *Born-Einstein Letters, 1916—1955,* London, 1971.

BORN, Max, *Einstein's Theory of Relativity,* New York, 1962.

BORN, Max, *Natural Philosophy of Cause and Chance* (The Waynflete Lectures, 1948), Oxford, 1949.

BORN, Max, *Physics in My Generation,* London, 1956, and New York, 1969.

BRAUNTHAL, Julius, *In Search of the Millennium,* London, 1945.

BRODETSKY, Professor Selig, *Memoirs: From Ghetto to Israel,* London, 1960.

BUBER, Martin, *The Knowledge of Man,* London, 1965.

BUCKY, Thomas Lee, "Einstein: An Intimate Memoir", *Harper's Magazine,* September 1964.

BYRNES, James F., *All in One Lifetime,* New York, 1958.


CAMPBELL, Lewis, and W. Garnet, *James Clerk Maxwell,* London, 1884.

CLARK, Ronald W., *The Birth of the Bomb,* London, 1961.

CLARK, Ronald W., *Tizard,* London, 1965.

CLINE, Barbara Lovett, *The Questioners: Physicists and the Quantum Theory,* New York, 1965.

COHEN, Harry A., "An Afternoon with Einstein", *Jewish Spectator,* January, 1969, p. 13.

COHEN, I. Bernard, "An Interview with Einstein", *Scientific American,* Vol. 193 (1955), p. 69.

COHEN, Morris Raphael, *A Dreamer's Journey,* Boston, 1949.

COHEN, Morris Raphael, "Einstein and His World", *The Menorah Journal,* Vol. 24 (Spring, 1936), p. 107.

COHEN, Morris Raphael, *The Faith of a Liberal,* New York, 1946.

COMPTON, Arthur H., "The Scattering of X-Rays", *Journal of the Franklin Institute,* Vol. 198 (1924).


DAMPIER, Sir William, *A Shorter History of Science,* London, 1945.

DE BROGLIE, Louis, *New Perspectives in Physics,* Edinburgh, 1962.

DE BROGLIE, Louis, *The Revolution in Physics: A Non-Mathematical Survey of Quanta,* London, 1954.

DE SITTER, Professor W., "Einstein's Theory of Gravitation" from: *Monthly Notices* of the Royal Astronomical Society, Vol. LXXVI, p. 702., 1916.

DE SITTER, W., "From Newton to Einstein," *Kosmos: A Course of Six Lectures on the Development of Our Insight into the Structure of the Universe,* Cambridge and Harvard, 1932.

DEUEL, Wallace, *People Under Hitler*, London, 1942.

DOUGLAS, A. Vibert, "Forty Minutes with Einstein," *Journal of the Royal Astronomical Society of Canada*, Vol. 50, No. 3, p. 99.

DOUGLAS, A. Vibert, *The Life of Arthur Stanley Eddington*, London, 1956.

DURRELL, Clement V., *Readable Relativity*, London, 1966.

EDDINGTON, Sir Arthur, *Relativity* (Eighth Annual Haldane Lecture, May 26, 1937), London, 1937.

EDDINGTON, Sir Arthur, *Report on the Relativity Theory of Gravitation*, London, 1918.

EDDINGTON, Sir Arthur, *Space, Time and Gravitation*, London, 1920.

EDDINGTON, Sir Arthur, *The Theory of Relativity and its Influence on Scientific Thought* (Romanes Lecture, May 24, 1922), Oxford, 1922.

EHRENHAFT, Felix, "My Experiences with Einstein" (unpublished).

EINSTEIN, Albert, *About Zionism: Speeches and Letters by Professor Albert Einstein* (Ed. & Trans: Leon Simon) London, 1930.

EINSTEIN, Albert, *The Fight Against War*, Alfred Lief, ed. New York, 1933.

EINSTEIN, Albert, *Ideas and Opinions*, London, 1964.

EINSTEIN, Albert, *Investigations on the Theory of the Brownian Movement*, Methuen, 1926.

EINSTEIN, Albert, *Lettres à Maurice Solovine*, Paris, 1956.

EINSTEIN, Albert, *Out of My Later Years*, London, 1950.

EINSTEIN, Albert, *The Theory of Relativity*, London, 1924.

EINSTEIN, Albert, *On the Method of Theoretical Physics* (The Herbert Spencer Lecture, June 10, 1933), Oxford, 1933.

EINSTEIN, Albert, *"The Origins of the General Theory of Relativity"* (First Lecture of the George A. Gibson Foundation in the University of Glasgow June 20, 1933), Glasgow, 1933.

EINSTEIN, Albert, *Why War?* London, 1934.

EINSTEIN, Albert, *The World As I See It*, London, 1935.

EINSTEIN, Albert, and Max Born, *Briefwechsel 1916–1955*, Munich, 1969. (*Born - Einstein Letters*, London, 1971)

EINSTEIN, Albert, and Leopold Infeld, *The Evolution of Physics*, Cambridge, 1938.

EINSTEIN, Albert, Erwin Schrödinger, Max Planck, H. A.

Lorentz, *Letters on Wave Mechanics,* ed. K. Przibram, London and New York, 1967.

EINSTEIN, Albert, and Arnold Sommerfeld, *Briefwechsel,* Basel and Stuttgart, 1968.

*The following are Einstein's more famous scientific papers:*

1905: "Über einen die Erzeugung und Verwandlung des Lichtes betreffenden heuristischen Gesichtspunkt", *Annalen der Physik* Ser. 4, Vol. 17, 1905, pp. 132–148.

1905: "Über die von der molekularkinetischen Theorie der Wärme geforderte Bewegung von in ruhenden Flüssigkeiten suspendierten Teilchen", *Annalen der Physik,* Ser. 4, Vol. 17, 1905, pp. 549–560.

1905: "Zur Elektrodynamik bewegter Körper", *Annalen der Physik,* Ser. 4, Vol. 17, 1905, pp. 891–921.

1905: "Ist die Trägheit eines Körpers von seinem Energieinhalt abhängig?" *Annalen der Physik,* Ser. 4, Vol. 18, 1905, pp. 639–641.

1907: "Die Plank'sche Theorie der Strahlung und die Theorie der spezifischen Wärme", *Annalen der Physik,* Ser. 4, Vol. 22, 1907, pp. 180–190 and p. 800 (Berichtigung).

1907: "Über das Relativitätsprinzip und die aus demselben gezogenen Folgerungen", *Jahrbuch der Radioaktivität und Elektronik,* Vol. 4, 1907, pp. 411–462, and Vol. 5, 1908, pp. 98–99 (Berichtigungen).

1909: "Über die Entwicklung unserer Anschauungen über das Wesen und die Konstitution der Strahlung", *Physikalische Zeitschrift,* Vol. 10, 1909, pp. 817–825.

1911: "Über den Einfluss der Schwerkraft auf die Ausbreitung des Lichtes", *Annalen der Physik,* Ser. 4, Vol. 35, 1911, pp.898–908.

1913: "Entwurf einer verallgemeinerten Relativitätstheorie und eine Theorie der Gravitation" I. Physikalischer Teil von A. Einstein. II. Mathematischer Teil von M. Grossmann. Leipzig, 1913, Teubner, 38, pp. Sonderdruck aus *Zeitschrift für Mathematik und Physik,* Vol. 62, 1913, pp. 225–262 (Physikalischer Teil, pp. 225–244).

1915: "Erklärung der Perihelbewegung des Merkur aus der allgemeinen Relativitätstheorie", *Preussische Akademie der Wissenschaften, Sitzungsberichte,* 1915, Pt. 2, pp. 831–839.

1916: "Die Grundlage der allgemeinen Relativitätstheorie", *Annalen der Physik,* Ser. 4, Vol. 49, 1916, pp. 769–822.

1917: "Zur Quantentheorie der Strahlung", *Physikalische Zeitschrift*, Vol. 18, 1917, pp. 121—128.

1917: "Kosmologische Betrachtungen zur allgemeinen Relativitätstheorie", *Preussische Akademie der Wissenschaften, Sitzungsberichte*, 1917, Pt. 1, pp. 142—152.

1923: "Zur affinen Feldtheorie", *Preussische Akademie der Wissenschaften, Phys.-math. Klasse, Zitzungsberichte*, 1923, pp. 137—140.

1924: "Quantentheorie des einatomigen idealen Gases", *Preussische Akademie der Wissenschaften, Phys-math. Klasse, Sitzungsberichte*, 1924, pp. 261—267.

and

1925: "Quantentheorie des einatomigen idealen Gases. 2. Abhandlung", *Preussische Akademie der Wissenschaften, Phys-math. Klasse, Sitzungsberichte*, 1925, pp. 3—14.

1928: "Fundamental Concepts of Physics and Their Most Recent Changes", *St. Louis Post-Dispatch*, December 29, 1928.

1929: "Zur Einheitlichen Feldtheorie", *Preussische Akademie der Wissenschaften, Phys.-math. Klasse, Sitzungsberichte*, 1929, pp. 2—7.

1933: *On the Method of Theoretical Physics*. The Herbert Spencer Lecture delivered at Oxford, June 10, 1933. Oxford, 1933.

1933: *Origins of the General Theory of Relativity*. Lecture on the George A. Gibson Foundation in the University of Glasgow, June 20, 1933. Glasgow, (Glasgow University Publications, No. 30) 1933.

1935: "Can Quantum-Mechanical Description of Physical Reality Be Considered Complete?" with B. Podolsky and N. Rosen. *Physical Review*, Ser. 2, Vol. 47, 1935, pp. 777—780.


EISENHART, Churchill, "Albert Einstein As I Remember Him", *Journal of the Washington Academy of Sciences*, Vol. 54 (1964) pp. 325—328.

EPSTEIN, Jacob, *Let There Be Sculpture*, London, 1940.

EVE, A. S., *Rutherford*, Cambridge, 1939.


FERMI, Laura, *Illustrious Immigrants: The Intellectual Migration from Europe 1930—1941*, Chicago, 1968.

FIERZ, M., and V. F. Weisskopf, *Theoretical Physics in the Twentieth Century: A Memorial Volume to Wolfgang Pauli*, New York and London, 1960.

FISHER, H. A. L., *The History of Europe*, London, 1936.

FITZROY, Sir Almeric, *Memoirs, Vol. II*, London, n. d.

FLAMMARION, Camille, *Lumen*, Paris, 1873.

FLEXNER, Abraham, *I Remember*, New York, 1940.

FLUCKIGER, Max, *A. E. in Bern*, Berne.

FRANK, Philipp, *Einstein: His Life and Times*, London, 1948.

FRANK, Philipp, *Interpretations and Misinterpretations of Modern Physics*, Paris, 1938.

FRANK, Philipp, *Modern Science and Its Philosophy*, Cambridge, Mass., 1949.

FRANK, Philipp, *Relativity — A Richer Truth*, London, 1951.

FREUD, Sigmund, *Letters of Sigmund Freud, 1873—1939*, London, 1961.

FREUNDLICH, Erwin, *The Foundations of Einstein's Theory of Gravitation*, Cambridge, 1920.

FURER, Admiral, *Administration of the Navy Department in World War Two*, Washington, D. C., 1959.


GAMOW, George, *My World Line*, New York, 1970.

GEORGE, Hereford, *The Oberland and Its Glaciers, Explored and Illustrated with Ice-Axe and Camera*, London, 1866.

GILPIN, Robert, *American Scientists and Nuclear Weapons Policy*, Princeton, N. J., 1926.

GOLDMAN, Nahum, *Memories*, London, 1970.

GORAN, Morris, *The Story of Fritz Haber*, Norman, Okla., 1967.

GOUDSMIT, Samuel A., *Alsos*, New York, 1947.

GOWING, Margaret, *Britain and Atomic Energy 1939—1945*, London, 1964.

GROSSMANN, Kurt R., "Peace Movements in Germany", *South Atlantic Quarterly* (July, 1950), Durham, N. C.


HAAS-LORENTZ, G. J. de (ed.), *H. A. Lorentz: Impressions of His Life and Work*, Amsterdam, 1957.

HADAMARD, Jacques, *An Essay on the Psychology of Invention in the Mathematical Field*, Princeton, N. J., 1945.

HAHN, Otto, *My Life*, London, 1970.

HALDANE, R. B., *The Reign of Relativity*, London, 1921.

HANNAK, Dr. J., *Emanuel Lasker: The Life of a Chess Master*, London, 1959.

HARROD, R. F., *The Prof*, London, 1959.

HARTSHORNE, Edward Yarnall Jr., *The German Universities and National Socialism*, London, 1937.

HEISENBERG, Werner, *Physics and Philosophy: The Revolution in Modern Science*, New York, 1962.

*Helvetica Physica Acta*, Supplementum IV, Basel, 1956.

HERNECK, Friedrich, "Über die deutsche Reichsangehörigkeit Albert Einstein", *Die Naturwissenschaften*, Heft 2, S 33, 1961.

HEWLETT, G., and E. D. Anderson, Jr., *The New World, 1939—1946*, University Park, Penn., 1962.

HOFFMAN, Banesh, *The Strange Story of the Quantum*, New York, 1959.

HOLTON, Gerald, "Mach, Einstein and the Search for Reality", (reprinted from *Daedalus*, Journal of the American Academy of Arts and Sciences) Spring 1968. Richmond, Virginia.

HOLTON, Gerald, "Einstein, Michelson and the Crucial Experiment", *Isis*, Vol. 60, Part 2, No. 202, 1969.

HOLTON, Gerald, "On the Origin of the Special Theory of Relativity", *American Journal of Physics*, Vol. 28, 1960.

HUBBLE, Edwin, *The Observational Approach to Cosmology* (The Rhodes Memorial Lectures, 1936) Oxford, 1937.

INFELD, Leopold, *Albert Einstein: His Work and Its Influence on Our World"*, New York and London, 1950.

INFELD, Leopold, "As I See It", *Bulletin of the Atomic Scientists*, February, 1965.

INFELD, Leopold, *Quest: The Evolution of a Scientist*, New York, 1941.

INGE, The Very Rev. W. R., *Diary of a Dean: St. Pauls 1911—1934*, London, 1949.

INGE, William Ralph, *God and the Astronomers*, London, 1933.

JAFFE, Bernard, *Michelson and the Speed of Light*, London, 1961.

JEANS, Sir James, *The New Background of Science*, Ann Arbor, Mich., 1959.

JEANS, Sir James, *The Universe Around Us*, Cambridge, 1930.

JONES, R. V., "Thicker than Heavy Water", *Chemistry and Industry*, August 26, 1967.

KARMAN, Theodore von, *The Wind and Beyond*, Toronto, 1967.

KISCH F. H., *Palestine Diary*, London, 1938.

KLEIN, Martin J., "Einstein's First Paper on Quanta", *The Natural Philosopher*, Vol 2., New York, 1963.

KLEIN, Martin J., "Einstein and the Wave-Particle Duality", *The Natural Philosopher*, Vol. 3, New York, 1964.

KLEIN, Martin J., *Paul Ehrenfest*, Vol. I., *The Making of a Theoretical Physicist*, Amsterdam, 1970.
KUZNETSOV, B., *Einstein*, Moscow, 1965.

LEMAÎTRE, Georges, "The Beginning of the World from the Point of View of the Quantum Theory," *Nature*, Vol. 127 (1931), p. 706.
LEMAÎTRE, Georges, *The Primeval Atom: An Essay on Cosmogony*, New York, 1950.
LIEF, Alfred (ed.), *The Fight Against War*, New York, 1933.
LINDEMANN, F. A., "Einstein's Theory: A Revolution in Thought", *Times Educational Supplement*, January 29, 1920.
LINDEMANN, A. F. and F. A., "Daylight Photography of Stars as a Means of Testing Equivalence Postulate in the Theory of Relativity" *Monthly Notices* of the Royal Astronomical Society. Vol: LXXII, December 2, 1916.
LODGE, Sir Oliver, "Einstein's Real Achievement", *Fortnightly Review*, DCLVII, new series, September, 1921.
LORENTZ, H. A., *H. A. Lorentz: Impressions of his Life and Work* (ed. G. J. de Haas-Lorentz) Amsterdam, 1957.
LORENTZ, H. A., Albert Einstein, H. Weyl and A. Minkowski, *The Principle of Relativity, A Collection of Original Memoirs on the Special and General Theory of Relativity*, New York, 1952.
LOVELL, Sir Bernard, *Our Present Knowledge of the Universe*, Manchester, 1967.
LOWENSTEIN, Prince Hubertus of, *Towards the Farther Shore*, London, 1968.

MACH, Ernst, *The Science of Mechanics*, Chicago and London, 1907.
MARIANOFF, Dimitri, and Palm Wayne, *Einstein: An Intimate Study of a Great Man*, New York, 1944.
MARTIN, Kingsley, *Editor; a Second Volume of Autobiography, 1931—45*, London, 1968.
MEITNER, Lise, "As I Remember", *Bulletin of the Atomic Scientists*, November, 1964.
MICHELMORE, Peter, *Einstein: Profile of the Man*, London, 1963.
MILLIKAN, Robert A., *The Autobiography of Robert A. Millikan*, London, 1951.
MILLIKAN, Robert A., *The Electron*, Chicago, 1917.

MILLIKAN, Robert, A., *Time, Matter and Values*, Chapel Hill, N. C., 1932.

MILNE, E. A., *The Aims of Mathematical Physics*, Oxford, 1930.

MILNE, E. A., *Modern Cosmology and the Christian Idea of God*, Oxford, 1952.

MILNE, E. A., *Sir James Jeans: A Biography*, Cambridge, 1952.

MOORE, Ruth, *Niels Bohr: the Man and the Scientist*, London, 1967.

MOSSE, George L., *Nazi Culture: Intellectual, Cultural and Social Life in the Third Reich*, London, 1966.

MOSZKOWSKI, Alexander, *Einstein the Searcher: His Work Explained from Dialogues with Einstein*, Berlin, 1921.

MOWRER, Edgar Ansel, *Germany Puts the Clock Back*, London, 1933.

NATHAN, Otto, and Heinz Norden (eds.), *Einstein on Peace*, London, 1963.

NEWTON, Sir Isaac, *Opticks*, New York, 1952 (based on the Fourth Edition, London, 1730).

NOBEL FOUNDATION, (ed.) *Nobel: The Man and His Prizes*, Stockholm, 1950.

NORDMANN, Charles, "Einstein à Paris" in *Revue des Deux Mondes*, Vol. 8, 7th series, Paris, 1922.

NORDMANN, Charles, "Einstein à Paris", *L'Illustration*, April 15, 1922.

NORDMANN, Charles, *The Tyranny of Time: Einstein or Bergson*, London, 1925.

NORTH, J. D., *The Measure of the Universe*, Oxford, 1965.

OBSERVATORY, The *A Monthly Review of Astronomy*, London.

OLLENDORF, Ilse, *Wilhelm Reich*, London, 1969.

OPPENHEIMER, J. Robert, "On Albert Einstein" (Lecture delivered at UNESCO Housé, December 13, 1965), reprinted in *The New York Review*, March 17, 1966.

OPPENHEIMER, J. Robert, *The Flying Trapeze: Three Crises for Physicists*, (The Whidden Lectures for 1962), Oxford, 1964.

PAULI, W., *Theory of Relativity*, London, 1958.

PEARLMAN, Moshe, *Ben-Gurion Looks Back in Talks with Moshe Pearlman*, London, 1965.

PLANCK, Max, *The Origin and Development of the Quantum Theory*, (Nobel Prize Address June 2, 1920) Oxford, 1922.

PLANCK, Max, *Scientific Biography and Other Papers*, London, 1950.

PLANCK, Max, *Where is Science Going?*, London, 1933.

PLESCH, John, *Janos: The Story of a Doctor*, London, 1947.

POLANYI, Michael, *The Logic of Liberty: Reflections and Rejoiners*, London, 1951.

POLANYI, Michael, *Personal Knowledge*, London, 1958.

PRZIBRAM, K. (ed.), *Letters on Wave Mechanics: Schrödinger, Planck, Einstein, Lorentz*, translated and with an introduction by Martin J. Klein, New York, 1967.

RAYLEIGH, Lord, *The Life of Sir J.J. Thomson, O. M.*, Cambridge, 1942.

REICH, Ilse Ollendorff, *Wilhelm Reich*, London, 1969.

REICH, Wilhelm, *Biographical Material: History of the Discovery of the Life Energy — the Einstein Affair*, Orgonon, Rangeley, Maine, 1953.

REICHINSTEIN, David, *Albert Einstein: A Picture of his Life and his Conception of the World*, Prague, 1934.

REISER, Anton, *Albert Einstein: A Biographical Portrait*, London, 1931.

RINGER, Fritz K., *The Decline of the German Mandarins*, Cambridge, Mass., 1969

ROBB, Alfred A., *The Absolute Relations of Time and Space*, Cambridge, 1921.

ROBB, Alfred A., *A Theory of Time and Space*, Cambridge, 1914.

ROLLAND, Romain, *Le Bund Neues Vaterland (1914–1916)*, Lyons and Paris, 1952.

ROLLAND, Romain, *Journal des Années de Guerre 1914–1919*, Paris, 1953.

ROSENFELD, L., *Niels Bohr: An Essay*, Amsterdam, 1961.

ROSENFELD, Leonora Cohen, *Portrait of a Philosopher: Morris R. Cohen in Life and Letters*, New York, 1948.

ROTBLAT, J., *Pugwash*, Prague, 1967.

ROZENTAL, S. (ed.) *Niels Bohr*, Amsterdam, 1967.

RUSSELL, Bertrand, *The ABC of Relativity*, London, 1925.

RUTHERFORD OF NELSON, Lord, "The Transformation of Energy", (Watt Anniversary Lecture for 1936 delivered before the Greenock Philosophical Society, January 17, 1936).

SACHS, Alexander, *Background and Early History, Atomic Bomb*

*Project in Relation to President Roosevelt,* Washington, D. C., 1945.

SAMUEL, Viscount, *Belief and Action: An Everyday Philosophy,* London, 1937.

SAMUEL, Viscount, *Essay in Physics,* Oxford, 1951.

SAMUEL, Viscount, *Memoirs,* London, 1945.

SAMUEL, Viscount, and Herbert Dingle, *"A Threefold Cord: Philosophy, Science and Religion." A Discussion Between Viscount Samuel and Professor Herbert Dingle,* London, 1961.

SCHILPP, Paul Arthur (ed.), *Albert Einstein: Philosopher-Scientist,* Evanston, Ill., 1949.

SCHONLAND, Sir Basil, *The Atomists,* Oxford, 1968.

SCHRÖDINGER, Erwin, *Mind and Matter,* (The Tarner Lectures, 1956), Cambridge, 1958.

SCOTT, C. P., *The Political Diaries of C. P. Scott, 1911–1928,* London, 1970.

SEELIG, Carl, *Albert Einstein: A Documentary Biography,* London 1956.

SEELIG, Carl (ed.), *Helle Zeit; Dunkle Zeit,* Zurich, 1956.

SHANKLAND, R. S., "Conversations with Albert Einstein", *American Journal of Physics,* Vol. 31 (1963), pp. 47–57.

SHAPLEY, A., *Through Rugged Ways to the Stars,* New York, 1969.

SHIRER, William, *The Rise and Fall of the Third Reich,* New York, 1960.

SMITH, Alice Kimball, *A Peril and a Hope: the Scientists' Movement in America, 1945–47,* Chicago, 1965.

SMITH, Jean, and Arthur Toynbee, (eds.), *Gilbert Murray: An Unfinished Autobiography,* London, 1960.

SMYTH, H. D., *Atomic Energy for Military Power,* Washington, D. C., 1945.

SOMMER, Dudley, *Haldane of Cloan: His Life and Times 1856–1928,* London, 1960.

SPEIGHT-HUMBERTSON, Clara E., *Spiritism: The Hidden Secret in Einstein's Theory of Relativity,* Kitchener, Ontario, n. d.

STEIN, Leonard, *Zionism,* London, 1925.

STERN, Alfred, "An Interview with Einstein", *Contemporary Jewish Record* VIII (June, 1945), pp. 245–249.

STRAUSS, Lewis, *Men and Decisions,* London, 1963.

STUART, James, *Within the Fringe,* London, 1967.

SZILARD, Leo, "Reminiscences", *Perspectives in American History,* Vol II, Cambridge, Mass. 1968.

TALMEY, Max, *The Relativity Theory Simplified and the Formative Period of Its Inventor*, New York, 1932.
TEMPLEWOOD, Viscount, *Nine Troubled Years*, London, 1954.
THIRRING, J. H., *The Ideas of Einstein's Theory*, London, 1921.
THOMSON, Sir J. J., *Recollections and Reflections*, London, 1936.
TOYNBEE, Arnold J., *Acquaintances*, Oxford, 1967.
TSCHERNOWITZ, Dr. Chaim, "A Day With Albert Einstein", *Jewish Sentinel*, Vol. I (September 1931).

ULITZUR, A., *Two Decades of Keren Hayesod*, Jerusalem, 1940.

VALLENTIN, Antonina, *Einstein: A Biography*, London, 1954.
VOSS, Carl Hermann, (ed.), *Servant of the People* (the letters of Stephen Wise), Philadelphia, 1969.

WATTERS, Dr. Leon L., "Comments on the Letters of Professor and Mrs. Albert Einstein to Dr. Leon L. Watters" (unpublished).
WEIL, E., *Albert Einstein: A Bibliography of His Scientific Papers, 1901–1930*, London, 1937.
WEISGAL, Meyer W., and Joel Carmichael, (eds.) *Chaim Weizmann: A Biography by Several Hands*, New York, 1963.
WEIZMANN, Chaim, *Trial and Error*, London, 1950.
WEIZMANN, Vera, *The Impossible Takes Longer*, London, 1967.
WEYL, Dr. Hermann, *The Open World* (Three Lectures on the Metaphysical Implications of Science), New Have, Conn., 1932.
WHITEHEAD, A. N., *Science and the Modern World*, London, 1926.
WHITROW, G. J., (ed.), *Einstein: The Man and His Achievement*, London, 1967.
WHITTAKER, Sir Edmund, *Albert Einstein, Biographical Memoirs of Fellows of the Royal Society*, Vol. 1, 1955.
WHITTAKER, Sir Edmund, *From Euclid to Eddington*, New York, 1958.
WHITTAKER, Sir Edmund, *History of the Theories of the Aether and Electricity*, 2 vols.: London, 1951 and 1953.
WHYTE, L. L., *Focus and Diversions*, London, 1963.
WILSON, Margaret, *Ninth Astronomer Royal: The Life of Frank Watson Dyson*, Cambridge, 1951.
WOLF, Edwin, II, (with John F. Fleming), *Rosenbach: A Biography*, London, 1960.

# References

Full details of the sources quoted, manuscript and printed, are given with bibliographical information in the "Sources and Bibliography" above, pages 593—609.

page

19 one of the follies of his life: Einstein-Plesch, February 3, 1944 (Material in hands of the Plesch family; afterwards referred to as 'Plesch correspondence').

20 "pas très Juif": private note by Lord Samuel of conversation, October 31, 1930; Samuel Papers, (House of Lords Records Office; afterwards referred to as 'Samuel Papers').

21 Genealogical details: "Der Stammbaum Prof. Albert Einsteins" by Rabbiner Dr. A. Tanzer, *Jüdische Familien-Forschung*, Jahrgang VII, December, 1931, and *Israelitische Kultusvereinigung Württemberg und Hohenzollern*. Genealogical trees of both the Einstein and the Koch families also exist in the Princeton archive (afterwards referred to as 'Princeton').

21 "my husband mystical": G. K. A. Bell, p. 1052.

21 "His mode of life": *Einstein: His Life and Times*, Philipp Frank (afterwards referred to as 'Frank'). p. 15.

22 "exceedingly friendly": Einstein to Bela Kornitzer, *Gazette & Daily*, York, Pennsylvania, September 20, 1948 (afterwards referred to as 'Kornitzer').

22 Ulm birth-place details: Stadtarchiv, Ulm.

23 "excellent, reliable, incorruptible": Max Born, Obit. Notices, Fellows of the Royal Society, Number 17, November 1948, Vol. 6, p. 161.

25 "marvellous memory": Janos Plesch, *Janos*, p. 200 (afterwards referred to as 'Plesch').

26 "Leonardo da Vinci . . . Einstein and Niels Bohr": News Letter No. 1 of The North Surrey Dyslexic (Word Blind) Society, September 1968, p. 3. Letter from Mrs. V. W. Fisher to author, November 9, 1968.

26 "A true story": Kornitzer.

27 "algebra is a merry science": Frank, p. 24.

28 Cäsar Koch details from documents in the possession of M. Jean Ferrard of Brussels, located by Dr. Jagdish Mehra of the University of Texas and brought to my notice by Professor Jean Pelseneer of the University of Brussels.

29 "could not . . . say that he hated it": Antonina Vallentin, *Einstein*, p. 8 (afterwards referred to as 'Vallentin').

29 "respect for Planck": Kornitzer.

30 "the happy comfortable . . . Einstein home": Max Talmey, *The Relativity Theory Simplified and the Formative Period of its Inventor,* p. 161. (afterwards referred to as 'Talmey').

30 "a pretty dark-haired boy": Talmey, p. 161.

31 "worked through the whole book of Spieker": Talmey, p. 164.

31 living matter and clarity . . . opposites: Einstein—Hedwig Born, January 15, 1927; *Born - Einstein Letters,* p. 95. (afterwards referred to as 'Born').

31 "biological procedures": Carl Seelig (ed.), *Helle Zeit — Dunkle Zeit,* p. 64 (afterwards referred to as *Helle Zeit*).

31 "they follow beams": "Comments on the Letters of Professor and Mrs. Albert Einstein to Dr. Leon L. Watters", unpublished MS, American Jewish Archives, p. 4 (afterwards referred to as 'Watters').

32 "the Hebrew mind has been obsessed": Abba Eban, *The Jewish Chronicle,* October 2, 1959, p. 33.

32 "the *arcana* of nature": George. *The Oberland and Its Glaciers, Explored and Illustrated with Ice-axe and Camera,* London 1866.

33 "to draw His lines after Him": Buber, *The Knowledge of Man,* p. 156.

33 "how God created the world": Esther Salaman, "A Talk With Einstein", *The Listener,* September 8, 1955 (afterwards referred to as 'Salaman').

33 "God is subtle but he is not malicious": for origin of phrase see pp. 370.

33 "God does not play dice": for origin of phrase see p. 327.

34 "something behind the energy": Gurion, *Ben Gurion Looks Back,* p. 217.

35 "your presence . . . disruptive": Frank, p. 27.

35 "the ordinary Italian": Harry A. Cohen, "An Afternoon with Einstein", *Jewish Spectator,* January 1969, p. 16.

36 "sensible trade of engineering": Hans Einstein, quoted Kornitzer, *Ladies Home Journal,* April 1951, p. 136.

36 A paper to Uncle Cäsar in Stuttgart. Undated letter and MS, Einstein Cäsar Koch, authenticated c. 1950 by Einstein, in possession of the Suzanne Gottschalk - Jean Ferrard family, Brussels. Pre-print No. of "Albert Einstein's 'First' Paper" by Dr. Jagdish Mehra, CPT - 82: AEC - 31 January 8, 1971.

38 "his influence to let Albert jump a class": Plesch, p. 219.

38 "entirely his own fault": Plesch, p. 219.

38 "supposed to choose a practical profession": Kornitzer.

39 a pleasant place: Einstein, *Aargauer Tageblatt,* February 19, 1952.

39 "pretty much the same to me": Seelig, p. 19.

40 "Sure of himself, his grey felt hat": Seelig, p. 14.

41 "he was by nationality a German": Andre Mercier, quoted G. J. Whitrow (ed.) *Einstein: The Man and His Achievement,* BBC Third Programme Talks, p. 17 (afterwards referred to as 'Whitrow').

41 "gave up his passport": Jens, "Albert Einstein", *Universitas* Vol. 11, Number 3, 1969, p. 243.

41 "formally ended Einstein's German nationality": Stadtarchiv, Ulm.

43 "When I was a very young man": Watters, p. 26.

43 "he did not care for large, impressive mountains": Hans Einstein, quoted Whitrow, p. 21.

43 Fräulein Markwalder: quoted Seelig, p. 36.

44 "It's in my blood": Seelig, p. 15.

44 "masculine good looks": Vallentin, p. 3.

45 "he was attracted to women who did physical work": Vera Weizmann, pp. 102 - 3.

45 "personal matters": *Observer*, London, April 24, 1955.

46 "I never saw him show jealousy": Dr. Thomas Lee Bucky, "Einstein: An intimate memoir", *Harper's Magazine*, September 1964.

46 "the experience of the exterior world": "Jubilee of Relativity Theory", *Helvetica Physica Acta*, Supplementum iv, Basle, 1956, p. 19 (afterwards referred to as '*Physica Acta*').

46 "not embarrassed by much learning": Morris Cohen, "Einstein and His World" — *The Menorah Journal* Vol. 24, Spring 1936, p. 107 (afterwards referred to as '*Menorah*').

47 saw mathematics as being split up: autobiographical notes in *Albert Einstein: Philosopher-Scientist*, Paul A. Schilpp (ed.) p. 15, afterwards referred to as Schilpp.

47 that more mathematics was required: Schilpp, p. 17.

47 "to construct an apparatus": Anton Reiser, *Albert Einstein*, p. 53 (afterwards referred to as 'Reiser').

47 excellent teachers: Schilpp, p. 15.

48 "Maxwell's work was not touched upon": Gerald Holton, "Influences on Einstein's Early Work in Relativity Theory", *The American Scholar*, Winter 1967/68, p. 63 (afterwards referred to as 'Holton').

49 "explanations of new discoveries fitted together": Sir William Dampier, *A Shorter History of Science*, p. 92.

50 "Maxwell's theory — not a part": Max Born, "Physics in the Last 50 Years", *Nature*, Vol. 168, 1951, p. 625.

51 in his spare time: Schilpp, p. 15.

51 "the last man": E. T. Bell, *Men of Mathematics*, Vol. 2, p. 581.

51 "These are the only realities": quoted Gerald Holton, "Mach, Einstein and the Search for Reality", *Daedalus*, Spring 1967, p. 659.

52 "not speculative in origin": typically, lecture, King's College, London, 1921, quoted *The Nation*, London, June 18, 1921.

52 "a long philosophical pilgrimage": Holton, p. 636.

52 "to warn you in your own interest": quoted "Erinnerungen an Einstein" by Margareta Niewenhuis von Uexkuell, *Frankfurter Allgemeine Zeitung*, March 10, 1956, also "Albert Einstein nach meiner Erinnerung" by Uexkuell, E.T.H.

53 put off scientific work: Schilpp, p. 17.

53 A further letter followed: Einstein-Hurvitz, September 26, 1900, quoted Seelig, p. 49.

54 the work served its purpose: Einstein — Hurvitz, September 23, 1900, Seelig, p. 48.

54 "happy in Switzerland": Infeld, *Albert Einstein*, p. 119.

54 "perfectly in agreement": Stadtarchiv, Zurich.

54 "The Zurich city fathers": Reiser, p. 65.

55 The people were humane: Einstein - Wisseler, August 24, 1948, Swiss National Library, Berne.

55 "opponents of military imperialism": *Menorah*, p. 53.

56 heard through a student friend; Einstein-Kamerlingh Onnes, April 12, 1901. Rijksmuseum voor de Geschiedenis der Naturwetenschappen, Leiden (afterwards referred to as 'Leiden').

56 teaching mathematics . . . at Winterthur: Einstein - Professor Alfred Stern, May 3, 1901, E.T.H.

58 "Albert was examined": Reiser, p. 65.

59 "Thorough academic education": Bureau Federale de la Propriété Intellectuelle, Berne.

60 "proved himself very useful": quotation from Haller and details of salary and gradings: Bureau Federale.

61 "as the principal achievement of Einstein's words and crudeness in style": reports, E.T.H.

62 "great deal of poverty": Talmey, p. 167.

63 "More severe than my father": "Erinnerungen an Albert Einstein, 1902 - 1909", Bureau Federale.

64 "first two papers": "Folgerungen aus den Kapillaritatserscheinungen" *Annalen der Physik*, Ser. 4, Vol. 4, pp. 513 - 23 and "Thermodynamische Theorie der Potentialdifferenz zwischen Metallen und vollstandig dissoziierten Loesungen ihrer Salze, und eine elektrische Methode zur Erforschung der Molekularkraefte", *Annalen der Physik*, Ser 4. Vol. 8, pp. 798 - 814.

64 "three more papers": Kinetische Theorie des Wärmegleichgewichtes und des zweiten Hauptsatzes der Thermodynamik" *Annalen der Physik*, Ser. 4, Vol. 9, pp. 417 - 33. Theorie der Grundlagen der Thermodynamik" *Annalen der Physik*, Ser. 4, Vol. 14, pp. 170-87 and "Allgemeine Molekulare Theorie der Wärme", *Annalen der Physik*, Ser. 4, Vol. 14, pp. 354 - 62.

65 "Walking in the streets of Berne one day": Einstein, *Lettres à Maurice Solovine* p. vi. (afterwards referred to as 'Solovine').

65 "Einstein is 1.76 metres tall": Seelig, p. 40.

66 eating . . . without comment: Solovine, p. x.

67 "a man's private life": Princeton.

68 "a modest unassuming creature": Seelig, p. 38.

68 "her dreamy ponderous nature": Seelig, p. 46.

68 "she has such a lovely voice": Seelig, p. 38.

68 "How it came about": Watters, p. 14.

69 "He was sitting in his study in front of a heap of papers": Dr. Hans Tanner-Seelig, E.T.H.

70 "one hand rocking the bassinet": Reichinstein, *Albert Einstein: A Picture of His Life and His Conception of the World*, p. 25.

71 "blazing rockets": Louis de Broglie in Schilpp, p. 110.

71 a resumé of things to come: Einstein - Habicht, early 1905, Seelig, p. 74.

72 "These motions were such as to satisfy me": *Phil. Mag.* (4), 1828.

72 M. Gouy: *Journal de Physique* (2) 7.561, 1888.

72 F. M. Exner: *Annalen der Physik* 2.843, 1900.

72 "On the Movement of Small Particles"; "Über die von der molekularkinetischen Theorie der Wärme geförderte Bewegung von in ruhenden Flüssigkeiten suspendierten Teilchen" *Annalen der Physik*, Ser. 4, XVII, 549 - 60.

73 "To appreciate the importance of this step": Max Born, *Natural Philosophy of Cause and Chance*, p. 63 (afterwards referred to as Born, *Cause and Chance*).

73 "the old fighter against atomistics": Sommerfeld, in Schilpp, p. 105.

73 "The accuracy of measurement": *Cause and Chance*, p. 63.

74 "like a bolt from the blue": de Broglie, *New Perspectives in Physics*, p. 134.

74 "end his scientific life in sad isolation": de Broglie, *New Perspectives*, p. x.

74 "On a Heuristic Viewpoint": "Über einen die Erzeugung und Verwandlung des Lichtes betreffenden heuristischen Gasichtspunkt", *Annalen der Physik*, Ser. 4, XVIII, 132 - 48.

77 "something fundamental . . . missed by both": Schonland, *The Atomists*, p. 70.

77 "clearness began to dawn upon me": Max Planck, Nobel Prize Address, "The Origin & Development of the Quantum Theory", p. 3.

77 "a discovery as important as that of Newton": Max Born, Obit. Notices, F. R. S., No. 17, November 1948, Vol. 6, p. 161.

79 "killing of two birds by one stone": quoted Milne, p. 54.

79 "a novel kind of complementary relationship": Bohr, "The Solvay Meetings & The Development of Quantum Physics" in *Essays 1958 - 1962 on Atomic Physics and Human Knowledge*, New York, 1963, p. 80.

80 "practically no convinced adherents": Millikan, *Autobiography*, p. 83.

83 "On the Electrodynamics of Moving Bodies": "Elecrodynamik bewegter Körper", *Annalen der Physik*, Ser. 4, XVII, pp. 891 - 921.

85 "a magnificently precise and beautiful science"; Oppenheimer, *The Flying Trapeze —Three Crises for Physicists*, p. 10. (afterwards referred to as 'Oppenheimer, *Flying Trapeze*')

85 "absolute true and mathematical time": Sir Isaac Newton, *Mathematical Principles of Natural Philosophy*, p. 6.

85 "Absolute motion is the translation from one relative place into another": Newton, p. 7.

87 "expressed intention only to investigate *actual facts*": Ernst Mach, *The Science of Mechanics*, tr. Thomas J. McCormack, p. 229.

87 "The last man to take practically all mathematics": E. T. Bell, p. 581.

88 "If Michelson-Morley is wrong": *A Threefold Cord*, Viscount Samuel & Professor Herbert Dingle, pp. 52—3.

88 "Trouton and Nobel had tried": *Phil. Trans.* A. Vol. 202, 1903, p. 165.

88 "Lord Rayleigh and Brace had looked": *Phil. Mag.*, December 1902, p. 678 and *Phil. Mag.*, April 1904, p. 317.

90 "happy in the knowledge of a good instrument maker": quoted L. Campbell & W. Garnet, *James Clerk Maxwell*.

90 "the enormous stream of discoveries": H. Bondi, *Assumption and Myth in Physical Theory*, p. 5, afterwards referred to as Bondi.

91 "for me personally . . . ": Einstein in Haas-Lorentz, *H. A, Lorentz* p. 8.

92 "a logical consequence of several simultaneous hypotheses": *Interpretations &* *Misinterpretations of Modern Physics*, Philipp Frank, p. 39.

94 a spatially oscillatory electro-magnetic field at rest: Schilpp, p. 53.

"all sorts of nervous conflicts": Alexander Moskowski, *Einstein The Searcher*, p. 4.

95 "time was suspect": Shankland, "Conversations With Albert Einstein", *American Journal of Physics* (afterwards referred to as 'Shankland'). 1963, 31: 47—57.

95 "I pestered him for a whole month": Sauter-Seelig, Seelig, p. 73.

95 "You are the second": "Erinnerungen", Bureau Federale.

95 sounding-board in all Europe: Einstein quoted Seelig, p. 71.

95 "Einstein the eagle": Besso, Seelig, p. 71.

96 "as impersonalised a piece of writing": Bondi, p. iv.

96 "but nobody had taken offence": Born, *Physica Acta*, p. 251.

97 "If you are on an escalator": Russell, *The ABC of Relativity*, p. 28.

97 "eternal struggle of the inventive human mind": Einstein and Infeld, p. vi.

97 "fey": Schonland, p. 56.

98 Something in this idea: Plesch, p. 207.

99 "the notorious controversy": Born, *Einstein's Theory of Relativity*, p. 254.

99 "It is as real as anything we can observe": H. A. Lorentz at Mount Wilson Observatory, quoted *Contributions from the Mount Wilson Observatory*, Vol. XVII Carnegie Institute of Washington, April 1928, Nov. 1929, p. 27.

99 "length is not a property of the rod": Eddington, quoted H. L. Brose, *The Foundations of Einstein's Theory of Gravitation* by Erwin Freundlich, p. viii.

99 Voigt— "über das Dopplersche Prinzip", Nachr. Ges. Wiss. Göttingen (1887), 41.

101 "Lumen": see "Lumen", Flammarion.

102 "because the old conceptions are so nearly right": Lindemann, "Einstein's Theory: A Revolution in Thought", *The Times Educational Supplement*, January 29, 1920.

102 "Nature always economical": Russell, *Observer*, April 24, 1955.

102 "gross change, a rather sharp change": Oppenheimer, *Flying Trapeze*, p. 22.

103 "the most fundamental terms in physics": Eddington, Romanes Lectures, 1922.

105 "a further consequential development": Lecture given Davoser Hochschule, printed *St. Louis Post-Despatch*, December 29, 1928.

105 "the harmony of the Universe": Reichenbach, quoted Vallentin, p. 106.

105 "the work of the individual": Speaking to Nat. Acad. Science, Washington, April 26, 1921, quoted *New York Times*, April 27, 1921.

105 "the desire to make physical theory fit observed fact": typically, lecture King's College, London, quoted *The Nation*, London, June 18, 1921.

106 "*only after 1905*": Shankland.

106 "The Michelson-Morley experiment had no role": Polanyi, *The Art of Knowing*, p. 11.

107 "the experimental works of those preceding me": *Jewish Observer*, February 22, 1955.

107 ripe for discovery: Einstein-Seelig, *Technische Rundschau* No. 20,47 Jahrgang, Berne, May 6, 1955.

107 "adopted Poincaré's Principle of Relativity": Whittaker, *Biog. Memoirs of Fellows of Royal Society*, 1955 Vol. 1., p. 42.

107 "a particularly welcome task": H. A. Lorentz, *Physikalische Zeitschrift* Vol. 11, 1910, p. 1234, quoted Born, *Physica Acta*, p. 225.

108 "The genius of Einstein": *The Times*, May 25, 1931.

108 a brief paper: "Ist die Tragheit eines Körpers von seinem Energieinhalt abhängig?" *Annalen der Physik*, Ser. 4, XVIII 639—41.

109 "gross Bodies and Light convertible": Newton. *Opticks*, p. 374.

110 "the dormant energy of a single brick": Thirring, *The Ideas of Einstein's Theory*, p. 92.

110 "It's foolishness is evident": Frank, p. 211.

111 "in almost every branch of nuclear physics": Oppenh imer, *Flying Trapeze*, p. 20.

111 "the introduction of a richer language": Frank, *Relativity, a Richer Truth*, pp. 29—30.

111 "Physical science does not . . . suggest": Jeans, *The New Background of Science*, p. 98.

112 "the viewpoint of a man, not from that of an angel": *The Tablet*, London, April 23, 1955.

114 He did not care: Seelig, p. 113.

115 "obsessional concentration . . . one of the keys to his (Churchill's) character": Stuart, *Within the Fringe*, p. 96.

115 "refuge in music": Whitrow, p. 21.

116 "the first lecture . . . was one by Planck on Einstein's work": Von Laue-Seelig, March 13, 1952, E.T.H.

116 "A new Copernicus": Infeld, *Albert Einstein*, p. 44.

116 "neither Born nor anyone else there had heard about Einstein": Infeld, *Albert Einstein*, p. 44.

116 "Einstein's reasoning was a revelation": Born, *Physica Acta*, p. 247.

117 "the results are not compatible with the Lorentz-Einsteinian fundamental assumptions": Kaufmann, *Annalen der Physik*, Vol. 19, 1906, p. 495.

117 Kaufmann could not apparently be faulted: Einstein, "Relativitätsprinzip und die aus demselben gezogenen Folgerungen", *Jahrbuch der Radioaktivität, und Elektronik*, Vol. 4, pp. 411—62 and Vol. 5, pp. 98—9 (Berichtigungen), 1907.

118 "Einstein kneeling in front of the oven": Seelig, p. 72.

118 explaining the deviations of the specific heat of solids from the classical law — Einstein: "Plancksche Theorie der Strahlung und die Theorie der spezifischen Wärme", *Annalen der Physik*, Leipzig (4) 22, pp. 180—90 and 800.

119 the law of causality: Frank, "Kausalgesetz und Erfahrung" (Causality and Knowledge), published in Ostwald's *Annalen der Naturphilosophie*, 6, 443, Leipzig, 1907.

120 "He approved the logic of my argument": Frank, *Modern Science and its Philosophy*, p. 10.

121 an example of academic red tape; and decision was revised shortly afterwards: Einstein-Plesch, February 3, 1944, Plesch correspondence.

122 "we feel compelled at the present juncture to grant a kind of absolute physical reality to non-uniform motion": Einstein, *The Theory of Relativity*, p. 62.

123 "displeasing to Einstein": Dr. Sciama in Whitrow, p. 34.

125 "aeroplane pilot in a cloud": Lindemann, *The Times Educational Supplement*, January 29, 1920, p. 59.

126 a reasonable theory of gravitation: Einstein, *Origins of the General Theory of Relativity*, George A. Gibson Lecture, delivered Glasgow, June 20, 1933, afterwards referred to as Gibson, p. 8.

127 "great and brilliant period": Weyl, *David Hilbert*, Obit. Notices, Fellows. of the Royal Society, No. 18, November 1944, Vol. 4, p. 547.

128 "whether he would ever have done it without . . . Minkowski": E. Cunningham, *Nature*, February 17, 1921.

128 "the natural laws . . . assume mathematical forms": Einstein, *Theory of Relativity*, p. 57.

129 "a mysterious shuddering": Einstein, *Theory of Relativity*, p. 55.

129 "a 'happening' in three-dimensional space": Einstein, *Theory of Relativity*, p. 122.

129 "from the engineer-scientist to the mathematician": James Jeans, quoted Leon Watters, p. 30, Vol. 4, *The Universal Jewish Encyclopaedia*, New York, 1941.

129 "The people of Göttingen": Frank, p. 249.

130 "so busy discussing relativity": Theodore von Karman, *The Wind and Beyond*, p. 51.

131 "every moment . . . servant of society": Statement for Curie Memorial Celebration, Roerich Museum, New York, November 23, 1935, reprinted *Einstein, Ideas and Opinions*, p. 76.

131 "never met a real physicist": Infeld, *Albert Einstein*, p. 119,

131 Axalp . . . where he and Einstein . . . to have met: Princeton.

132 "presumptuous on his part": Planck, *Where is Science Going?*, London, 1933, p. 16.

132 "special relativity left to minor prophets": Born, *Physics in my Generation*, p. 197.

132 "one of the landmarks": Pauli in Schilpp, p. 154.

132 A profound change in contemporary views . . . Einstein: "Entwicklung unserer Anschauungen über das Wesen und die Konstitution der Strahlung", *Physikalische Zeitschrift*, Vol. 10, 1909, pp. 817–25.

133 "two facts . . . so overwhelmingly new and surprising": Meitner, "As I Remember", *Bull. Atomic Scientists*, November 1964, p. 4.

134 "absurd to appoint me": Frank, p. 95.

134 "I hope to have achieved this": Fritz Adler—Viktor Adler, November 28, 1908. Adler Archives, *Verein für Geschichte der Arbeiterbewegung*, Vienna.

134 "Einstein was not mentioned": Fritz Adler-Viktor Adler, April 16, 1909, Adler Archives.

135 "His departure means a loss": Haller-Federal Council, July 12, 1909, Bureau Federale.

135 Sending his Dienstbüchlein: Einstein—Chavan, October 19, 1909, Max Fluckiger *A. E. in Bern*, p. 27.

136 "In my relativity theory": Frank, p. 96.

136 "spend all his time in more solitary pursuits": Note by Lord Samuel, October 31, 1930, Samuel Papers.

137 he made this clear: Einstein-Besso, November 19, 1909, Besso correspondence.

138 "The more I speak with Einstein": Fritz Adler-Viktor Adler, October 28, 1910, Adler Archives.

139 The details of Einstein's move to Prague are provided mainly by the Adler letters and are supplemented by Frank, pp. 98—101, who as Einstein's successor gives the most reliable general account of the move.

142 He was having a good time: Einstein-Chavan, July 5, 1911, Seelig, p. 129.

143 Einstein-Pick correspondence: Princeton.

143 "the relation of the Jews to the other Germans": Frank, p. 106.

144 "The problems of nationality": Frank, p. 107.

145 "Once in his strolls": Marianoff and Wayne, *Einstein: An Intimate Study of a Great Man,* p. 49. afterwards referred to as Marianoff.

146 "another paper for the *Annalen der Physik*": "Über den Einfluss der Schwerkraft auf die Ausbreitung des Lichtes" (On the Influence of Gravitation on the Propagation of Light), *Annalen der Physik,* Vol. 35, (ser. 4.) 1911, pp. 898—908.

146 "bodies act upon light": Newton, *Opticks,* p. 339.

146 Soldner: *Astronomisches Jahrbuch,* Berlin 1804, p. 161.

149 "Einstein all calculation": Chaim Weizmann: *Trial and Error,* p. 153. afterwards referred to as Weizmann

149 "They have too much sense": Eve, p. 193.

149 "I well remember my co-secretary": original draft of obituary published *Daily Telegraph,* April 22, 1955, Cherwell Archives, Nuffield College, Oxford (afterwards referred to as 'Cherwell Archives').

149 "I got on very well with Einstein": Birkenhead, p. 52

149 "Lindemann formed an opinion of Einstein's character": Birkenhead, p. 37.

150 Einstein contributed a paper: "Zum gegenwärtigen Stande des Problems der spezifischen Wärme", *Deutsche Bunsengesellschaft,* Abhandlungen nr. 7, pp. 330—64, 1913.

150 "the clearness of his mind": Curie-E.T.H., November 17, 1911, E.T.H.

150 "the wish of his first wife": Frank-Seelig, May 13, 1952, E.T.H.

150 "to lecture on experimental physics": Hans Einstein statement to author.

151 Correspondence between Einstein and Utrecht: Univ. of Utrecht. Collection Julius papers, correspondence Julius, University Museum, Utrecht, vacature Windt, 1911.

151 "artistically fine-spirited man": *Astrophysical Journal* Vol. 63, 1926, pp. 196—8.

152 The prospect of returning to Zurich: Einstein-Grossmann, November 18, 1911, Seelig, p. 132.

152 "despite my long silence": Lorentz-Einstein, December 6, 1911, Leiden.

153 a further misunderstanding: Klein, *Paul Ehrenfest,* pp. 183—4.

153 "I much admire the work": Mme. Curie-Professor Weiss, November 17, 1911. E.T.H.

154 "The role of mathematical physics": Poincaré—E.T.H., undated E.T.H.

154 "Your coming would be welcomed": Pegram-Einstein, January 9, 1912, Columbia University

155 "he infected his students with his own enthusiasm": *Nature*, Vol. 132, October 26, 1933, p. 667.

156 "I can still see Einstein": Von Laue-Seelig, March 13, 1952, E.T.H.

156 about a trip to the Alps: Einstein-Curie, April 3, 1913, Bibliothèque Nationale, Paris.

157 "that is absolute nonsense": Levy, in Whitrow, p. 43.

157 "opposed to all metaphysical undertakings: Full text of manifesto quoted *The Journal of Philosophy, Psychology and Scientific Methods*, Vol. ix, No. 16, August 1, 1912, p. 419.

158 "Einstein and Grossman published jointly a paper": *Zeitschrift für Mathematik und Physik*, Vol. 62, 1931, pp. 225—61.

158 "were not compatible with experience": Gibson, p. 11.

159 "as matter-of-factly as others speak of sandwiches": Goldman, p. x.

159 "German-speaking men of science": *Nature*, Vol. 175, May 28, 1955, pp. 926—7.

159 "the blackboard moves": Felix Ehrenhaft, "My Experiences with Einstein", unpublished MS (afterwards referred to as 'Ehrenhaft').

161 "leaning directly on Einstein's treatment": Bohr, p. 84.

161 "he once had similar ideas": Hevesy-Rutherford, October 14, 1913, Rutherford Papers, University of Cambridge.

161 "it means the end of physics": Bohr in *Nauka i Zhzn* (Science in Life) 1961, No. 8, p. 77, Kuznetzov, p. 271.

161 "a stream of knowledge": Planck, Nobel Prize Address p. 16.

162 "a half-good-natured, half-cunning expression": Frank, p. 131.

162 "Einstein asked Mach": Bernard I. Cohen, "An Interview wirh Einstein", *Scientific American*, Vol. 193, 1955, p. 73.

163 "to cancel my contemplation": Mach, *The Principes of Physical Optics*, vii.

163 "un bon mechanicien": *Bull. Soc. Phil.*, Vol. 22, p. 111.

164 To discover whether light was . . . bent: *Forschungen und Fortschritte*, Vol. 37, 1963 quoted in . . . "Mach, Einstein and the Search for Reality", Gerald Holton, *Daedalus*, Spring 1968, p. 645.

164 Details of Einstein's early friendship with Freundlich are contained in a long series of letters between the two, including the following until recently held by Frau Freundlich:

164 welcomed the help: Einstein-Freundlich, September 1, 1911.

164 if the speed of light was affected: Einstein-Freundlich, August 1913.

165 "a nice letter from Einstein": Freundlich-Frau Freundlich August 26, 1913.

166 "No possibility of detecting the effect": Hale-Einstein, November 8, 1913, Hale Papers, California Institute of Technology.

167 Willing to contribute: Einstein-Freundlich, December 7, 1913.

167 "at a profound disadvantage with the Germans": Haldane p. 232.

168 "the weakness of human beings for decorations and titles": Plesch, p. 129.

169 gone to Berlin: Princeton, Einstein-Besso, March 26.

170 "The devastating results of this new interpretation": Statement dated Berlin, June 12, 1913, E.T.H.

172 "Einstein will move to Berlin": Nernst-Lindemann, August 18, 1913, Cherwell Archives.

172 "personal factors": Frank, p. 136.

173 "when a great idea is at stake": Reichinstein, p. 28.

173 "the true artist will let his wife starve": Shaw, *Major Barbara*.

174 "Prussian nationality acquired in 1913": Dr. Ernst Heymann, April 1, 1933, quoted Einstein, *The World As I See It*, p. 86.

174 no change in his nationality: Einstein to Academy, March 23, 1923 (18 Akad. Arch. II: IIIa, Bd. 23, B197) quoted Herneck, *Naturwissenschaften*.

175 "errors of thinking": Gibson, p. 11.

175 "Kieks": Rudolf H. Hertz—author, April 12, 1969.

175 "a farewell supper at the Kronenhalle": Kollros, *Physica Acta*, p. 280.

175 determined to keep . . . clear as possible . . . of . . . bureaucratic machinery: Einstein-Plesch, February 3, 1944, Plesch correspondence.

176 "honoured to receive him in their homes": Frank, p. 153.

176 "kneel down on the floor": Samuel, *Memoirs*, p. 254.

176 He was confident: Einstein-Besso, March 1914, Holton, *Daedalus*, p. 652.

179 "problem from the Ordnance Department": Morris Goran, *The Story of Fritz Haber*, p. 66. afterwards referred to as Goran

179 "they stunk first": Sommerfeld quoted Schilpp, p. 103.

179 "lack of a higher military title": Goran, p. 75.

179 "I am a sergeant": Goran, pp. 75—6.

179 "a few educated Germans": Fritz K. Ringer, *The Decline of the German Mandarins: The German Academic Community 1890—1933*, p. 180.

181 Koppel providing his academic salary: Einstein-Freundlich, December 7, 1913, Freundlich correspondence.

181 his academic pay: Einstein-Hedwig Born, September 1, 1919, Born letters, p. 12.

181 "Manifesto to Europeans": quoted Otto Nathan and Heinz Norden, *Einstein on Peace*, afterwards referred to as Nathan and Norden p. 4-6.

181 Nicoli gives him credit: George Nicoli-Einstein May 18, 1918, quoted Nathan and Norden, p. 7.

182 "Einstein . . . very active": Kurt R. Grossmann, "Peace Movements in Germany", *South Atlantic Quarterly*, July 1950, p. 294.

182 "Equivalent to treason": Grossman, p. 294.

183 " . . . wrote with a mixture of resignation, pity and disgust" Einstein-Ehrenfest, August 19, 1914, Princeton. Einstein-Ehrenfest, December 1914, Princeton. Einstein-Lorentz, August 2, 1915, The Hague Einstein-Ehrenfest, August 23, 1915, Princeton.

183 "brilliant physicist and mathematician": Rolland, diary entry September 16, 1915 quoted *Journal des Années de Guerre, 1914—1919* Romain Rolland, Paris 1953, pp. 510—15. (afterwards referred to as 'Rolland').

186 "The Kaiser meant well": *Saturday Evening Post*, October 26, 1929.

186 "the worst side of his own nation": Rolland, p. 514.

186 the cause of war . . . the nature of homo sapiens: "Das Land Goethes 1914 —1916" Berliner Goethebund, 1916, Dokument-sammlung der Preuss. Staadts-bibliothek, Berlin-Dahlem.

187 Einstein and Ehrhardt: *Interavia* Vol. X, No. 9, 1955, pp. 684—5, Einstein to Ehrhardt, September 7, 1954.

188 irrevocable decision: Einstein-Besso, July 14, 1916, Besso correspondence.

189 Adler-Einstein correspondence: Princeton.

190 "Adler was mentally deranged": Frank, p. 212.

190 "follows no set rules": Plesch, p. 206.

191 "his utter independence": Hedwig Born, *Helle Zeit*, p. 36.

191 "thankful every hour of my life": Bucky, *Helle Zeit*, p. 65.

192 "My first wife did": Salaman.

192 "women . . . attached to their furniture": Frank, p. 156.

193 His letter was long and pessimistic: Einstein-Rolland, August 22, 1917 Rolland, p. 1205 (given as Wednesday 21st, but Wednesday was the 22nd).

193 "the extreme injustice": Rolland, p. 1303.

193 financial details: Einstein-Besso, May 15, 1917, Besso correspondence.

194 The move to Haberlandstrasse: Einstein-Besso, September 3, 1917, Besso corres-pondence.

194 "look after his outside affairs": *Manchester Guardian*, June 14, 1921.

194 "he has a good wife": Dr. Chaim Tschernowitz, "A Day With Albert Einstein", *Jewish Sentinel*, September 1931.

195 divorce papers and evidence before tribunal: Einstein-Besso, December 12, 1919, Besso correspondence.

196 made their way to the Reichstag: Born Letters, p. 150.

198 the most exacting . . . period of his life: Einstein-Sommerfeld, November 28, 1915, quoted *Briefwechsel Albert Einstein/Arnold Sommerfeld*, p. 32 (afterwards referred to as 'Sommerfeld').

198 "the greatest feat of human thinking about Nature": Born, *Physica Acta*, p. 253.

198 "not merely a background for events": Wolfgang Yourgrau, "On Invariance Principles" in *Entstehung, Entwicklung und Perspektiven der Einsteinschen Gravita-tionstheorie*, Berlin, 1966 (report of Einstein-Symposium 2—5 November, 1965).

198 "I want to reflect": *Aufsätze und Vorträge über Physik und Erkenntnis-theorie*, Braunschweig 1961, p. 88.

200 "when the blind beetle": Seelig, p. 80.

201 "last nail in the coffin of absolute space": E.T. Bell, p. 561.

201 "responsible for a great deal of popular misconception": Sir Edmund Whittaker, *From Euclid to Eddington*, p. 39.

202 "the expression 'Raum-Krummung', space curvature": Talmey, "Einstein's Theory and Rational Language", *Scientific Monthly*, Vol XXXV, p. 254, 1932.

203 "found by Flinders Petrie": O.G.S. Crawford, *Archaeology in the Field*, London 1953, p. 269.

203 "the assumption of hypotheses": Einstein, *Theory of Relativity*, p. 103.

203 He hoped would account . . . for the changes: Einstein-Habicht, December 24, 1907, Seelig, p. 76.

204 full agreement between Theory and experience: Einstein-Mrs. Whitney, July 15, 1926, Stanford University.

204 "I did not . . . doubt": Moskowski, p. 5.

204 "Schwarzschild published a description": Berlin, Sitz. (1916) p. 189.

205 "L.F. Jewell": *J. Phys.*, vi (1897) 84.

205 "a recent experiment conducted at Harvard": Oppenheimer, *Flying Trapeze*, p. 27.

206 "to use tensors as a tool": A. Vibert Douglas, *The Life of Arthur Stanley Eddington*, p. 39. afterwards referred to as Douglas.

206 "an enormous progress": de Sitter, Wilhelm, "Einstein's Theory of Relativity", *Monthly Notices*, Royal Ast. Soc. Vol. LXXVII, December 2, 1916.

207 "a view to testing Einstein's theory": F. A. Lindemann and A. F. Lindemann, "Daylight Photography of stars as a means of Testing the Equivalence Postulate in the Theory of Relativity", *Monthly Notices*, Royal Ast. Soc. Vol. LXXVII, December 2, 1916.

207 "wait some thousands of years": Eddington, *Space, Time and Gravitation*, p. 113.

208 "an unusual number of bright stars": *Monthly Notices*, Royal Astronomical Society, Vol. LXXVII, Greenwich, March 2, 1917.

208 "two important papers": "Quantumtheorie der Strahlung", *Physikalische Zeitschrift*, vol. 18, pp. 121−8, and "Kosmologische Betrachtungen zur allgemeinen Relativitätstheorie". *Preussische Akademie der Wissenschaften, Sitzungsberichte*, 1917, pt. 1, pp. 142−52.

210 "a superstructure including other principles": Hubble, "The Observational Approach to Cosmology", The Rhodes Memorial Lectures, 1936, p. 53 (afterwards referred to as 'Hubble').

211 " . . . all must see the universe alike": Hubble, p. 53.

212 "The whole universe": Moskowski, p. 127.

213 "Friedmann noticed": Gamow, pp. 149−50.

213 "It solved the mysterious fact": Born, *Physica Acta*, p. 254.

216 An allied victory . . . a lesser evil: Einstein-Lorentz, August 1, 1919, The Hague.

217 to plead with the Allies: Einstein-Ehrenfest, December 6, 1918, American Philosophical Society.

218 an incident recalled by Hermann Weyl: Weyl-Seelig, May 19, 1952, E.T.H.

219 understanding among the Germans: Einstein-unnamed correspondent, August 17, 1919, Nathan and Norden, p. 31.

219 "Einstein . . . in no way German": Lorentz-Solvay, January 10, 1919, Solvay archives quoted unpublished MS "Historique des Institute Internationaux de

Physique et de Chimie Solvay depuis leur fondation jusqu'a la 2e guerre mondiale" by Jean Pelseneer, p. 37 (afterwards referred to as Pelseneer).

220 "you must not deceive yourself": Lorentz-Einstein, May 4, 1919, The Hague.

220 "Germans will not be invited": Lorentz-Einstein, July 26, 1919, Leiden.

220 "Einstein . . . who spent the whole war in Berlin": Brillouin-Tassel, June 1, 1919, Solvay Institute documents.

221 "an exception made for Einstein": Tassel-M. Huisman, March 23, 1921, Solvay Institute documents.

221 "the only German invited is Einstein": Rutherford-Boltwood, February 28, 1921, quoted Badash, p. 342.

221 Einstein accepted with great pleasure: Einstein-Lorentz June 15, 1920, The Hague.

221 Lorentz informed Rutherford: Lorentz-Rutherford, December 16, 1920, Rutherford papers.

221 not right for Einstein to take part: Einstein-Lorentz, August 16, 1920, The Hague.

221 "I am able to write to Einstein": Lorentz note on telegram quoted Pelseneer, p. 41.

221 "feelings . . . should be gradually damped down": report Lorentz-Solvay, Pelseneer, p. 41.

222 booklet . . . startled Einstein: Einstein-Lorentz, September 21, 1919, The Hague.

222 the offer came from Ehrenfest: Einstein-Ehrenfest, September 12, 1919, Klein, *Paul Ehrenfest*, p. 311.

223 "Eddington found star displacement": Lorentz-Einstein, September 22, 1919, Leiden.

223 "experimental confirmation has been ample": *Monthly Notices*, Vol. LXXVII, February 1917, p. 377.

223 "an end . . . of boycotting German Science": A.S. Eddington, quoted Obit. Notices, Fellows of the Royal Society, No. 8, Vol. 3, January 1940, p. 167.

224 "Eddington will go mad": Douglas, p. 40.

224 "programme of photographs on faith": Douglas, p. 40.

224 "We developed the photographs": Douglas, p. 40.

225 "This . . . Eddington never forgot": Douglas, p. 40.

225 "The clock no question makes": Douglas, p. 43.

225 "definitely confirming . . . value of deflection": Wilson, p. 193.

226 Knew nothing about the . . . measurements: Einstein-Hartmann, September 2, 1919, Leiden.

226 pass on the good news from H. A. Lorentz: Einstein-Pauline Einstein, September 27, 1919, Nathan and Norden, p. 27.

226 "I have heard of Eddington's results": Lorentz-Einstein, October 7, 1919, The Hague.

228 "that of the Greek drama": Whitehead, *Science and the Modern World*, p. 13.

228 "a whole new Continent": quoted *The Times*, November 8, 1919.

228 "no need to observe an eclipse": Eddington, 8th Annual Haldane Lecture, May 26, 1937.

232 "these . . . are sold for the benefit: *Daily Chronicle*, January 15, 1920.

232 "talk of nothing but Einstein": Lawson-Berliner, November 1919, Nathan and Norden, p. 27.

233 "After the lamentable breach": *The Times*, November 28, 1919.

234 "I was myself a sceptic": Dyson-Hale, December 29, 1919, Hale Papers.

234 "too much for my comprehension": Hale-Dyson, February 19, 1920, Hale Papers.

235 the tendency to draw scientific men away: Rutherford-Hale, January 13, 1920, Hale Papers.

235 "a typical case of mathematical development": Rutherford Presidential Address, British Association, 1923, Eve, p. 296.

235 "a magnificent work of art": Rutherford, Royal Society of Arts, 1932, Eve, p. 353.

235 "he never seemed particularly enthusiastic on the subject": Rayleigh, p. 202.

236 "an individualist . . . can have a universe of his own": Thomson, p. 431.

236 "like the Mad Hatter, experience time standing still": Douglas, p. 117.

236 "the really essential physical considerations": Robb, *A Theory of Time and Space*, p. 1.

237 "Hymn to Einstein": Robb, Rutherford Papers.

239 "all England has been talking": Eddington-Einstein, December 1, 1919, Princeton.

239 would be going to England: Einstein-Born, January 27, 1920, Born Letters, p. 22.

239 "a rebuff from reaction": Eddington-Einstein, January 9, 1920, Princeton.

240 "universal theme which had taken possession of humanity": Moskowski, pp. 13—14.

241 "to those who have the vision": *Nature*, Vol. 106, p. 337, November 11, 1920.

241 "crowd . . . queued up on a cold . . . night": Infeld, "Einstein", *The American Scholar*, Vol 16, 1946—7.

243 "People were weary of hatred": Infeld, *Quest*, p. 264.

243 "the dethronement of time as a rigid tyrant": E. Schrödinger, p. 82.

245 Correspondence on proposed Freedom of Ulm; Stadtarchiv, Ulm.

245 first meeting with Bohr: Einstein-Ehrenfest; Seelig, p. 185.

246 "my admiration for Einstein": Bohr in Schilpp, p. 206.

246 "the first . . . opportunity of meeting Planck and Einstein": Bohr-Rutherford, July 27, 1920, Rutherford Archives.

247 "the man who introduced the idea": *Nauka i Zhzh* (Science in Life) 1961, No. 8, p. 73, quoted Kuznetzov, pp. 279—80.

247 "certain difference in attitude and outlook"; Schilpp, p. 206.

247 "one of the great experiences of life": Bohr-Einstein, June 29, 1920, American Institute of Physics.

268 Swearing into Weimar and Prussian constitution: dates given by Herneck.

248 anti-Semitism was strong: Einstein-Ehrenfest, December 4, 1919, Nathan and Norden, p. 37.

249 "secret groups round Krupp": Grossmann.

249 "a high opinion of Einstein's photo-electric paper": Laub-Seelig, September 19, 1959, E. T. H.

250 "a University lecturer": Infeld, *Die Wahrheit*, March 15—16, 1969.

250 "My Answer to the Anti-Relativity Theory Co. Ltd.": *Berliner Tageblatt*, August 25, 1920.

251 "not very happy": Sommerfeld-Einstein, September 3, 1920, Sommerfeld, p. 68.

251 "rather unfortunate reply": Hedwig Born-Einstein, September 8, 1920, Born letters, p. 34.

251 "men such as Lenard and Wolf of Heidelberg": Von Laue-Sommerfeld, August 25, 1920, Sommerfeld, p. 65.

251 "With real fury": Sommerfeld-Einstein, September 3, 1920, Sommerfeld, p. 65.

253 "referred to his lecturing at Oxford": Everett Skillings, "Some Recent Impressions in Germany", *The Oxford Magazine*, Vol. XXXVIII No. 23, June 11, 1920.

253 "need of a first-class applied mathematician": Jeans-Rutherford, September 1 1920, Rutherford Papers.

254 He was . . . tormented: Planck-Einstein, September 5, 1920, Princeton.

254 "Most respected professor": Haenisch-Einstein, quoted *New York Times*, September 1920.

255 Bad Nauheim meeting: as with the famous confrontation between T. H. Huxley and Bishop Wilberforce at the Oxford meeting of the British Association in 1860, no complete verbatim record of the Lenard-Einstein exchange appears to have survived. Eye-witness accounts, recalled after half a century, are conflicting. The overall impression is that Planck just managed to keep the occasion in hand.

255 "guaranteed a very large sum": Ehrenhaft, p. 3.

255 Lenard, Einstein and (p. 310) other speakers: *Physikalische Zeitschrift*, Vol. XXI, 1920, pp. 666—8.

255 "When Lenard began": Dr. Friedr. Dessauer-Seelig, September 9, 1953, E. T. H.

255 "the simple understanding of the scientist": Lenard, *Physikalische Zeitschrift*.

256 Einstein "provoked into making a caustic reply": Born letters, p. 36.

256 He would not allow himself to get excited: Einstein-Born, undated, Born letters, p. 41.

257 "the closest human and scientific ties": Frank, p. 206.

257 "presented him to the fifty or sixty thousand people": Grossmann.

257 Founder member of the Republican League, *New York Times,* January 9, 1921. 3 : 3.

258 "That power/Which Erring men call Chance": Milton, *Comus*.

260 thorns in the side: Einstein-Plesch, February 3, 1944, Plesch correspondence,

260 "Calm yourself": Frank, p. 211.

261 "Einstein stayed in my house": Ehrenhaft, p. 5.

262 his English was practically non-existent: and following Manchester correspondence, Manchester University archives.

263 "the excellence of his diction": *The Manchester Guardian*, June 10, 1921.

264 "The man in the street": *The Manchester Guardian*, June 10, 1921.

264 "a more condensed distribution": Eddington-Lindemann, April 24, 1932, Cherwell Archives.

265 "admiration for the power of systematic reflection": Haldane, p. 283.

265 "Haldane is doing for Einstein": Lodge, "Einstein's Real Achievement", *Fortnightly Review*, DCLVII, New Series, September 1, 1921, p. 353.

265 "a poor compliment": Eddington, 8th Haldane Lecture, 1934.

265 "a cloud descended": Sommer, p. 381.

265 "make a market for us": Haldane-John Murray, May 12, 1921, John Murray Archives.

265 "Will you do me the honour": Haldane-Einstein, Princeton.

265 Haldane's comments to his mother on the Einstein visit are taken from the Haldane correspondence in the National Library of Scotland. Sources for the dinner-party on the 10th, include G. K. A. Bell and Sommer. Randall Davidson appears to have made a detailed record of the meeting.

266 "neither head nor tail of Einstein": Sanderson-Thomson, April 7, 1921, quoted Rayleigh, p. 203.

267 "typical scientific lion": Randall Davidson, quoted G. K. A. Bell, p. 1052.

267 "it is purely abstract-science": G. K. A. Bell, p. 1052.

267 "relativity... widely misunderstood": *Saturday Evening Post*, October 26, 1929, p. 17 et seq.

267 "clergymen are interested": Philipp Frank, "Einstein's Philosophy of Science": *Reviews of Modern Physics* Vol. 21, No. 3, July 1949, p. 349.

268 "My husband mystical": G. K. A. Bell, p. 1052.

268 "Mysticism is in fact": Seelig, p. 79.

268 "The non-sequitur is obvious": Eddington, 8th Haldane Lecture, 1937.

268 "events . . . of the Norman Conquest": Sir Almeric Fitzroy, *Memoirs*, Vol. II, London n. d., p. 756.

269 "his palatial residence": Kuznetsov, p. 237.

269 "Feeling against Germany": Barker, p. 136.

269 "no notes, no hesitation": *The Nation*, June 18, 1921.

270 "not speculative in origin": *The Nation*, June 18, 1921.

270 "the harmony of the Universe": Reichenbach, quoted Vallentin, p. 106.

271 "Each of these two nations": *The Nation*, June 18, 1921.

271 "the German Ambassador was right": Haldane-Lindemann, June 15, 1921. Cherwell Archives.

272 "no room for question that Einstein 'explained' gravitation": Sampson-Lindemann, June 16, 1921, Cherwell Archives.

273 "a markedly unfriendly feeling": *New York Times*, July 2, 1921.

274 no right to reproduce what he had said, Einstein-Sommerfeld, January 28, 1922, Sommerfeld, p. 99.

277 The two fullest accounts of Einstein's Paris visit are given by Charles Nordmann in *Revue des Deux Mondes*, Vol. 8 (7th. Series) 1922, and *L'Illustration*, April 15, 1922.

277 "impression of astonishing youth": Nordmann, *L'Illustration*.

279 "I see red": quoted Jaffe, *Michelson and the Speed of Light*, p. 101.

279 "Mach was a good mechanic . . . a deplorable philosopher": *Bull. Soc. Franc. Phil.*, 1922, pp. 92—113, Vol. 22.

280 "Relativity is an interesting word": *The Times*, April 3, 1922.

280 "all the students of the world": Nordmann, *L'Illustration*.

281 "another movie on the same terms": Cohen, *A Dreamer's Journey*, p. 189.

282 "get in touch with one another across frontiers": quoted Einstein, *The Fight Against War*: ed. Alfred Lief, p. 13.

283 "Madame Curie wrote": Curie-Einstein, July 7, 1922, Curie Laboratory archives.

285 Einstein's nationality: a major source is Herneck in *Die Naturwissenschaften*, which quotes extensively from Government and Academy documents.

285 "The Swiss Ambassador was surprised": Nadolny, quoted Herneck.

286 "Award received by German Ambassador": Nobel Foundation.

286 "handed over at Einstein's request by Swiss Ambassador": Princeton.

286 Ministerial report of January 13, 1923: quoted Herneck.

286 He gave them on March 24: Einstein-Ministry, March 24, 1923, quoted Herneck.

286 "Einstein . . . always appears as German": report of German Consul-General, Barcelona, May 2, 1923, Deutsches Zentralarchiv, D. D. R.

287 Einstein statement: February 7, 1924, quoted Herneck.

287 "a material side to the Nobel Prize": Lorentz-Einstein May 1, 1923, Leiden.

287 A Japanese publisher: Einstein-Plesch, February 3, 1944, Plesch correspondence.

291 "when I say it three times": Douglas, p. 44.

291 "reluctance of many leading men of science": Douglas, p. 44.

292 "still controversial": Born, *Physica Acta*, p. 225.

292 "alleged trip to Russia": Frank, pp. 245—6.

292 "Blumenfeld has . . . told the story": Blumenfeld has described his recruitment of Einstein into the Zionist ranks in his autobiography, *Erlebte Judenfrage*; in a lengthy article in the Belgian Zionist paper *La Tribune Sioniste;* and in various documents now in the E. T. H. They differ in wording, but not in significant detail.

293 leaving the country . . . and cancelling a dinner date with Planck: Princeton.

300 "Poor old Joffé'': Plesch, p. 235.

300 "never mind the dust and disorder": Plesch, p. 201.

301 "the salaries of scholars and teachers": *New Leader*, October 6, 1922.

301 "grievous privations": *Oxford Magazine*, Vol. XXXVIII, No. 23, June 11, 1920.

302 "Seven more books on relativity": *Nature* Vol. 109, June 17, 1922, pp. 770—2.

302 "old ideas . . . in the melting pot": Douglas, p. 42.

303 "Poor people beg for money": Reiser, p. 202.

304 "the great Pyramid of Egypt": Speight-Humbertson, *Spiritism: The Hidden Secret in Einstein's Theory of Relativity*, p. 23.

304 "When you are twenty": Letter to author, October 22, 1968.

305 "his great kindness": Infeld, *American Scholar*.

306 "already disclosed the secret": Ehrenhaft, p. 11.

306 "I retire to the back of my mind": Marianoff, p. 85.

307 "dressed in a dark suit": "Einstein: An Intimate Memoir" by Thomas Lee Bucky, with Joseph P. Blank, *Harper's Magazine*, September 1964, p. 43.

307 "I want nothing from anyone": George Sylvester Viereck, "What Life Means to Einstein", *Saturday Evening Post*, October 26, 1929, pp. 17, et seq.

308 "Einstein could do that": statement Frau Freundlich to author.

308 "Anything is allowed to Einstein": Tatyana Ehrenfest-Afanassjewa-Seelig, June 4, 1952.

309 Einstein Tower: for details see: "How I came to Build the Einstein Tower", Erwin Finlay-Freundlich, *Physikalische Blätter*, Vol. 12, 1969.

310 "Einstein looking at me": Salaman.

311 "crest of the wave": A. S. Eve & J. Chadwick, Obit. Notices, Fellows of the Royal Society, No. 6, Vol. 2, January 1958, p. 422.

312 "discussions with him were . . . unforgettable": Herzberger—author, January 22, 1970.

312 "Physics melted in his mouth": Gabor—author, November 15, 1969

313 "it can be used to set up violent explosions": Leo Szilard, *Reminiscences*, p. 102, afterwards referred to as Szilard.

313 who created intellectual and spiritual life: Einstein-Professor Donnan, August 16, 1933, Szilard Papers.

315 "Ten years of my life": *Review of Modern Physics*, Vol. 21, No. 3, July 1949, p. 344.

315 "X rays . . . consist of discrete units": A. H. Compton, *Journal of the Franklin Institute*, Vol. 198, 1924, p. 70.

316 the whole theory would collapse: Einstein-Millikan, July 13, 1925. Millikan Papers, California Institute of Technology.

316 "sent Miller home": Polanyi, *The Logic of Liberty*, p. 11.

316 "completely lost faith": Born letters, p. 74.

317 "The Einstein & The Eddington": Professor W. H. Williams: poem was discovered among Eddington's papers by Professor A. Vibert Douglas when writing his life and is published in her biography, p. 116.

320 "he gropes his way in loneliness": Born, in Schilpp, p. 163.

321 very loath . . . to abandon complete causality: Einstein-Born, January 27, 1920, Born letters.

321 "after a long absence": de Broglie, *New Perspectives in Physics*, p. 80.

322 "purely on grounds of intellectual beauty": Polanyi, *Personal Knowledge*, p. 148.

322 "in the months that followed": de Broglie, *New Perspectives in Physics*, p. 139.

322 "two papers for the Prussian Academy": "Quantentheorie des einatomigen idealen Gases", *Preuss. Akad. der Wiss., Phys.-math. Klasse, Sitz.*, 1925, pp. 3—14, and pp. 18—25.

323 "the scientific world of the time": de Broglie, *New Perspectives in Physics*, p. 140.

323 "to exterminate mankind": Schrödinger, "Our Image of Matter" in *On Modern Physics*, London, 1961, p. 43.

324 "the top of Fujiyama": L. Rosenfeld, *Niels Bohr*, p. 15.

325 "a given experiment . . . cannot do both": de Broglie.

326 "the monumental stability of an enormous life insurance company": Schonland, p. 188.

326 "is no objectively existing situation": Born, "Physics & Metaphysics", *The Scientific Monthly*, Vol. 82, No. 5, May 1956, p. 234.

326 "unhappy over what they have been forced to do": Oppenheimer, *Flying Trapeze*, pp. 5—6.

327 "A new fashion . . . in physics": Frank, p. 260.

327 "A good joke . . .": Frank, p. 261.

327 He was convinced that God did not throw dice: Einstein-Born, December 12, 1926, Born letters, p. 91.

328 "came to the conference with great anticipations": Schilpp, p. 211.

328 "an impossibility of any sharp separation": Schilpp, p. 210.

329 "Einstein mockingly asked us": Schilpp, p. 218.

330 "his sweet disposition . . . his general kindness": de Broglie, *New Perspectives in Physics*, p. 182.

331 "Einstein, who had forgotten to apply his own general theory": Cline, p. 240.

331 "On Mondays, Wednesdays and Fridays": Sir William Bragg, "Electrons and Ether Waves", 23rd. Robert Boyle Lecture, Oxford, 1921, p. 11.

331 "The advancing sieve of time": Lawrence Bragg—author, May 30, 1970.

332 "power to restore unison": *Nature*, Vol. 119, 1927, p. 467.

332 "the right to go to the limit": Born, *Physica Acta*, p. 259.

333 "we all dance to a mysterious tune": *Saturday Evening Post*, October 26, 1929, p. 17 et seq.

334 "faith in unbroken causality is threatened": "Fundamental Concepts of Physics and Their Most Recent Changes": Translation of the Davos Hochschule Lecture published in the *St. Louis Post-Despatch* December 29, 1928.

334 "Einstein never took any exercise": Plesch, p. 216.

334 rowing in a sailing-boat: Einstein-Plesch, February 3, 1944. Plesch correspondence.

336 "pacifism . . . an instinctive feeling": *The Christian Century*, Paul Hutchinson, July/August, 1929.

337 refuse to do war service: *Die Wahrheit*, 1929, quoted Lief, p. 26.

338 "not as representatives": League Archives.

338 "a conversation with leading members": Murray-Russell, May 4, 1955, Smith and Toynbee, p. 200.

339 "the example of . . . Newton": *Menorah*.

339 He had no desire to represent people: Einstein-Comert, July 4, 1922, League Archives.

339 "your letter which has caused me great disappointment": Curie-Einstein, July (date unclear), 1922, Institut de Physique Nucleaire, Paris.

340 "Einstein resigns": Nitobe-Murray, League Archives.

340 "resignation . . . cannot become definitive": Bergson-Nitobe, League Archives.

340 "your sudden and motiveless retreat": Comert-Einstein, April 10, 1923, League Archives.

342 "As a convinced pacifist": Einstein-League, March 21, 1923, League Archives.

342 "a condemnation, without appeal": Comert-Einstein, April 10, 1923, League Archives.

343 If he were not elected: Einstein-Murray, May 30, 1924, League Archives.

343 the offer was magnanimous: Einstein-Drummond, June 25, 1924, League Archives.

344 "guided by narrow nationalism": speech at inauguration of Institute for Intellectual Co-operation, June 26, 1926.

345 "we had no funds": Smith and Toynbee, p. 202.

346 "immense intellectual power, perfect good will": Smith and Toynbee, p. 200.

346 "very reluctant to believe evil": Murray-Bertrand Russell, May 4, 1955, quoted Smith and Toynbee, p. 200.

347 "a horror of platonic declarations": Steinig-M. Bonnet, October 29, 1931, League Archives.

350 useless to discuss rules of war: Einstein-Women's International League for Peace and Freedom, January 4, 1928, quoted Nathan and Norden, p. 90.

350 "Einstein considered . . . governments . . . justified": *War Resistance*, Vol. 2, No. 23, 4th Quarter, p. 11.

350 "to meet Einstein at his lakeside summer house": *War Resistance*, Vol. 2, No. 23, 4th Quarter, p. 11.

351 "Even if only two per cent": Speech: Ritz-Carlton Hotel, New York, December 14, 1930, quoted Lief, p. 35.

351 "there are two ways of resisting war": *The New World*. July 1931.

352 suggesting he should be replaced: Einstein-Montenach, April 20, 1932, League Archives.

352 "I was not suitable for doing useful work": Einstein-Montenach, April 20, 1932, League Archives.

352 "his colleagues . . . would greatly appreciate": Montenach-Dufour Feronce, League Archives.

352 "This little corner of Balfourian jobs and gentility": quoted Kingsley Martin, p. 94.

353 "I believe (it) should take place": *Paix Mondiale*, November 17, 1931.

353 Henderson "engineered" Einstein's appearance: "The Comedy of Peace", *Pictorial Review*, February 1933.

354 "One does not make wars less likely": quoted Nathan and Norden, pp. 168-70.

355 "This is not a comedy": Einstein quoted Konrad Bercovici *Pictorial Review*, February 1933.

356 a bad speaker: Blumenfeld-Weizmann, March 15, 1921, E. T. H.

357 "the movement . . . came to a standstill": Leonard Stein, *Zionism*, p. 98.

357 "denied that the Jews were a nation at all"; Stein, p. 82.

358 "the . . . community which . . . controls the loan market of the world": Fisher, p. 1147.

361 "put down 'Palestine' for the next War Cabinet": Scott, entry for September 28, 1917, p. 306.

361 "Weizmann's relationship with Einstein . . . remained ambivalent": Isaiah Berlin, in Weisgal and Carmichael, p. 41.

362 "I approached . . . Einstein": Weizmann, p. 331.

362 "I was to stir up Einstein": Blumenfeld, see note to p. 292.

363 "Haber had done all he could": Weizmann, p. 435.

363 "Telegram Weizmann that I agree": Blumenfeld.

364 "a letter which Blumenfeld wrote to Weizmann": March 15, 1921, E. T. H.

365 "Overbearing and politically ruthless"; Weisgal and Carmichael, p. 41.

365 "Einstein . . . gay and flirtatious", Vera Weizmann, pp. 102-3.

365 "I was fully convinced he understood it": Weizmann-Ossip Dymow, quoted Seelig, p. 81.

365 New York arrival; the main record of Einstein's day-to-day activities is taken from the *New York Times*.

368 "To every person in America": Frank, p. 219.

369 "I was asked to translate": Morris R. Cohen, *A Dreamer's Journey*, p. 187.

370 "a new theory of Eternity": Shapley, p. 78.

370 "God is subtle": the famous remark, later to be carved into the mantelpiece of a Princeton University common-room was, says Miss Dukas, overheard and remembered by Professor Veblen.

371 "We escaped . . . by a narrow margin": Boltwood-Rutherford, July 14, 1921, Badash, p. 342.

371 "the Club has made difficulties": Weizmann-Einstein, June 30, 1922, Weizmann Archives.

373 "insisted on travelling second-class": F. H. Kisch, p. 29.

373 "outer gates were stormed" and "made happy by the sight of the Jewish people": *Palestine Weekly*, February 9, 1923.

374 "Interview with Deedes", F. H. Kisch p. 30.

374 "attended the first lecture": Bentwich, *Mandate Memories*, pp. 88–9.

374 "a Hebrew that was evidently unfamiliar"; Samuel, *Memoirs*, p. 253.

375 He was impressed: Einstein-Weizmann, February 11, 1923, Weizmann Archives.

375 "I am tenfold happier": *Palestine Weekly*, February 23, 1923.

375 "rouse the Jewish world": *Palestine Weekly*, February 23, 1923.

375 "no genius of rank . . . save a mathematician": Bentwich, *Wanderer Between Two Worlds*, p. 133.

375 "writes just like a professor"; Bentwich, *Mandate Memories*, p. 88.

376 "a simple German housewife", Frank, p. 243.

376 "good . . . embodied and continued in the next theory": Einstein quoted note by Samuel, February 5, 1923, Samuel Papers.

376 "Ramassez plus d'argent": Kisch, p. 30.

377 "the first political aim": Bentwich, *My Seventy-Seven Years: An Account of My Life and Times*, p. 99.

378 "many financiers from America": Hebrew University Report.

378 asked for the withdrawal: Einstein-Magnes, December 29, 1925, Weizmann Archives.

378 Magnes declined: Einstein-Magnes, March 6, 1926, Weizmann Archives.

379 "my colleagues and I . . . were most upset": Weizmann-Einstein, July 9, 1926, Weizmann Archives.

379 to complain in stronger terms: Einstein-Weizmann, January 8, 1928, Weizmann Archives.

379 "Our income . . . entirely from voluntary subscribers": Weizmann-Einstein, June 8, 1933, Weizmann Archives.

379 Einstein's resignation: Einstein-Weizmann, January 8, 1928.
Einstein-Weizmann, June 14, 1928.
Einstein-Weizmann, June 20, 1928.
All Weizmann Archives.

380 "of an unusually momentous character": Weizmann-Einstein, May 29, 1929, Weizmann Archives.

380 "I am the Jewish saint": statement to Simon: visit to Markwalder: personal information.

380 "the brave and dedicated minority: Einstein, quoted official report, 1. Council-Sitzung: Eroffnungsreden, p. 578.

381 "Arabs who had murdered Jews": Brodetsky, p. 137.

381 Some ways of co-operating with the Arabs: Einstein-Weizmann, November 25, 1929, Weizmann Archives.

382 "very patient in his suffering": Reiser, p. 200.

382 "only just beginning to think": *Nature*, Vol. 123, March 23, 1929, p. 464.

383 "master of the intellectual world": Mercier, "Sur L'Identification des Theories Physiques" in *Entstehung, Entwicklung, und Perspektiven der Einsteinschen Gravitationstheorie*, Berlin, 1966 (report of Einstein Symposium November 2—5, 1965).

384 a preliminary paper; "Zur affinen Feldtheorie", *Preussische Akademie der Wissenschaften, Phys-math Klasse, Sitzungsberichte*, 1923, pp. 137—40.

384 "his position was assured"; Taub, quoted Whitrow xii.

384 "the outline of a unified field": "Neue Möglichkeit für eine einheitliche Feldtheorie von Gravitation und Elektrizität, *Preussische Akademie der Wissenschaften, Phys-math. Klasse, Sitzungsberichte*, 1928, pp. 224—7.

384 "the dream of his life": Elsa Einstein-Hermann Struck, December 27, 1928, quoted Stargardt Auction Catalogue, November 1969.

384 the unified field paper: "Einheitliche Feldtheorie", *Preussische Akademie der Wissenschaften, Phys.-math. Klasse, Sitzungsberichte*, 1929, pp. 2—7.

385 "a non-mathematical explanation is out of the question": *Nature*, Vol. 123, February 23, 1929.

386 "I cannot readily give up the affine picture": *Nature*, Vol. 123, February 23, 1929, p. 281.

386 "an agony of mathematical torment": *Helle Zeit*, p. 51.

386 the author of the book, Reiser, p. 11.

387 factual contents . . . personal information from Einstein: Kayser-Seelig, October 31, 1955, E. T. H.

387 forbade its publication in German: Reichinstein, p. 251.

387 "I had to explain to Boess": Plesch, p. 224.

388 "the decisive power", Frank, p. 270.

389 "we have spent most of our savings": Elsa Einstein-Frank, Frank, p. 270.

390 O'Connell, Goldstein, and Spinoza's God: *New York Times*, April 25, 1929.

391 "the 'Authorised Version'": *The American Hebrew*, September 11, 1931.

391 "The conversation drifted back and forth": Tschernowitz.

391 "The kind of work I do": Frank, p. 147.

392 "I arrived at his house about three o'clock": *Die Wahrheit*, Berlin, March 15—16, 1969.

392 "then Einstein spoke": Plesch, p. 210.

393 "by giving favours to Jews": Whyte, p. 99.

394 "grim signs of the rising anti-Semitic flood": Bentwich, *My 77 Years*, p. 95.

394 the difficulty . . . the 'jüdischen Nationalität: Rosentiel-author, December 2, 1968.

395 Draft letter to Planck: Einstein-Planck, July 17, 1931, Princeton.

397 "the Queen's own notes in her agenda book": Royal Archives, Brussels.

397 sat down with Royal family to a frugal dinner; Einstein-Elsa, quoted Nathan and Norden, p. 662.

397 "the pockets of a school-boy": Vallentin, p. 81.

398 for the pleasure of talking with him: Einstein-Eddington, quoted Douglas, p. 102.

399 "Je suis model" and "pas très Juif": note by Samuel, Samuel Papers.

399 "the impression of a monkeys' assembly": Vera Weizmann, p. 113.

399 "when I first met Einstein . . .": Fleming-Allan Balch, December 5, 1934, Millikan Papers.

400 religious thought "an attempt to find an out": Ernst G. Strauss, *Encyclopaedia Americana*, New York 1969, Vol. 10, p. 42a.

400 "he had no belief in the Church": Born letters, p. 203.

400 "something behind the energy"; quoted Pearlman, p. 217.

400 "they quote me for support of such views": Lowenstein, *Towards the Farther Shore*, p. 156.

401 "An impersonal God . . ." William Kent, "Einstein's Reflections on Life and Religion", *The Western Humanities Review*, Vol. IX, Summer 1955, No. 3, p. 189.

401 "at opposite ends of the range": Sheen, Krass, *New York Times*, November 16, 1930.

401 "a sad commentary on . . . commercialism . . . and corruption": *New York Times*, November 23, 1930.

402 "I want to be left alone": *New York Times*, December 3, 1930.

402 "one should not speak publicly": *New York Times*, December 17, 1930.

403 "to define the fourth dimension", *New York Times*, December 12, 1930.

403 "five crowded days": details, *New York Times*.

405 "the dear Lord knows very well": Hedwig Born-Einstein, February 22, 1931, Born letters, p. 110.

405 "the greatest mind in the world": Upton Sinclair," As I Remember him", *Saturday Review*, April 14, 1956.

405 "New observations by Hubble & Humason": *New York Times*, January 3, 1931.

407 "symmetry . . . nearly as important as truth": North, p. 118.

409 "the back of an old envelope": as with many stories of the Einsteins in Pasadena, this is firmly believed even though evidence is lacking.

409 "if I may take refuge behind Einstein": Inge, *God and the Astronomers*, p. 50.

410 "Financial position . . . extremely difficult": Cable—Weizmann-Einstein, February 4, 1931, Weizmann Archives.

410 the Rhodes lectures: the Princeton Archives, the Cherwell Papers, and the present Warden of the Rhodes Trust are the main sources for details of Einstein's negotiations with the Trust.

411 he therefore asked to be excused: Einstein-Haldane, June 8, 1927, Rhodes Trust.

411 Perhaps a four-week visit in the Summer would do: Einstein-Lindemann, August 8, 1927, Cherwell Archives.

411 Trustees "put in the difficult position": Fisher-Einstein, October 14, 1927, Princeton.

411 "his health seems quite restored": Lindemann-Lord Lothian, October 4 and 13, 1930, Cherwell Archives.

411 "every care that he has all he wants": Lindemann-Mrs. Einstein, February 24, 1931, Cherwell Archives.

412 the Oxford Luncheon Club had written to him: Einstein-Lindemann, March 23, 1931, Cherwell Archives.

412 "My husband took a good deal of trouble": Mrs. Haldane, *Manchester Guardian*, April 28, 1955.

412 "The first lecture . . .": Einstein's Rhodes lectures have never been printed. They are summarised in *Nature*, Vol. 127, pp. 765, 790, 826.

413 "The far-away thought behind that far-away look": Toynbee, *Acquaintances*, p. 268

413 "his great interest in music": Whitrow, p. 58.

413 graphic and pessimistic account: Einstein-Lindemann, June 9, 1931, Cherwell Archives.

414 "He . . . proved so stimulating": Lindemann-Lord Lothian, June 27, 1931, Cherwell Archives.

414 "proposed that Einstein should be made a Research Student": details from Christ Church, Sir Roy Harrod, C. H. Collie, Cherwell Archives.

414 Einstein thanked him in doggerel, translated by J. B. Leishman, *The Times,* May 17, 1955.

415 "able to visit Oxford for something like a month": Lindemann-Einstein, June 29, 1931, Cherwell Archives.

415 Einstein . . . delighted . . . to keep in touch with Oxford: Einstein-Lindemann, July 15, 1931, Cherwell Archives.

415 "Fleming read *not* his own letters": Noyes-Hale, October 8, 1931, Hale Papers.

416 "commitment of twenty thousand dollars all inclusive": telegram—Barrett-Millikan, Millikan Archives.

416 "the seven thousand dollar figure which we talked about": Millikan-Einstein, October 11, 1931, Millikan Papers.

416 decided to remain in Germany for the winter: Einstein-Millikan, October 19, 1931, Millikan Papers.

416 Elsa wrote to Millikan: Mrs. Einstein-Millikan, November 14, 1931, Millikan Papers.

417 "I drove over to the Athenaeum": Flexner, p. 381.

417 "I had no idea that he would be interested": Flexner, p. 382.

418 "in one swoop": Lief, p. 56.

418 "we entered into relations of easy intimacy with him": Harrod, p. 47.

418 "some mathematical proposition which he took well established": Harrod, p. 48.

419 the proof about prime factors: Einstein-Lindemann, June 19, 1944, Cherwell Archives.

419 "a glow of triumph": Birkenhead, p. 140.

419 "I have examined the affidavits": Birkenhead, p. 140.

419 "I would not presume to offer you a post": Flexner, p. 383.

420 "a people that refused an Einstein": Mowrer, p. 238.

420 "The military dictatorship will suppress the popular will": Frank, p. 273.

420 "I found him seated on the veranda": Flexner, p. 384.

421 "Let Mrs. Einstein and me arrange it": Flexner, qouted *New York Times,* April 19, 1955.

421 "Whatever doubts and thoughts we had": Weyl-Seelig, May 19, 1952, E.T.H.

421 "you are establishing in Princeton a theoretical research Institute": Millikan-Flexner, July 25, 1932, Millikan Papers.

422 "annual residence for brief periods at several places": Flexner-Millikan, July 29, 1932, Millikan Papers.

422 "maybe a solution will be found": Mrs. Einstein-Millikan, August 13, 1932, Millikan Papers.

422 "leave of absence from the Prussian Academy": *New York Times*, October 16, 1932.

423 "to a request for you to rejoin the Board of Governors": Weizmann-Einstein, November 8, 1932, Weizmann Archives.

423 Einstein was delighted to hear the news: Einstein-Weizmann, November 20, 1932, Weizmann Archives.

423 "funny if they didn't let me in": *New York Times*, December 4, 1932.

424 "you will never see it again": Frank, p. 273.

425 "to cover the expenses of Professor Einstein in America": Wilber K. Thomas, Oberlaender Trust—Millikan, January 14, 1932, Millikan Papers.

426 "aiding and abetting the teaching of treason to the youth of this country": Fried-Millikan, March 4, 1932, Millikan Papers.

426 "Einstein has been exploited by all sorts of agencies": Millikan-Fried, March 8, 1932, Millikan Papers.

427 "a skill which . . . would help to relieve their minds": Millikan-Thomas, January 16, 1933, Millikan Papers.

427 "some wholly non-representative groups of so-call 'War Resisters' ": Millikan-Thomas, January 24, 1933, Millikan Papers.

428 "Einstein was only nodding. He seemed somewhat ill at ease": Watters, p. 3.

428 "the obstacle of the black dress suit": *Bulletin* of the California Institute of Technology, Vol. XLII, No. 138, February 1933, pp. 4—12.

429 a brief poem: Einstein-H. M. Queen Elizabeth, February 19, 1933, Royal Library, Brussels.

429 "The success of our banquet . . . if we were to replace Professor Einstein's presence": Earl C. Bloss-Millikan, February 18, 1933, Millikan Papers.

429 "efforts of all kinds of radical groups to exploit him": Millikan-Oberlaender Trust, January 16, 1933, Millikan Papers.

431 "As long as I have any choice in the matter": Interview—*New York World Telegram*, Evelyn Seeley, March 10, 1933.

432 "would not leave us": Lola Maverick Lloyd, *Unity*, March 27, 1933, p. 59.

432 helping to save European civilisation: Einstein-Nahon, July 20, 1933, *La Patrie Humaine*, August 18, 1933.

433 "rumours that Einstein's genial gullibility had been taken advantage of": Edwin Wolf II with John F. Fleming, *Rosenbach*, p. 380.

433 "a visit to Princeton": details from *New York Times* and Jewish Telegraphic Agency.

437 Details of Berlin meeting, August 16, 1933: German Foreign Office, Bonn.

439 "taking over my small house in London": Locker-Lampson-Einstein, March 25, 1933, Princeton.

439 Planck's reply: Planck-Einstein, March 1933, Princeton.

440 "The Prussian Academy of Sciences heard with indignation": The correspondence with the Academy has been published in various versions. That used here follows the text used in *The World as I See It*, pp. 85—92.

441 "we are all very proud of the part you have played": Wise-Einstein, May 9 ,1933, Wise, *Servant of the People*, p. 187.

441 "less important that a professor make discoveries": quoted Fermi, *Illustrious Immigrants: The Intellectual Migration from Europe 1930—41*, p. 51.

441 "a scene . . . not . . . witnessed . . . since the late Middle Ages": Shirer, p. 241.

442 "the task of the universities": Professor Ernst Krieck, quoted *Science*, May 23 1933.

442 "reverential greetings to the Chancellor": *Science,* Vol. 77, No. 2005, June 2, 1933, p. 529.

443 "not yet hanged": Private information.

443 "the dangerous influence of Jewish circles on the study of nature": Lenard, *Völkischer Beobachter.*

443 "one of the hideously anti-Semitic cartoons": Letter from owner to author.

444 Einstein's commitments elsewhere: Einstein-Langevin, May 5, 1933, Nathan and Norden, p. 221.

445 Einstein was not enthusiastic: Einstein-Szilard, April 25, 1933, Szilard Papers.

445 "he is still at some sympathy for his original plan": Szilard-unknown correspondent, May 14, 1933. Szilard Papers.

445 "the kindest are not always very practical": Frank, p. 333.

446 "on my arrival in Cairo the following day": Weizmann-Einstein, May 3, 1933, Weizmann Archives.

446 already unburdened himself to Samuel: Einstein-Samuel, April 4, 1933, Samuel Papers.

446 "Einstein had told the Jewish Telegraphic Agency": J. T. A. Bulletins.

447 "it was deplorable that this university": *Jewish Chronicle*, April 8, 1933.

447 "the action you have thus taken . . . so surprising, and so unjust even": Weizmann-Einstein, May 3, 1933, Weizmann Archives.

448 "his reply to Weizmann": Einstein-Weizmann, May 7, 1933, Weizmann Archives.

448 he might come in June: Einstein-Lindemann, May 1, 1933, Cherwell Archives.

448 "I was in Berlin for four or five weeks at Easter": Lindemann-Einstein, May 4, 1933, Cherwell Archives.

449 "Shrewd persons": Frank, p. 318.

449 "Certainly by le Chanoine Lemaître": Dr. M. Gottschalk, *Bull. de la Centrale d'Oeuvres Sociales Juives*, June 1955, p. 4.

450 "I can almost see Einstein now": C. H. Arnold-author, October 8, 1968.

450 "suggesting that Weizmann and he should meet": Weizmann-Einstein, June 4, 1933, Weizmann Archives.

450 "a three-page letter": Weizmann-Einstein, June 8, 1933, Weizmann Archives.

451 firmly standing his ground: Einstein-Weizmann, June 9, 1933, Weizmann Archives.

452 "Einstein has severely criticised the university": *New York Times*, June 30, 1933.

452 "Dr. Weizmann . . . has misled public opinion": Einstein, Jewish Telegraphic Agency, July 3, 1933.

452 "made peace with the Hebrew University": Weizmann, *New York Times,* July 5, 1933.

453 "things could never be the same": Bentwich, *Judah L. Magnes*, p. 168.

453 "a more or less decorative figure": Voss, pp. 206—7.

453 "Even the events in Germany": Magnes, *Reply to the Report of the Hebrew University Survey Committee.*

454 "(His) faith has the stirring and driving quality": *Menorah.*

456 "you should come here for a month or more": Hewlett-Johnson-Einstein, June 3, 1933, Cherwell Archives.

456 "I saw that it was a Peace Congress": Gottschalk, *Bull. de la Centrale d'Oeuvres Sociales Juives,* June 1955.

457 "the fusing of small professional armies": Lord Ponsonby-Runham Brown, February 6, 1933, quoted Nathan and Norden, p. 225.

457 times were out of joint: Einstein-Hugenholtz, July 1, 1933, Nathan and Norden, p. 226.

458 "The husband of the second fiddler": quoted Nathan and Norden, p. 227.

459 he had decided not to intervene: Einstein-H. M. King Albert, July 14, 1933, Royal Archives, Brussels.

459 "responsive to what you say about Belgium": H. M. King Albert-Einstein, July 24, 1933, Royal Archives, Brussels.

459 "would rather be hacked in pieces": Einstein, *Ideas and Opinions,* p. 10.

459 cheerfully accept military service: Einstein-Nahon, July 20, 1933. *La Patrie Humaine,* August 18, 1933.

460 "The apostasy of Einstein": Press Service of the International Antimilitaristic Commission.

460 "Until a year and a half ago": Einstein public statement at Le Coq, Nathan and Norden, p. 234.

460 "a sword of peace": quoted Kingsley Martin, p. 94.

461 "to guard ourselves from thinking": Wilfred Trotter, "Has the Intellect a Function?", *The Lancet,* i, June 24, 1939, p. 1419.

462 "seen Einstein . . . bringing him to England": Locker-Lampson-Lindemann, July 20, 1933, Cherwell Archives.

462 "I do not . . . possess a drop . . . of Jewish blood": Locker-Lampson, House of Commons, July 26, 1933.

462 "Einsteinian Jew Show": *Völkischer Beobachter.*

463 "I did not write a word of it": quoted Press reports, Britain and America.

464 "I implored him to resign": Ellen Wilkinson, quoted *Daily Express,* September 12, 1933.

464 "When a bandit is going to commit a crime": Jewish Telegraphic Agency.

464 "the professor is taking everything quietly": Jewish Telegraphic Agency, September 8, 1933.

465 "a small boarding house": information on Einstein's third, and final, journey to England in 1933, provided by Locker-Lampson's widow; Sir Walter Adams, former secretary of the Academic Assistance Council: the Rutherford Papers: contemporary newspapers and other sources cited.

465 "I shall become a naturalised Englishman"; *Daily Express,* September 11, 1933.

466 "Three wonderful people called Stein": It has been impossible to trace the printed source of this. It may well be a folk-creation, springing from "Precious Steins", 15 lines which appeared in *Punch,* September 11, 1929.

466 "a mixture of the humane, the humorous and the profound"; Epstein, pp. 77—8.

468 "made to become a double symbol": *New Statesman,* Vol. VI, October 21, 1933. p. 481.

469 "For more than forty years": Goran, p. 161.

469 "things of value": Haber-Kaiser Wilhelm, Bentwich, *The Rescue and Achievements of Refugee Scholars,* p. 4.

469 "a position at the Hebrew University"; Frank, p. 292.

469 "did not want to shake hands": Born, *Universitas,* Vol. 8, No. 2, 1966, p. 104.

469 "the climate will be good for you"; Weizmann, p. 437.

470 "I see that Einstein has resigned": Rutherford-de Hevesy, April 3, 1933, Eve, p. 371.

471 Lord Rutherford was in the Chair: details from official and Press accounts of the meeting: also Sir Walter Adams to author.

472 "it is possible . . . to do more harm than good": Bragg-Rutherford, May 4, 1933, Rutherford Papers.

472 "no implication . . . of hostility to Germany": Adams-Rutherford, Rutherford Papers.

473 "a great scientist should lend his name": Dufour-Feronce-Sylvestor, September 27, 1933, Beaverbrook Library.

474 "The value of Judaism": *New York Times,* Oct. 1933

474 looked forward to their next meeting: Einstein-Lindemann, October 5, 1933, Cherwell Archives.

475 "Einstein's boat was not yet at the pier in New York": Rev. John Lampe, July 7, 1956.

479 "leaving the physical world": Cline, p. 15.

479 "Do you want to commit suicide?": Plesch-Einstein, September 22, 1947, Plesch correspondence.

480 "never known a place that to me was a homeland": Watters, p. 26.

481 "his divided attitude towards contact": Frank, p. 325.

482 "but I *am* Dr. Einstein": Eisenhart.

482 "We are slaves of bathrooms": Infeld, *Quest,* p. 293.

482 "his choice was Moses" and "my husband always says": private source.

483 "Colonel MacIntyre . . . telephoned the Institute": Report to White House Social Bureau, December 7, 1933, Roosevelt Library.

483 "with genuine and profound reluctance": Flexner-Roosevelt, November 3, 1933, Roosevelt Library.

484 never received: Einstein-Mrs. Roosevelt, November 21, 1933, Roosevelt Library.

484 the original of the doggerel: The copy in the Roosevelt Library in Elsa's handwriting, was translated by the Department of State Translating Bureau which provided a close and a rhymed version and were "careful not to fold or otherwise tamper with the original sheets". The original card, written by Einstein and addressed to Queen Elizabeth, is in the Royal Library, Brussels.

484 "a letter from Representative F. H. Shoemaker": Shoemaker-Roosevelt, December 1, 1933, Roosevelt Library.

485 "many different circumstances", Jewish Telegraphic Agency.

486 "discussed with Lindemann from November 1933 onwards": Princeton and Cherwell Archives.

486 written to Mrs. Roosevelt: Einstein-Mrs. Roosevelt, December 21, 1933, Roosevelt Library.

486 his mind . . . not yet . . . made up; Einstein-Born, March 22, 1934, Born letters, p. 122.

486 "news from me concerning our friend A. E."; Schrödinger-Lindemann, March 29, 1934, Cherwell Archives.

487 the Governing Body considered his request: Christ Church Records.

487 if he came to Oxford he would also have to visit Paris and Madrid: Einstein-Lindemann, January 22, 1935, Cherwell Archives.

487 "I recalled that . . . I had mentioned a somewhat rare book": Watters, p. 5.

488 "one flower is beautiful"; Watters, p. 20.

489 "Einstein . . . came back with my chauffeur"; Watters, p. 10.

489 "never enjoyed the companionship": Watters, p. 26.

490 "Liszt's Lorelei . . . played on the Ampico": Watters, p. 20.

490 "his letters to and from Bucky": the collection of letters is owned by the University of Texas at Austin.

490 "a signboard showing at what time each country": Watters, p. 19.

490 "the one thing . . . it hurt him . . . to leave behind": Plesch, p. 224.

491 "was . . . too snobbish": Bucky, Helle Zeit, pp. 60—5.

491 "the Herr Professor does not drive": Harry A. Cohen.

491 "a child-like delight": Bucky, Helle Zeit, pp. 60—5.

491 "Burgess had made a number of drawings": Watters, p. 21.

492 "Suddenly cried out 'Achtung' ": Watters, p. 21.

492 "we tramped together along the beaches . . .": Einstein: An Intimate Memoir by Thomas Lee Bucky and Joseph P. Blank, Harper's Magazine, September 1964, p. 43.

493 "You know how to be gracious": quoted New York Times March 12, 1944, VI, p. 16.

493 "Einstein's thoughts . . . being misrepresented": Weizmann-Einstein, April 28, 1938.

494 "born from a mother earth and bound up with blood": Shirer, p. 250.

494 "True physics . . . the creation of the German spirit": Shirer, p. 250.

494 "the founders of research in physics . . . were almost exclusively of Aryan": Nature, Vol. 141, April 1938, p. 772.

494 "the probably pure-minded Jew, Albert Einstein": Lenard, Deutsche Physik, Vol. 1, 1934.

495 "the world view of German man": Bruno Thurring reprinted in Deutsche Mathematik, ed. Theodor Vahlen, Leipzig 1936, pp. 706-11.

495 "I hate them so much . . . I have to go back": personal information.

497 "private evening of chamber music at his house": Shapley, p. 111.

497 "always going — but never gone": Shapley, p. 112.

497 "I still would not believe it": Lindbergh-author, December 12, 1969.

499 "The individual counts for little": Watters, p. 27.

500 "never ask the Professor to do that": Mayer-author, December 4, 1968.

500 "I give her my understanding": Eisenhart.

500 "little time to fulfil the duties": Watters, p. 150

500 Einstein could well have taken lessons: Mrs. Einstein-Watters, September 10, 1926, American Jewish Archives.

501 "more like a historic relic": Infeld, *As I See It*, Bull. At. Sc., February 1965, p. 9.

501 "two such relics from times past": Born, *Physics in My Generation*, p. 164.

501 "he had a right to that failure": lecture to UNESCO, Paris, December 13, 1965, printed *New York Review*, March 17, 1966.

502 "beauty for him was, after all, essentially simplicity": Rosen-author, January 26, 1970.

502 "the nature of science": Hoffman-author, March 24, 1970.

503 "God never tells us in advance": Mattersdorf-author, May 7, 1969.

503 "to save another fool": Mitrany Statement to author.

504 "Can Quantum-Mechanical Description of Physical Reality be Considered Complete?": *Physical Review*, Ser. 2., Vol. 47, pp. 777—80.

505 Bohr published a paper: "Can Quantum-Mechanical Description of Physical Reality be Considered Complete?" *Physical Review*, Vol. 48, October 15, 1935, p. 696.

505 "I have used this opportunity": Bohr-Rutherford, June 3, 1935, Rutherford Papers.

505 "he grinned like a small boy": A. E. Condon, quoted Samuel Rapport and Helen Wright, *Mathematics*, New York, 1963, p. 90.

506 "his result had a somewhat broader sense of validity": Eisenhart.

506 "Elementary derivation of the Equivalence of Mass and Energy": American Mathematical Society, *Bulletin*, Vol. 41, pp. 223-30.

507 "we shall do it": Infeld, *Quest*, p. 311.

508 "my physical powers decreasing": Watters, p. 39.

512 "a wave of atomic disintegration": Sir William Dampier-Whetham-Rutherford, July 26, 1903, quoted Eve, p. 102.

512 "radical process . . . now in the range of the possible": Planck quoted in Born's obit., p. 5.

513 "Rutherford's warning to Lord Hankey": Clark, *The Birth of the Bomb*, p. 153.

513 "The destiny of Man has slipped": Desmond McCarthy, *New Statesman*, Vol. III, May 7, 1932, p. 585.

514 "an element which is split by neutrons": Szilard, *Reminiscences*, p. 100.

514 "I assigned this patent to the British Admiralty": Szilard, *Reminiscences*, p. 102.

514 "the threat of the concentration camp": the story of Lise Meitner's escape from Germany is told in Otto Hahn's *My Life*.

515 "two fairly large nuclei flying apart": Clark, *The Birth of the Bomb*, p. 15.

516 "Clever these physicists": Oppenheimer, *Flying Trapeze*, p. 52.

516 "Tizard met the company's president": Clark, *The Birth of the Bomb*, p. 23.

516 "building of 'a uranium device' ": *Naturwissenschaften* Nos. 23/24, June 9, 1933.

517 "the show was going on": Dr. Vannevar Bush, *Boston Globe*, December 2, 1962.

517 "New Material": Leo Szilard's archives are the most important single source of fresh information on the Roosevelt letter. Another is Alexander Sachs.

518 "Both Wigner and I began to worry": Szilard, pp. 111—12.

518 Einstein "had not been aware": Szilard-Seelig, August 19, 1955, E.T.H.

518 "That never occurred to me": Szilard-authors of *Einstein on Peace*, quoted p. 291.

519 "that he himself had discussed chain reactions": statement Wigner to author.

519 "deeply involved in his own work": Professor Aage Bohr — author, September 23, 1970.

520 "a surprising conclusion": Clark, *The Birth of the Bomb*, p. 39.

520 "any immediate use . . . is impracticable": Message Bohr-Chadwick quoted Cockcroft, *Obit. Notices, Fellows of the Royal Society*, Vol. 9 p. 45.

520 "a surprise for him on his arrival in England": Professor Aage Bohr-author, September 23, 1970.

520 "I did not foresee it would be released": Einstein, "Atomic War or Peace" *Atlantic Monthly*, November 1945.

520 "scarcely believe the universe was constructed this way": quoted Clark, *Tizard*, p. 301.

520 "do you really think the universe was made in this way?": Clark, *Tizard,* p. 301.

521 "my colleagues knew I was opposed", Born-author, 1960, quoted Clark, *The Birth of the Bomb*, p. 83.

521 "one great mistake of my life": Einstein to Pauling, recorded same day in Pauling's diary; Pauling-author, July 28, 1969.

521 "Before contacting the Belgian Government": Szilard-Seelig, August 19, 1955, E.T.H.

521 "the danger to the Belgian State": Szilard Papers.

522 "the real warmongering": Sachs before Special Committee on Atomic Energy US Senate, November 27, 1945; *Background to Early History, Atomic Bomb Project in Relation to President Roosevelt*, Washington, D. C. 1945, pp. 553—73 (afterwards referred to as Senate).

522 "Szilard had a final formulation": Teller-author, May 19, 1969.

523 "Bernard Baruch or Karl Compton": Szilard-Einstein, August 2, 1939, Szilard Papers.

523 "not to be too clever"; Einstein-Szilard, undated but apparently August 9, 1939, Szilard Papers.

523 "Lost in the heavy mail": Lindbergh-author, December 12, 1969.

524 "Lindbergh is not our man": Szilard-Einstein, September 27, 1939, Szilard Papers.

524 "Sachs confessed": Szilard-Einstein, October 3, 1939, Szilard Papers.

524 "National public figures . . . punch-drunk": Senate.

524 Sachs read his covering letter: Hewlett and Anderson, p. 17.

525 "pressure — by Einstein and the speaker": Senate.

525 "their accessibility . . . to Germany constituted an important problem": Senate.

525 the letter . . . written to Sachs: Einstein-Sachs, March 7, 1940, Senate.

526 "there had to be secrecy against leaks": Senate.

526 "the matter should rest in abeyance": Senate.

526 "a time convenient to you and Dr. Einstein": Roosevelt-Sachs, April 5, 1940, Senate.

526 "perhaps Dr. Einstein would have suggestions to offer": Senate.

526 "the great shyness and humility of that really saintly scientist": Senate.

526 "a polite letter of regret": Szilard-Einstein, April 19, 1940, Szilard Papers.

526 the third (letter) that Einstein had signed: Einstein-Briggs, April 25, 1940, Senate.

527 Government Committee "was to retard rather than advance"; Compton, p. 29. Bush "had a long conversation with the President"; Baxter, p. 427.

528 "in 1940 it was still difficult for us": Compton, p. 60.

528 "gave Bush and Conant what they had been looking for": Hewlett and Anderson, p. 43.

529 "detailed case they made to American scientists": Boorstin, p. 862.

529 "Bush turned to Einstein for help": Aydelotte-Bush, December 19, 1941; Bush-Aydelotte, December 22, 1941; Bush-Urey, December 22, 1941; Urey-Bush, December 29, 1941; Bush-Aydelotte December 30, 1941; U. S. Atomic Energy Commission, Documents Nos. 327—31.

530 "Roosevelt . . . did not mention it": Bush-author, December 27, 1968.

532 "He never lived at my house": New York Times, August 5, 1944.

532 "stressing the important work": Julius-Loeb-Roosevelt, May 15, 1944, Roosevelt Library.

533 "silence about the fund-raising": memo W. D. H.-Judge Roseman, May 27, 1944, Roosevelt Library.

533 Einstein's English had been pretty badly broken; Shapley, p. 132.

534 "fight against the Fascist pestilence": Reich-Einstein, December 30, 1940, Reich, not paginated.

534 "Einstein was easy to talk to": Ilse Ollendorff Reich, p. 58.

535 links with the Navy: Einstein-Bucky, July 26, 1943 and August 13, 1943, Bucky correspondence.

535 "Einstein . . . disturbed because he not active in the war effort": Bush-author, December 27, 1968.

536 "persons which it would not otherwise have attracted": Furer, p. 147.

536 "signed on as a scientist"; dates and details from National Personnel Records Center, General Services Administration.

536 "I took a morning train to Princeton": Gamow, p. 151.

537 "project moved from the top of the priority list": Gamow, p. 151.

537 "defended . . . with the sacrifice of human lives": Born letters, p. 147.

537 "a more accurate means of antiaircraft fire": "Einstein: An Intimate Memoir", Thomas Lee Bucky and Joseph P. Blank, *Harper's Magazine*, September 1964, p. 43.

539 "uranium industry in 1943": *U. S. Minerals Handbook*, 1943, p. 828.

539 "enlivened discussions on bomb assembly": Gowing, p. 264.

540 influential scientists: Einstein-Bohr, December 12, 1944, diplomatic source.

541 "a letter from Kapitza": the fullest account of the Kapitza incident, the meetings with Churchill and Roosevelt, and the Hyde Park aide mémoire, is given in Gowing, pp. 350—60.

542 Bohr memorandum, December 1944: diplomatic source.

543 "a meeting in Munich": details and quotations, Goudsmit, p. 152.

543 "before Einstein": Goudsmit, p. 153.

544 "the war situation was already "too tense": Heisenberg, "The Third Reich and the Atomic Bomb", *Frankfurter Allgemeine Zeitung*, December 1967, reprinted, *Bull. At. Sc.*, June, 1968.

545 "a serious attempt to produce atom bombs in Germany . . ." Heisenberg, "The Third Reich and the Atomic Bomb".

545 "I had them brought to Farm Hall": R. V. Jones, "Thicker Than Heavy Water", *Chemistry and Industry*, August 26, 1967, p. 1419.

545 "how would the bomb be used": Szilard, p. 123.

545 "trailed by . . . Intelligence agents": Byrnes, p. 285.

546 "a possibility . . . not entirely in the Utopian domain": *Contemporary Jewish Record* VIII, June 1945.

546 "an overwhelming superiority in this field". Szilard memorandum, Szilard, p. 147.

546 "scrambling his technology": Hewlett and Anderson, p. 342.

546 "I decided to transmit the memorandum": Szilard, p. 124.

547 "hope you will get the President to read this": Szilard, p. 124.

547 "Truman asked me to see Szilard": Byrnes, p. 284.

547 "statesmen who did not realise": Hewlett and Anderson, p. 342.

548 "The World is not yet ready": *New York Times*, August 7, 1945.

548 "Oh weh": Nathan and Norden, p. 308.

548 "the professor thoroughly understands": Dukas, quoted *New York Times*, August 8, 1945.

548 "science did not draw on supernatural strength": Einstein interviewed Richard Lewis, *New York Times*, August 12, 1945.

551 "Atomic War or Peace": by Einstein and told to Raymond Swing, *Atlantic Monthly*, November 1945.

552 "This foreign-born agitator": Congressman John Rankin, October 5, 1945. "no hope of reasonableness in the Soviet Government": Russell-Einstein, November 24, 1947, Russell Archives, McMaster University.

553 "Russians . . . stationed in America": Interview June 22, 1946: Thomas-Einstein, June 26, 1946, Einstein-Thomas, June 27, 1946: Perkins Library, Duke University.

554 "Open Letter to the General Assembly": Einstein, *United Nations World*, October 1947.

554 "Dr. Einstein's Mistaken Notions": *New Times*, November 26, 1947.

555 "What happened next": Kimball Smith, p. 325.

555 "A nation-wide campaign to inform the American people": this, and other appeal quotations, are taken from the Emergency Committee papers, University of Chicago.

555 "a great chain-reaction of awareness": Michael Amrine, "The Real Problem is in the Hearts of Men", *New York Times*, June 23, 1946.

556 "pledged word of treaties, public opinion": Abbot-Einstein, May 3, 1947; Emergency Committee.

556 "refuse to submit to any kind of disarmament": V. H. Van Maren-Emergency Committee, April 29, 1947, Emergency Committee.

557 "I do not remember that Einstein had any influence": Weisskopf-author, May 14, 1970.

557 "that natural and convenient converse with statesmen": Oppenheimer, *On Albert Einstein*.

558 "suggested draft letter to Professor Einstein": undated (pencilled December 1945), Weizmann Archives.

558 "finally wrote on December 28": Weizmann-Einstein, Alexander Sachs.

558 during the walk they discussed the proposal: Sachs-author, May 7, 1970.

561 "on tap but not on top": The phrase is credited to the British junior minister who said: "We must keep the scientists on tap but never let them get on top"; Sir Thomas Merton, "Science and Invention", *The New Scientist* Vol. 25, p. 377. "Einstein . . . passionately defended the intellectual and moral freedom": Nathan and Norden, p. 541.

562 intellectuals should refuse to testify: *New York Times*, June 12, 1953.

562 "the unnatural and illegal forces of civil disobedience": *New York Times*, June 12, 1953.

562 "worry that Dr. Einstein's name . . . exploited": Thomas-Seelig, July 28, 1955, E.T.H.

563 "The Germans are cruel": Harry Cohen.

563 "The Germans can be killed or constrained": *Free World*, VIII 1944, pp. 370—1.

564 If the Ruhr were left to the Germans: Einstein-Council for German Democracy, October 1, 1945.

564 no wish to have . . . dealings with the Germans: Einstein-Sommerfeld, December 14, 1946, Sommerfeld, p. 121.

564 Germans' mass murder of the Jews: Einstein-Heuss, January 16, 1951, Nathan and Norden, p. 578.

565 a land of mass-murderers: Einstein-Born, October 12, 1953, Born letters, p. 199.

565 "they are no mass-murderers": Born-Einstein, November 8, 1953, Born letters, p. 204.

566 He wrote consolingly and without bitterness: Einstein—Frau Planck, Princeton, November 10, 1947.

566 raise funds for the Haganah Organisation: Einstein-Kocherthaler, May 4, 1948, Kocherthaler correspodence.

568 "fall victim to a great lie": Adolf Hitler, *Mein Kampf*.

569 considered leaving the United States: Kocherthaler broadcast 1968, German language radio, Montevideo, Urugvaj.

569 "he said he was too old": Brodetsky, p. 289.

570 "an impressive Rembrandt": Max Gottschalk, *Bulletin de la Centrale d'Oeuvres Socialist Juives,* June 1955.

570 no doubts about how they regarded him: Einstein-Habicht, Summer 1948, Seelig, p. 209.

571 did not attempt to put forward a logical defence: Einstein-Born, March 3, 1947, Born letters, p. 158.

571 "tiring if I had understood them": private information.

571 "what ideal qualities the Trustees should seek": Strauss, p. 271.

572 "just been downstairs to see Einstein": Abraham Pais, "Reminiscences of the Post-War Years" in Rozental, p. 224.

572 "what had been a monologue became a dialogue": Dr. Mitrany, statement to author.

573 "Einstein—Einstein": Pais, p. 225.

574 "Like Chinese, you have to study it": Infeld, quoted New York *Herald Tribune,* January 1, 1950.

575 "His routine was simple": Details of Einstein's post-war life are taken from conversations with Miss Helen Dukas, letters from Miss Dukas to Seelig (E.T.H) and the more reliable of the correspondents who visited him.

576 "dumped the contents of a very large wastebasket": Eisenhart.

577 "various objects of religious art". Douglas, *Forty Minutes with Einstein.*

577 "Her manner of speaking and her sound of voice": Frank, p. 351.

578 "The Presidency in Israel is a symbol": Pearlman, p. 203.

578 "Herr Gott. What is wrong now": Mitrany statement.

578 There is some conflict of evidence about the details of how the offer of the Presidency was made, as remembered by those directly concerned. The main facts are clear.

578 "Einstein was visibly moved by the splendour and audacity of the thought": Eban, *The Jewish Chronicle,* October 2, 1959.

579 "Acceptance would entail moving to Israel": Eban-Einstein, November 17, 1952, Nathan and Norden, p. 572.

579 Einstein felt bound to refuse: Einstein-Eban, November 18, 1952, Nathan and Norden, p. 572.

580 "I made one great mistake": Einstein-Pauling, quoted in Pauling's diary.

580 repudiated materialism: message to American Friends of The Hebrew University, 1954, quoted Bentwich, *Hebrew University*, p. 148.

580 "the only thing . . . is to go on working": Einstein-Hermanns, interview by William Miller, *Life,* May 2, 1955.

580 "the beauty and brilliance of Eddington's writing": Douglas, *Forty Minutes with Einstein.*

582 "I cannot prove there is no personal God"; "the brotherhood of man"; "never lose a holy curiosity": Einstein-Hermanns, interview by William Miller, *Life*, May 2, 1955.

583 "A lot of work will have to be done": Freundlich, *Physica Acta*, p. 112.

583 "Of the three observable consequences": Born, *Physica Acta*, p. 225.

583 "every theory is killed": Einstein quoted note by Samuel, February 5, 1923, Samuel Papers.

584 "opposed the First World War": Russell, quoted Nathan and Norden, p. xv.

584 "eminent men of science ought to do something dramatic": Russell-Einstein, February 11, 1955, Russell Archives.

585 a public declaration by a small number of scientists: Einstein-Russell, February 16, 1955, Russell Archives.

585 "we urge the governments of the world to realise": Russell-Einstein, April 5, 1955, Russell Archives.

585 "he had written to Russell" and "he was on the porch of his house": Paschkis-author, January 5, 1969.

586 He would like to help: Einstein-Israeli Consul, April 4, 1955, Nathan and Norden, p. 639.

586 "Professor Einstein told me": Abba Eban, *The Jewish Chronicle*, October 2, 1959.

587 He agreed . . . and he signed the document: Einstein-Russell, April 11, 1955, Russell Archives.

588 almost failed to recognise him: Margot Einstein-Hedwig Born, Born letters, p. 234.

# Index

# INDEX